CW01499591

PENGUI

THIS IS NOT

YASHPAL (1903–76) began to write while serving a life sentence for his participation as a comrade of Bhagat Singh and Chandrashekhar Azad, in the armed struggle for India's independence. What he wrote formed his first collection of short stories, *Pinjare ki Udan*, published in 1938. After his release Yashpal dazzled Hindi readers with the political journal *Viplava*, which he founded and published with the help of Prakashvati, a revolutionary whom he had married in prison. He wrote more than fifty books including collections of short stories, novels, essays, a play and memoirs of his revolutionary days.

Yashpal died in 1976 while writing the fourth volume of his reminiscences.

ANAND, a former print and broadcast journalist, has translated *Divya*, Yashpal's other major novel, into English, as well as his short stories into English and French. He was the editor of the fourteen-volume *Collected Works of Yashpal*, published in 2008. He has also translated Canadian writers Alice Munro, Mordecai Richler and Hugh MacLennon into Hindi.

HARISH TRIVEDI is professor of English at the University of Delhi and has been visiting professor at the universities of Chicago and London. He has co-edited *Post-colonial Translation: Theory and Practice* and has translated from Hindi into English a wide range of poetry and short fiction as well as a biography, *Premchand: A Life*.

This Is Not That Dawn

YASHPAL

Translated from the Hindi by
ANAND

Introduction by
HARISH TRIVEDI

PENGUIN BOOKS

PENGUIN BOOKS

USA | Canada | UK | Ireland | Australia
New Zealand | India | South Africa | China

Penguin Books is part of the Penguin Random House group of companies
whose addresses can be found at global.penguinrandomhouse.com

Published by Penguin Random House India Pvt. Ltd
7th Floor, Infinity Tower C, DLF Cyber City,
Gurgaon 122 002, Haryana, India

Penguin
Random House
India

First published in Hindi as *Jhootha Sach* by Viplava Karyalaya 1958, 1960
First published by Penguin Books India 2010

Copyright © Viplava Karyalaya 1958, 1960, 2010
Translation copyright © Anand 2010
Introduction copyright © Harish Trivedi 2010

All rights reserved

10 9 8 7 6 5 4 3 2

This is a work of fiction. Names, characters, places and incidents are either the
product of the author's imagination or are used fictitiously and any resemblance
to any actual person, living or dead, events or locales is entirely coincidental.

ISBN 9780143103134

Typeset in Perpetua by R. Ajith Kumar, New Delhi
Printed at Repro India Ltd, Navi Mumbai

This book is sold subject to the condition that it shall not, by way of trade
or otherwise, be lent, resold, hired out, or otherwise circulated without the
publisher's prior consent in any form of binding or cover other than that in
which it is published and without a similar condition including this condition
being imposed on the subsequent purchaser.

www.penguinbooksindia.com

To the memory of my mother Prakashvati
who, more than any other,
wanted to see this work
by my father,
in English translation

These tarnished rays, this night-smudged light
This is not that Dawn for which, ravished with freedom,
we had set out in sheer longing
                    —'Dawn of Freedom', Faiz Ahmed Faiz
              (Translated from the Urdu by Agha Shahid Ali)

Contents

Contents

Introduction

I. Life and Works

FOR HALF A CENTURY NOW, HINDI READERS HAVE BEEN OF THE VIEW THAT THIS novel is the greatest Partition novel ever written. Yashpal's *Jhootha Sach* (2 vols, 1958, 1960; literally, The False Truth), beginning in the early 1940s in Lahore and carrying its populous cast of characters forward up to 1957 in Delhi, has an epic sweep, a degree of verisimilitude, and a range of human concerns that no other novel on this cataclysmic theme in any language can begin to match. The vast Anglophone discourse on Partition and its literary representations, which got a new fillip in 1997 when it was the fifty years not so much of Independence as of Partition that emerged as the focus of attention at least in intellectual and academic discussions, will need to be substantially recast now that this novel becomes available in English. So far, it may even seem, it has all been a bit like talking about *Hamlet* without the Prince of Denmark.

A Revolutionary Life

Yashpal led the kind of dynamic and dramatic life that could itself be the stuff of fiction. Born on 3 December 1903 in Ferozepore Cantt in Punjab where his mother worked in an orphanage, he was educated initially, from age seven to fourteen, at the Gurukul Kangri, an Arya Samaj institution where he imbibed reformist Hindu values as well as an intense hatred for foreign rule. After further schooling in Lahore, he went for his BA to the National College there where he met Bhagat Singh, Sukhdev and Bhagvati Charan, and became with them a prominent member and then leader of what later came to be called the Hindustan Socialist Republican Association/ Army (HSRA) which worked for liberating India through revolutionary armed struggle. After his more famous comrades had shot dead the British police officer Saunders in Lahore on 17 December 1928 and thrown bombs in the Central Assembly in Delhi on 8 April 1929, Yashpal himself on 23 December 1929 detonated the bomb which blew up the dining car of the Viceroy's special train while Lord Irwin, two carriages away, was thrown out of his bed to the floor.

After Chandrashekhar 'Azad' died in a shoot-out with the police on 27 February 1931, the HSRA regrouped with Yashpal being elected as its commander-in-chief. On being ambushed by the police in the house in Allahabad of an Irish woman sympathizer who had taken the name Savitri, Yashpal ran out of ammunition and was arrested on 23 January 1932. He was subjected to ideological interrogation and attempts at persuasion by the British police officer with whom he had before being arrested exchanged bullets and by a loyal Indian police officer with whom he traded verses from the Bhagavad Gita, each of them citing *shlokas* which supported their own respective beliefs. Defended in court by his lawyer Shyam Kumari Nehru, a niece of Jawaharlal, Yashpal was sentenced to fourteen years' rigorous imprisonment.

Meanwhile, for some years before his arrest, he had developed a relationship with another member of his revolutionary group, Prakashvati, and now from jail he wrote to her offering to release her from all bonds so that she could lead her own free life. In response, she petitioned the authorities to be permitted to marry Yashpal, and as nothing could be found in the jail regulations to deny such an unprecedented request, they were married in jail in a brief civil ceremony conducted by the Deputy Commissioner on 7 August 1936, following which Yashpal returned to the barracks and Prakashvati to study dentistry in Karachi. As a result of the elections held under the newly passed Government of India Act, a Congress Government came to power in the United Provinces in 1937 and one of its first acts was to order the release of all political prisoners, including, after some initial objections from the British Governor, a violent militant such as Yashpal. The HSRA was by now virtually disbanded and defunct, and his release on 2 March 1938 marked the end of Yashpal's life as a revolutionary.

Literary Career

Barred from entering Punjab, Yashpal now decided to make Lucknow his home, and he took to writing as his new calling, wishing to use it as a medium for the same political ends. He founded a Hindi journal titled *Viplava* (i.e., revolution, or more accurately, cataclysm, with the same etymological connotation of a deluge that drowns out the old order), which he described as 'the avant garde of the Indian National Movement'. His wife set up a publishing house called Viplava Karyalaya in 1941 and a printing press—Sathi Press—in 1944. Prakashvati stood by him not as a romantic muse but rather as a more sturdy and pragmatic partner who helped Yashpal find the creative and intellectual space for going on to write seventeen collections of short stories, twelve novels, and over twenty other books of essays, political analysis and travelogue.

Probably wisely from an artistic point of view, he did not, except in his first novel, turn his experiences as a revolutionary into fiction; instead, he wrote them up as a detailed factual account or personal testimony under the title *Simhavalokan* (3 vols, 1951, 1952, 1955; literally, A Lion's Eye-View but idiomatically and more modestly, A Backward Glance); this is available in selected extracts in English translation together with a linking commentary by Corinne Friend under the title *Yashpal Looks Back* (1981). (For further bibliographical information on English translations of Yashpal's works and for a selection of his photographs, see www.viplava.com).

On the postage stamp that was issued in his honour, Yashpal is described as 'writer and patriot'—except that the parallel Hindi text, '*krantikari va lekhak*' (revolutionary and writer) seems rather more accurate both in terms of chronology and political category. It is a rare conjunction, matched in Hindi perhaps only by Satchidanand Hiranand Vatsyayan 'Agyeya' (1911–87) whom Yashpal mentions as a younger and technically expert member of the HSRA, who wrote an autobiographical novel he had first sketched out in jail, *Shekhar: Ek Jivani* (2 vols, 1942, 1944; Shekhar: A Life), and whose reputation as a novelist and poet in Hindi, I think, stands even higher than Yashpal's. One wonders what would have happened to revolution on the one hand and literature on the other had some other revolutionaries with a marked literary inclination and talent lived on, such as Bhagat Singh or Ramprasad 'Bismil', author of '*Sarfaroshi ki tamanna ab hamare dil men hai*' (We have now decided to put a price on our heads), perhaps the most defiant and moving of all the revolutionary poems in Hindi/Urdu.

Yashpal's first published book was *Pinjre ki Udan* (1938; The Flight of the Cage), comprising short stories written in jail. As with many Indian (as distinct from Western) writers, his numerous short stories are regarded as constituting quite as important a part of his oeuvre as his longer fiction. Of his twelve novels, five are regarded as 'short novels' (but only relatively, for they are still on average over 200 pages in length) while the others are more extensive in scope. His other works include collections of essays and accounts of his travels to several Western countries including several times to the Soviet Union, to several other communist countries of the Eastern Bloc, and to Mauritius.

Most of Yashpal's fiction show a committed and urgent engagement with contemporary issues and reality. The three predominant themes that can be said to run throughout his work are revolution, romance and gender equality, and they all come blended together in most of his major fiction, though not always in artistic harmony or with thematic cogency. Four of his early novels are all concerned with the evolving political situation in the country while they also explore the complexity of man–woman relationships including the place of sex in them. *Dada Comrade* (1941) depicts under thin disguise some aspects of Yashpal's own experiences as a revolutionary including the phase in which he was sentenced by the central committee of the HSRA to be executed but was later exonerated and restored, and his subsequent journey to communism; in a much controverted scene, its heroine appears in the nude before the celibate hero at his request. *Deshdrohi* (1943; Traitors) attempts to exonerate workers of the Communist Party from the charge of betraying the nation in 1942 when, following the Party line, they supported the British. *Party Comrade* (1946; reprinted as *Gita*) is centred on the naval mutiny that took place that year, and *Manushya ke Roop* (1949; The Many Faces of Man) shows how characters who are influenced in their conduct by ideology are still subject to their circumstances. These skeletal summaries do not reflect the fact that Yashpal fleshes these novels out with lively characterization, dramatic situations, and a variety of romantic relationships that were thought to be distinctly boldly depicted when these novels were first published and which, in the varying views of different critics, either sweeten or dilute the political content.

With all his concern about the contemporary political situation, Yashpal also wrote three novels set in the remote past. These are interspersed over a wide span of his career and while they illustrate his extraordinary range, they all focus on women characters and serve to reinforce his political convictions and worldview through historical recontextualization. The first and the greatest of these is *Divya* (1945), named after the heroine and set in the times of the rise of Buddhism and its contestation for religious hegemony with traditional Hinduism depicted as hide-bound by its caste system and Brahmin supremacy. Divya is shown as fighting against various kinds of oppression and for her right to social equality and sexual freedom, and she finally decides to go with Marish, a follower of the materialist philosophy of Charvaka, who appears to be the novelist's spokesman.

In *Amita* (1956), written during the Cold War against the background of efforts to promote 'world peace' both by the Soviet Union and Third World leaders and indeed dedicated to Prime Minister Nehru, the climactic episode is the change of heart by Emperor Ashoka after his military victory over Kalinga as a result of his confrontation with the heroine, the child princess of that kingdom. It has been pointed out that this is perhaps the only work by Yashpal in which he is, even if unwittingly, sympathetic to Gandhian values including ahimsa which he had resolutely opposed throughout. In *Apsara ka Shap* (1965), earlier published serially as *Shakuntala*, Yashpal interrogates the version of the story presented by Kalidasa by eliminating the supernatural excuse for Dushyanta's rejection of Shakuntala, ascribing his conduct instead to pragmatic reasons of statecraft and political alliances, and by altogether diminishing his heroic stature.

Not all of these works, and some others not mentioned here, are equally successful as artistic creations, partly because Yashpal was in all senses of the word a professional writer, obliged to write constantly if only in order to make a living while maintaining at the same time a conscientious level of imaginative creativity. Yashpal had already won a place for himself in the front rank of Hindi fiction-writers when, through a fortuitous configuration of circumstances, he began in 1956 to write *Jhootha Sach* in which he would excel himself and produce a classic worthy to rank among the great Indian novels. Having found his stride, he then attempted another novel of comparable ambition and scope which is set chronologically before the time-span of *Jhootha Sach* even though it was published considerably later. This was *Meri Teri Uski Baat* (1974; My, Your and Her Story), which traces the political trajectories of a close group of Hindu, Muslim and Christian young men and women, starting in 1928 (though extending through flashbacks up to the Rowlatt Act of 1919 and even earlier) and going up to the critical year of 1942.

Usha, the heroine of this novel, begins with admiration for Gandhi, soon shifts allegiance to the charismatic and recently bereaved Nehru, has sympathy for Subhas Bose in his strife with Gandhi, and ultimately becomes a communist, while the hero finds his ideological resting point in the Congress Socialist Party. Once again, Yashpal weaves intricately the warp and woof of the political fabric of the nation in all its ideological colours, though some of the shades are predictably more prominent than some others. This was to prove to be his last novel and was awarded the Sahitya Akademi Prize in 1976, days before Yashpal passed away on 26 December that year. With all his vocal criticism of the Congress and the government, he had already been awarded the Padma Bhushan in 1970.

II. The Great Partition Novel

The first volume of *Jhootha Sach* is set in Lahore, a city Yashpal had known well in his youth but had not visited ever since, leaving it in 1931 except on a brief clandestine trip in the mid-1940s; it was, of course, closed to Indians after Partition. In 1955, however, when planning his second visit to the Soviet Union, Yashpal was unexpectedly granted a visa to travel through Pakistan and saw his beloved city again. And he wondered:

Is it the same Lahore that I had last seen in 1945 for a couple of days and whose grandeur still lived in my imagination? Instead of a fairground, it seemed to be a graveyard....The shops were deserted, and the devastated city lay under a pall of gloom. (Yashpal, quoted in Madhuresh, *Yashpal* [Panchkula: Aadhar Prakashan, 2006], p.193; my translation)

Apparently, this visit back became the *donnée* of Yashpal's greatest novel:

I felt constantly agitated. My Panjab and Lahore were gone; could not one preserve even a memory of them? And the anguish of penitence at the folly of collective madness due to communal ill-will? (as above, p. 194)

Lahore and the Motherland

Such an originary impulse accounts for one of the outstanding achievements of the novel: its intimate and loving evocation of Lahore. The first volume of the novel is titled 'Vatan aur Desh', *vatan* being the land where one is born or one's motherland, while *desh* is the nation. It is the forcible split and unnatural dichotomy introduced by Partition between these two normally synonymous terms that lies at the heart of the novel. Nor is vatan evoked here in grand and vast terms. In an artistic masterstroke, Yashpal identifies vatan above all with just one narrow street in Lahore, Bhola Pandhe's Lane, near the Shahalami Gate, with all its buzz of domestic chores, family quarrels, the daily office-going and college-going, the occasional clandestine romance and the ritually celebrated arranged marriages. This tightly knit and fully integrated community inhabiting the lane knows no difference between Hindus, Muslims and Sikhs, at least not until the immediate build-up to Partition.

This '*gali biraadari*', as Yashpal calls it in Hindi (i.e., same-street community or fraternity) constitutes the emotional and imaginative core of the novel. First glimpsed in its humdrum and cheerfully quotidian aspect at the beginning of the novel, it soon develops splinters and is then devastated out of recognition as its inhabitants flee helter-skelter to save their lives. As and when they are later reunited hundreds of miles away in strange Indian cities across the newly drawn border, they instantly reaffirm their old-street loyalty than which they seem to know no greater bond. This little lane is what Partition has parted them from; having to leave their homes here is what has split their lives asunder. This is probably among the most vividly and vibrantly evoked locales in the whole modern literature of the subcontinent, and such depiction is made the more poignant by the fact that all too soon it is irrevocably gone and lost forever. The emotional impact of the novel seems to be in direct proportion to the imaginative completeness with which Yashpal created this core location, for the rest of the novel seems to follow naturally and inevitably from it. It is possible to map the lanes, roads and various neighbourhoods of Lahore accurately enough from this novel, as it is in the case of Joyce's Dublin which was also recreated from memory in exile, with the difference that in this case, the geographical verisimilitude exists not only for its own sake (or indeed for art's sake) but also serves to undergird the imaginative authenticity of the historical tumult.

Such scrupulous specificity of space is fully matched by Yashpal's plotting of fictional time. The main characters are quickly introduced and then, all of them are shown to live under an air of tense apprehension as more and more dire news follow in rapid succession. The hero Jaidev Puri is himself a writer and an engaged journalist who serves as an antenna for political developments on the fiercely contested national stage. The year 1946, resonant with urgent political sounds of all kinds of import, gives way to 1947, and now each day seems to dawn with some new foreboding. Over the last few months in the run-up to Independence, from May 1947 onwards, almost each successive development is flagged with a precise date by Yashpal: 4 May, 11 May, various dates in June when the deadline for transfer of power is still believed to be June 1948 as announced by Attlee, and then from late July almost every alternate day is marked by unforeseen events that gather pace to sweep the characters literally off their feet. It is as if the whole cast of the novel were holding their breath and listening to the ticking away of a time-bomb.

In contrast, the second volume of the novel, covering a whole decade from 1947 to 1957 and set in Delhi, Jalandhar and Lucknow with many spatial intersections, unfolds at a markedly slower pace, to convey mimetically the effect that while lives can be uprooted and devastated in virtually a moment, before one knows what has happened, it takes forever to pick up the pieces that are left and to rearrange them in some residual pattern of survival. In the novel's compositional harmony and rhythm, the sweeping *drut* of the disaster is followed by a long *vilambit* of rescue and recuperation. The novel carries on until 1957 for one other strategic reason, which is that Yashpal wishes to show a corrupt Congress minister losing in the general elections held that year!

Men and Women

The novel begins with the death of an old woman and though the laid-down rituals of mourning that follow are somewhat comically treated, the death and the change in domestic order is a premonition of many more deaths and the change in the political order that will swiftly follow. It is significant that it is a woman who dies and not some old patriarch, which is the figure more familiarly deployed in fiction to signal the change of an era. Throughout his fiction but most notably in this novel, Yashpal creates a whole range of strong women characters, with Tara, Kanak, Sheelo, Urmila and Banti the foremost among them, who are nearly all distinctly attractive in traditional feminine ways but who turn out to be far more than that. Being women, they are, predictably, the main victims of the catastrophic events and they suffer the most, but then, unusually, they also pick themselves up and with sheer grit and determination and a sturdy independence of mind and action, they build a new life for themselves—except Banti who dies protesting against hypocritical male norms of family honour.

In a large number of cases, such reconstruction of their lives involves not only overcoming adverse public circumstances but also taking a decision to liberate themselves from the men thrust upon them by arranged marriages, and boldly marching out in defiance of all convention to forge new bonds with other men these women have themselves chosen to love. Their valiant actions in the public sphere are fully matched by their hard-won autonomy in that inner domain which is equally the arena of sexual politics.

Correspondingly, it is the men in Yashpal's scheme of things here who behave abominably (Somraj, Mohan Lal), or give in and resign themselves with a forced cheerfulness to the circumstances (Pandit Girdharilal), or betray weaknesses of character which subject them to moral degeneration, as in the case of the hero Puri and his political patron Sood. There are, of course, a few good men like Ratan and Gill and above all Dr Pran Nath who play positive roles in private and public life and also help and support the women in various ways—and that is how they prove themselves worthy of the women who choose them.

The novel depicts the gradual fall of the hero, Puri, from his high ideals and principles to devious self-serving practices. In contrast, in what proves to be the central strand of the novel, it also shows the rise of his sister Tara from the depths of the misery and degradation inflicted on her by men to becoming perhaps the most impressively successful of all the fractured and dislocated humans who have been washed upon a strange land and left stranded by the hurricane of history. In her quiet but resolute way, she embodies best the unbreakable spirit of the Punjabi refugee of whom we glimpse numerous other nameless examples inhabiting and indeed swarming the streets and public spaces of Delhi in this populous novel. They are not '*sharanarthis*' (refugees) but, as Yashpal calls them, '*purusharthis*', a term that connotes determined pursuit of a high goal worthy of a true man. In this sense, Tara, with all her innate grace and courtesy, proves herself to be as much of a purusharthi as any man in the novel.

This is the more remarkable because she has suffered as no other character has in what is virtually a sea of suffering. Her abduction and rape seem to constitute perhaps the nadir of all the cruel and dastardly acts committed in the whole novel—except that she is a little later herded together with a number of other women who, we discover, have suffered a similar or even worse fate as they now sit half-naked and starving in the enclosure where they have been locked up and tell their grievous tales to each other.

Artless Art

This whole episode, with its multiple narratives of several raped women whom their ill fortune has momentarily brought together, is presented by

Yashpal in his usual plain prose and seemingly flat style (*sapaatbayani*), with his unblinking narratorial eye not failing to register some little jealousy and class envy among the women even in this extreme situation. But this is because Yashpal tells the whole and unadorned truth with an apparently artless art which is deceptive in its cumulative effect. He appears to follow closely the curve and trajectory of events and to imitate the tenor and sweep of life itself, though this is of course a careful artistic construction. Shortly after the novel was published, Kunwar Narain, a Jnanpith-award winning poet, had acutely enough observed that it lacks any element of poetry and the critic Ram Svarup Chaturvedi has pointed out that in this whole vast narrative, there are few moments when a character stops and reflects on what she or he has experienced. But then, they all seem so constantly buffeted and tossed by the workings of circumstances that they are busy enough just keeping themselves afloat, and as for poetry—as Wilfred Owen said of his poems of World War I—'the poetry is in the pity'. It is not the pity of the author for the characters or the pity of the hapless characters for themselves, which are hardly ever in evidence, but the pity that events have turned out in as they have.

Nevertheless, even in this unremittingly realistic and at places naturalistic flow of the narrative, one may discern a design or pattern that heightens the intensity of the experience. Tara is abducted and raped by a Muslim goonda but, in Yashpal's ordering of events, this is but moments after she has walked out on her no less brutal and abusive Hindu husband on her wedding night. There is irony in the fact that it is a Muslim young man she had loved and wanted to marry and she is now raped by a Muslim. After carrying her home and dumping her on the floor, her abductor Nubbu goes out and lies down and slowly smokes one cigarette and then another and only then saunters in to rape her, with the kind of impersonal cold-bloodedness that we find in Manto's short stories such as 'Open Up' or 'Cold Meat'—except that this scene has none of the charged theatricality of Manto.

As Nubbu rapes Tara, his wife sits outside the door cursing him to hell. The sub-human Nubbu is not dignified by the author with a formal proper name; in fact, he is during the act of rape pointedly and repeatedly called just the '*mard*', and his motive for the act is not only to violate a Hindu woman but also to make money, first by stripping her of all her jewellery and then by selling her off for twenty-five rupees. After the rape, Tara is surrounded by sympathetic Muslim women, and then taken home and looked after by another Muslim, Hafiz-ji, who is a *hafiz* or custodian not only of the Koran (which one must have by heart to earn the title) but equally piously of this woman of another faith; she in turn observes with him and his family the daily fast for ramazan. Hafiz-ji does later suggest to her that she should convert to Islam, and she seems half willing, for she does not care much for either faith. When thrown together with those other raped women, she recalls Hafiz-ji's offer and wonders what good remaining a Hindu has done her and whether she might not have been better off turning a Muslim.

Too many subtle ironies attend upon this climactic scene and enrich its meaning for it simply to have 'happened' without consummate artistic mediation. Another similarly layered and nuanced aspect of this novel is the apparently plain enough language used by the narrator as well as by the characters. Language is, of course, not only a medium here but also a major plank of the agenda of communal division, as is openly enacted and debated time and again in the novel. All the characters in Lahore whether Hindu or Muslim or Sikh speak Punjabi and several words in their speech and even in the author's own narrative are translated within brackets into Hindi by the author himself. The language of formal discourse and literature is Urdu; Puri is an Urdu journalist, and it is only a few women who are proficient in Hindi. Language in this novel is thus not a cause of division but an emblem of shared community, and most characters can speak any of the three languages named above, as well as English, according to the demands of the social situation while the highly anglicized senior bureaucrat Rawat can even quote Kalidasa in Sanskrit. A nicely discriminated deployment of such multilingual polyvocality becomes a means of characterization in the hands of the novelist.

Narrating the Nation

In two interrelated postcolonial formulations, the nation is theorized to be an 'imagined community' (Benedict Anderson), and the novel is acclaimed as the literary genre peculiarly suited to 'narrate the nation' (Homi Bhabha).

Even without the benefit of these recent assertions, and in fact ever since Gandhi in 1918 declared Hindi to be the national language, a number of major Hindi novelists have shown a keenness to take up the burden of narrating the nationalist movement and the liberation of the nation, including Premchand (*Rangabhumi*, *Karmabhumi*, *Godan*), Bhagwati Charan Varma (*Terhe-Merhe Raste*, *Bhoole-Bisre Chitra*) and Satchidanand Hiranand Vatsyayan 'Agyeya' (*Shekhar: Ek Jivani*), to name only the foremost.

It is Yashpal's particular distinction that he has in this epic novel narrated not one but two nations, which are not so much India and Pakistan of the two-nation theory (for he leaves Pakistan well alone), but the vatan and the desh. In his narration, the vatan, or the organic and 'knowable' community, has to be left behind for the desh, the 'imagined community', to come into being and to march on to its future (in the sub-title of the second volume, 'Desh ka Bhavishya', The Future of the Nation). It is a sombre and sobering narrative but not ultimately a tragic one, for most of the characters heroically fight the tumultuous circumstances and forge a new life for themselves in the new nation—above all Tara, who at the end of the novel is an undersecretary with the Government of India.

Such is the overwhelming nature of the historical material out of which this novel is shaped that Yashpal seems to keep in abeyance or at least under artistic control even his familiar ideological predilections. Apparently, he had thought of not Tara but Kanak as the heroine of the novel in which case it might have ended with her marrying Gill, the Marxist activist. As a confirmed 'terrorist' turned communist (though he never formally joined the Party), Yashpal had a long-standing quarrel with Gandhi which was not only ideological but almost personal. When Yashpal had bombed the Viceroy's train, Irwin was travelling to Delhi to meet Gandhi, a meeting which did go ahead on the same day as scheduled, and Gandhi wrote in the next issue of *Young India* (2 January 1930) an article condemning the bombing under the title 'The Cult of the Bomb', in response to which the HSRA published 'The Philosophy of the Bomb' drafted by Yashpal. A visit by Yashpal to Gandhi's ashram in Sevagram and a conversation with him did not help to settle any of the issues between them, and a particularly trenchant tract by Yashpal, titled *Gandhivad ki Shav-Pariskha* (Gandhism:

A Post-mortem), was published at the height of the differences between Gandhi and the communists in 1942. But one would guess none of this from the novel which has many characters critical of Gandhi but also acknowledging the unique power and influence that he wielded, as in the powerfully realized scene set in the evening of the day Gandhi broke what was to be the last of his fasts on 18 January 1948. Nehru comes in for criticism too in the novel but, nevertheless, Tara and the man she finally marries, both work for the government. The nation is a going concern, the *desh* clearly has a *bhavishya*, and the somewhat perfunctorily stuck-on populist conclusion only reinforces the message: 'The people are not inert. Nor are they always silent. The future of the nation is not in the hands of leaders and ministers; it is very much in the hands of the people.'

In the title of a memoir of Yashpal after his death, Bhisham Sahni called him the 'Harbinger of a New World Order'. Sahni was a cosmopolitan Marxist writer who had lived for six years in Moscow, taught English literature in a college of the University of Delhi for a living, and would himself go on to write *Tamas*, one of the most highly acclaimed novels on the Partition. He went on to say:

> Over the last fifty-odd years…world literature has given us many great and engaged writers who include figures such as Pablo Neruda, Nazim Hikmet, Louis Aragon, Faiz Ahmed Faiz and Mahmoud Darwish.Yashpal stands in the same distinguished rank as them. (Sahni, in Madhuresh, ed., *Krantikari Yashpal* [Allahabad: Lokbharati, 1979], p. 37; my translation)

By many other Hindi writers and critics, this novel by Yashpal has been often compared with *War and Peace*, so much so that, with his eyesight failing, Yashpal arranged for someone to come and read Tolstoy's great work to him—perhaps to figure out what the fuss was all about. Now, readers in English will have the joy of reading Yashpal's magnum opus and of figuring out these lofty and enviable comparisons for themselves.

Harish Trivedi

Translator's Note

ALTHOUGH *JHOOTHA SACH* HAD BEEN TRANSLATED, FIRST INTO RUSSIAN AND then into Chinese, years ago, and into nearly all major languages of India following the novel's publication in Hindi in 1960, its English translation had lagged behind for reasons that had more to do with the novel's politics than with the logistics of translating a book of this size. I, therefore, feel privileged to be able to present to the English-reading public the long-awaited translation of one of the landmark works of Hindi literature.

I was reminded of the need for an English translation of Yashpal's best-known work every time I came across references to a few English and translated novels as the sum total and the representative of Indian writing on the Partition. Those who read Indian writing only in English apparently could not have known that *The Journal of Asian Studies* had called *Jhootha Sach* 'the most significant novel about the partition of India' in any language.

It was evident from the widespread celebration of Yashpal's birth centenary all across India in 2003 that there was a resurgence of interest in his writings and that a reappraisal of his work in the present-day context was going on in India and abroad. For me, the realization that it was time to begin my translation—akin to an epiphanic moment —came, I distinctly remember, during a national seminar on Yashpal organized by the Sahitya Akademi in Kolkata in December 2003 when one of the speakers, in his presentation at the event, mentioned that Bhisham Sahni, the eminent Hindi writer famous for his novel *Tamas* on the theme of India's Partition, had once said that 'The only novel about the Partition is Yashpal's *Jhootha Sach*; everything else is merely a footnote.'

Therefore, I was particularly gratified that my translation was well on its way four years later when *Kadambini*, a literary magazine published by the Hindustan Times group, carried the results of a survey of prominent Hindi litterateurs, critiques and scholars to determine the most influential writer of the second half of the twentieth century. They placed Yashpal on the top of a list of the best of Hindi literature.

A novel with as vast a canvas and being as rich in detail as *Jhootha Sach* involves serious decisions about the strategies and methodology of translation, particularly of culture-specific concepts, neologisms and metaphors. Those decisions were, for the most part, made easy by the fact that Yashpal, in the seven books that he had translated into Hindi in his life time, had concentrated on the effective communication of the meaning of the original text rather than a word-to-word translation. Keeping Yashpal's approach in mind and the books translated by him as the model, I freely used the metaphors of the target language, keeping the language supple; I did an English version rather than a literal translation. Having met several people and having witnessed some incidents described in *Jhootha Sach*, especially in 'Desh ka Bhavishya', also helped in conveying the intended meaning of certain passages.

I owe a great deal to Bernard Queenan for making the translation of *Jhootha Sach* a reality. The time he spent as a British Army officer in India during the dying days of the Raj helped immensely in translating the descriptions of the events leading to the Partition from the point of view of—as I jokingly called it—the sahib log. His enthusiasm and commitment to help never flagged, and it is indeed very sad that he did not live to see our joint endeavour reach fruition. Without his help, as in the case of my translation of Yashpal's *Divya*, this work too would have been unforgivably full of errors.

This Is Not That Dawn, from Faiz Ahmed Faiz's poem, is the title of this English translation. Little is known of Yashpal's contact with Faiz, except for a memorable photograph taken in Tashkent in 1958, in which, sitting across a food and beverages-laden table at a friend's home, they seem to be enormously enjoying each other's company. It's possible that Yashpal would have written about his comradeship with Faiz in the fourth volume of his reminiscences that he could not finish.

Anand

Spring 2010

Part I

~

Homeland and Nation

Chapter 1

BOTH DAUGHTERS-IN-LAW WERE PRESENT WHEN THE OLD WOMAN BREATHED her last.

The elder told the younger to announce the death of their mother-in-law with a scream of unbearable pain, mindful of the ritual at the hour of terrible grief.

The younger one was at such a loss that she could not do this right. To observe the tradition properly, the elder went to the window herself and cried out in the required loud, heart-rending voice, as an eagle might cry in agony when pierced by an arrow.

The people in the gali were awakened from their sleep. Meladei, Kartaro, Basant Kaur, Purandei, Jeeva and other neighbours came quickly. The women began to wail and beat their chests. In between their cries of grief, they would console themselves, 'The old woman's time had come. She'd had the good fortune to see the faces of her grandchildren, a reward for her actions of her past life, no doubt.'

The men were gathered on the chabutaras, the raised platforms, beside the front steps of the house. They all mourned the loss of the mother of Master Ramlubhaya and Babu Ramjwaya, and of her guiding presence. They consoled her sons by reminding them that human beings were mortal and it was an impermanent world.

The old woman had lived mostly in the home of her older son, Babu Ramjwaya who worked at the railway parcels office, where he had been employed for twenty-six years. He had bought two dilapidated houses in Uchchi Gali in the neighbourhood of Peepul Behera, and had two new three-storey houses built there. Then, getting greedy, he had even rented out half of his own house.

Ramjwaya's elder son was already married. He and his new bride took over one room of the house. But, even though everyone else in their household was well taken care of, there was no room for the old mother. What would an old woman need a little extra room for, they all thought.

Ramjwaya's wife had a testy temperament which only increased after becoming the owner of two houses. If the mother-in-law ranted with the irritability of old age, the daughter-in-law, who had recently become a

3

mother-in-law herself, could not rest easy without delivering some angry, biting retort. Whenever there was such an exchange, the old woman would think back on the merits of her elder son's first wife. She would then put all her clothes in a small bundle and go to Bhola Pandhe's Gali to the house of her younger son, Master Ramlubhaya, with her bundle under her arm. After a few days, Ramjwaya would go and bring his mother back again, or the old woman would grow annoyed by the lack of space in the house and return to Uchchi Gali to see her elder son's children. But when she arrived at the younger son's house in the winter of 1946, she came down with a bad cold, which turned into pneumonia. Both sons did all they could, but their mother's time had come.

Master Ramlubhaya was a teacher at the Dayanand Anglo-Vedic (D.A.V.) School. Belonging to the reformist Hindu Arya Samaj movement, he was himself a reformist in his beliefs. According to him, the rituals performed to assuage the grief and to cleanse the house after their mother's death were hymn singing and the havan ceremony. The women of the gali were dismayed when they heard about the proposal to sing subdued bhajans and to perform the fire ceremony, instead of the customary mourning ritual of syapa. They raised objections saying, 'Goodness, how can this be allowed? She was a good woman, she had grandsons and granddaughters … and she'd even seen the face of her grandson's bride before she died. If her bier isn't decorated properly and a syapa not held, what will be done when a young person dies?'

The old woman had died in Master Ramlubhaya's house, so her bier was carried out from his doorway. But she was also Babu Ramjwaya's mother, so when it came to whether or not the old woman's last rites were to take place with the established decorum his honour was in question as well.

The expense of providing the elaborate decorations needed for the bier of such a fortunate woman was not within the reach of a poor schoolteacher. Ramjwaya also felt distressed and ashamed that his mother, who had lived in his house in the city, had died in the home of his younger brother. Thus, though their mother's last rites were performed in his younger brother's house in Bhola Pandhe's Gali, Ramjwaya took care of all the expenditure and provisions so that he could make an appropriate show of respect towards his mother.

Masterji lived on the top floor of a rented house. There was a common faucet in the aangan, the inner courtyard, and the rooms around it contained the landlord's cloth warehouse. There were only a large room, a kitchen and a veranda upstairs. But in accordance with tradition, the syapa gathering could not take place on the top floor. The in-laws of Babu Ramjwaya and Masterji, and other relatives from their ancestral village were expected to come. In the house adjacent to Masterji's lived the postal worker Babu Birumal and the insurance company clerk Tikaram. There was a three-foot-wide path that ran next to the two houses, at the end of which was another small courtyard. All the gali ceremonies and mourning gatherings took place in this open space. The straw mats for the syapa ceremony were spread out here.

Upon hearing the news of the old woman's death, the sisters of the Buddh Samaj arrived. This group advocated eradicating outdated rituals from society, replacing them instead with socially uplifting customs. The sisters asked the family to shun the evil custom of syapa, and to sing devotional bhajans urging detachment from the world. The elder daughter-in-law refused to listen to the sisters, saying, 'How can we abandon our old customs and be embarrassed in front of everyone? People will talk about us and say we were afraid of spending money...'

So Ramjwaya's wife sent for Kaula the naun. Kaula was considered to be an expert at performing syapa. In keeping with custom all the women who participated in the syapa, wore black lehangas and large cotton chadars made of thick muslin, coloured with diluted ashes. The women from the community and acquaintances came in ordinary clothing. Of the women in the family, only the young unmarried ones and recent brides were exempted from wearing mourning clothes. When mourning an old man or woman, the family usually made some sort of display to show the success in the life of the deceased. The ritual on such occasions was for the old person's unmarried granddaughters and granddaughters-in-law to dress up in special jewellery and clothing and sit near the circle. The naun sat between both the daughters-in-law. The other women sat in orderly circles, so that the ones with the closest relationship to the deceased were nearest to the daughters-in-law, and those with more distant ties further away.

Kaula the naun introduced the first cry of the mourning chant, 'Say the name of Ram, dear sisters.' The women imitated her in unison.

The naun chanted laments remembering the old woman, 'Who had a full and flourishing family, beloved mother.' The women took up the refrain, 'Hai-hai, beloved mother.'

The naun said, 'Who ruled over the household, beloved mother.'

The women repeated, 'Hai-hai, beloved mother.'

The naun said, 'Mistress of many houses and gardens, beloved mother.'

The women followed, 'Hai- hai, beloved mother.'

Then the women began to beat their chests with their hands in a steady rhythm. The naun called out the words of the mourning litany in a pain-filled, tremulous voice, and the women kept saying 'hai-hai, hai-hai', beating their chests with both hands. There was a definite pattern in this tradition of mourning and breast-beating. The women's hands fell sometimes on their chests, sometimes, in sequence, on their thighs and chests, then on their thighs, chests and cheeks. In accordance with signals from Kaula, this performance was enacted in a slow rhythm, sometimes more quickly and then at times at an intensely fast pace; sometimes the women were seated and sometimes they stood.

The naun led this ceremony with alertness and discipline. If a woman fell out of rhythm, the naun could eject her from the gathering. If someone with closed eyes or, on the other side of a wall, heard the women, it would have seemed to them that a squad of well-drilled soldiers was doing the quick march, about-turns and marking time.

The intensity of a syapa is always proportionate to the grief caused by the bereavement. The grief is enhanced for a death that has occurred in the fullness of youth and less so for the death of an old person. The death of Ramjwaya's mother was an occasion where the joy was greater than the grief. But no slackness was shown in the performance of the ceremonies. Whatever negligence the old woman faced in her lifetime was compensated for with respect after her death.

Each stage of the refrain and the chest-beating lasted for four or five minutes. During the intervals, when they rested, the women talked about syapa ceremonies that they had attended in the past, and also probable marriage engagements. Distant relations and other women from the community who came would sit close to the mourning women and talk about other things, or work on the handiwork they had brought along. Their presence was taken as their participation.

A dhurrie was spread out on the chabutara to make a reception area for the men so that they could observe the mourning. Both brothers had shaved their heads and faces. The brothers sat in the midst of their guests, heads bowed. The redness of weeping lingered in their eyes. People came and sat near them quietly for a minute or two at first. Then the visitors would begin to talk about the love and kindness of parents. They expressed sympathy for the two brothers now that the shade and shield of their mother's guiding hand had been lifted from their heads. They would go away after repeating the precept of obtaining peace of mind through indifference to worldly things.

Babu Ramjwaya and Masterji would join their palms together and say, 'Please come again,' and thank them for their condolences. This was the sign for the guests that they could get up and leave; they would not go away until they received this kind of signal from the mourning family two or three times.

In this practice of mourning, all these efforts of vigilance, care and control were necessary so that the bereaved minds would not have a chance to dwell over the shock of grief. Grief was thus turned into a ritual duty as also a psychological remedy for mastering it and then releasing it.

On the fourth day after the death, the final rites were carried out. Ramjwaya's daughter-in-law came dressed in jewellery and special clothing. Masterji's daughter Tara, and Ramjwaya's daughter Sheelo, also had to wear new, colourful silk clothing and sit near the mourners for a while.

In the afternoon, Sheelo and Tara took their little brothers and sisters to Masterji's house to chat and have something to eat and drink. They asked Sheelo's sister-in-law to come with them too, but she said she had a headache and went back home.

Sheelo usually liked to nibble on salty or sweet tit-bits as she chatted. Because she got engaged six months ago, she had received two rupees at her grandmother's funeral rites. Poor Tara was not engaged yet, so she didn't get any gift or money. Before leaving for Tara's house, Sheelo went to the bazaar at the entrance to the gali and bought two annas' worth of freshly fried *mongra* in leaf cups.

Tara's house was empty. Her elder brother Jaidev was away at college. Tara gave a rubber doll and a rattle to her one-year-old sister, spread out a straw chatai and lay down next to Sheelo. They placed the leaf cups between them, and chewing on the snacks, they began to talk.

Sheelo said, 'You know, my Bhabhi got a lehanga, a dupatta and five rupees! Still she kept complaining. She wanted ten rupees instead. And you saw that when we asked her, she didn't come to your house. Said she had a headache. What a liar! When she gets home she'll go to her room with my brother, close the door, and do you-know-what. She's so shameless that she doesn't even care what time of day it is.'

'What?' Tara asked.

'Oh!' Sheelo smiled and said in a knowing voice, 'I peeked through a crack in the door and saw them. Haven't you ever seen it?'

Tara's face reddened with embarrassment, 'There's only one room in the house. Brother and Masterji sleep in the veranda. One night when I woke up to go to toilet ... ' Tara hid her face with both hands.

Overcome with laughter and embarrassment, she could hardly speak, 'Hai, how to tell you! Hari, he's only a child, and little Peeto who lives right across from our house; the girl who was wandering around without any shirt just now. Hai, how can I say it? They began to do... whatever in Peeto's aangan. When Kartaro Auntie saw them, she dragged Hari over to mother and started to fight with her, "What're you teaching the children? Have you no shame?"'

'Mother shot back, "It was probably you who taught them. Your Peeto is older than my boy." They had a big fight.

'When Masterji came and heard, he gave Hari one good thrashing. He shouted at mother too, "Why don't you put some underwear on that boy?" That's what our house is like. Peeto's house is just as small. These poor kids see things and think it's just a game. I get so embarrassed, it's so shameful.'

Sheelo added her bit in a conspiratorial tone, 'Guess what? I've seen father and mother too.' She asked after some thought, 'Are you afraid of boys?'

Tara replied, 'Some boys are bad. They tease so much I can't stand it.'

Sheelo said, 'You know Baldev from our gali, I really like him. He's so shameless, he winks every time I look at him.'

They heard the sound of footsteps coming quickly up the stairs. Sheelo asked, 'Your brother?'

Tara said, 'It's probably Ratan.'

The door to the room was already open. Ratan, the son of Babu Govindram, the neighbour from the other half of the house, peered in with books under his arm, and asked, 'Auntie hasn't come back from the mourning yet? My mother isn't back as well.'

Tara answered back curtly, 'How can they be back so soon?' Ratan went away.

Sheelo had met Ratan several times before at Tara's house. He was studying in the eleventh standard, and was about three years older than Tara. He was fair and tall and beginning to show a moustache.

Sheelo smiled and looked into Tara's eyes, 'My, he's turned out to be a real good-looker. Doesn't he talk to you?'

Tara's face became serious as she said, 'He's really bad news. Always staring. When we meet on the stairway, he starts acting smart. I tell him: "Shame on you! Go to hell! Don't you dare touch me! I'll scream and tell your mother!"'

Ratan and Tara had both been born in this same house. As kids, wearing only underpants, they played hide-and-seek, hopscotch and other games with the children of the gali. As they got older, they began to spend less time together. Once when Tara was eleven, she was coming home from school when some boys from another gali pushed her and made her drop her schoolbooks. When Tara came into the gali crying, Ratan who was also returning home from school, saw her and asked, 'Did someone hit you?'

Fresh tears began to flow from Tara's eyes.

Ratan grabbed Tara by the arm and said, 'Come on, show me who.'

Tara went back with Ratan to exact revenge. Ratan swore at the boys and challenged them. The boys from both sides put their school bags down on the street in the bazaar and had a scuffle. Tara looked on with pride. The people in the bazaar separated the boys and stopped the fight.

Panting, Ratan warned them, 'You'd better watch out when you touch a girl from our gali else I'll bust your heads open!'

When Ratan came home, blood was oozing from a wound on his head. He told his mother, 'I fell down at school, it's nothing really.'

Tara thought of Ratan as someone of her age and her gali companion. Ratan was closer to her than the other boys in the gali, and he was more refined and more educated than Bir Singh and Meva Lal. A kinship had developed between them. Two years later, Ratan had started to be a little playful. Tara scolded him, but she didn't mind at all. She knew he liked her.

They heard a call from Ratan's house, from the other side of the staircase, 'Tara, there's no daal or vegetables here for me. If there's any in your house, give me some too.'

Tara looked at Sheelo meaningfully, 'See what trouble he gives me! Why should I go?'

Sheelo said, 'Oh come on, I'll take it to him. Tell me where the vegetables are.'

Sheelo put some vegetables left over from the morning in a bowl, went to the other side of the stairway and called, 'Where are you? Here are your vegetables.' She gave him the food and returned.

Tara and Sheelo continued to talk for a while. Tara's mother could not leave the mourning till after sunset. Tara told Sheelo to watch her baby sister and started kneading the dough for the chapattis for dinner. Sheelo sat near her and told stories about different fights that had happened in her gali. A little while later, Sheelo said lifting the baby girl, 'I'm going to take Munni and sit upstairs. I need some fresh air and Munni can play there just as well. You cook the chapattis.'

Tara put the daal on the fire and began to roll the chapattis. Soon she had made the chapattis, scattered the coal to lower the heat, washed the kneading tray and the rolling pin and board and put them away. Then she climbed the stairs leading to the open roof to talk to Sheelo.

Munni was sitting on the roof in a pool of her own pee, biting her squeaky rubber doll with her two rice-grain-like little teeth, and cooing happily to herself. Tara did not see Sheelo anywhere. She walked ahead without calling out and peered on the other side of the barsati, and immediately turned back in shock. Ratan had Sheelo in his arms and was kissing her on the mouth.

They were startled on hearing Tara gasp. Tara didn't say anything; she just picked up Munni and went down, her feet thudding on the stairs.

After a few minutes Sheelo came downstairs as well. Tara didn't speak to her. Sheelo said pleadingly, her eyes downcast, 'He just grabbed me.'

'Get out of here, you liar!' Tara turned her face away.

When Sheelo sat down quietly with her head bowed, Tara could not stand it anymore. She moved closer to Sheelo and said, 'Have some shame, you stupid girl! You're already engaged.'

'So what?' Sheelo replied, head down, raking the cement filling between the bricks with her toenail, 'I hardly did anything.'

'What didn't you do?' Lowering her voice, Tara said angrily, 'If someone from the gali had seen you, they would have cut off all your hair and broken his bones too, you idiot. And they would have thrown us out of the gali. You're so shameless!'

After that evening, Tara began to detest Ratan. In the past Tara's scowling had had little effect on Ratan; her tone would give her away, that there was no bad feeling behind it. But now there was loathing in Tara's eyes. She was angry with both Ratan and Sheelo. They had both fooled her.

At their grandmother's mourning ceremony, Sheelo had been given some money. Tara's mother thought nothing of the present of two rupees and two sets of clothes, but it was proof of the fact that the elder daughter-in-law's daughter was engaged while Bhagwanti's daughter was not. It didn't matter that Tara was only two-and-a-half months older than Sheelo; she was still older. Tara was also two years ahead of Sheelo in school. Even though she was just fifteen, people thought she was older at least by a couple of years. She was even the same height as her elder brother.

Tara's mother was unhappy about her husband's unrealistic ideas. What need was there to educate a girl so much, and so quickly? Who would be tempted by the dowry of a poor schoolteacher's daughter? Masterji's expectation that his daughter's intelligence and education would attract a bridegroom was being proven false. Only the wife of her husband's elder brother could be of any help to Tara's mother in such a difficult situation. For this reason, even at the risk of neglecting all her work at home, Bhagwanti went to her sister-in-law's house to lend a hand in the making of papad and *bariyan*, and to spin cotton stuffing from old quilts for making dhurries.

Sheelo's mother was two years younger than Tara's mother, but being the wife of the elder brother, her status was that of the senior daughter-in-law. A woman's standing is the reflection of her husband's social position. Ramjwaya's first wife had died after giving birth to a son. Ramjwaya's second marriage brought Sheelo's mother into the family. As is customary, she got more care and attention.

She had a fondness and taste for dressing up. She would not go out without wearing silk. Tara's mother's clothing and behaviour appeared lacklustre and inferior when she walked beside her elder sister-in-law. Wrapped in a thick muslin chadar and wearing a discoloured silken lehanga or shalwar, Tara's mother seemed five years older than her age. She had been wearing the same two one-tola gold bangles on her wrists since her marriage. Sheelo's mother wore two tissue-paper thin, well-starched 'chhabbi' brand muslin dupattas together that looked white and frothy as foam. Different gold bracelets and bangles appeared on her wrists. Her smooth glowing face and her pride in her youthfulness made her look even younger. She also carried herself with authority.

There was the same contrast between Master Ramlubhaya and Babu

Ramjwaya. Masterji always had a worn look, and wore a round brown hat and a coat that buttoned up to the neck. Out of thriftiness he always shaved his own beard; moreover, he only had Mondays and Thursdays off from school, and he never bothered to shave his chin on those two days. His moustache, two-thirds white, covered his lips, and after drinking water he always had to wipe it dry.

Babu Ramjwaya was issued a summer and a winter uniform by the railway, but for social occasions he did not wear the company's clothing, wearing his own instead. He wore a starched turban of fine muslin, a very white starched shirt with a collar, and loose pajama trousers. The red silk brocade ends of the pajama waist-cord peeked out slightly from under the edge of his shirt. He wore a coat with a collar, cotton or wool, according to the season. He had never worn a necktie or Western-style trousers. The barber shaved his chin every other day, and trimmed his salt-and-pepper moustache along the line of his upper lip to keep it looking neat. There was always a certain smoothness to the skin of his face.

Lala Sukhlal Sahni had come to express his condolences at the mourning for Babu Ramjwaya's mother, and his wife had come for the syapa ceremony. Lala Sukhlal had no family relationship with Ramjwaya; rather, they had a deeper, professional relationship. Ostensibly, Sukhlal transported goods towards the east and the west of Lahore, but he had other dealings as well. One of his businesses had to do with the forwarding of parcels sent by rail.

When Lala Sukhlal Sahni's wife Jayarani came to the syapa ceremony, she already was in a state of mourning. Three months earlier her daughter-in-law had passed away. The talk of her daughter-in-law's sickness and death led to hushed hints and suggestions for a second engagement for her son Somraj.

Jayarani said to Sheelo's mother, 'Bahin, you know, there's no shortage of girls for our son. We'd not even returned home after cremating her body when offers had already come from five places. But I won't rush things, this time. The poor girl had a good nature, and her parents didn't give a bad dowry either, but the truth is that the boy's heart wasn't in that marriage. She was a little simple and her features and figure were rather ordinary. The boy just didn't want to stay at home. The poor girl got the influenza, that fever of colds and coughs. We consulted all the doctors from Vacchovali and Mall Road, but who can erase what God has written? This time, whatever happens, I'll select a girl only after a thorough inquiry, and only one with a pretty face and shapely figure. I'll show her to the boy somehow; that'll be the only suitable way. You know boys nowadays! I don't care much about the dowry. I'll accept whichever girl the boy looks at and says yes....'

Seeing an opportunity, Sheelo's mother said, 'My younger brother-in-law is a schoolteacher. He's a good soul but they're poor. Won't be able to give a big dowry, but believe me, the girl's face is one in a thousand; so fair that it becomes dirty if touched by anyone's hand. Her eyes are lovely and shapely, like slices of mango. She's only two months older than my Sheelo, but a couple of inches taller. Just like a jewel, and she's studying in the tenth standard. Always stands first in her class, but my sister-in-law, poor thing ...'

Only a few days later, Sukhlal Sahni's son Somraj went away for a while on some business, and nothing could come of this proposed match for a whole year.

In 1943, Tara passed the matriculation exam with a first division. Her brother Jaidev insisted that she should be allowed to study up to BA level. Jaidev was in the second year of his MA at Dayal Singh College. Tara also took admission there. But only two months later, Jaidev was sent to prison for being a part of a secret political movement. Tara attended college without her brother.

Two years later, Tara appeared for the Intermediate examination. Every day she had to go to the examination hall at nine o'clock in the morning. One day Sheelo came early and said, 'Today I'm going to accompany you.'

There was a twinkle of mystery in Sheelo's eyes. She was not able to suppress her smile.

Bhagwanti looked at Tara's clothes and commented, 'What's this, you're going out wearing such wrinkled clothes? Comb your hair carefully.' She took out Tara's best shalwar, kameez and dupatta, and asked her to wear those.

Tara was by nature clean and tidy. Her mother had never commented on her clothes before. Masterji liked simplicity. Tara could not understand the need to put on such clothing to go to an exam, just as she could not understand Sheelo's secretive smile. She changed her clothes on her mother's insistence, suspecting she would be late if she argued about it. While they were going down the stairs from her house, she asked, 'What's the matter? Why aren't you telling me what is up?'

'Today, on the street, he'll see you. When he sees me with you, he'll recognize you. I'll warn you. You also get a look at him,' Sheelo said. Tara didn't like this. She had begun to think differently about her life.

Two Sundays before, Tara's classmate Amrita had gone to her ancestral home in Ambala Cantonment. When she came back she told them that she'd been called for her engagement. Amrita's parents had modern and liberal opinions. Before the engagement, they had invited the boy for tea at their house and introduced Amrita to her future bridegroom. Although both were shy and nervous, they'd even had a little conversation. When the boy and girl agreed, the date of the engagement was fixed. The girls had insisted that Amrita give a party, and she had given quite a lavish one for six girls at the Standard restaurant.

Gurtu and Sneha were the gossipy ones in their group. Gurtu asked Amrita, 'What did you find out about that boy in an hour?'

Sneha answered for her, 'What does it matter what she found out? Boys are all the same. She saw that he was good-looking, and that he's a lieutenant in the army. What more could she want?'

Krishna said, 'Amrita's fate has been decided. When her lieutenant gets some leave, they'll get married. She'll keep house, she'll have children. They'll bring them up and then they'll worry about marrying them off.'

Amrita asked, 'And when you become a doctor, you won't get married?'

Sneha said, 'As soon as she has a child, she'll forget all about doctoring!'

Tara felt compelled to say, 'That's right, a mother never has any free time when she's taking care of children. She becomes completely wrapped up in that alone.'

Krishna replied, 'We'll get an ayah, what's wrong with that?'

Surendra joked, 'Will you get an ayah for your child when it's still in your womb?'

Sneha interrupted, 'Then why not an ayah in place of you...?' All the girls burst out in laughter.

Surendra said thoughtfully, 'That's really a girl's problem and tough luck. When one has children, one's life becomes completely devoted to them.'

Amrita interrupted her, 'So you don't want children? What about a husband?'

Surendra agreed, 'Sure, a husband is necessary.'

Sneha asked, 'In college only the girls give engagement parties. Why don't boys do the same?'

Gurtu said, 'The boys don't talk about it. The more girls those idiots can make friends with, the better they like it. For a girl, just one friendship with a boy and she's had it.'

Krishna explained seriously, 'The thing is that boys wants to play around and girls want to settle down.'

Gurtu complained, 'What do boys get out of marriage anyway? They might suffer under the yoke of marriage, but also feel good about being the lord and master. They can do what they want, who stops them? Girls do indeed gain prestige and a licence of respectability from marriage. But a woman's womb is her greatest curse.'

Surendra suggested, 'There should be marriage but no children.'

'And remain an object of ridicule for your entire life?' said Amrita. 'People would call you infertile.'

'Oh my, that's even worse!' Sneha exclaimed.

Surendra said, 'Come on, what's all this talk? As if love and companionship for life mean nothing!'

'What kind of love is that?' Gurtu objected, glancing towards Amrita, 'Your parents said: Love this boy! As soon as you had permission, or got an order, you fell in love!'

Surendra said, 'I'll never act like that. I'll choose my companion all by myself.'

Tara agreed with her. Surendra continued, 'The real thing is falling in love. When you've got married, you're bound for life!'

Amrita said, 'Love hardly ever happens in any special way! Love just happens.'

Tara faced the very problem only one week later.

When Sheelo and Tara came out of the Shahalami Gate, they walked through the walled garden towards the Lohari Gate.

'Look at that boy up ahead. The one in the silk suit, he's looking in our direction!' Sheelo said, pressing Tara's arm.

After one glance, Tara couldn't look at him again; she had to lower her eyes. She didn't like the way the boy was rudely staring at her.

Tara studied alongside boys in the college. She had seen good boys and bad boys. Among themselves, Tara and her girlfriends called the kind of boy who stared 'stupid', 'rude' and 'girl gazers'. Such boys disgusted them and they made fun of them. They avoided the 'girl gazer' kind of boys, such as Avinash, one of the BA students. If he saw some girl standing alone, he would approach her and ask very quietly, 'It's the —th of this month today, isn't it?' This was a trick to make other guys believe that the guy was very friendly with that girl. Tara liked the spontaneous and easy manner of some boys, like the ones who participated in college societies, debates and the Student Federation; like Asad bhai saheb, the MA student at the Christian College—direct, spontaneous, friendly and respectful.

Though Tara had said several times at home, in front of her mother, 'I won't get married. I'm going to keep on studying up to MA level,' nobody paid her any attention. Nobody even asked her about it. One day she heard that her mother had gone to the Banni Hata mohalla and had given eleven rupees to a family as a goodwill token for her daughter's engagement with some boy. That day Tara had wept all day, especially when no one was around. She thought, it couldn't have happened if my brother was here. She would have been able to explain to him somehow; her brother could not agree to an engagement that was against her wishes.

When Tara had been admitted to Dayal Singh College she thought she would only make friends with girls, but at the beginning of her second year, her opinion and behaviour changed. She enjoyed the company of Surendra, Zubeida, Sneha, Gurtu and other girls in the college who took part in political meetings and the Student Federation. These girls would neither shy away from boys nor avoid them.

Surendra Kaur had become Tara's closest friend. Surendra's brother Narendra Singh had been Jaidev's classmate. He had passed his MA and was studying in the Law College. Narendra Singh was one of the leaders of the Student Federation. Surendra took a very active role in the Federation's work. Tara also began to attend those meetings in the company of Surendra. In the meetings they discussed the international implications of the Second World War. The invasions by Germany and Japan were described as Fascist invasions. India's interest, it was explained, lay in the victory of America and Britain and the defeat of Fascism, of Germany and Japan, under Russia's leadership. They discussed ways to fight the invasion of India by Japan so that the leaders of the Indian nationalist movement could lead the war against Fascism. Whether or not Tara understood anything, she liked their company.

Dayal Singh College subscribed to the Brahmo Samaj ideology. The college professors did not favour sectarian ideas, social conservatism or fanaticism. They advocated tolerance and acceptance of all human beings, and held that God was one and the same in all different religions. The last day of the term in the first year, before the summer vacation began, had left an indelible impression on Tara's mind. The college had organized a picnic at the Tomb of Jehangir, where Hindu, Muslim and Sikh students sat together taking food from each other's hands, and some had even eaten from the same leaf plates. Tara felt a thrill of pleasure in these efforts that pushed differences aside and created a sense of unity.

Tara was attracted to members of the Federation, and to those who were called Communists, for the very reasons they were criticized by society. These people were notorious for ignoring religious differences and social conservatism. In their debates they were always in favour of equality of rights between men and women, and for self-determination inside the bonds of marriage. In their company, Tara, like her brother, also began to argue against outdated conventions. She felt encouraged when her arguments and her quickness of mind were appreciated.

Tara had tolerated Masterji's discipline and religious beliefs since childhood. Masterji forced her and her elder brother Jaidev to get up every morning at the crack of dawn and bathe. He would have them come and sit near him and sing morning and evening bhajans. He had the same kind of rules concerning dressing and other forms of conduct. Jaidev had to have the hair on his head cut short with clippers, and to wear a coat that buttoned up to the neck. After he'd gone to college, Jaidev broke free of these rules. Tara had been ordered to wear her hair in a single braid. She had to keep her head covered when she went outside the house. She wanted to wear a fitted kameez that showed her waist, a shalwar that was wide at the ankles, and cover her head with a dupatta of gossamer-fine cloth, but she was made to wear a loose, shapeless kameez and a shalwar that tapered at the ankles, and she was given a dupatta made of thick cloth. Everybody else in the gali always sang film songs and ghazals, but in Masterji's house that was forbidden. However, after Tara enrolled in college, family control over her was relaxed as well.

Sometimes Tara thought that her father's discipline and rules were too stringent, but then she worried that her own inclinations might be sinful, and she would check her thoughts. In the company of her classmates and friends in the Federation she came to understand that she didn't have to feel guilty about her preferences and tastes. She began to acquire a sense of self-respect. Sometimes she sat in restaurants with Zubeida, Asad or Zuber, and felt the satisfaction of freedom from meaningless conventions, because she was eating and drinking in the company of a Muslim. Conversing without embarrassment or walking with one of the boys in the group, she had a feeling of equality and self-confidence. But in her gali, Tara continued to behave as before, out of deference to her father and the neighbours. In college, that kind of behaviour seemed ludicrous.

Chapter 2

JAIDEV PURI WAS IN THE SECOND YEAR OF HIS MA IN 1943 WHEN HE WAS arrested and sent to prison for taking part in the anti-war movement. He was distraught at the thought of not being able to help his family face the hardships of wartime, but he could not let pass this sacrifice for the freedom of his country. He was convinced that he would soon gain his freedom in a free India, where his troubles would also end along with the woes of the motherland.

Puri made good use of the time spent in Multan Jail. Before his imprisonment, his ambition had been to apply for the position of a lecturer in some college after passing the MA exam with first division, and to earn a name as a writer. His literary talent had impressed his friends. In his student days, he had published essays, full of sentimental pathos, and some short stories in several magazines in Lahore. While other political prisoners spent time massaging themselves with oil and cooking food smuggled into the prison, Puri read and wrote. He would read his own writings with a critical eye, and rewrite them. In the close to two years he spent in the prison, he had finished a collection of short stories after rewriting and polishing them several times. This work, he hoped, would help launch his literary career.

Puri was released from prison in the second week of May 1945. An irony of fate, his freedom was not due to the success of the August 1942 revolution in India and the ouster of British rulers, but in celebration of the victory of Britain and its allies in the Second World War. Even with the country still under the British yoke, Puri was happy and relieved to be out of prison.

Though he had missed his family and worried about them, he had few worries of his own in the prison. Food and clothing were not all that great, but they were provided free. Political prisoners did not suffer any shortages of food or clothing. But on his return he found that the family's circumstances had changed in his absence.

Puri had been back home for three days when his mother said to him, with some hesitation, 'Your father has to do some tutoring after school. I can't stand in the queue at the ration shop with the baby in my arms. Can't ask Tara; there are all sorts of people in that crowd. Usha too has grown up. Can you get a rupee's worth of sugar? The bazaar rate is a rupee and a half for a seer.'

To stand in that queue for nearly two hours was tormenting for Puri. He, who was ready to make any sacrifice for his country, had to struggle for a rupee's worth of sugar; but there was no way out. The war was over, but prices kept on rising. Cloth prices were no different. Masterji was still making do with the same old striped cloth jacket that he had when Puri was sent to prison. Shalwars that his mother, Usha and Tara wore had been patched and mended repeatedly. His mother and sisters cared for their street clothes more than they cared for their skin. Puri could see that the blue striped khaki trousers his younger brother wore had once belonged to the neighbour's son. When Ratan grew out of them, his mother had quietly given them to Bhagwanti.

The ration allotment was for eleven yards of cloth per person every three months. Wheat was two-and-a-half seers per rupee. It could be had at three-and-a-half seers for a rupee at the ration shop, but that meant an hour and a half of standing in the queue. Memories of twenty seers of wheat and one seer of ghee for a rupee only eight years before seemed like details of history from the time of the Mughal emperor Akbar.

Postal worker Birumal's mother was going through the gali below Puri's house one morning with half a lauki in her hand when Bhagwanti called out to her from her window, 'Sister, how much did that cost you?'

Jaidev could hear the craving in his mother's voice. Birumal's mother replied, 'Six annas a seer, sister. Six paisas for a seer used to be too much for this lowly gourd. Sister, we have been cooking daal every day for such a long time. Felt like having a vegetable for a change.'

Jaidev remembered a woman from a nearby village hawking her produce the previous evening in the gali, 'Ghee for sale! Home-made ghee from our own buffalo.'

Several gali women asked the price, but who could buy ghee at four rupees a seer?

The woman was annoyed, 'You just ask the price, no one buys anything. I used to sell as much as ten seers of ghee in these galis. What kind of people live here now!'

Sardar Khushal Singh's wife, Kartaro, said from her window, 'The ghee-eating days are over. Now one has to buy small amounts of ghee only when the doctor prescribes it. The smell of ghee is enough for us now, sister.'

Jaidev knew that families of Birumal, the insurance company clerk Tikaram, and Khushal Singh were facing hard times. Only two days before, Tikaram's wife had been asking Tara to sew pajama trousers for her young boy out of her husband's old and torn pair. Khushal Singh was fond of starched turbans of fine coloured muslin; his turban was now mostly in tatters.

The worst of the lot was the old Brahmin woman Purandei. This poor illiterate widow worked as a chaperone for girl students of the Aryaputri Pathshala in Sheesha Moti Bazaar. Both her father's and her husband's families were well-to-do. But after she became a widow, her husband's elder brother took over her side of the house and threw her out. She moved to Lahore from her hometown because she felt ashamed to work for a living in the midst of her community. Her daughter Sita, almost a young woman at fifteen, was in the eighth grade at school. The enlightened, socially responsible management of the school, even in those hard times, paid Purandei only twenty rupees a month. She could, if she had to, eat just dry bread in her house, but she needed clothes to cover herself, and more so her young daughter.

Doctor Prabhu Dayal's wife Pushpa said to Bhagwanti one day when they were alone, 'I am not very friendly with Purandei and Sita. I'm new to this gali, and they won't be comfortable with me. The shalwar Sita had on was so torn that she was crying over it. She couldn't go to school today for that reason. I have a shalwar that I've worn only twice, it is of a good material. It doesn't fit me any more, but it will fit her. Don't tell her it's from me, no one will know. That girl is pretty. If a match is found for her, the poor widow will have one less worry.'

A narrower gali branched off towards the Mochi Darwaza bazaar from Bhola Pandhe's Gali. Mostly Muslim railway workers and artisans lived there. Passing through it, Jaidev noticed that none of the cheap sacking curtains covering the entrances to the rooms was intact. The kurtas, shalwars and lungis worn by men would invariably be torn and soiled; the chadars and burkas of the women even more so.

Only the family of Babu Govindram, head clerk at the Public Works Department, who shared the dwelling with Jaidev's family, was better off than before. Ratan's mother was sporting new gold bangles. Their house had a new electric fan.

Bajaj Dewanchand would sit on the chabutara below and comment, 'Grass is sprouting on barren rocks in this time of war. He who never earned a paisa, too has made a tidy sum.' Ghasita Ram, the iron dealer, had bought off the crumbling dwelling of a family of gujjars, milk sellers, next to his house, and had begun to construct a new one over it. Rumour had it that Babu Ramjwaya was thinking of buying another small house in the Sareen Mohalla.

Khushal Singh would throw a curse at everyone, 'All these blackmarket-wallahs sleep with their own mothers!'

Besides teaching at the school, Masterji had always been a tutor at the mansion of Seth Gopal Shah. Sometimes he took on another pupil. Now even though he had three, sometimes four, pupils for tuition, the family was barely scraping by. The increasingly pale and withered faces of Bhagwanti and Masterji betrayed the strain of feeding the family. Tara's constant sulking was also adding to the household's tension.

The Intermediate exam was over and Tara had passed with a first division. Masterji was not willing to let her study for her BA. He thought: Jaidev would resume his MA studies after he was free, his other son and daughter were also attending school. How much could he afford? Education was a more noble pursuit than making money, but without money education could not be had.

Jaidev's family had never had money. He had spent his months of imprisonment buoyed up by pride in his sacrifice, dreaming of making good solely on his talent once he was out. On his return from the prison, he found the hardships at home appalling. He told his father that he would not go back to college.

He did not have much use for the master's degree. After being incarcerated by the British for his political beliefs, he found it humiliating to ask the government for a job. There was no hope of a government job anyway. He decided to find employment with a newspaper.

Jaidev had received the news of Tara's engagement while in prison. Sheelo had also told the family that Somraj, Tara's fiancé, had dropped out of his BA exam. Tara would withdraw into herself every time there was any mention of her engagement and weep silently. Bhagwanti and Masterji thought that if Tara's fiancé was not going to get a BA degree, it wouldn't be proper for her to get one either.

Jaidev knew a bit about Somraj Sahni, a student of the Sanatan Dharma

College, and considered this engagement unfair to Tara. To correct this injustice meted out to his sister, he decided to get her admitted into the first year of the BA course. It was neither fair nor Jaidev's wish to burden Masterji with this extra expense. He was confident that he would be able to earn enough in the future, but the college fee had to be deposited soon. He went to his former classmate Kalicharan Kaul to borrow money. Kaul was a kind soul, an industrious and bright student who'd always done well in his studies. Jaidev had hoped that he had found a good job after earning his MA degree.

Jaidev found Kaul in a dejected state. He had applied for a number of jobs in the past nine months. He had letters of recommendation from well-known people such as Doctor Radhey Behari, Seth Gopal Shah, Barrister Chawla, and Raibahadur Dinanath, but nothing worked.

Kaul was bitter, 'There's no employment for us in this Unionist ministry. Muslims and Jats, even if they have third-division BAs, have no problem finding jobs; a Hindu, even with an MA first division, has no chance.' Other friends had similar stories of economic hardship for Jaidev.

Jaidev had always heard his father praise Pran Nath, PhD. Masterji mentioned, always with a certain pride, how he had tutored the young Pran Nath for eight years. Masterji had been a tutor to the family of Seth Gopal Shah for the past twenty-five years. His salary had been eight rupees a month for the first five years; this was increased to ten rupees a month for the next five years. Now there was an increment of one rupee every year. The value of education was counted in rupees in the Seth family, but Pran Nath was not like the rest of the family.

Nath had returned to India in 1939 with a PhD in economics from Oxford University. Some of his articles had been published in the British *Economist* before his arrival. Eminent British scholars had lauded the brilliance of his work and compared his theories to those of the leading British economists. He had been appointed as a professor in Punjab University. Nath was about seven years older than Jaidev. Jaidev used to attend the doctor's lectures in preparation for his MA examination. After war broke out, the governor of Punjab appointed Professor Pran Nath as his advisor on economic affairs. He still held that position.

Doctor Nath had the utmost respect for Masterji. Upon hearing of Jaidev's arrest and imprisonment, he had come to visit him without caring for his position or that he was the governor's advisor, and had implored

Masterji to come to him if he needed money for legal expenses.

With no other recourse, Jaidev went to the doctor's house. Nath praised Jaidev's stories in the magazines, and asked him about his time in prison. As they were talking, the Doctor reminded Jaidev, 'Puri, do you remember; I had said that Germany's economy would not be able to support their war effort for long…'

It was well known in the university that the Doctor had little time for the communists and their meetings, but he was influenced by Marxism and believed in radical change. He often criticized communists for being doctrinaire. After some time he asked Jaidev, ' So, what brings you here? Something I can do for you?'

'Doctor Saheb, I would like to borrow one hundred rupees,' Jaidev said after some hesitation.

Nath thought for a moment. Then he took out ten ten-rupee notes from a cupboard and handed them to Jaidev. 'Hope you'll put them to good use.'

His meaning was clear. Jaidev had once come to the doctor in 1942 to ask for help for the underground revolutionary movement. He was not sure of the doctor's help, but knew he would not be handed over to the police. To remove any trace of doubt from the doctor's mind, Jaidev explained, 'This is the fee for my sister's admission to the BA course. Once I get paid for my writings, I shall return it.'

'Um,' said Nath, taking out a cigarette from the tin. 'Your sister Tara is that old?'

'Yes, she passed the Intermediate exam in the first division.'

'Good. She looks bright. I saw her twice at your place. She must be given a chance to study. But why doesn't she work to support herself? Three-month-long summer vacations have begun. Why doesn't she work as a tutor? She will also gain some self-respect this way.'

Without waiting for Jaidev's answer he continued, 'Ask her to come here. I have three- and four-year-old nephews and nieces. Tara can tutor them for an hour or so during the vacations. She will have other expenses at the college. If one cannot dress and act like their friends and classmates, it often leads to an inferiority complex. That is not a good thing to happen.'

Jaidev had faced the same problem, he could not but agree.

Master Ramlubhaya was being ground between two millstones: his regular job and his tutoring work. Jaidev had not been able to find work to support himself, and this was nagging his conscience and gnawing at his self-respect.

Before going to jail, Jaidev had sometimes filled in for his father at tuitions when Masterji was tired or unwell. Masterji had taken on another pupil in the last two months. He could not say no to this extra income, even if the strain gave him headaches or made him doze off while teaching at school.

Lala Badhawa Mull Narang's son Jagdish Chandra had been Masterji's pupil. He was never serious about his studies; Lalaji, therefore, often had Masterji as his tutor. Jagdish somehow got through his BA and took over his family business selling electric machines. His younger sister Urmila had given up her studies after failing the high school examination. Urmila's mother, more than her father, wanted her to pass her matriculation exams. Times were such that parents of prospective grooms, especially from good families, wanted to know about the girl's education. Urmila's mother knew her daughter was playful and impertinent. She wanted someone she could trust to tutor her. Narangji personally came to speak with Masterji.

The Narang family had moved away from Khooh Tillian to Manso Gali three years ago. Manso Gali was a little far for Masterji to walk. Narangji offered to pay his tonga fare too; in all twenty-five rupees a month. Masterji taught the eighth grade students at school, but he could tutor students up to high school in all subjects except English. Narangji was willing to hire another tutor to teach English to his daughter.

Jaidev had been back from jail for only two weeks when his father came down with high fever; it lasted for three days. Masterji was not so much worried about being absent from tutoring jobs that paid ten or fifteen rupees a month as he was troubled by not being able to go to Narangji's place. Her father wanted Urmila to appear in the September examination.

When Masterji had been Jagdish's tutor, Jaidev had filled in for him on several occasions. Narangji had noticed that Masterji son's was intelligent and diligent. When his father asked him, Jaidev borrowed Ratan's bicycle and went to tutor Urmila. He found that Narangji, Urmila's mother and Jagdish all knew about his work being published in reputed magazines, and were concerned about the time he had spent in jail. They talked to him with affection and served him tea and snacks. During the week he tutored Urmila, Jaidev was mindful of his responsibility.

One day Urmila's mother asked him, 'Son, Jagdish told me that you also can teach English.'

When Jaidev said yes, Urmila's mother spoke to him trustingly as if he were her son: Urmila's father had not been keeping well. June had begun. The family wanted to spend the three months of summer at the hill resort of Murree. She was worried about her daughter's tuition being interrupted. Urmila's mother suggested, 'You must have suffered during your time in prison, you too can do with some rest and change. Masterji cannot get away from his job at school. You can teach English to Urmila. You stay with us and eat with us too. For us, there's no difference between you and Jagdish. Our Murree house is quite spacious. We will pay you fifty rupees per month. Once in a while, if you feel like it, you can tutor Urmila's younger brother Praveen.'

To be able to spend some time at a hill resort and earn some money in the process did not seem like a bad idea to Jaidev. He had been whiling away his time in Lahore. He would be able to write in peace in the cool and quiet of Murree. His parents gave their approval, what objection could they have! Jaidev gathered his finished and unfinished writings, and went to Murree with the Narang family.

Urmila's mother knew that her daughter was not fond of studying. She was going on eighteen, but her young, doll-like figure made her look sixteen. It was time for the girl to get married, but she wanted Urmila to finish high school. In Murree, she treated Jaidev like a member of the family. He was given one of the good rooms at the front of the house. She would ask him to come along when she went out for a walk. She had told Jaidev that he would have to be a little firm with Urmila, making sure that she studied the books and did the homework. Jaidev talked and behaved freely with Urmila, but became stricter while tutoring her.

In spite of being intelligent and talented, Jaidev had a short height. Up to the age of fourteen or fifteen, he could pass as a twelve-year-old and travel by paying half fare. His face was still soft as a boy's. He was only half an inch taller than Tara, and they looked the same height when walking together. When he became aware of not being as tall as other boys of his age, he began to walk erect and to keep his back straight. That soon became his posture. To appear older, he began to grow a thin moustache. When he sat with Urmila for her lessons in the dining room that was divided by a curtain, he kept his spine straight in an attempt to exude authority.

Urmila used to address him as 'Masterji', but the tone of her voice had gradually become intimate and friendly. Beyji, Urmila's mother, was right, Jaidev found. He would ask her to concentrate on her lesson, but her chatter would not stop. When Jaidev would be explaining something from her study book, her attention would wander and she would begin to talk about a school friend or tell a joke or ask an unrelated question. Or remember an incident from last evening's outing.

Jaidev would stop her, 'Pay attention here.' Or, 'It's time to study. We can talk about all that later.'

Urmila would insist, laughing, 'No, first tell me this.' Or, 'Listen to this first.' She would break into giggles when Jaidev tried to be strict. Jaidev had to make an effort to ignore the playful antics of this young and attractive girl. He was mindful of the respect given to his father and the trust placed in him by Urmila's parents.

True to her name, Urmila was fickle like a wave. She could not be called beautiful, perhaps, in the classical sense. A round face over a short neck, a nose that was not shapely, but wisps of golden-brown hair surrounding her fair face and large, cowrie-like eyes gave her a look that was compelling. Her ordinary features were overshadowed by her ebullient youthfulness and her brash behaviour.

Jaidev was conscious of his position as her tutor. That did not stop him from noticing the invitation in her eyes, and he would sometimes return her glance. But it happened only when they went to the bazaar for a walk, or when Beyji's back was turned. He kept his distance when they sat for her lessons.

They were studying algebra. She would not concentrate on the problem he was teaching her to solve. After asking her to concentrate for the third time, Jaidev was a little peeved, 'I'll tell your father that you don't listen to me.'

On a previous occasion, when Jaidev had threatened her in the same way, she had replied, 'Go ahead! You'll no doubt enjoy it if I'm scolded.'

That day she shot back, 'Why do you try to intimidate me by reporting to father or mother as if I were my younger brother? This is between you and me. What has father or mother to do with it! Can't you speak for yourself!'

Jaidev lost his temper, 'I'll slap your face! Remember that!'

'Go on! Slap me!'

Jaidev took a deep breath to calm himself. 'All right, pay attention. $a^2+3a+2=(a+1)(a+2)=(a^2+a)+(2a+2)$.'

'Slap me first!' She thrust her face forward.

'I am sorry. Please pay attention.'

'No, first slap me. Why did you threaten!' She snatched the math book open between them, closed it with a thud, and offered her cheek to him.

Jaidev could not restrain himself. He hit her hard. The room reverberated with the sound. The imprint of his fingers showed on Urmila's fleshy fair cheek.

Urmila was stunned; two heavy droplets appeared in her large eyes. She bit her lower lip to stop crying. She closed her eyes to collect herself. Both of them remained quiet for a few seconds.

Jaidev was filled with remorse. His anger melted away and his mind and body became taut with excitement. He wanted to hold her in his arms and to kiss her cheek to soothe her. Trying to compose himself, he said, 'I'm very sorry. Let's continue.'

'Hit me again,' Urmila thrust her face even further.

Jaidev accepted defeat. He got up and went to his room. He lay down, thinking: Everyone would notice that mark on her cheek. What now? What will they say? What have I done?

He heard loud noises from the room next to the one in which they had sat. Praveen was being reprimanded for hitting his sister, and he was shouting in protest. There was the sound of two slaps. The boy again protested his innocence in a tear-filled voice.

What a cunning, bold girl! What she can't do! What am I to do!

In the evening Beyji was going for a walk to do some shopping in the bazaar. As usual, she invited him, 'Jaidev, son, let's go for a walk.' Urmila was her usual self, talking and joking as before. The mark of the slap was all but gone.

They stopped at the fruit seller at the insistence of Praveen. As Beyji was helping the boy to pick ripe plums, Urmila looked into Jaidev's eyes with affection and comfort. Jaidev breathed easy.

Next day Jaidev began the lesson with a serious face, 'Did you write the paraphrase for the poem "Perfect Life?" Let me see.'

'Slap me first,' said Urmila.

'Show me what you wrote.'

'No, slap me first.'

'I made a mistake. I won't do it again.'

'Why won't you?'

'That was not right.'

'Then why did you do it yesterday?'

'Because I was angry. I'm sorry. Let's study.'

'You're not angry now?'

'Not any more. Please study.'

'How do you feel now?'

'I don't feel anything.' Jaidev said impatiently, without looking at her.

'You're still angry.' Urmila smiled.

'I am not.'

Urmila recited a couplet she had heard somewhere, 'He gets angry when I say I love you; I love him more when he gets angry.'

Jaidev took a deep breath and looked at her. Urmila held his gaze.

'Don't you want to study?' He asked her softly.

She shook her head.

'What do you want to do?'

'Told you already.' Urmila's face was flushed crimson like the inside of a watermelon. Pulled by the passion of this young attractive girl, Jaidev lost his foothold on the rock of propriety. He felt himself being lifted into the air and carried away; his blood was surging to his face.

'How?' He asked.

'Don't you know?' Urmila's voice was hoarse with excitement.

'No.' Jaidev was holding on against being swept away.

'Want me to tell you?' Her throaty voice excited him even more.

'Yes.'

'Close your eyes.'

Jaidev pressed his knees together to hold himself back. With one hand he clutched the desk, with other he held his chin. He closed his eyes.

A kiss on his cheek made him open his eyes. Urmila's breathing quickened; there was an irresistibly inviting a pinkish glaze of passion in her bright shining eyes. Jaidev used all his self-control to hold back, but his hand crept to Urmila's arm.

'Come here, Urmi!' Beyji's voice from the other side of the curtain hit them like a whip.

'Damn it! She must have seen us! You go!' Urmila whispered urgently and pulled away.

Jaidev could not move. Urmila went away, trembling with fear.

Jaidev could hear someone being slapped on the other side of the curtain. He got up and went to his room. He paced around his room in agitation without knowing what to do? He lay on the bed for a while, and then sat up. He went out towards the bazaar. When he returned in the afternoon he had made up his mind. He had found out the time of the next bus to Rawalpindi. He began to collect his few clothes.

He was packing his bag when Praveen came, 'Masterji, Beyji is calling you for tea.' The boy told him quietly, in a sad voice, 'Sister got a good thrashing. Beyji beat her with the curtain rod. Don't tell father.'

Beyji looked upset. She gave Jaidev a cup of tea and some snacks, and said, 'Son, where did you go at lunchtime? Did you eat something?' She could not hide the distress in her voice.

Jaidev was expecting a different reaction from her. He sat quietly for a few moments, his head down, and then said in an apologetic and guilt-laden voice, 'I'm going back to Lahore in the evening.'

'Why, son?' she asked. 'I said nothing to you, did not blame you. The fault lies with us; it's our fate. Don't say anything to her father. When he is angry or hurt, his blood pressure shoots up.'

Jaidev bit his cheek to stop tears welling up in his eyes.

He did not see Urmila for the next three days. Once he caught a glimpse of her back, but her head and face were wrapped in her dupatta. On the fourth day Praveen told him, 'Masterji, sister is waiting for her lessons.'

Jaidev looked briefly at Urmila sitting at the desk. There was a dark welt on her forehead, below her golden hair. A bandage was tied round her left arm. Without looking at her, Jaidev said, 'Read the same poem.'

'You're heartless. Don't you want to see what happened to me?' He heard.

Puri had decided to keep his cool. He said in stern voice, looking at the book, 'You want the rest of your bones broken?'

'I was beaten up; why are *you* scared?'

'So?' He looked at her.

'Let them beat me again if they want. What's to fear now? I didn't take that beating for nothing.'

Jaidev closed his eyes and thought. His blood was racing again, a sour taste in his mouth. With his eyes on the book, he began to explain the meaning and context of the poem.

'Won't listen! Won't study! Won't listen!' Urmila kept interrupting him.

Jaidev got up and went to his room.

Around noon there was a knock on his door. Beyji came in. Her eyes were swollen from wiping away tears. She held out five ten-rupee notes, and said, 'This was owed to you.' She gave him another note, 'Here's your fare.'

She was leaving when Jaidev said with some discomfort, 'You didn't have to. I could be of no service to you; only caused you embarrassment.'

'Don't say that.' Beyji turned around and dabbed her eyes again with the aanchal of her sari, 'I asked you. I should be sorry. Whom can I fault when our coin is tainted? Son, please keep all this to yourself.'

Jaidev's family was surprised to see him return from Murree. People of the gali questioned him too. Jaidev said nothing, but he was full of bitterness. His thoughts kept turning back to Urmila. *I wasn't man enough ... She was so pretty ... couldn't we get married? Beyji wouldn't have objected. She was so passionate and intense. But I was their employee. Marriage is more than sex. My feelings for her were purely physical. She nearly caught me. She really forced herself upon me.*

Jaidev remembered his ideal of a suitable life companion, of a spouse with an intellectual and artistic bent. 'Saved myself from getting trapped in that quicksand just in time,' he told himself.

Chapter 3

JAIDEV PURI HAD SENT THE STORIES HE'D WRITTEN IN JAIL TO SEVERAL PLACES for publication. He was already known as a young, promising writer, but these four stories had been specially praised and noticed. Two of them had appeared in the Sunday editions of *Pairokaar* and *Nishat*. All this praise had gone to his head, and although he had no job and no money in his pocket, he now began to hold his head even more proudly over his habitually erect back.

An introductory note about the author published with his story in *Pairokaar* said in florid, Farsi-heavy Urdu, 'This publication has the honour of presenting, for the enjoyment of our readers, a story by that incomparable chronicler of human nature, Jaidev Puri, writer par excellence and foremost among new writers. Jai Puri is still young, but his literary maturity has left its mark on the forefront of world literature.'

Emissaries of various newspapers and magazines would seek out Jaidev and convey personal requests from their editors for his short stories, light essays and humorous sketches. No one ever talked of any payment for his work; as if they did not want to insult the writer by equating his immense talent with a few measly rupees. But Puri kept rolling in the throes of torment because he was unable to earn anything to help his family.

What's the worth of my talent, he'd ask himself, if I have no place to work, not even a writing desk to practise that talent! I sit twiddling my thumbs while my father breaks his back working. My mother is overworked, always tired and short-tempered. My sisters worry over their clean clothes as if their lives depended on it. I don't have proper, decent clothes for going out. Should I go and ask for work in some newspaper, he thought many times, those people are the least likely to refuse me. But buoyed up by the good reviews and compliments his stories had received and awash in a feeling of self-worth, he waited for a job to be offered to him. The problem was: what would he do until that offer came?

Puri got a novel to translate from Adayara Munavvar, an Urdu publisher. He completed a part of the work in a week's time, hoping for payment, but the publisher was not too anxious to bring it out. Lekhram Sharma, a sub-editor at *Pairokaar* and an old acquaintance of Puri, knew about his dilemma. Beside his newspaper job, Sharma occasionally did translation work for Naya Hind Publications. He suggested to Puri, 'Why don't you meet Pandit Girdharilal, the owner of Naya Hind? There might be a chance of some tutoring work. You have a good knowledge of Hindi.'

Kanak, the second daughter of Pandit Girdharilal, was studying for her MA in English literature and wanted to sit for a Hindi exam. There was a recent wave of interest in Punjab, especially among women, to learn the Hindi language. Puri, too, had passed the Prabhakar, an exam of competency in Hindi, when he was in the first year of his MA.

Pandit Girdharilal was an old nationalist of liberal views; his daughters could wear sari in public. Under her father's influence, Kanak had begun to lean towards the Student Congress, the youth wing of the Congress party. She had often taken part in demonstrations and meetings at the time of the 1942 movement. Clad in a fine white khaddar sari, she stood out from the rest of the crowd. Puri had noticed her, but they'd never had occasion to speak to one another.

Panditji knew only Urdu and English. He was interested in literature; rather his interest in literature had led him into the publishing business. Kanak had been taught some Hindi at school, but her bent had been towards Urdu. She wanted to do her MA in English literature, and then pass the Munshi Fazil exam in Urdu. In a surge of nationalist feeling, she decided to appear for the Hindi Prabhakar exam.

Puri received a message that Panditji wanted to consult him about guiding Kanak in the study of literature, especially in the Hindi language. He found Kanak to be interested in literature and particularly respectful towards him as her tutor. She had read all the short stories and some poems that Puri had published; she had even read two of the stories to her literature-loving father. She introduced Puri to Mahendra Nayyar, her brother-in-law, as if it was Nayyar's good fortune to meet him. Nayyar had a law practice in the high court, and lived in his own bungalow in Model Town.

Panditji broached the subject in a roundabout way. He was aware, he said, that time given by anyone with Puri's reputation was worth a lot. Would Puri be able to help Kanak study Hindi language and literature three times a week, or whenever it was convenient for him to teach? Considering his time was valuable, what would be an appropriate sum to help the girl, whom he should regard as his sister, gain some appreciation of literature?

After he got a little acquainted with Kanak, the idea of being in her father's pay became unpalatable to Puri. The bitter experience of tutoring Urmila was still fresh in his memory. His feeling of self-respect overrode his need for money. He agreed to tutor Kanak occasionally on the condition that no mention of money was ever made.

Puri began going to Gwal Mandi to tutor Kanak nearly every other day. Panditji was respected both in political and publishing-literary circles. Puri was pleased to gain entry into a well-regarded family. But he took care that neither Kanak's family, nor his own got to know anything about his financial situation. He would dress in his best trousers and shirt while visiting them. His shoes would be polished.

Panditji's press and warehouse were on Kele Wali Sarak, but his own office was on the ground floor of his residence in Sadhuram's Gali. The family's living room was next to his office. When he finished his office work around six and sat down for tea in the living room, he would call Kanak and his youngest daughter Kanchan to join him. Kanak's mother was quiet and withdrawn, and seldom spoke more than two sentences at a time. If all the kitchen work were over, she would begin to wash clothes. When there were no dirty clothes, she would mend the washed clothes and sew on buttons. Or she would just pick and clean enough spices, lentils and grain for grinding to last the family a month. She always seemed busy. When she did not feel well, she would lie down in the aangan, cover herself and stay there until she felt better. She refused to join the rest of her family in the living room. She belonged to a different generation and was not willing to change.

Puri tutored Kanak in the living room. Panditji had brought up his daughters Kanta, Kanak and Kanchan in liberal tradition. They did not shut up or feel embarrassed in the company of men. When other families hired a young man to tutor their girls, an older relative would sit beside the girl to keep her company, and more to keep an eye on the male tutor. No such thing happened at Panditji's house.

Puri began to visit Panditji's house not as a paid tutor, but as someone of equal standing and status, and a welcome guest. He would turn up at five or later, if that suited him. Panditji had instructed that tea should be served to him. Sometimes Panditji would join Puri and Kanak, not to keep watch, but to enjoy poetry in the Brij dialect or the works of poets from other times. He would listen intently and say *wah wah* in appreciation. Sometimes he would compare a couplet or the lines of a Hindi poem with an Urdu sher or lines from a ghazal. This would lead to a discussion on the finer points of literature, and from there on, to current political issues, Puri's jail experience and many other topics. Sometimes Kanak would show Puri an article or short story she had written, and ask his advice.

Puri had been tutoring Kanak for only two weeks when the thought of seeing her in the evening began to fill his days. The memory of Urmila and the rage in his heart against women were blown away by the cultured and sophisticated behaviour of Kanak, just as earth scorched by the blazing sun of May and June is turned green and fertile by the monsoon rains. It was not that Puri had not felt attracted towards any other girl before meeting Kanak, but her company washed away even the remnants of bitter memories as the rising sun dispels the lingering mist of early dawn.

Was there any girl who did not appear attractive in the flower of her youth! But Kanak's charm had a special appeal. She had a glowing, light tan complexion, a slim but developed figure that made her look tall. Her easy, unselfconscious manner left a lingering impression. The prestige and status of her family made her charm and elegance appear twice as attractive to the ambition-filled heart of Puri.

Aware of his own feelings towards Kanak, he would try to gauge how she felt for him. Then he would feel depressed and ashamed by his unemployment and the differences in their social and economic status. To be able to stand next to her and feel her equal, he needed the firm ground of employment beneath his feet.

Two months had now passed since his release from prison. His sixth short story had been published, and had received attention and praise like his earlier works. Editors of magazines and newspapers would ask him for his writing, but not if he needed a job. How long can I wait to be asked? he thought. Going to Kanak's house made his own family's poor circumstances more unbearable.

Feeling helpless, Puri went to Dr Prabhu Dayal, who lived across from him. The doctor had moved to Bhola Pandhe's Gali just before Puri's imprisonment. He had passed the MBBS examination in 1942. He could have easily found a good job in the army, but owing to his nationalist feelings, he was trying to set up an independent practice. He took part in the Congress party activities and worked as an assistant to Dr Radhey Behari; he was also helping the organization to prepare for the coming elections.

Dr Radhey Behari had written a letter to the Rent Control Office, and in spite of the wartime housing shortage, a spacious house was allotted to Prabhu Dayal at a very low rent. Dr Radhey Behari was one of the main leaders of the Congress party, and an influential member of the Punjab Legislative Assembly. Ministers in Sir Khizr Hayat's government sought his advice. His word was considered a command in the Hindu community.

Puri went with Prabhu Dayal to Dr Radhey Behari's office. Prabhu Dayal introduced Puri by mentioning his loyalty to the Congress party's programme and how he had been sent to prison for taking part in the underground movement. He also talked about Puri's standing as a writer, and his own concern about Puri's economic troubles. Dr Radhey Behari heard all this, and said, 'I'll see what I can do.'

Prabhu Dayal took Puri to Dr Radhey Behari's house again one afternoon, when he was alone. He repeated what he had said about Puri's work for the Congress party, the incident of his being sent to prison, and his literary reputation, and without mincing his words said, 'Before going to jail, he was with the socialist faction. The elections are coming, and it'll be better if he stayed with us. Why should others benefit from his skill?'

Dr Radhey Behari was the chairman of the board of directors of *Pairokaar* newspaper. He dictated a letter to the typist for the chief editor of *Pairokaar*, Karam Chand Kashish.

The editor of *Pairokaar* called Puri in as soon as his arrival was announced. In spite of the importance of his position and the difference in their ages, Kashish stood up to receive him and extended his arms in welcome. After shaking Puri's hand, he held on to it for several seconds to show his affection and respect, saying, 'Welcome! Welcome! Please have a seat.' He made Puri sit down before settling back in his own chair. He offered him a cigarette from his cigarette case.

Puri did not smoke, out of deference to his father and also because he had had no chance to learn the habit. He had only smoked a couple of times before now. He lit the cigarette without hesitation and blew out the smoke. The screen of smoke will help in talking to the shrewd editor, he thought.

Kashish asked, 'Mister Puri, your pleasure is my command. What will you have: tea, coffee or a cold drink?'

Puri was a bit flustered. He was not accustomed to such fine treatment except at Kanak's place.

'Please don't bother,' he said, 'I don't want anything at the moment.'

'How can that be!' Kashish protested, repeating his offer with twice the vehemence. 'A promising and talented writer like you honours us by coming to this office, and we can't have the good fortune of serving him tea! Well, would you like some cake or mithai with your tea?'

Puri had said no. He had to stick to his refusal, 'I just had tea at a friend's place.'

'That's all right.' Kashish said. 'Maybe later; there's no hurry.' He placed his elbows on the desk, entwined the fingers of both hands, and leaned towards Puri. His burning cigarette remained in the ashtray. He said again, 'Puri saheb, tell me what you have for us. We'll be publishing a special number on the occasion of Dussehra.'

In this torrent of praise Puri had no heart to show the letter recommending him for employment. He began to say, 'I want to help you as much as I can...'

Kashish struck the desk with his fist in excitement, and asked eagerly, 'What are you writing now? I want something that will touch the readers, capture their hearts.'

Puri tried to come back to the subject, 'Editor saheb, I have to think of my time and of the circumstances...'

Kashish interrupted him, 'Time! Inspiration comes to an artist like this.' He snapped his fingers together. 'Then it's only a question of putting it to paper. I too write like that.'

Puri shifted in his chair, 'One can't get inspired when one is involved in other work. I want to earn my living through writing, beginning with your paper.' Before Kashish could interject, he added, 'Dr Radhey Behari has given me a letter for you.' He placed the envelope on the desk.

Kashish's face became serious at the name of Dr Radhey Behari. He took out the letter and read it. Placing the letter on the desk, he took off his glasses and began to rub his eyes with the cushion of his palms, as if now the mind rather than the eyes were needed. He lit a fresh cigarette, blew out the smoke towards the ceiling, and said, 'My friend, it's no joke to serve literature and politics.' His voice now had a different tone. The door to his office opened and he paused. A young man wearing pajama and shirt and holding sheets of paper stepped in. Kashish asked him, 'Yes, bhai?'

'There is no space on the second page for all three reports. Can Dattatreya's statement be moved to the third page?' he asked.

'Have a seat,' Kashish gestured with his hand for the man to sit down. 'Do you know Mister Jai Puri.'

The man nodded.

'Mr Puri wants to join our newspaper. I was explaining to him how anyone wanting to serve literature or politics takes on a grave responsibility. Service entails sacrifice. What do Mahatma Gandhi, Pandit Nehru and Sardar Patel gain from serving the nation? A writer can express his view, that's how his service is rewarded. We all know journalism means hard work and sacrifice and very little pay. It's nothing but poverty and penance, isn't it, Indranath-ji?

'Journalism is unrelenting hard work, and one must learn it,' Kashish went on. 'All great writers spent their lives learning their craft. Take Tolstoy, for example. Did you know, he revised the first collection of his short stories a hundred times! There is no lack of talent in young men of today, it's there, but the element of hard work is lacking. They don't want to learn; all they want is instant fame, status and riches. If you don't learn to, you won't be able to drive a motorcar. You'll cause an accident, you certainly will. A motorcar is not that important, but politics is all about the ship of state. The journalist can, if he wants, save or capsize the ship. It's a tremendous responsibility!' Kashish spread his arms to balance the heavy burden of responsibility.

'You're right, sir!' Indranath said, 'each word must be weighed before it is written.'

'All right,' said Kashish in a low and grave voice without looking at Puri, 'You can work here but you'll have to learn. Go and see Babu Banarasidas. You may start today, but the salary will be decided after seeing what you can do.'

He put on his glasses, shuffled some files and papers on his desk, and said to Indranath, 'Listen, do the layout as you want. Just give proper importance to that statement by Sardar Patel.' The grand offer of tea to Puri was not repeated.

Indranath got up, and so did Puri. He had been welcomed as an honoured guest, as an independent writer. He was leaving as a paid subordinate to Kashish. This was bitter medicine, but with a source of livelihood now at hand, swallowing it had been less difficult.

Puri's hours at *Pairokaar* shifted from ten in the morning to four in the afternoon for one week, from four to nine in the evening the second, and from nine to two a.m. in the third week. A newspaper has to be in the hands of its public when they wake up in the morning, at the same time that other competing newspapers reach their readers. The editorial and production staff of a newspaper works with that deadline in mind; they cannot, therefore, keep regular office hours. As the city sleeps, the journalists work all night at their desks under bright lights. The presses roll at great speed to print their reports. At daybreak, the newspapers prepare a digest of the events of the past twenty-four hours from every corner of the world for the townspeople. All this work goes on without a hitch. The reason being the owner or the chairman of the board or the managing editor of the newspaper tells a host of underpaid sub-editors, reporters and machine operators what to do, and instructions are understood and orders carried out, irrespective of the difficulties and inconveniences, by subordinates who have mouths to feed.

As citizens stir from their sleep in the morning the newspapers are ready with their offerings, each in a distinctive style and colour. The skill of the journalist lies in putting his likes and dislikes aside, and in shaping and colouring the news in accordance with his employer's directives. Thousands read what he has written, but as he is anonymous, the question of his convenience or comfort does not arise. Sub-editors work like machines to prepare something to print on other machines. The work was Puri's choice, but the choice of time of work could not be his. When he would eat or sleep was decided by the needs of the newspaper. Some day he would be the chief editor and work his own hours, but that day was still years away.

Puri was unable to go to Kanak's house for days, but he did, whenever the opportunity presented itself. And when they did meet after these intervals, it was difficult to talk only about similes, metaphors and comical allegory in some poem. Kanak could not help complaining about not seeing him for so many days. Puri too liked telling her about his work and the people at the office. Her easy and unselfconscious manner and her enthusiasm for literature were giving way to listening to him in respectful silence. She did not any longer want to ask him to expand upon an interesting or complex couplet or quatrain. He must be exhausted after work, she would think. If Panditji got up in the middle of their evening tea for some reason, they would sit quietly for some time, and then both of them would be embarrassed by their silence.

Winter had begun. Puri found time to visit Kanak one afternoon, but only after darkness had descended. He found Panditji sitting in the living room, wearing his turban and holding his walking stick, ready to go out. 'Come, my boy,' he welcomed Puri loudly and fondly. He asked after Puri and praised several articles published in *Pairokaar*, thus, indirectly, complimenting Puri's work. He told Puri that a parcel full of Hindi books for Kanak had arrived.

Soon there was the sound of footsteps coming down the stairs next to the living room. Kanak came into the room wearing a silk sari, carrying a long coat. Her face lit up when she saw Puri, but also sadness came into her eyes. She seemed to hesitate for a moment. Her younger sister Kanchan, dressed for going out, followed her into the room.

Panditji knocked with his stick on the floor, 'Kanak dear, since Puri is here, you stay. Kanchi and I will go to Chaddha's house. You can meet Vimla some other time. Your study comes first.' He looked at Puri, 'My boy, it was me who asked her to come along. But study is more important. Work is always first.' He had a habit of saying his final sentences in English.

'No, no. You all are dressed to go out. Please go ahead. I'll come again tomorrow.' Puri said considerately, not wanting to spoil the family outing.

Kanak looked helplessly at her father.

Panditji said decisively, 'No, no, my dear fellow. Friends can be visited any time. Work is always first.' He got up. As he was leaving, he said, 'Get Puri some tea, dear.' He smiled at Puri, 'You must be tired after work. You're very hard-working, I know.'

Kanak put her coat on the back of the sofa, and sat in the chair next to Puri. Being alone again made them silent. Each waited for the other to break the silence, but neither knew how.

'Why are you so quiet?' asked Puri.

'No, I'm not,' she said. 'You say something.' They again fell silent, enjoying each other's presence.

Kanak remembered, 'Let me get tea.'

'What's the hurry?' Puri said. His emotion-laden voice sent a shiver through her body. She kept her eyes averted, and looked at the border of her sari as if searching for a special thread.

Seeing her quiet, he asked, 'You feel like having tea?'

Kanak lifted her eyes for a moment, shook her head to say no, and resumed her search with trembling fingers for that special thread.

'You have a strange look in your eyes,' Puri found enough courage to use an intimate tone.

Every fibre in Kanak's body tingled with excitement. She could look at him only for a second. 'My eyes have a strange look? What about yours!'

What Puri had decided never to say came to his lips involuntarily, 'Can I say something?'

Kanak nodded, full of anticipation.

'You won't mind?'

Kanak looked into his eyes and shook her head to assure him that she would not.

'You promise?' Puri wanted more assurance.

'For what?'

'That you won't be angry.'

'I won't be.'

'Give me your word.' Puri held out his hand.

Kanak gave him a quick, upward look, then lowered her eyes. Her face was flushed. She placed her hand in his.

'You've given me your word. You won't break the vow?' Puri asked in a trembling voice.

Kanak looked straight into his eyes, 'Never.' Having said what she felt in complete sincerity, she became serious. She let her hand stay in his.

To acknowledge the sincerity in her voice, he raised her hand and touched it to his forehead. He tried to control his voice, 'I've asked you for a serious commitment. I know I may not be worthy of it. What do I have? Neither enough money, nor a status befitting you.'

Suppressing tears of happiness welling into her eyes and with quivering lips, Kanak said, 'How can you say that! It's me who's not worthy of you. You're a great artist, a writer.' Unable to control herself, she covered her eyes with her aanchal and ran towards the kitchen.

Kanak told the servant to make tea, and returned with a book in her hand. She opened the book, placed a pencil between the pages to mark the place, and came and sat near Puri. Exercising her new-found right over him, she protested, 'Why did you make that strange mention about being worthy?'

Puri was never able to be completely at ease in the affluent surroundings of her home or to forget his own poverty in the face of her easy, confident manner. He said, 'You're so kind and big-hearted, not telling you the truth would be a crime. I have very little money. My salary is only one hundred

rupees a month, but I have confidence in my ability to do better in future.'
Puri felt a relief pouring out his heart to Kanak about his economic
situation.

Kanak's eyes again brimmed with tears, 'What's money? I am not
concerned with money. Everyone is aware of your talent and your
capabilities?'

After that evening, they began to meet outside her home too. If Puri was
busy in the evening, Kanak left the college and met him in the afternoon.
The restaurants were mostly deserted at that hour. They would usually meet
at the Standard on Mall Road. Never having felt any shortage of money,
she was not concerned about it. Her family might not be rolling in riches,
but she had no wish to amass wealth. Two of her friends were from rich
families, and came to college in a motorcar. Kanak always had enough in
her purse to hire a tonga. She would have happily taken the bus.

Kanak began to form a picture of her future in her mind. She had
dropped the idea of appearing for the Munshi Fazil exam in Urdu literature
after completing her MA. She now wanted to get into journalism, and
eventually start her own literary magazine with Puri. She had no doubt that
one day Puri would become a world-famous writer. Just like Premchand,
Sharatchandra, Gorky, Hardy and Maugham. Their house would be
surrounded by a small garden, a study with two desks in it...

Chapter 4

IT DID NOT TAKE PURI LONG TO PROVE HIS WORTH AT *PAIROKAAR*. HE WAS GIVEN
the job of translating the news from English that the teleprinter spewed
out, and was soon asked to write editorial comments and opinion pieces.
His views began to carry weight among his colleagues, and this sometimes
resulted in minor differences of opinion with Kashish.

Kashish often reminded Puri, 'Puri saheb, our paper has not published
any of your short stories for a long time. You work for *Pairokaar*, your
stories gets published in *Aarsi*. For us you're a story-writer above all.' Puri
did not expect to be paid for his stories published in *Pairokaar,* so he sent
them to other periodicals.

In his piece on the February 1946 Sailors' Mutiny, Puri had made some
barbed comments against the leaders of the Congress party and the Muslim
League for their lack of compassion and support for the sailors. Readers
had appreciated his comments, but Kashish had warned him: The popularity
of the newspaper matters, but a political newspaper must not be swayed
by public sentiment; its role rather is to give a direction to that sentiment.

The article also brought many of his friends back to Puri. These were
members of the Student Federation and the Communist Party—Manzoor,
Narendra Singh, Asad, Pradyumna, and others. They commended Puri for
his views and invited him to a meeting at the Bradlaw Hall organized in
support of the sailors of the Bombay revolt. Puri gave a spirited speech at
the gathering. The comrades began to hope that they had found a fellow-
traveller in Puri. But there were some differences that would distance him
from them. Puri saw differently from the communists on the right to self-
determination for religious communities. For Puri such a demand meant
placing Hindus and Muslims on either side of a sectarian divide, which
would result in the partition of the country into Hindustan and Pakistan.

The communists thought that the right to self-determination was the
only way to sectarian harmony and to avert the partition of the country.
They organized study circles to discuss this delicate issue. Tara and Kanak
would occasionally show up at these meetings in the company of Surendra
and Zubeida. Sometimes Puri talked to Tara at home about reports and

statements published in the newspapers, but always very briefly, and many questions remained unanswered. Puri could sense that she was beginning to lean towards the communists' viewpoint, and was not pleased.

It was an April evening in Lahore. The city folk had put away the heavy quilts of winter and were enjoying the breezes of spring. Young women had shed the thick clothing that hid the curves of their bodies and were flitting like butterflies on Lawrence Road, and in the gardens of Anarkali and Mall Road outside the walled city. Their bright clothes competed with the flowers in the gardens and the flowers beds. Young men, their chests and shoulders braced in hope of brushing against the girls in passing, roamed the streets. That week Puri was working from nine to two in the morning. In the evening, he had met Kanak in Lawrence Garden and discussed their future plans together. His heart was filled with hope, and he now wanted to get to work.

Indranath handed him the day's reports and suggested, 'Give a banner headline to the news of the Senate Hall altercation.'

The news was: That day in the last session of the BA examinations at the university, the invigilating officer Professor Deen Mohammed objected to cheating by a student of the Sanatan Dharma College, Somraj Sahni, and ordered the student to surrender the answer book to him. When the student refused to comply with the order, the professor asked him to leave the Senate Hall. Before the chaprasis and guards could eject him, the student beat up the professor and left the Hall.

Puri read the whole report in one breath, frozen in his seat. Tara was foremost in his mind. He put the report away and thought, his chin cupped in his hands: If he deleted the news completely, he would have to answer to Kashish, but he himself felt disgust, not sympathy, towards Somraj

Puri edited the news report to omit the words 'Sanatan Dharma College' and 'Sahni' from the name of the student. Instead of 'saw him cheating' he wrote 'mistook him to be cheating'. He changed the headline from 'Altercation at the Senate Hall' to 'Confusion at the Senate Hall'. He found it difficult to concentrate on the work at hand, and had to stay an hour longer to finish it.

Masterji had relaxed the rule of waking up at dawn for Tara and Puri. They both had to study until late at night for their examinations, and were now allowed to get up late in the morning. The time Masterji thought proper to get up from the bed, those last vestiges of early morning sleep were the sweetest for Puri. Khushal Singh, his neighbour who ran the store selling papad and bariyan, would begin to sing *asaavari* at that hour:

Mother, the time to play is very short.
I got so engrossed in play that
I forgot all about my home and family…

Khushal Singh had an ear for music and he sang the morning-time song with such feeling that the people of the gali did not mind having their sleep disturbed by his voice. Everyone wanted to linger in bed, listening to his song with eyes closed in the languor of the early morning, but Masterji would begin to chant at the same time his morning bhajan in a loud and shrill voice:

Begetter of the world, mother of the world, we salute you…

That day Puri got up as soon as he heard the newspaper vendor arrive, and went to get a copy of *Pairokaar*.

Masterji had finished his bhajan and was about to close his eyes to pray when Puri showed him the newspaper report and said, 'This news is not good.'

Masterji read the news and his mouth opened in surprise. He said after a few moments, 'It can be about some other person.'

'It was Sahni, from Sanatan Dharma College. I edited out the name,' Puri told him.

'He won't get through this year again,' Masterji was worried.

'Not only will he not pass the exam, this may go even further,' Puri said.

'As God wishes.' Masterji looked at his son with a worried expression, 'This may be serious. He might be punished for punching the professor.'

'He should be,' Puri said without sympathy. 'Professor Deen Mohammed will file a complaint with the registrar. He won't keep quiet.'

'What's in the newspaper?' called Bajaj Dewanchand from the gali below. His wobbly voice showed that he was chewing on a *datun* to clean his teeth.

'Hindu student beat up Muslim professor!' replied Tikaram.

'Bravo!' said Dewanchand. 'He must have hassled the poor boy. These Mohammedans…' He spat out a particularly vulgar expletive.

'Masterji! What're you doing?' Babu Govindram called out.

'I'm coming, bhai saheb,' said Masterji, trying to hide the distress in his voice, and went downstairs.

Babu Govindram was holding a copy of the daily *Chhatrapati*. It had published the same news with the name of Somraj Sahni, a student of the Sanatan Dharma College. Being Masterji's neighbour Govindram knew about Tara's engagement. He said to Masterji in sympathy and concern, 'What bad luck has befallen you! How could you know? Tara is such a bright girl and the boy has done this!'

All Masterji could say was 'As God wishes.' and hang his head in despair.

Everyone in the family had heard the news, but no one talked about it. Tara became quiet and withdrawn. She did not eat anything, nor did she go to college. 'I have a headache,' she said, and stayed in bed the whole day. Her friends at college did not know about her engagement, but she still wanted to jump into the well in the gali and kill herself in shame and embarrassment.

At the school Masterji's colleagues had but one topic of conversation. Some of them were upset with such a travesty of discipline. Most of them agreed that if university professors were insulted in this way, an ordinary schoolmaster would not be safe walking alone on the street. Such students should be flogged in public, they should be sent to jail as punishment. As an example to others, they should be expelled for life from the university. Masterji said nothing, only let out sighs of remorse.

The next day's newspapers again carried different versions of the report. The city correspondent of *Pairokaar* reported: Professors from all colleges and the university have appealed to the university registrar for quick and proper action to discourage undisciplined behaviour at the time of examinations.

The daily *Siasat* gave the news a pro-Muslim slant: Senate Hall altercation accused at large! Summons served on Somraj Sahni, a student of the Sanatan Dharma College, to appear before the magistrate's court. Reliable sources have confirmed that the accused is still a fugitive. The police have launched a massive manhunt.

The daily *Chhatrapati* published another version of the news: Proof of sectarian cronyism! More revelations in the Senate Hall affair! A member of the Rashtriya Swayamsewak Sangh harassed by a professor belonging to the Muslim League. Reliable sources have confirmed that Professor Deen Mohammed, a follower of the Muslim League, had long held a grudge against the Sanatan Dharma College student Somraj Sahni. The student could not escape being a victim of Muslim fanaticism. What else to expect from a Muslim League government?

After school Masterji went to his job to tutor the boys at Seth Gopal Shah's mansion. On his return he was told that Babu Ramjwaya had sent for him. Babu Ramjwaya seldom picked up a newspaper. He got the news from his neighbours. He rebuked his younger brother for his stupidity, 'Why did you not go and meet Lala Sukhlal after you got the news? Have you no concern about your relations with his family? He is their son, but he's your daughter's fiancé too. You must go and ask after the boy.'

Ramjwaya took Masterji to Lala Sukhlal's place in Banni Hata. A couple of other men sat commiserating with him. Ramjwaya said, referring to the Senate Hall affair, 'After Ramlubhaya heard the news, the poor man couldn't eat anything. The situation is not clear. What exactly happened?'

Sukhlal hurled abuse at Professor Deen Mohammed, 'He has the nerve to insult *my* son! Who cares for that registrar! I too have contacts in Governor Lord Jenkins' office. That mother-fucker registrar will file a criminal charge against my son! He doesn't know me yet. If I don't give him a shoe beating on his own doorstep, you are free to believe that my father was an untouchable bhangi! What do you know! Not a single Muslim will be left alive in Lahore. We're Surajvanshis, we'll die but we won't go back on our word!'

Ramjwaya asked with some hesitation, 'The boy is not upset, is he?'

Sukhlal said nonchalantly, 'I don't care a fig about this darned BA! My boy's not going to be a clerk or a petty accountant, you know!'

After the Second World War, the British government had sent three emissaries in 1946 to arrange the handover of power to Indians. The Cabinet Mission was meeting at Simla with the representatives of the Congress party and the Muslim League. The future of the country hung on the outcome of the possibility of an understanding between the former and the latter, between Hindus and Muslims. The people of Lahore seemed oblivious of the fateful moment in their preoccupation with the Senate Hall affair, the quarrel between a Muslim professor and a Hindu student. The matter of cheating at an exam had grown into a matter of religious tension between two communities. At the time of the legislative elections two months earlier, Lala Sukhlal had campaigned vigorously for Dr Radhey Behari. He was also Dr Radhey Behari's right-hand man and his chief lieutenant in the Hindu Mahasabha and the Rashtriya Swayamsevak Sangh organizations. Doctor Saheb's advice to Chief Minister Khizr Hayat Khan was that since the affair had become a sectarian issue the Hindus would be distrustful of his government unless the matter was hushed up.

Sir Khizr, the chief minister of Punjab, was in an uncomfortable position. After the 1946 elections, the number of Congress party and Muslim League members in the House had increased while that of his own Unionist Party had gone down. He could stay in power only with the support of the Congress members. The League's behind-the-scene machinations were to bring his ministry down. He also had to deal with the question of undisciplined behaviour, and upholding the prestige of the university. The registrar of the university, Madanmohan, was bent upon moving the high court unless an equitable solution of the Deen Mohammed affair was found. Any agitation at this time could worsen the already delicate situation; the Congress party faction too had to be appeased. The government decided to appoint a committee to investigate the matter.

Puri told his family that he had learned from reliable sources that Professor Deen Mohammed had been posted away from Lahore as the principal of Peshawar College. The professor was apparently satisfied, and had accepted the promotion as a testimonial to his diligence. Members of the investigative committee wanted to put off any decision indefinitely.

The elder sister-in-law chided Tara's mother, 'What's the use of sending your daughter to college? Her education is already equal to her fiancé's! Is she going to work as a clerk or a schoolteacher after her marriage? Will she sing lullabies to her children in English? Only those living on Mall Road and in Gwal Mandi send their daughters to college. You know, we got our Sheelo married off right after high school. See how nicely she's settled in at her in-laws! One's daughter is like another's property. When the boy's not a BA graduate, letting Tara study for her BA would make a laughing stock of you.'

Tara's mother agreed with her. Masterji had no recourse but to agree. 'How can anyone go against God's will?' he said. Tara had been allowed to join the BA programme only at Puri's insistence. She could now be persuaded through her elder brother.

When Puri sat down for his meal, his mother called Tara over before broaching the subject, 'You tell her, son! If her in-laws don't want it, what's the point of continuing her studies? We can't afford to displease them!'

Tara sat silently facing the wall.

'Let them be displeased,' said Puri, disappointing his mother's expectations.

His mother gasped and looked at her boy whom she had regarded as serious-minded, 'And what if they call off the engagement?'

'That'll be better. We'd be saved the trouble of doing so.'

'Who'll care for the poor girl all her life?'

'If she's a burden for you, I can take over her responsibility.' Puri said angrily. 'She's a first-division student, and he cheats at exams.'

Seeing no point in going any further with the conversation, his mother got up. Puri looked at Tara and said in English, 'You're worrying your head for nothing. Concentrate on your books. So many changes are taking place in the world, but our parents cannot look beyond their own problems. Marriage is not the end of life. When you're ready, there won't be a shortage of boys willing to marry an eligible girl like you.'

His comforting words brought tears to Tara's eyes. She felt as if some indescribable fear clutching at her heart, mind and body had suddenly been lifted.

The June heat turned their one-room house into an inferno. She spread out a mat on the veranda, lay down on it and thought: If Somraj hadn't been caught cheating or if I remain engaged to that man, continuing my studies is improper only because he does not have his BA degree. A woman is not born inferior to a man, she becomes that through social pressures.

She remained lost in thought: If I ever get married, it'll be to a really intelligent and capable man. How can I marry someone I don't consider my equal? A woman's worth is measured by her ability to find a mate. Why does a woman always have to play second fiddle? If a woman can't look up to a man, why should she think he's right for her? How can she love and respect him?

The naming ceremony of Surendra's nephew was on the first Sunday in July. She had invited Tara with affectionate insistence. Tara went to her place near Amritdhara in Gwal Mandi at eight in the morning. Dhurries and cotton sheets had been spread out for the guests on the floor of a large room. In the right-hand corner, an old granthi, the Sikh priest, was reciting from the Guru Granth Sahib placed before him on a low table. This book of scripture rested on a cushion of silk. Surendra's father sat beside it, waving a white flywhisk over it slowly and with apparent devotion. Men sat on one side of the room, women on the other, separated by a two-foot wide aisle.

Since Tara had arrived a little late, the place she found was next to the divide, beside the men. Surendra caught her eye and made a gesture to cover her head with her dupatta. Surendra never covered her head outside her home. Next to Tara sat Gurtu and Kanak, their heads covered with a dupatta or a corner of the sari. They smiled at her. All the women had their heads covered. Most of the men present were Sikh, with turbans on their heads. Some Sikhs with short hair wore turbans too. A modern gentleman had come wearing a Western-style hat. He could not leave his head uncovered, and sat with the hat on his head. Another person who had neither a turban nor a hat had covered his head with a handkerchief.

Asad Ahmed, a friend from the Student Federation, had arrived just after Tara. She was glad to see him. Asad had a nice sense of humour. When he spoke at a meeting or at the Study Circle, he was always brief and to-the-point. After the meetings, at times, they walked together up to the Shahalami Gate, and if she needed him to escort her, she could ask him without hesitation. Many people were sitting near the entrance, so Asad had to cross over to the centre of the room, where Tara was sitting on her side of the aisle. They saw each other, and exchanged nods of greeting.

Asad had short, curly hair. He never wore a hat or a turban. He was not familiar with the customs of a Sikh ceremony, but when he saw that others who sat facing the Granth Sahib with their hands joined reverently, he too put his hands together.

A Sikh gentleman sitting next to Asad nudged him and motioned him to cover his head. Asad looked at others around him, and when he saw the man with the handkerchief on his head, he too put his hand into his trousers pocket to take out his own. There was none. Tara watched all this, trying not to smile. Asad, flustered at not finding his handkerchief, excused himself and was getting up when another Sikh gentleman took out a new, flower-patterned silk handkerchief from his pocket and handed it to him. As Asad covered his head with the handkerchief loaned to him, his eyes met Tara's. A smile crept to her lips. Asad was trying to hide his embarrassment. They both averted their eyes to stop laughing.

Having finished his incantation of the scriptures, the granthi announced, 'The gathering prays to the Granth Sahib that they should learn the first letter of the lad's name.'

He again opened the Granth Sahib at random. He looked at the first letter on the page, and said, 'The Granth Sahib commands that the first letter of the lad's name be a T. The gathering may suggest a name beginning with a T.'

Names beginning with a T were called from all sides: Tej Singh, Tara Singh, Tota Singh, Takht Singh. One Sikh gentleman suggested Tope (cannon) Singh. Asad found it difficult not to smile at some suggestions.

The gathering approved Tara Singh. Asad leaned towards Tara and whispered, 'The lad's now your namesake!'

Huge salvers heaped with sweet halwa were brought in. The granthi stood up and led the gathering in a prayer, all standing with their hands folded in supplication. A small portion of the prasad was placed in a vessel as an offering before the Granth Sahib. Narendra Singh and another youth carried a salver over to the men's side, Surendra and her sister to the women's side, and began distributing handfuls of halwa to the guests. Asad was intrigued: no plates, no cups, no leaf plates, not even pieces of paper to hold the prasad. Everyone accepted the ghee-drenched halwa reverently into his or her hand. Narendra Singh reached Asad with his salver. Asad motioned him with his eye to pass him by. Narendra Singh motioned back that he could not refuse the offered prasad.

Asad could not but accept the halwa. In his awkwardness he watched Tara to see how she handled the situation. Tara and her friends had small hands, and they had succeeded in accepting a smaller portion of halwa. Asad again whispered into Tara's ear, 'That's the punishment of having big hands.'

'I'd call it the reward,' she replied.

'Want to exchange?'

'Uh-uh, be content with what you get.' She hid her hands.

Tara and her friends ate their portion of halwa, but with some difficulty. The problem now was how to clean their ghee-smeared hands. Most Sikh gentlemen were content with wiping the hands on their long full beards. A few used handkerchiefs too. Tara and her friends somehow managed with their tiny women's hankies. What was Asad to do? He could not soil the silk handkerchief someone had graciously loaned to him! He sat quietly with his hands spread out in front of him, waiting for a chance to slip out.

Tara was enjoying Asad's predicament, and he was trying to keep a straight face. Tara threw her handkerchief to him; Kanak and Gurtu gave theirs too.

Nodding at Narendra Singh, Asad said, 'The idiot had heaps of halwa to eat; couldn't he arrange for plates or leaf cups?'

Tara said, 'This is prasad. It has to be accepted in bare hands. You defile it by accepting it in anything else.'

As others were leaving, Narendra Singh and Surendra asked their friends from college and from the Student Federation to stay behind. Once he was alone with his friends, Asad threatened the siblings in mock anger, 'Why didn't you warn me beforehand? I too would have worn a large turban, and carried a towel in my pocket. Well, one day I shall take you smart alecks to a mosque under some pretext, and make you do all that bowing and getting up again!'

Narendra Singh took out the new issue of *People's Age*, the Communist Party organ. They gathered around him, and began discussing how the British government's intentions were far from honest, and its representatives were making hollow promises to the Congress and the League just to pacify them. If the Cabinet Mission proposals were to be believed, how would the League get its Pakistan and how would the Congress party be able to keep India undivided? Singh's suggestion was that during the summer break, they should try to convince their friends and fellow-travellers that only a rapprochement between the two would put a stop to the division of India.

When Tara left for home, Asad came out too. As they walked together, they were talking about the incident of Asad attending a Sikh ceremony with his head uncovered. He said, 'Do you see how such little things as these customs and beliefs are keeping our two communities apart? Is this the only way to preserve one's traditions? The more we mingle, the better. Some of these beliefs and practices may survive, but others will surely change.' Tara listened, muttering in agreement.

Asad asked, 'Do you have a Muslim girlfriend?'

'I see Zubeida often,' said Tara.

'Have you been to her home?'

'Not so far.'

'I'll ask her to invite you for tea some day. You too ask her to come and visit you.'

'It won't be possible for me,' Tara said with some hesitation.

'Why? Does your family not eat with Muslims or invite them over? Puri doesn't believe in all that,' Asad was surprised.

'Our family doesn't behave the same as I and my brother do. Our place is rather cramped too.' Her embarrassment increased.

'Let's forget it. But if I come to your home, would your parents be able to guess that I'm not a Hindu, just by looking at me or from my behaviour? I have been to Dr Nath's place and had tea with him several times. His family is an orthodox Hindu one.'

'You visit him often?' Tara wanted to know.

'Well, we, Puri and I, have been his students. Actually, I am on my way to his place now. He is the economic advisor to the governor, but still very approachable. He gives tutorials now only to MA students. Have you been to his place with Puri?'

'I'm tutoring the family children during the summer break. I go there between half past four for an hour. If I didn't have this tutoring job last year, I wouldn't have been able to go to college.' Tara did not mind telling Asad about her situation. And what truth can be more personal and embarrassing than for white-collar, lower-middle-class people to confess their difficulties with money?

Chapter 5

'Here they are! Come and get them! Green-skinned bananas! Guavas from Allahabad! Pomegranates grown in Kabul and Kandahar!' The loud and oft-heard cry of the fruit peddler reached every nook and entered every cranny of the houses in Bhola Pandhe's Gali.

There was a ripple of response among the women sitting on straw mats and low stools on the chabutaras in front of the houses. Most of them had some piece of work in their hand. In the cloying, sticky heat of August they wore blouses and cotton dhotis of flimsy muslin; the older ones made do with only a dhoti around their bodies. Young girls with budding bodies and women wore shalwar and kameez. For a woman, the need to cover her body waxes and wanes like the temperature at different hours of the day. In the morning of her life, a girl is not shy about her body. As she becomes older, she begins to see her body grow into that of a woman and realizes that the fulfilment of her life is in attracting a male; and she begins to act demurely, to increase the pull of her attraction. In her youth and before she is married, the need to be coy and attractive reaches its peak. When the desire to attract bears fruit in the form of her marriage and marriage results in progeny, that shyness about her body begins to wane. In the twilight of her life the same lack of shyness about her body, as in childhood, returns.

Most middle-class and lower-middle-class people lived in the galis of Lahore, and the afternoons in the galis belonged to the women. The galis were rather narrow, not more than four to five feet wide. Women sitting on a chabutara on one side could converse easily with someone on the other. The men would be at work in offices, in their shops or other places of business. The women felt free about their behaviour and clothing. If a male had to come back to the gali for some reason, he would clear his throat loudly to warn the women. They would rearrange their clothes, find their vagrant dupattas and aanchals, or just turn their back towards the gali. Young children, wearing just enough to cover their genitals, played hopscotch or island by drawing lines on the brick surface of the gali with charcoal or a shard of a clay pot. Hawkers, peddlers and haberdashers were from the lower, servant class; the women did not bother if they came and went.

That afternoon in Bhola Pandhe's Gali, the tongues of the women and their hands worked swiftly. Usha was sewing something on a hand-cranked sewing machine that she had borrowed from Meladei. Birumal's mother was working a spinning wheel. Kartaro was knitting cord, using the back of an upturned cot as a frame. Meladei was weaving nivar on a cotton-webbing frame. Purandei sat with skeins of silk in the making. Kartaro's daughter Peeto embroidered, another woman rolled balls of cotton thread, and the ones with nothing to weave or sew shelled melon and pumpkin seeds. These jobs were done for the household, or as odd jobs for merchants. The gali women were known to earn enough money from such small jobs to buy an occasional gold ornament. Only the woman with the water well in her house, called the Woman-of-the-Well, sat idly with hands on her knees and her back against the wall, talking to herself. She was eighty-seven years old.

The conversation revolved around finding eligible matches for Meladei's son Ratan and for Bhagwanti's son Jaidev. These young, strapping men with jobs were refusing to listen to any proposals for marriage. Whenever there was any talk of finding a bride, Ratan would retort angrily and Jaidev would say that he'd rather wait a little longer.

The mothers of the two boys were airing their frustration, expressing their inability to convince their sons, and the Woman-of-the-Well was talking without care, whether anybody was listening or not, 'All this is your own doing. Marrying your sons at such a ripe age! In my day, boys got married off at eighteen if not sixteen. Say what you want, I know the boys have been bewitched by girls who go about with their hair plaited into braids.'

Sita and Usha were making eyes at each other and laughing quietly at the old woman's familiar tirade.

When they heard the fruit peddler's cry, Kartaro and Meladei covered their shoulders and legs, bared due to the heat. Sita and Usha, wearing shalwar-kameez, pulled on their dupattas.

The peddler stood at the mouth of the gali balancing a huge basket on his head. He held it with both hands and lowered it to the ground with a loud grunt. On his shaven head, to balance his heavy-laden basket, was a coil of tightly wound cloth. To keep from getting caught between his lips, his bushy moustache was trimmed along the line of his upper lip, but hung down like the wings of a bird at the corners of his mouth. His close-clipped beard had been shaped with a razor. His trademark, the long blue lungi that covered his toes, and the loose kurta of artificial silk hanging from his broad muscular shoulders proclaimed that he was a *rai*, a Muslim peddler of fruit and vegetables.

The man placed his basket on the pavement of the gali, and sang out in a friendly voice, 'Mothers, sisters, daughters, ladies … the fruit peddler is here!'

Several children, sitting next to their mothers, playing with toys or with any odd thing they could lay their hands on, reacted to his call. Before their mothers could refuse, they asked in a plaintive voice or with tears in their eyes, pulling at their mothers' clothes, 'Want banana … want guava.'

Having her aanchal pulled by her baby daughter pleading for a guava irritated Bhagwanti, 'This darned peddler shows up every day!'

Purandei asked, eyes on her skeins, 'How much for the guavas?'

Before the rai could reply, some woman admonished him in a loud voice from the bazaar, 'What's this nonsense! How can you block the entrance to the gali? Stay in the bazaar! Whoever wants to buy something will come and get it from you.'

The women looked towards where the gali branched off from the bazaar. A respectable-looking woman in a white dhoti and white chadar, and a young woman in a white khadi shalwar-kameez, were shouting at the rai for blocking the entrance to the gali.

The rai ignored the angry protestations good-humouredly, slid his huge basket about a foot to one side, and said, 'May your children prosper, lady, who's blocking the way? Here, see this passage … enough for an ox cart to go by.'

There was enough space to step into the gali, but both the women kept on insisting for him to pull back his basket onto the road of the main bazaar. In reply to their threats and complaints, the rai blessed them with a long life and prosperity, and moved his basket another inch or two away.

The women of the gali watched this argument with some surprise and with expressions of annoyance on their faces. Why were these women shouting at the peddler who came to their gali every day? Why didn't they mind their own business!

The imperious and sharp scolding of the visitors prevailed. They made the rai remove his basket and walked on towards the women in the gali. Ratan's mother whispered to Jaidev' mother, 'Why did they scold the poor fellow… and make him remove his basket?' The women visitors reached the chabutaras where the gali women sat.

The young woman placed her finger on her chin in a gesture of dismay, and said in an angry voice, 'Sisters, it's really sad!'

A hush had descended on the gali. Seeing the reaction of their mothers, mewling and whimpering children too had become quiet in the presence of the respectable-looking visitors. In reply to the questioning gaze of the gali women, the young woman said, 'Sisters, haven't you heard? In Calcutta, Muslims have murdered thousands of our Hindu brothers, they have raped and mutilated hundreds of women from Hindu families. It is indeed sad that these people still come to peddle their stuff in your gali.'

The older woman spread her hands to show the extent of her disgust, 'May they mourn for their own children, these Muslims feed on us and then stick a knife into our stomachs. Have you people lost your senses!'

Kartaro said, 'Bahinji, we don't want to buy from these Muslims, may their wives become widows. We would buy any time from our Hindu brothers, but those good-for-nothing Hindu peddlers don't come this far. If they do, they charge us double.'

The young women said, 'Sister, Hindu peddlers don't come here; do you know why? These Muslims have control of the wholesale market at Mewa Mandi. When Hindus want to buy goods, Muslims jack up the prices. So what if you pay two paisas more to our own people. If we feed these cursed Muslims, one day these same people will stab us in the back. All the women in our mohalla have taken a vow never to buy anything from a Muslim.'

Kartaro yelled at the rai, gesturing with her arm for him to leave, 'Go away, man! No one wants to buy anything. And don't show up here in future.'

Reassured, the young woman introduced her elder companion, 'She is Mata Ishwar Kaur-ji of Vachchovali gali. You must have heard her name. We want to speak with all you sisters on behalf of the Hindu Defence Committee.'

'Sure, what else! Hindus will now peddle fruits,' they heard in a shrill, loud voice.

All eyes turned to the Woman-of-the-Well. Startled, the visitors also looked towards the source of the voice. The women kept silent, some covered their lips with a corner of their clothing to hide their smiles. On the last chabutara towards the bazaar sat the Woman-of-the-Well, her hands framing her face, her emaciated legs showing through the folds of an old black lehanga. Without looking at any one she continued, 'Now Hindus will sell vegetables and fruits and demean themselves to do the job of a rai and kunjara, they will work as gujjars and sell milk, will do the lowly job of washing other people's clothes as dhobis do, will make shoes, and defile their caste by being dyers of cloth.'

Ignoring the old woman's outburst, Meladei said to the visitors, 'You are heartily welcome, please take a seat.'

From her side of the gali, Kartaro offered her low stool to the elder woman and sat down on the bare floor of the chabutara. She said, 'Bahenji, don't pay attention to what the Woman-of-the-Well says. She rambles on like this; no one minds what she says.'

Without caring if anyone was minding her words, the old woman went on, her elbows on her knees and her head in her hands, 'Hindus will become potters, as kalaigeers they will tinplate kitchen utensils. They are doomed. Turn away from your family profession, and you defile your caste. Both the communities have discarded their dharma, their age-old professions. The Muslims will make mithai and sweets; will be cloth merchants. Who's ever heard of a Muslim halwai or cloth merchant? If Hindus drink water piped into their homes, water touched by the Muslims, how can they save their religion? Whoever drinks the piped water, can commit any crime and will stop at nothing. Send your girls to school, give them education in English, let them wear spectacles, let them braid their hair, let them wear dhotis or let them go naked, what's the difference? What's more, now women look at themselves in the mirror just like whores! Did any decent household have a mirror in my time? Now our dharma is lost, so is our karma, and we have no shame left any more.'

The women felt uncomfortable at such rambling in front of the visitors to their gali. Meladei spoke apologetically for everyone, 'Bahenji, no one listens to what that woman says. Her mind is not right.'

Kartaro, Bhagwanti and others too chipped in, 'Yes, of course! Who cares what an old woman, a grandma or a great-grandma says?'

Meladei went on, 'Bahenji, the water well of the gali is in the house that belongs to her. Her grandsons have built new houses in the Anarkali bazaar, but she doesn't want to part from the water of her well. The first house in the gali belonged to her family. She has no eyesight left and can barely stand up straight, but has all her teeth intact. Says that teeth fall if one drinks piped water. Her house has no electricity or piped water. Lights a mustard oil lamp every night. Who would choose to live in a house like that; she's got tenants only because of the housing shortage. She always talks about the times when Sikh kings ruled, regards it as sacrilege to wear anything other than a lehanga and chadar. Her grandsons have a shop in the Anarkali bazaar selling glass and ceramic wares. She refuses to drink water even from their hands.'

The wife of Bajaj Dewanchand interrupted Meladei, 'She doesn't trust her grandsons either to do anything for her after her death. She has already had all those rites performed, has donated a cow to a Brahmin, pooja and prayers done so that her soul may rest in peace, everything so that she may go straight to heaven when she drops off.'

Kartaro began to laugh as she spoke, 'The poor soul has spent all that money on her life hereafter, but what if Yamraj or his angels of death failed to recognize her? She still buys milk only from a Muslim gujjar and vegetables from a Muslim rai; says these occupations are a Muslim's dharma.'

Gyandevi, the representative of the Hindu Defence Committee came to the point, 'Sisters, you all know, as we do, this was all in the newspapers, that the Muslims have killed five thousand Hindus in Calcutta. What are we going to do about it?'

Kartaro butted in to express her agreement, 'Yes, yes, don't we know!' She pointed at Bhagwanti, 'Her son writes in a newspaper, he's one in a thousand. Pushpa's man, the doctor, also said that the Muslims had slaughtered ten thousand Hindus.'

The young woman nodded, 'Yes, sister, who knows what these devious people won't do? They've killed probably more than ten thousand. The wily English are on their side, they don't allow the facts to get through. The accursed Muslims have dishonoured thousands of Hindu women, our sisters, daughters.'

Kartaro again interrupted her, 'Yes, I know. Listen, Peeto's dad also said the same thing. These wretched people, they let all hell loose. Each Hindu woman was ravaged by hundreds of Muslims.'

Jeeva, wife of Bajaj Dewanchand said with a shudder, 'Sister, I've heard that they cut off women's breasts.'

Birumal's mother said, 'I heard that they eat Hindu children.'

The Hindu Defence Committee workers did not want to waste time in dispelling the rumours. Gyandevi said, 'The Defence Committee is asking for donations of money and clothes to help our Hindu community in Bengal. Those rotten Muslims have taken everything from Hindus there, even clothes off their women. Without any clothes, those naked daughters and sisters of Hindus couldn't go out to fetch water from the well, and died of thirst and hunger. Many Hindu women committed suicide in the shame of such humiliation.'

Her eyes moist with sympathy, Basant Kaur said, 'May Guru Maharaj destroy everything belonging to such cruel people.'

Gyandevi went on, 'The Committee is sending cash, clothes and provisions to help the Hindus. You all should help by doing what you can.'

Meladei sighed deeply to show how pained she was, 'Yes, bahenji, why wouldn't we help our brothers and sisters? They're no strangers. Their honour is our honour! We'll do what we can.'

Some other women too dabbed at their eyes.

Gyandevi explained, 'Women of Bengal don't wear shalwar or lehanga. They wear dhotis, dhotis are needed for them.'

Usha, younger daughter of Bhagwanti, asked in bewilderment, 'Even young girls go to school wearing dhoti?'

Bhagwanti scolded her, 'Shut up, don't interrupt when elders are talking. Every land has its own customs.'

'Yes, it's a matter of custom,' interjected Basant Kaur. 'In Rawalpindi, where I come from, such a revealing dress would never be tolerated. No woman can dare to be seen outside her home or in the bazaar in a dhoti or a sari.'

Meladei said in a worried voice, 'The price of dhotis is sky-high right now. A dhoti that used to cost three rupees is now sold for thirteen. Well, I'll see what...'

Kartaro waived her hand to attract attention, 'Fine-quality dhotis won't do. The women from the East don't wear a petticoat under the dhoti. I saw them in Haridwar. I could have died of shame.'

Gyandevi wound up the discussion. 'You collect cash and clothes from your gali. Make a list of who gives what. The Committee's representative will collect it from you and give you a receipt. You should organize a defence committee in the gali. We'll soon face the same threat here.'

Meladei said, 'Bahenji, rest assured. We have many educated girls in the gali. There's Pushpa, and Tara, they can read the newspaper in English. Our parents didn't let us study. Letting us get past the eighth grade was considered more than enough; now most of the girls pass high school. Pushpa has studied up to the twelfth grade, Tara's in her BA.'

Gyandevi said, 'Where are those girls? Call them! Girls like them are needed.'

Bhagwanti was always careful to keep other people from saying that Tara's parents had sent their daughter to college because they wanted to imitate rich people or put on airs. She said, 'Sister, what can we do? We're poor people. When you look for a match for your daughter, they ask about the girl's education before they talk of the engagement ceremony. Times have changed.'

Gyandevi repeated, 'Call the girls.'

Bhagwanti turned towards the window of her house on the upper storey and called, 'Tara, come down here for a minute.' She turned to the other women, 'The poor dear hardly finds time to study. She tries to catch up in the afternoon when it's quiet. Today her cousin Sheelo has come from her in-laws' place. She must be with her.'

Meladei called at another upper storey window across the gali, 'Pushpa! Come out for a minute. One should sit with their neighbours once in a while.'

'She won't come,' said Kartaro, 'she's angry. Quarrelled with her hubby this morning.'

Basant Kaur put her hand to her lips as if she had been rendered speechless, 'Oh dear, too bad! Hardly eighteen months have passed since their marriage, and tiffs and arguments have already begun!'

'Yes, what else!' said Kartaro. 'Just look at these young educated kids. Believe me, these educated girls don't know a thing about taming a man. Soon after the marriage, they open up, show every inch of their body. Going out with their hubby to the bazaar, going to the cinema with him, he's had his fill in a month. We'd let months or even a year pass before we showed him half of our face.'

'What is it, mother?' asked Tara as she came down the stairs. Sheelo was with her.

'Shut up!' Meladei said to Kartaro. 'Watch your language before grown-up girls.' She lifted a corner of the mat where she sat, took out some change and spoke to Kartaro's ten-year-old daughter Peeto sitting nearby, 'Child, run and get two anna's worth of hot sweet *boondi* from Mohan and two anna's worth of eggplant pakoras from Iqbal. Get a paisa's worth of ice, too.'

'No, no, no! That's not needed, sister!' Gyandevi raised both her hands in protest.

'No bahinji, its nothing,' said Meladei. 'You have to have a glass of cold water. You've come this far in such heat.'

Peeto took the eight-anna coin from Meladei's hand and flew off like a swallow, her chunni trailing behind her.

Gyandevi looked at Tara and Sheelo, 'Come, girls, sit here. Girls like you should take on the task of organizing the women of the gali.'

Kartaro attempted to explain on behalf of Gyandevi, 'Listen, girls, bahenji was telling us how in the Bengal of Calcutta, the Muslims have killed ten thousand of our Hindu people. They also stripped our Hindu sisters and mothers naked in front of everyone in the bazaar, and hundreds of rotten Muslims took turns.'

'Be quiet! May your tongue fall out! Shame on you!' Meladei hissed at her. 'Don't wag your tongue before young girls. Bahenji was asking us,' she said to Tara, 'to collect donations of cash and clothing from the gali. You can make a list of what we get.'

Tara had bowed her head demurely on hearing something that was not supposed to be said in her presence. She said to Gyandevi, 'I'll keep a record.'

Gyandevi said imperiously, 'Sure, you can do that. You must have seen in the newspapers …'

Kartaro could not stop herself, 'It's her brother who works at the newspaper.'

Gyandevi continued, 'The Muslim League declared open war on 16 August in Bombay on Hindus. Those damned people say that they want Pakistan, want to carve half of Hindustan into Pakistan. Want Punjab to be a part of Pakistan. Will throw Hindus out of here.'

Basant Kaur said, 'Throw us out! Punjab is not their father's property; it has always belonged to Hindus and Sikhs! The rotten Muslims ruled in Delhi, Agra and Lucknow. Punjab was always ours.' She was the wife of the postal clerk Birumal, and had studied up to the tenth grade.

Ishwar Kaur shook her clenched fist, 'Punjab belongs to us and to keep it ours we must fight the Muslims. You all saw the huge procession that the Muslims marched in on 16 August. The battle has begun in Bengal, now it will begin in Punjab too.' She lowered her voice conspiratorially, 'The rotten Muslims are preparing for war. They're making gun barrels from water pipes. Their women now carry daggers and knives. We're still asleep. You all should tell your men to go to *akharas* to exercise and train, ask them to learn to fire a gun or use a sword or a club. How else will you save your belongings?'

Jeeva chipped in, 'What is there in a wretched Muslim's home? Four earthenware pots, one hookah and a burka! That's why these hotheads are all so keen!'

Gyandevi tried another explanation, 'We should be strong enough to protect our religion and guard our properties. The Hindus have turned into a mimosa plant that closes up when touched. All we know is how to earn money, then lose it and remain compassionate. We sisters should be ready to defend ourselves. Anyone tries to molest you, slit his stomach open. Look at the Rani of Jhansi and at Padmini, and look at us! All girls and young women should carry a kirpan.' She showed a kirpan strapped under her clothes, and challenged, 'I dare any one to lay his hands upon me!'

Tara's younger sister Usha and Meladei's daughter Dammo were thrilled, 'We too will carry a kirpan!'

Tara said lightly, 'Who would you use it on, stupid?'

'Use it to cut off their husbands' noses,' answered Kartaro.

'Hai, may everyone keep safe and healthy! What do kids have to do with kirpans and daggers,' said Purandei sorting out her skeins.

'Sister, such talk turns children into cowards,' Gyandevi told her.

'Bahenji, it's the British who are causing all this strife.' Tara began in a quiet voice.

Ishwar Kaur at once contradicted her, 'But why do the damned Muslims fight us at the urging of the British? They don't have to.'

'The Hindus too can be instigated,' Tara said boldly. 'We were just talking about preparing for war.'

Gyandevi, Kartaro and Basant Kaur all spoke together, 'It's the Muslims, may they die childless, that start the fight. Poor Hindus don't. Who wants to fight? If someone attacks us, won't we fight back? We'll drink their blood!'

'Auntie, you'll drink their blood?' Tara again said quietly. 'You don't even drink water from their hands!'

Kartaro threw aside all decorum in the rage to express her loathing. She brought her foot forward and stamped it on the chabutara, 'My shoe will drink water from their hands!'

'You called, bahenji?' Pushpa said coming down the stairs. She looked sullen and everyone noticed it. She sat next to Kartaro on the chabutara.

Meladei mentioned the Hindu–Muslim conflict, and then said, 'What happened, girl? Why this dour face?'

Kartaro answered for her, 'Fought with the doctor.'

'Stop it!' Pushpa turned her face away.

'Everyone look at that lying face!' Kartaro pointed at her. 'Listen, what do you want to hide from your gali neighbours? Look at these educated girls! Sister, it's your neighbours who hold your hand when you're in trouble. Husbands are useless at such a time!' She felt Pushpa's abdomen, 'Mare in foal yet?'

Pushpa's face flushed with embarrassment. She shrank back.

Peeto brought sweet and savoury snacks in two leaf cups, and a chunk of ice tied in the corner of her chunni. Meladei handed the ice to her daughter Dammo, 'Go and make ice water and fill four glasses. Bring two plates too.' She turned to Pushpa, 'So, what was the quarrel about?'

Pushpa had to confess, 'Auntie, nothing much. He leaves early for the hospital. I got up late today. Was having a wash. The servant lad made paranthas and served him on a dirty plate. He threw away the plate in anger, and left without eating. He could have called me.'

'Hai! Hai!' Kartaro put her hands on her head in mock dismay. 'You ask your servant to feed your husband? See what education does to you! Hey, these are the ways to keep your man hooked. Even a dog obeys the person that feeds it.'

Basant Kaur said, 'My friend, a husband-and-wife tiff and clouds in the month of October don't last.'

Tara said to Gyandevi to change the topic, 'Bahenji, the Hindu–Muslim conflict is nonsense. Where will the two go if they fight one another? Their country is one! Our real fight is with the British oppressor.'

Ishwar Kaur replied vehemently, 'Don't be so simple, beti! The Muslims are the ones behind the demand for Pakistan. What'll we do with the country if we lose our homes and native land? For the British, Hindus are the same as Muslims. Since Khizr and Sikandar formed the ministry in Punjab, can a Hindu get a job in any department? It was unheard of for a Muslim to work as a babu in some office. They used to work as peons, drive tongas or do other menial jobs.'

Gyandevi intervened to end the argument, 'There should be an iron gate at the entrance of the gali. You all should be ready to defend yourselves.

Whatever donations are received for Bengal, these girls will keep a record. The Committee will issue a receipt for all donations.'

Tara began to get up, 'Whatever needs to be recorded, Pushpa bahin will do it or I'll do it. I have to go to my tutoring job, I'll be late.'

'Yes, sure, beti, you go ahead.' Meladei said, 'Let the menfolk return. Let Masterji, Ratan's father, Jaidev come back, doctor sahib and Sardarji too. It's proper to ask the men before making any decision.'

Sheelo climbed the stairs with Tara to her house. Tara went to a corner of the room, washed her face over an area that led to the drainpipe, and removed her neatly folded clothes from a rope slung across the side of the room. She closed the window that opened into the gali.

'Oh, it's hot!' Sheelo said. 'You shut off the air.'

'I'll open it; let me change my clothes first.' She said. 'That stupid Biru peeps at me through the window. He's just a pup, but has learned all the bad ways of a goonda. I haven't told anyone yet, I feel so embarrassed. But if I do blurt it out someday, I know the gali people will thrash the idiot. We only have one room. It's very inconvenient to change clothes when father and brother are at home. Sometimes the dupatta slips off the shoulder without one knowing.'

Sheelo was looking hard at Tara's breasts and at the bra that covered them as she changed her clothes. She said, 'Your body is no good. Look at mine, it's imported. I'll give you mine, you can sew one like it yourself.'

'No baba no, what I have is fine for me. As it is, mother is always nagging me about wearing such tight clothes,' Tara said. 'What do you care? You're married, you can do what you want. Listen, I'll be back around half-past-six. Mother will find someone to escort you.'

'I'm not leaving yet.' A sparkle came to Sheelo's eyes and she turned her face away, 'I have to go back to my in-laws the day after tomorrow. Now that I'm here, let me see Ratan just this once.'

'You always say,' Tara took a deep breath, 'that Mohanji is such a good person. That he really treats you well!'

'So what! What if he does treat me well?' Sheelo said. 'Old infatuations die hard. Can't one have one's own wishes and desires after marriage? At home my husband is always after me: don't eat this, this won't suit you, you'll get a cold, your stomach will be upset; where did you spend those four annas? He neither laughs nor shows anger.'

'Aren't you scared?'

'When I should have been, I wasn't. Now that's history. Ratan's the real father.' Sheelo smiled.

'What do you mean?' Tara gasped.

'It's his.' Sheelo said, lowering her gaze.

Tara felt so disgusted that she could hardly breathe. She managed to ask, 'How?'

'Don't you remember, I was once here around noontime? When you came back from the college in the evening, you went to drop me off at Uchchi Gali.'

Tara was speechless. She felt faint at the thought of Sheelo and Ratan committing such a sin in her house.

'When does he get back?' Sheelo asked.

'How should I know!' Tara said angrily.

'Save your anger!' Sheelo said. 'We'll see when your time comes. You don't care for that Somraj either. Sister, such things are ordained by fate.'

'I want nothing to do with that man. I'll never get married to him,' Tara said, heading for the stairs.

Her dislike for Sheelo's shameless behaviour was rekindled. Ratan, she had begun to loathe even before her own engagement.

When Tara stepped into the gali, Ishwar Kaur and Gyandevi had left. Most of the women had wound up whatever they were doing, and had gone to their homes to get the evening meal together. Tara came into the Machchi Hatta bazaar from her gali and turned towards the Shahalami Gate. She walked with downcast eyes, keeping on the left side to avoid the bustling crowd and packs of unruly cattle being herded back to their shed after grazing in the fields. What Sheelo said had disturbed her. Deceit is sin. Despite such shamelessness Sheelo was good and virtuous in the eyes of everyone whereas her own intentions were questioned because she didn't want to get married. But I won't give up, she thought. Asad bhai said that he'd go to Dr Nath's after Tuesday. He might be there today. He should be told about all this, about these people fanning the flames of riot in the galis.

Inside the entrance of Seth Gopal Shah's mansion, there were verandas on both sides. In the verandas were seats for the account clerks. The cotton-filled seats, hardened after years of use, were covered with ink-stained, dirty white sheets and large bolster pillows lay on them against the wall. Both the munims sat cross-legged on the mattresses, facing the ledgers bound in red cloth. Tara always walked straight into the aangan beyond without looking at them. On the right and the left side of the aangan were broad stairways to the upper floor. She took the stairs on the left to an upstairs room.

She found the room empty.

The rear of the room opened on to a veranda. She went out and called out, 'Kikka! Gulli! Where are you? Come, children.'

There was no response.

Where were the children? Tara wondered. Somebody should surely have heard her, and said something in reply. She looked down into the aangan and called out for Karmo, the old woman servant.

The house looked deserted. On one side of the aangan, Chaitu the servant boy was creating a racket as he washed the floor with water from a tin bucket. Tara called out to him and asked about the children.

Chaitu said, 'The kids are in the other wing of the house. They won't come. Maaji has said that they don't need a tutor any more.'

Tara's heart missed a beat. She was walking towards the stairs when she heard someone call her, 'Tara, is that you?'

Dr Nath came towards her. He rephrased Chaitu's message, 'You're looking for the kids? They've all gone to Vachchovali. Come this way. Asad too is here, we'll all sit together.'

Nath's words did not have the ominous tone of Chaitu's, but Tara's mind was still on the servant's words. The wing of the house they went to belonged only to Nath. No women lived there. Tara felt a little embarrassed, however she could not but follow the doctor.

Tara had tutored Kikka, Bholi and Gulli, three- and four-and-a-half-year olds, for three months the previous summer. More than tutoring, it was playing with colours and doodling with crayons on paper. Tara knew it was meant to help her with her college fees. The previous year, Nath had gone to Simla after appointing her as tutor and paying her one hundred rupees in advance. The war was over, but the governor of Punjab sent for Nath for his advice now and then.

This year Tara had asked Puri to remind Dr Nath about the tutoring. She would be able to save some money, she thought, for her winter clothes. Nath was not needed in Simla as he was last year, and she sometimes saw him at the mansion when she went to tutor the children. Nath would ask after her, and sometimes invite her to stay for tea. The women of the house had received Tara cordially and were friendly towards her. But when they heard that she went to Nath's side of the house alone and had tea with him, they began to treat her like a pariah. Now when Tara met them, they would look askance at her and exchange meaningful smiles. Tara felt hurt and ostracized.

Tara had told Asad about her tutoring the children of Nath's family. They met twice at Nath's place; during the vacations there was little other chance of meeting at the house of some friend from the college or the Student Federation. Asad would sit with Nath and wait for her to finish. He would then leave with her and they would walk together up to her gali.

Tara knew that the family of Seth Gopal Shah was among the wealthiest in Lahore. In the right wing of the mansion, with three huge inner courtyards, lived Nath's aged father, and the families of his other sons. The left wing held Nath's quarters. He lived alone, and his servant and his kitchen too were separate. Tara also knew that when Nath was a boy, Masterji had come to this mansion for eight years as his tutor, and that he regarded Masterji with reverence. Upon returning from England, he had come to visit Masterji at his home to pay his respects. Tara still had a vivid memory of Nath being dressed in a bright white shirt and trousers, and how Masterji was flustered when such an eminent guest arrived. Her father had called for something to be brought for the guest to sit down, but Nath sat next to Masterji on the straw mat spread out on the floor. Everyone in the gali knew of this visit.

Nath led Tara to a veranda in his wing of the mansion. When Asad saw Tara, he stood up and greeted her with a 'Namaste'.

Nath asked his servant to bring tea, and said to Asad as he took his chair, 'Yes, go ahead. You can speak freely before Tara.'

'Yes, I know I can,' said Asad. 'Dr Saheb, I was saying that these fanatics are poisoning people's minds in both Hindu and Muslim neighbourhoods. In the mosques, the mullahs are preaching to the faithful and issuing fatwa for jihad in the name of the Prophet. They are making plans to collect arms and ammunition. If riots break out here, the carnage will be worse than in Calcutta. If Khizr chooses to remain oblivious to all this, the governor should be told.'

'The bureaucracy is not troubled by sectarian riots.' Nath said. 'The riots would diminish the influence of the League and the Congress. Tell this to your leader Fiqar; he left the Congress and joined the League. Tell this also to Ibrahim, the leader of the railway union. The Muslims trust these men.'

Asad leaned forward in his chair, 'They are doing what they can. The government too needs to act firmly.'

Tara ventured to say, 'Some women from the Hindu Defence Committee were inciting similar trouble in our gali today.'

'I know, this is happening not only in this town but in the whole province,' Nath said in agreement. Running his fingers through his hair, he looked at Asad, 'Sir Khizr can't do much at the moment. Several members of his Unionist Party have defected to the Muslim League. If he puts any pressure on the League, he might face desertion by the rest of the Muslim members. He doesn't want to take that risk. His ministry is on its last legs; let's see how many days it can drag on for.'

Asad tried again, 'You can speak to the governor, Sir Evan Jenkins. You're his advisor.'

Nath motioned him to listen, 'I am an advisor on economic affairs. I cannot offer unsolicited advice. The governor too knows that the Unionist ministry won't last. The results of the recent elections clearly show that. The governor had asked me to report on the economic reasons for the current unrest among the farmers of Punjab. He knows that the farmers are seething for a change in the current land distribution system. The Unionist ministry cannot keep them quiet. Any administration depends on the prevailing system of land ownership and distribution. The way to make farmers forget their dissatisfaction with the government is to get them enmeshed in some sectarian nonsense. If the League and the Congress don't continue to fight each other, the administration can't keep either of them down. Jenkins wants to prove to the Cabinet Mission that Indians are not fit to have the government handed over to them. If the League and the Congress can work together, what's the point of having a Britisher as the governor?'

As they sipped tea, Nath expanded on his views, 'The British are now eager to divest themselves of the burden of ruling India, but the British bureaucracy in India is not in touch with the international situation and the crisis in Britain's economy. The bureaucracy does not want to give up being the rulers of India.'

When they finished their tea, Asad looked at Tara to see if she was ready to leave. Tara faced a dilemma: she wanted to leave with Asad, but she also wanted to know more about the message given to her by the servant.

Asad asked for Nath's leave. Nath guessed Tara's dilemma and said to her, 'Tara, stay behind for five minutes if you're not in a hurry. I want to ask something about the kids you tutor.'

Tara could not say no. Asad left without her.

'You wanted to leave with Asad,' Nath smiled. 'I asked you to stay. Hope you're not annoyed.'

Tara was disconcerted that her secret was out. She had not even acknowledged this secret to herself, not so plainly and unequivocally. She was at a loss for an answer.

Nath did not wait for her to answer. He said in English, 'When Puri was here the other day to ask about your tutoring job, he mentioned that your father's elder brother had gotten you engaged to some oaf. Did you both not oppose it?'

Tara sat quietly, with her head bowed.

'You like Asad, he's a good chap. Do you believe in social restrictions?'

Tara was silent.

'To be in love is a pleasant feeling. You feel alive. You're what... nineteen? Twenty?'

'Nineteen.'

'Stay in love all you want, but marry only after finishing your studies.'

She regarded Nath with respect. Hearing him say these words caused her a lot of embarrassment.

Nath shifted in his chair, and said, 'This is your final year of BA. You probably waste too much time in tutoring the children.'

Tara was alarmed with the possibility of losing her job, 'No, there's no such problem.'

Nath thought for a few moments, 'You were hired for three months. You're owed that much; you mustn't lose any salary. If you've been told not to continue, you won't feel like working either.'

'That's true,' she lifted her eyes, 'but I'll accept salary only for the time that I've worked.'

'That wouldn't be fair!' Nath said with irritation, 'You're not leaving of your own free will. We should have given you notice, or you ought to be paid the rest of your salary. It wouldn't be proper.'

'We don't need legalities in this case,' she said out of politeness.

'The atmosphere of this place is not suitable for you.' He averted his eyes. 'Do you know why you were given that message through Chaitu? Maybe you guessed, it was because by mistake I praised you before the women.'

Tara looked at him in surprise. Nath was looking away. He went on, 'They think I am attracted to you, and that perhaps I'll marry you.'

Tara bowed her head again. How could he say such a thing!

Nath continued, still not looking at her, 'You're nineteen, I'm thirty. These women can't imagine why a nineteen-year-old would consent to marry a thirty-year-old middle-aged man. But is it their fault? They can't imagine that a woman can have a say in whom she marries or what she wants to do. They can't see either that I can like you without any thought of sex.'

Every fibre in Tara's body quivered. She was glad that he was looking the other way. Nath continued, 'But can we blame these women for such thinking? The poor souls don't know anything beyond sex and marriage. Aren't the women of their class—the class whose status rests on wealth— valued only for sex? Servants and maids do the housework for them. Men have all the freedom to get sex wherever they want; women of the family serve only as begetters of undisputed heirs for the property. Their dharma, their mission in life, is to obey and follow their husbands. They've been taught not to think beyond that. For them, the only capable woman is one who doesn't let her man slip through her hands. They are not envious of your mind; they are jealous of the attractive woman in you.'

Tara listened in amazement. What is he saying? She knew Doctor Sahib was expressing his own annoyance and hurt, so there was no question of impropriety or indecorum. What he had said had shaken her, but the feeling was not unpleasant.

Tara stole a glance at Nath. She had always looked upon him as a scholar and a person of distinction. For a university student, he was the epitome of all the prestige, position, success and money that could be had. She had always felt obliged and beholden to him; now she felt sympathy for him.

'You can't possibly imagine the reason, the story, behind all this,' Nath said in an agitated voice. 'The reason is not any concern for me, but a concern for the ownership of this house and property. My grandfather had willed this part of the house to me, but if I want I can legally claim half of the entire family property, and the other half will go to the rest of them. All this fuss is about property.'

Tara looked again at Nath. There was anger in his eyes. He said, 'The truth is that my grandfather regards me as his grandson, but my mother's husband—my grandfather's eldest son— does not want to accept me as his son. He left my mother here with his family. He used to look after the family business in Kashmir. He kept a mistress; therefore, my mother could not be taken there. I am in truth the child of my grandfather's second son. My grandfather's eldest son was angered by my birth, and he married for a second time. My grandfather's second son had only daughters from his marriage. If my grandfather wants to divide the family property between his two sons, then I am the sole heir of one of the sons, the same property mess again! My grandfather's eldest son is the legal heir to the property. The eldest son had two wives: I am the sole offspring from the first. The second wife had five sons. My mother's husband did not want to share his inheritance with me. All this quibbling saddened my grandfather. He didn't let the secret out, for the sake of the family's prestige. I may not be the son of his eldest son, I was still his grandson. He was very fond of me. I was his first grandson. If he had not made me sleep in his room, my stepmother or even my own legal father would have murdered me so as not to share their inheritance. I was poisoned once while my mother was still alive, but I was saved. Here, look at this.'

He showed marks below his ear and on his arms, 'These are burn marks from my childhood. They tried to finish me off by pouring boiling water on me. As long as I stay a bachelor, they are assured that the property will remain in the family, that after my death the mansion too will go to my brothers or to their offspring. If I marry, my children will be able to claim the half of the whole property.'

Tara had not asked for her previous month's salary. She would collect for all three months together, she had thought. She wanted to have a winter coat; she was the only student in the college without one. Not having a coat was not her fault, but she still felt the embarrassment of her poor circumstances. Nath handed her a hundred rupee note for her three months' work. It was ten rupees more than what was owed to her, but she did not know how to tell that to a person as eminent as he was.

Nath looked at her fondly, and said again in English, 'Don't get me wrong. Hope we'll meet again.'

Nath was on Tara's mind as she walked back to her home, he too is miserable and helpless, he too is constrained by the concern for his family and bound by the mores of society. He can, but will not fight back. She remembered how he had so casually said, 'I like you.' He's really a gentleman.

The thought led to the other things Nath had said about Asad. Nath's words echoed in her mind and pierced her heart like an arrow. What she felt in her heart made her flush. How deep this secret was buried in her heart! She had never admitted it, not even to herself.

Tara tried to reason: What could Doctor Sahib have seen in her behaviour to guess her secret? Could others suspect the same? But what's wrong with that? Nothing immoral, like the Sheelo–Ratan affair!

She stopped in her tracks. Lost in thought, she had walked past the entrance to her gali. She turned round, and went back.

When she reached home, her mother was alone and busy in the kitchen. Tara asked, 'Has Sheelo left? Did you escort her to her home?'

'No, she's still here,' said her mother. 'It's hot down here. I told her to sit on the roof, in the open air. You go and drop her at Uchchi Gali. Change your clothes after you return.'

The sun had set. As Tara began to climb the stairs, she was uneasy that Ratan might be there too. She climbed with noisy steps, and cleared her throat near the top. When she came out into the open, Sheelo was lying on a charpai staring into the sky. Usha was there too, with Munni in her lap, showing the child the kites the neighbours were flying.

'You're still here,' she asked Sheelo, and sat beside her on the charpai. Sheelo looked sad. Her eyes were puffed up from wiping away tears. Tara forgot her anger of two hours ago, 'Hai, what happened?'

Sheelo's mouth quivered. She bit her lip and covered her eyes with her aanchal. She let out a deep sigh and turned her back.

Tara did not want to question her in front of Usha. She said to Usha, 'My good sister, take one paisa from mother and get some ice. I'm really thirsty. Sheelo too would like a glass of cold water.'

Usha went down. Tara put her hand on Sheelo's forehead and asked, 'Tell me, what happened?'

Tears flowed from Sheelo's eyes and she dabbed them with her aanchal. 'He's angry with me.'

'Why?'

'When I told him that the child was his, at first he kept quiet. Then said: If that's so, let's go away from here together. I said: I can't do that! I may be married, but I am still yours. He said: Wah! My child will be someone else's. I won't accept that!'

Tara and Usha were returning after dropping Sheelo off at her house when they came across Ratan on his way to the bazaar. Usha inquired, 'Bhai, where are you going?'

'Nowhere, just walking around,' he said briefly and kept going.

Tara was quiet too. She had felt that Ratan's face was pale with a shadow of worry and anxiety. After what Sheelo had told her, Ratan did not seem as bad a person as before. He is not so shallow after all, she thought. Asad too came to her mind, but he is totally different, she thought.

Chapter 6

THE COLD HAD TURNED BITTER. A FOG DESCENDED SOON AFTER SUNSET, HELD down the smoke from kitchen fires and covered the city like a canopy. Frost nipped at ears and noses. Puffs of steam rose from the mouths of the pedestrians in the bazaars and on the roads. Breath from the nostrils of horses straining to pull the tongas looked like jets of steam from boiling kettles. Eyes smarted from the smog. But the bright lights of the stores in Anarkali penetrated the smog and lit up the people thronging the bazaar.

Every evening the bazaar also saw people taking part in processions, shouting: 'Allah-u-akbar! Muslim League zindabad! Down with the Khizr government! Long live Quaid-e-Azam! We want the League government! Hindu–Muslim unity zindabad! We must have Pakistan!' The processions were thin, some volunteers of the Muslim League, a few Muslim students or a handful of Muslim youths from middle-class families carrying green flags.

Hindus in Lahore were uneasy worrying about what turn the rising League movement might take. Editorials in the Hindu press and in the Congress party newspapers cautioned the administration to keep watch on the situation. Puri had written twice in *Pairokaar*, 'A storm of sectarian-inspired politics and of sectarian violence and hatred is gathering on the horizon. This storm will end civic peace and security. No one will remember these sermons for Hindu–Muslim unity when the storm breaks.'

Soon the League processions became larger. Railway workers began to appear in the processions, and they chanted slogans of a different sort: 'Unite Hindus–Muslims! Down with the Khizr government! Down with the establishment! Hindustan zindabad! Pakistan zindabad! Long live Quaid-e-Azam! Install a democratic government! We want the right of self-determination! Workers of the World, Unite!'

Puri wrote in *Pairokaar*, '... The change in the mood of the processions will give some comfort to peace-loving citizens. We do not oppose a democratically constituted ministry or even a coalition of two political parties. Nonetheless, we want to warn the political parties involved in the movement that the demand for Pakistan is based on a sectarian division of the country. At the root of such a demand are religious intolerance, enmity

and hatred for other communities. Such tendencies will neither foster unity
nor bode well for civic peace.'

Zubeida and Gurtu met Surendra, Krishna, Sneha and Tara at Dayal Singh
College and told them, 'Narendra bhai has sent a message that a procession
of Muslim women will march from Lohari Gate at four. If you all join in,
it won't appear just a sectarian show. We won't let them shout sectarian
slogans. Some Federation comrades will come along too.'

Surendra agreed and asked Tara to accompany her. Tara knew how her
brother felt about such marches, so she said, 'I'll accompany you to the
Lohari. We'll see after that.'

In front of Lohari Gate, where Railway Road intersected Anarkali,
Narendra Singh, Asad, Pradyumna, Zuber and Dhanpat were waiting
along with several others from the Student Federation. Some communist
workers were present too. On one side, encircled by the volunteers of
the League, were twelve Muslim women wearing burkas and another five
without burkas about to march in the procession. Surendra, Zubeida and
Gurtu joined them. Seeing Sneha and Tara hesitate Narendra Sigh invited
them, 'Comrades, you come along too.'

Tara saw that Asad was looking at her. He said, 'The more Hindu women,
the better.' As Tara walked towards the group, Sneha joined her.

The girls from the Student Federation were at the head of the march.
They began to walk, chanting: 'Reinstate civil liberties! Hindus, Muslims
and Sikhs unite! We want democratic government! Long live Congress–
League unity! Quaid-e-Azam zindabad! Mahatma Gandhi zindabad!' The
girls shouted the slogans in their high, female voices, and their colleagues
and the comrades repeated them in a loud and powerful unison.

The procession had gone only about 100 yards on Ganapat Road when
a scream from a woman was heard.

With the scream came shouts of 'Grab him! Hold him!' Narendra Singh,
Zuber, Pradyumna and some League volunteers ran after and caught a man
in a white Gandhi cap, and gave him several punches.

The man in the white cap yelled, 'Save me! The Muslims are after
me!'

Another shout was heard, 'The Muslims are attacking! Come on! Hit
back!'

From one side someone called, 'Come on! Kill the bloody Hindus!'

In the melee, some rushed forward to fight and most others turned to run away. Lathis were brandished. On Anarkali Road shops were owned both by Hindus and Muslims. The bazaar rang with the sound of running feet.

Zuber could raise his voice like a megaphone. He shouted, 'Friends, this is no Hindu–Muslim riot! Some goondas have created this mischief!'

The office of *Pairokaar* was at the junction of Anarkali bazaar and Ganapat Road. Many office workers came out of the building at the sound of the commotion. Puri too climbed down the stairs. He saw that several League volunteers and Student Federation members were holding a man by his arms and shirt collar. The man was trying to wriggle free, saying, 'Watch out! Don't you dare touch me! I've done nothing! I don't know anything!'

Puri said with surprise, 'This man is police constable Waheed! He used to escort me from prison to the court!'

The uproar grew. The burka-clad women began to beat their chests in syapa style and curse, 'Police dogs hai-hai! Kizr government hai-hai!'

Puri went into the crowd and said to Tara and Gurtu, 'What's this nonsense! You're marching to support the demand for Pakistan?' He knew Gurtu from the time of the 1942 Quit India movement.

'Bhaiji, this is…' Tara began to say when Asad jumped in, 'We are marching to demand the reinstatement of civil liberties. And for democratic government and Hindu–Muslim unity!'

'That's not right!' Puri shot back in English, 'In a procession of Muslim women yesterday, there were calls of "We must have Pakistan! Don't forget the carnage of Muslims in Bihar!" Do you want me to show you the *Siasat* and *Zamindaar* newspapers?'

'Others were behind what happened yesterday,' said Asad. 'We won't allow any slogans asking for the break-up of the country.'

'You communists support the creation of Pakistan! Isn't that breaking up the country? This march is a front for that demand!' Puri said forcefully.

'We oppose any partition of the country!' Asad replied equally forcefully. 'What does the demand for Pakistan mean? Only that there would be a Congress ministry in one province of Hindustan and of the League in another province. This is a demand for self-determination! The Congress is willing to accept the break-up of the country. We oppose that.'

'The Congress has been driven into a corner!' Puri conceded. 'Otherwise, the League won't allow an independent government anywhere.'

'We only want to impress upon the people and the politicians that the Congress and the League should join forces.'

Puri shook his head in disagreement and looked at Tara, 'I can't approve of this.'

Asad put his hand on Puri's shoulder, 'If they say anything like "We must have Pakistan" or "Don't forget Bihar", we won't march with them.'

"Well, look after Tara. See her home." Puri said to Asad and returned to his office.

While Puri and Asad were arguing, Pradyumna stood on the extension for seating customers in front of a store and began to address the crowd, 'Hindu, Sikh and Muslim brothers. You have seen with your own eyes how the British government and its toady dogs conspire to make the two communities fight. Our Hindu and Muslim sisters are marching together in this procession. They are protesting Khizr's dictatorship and his draconian laws to deny us our civil liberties. Friends, the Congress, the League, the Hindu Mahasabha and the Akali party are all against these draconian laws. Friends, unite to strike down the government of this sycophant Khizr, and support the joint ministry of the Congress, the League, the Mahasabha and the Akalis.'

The crowd packing the Anarkali bazaar made way for the women in the procession. The procession crossed the bazaar and proceeded to Mall Road, went past the high court and the general post office, and reached the assembly hall after about an hour. Once there, the burka-clad women beat their chests for a few minutes, 'Khizr toady hai-hai! Cruel laws hai-hai! British government hai-hai!'

Zubeida also shouted, 'Hindu–Muslims are brothers! Congress–League unite!' The women repeated the slogans.

The League volunteers hired some tongas to take the burka-clad women to their homes. Zubeida, Surendra, Tara and Sneha walked with Narendra Singh, Asad and Zuber towards Lower Mall Road. Pradyumna, pushing his bicycle, went with Gurtu to drop her in the Old Anarkali area. When they reached Nisbet Road, Narendra Singh, Surendra, Zuber and Sneha went through Shabadar Mali Gali to Kele Wali Sarak. Asad had the responsibility of first dropping Zubeida on the road leading to Neela Gumbad, and then escorting Tara up to the Shahalami Gate.

Tara, Asad and Zubeida walked alongside the Medical College and reached Hospital Road, past the road that led to Neela Gumbad. Tara reminded Zubeida, 'You were so busy talking that you forgot the way home.'

Zubeida pretended not to hear. Tara repeated her warning.

Asad said, 'It's all right. We're not very far.'

They saw Pradyumna coming on his bicycle. He dismounted when he saw them. Pradyumna and Zubeida walked back together towards Nisbet Road. Tara understood. Surendra and Gurtu had told her about their mutual affection.

After they left, Asad said, 'Don't talk about them to anyone.'

Tara replied, 'I heard that Zubeida's parents are quite liberal. That they didn't mind.'

'Yes, they're decent people. They mind, but not so much as to harass their daughter to death,' Asad said. 'Zubeida's mother was a Christian before marriage. She worked as a nurse. She knows one can be from a different religion, and still have human feelings. There are others, some fanatics of Islam who are not concerned with the girl's feelings or her happiness. They're worried that if a Muslim girl weds a Hindu, it's a victory for the Hindus. Let this Hindu–Muslim conflict cool down, then we'll get them married with the traditional pomp and ceremony.'

'Yes,' Tara said in agreement.

Asad continued, 'If Hindus and Muslims entered into marriages and relationships despite their religious and communal differences, there'd be little strife. Then the religion or the sense of community would have some meaning. At present, you merely adopt the religion of your family. The difference between two faiths has separated two people. My grandfather was a Hindu. We're from Gurdaspur and my mother still lives there. My grandfather must have been quite a romantic, he converted for the sake of my grandmother. How about me becoming a Hindu for some Hindu girl?'

'Sure! Why don't you!' Tara looked at him with shining eyes.

'Do you believe in this Hindu–Muslim distinction?' Asad asked.

'Not at all.'

'Then why bother to convert? To do that or choose another religion would be to give unnecessary importance to the difference. It's better to ignore it.'

'Yes, you're right.'

'Achcha, let's go through the garden of the Chardewari.'

They walked towards Shahalami Gate through the garden.

Asad asked, 'Why are you so quiet?'

'I was just listening to you.'

'What do you think?' Asad asked, 'Will the decision about whom you marry be yours or your parents'?'

His question shook her body and mind. She could not say anything.

He did not wait long for her answer, and said, 'Maybe the question has never come up?'

Tara kept silent. What does he know about my problem? she thought. She felt it was unkind of him to speak as he had, but when she replied, it was to ask a question, 'Why do you ask?'

'Sorry. My question upset you. I'm sorry.'

Tara had felt hurt, but she said nothing.

They walked through the narrow bazaar. Bhola Pandhe's Gali was only a few steps away. Not to upset Asad with her silence, Tara said, 'Tell you another time. Namaste.'

She turned into her gali without waiting for his reply.

A fog had come before her eyes in her attempt to answer Asad, and she failed to see a brick that had been left behind by children playing in the gali. She stumbled over it and regained her balance with difficulty. A buffalo that Bajaj Dewanchand kept for milk was still tethered on one side. As she tried to squeeze by, it swung its urine-drenched tail and splattered her shalwar.

Tara climbed the stairs to their one-room house. Her mother welcomed Tara with silence. Since the day she had told her son to ask Tara to stop going to college so as not to displease her future in-laws and her son had refused to side with her, she had kept up a hurt silence. She spoke to Tara when she had to, and that only abruptly.

Tara placed her books on the tin trunks stacked beside the wall, and went up to the roof. There was no one there in the chilly winds of December. She wept for a few minutes and that lightened her heart. Asad's question had been an invitation to open her heart. 'I'll tell him everything,' she decided.

Seeing the League campaign grow, the Khizr ministry placed several cities of Punjab under Section 144 to curb demonstrations and public meetings. In Lahore the League launched the satyagraha movement against the government's restraining order. Few expected the League volunteers to remain passive in their demonstrations like those of the Congress, and continue their peaceful protest. It was feared that the League volunteers would resort to violence when provoked, and thus give the administration an excuse to use force to suppress them. Sir Firoze Khan Noon, Iftkharuddin,

Gaznafar Ali Khan and other prominent leaders of the Muslim League had been sent to prison for leading the satyagraha movement, but the League workers continued their peaceful marches against the government ban. The police would intercept their processions and beat them up with lathis, but the volunteers would refuse to turn violent, and court arrest by merely shouting: 'Allah-u-akbar! Muslim League zindabad! Down with the Khizr ministry! We must have Pakistan! We demand the League ministry! Hindus–Muslims unite!'

Members of the Railway Labour Union and the Student Federation mostly stayed away from these demonstrations. The annual college examinations were drawing near. Tara spent as much time as possible in her studies. Still she would go to a study circle meeting if she heard one was being held. She would often see Asad there, but there was seldom an occasion for a talk just between the two of them.

Surendra had not come to the college for a week. Tara heard that she was not well. Tara had two periods off one day, and she went to Gwal Mandi to visit Surendra.

Tara met Surendra's mother as she entered their house on the first floor. She chided Tara affectionately, 'Daughter, some friend you are of Surendra! Didn't care to ask about her. She's had a fever for some time now. She's always talking about you all. The fever lasted for three days. She got better only the day before yesterday.' She took Tara into the next room where Surendra lay on her bed.

Surendra's healthy pink complexion had paled because of the fever, and her large eyes looked even larger. Her eyes brightened when she saw Tara, but she turned around and buried her face in the pillow.

Tara sat on her bed, and tried to hug her to placate her. Surendra protested, 'Go away! I don't want to talk to you, or to anyone else! All you comrades who pose as close friends! Nobody would have bothered even if I'd died!'

'Hai, I only found out yesterday,' Tara apologized. 'I saw Sneha at the college, but she said nothing about you. I only heard when I went to the Study Circle; I hadn't been there for several days. With the exams looming large, I can't afford to go out much.'

'Who else was there?'

'Narendra bhai, Pradyumna, Asad bhai; Gurtu was there too. Pradyumna bhai and Zuber got into an argument.'

'Did anyone ask about me?'

'Who?'

Surendra remained silent.

'Who?' Tara asked again.

Surendra again hid her face behind her pillow. Tara pulled her arm and said, 'Tell me, my dear. Trust me.'

Surendra pressed Tara's hand into hers, 'No. First you swear to me that you won't tell anyone!'

'All right, I swear.'

'Did Asad bhai leave with Gurtu after the meeting?'

'No, I think he went with Narendra bhai to the Communist Party office.'

'Is there something between Asad bhai and Gurtu?'

Tara hesitated, thought for a moment and said, 'I don't know... I haven't noticed anything.'

'You're sure!'

'How can I tell? But I don't think so.' Tara did not like being questioned. Surendra's jealousy towards Gurtu was making her miserable. '

'When you see him next, tell him that I'm ill'. Can't he visit me once?'

'I will,' Tara agreed.

It became difficult for her to sit next to Surendra. She made an excuse, 'My mother asked me to return home soon. She's not well.'

On her way back, Tara's head swam with suspicion. 'Is that thing about Gurtu that Surendra suspected true? Why would Surendra complain? Why did he say all those things to me? You can't trust men, they want every woman they can get. He just acts gentlemanly.' She felt sad and empty.

She could not concentrate on her books. At night she lay wide awake next to her sister on the bed that they shared. Next day her thoughts kept returning to Asad. 'Why did he say all those things to me? I won't talk to him again.' A sense of having lost something niggled at her heart.

She came across Asad twice at the college. The Student Federation was campaigning for the reopening of talks between the Congress and the League. Narendra Singh, Asad and Pradyumna came often to Dayal Singh College. She lowered her gaze whenever their eyes met. The next week, in spite of herself, she went to the Study Circle. Once when they were face-to-face, she spoke to him in a normal tone, passing without meeting his gaze.

'Tara Singhji!' Asad called. Since the day of the naming ceremony of Surendra's nephew, he had sometimes called her that in jest. Tara turned around and saw that Surendra was with him.

'Why are you leaving? We're all going the same way.'

'She's the studious type. She'll go home and learn all her history book by heart,' added Surendra.

'I thought you might all stay a bit longer,' Tara said.

'We're leaving too.' Asad and Surendra left with Tara. As they walked, Asad began telling of an argument between some friends at the Student Federation.

When they reached the square before Medical College, where the road branched off towards Gwal Mandi, Asad said to Tara, 'If you're not in a hurry, let's first see Surendra home. I will drop you off at your gali and then go home.'

'No. Let's first drop Tara at Shahalami. You go back through Kele Wali Sarak,' insisted Surendra.

'I'll walk alone, Shahalami is just across from here,' said Tara.

'No, let's first see Surendra off. I also want to see Puri for a minute,' Asad said decisively.

When they reached the stairs to Surendra's house, she asked them both to come up. Asad made an excuse for both of them, 'Not this time. We'll both be late.'

Seeing that he wanted to be alone with her, half the anger and hurt in Tara's heart melted away. Asad asked when they were alone, 'What's the matter? Have I been rude to you?'

'Who said so?' Tara said looking down, pretending to sulk.

'I felt you were avoiding me. Is that true?'

'You disappointed Surendra,' Tara said, biting her lip. 'She wanted to be with you, didn't you notice?'

'I thought so, but I didn't want to lead her on.' Asad said. 'You haven't answered my question?'

Tara said nothing.

Asad said in English, 'I'm eager to hear your reply.'

He said that with a feeling that sent shivers through her body. There was no need for an answer, but what woman can pass up a chance to affect mock anger? 'I didn't want to stand in her way,' she said, her head still lowered, and feeling nervous again.

'In whose way? Speak up!'

'I've made a promise not to tell.'

'To whom?'

'To Surendra.'

Asad thought for a moment, and asked, 'Does this concern you or Surendra?'

Tara was nonplussed. Had she said too much? She tried to explain, 'It's one and the same thing.' She realized she had made it worse. She felt more embarrassed.

They walked in silence for a few steps before Asad said, 'If you don't mind, let's sit somewhere and talk.'

'Where?'

'In some restaurant.'

Tara had been to the Standard only twice; once with Gurtu, and another time for Amrita's party. She had had tea several times in the company of men and women at her college cafeteria. To go to a restaurant with a young man seemed like taking a big step. What if somebody saw them? But in that state of feeling vulnerable, she said without thinking, 'Achcha.'

As they walked towards Mall Road, Asad said, 'Breaking a promise to deceive someone is one thing, but one should not feel they are facing a dilemma if one has to do it to clarify or to explain something.'

They sat in a booth on the mezzanine of the restaurant. Tara slowly divulged Surendra's suspicions about Gurtu, and her message to Asad.

Asad watched in silence as she poured tea into cups. Tara felt awkward but elated that her doubts were proven wrong. Asad said, 'Wouldn't it be better if you trusted me rather than believing what others may tell you about me?'

Tara busied herself with making whirls in her cup with a spoon. 'What do you mean, believe what?' She shot him a glance.

Asad lifted the saucer with the cup as he replied, 'I was very distressed to see you angry.'

Tara took a deep breath. She tried to find courage to look at him, but could not. She looked into her cup as she sipped the tea. She could feel Asad's eyes on her face, and tiny spasms of sensation all over her body.

She heard him say, 'I thought I'd never express my feelings for you out loud, but you made me confess.'

She looked at him, for several long moments, then closed her eyes; as if to let herself absorb what she saw.

'Can I tell you something?' she said in an unsteady voice. Her face was flushed. Neither of them said anything.

'Of course,' said Asad finally, placing his cup back on the table.

'I don't think I can.' Her face flushed to crimson.

'Tell me,' he insisted.

As she poured tea for the second time, she told him slowly and haltingly, 'That day when you were at doctor sahib's, you know what he said after you left?' She stopped.

'What? Tell me!' Asad asked with some trepidation.

She raised only her eyelashes, 'He said to me…,' she faltered.

'Go on!' Asad encouraged her.

'That I liked you.' Tara said with some effort.

Asad's eyes twinkled. 'What did you say?' he asked.

'What could I say? I almost died with embarrassment!' she said, and asked, 'But why would he say such a thing?'

'Did you mind?'

'No, but how could he know about that?'

They talked about Nath for some time. Asad changed the topic, 'That day when I asked you, whether you or your parents would decide whom you should marry, you answered that you had something to tell me.'

Tara told him about her engagement to Somraj, and said, 'My brother wants that engagement annulled.'

'Sure, he would want that. What else could he say?' After a few moments' silence he said, 'You didn't say who would decide?'

Tara just stared into the empty cup.

'Don't want to tell me?' His voice shook.

She bit her lips before answering, 'What's the use? What difference would my decision make?'

'Then whose decision?' he asked tensely, 'Your parents'?'

She said nothing.

'Answer me!' Asad's voice was heavy with emotion.

She looked into his eyes for a second. 'Yours!' she blurted out and lowered her head even more.

Asad's breathing became shallow. After some thought, he said, 'Do I have to tell my decision? But there is a deep chasm of religion, community and families in between.'

'That's true.'

'Can you cross it? Are you sure?' His voice had deepened.

Tara said nothing for some time, then looking at her nails, said earnestly, 'I'll cross it if you hold my hand.'

Asad mentioned Puri, 'He and Kanak seem quite serious about each other.'

'Why do you say that?'

'I've seen them together several times. They sometimes come here in the afternoons. One can't hide that look. Kanak is a nice girl.'

'Yes, she's quite sincere. But Gurtu said something else about her.' Tara said in a secretive tone, 'They are old friends.'

'Must be about Samuel. He was a crook. We are the ones who exposed him. Kanak was quite sincere about him. She was really shocked. She's impressed with Puri's writing. Don't you think Puri is a little short for her? They look about the same height.'

'Yes, my brother's height is on the short side. But that doesn't matter. What impresses Kanak is that he's a genius in his field.'

'No doubt!' Asad agreed, and said, 'Does he get a chance to do original writing in the midst of all that newspaper work?'

'On days he's on afternoon or night shift, he works on his own writing.'

'I was wondering if there would be any chance of practising law after I finish my course. There might be some possibility in Gurdaspur, but I don't want to leave Lahore.'

'Of course not!' Tara asserted with a smile.

'It'll be good if I find a job at some college. There might be some chance at the Islamia College, but I don't want to work there. Sometimes I get an urge to try journalism.' He asked in the same breath, 'You'll enrol in the MA course, right?'

'I do want to, but it might not happen.' Tara told him about the problem in arranging fees for her admission to the BA programme, and how her parents wanted her to stop studying after her engagement. 'It was possible because of my brother's support, but I don't know about the future.'

Asad held his thumb between his teeth as he pondered. 'You should join the MA programme,' he said. 'That would be the best way to end your other problem. You did economics with honours. So why don't you try for a scholarship in that subject? I too got a scholarship for my MA studies.'

'I don't know if I'd qualify. One will also need books … and then one has to get a top position in the BA examination, and not only in one's college. That won't be possible without some tutoring,' Tara expressed her difficulty.

'You can do it. There's a way. Doctor Nath sets the question paper for the BA honours examination. You know what I did? I would go to see him every week for his advice, and he would ask me to study what he thought was important. His guidance, you know, can be very valuable. He won't refuse you. Go and see him on Sundays. I'll help you too. I'm tutoring a BA student even now.'

'That's not possible either.' Tara told him about the reason behind the termination of her tutoring job. 'How can I visit him now?'

'Never mind. If Puri or I ask the professor to help you, he might find time for you at his university office. I'm ready. You talk to Puri. Soon the college will close for the preparatory leave. If Puri agrees, I can come to your place.'

'There's not enough space even to sit at our place.'

'Then come to your college library, that won't be difficult for you.'

'If I don't get the scholarship, what would my brother say?'

'Well, we'll at least have an excuse to meet,' Asad said smilingly.

'Anything for that!' Tara agreed. 'Achcha, I'll speak to my brother.'

When she reached home, Tara found her mother in a bad temper. Munni was unwell because she was teething, and did not want to let go of her mother. Usha was neither willing to look after the child, nor help in the kitchen. She was busy doing her homework. Masterji was due back from his tutoring job.

Tara told her mother, 'You look after Munni, I'll see to the kitchen.' She changed her clothes and began cooking the evening meal. She was so distracted by the day's events that while shelling peas for cooking, several times she discarded the shelled peas and put empty pods into the pot.

Tara cooked the meal. Masterji returned tired and hungry from his job. He changed his clothes, tied a lungi around his waist, washed his hands and face, and came to the kitchen, all the while mouthing, 'God, you are our protector.' Tara served him a hot meal. Munni had dozed off. Tara's mother came and sat next to her husband, the child in her lap. A wife can at leisure talk to her husband while he eats his dinner. She spoke about her sister-in-law's visit, 'Bharjai came again this afternoon. Tikaram's wife also wanted an answer from us about her sister-in-law's daughter. She's the only child, owns a house and has some property to her name. Why don't you speak with Jaidev? When I talk to him, he always asks why I am in such a hurry!'

Masterji chewed his food slowly and said, 'We both spoke to him the other day. Who knows what he wants? Let's wait a bit longer.'

'How can I wait? What can I say to bharjai? She had so many complaints against Jaidev. She wondered if he wanted to marry someone from the family of a barrister or a judge? The women from the gali don't give me a moment's peace. They all ask, he's already twenty-five, so why won't he agree to marriage? He probably has someone in mind, or wants to choose the girl himself. I can't answer to everyone.'

Masterji chewed as he listened. He said, 'What's the harm if there is someone he likes? Has he said any such thing?'

Tara was quiet as she rolled the chapattis and cooked them over the fire. When Masterji would finish eating one, she would put another in his thali. She said, 'Pitaji, ask Tayaji to speak to brother himself. Let brother answer him.'

'Yes, that's right,' said Masterji to his wife. 'Say so to your sister-in-law.'

Masterji let out a resounding belch, saying 'om' at its end. He got up from his place, and went to lie down on a charpoy in the veranda, muttering 'God, you are our protector.'

Tara found the opportunity to tell her mother, 'Ma, don't agree to any proposal from anyone. Brother won't agree unless he has seen and spoken with the girl.'

Her mother replied as if telling a secret, 'They don't mind if he wants to look at the girl. She goes to the Rani Burdwan School. He can see her on her way. You too can see her.'

'You call that knowing a girl?' Tara expressed her dissatisfaction, 'Neither a chance to speak to her, nor to ask her anything. What can one know in just one glance? Nowadays boys and girls meet several times and talk with each other before getting engaged.'

Her mother waved her hand in disgust, 'Rubbish! That's flirtation, not engagement! Such behaviour is fine for those who live in Anarkali, Mall

Road and Gwal Mandi. What would the people living in our gali think?'

'Wah, what's wrong with that! Brother will only consent to that type of arrangement,' Tara said knowingly as she scraped the dried dough from the kneading tray.

'You know something about this matter, don't you?' Her mother put her hand over her lips, and whispered to Tara, 'Tell me, who's the girl, what's her caste?'

'What do I know?' Tara smiled. 'The girl is pretty, she's an MA student.'

'What caste?' Her mother lowered her voice even further.

'Swear to me!' Tara looked into her mother's eyes. 'Don't let my brother know that I told on him. They're very nice people, and well-off. They're Duttas.'

'Dutta!' Her mother's eyes rose in surprise to meet the furrows on her forehead. She placed her hand on her cheek and said, 'Hai, Duttas are Brahmins. There is no match between Brahmins and Khattris! That can't be!'

'What do you know, Ma! The elder sister of the girl was married into a Khattri Arora family.' Tara corrected her mother. 'Hindus are getting married to Muslims nowadays. Mahatma Gandhi's son married a Brahmin girl, and Pandit Jawaharlal Nehru's daughter married a Parsee. What's the difference between a Hindu and a Muslim and a Parsee? They're all human beings.'

'You think I don't know all that?' Her mother moved Munni from her lap to her shoulder, 'Lala Harkishan Lal, of Peepal Bank, married a Muslim woman. Dewan Chaman Lal married one too. But, Tara, that's another matter. They're rich people. We cannot marry outside our community and our people.'

'Different how? Do they have wings?' Tara could not keep quiet. 'My brother is equal to anyone.'

Someone was coming up the stairs. Tara recognized her brother's footsteps, and fell silent.

'Bhaiji, have your dinner. Eat while it's hot,' she said as he came into the room.

'Yes, all right,' Puri began to change from trousers into a lungi. He was careful not to spoil the crease of his trousers by sitting cross-legged on a mat. He wore that suit whenever he went to meet Kanak.

The loud, angry voice of Tikaram was heard from the gali below, 'What's the meaning of such shameless behaviour! I'll break your head open! You can't insult the poor woman because she's a helpless widow.'

Ghasita Ram, the hardware store owner, replied in an apologetic voice, 'Look, you're blaming me for nothing. I said nothing to anybody. I was...'

Tikaram's wife Jeeva shouted in a voice shrill as a cicada, 'Who are you to offer her daughter mithai and other sweet goodies? Your own daughter Dhanno is of the same age. Are you not ashamed!'

The voices of Mewa Ram and Doctor Prabhu Dayal were also heard.

Instead of sitting down on the mat, Puri went downstairs. Masterji too got up to investigate. Usha and Hardev looked out of the window. Bhagwanti said to the kids, 'What's that got to do with you! Tara, serve them too.'

Amidst all this clamour, Khushal Singh's voice rose in a roar, 'Lalaji, you don't seem content with your black money. You have lost respect for others. Making passes at the girls from your own gali! Looks as if we'll have to lighten the earth of your burden.'

Puri's serious tones were heard, 'Chachaji, what's the matter?'

Ratan's voice rose too, 'Brother, Lalaji seems to be asking for some roughing up. He doesn't act his age.'

Tara's mother, Munni in her lap, went to her window and called, 'Peeto's mom, what happened? What did Ghasita bhai do?'

Kartaro replied from across the gali, trying to keep her voice low, but even Tara could hear her, 'This scoundrel keeps giving mithai to Purandei's daughter on the sly. Purandei has already beaten up her daughter a couple of times for accepting. What can the poor widow do except blame the gods for her misery!'

Pushpa too joined in, 'What's his idea in making a pass at a girl from our gali!'

'But the girl is no child either. She's not less than sixteen, if a day. Why does she accept anything from him? Doesn't she understand!' Basant Kaur objected.

'You don't know him, he's such a bastard. He tries to kiss her cheek as he pretends to pat her head. What could she say to a man that old?'

'She's young after all! Even if she is greedy, shouldn't this old geezer have some shame? His own daughter is as old as she is; he should treat Sita the same as his Dhanno.'

Tara pricked up her ears to catch the voices from the gali.

'... If he wants to do some hanky-panky, why doesn't the lout find someone outside the gali?' asked Rampyari.

'... He should show some respect for the daughters and sisters from our gali.'

'Ghasita is bad all right, but...' Basant Kaur paused before continuing, 'you know the saying that when you keep a cat for catching mice, it will steal your milk too. She's always at his house to borrow buttermilk. I know that she borrows money from Ghasita Ram. When he asks her to return the loan, she laughingly tells him, "You have enough, Lalaji."'

Kartaro commented, 'He's a black marketeer. He'll get the mother and grab the daughter in interest.'

'Ram, ram, ram,' said Tara's mother. 'Such a person will shame the whole gali. And we thought she was so helpless and poor.'

Tara heard all this as she cooked the chapattis and gave them to Usha and Hardev. She was thinking about her afternoon ... 'Let me finish my studies and escape from this gali.'

Kartaro again said, 'Bahin, she must be hard up. If she wasn't, she would not have settled for this Ghasita who looks like a sack of leaking molasses. She would have latched on to someone decent.'

'Quiet, you loud-mouthed shameless hussy!' Tara's mother shouted at her and returned to the room.

That evening was full of quarrels and arguments.

Ghasita Ram hid in his house to escape the wrath of his gali neighbours. Masterji, Babu Govindram and Puri went back to their homes. Ratan bolted the gali door from inside before climbing the stairs to his side of the house. Puri was about to sit down on a mat in the kitchen for his dinner when the lock chain on the outside of the door was rattled and a call was heard, 'Jaddi! Jaidev beta! Tara!'

Bhagwanti had put Munni to bed on Masterji's charpai in the veranda, and was returning to the kitchen. She and Tara exclaimed simultaneously, 'Bhraji! Tayaji!'

Bhagwanti said, 'Hardev, run down and open the door.' She walked back to Masterji's charpai and told him about the visitors.

Usha pulled a charpoy into the room from the veranda and covered it with a dhurrie. Puri too came into the room from the kitchen.

Babu Ramjwaya's visit to his younger brother was no small matter. Jaidev bent and made a gesture to touch his feet. The girls joined their palms and said namaste to him. Bhagwanti covered her head with her aanchal and touched his feet. Masterji too said namaste to him and directed him to the dhurrie-covered charpoy.

Bhagwanti said to Usha, 'Bring some embers from the kitchen in a brazier and put it next to Tayaji.'

Babu Ramjwaya was wrapped in an expensive Kashmiri shawl. Tightening it again over his body, he said, 'No, child, I don't need it. It's not so cold tonight. My shawl is quite warm.' He asked everyone how they were getting along. Tara remained seated in the kitchen. Usha, Hardev and Puri stood beside him.

'How about you, editor sahib?' he said to Puri sarcastically. 'I sent so many messages for you, but you had no time to come to Uchchi Gali. I thought, if sahib can't come, I'll go and see him.'

'Tayaji, last week my office duty was from two in the afternoon to nine at night. Today is the first time I'm on my day shift.' Puri said by way of apologizing. 'I was thinking that tomorrow evening I would go and pay my respects...'

'Well, yes, you're an important person now. How can you have free time!' Ramjwaya did not let him finish. 'I wish that you have even more success. May your fame and reputation grow even greater. But you must also think about settling down. What do you have to say, master?' He looked at Masterji for his yes.

'Yes, Bhaiji is absolutely right,' said Masterji.

'So, tell me, what should we say to the Khosla family about that matter?' Ramjwaya asked Masterji, but aiming the question at Puri. 'Sheelo's mother came to see you this afternoon. She says you people say neither yes nor no. What's going on?'

'When you're handling this business, we don't have to do anything. The boy's in front of you. He says it's been only a year since he found work. He wants to establish himself and get a couple of promotions first.' Masterji turned towards Puri, 'Speak up, son, answer Tayaji.'

'The one who does anything is He.' Ramjwaya raised his hand heavenwards. He said to Puri, 'My dear fellow, there's a time and right moment for everything. Sure, you'll get promotions. Why Master, when we got married our salaries were thirty rupees a month. You are getting a hundred now, but bhai, in those days twenty-five was better than a hundred now. Well, God will take care of everything. Lakshmi, the goddess of wealth, showers her blessings on both husband and wife. If Fate has so decided, a hundred will become two hundred the moment the bride steps into this house. She'll bring Lakshmi here, don't you know!'

'Tayaji, what's the hurry, by next year...'

Ramjwaya stopped Puri, 'What! Look at this crazy boy, he's talking about next year. The girl's parents will save her for you?' He looked at Masterji and spoke a little more emphatically, 'You have a daughter to marry off. I'm worried about her. Get him married, then get her married using what you get in his dowry. Otherwise what do you have as cash?'

'That's true,' Masterji acknowledged, and Bhagwanti too agreed, 'What Bhraji says is right.'

Ramjwaya spread out the fingers of his right hand to make his point, 'I had to count out eight thousand for Sheelo's marriage. Even if you don't do much, for the ceremony's sake you'll have to put some ornaments on her wrists and neck, give her at least eleven or thirteen sets of clothes, receive and feed the groom and his relatives who come in baraat. Not less than four thousand in these days. We'll have to do things in keeping with our family's standing. Where will you get the four thousand?' Ramjwaya asked. 'You won't find a better match than this. It's his good luck,' he pointed at Puri. 'She's the only daughter with no other siblings. Has a house in her own name. Her mother will give her all her jewellery and possessions, and they're willing to give five thousand in cash. That's why I'm trying so hard to fix up this match. You'll be able to get your sister married properly.'

'Tayaji, I can't marry someone just to get a house and property!' Puri leaned against the wall.

'Oh, you want to marry some pauper's daughter? How will your sister get married?' Ramjwaya looked at Masterji, 'Just look at what he says! Mister big editor sahib!' He again addressed Puri, 'When we educated you and brought you up to manhood, did we spend nothing? Or did you grow up on your own? Will the girl's family not benefit from your abilities! If the girl's parents want a good match for her, shouldn't they contribute something towards making you capable so that you can keep her in comfort for the rest of her days? Did we give a dowry in Sheelo's wedding or not? Your father worked hard all his life for this day, and you want to dash all his hopes? Do you have the key to the treasure of King Qarun? If you do, why don't you cough up thirty–forty thousand, eh? If my son Kishor Chand talked back to me like that, I'd break his jaw!' Ramjwaya was livid with anger.

Puri clasped his arms to bolster his courage, and said, 'You're right, Tayaji, but it's all about the girl. I don't know her... how she looks, her nature.'

'What rubbish you talk!' Ramjwaya raised his voice a notch, 'What does a girl look like! What's there to know or see? You want to marry some girl from a decent family, or some slut working the streets of Anarkali or Mall Road? Who wants to know or meet the girl before marriage? It's her family that matters, their status that's of value. We've checked out all that. When it's your turn, you see all you want!'

Puri again said, 'How old is the girl? She shouldn't be too young.'

'More of the same nonsense!' Ramjwaya said, 'You want to marry an old hag! The younger she is, the better. Who knows anything about a girl's character when she's older? People search for young girls. She will stay young for you longer. Today she's sixteen, tomorrow she'll be seventeen, and next she'll be eighteen. We married Sheelo off when she was seventeen. You've got a twisted mind.'

Puri refused to back down, 'If she's sixteen, then what education can she have had? How can I marry someone like her? The girl should have some idea of what she's getting into ...'

'You want a girl who has a BA degree? Will the girl who is BA produce babies that are already educated?' Ramjwaya's anger boiled over.

Masterji lowered his head. Bhagwanti turned her back towards the conversation and motioned Usha to leave the room. In the kitchen, Tara too hung her head.

Ramjwaya looked at Masterji and said, 'If he doesn't agree, why should I break my back? But then it's your problem. I'm doing all this so that you get something to marry off his sister. So that you get some reward for working hard all your life. Lala Sukhlal is sure to ask for an early marriage. It's been eight or nine months since that business with his son. If the government wanted to take action, it would have done so by now. All right, I'm leaving. Everyone holds their fate in their own hands. I hope I don't get my fingers burned trying to help you all.'

As Ramjwaya got up, Masterji too rose to his feet to escort his brother to Uchchi Gali, but Jaidev told him, 'Its cold outside. I'll go with Tayaji and see him home.'

When Tara saw her brother hold his own against the tirades and scoldings of
Babu Ramjwaya, her faith in her brother and also in her own self-confidence
grew stronger. Next day she told him in English while their mother served
him his meal, 'Asad bhai suggested that I try for the scholarship. His
suggestion was that if you spoke with Professor Nath about giving me some
guidance, I could go to see him at his office in the university.'

Puri said, 'It's a good idea, but you should have thought about it sooner.
It wouldn't have been difficult for you. If I ask the professor, he won't say
no to me, but you don't even have two months' time left. One should begin
six months in advance. Some even take help from tutors. How would you
manage now?'

'Bhai said that he could give me some time each day until the
examinations.'

'Who, Asad? He charges for tutoring. Sixty rupees, I heard.'

'Not from me. He himself offered to help.'

'Why? Does he want to recruit you? These communists can use any ploy.'

'He can't force me. It's a matter of one's wish and belief too.'

'You must be half way to party membership by now. They probably
already regard you a fellow-traveller.' Puri taunted and then asked, 'Where
will he tutor you, here?'

'It'll be better at the college library. I could go there in the afternoons.
It will be preparatory leave in a few days' time; then we'll see what time
is convenient.'

'What objection can I have, but the time is short. You may try. I will ask
Kali for the textbooks by Marshal and others. If you want I can speak with
the professor even today.'

Tara poured her heart and soul into her studies. Asad began to teach her
economics for about an hour in the veranda of the library. Tara's classmate
Bal Mukund saw them, and asked Asad's permission to join in. Bal Mukund
was very poor. He was supporting himself by tutoring work. He was good
at his studies, but seldom got enough time to study. Asad could not refuse
him.

One day Bal Mukund could not come. That day Tara and Asad talked
mostly about things other than economics. Tara said, 'Your tutoring me
has done some good for Bal Mukund too.'

'It's good for me too,' said Asad. 'When he's present, we can't wander
off.'

'Yes, we work hard when he's here. See, we hardly studied today!' She laughed shyly.

'You mean we won't study every time he's not here? I'm not that lenient, and you too are not so naïve. Once in a while is a different matter. Achcha, let's begin.'

'You're different. A man and a communist at that; no wonder you are as hard as a rock.'

'What do you mean?'

'Well, out of sight, out of mind. When I'm home and I think of you, I can hardly concentrate.'

'Sure, I'm not human, you suppose. What do I have that you can think about or like in me? Some refer to me in jest as the Moor, and to you as Desdemona.'

'Really!' Tara's face flushed. 'Who says that?'

'Some smart alecks such as Zubeida, Narendra Sigh, Mahajan.'

'Hai, and we don't even go out together like bhai and Kanak.'

'People can be jealous.'

'Who's jealous? Surendra?'

'No, not her. She's the understanding type. Others like Khanna, Hira Singh. Try not to avoid them.'

'I don't avoid them, I just keep to myself. Otherwise, you know ...'

'Listen, about being together, I think that after passing my law exam I should go to Gurdaspur and work as an apprentice. Once I have some money, I want to start building a nest for us. You need a nest if you want to get married. Birds do the same thing. I don't want to wait very long.'

Tara looked into his eyes and gave her silent approval.

'Have you ever sounded Puri on this matter?' Asad asked.

'Not yet,' Tara said after a few moments. 'But bhai is the intellectual type, he dislikes anything sectarian. If the situation with Kanak pans out, our problem will be solved.'

Chapter 7

PURI WAS ROUSED GENTLY FROM THE DELICIOUS LANGUOR OF HIS MORNING sleep. The sweet strains of Khushal Singh singing the morning chant wafted through the window. Just then Masterji, on the charpoy next to him, began to sing his morning prayer in a harsh shrill voice which interrupted the flow of melody from across the gali. Puri tried to ignore Masterji's bhajan and concentrate on Khushal Singh's song, waiting for it to end before getting up.

'Sir Khizr's resignation accepted! The governor assumes control of the government!'

The loud cry of the newspaper vendor pierced the morning quiet. That week Puri had been working on the day shift and had no way of knowing about the events of the night. He sprang from his bed and went down to the gali.

Doctor Prabhu Dayal subscribed to *Pairokaar*. Govindram bought either the Hindi daily *Chhatrapati* or *Pratap*. The newspaper vendor had wedged the newspaper in the door to the doctor's house. Puri removed the paper. The news came as a shock to everyone.

It read: At 10'o clock last night, Sir Khizr, chief minister of Punjab and leader of the Unionist Party, resigned from his post. The governor has accepted his resignation, and has taken over the powers of administration. All the ordinances promulgated by the Unionist ministry would remain in force.

Puri went to the bazaar and bought a copy of the Muslim daily *Siasat*. It had a different version of the news: Sir Khizr recognizes the claim of the League! Speculations about the identity of the members of the League ministry led by the Khan of Mamdote abound. The enemies of Pakistan suffer defeat. The way is cleared for a League ministry!

Hearing the commotion in the gali, the doctor came downstairs with sleep-laden eyes. He had to believe the news after reading it. He was furious, 'So Khizr finally succumbed to the League's pressure tactics. He has cleared the way for the League. All the policemen are Muslims. How mercilessly they beat the Congress volunteers in their demonstrations and just make a pretence of beating up the League volunteers.'

Masterji too had come down. He said, 'Whether they're Unionists or from the League, they're all Muslims and in cahoots with each other.'

Govindram was very upset by the news. 'Now the mullahs will rule, with no holds barred,' he said. 'We can forget about justice and fair play. The Muslim ministers did what they wanted during the Unionist ministry anyway.'

Puri suggested, 'The governor would rather let the turmoil continue. But it's unlikely that he'll yield to the demand for Pakistan. The ordinances banning the League demonstrations are still in force. Khizr at least was concerned about his ministry's image.'

Govindram said vociferously, 'Spare us all this glib journalistic talk. I'm telling you what I see. One could expect justice and fair treatment in the war years. Since the governor handed over the administration to the ministers last year, the government jobs have all gone only to Muslims and those from the caste of Jats.'

Since Puri was on day-shift, he walked with Tara up to Shahalami Gate. Tara's college was closed, preparatory to the examinations, but she was going to study at the library. After passing Shahalami Gate, Puri meant to go through Chardewari garden to Anarkali, and Tara was going on Nisbet Road.

Tara and Puri had not yet crossed Shahalami Gate when they heard the distant roar of slogans being shouted. As they crossed Shahalami Gate, a huge Muslim League procession carrying hundreds of green flags came along Railway Road towards the Lohari Gate. Early March mornings in Lahore retain some traces of cold. But the faces of the marchers were flushed with excitement and shone with sweat from the strain of shouting. Their slogans had a different tone: 'The news is out, Khizr is our brother! Allah-u-Akbar! Muslim League zindabad! Pakistan or Death! We want a League ministry! Long live Quaid-e-Azam! Don't forget the Bihar massacre!'

It was not possible to cross Railway Road because of the procession. Inside Shahalami Gate a crowd of tongas, bicycles and pedestrians had jammed the bazaar, waiting to go towards Gwal Mandi, Medical College, Nisbet Road and Mall Road. The congestion was growing quickly.

As in the past, the marchers did not chant, 'Down with imperialism! Down with the British government! Long live democracy! Hindu–Muslims unite! Down with Khizr! Toady Khizr hai-hai!' Instead, they cheered the Unionist leader, 'Khizr zindabad!' and 'Khizr is with us!' In place of their usual inclination to fight oppression and court arrest, they seemed defiant and ready for a showdown. Their manner did not invite sympathy for their cause, but held a menacing tone.

Puri did not follow his usual route, but stayed close to Tara. He said, 'It looks like trouble out there. Better if you go back.'

Tara said in desperation, 'I must go to the college library and take notes from the textbook by Smith. There's hardly any time left before the examinations.'

After the procession had gone past, Puri said, 'Take a tonga. See how the situation looks when you return home. Ask someone to escort you, or hire a tonga again.' He took out some coins and gave them to Tara.

Puri followed the marchers through Anarkali bazaar up to Ganapat Road. His office was buzzing with guesses of what might happen next. Puri began to read through the sheets fresh off the teleprinter. He picked up the statement by Sir Khizr about his resignation and was about to read it, when he heard Narendra Singh call through the open door, 'So, Puri bhai, what's going on?'

Puri looked up and said, 'Come in.'

Singh asked, 'Any new development?'

'Yes, Khizr's statement about his resignation,' Puri said as he read the news. He explained to Singh, 'Khizr says that according to Clement Atlee's proclamation of 16 February, whichever political party holds the majority in a particular region of India in June 1948, the British government will hand over the administration to that party. Therefore an opportunity should be given to form new ministries.'

'Why, doesn't Khizr want his Unionist Party to rule?' Singh seemed unconvinced, 'Is he dissolving the Unionist Party?'

'The statement was issued by Governor Jenkins, not by Khizr. It simply means that now there will be an opportunity and a provocation for a free-for-all among the parties,' Puri said. 'Khizr submitted his resignation at ten o'clock last night. The newspaper is put to bed around two or three in the morning. In the period in between, the governor had enough time to consult Delhi, accept the resignation, and get the statement published in the official gazette? Obviously, everything had been planned.'

'Listen,' Singh said in English, biting the nail of his index finger thoughtfully, 'you know that Khizr asks Dr Radhey Behari's advice in every matter. He must have discussed his resignation with his Cabinet. The

Congress has only two ministers in the Cabinet. What did they have to say? Will the Congress collaborate if the League forms the new ministry?'

The teleprinter again came to life. Puri and Singh bent over the printer and began to read to the news as it was typed out: 'The governor has invited the Khan of Mamdote, leader of the Muslim League and of the majority party in the assembly, to form the new ministry. The new ministry has to be in place before the Budget session of the Punjab Legislative Assembly, scheduled for 3 March, begins.'

'That's right!' Singh said, 'Unless there is a council of ministers responsible for the administration, how can the working of the Assembly go ahead?'

The printer typed another line of news: The Khan of Mamdote is expected to announce the names of his new ministers at the Assembly session.

Kashish and Banarasidas had not yet arrived. Puri went to another room and called Dr Radhey Behari's number to learn of any new developments. When he came back he said to Singh, 'Khizr didn't talk to any of his ministers before submitting his resignation. Dr Saheb has gone to Sikh Missionary College to seek Master Tara Singh's advice. From there he'll go directly to the Assembly House.'

Indranath and Bhagat Ram came in. An animated discussion began: What now? Will the ministry have only Muslims in it? Puri looked at his watch and said to Singh, 'It's already eleven. The Assembly session should be beginning about now. Stay around if you want, or go and see Fiqar, to sound him out on what they're thinking in League circles. Will there be any Hindu or Sikh members in the new Cabinet?'

Singh left, but Indranath, Bhagat Ram and Puri could not go back to work in the newsroom. What would happen next was anyone's guess.

The telephone rang around 12.30. Indranath answered and told the rest: The Khan of Mamdote has not yet been able to submit the names of his ministers to the governor. Therefore, the governor was not willing to hand over the administration to the leader of the Muslim League. The Assembly session had been postponed for the day. Members of the League and other parties were holding meetings in their chambers. Master Tara Singh and a few other prominent leaders had been invited to some of these meetings. The press had not been allowed in, but from the noises heard outside it seemed that both sides were having heated discussions. One guess was that the Opposition considered Khizr's resignation to be unconstitutional, and had decided not to allow a League ministry in any circumstance. The League was bent upon forming the ministry and taking over the administration. Large crowds of League supporters had gathered in front of the Assembly, and were chanting slogans in support of the League's ministry and the formation of Pakistan. A contingent of armed police had surrounded the Assembly building.

Puri quickly prepared a news report at the suggestion of Bhagat Ram. The headline ran: First failure of the sectarian ministry! The essence of the story was: Would the ministry formed by one sectarian party be practical and acceptable to the people? Could such a ministry alone restore peace and order?

Bhagat Ram suggested that the editor might want to publish a supplementary edition on the basis of this news and other developments being filed from the Assembly. Puri went to see the editor.

Kashish put the lighted cigarette he was holding on the glass top of his desk and read the story carefully. He took off his glasses, rubbed his eyes and said in English, 'Good idea. It calls for a supplementary. There'll be more sensational news around 2.30. It'd be big news if the Cabinet is formed, and also if it's not formed. It's a matter for a supplementary. Ask Babu Banarasidas if there are any standing advertisements for supplementaries.'

'Today is his day off.' Puri reminded the editor.

'Oh goodness!' Kashish slammed in his fist on the desk, 'Gulab Singh must be there in the advertising section. You too can consult the file of National Publicity, and telephone them for advertisements of Bhalla Shoe, Karnal Shoe, Kanha Chand, Khem Singh Hosiery. You all should learn how to do this. The supplementary can't go to press unless there are advertisements worth at least two or three hundred rupees. Go, hurry up! Make haste!'

Banarasidas kept Puri away from the secrets of the advertisers' file. In his absence, Puri, Gulab Singh and Indranath began to check the file and telephone to arrange advertisements for the supplementary.

The *Pairokaar* correspondent Mahesh called again at 2 o'clock with further news: Master Tara Singh pulled out his sword on the steps of the Assembly house in front of the supporters of the Muslim League. When Master Tara Singh came out of the building along with the members of the Congress Party, the Akali Dal and the Hindu Mahasabha, the thousands-strong crowd of Muslim League supporters rent the air with calls of: 'Nara-e-Haideri ... Ya Ali! Pakistan zindabad! Muslim League zindabad!

Pakistan or Death! We will spill blood for Pakistan! The League will form
the ministry!'

Master Tara Singh and other Hindu–Sikh members faced the crowd.
Master Tara Singh gave the Sikh war cry in a thundering voice: '*Jo bole so
nihaal, sat siri akaal!*', 'Death to Pakistan!'

The crowd of Muslims responded with a deafening roar of slogans and
surged forward threateningly. Master Tara Singh pulled out his sword and
challenged the crowd: 'Any of you, who has the guts come forward! Let's
settle it here and now!'

Armed police intervened and kept the two sides away from each
other.

In a joint statement, the Congress, the Akali Dal and the Hindu
Mahasabha had unanimously declared that the dismissal of the Unionist
ministry by the governor was unconstitutional. Therefore, they would not
allow a League ministry in any circumstances.

Bhagat Ram went to Kashish with the news.

'Good, we must have a supplementary,' Kashish gave the order.

Only half a page of advertisements could be arranged. Kashish was not
happy. He lectured Puri, Bhagat Ram and Indranath, 'Advertisements are
the fuel of the ship of journalism.' So that the *Pairokaar* supplementary
would not lag behind other rival papers *Chhatrapati, Siasat, Pratap* and
Zamindaar, he ordered the printing to begin.

The *Pairokaar* supplementary carried a notice from the president of the
District Congress Committee: Sir Khizr Hayat Khan's resignation and his
renunciation of the power of administration had resulted in an ominous
and dangerous situation. The public was asked to come to a meeting on
the grounds of the Bharat Insurance Building at 6 p.m., and participate in
a discussion on the national implications of the situation.

Puri could manage to reach the meeting only by half past six. A sizeable
crowd had gathered. Comrade Kapoor, the president of the District
Congress Committee, was addressing the gathering from the dais: 'Ladies
and gentlemen, keeping the purpose of the meeting in mind, may I ask you
to express your views on the situation created by the resignation of the
Unionist ministry, and on what our responsibility might be towards our
country and people as well as towards maintaining peace and order. The
purpose of this meeting will be defeated unless we consider the gravity
of the situation with restraint rather than emotion and anger. I request

those wishing to address the gathering to do so after asking permission from the chair.'

The speakers spoke as the mood took them, without bothering to ask for permission. None of the prominent Congress leaders, neither Dr Gopi Chand Bhargava, nor Bhimsen Sachchar, nor Dr Radhey Behari were present. There were some Congress workers and volunteers milling around, but the Rashtriya Swayamsewak Sangh members outnumbered these. Ratan too was present.

A man climbed on to the dais, shook his clenched fist and declared, 'Punjab is ours. We'll never allow a Pakistan in Punjab. We care nothing for the League or the Congress! As long as the blood flows in our veins, we won't let the League form the government. Whoever wants to fight, come forward! Don't hide like cowards.'

The gathering cheered and clapped. Someone invoked the name of Hanuman to pep up the throng, 'Nara-e-Bajrangi!' The crowd responded with the Hindu war chant, 'Har Har Mahadev! Victory to Bajarangbali!'

The chairman thumped the table in protest against this outburst, but the man ignored the warning and continued to speak.

Another speaker said, 'Right from the time of creation, this country was known as the Aryavarta. This is the land of the gods Ram and Krishna. The Vedas called it Panchnad, the land of five rivers. How can Pakistan be formed here? Those who want Pakistan should go to Arabia. The policy of Gandhi and the Congress has always been detrimental to the Hindus. The Congress has always sacrificed the rights of the Hindus to appease the Muslims. Now the League and the Muslims have the gall to demand half of the country. The Congress leaders have acquiesced so that they can hold positions in the government, but the League and Jinnah would next demand control over all of India. What the Mughal tyrant Aurangzeb failed to do, Mohammed Ali Jinnah wants to accomplish! To mock us they shout slogans: We'll get Pakistan with a smile! We'll get Hindustan by bloodshed!'

The crowd booed and chanted, 'Shame! Shame!'

The speakers asked the audience, 'Are you going to take all this lying down?'

'Never! Never!' The audience roared back. They began to chant again, 'Victory to Bajrangbali! No formation of Pakistan! No partition of Hindustan!'

The chairman thumped the table and interrupted the speaker several times, 'Sir, please speak on the issue before this gathering.' But the speaker continued to extol the greatness of the indestructible Hindustan.

After the speaker finished, the chairman got up and addressed the audience, 'Friends, first of all, I ask for your forgiveness, and may I go on to say that this meeting is progressing in a highly irregular way. The City Congress Committee organized this event, but the speeches here do not conform to the Congress policies. I am, therefore, compelled to close the meeting.'

Mahesh, the city correspondent of *Pairokaar*, came to Puri and asked him, 'What are we to report of these speeches?'

'Better to ignore them. Just report what Comrade Kapoor said. Kapoor was wise enough to close the meeting.'

Comrade Kapoor climbed down from the dais. The volunteers began to roll up the dhurries and floor coverings on the dais. From behind the wall of audience around the dais, came the sound of the Sikh war cry ... '*Jo bole so nihaal, sat siri akaal!*' And then, 'Vande Mataram! Har Har Mahadev!'

The audience turned round. The short-statured Master Tara Singh, in his steel-grey turban and with a sword hanging from his belt, and Dr Gopi Chand Bhargava, his dhoti flapping, were walking towards the dais. Seeing them approach, the Congress volunteers stopped removing dhurries and floor coverings.

Puri turned and said to Mahesh, 'Now there might be something worth reporting.'

Master Tara Singh began his speech without waiting for the chairman's permission, 'We shall never tolerate a Muslim government in Punjab. Don't forget history. The Sikh race came into being by fighting the Muslims. If we have to live under Muslim rule, why did Govind Singh, the tenth guru, appear in his avatar?'

His words made Puri's hair stand on end. Master Tara Singh continued, 'The League thinks that by dislodging the Unionist ministry and forming its own, it will lay the foundation for Pakistan. It should drop that illusion. We'll not let the League ministry function for even a day in Punjab.'

Puri tuned round when he felt a hand on his shoulder, and saw Narendra Singh and Asad. The words sprang from his lips, 'This man is breathing fire!'

'Don't you know what he did in front of the Assembly hall?' asked Singh.

Mahesh began to relate the incident, 'Master Tara Singh was infuriated and brandished his sword on the steps of the Assembly building. It's sure to have repercussions.'

Dr Gopi Chand Bhargava was next on the dais. He said, 'Trust us, we'll never allow the formation of a Pakistan. The League's machinations caused the downfall of our Unionist ministry. We will not allow its ministry to survive. We'll fight the League at every step inside the Assembly chamber. You people fight the League in the streets.'

Asad said with a smile, 'The bania is crafty. He would fight sitting safely in his Assembly hall chair. We'd have to fight bloody battles in the streets. These people have no bone to pick with Khizr, who masterminded all this. They have no desire to expose the conspiracy hatched by the governor and that toady Khizr. They just want to oppose the League. Khizr held the majority in the House. So why did he resign? If he could no longer bear the burden of the administration, he should have discussed this matter with his Cabinet, and with the Unionist Party executive. His resignation goes against any parliamentary procedure and traditions. The Congress members in his Cabinet should protest against that, but they're concerned with only issuing threats to the League. How could the League break up the Unionist ministry? It was broken up by the governor and Khizr.'

Narendra Singh said, 'Khizr has shown himself to be the smartest. The Congress and the Hindus consider him to be their ally. The League supporters shout, "Khizr is our brother." Jenkins has always regarded him as a trusted crony.'

Puri, Asad and others had walked past the Bharat Insurance Building, towards the junction of Anarkali and Mall Road. Asad called out to a man coming from the direction of Lucky Lines on a bicycle, 'Hey, Abdul! Where are you off to?'

'I'd come to see the Congress procession on Mall Road. The buggers were exposed today,' replied Abdul in a hoarse voice.

'What's wrong with your voice? Were you in this morning's march?'

'Of course!'

'I heard that the news is out, that toady Khizr is now your brother. Has he joined the League?' Asad asked.

'After all he's a Muslim, not a kafir like you,' replied Abdul. 'The Congress finally showed its true colours today; soon it'll be the turn of you communists to be exposed.'

'What d'you mean true colours?'

'Haven't you heard?' Abdul said in disbelief. 'The Congress minister in the Unionist Cabinet led a march on Mall Road this evening. The Congress people have torn off the green from their tricolour flag. We're glad that they've admitted that the Muslims are not with them. Quaid-e-Azam has always said that the Congress could never be a representative of the Muslims, that it was a organization of and for the Hindus.'

'Are you telling the truth? You saw the torn flag, or just heard about it?' Asad asked in a troubled tone.

'Saw it with my own eyes, and along with thousands of witnesses. I followed the procession up to the Assembly hall. Tara Singh pulled out his sword and shouted a challenge, "Come on, whoever is brave enough!" The long-haired bum doesn't realize the power of Islam, that's why he's making threats with his knife. He supposes that his threats will bring in the government of the Congress and the Akalis. The Muslims will rule in Punjab! Who can stop the march of the true religion?'

Puri, Asad and Narendra Singh walked in silence through Anarkali bazaar. Nobody had anything to say. When they were halfway across the bazaar, Asad spoke, 'I heard that some progressive elements of the League have sent a proposal to Jinnah saheb about forming a joint ministry with the Congress. In view of such erratic behaviour by the Congress, who knows what will come of that? No other party except the League would be able to form the ministry at the moment. The tussle between the League and the Congress has turned into a confrontation between Hindus and Muslims. This stalemate can't be resolved by another round of Assembly elections. Whoever is a Unionist or an independent candidate at present, he too would turn into a Hindu or a Muslim. The policy of holding elections on sectarian–religious basis introduced by the British is now bearing fruit. This conflict can either be resolved by mutual agreement, or by the swords of Tara Singh and the head imam, Allama Mashriki. It means that either the Hindus or the Muslims pack up and leave Punjab, or that both should live forever under British rule.' Puri and Narendra Singh listened in silence.

When they reached the Shiv temple in Anarkali, they found a gathering of about 150 people in the middle of the road. Shanno Devi, a well-known leader of the Congress, stood on one of the extensions for seating the customers in front of a store, and was working up to the climax of her speech, 'My Muslim brothers, the whole record of the Congress is before you. The Congress has never stood in the way of any reasonable concession requested by the Muslim community. If you want a separate Pakistan, or a ministry formed by the League, that too is possible through mutual talks. Those who believe in fighting are pushing the country towards political suicide.'

In the audience were Sharma-ji and Sodhi from the left wing of the Congress, and Hajara Singh, Pradyumna, Ibrahim and others from the Communist Party. They asked Asad and Narendra Singh to stay behind. Puri returned home.

On the morning of 4 March, there was again a ring of excitement in the cries of the newspaper vendors. The news headlines were sensational. The *Chhatrapati* daily newspaper read: Disappointment in League circles! The governor of Punjab refuses to allow the Khan of Mamdote, leader of the League in the Assembly, to form the new ministry without Hindu and Sikh members.

The *Siasat* daily said: The Congress and the Hindus refuse to recognize the democratic rights of the League. Master Tara Singh threatens to resolve the issue by the sword. The Congress and the Akalis insist on leaving the fate of Punjab in the hands of the governor.

Nearly every Hindu newspaper carried the news of street demonstrations in several cities of Punjab against the League ministry, and the news in the Muslim press described the mood of joy following the break-up of the Unionist ministry, and of marches in support of a League ministry. The papers also carried the news of processions planned and organized jointly by all parties of the Hindus and the Sikhs.

The people of Bhola Pandhe's Gali were pleased with the governor's decision. Babu Govindram said, 'Khizr's ministry had plenty of Muslims in it. Khizr is a little less sectarian than the rest of the pack. The League wants to have a tyrannical, anti-Hindu rule similar to Aurangzeb's. The British won't tolerate such injustice.'

Masterji gave his opinion, 'If the League comes to power, Urdu will be made compulsory in all the schools just as the Koran, a compulsory textbook. Just watch.'

Puri tried to reason, 'That can't happen if there's a joint League–Congress ministry. The Unionist ministry had a mix of Muslims, Sikhs and Hindus. The League ministry will also have some Hindu members. The difference is that the Unionists were pro-British, and the League Muslims are anti-British. Jinnah and other leaders of the League are political Muslims, not religious Muslims. They're just power-hungry. There can't be separate laws for Hindus and Muslims.'

Masterji stopped him, 'Don't you know that Hindus and Muslims have different laws relating to marriage and inheritance? Their holidays are different too. Under a League government, there would be no holiday for Diwali, and four holidays each for Id and Muharram, for what you know!'

Doctor Prabhu Dayal had returned late at night, and therefore came down to join the others a little later. He said in a conspiratorial voice, 'Bhai, it's all the fault of our Hindu and Congress leaders. Doctor sahib told us last evening what Khizr had been saying for the last two months: Just have a minor Hindu–Muslim riot at the time of a League procession, and I'll straighten out these mischief-makers in no time. The Congress leaders were hoping for a rapprochement with the League. How long could the governor wait? He will himself deal with the leaders now. That's why he told the Khan of Mamdote that the Cabinet must have some Hindu and Sikh representation, or he can't form a ministry.'

Mahesh came to the office of *Pairokaar* around noon from Golbagh. Police had opened fire on the meeting of Hindu and Sikh students. He said, 'The police began firing at the crowd without any warning. Some pedestrians going along Upper Mall Road outside Golbagh were also fired upon, and a student watching from the veranda of the boarding house of Government College beside the road was shot dead. The crowd at Golbagh has dispersed, but this matter won't end there.' Mahesh had also heard about clashes in Mazang and Neela Gumbad. A curfew was likely to be imposed soon; therefore he wanted to make the rounds of those areas too.

Puri suddenly remembered. He said to Indranath, 'My sister had gone to the library of Dayal Singh College. If the disturbances spread or the curfew is imposed, it won't be easy for her to return home. I'll just go up to the library. If she's left, I'll come back at once, or take her home and come back immediately.' He borrowed Indranath's bicycle.

Tara was still at the library. There were about ten other students there, and Asad. Everyone was worried. A student of Dayal Singh College, Nihal Chand, had been wounded in the Golbagh shooting. At the library, Puri got the news of knife attacks at Delhi Gate and Mochi Gate.

Asad told Puri that Tara had been about to go home, but they asked her to wait when the news of the disturbances came. Bhardwaj, an MA student, was also at the library. He had his own motorcar. Bhardwaj agreed to drop Tara at her gali inside Shahalami bazaar.

Puri returned to the office. He gave Bhagat Ram and Indranath further news about the escalating conflict. Bhagat Ram was concerned, 'Who knows where it might break out again?' His house was in a Muslim area in Kila Gujjar Singh. 'Who knows what will come out of the shenanigans of Master Tara Singh and Dr Bhargava?' Puri and Indranath had similar views on the situation.

Since he had taken an hour's leave, Puri could not get out of his office before 5 p.m. The flow of traffic along Railway Road was normal. He walked through Chowk Matti and Papar Mandi up to Machchi Hatta on his way home, and saw huddles of agitated and frightened people at several places. He also heard people talking of clashes at Mochi Gate behind Pari Mahal.

As he entered the gali, he saw a group of women bending over something in front of Ghasita Ram's house. Someone was crying in pain. Kartaro and Rampyari were weeping and the faces of others were streaked with tears. The women made way for Puri. Dauloo mama lay on the floor covered in blood. His old kurta, tinted with all the colours thrown at him at the time of Holi, was now smeared only with red. A makeshift, blood-soaked bandage was tied to his abdomen. Near him lay containers and tumblers filled with water.

Ratan's mother said to Puri, 'Son, take mama quickly to the hospital!'

Chaitu, Pushpa's servantboy, had been sent to look for a tonga. Peeto had summoned her father and brother from their shop. Khushal Singh too had run off towards Shahalami to get a tonga. Bir Singh had gone to telephone Dr Prabhu Dayal at his hospital, Puri at his office and Ratan at the railway goods clearing agency. As it happened, Puri reached the gali ahead of the other two.

The women said: About half an hour before, Dauloo came into the gali from the direction of Mochi Gate, howling 'They've killed me! The Muslims have killed me!' and fell to the ground. The women first screamed and ran off to their houses. Then they cautiously came out and tried to stop the flow of blood by placing dry and wet rags over Dauloo's wound. But the blood continued to flow, and Dauloo's groans became weaker.

Puri placed his hand on Dauloo's sweat-soaked forehead and called, 'Mama... Dauloo mama!'

Dauloo opened his eyes. 'Water... water,' he whispered amid his groans.

Rampyari, the wife of Bajaj Dewanchand, sat huddled over him. She put a tumbler of water to his lips.

Puri again called, 'Mama... Dauloo mama!' His eyes had filled with tears.

'Child...' Dauloo replied weakly. He looked at Puri with tears streaming from his eyes and cried, 'I'm going to die.'

Puri tuned to Rampyari impatiently, 'Where's Chaitu? Should I go for a tonga?'

'Ratan's here,' the women said and moved aside.

'Mama... what happened?' Ratan crouched over him.

'Child...' Dauloo opened his eyes again and cried, 'I'm going to die.' He put his arm around Ratan's neck.

Tears flowed from Ratan's eyes.

The tonga arrived.

Khushal Singh helped Ratan and Puri carry Dauloo to the tonga. All three went to hospital with the bleeding man. As they left, the children of the gali were weeping, and the women were wiping away tears.

The hospital's emergency ward was filled with wounded, sitting and lying on beds and on the floor, groaning with pain and crying for help. There was bustle and urgency everywhere. The doctors were busy talking with police officers. The compounders and male nurses were muttering in frustration, 'Sixty-three have been brought since this morning. Why do they bring the dead here? The hospital gets involved in police investigations.'

Ratan and Puri would talk to one person, and then plead with another. Nobody paid any attention. An old Muslim with a henna-dyed beard and tears in his eyes, waved a sheaf of currency notes at everyone in sight, begging them to attend to his young son. He did not know how to offer a bribe. All he got in return were rebukes.

Dr Prabhu Dayal arrived after about an hour. At his request, Dr Yunus, the doctor on emergency duty, examined Dauloo. Dauloo was immediately taken to the operating theatre. He was already unconscious. It took only a small dose of anaesthetic to put him to sleep. His wound was examined. It was deep and serious. Dr Yunus began to put in stitches.

A nurse was holding Dauloo's wrist to feel his pulse. She said, 'He's sinking.'

He was immediately given an injection. The doctor said, 'He will have to be given a blood transfusion.'

Puri and Ratan offered to give their blood for Dauloo. When they were told that only blood sterilized by the hospital could be used, Ratan paid twenty-four rupees, the price of eight ounces of blood.

Out of consideration for Dr Prabhu Dayal, Ratan and Puri were allowed to stay at Dauloo's bedside until he regained consciousness, but Dauloo did not come out of his coma. Ratan wanted to take his body back to the gali for proper last rites.

Dr Yunus explained to Puri the legal implication of their case. According to the law, the hospital was obliged to report the death of someone suffering from a stab wound. The corpse would then be handed over to the police. Unless the civil surgeon or one of his deputies performed the autopsy to verify the cause of death, the police could not hand over the body for the last rites. There were already eleven corpses in the morgue. It was necessary to declare that the body could not be identified. Otherwise the people of the gali would be harassed in the investigation. Dauloo's body was left at the hospital.

As Puri and Ratan came out of the hospital, the news of the approaching curfew was being announced on a loudspeaker. Someone at the hospital gate told them that several cases of arson had been reported from the Delhi Gate and Chowk Matti areas, in the wake of ferocious riots.

All the shops were closed in Shahalami bazaar. When Puri and Ratan reached their gali they found many people waiting outside their houses for news of Dauloo. Ratan burst into tears when he saw them. The news spread quickly. Men came and sat on the chabutaras. Women stood in doorways or at windows. Rampyari, Jeeva and Kartaro began to cry aloud. Almost every woman was wiping her teary eyes with her aanchal.

The Woman-of-the-Well was sitting in her doorway, her back against the open door. She said, 'Dewanchand's father had hired the poor man as his servant. He was quite a strapping lad then. Used to carry bales of cloth for them and milk their buffalo. He was a good man. Scrupulously honest and decent. Never said a bad word to anyone. Which boy or girl from the gali has not played in his lap.'

Dewanchand said, 'I used to study then at Pandhe's school. Hadn't begun to look after the shop yet. Father had given him a room for free, and I never asked him for any rent either. The poor soul was from somewhere near Vaishno Devi in Jammu. I owe him one hundred and fifty rupees. If you all say so, that sum can be donated to some temple or to a cow shelter or wherever you all decide.'

All the young men and women and children of the gali had grown up with Dauloo mama around. Only the Woman-of-the-Well, Masterji and Govindram called him by his name; the rest addressed him as mama. He would hoist the children onto his shoulder and amuse them by making funny noises. Whenever a baby was born to someone in the gali, they would congratulate him and tell him that he now had another niece or nephew.

Dauloo would smile showing his toothless gums, and say with pride, 'You're telling me? You've all shitted and peed on me!'

Ever since Puri was very young, he remembered Dauloo selling things from his tin box in the galis of the neighbourhood. The box held many titbits for children: pieces of pateesa sweet, peppermint and other candies, sour mango leather and dried tamarind in their season, and churan, the tart mix of pulverized spices. The women of the gali, Meladei and Basant Kaur more than others, were constantly accusing Dauloo mama of giving their kids mango leather and dried tamarind on the sly to make friends with them. They would complain: 'What a way to show your affection, mama! We're fed up with having to treat them for sore throats.'

Meladei's son Ratan, her second son Vijay and daughter Dammo had sweet voices and were particularly attached to Dauloo. He would teach them folk songs from the hills sung in his own language. If Usha and Hari imitated the singing, Masterji would shout at Dauloo for teaching children nonsensical songs.

Children living in the galis of Machchi Hatta, Kanjar Phalan, Vachchovali and Rang Mahal and also in the galis around Mochi Gate knew that Dauloo jabbered angrily if anyone said 'banana' in front of him. Children would begin to chant 'banana, banana' on seeing him, and Dauloo would curse them in his own particular way. The first part of the curse would be audible, and the rest would be lost in angry gasps and the breath escaping from his toothless mouth. The neighbourhood children often played a game. On seeing Dauloo approach with his box, they would ask their mothers for a paisa or two. They would show him the money from a distance, and ask with a serious expression, 'Mama, I want to buy something.'

Dauloo would reply, 'Come here, child! Come here, baby!'

The children would come closer and ask, 'Mama, you have bananas?'

Dauloo would begin to curse them and beat the ground with a stick to scare them off.

The children would scamper off laughing in every direction. Dauloo would chase some for a distance when another child would come up from behind and shout, 'Mama, banana!' After playing this trick a couple of times, they would buy stuff worth a paisa or two.

As in the previous years, that year too the coloured water prepared for the celebration of the Holi festival were thrown at him before anyone else, turning his kurta into a collage of red, blue, green and yellow. The words 'stupid' or 'ass' carved into potato halves were first stamped as a joke on Dauloo's back. And now, he was also the first victim of the bloodbath in the neighbourhood.

Remembering him, Masterji said, 'He felt no greed or jealousy. He treated everyone with love. That's the true way to worship God.'

The gali people unanimously decided to claim Dauloo's body from the hospital, and to cremate it with all due rites.

Puri climbed the stairs to his house. Tara and Usha were both sitting close to the light, studying for their exams. Hari too was sitting on the ground on a mat and writing in an exercise book before him on a low desk. Their mother sat with Munni in her lap, mending the hem of the baby's frock.

When Puri came in, mother said to her daughter in a tear-filled voice, 'Usha, serve food to your brother. Munni will begin to cry if I get up.'

Usha usually did not do anything unless asked repeatedly, but Dauloo's death had softened her too. She placed her open book on the mat and got up to serve the food without a word. Everyone was sad. The whole gali was quiet in mourning.

As he changed his clothes, Puri thought: When someone dies, you express your feelings of loss and grief to their relatives. The feeling of grief at the death of Dauloo mama was not for show. It was everyone's personal grief. He had not belonged to anyone, but to everyone.

As the curfew ended at 5 o'clock in the morning of 5 March, the newspapers were delivered late. The front pages carried the news of the League's failure to form a ministry. There was also news about the formation of the Anti-Pakistan League by the Hindus, the Sikhs and the Congress Party to oppose the demand for a League ministry and for Pakistan. Master Tara

Singh had been unanimously appointed 'the dictator' of the new league.
There were also reports about widespread riots in Rawalpindi, and of the
success of the police in controlling the situation there, about firing on the
meeting of Hindu–Sikh students in Lahore, about the incidents of rioting
and arson in Chowk Matti, and also about sporadic knife attacks in Mazang
and near Delhi Gate.

The Chowk Matti incident was described in the Hindu newspapers as an
attack on a peaceful march of Hindus passing through a Muslim mohalla.
The Muslim papers reported it to be an unprovoked attack by Hindu
mobs on Muslims. There were eighteen murders and over a hundred were
wounded in Lahore in one day.

The gali people were pleased that the League ministry could not be
formed. The spectre of Pakistan was on everyone's mind, and anger against
the League and the Muslims for the events of the previous day was brewing.
They sat together, read the newspapers, expressed their views and discussed
the events as usual. But Puri did not say a word to anyone.

Karam Chand Kashish was the director–editor of *Pairokaar*, and Banarasidas
Sondhi its managing editor. They both had other, more important work to do
than write for the paper. The three assistant editors, Bhagat Ram, Indranath
and K.K. Chaddha, took turns writing editorials and commentaries. Puri
was a sub-editor, but he was often given the responsibility of writing
an editorial. The rest of the editorial staff worked in the newsroom,
translated news into Urdu and edited copy. Before the copy was given to
the calligraphers, Kashish and Banarasidas would sometimes glance at the
editorials, commentaries and the lead articles; they were sent to the litho
presses even if they could not read them beforehand.

Bhagat Ram had a bad cold, his eyes were red and watery. He had
wrapped hot, freshly roasted chickpeas (that Sewa Ram had brought him
from the bazaar) in a handkerchief, and was inhaling the vapours and
putting the poultice to his forehead to relieve the congestion and be able
to work. He had taken several days off in the past month on the occasion of
the birth of a new child, and then because of the infant's sickly condition.
The assistant and the sub-editor usually shared the workload, but it was
Bhagat Ram's turn to write the editorial on 5 March and he did not have
the courage to ask Banarasidas for another leave from the office. He looked
pleadingly at Puri, 'Puri, my friend, you can see my condition. Why don't

you write today's editorial? I'll do it when it's your turn. Write something on Comrade Kapoor's appeal for peace between the communities. What do you think?'

Puri thought for a few moments. He would not be able to join the funeral procession for Dauloo, but he would have a better opportunity to express his feelings for him.

When Puri left his office at 5 o'clock, he thought that Ratan, Mewa Ram, Bir Singh and others must have left with the bier for the Ram ka Bagh cremation ground. Perhaps they were back by now. He was often tired after finishing work. He had a vocation for writing, and had thought that writing for a newspaper would be easy and not a burden, but the previous year's experience had taught him that it was another matter to write according to one's imagination, inspiration and inclination. But to write on a given subject with a certain perspective and within a limited number of words was frustrating rather than heartening. However, today he had written and expressed what he felt in his heart, and that made him feel fulfilled.

He had gone to Kanak's house two days before, on Sunday evening. Her brother-in-law Nayyar was there, and sat in the living room with them. Nayyar had come to ask Panditji's advice about buying some land to build a house. What could Puri add to that conversation? He asked Kanak indirectly if they could go out, but she did not catch the hint. Puri did not feel comfortable in Nayyar's presence; he always looked at Puri unseeingly. Puri realized that it would be difficult to talk alone with Kanak that evening, and had excused himself after a while.

Today, Puri wanted to go back home, wash his face and change his clothes, and go to Kanak's house. When he reached the gali, he saw Masterji sitting on the chabutara below their house. The schools were closed for preparatory leave before the examinations. He looked sad. Since everyone in the gali was in mourning for Dauloo mama, Puri found that natural.

'Son, I have very bad news,' he said as Puri came by. 'The son-in-law of Badhawa Mull Narang was murdered last night.'

'How did you find out?' Puri blurted out in shock and disbelief.

Masterji told him the source of the news, and said, 'Son, people don't mind if one doesn't send good wishes on a happy occasion, but it wouldn't be proper to fail to visit them at the time of a bereavement. Have some water or tea if you want, but let's go to their house as soon as possible.'

Urmila had been married to a wholesaler of stationery goods, Kewal

Krishna, the son of Daulat Ram Chaddha of Bhati Gate. As the tutor of Narang's daughter Urmila and son Jagdish, Masterji had received mithai in invitation to attend her wedding. Masterji had gone to give his blessings to Urmila. Puri had found an excuse not to go, but an excuse now would be improper. There was no chance of visiting Kanak.

The month spent at Murree came alive in Puri's memory. Brash and irrepressible Urmila, with flirtation in her eyes. Married yesterday, today a widow; such were the consequences of this Hindu–Muslim conflict. That pinkish glaze of passion in her eyes, with those lovely tears… those eyes would now be shedding tears of grief. The song of love that the cheerful girl wanted to sing was drowned in her fate.

Lala Badhawa Mull Narang sat in mourning with his eyes closed, his hand on his forehead, surrounded by people. There was but one topic of conversation: Only two months had passed since the wedding. The family could have waited for two more months. Who can change what is ordained by Fate. The bride had spent hardly any time with her in-laws. Once she had stayed for two days, then for four. She had been at her own parents' mostly, the poor thing. When they heard the news, the crying parents took the daughter back to her in-laws. They would bring her home after the mourning period; how can she remain there now?

Puri spent the night thinking about Urmila's lust for life, and her dark, sorrow-filled future. He tried to imagine how she might have behaved with her husband after the marriage. Maybe she had fallen in love with other men too before she got married. She longed for love, and to be loved. Now, as a widow, she had become unworthy of giving or receiving love for the rest of her life.

On the morning of 6 March, the inhabitants of Bhola Pandhe's Gali and of other galis in the neighbourhood were surprised to see a sidebar column entitled 'Dauloo Mama' beside the editorial in *Pairokaar*. Doctor Prabhu Dayal read it aloud:

Dauloo mama, how many children in how many galis in the town of Lahore called you 'mama' because they regarded you as an uncle. Every day of your life you made hundreds of children laugh, and now you have left them crying bitterly for you. What cruel Fate took away the source of laughter of these innocents? Whose enemy were you, mama? Mama had nothing to do with the Unionists, nor did he belong to the League. He was a human being, just a human being. His murder was the murder of human values. Who's behind this craving for the blood of humanity? Dauloo mama had no quarrel with any one, not even for a place to sleep or for a piece of bread. In whose path was he an obstacle to power and glory?

Mama, when God asks you the name of your murderer, whom would you point at? Does He not know that those leaders behind the incitement to your murder use innocents like you as stepping-stones to the seat of power. Will the public not someday judge those leaders for making a mockery of human ideals? Can the deception and the betrayal of the ordinary people for selfish reasons be called protecting religion and democracy?

Ratan clutched Puri's arm and whispered in a decisive tone, 'Bhai, I swear that I will avenge the murder of Dauloo mama!'

Puri could not say anything in reply. The same incident had such a different effect on him and on Ratan.

Doctor Prabhu Dayal next read the editorial to everyone:

To the leaders of the League and the Congress! Both your organizations owe their origin to the desire to free the country from slavery. Today, all of you are in the dock for handing over the administration of Punjab to the governor. Today you are all claiming a lackey of the imperialist power and an inveterate turncoat as your ally, and the anti-imperialist forces to be your enemy. The very same person who ordered lathi-charges on peaceful demonstrations of the League, is being called 'a brother of the League'. What has happened to the slogans of Hindu–Muslim unity of the past two months, and of the promises to end the draconian laws of the imperialist masters? The same Khizr who put the Congress leaders in prison during the War and sold out to British imperialists, today has become a blood brother of these Congress leaders!

Remember that the Congress has been as much a representative of the Muslims since its inception as of the Hindus. By tearing off the green colour from its flag the Congress has cut off one of its hands. To fight the foreign aggressor by forming a united front, Mahatma

Gandhi and Pandit Nehru are willing to join hands with the League in forming a national government, but in spite of the League's majority in the Punjab Assembly, the Congress leaders are reluctant to join its ministry here. If the Muslims have the confidence in the Congress governments in eight provinces, why won't the Hindus accept one League government? The downfall of the Unionist ministry is the defeat of imperialism and its henchmen. This defeat is a victory for the Congress demand for democratic and civic liberties. Fomenting age-old enmities or threats to break up ministries formed by other political parties will not solve any problem. Passive resistance of satyagraha to violent suppression by the imperialists, but brandishing swords to threaten the League, does such double-faced behaviour represent your diplomacy and courage? Is the killing of so many innocents in one day not enough for you? Don't let the enemy turn you into human torches so that he can dance in their light.

The gali people heard this in silence. They did not curse or blame the League as they had done in the days past. Puri did not disclose that he had written the editorial, but Tara guessed so. In praise of the article, she said, 'I'll ask everyone at the college to read the editorial.'

All of Puri's acquaintances who read the editorial had something to say about it. Some liked its bold and direct language, others praised its message for unity and peace while some others praised Puri's writing style. The communists too came to pat him on the back, and to explain to him the strategy of inspiring a bourgeois democratic revolution by uniting different factions of society. Some of Puri's colleagues at *Pairokaar* were ambivalent, but Bhagat Ram was particularly concerned. He had heard that Sondhi had not liked the editorial. Puri didn't care, what did one person's opinion matter?

Puri felt buoyed up by this acknowledgement of his abilities and the power of his pen. When he returned home from the office, the previous day's idea of visiting Kanak was on his mind. He washed his face, changed his clothes and went to Gwal Mandi.

He reached Kanak's place at 6 o'clock. As fate would have it, her elder sister Kanta and Nayyar were present. Kanak rose from her chair to welcome him. Kanta had met Puri only a couple of times, and paid little attention to his arrival. Nayyar sat slouched in his chair; he did not move, but acknowledged Puri's namaste with a nod of his head.

As Puri took a seat, Kanak said excitedly, 'Today your piece was really powerful.' She turned to Nayyar, 'Did you see Puri-ji's editorial?'

'Where?' Nayyar asked without enthusiasm.

'In *Pairokaar*.'

'I read the *Tribune*.'

'Want me to read it to you?' she asked, but did not get up to bring the paper. Puri did not like this cool response to his writing.

Kanak's enthusiasm had been deflated by the memory of an incident a few days ago. Puri had told Kanak about the indifference shown by Nayyar towards him, and Kanak had replied, 'Why do you bother about his behaviour? He doesn't have time for art or literature. He only knows about legal matters and law courts, his concern is only with money and property.'

Kanak made excuses for Nayyar, but let her brother-in-law know about her annoyance. As in any modern family, the brother-in-law playfully teased, argued with and baited his wife's sisters. Kanta had no brother, and that brought her husband even closer to her sisters. Kanak shared some of her secrets only with him. Being three years younger than Kanta, she was closest to and most intimate with Nayyar. Which young, unmarried woman would let go of the occasion to learn, from a safe distance, a bit about flirtation and seduction from her sister's husband? Nayyar too would rather talk to Kanak than to her elder sister about certain matters.

Kanak asked her brother-in-law, 'Why are you so cold towards Puri-ji? He's our guest, we're also grateful to him for his help.'

Nayyar showed surprise at her criticism. He said, 'What can one talk about with him? He always seems nervous, out of place. He's not used to the company of cultured people.'

Kanak's defence of Puri gave Nayyar the opportunity to express a grudge he had been nursing for some time. He had felt that Kanak was moving away from him and inching closer towards Puri. He looked hard at her and asked, 'Is that a feeling of respect for your tutor, or is there something else?'

'Yes, there is!' Kanak wanted to say, but she held back. She did not want to take such an important step without consulting Puri. She had not talked to him about letting her family know of her plans. Instead, she said to Nayyar, 'You always see something where there's nothing.'

'What did I see?'

'Why, are you jealous?'

'Jealous?' He turned his curiosity into a question, 'Have I any reason to be jealous?'

'I don't want to talk to you. You always twist things around.' She was angry and did not talk to him for two days. She decided that until she consulted Puri about broaching the subject of their affair to her family, she would be careful with her 'devious' brother-in-law.

Puri sat with Kanta and Nayyar, but they said little to him. There was no particular topic of conversation, but still Kanak was careful to speak with Puri and also to her sister and her husband. The conversation turned to the riots and then to Nayyar's Muslim neighbour Mirza. Panditji was still in his office, trying to wind up his work. Nayyar was going to take all of them back to his house in Model Town.

Puri was uncomfortable at being ignored by the company. He got up and asked to be excused. Kanta and Nayyar made no show of asking him to stay. In the circumstance, Kanak did not ask him to stay either, and let him leave.

Puri was furious as he came out of her house. What's the matter, he thought, why this insulting and indifferent behaviour? Kanak had behaved oddly last time too. He wouldn't visit her in future. No, he would meet her outside and demand an explanation.

He felt upset by Kanak's demeanour till he drifted into sleep that night.

On 7 March, as Puri stepped into the office, he found Bhagat Ram waiting for him. Bhagat Ram motioned Puri to follow him to the balcony that overlooked the bazaar. He was obviously worried.

'It's a disaster!' Bhagat Ram pointed towards Kashish's office and said, 'He says that we have betrayed the Congress and the Hindus, that filthy columnists have infiltrated *Pairokaar*. He says that he was suspicious of you from the beginning, that you stabbed the Congress in the back last year at the time of the sailors' revolt. He is also angry with me that I let you write the editorial. You know I wasn't well, I didn't even read what you had written. You could have written all that the next day.'

'I'll take the responsibility for what I wrote,' Puri said to soothe Bhagat Ram.

Kashish sent for Puri. When Puri entered his office, he found Kashish waiting with a grave expression on his face, ready for an encounter. On his head was a starched and ironed white Gandhi cap. His fingers were intertwined; he was sitting erect and well back in his chair. On his desk was the editorial written by Puri, marked in places with a green pencil.

In reply to the namaste offered by Puri, he pointed to the editorial on the desk and asked, 'What foolishness is this?'

Puri tried to answer calmly, 'Panditji, in my opinion I didn't write anything foolish. It was an appeal to douse the raging fires of communal disturbance. I thought that was in line with the policy of the Congress.'

'Oh, very clever! You think I can't see how you've stabbed the Congress and the Hindus in the back, behind a show of sorry sentiments.'

Puri swallowed this deliberate insult and said, 'In my view I didn't write a word against the policy and the interest of the Congress.'

'To accuse the Congress leaders of bloodshed and provocation, to call them devious and dishonest, is that in the interest of the Congress?' Kashish asked sharply. 'To suggest that it yield to the pressure from the League, is that in the interest of the Congress?'

'I wrote all that on the basis of facts. I heard the speeches, and the newspaper reported the same. I didn't ask the Congress to surrender. I have also pointed out the folly of the League,' Puri tried to explain.

'Oh, very clever! You'll tell both the Congress and the League what to do? You've come here to teach your bosses how to write! Spare us your devious ways. Go back and show your tricks to people from whom you learned them!' Kashish said threateningly.

Puri could not hold back, 'Sure! I don't want to work at a place where I have to suppress the facts!'

'Is that so?' Kashish said sarcastically. 'You already have some agreement with the League. Get out! We don't need traitors here!'

Puri got up in anger and shouted back, 'You're the traitor!'

Kashish's eyes became red with rage. He pressed a switch on his desk. A bell outside his office door rang. Puri went on, 'You've betrayed the Congress, the country, your people. I spit on your job!'

In the next room others were inquiring from the peon about the uproar in Kashish's office. The peon came running at the sound of the bell.

Puri had opened the door; he got out before the peon could enter the office. He heard Kashish yell, 'Throw this man out! He's not allowed back in the office.'

Chapter 8

THE NEWS OF JAIDEV PURI LEAVING HIS JOB AT *PAIROKAAR*, OR OF HIS BEING FIRED from the newspaper, spread quickly among the journalists of Lahore, but not a single report of the incident appeared in the press. The newspapers might have differed in their political affiliations and sectarian beliefs, but there were no disagreements among them about keeping employees in line.

Manzoor, Hira Singh, Asad, Narendra Singh and Mahajan did their best to organize a united show of protest by the journalists of Lahore against the unjust treatment of Puri by his editor. A number of assistant and sub-editors were in sympathy with Puri's views. These sympathizers were willing to voice their support, but on condition that all the journalists from all the newspapers joined them. Few of Puri's friends were confident of his getting any kind of general support. A section of the city's journalists found Puri's right to express his opinion to be morally justified, but harmful to the commercial interests of the paper. Puri, in their opinion, should have toed the line. There were some others who thought that Puri's comments amounted to bad political judgement. The communists did not succeed in uniting the journalists in support of Puri.

On the evening of 8 March, curfew was imposed in the Bhati Darwaza, Delhi Gate, Said Mittha and Mazang areas after rioting went out of hand in those neighbourhoods. The communists waited two days before calling a meeting of the city's Printing Press Workers Union, and had a motion passed in support of Puri's call for communal harmony and condemning the injustice done to him by *Pairokaar*.

The union meeting was held in the evening outside Chardewari, in a garden near Mori Gate. Several people spoke, and then Asad stood up to praise Puri's journalistic and literary abilities. Citing his courage, Asad said that this exemplary journalist and writer had empathy for others' suffering. Asad read Puri's editorial from *Pairokaar* to the gathering, and asked, 'You be the judges: is this an appeal for Hindu–Muslim unity or an attempt to besmirch someone's reputation?'

Asad declared, 'We intend to send a copy of Puri's article to Mahatma Gandhi, and ask for his opinion as to whether the writer is guilty of slander.

We hope that the *Pairokaar* management will honour Mahatmaji's verdict. The newspapers demand freedom of the press from the government. We ask, do they give their journalists the same freedom to express their views? Is freedom of the press and of speech meant only for the owners of the newspapers? What about freedom of expression for those who do not own a newspaper or a printing press? Such one-sided freedom will not be in the public good, and will also serve the interests of the newspaper bosses.'

Asad appealed to the public, 'The sacrifice made by Comrade Puri for the sake of communal peace should not be in vain. The workers of Lahore should raise their voices in support of his demand that the Congress, the League and the Akalis stop playing into the hands of the British imperialists in the hope of getting ministerial positions, and that they work together to form a common front to take back the administration from the governor.'

Hira Singh and Pradyumna also spoke. The gist of their speeches was that British imperialists, who manipulated the two Hindustani peoples by their 'divide and rule' policy, were the enemy in the struggle for independence. But greater and more dangerous enemies were those who were turning the struggle for political autonomy into a sectarian confrontation. The independence and unity of India rested on harmony between Hindus and Muslims. The negative consequences of gaining the political upper hand by inciting communal hatred and rivalry, and of working hand in glove with British civil servants, were obvious to everyone.

'Friends, terrible news has come of widespread riots in Amritsar earlier today. The commercial hub of Punjab is in flames. The people behind this conflagration are safely ensconced in their palatial houses, leaving you and me to be the victims of this inferno of hatred. Our brother Puri was doing something sacred; he was working, fearlessly and selflessly, to defend the man in the street. We appeal to all journalists of the country to follow Comrade Puri's example. The struggle for our country's independence and for uplifting the masses cannot be safe in the hands of leaders who want to incite sectarian hatred for their own devious ends. The working class must strive for the unconditional unity of the people. We, the workers of this country, in one united voice, offer our praises to Comrade Puri for doing his duty. Victory to Comrade Puri!'

Puri was deeply moved by these generous tributes. When he stood up to express his thanks, he had to make an effort to control his emotions and clear the lump in his throat, 'I am much obliged to you, my friends, for your recognition of my efforts. For the sake of my conscience, I am willing to walk away from hundreds of jobs if need be. Hindu–Sikh–Muslim unity is the first step towards gaining freedom from slavery under foreign domination. The Congress has always stood, and will always stand, for this ideal. Subhash Bose's Indian National Army was a living proof of the strength of our unity. I pledge my word here before you all that I'll never shirk from sacrificing my life for that ideal.' The audience cheered and clapped.

After news came in of bloody riots, looting and arson in Amritsar, a group of communist workers went there to help with peace efforts. They asked Puri to go with them. Puri was shaken by the enormity of the destruction in the carnage. Their efforts quickly succeeded in restoring peace. Enemies of the previous day embraced their opponents and asked for their forgiveness. Puri felt hopeful.

The communists, some Congress workers who opposed sectarian discord, the socialists and other liberal-minded people, launched a movement for communal and civic harmony in Lahore. They held meetings in various parts of the city and began peace patrols with the help of the Railway Workers Union. Puri was always invited to these meetings, and he too participated with a sense of purpose. Sitting idle at home was intolerable for him. He was always treated like a leader and a hero at these meetings. The recognition of his sacrifice encouraged him, but this feeling alone could not meet the needs of his daily life. The long faces of his mother and Masterji bespoke their regrets about his losing the job. They had become an object of sympathy and pity for the gali people. Puri felt like a limb cut off from a tree, its leaves and shoots gradually withering away.

At the suggestion of Asad and Pradyumna, Puri had sent a copy of his *Pairokaar* articles and a description of the treatment meted out to him to Mahatma Gandhi by registered mail. With Gandhiji's moral support, he hoped to gain some standing in political circles. But three weeks passed without any answer. His communist friends had asked like-minded staff workers of other newspapers to look for a job for Puri, but that effort too proved fruitless.

Puri was deeply frustrated by the resulting lack of money, more so since he had grown accustomed to a certain lifestyle in the past year. He had bought several things on credit on the assurance of getting one hundred rupees at the end of each month. The shame of not being able to settle his debts was as painful as an insect boring into his skull.

Pairokaar owed Puri his salary for February. But he could not bear the thought of going to the office and demanding it. Bhagat Ram and Indranath had warned him not to expect his outstanding salary to be delivered to his home. Kashish was not even willing to hear the mention of Puri's name. Puri found it maddening that he could not afford to hire a tonga, have his shirts laundered or even get a haircut. He used to hand over most of his salary to his mother, and the family scraped by on the combined salaries of father and son. How could he ask her for money now, when he was not earning a single rupee? The hot months of summer had begun. The middle-class people of Lahore wore either white shirts and trousers, or white linen suits. Such elegance had now moved beyond Puri's reach.

In those days of difficulty and anxiety, Puri often thought about Kanak. The memory of her indifferent behaviour in the presence of Nayyar still gnawed at him. He wanted to tell her about his misfortunes, but meeting her would mean telling her about losing his job. This predicament was making him drift like a leaf blown down the street in a windstorm. He thought it better not to go and see her in his impoverished situation, and risk a blow to his self-respect.

Puri had the ability and the inclination to work. In fact, he desperately wanted to work, but the chance to do so was being denied him. And this denial meant a half-empty stomach, a lack of clean clothes and the frustration of being unemployed. There was no hope of finding work with any Lahore newspaper. He often thought of going to another city, but could not muster the courage to try his luck without some assurance of work. Gather your wits, he told himself, you're better known in the field of literature and journalism now than when you were just a beginner at *Pairokaar*. He decided to become a freelance writer.

He wrote two satirical articles on Kashish and titled them: 'The Wily Writer', and 'Mr Big Editor'. One was published in *Sitara*, the other in *Bhanmati*. Despite widespread praise, all Puri got for them was ten rupees each.

Puri pondered: Is literature and art worth so little? At least 4,000 or 5,000 persons must have read my articles. He reasoned: What more can I expect? I write just to entertain the readers. What more should an entertainer expect? Like other street jugglers and pavement artists, if I stood and read aloud my work in the garden outside Chardewari, maybe people would throw a paisa or two to me. I might be able to earn fifty rupees a day, but being a white-collar gentleman, I can't bring myself to do that. He smiled at himself: I am penniless, but I still want respect. That's the height of my folly. Prestige is measured by one's means. For my means I must depend on magazines and newspapers.

In his distress he would think: What a miserable profession I have chosen! The fame of an artist or a writer is like a hollow drum: its sound reaches far and wide, but there's nothing inside. But what else could I have done? Take a job earning forty or fifty rupees a month at some school or as a clerk with the railways? For him that thought was even more humiliating.

Pandit Girdharilal had great regard for Puri's talent. Pride had not allowed Puri to accept money for tutoring his daughter or to reveal his own modest circumstances. He would have preferred to commit suicide rather than admit his being penniless to Kanak's family and ask them for a handout.

Seven or eight months earlier, Pandit Girdharilal had asked Puri for the manuscript of his short stories. Again, it would have hurt Puri's pride to remind him unless Panditji talked about it first. He felt it was beneath him to show any eagerness to have his writings published as a book. He would despair and think: Nothing earns respect like having money; all show of friendliness is mere pretence.

Puri knew the owner of Adayara Munavvar, the Urdu publishing house. He got from him the work of translating an English novel into Urdu, at eight annas per page. Despite the efforts for peace, there were sporadic incidents of rioting, violence, arson and knifing. On days home due to the curfew, Puri would work hard and translate, sometimes more than 20 pages of the novel. He would feel happy that he could earn at least ten rupees at the end of the day; 300 rupees per month!

Puri managed to translate half the novel in a week and took the manuscript to the publisher in the hope of a payment of seventy-five rupees. The owner of Adayara Munavvar, Ghaus Mohammad liked the translation, but he was, as Puri found, in no hurry to publish the book. He had given the job to Puri mainly to help out a promising writer. Puri swallowed that remark for the sake of future business relations with the publisher. Ghaus promised to pay a part of the money in a couple of days. Puri lost interest in finishing the translation. He thought, what's the value of an art that has no buyer!

Another month passed. No political party, either on its own or in coalition, succeeded in forming a government. The administration remained in the hands of the governor and his cadre of civil servants.

The League's demand for Pakistan had become increasingly vociferous and militant. The Anti-Pakistan League, under the leadership of Master Tara Singh, roared to match its stridency. The newspapers were full of reports of terrified Muslims fleeing westward from their ancestral homes in eastern Punjab, and of frightened Hindus on the other side uprooting themselves to settle in eastern Punjab. Everyone seemed to be waiting for the lid to blow. At the time of the Quit India movement in 1942, most people would break out in a cold sweat at the mention of swords, firearms or other weapons. Now Puri frequently heard about Lahorites hoarding swords, spears and guns. Some were having crude flintlocks made out of plumbing pipes. It was widely rumoured that in the name of defending Hindus and for the defeat of Pakistan, one could buy as many guns as one wanted for about Rs 200 each from Lala Madho Shah and Lala Sukhlal.

In spite of the efforts of the communists and the committees for the maintenance of peace, some part of the city would always erupt in riot and flames and a curfew would be imposed. The University and the colleges were closed for preparatory leaves for the examinations. Tara had been warned not to go out because of the possibility of riots breaking out at any time. In desperation she thought, it's me who has to take the brunt of the stupidity, fanaticism and rivalries of other people. But she was helpless. On those days Puri too was forced to stay home and work on his writing or on his translation. When the curfew was relaxed, the communists would organize a meeting or a march in support of communal harmony. Puri always took part in such demonstrations.

Tara would find some excuse to go out with him to hear him speak. Asad had guessed Tara's difficulty, and he was always present on such occasions. They got a few minutes to talk together while Puri gave his speech. After the meeting, Asad would walk with them through Shahalami to Bhola Pandhe's Gali, and continue on his way through Rang Mahal to Delhi Gate.

Tara had reason to be nervous on a couple of occasions. Her brother had high regard for Asad, she knew, but she also felt that he did not like her being too close to him. Puri's anger and irritation seemed to have grown in the past few days. She had a suspicion as to why, and could not blame her brother. She began to act more cautiously.

Her hunch was right. Puri had not been able to visit Kanak for a month.

He was in two minds: he wanted to meet her because of his feelings for her, but he held back because of his shame at being jobless. He had hidden his tender feelings under his resentment for her indifference and coolness at their last two meetings. In his rage he would remember the rumours about her 'loose' behaviour. In that mood of resentment he would think: First she pledges her everlasting love, and then shows such indifference! Maybe something is brewing between her and the brother-in-law! Who can trust such girls?

Puri began to despise any indication of a girl being too forward with men. He could disregard the remarks about Kanak's spontaneity as the result of her sophisticated upper-class background, or accept it as the effect of her being attracted to his own forceful personality. But for his sister to behave in the same way could tarnish his own and his family's honour. He did not want to let that happen. Tara began to take pains not to allow even the slightest slip-up.

After the news of Puri losing his job became known, the gali people had commiserated with him and cursed his boss's unfairness. They would hush up in sympathy whenever he was around. Ratan's brother Vijay was very fond of singing the *tappas* of Punjabi folk songs. He could learn the tune and the words of a song just by hearing it once, and would often break into song at any moment. Neighbours called him the 'phonu-graph of the gali'. One morning when Puri was working at home, Vijay began to sing a *tappa* in a loud voice: 'As she climbs on to the train, the guard blows his whistle meaningfully at her.'

Vijay was in the middle of the refrain when his song was cut short. Puri heard the boy's mother scold him, 'Be quiet, you bad boy! You've grown so tall, but have learned nothing. Your next-door neighbour has lost his job, and you continue to sing at the top of your voice.' The boy lowered his voice and hummed his song.

The sympathetic silence for Puri's problem lasted only a few days, but he could feel that Ratan, Bir Singh, Tikaram and others had drawn away from him. These men huddled on the chabutaras in the mornings and evenings talking in conspiratorial tones, but fell silent when Puri came near. Puri felt awkward, but he knew the reason. These men had joined the Anti-Pakistan League, and were helping to sabotage the efforts being made towards the inclusion of Punjab in Pakistan. After Clement Atlee's proclamation of 16 February and the resignation of Sir Khizr, the possibility of the formation of Pakistan had ceased to be a matter of bigger demonstrations, different opinions and discussions on the formation of the next government. It had, instead, become a confrontation between the two communities: the Hindu resistance to the Muslim demand for Pakistan, and the Muslim insistence on creating it. Puri was in favour of Hindu–Muslim unity. How could he be close to these men?

Puri again went to see the publisher for payment for his translation work. Ghaus Mohammad had no money on him, but promised to pay Puri something after three days. He also made another offer to Puri: to compile a history textbook for a lump sum of 500 rupees. Professor Shah of the university had suggested the names of three history books in English. Puri's job would be to glean information from these books, and rewrite it in Urdu in about 300 pages. The textbook was to carry Professor Shah's name as the author, and several established writers had refused the offer for that reason. Ghaus Mohammad was going to give Rs 8,000 to Professor Shah, but pay only Rs. 500 to the ghostwriter.

Puri smiled cynically when he heard the offer, 'Mianji, such black marketeering in the field of learning and education?'

Ghaus Mohammad said without embarrassment, sweetening his words with typical Lahori terms of endearment, '*Sohanyo*, this is business. It's not my idea, but the university professor's who is blackmailing me. A payment of eight thousand rupees for his name on the book is the price of having it prescribed as a textbook. *Motiyanwalo*, don't I know that an educated young man like you could write a better book than his. But, yaar, the book would be useless to me if it didn't become a textbook. I don't sell knowledge; I sell textbooks. If I don't cough up the money, Pandit Girdharilal will offer Shah ten thousand. I too have to survive in this business. Badshaho, if you live in a coal mine, why complain when your hands get dirty?'

A chance to earn Rs 500 for two months' work was no ordinary matter for Puri, but being a ghostwriter seemed like closing the door on his future as an author. Ghaus again said, 'Well, think about it. Let me be frank, Masood agreed to do the work, but I like your language and style better. I'll wait for you until Friday. When you come to collect your money, borrow these three books and look them over. For this work, I'll pay you the moment you hand me the manuscript.'

Puri went to see Ghaus Mohammad on Friday after sunset. The publisher's office was at his residence in Noora Bhishti's Gali, inside Mori

Gate, a predominently Muslim area. Even the cloth-sellers and sweet-makers were Muslim. Usually after sunset was the busiest time for shopping, but Puri was surprised to find the bazaar deserted and most shops closed.

Puri heard Ghaus Mohammad's voice before reaching his office. They saw each other through the open window. Puri raised his hand to his forehead in salaam. Ghaus replied in the same way.

The front door was open. Puri asked, 'May I come in?' and went inside. Ghaus silently motioned Puri to sit on a modha, the low stool made of wicker and jute. He was sitting on a bed-like *takht* and speaking angrily to a man sitting beside him on another modha. The man got up as soon as Puri entered. Ghaus bid him farewell rather brusquely.

Puri found Ghaus showing an uncharacteristic reserve and calm in his speech. He did ask people to come back several times before making a payment, but he was always a sweet-talker. He would effusively welcome his visitors with, 'Come in, sohanyo! Welcome, motiyanwalyo! Good to see you, bhadshaho!' His kohl-lined eyes, would shine in welcome, over his fair-complexioned face , framed by a fringe of trimmed salt-and-pepper beard. To some he would offer mithai, tea and lassi. He was particularly proud of lassi blended with *pera* sweet, and the vermicelli *faluda* from Fazaldin's shop in his neighbourhood. He would walk his visitors to the end of the gali, hold their hand in both of his and shake it many times before letting go, bidding them *khuda hafiz* before they left.

Puri sensed from Ghaus's reaction that he was surprised to see him at this time. But Puri needed his payment, and sat down with the resolve of not leaving unless he got it.

After the other visitor had walked away some distance, Ghaus motioned Puri to come to the modha near him and, scratching his beard, asked in a grave voice, 'How did you reach here? Didn't you notice anything in the bazaar?'

Ghaus spat out his habitual swearword, and pointed at Puri's trousers, 'This dress is the best! Doesn't reveal if one is Hindu or Muslim. That's why no one stopped you. Me, I have this,' he again uttered the same expletive and grabbed his beard, 'the divine radiance, the signpost of being a Muslim attached to my face.'

'Anything the matter?' said Puri. 'Many shops were closed.'

Ghaus kept on holding his beard, 'May Allah forgive their sins! These dimwits murdered a poor man. Near that end of the gali,' he pointed towards Mori Gate, 'a cobbler from somewhere to the east, maybe the United Provinces, used to sit. They killed him. I saw him lying in a pool of blood on his spot on my way back. He was still alive, and moaning. I've been feeling sick since then. His body lay there for four hours; the police carted it away just now.'

'No one took him to the hospital?' Puri asked.

'I've had enough of being a Good Samaritan. A good plot for a story for you to write. You were here last on Monday. After that I went with Mian Mohsin to help him on an errand up to Bhati Gate. Right before our eyes, a man slit the stomach of a Sikh villager who must have been unaware of the tension in the city, and melted into the crowd. We took the Sikh on a tonga to the Bhati Gate police station, thinking they would take him to the hospital.

'The head constable began to interrogate us. He asked us about the cash and other stuff belonging to the Sikh?

'We were flabbergasted. I said: We brought him here because he was injured. You're accusing us of a crime!

'The head constable said: Mister, that's the seasoned criminal's ruse to avoid being blamed for a crime. Please remain here. You may go after we've conducted an investigation.

'It was scary, you'll agree. Anyway, I said to the head constable: Very well, my good man, allow me to make a telephone call. Let me ask Additional Magistrate Bakar Hussain to bail me out.'

Ghaus smiled, 'Then, mian, the head constable got up from behind his desk. He saluted me and begged my pardon for being rude. He said: Shaikhji, how many can we take to the hospital? The inspector general saheb orders us to do only policing work and not get involved in this mess. If someone needed medical help, he said, they'd reach the hospital by themselves. The job of the police is not to transport corpses. Just stick to your official duties.'

'Mianji, it's obvious that the British are making us fight,' Puri said in agreement.

'That poor easterner became a victim of the communal hatred. Today around noontime, some goonda threw a firecracker inside Bhishti ki Maseet mosque. No harm was done. You know, Muslims live in Bhishti ki Gali, and around the mosque all the houses belong to Muslims. The rumour spread that Hindus had dropped a bomb from an airplane. That some jinn threw the bomb. The savages murdered the innocent man. He had been sitting near the entrance of the gali for the last four years. Was that poor bugger denying them their Pakistan? What savagery, *tauba!*'

Puri thought for a moment. He felt shaken, but he still said, 'Mian, I'm really in need. I've come for my payment.'

'Um,' said Ghaus holding his beard. 'The situation is really bad. It's better that I escort you up to the S.P.S.K. Hall.'

Puri waited in suspense for a few moments. Then he said, 'So Mianji, I'll take leave of you.'

'Yes, let's go. *Lillah...*' said Ghaus getting up. He saw disappointment on Puri's face, and said, 'I have your money inside here.' He patted the achkan over his breast pocket, 'You can have it when we reach a safe place. If some one knifed you on the way, the money would be neither yours nor mine. I won't stand around to take it out of your pocket.'

Puri felt a shiver of fear, but said nothing and walked out with Ghaus.

When they reached the bridge near the S.P.S.K. Hall outside Mori Gate, Ghaus handed the cash to Puri and said, 'I won't go beyond this point, brother. Khuda hafiz.' He held Puri's hand in his own, 'Puri yaar, do that history book for me. I'll pay fifty rupees more, just for your sake.'

'Mianji, you know; this is taking unfair advantage of us poor writers.' Puri expressed his reluctance. 'You always want us to remain nameless.'

'Yaar, I've thrown in fifty more, just because it's you. Think of future business between us. I'll wait a couple of days for you to make up your mind. When it's quietened down a bit, come and get the English books.'

'Mianji, don't mind, but I won't be able to help you,' said Puri, and put the cash in his trouser pocket. He did not cut through the Chardewari garden as usual, but went towards Shahalami by Railway Road beside the S.P.S.K. Hall. The flow of motorcars, tongas, bicycles and pedestrians on this road was normal. There was no visible effect of the incident inside Mori Gate. By adding fifty rupees to his original offer, Ghaus had put Puri in a terrible dilemma: whether to maintain his self-respect and dignity as a writer, or live with the stigma of unemployment and the need for money to help his family. He was intensely aware of his own vulnerability. But yielding to those who took advantage of the circumstances of people like Masood Khan and himself would have meant harming and sabotaging his future. And if somebody can make him do something to his own detriment, he can also easily be persuaded to sell his conscience to the detriment of society or country. He suddenly recalled what constable Waheed was doing that day at the demonstration in Anarkali! What, for that matter, does Kashish do in the name of the Congress? The person behind today's bomb incident at the mosque too would have been someone similar, he thought. And why do Indians work in the police forces of the British Raj, for the sake of money! Let Ghaus wait, I won't destroy my future by being a ghostwriter.

The crowd had thinned in the bazaar. As Puri stepped into his gali, he saw three men running to enter it from the other end. He made out in the light of the street lamp that they had wrapped pugrees around their heads so as to hide their faces. Puri recognized them. Mewa Ram, Bir Singh and Ratan went into their houses. They too had seen Puri. Puri was surprised and alarmed, but he chose to say nothing. Ratan had a pistol in his hand, the other two had daggers.

His mother asked as he came up, 'What happened? There were loud explosions in the bazaar.'

Puri thought for a moment before replying, 'I didn't see anything in Machchi Hatta bazaar.'

Usha said, 'The noise came from the Mochi Gate side, mother. There was some screaming too.'

Puri went to the window. He heard the noise of people screaming in the distance, somewhere behind Ghasita Ram's house. He took off his shirt and trousers, tied on a lungi, and was about to sit down in his undervest for his meal in the kitchen when he heard Ratan call, 'Puri bhaiji!'

Puri went to the stairs and asked, 'What is it?'

'Bhaiji, I kept my promise. I avenged Dauloo mama's murder.' Ratan seemed rather agitated.

Puri had guessed right. He said, 'You've probably killed a few other Dauloos. We don't know who killed Dauloo mama. Now they'll come to take revenge.' He took a deep breath and changed the subject, 'It's not the average man like Dauloo mama who wants Pakistan.'

'Bhaiji, we can't let our throats be cut in silence.'

'Jaggi! Tara!' Babu Ramjwaya called from below.

'*Pairipaina*, tayaji.' Puri greeted Babu Ramjwaya standing at the foot of the stairs, cutting short his reply to Ratan. He told the others inside the house, 'Tayaji is here.' Ratan too turned towards Babu Ramjwaya and touched his feet.

Hari went and told Masterji who was resting on the roof.

It was the second week of April. Masterji had less tutoring work now that the exams were over. This year the exams were being held at irregular intervals because of the rioting. After he returned from his year-long tutor's job at the mansion of Seth Gopal Shah, Masterji had gone to lie down in the open. He came down as Usha pulled a charpoy into the room. Tara was studying in the veranda on a mat near a table lamp, she shut her book.

When Babu Ramjwaya had something to say to Masterji, he sent for him to come to his house in Uchchi Gali. He came to Masterji's house only if there was some special reason. His visits to his younger brother's home always created a stir, as it had done two months ago when he came to talk about the proposal from the Khosla family for Puri's engagement.

'Ratan, son, I must talk to you,' Ramjwaya said to Ratan as he came up. 'Lala Sukhlal has sent a message for you.' He looked left and right for a place to talk, then said, 'Come, let's go up to the roof.'

Puri had some inkling of what his tayaji, wanted to say to Ratan. Tayaji had sent for Ratan on two occasions before this. Once Puri was surprised to see Ratan come home for lunch with a suitcase in his hand. On another afternoon, Puri was working at home when the ink in his fountain pen ran out. There was no ink in the house, so Puri walked to Ratan's side of the house with his pen in his hand. He saw Ratan holding a rifle and explaining its mechanism to Bir Singh. Ratan had had some arms training in the University Cadet Corps. Puri did not want to be a party to all this, so he did not ask any questions.

Puri figured out the mystery on his own. Ratan had been very busy at his uncle's agency that cleared goods and consignments from the railway's parcel office and warehouse on behalf of the city's businessmen and traders. Babu Ramjwaya was a clerk at the parcel office. Puri had heard rumours about the shady dealings between Lala Sukhlal and Babu Ramjwaya. Sometimes parcels sent by railway to and from Lahore would get lost. Lala Sukhlal would get the claims for such parcels settled after taking his cut.

Lala Sukhlal also helped to bring in consignments of goods that could not be shipped through official channels. Such parcels disappeared from the parcel office without a trace. These contained arms and ammunition smuggled into the city from East Punjab. Ratan helped out in this dangerous work as his duty to the community, and as a service to the cause of saving Hindus from Muslims, and to ensure the death of Pakistan.

While Babu Ramjwaya talked with Ratan, a sheet over a *khes* were spread for him on the charpoy in the room below. Masterji sat at the foot of the bed, leaving the head for his elder brother. Sitting in the kitchen, Bhagwanti covered her head in respect for an elder person. Haridev ran off to the bazaar to get a paisa's worth of ice to make a cold drink of water for his uncle.

Ramjwaya finished his talk and came down. Masterji got up from the charpoy and greeted him with a namaste. Bhagwanti came from the kitchen and squatted before him to touch his feet. Puri took his usual stance nearby, his back to the wall.

Ramjwaya greeted everyone with 'Bless you! Have a long life,' and sat down. 'Everything's okay,' he asked. 'Is Munni asleep? Did she cut another tooth?'

Bhagwanti called to Usha, 'Get the fan. Tayaji must be feeling hot.'

Ramjwaya said, 'No, no. There's no need. It's not that warm yet.'

Usha waved a fan at him.

Ramjwaya told her, 'No, stop. Girls are not supposed to do such things. Girls are like goddesses. Let go, *beta*.' He scolded Haridev affectionately, 'What're you doing, you idiot? Grab the fan.'

Haridev took the fan from his sister. He began to wave the fan vigorously, as if to blow his uncle away.

Ramjwaya seemed somewhat worried, and in a bit of a hurry. Bhagwanti said in a quiet voice, 'Have a chapatti. I'll serve you a hot one.'

'No, no.' Ramjwaya refused her offer. 'I have no appetite yet. Had some milk when I returned from the office. Went first to Lala Sukhlal before coming here. He'd sent a message for me.'

Tara stiffened silently and looked at her feet at the mention of Sukhlal's name. Puri too was alarmed. Ramjwaya went on, 'They must be waiting for me at home for dinner. Well, you haven't told me what your plans are, what preparations you have made? Will you do that at the eleventh hour, when the groom's party is on your doorstep?'

'We'll do whatever you tell us.' Masterji said timidly, in an apologetic voice.

'But when will you do it?' Ramjwaya asked. 'Your daughter was engaged two years ago. She's twenty years old now. And you're waiting for me to say when? Did you ever ask me?'

Masterji kept silent. Tara turned her face towards the wall. Puri crossed his arms on his chest to brace himself for what was coming.

Ramjwaya went on, 'The wedding should have taken place long ago.

Because of that nonsense about his exam, Lala Sukhlal had sent his son somewhere to what's-it's-name, Lucknow or Kanpur. He's back. Lala was asking for a marriage date in late May. I begged him with folded hands, we're poor people. We've nothing in the house, we have to make all the arrangements. Give us some time. He has agreed for some auspicious day in the month of sawan.'

Tara felt as if she had been struck by a heavy blow. Masterji said hesitantly, 'We weren't ready for so early a date.'

'You call that early? My dear soul, the girl is past nineteen, almost twenty years old. She's two months older than Sheelo; isn't she? Does a girl that age stay with her parents? God has already given Sheelo the gift of a boy. Have you no fear of your religion and community? What's wrong with you? You're behaving like angraizi-Christians.'

'She has to pass her exams. There was a notice in the newspaper that the exams will be held late because of the riots,' Puri said.

'What exam? She needs to get married not sit for her exam,' Ramjwaya raised his voice. 'I thought she wasn't going to college. I'd told her not to. The boy's not passed the BA exam, and she wants her BA degree! What nonsense! No exam, as I said before.'

Tara lowered her head.

'Tayaji, how can we arrange a marriage at this time?' Puri spoke politely. 'I have no job. There's a severe strain on our finances as it is. I'm trying for another job. She's done her studies; let her sit for the exam. The exam isn't far off. The marriage can take place after that.'

'I said, her in-laws don't want her to have a BA degree. Do you follow me or not?' Ramjwaya was now angry. 'What if they refuse to accept the girl in marriage?'

'They can do what they like,' Puri said what he thought was reasonable.

'I don't want to get married.' Tara mustered enough courage to mumble in support of her brother.

'Don't want to get married?' Ramjwaya was dumbfounded. 'What do you want to do, spend all your life as an old maid and a burden to your parents?'

'I want to pass my exam,' Tara replied, her head bent.

'Don't interrupt!' Tara's mother scolded her. 'Go and sit outside. Usha, go and make chapattis in the kitchen.'

Tara wiped her tears and went out of the room with Usha. She sat against the veranda wall, with her head on her knees. She could hear her uncle's angry voice from the room, 'You people have your noses in the air! You're acting like those angraizi-Christians, trying to imitate people of Gwal Mandi and Model Town. You don't realize your limits. As the old saying goes, when the horses were being shod, a frog held out his foot and said, fix a horseshoe on this too.'

Puri again tried in a polite tone, 'What I was trying to say is that it'd be easier for us once I have a job.'

Ramjwaya said scornfully, 'What about your job! If you were that concerned about your job, about your family, you wouldn't have talked back to your boss. You would've listened to me. I offered to get you a job. My son Kishor's got a job. He brings in sixty-five rupees with his monthly salary and fifty–sixty extra on the side. But you wanted to be a leader, give lectures. If you were that concerned about your parents and family, you'd have listened to me. Who knows what Fate has in store for you? The Khosla family of Hira Gali was offering a dowry worth ten to twelve thousand. Were willing to transfer the ownership of the house to the grandchildren. All that property is worth more than forty-five thousand. They have only one daughter. Wanted the property to remain in the family. What could've been better than that, tell me? They were ready to give *shagun* to seal the engagement. What could I do when you lost your job? Had you followed my advice, the poor master would have seen some reward for his lifelong toil. You sank your ship, and now you want to drown your sister too. You don't have a paisa to your name, how can you take responsibility for somebody else?'

Puri said, looking down, 'I'm not sitting idle, I'm trying to work from home. I can only do what I know how to do. All I said was that Tara's not a baby. We must listen to what she has to say.'

'Not a baby! Wait a bit longer and she'll be an old woman by then.' Ramjwaya looked at Masterji, 'Are you ready to keep your daughters as old maids? Willing to feed them all your life?'

'No, bhaiji. They're your daughters too. I'll do what you say. All I want is to somehow get rid of this responsibility that God has given me,' Masterji said in a guilty voice.

Ramjwaya lowered his voice, 'I was shocked to hear something. Someone spread the rumour that your family doesn't like Lala's boy. That you said the engagement might be broken. You don't know Lala Sukhlal. If he gets mad, he can have you given a shoe-beating right in the middle of the bazaar. He would go after even the last person in our family. I touched his feet and swore to him that some enemy of ours was behind that gossip.'

'Who doesn't know the truth about Lala's boy?' Puri said in spite of himself.

Ramjwaya shouted at him, 'Shut up, you shameless good-for-nothing. Aren't you ashamed of yourself?'

Masterji also shouted at Puri, 'Why don't you shut up. Who's asking for your advice? Why do you want to shame us?'

Ramjwaya continued to fume, 'And this is the talk of a so-called educated person! You want the girl to be married twice. What's the difference between an engagement and a wedding? When the decision is yours, do as you wish. We arranged this engagement and we'll arrange the marriage too. Don't you dare talk back to me!'

Tara sat in stunned silence. She heard the sound of the door to the stairs opening, and someone going up. Her brother had gone to the roof in defeat, she guessed. She stuffed a corner of her dupatta into her mouth to stifle her crying. Ramjwaya and Masterji were quietly discussing the marriage arrangements and about the disposal of their modest ancestral property in Naroval village. When Ramjwaya left at nine, Masterji went with him up to Uchchi Gali.

Usha came from the kitchen and said to her mother, 'I'm done making chapattis.'

Munni had gone to sleep on the mat. Bhagwanti said as she transferred the baby to the charpoy, 'Serve you brothers and sister before your father returns.'

Usha said to Hari, 'Call bhaiji.'

Puri came down in response to Hari's call and said he wasn't hungry.

Usha called Tara, who replied with a whimper, 'I don't feel hungry. I won't have anything.'

Her mother too retorted in anger, 'Usha, she doesn't have to if she's not hungry. Serve Hariya. You too eat.'

Puri went to Tara who sat weeping in the veranda. He felt himself responsible for her grief. Had he been employed, his right to speak on behalf of his sister could not have been ignored. Tara's desperation and tears were an insult to him, and he felt disgusted with himself. He said to Tara in English,

'What's the point of crying? The exams are at the end of May. The date of the marriage would fall some time in late July or August. The situation may change before that. I have a good offer of work. Let's wait and see.'

Her brother's words lacked conviction.

Bhagwanti thought that by refusing food and speaking in English, her son and daughter were showing their resentment and conspiring against the elders of the family. How much it would pain their father to see such defiance! He had devoted his whole life to them, and all he got in return was pain and suffering. She had high regard for her grown-up, highly educated children, but she had to say something in disapproval of their unreasonable behaviour, 'You're both venting your anger, but you don't realize that you shouldn't have talked back to Tayaji. You've no respect for your elders. What's the use of being educated?'

'He showed no respect for me when he called me worthless and good-for-nothing! I didn't ask him for anything.' Puri shot back in anger.

'He's the eldest of the family and that's his right. Whatever he said was proper, and for your own good.' His mother stood her ground. 'You shouldn't have barged into the conversation. He was talking sense.'

'How can you say that? It doesn't make any sense not to let her sit for the exam,' Puri tried to silence his mother.

'I don't want to get married. I'll sit for the exam,' Tara said in support of her brother.

'*Phitemunh*! Quiet! You talk like a shameless hussy that everybody will spit on. I gave you birth so that you may blacken my womb!' Tears came to Bhagwanti's eyes. Even in her anger she was careful to speak in a low voice so that her neighbour Meladei might not hear. She looked at her son, 'We don't want her to sit for the exam. What's the use? She should be married off.' She pointed at her daughters, 'Don't you see them, the fruit of our karma, these three millstones around our neck? Your father is wasting his life worrying how to save his honour and dharma. You're the oldest, most responsible of my children, yet you're ruining all our efforts. What do you know? You were in prison. For a whole year I massaged the feet of my sister-in-law and slaved away for her so that my daughter might get married. You want to throw all that away?' She began to weep.

'Ma, how can you say that!' Puri said. His tone was less strident, 'What's all this about marriage proposals. We'll do something when the time comes.'

'What'll you do?' His mother gestured angrily with her hand. Now that she had a chance to say something to her grown-up son and daughter, she wasn't holding back, 'What can you do? Suppose you find work, suppose you earn two or three hundred every month; what'll that amount to in a year or two, I ask? The younger one has turned sixteen. Have you done anything for her? You refused the proposal for your own marriage. That's what you decided. Good! It's different with boys. If my nineteen-year-old daughter, big as a she-camel, remains unmarried, I can't look anyone in the face.'

Puri stood silently with his back against the wall. His mother covered her face with her aanchal and sobbed. Tara sat, chin on knees, listening to what she felt were the preparations for her sacrifice. The voice of her brother in her defence had been silenced.

They were roused to action by the sound of Masterji's steps on the stairs. Bhagwanti wiped her face with her aanchal and her tone changed, 'Ushi, serve your father immediately.' She went into the room.

Puri went and sat near the table lamp, and began looking at Tara's book. Tara moved to the other side of the veranda.

Bhagwanti said to Masterji in her normal voice, 'Have your meal. Ushi'll serve you. It's quite late.'

Masterji was a little breathless from climbing the stairs. He took deep breaths, mumbling to himself 'Hari om tatsat. God, you're our only hope.' He asked, 'Why, have Jaggi and Tara eaten?'

'Everyone's eaten. Have your meal,' Bhagwanti said.

Masterji washed his face, and mumbling the same words, came into the kitchen and sat on the mat before his thali. From the light in the veranda it was obvious that Puri and Tara were there. He took a mouthful and asked, 'Where are kakaji and Tara?'

'They're reading in the veranda,' Bhagwanti replied.

Without addressing anyone, Masterji began to sermonize so that his son and daughter could hear, 'We should have cool heads. We should bend before God's will. He's the one who decides everything. Vanity is of no use.'

Maybe I should hang myself with my dupatta to fulfil God's will, Tara thought.

'Allah-u-Akbar! Ya Ali!' Very loud shouts and slogans from the direction of Mochi Gate could be heard. At the same time, there was banging on the doors of the houses opening on to the gali and the terrified screams of women. Ghasita Ram called out in a frightened voice, 'The Muslims have attacked!'

The food in Masteji's hand fell back into the thali.

Puri leaped to the window and saw that a small mob with burning torches, lathis, spears and daggers had invaded their gali. They were trying to break down the doors of the houses of Panna Lal on one side, and of Mukund Lal and Harbans on the other, and set them on fire. They were hurling stones and chunks of bricks at the windows and shouting threats: 'Ya Ali! Come on! Come out you sneaky bomb-throwers! You mother ... you sister ....!'

Moments later, pandemonium broke out in the gali. Puri saw Harbans, Khyali Ram, doctor Prabhu Dayal. Mewa Ram and others peeped out of their windows. From a window to his right came Ratan's shout, 'Grab your lathis and go down into the gali!'

Puri called out, 'Throw bricks down from the roof tops.'

Prabhu Dayal, Mewa Ram, Bir Singh and Mukund Ram too repeated Puri's call, 'Pull down the latrines! ... Throw down bricks!'

Puri shouted at Tara, Usha and his mother, 'Go to the roof at once and pull down the latrine walls and throw the bricks at the attackers.' After the news of rioting in the galis of Bhati Gate and Said Mittha, the women had been told about this method of defence.

Puri went to Ratan's door and called, 'Give me something too!'

Ratan was removing a small box from an almirah. He put it down carefully, and handed Puri a lathi kept beside the door. Puri went down, taking the stairs two at a time.

Mewa Ram and Bir Singh with hatchets in hand were the first to reach the gali. Bir Singh too challenged the crowd by yelling imprecations about the mothers and sisters of the attackers, 'Come on, you ...!'

Tikaram, Puri and Manohar, swinging their lathis, faced the invaders. Prabhu Dayal, Mukund Lal and others too had reached the gali. Terrified women were screaming all around. Mewa Ram gave the Hindu war cry, 'Nara-e-Bajrangi!'

'Har Har Mahadev!' Puri roared with others.

Women were crying and yelling at the top of their voices, but were also pelting the attackers with bricks from the rooftops. The bricks fell in such numbers that neither the attackers nor the defenders were able to take a step forward. Both sides were shouting 'Ya Ali!' and 'Har Har Mahadev!' and hurling curses and abuse at each other.

Rampyari's voice was heard from the window of Dewanchand's house, 'Hey Shamoo! Stop! Come back upstairs!'

Someone called from the rooftop of Panna Lal's house, 'Mewa! Puri! Biru! Watch out!'

There was an explosion in the midst of the attacking crowd, and a giant flame leapt skywards.

Hai! Oh! Ooo! came the screams. The attackers turned round and fled, stumbling and bumping into each other. The gali was filled with acrid smoke. Several people sneezed.

Prabhu Dayal, Puri and Mewa Ram called out to the women on the rooftops, 'Stop! Enough! Don't throw any more bricks!'

The women of Ghasita Ram's house continued to cry and scream. Ghasita too was yelling, 'Fire! Fire! My house is on fire! Help me!'

The doors to his house were on fire. Some firewood stacked on the landing had also caught fire. It was impossible to pass through the entrance to the house.

Panna Lal's house adjoined Ghasita Ram's. Some men went over to Ghasita Ram's house from Panna Lal's roof, and pulled out women and children. Women from all the houses were passing bucketfuls of water to men to douse the flames. Everyone in the gali was doing something to extinguish the fire. Water was being thrown from the windows and the rooftops of the houses situated on the opposite side.

Puri ran towards Rang Mahal to summon the fire engine.

The attackers had retreated towards the bazaar of Mochi Gate, but one man from that mob remained lying on the gali floor. It seemed as if a small bundle of clothes had burst open. A hit from a brick from the rooftop had smashed his head like a melon dashed to the ground. Trickling blood formed a puddle all around.

Doctor Prabhu Dayal pointed to the corpse and said to Mewa Ram, 'Bhai Mewa, remove this nuisance at once. If the police found this body here, the whole gali would have to bear the consequences. Take him back to his own gali.'

Mewa Ram put down the bucket in his hand and called, 'Ratan bhappa, come quickly with your musical instrument.' He said to the doctor, 'Right now, badshaho, he goes back to his home.'

Ratan put down the water pot he was holding and pulled out a pistol from his waistband. He grabbed one leg of the dead man and Mewa Ram the other. They dragged the corpse like a dead dog past Ghasita Ram's house up to a gali inside Mochi Gate.

The fire engine reached the gali in about fifteen minutes. The gali people had not let the fire spread. In no time, the firefighters bathed the houses of Ghasita Ram and the others next to it with long-reaching powerful jets of water.

The chaos was over in less than an hour. But it looked as if the gali had been ravaged by a storm. Mud, water and bricks covered the ground. Blood mixed with the mud in front of Harbans's house.

The men of the gali stood or sat on their chabutaras discussing the damage done to Ghasita Ram's house. Ghasita Ram and Panna Lal were examining the walls of their houses damaged by the fire and the explosion. Kartaro, Basant Kaur and other women were telling each other about the shock they had felt from the blast.

Khushal Singh patted Ratan on the back, 'Bravo, you fearless boy!'

Babu Govindram's chest swelled with pride. He said, 'No bhai, all the boys fought bravely.'

The doctor corrected him, 'Mewa, Puri, Harbans, Manohar and Tikaram were equally brave. They were the first ones to face the attackers.'

The women at their windows had a new subject. Pushpa said, showing her hands, 'Look at these blisters from throwing those *khasamkhani* bricks.'

'Death to *bachchepitte*, these mourners of their own children,' Kaula cursed. 'All my bangles have been smashed from hurling bricks.'

Meladei said from her window, 'Did you all hear what Rampyari said? She was telling her son to stay home. That good soul isn't the only one with a son. She wants her son to cower at home, and other lads to jump into the fight. Haven't we all gone through the pain of giving birth!'

Kartaro echoed Meladei's sentiments in an angry voice, 'Yeah, she's the only one to have suffered birth pangs. We just pissed our babies out.'

Rampyari shot back from her window, 'I didn't ask any one to go and fight. Those who have a few big strong sons, let them send their sons to fight. I've only got one son.'

Bhagwanti was incensed. She looked out of her window and yelled at Rampyari, 'Watch out, you slut! Don't count other people's children!'

Curses were also hurled from other windows at Rampyari.

The men standing around or sitting on chabutaras called to their respective windows, 'Hey, shut up! Stop this nonsense!'

Dewanchand raised his voice to he heard, 'Now we must put an iron gate at the mouth of the gali next to Ghasita Ram's house.'

Puri said, 'The municipal corporation will object. For ages this has been the route from Machchi Hatta to the bazaar at Mochi Gate.'

Tikaram said, 'What route? No one comes this way from up there, or takes this road to get up there. Only Muslim families live in the gali on the other side.'

The Woman-of-the-Well had been stunned by the explosion. Nobody had thought of looking after her. She slept very little, and could not stay indoors after the bedlam outside her house. She opened her doors, sat in the doorway and began her rant, 'Ramji, take me away from this world. I have lived eighty years and seven, but this is the first time I've seen such fighting in the gali. You all are responsible for all this. When there are no relationships, no business or bonds between Hindus and Muslims, no consideration for each other, they will fight each other. What else. My days in this world are numbered. Ramji, please take me away. Who knows what's to come next! Hai Ramji...'

No one paid attention to her. The gali people were busy talking about a new iron gate at the western entrance. Khushal Singh proposed that a watch be kept for the rest of the night, one from the right end, and another from the left.

The nights in Lahore in the middle of April are not all that warm, but Puri had been sleeping on the roof. Ratan followed Puri to the roof. Ratan had been addressing him as 'Puri bhraji' in previous days. As he went up with Puri, he again called him 'bhappa' or brother.

Ratan said, 'These Muslims must have had some guts to attack us. Now they'll rue the day. And that's not the end of it. Tayaji told me that a large shipment of arms is due soon. There should be some "pieces" in the gali for such situations. Now everyone will be clamouring to buy weapons.'

Puri checked him, 'Bhappa, this'll never end if it goes on like this. The Muslims also have ways to get weapons. After all, we all have to live side by side.'

'Bhappa, if they want Pakistan, how can they live next to us?' Ratan asked.

'Those responsible for fanning the flames of communal hatred have done their job. If some gullible people have become their prey, we should tell them that they're wrong, not shoot them dead.' Puri wanted to say more, but saw that Ratan was not willing to listen.

Early next morning, children from the gali houses carried back the bricks thrown from the rooftops. The missiles had been taken from the makeshift, single-brick walls of the dry latrines and, therefore, needed in the morning.

The puddle of mud and blood was washed away with bucketfuls of water. There were some tiffs between families over the bricks. The latrine walls on the rooftops of Tikaram and Birumal were a few bricks short. They suspected that Kartaro's daughter Peeto had carried off some extra bricks.

Jeeva said sarcastically from her window without naming the brick-thieves, 'May God pity those who covet other people's bricks and stones.'

Kartaro turned around and said, 'Tell that to those who took your bricks. Guru Maharaj will punish the false accusers.'

Tara heard the exchange and said without addressing anyone, 'I wonder whom and how many God will punish! Will He punish those who attack and burn other people's houses, or will He punish those who tie the hands and feet of other people and throw them in a well to drown?'

No curfew was in force that day. By 10 o'clock in the morning, most men had left for work. Only Puri, the doctor and Babu Govindram knew anything about the workings of the police and law courts. It was decided that if the police came to investigate while these three were away, the women should simply deny knowledge of any incident. The other men should do the same.

After being accused by Babu Ramjwaya of sitting at home twiddling his thumbs the previous night, Puri had decided to go to Ghaus Mohammad first thing in the morning and agree to compile the history book. He hadn't eaten anything the night before and had to take an active part in the melee. He was weak and hungry in the morning. Masterji and Haridev had had their meal. Usha was across at Pushpa's. Puri was about to ask his mother for his meal when he remembered Tara who was still lying in the veranda, her face covered with her dupatta. She hadn't eaten the night before either.

He went to her and spoke in English, 'What's the use of shedding tears? I'll discuss this with father. Mother doesn't understand any of this. Tayaji shoots his mouth off the way he does; what did he not say to me that day!

He taunted me for not having a job. Well, I'm on my way to accept a new assignment. I got only hundred a month at *Pairokaar*, but this man Ghaus is offering me 550 rupees for something I can do in two or two-and-a-half months. Not bad, eh?'

He tried to take her mind off her grief. 'I just can't figure what's going on in the city.' He told her about the bomb blast at the mosque, and the murder of the poor cobbler. He also recounted how he saw Ratan, Mewa Ram and Bir Singh running back into the gali from the Mochi Gate bazaar side, and the attacking crowd cursing the bomb-throwers. He said, 'Did you notice something about last night? A house was set on fire, the fire engine came, but the police and the government remained oblivious. Nothing seems to result from the efforts for peace and order by organizing peace committees. Either the communists should work with all their might—they control the 45,000-strong Railway Union— or let the people face whatever may come. Why should I waste my time? I'll go to the party office too and discuss this with the comrades.' Tara was the only one in the gali with whom he could talk about such matters.

At the kind words of her brother, the grief that had been collecting in Tara's heart flowed out in her tears. She told him, 'I'm coming,' and sobbed quietly for a few moments. She thought of finding some excuse to go out with her brother. Maybe she would see Asad at the party office. Her tears flowed again. How could Asad know about what she was going through? But accompanying her brother did not seem possible. She was not feeling well either that day.

When Puri returned home in the evening, he was told the police had come to investigate. No one told them anything, but at the sight of the fire-damaged house of Ghasita Ram and the blast-damaged wall of Panna Lal's house, both men were taken to the police station. Bir Singh had come home for some reason; he too was taken away. The police had taken a note of names and addresses of the gali families. It being Saturday, Babu Govindram, Tikaram and Birumal had returned early in the afternoon. They had gone to bail out and put up sureties for those in police custody. Everyone had become quiet after the arrest of three men from the gali. The children, too, were not playing.

Chapter 9

THE WALLED CITY OF OLD LAHORE WITH ITS MAZE OF GALIS WAS MORE vulnerable to rioting, knifings and arson than the outlying areas of Mall Road, Anarkali, Nisbet Road and Gwal Mandi. Outside the walled city, the flow of traffic and everyday activities of life went on unabated. The calls of Hindu and Muslim peddlers selling iced sherbet drinks, fruits, chunks of sugar cane, vegetables and mithai were as loud and prolific as before. The people living around this place were, of course, haunted by the spectre of incidents in the Old City. The threat of fresh clashes cast a pall over their lives.

Puri had not come to see Kanak for over five weeks and she pined away thinking of his coldness towards her. For her, the mayhem in the city, the arson, the killings—all seemed to pale beside her own suffering. 'What's to fear from death?' she'd ask herself. For some days she remained in a huff, sulking, stubbornly waiting for him to be the first to make an approach. She rehearsed in her mind how, when he came, she would not say a word, but punish him for his cruelty by just shedding tears silently before him. But when he did not come, she accepted defeat. She was anxious to find him. She was like a dog lost in a crowd in a desperate search for its master.

Kanak had come to know about Puri's walking out on his job rather than compromise his independence and principles, and about the motion to support him proposed at the union meeting. She found this out from Surendra and Zubeida. She also found out that Puri had put all his work aside in order to take an active part in the peace committees formed by Manzoor, Narendra Singh and other communist workers. Surendra told all this to Kanak in a tone that gave the communists all the credit for Puri's participation in the peace efforts, and in one which suggested that she was closer to Puri than Kanak.

Kanak had become a bit wary of the communists after her differences with them over the 1942 Quit India movement. It had particularly vexed her that to get news of Puri and to have a chance to meet him, she had to depend on Zubeida and Surendra. She could have asked Tara, but none of the girl students living inside the old walled city had come to college because of the rioting. Tara's college was closed, anyway, in preparation for the examinations. Kanak would just sigh in desperation at her helplessness. She was not the type to ease her pain and suffering by moping about and weeping quietly. In her admiration for Puri's noble sacrifice, she was even more eager than before to meet him, but he had managed to avoid her.

Surendra's garrulous and over-friendly manner often piqued Kanak. Zubeida was different, reserved and matter-of-fact. When Kanak showed interest in meetings and marches in support of communal harmony, both of them began to visit her home. Kanak's house was on the route Surendra followed every day, and she would drop in every second or third day for a chat. Once she said casually, 'Puri bhai speaks wonderfully on the issues of Hindu–Muslim unity. He was at our place the other day, talking for a long time about communal tension.' Kanak felt snubbed by the fact that Puri had passed by her house, but had not even stopped to say namaste. What wrong had she done? She wondered. She too was willing to help in the efforts towards peace and communal harmony, but she wished Puri would speak to her about it, even once.

Surendra told Kanak that Puri would be taking part in the march organized by the Student Federation on 30 March, and would also speak at Bradlaw Hall. She hired a tonga and rode past the crowd that had gathered to march in the procession. She saw Puri twice, but he was surrounded by people, and she could not catch his eye. In her anxiety she thought of writing him a letter. She knew his address at Bhola Pandhe's Gali, but was not sure who might open the letter. Puri had told her that his parents were quite old-fashioned in this respect.

A doubt niggled at Kanak's mind that someone had turned Puri against her. She suspected Surendra, after hearing such effusive praise of Puri from her. Surendra had seen her a couple of times in the Gwal Mandi bazaar with the younger brother of Kanta's husband, and had given her a knowing smile. Rajendra Nayyar sometimes took Kanak to Model Town to meet her sister in his brother's car. Kanak was not particularly fond of him; Rajendra talked of little other than his hosiery business and bridge games.

Kanak habitually glanced at the daily newspapers. She read in the city news column of *Pairokaar*: 'Bomb blast and fire at Bhola Pandhe's Gali. A bomb was thrown at the gali and houses were set on fire. Some gali residents had been taken into police custody after an investigation of the incident.'

Kanak could not contain herself. Panditji was in his office early that day attending to some work left over from the day before. She read the news to her father and reminded him that Puri's house too was in Bhola Pandhe's Gali.

'Oh, really!' Her father took off his reading glasses and placed them on the desk. He held his chin as he reflected upon the implication of the news, 'Yes, we haven't heard from Puri for quite some time.' He thought for a few moments, before himself providing the answer, 'He must be busy. He's a good boy, very hard working.'

Stung by her father's indifference, she said, 'We must enquire how he's doing, don't you think?'

'Enquire?' Panditji said scratching his head. 'Yes, of course, although it wont be easy to find someone in those galis. Well, if Vidhichand has some work in the Lohari Gate area, I'll ask him to pass by Bhola Pandhe's Gali.' He put his reading glasses back on and went back to the papers in front of him.

Kanak seethed in frustration. She returned to her room, thinking over what she could do. She went back to her father after a few minutes, 'Pitaji, I have to go to Shanti Bhasin's place. I shall be back by lunch time.'

'What, beta, when there's such trouble outside?' He moved his eyes from his papers to her.

'It's not so bad on Nisbet Road, Pitaji. I'll be back soon.'

She changed into her going-out clothes and hired a tonga in the Gwal Mandi bazaar and gave directions for Bhola Pandhe's Gali, inside the Shahalami Gate.

The tonga could not wait for Kanak's return near the entrance to the gali in the narrow bazaar of Machchi Hatta. She noted its serial number, and asked the driver to wait in the Rang Mahal square just a few paces ahead.

Children skipping and playing hopscotch in the gali ran ahead of Kanak and showed her the stairs leading to the house of Jaidev Puri and Tara.

The heated words between Puri and Babu Ramjwaya about Tara's marriage two evenings before had left everyone quiet and gloomy in the family. Their sadness did not last long in the aftermath of the pandemonium caused by the attack on the gali. But Tara, the focus of the family row, could not forget her woes like everyone else. The suggestion of her taya lay open before her like the jaws of a trap whose clutch would finish her off. Her only support so far had been her brother; but he too had failed to stand his ground that evening.

Puri had again reminded Tara not to fall behind in preparation for her exams. She lay on a mat next to the wall in her home, trying to concentrate on the book in her hand, but her mind was elsewhere. Girls normally wear ordinary clothes when at home. With her small wardrobe, Tara wore indoors what was not fit to wear outside. She looked even more dishevelled in that distracted state of mind, with a slight ache in her body and head, her hair and clothes tousled. Since no male was present, she had no dupatta around her shoulders. She kept thinking of Somraj being caught cheating in the exam, and of him staring at her on her way to college. Then she heard Asad's words and his face came up before her eyes: 'Would you be able to cross the deep gulf of faith, community and religion?' And her answer: 'Yes, if you hold my hand.' She desperately wanted to meet Asad and ask him about what she should do in the face of all that had happened.

She heard the sound of footsteps on the stairs. Must be Pushpa or Sita coming to see Ratan's mother, she thought. Then she heard someone call, 'Tara bahin!'

Tara turned her head as she lay on her back, and saw Kanak peeping from behind the landing door.

For a moment Tara was left paralysed at the embarrassment of being seen in such an unkempt condition, by her brother's girlfriend on top of that. Then she sprang up from the mat. 'Come on in,' she said.

Kanak stepped in with a friendly smile.

'Wait a second, I'll get you a stool to sit on.' Tara said, afraid that her guest's clothes might get dirty and wrinkled from sitting on the mat. Kanak's clothes still smelled freshly laundered and ironed.

'No, no. It's all right.' Kanak held Tara's hand, sat down on the mat against the wall, and made her sit next to her. Tara felt guilty at this exposure of her poor living conditions as if the family's financial hardships were her fault. At that moment her mother came in to hang some washing she had done in the kitchen on a clothes line beside the veranda. Her mother was wearing only a petticoat and a blouse. Tara felt even more embarrassed. She said to her mother, 'You've done enough. Time to stop.'

Kanak said namaste to Tara's mother, and said, 'My mother too does all sorts of chores the whole day. Housework demands so much time.' She turned to Tara, 'Today there was some news about an attack in your gali. We all felt anxious when we read the newspaper. Surendra and Zubeida too wanted to come for a visit. I'd come to meet the Chaddha family outside

Shahalami and thought I'd look you up. There were reports of a bomb explosion and of houses being set on fire. Hope no one was hurt.' Kanak also told her of another report of a death and nine injuries in a bomb blast in a gali near the Mochi Gate bazaar.

Tara couldn't but tell her, 'The boys from our gali were the ones behind the bomb attack at Mochi Gate. Bhai tries his best to discourage them. What else can he do?' She briefly described the incidents of the other night. She also described their dilemma, 'Bhai is working so hard for peace and communal harmony, but we had to defend ourselves. Three men from the gali are in police custody. Bhai and several others have been trying since this morning to get them out on bail.'

'He...' Kanak began.

Tara looked at her.

Kanak gathered her wits and changed the subject, 'Yeah, how are your preparations for the exam?'

'What preparation!' Tara said unhappily, biting her fingernail, 'The exam has been postponed once. Who knows if it will be held at all? If it is, I don't know if I'll be able to show up for it.'

'Hai, how can you say that? Everyone tells me that you're one of the best students.' She asked, 'You'll join the MA programme, yes?'

Tara's face fell, 'That's not my kismet.'

'How so?' Kanak said. 'When students like me who pass in the third division can do an MA.'

Tara hung her head as if to hide her humiliation, and replied, 'No such luck for me. My parents won't agree...'

'But your brother will definitely support your studying.' Kanak said with assurance. She wanted to hear about Tara's brother.

'How can he?' Tara took a deep breath. 'He has his own troubles. He lost his job; I'm sure you know about that. We were hard up even with his salary. Bhai had got some translation work from a publisher, but he had to choose between doing the translation and spending time helping in the peace efforts. He still manages to work whenever he can. He had done translation worth one hundred and fifty rupees for the manuscript he got from Adayara Munavvar. He was paid only half the amount, and this only after repeated visits to the publisher.'

Tara wanted to praise her brother in front of Kanak. She said, 'Bhai has been very upset ever since he lost his job. The editor of *Pairokaar* held back his last month's salary. Bhai isn't one to beg. That's his way; he may suffer in silence, but he won't take insults from anyone. You know, all kinds of things happen in a home. In his present state of mind, he feels very hurt when someone from the family criticizes him. You know how intelligent he is, but when there's no opening for him what can he do?'

Kanak felt proud about Puri leaving his job for the sake of his principles and honour. She had paid him tributes in her heart for his uprightness too, but she had never thought about the monetary aspect of the job; as if Puri was working only to satisfy his creative urges and his bent for writing. Tara's words brought home the enormity of his situation, along with a feeling of guilt for not thinking about it before and for not helping him.

Tara suddenly remembered, 'Do you want some lassi? Or would you rather have tea?'

'No, no. Nothing.' She put her hand on Tara's shoulder to stop her from getting up. 'I had a late breakfast. But I could have a glass of water.'

Tara called Usha to ask, 'Where's Hari? Can you get some ice?'

Usha too was not in her going-out clothes. Tara told her, 'Ask Vijay, or call Peeto from across the gali.'

Kanak protested, 'Don't bother about the ice. My throat is a bit raw. Plain water would be just fine.'

Usha went to the kitchen to ask her mother for a paisa for some ice. Bhagwanti first asked about the need for ice, then said, 'There are some coins wrapped in a handkerchief on the top shelf of the cupboard. Take one paisa.'

Kanak heard all this and the evidence of their adversity sent a shiver down her back.

Kanak took up the thread of the conversation, 'Pitaji frequently remembers him ... Puriji.'

Tara's ears picked up the first inadvertent reference to her brother and she liked it. Kanak went on, 'Pitaji is full of praise for Puriji's writing. He asked about him several times, and said that he hadn't visited us for some weeks.'

Tara said, 'Bahin, my brother has no time. That Urdu publisher too wanted him to do something soon, but he...'

'Wah!' Kanak cut her short to complain, 'He went to Surendra's. Zubeida and Surendra both told me. Neither of you has time to come to my place. Very well! I know I'm not an important person or a leader, but my house is right on the road to Surendra's. So when will you both come to see me?'

'Hai, don't say that.' Tara felt Kanak's desperation. She said, 'Bhai is not as fond of anybody else as he is of your family. It's just that he's got too much on his hands with the peace committees. You know the unrest in the city. I don't go out at all. Bhai definitely has to go in your direction tomorrow. Ibrahim from the Railway union sent a message for him earlier today. They want bhai to be at the party office tomorrow at three o'clock.'

Kanak looked at her wristwatch and got up, 'I'll go now, the tongawallah must be wondering what's happened to me. Bahin, you must sit for the exams. Give namaste to Puriji from me, and my father's message that we haven't seen him for some time.'

Pandit Girdharilal gave Kanak twenty rupees and Kanchan fifteen every month as pocket money. Kanchan thought it unfair, but her father would affectionately wave aside her complaint, 'But beta, you're three years younger than Kanak.' Kanchan often borrowed small amounts from Kanak, and her father had to make up for that too. Panditji never said no to his daughters if they wanted to buy clothes. Kanchan still liked to save up her money and buy something special for herself.

The sisters had got their pocket money for April ten days before. Kanak had few places to go to now, with the growing unrest in the city, and had seventeen rupees in her purse. Her sister Kanta had come the evening before and had left Kanak fifteen rupees to buy fine lace borders for Kanta's white voile saris. Thirty-two rupees still did not amount to much. Kanak pondered over the problem until the following afternoon, and, with some trepidation, went to see her father. His assistant Vidhichand was also in the office. She quietly asked her father to come to the living room.

When Panditji came in, Kanak told him with a grim expression of regret, 'Zubeida gave me seventy rupees for safekeeping. They had received the amount as donations for the peace committee. I seem to have lost the money when I went out.'

'Oh! How did that happen, beta! You shouldn't have accepted it for safekeeping, and if you did, you should have been more careful. You must realize your responsibility. When did it happen?'

'The other day when I went out with her.'

Panditji searched his memory for the day, and said, 'That was a while ago, why didn't you tell me before? How do you know you lost it outside? Are you sure?'

'I wasn't carrying my purse that day.' Kanak said, and pointed to the neckline of her blouse, 'Just kept it here. Never lost anything before.'

'That's bad, it's really bad.' Panditji said regretfully. 'When Zubeida comes next time, ask me for the money to give to her. And take care in future. You should learn to look after money.'

Kanak said looking at her hands, 'I bumped into Zubeida yesterday on my way to Shanti Bhasin's place. I promised to give her the money today. She also wants to talk to me.'

'Achcha, I'll give it to you now.' Panditji returned to his office, withdrew a key from his desk drawer, and asked Vidhichand to take out seventy rupees from a safe. He handed the money to Kanak repeating his lecture about handling money carefully. He said, 'Let me know after you've paid Zubeida back. All right, beta!'

Tara had told Kanak that Puri had been called to the party office on Tuesday at 3 o'clock. It was difficult to guess how long he would stay there. Kanak left home at 2.30 in the intense April sun on the pretext of meeting Zubeida. The bazaars were deserted in the heat of the afternoon sun. The owners dozed off behind the partly closed doors of their shops. Driven by the burning rays of the sun, the shadows too had sought refuge under the shop awnings and in foot-wide strips at the base of walls. The cries of street vendors hawking sugar cane pieces, watermelon slices and iced sherbet drinks had been quieted by the scorching glare. The tarred surface of the roads had softened. Kanak walked along leaving the imprints of her sandals on that softened surface, hoping to catch Puri on his way to the party office.

The office of the Communist Party was near the intersection of McLeod Road and Nisbet Road. Anyone coming towards the office from the direction of Shahalami would come along Nisbet Road. Kanak had set her mind on meeting Puri. She wanted to pour out her heart to him.

She walked through Gwal Mandi to the square in front of the Medical College. It was twenty-five to three; she was in two minds about what to do next. She decided to hire a tonga and go along Nisbet Road to McLeod Road. If she did not see Puri on the way, she would then go towards Shahalami. Kanak was about to hail a tonga when she saw him coming towards the square.

Puri seemed lost in thought. Kanak called out when he came closer, 'Namaste. Where're you going? Trying not to see me?'

Puri was startled by her call, 'Oh, it's you! Namaste! Why wouldn't I want to see you? I was going to the party office.'

Puri knew about Kanak visiting his home. He had asked Tara minutely about where Kanak had sat, what she had seen and what she had talked about. He felt naked and exposed now that the truth of his situation had been disclosed.

He said again, 'I've to be at a meeting soon.'

'Come with me first.' Kanak insisted.

'Where?'

'I want to talk to you.'

'Very well. Let's walk together and talk.' Puri agreed.

'No, let's not walk. Look at the sun! Let's take a tonga.'

'The sun is hot…' Puri began awkwardly. He felt in the pockets of his wrinkled trousers, 'I just walked out. Seem to have forgotten my wallet at home.'

'How can you say that?' Kanak asked with a loving reproach. 'What's this!' She showed him the purse in her hand.

'All right.' He acknowledged timidly. 'But I have to be at the meeting. It was me who had asked for the meeting to be called.'

'Whatever. But come with me for a bit. I've been waiting here for you.'

Puri could not say no. 'Where do you want to go?'

'Anywhere you want. How about the Standard?'

Puri again averted his eyes in embarrassment, 'I told you, I don't have…'

'What's the matter with you? This purse is yours.' Kanak said tenderly.

Puri was defeated. He called a tonga and they both climbed into it. The tonga went towards Mall Road.

Puri said to the tonga driver, 'Go towards McLeod Road.' He looked at Kanak, 'We'll go to the Venus on McLeod Road. It's nearer to the party office.'

Kanak nodded her head. 'What's happened to you?' She again asked.

'What do you mean?'

'Why are you so formal with me? Wait till we reach the restaurant, then I'll explain.' She grabbed the arm support on her side of the tonga to control herself. Puri, holding on to the post on his side, was thinking about a plausible justification of his behaviour.

They sat in a booth at the Venus restaurant. Kanak said, as they sat down, 'Order some tea.' Puri told the waiter to bring tea.

'What's happening to you?' She repeated her question.

'Why?'

'Did you think I was dead? Is this what you meant when you held my hand and promised never to break your promise to me? Why have you been avoiding me for a whole month and half?' Her tears fell on the tabletop.

Puri did not know what to do. The waiter could come back at any moment. He said nervously, 'Kanni, take a grip on yourself. Think of the waiter.'

Kanak took out a handkerchief and dabbed her eyes.

'Kanni, consider the situation from my position, my point of view.' He tried to reason with her.

'Consider what? Why didn't you tell me? You didn't think I was worth anything, worthy of your trust!'

'Please, first wipe your eyes.' Puri said. Kanak had left nothing for him to say.

There was the sound of the waiter approaching and the tinkle of cups on the tea tray. Kanak opened her purse and began searching for something to hide her tears.

The waiter placed the tea and a pastry stand on the table and went out.

Tears were still rolling down Kanak's cheeks. Puri choked back his own, and said, 'You thought I was ignoring you? You don't know about my suffering, about the agony of being away from you. Think of my position. The ladder I had begun to build to reach you has been knocked down. In the eyes of the world, I'm just another person without a job, now an object of derision because I'm striving to scrape together a living.'

Kanak interrupted him, 'Why do you say that? Who doesn't know the truth? You left your job for the sake of truth and justice. Everyone respects you for that.'

Puri said stirring his tea, 'Whether I left my job or I was made to leave doesn't matter. If some woman drowns herself in a well to escape being raped, will that be considered as an escape? The result of being unemployed is just the same, irrespective of my principles. It is also true that, maybe, I can earn more now, but by remaining anonymous. Is that any less painful?'

'To make sacrifices for your ideals is no light matter.'

'What ideals? I'd been working all this time for my ideal of communal harmony, and last week I had to fight off a mob to defend myself, and defend the people of my gali. My hair stands on end when I think of it. I also know that my own gali people were at fault.'

'But you weren't thinking of yourself when you gave up your job.'

'That's my weakness, my disadvantage. You have to be self-seeking to earn respect from people and keep a position in society.'

'What are you saying? Everyone is all the more respectful of you because of your self-sacrifice. I consider it an honour to be the dust under your feet.'

'You're just saying that out of the goodness of your heart. I want to be worthy of such praise.'

'Don't make fun of me. I'm begging at your feet. You gave me a place in your heart, and you can't throw me out now. You may kill me, but you won't be able to get rid of me.'

'I didn't feel worthy of you. That's why I was staying away from you. I'm just trying again to be deserving of your affection. I don't want you to get hurt because of your feelings for me.'

'What nonsense is that!' Kanak was upset. 'Would you have left me if we were married and you had lost your job?'

Puri felt good on hearing that, but continued, 'First, I want to be worthy of marrying you.'

'Don't say any such thing.' She said with hurt in her voice, and looked into his eyes, 'You still haven't made up your mind about me? What do you mean?' Her tears began to flow again.

'Wipe away your tears.' Puri said softly.

'I won't. I won't. What do you care?' She bit her lips. Tears continued to roll down her cheeks.

Puri had to get up and go to her. He held her head in his hands and wiped off her tears with his shirtsleeve. Kanak did not stop him. His blood was racing. He bent and kissed her eyes. She shivered slightly, and put her head on his shoulder. He could not help but kiss her lips.

She put her arm around his waist and said with a pout, 'Why did you tell me all that rubbish? If you do it again, I'll cry myself to death. You took my hand in yours; that's *panigrahan*, the sacred marriage rite. Whether I was worthy of you or not, you should have thought before performing panigrahan. Now you can't go back on it.' A smile came to her tear-stained face, like the rays of the rising sun on a cluster of dew-laden flowers.

'I did make a vow by holding your hand, but have you spoken to your father?' Puri asked.

'What's there to tell him? Had you mentioned something to him, I would have responded. Pitaji didn't ask me any questions. I want my intentions to be known. Pitaji probably wants me to finish the MA course first.'

'You'd better go through with your MA. I won't be able to think of marriage for a while.'

'The same talk again!' Kanak scolded him lovingly. 'It'd be better if my family knew about it. I can't go on like this, acting like a criminal.'

'Why, what's the problem?'

'Trying to hide it from everyone. My family will suspect something; why wouldn't they?'

'Why? What have they said?'

'They said that it wasn't just regard for my guru that I felt for you, but something more serious.' She looked into his eyes and smiled.

'Who said that? Your brother-in-law?'

'He did, and others will too, eventually. Why wouldn't they!'

'What did you tell them?'

'I was about to say, yes, there's something more, but I hadn't consulted you, so I had to shut up. I just said, don't talk nonsense. But this can't go on. I can't just go on pretending. That day I couldn't even ask you, why you were leaving so soon, and when would I see you again? There should be something firm, as there was with my elder sister. I wouldn't mind waiting, if it was like that.'

Puri gave it some thought before saying, 'Not just at the moment. Wait a while. I'll get things under control soon.'

'But will we meet? Will you come to my place? Why don't you speak with Pitaji? You gave him the manuscript of your collection of short stories.'

'What should I talk to him about? Tell him that I'm an unworthy suitor of his daughter, not even able to support himself?'

'What d'you mean by unworthy?' Kanak protested. She suggested, 'Come for a visit as before, as you used to. You must.'

'I don't feel like it in my present situation.'

'Do you want me to work for the peace committees? That'd give us a chance to meet once or twice a week.'

'You can, if you want to, but I'm not too hopeful about their efforts. Will people listen to the leaders of the Congress, the League and others, or to us? I've been thinking of going to Delhi, if nothing works out here.'

'You'll go to Delhi? That far? Will you write to me?'

'What could I write in a letter?'

'That you're well, a couple of sentences to comfort me. I've been waiting for your letter these past days too. Write to me if you can't come.'

'Achcha.' Puri looked at the wall-clock over the booth, then at his wrist watch, 'It's nearly four o'clock. They must be cursing me. I'd asked them to call the meeting.' He pressed the bell to summon the waiter.

'To me, this meeting is like a *saut*, your other wife.' Kanak complained smilingly. She said, 'Honoured Sir, I don't mind you having another wife. Just leave me a place at your feet.' She took out several ten and five-rupee notes from her purse and offered the cash to Puri.

'What's all this for? Give me just two rupees.' Puri said, 'The bill won't come to more than one or one-and-a-quarter rupees.'

'Keep it. You might need it.'

Puri's face took on a grim expression. The waiter had arrived with the bill on a tray. Puri placed a note on the tray, and said, 'Bring the change.' He said to Kanak after the waiter had left, 'No, I don't need it.'

'What's wrong?' She asked earnestly, 'Keep it. For my sake.'

Puri said in a serious voice, 'It's true that you know about my difficulty. I'm in need too, but I'll feel worse if I take this. It'll amount to my admitting my defeat. In fact, I'm not so hard up now. It's the shame of being unemployed that's most hurtful.'

'I didn't need the cash.'

'You're throwing away what you don't need. You want me to pick it up because I'm broke?'

Kanak said, with hurt and disappointment, 'Why do you say such things?'

'Don't insult my self-respect.' Puri said in English.

The waiter returned. Puri left four annas for him as a tip, and pushed the rest of the money towards Kanak.

She felt wounded as she put the money back in her purse.

They came out of the restaurant. Puri hailed a tonga for Kanak to return to her home, and walked towards the party office.

As the tonga went towards Gwal Mandi, Kanak was happy to have been close to Puri after such a long time, but she also felt troubled by another thought, 'Why did he refuse to accept help from me? If I can belong to him, then why can't what I have belong to him? Just because I'm a woman? Don't I have the right to help him and share his troubles? He'll have to accept my help. If he doesn't, I'll split my head open on the floor in protest in front of him. Won't we both earn money together after our marriage? Will he then see any difference between what's his and what's mine?'

When she reached home, Muttu Baba was teaching sitar to Kanchan. He came twice a week. When Kanchan had her lessons, Panditji would have the door connecting the living room with his office closed to shut out the sound. Kanak climbed the steps straight to her room, lay down on the bed without changing her clothes, and using her right arm to pillow her head, closed her eyes and placed her left arm over her forehead. Her thoughts kept on returning to Puri's refusal to accept her help. The sitar playing downstairs had reached a crescendo, drowning out all other sounds. Her surging thoughts so much merged with the music that she was oblivious when the playing ended.

'Kanni!' Kanchan called her, sitting on the bed. She was three years younger than Kanak, but had called her 'Kanni' since her childhood.

'Yes?' Kanak replied, jolted out of her reverie.

'Did you borrow any money from Zubeida?' Kanchan asked.

Kanak thought for a moment before replying, 'Why, what happened?'

'When you were out in the afternoon, Zubeida and Surendra came looking for you. When I said you'd gone out, they asked if you had gone to the meeting at the Communist Party office. They had come to take you along. As they were going back, Pitaji sent Vidhichand after them. Pitaji told them that you had gone to Zubeida's house, and asked if Zubeida hadn't seen you heading that way.

'Zubeida said that she was at Surendra's house.

'Pitaji told Zubeida that you'd gone to return the money that you'd borrowed from her. Maybe you missed Zubeida on the way. So he wanted to return Zubeida seventy rupees because she might need the money?

'Zubeida was surprised. She told him that you didn't owe her anything. Pitaji wanted to give her back the money, but she refused to accept it.'

Kanak took a deep breath and said nothing. She was thinking: Why did Zubeida have to show up here today of all days? What would she do now? Pandit forgave everything but a lie. What would she tell him?

'Did you ask her not to tell Pitaji?' Kanchan asked.

When Kanak gave no answer, Kanchan got up and went out. Half an hour later Jaggi the boy servant came to tell her, 'Tea is served. Pitaji is waiting for you.'

Kanak knew that the hour of judgement had struck. To ward off the moment, she picked up a book from the bedside table and said, 'Tell Kanchi to make tea for Pitaji. I'm busy reading.'

She knew that she would have to face her father again at 8 o'clock at the dinner table. She went down at 7.45 and said to her mother, 'Mom, I didn't have any tea. I'm hungry. Give me my dinner.'

She had a sinking feeling at the thought of having to explain her lie to her father. She was trying to postpone the moment of truth, but knew that that time would come sooner or later. Panditji sent for her again at nine. She had to go. Panditji was waiting in the stuffy, hot office so as to be able to speak to her in private. He asked her to sit on the chair to his right, and said, 'Kanchi must have told you that Zubeida came here. I wanted to pay her back, but she refused.'

Kanak had brought the money with her. She put it before him and sat looking down.

'It's not about the money, beta, you keep it. I just wanted to know why you needed it?'

Kanak said nothing.

Panditji said without reproach or anger, 'Beta, if you needed money, you should have simply said so. You've never done such a thing before.'

Kanak sat on in silence.

Panditji said again in the same calm tone, 'Beta, you know that you could have said: "I need some money, but I can't say why." I wouldn't have minded that, but I did mind being lied to. All I have is yours. You had to hide something from me. That's really sad.'

Kanak hid her face in her aanchal, but the shaking of her shoulders showed that she was sobbing.

Panditji said with a note of sadness in his voice, 'Beta, you're obviously not yourself at this moment. Go and rest. Come and talk to me tomorrow, or whenever you feel better. I'm not angry, beta; I'm only sad.'

Kanak went to her room and threw herself on the bed, weeping uncontrollably. She had not imagined she would be found out by her father so soon.

It took her an hour to compose herself. She went downstairs again. Panditji slept alone in a room next to his office. He was reading by the light of a bedside lamp, and a table fan hummed in a corner. He did not hear Kanak come in. She moved a chair to show that she was there.

He looked at her and said, 'Come, beta.' and moved aside to let her sit on the bed.

Kanak's spoke in a voice heavy with tears. She kept her eyes on her fingers, fiddling with the border of her sari, 'I met Puriji's sister Tara. She's going to sit for her BA finals. Their family's finances are in a really bad shape. He has lost his job at *Pairokaar*.'

'Yes, I heard about that too,' he said. 'Kashish is a mean fellow. Dr Radhey Behari is no better; very unscrupulous. Oh, I see, Puri's sister needed the money. You should've given it to her. I'd have been happy.'

'They wouldn't accept the money,' Kanak said looking at the border of her sari.

'Who ... his sister?' Panditji asked after a moment's pause.

'No, Puriji.'

'You wanted to give it to Jaidev?'

Kanak nodded her head silently.

Panditji thought quietly holding his chin, then spoke in a tone of concern, 'You didn't say anything to me about helping Jaidev. He's a decent intelligent fellow. He's tutored you all this time. We're obliged to him; in a way we're indebted to him for his help. He never said a word to me.'

Kanak felt a little bolder. She said, 'It's a question of self-respect for him. He'd never ask anybody for help.'

Panditji sat thinking.

Kanak said after a moment's silence, still looking at the fringe of her sari, 'Pitaji, ask him to come and talk to you.'

Panditji replied with a thoughtful 'um'. He said, 'Achcha, beta, now go to bed.'

Kanak climbed the stairs back to her room with more confident steps. She had handled the situation cleverly, she thought. She fell asleep as soon as she lay down. The day's events had exhausted her mind and body.

Panditji had easily seen through the web of lies his daughter had so cleverly woven in her youthful naïvety. Why did she have to do all this behind my back? he wondered. Kanak had not called Puri bhaiji as she had done in the past. Panditji had always had to be a little more careful with his 'extra smart' daughter. She had shown a lot of promise, but was also emotionally fragile. Three years ago she had been willing to give up everything for a lecturer at the Christian College. He was married, and Kanak found out in time that he was leading her on.

Puri was satisfied with the result of the meeting held on Tuesday at the office of the Communist Party. On the very next day, the Railway Workers Union and the Student Federation jointly launched the Militant Peace Movement, led by Comrade Ibrahim to restore civic peace. Their processions were far bigger than those organized by the Muslim League and the Anti-Pakistan League. The dust raised by these processions hovered like a cloud over the column. Their slogans were: 'Congress–League–Akalis unite! Hindus–Sikhs–Muslims are brothers! Death to sectarianism! Down with imperialism!' These slogans were shouted with such force that those who heard them were both warned to keep the peace, and cautioned against breaking it. The Union formed peace patrols with the help of residents of various districts in the city, and it seemed for a while that civic peace might return once more.

Puri had thrown himself heart and soul into the compilation of the history textbook for Ghaus Mohammad. He slept on the roof at night because of the hot weather. He would begin work in the morning as soon as there was enough light to read. Summarizing the information from the three books recommended by Professor Shah and rewriting this in Urdu was not an easy task. In his first session, from six to eleven in the morning, he read the original in English, and then rewrote it in Urdu. At the most, he was able to write only five or six pages of his manuscript in one sitting.

Tara could help him in this work as history was one of her subjects in the BA, but she did not know any Urdu. The movement for civic peace that Puri had helped to start was growing, but he could not give as much time to the movement as before. Some days he would try to write three or four pages more in the afternoon. His heart's desire was to get those 550 rupees from Adayara Munavvar, and thus, prove his right to be heard by his father and his uncle.

If he continues to get work like this, he thought, why bother to find another job? 'The publisher will make a profit of 20,000 rupees, he will also spend 10,000 rupees to buy someone's name as the author of the book, but he will pay me only 500. However, cash is cash.' He would let them exploit him for the moment, if that resulted in his survival. If he could put an end to his exploitation by making compromises sooner or later, he was ready for that too.

The city was mostly quiet. Puri was giving all his time and attention to his work, but Tara's desperation and anguish knew no bounds. Masterji and Bhagwanti often talked about the selling of their part of the house in Naroval village to Babu Ramjwaya, in order to meet the expenses of the wedding. They talked about buying clothes and jewellery for Tara. Bhagwanti went to her sister-in-law's to consult her, and Sheelo's mother herself came to see how things were going.

To begin the preparations for the wedding, Bhagwanti bought silk materials and lace borders for two sets of bridal shalwar-kameez. Meladei, Pushpa, Rampyari and Jeeva sat with Tara's mother to decide on the style and fashion of the clothes. They talked among themselves so that Tara could hear, 'Who can cut and sew better than Tara? What could be better than her designing the clothes according to her own taste? Nowadays, many girls help make their own trousseau. There's no shame in that.'

To Tara, the bridal dress being prepared for her had all the appearance of a shroud for a corpse. When everything was made ready, they would swathe her body in that shroud and hand it over to that goonda—her bridegroom. Her brother just stood by in silence. With teeth clenched, she said to herself: 'No, I'll never let that happen. I'll run away from home. As it is, they're pushing me out. Asad had asked: Would I be able to cross this gulf between our faiths, communities and families? I did say to him that I would, if only he held my hand. I'll tell him that the time has come to give me that support. We'll go somewhere together, anywhere.'

In his anxiety to finish the textbook as soon as possible, Puri seldom went out. Tara was on tenterhooks all week, waiting for her brother to go to a demonstration or to some meeting. She wanted to go along too, to try to find Asad to talk to him and decide what she should do.

It was past eleven in the morning. Puri sat and worked on his history book in the shade of the barsati on the roof. Usha came up to tell him that Vidhichand from Naya Hind Publications had come for him. On his way downstairs, Puri put on a shirt which he took from the rope slung across one side of the room that held their clothes, and with the fountain pen in his hand to show that he was working, went down to the gali.

Vidhichand said that Panditji Girdharilal has sent a message that he would like to speak to Puri about the collection of his short stories. Vidhichand had met Puri before, he added by way of emphasis, 'Panditji had asked me to call you the day before yesterday, but I couldn't come till now. Come over to his office today, if you can.'

'Bhai, I'm really busy, can't say about today.' Puri said, scratching his head with his pen. 'That manuscript for Adayara Munavvar is due soon. If I'm in your neighbourhood in the evening, I might stop by.'

When he went back upstairs, Puri said to Usha, 'Ushi, launder a shirt and trousers for me.' He told Tara, 'When they're dry, just iron them at the neighbour's or at Pushpa's.'

'Ushi, do it now,' Tara said quickly. 'I'll iron them nicely. Bhai, I'll come with you. Kanak had come here to see me and I should return the visit. I haven't seen Surendra for such a long time. She must be annoyed with me!' There was a chance of meeting Asad at Surendra's. 'Everyone but me seems to be going around. I've been stuck here for the past month. The farthest I go is across the gali. I need to stretch my legs too.'

'All right.' Puri agreed, and then realized that it might not be such a good idea to let Tara visit Kanak. Her contact with Kanak's family would just reveal more of his own desperate circumstances. And what if Tara talked about being married against her will? What impression would that leave? He said after some thought, 'I won't stay for more than five minutes at Panditji's. I also want to go to the party office. I've to go out again tomorrow or the day after. You can go to Surendra's then.'

Tara felt excited at the mention of the party office. She said, 'Bhaiji, that's even better. I'll go the party office with you. Zubeida is sure to be there.'

'No, what would you do in that crowd?' Puri ended the discussion.

Tara felt as if a rock had fallen on her heart. But she could not object; she was only a female. She sighed with despair and thought, let's wait till tomorrow. I'll ask Surendra to take me to the party office.

Puri had been called by Pandit Girdharilal, so he went in through the office door. Panditji welcomed him heartily. He asked after him and complained that he showed up like the Id moon—only once in a long time. He said, 'Kashish and Dr Radhey Behari are both self-serving opportunists. No wonder a decent, upright young man like yourself couldn't get along with them.' He took off his glasses, put them down carefully, and said rubbing his chin, 'Yes, now, about your story collection—bhai Vidhichand,' he looked at his assistant, 'get me the manuscript of Puriji's short stories.'

He again looked at Puri, 'These are fine stories, of very high calibre. The test of the skill of a writer, in fact, is in the short story. The shorter the better, but, barkhurdar, there's no market for short stories. The product might be very good, but what use is it when it won't sell.'

'Of course,' Puri acknowledged solemnly.

'The market for short stories,' Panditji said, still stroking his chin, 'has been spoiled by the magazines. I mean, they can give the reader ten or twelve short stories at a price of five or six annas. Their profits and costs are covered by the advertisements. If we publish those stories, we'll have to price them at one or one-and-a-half rupees. Who'll buy from us? It's bad, very bad.

'The professional writer suffers. The amateurs are happy to get their work published free in the magazines. A magazine editor can employ one or two persons to translate from English. A few good stories from literary writers like yourself at twenty or twenty-five rupees each, and he has a story collection for only two hundred to two hundred fifty rupees a month. It's a great injustice to writers. I've been down that road. It's very sad.'

Did he call me to give this lecture? Puri thought. He had sensed that Kanak was in the living room. He waited for Panditji to finish so he could speak with her.

Puri agreed with Panditji, hoping to end the talk, 'You're absolutely right.'

Kanak could not hold back. She stood in the connecting door, said 'namaste' to Puri, and called, 'Come to the living room before you leave.'

'Who's that? Kanni!' asked Panditji. Running his hand over his close-cropped hair, he said, 'The market is for textbooks at present. People have no taste for literature any more. Who can blame them? Where can anybody find money for books when they have difficulty just meeting their daily needs? A novel, however, has more sales potential. Mister Puri, suggest the name of a good novel. Not necessarily from English literature, that context is too foreign. Our readers can't absorb it easily. Either from Hindi, or even better a Hindi translation of a Bengali novel, but some quality work. Let me think, what was the name? Kanchi had sent for it on your advice. She read aloud some passages to me too. That was very good.'

'*A House Built upon Sand*,' Puri reminded him.

'Yes, of course, *A House Built upon Sand*,' Panditji said with a smile. 'The title is full of meaning, isn't it? Kanchi read out parts of it to me. But, tell me, is the rest of it as interesting?'

'Very engrossing,' Puri assured him. 'And purposeful. Schocken is considered to be one of Austria's finest writers. The translation into Hindi has also been very successful.'

'Oh, is that so? It's a translation. Bhai Vidhichand, ask Kanchi to get us that novel,' he asked Puri again, '*A House Built upon Sand*, right? Yes, ask her for that novel. Barkhurdar, will you be able to find the time to translate it?'

'I'm working on something for Adayara Munavvar at present,' Puri replied, 'A textbook.'

'That's good, that's fine,' Panditji said. 'On what subject?'

'History,' Puri said. 'It's time-consuming work. Professor Shah of the university is a member of the textbook committee and he's the one behind it. His name will appear as the author.'

'That's bad,' Panditji commiserated. 'He'll ask the publisher for at least five or six thousand rupees; you won't get more than four or five hundred. That's the practice, they all do the same thing.'

'Yes,' Puri had to accept the embarrassing fact. 'I had no option.'

'Such work is indeed time-consuming. Not less than three or four months' labour, if it's done properly. That's cruel! But what alternative does the publisher have? Otherwise it won't become a prescribed textbook. I'll keep in mind that you can do such work. That's good.' He turned towards Vidhichand, 'Yes, how many pages in the book?' He handed the book to Vidhichand.

'Three hundred sixty-eight,' Vidhichand said after checking.

'Three hundred and sixty-eight,' Panditji repeated the figure in English. He thought for a while, then asked, 'Well, Mr Puri, tell me, what's the current rate of good translation work from Hindi into Urdu?'

He had charged Adayara Munavvar, Puri recalled, eight annas per page for translating the English novel into Urdu. He pretended to try to remember the correct figure, then to do justice to the dignity of writers and translators, said, 'One rupee per page, I'd say. It can be done for less, but you asked about the rate for really good translation. A well-known translator might ask for even more.'

'How about twelve annas a page?'

'Twelve annas is decent too. Quite appropriate, actually. Depends on the person doing the work.'

'No, no, barkhurdar, it's you who has to do it. Why should I have to ask anyone else? That's why I chose something recommended by you, so that you might have some interest in the work.'

'I'll obey your order to do the work, but there's no question of payment to me.'

'No, no. That's not proper. No work without payment. There should be a suitable reward for your time and effort. Bhai Vidhichand, how much would three hundred and sixty-eight pages come to, at twelve annas per page?'

Vidhichand said after calculating with pencil on paper, 'Two hundred seventy-six rupees, sir.'

Puri had time to think. He said, 'Panditji, I think I'll finish this work first. I'll be able to devote all my time to the history book afterwards.'

'Barkhurdar, whichever way you prefer,' Panditji said. He took the book from Vidhichand and placed it before Puri, 'I could give you a cheque, but that would mean the hassle of cashing it. Vidhichand bhai, give Puriji one hundred rupees, and get him to sign a receipt for an advance.'

Panditji's smile almost caused his eyes to disappear in the folds of his cheeks. Through half-shut eyes he looked at Puri, 'I hope you don't mind. It's only for accounts. The income tax people want every little detail. What can I tell you?'

Puri was at a loss for words, with the emotions surging in his heart. He managed to get out, 'Panditji, what's the hurry with payment? Leave it for now. We can settle up later.'

'Arrey, barkhurdar,' Panditji said in a laughing voice, 'I do know you don't care for money. You're a real jewel. But, business is business.'

Puri signed the slip of paper shyly without looking at it, took ten notes of ten rupees each from the hand of Panditji, and stuffed the money in his trouser pocket without counting it.

'Do count the money,' Panditji said.

'It's all right,' Puri said smiling. 'It's just my reward for following your order.'

'Oh, you're a fine fellow. You're a gem,' Panditji said.

Puri found the words to say, 'I'll just say hello to Kanakji.'

'Yes, sure, why not? The sisters must be waiting for you. You came here after such a long absence.' Panditji waved in the direction of the living room.

Puri stepped into the living room and saw that Kanak's eyes and face lit up with joy. His face too brightened at the sight of her. She was sitting at the corner of a sofa. Puri took the chair next to it.

She pretended to sulk, 'I don't want to talk to you. You didn't come because of me, but because Pitaji sent for you. It would be all the same for you if I died.'

Kanchan came in, 'Oho, Puri bhaiji's come after such a long time.'

Kanak asked her to bring tea.

Puri's spirits were high because of the money in his pocket. But he wondered if Panditji had shown kindness to him at the urging of Kanak, or if he had paid Puri off for the obligation of tutoring Kanak all those months without accepting money. He asked Kanak, 'Did you say anything to your father about translation work?'

'We didn't talk about it,' Kanak said sincerely.

Puri was satisfied that the work had been given to him not as an act of kindness, but in recognition of his talent.

'What were you talking about for so long? I've been waiting here forever.' Kanak complained.

Panditji came in before Puri could answer, 'Is someone getting tea for Puri?'

Kanak said, 'Kanchi has gone for it.'

Panditji sat next to Kanak on the sofa and talked about the situation in Lahore and Punjab. The city had been quiet for over a week, but he was not hopeful for peace. The probability of a Congress–League–Akali coalition in Punjab had evaporated with one word from Jinnah Saheb. His decision was that the Congress must give half the positions in the national government to the Muslim League, and share the other half with the rest of the non-Muslim parties. Otherwise, the Muslim League might form a coalition with the Akalis, but not with the Congress in Punjab.

Panditji's view was, 'The League would make absurd demands. Attlee has encouraged them by declaring that Britain will only accept a plan that has the support of the League. If you believe in democracy, the question doesn't arise as to what the League or the Congress wants. Go along with whoever is in the majority…'

Puri agreed with Panditji's views. In his presence, Puri and Kanak had no chance to talk about themselves. Puri could not sit forever. He got ready to leave.

Kanak said, 'Wait a minute.' She turned to her father and said, 'Pitaji, I'll go up to Shahalami with Puriji. I have some things to discuss with Sarla Sharma.'

'Achcha, beta,' Panditji had to agree. 'Be back soon.'

Kanak changed her clothes quickly and went out with Puri. As they both reached the bazaar, she asked, 'What did you two talk about? Tell me.'

'Nothing special. Just about some translation work.'

'Oh, as if I couldn't hear,' Kanak flashed her eyes at him.

'What did you hear?'

'You're a fine fellow. You're a jewel,' She glanced at him sideways.

'He said it just like that,' Puri said modestly.

'Why just like that! I'm sure he meant it. He praises you behind your back too.'

'Praises me for what? In what connection?' Puri was curious.

But Kanak would not tell him. They had reached the bazaar of Gwal Mandi. She said, 'I'll tell you. Let's go for a walk. We can talk as we walk along.'

The sun was dipping behind the wide expanse of the city, its rays catching only the tops of the tall buildings. The breeze was pleasant. Many people were going for a stroll on Nisbet Road towards Mall Road and Lawrence Garden. Puri and Kanak turned on to Nisbet Road.

Kanak guardedly related the story of her asking Panditji for money to return to Zubeida, and of Zubeida's showing up at her house in her absence. She said, 'I was in a fix. I had to confess to him, but Pitaji had only good words and praise for you.'

Puri's shoulders sagged a little, 'I didn't want a handout. To feel pity is one thing, to feel respect is another. You can't respect the one you pity. I have good chances of getting more translation work. I wanted to solve my problem and be worthy of you in his eyes, without telling him about my problem.'

Kanak said sincerely, 'You don't know my father. For him, a man's measure is his talent, not his money. He has always told us, "Depend on your skills and capabilities, not on your family or riches. Your fortune may melt away if you have no skills. If you have talent, you can build a palace of gold."' She smiled meaningfully, 'He will leave everything to his daughters. He thinks you're clever, calls you a jewel, he seems satisfied that he's found what he was looking for.'

Kanak wanted to make up for her gaffe. She wanted to remove every trace of humiliation from his mind because of her action. They walked and talked for a long time, but still so much remained. From Nisbet Road they went to Mall Road, then through Lawrence Garden to Kashmir Valley.

Kanak did everything to reassure him, so that Puri wouldn't continue to feel slighted.

Puri's hurt pride was gradually soothed. His imagination took off. What Kanak had said was, after all, not implausible. He might some day have to manage the publication and Naya Hind Press of Pandit Girdharilal. His own writings would add to the worth of the business. Why not a magazine or a newsweekly? To be in control of a newspaper would give him so much power. That'd be the time to confront Kashish and Dr Radhey Behari. If Panditji wanted to test and evaluate a person before handing out such responsibility, that was his prerogative.

Their conversation ran on and on, with each confiding more and more in the other. Kanak thought of the time. Puri looked at his watch. It was nearly eight. Kanak was uneasy. It was late. Kanta and her brother-in-law might be visiting, she remembered. Then she saw the passage shaded with grape vines in Kashmir Valley. She led the way to it. Away from the light, she took Puri's hands into hers and asked, 'No more anger, I hope.'

'No. It's not anger. Maybe you understand the whole situation better than I.'

Kanak came closer and stood with their bodies touching, 'Tell me the truth.'

Puri took her in his arms, and in reply kissed the lips she offered.

They walked with brisk steps, holding hands, towards the exit of the garden and the tonga stand. Puri said, 'What might people think seeing us together?'

'The right thing,' was Kanak's answer.

Chapter 10

JAIDEV PURI KNEW THAT THE TRANSLATION OF *A HOUSE BUILT UPON SAND* WOULD be simpler and less demanding than the compilation of the history textbook. In the morning, with a fresh mind, he worked first on the textbook. In the afternoon he read a few pages of the novel. As a writer himself, he realized that to rewrite the well-crafted story in another language and style would be a real challenge. This he found very agreeable. After translating four pages of the novel in two hours, he thought of a new approach. Instead of reading a paragraph from the original and rewriting it in Urdu, it would be easier to write it straight into Urdu if someone read the Hindi version aloud to him. It would just be a matter of changing the script and a few words, since Hindi and Urdu shared the same grammar and syntax.

It was stiflingly hot in the room. Puri was working in one corner of the veranda, and in another Tara lay stretched out on a mat studying for her exam.

'Tara!' Puri called. 'I'm thirsty. Bring me some water.'

Tara brought him a glass of water. She looked troubled and depressed as she now did most of the time. As she went back after handing him the glass, Puri said, 'Studies going well?'

'I'm coping as well as I can,' she answered, wiping her wet hands on the dupatta around her shoulders.

Puri drained the glass. He said, 'I've an idea. You've been reading your textbook for quite some time. If you think you've had enough for a while, why don't you read this novel in Hindi aloud and I'll rewrite it in Urdu? The sooner it's finished, the sooner I'll get paid.'

Tara agreed. She had not read the novel, so she read through the first four pages, which caught her interest. She began to read aloud to Puri. She became so engrossed in it that she began to read faster than Puri could write. Until now, she had not had much time to read novels.

Tara read aloud to Puri till 7 o'clock in the evening, and with her help he was able to translate nine pages in three hours. He felt so encouraged that he could not stop himself from sharing his excitement with Tara. This was their secret, and he wanted it to remain between them. He spoke to her quietly in English, 'It took some of your time, but I've managed to do work worth seven rupees in this short period. I've already accepted one hundred rupees in advance for this work. I spent five hours on the history textbook in the morning, and completed four pages of that too, which is worth another six or seven rupees. I want to be through with this by the first week of July. All in all, about seven or eight hundred rupees. Once I've established my contacts and more work begins to come my way, I'll be able to face up to tayaji. I can't do that now. I know how you feel at being forced to marry a man like Somraj. This is sheer injustice. I can see what's going on, but how can I say anything now?'

Tara stared at the floor as he spoke. She wanted to ask him: What's the good of speaking out and why would anyone listen when it's too late? Why not say it now? She also thought: He knows it's not fair to me. If he can't tell the family, he can help me in some other way. With my brother willing to help, everything is possible. She told herself: He'll solve his own problems in the end, but then Kanak's people are liberal-minded, and not so orthodox in their outlook.

For the next three days Puri worked on the textbook in the morning, and at the translation in the afternoon. On the evening of 30 April, a messenger came from the Communist Party office, with a letter for him from Comrade Manzoor. It was a request for him to speak on communal harmony and goodwill at the May Day rally the next evening.

Tara went to the rally with her brother. Asad too was present. This was their first meeting in a month, but what could she tell him in the midst of so many people and with her brother nearby. There were only five other girls and all of them were asked to sit on the dais behind the chairman of the rally. Surendra had not been able to attend.

Tara's chance came when Puri got up to speak. Asad came up behind where she sat. His eyes held many questions.

'I can't say anything now,' she said to him in a hurried whisper.

'What's up?'

'It's a matter of life and death!'

'How do we meet?' Asad asked.

'I can come to Surendra's.'

'When?'

'Soon. I'll try next week.'

Puri was a good speaker, and always spoke brilliantly on the issue of civic peace. Asad, Manzoor, Narendra Singh and others too congratulated him on his speech.

Tara asked Narendra Singh, 'Bhaiji, couldn't Surendra come?'

'She has fever again,' Singh replied. 'It's malaria. She won't take quinine, so what can anyone do?'

Tara spoke rather loudly so that her brother could hear, 'Tell her that I'll come to see her for sure in the next couple of days. First I couldn't go out because of the unrest, and also I barely get time away from my studies.'

On 5 May, Tara said to her brother as she began to read aloud to him, 'Bhaiji, I've given my word that I'd go and visit Surendra today. Are you going in that direction around 5 o'clock, or should I go by myself?'

Puri said, 'Help me finish twelve pages by five o'clock, and I'll get through a hundred pages of the translation. After that I'll go with you, or you can go on alone.'

They managed to finish by five. Puri said, 'Everything seems normal up towards Gwal Mandi. You go to Surendra's. I'll go and show what I've done on the history book to Ghaus Mohammad. I want to be sure that he's satisfied; he might want to have the manuscript checked by someone else.'

Tara got what she wanted. She said to her mother, so that she would not object, that her brother knew that she was going alone to Surendra's for an hour or so.

Puri left. Tara had begun to put a waist cord in a laundered shalwar, when she heard Usha's excited voice, 'Ma! Tara! Sheelo bahin is here. She's brought her baby too. Hai, he's so cute, rosy just like a doll. Has lovely round, blue eyes.'

Usha called her sister, who was four years her senior, 'Tara' like everyone else. Sheelo was three months younger than Tara, but Usha had begun to call her Sheelo bahin or bahinji out of respect to her married status.

Tara flinched; the shalwar fell from her hands. A sinking feeling washed over her. Sheelo had come to her house for the first time with her son. She could not leave now. She had to jump up and show her delight by holding the baby to her breast and kissing him over and over.

In the month of March, when the rioting was at its peak, a son had been born to Sheelo. Masterji, Bhagwanti and Tara had gone to visit and congratulate her in-laws. It was not safe to take the usual route through the bazaars, and they had to pass through Hindu areas to reach the house of Sheelo's in-laws in Sheesha Moti. Forty days after the baby's birth, Babu Ramjwaya's daughter was allowed to go to her parents' house. Everyone from Tara's family had gone to visit her there too. At that time, as she held the baby, Tara had said to Sheelo, 'Hai, he's really pretty, much more than you.'

Making sure that no one was around, Sheelo had replied. 'Why wouldn't he be? Just think of the seed that produced this fruit. I'll come to your house and show Ratan his son. I'll see how he can ignore me then.'

The gali women began to gather at Bhagwanti's house as the news of Sheelo and her son's visit spread. Sheelo's body had filled out. Everyone noticed the glow on her face and the sparkle in her eyes. Her old clothes had taken on a nice, snug fit, but there was hardly any difference in her waistline. Kartaro said teasingly, 'Your body always blooms after the first birth. Wait till you have more.'

Tara dropped her gaze to show her embarrassment. Bhagwanti swore at Kartaro, 'Aren't you ashamed to talk like that when there are unmarried girls present. Think of your own daughter.'

Kartaro did not shut up. She nodded towards Tara, 'Her time has come too. How long now, three months if not two.'

Bhagwati said angrily, 'Phitemunh! Shut up!' Kartaro laughed even louder.

After the women left, Sheelo said to her aunt with a grim face, 'Chachi, there is something else. When my husband came to see me yesterday from Sheesha Moti, he was very upset. He had run into Somraj somewhere in the bazaar. They both were classmates, you know. Somraj said to him: I heard that your sister-in-law tells everyone that she doesn't like me. Tell me if that's true. If it is, tell her to forget about marrying me. But before that, I'll take her by her braid and teach her a lesson right here in the bazaar. I know how to handle the likes of her, these college students.' Sheelo gave Tara a worried look, 'Did you go to some kind of meeting at Mori Gate? Somraj probably saw you there somewhere.'

Bhagwanti cringed when she heard this, then broke into a litany of curses, 'These gossip-mongers, these bachchepitte, *randichadne*, may they be without sons for seven generations. My daughter never uttered a word. She's so quiet that you'd think she had no tongue in her head.' She said to Sheelo, 'Daughter, you tell your husband to make sure that Somraj knows the truth. There are mean people in this gali, who can't bear to see anyone happy. God save us from such neighbours. May they burn in hell for seven generations! When your husband comes again, call me; or maybe I better go with you to Sheesha Moti to see him.'

Tara sat with bated breath, pretending not to hear. She was not supposed to have a say in this matter. Her mother turned to her and said, 'Stay home from now on. And don't dare take a step out of the gali.'

Pushpa called to Tara from her window, 'Bring your cousin over. She and I are in the same boat. We'll chat for a while. You come too.' A daughter had been born to her at the end of February, just a few days before Sheelo gave birth. The two of them had become pals. Pushpa sent her servant to the bazaar for some mithai as a treat for Sheelo.

Seeing Tara silent at Pushpa's house, Sheelo said to her, 'Arrey, why such a long face?' She told Pushpa about Somraj's anger and began to console Tara, 'Don't you see why he gets angry with you? Why, it's because he loves you. He's no man unless he flies off the handle and gets angry with you. You have to knuckle under him. If he can't scold you, he can't love you either. A quick temper is becoming in a man.

'My man is just a lump of dough. Always afraid of getting sick, of catching something. I wish that sometimes he'd shout at me so that I could sulk and then he'd have to butter me up. As things stand now, I may stay in a huff and not eat anything the whole day, but he won't guess a thing. All he will have to offer is to ask me to eat something or I'll get a queasy stomach.'

'Arrey, what should I tell you about my doctor?' Pushpa asked with a meaningful smile. 'First he makes me cry, then does such things to humour me that I just can't tell you.'

Pushpa talked about her husband, and Sheelo told ribald tales of her elder brother and his wife. They both laughed loud and hard. Since no elder was around, Tara did not need to act coy. But she wasn't listening to them either. Once or twice she just spread her lips in a smile.

Sheelo looked out of the window at the sky, and said, 'Let's go back to your place.'

Tara caught the hint. She too said, 'Yes, let's. I have to help my mother in the kitchen.'

When they went back, Tara's mother fondly told Sheelo, 'You can't leave just now. Have dinner with us, then I'll send you home with someone to keep you company till you get there.'

In the month of May in Lahore, it is bright on the rooftops till 7.30 or 8 o'clock in the evening. Sheelo said, 'Chachi, the baby will be uncomfortable in the heat down here. I'll take him to the roof.'

'Yes, sure,' Bhagwanti agreed, and called out to Usha, 'Go up on the roof, girl, and spread a dhurrie on a charpoy for the baby.'

Usha did so without complaining for the sake of her newborn nephew, and came back downstairs. Lying on the bed on his back, Sheelo's forty-five-day old son gazed at something invisible up in the blue sky, his tiny toothless mouth letting out gurgles of joy. He waved his chubby feet and hands around, filling his mother, and Tara too, with joy and pride.

Sheelo said, looking at her son, 'Say, isn't he cute? Would Ratan be able to resist holding him? Why won't he speak to me?'

They heard Vijay calling Ratan from his side of the house, 'Bhappaji, sister Sheelo's here. She's brought her baby too.'

Tara rose to go downstairs, leaving Sheelo alone on the roof. She heard Ratan speaking to his mother on the other side, 'Jhhai, I'm ready to eat if you've made the chapattis.'

His mother replied, 'I'm almost finished. But first, go and look at Sheelo's little boy. Your sister has come for the first time with her baby.'

Ratan came to Tara's side and called, 'Auntie!'

His eyes met Tara's. She said, 'Sheelo is upstairs in the fresh air with her son.'

Ratan climbed the stairs with slow, measured steps, as if in no hurry.

Tara went and lay down in the veranda. Once upon a time, Ratan used to fly to Sheelo's side at the mere sight of her, or at the sound of her voice, she thought. It's not the same now. But he did ask Sheelo to elope with him. And why hadn't she, if she really loved him? Her love should have given her courage. Why put up with someone for whom she has no feelings? She's being dishonest to both men, Tara thought.

Soon she heard Ratan's steps coming back down. Tara had been appalled by Sheelo's duplicity, but she was also curious to know what Ratan might have said to her. She went to the roof and saw Sheelo wiping away her tears.

'What happened?' Tara asked gently.

Sheelo burst out crying.

'Tell me,' Tara insisted.

'He refused to listen to me,' Sheelo whimpered. 'He didn't even touch my baby.'

'What did he say?'

'He said, "Come away with me." Said that he'll be responsible for whatever happens; he will do whatever he has to to support me. He accused me of giving his child to another man, of letting him down. He said that that's not true love, that he and I should be willing to bear the consequences of our love.'

'He's right,' Tara blurted out.

'Sure, you can say that. Because it's not you who's had to deal with the problem.'

'What problem? Why put up with someone you don't love?' Tara said. 'He's right. If one's really in love, one must face the consequences, come what may.'

'Isn't that what I've done?' Sheelo cried angrily. 'It's me who comes running to see him. He's the one running away scared.'

'It's you who's scared!' Tara declared flatly. 'You love him, you bore his child, you should be with him. You're turning love into something sinful.'

'You're talking nonsense!' Sheelo said in irritation, 'The dharma of love is one thing, and the obligations of family and marriage another. There's a time and place for both. Love happens just like that. The ancients did the same. Lord Krishna had Radha as his beloved. He loved her milkmaid friends, the gopis too, but did he leave his wife Rukmini for them? No! Neither did he desert his family when he went to stay with Kubja. Heer and Ranjha did the same, despite their legendary love for each other. If you run off without any thought for your own people, you bring shame on the families. That is not the thing to do. If God gives you a slice of happiness, you should be content to accept it as your share,' Sheelo sighed deeply during her little speech to Tara. She had never spoken with such seriousness.

Sheelo's sermonizing did not convince Tara. There was no point in arguing with her simple-mindedness. She decided to be bold and ask something that Sheelo would understand, 'If you don't like Mohan, why do you let him make love to you?'

'It's not a question of like or dislike. That's his right.'

'To hell with such a right!' Tara touched her ears in a gesture of penitence. 'If you care so much for his rights, then why are you involved with Ratan? Let him go!'

'You're talking a load of rubbish again! You don't fall in love of your own free will. Arrey, love can overcome anyone, even the gods; not to say anything of us mere mortals? Don't get me talking, my dear. I don't know about you, but can anybody claim to be without sin? I know all about my father, my mother too. After a while, they all act innocent. That's sinful. It's not love but some kind of game. That's not for me. I'll be faithful to him all my life. What do you know about me?'

Tara was returning home with Usha and Haridev after dropping Sheelo off at her parents' house. She thought with a heavy heart: Deception and loving someone on the sly is the dharma for Sheelo. I can't live like that. I'd have decided my future today, but Sheelo spoiled everything by showing up at the last moment.

When Puri reached home about 8 o'clock, Tara had not yet returned. His mother said, 'Sheelo came round with her baby. I gave her two rupees in shagun, as a good omen for her son's first visit here. I did the right thing, huh?' Bhagwanti had begun to tell him lately about such family matters.

'You know better. All that's for the women to think about,' he replied.

His mother also told him what Sheelo had said about Somraj's threats. She said, 'I let Tara go up to Uchchi Gali because Sheelo insisted, but I've been shaking with fear since I heard that.' Bhagwanti was still talking when she heard the sound of someone climbing the stairway. Tara was the first to come into the room.

Their mother wanted Tara to hear what she was telling her eldest child, 'I've told her that there's no need to go out of the gali. She's not a child anymore.'

'What do you mean by that?' Puri interrupted her. 'She's in her own home. Who's he to object to her coming and going? If Tara wants to go somewhere, I'll go with her. I'll see who dares to stop her in the bazaar.'

'If they don't like my ways, why are they after my life? Is there no other girl for them in the whole wide world?' Tara asked angrily, without looking at anyone, and sat down with a scowl on her face.

Bhagwanti gaped at Tara, horrified. Muffling her voice with her hand, she scolded her, 'Is she in her right mind? Just listen to what she's saying.'

Puri said nothing beyond asking his mother to give him his dinner.

Puri had another reason to object to Somraj's high-handed manner. On the evening he had stayed out late with Kanak in Lawrence Garden, she had made him swear, when they parted, that he wouldn't torture her by not meeting her. 'If you don't want to come to my house,' she had said, 'we can meet at the same spot on Nisbet Road. I'll write to you if I have another place in mind. You send me a letter in a sealed envelope, and I'll come whenever you tell me.'

One evening he had wound up his business at Adayara Munavvar by 6.30 and reached Nisbet Road for his appointment with Kanak. He waited at the meeting place, then went from one end of Nisbet Road to the other, and then retraced his steps. She was nowhere to be seen.

This was the second time that she had failed to keep a date with him. Once he had written and asked her to meet him on the Mall Road on Tuesday morning at 11 o'clock. Then he had sent a letter to tell her to come to Nisbet Road on Friday evening between 6.30 and 7. She had not replied or written to him about any change in her plans. He had begun to suspect that she was somehow prevented from meeting him. With her renewed assurances of love for him, he had once again begun to trust her. In his frustration he thought: How unfair to put such constraints on a free-spirited young woman.

His reply that night had silenced his mother, but had also sown the seed of doubts in Tara's mind. Tara's ears pricked up as she noticed how he had changed his way of talking. 'She's in her own home,' he had said. What had happened to change his declaration that her parents did not have to worry if Somraj's father broke his son's engagement to Tara?

Thoughts whirled around in her mind as she lay down to sleep: These were all excuses to make it easier to get her out of this house. She remembered Masterji's intention of selling his part of the ancestral village house, and taking a loan against his provident fund. Her parents were apparently willing to sacrifice everything of their own to ensure her destruction. 'Why do they see me as a burden on them? Now that I've given up on my brother, I must do something for myself, and do it at once.'

When she woke up the next morning, the thought of changing her circumstances was still on her mind.

Puri too was frantic with apprehension after his two failures to meet Kanak. He desperately wanted to go to her house to know the reason, but thought it below his dignity to go there without a plausible reason. He looked for a credible excuse to pay a visit. He thought that it would be better to translate half of the book and take it to show to Panditji. If Panditji could give him 100 rupees as advance payment, he reasoned, he might also hand over half of his final fee, another forty rupees. Even if he didn't, he would see that Puri had already completed more than one hundred rupees' worth of work.

He had been thinking of putting off work on the textbook for a few days, and asking Tara to give more time to the translation of the novel. Tara herself came to him and mumbled nervously, 'Bhaiji, I couldn't go to Gwal Mandi yesterday. I feel bad because I told Narendra bhai that I'd come. I want to go some time today.'

'Listen,' Puri said. 'Not today. If I work only on the translation with your help, we can finish half the book in two days. We can go the day after tomorrow, and I'll hand over the manuscript to Pandit Girdharilal at the same time.'

Whenever she thought of her decision and her course of action, her head would spin and she would feel a shiver. While reading aloud to Puri from the novel, she was so distracted and preoccupied with what was to come that she kept on missing the continuity to the next line on the page. She would picture in her mind's eye, her brother coming to Surendra's house on his way back, and his puzzlement at not finding her there. How would her mother and Masterji react? ... But, they're the ones who paid no heed to my cries and forced me to run away from home. Am I not to resist as the noose is tightened around my neck? Can't I run away to save myself if someone keeps pushing me towards the sacrificial altar? If I do run away, it'll be good for all of us. At least my parents won't have to sell the village house or take a loan. What about the money needed for my sisters and brothers? ... It had also crossed her mind that she might have to stay at home for another few days, that Asad might ask her to come to meet him again in a day or two. 'I'll find another excuse to go out,' she thought.

The translation of half of *A House Built upon Sand* was finished in the afternoon of 5 May. Puri went out for a short while, came back and immediately began revising the manuscript. He did not want to risk leaving a single mistake. He again took up his revision early on the next day. At about 4 o'clock in the afternoon, he and Tara went together to Gwal Mandi. He turned into Shaduram's Gali, and Tara walked alone towards Surendra's house. That's what she wanted. To be alone.

Puri had gone to Panditji's house ostensibly to show him the translation, so he went in through the office door. Panditji was on the telephone with some paper merchant. He signalled for Puri to take a chair. Puri waited for him to finish, but his ears were cocked to catch any sound coming from the living room. Once he turned around to look when he thought he heard something, but whoever it was, had gone past. Kanak or Kanchan, he couldn't be sure.

Since he was talking on the telephone, Panditji had not been able to welcome Puri in his usual expansive style. He hung up, gave him a broad smile and said, 'So, barkhurdar!' He asked several questions about Puri's health.

Puri had placed the folder with the manuscript on the desk. He said, opening it, 'Panditji, I've managed to finish half the novel. Why don't you look at it and tell me what you think?'

'You've brought the translation? So soon? Let me see.' He held out his hand.

He took the folder from Puri, read half of the first page, turned over fifteen or so pages and read another half page, leafed through twenty-five more sheets to read a paragraph, and then a paragraph at the very end. He put the manuscript back on the desk seemingly satisfied, and said, 'Good! Very good! Fine work, wonderful expression. You're a master, barkhurdar, no doubt of that. Very good.'

Panditji took off his glasses and put them on the desk, ran his fingers through his closely cropped hair as he looked at the ceiling, and called out, 'Bhai Vidhichand, how's that title page coming along? The printing press has been working to get the colour of that page right since this morning. What's going on? Why don't you get on your bicycle and go there to find out the reason. Ask Sawan Mull what problem is holding up the printing? If the block for the page has to be replaced, why can't they begin work on something else? This is sloppy work!'

'I'll go,' said Vidhichand and left.

Panditji stroked his hair for a few moments more before turning to Puri, 'Your translation is excellent. Barkhurdar, you are a creative writer. For you translating someone else's work can't mean the same as creating your own. It's a waste of time for you. First make a name for yourself and get your stories published in magazines. Then come out with a novel. You need a good publisher to back you up.' He stroked his chin in silent contemplation.

Puri was encouraged by these words, and by this show of concern and sympathy for his future.

'You did this in a very short time,' Panditji said, again by way of praise.

'If you like, I can work harder and finish the whole thing in a week,' Puri said to show his goodwill.

'No, no, no! You don't have to sweat it out. Take your time, do it when you get some free time or when you feel like it. Do it as a pastime. This is the time for selling textbooks. Even if I decide to hand it over for printing, I won't be able to publish it any time before October or November.'

Puri was beginning to get uncomfortable with the tone of his voice. Panditji went on, 'Of course, it's a different matter if you need money. You can come to me without hesitation.'

It became obvious to Puri that Panditji had given him the work to help him out, but he had made that obvious without meaning to hurt him. What could Puri say to respond to such kindness? Panditji picked up a glass paperweight from his desk, and looked at it intently, trying to concentrate on his words, 'You're like family. There's something I wanted to speak to you about. It's good that you came.'

Puri felt alarmed.

'It's about Kanak,' Panditji uttered almost inaudibly. Puri held his breath, as if the future of his relationship with Kanak hung in the balance and the next word from her father could tip the balance in his favour or against him.

Panditji thought for a few moments staring at the paperweight, then said firmly in English, 'You have always regarded Kanak as a younger sister. Now it's up to you to honour that relationship.'

With that sentence Panditji disarmed Puri, taking the starch out of his courage and his will to protest. He continued to speak in English, 'She's just over twenty. What does a girl that old know about life? What I mean is, that to be able to solve the problems faced by young people of her age, she needs some worldly experience. She's done her BA. That's a certain achievement, but not a very important one. She's intelligent, and has a literary bent for which you deserve credit. What she knows about life she has learnt from books, not from experience. You know how one can be easily swayed by emotions at her age, and regret such feelings later on. You know that quite well.'

Seeing Puri sit in silence, Panditji laughed as if he had no doubts of Puri's agreeing with him, 'Heh, heh, heh! You're a writer; you have imagination. You know what I'm saying.'

Puri did know what he was saying. He felt so upset he could hardly breathe. Panditji's words fell on him like the blows of a mailed fist wrapped in a velvet glove of affection and politeness.

He went on before Puri could respond, alternating between Urdu and English, 'These are natural, human failings. At one stage in their lives, all young men and women feel that romance is the goal of life. They are swayed by their emotions. But romance is an illusion, just a dream. When one begins to turn such dreams into reality, the result is bitterness and disappointment. You know what I mean. A commitment made in the romantic folly of youth means nothing.'

Puri wanted to protest in self-defence: Sure, she may be twenty-one, but what she said to me was not childish prattle. As if I'm the wily hunter, and she's my unsuspecting quarry.

Panditji went on as if there was no question of Puri's disagreement, 'Maybe at her age she's not too young for marriage. In our family too, girls are married off at sixteen or seventeen, but it's the girl's parents who make those decisions. It's another matter when a girl wants to have a say in whom she marries and when; don't you think? And marriage has a social and economic aspect, a wider implication. It may not survive outside that particular social and economic framework. The way someone has been brought up counts for a lot. You know that quite well. You're very wise.'

Panditji continued to speak without giving Puri a chance to get a word in, 'I'm not the one to impose unnecessary restrictions on my daughters about whom they should meet or talk to. You've seen that for yourself. I don't want them to feel awkward in social situations. But if any social interaction can create or lead to misunderstandings, such interaction is best avoided. Why let people's tongues wag? People recognize you. You have a reputation. Kanak too is known in many social circles. Why should people point the finger at both of you for nothing?'

'I'm fully aware of my reputation and social standing,' Puri forced out the words.

'Of course. Certainly. I know that you're a responsible young man,' Panditji said, as if confiding in him, 'That's why I'm sharing my concerns with you. I think this matter should end here. Stop seeing Kanak for a while in the best interests of both of you. I know I can trust you in this matter.'

Puri's face fell. It took a few moments for him to gather enough courage to say, 'Please forgive me. Although I've been careful not to be the first to start anything that might give Kanak any wrong notions about my intentions, still I have in a way given my word to her about us.'

'Oh-oh-oh! No, no, no!' Panditji did not let him continue, 'I'm not putting any blame on you. Anyone can say such silly things when they're young; such is the folly of youth. Forget that bit. I'd meant to say something in the interests of your future. What I mean is, you should avoid what is not suitable for you. Why get into trouble?'

Panditji had used very subtle language to tell Puri that he was unsuitable for Kanak. An insulted Puri shot back, 'You may have your own ideas on who's suitable or unsuitable, but may I ask what is your basis for weighing somebody as suitable or not? How do you measure a person's worth?'

'Oh-oh-oh! No, no, no!' Panditji waved both his hands to emphasize his disagreement. 'Barkhurdar, I have already said that you're a talented, hard-working and responsible young man. What I meant was the overall situation, status … class consciousness … things like that. You know … I mean … keep away from what's not suitable for you.'

'What you mean is money!' Puri raised his voice angrily. 'You're probably well off, but I never came to your house uninvited. I tutored your daughter, but never took a paisa as fee. You don't want the translation done, I'll return your hundred rupees. But you've no right to put me down. And it wasn't me, but Kanak who first…'

Puri controlled himself and fell silent on seeing the expression on Panditji's face.

Panditji spoke slowly, choosing his words carefully, 'Barkhurdar, I am pained to see that you've misunderstood me. I have a great and a deep respect for you. I'm telling you this because I consider you as my esteemed friend and associate. I acknowledge my indebtedness to you, and now I'm asking for your help once again. What do one hundred rupees mean to a promising young man like you? You probably can earn that much in one day. You can have any sum of money from me, whenever you say so.'

'No, sir, thank you very much.' Puri replied through clenched teeth. 'But if you'll allow me, I'd like to speak with Kanakji just once for a few minutes about your ideas of …'

'Oh-oh-oh! Barkhurdar!' Panditji interrupted him, 'Why only once? You may speak to her as often as you like. She's like a sister to you, after all, but at this time… I mean … at this time it may not be proper because she'll just feel sorry and humiliated for her mistake. And, as I've said, it's better to let bygones be bygones.'

'Namaste!' Puri said sharply as he got up, and leaving the manuscript on the desk, went out of the room.

'Namaste, namaste, namaste … barkhurdar!' Panditji repeated until Puri was out of the room. He was sure that he had avoided hurting Puri's feelings.

Puri was seething with anger as he left the office of Naya Hind Publications. Unable to think of anything but the insult to which he had been subjected, he walked with hurried steps along Amritdhara Road up to the gali where Narendra Sigh's house was. He did not want to see or talk with anyone in his state of agitation. He kept on going and reached Kele Wali Sarak. Thoughts churned about in his mind, 'I knew this was going to happen, that's why I was avoiding that house. It's all my fault. I made the mistake of believing Kanak. She misled me into going to see her father, and just think how brutally I've been humiliated. If she's so smart and confident of being able to handle everything, why didn't she come into the office? I should have known she was playing games with me. Didn't they tell me that she was like that? I've let her pull the wool over my eyes.'

But was she also trying to fool me that evening in the Lawrence Garden? Puri wondered. It didn't seem that way. Has she been brainwashed by her father? Has she begun to see everything from his point of view? What made her say those beautiful words, and what did she base them on? When he realized that, lost in his thoughts, he had reached the railway station, he turned round and went back.

When Tara reached Surendra's house, she welcomed Tara with mock anger, 'You bad girl, I'm not going to talk to you. My brother told me on May Day that you'd come in a couple of days. You call this long time just a couple of days? Go away!'

Surendra chattered on without giving Tara a chance to say anything, 'Neither do you visit anybody, nor do you invite anyone to your house.' She spoke so that her mother could hear, 'Ma, she's studied her textbooks so much that the pages have turned white. Always gets the highest marks. Hasn't told anyone where her house is, in case other people may come and interrupt her studies, and she might have to make them a cup of tea. Ma, don't you offer her anything to eat or drink.'

'Keep quiet, silly girl. Why wouldn't I?' Surendra's mother replied. 'Isn't she my daughter too? Nice girls are like that. She's not like you and your brother. He thinks he's in charge of everything. And you roam all over the town like a *nagar-naun*, behaving as if you were a bigger leader even than he.'

'Ma, you too have begun to sing her praises.' Surendra pouted. 'She's very deep. She knows the *vashikaran* mantra that puts magic spells over everyone and holds them captive. Watch out for her.' Surendra looked sideways at Tara.

Her mother got up, 'You sisters keep me out of your childish squabbles! Tara beti, will you also have the red-coloured hot water, what they call tea, in this heat, or sherbet? I could make you some sherbet with *phalsa* berries'

'What's the hurry, ma?' Surendra said. 'She's not a guest. If she wants something, she'll ask for it.' Tara explained that she'd meant to come one day as promised, but her cousin had come to visit with her first-born child.

'I know the truth!' Surendra whispered knowingly.

'What do you know?'

'Why you've come here.'

'Why then?' Tara showed her surprise.

'Stop pretending,' Surendra said, keeping her voice down. 'He comes here every morning and waits for you. This morning too. Said that he'll wait one more day, and if you don't show up, he'll take me along and go to your place to ask about you. He knows which gali to go to, and where your house is in it.'

'Who does?' asked Tara, raising her eyebrows in puzzlement.

'Hai, your playing innocent will kill me. You're really a deep one, you sly thing. You've picked the real pearl out of a basket of imitations, and you want to keep it a secret?'

'Tell me. Stop talking in riddles,' Tara showed her irritation. 'Who was asking about me?'

'You don't really trust me, do you?' Surendra said, with a twinkle of mischief in her eyes.

'Don't tease me, please. Tell me. I beg of you. You're my best pal,' Tara said, accepting defeat.

'Whom did you promise on May Day that you'd come to Surendra's house?'

Tara tried to keep up her pretence. 'Who?'

'All right. Keep it up. I'm not telling you anything,' Surendra gestured with her thumb in refusal.

Tara's face turned crimson. They were both sitting on a dhurrie on the floor. She put her hand on Surendra's feet, and said, 'Please tell me. Here, I'm touching your feet in appeal.'

'Yes, touch my feet, call me sister-in-law,' Surendra turned serious. 'That's my right.'

'Hai, have some shame! What are you saying?' Tara was embarrassed.

'Well, Asad bhai has adopted me as his sister. He's asked me to tie a *rakhi* on his wrist, and formally became my brother. He said that he found this custom of sisters tying a thread on their brothers' wrist very pleasant and meaningful.'

Tara sat in thought, her chin resting on her fist.

'What's troubling you?' Surendra said. 'Asad bhai too seemed very upset.'

'I don't know how to explain,' Tara said. 'I don't know what to say.'

'What is it? Give me some idea, so that I can help.'

'Let me first talk to him. Then I'll tell you.'

'Don't you have faith in me?' Surendra said grumpily.

'It's not that, but there's another problem. Please don't feel bad about it, sister.'

'Whatever you say.'

'Can't I meet him anywhere now?' Tara asked uneasily.

'My brother has gone with Asad, Pradyumna and others to the railway workshops. They hold a meeting every day outside the workshop gate. They return around eight o'clock in the evening.'

'Then it's not my lucky day.'

'Come tomorrow. At what time can you be here?'

'Can't come tomorrow.'

'Why?'

'It's all very complicated. I came today with my brother. I can only come if he's with me.'

'What's so complicated about that?'

Tara was thinking: If they translated three pages every day, the rest of *The House Built upon Sand* should be finished by the eleventh of that month. Her brother might come this way again, to deliver the manuscript. 'Maybe on the twelfth, I can come at the same time,' she said.

They talked about other matters. Surendra told her that she had received a proposal of marriage from a captain in the army from the town of Ludhiana. She said 'no' to her mother. Her mother had asked: Do you want to get married or not? Surendra's brother said: Ma, wait a while. Let's wait until she herself asks for it ten times over. She'll come round in the end. 'I was really embarrassed.' Their talk turned to the friendship between Zubeida and Pradyumna.

'Narinder S-e-e-ngh!' A call came from the gali.

'Bhai's here,' Tara said and walked towards the window opening onto the gali. Surendra followed her.

'Come on up,' Surendra said looking down from the window.

As they headed towards the landing, Tara took Surendra's arm and said, 'Ask me again in front of my brother. Insist that I come.' She fell silent as the sound of steps neared the top of the stairs.

Tara asked her brother, 'It seems that you had quite a long talk. Did Panditji read many pages? What did he think of it?'

Surendra led Puri to the room where there was a sofa.

'He seemed to like it,' Puri said, as he sat down.

'What do you mean by "seemed to like it"?' Tara asked.

'Nothing. I mean, he liked it.' Puri closed the discussion by asking, 'Narendra isn't at home?'

'He goes out every evening for the gate meeting at the workshop,' Surendra said.

'They're all really working hard.' Puri said, wiping the perspiration from his forehead with his handkerchief.

'Will you have tea, bhaiji?' Surendra asked.

'No, no. I've just had tea.' Puri replied.

'Wah, we both were waiting for you to have it with us. I forgot that Kanak's father wouldn't let you off without offering you tea. He must have put his arm round your shoulders, saying : Barkhurdar, my boy, how can you leave without having tea? What would your sisters think? I might get a cup too when Kanni and Kanchi bring one for you ... Kanak's father is very affectionate.'

Puri smiled, but said nothing.

Surendra went on, 'Even if you had a cup, so what? You must have lost twice that much in perspiration.'

As Tara and Puri got up to leave, Surendra asked Tara, 'When will you

come again?' She said to Puri teasingly, 'I know writers want to chat only
with other literary-minded people; and I'm not a literary type. But bhaiji,
the Gwal Mandi bazaar doesn't end at Shaduram's Gali. There's also our
Jeeva Gali. Tara, don't forget to bring him along.'

'Have I ever failed to show up when you have invited me?' Puri said.
'I've been here almost every time. It's just that I've a bit of a workload in
the past few days.'

'That load was lightened when you had go to Shaduram's Gali?' Surendra
added, teasing him again.

Tara hid her smile.

'Pandit Girdharilal's work was like a load on my conscience. I've thrown
off that load today.' Puri said, turning her jokes into a fact.

Before parting with Tara downstairs, Surendra said again, 'Don't forget
to come on the twelfth, or else!'

She's a *jatni* after all, Tara thought. 'When I asked her to call me on the
twelfth, she just parroted the words after me. She could've asked us to
come a day or two earlier.'

Puri was quiet as they walked home. Tara asked, 'How's Kanak? I'll go
to see her too, next time.'

'Don't know. Haven't seen her,' Puri replied curtly.

Tara did not know what to make of his answer. She said, 'Maybe she had
gone out. What did her father say about the translation?'

'Praised it.'

'I'll help you finish the rest. It should be four or five days' work. Then
you'll be able to give all your time to the history textbook.' Tara was
preparing the ground for coming back to Surendra's on the twelfth.

'There's no need to finish the translation now.'

'Why? It's such an interesting novel.' Tara said in surprise.

'Girdharilal talked as if he was having it translated only to help me out.
I don't need such patronage,' Puri said in a sharp tone.

'Who asked him for his patronage?' Tara said, out of sympathy for her
brother's feelings. But anxiety swept over her mind. What excuse would
she now have to go to Gwal Mandi?

Tara's family had begun to get her trousseau together in earnest. Sheelo
sometimes came and lent a hand. She brought her infant son along, so

that she would not have to hurry back home. She found Tara's indifference towards her trousseau infuriating. Sheelo often talked about the approaching wedding, 'Your in-laws are not such bad people…'

Irked by Tara's apathy, Bhagwanti too sometimes mumbled irritably or aimed a jibe at her daughter. Tara did not want to start a quarrel, nor did she want to risk losing the opportunity of going out with her brother. Therefore, after being asked several times, she too would contribute something to the work of preparation. In her heart she would tell herself: 'I know my family will say all kinds of horrid things when I'm gone.' And she would answer herself: 'They are the ones who forced me to elope. Let them say what they want.'

Puri was surprised at seeing Tara take part in the preparation of her trousseau. He did not say anything, but felt relieved of a burden. He had felt guilty at not fighting the injustice being forced on Tara; now she herself had freed him of that responsibility. He too asked a couple of times of his mother and Masterji, 'Let me know if I can do anything to help.'

His mother said with relief, 'It's you who has to do everything. Who else can?'

But Tara had also heard him. Why had he said that? He's had a change of heart? The ground beneath her feet had opened, she felt, and she was falling into a dark bottomless pit. She suppressed her sighs of desperation with clenched teeth, and told herself: There's no hope or help for me from anyone now. I have to fend for myself.

To lighten her distress, Tara would say to herself: What's the use of worrying like this? Why should I continue to torture myself? But whenever she tried to turn her back on her worry, it came back with greater intensity. Why did my brother say that? Only two days ago he was telling me not to worry. She reasoned with herself: I too am pretending to lend a hand to avoid unpleasantness. Probably he's just doing the same. Doesn't he know what's going on? She thought she had found an answer.

Pandit Girdharilal had cunningly dealt a shrewd blow to Puri's self-respect. Smarting from the insult, Puri did not want to go near Panditji. Still, it was not easy to avoid thinking about Kanak's willingness to yield to him, and of her promises of love. He was quite sure that either Kanak or Kanchan had seen him sitting in Panditji's office. He also found it difficult to believe that Kanak had known nothing of his visit. Why, then, had she not asked him to come to the living room as before? Has she been affected so much, and so soon, by her father's lectures? The old saying was right: It's never wise to trust a woman!

Puri's mind was seething like a vat of boiling oil. Was Kanak a part of the scheme to get me the translation work, so that I could be put down? Puri did not believe so, but still he thought: If she was, I'll get my own back by jilting her. She'll have to explain herself to me. Could it be that she now finds it embarrassing and bothersome to meet me? These women!

He knew he had to meet her and ask her for a satisfactory explanation. But he wanted to meet her outside her home. He also wanted her to make the first move to meet him. To give her that opportunity, Puri put aside work on the textbook and passed by her house at 9 o'clock in the morning, on his way to the office of his friend Chopra. In the depths of his heart he believed, perhaps wrongly, that Kanak would not be able to resist coming out and meeting him if she saw him passing by.

Chopra, a sub-editor at the *Tribune*, was an old acquaintance. Puri asked him if he could borrow a report from the newspaper's library. He went back in the evening to collect the report. And again the next evening to return it. The third time he saw Kanchan on her way out of the house. She smiled and said namaste to him as if he was just another acquaintance, and kept on walking. Kanchan saw him at her doorstep and did not ask him to come in. What could be more humiliating for Puri?

Everyone in the family had ganged up to insult him, Puri told himself. He took Kanchan's insolent behaviour to heart. He vowed that he'd avenge this insult dealt out to him, question Kanak harshly for an explanation, and make her shed tears of remorse in front of him.

Puri was working on the history textbook in the morning of the next day. It was close to 10 o'clock. Bhagwanti was finishing off kitchen chores so that she could do some sewing work on Tara's wedding clothes. Tara sat looking at her textbooks on a chatai in the veranda, sunk in the depths of her worries. There was no sense in preparing herself for exams that were now only two weeks away. Her parents would certainly object, and she wouldn't be allowed to sit for them. Then again, who knew where she'd be after 12 May, and whether she'd be in a position to present herself for the examination? How completely her family was destroying her life and her future!

'Tara,' she heard her brother call. 'Bring me a glass of water.' He had an uncapped fountain pen in his hand. Tara had noticed an edge of nervousness and unease in him since the day of his meeting with Pandit Girdharilal.

She looked up at him from her book, and got up to get him the water.

'You wanted to go to Surendra's?' he asked.

Tara nodded.

'Achcha, we'll go around four or five this afternoon. You also wanted to meet Kanak?' He began to drink from the glass she had fetched.

Tara understood his motives; he wanted news of Kanak. But Surendra had asked her to come on the twelfth, and would have told Asad to be there on that day. Nobody would be there today. She said apprehensively, 'Bhai, Surendra invited me for the twelfth, not today.'

Puri removed the half-empty glass from his lips, and said kindly, 'I've to go in that direction today. You can meet Kanak today. We'll go to Surendra's again on the twelfth. Two visits in the same evening will stretch for too long.'

Tara was willing to help and assist her brother in any way, if it ensured her going to Surendra's on the appointed day. Their motives might be similar, she knew, but there was a world of difference between them. He could ask for her help without hesitation, but she was compelled to adjust herself to suit his convenience. Women perhaps have to become deceitful for want of such simple freedoms, she thought.

Tara had been steadfast in her resolve to present herself for her exams, but she had another, secret plan in mind. She couldn't keep up pretences any longer, sitting in front of an open textbook. The thoughts racing through her mind overwhelmed her with their intensity. To clear her head she would sit with her mother, Meladei and Pushpa, listening to their chatter, hemming her trousseau.

Puri had been working in the veranda in the afternoon, sitting on a chatai. Usha sat near him, bent over her homework on another chatai. Puri called, 'Tara, it's four-thirty. Get dressed if you want to go out. Give me my shirt and trousers that you've ironed.'

Tara put down the garment in her hand. She gave her brother the clothes she had ironed at Meladei's. Her mother could hear that Puri had asked her to come along; Tara didn't have to explain anything to her. She went to the kitchen, washed her face in a corner over the small drain, and began to comb her hair before changing her clothes.

Since the women were using the room, Puri had to change his clothes on the veranda. He was tying his shoelaces when he said in a startled voice, 'What's that?'

'*Agg da bamba,* the fire engine!' Usha said, raising her head. The faint clanging of a bell that they had heard receded into the distance.

'It's somewhere far away,' Meladei relayed her guess from the room. 'You go ahead, wherever you have to get to.'

Usha could not restrain her curiosity. There was the thud of her feet on the steps going upstairs, and she called out, 'Tara! Ma! Auntie! Come and look!'

The women dropped whatever they were doing and went up to the roof. Tara followed them, comb in hand. Puri too went up.

There was a pall of smoke over the eastern horizon. Several three-storey houses towards the east dwarfed Puri's house. A huge spiralling column of dense black and brown smoke churned upwards from an unseen source somewhere behind the building right in front of Puri's house and spread out across the sky. Clouds of denser smoke followed in its wake.

Usha yelled at Kartaro and Rampyari to come up to their roof and look at the spectacle.

The women were making guesses about the location of the fire. One thought it was the railway station, others guessed it was at Delhi Gate or Kashmiri Mohalla or Akbari Mandi. Puri agreed that Akbari Mandi was the most likely place, and said, 'The fire seems to have spread. Must have been going on for some time.'

Usha said to Pushpa, 'Let's go to Dhanno's roof, bahinji. We'll have a better view from there.' The rest followed them downstairs.

Puri said in a worried voice to Tara when they reached the room below, 'Should we leave or not? It would be a different matter if the fire were an accident. Otherwise...'

Dewanchand called in a loud voice from the gali, 'Shyam! Where are you?' He warned the children playing in the gali in the same breath, 'Careful, all of you. No one's to go out of the gali. The curfew is on.'

Shyam's mother called her husband from her window, 'Go quickly and look for Shyam in the bazaar. He's gone to buy mithai from Mukund Lal's shop.'

Bhagwanti and Meladei called from their windows, 'Bhai, what's happened? And where was it?'

'There were huge riots at Delhi Gate, and a big fire is burning in the

Akbari Mandi. The police are patrolling the bazaars. The curfew has been imposed.' Dewanchand said hurriedly and ran off to look for his son.

Masterji had left only minutes before, for his tutoring job at Seth Gopal Shah. Govindram, Beeru Mal and Tikaram had not returned from their offices. Some announcement was being made over a loudspeaker. What was being said was unclear, since it was some distance away, but it was obviously about the curfew. For the past three weeks the curfew siren had not sounded.

The women assembled on the chabutaras in front of their houses. Puri said to his mother, 'I'll go and get father. It's quite safe at the place where he is.'

Bhagwanti's heart sank, but she could not refuse. She pleaded, 'Kakaji, be very careful. Don't go through Machchi Hatta. Take the Vachcho Wali and the Haricharan Steps route, and come back the same way.'

Meladei said, 'Vijay has gone over to his uncle's in Said Mittha. Hope he stays there. And you know about Ratan, how careless he is. I won't rest until I see them both.'

Every mother thought that her own son was the most vulnerable, and every wife was afraid for her husband and her children. Their men straggled back home one by one. When the son or the husband of a woman arrived, she would quietly leave for her home to busy herself in her kitchen. Men now sat on the chabutaras, recounting what they had heard about the incident. Some women listened at their windows. Puri and Masterji too came back.

Birumal said, 'Only the Mall Road is open to traffic. The curfew covers Nisbet Road, Gwal Mandi and Anarkali. There has never been a curfew as wide as this.'

Doctor Prabhu Dayal said, 'I telephoned the hospital. Seventy injured have been admitted so far. Most are Hindus.'

Puri had been able to telephone to his sources for news from the mansion of Seth Gopal Shah. He said, 'There was a huge explosion at the railway workshop at the time of the one o'clock break. Three were killed and twenty-two injured. The workshop has been closed. Wherever the workshop employees went, the disturbances spread to those areas. It would be difficult to avoid a large-scale riot now. The forty-five thousand members of the Railway Union have so far been opposed to the riots. That's why there was peace in the city recently. Now these men are out of control. Shahji said that the damages amounted to over one-and-a-half crore at Akbari Mandi alone. The fire is still raging there.'

'It's the Hindus who must have suffered the damage,' Ghasita Ram let out a long sigh.

'The Muslims looted the grain stores before the fire started. Many of them carried away rations enough for two years,' Masterji added what Puri had avoided mentioning.

'They're always looking for an excuse for looting,' Dewanchand said.

'Hindu or Muslim, whoever exploded the bomb, did a cruel thing,' Masterji said.

'God is one for all. You may call Him whatever you want,' Govindram said. The mention of God's name ended their discussion.

When Puri went upstairs to his house, he repeated to Tara his fear of the spreading riots, and said, 'The party comrades used to hold a gate meeting at the workshop every day.'

Tara's heart missed a beat as she remembered that Asad too used to go to the workshops. Puri continued, 'But the meeting was at four o'clock. They wouldn't have gone if the riots had broken out before that.'

Tara did not reply. Previously the curfew had sometimes lasted up to two days. She thought, 'Wonder what'll happen tomorrow? My bad luck!' She had planned so much for the next day.

It was stifling and hot inside the house at night, but cool and pleasant on the roof. Masterji's family had more space to sleep on the roof this year. Ratan had bought another electric table fan, and all of Babu Govindram's family slept indoors. Now charpoys could be set up on the roof for everyone in Masterji's house.

Whenever he could, Puri gave an hour to the history book at night, doing his work in the light of a table lamp in the fresh air. Working was the best cure for his troubled mind, and the hope of receiving 500 rupees from Ghaus Mohammad after finishing the work was an added attraction. The sky in the direction of Akbari Mandi still held a dirty glow. No smell of burning filled the air because the breeze was blowing towards the fire.

Masterji and Hari were sleeping on a large charpoy while Tara lay alone on a smaller one. Usha, who did not want to share a bed, was sleeping on the floor on a chatai. Munni slept on a length of dhurrie on another charpoy. At 11 o'clock Bhagwanti was still downstairs finishing off one last chore.

'Oh, what's that?' Masterji shrieked in a frightened voice. Puri raised his head from his work. He saw that some flaming object had fallen near Masterji's charpoy. It stank of oil and resin. Puri went up to it and saw that the flames came from a rag tied to a bamboo stick fashioned into an arrow.

'Tara! Bring some water!' Puri called.

'What?' Tara asked with a start, and went down immediately to bring water. Puri picked up the flaming rag by the other end of the stick, and carried it away from the beds, to near the latrine and doused it with bricks pulled from the latrine wall. Then he went and called out to Ratan.

Puri and Ratan decided that an arrow, with the rag on its head, had been shot from a bow. Puri turned the lamp off, 'Maybe some one saw this light and shot the arrow to start a fire.'

'Look! Look at that!' Tara yelled. Another arrow with a flaming head was soaring into the eastern sky.

Puri and Ratan called out to other houses of the gali that they should be on guard and keep buckets of water on their rooftops. Some people living near the Mochi Gate were shooting arrows with burning rags tied to them, they said.

Tara corrected them, 'That arrow had been shot towards the Mochi Gate.'

'Om! Om!' Being woken so abruptly shook Masterji. His heart was still racing. He was uttering prayers to calm himself, 'Om! Om tatsat! You are our Saviour! You are our Protector!'

'What happened? What's the trouble?' Dewanchand, Prabhu Dayal, Tikaram and Khushal Singh began calling from their rooftops.

Govindram, Meladei and Bhagwanti had come up to see the flaming arrow. Everyone gathered on the roof now was scared that another arrow might land at any moment. Puri said, 'This is their revenge for exploding a bomb at the holy hour of namaz.' Meladei said, 'May these heartless murderers go to hell, those who throw bombs at people praying to God. It's not them, but helpless folk like us, who suffer the consequences. God will punish those who set fire to other people's houses.'

Bhagwanti asked, 'What have we done to anyone that they're setting our homes on fire?'

'How will the person know where his arrow will land?' Ratan replied by way of calming her.

'Yes,' Tara muttered. 'They just want to burn somebody's house. Anybody's house.'

Mewa Ram came over from two rooftops away by climbing over the low dividing walls. He too tried to calm the others, 'Bhai, anything can happen in battle, in times of war.'

'This is something no human being would do,' said Govindram.

They heard shouts of 'Hai! Hai! Ho! Ho!' and screams coming from the north-east. Then smoke poured out from where the shouts had been heard. Some house had apparently caught fire. Everyone gathered on the rooftops turned their heads in that direction.

The sound of a fire engine alarm came from the direction of Rang Mahal.

Govindram and Meladei turned towards the staircase. Bhagwanti said to her family, 'All of you come down too. Anyone can try to set this house on fire again. God saved us all this time.'

'If anybody tries it, we'll handle things. We can look after ourselves,' Puri replied.

'Girls, you go down.'

'Why? Can't we look after ourselves?' Tara asked.

'Just listen to her...' said Bhagwanti.

Meladei had begun to go downstairs. She turned back and said, 'Of course, you can look out for yourselves. But you girls are handicapped with your dupattas and shalwars.'

'What difference would it make even if I died?' Tara remained sitting on her charpoy.

'You will put a jinx. Keep quiet and don't bring bad luck,' Bhagwanti scolded her.

'Is just talking so bad, when Fate is playing such dirty tricks?' Tara said, with a sideways glance.

'Go downstairs if Ma tells you to,' her brother said.

'I can't sleep as it is. Why should I suffer in that heat downstairs?' Tara's tone showed that she wouldn't budge.

'Let her stay here then,' Puri intervened. 'Besides, someone must keep watch on the rooftop.'

Mewa Ram had returned to his roof. He called out, 'Look there, up that way. Towards Pari Mahal.'

Smoke was billowing up in that direction, and screams and cries could be heard.

'Yaar Ratan, listen!' Bir Singh said from his rooftop across the gali, trying to keep his voice low, 'Can't we shoot back an arrow with a *dabba* tied to it? That would be some fun.'

'Shut up, you moron!' Ratan rebuked him. He looked at Puri, 'A stupid person's friendship is always a headache.'

'What's a dabba?' Tara wanted to know.

'A home-made bomb!' Puri replied with disgust, and said to Bir Singh, 'What if someone else fired an even bigger dabba at you?'

Ratan asked Puri, 'Do you want me to sleep on the roof?'

'No, I don't think so,' Puri replied. 'I'll call you if there's any need.'

Masterji, the doctor, Tikaram, Khushal Singh and Govindram quickly reached a decision that two men, one at the right and another at the left end of the gali, would stand watch in two-hour shifts until the morning. In the surrounding galis, a lot of hubbub and shouting was still to be heard.

Puri pushed Masterji's charpoy under the awning of the barsati, and lay down on another charpoy in the open. Tara and Usha too lay in the open, wrapped in their dupattas. There was no sleep for Tara. She looked at the twinkling stars in the night sky through the gossamer covering of her dupatta. She could still hear people screaming and calling out loudly from the direction of Delhi Gate, Peepul Behera and Pari Mahal. The sound of the neighbours' voices from their rooftops showed that they too were unable to sleep because of their fears.

Tara could not put Bir Singh's threat of shooting an arrow with a dabba tied to it out of her mind. 'Why do they want to kill poor, innocent Muslims?' She reflected that Ratan and his cronies had already thrown a bomb into a Muslim gali, and someone had set one off at the time of the Muslim prayers, and still they didn't have enough. Why do they consider all Muslims to be evil-minded and wicked? Behind closed eyes she saw images of several Muslims, of rais, and the khaki-clad tongawallahs who called out to warn others as they rode through crowded bazaars: 'Watch out, lady, may your children live long! Make way, daughter! Good sister, hey mother, look out!' And those working for communal harmony, Asad, Zubeida, Manzoor, Zuber … Asad … Asad. 'My brother agreed to go to Surendra's tomorrow, but now there's this curfew. My movement is restricted by it; he can go whenever he wants. A man can sleep in the open; it's the woman who must cover herself. There's either a taboo or a restriction on everything that a woman wants to do.'

The curfew imposed at 4.30 in the afternoon of 11 May was lifted at 5 o'clock in the morning of 14 May. The city people were most inconvenienced by the absence of *mehtars*, the cleaners that removed the night soil from the rooftop latrines. The gali floor was covered with droppings from the buffaloes of Dewanchand and Ghasita Ram. The newspapers delivered on Monday morning were full of reports of bloody riots and cases of widespread arson throughout the city on the previous afternoon. Hari, Ratan, Bir Singh and Puri had gone out and verified that contingents of armed police were stationed in bazaars, at the intersections and near the entrances to galis. Policemen were sitting on charpoys in a temporary camp in the Rang Mahal square. Puri had even been to Uchchi Gali to inquire after his uncle's family.

Masterji did not go to his job after the lifting of the curfew on Monday, nor were Usha and Hari allowed to go to school. Since his worrying over the unrest in the city was not going to bring any change in the situation, Masterji was discussing his other constant worry with the children's mother— the expenses of the forthcoming wedding. His application for the loan of one thousand rupees from his provident fund had been approved, and he was to receive the money in the first week of June. The first gift they wanted to buy for Tara was the customary brass bucket with a lid and a variety of kitchen utensils inside it. Tara could hear them, but she was not paying attention to what they were saying. She was thinking that perhaps the curfew had been lifted in the Gwal Mandi area. That Asad might have gone to Surendra's. That she'd have to find another occasion to meet Asad.

Puri was unable to concentrate on his work. At 11 o'clock he made another hour-long sortie to assess the situation. Tara, to be away from the others in the house, was again sitting on the chatai in the veranda with an open book. Puri sat down next to her with his back against the wall, and asked, 'What are you studying?'

'I'm going over the period of Aurangzeb's reign.'

'I've rewritten that part for the textbook. I just walked to the Gwal Mandi intersection. It seemed peaceful, but you can feel a certain tension. Didn't see any women on the street, except one or two in motorcars. It's not safe yet for you to go out—maybe tomorrow.'

Tara agreed, and thought, she'll have to think it out all over again. She was so decided about the twelfth that she had not done her daily laundry on the eleventh, and had prepared two suits of clothes instead of one for the twelfth.

Puri went out again on Tuesday afternoon to check the streets and the bazaars, and on return told Tara quietly, 'We'll leave after four.'

He hired a tonga outside the Shahalami Gate, something he had never done before for the journey to Gwal Mandi and Amritdhara. He halted the tonga outside Shaduram's Gali, and said to Tara in English, 'You go and meet Kanak first. Don't be too long. If you see Panditji, don't tell him that I'm waiting outside. I don't want to meet him. If Kanak asks you to stay, tell her that I'm waiting for you.'

Tara knew what he meant, nodded her head, and walked into the gali.

Puri had gone over his plan minutely. Why wouldn't Kanak come out, once she knew he was waiting outside? If she didn't, that would be the end of it all. He was sure that when Tara returned, Kanak would be with her. Surendra's house was only a short distance away, he thought, Tara could walk to her place. He'd ask Kanak to accompany him. Let Girdharilal try and stop her! He was dying to interrogate her, in the severest way, for an explanation of the insult meted out to him. He could already see in his imagination the tears rolling down Kanak's face.

Puri got a rude shock. Tara returned alone from the gali. He was too thunderstruck to ask her anything. She sat next to him in the tonga and said, 'What a strange family! There was no one in the living room, so I went into the aangan. Kanak's mother said that Kanak had gone to her sister Kanta's house in Model Town. She telephoned her father in the morning to say that she'd be back home by five o'clock. Her mother doesn't know me, but she still said, "*Balli*, dear, do sit down. Kanak will be back soon. Have something to drink." I said that I'd come again, that my brother was waiting for me outside. As I was going out, Kanchan came down the stairs. She knows me well, but she just said "namaste" as if I was a stranger, and asked whom I had come to see.

'When I told her that I wanted to meet Kanak, she said that her sister was out, and that she didn't know when she'd be back. What strange behaviour!'

Kanak's absence had put Tara in a difficult situation. She thought, 'What if my brother stays with me everywhere I go?' That would be another day lost. How long would she be able to tempt fate? Her mind went blank.

Puri had hired the tonga for a set period, therefore the tongawallah was driving along at a leisurely pace towards Amritdhara. Puri, his eyes closed, was deep in thought. He had made up his mind by the time the tonga reached Jeeva Gali. He asked the driver to stop, and said to Tara, 'You go ahead to Surendra's; I've nothing to say to her. I'll come along after a while to pick you up.'

Tara let out a sigh of relief. 'Achcha,' she said, and walked quickly into the gali.

Puri looked at his wristwatch. It was close to 5 o'clock. He did not want to miss seeing Kanak that day, even if that meant speaking to her in the middle of the street. Kanak's mother had told Tara about her daughter returning around 5 o'clock from Model Town.

On his way back after letting Tara off, Puri did not see Kanta's car parked outside Shaduram's Gali. The road from Kanta's house in Model Town passed through Chauburzi. He'd watch for all the cars, he thought, coming towards Gwal Mandi from Chauburzi through Nisbet Road and Ferozepur Road. He would try to spot Kanta's tan-coloured car. On seeing him, Kanak would ask the car to be stopped. Or, he himself would signal for the car to stop. He did not care what anyone might think; his reputation had already been blackened.

He asked the tonga driver to go towards Chauburzi, and peered into every vehicle, particularly the automobiles, that passed by. He did not see Kanta's car, or Kanak. The car could have gone to Gwal Mandi via Anarkali, he realized, or even along the road that went by Bahawalpur Jail. In desperation he asked the tonga to turn around. He let the tonga go in the Gwal Mandi square, but did not give up on his resolve to meet Kanak and ask her for an explanation.

It was a few minutes to 6 o'clock. If Kanak was not back yet, he thought, she should arrive within the next half-hour. Why not ask Tara to go to her house again? Kanak's mother had invited her back. Let's try once more, whatever the result. As he went towards Kanak's house, Puri saw Kanta's car parked outside the gali. He began to walk briskly towards Jeeva Gali. He wouldn't go up, he decided, but would call from the gali and ask Tara to come down quickly.

After he had called Narendra Singh's name at the house twice from the gali, Surendra's ten-year old sister Mahendra looked out of the window and said, 'Bhaiji's not home.'

Puri said, 'Munni, my sister Tara has come to meet Surendra. Ask her to come down quickly. Tell her that her brother is waiting in the gali.'

Mahendra pulled back from the window. After a few moments, Surendra's mother looked out and said, 'Surendra and Tara are out. Maybe they've gone to the party office to look for Narendra.'

'When?' Puri was not ready for this unexpected news.

'Several other people were here when Tara came. They all left, one after the other.'

Puri felt very annoyed at not having Tara's help at such a critical time. As he walked back towards the square, his anger kept growing: What's Tara doing? She'd come to meet Surendra; so why had she gone to the party office?

Kanta's car was no longer parked outside the gali. They had dropped Kanak off. He thought of another plan. He hired another tonga. He would pick up Tara from the party office and ask her to go to Kanak's house and he himself would wait outside the gali as before. He had put four rupees in his pocket with the idea of going to a restaurant with Kanak and speaking with her at length. All that money was being wasted on hiring tongas, but what could he do?

He asked the tongawallah to go quickly to the party office on McLeod Road. As he got down from the tonga outside the office, he saw Hira Singh and Parmanand coming out of the gate in the boundary wall of the two-storeyed building.

'Did Tara come here with Surendra?' he asked them.

'Surendra is upstairs,' Hira Singh replied. 'Tara left with Asad. You had sent for Asad, hadn't you?'

'What?' Puri said in surprise. He thought for a moment, then had to say, 'Yes, yes, but I got delayed.'

To avoid more questions Puri returned to his tonga and climbed back into it. He was puzzled: 'I sent for Asad? When? Tara is alone with Asad? Is that Surendra's doing? What are these shady goings on! What's Tara up to?'

Maybe he should go inside and ask Surendra, but then he thought, what if she gave the same answer?

Puri was sitting in silence, so the driver asked, 'Where to now, babu?'

Puri's brain finally clicked into gear again. Wherever Tara was, he thought, she'd come back to Surendra's. 'Amrtidhara,' he replied.

The driver turned his horse around, flicked the reins over its back to smarten it up, and called to it, 'Get going, lad! And God go with you!'

The tonga was going past the Venus restaurant when Puri called out to the driver, 'Stop! Stop!'

Tara was coming out of the restaurant, followed by Asad.

Tara was climbing the stairs to Surendra's house when she heard gabbling voices and laughter. Her steps slowed at the realization that a crowd was present. She saw Hamid, Zuber, Sneha, Zubeida, Pradyumna and Surendra; Narendra Singh and Asad were missing. Surendra waved to Tara to call her over to where she was sitting.

Hamid was just saying to Zubeida, 'If you forgot your bag at the party office, you can pick it up tomorrow when you go back.'

'Arrey bhai, my burka is in it,' Zubeida replied anxiously. 'How can I go anywhere inside Bhati Gate without wearing my burka? When we are about to leave, get on your bicycle and fetch it. You're such a sweet boy.'

'Go, yaar, and get it!' Pradyumna slapped Hamid's back to encourage him to listen to Zubeida. He turned to Surendra, 'Meanwhile, dear sister Surendra Kaur-ji, could we please have a cup of tea?'

'This is no time for tea!' Zubeida objected.

'If you ask me, it's quite the right time for tea,' Zuber said.

'It is indeed the time for tea,' said Pradyumna. 'Then we're off to Bagwanpura. Do you imagine our mothers and sisters will be waiting there to serve us tea! In our attempts to bring peace, we may ourselves be left to rest in peace. Who knows? If we're going to die, let's at least have some tea from sister Surendra Kaur before that.'

'You do shoot your mouth off, don't you?' Zubeida said in irritation.

Zuber said, '*Bebe*, sister, you told us yesterday that your aunt's daughters volunteered to go and bring guns and other arms from Bahawalpur. Will those guns be used for halal killing of chickens?'

'That's enough! Stop talking rubbish!' Zubeida told him.

'I'll ask my mother to give you all tea,' Surendra said. 'I have to go with Tara.'

'Wah, Kaurji, what's the fun of having tea when you're gone!' Pradyumna said teasingly.

'Why, do you plan to put me instead of tea leaves in the teapot with boiling water?' Surendra shot back. 'I've got to go.'

Zubeida interrupted her, 'Hai, *sukhkhi-sandi*, may everyone stay happy and healthy. You're all always talking about unhappy things.'

Surendra finished her sentence, 'I have to go to the party office with Tara.' She held Tara's arm and led her to the door.

As they both went downstairs, Surendra said, 'Asad bhai came around at three o'clock. Couldn't stay long. They're all going on a peace mission to Bagwanpura. Asad bhai is looking after the organizing side at the office. He asked you to come over.'

Asad was sitting at a table talking with Hira Singh, Parmanand, Chopra, Mahajan and a few others. He said to Surendra and Tara, 'Wait a second.' He finished whatever he was saying to the others, and said, 'I'll be back in fifteen or twenty minutes. Puri has sent for me.'

He went down with Tara. After they reached McLeod Road, he asked, 'What's the matter? You seem very worried.'

'Yes,' Tara could not say anything further.

'I went to Surendra's yesterday, and also the day before that, hoping that you'd come. I was there several times before that too. Once I passed through your gali, but didn't ask for you at your house, thinking that if Puri was at home, he'd come down alone, and if he wasn't, you still wouldn't be able to come down alone.'

'Yes,' Tara managed to get some words out of her tensed throat. 'Let's sit down somewhere and talk.'

Asad and Tara walked to the Venus restaurant nearby.

Inside the restaurant, Asad raised the curtain of a booth for Tara to go in first, and asked, 'Do you want tea or coffee?'

Tara waved her hand without speaking.

The waiter came. Asad said to him, 'Two cups of coffee.'

'Tell me now, what's bothering you?' he asked, leaning on the table between them.

Tara's desperation and anxiety gathered into her eyes and showed on her face, 'Where do you want me to stay? I've left home.' She had neither the time nor the patience to talk in roundabout terms.

'What?' As he bent forward, Asad's face froze in surprise.

'I can't go back now. They're getting the trousseau ready for my wedding. My tayaji has told me not to sit for my exam, and has forbidden me to leave the house. We were told that Somraj had threatened that if I refused to marry him or continued to go around alone, he'd shame me in front of everyone in the bazaar. Today I somehow managed to get out of the house. Even that won't be possible in future.' She looked into his eyes as she spoke.

Asad bit his lip. He clutched his hair in his right hand, and rested his elbow on the table. He said, after a few moments' thought, 'What did Puri say? He was against your marrying Somraj.'

'He didn't say a word. He doesn't have the guts any more. Ever since he lost his job, he's unable to stand up to anybody. He's even helping to get the trousseau together for me. He's changed. He's worried about his own problems.'

'What do you mean?'

'He has no job. And Kanak's family has probably told her not to meet him. He's very frustrated.'

'All the more reason for him to help.'

'No, no,' Tara stopped him. 'He's only concerned with himself. He takes no stand when it comes to me. He doesn't have the confidence that he had before.'

Asad thought for some time, his hand holding his hair. The waiter placed the coffee cups on the table.

Asad took a deep breath, 'Tara, what are we to do now?' He thought for some moments more before continuing, 'Where could I put you up at such short notice? It'll cause a storm. You know about Pradyumna and Zubeida. The party has refused to give them approval to marry for the time being. They've been told to cool off for some time. At this time I can't bring up any questions of us. I can't do anything without the party's permission. It's against the rules and, in the present situation, against common sense.'

'But what am I to do? There's no other way out for me.' Tara looked into his eyes. 'Didn't you tell me?'

'I did, and I'm saying it again now.' He leaned closer to her, and said, 'But I'll have to get the party's permission. Just look at the situation in the city. All our efforts have gone for nothing after that outrage at the workshops. Where would you be able to live, away from home?'

'Outside Lahore, in some other city?'

'Who would give me permission to leave Lahore at this time? How can I even ask for permission. How did you reach the party office?'

'I went to Surendra's place with my brother.'

'That was dangerous! Puri would ask Surendra where you went? The party would be involved for no reason.'

'The party is everything to you! Don't I mean anything at all?' Tara's tears rolled down her face and fell into her coffee cup.

'Listen, *jaan!*' Asad said tenderly. 'Don't be so down-hearted. We have to think about the times and our situation. You are mine and I am yours, but I have to be loyal to the party also. We have to get over this problem. We have to wait until the time is ripe. Have some patience. Let things cool down a bit. We'll find a way.'

'I may not live that long,' Tara lowered her eyes.

'Don't say that. We're all facing very tough times. We all have a duty to defuse the tension, or none of us may come out of this alive.'

'It's not possible for me to go on living now.' She dried her tear-filled eyes with a handkerchief crumpled in her hand.

'I know you're in a terrible situation, but be brave. Weren't you brave enough to want to leave home? You do have courage. *Meri* jaan, use that courage now to face your family, to bear with them a bit longer.'

'I wouldn't have asked for your help at this time if I could do that.'

'You're right. We all know that in our society a woman's life is nothing but pain and tears. We must be ready to break those chains, even at the cost of our lives. But at this time, we must think first of our people and our nation, before dealing with our individual emotional problems. We're all in danger. We have to face this collective problem first, and only then our individual problems.'

'How long will that take?' Tara let out a deep sigh as she asked the question.

'How can I say, jaan?' He said tenderly in Punjabi. 'If I could help you, I'd do so right now. I wish we didn't have to part even for a moment, but we can't ward off the threats and the danger just by wishing them away. It might take any length of time, four, six months, a whole year. I hope not, but it may take my whole lifetime.'

Tara dropped her head in disappointment.

Asad continued in a soothing tone, 'Trust me, my love, you're with me, every breath I take. It's our misfortune, nothing more, that we're in this jam. Ninety people have lost their lives since last night. What can I say about that idiot Somraj! Even your parents had to create a problem for you at this very moment. I went to visit the family of a young man killed in the bomb explosion at the workshops. He'd got married only last month. His wife's hands still carried the henna dye from the time of her wedding. I can still see his mother and his new bride weeping and beating their chests in mourning. Even if it means having a heart of stone, my love, there's no way out for us but to control our feelings.'

Tara listened in silence, her head bowed.

'What do you say?' Asad asked.

'For me, there's no other way out but to kill myself,' she replied, still looking down.

'Don't say that, my love,' Asad said. 'Your killing yourself will achieve nothing. Otherwise I would have killed myself first, or even died with you. At this time it might backfire. It might put other people's lives in danger.

'We believe,' he said in a grave voice, 'that we're fighting for justice and the right to exist. To sacrifice your life in the cause of justice might be noble, but why let yourself be a sacrificial victim on the altar of injustice? We must fight for justice always. If death comes, let it be in the fight for justice, not in surrender to injustice.'

Tara remained silent.

'What do you say?'

'I have nothing to say about anything.' She swallowed her tears and again wiped her eyes. 'Let's go,' she said.

'All right,' Asad said. 'We can't stay here, anyway. The others are waiting for me. But give me your promise that that you'll help me and yourself too, by being patient and strong in this trying time.'

'Don't ask me for anything.'

'Why do you say that, my love? Listen, we all feel that we have to stand up for what is just and right. I'm sure Puri would help us in finding a way out if he was told about it.'

'I don't know.' Her eyes again brimmed with tears. She bit her lip in an effort to control herself, and said, 'I've told you everything about my family and my neighbours. They all think that it's their duty and obligation to send me off to be sacrificed.'

Asad said after some thought, his head bowed, 'Tara, don't think of me as a weak person. I promise you that I'll fight to the end to be with you, and I'll face whatever may come my way to make you mine. I have faith in you that you too will somehow find the courage to face up to things.'

Tara remained silent, her head down.

Looking intently at her, Asad said in English, 'I have faith that you'll be brave enough to overcome this problem.'

Tara shook her head in a firm denial.

Asad took a deep breath, and said, 'Why don't you let me speak to Puri? He can't just go on ignoring this injustice to you.'

'I don't have much hope. I kept quiet at first because he assured me of his support. Now he's changed. I told you that he even helped in the preparations for the wedding. He surely doesn't mind using me as a messenger to Kanak. Something's not quite right between them, I think.'

'Has she changed her mind, or is it her family that's creating some problem? They didn't seem to be the interfering type.'

'Who knows?'

'Anyway, what's wrong with speaking to Puri?'

'I can't stay at home if he refuses to help.'

'Does he suspect anything between us?' Asad asked in English.

'I'm not sure.'

'Can he refuse to help?'

'Yes.'

'Couldn't I just talk about the injustice done to some girl or other, maybe to someone's sister?'

'I've no hopes, but I do have some misgivings about him.' She shook her head diffidently as she spoke. 'Let's go,' she said under her breath, and pushed her chair back to get up.

'Have some coffee before you leave,' Asad pushed aside her cup and slid his untouched cup before her.

Tara shook her head in refusal.

'Just one sip,' he insisted.

She again shook her head.

Asad remained quiet for a few seconds, and then picked up her cup in which tears had mixed with the coffee. He said looking at her, 'Tara, I swear that I shall never forget your tear-filled eyes. I will wait for that day when I will see your eyes smiling, and the hope will give me the courage to wipe the tears from the eyes of innocent, suffering people everywhere.' He put the cup to his lips.

'What are you doing?' Tara finally broke her silence. Asad drained the cup, and put it back in its saucer. He said, 'Tara, trust me. Try and find a way for us to meet. I'll try too.'

Tara stood up. Asad went up to her, and put his arm around her shoulders.

Tara said haltingly, 'If that's possible, if I'm alive ...I can't promise.'

Tears were again welling up in her eyes, but she bit her lip to hold them back and to control herself. She went out of the booth ahead of Asad.

Asad walked to the cashier to pay for the coffee. Tara began slowly walking towards the door. Asad paid up, then reached the exit by taking long steps to reach before Tara, and opened the door for her. As they reached the pavement, Asad and Tara saw Puri in a tonga going along the road. Puri had already seen them. The tonga came to a halt. Puri's eyes were still on them. His face was flushed with anger.

Tara suppressed a chill creeping up her spine. Asad too was at a loss, but called out 'Hello!' and walked towards Puri. Tara, her head bowed, followed him.

Puri got down from the tonga. He did not smile or reply to Asad's greeting. In spite of Puri's cold, hard stare, Asad asked, 'Where are you coming from?'

Puri turned his eyes away without answering him.

Asad felt insulted, but tried to lighten the awkwardness of the situation. He glanced at Tara, and said, 'We came here for a cup of coffee.'

Tara, visibly shaken and nervous, was still looking down. Asad said in English, 'Tara's very upset. We were talking about her problem.'

Puri had been able to control his anger and surprise to some extent. He replied sarcastically in English, 'Is that so? She's my sister, or so I thought, but I see that you know her better than I do.'

That riled Asad, but he said in a conciliatory tone, 'I don't mean to be rude, but it's not all that unusual for someone other than a brother to understand the problems of a sister.'

'Oh really? I'll try my hardest to understand her problems.' Puri said curtly, and again looked away.

Asad swallowed the insult and said, 'If you're in a hurry now, maybe we can meet some other time and talk about this.'

Puri said, without looking at him, 'Thank you.'

'Goodbye,' Asad said, ignoring Puri's rudeness. He could not linger around further and began walking towards the party office.

Tara had been standing in silence. Puri ordered her, 'Get into the tonga.'

When the tonga had gone only a short distance, Puri—still smouldering from the encounter— spoke in English so that the tongawallah would not understand, 'What game are you playing?'

'What do you mean by "game"?' Tara protested in English. Her head was still bowed.

'You'd come to meet Surendra.'

'I did go to the party office with Surendra.'

'There's no doubt whom you'd really come to meet.'

Tara had nothing more to lose, and therefore refused to accept his accusation tamely. She said, 'You too have meetings with somebody. Don't I know?'

'That's my own business. What is that to you?' Puri's tone became harder.

'This too is my own business.' She did not hold back.

Puri squirmed with anger, 'You used me as an excuse to get out of the house. And you came with me as escort, remember!'

'Didn't you send me to Kanak's for the same reason?'

'Didn't you first ask to go to Kanak's yourself?'

'I didn't ask you today.'

'But you did in the past.' There was no conviction in his reply, but he still said that to justify himself.

Tara kept quiet. Puri too remained silent, seething with indignation. Tara felt she was being carried back to her home against her will just like an animal being dragged away for sacrifice. She had but one wish, that at the very moment she could somehow kill herself, that she could jump in front of a passing motorcar and die, but each clop from the horse's hooves was carrying her back nearer home.

Finding it hard to contain his anger, Puri said, 'I don't want to be held responsible for your behaviour in future.'

'That suits me just fine,' Tara shot back curtly. Infuriated with each other, they both sat without saying another word.

The tonga went past the road leading to the Gwal Mandi. How could Puri ask Tara to go to Kanak's house in the present situation? Tara was being deliberately malicious and unkind, he thought. She was going back on her word and letting him down, and he could do nothing about it.

In the evening, hired carriages were not allowed to enter Shahalami Gate because of the dense crowds in the bazaar. Puri and Tara had to get down from the tonga outside the gate. They walked side by side; Puri silently fuming at the wrongdoer he had unmasked, Tara silent with the guilt of having been caught red-handed.

Babu Govindram was smoking a small hookah on the chabutara below his house. Masterji was talking with him. Puri and Tara, still in silence, climbed the stairs one behind the other.

In the daylight that still remained, Bhagwanti, with the help of Pushpa, was sewing some embroidered *gota* lace on Tara's trousseau. Usha was cooking the evening meal in the kitchen. Bhagwanti said to Puri, 'You've both been out for a long time.'

Puri grunted in reply, picked up his lungi and went towards the veranda to change. Tara looked into the room, and went straight to the roof.

Most houses in Punjab had rooftop latrines, and it was not unusual for someone returning home to go straight to the roof. Tara pulled out a charpoy and lay down in the fresh air. She was too disturbed to sit or talk with anybody. A suicidal person does not like to be with other people. After what had transpired between her and Puri, what else could she wish for but death?

Puri had taken off his shoes and was changing his clothes. Pushpa called from inside the room, 'Say, bhai, where did you take your sister for your outing? You might invite us to go along with you from time to time.'

'What outing? We just went out for a while.' He replied, folding his trousers carefully to keep the creases sharp.

'I just thought I'd ask.' Pushpa went on, 'You've been getting the dowry together to present to your sister. Tell me, how far off is the day when you yourself would be ready to receive one?' Her voice rang with teasing banter, inviting a response.

'Yes.' Puri's tone showed that he was in no mood for jokes.

He changed back into his street clothes, put his shoes on and called out to his mother, 'I'll be back soon,' and went downstairs.

Puri, already quite distressed by Kanak's strange behaviour, was even more troubled by Tara's actions and her unrepentant attitude. That he could not share his pain with anybody rankled with particular intensity. He wanted to deal with Tara's improper and shameless behaviour without telling his parents. It was not easy for him to hide his concern and frustration from the others in the family.

Pushpa was threading her needle. Snipping the thread from the spool with her teeth, she asked, 'Where's Tara—still on the roof?'

As birds flying in the sky instinctively know about the approach of rain and storm, a mother too can feel the moods and whims of the children she has known and cared for since their birth.

'They must have quarrelled, what else!' Bhagwanti replied. 'Both may seem to have become adults, but in temperaments they're still children.'

'Hai, why would they quarrel?' Pushpa wanted to know.

'Oh, perhaps the brother said, "Let's go this way," and the sister replied, "No, let's take the other way." That's enough ground for a falling-out.'

'I've never seen them quarrel.'

'Wah, they quarrelled so badly when they were small that I'd lose all patience with them. He would beat her without reason, and she's just as strong-willed. She'd bite him and swear at him like mad. They may seem mature and highly educated now, but their natures haven't changed. Tara is the secretive type; she doesn't say much, but she doesn't forget things and nurses her grudges for a long time...'

After he passed out of high school and went on to college, Puri stopped hitting Tara, even when he was very angry with her. Usha had turned eleven, and she was there if he wanted to slap someone. When Puri was sent to prison, Tara regarded his courage and patriotism as reflecting credit on the family. Whenever she sent the family letter to him in prison, she addressed him as 'Respected Bhaiji' or 'Honoured Bhai'. When he came back from prison, instead of calling him 'Jaddi' as before, she began to use 'bhai' or 'bhaiji' to address him. The squabbles, playful scuffles and horseplay of the past were now happy memories. They agreed on most things. Brother and sister formed a united front against the narrow-minded and conservative outlook of their family and of the people of the gali. Tara respected him for what she thought to be the exceptional brilliance of her brother.

She came downstairs from the roof after half an hour. Her mother gave her one look and said, 'Come here.'

Tara was removing clothes to change into from the slung rope that was their collective wardrobe. She asked, 'What for?'

'Come here, I said. How're you feeling?' She held out a hand to touch Tara.

'I'm all right. I just have a headache.' Tara went to her and let her mother touch her arm.

'See, she has fever!' Her mother raised her eyebrows. 'Pushpa, feel her arm and tell me.'

Pushpa agreed with Bhagwanti after feeling Tara's arm, 'Yes, she's running a fever.'

'She must have been wandering around in the sun. Her brother is just as thoughtless. He should remember that girls can't gad about all over the place like boys.' Bhagwanti said. 'Go to the veranda and lie down on the charpoy. Your face is so pale. Why did you go out in the first place?' A thought occurred to her, and she said, 'If you couldn't walk, you should've asked your brother to hire a tonga.'

Tara did not feel like explaining. She changed her clothes, tied her dupatta tightly around her head, and lay down. 'It's good if I have a fever,' she thought, 'it saves me the bother of answering every silly question.'

Puri returned home around eight. The curfew was to begin at 8 o'clock. As she gave him dinner, his mother said, 'Tara has a fever. The two of you should take care not to be out and about so much, away from home. You're not kids any more.'

Puri thought, 'I know what's behind her so-called fever.' To answer her accusation, he said to his mother, 'She's the one who insisted on going out. And most of the time she stayed at her friend's house, and hardly went anywhere else.'

As on every other night, Puri was working on the history textbook on the roof in the light of a table lamp. He had shaded the lamp in such a way that its light would not disturb the others sleeping on the roof. His mind was so uneasy after the day's events that his eyes would read a paragraph of text in English, but his brain would not register a single word. When he tried to write, the pen clung to his hand without touching the paper.

'It's not good for you to sleep in the open if you have a fever! Why don't you listen to me?' He heard his mother say.

He shaded his eyes from the light and saw that Tara had come up to the roof and was lying on a charpoy. Tara answered her mother, 'Must you always make a mountain out of a molehill? I have hardly any fever. I just can't breathe in that stifling heat downstairs. I'll feel better up here.'

'Achcha, cover yourself with a thick sheet. I'll bring you one.'

Puri's lips tightened in disapproval. 'What does she want to achieve by this display?' he wondered. 'Women! So much deception and slyness behind that façade of frailty! I've just seen two examples. How Kanak first pretended to give her heart to me, then got me to accept money doled out by her father so that she could put me down. She is acting as if Model Town is as far from Gwal Mandi as some foreign country. Makes her father dance

to her tune, and now she tries the same thing with me. Deception, thy name
is woman! And Tara! What's she up to, in her sly way, behind her pretended
modesty and innocence, and her opposition to marriage? Couldn't find
anybody but a Muslim to get entangled with! Wants to blacken the family
name! What cheek she showed to me! Such insulting behaviour! I'll make
sure that she gets rid of that attitude.'

Once again, Puri could not concentrate on his work the next morning.
All his problems seemed to be closing in on him. Kanak had made him
feel that he was not worthy of her love because she belonged to a higher
social class, and Tara was sullying his and his family's honour. He had no
money, no social standing, not even a job; the only thing he could cling to
was his reputation. He wanted to keep it intact, and Tara was bent upon
dirtying it. A man is less concerned about his own philandering becoming
public knowledge as about the disclosure of the misbehaviours of his
womenfolk—mother, sister or wife. Kanak had hurt him and slipped out
of his reach. His impotent rage against Kanak could only be vented upon
Tara. His growing ill humour was clouding his mind.

Through that state of fogginess and confusion, the words that Asad
had used shone like a flash of lightning, 'Someone other than a brother
might understand the problems of a sister.' What does Asad claim to be, a
husband or a lover? The utter gall of the man! He's challenged me! I must
do something immediately ...' He put his pen down and pressed his hands
to his temples.

In summer, the schools began at 6 a.m. Masterji, Usha and Hari were
at school. Puri's unquiet mind could not focus on his work, and that made
the heat below the corrugated tin roof seem all the more unbearable. The
rivulets of perspiration running down his back, had not bothered him
before, as he worked under the roof barsati, but they felt unbearable today.
He stopped working at 9 o'clock and went downstairs. He got his towel
and an *angauccha* to wrap around his waist while having his wash, and was
going to the common faucet on the ground floor aangan when his mother
called out to him for his help, 'Just look at the girl! How much more
will she torment me! Had nothing to eat last night. I bought this *beedana*
and *banafsha* sherbet from the bazaar especially for her. Having an empty
stomach in this heat will surely make her sick. What'll I do then? But she
refuses to touch it!'

Puri turned around and saw Tara lying on a charpoy in the veranda. Her mother was standing near the head of the charpoy with a glass in her hand. He went to the veranda. He put both his hands on his hips to give himself an impressive posture, and called out in a commanding tone, 'Why won't you drink this?'

Tara got up without saying a word. She took the glass from her mother and drained it in a single draught. She put the glass on the floor, lay back down on the charpoy, and covered her face with her dupatta.

His mother was not pleased at his roughness. She said softly, 'She's not well. Don't speak so harshly to someone who's sick.'

She picked up the glass and went away. Puri stood in angry silence next to the charpoy. After a few moments he said to Tara in English, 'I know you're not asleep. There's something I want to talk to you about.'

Tara rose and sat hunched up at the foot of the charpoy. Puri sat on its edge, resting his weight on his hands. Keeping his voice down, he again asked in a firm tone, 'What's the idea of this silent treatment?'

'It's not like that,' Tara replied, her head bent.

'That's how I see it. What problem were you talking over with Asad?'

'No problem.'

Puri's anger surged up again at this obvious lie, but he suppressed it, so as to be able to pry out her secret, 'Was he telling a lie? He said in front of you that you were upset. What did you tell him?'

Tara gave no answer.

'You can't just keep mum.' He chided her. 'You went out with me. I have to know what happened because the members of this family, and I too, have a certain responsibility towards you. You must have told him something—must have said what was bothering you.'

Tara did not want to talk about the incident. She said, 'Nothing in particular.'

Puri thought for a moment how to rephrase his question in order to trap Tara, and asked in a level tone, 'It's my duty and the family's too, to help you solve your problem. You need money? Is something wrong with you, physically?'

Tara shook her head in denial.

'What's so secret that you can tell it to him, but not to me?' He pressed on.

Tara, caught in his web, had to own up, 'You know everything.'

Puri made a show of thinking, and said, 'I don't know what you mean. Explain yourself.'

Enraged by his persistent needling, she replied, 'It's easy for you to say that you can't remember. Didn't you say that this match was no good for me, that we should let the engagement be broken? That you didn't have a good opinion of Somraj? And now you're asking Ma how you can help in preparing the trousseau. Why would you want to remember what you'd said earlier?'

When they were young, Tara had responded to Puri's punches and blows by biting him and by cursing him that he might die and leave his wife a widow. When she could not fight back physically, she would scream and cry so that their mother would intervene. In the previous four or five years she had become so shy and reserved that people seldom heard her complain. Her brother often talked proudly of the sharpness of her mind and her good manners. Now this same brother was trying to entangle her in the web of his questions, and she had fought back by calling him a coward and a liar! Puri was alarmed by her reaction.

To counter the bitter truth she had blurted out in anger and to deny the charge of not carrying out his duty towards her, he took a few moments to collect himself, and said, 'You're accusing me of not keeping my word. How could I object after seeing you willingly help them in getting together your trousseau?'

Staring into her brother's eyes, Tara let out a deep breath of despair, as if life itself would go out of her body with that breath. Stunned into silence, she just looked at him in disbelief. Her eyes said, how could you twist the fact of my helplessness?

Puri could not resist a touch of *Schadenfreude*, 'My opinion of that man Somraj is a secondary consideration. If you didn't want to get engaged, you should have refused before they formalized it.'

'Didn't I oppose it?' Tears filled her eyes as her body shook in anger.

To overcome her attempt to fight back, Puri said in a distracted way, 'I don't know. I was in prison at the time. Don't hold me responsible. They couldn't push me into an engagement even with an offer of a dowry worth thirty or thirty-five thousand rupees. If you had refused to go along, the engagement would never have taken place.'

'I would have, if you hadn't misled me into thinking that you too were against this marriage.'

'Did you expect me to go on objecting even when I could see you helping with your trousseau?' Puri asked.

Tara, her eyes brimming with tears, gave him a look of surprise and incredulity, but Puri was not moved. He felt he had recognized the devious, licentious nature of woman. He was now punishing one woman for sullying his own and his family's honour, and, at the same time, ridding himself of the guilt of not protesting the injustice being done to her. He pressed on, 'Your refusal of this marriage is a complete deception after you first accepted the arrangement, and made the family take out the loan that we could ill afford. And to top it all, you blame me for not supporting you. You just wanted to play a game, you want flirtation, not marriage. Does that come naturally to a woman?'

Tara joined her hands to beg him to stop, 'Forgive me. I've nothing to say. Don't mind me. Whatever becomes of me, just let it happen.'

Puri had wrestled the adversary that had dared to defy him to the ground, but his opponent was resisting him by answering him back. He hit again, 'I still want to know, what was the purpose of discussing this problem with that fellow? What has he to do with this? What can he do about it? Have you no concern for the family honour?'

In self-defence, Tara retreated behind a wall of silence.

Puri said, 'I want an answer to my question.'

Tara gave none.

He felt in Tara's silence an insulting defiance and refusal to accept his authority. With his pride stung at one time by two women, the desire to take revenge was raging like a fire in his mind. He had rendered his adversary helpless and mute. Now he wanted to draw blood from the defeated opponent and to hear the cries for mercy, to slash with the sword of vengeance. He chose his words carefully before going on, 'I know the truth even if you don't tell me. I'm not lacking in imagination. You both had on your faces an expression of being caught red-handed. I know that you both were eloping.'

Tara jerked round and bashed her head on the corner post of the charpoy, and raised her head to bash it again.

Puri put his arm around her to pull her back, and threw her on the charpoy. She gave a slight moan and lay motionless.

'What's happened? What's happened?' Bhagwanti cried, as she came running from the kitchen. Puri examined Tara's face as she lay unconscious. Blood trickled from a gash on her forehead.

His mother asked with alarm in her voice, 'What's happened? Did she fall? Hai, my daughter!' She began to weep seeing the blood.

Puri shouted at her, 'Stop your howling! I'll explain what happened. First bring some water in a cup and a piece of clean cloth. The wound isn't serious.'

His mother tore a strip from an old garment, and carried it in, along with some water in a cup. Then she sat on the floor beside the charpoy and began to cry. Puri again spoke to her sharply, 'What is the use of crying? I told you it's only a scratch.'

Puri washed Tara's forehead with a wet rag, then bandaged her forehead with it. Not much blood was to be seen on her forehead; most of it had seeped into her hair.

Tara was still unconscious. Ratan's mother came over when she heard Bhagwanti cry, and asked with concern, 'What's happened?'

Puri replied, 'She was talking with me. Said she was going to the roof for a minute. Fell in a faint as she stood up. Must have passed out.'

'Hai, why didn't you grab her? Don't you know she hasn't eaten anything since yesterday evening? Had a fever too. Anybody can faint in this heat if they haven't had anything to eat. You boys have no feeling for anybody.' His mother shed tears as she gently stroked Tara's hands and feet.

'I tried grabbing her as she fell. How could I know that she'd just collapse? I'll ask the doctor to put some ointment on her wound when he returns home. It'll heal in a couple of days.'

'I hope it doesn't leave a scar.' His mother was worried about her daughter's looks, even in her grief.

As Tara came round, her mother asked her tenderly, 'Hai, did you pass out? Why didn't you call me if you'd no strength to go up to the roof? Come on, hold on to me, I'll take you upstairs.'

Tara realized that she was supposed to have got up from the charpoy to go to the roof, but had passed out and fallen, injuring her forehead. She accepted the story as true.

What could she say? She was not worried about a scar on her forehead, but the thought of why she had to cut open her forehead sickened her. What else could she have done to silence her brother as he levelled those accusations? Even if his accusations were true, what else could she, a woman, do to save face? He, of course, wasn't concerned with losing face when he sent a message through her to another woman, Kanak, under the pretence of a casual visit. 'His, and the family's honour, would continue to hang in the balance unless I was sacrificed to save it. That's what he meant by his big talk of fighting for truth, justice and his country, and for the sake of Hindu–Muslim unity! But who cares how I feel or what I want? And if I do say what I want, where could I go? Men can spend the night roaming the streets, or on a bench in a park ... And how would I face anyone with this telltale scar on my face showing that I was trying to escape an injustice?'

Meladei had the medicinal herb *shilajit* in her home for such emergencies. A tiny amount of it was given to Tara in a cupful of warm milk mixed with some ghee.

Puri too was shaken by Tara's gashing wound. He felt a pang of remorse at being cruel to her. He was at a loss what to do next. Kanak's face, streaked with tears and showing remorse, swam before his eyes. He went down to the aangan to take a bath. As he lay down after having his meal, thoughts of the previous evening returned to his mind: Such hypocrisy! To disarm and put down others with the threat of harming oneself! What a weird, conceited way of arguing! Doesn't it amount to suppressing truth and justice by accusing others of violence? ... What a cunning use of satyagraha!

Pushpa, Rampyari, Kartaro and other gali women had come to ask after Tara, who just lay there without saying anything. Bhagwanti would recount for her visitors how her daughter had collapsed after she had a fainting fit. They were all sorry to see her hurt, but even more concerned because it might leave a scar on her forehead. 'Such a pretty forehead,' they said, 'it's a pity that she'll have a scar, and that too just before her wedding! Hope her in-laws don't hear about this! Who can know God's will?'

Bhagwanti would reply, 'He does what He thinks best. Bahin, who can go against His will?'

Puri called the doctor to come over after he returned home. Prabhu Dayal removed the bandage to examine the wound, and advised, 'Better to have one stitch on the cut. Otherwise it'll take longer to heal. The wound is less likely to leave a scar if it's stitched properly.'

Tara said indifferently, 'No need for a stitch, it'll heal by itself. Stitches will hurt.' But she had to yield before the wishes of others. Bhagwanti, Usha or Haridev would wave a hand-held fan over her as she rested. The sewing work for her trousseau was put aside for a day or two.

The wedding of Ghasita Ram's daughter Dhanno was only three weeks away. The gali women took turns in helping Dhanno's mother, Basanti, and Tara's mother. Basanti had her hands full with preparing Dhanno's trousseau, as well as the cleaning and grinding of the spices for the wedding feast.

Tara moved from her charpoy next day to a chatai on the floor. A nauseating smell of antiseptic came from the bandage on her forehead. If anyone came and spoke to her, she'd just say, 'It hurts when I talk.'

In the afternoon, Basanti came to invite Bhagwanti and other women of the gali. 'Dhanno's wedding is on the fifteenth of jyeshtha month,' she said. 'We'll have a musical party and singing today. Bahin, send your daughters early so that they can join in the singing. We'll wait for all of you.'

Bhagwanti offered her congratulations and said, 'Why wouldn't we come? We will, of course. Dhanno's like my daughter. You know Tara's hurt her head. She probably won't be able to come today.'

Usha held Basanti's hand and said, 'Auntie, I'll play the dholak. I've learned how. It was I who played it at the singing party when Sheelo bahin's family held the celebration for the birth of her son.'

Basanti placed her finger on her cheek in wonder as she replied, 'Really, Usha! Let's go to Uchchi Gali this evening. I must invite Sheelo and her mother too. The gathering won't be the same without Sheelo.'

On the occasion of Tara's engagement, Sheelo had sung all night in Bhola Pandhe's Gali. Not only was she fond of singing, she had a good voice too. She liked to sing long, sad songs with a depth of feeling that touched everybody. Few girls, or even women, knew as many songs as she did.

Puri tried to lose himself in his work. It was the only way for him to save himself from sinking into despair. He had never held a sum as large as 550 rupees in his hand. He had not been able to do any work the previous evening, nor the day before, and was trying to make up for that loss by working late, even after sunset.

'Hey brother Jaddi! Did you hear of this new development?' Tikaram called from the gali below.

As she lay in the veranda, Tara was alarmed by Tikaram's call. Everything, she felt, was aimed at harming her and ruining her life. She pricked her ears to know what this new development was. Tikaram's voice came again, 'Look at this newspaper special. The Congress has agreed to the formation of Pakistan!'

Puri was always called to join in whenever the gali people discussed a newspaper report or any other political question.

As Puri went downstairs, Ratan called out in an angry voice that dripped sarcasm, 'Bhappaji, you used to say that Hindu–Muslim unity would block attempts to create Pakistan. Now the Congress too has yielded to the demand for Pakistan. This is what happens when you talk of conciliation!'

Tikaram began to read aloud from the newspaper's special edition.

With the increase in cases of arson in the city, the workload at the insurance firm where Tikaram worked had also increased. He returned late from his office every evening. He had bought the special editions of *Pairokaar* and *Siasat* on his way home. He was reading so loudly from both the newspapers that even Tara could hear him from where she lay.

Both newspapers had reported that the Congress had accepted in principle the partition of the country, but was not willing to let the whole of Punjab and Bengal be included into Pakistan. Only the Muslim-majority areas of West Punjab and East Bengal could be given to Pakistan. Neither could any part of the United Provinces become a part of Pakistan, nor any other province where Hindus formed the majority of the total population.

Siasat also carried a statement by Quaid-e-Azam Jinnah, on behalf of the Muslim League, opposing the splitting up of Punjab and Bengal and demanding a corridor connecting the two provinces as an additional territorial claim for Pakistan.

Puri attempted an explanation, 'The formation of Pakistan would probably mean a Muslim League government in Punjab. Whoever forms the ministry, Hindus and Muslims will have to live side by side in the galis and districts of Punjab. What does it matter to us whose ministry it is? Our concern should be about maintaining good relations with our Muslim neighbours.'

Tara could hear her brother talk from where she lay in the veranda. She thought in disgust: 'What a hypocrite! Just listen to him talk of relations with Muslims! People like Ratan are at least more honest; they don't pretend to be friends with those they regard as enemies. I'd rather be dead than have anything to do with such a devious, poisonous person. I must do something ...' She felt as if she had moved another step closer to death.

Tara's ears again picked up the thread of conversation from the gali. Masterji was back from his tutoring job. Vijay had brought Babu Govindram his portable hookah as he relaxed on the chabutara. A discussion had begun as to whether Lahore would remain in India or go to Pakistan? ... What if the Muslims were 51 per cent of the population in the city? The Hindus owned over 80 per cent of the real estate.

'That's the reason why the Muslims are afraid of the Hindus,' Puri said.

'Muslims fear Hindus?' Govindram objected. 'The Hindus didn't get hold of so much by stealing it from the Muslims!'

'If they didn't steal, did the Almighty send them the money to buy the property of others?' Khushal Singh asked. 'Didn't we all see how Ghasita Ram got hold of two houses from those Muslim tinsmiths, the *kalaigeers*, in their gali in next to no time.'

'He bought them, and didn't grab them by threatening with a lathi. He paid them handfuls of cash,' Dewanchand explained.

'Chachaji, money can sometimes hit harder than a lathi,' Puri said quietly.

'Wah, what an apt remark Jaddi's made!' Khushal Singh said. 'It shows when someone's had an education.'

They were still discussing the news reports when Doctor Prabhu Dayal returned home around 8 p.m. 'Did you read the news?' Babu Govindram asked him without removing the mouthpiece of hookah from his lips.

It was obvious from his silence and the glum look on his face that the doctor had indeed seen the newspapers. They all knew that the doctor's ancestral home was in the Sargodha district, west of Lahore. Puri addressed him on behalf of all those sitting on the chabutara, 'Doctor sahib, didn't Gandhiji assert that Pakistan would be created over his dead body? You and Dr Radhey Behari were quite sure that the British would not accept the League's demand for Pakistan. What happened?' Puri was attempting to restore his image by redirecting the remark Ratan had earlier aimed at him.

'Why blame Gandhiji?' Prabhu Dayal answered, but with less than the usual conviction in his voice. 'This was decided by Pandit Nehru, Sardar Patel and the Congress Working Committee. Gandhiji had nothing to do with the decision. He had made it absolutely clear that Nehru and Patel were responsible for running the government. They may have had to take into account the advice of so many people whom I don't know about. I don't wish, in my ignorance and naïvety, to pass any judgement on their actions. How can Gandhiji be held responsible if it was Nehru and Patel's decision?'

'Remaining true to your principles must also mean something,' Ratan contradicted him in a loud voice. 'If the partition of the country was against the Congress's stated principles, how could the Congress justify partition, even if Patel and Nehru approved it? Nehru and Patel themselves were against the partition of the country until just a few days ago.'

Puri supported Ratan, 'What can one say of Nehru and Patel? They're like weathervanes. While in Ahmedabad Jail in 1945, they claimed that the Quit India movement of 1942 was against the policy of the Congress. After they formed the ministry in 1946, they blatantly took credit for the same 1942 movement.'

The doctor did not dwell upon the loss of his ancestral home, 'The real issue is the independence of the country and its future. What option did Nehru and Patel have? Refuse to accept the partition of the country and let it go to the dogs? It's the British who are quietly encouraging the League to make absurd demands. Let's first deal with the British, and then we'll take care of the League too. In the game of politics, bhai, one has to make all sorts of compromises.'

'And that's the true meaning of Gandhiji's pet principles of truth and non-violence?' Ratan asked sarcastically.

Khushal Singh liked Ratan's crack at the Congress. 'Ratan is right! We too would like to know the true meaning of that kind of truth and non-violence! Jinnah is more honest by comparison. He tells you the facts face-to-face, after giving you a slap. Only Master Tara Singh can answer Jinnah.'

Ignoring these comments, the doctor said to Puri, 'Let's go to Dr Radhey Behari and find out how all this happened?'

Puri replied, 'Am I to go to Dr Saheb's? He's probably still annoyed with me after that incident at *Pairokaar*. But if he and others had been able to form a Congress–League coalition ministry, all this surely could've been avoided.'

'How could that be?' the doctor asked. 'Jinnah refused point blank. An interim ministry barely works. You know that. Jinnah's condition for his support was that the ministry should have only League members. But you come along with me. Why are you hesitant? You don't owe him anything. Let's see what he says to you now. I'm afraid that we may have let Lahore slip through our fingers. Mark my words.'

Bhagwanti was in her kitchen. She came to the window and called Puri, 'Kakaji, have your dinner before you go. We have to go to Basanti's for a while. It's the first day of the singing party at her place.'

Puri quickly finished his dinner and went to Dr Radhey Behari's house with Prabhu Dayal. Bhagwanti cleaned up the kitchen, and as she and Usha were leaving for Basanti's place, she called out to Pushpa, 'Come Pushpa, let's spend some time at Basanti's.'

Pushpa looked out of her window and replied, 'Bahinji, give my excuses to Basanti bahin. My daughter's not well; she keeps waking up and cries loudly. Can't leave her in the care of my servant boy. It wouldn't be proper to take her with me, either.'

Bhagwanti said in agreement, 'No, no. You stay with your baby. You can go tomorrow.' She and Usha left.

Masterji and Babu Govindram were resting on charpoys upstairs and talking in the open air. The city had had no curfew for the past two days. Ratan too was out somewhere. Hari and Vijay were playing with other children under the street light in the gali.

Tara was alone in the house. She lay on a chatai, preoccupied with her never-ending worries. She thought about her meeting with Asad at the Venus restaurant, and her brother's reproaches afterwards. The sound of gali women singing the auspicious *suhag* song floated up from the direction of Ghasita Ram's house:

Jayeen jayeen ve bavala us nagari ...

Tara got up and called out from her window in the direction of Pushpa's house, 'Pushpa bahinji! Pushpa bahin!'

'Is it you, Tara?' came the reply. 'How're you feeling?'

'I'm all right. Are the doors to your house locked?'

'No, the chain is not on. My servant boy has gone out. You want to come over? Will you be able to climb the stairs alone? Come along.'

When Tara reached her place, Pushpa said, 'Come in. Are you well?'

'I want to borrow some kerosene,' Tara showed her the empty bottle. Pushpa had a Primus stove in her kitchen. She preferred using it to lighting a fire, and kept a can of kerosene in storage. Bhagwanti borrowed small amounts of kerosene now and then from Pushpa. It made starting a fire easy.

'What'll you do with kerosene at this hour?'

'My mother put out the kitchen fire. I just wanted to warm some milk.'

'You should've brought the milk here and warmed it over the stove,' Pushpa noticed that Tara looked very depressed, and did not raise her eyes.

'I'll warm it at my place.'

Tara knew where the can of kerosene was kept. The can worked with a simple, handpump made of tin tubing. Pushpa could hear the sound of the creaky pump working. How much kerosene did Tara need? she wondered.

Tara was quietly going towards the stairs with the bottle held under her dupatta. Pushpa grabbed her arm, took the bottle from her hand and raised it against the ceiling light. She saw that the bottle was full.

'What do you need so much kerosene for?'

Tara stood without answering, looking down.

Pushpa's eyes widened when she understood. 'Hai, you were...!' she said, and fell silent. She put the bottle away on one side, pulled Tara close to her and put her arm around her, 'What is it? Tell me.'

'Nothing. Just wanted to warm some milk.'

'Taro, have you gone mad! What happened?' She held Tara by both her arms and shook her, then led her to a bed. She made Tara sit beside her, and gave her a hug, 'I think I know what's going on. Did you quarrel with your brother, or with your mother?'

Tara shook her head without looking at Pushpa.

'Look at me!' Pushpa insisted.

Tara could not meet her eyes.

'Should I call Bhagwanti bahinji and tell her?' Pushpa scolded her.

'No, no.' Tara begged her with joined hands.

Pushpa broke into tears as she held Tara close. Tara remained silent and unmoved for a few seconds, then she too began to cry.

'Swear with your hand on my head that you'll tell me the truth,' said Pushpa.

'Don't you know?'

'Then why have you kept quiet until now? Should've opened your mouth long before.'

'I didn't keep quiet. I did speak out before.'

'What? We never heard you say anything!' Pushpa was obviously surprised. 'I could speak with your mother, but now, when all preparations are over, how will she feel?'

'There's no need. It's no use now.' Tara let out a deep sigh and sat still as a stone.

When Tara returned home after about an hour, she left the bottle of kerosene behind at Pushpa's house.

Next morning the news spread quickly in the galis and neighbourhoods.

From the top of tall buildings owned by the Hindus in the Sareen Mohalla, shots were fired just before dawn at clusters of one-storeyed houses of Muslims in the neighbourhood. Seven people sleeping on the roofs of their houses had been killed. There was also news of knifings and of kirpan attacks near the Badshahi Masjid and the Bawli Saheb areas. The curfew was not yet in force, but most bazaars in Lohe ka Talab, Tibbi Bazaar and Rang Mahal had been closed.

Sheelo's husband Mohanlal asked her not to go to Bhola Pandhe Gali during such unrest. Sheelo insisted, 'Around the corner is the bazaar with shops owned by Hindus. Then the rest of the way is through galis. Drop me off. I can ignore the invitation to the singing party, but Tara has been injured, and I can't refuse to go to see her.'

Mohanlal replied, 'Good soul, I don't think it's wise to go anywhere in the present situation. If you want to go alone, go ahead. I'm staying here.' Mohanlal didn't even go to his office that day. Sheelo sat fuming with frustration. How could she go ahead and show that she was bolder than her husband? It would be an insult to her, if her husband's cowardice became known.

Sheelo could not attend the singing party at Ghasita Ram's house, but no singing could be held that evening in any case. The gali women had assembled on Ghasita Ram's roof instead of the stuffy, hot indoors. Later in the evening, an arrow with an incendiary head had fallen on the roof of Mukund Lal's house. This arrowhead was different from the one that had fallen on Masterji's roof. The rag tied on its head was wrapped tightly like a bandage, and had caught fire after hitting the roof.

Ratan and Bir Singh had gone over to look at the arrow. Bir Singh exclaimed with surprise, 'Just look at this! Who taught these sister-lovers our technique?'

On the night before, Ratan, Mewa Ram, Bir Singh and Tikaram had gone to the rooftops of Panna Lal, Prabhu Dayal and Khushal Singh, and had used large bows to shoot arrows with similar incendiary heads in a south-easterly direction. The arrow that had fallen on Mukund Lal's roof had caused no damage, but the women did not want to sit any longer in the open air, nor did they feel much like singing.

Next day, Mohanlal had to go to his office in the secretariat. He was still afraid of going out because of the disturbances, but was also afraid of being absent from his desk. For him, there was something to fear everywhere.

Sheelo came with him as far as the Uchchi Gali. Once there, she pleaded with her mother to take her and her son to Bhola Pandhe's Gali.

Tara was still moody. Sheelo's mother expressed her worry to Tara's mother about her daughter's scar. Bhagwanti, her voice heavy with worry, told her *jethani* about a matter of even greater concern, 'Bhahinji, I've been trembling inwardly with fear that her mind may have been affected by the fall. Although the doctor did say that her wound was superficial, and needed only one stitch she's been silent since that day.'

'Hai hai, sukhkhi saandi. May her enemies suffer disgrace! You shouldn't even think about such bad things,' Sheelo's mother said. 'You couldn't find a girl with such a brilliant mind on all seven continents. Some bad person has put the evil eye on her. Have you turned seven pods of dry red chillies round her head and thrown them into the fire to ward off the evil eye, yet?'

'God help us.' Bhagwanti's eyes became watery with tears. She looked at Sheelo and said, 'Let's see if she talks to you. If anyone tries to talk to her, she just says that it hurts her to talk, and turns her face away. I'm so scared that her brain may have been damaged in some way...'

Sheelo went to the veranda and sat next to Tara. She had heard about the incident from Tara's mother, but asked Tara again to tell her about how she fell and hurt her forehead. Tara replied, 'My mother has already told you. I don't know any more. I just fainted, they tell me.'

'But why did you faint? Why weren't you eating? Nobody faints just like that.'

'Well, if it happened, it happened. What else can I tell you? Don't ask me questions. Tell me about yourself,' Tara pleaded with her.

'What's there to tell about me? Listen, I didn't tell this to chachi, but the elder sister of your fiancé came to our place from Sheesha Moti...'

Tara signalled with her hand to ask Sheelo to stop, 'Talk only about yourself.'

'Hai, you two gossips are sitting here!' Pushpa came onto the veranda. She sat down on the chatai with Tara and Sheelo, and said in a low voice, 'Come to my place. We'll sit and chat there.'

Tara looked at Pushpa with eyes that begged: Let it go! Leave me alone!

'Why, what's the matter?' Sheelo asked suspiciously.

'Can't talk here. Let's go to my place. I came to ask you both over,' Pushpa said.

'Leave me out of it. Don't insist,' Tara pleaded.

'Why, am I your enemy?' Pushpa whispered to make sure that Bhagwanti and Sheelo's mother could not hear her. 'The way you're clamming things up in your heart, who knows what you might do? Let us sisters talk among ourselves. You won't even talk to us?'

Sheelo wrinkled her brow in puzzlement and looked at Tara and then at Pushpa.

Tara had to give in. Pushpa said to Bhagwanti, 'Bahinji, get the sewing machine and the cloth out. We'll be back in no time. Sheelo wants to have a look at my munni.'

Bhagwanti said to Pushpa, 'Make sure to hold her arm as you go down the stairs.'

Pushpa told Sheelo of the incident of Tara trying to borrow the bottle of kerosene as Tara listened. She asked Sheelo, 'If she's so desperate now, what might she not do at her in-laws? Or, what if she swallows something tomorrow? Tell me, how she's going to be able to bear living with Somraj? Now that we know about it, we can't push her down the well to her death. Can't your mother do something about it?'

Sheelo sat with chin on her drawn-up knees in dumb silence. She just stared at the floor.

Pushpa goaded her for an answer, 'Tell me, *adiye*.'

Sheelo let out a deep sigh and remained sitting without speaking. Tara sat with her head bent in embarrassment.

After sitting quietly for several moments more, Sheelo looked at Tara's averted face, and tears began to roll down her cheeks. Tara looked at Sheelo when she heard her sob, and also began to cry.

Pushpa too wiped her tears, and reminded them, 'Crying won't solve anything.'

Sheelo said nothing. She turned towards the wall, bent her head into her chest, and wept bitterly. Tara too began to sob. She bent over Sheelo, and trying to take her into her arms, said, 'How long will you go on crying over my bad luck? Stop crying.'

In a cradle nearby, Pushpa's baby daughter screwed up her face, closed her eyes, and thrusting up her tiny feet and fists, burst out crying.

Pushpa got up, looked at her daughter, and said, 'Let me change her, and give her a bath. The heat must be bothering her. Didn't get time to bathe her.' She picked up her daughter and went over to the aangan that was covered with a grille.

Tara held Sheelo close and said, 'Enough! Don't cry any more! If you do, may you see me dead.'

'You might have really died! You'd almost made sure that I wouldn't see your face again. To hell with you, you wretch!' Sheelo cursed angrily. 'I've never hid anything from you. And you couldn't trust me even a little bit! Are you that full of having a BA degree? Go to hell! I don't ever want to see your face again! Kill me! Kill all of us!' She slapped her forehead in rage.

Tara put her hand over Sheelo's lips, and hugged her hard, pinning her arms. She then held her cheek over her mouth to stop her from speaking.

After she regained her composure, Sheelo said, 'First swear on my baby that you'll tell me the whole truth. Only then will I speak to you.'

Tara said lovingly, 'May he live a hundred years! Don't say that! I'll tell you. What is there to hide now?'

'How did you hurt you forehead? Tell me the truth.'

'My brother said something, and I had to do something to stop him.'

'What did he say?'

Tara told Sheelo why Puri had asked her to go with him. She too had wanted to see someone, and had gone to keep her appointment from her friend's house. As she came out of the restaurant with him, her brother was passing on a tonga. He accused her of having been caught in the act of trying to elope.

'Tell me honestly, and you've sworn on my baby, were you really going to elope?' Sheelo stared hard into her eyes.

Tara hung her head and kept silent.

'You never gave me any hint of this.'

Tara said nothing.

'Do you really want to elope?' Sheelo asked after some thought.

Tara shook her head.

'How is that? You want to go left, then you want to go right! Then why did you advise me to elope with Ratan?'

Tara said nothing.

'Why don't you want to? Tell me the truth. I'm sorry that I didn't listen to Ratan. Had I known all this I'd surely have run away with him. Now it's too late. But I'll do anything to help you. Love is no sin. When Lord Krishna saw that his sister Subhadra was in love with Arjun, didn't he himself tell her to elope with her love? That's the tale in the Mahabharata, we all know that. Just tell me the truth. Don't worry about what I might think.'

Tara shook her head.

'Damn you to hell! You're really weird. You gashed your head, you had the guts to set fire to yourself, but you don't have the guts to run away with him. You've just told me that you were all set to run away. I say, elope if you want to. You're still unmarried; that would be no sin.'

Tara kept her silence.

'Is he willing to keep you?' Sheelo asked after a few moments.

Tara again shook her head.

'Be damned to you, then, and him too!' Sheelo said irately. 'Shame on you for loving such a wimp, and shame too on a man who says he loves you but hasn't the guts to stand by you. Somraj is a hundred times better than he is. He's mad about you, and that's why he says that he won't rest until he's made you his own. He asks how you can change your mind after saying "yes" to him. Says that he said "yes" only after knowing that you had said "yes" first.'

Tara did not want to defend Asad in front of someone who did not know him. Nevertheless, she tried to explain to Sheelo, 'No, he does have guts. He just says that we should let this Hindu–Muslim conflict cool down a little first.'

'Forget that!' Sheelo said scornfully, 'That conflict is never going to end. It's been there since I was born. There will be Hindus and there will be Muslims, and so will be the problems between them. Shame on that weakling of a man! He's bothered about the conflict, not about you. And that's what you call love! Love is when you're blind to everything else, to the whole wide world. Love is when you cross the river holding on to an unfired clay pot, like Sohini in the legend, without thinking about risking your life.'

Tara attempted to pacify her, 'It's not like that. Actually, I just don't want to get married. I want to study for my MA degree. Who needs marriage?'

Bhagwanti called from across the gali, '*Nee* Pushpa, are those girls going to be stuck there forever? Tell them to come back now.'

'They're coming, bahinji,' Pushpa called back, and came to sit with Tara and Sheelo.

'You're crazy!' Sheelo said. 'Who questions the need for marriage and family? People are born, people get married. That's life, and if we're born, we have to live. We'll suffer if that's our fate, but why be afraid of that? Some women have the bad luck of being widowed while they're young.

Just like Biddi bua; it's all the result of our actions in our previous life.'

'Biddi bua's case is different.' Tara made an attempt at explaining her viewpoint, 'Nowadays some women take another track, they become doctors or professors. Others don't marry at all. They don't suffer any consequences either.'

'They're not like us. Their customs and ways of life are different,' Sheelo replied. 'We have to live with our own kind. You've had education, so you've begun to think like one of them, but your family and your people are different. People like us have to go along with people like ourselves, and not break away. If someone chooses to become a *jogin* and renounce the world for her love, that's another matter. Otherwise we must follow the customs of our own community.'

Tara kept quiet. Sheelo's philosophizing was unusual for her. 'What a naïve approach to life!' Tara thought. It was as if the very bricks and mortar, imbued with the culture and spirit of the galis, were speaking through Sheelo. She remembered that Asad too had asked, 'How can we escape from our circumstances?' Sheelo is essentially saying the same thing. 'Why did I remain quite for so long? Because I trusted my brother. If I raise my voice now, he'll be the first to brand me a rebel. Nothing has happened to change the circumstances of my family and community. So how can those be changed in a hurry now? It's possible for Zubeida and Pradyumna, because Zubeida's mother has set the precedent. And Pradyumna's family too is different; he lives in a bungalow, the son of a doctor. Doesn't have to care for the opinions of any gali or the people of the neighbourhood.'

For some time, the three of them sat in silence. Sheelo said again, 'Somraj and his sister came to my in-laws' place. Both were mad. Who knows how they came to know of your refusal to get married? I think it's the doing of Rampyari and Purandei. They're both sneaky. All they do is tattle here, gossip there. Somraj blew his top, "I don't have to get married. I don't give a shit for this marriage, but I won't let that girl off the hook. She has insulted me. Her mother and her *tayi* came to our house a hundred times and grovelled before us, to get us to accept the proposal. I let go dowries worth thirty and forty thousand for her, and she dares to look down her nose at me! I'll be damned if I won't take revenge for such a humiliation."

'I gave them a piece of my mind. I said, "We're a poor family. Why don't you admit that you're looking for a big dowry, and just want some excuse to break off the engagement? Say what you like, but the whole gali and the whole neighbourhood knows about my sister. If she says 'yes' once, she won't say 'no' afterwards even if someone cuts her head off. She never said 'no' to the marriage, but she did beg her family to let her finish her BA. My father asked, 'What do you need a BA degree for? Your fiancé doesn't have one.' My sister replied, 'My fiancé is like a god to me, it doesn't matter if he has a BA or not .' "'

Pushpa broke into laughter, 'You're bad. You really know how to tell the tale!'

'Hai, I swear to you, what else could I say?' Sheelo said. 'They were bent on shaming her in the bazaar. I stopped him in his tracks, "Tell me about yourself. Everybody praises my sister and says that she's blameless and pure like a devi, but what about you? Maybe you're mixed up with someone else, maybe you've chosen another girl. If so, you'd better come clean. My poor sister will just accept it as her lot in life. You men are all the same."'

Sheelo said that Somraj's sister replied, 'There's nothing to it. Somraj turned down a number of offers before agreeing to your family's proposal. Why shouldn't he feel annoyed? He has reason to be.'

Sheelo went on, 'I still say that Somraj is a hundred times better for you. He's upset that he's fallen for you. Adiye, who better for a woman than one who loves her? If he doesn't have a BA or an MA, so what? My husband has a BA, but what has come of that? All he does is push a pen in some office. He almost peed in his pants yesterday when I asked him to bring me here.'

Tara was silent as before.

Tara's bandage was removed after three days, and a small square of adhesive plaster was stuck over the wound. That too came off after a couple of days. A tiny star of reddish-brown lines, was left behind on her forehead as the symbol of her protest. To Puri the scar was like an eyesore. It reminded him of her accusations of his cruelty, and her proclaiming her own martyrdom. Tara was shifting the blame of her own wickedness onto him. This stain on his honour and dignity troubled Puri; it was an irritant that took his mind off his work time and again. Isn't suppressing the truth by the false pretence of non-resistance, he wondered, crueller and more heinous than suppressing the truth by the use of violence? He had to yield before his sister's manoeuvring only because of his kindness and concern for her. Otherwise she could have banged her head as much as she wanted! And the dishonour to the family's name? If she had committed suicide so that her shenanigans would not be exposed or had she eloped, and that too with a Muslim, how would his family have faced up to their relatives and the people of their gali? His anger over her action to blacken the family's reputation took a permanent hold on his heart.

Whenever he thought of Tara's misdemeanours, his thoughts would invariably turn to Kanak, whom he had begun to see as a reflection of Tara. Kanak's heart-warming smile, her passionate eyes looking into his own, her letting him take her into his arms and assuring him that she was his ... that her father had called him a 'jewel', that someday he might have to take over Panditji's assets. How treacherously deceptive was the maddening scent of Kanak's hair! Her doing an about-face under her father's influence! Kanak seemed to him to be even more devious than Tara. He had really been taken for a ride ... she was playing little games! She needs someone, anyone, to flirt with. Perhaps, even now, she's gadding about in the car with her brother-in-law, or his younger brother! How can women be trusted?

The newspapers carried grim reports of growing tensions and confrontations between Hindus and Muslims, and of the dimming of prospects for any rapprochement between the Congress and the League. In the third week of May, a forty-eight-hour curfew was imposed again after clashes in the neighbourhoods of Bagwanpura, Kele Wali Sarak and Bhati Gate. In its wake came the news that due to the disturbances in Lahore and throughout the province, the BA and MA examinations were being postponed until further notice.

Usha placed three textbooks before Puri and said, 'Tara says, who knows when the examinations will be held, that there is no point in keeping these borrowed books.'

It was announced in the first week of June that the western half of Punjab would be included in Pakistan. Most people imagined that the dividing line would be somewhere near Lahore. The hot topic of discussion and of speculation now was whether the city itself would go to Pakistan, or remain in India. The declaration rekindled the smouldering fire of riots in the province. Several Muslim neighbourhoods in Rajgarh, near Krishna Nagar and Dev Nagar, were attacked during the night. A hundred or so persons were killed, and scores of Muslim homes were reduced to ashes. Great numbers of Muslims began to flee Lahore for safer havens in the west.

Puri had borrowed the textbooks for Tara from Kalicharan. In the aftermath of the conflagration in Rajgarh and the curfew, he could not go to return the books. He waited for things to calm down before going to Kalicharan's place in Doongi Gali, past Sareen Mohalla. Most of the galis and neighbourhoods on his route belonged to Hindus. In the Doongi Gali, almost all the houses that had once belonged to Muslims had now been sold to Hindus. Only a handful of the remaining dilapidated houses were occupied by Muslims.

A tonga stood at the entrance of the Doongi Gali. On it lay a roll of worn-out bedding tied with rough *moonj* cord, a gunny sack filled with various household articles, and two oblong cans— that once had held kerosene but were now fitted with lids—to be used as storage boxes. Puri had to squeeze past the tonga to enter the gali. He saw that Kalicharan and his neighbour Comrade Rajbans Mahajan, whom Puri knew, were barring the way of a poor Muslim family ready to move out of the gali. Mahajan had his hand on the shoulder of an old woman and was holding her back. She was wearing an old, faded, torn burka, with its veil pulled back over her head. Kalicharan held an old man by his arm and was speaking as if explaining something to him. The old man's beard was dyed with henna, and he was carrying a cheap clay hookah in his hand. Two other burka-clad women stood with their backs against the wall. The outlines of their figures suggested they were young. A boy, about seventeen, a flower-painted tin trunk in his hand, stood watching.

Over the threshold of the nearby house hung a sacking curtain. An old man, with a clipped beard and long, untrimmed moustaches sat on the doorsill. A woman stood looking from behind the curtain, her dupatta covering all her face except her eyes. In front of the next house, a Muslim youth, in a vest and multicoloured lungi, watched the scene with curiosity and apprehension. Behind him stood an old woman in a soiled and patched shalwar, her henna-dyed white hair covered with a torn dupatta, her hands supporting her bent back.

The old woman on her way to the tonga was saying, with her hand raised in emphasis, 'Bansi, my son, we've no reason to fear you, but when most people of our community and religion have left, how can we remain behind? Tell me, how long will you be able to tell others in the gali not to leave? Yesterday evening, Shadi Lal—may Rabba give him good sense—warned my husband, your taya, in the bazaar that we should leave the gali within twenty-four hours. Don't you know, it was I who brought the wretched boy out of his mother into the world and cut his umbilical cord. When he got sick from a sore throat, his mother Guro would ask me to apply the *chutki* to soothe his throat. That little devil used to call me bua. Nisso used to go to his home everyday to ask for buttermilk...'

Mahajan pleaded in a loud voice, 'Tayi, are you trying to bring shame on us! If you wish,' he lowered his head before her, 'hit me on the head with your slipper. Before anyone dares to harm you, they'll have to cut our heads off. For us, what's the difference between our Vimla and your Nisso!'

Mahajan looked at one of the young women, 'Look at her, all ready to move out of the gali in her burka! Don't you remember how you used to steal the strings of my spinning tops to use as the waist cord of your shalwar! Look at this,' he showed the others a scar on his elbow, 'the mark where she bit and clawed me like a cat.' The young woman bent her head and lifted her hand under the veil to wipe away her tears.

Mahajan went on, 'Have we forgotten that any woman living in the gali was to be regarded also as our mother or sister! If Nisso leaves this gali, it'll be only when she's carried off in a *doli* palanquin after her wedding.'

Grasping his beard, the old man sitting on the doorsill of his house said, 'Mama Imambuksh, we're still here. If we can't trust our longtime neighbours, whom can we trust?'

Kalicharan took the old man's hand into his own, and said in a calming tone, 'Taya, all this madness won't last more than a couple of days. Those who have fled will return soon too. What if there's a Pakistan or there's a Hindustan? We're Lahorites, neighbours of Doongi Gali. Go back to your house. If your shop was burnt down, Rabba willing, there'll soon be another one. Put your trust in Allah.'

Mahajan hurled curses for all to hear, 'Only these sister-loving sons of a monkey Britishers can get us to exist side by side? Why can't we live together on our own?'

Mahajan's mother was looking down from a window above. She said to the old woman, 'Bebe, you yourself are sensible enough. Just think, where would you go wandering around in a strange country with young daughters?' She pointed at old Imambuksh, 'Brother gets fits of asthma. Could he risk travelling? Think again. What's gone wrong with your mind?'

She said to the old woman who stood with her hands supporting her back, 'Fatan bhabhi, why don't you put some sense into bebe?'

Fatan replied in a shrill but frayed voice, 'Bansi's mother, you can ask

Shadan yourself. She asked us to go with them. I said, I came into this gali after my wedding in a doli carried on four shoulders; I'll leave this gali only when I'm dead, on a bier resting on four shoulders. Whoever wants to leave, can leave. I'm staying put.'

Mahajan said to Imambuksh's grandson who was watching all this in puzzlement, 'Hey Samadaya, go back home with your sisters, and take back your *trunky* too.' He called out to the youth in lungi standing silently on one side, 'Hey Dulley, stop staring like an owl! Carry taya's stuff back from the tonga to his house.'

The tongawallah cried in protest, 'Badshaho, have some mercy on me! Is this God's curse on me, or what? People are so scared these days that hardly anyone goes out of the house. This was my first fare since this morning; I had to crawl half a mile through the galis to get here. I've been waiting for over half an hour, and now you're sending me away.'

Kalicharan shut up the tongawallah, 'Shut up, mian. Keep your shirt on! You will be paid your twelve annas, you don't have to kidnap our gali people for that!' He called to someone inside his house, 'Hey Mattu, bring me twelve annas from the pocket of my jacket.'

'*Shava, putro, shava* !' Fatan raised her hand in blessing. 'May you have long lives! May your children be like you!'

Kalicharan had signalled to Puri to wait for him. He took Puri to his living room. Mahajan too went with them. He began to describe how other terrorized Muslims were fleeing the neighbourhood. His tone was sad, 'Yesterday, another man, Gokul, was telling these people, "Better become a Hindu if you want to remain here." Do you know what answer Fatan bua gave him? She said, "I've lived here as a Muslim for four-and-sixty years; why can't I do that now? Your father never dared to speak to me like this! Whose son are you?"' He added dejectedly, 'Who knows if any Hindustan–Pakistan gets created? I see Punjab remaining forever in the grip of the British.'

'Why, is there a separate policy for Punjab? Attlee's statement of 16 February was for all of India.' Puri tried to guess what Mahajan meant to say.

'That very statement by Attlee is good reason to worry,' Kalicharan said.

Puri considered Kalicharan to be a serious-minded and thoughtful person. Unlike Mahajan, he was not a member of the Communist Party.

Wanting to know his opinion, Puri asked, 'How come?'

'Attlee had announced that no matter which political party is in the majority in any province in June 1948, the government would be handed over to that party. The governor of Punjab is scheming to make sure that no political party can form the ministry in the province until then. If that's the case, then according to Attlee's statement, the administration of the Punjab will remain in the hands of the British.'

'Aren't you thinking too far ahead?' Puri expressed his doubt.

'How far ahead?' Mahajan began with his habitual swearword. 'March is over, April and May too, it's June now. The governor has so far been successful in not allowing the formation of any ministry.

'Bhai, my view is that whoever is in the majority, let them form the ministry. Give them a chance, then wait and see what happens. What right does the governor have to impose his will on who should and shouldn't be in the ministry? To hell with them, if they can't govern India any more. Who're they to decide to partition it? Leave it to the Indians; they'll carve it up as, and if, they want to. Why was Khizr asked to resign? You say that the Unionist ministry couldn't guarantee civic peace? Well, the situation has deteriorated in the three months since its downfall, and is getting worse by the day. It was army explosives that were used to blow up the railway workshop. A very large number of homes now have some kind of a firearm. You call what we've got peace? Why can't the administration restore peace and order with such a large police force and army at their disposal? If Kidwai could put down the Khaksar movement in the United Provinces, why can't that be done here?

'The truth is,' Mahajan continued in a conspiratorial tone, 'The Punjab governor belongs to Churchill's Conservative Party. He has his own policy for Punjab. He thinks, even if Attlee and Mountbatten agree to hand over India to the Congress and the League, he still might be able to hold on to Punjab, especially the western Punjab. You know, Punjab has a strategic and important position in international politics. The British want to keep an eye on the Soviets, my friend!' Mahajan grabbed Puri's hand to emphasize his point.

'Arre yaar, you see Soviets under every bed,' Puri refused to believe him. 'You are talking as if you were a personal friend of the governor!'

'Hey, how can you say that?' Mahajan seemed surprised at Puri's ignorance. 'That's how Professor Nath sees it. Didn't you know? What do you say, Kali bhai?'

'Yes, yes,' Kalicharan said in agreement. 'After the official statement of 4 June about partition and what provinces might go to Pakistan, I went with Asad and Pradyumna to the professor's place. You know, he meets and talks with all kinds of people. The British bureaucrats, it seems, are not too pleased with the plan of Attlee and Mountbatten. They still somehow hope to prove that it would be foolish to hand over self-rule to Indians. The British know that after partition, both parts of the country will be unable to function. Up till now India has been developed as a single country. Now Pakistan will lack the ability to produce industrial goods, and the rest of the country will be short of raw materials. It's a clever move. Where will the cotton crop and other produce from western Punjab, and the jute grown in East Bengal go? To Britain! It'll revive their dying industries.

'Western Punjab and East Bengal would face even more problems,' Kali continued. 'The military secretary of the governor remarked jokingly that until now there was one North-West Frontier, which cost millions of rupees to guard. After partition, India would have two frontiers, and Pakistan would have four!'

'But the partition of India has been accepted in principle,' Puri said with some concern.

'Professor Nath said that if both the halves became autonomous but formed a federation, it wouldn't be all that harmful. But Attlee's policies are encouraging the League to separate. The British are interested in dividing up India in a way that will serve their own interests.'

After he returned from Doongi Gali, Puri could not get back to work on the history book. He desperately wanted to talk with Tara about what he had heard from Kalicharan and Mahajan on the future of Punjab. But brother and sister had not spoken to one other, except in monosyllables, since the day Tara had injured her head, and that only so that others might not suspect that they had quarrelled. So, Puri began to write a play based on what he had witnessed at the Doongi Gali. He kept at it until after sunset, when he heard Prabhu Dayal's voice indicating that the doctor had returned home. Puri went to the doctor's place taking Ratan along, and recounted to them what he had heard about the British Civil Service conspiring to keep both Hindus and Muslims from forming a ministry in Punjab.

Ratan listened patiently, then shook his head in disagreement, 'Both of them are our enemies. We've got to get rid of both of them.'

'How many will you get rid of?' The doctor asked. 'Who are Muslims now? Those who were Hindus only a short time ago. And what if more Hindus convert to Islam?'

'Times have changed. It's not the reign of Aurangzeb any more,' Ratan answered.

'If not Muslims, the untouchables and outcasts will become the problem...'

Puri cut the doctor short. 'They're already a problem. If you exploit any people, they'll revolt as a class, become hostile and turn into your enemy.'

'Bhappa, you bring communism into everything!' Ratan said with irritation.

'This is history. And I'm not a communist.'

Ratan turned his head away in disagreement. Puri gave up.

Puri could not do much work the next day either. The bridal procession was due to arrive that evening for the wedding of Ghasita Ram's daughter. Puri was expected to lend a hand at their house. Mukund Lal and Khushal Singh were the self-appointed organizers for any such special occasion in the gali. Mukund Lal told Puri to go to Lohe ka Talab to arrange for tents and gas lamps. And to make sure to hire everything from a Hindu and not a Muslim supplier.

Puri found some time in the afternoon to work on his play 'Doongi Gali'. Around 4 o'clock, Ratan called 'Puri Bhappa!' and came in. He said to Puri, 'The groom's party will come this evening from Kashmiri Mohalla. There are two mosques on the route, and shops belonging to Muslims, as you know. It'd be a shame on us if anyone in the procession were attacked on the way here. You know that the other day some person going in a bridal procession to Shahi Mohalla was knifed in Hira Mandi. Tell me, bhappe, what should we do?'

'You tell me,' Puri put his pen down.

'I think that three or four of us should accompany the baraat from Kashmiri Mohalla to here. We should get there by five-thirty.'

'I'll go with you.'

'Bhappe, some places on our route are rather unsafe. What if any of us get killed trying to protect the people in the groom's party? I already have two sets of body armour, I'll get one more. Listen, you go out often. Why don't you buy one instead of having to borrow it each time? Mewa Ram, Bir Singh and Dewanchand have all got one.'

'What's a suit of armour? What does it look like? I have never seen any.'

'Wait, I'll show you.' Ratan leaped to his feet, went to his half of the house, and came back with a sleeveless shirt made of galvanized tin. He opened it up—a breastplate and a backplate made from light-gauge sheet metal that could be fastened on the side. Ratan said, 'The one that Dewanchand got is quite heavy. I got this from Husaini, the tinsmith; the same one who used to sell us those things to squirt coloured water at the time of the Holi festival. He told me that lots of Muslims were buying these. Here, see, how light it is! If we've to go out at night, we put this on under our shirt. It would stop a bullet from a small calibre pistol.'

Puri replied with a laugh, 'No, bhappe, I can't bear to put on this tin shirt in this heat, nor do I have the money to buy it.'

Ratan said, 'All right, don't buy one, but at least wear one when we go to Kashmiri Mohalla.'

'No, I don't need all this hassle,' Puri did not want to pursue the subject. 'I'll just go like this.'

'No, bhappe!' Ratan objected. 'Why should a Hindu die for nothing? Before he falls, let him first kill four others.'

To end the argument, Puri agreed to wear one.

Chapter 11

IN THE LAST WEEK OF APRIL, WHEN PURI LEFT PANDIT GIRDHARILAL'S HOME after meeting with him, Kanak had gone out with Puri under the excuse of making a visit to her friend Sarla Sharma near the Shahalami Gate. She had been anxious to speak with Puri, and while talking they walked towards Lawrence Garden, in the direction opposite to the Shahalami Gate. Their conversation lasted a long time and Kanak was uneasy because the gathering darkness indicated that it would be late before she arrived home, but how could she just leave without saying all she wanted and without reassuring Puri? Returning from Lawrence Garden in a tonga, they discussed where and how they would meet in future.

When Kanak saw her sister's car parked near the entrance to her gali, she bit her lip apprehensively. She had told her father that she would return early. She had remembered, that her sister and brother-in-law were due to visit that evening. But they usually came late in the evening, and stayed for dinner. After receiving Kanta's telephone call in the morning, Kanak told Kesari the cook to buy and cook some mutton for dinner.

At first, when Kanak and Puri had begun going out together, they used to ask Kanchan to come along. Kanchan too enjoyed those outings of fun and frolic. Soon they began to forget to invite her. Kanchan would not invite herself, but she did resent not being asked. Left behind at home, she would read or sew. On that evening she first picked up a copy of the *Naya Zamana* magazine from the living room and lay on her bed reading it. Then she began to embroider the neckline of her new kameez.

When Kanchan heard the sound of the horn of her sister's car, she put aside her embroidery and ran down the stairs to be the first to welcome her baby niece. She did not see the child in her brother-in-law's arms, and exclaimed in disappointment, 'Hai, you didn't bring Nano today?'

'We had some errands to do in the bazaar. Had to leave her at home,' Kanta replied.

Nayyar asked as he stepped into the living room, 'Is Kanni back yet?'

Panditji put aside the magazine he was reading, screwed up his eyes and asked in some concern, 'Why do you ask? Did you meet her?'

'She was at the far end of the Lower Mall Road. With what's-his-name, Puri,' said Nayyar, sitting down. 'We were passing through. We spent quite some time in the Anarkali bazaar. She should be back by now.'

Panditji began to stroke his chin with his hand. 'Hmm,' he said. Then added, 'She should get here any moment. She's probably on her way back.'

Kanchan looked at her father and took a deep breath. Panditji had called her about half an hour before to ask, 'Kanchi, do you girls have this month's *Naya Zamana* upstairs?'

When Kanchan brought the magazine to him, her father voiced his concern that Kanak hadn't come back from visiting her friend Sarla Sharma near the Shahalami Gate. He was nervous about any young woman staying out late in these times of unrest and conflict. 'And now jijaji says that he saw Kanni and Puri on the Mall Road!' Kanchan remembered that Kanak hadn't explained the mystery behind the loan that she said she took from Zubeida, and had had a long conversation with Panditji one night. Kanchan could guess the reason for her father's concern.

Panditji asked Kanta several things about Munni, his little granddaughter. Then he talked with his son-in-law about a court case that Nayyar was contesting for some client from the town of Moga. Kanta then went inside to the aangan to see her mother. Kanchan was sitting next to her brother-in-law. When there was a break in the conversation, she said with a reproachful pout, 'Jijaji, you've forgotten to bring me flowers again. You're no good! I'll never visit your place now, I swear.'

Nayyar playfully tried to make up for his oversight by telling her about the wonderful flowers blooming in his garden, and why she should come there to enjoy them. He also promised to perform several little services for her as penance. His younger sister-in-law was about to turn eighteen, but to tease her he spoke to her as if she were still eleven.

Panditji took up an old topic of conversation with Nayyar about buying some land in Model Town, and about his idea of building on it a comfortable and airy small house with a garden. Kanchan also had something to say on that subject.

Kanta returned from talking with her mother. She looked at the clock on the living room wall and asked, 'Kanni isn't back yet? What's holding her up?' She wanted to get back home to her daughter.

Kanchan held her breath as she tried to catch her elder sister's eye. Her

father was already fretting over Kanak being late, and she did not wish him
to be reminded of it. But Kanta's gaze was upon Panditji. She had begun to
tell about a new, wheeled baby walker that a friend had sent from Bombay.
And how her Munni, although still too young to walk, could now roll her
way around the room, sitting in that contraption.

After she finished describing the walker, she again said, 'It's getting quite
late, pitaji. Let's have dinner. Kanni should arrive any minute now.'

Panditji again grunted in reply. Then he said, 'Yes, she should. She should
be here by now. Yes, let's begin.'

Nayyar said impatiently, 'It *is* late. That Puri won't let her go until he's
finished gabbing. He talks on and on just to hide his nervousness.'

Panditji cut him short, 'Kanchi, tell Kesari to serve dinner. Don't know
why Kanni's so late?'

Kanchan got up and went inside. Her sister's behaviour had upset her
too. She had noticed how Kanak had been acting distracted and stressed
lately. She knew the reason behind it, but that knowledge had not made her
sympathetic to Kanak's problem. She knew that no one else in their family
was fond of Puri. Her father's anxiety troubled her especially.

By the time Kanchan returned to the living room after seeing to the
dinner, Kanak had arrived and was explaining defensively, 'Jijaji, I got held
up. Couldn't help it. I'm really very, very sorry.' She went and sat next to
Nayyar on the sofa.

Nayyar pointed to his watch and said, 'A little late? Is this some kind
of artsy-fartsy act that your guests wait for you at your home while you
discuss highbrow stuff with your friends on the Mall Road?'

Kanak sidled closer to her brother-in-law and laid her head on his
shoulder to humour him, 'You a guest? Isn't this your home too? You weren't
waiting at the roadside or somewhere out in the sticks.' She jumped to her
feet and sat on the armrest of Kanta's chair and began to complain about
her not bringing her little daughter.

The next day Kanak noticed that her father was rather quiet. She tried
to make him laugh when they were having lunch, but he merely forced a
smile. His expression remained solemn in the evening too. When his grave
attitude continued the next day, Kanak asked Kanchan, 'Kanchi, what's the
matter? Pitaji seems a little sad.'

Kanchan was waiting for a chance to explain. She replied, 'I hadn't said
anything because I thought you might think it wasn't my business. Two days

ago, you told pitaji that you were going to Shahalami to see Sarla Sharma, but jijaji told us that he saw you with Puri bhaisaheb on the Mall Road. Kanta bahin and jijaji kept on asking where you were. Pitaji changed the subject, but he clearly was hurt. You know how he insists on being told the truth.'

'Where's the lie in all that?' Kanak replied. 'I did say I was going out. What does it matter whether I went to Shahalami or to the Mall Road? The same thing can be said in so many different ways. Pitaji saw me leave with him.'

'But Kanni,' Kanchan said, 'you know pitaji's not narrow-minded. We should have some consideration of how he feels.' She wanted to delve deeper into Kanak's secret.

'I do care for his feelings,' said Kanak.

Kanak felt slighted by what she thought was her father's unjust reaction. 'Am I not free to talk or meet with whomever I choose?' A wave of resentment rose in her heart, 'I'm not a baby any more! Soon I'll have to decide what to do with my own life. I won't always live with my family.' She was annoyed with Nayyar too. 'Who's he to spy on me? He's probably feeling snubbed now that I don't go out gadding about with him.'

Kanak was ready to fight for her right to personal freedom, but she also had to yield to her father's right to affection for her. To lessen his anger, she brought his afternoon tea to the living room. She told Kanchan that she had something to discuss with him in private.

As she handed the cup of tea to her father, Kanak began asking for his pardon in an embarrassed voice, 'Pitaji, I returned quite late in the evening the day before yesterday. As we were going towards Shahalami, I met Nanda Malhotra going the other way. She insisted that I walk with her for some distance. I didn't want to return alone, so I asked Puriji to come along too. I didn't know it'd take so long.'

'It's all right, beta,' Panditji said, with cup in hand. 'You are quite sensible. But, you see, one has to be more responsible as one gets on in life. One has to consider the opinions of others too. Usually, it doesn't make for a healthy outlook on life to put down rules about which boys and girls you can keep company with, but at your age, when emotions rule the heart, you ought to be more careful and selective. Your going out alone with a young man may appear unusual to some people. Probably it does. My suggestion is that you take Kanchi along, when you go out. You'll have company, and she too will get a chance to meet some people. Right?' Her father waited for her response.

Kanak remained silent.

Panditji went on, 'You've been brought up in a free and wholesome atmosphere, but someone who hasn't had much contact with girls till recently may misinterpret such a friendship. And once you've finished your MA, we must begin to think about your marriage too.' He laughed his whinnying laugh, 'To find a match for you we'll have to consider his social position, his personality, his family connections—all those things.' He switched to English, 'Puri is a good lad, but you and he belong to completely different classes and backgrounds. You must also consider the build and physique of a partner. So that he doesn't develop any wrong ideas. I suggest that you stop seeing him altogether for a while.'

Kanak was about to blurt out her secret, but she choked it back. 'I'll tell him another time,' she thought.

Panditji continued to speak gravely in English, 'Listen to me, beta, I'm thinking of nothing but your best interests and your happiness. I hope you won't forget what I've said.'

Kanak made an effort to suppress what was in her heart, and got up with the resolution to find a way in the long run to tell him what she wanted. Her heart was heavy and it was an even greater torture that she had to hide her true feelings. The following morning she remembered that she was to meet Puri that evening between 6.30 and seven on Nisbet Road. But after yesterday's talk with Panditji, she dared not to? And she was not willing to take Kanchan along, either. She would, she decided, write a letter to Puri and apologize for not being able to keep the rendezvous.

When Kanak and Kanchan needed envelopes and postage stamps, they would ask Vidhichand for them. He was a relative of Pandit Girdharilal, and had been working for him for over twenty years. Both the girls addressed him as 'uncle'. Kanak went to him soon after he arrived in the office at nine in the morning, and asked for an envelope and stamps.

Kanak returned to her room and wrote a letter to Puri. It was not easy to write to him. He himself was a writer, who looked for the hidden rather than the obvious meaning. He would have taken her father's objection to her meeting him as an insult. So Kanak wrote:

'My own one, something has come up. You know how unexpected things can happen in a family. I won't be able to get out this evening. You will get this letter tomorrow morning. Maybe I'll get a note from you today or tomorrow. I will meet you wherever you say. If you don't give me a place and time before Saturday, we will meet at 2 p.m. on Saturday in the Standard restaurant. I will be dying to see you ... Kanni.'

All the family's mail was delivered to Panditji's office. When there was something for Kanak or Kanchan, Vidhichand would come into the aangan and call out, 'Munni!'

Kanak or Kanchan would answer, 'Yes, chachaji?'

'There's a letter,' Vidhichand would say, and hand it over.

Panditji had gone out on Friday afternoon. Kanak was desperate for a letter from Puri. She went to the office to inquire, 'Chachaji, any letter for me?'

'For you? Yes, I gave one two days ago to the junior munni.'

'I got that one.' Kanak asked, 'But since then?'

'That's the only one bhaisaheb gave me for you. I put all the mail on his desk. He goes through it first.'

Disaster! The letter must have arrived, Kanak thought, but had not been given to her.... 'These people are bent on making life impossible for me!'

She waited for a letter on Saturday as if her life hung in the balance, but none arrived. She was finding it impossible to behave normally. She did not want to have lunch, but forced herself to eat something. She said, just for the sake of appearances, 'This raita is really tasty. Hai, I have a huge appetite these days. That's why I've put on so much weight.'

'Look at her! She thinks she's put on weight!' Panditji said. 'Your college has closed down. Kanta is going to the hills in June. You both should go with her.'

'No, pitaji. I don't like the Mussourie hills. There are hardly any nice walks there. I like Simla better,' Kanak knew that Panditji could not arrange to send her to Simla.

After lunch, Panditji went to his room to rest. It was only quarter past one. Kanak went to her room and lay down on the bed. She did not want to arrive early, because it was improper for a woman to sit by herself in a restaurant. But the fear of being late would not let her rest either. She forced herself to stay in bed for ten more minutes. Before opening the wardrobe for her outdoor clothes, she glanced at Kanchan to check if she was asleep. Kanchan's eyes were wide open; she was reading some magazine.

Kanak felt irritated. She knew Kanchan was bound to ask her where she was going. That could not be helped. She got up quietly and opened the wardrobe. But the rustle of her starched clothes caught Kanchan's ear and she asked, 'Hai, where to, in this scorching sun?'

'To Sarla's,' Kanak said, before recalling that she had used the same excuse last time when she went out with Puri. 'These people have got me all confused with their questions,' she thought.

'Wait till the sun goes down a bit.'

Kanak did not reply. She changed her clothes, put a dupatta around her shoulders, and left. When her tonga, passing through the bazaars and streets deserted and dozing in the blistering heat, arrived at the Standard restaurant, it was only two minutes past two o'clock. Puri was not in front of the restaurant, or anywhere around. Kanak took a few moments to decide what to do next. She had some coins in her purse, but still asked the tongawallah, 'Bhai, do you have change for a rupee?'

It was her luck that he did not. Kanak handed him a rupee note and said, 'Get change from one of the shops.'

The driver had to park the tonga beside the foyer of the restaurant, and went off in search of change. Kanak hoped with all her heart that Puri would arrive before the driver's return.

The tongawallah came back, grumbling, in a few minutes 'Everyone's asleep this afternoon. They refuse even if they do have change.' Still no sign of Puri. Seven minutes past two.

Kanak was now desperate 'He should realize that I can't stand around alone and wait. What a mess! Maybe I should go back,' she thought. Then she thought of the risks she had taken for this meeting. Probably he could not help being late. She just couldn't go back until the last moment.

She went inside the restaurant. For the sake of decency, the waiter raised the curtain for her to sit in a cubicle. Kanak thought, how would Puri know that she was in the cubicle? She said, 'No, I'll sit here ... outside.' She asked the waiter for two cups of coffee.

Only two other tables were occupied, in the quiet of the afternoon. Two young men at one, three at another. To overcome the embarrassment of being alone, she said to herself, 'I don't care. What's my crime?'

When the clock showed twenty past two, she began to get a sinking feeling ... 'Didn't he get my letter? Or, could there be another reason? The life of the city had almost returned to normal during the past two weeks. It's not possible that he won't come after getting my letter.' She waited for another five minutes. Then remembered that Panditji returned to the office after his siesta at 3 o'clock, or even a few minutes before.

On her way back home, just as she reached the intersection of Gwal Mandi, Kanak thought, I should have gone up to Bhola Pandhe's Gali to inquire. She looked at her watch. Twenty to three. There was no time. She wanted to be back home before Panditji returned to his office. She was sure that unless someone asked Kanchi directly, there would be no reason for her to say anything.

Kanak was taken aback when she entered the living room. Panditji was sitting on one side, and facing him sat a gentleman, a stranger. On the table in between were sliced bread, biscuits, some mithai, fruits and a pot of tea. Enough food for a full meal.

'Come, come,' Panditji called to her, and introduced her to the guest, 'My second daughter Kanak. Come and sit down, Kanni.'

Kanak said namaste and took a seat.

Panditji continued, 'She's in the first year of her MA, in literature. She's very fond of literature. English, Hindi, Urdu, all of them. She writes well too. Has published four or five stories.'

Panditji introduced the guest to her, 'Professor N.C. Mathur, D Litt. He edited this year's *Selected Prose*, the textbook for Delhi University's Intermediate examination. He's a great scholar.'

Kanak smiled and said, 'Sir, it is a delight to meet you. See you later,' she said namaste again, and got up.

She went to her room and called, 'Jaggi, bring me a glass of water.'

Kanchan was sitting on a dhurrie on the floor, sewing a kameez on a sewing machine. She said to Kanak, 'The sun's really hot, isn't it? You went out without an umbrella, too.'

'I took a tonga,' Kanak ended the conversation.

Jaggi the servant boy came with the glass of water, climbing the stairs playfully. Kanak went out to the balcony though the aangan, so that Kanchan would not listen. She asked Jaggi as he handed her the water, 'Where did you mail that letter, the day before yesterday?'

Jaggi was from the Kangra district, and perhaps eleven or twelve years old. His job was to wash the kitchen utensils and keep the floors swept all day. His clothes were always dirty and soiled, his face unwashed and grimy in patches. His fair skin showed under the layer of dirt. He wiped his wet hands on his dirty shirt, and looking at Kanak with his large, blue eyes, said, 'I didn't mail it.'

'What?' Kanak's heart missed a beat.

'Panditji asked me to give it to him, so that the peon could take all the mail directly to the main post office.'

Kanak went to her bed and lay down with her head clasped in her hands. Such treachery, she thought. 'I've become a condemned prisoner? Pitaji must be upset, must be thinking that I lied to him.'

While Kanak was going upstairs, on getting back home that afternoon, she was full of dread and foreboding. Although her father lectured her about her comings and goings, she had slipped out of the house only two days later while he was asleep. He had even caught her red-handed as she tried to sneak back in.

But she felt no compunction in the face of her father's meanness. Panditji's action now spurred her to fight for the privileges and freedom to which she had become accustomed since childhood.

'This will have to be resolved one way or the other,' she told herself. And once it was out in the open, she would have to decide her future in this house as well. Maybe it was time to break her ties with her family. Or, was it the family that was making her leave their fold? As she lay on her bed, thoughts raced through her head behind her closed eyes. One thought kept coming back to her, that now she would not hesitate to tell everything to her father.

She heard the *tun-tun* of the sitar as Kanchan's teacher Muttu Baba tuned the instrument before her lesson. Then a tune was played. The sound of the sitar gave her courage and helped in her thinking. The sitar playing came to an end and with it she suddenly realized that she was exhausted after her bout of intense thinking.

After a while, she heard Kanak call, 'Kanni, come down for tea. Pitaji's waiting.'

When Kanak did not reply, Jaggi came up with the message. She said to him, 'Tell them that I've a headache. Kanchi will serve tea.'

Kanak strained her ears to hear the reaction to her mute defiance. She was apprehensive about being asked about going out quietly in the afternoon. First it was her mother's voice, 'She has a headache? I'll massage her head with some ghee. Those scented hair oils are no good.' After twenty-eight years in Lahore, her mother had not given up the habits and practices of her home village. Her daughters jokingly called her 'nineteenth century'.

Then came her father's voice, 'It's probably a sunstroke. Tea might make the headache worse. Better if she doesn't have it. Make her some sherbet from phalsa berries.'

'Really!' Kanak thought in anger. 'How come such concern for my headache? Everyone is coming out with a cure.' She lay as before, her eyes shut.

She opened her eyes when she heard Jaggi's voice. He stood beside the bed, with one hand holding a glass full of purple-coloured sherbet balanced on the palm of the other hand. 'Lots of ice in it,' said the boy, his eyes shining as if he was sharing some secret.

'You drink it,' Kanak was about to tell him, but she checked herself. How would they know about her protest and frustration if Jaggi took back an empty glass? 'Put it here on the table,' she said, 'no, wait, take it back. Tell them I don't want it.'

Jaggi looked at her with disappointment and surprise. There was disbelief in his eyes, that some one could refuse a glass of sherbet with so much ice in it. Balancing the glass carefully on his palm, he went back downstairs.

Around eight in the evening Kanak was called for dinner. She replied, 'I don't feel like it.'

This time Kanchi came up, 'Come on, Kanni. What's the matter? What'll pitaji think?'

'What's there to think about? I can't force myself to eat if I don't feel like it,' Kanak said dryly. Kanchan went back downstairs.

Kanak's mother came up next. She felt Kanak's pulse to make sure that her daughter didn't have fever. She asked, 'What's the problem? You have a headache? Body ache? Your stomach's upset? Everything all right?'

'It's nothing. Just a headache. Don't feel like eating,' Kanak turned her back.

'Come down for a bit. Have some *khichari*. Your father had it made for you. Eat a little. You'll get bilious attacks from staying hungry. Come on, your father's waiting.'

As Kanak came down to the dining table, her father said, 'Come, come! Why don't you have any appetite? I've been watching for the last month. You're getting paler and paler. Have you checked your weight lately? Both of you should go on morning walks with me. It's been so hot this year.'

Kanak just sat and traced lines with her spoon in the rice-and-daal dish on her plate, and hardly touched the yogurt.

Panditji instructed Kanchan, 'Make sure she takes a glass of milk at bedtime. Don't put any ice in it. You girls have ice the whole day long. Ice has a warming effect. Cool the milk instead by placing it in a potful of ice.'

When Kanak refused any breakfast the next morning and sent back a glass of lassi too, the mood in the house became grave.

Her father came to the aangan, and looking up towards her daughters' room, called, 'Kanni beta, what's the matter? Let me take you to Dr Malkani after breakfast.'

Kanchan was in the room with Kanak. She had no reason for not eating. Without waiting for her father to come to breakfast, she had asked Kesari to cook her a parantha. Then she had a glass of lassi, and by 8 o'clock was already at work at her sewing machine. She also said to Kanak, 'Kanni, don't be difficult. Have something to eat. Think of pitaji.'

'What if I don't feel up to it?' Kanak said with some irritation, 'Pitaji wants me to consult a doctor for no reason. I'm bothering no one. Why can't you all leave me alone?'

They heard the voices of Mansa bua and of Phula, the wife of Vidhichand, from the aangan below. Both of them went to the Ravi River for their morning dip. On Sundays there was no reason to hurry home, so they would stop to pray at the temple of Sheetala devi. Then they would visit Pandit Girdharilal's wife, give her some *prasad*, and go home after having a glass of fresh buttermilk.

When Phula heard about Kanak not feeling hungry, she began to tell Kanak's mother how to cure loss of appetite because of the hot weather, 'Bahinji, soak some dried plums overnight in water in a fresh clay pot. Give that water to your daughter to drink. Why bother running to doctors for such small matters!'

Mansa bua said in a loud voice, 'What would a doctor do for this problem? It's not the hot weather. It's her age.'

Kanak felt annoyed by her remark. She looked at Kanchan sitting in front of the sewing machine. Kanchan kept her eyes on her sewing, but she was smiling.

'All right, bua. That's enough. Let it be,' Kanak's mother tried to play down the woman's words.

'Why should I let it be? You people can't bear to hear the truth.' Mansa bua spoke even more loudly. 'Have you forgotten the time when you were young yourself? At her age, even after having three children, when you had to spend a couple of months at your parents' house, it would drive you up the wall.'

Kanak was now angry at the loud-mouthed bua. She looked back at Kanchan, who had stopped sewing and buried her face in the folds of the dress with embarrassment. Kanchan's laughter infuriated Kanak. She thought, 'Fine, so what's wrong? If they think I am ready for marriage, let them marry me off. I'm ready too.' She began to imagine herself and Puri living as a married couple.

'All right, bebe! Here, have a glass of lassi,' said Kanak's mother to silence the woman.

After a few minutes, the mother called, 'Kanchi, come downstairs.'

When Kanchan returned to the room, she was carrying a glass of cold lassi. Condensation had misted the outside of the glass. Little blobs of churned butter floated on the surface. She said, 'Mother says you should drink what she's sent. Otherwise pitaji will come up and make you take it.'

Kanak sat up on her bed. 'Why is everyone being so cagey?' she thought to herself. 'Such pretence of affection and concern for me! Nobody wants to talk about the real issue.' But she said, 'Everyone insists that I force something down my throat. Nobody wants to know how I feel.'

'All right. Tell me, how do you feel?' Kanchan asked.

'I'll tell pitaji, of course, when he asks. You go and tell him that I don't need any doctor. I'm fine,' said Kanak, thinking. 'What more can I say?'

Around eleven in the morning, Kesari called from downstairs, 'Kanchi bahinji, Nano has come.'

Kanchan looked at Kanak and asked, 'Aren't you coming downstairs?'

'I'll come down shortly,' Kanak replied.

Kanchan left her sewing and ran downstairs. Kanak stayed in bed. 'I've really pushed matters a long way,' she was thinking, 'but now I must see things through. It can't wait now. Pitaji has read my letter to Puri. His reply must have come back too. They're pretending not to know anything. I won't take it any more!'

Kanak knew that her sister and brother-in-law must have come too, but nobody had called her to come down. All she could hear was Kanchan playing with Nano. Then she heard Nano crying, and Kanchan trying to soothe her after the child had apparently fallen, 'Hai, look at this ant! It was crushed too. Look, Nano, all these ants crushed by your fall.' Still no call for Kanak. Over fifteen minutes had gone by. Kanak found it difficult to lie still. She picked up a magazine lying nearby, and began to read it in frustration. She could not concentrate, but told herself, 'I won't go down unless they call me.'

Until eight or nine months before, Mahendra Nayyar and Kanak often indulged in a little banter. Nayyar would sometimes jokingly call Kanak *aadhi sarkar,* half wife, and pull at her hair-bun in fun. Kanak would show her irritation, 'Jijaji, I'll belt you one back!' but her tone and laugh would belie her threat. Sometimes she too retaliated with a playful slap or a light punch on his back.

Nayyar would say, 'It's not my fault! It's as the old saying goes, "A younger sister-in-law is one's half-wife!" Kanak did not mind such antics and banter as she found his attention amusing and pleasing. But after she had confessed her feelings to Puri, she began to find Nayyar's mock flirtation insulting and his attitude towards her a bit patronizing. She could not bear to be touched by anyone other than Puri. She would retaliate with a disapproving look rather than with pleasure. Kanak's coolness piqued Nayyar. The reason for the change in her attitude was easy to guess.

When Kanta's family gave their approval to her attraction to Mahendra and to their friendship by announcing their engagement, she began to feel bashful before her family and friends when he was around. Kanak and Kanchan had heartily accepted him as the brother they never had. After his marriage to Kanta, Nayyar not only became a brother-in-law but also a friend for her younger sisters. Eighteen months after their marriage, during the months when her pregnancy and the birth of her child had confined Kanta to her home, Kanak had become Nayyar's companion and confidante. There were many things that they could tell only to each other, and there was always something to chat about. After Puri's arrival, Kanak could neither give Nayyar the same companionship and attention, nor did she find his company as pleasing as before. She expected his approval when she praised Puri in front of him, and ended the conversation abruptly when he refused to accept his brilliance. None of this made Nayyar feel particularly kindly disposed towards Puri.

Nayyar ignored Puri in the same way that a fancy pedigree dog from a big house treats the street mongrel, like a pariah, without caring to fight or even stopping to growl. When Kanak told Nayyar about Puri's appointment as sub-editor at *Pairokaar*, all he had inquired about was his salary. Since then, every time Nayyar met Puri, a slight nod was the only sign he gave of their acquaintance. At the mention of Puri, he had once said jokingly to Kanak, 'He's just your tutor in the same way as Muttu Baba is Kanchan's sitar teacher.'

Nayyar's remark had hurt Kanak, and she had a heated discussion with Nayyar about Puri. Nayyar said, 'He has an odd arrogance and affectation in his behaviour, and he lacks confidence, like someone travelling on a train without a valid ticket. Haven't you noticed that? He seems very unsure of himself and nervous, as if he's undeserving and may be thrown out as a gatecrasher at any moment. He seldom has the courage to start a conversation.'

'But you can't have an intelligent conversation about literature or art with him either. What can he talk to you about? You don't understand politics, except what you read in newspapers. Of course, he can't make social chit-chat or carry on a silly conversation, because he doesn't move among that kind of people. That's not his fault, or his lack of personality. If you don't like Puriji's company, he's not exactly desperate for yours, either.' Kanak could not hold back without exacting some revenge for the insults meted out to Puri.

Nayyar had thought that once Kanak's passion for literature and her ambition to become a writer was over, the thick clouds of respect for her guru that were befogging her mind would be swept away. But when a whole year passed and nothing like that happened, he asked, exercising his right to the *jija-sali* intimacy, 'This devotion for your guru hasn't turned into anything else, has it?'

Knowing his dislike for Puri, Kanak replied with a stony stare, 'Absolutely not.'

In the weeks following the riots that had swept the city in March, Kanak had become so increasingly restive and impatient that it often attracted attention. Kanchan had kept her surmises to herself. Nayyar had attempted to question Kanak on the basis of his old intimacy, but Kanak had given nothing away. Nayyar had his suspicions, but in the absence of any evidence, had kept quiet.

'So Kanni, why are you being so canny with your favours?' Nayyar asked as he stepped into her room. Kanak was stretched on the bed, and he sat down beside her.

Kanak moved to one side to give him room and closed the magazine she was reading. She said, 'I'm not being canny.'

Panditji had told Nayyar about the letters she had written, the ones she had received, and about her silent defiance. He knew why Panditji was worried. He also had proof of his suspicions now. He had come to see Kanak and to resolve the matter as a member of the family.

To remind Kanak of their old intimacy, he nudged her in the back with his elbow, 'What's the matter with you?'

'Jijaji, I've told you that I don't like these touchy–feely jokes!' Kanak said irritably.

'I'm sorry!' Nayyar apologized. His face became serious. He removed his elbow. He moved away a little towards the edge of the bed and asked seriously, 'What's wrong? You feeling all right?'

'More or less.'

'Anything physical?'

Kanak shook her head in denial.

'Anything tugging at the heart strings?'

Kanak did not reply.

'Listen, Kanni,' Nayyar said sympathetically, 'how can your problem be solved unless you talk about it? If you do something without telling us, it will come out sooner or later.'

Kanak put aside her magazine, sat up and pulled the hem of her kameez over her knees, 'Pitaji is being unfair to me.'

'How is he being unfair?' he asked gently.

'He's keeping my mail from me.'

Nayyar asked, after a moment's thought, 'You mean he doesn't give you the letters that come for you?'

'Yes, and he kept the one I had asked to be mailed.'

'Who wrote to you and whom did you write to?'

'To Puriji,' Kanak said firmly.

'To Puri? But he comes here to visit you at home.'

'How can he? You all treat him with such disrespect.'

'What? I don't think I've ever shown him any disrespect. Anyway, it's a matter of personal opinion. We have to have a serious talk about this. Come to Model Town with us. We'll have more time there. Some fresh air will be good for you, too.'

Kanak finally ate something with her sister and jija at their home. She was now even more determined to fight for her rights. They talked several times, briefly, about what was bothering her. It was clear what her problem was. On the fourth day, after afternoon tea, all three drew up chairs in one corner of the lawn to have a heart-to-heart talk.

'You will agree that pitaji, and both of us too, are only concerned about your happiness, and that pitaji and we too have some experience and common sense.' It was Kanta who brought the topic up.

Kanak said, 'That same argument is made by those very people who marry off their daughters when they're fifteen and think it outrageous when their daughters utter even one word in protest.'

'But you know we're not like that,' Nayyar took over. 'We accept that when you decide to marry is essentially your prerogative, and that our agreement is necessary only as a sign of our concern for you.'

'How does it matter what I want, when you can all decide to ignore it?'

'No, that's not true. What you want comes first. There's no question of what we want or agree to, unless you say what you want first,' Nayyar explained.

'You know what I want, but you don't give a damn since you don't agree with it,' Kanak said heatedly. 'What you all want is that you choose someone for me, and I simply say yes, so that you all can say that everything was done just as I wanted.'

Nayyar stayed calm, 'Achcha, whatever you say. What I mean is that if our choice depends on your consent, your choice should also have our consent. Then the situation will balance out.'

Kanak became agitated, 'How will it balance out? You're invading my privacy and trampling on my rights. You cut my rights in half, and try to tell me that the two sides are equal. It's like the British saying that their rights and the Indians' rights are equal when it comes to deciding the future of this country. Or the Muslim League claiming the same rights as the Congress over all the provinces of India. Would you accept that? It's my whole life that's at stake, so what does any other consideration matter?'

Nayyar sounded resentful, 'How can you say such a thing? The question of our permission wouldn't arise unless we were concerned about you as family. Do you suppose that pitaji or any of us stand to profit in some way from your marriage? We see that your choice is not in your best interests. If it had been, we'd have been very pleased.'

'It's me who is getting married. What if you don't approve of my choice?'

'You speak as if we have no connection with you. You mean our advice goes for nothing? Isn't it a shortcoming in Puri's personality that he can't fit in with us? He comes from a different class. We want you to marry at you own level, or even higher. If you're bent on ruining your future, how can we stand aside and just look on in silence?'

'I've chosen him to make a success of my life,' Kanak said, dropping her gaze.

'I can't see what success he'd be able to bring to you,' Kanta objected. 'Standing next to you, he doesn't seem suitable for you. Hardly reaches up to,' she looked at her husband, 'his chin. The rest of his physique, too, is skinny; as if he was made up from leftovers during the wartime shortages when there wasn't enough of anything.'

'That's enough, bahinji!' Kanak stopped her angrily. 'What right you have to criticize others? How would you feel if I said that jijaji looks like a walking beanpole?'

'Hai, may he have my life!' Kanta laughed. 'I now must wave seven pods of dry red chilli round his head and throw them into the fire to ward off the evil eye.'

Kanak was determined not to let laughter sidetrack her, 'All you can see is someone's outsides. Just someone's wealth, car, bungalow, social standing.'

'Achcha baba, what do you see in him? Won't you be married to his body?' Kanta asked, as she leant her chin on her closed fist.

'Why, what about his literary talent, his sense of dignity, self-respect, his generosity? Does all of that go for nothing?' Kanak replied.

'You've discovered all that in such a short time?' Kanta joked.

'A person's qualities can't remain hidden for long,' Kanak said without hesitation.

'Listen, Kanni,' Nayyar said affectionately and with a serious expression. 'I admit he's a brilliant writer. I too can appreciate good writing. I took literary studies in my BA courses. He has talent, I agree. And some day he might even become a great writer. But what matters more in a marriage is not such qualities and abilities, but a person's social status and personality. Kanchi is fond of music. His teacher Muttu Baba has plenty of musical talent, but should Kanchi marry Muttu Baba? Tell me, would you approve if Kanchi were to do that? Other people have other talents. You may have respect for someone's talent, but you marry somebody with a view to making your marriage work. Do you follow me? Did you know about Tolstoy, that his wife tried to commit suicide several times because of his abuse? Tolstoy had no lack of literary talent and brilliance. Just think! Art is one thing and human qualities something else.'

'I do respect him for his human qualities,' Kanak replied with her head down.

'Listen,' Nayyar's tone became grave, 'You've known him for one year at the most. If my guess is right, the attraction between you two can't have lasted longer than seven or eight months. And that too with times in between when you couldn't see or meet one another. You may have met once in two weeks, or maybe twice in one week. In the past two or two-and-a-half months, there's been no meeting because of the riots in the city. It's quite difficult to know a person in that much time, especially when the other person is doing his best to create a good impression. Try to know the inner qualities of a person.'

'You people don't give anybody a chance for closeness to get to know the other person.'

'If you've made up your mind, what's the point of getting to know him any better?'

'Yes, my mind is made up,' Kanak said bluntly.

Kanta said pleadingly, 'You won't listen even to those who wish you well. You won't even learn from the experience of those who have been through more than you.'

'Bahinji, if all the people in this world listened to what their elders had to say, we'd still be living in the times when the Sikhs ruled the Punjab. Don't mind my saying so, but Mansa bua is the eldest in the family, but would you pay any heed to what she has to say to you?'

Next day Mahendra Nayyar had to go to the office of his senior lawyer at eight in the morning. Later in the day, both sisters were talking while lying on the bed together. Kanta said, with tears in her eyes, 'I could not tell you of this in front of my husband? Last Sunday we went over to your house after pitaji phoned us. Mahendra sat in the living room, but I went to pitaji's room. He was crying. He said to me, "Beta, you know, all children are the same for their mother and father. But, don't mind my saying so, I had expected better things from this daughter of mine. And she's the one who's causing me the most problems."

'He said, "Have I worked so hard all my life and built up so much, so that one day I could see Kanni destitute and homeless with that man? I'd be happy if I saw you all succeed in life. What else can I wish for? My daughter has ceased to trust me. She has to lie to me, and write letters without telling me. Why would I have objected if the man she fell for was any good?" You know pitaji never stood in my way. He said, "All I can wish for is that Kanak gets married, but how I can accept that man as my son-in-law?"'

Kanak began to cry, and wept for a long time. She said to her sister that afternoon, 'I wish I could drown or kill myself. You know how much I love pitaji, but I can't do anything else in this matter. Or, maybe I should forget about getting married.'

Kanta said, 'Pitaji said that he'd rather you stayed single than ruin your future in this way. Listen, Kanni, none of us likes that man. He appears to be always on guard, never his own self.'

'That's just my bad luck, isn't it?' Kanak replied and sank into silence.

Kanta had hoped that Kanak's affection and regard for her father would bring her round. Next day when Kanta brought up the subject again, Kanak said calmly, 'Bahinji, don't mind my saying so, but I must tell you this. You don't love pitaji any less than I do, but still you left him after your marriage and moved to your husband's house. In fact, today no one matters to you more than your own Nano. Pitaji too brought us up without caring for the ways of his own parents. It may sound heartless, but I'm helpless in this matter. That's what life is all about.'

'How can you be so insensitive?' Kanta interrupted her.

'I knew you'd say that. You can say what you want. I don't mind giving up my wishes for pitaji's sake, but what about the promise I gave to Puriji? He must be on tenterhooks. What if he does something desperate? Wouldn't you do anything for jijaji? Why shouldn't I?' Kanak again broke into tears.

Kanak could not face her father after finding out that he knew all her secrets and how her rebellious behaviour had hurt him. She continued to stay at her sister's house. She did her best to control her feelings, but that was not always possible. Thinking that she might be accused of not being straightforward, she said to Kanta bluntly, 'I'd like to write him a letter.'

Kanta did not know what to say. How brazen this girl had become! She thought, 'People used to point their fingers at Nayyar and me, during our courtship, called us shameless, but just look at her!' 'Wait till evening. No harm in asking your jijaji too,' she replied.

Nayyar was told of the problem in the evening. He and Kanak walked around the lawn as they talked, 'Kanni, I find myself in a strange fix. The problem is that I respect your rights, but pitaji has the right to worry over your best interests and so do we. I don't want to give up that right. That would amount to dereliction of my duty, and a terrible thing to do. I say this not only as your brother-in-law, but also because I feel affection for you as a sister and a friend. Once you too used to say that it was me whom you trusted most.' His tone became gentle, intimate, 'I don't want us to turn into lifelong enemies by taking opposite sides. And for that I'm ready to let your rights override mine. I want to help you, but I too need your help. Won't you give us a little right to worry about you?'

'Why, of course, jijayee. I'm asking you for only one thing,' Kanak stopped and said to Nayyar tenderly.

'All right then. Give me your word of honour.'

'No, jijayee.' Kanak shook her head, laughing. When she felt affectionate towards Nayyar, she sometimes shortened 'jijaji' to 'jijayee' or even to 'jiyaee'. She switched to English, 'You're very clever. You can trap me easily in the web of your words. Spell it out for me, first.'

Nayyar did not laugh. 'Listen,' he said as he continued to walk, and held her arm to make her walk alongside, 'When we asked you to come here with us, we promised pitaji that we'd convince you to think of what was good for you. Meaning not to write to Puri or meet him ...'

'That's no good to me!' Kanak cut him short. 'Kill me first, then you won't have to worry about what's good for me.'

'Listen to what I have to say,' Nayyar went on. 'I am putting a limit to what I said before, and what I thought was right. We think that you got involved with him just because of your fondness for literature. But you haven't had enough time to know and understand him, and what troubles us is that you've made a decision in an over-emotional state of mind.'

'I've done nothing wrong.'

'Right or wrong, that's a matter of opinion. I meant by committing yourself to him.'

'Jiyaee, a commitment to someone else is also a commitment to oneself,' Kanak said with a smile.

'Well, just let me finish. I think that whatever commitment you may have made, you—and we as well—should have more time to get to know and understand that man. Maybe we are at fault. Let's also make another attempt to get to know him. Since you want to get married to him, why can't we begin to appreciate his qualities too? Anything wrong in that?'

'Because you're all prejudiced against him,' Kanak said firmly without flinching. 'And that's your own doing. I put my greatest trust in you, and you're the one behind all this. Everyone in the family had a high opinion of him. When you run him down, the others just go along with you.'

'What you're saying is not true,' Nayyar explained patiently. 'But even if it were, whatever I did was out of my concern for you, not because of any animosity towards Puri. You trusted me because of my regard for you. I didn't want our plump pet pigeon to be lured away by a crow...'

'Oh, do be quiet!' Unable to hide her glee, Kanak punched his arm and said affectionately, 'You deserve a good beating.'

'Well,' Nayyar kept his serious demeanour, 'You did accuse me of prejudice. Take it as my attempt to clear myself of blame.'

'How?'

'Give us some time. I'll convince pitaji that he himself should invite Puri back. You'll be completely free to meet him when and wherever, every day if you wish. But on the condition that you behave properly and no scandal comes out of it. If your decision is the same after a year of all this, there would be no opposition from us. You agree?'

Kanak seemed satisfied, 'When will you take it up with pitaji?'

'By persuading pitaji I meant giving him a feeling of confidence and trust about that man. Personally, I've never tried to find out anything about him. I've read a couple of his short stories and an article or two, after you asked me to, and I liked them very much. I've a feeling that anyone who has such a way with words can easily lead an immature girl astray.'

'See, the same prejudice!' Kanak again threatened him with her fist.

'Well,' Nayyar remained serious as before, 'I too should know more about him and find an excuse to meet him again. But until then, as a proof of your regard for pitaji and us, you should neither write to him nor make any attempt to see him.'

Kanak said nothing.

'I think it'll take about three months,' Nayyar continued.

Kanak's eyes widened in amazement, 'Three months! You don't realize what a torture that would be for me, and an even bigger one for him. How would he know about your terms? And who knows, you might just say after three months, "Sorry, pitaji doesn't agree."'

'No, that won't happen,' Nayyar assured her. 'Agree to a three-month interval. We'll try to find out what we can about the man in that time. And tell you about our findings. If, after that time, we and pitaji still don't see eye to eye with you, or aren't able to change your mind about him, I won't consider it right to object to your meeting him.'

'Why must I suffer this torment for three months? You can make whatever inquiries you want. Leave us alone to do what we want,' Kanak said heatedly.

'That has become necessary because of your behaviour. Before you gave your word to him, you didn't think it proper to know our opinion, or pitaji's or the family's, or ask for our go-ahead. Was that proper? Why did you presume that we'd oppose you? Were you already convinced that we'd not approve of him?' Nayyar said as if cross-examining her like a witness in court.

'Absolutely not.'

'Then you should've asked us. Even if we hadn't agreed with you, at least we couldn't call your behaviour improper.'

'Improper in what way?' Kanak did not say anything more.

Nayyar said forcefully, 'Now there's only one way to resolve all this. Give us some time to make up our minds. Get rid of whatever concerns pitaji may have about your good name being dragged in the mud. Let us be sure that you'll give up anything for the sake of your love. Till now we thought it was merely a girlish crush.'

'So what if you do think it's just a crush.'

'Don't mind my saying so,' Nayyar raised his finger to warn her, 'But didn't you have a crush on someone before?'

'Why bring up that incident? I did admit my mistake then. Who doesn't make mistakes? How about you? Should I jog your memory?'

'I can make a mistake. So can anyone. So can you.'

'But I can't be afraid to make mistakes all my life. If I'm making a mistake again, don't stop me. Do you want me not to make a decision for fear of making a mistake? If I'm stupid, let me suffer the consequences.' There was anger in Kanak's tone.

Nayyar kept his voice normal, 'That means that even if you can have our help and support, you don't want it or care for it. You think it better to be disowned by your family. Does he think the same?'

'He doesn't care about all these old-fashioned ideas and ...'

'He doesn't care because he can't do anything about it. Isn't that the same thing as just not caring about it? Because, if he really doesn't care, it means that either he's not all there, or is mentally deficient. Did you ever ask him about it?'

'No, there was no occasion to.'

'I get it. My guess is that he thinks that your family would come around in the end. Or maybe he'll change his mind once he finds out that your family will disown you. Could it be that he wants your family as well as you?'

'You and your family considerations! I know that he'll give up everything for my sake.'

'If that's so, what's the harm in accepting my suggestion, and in having your family's support behind you? Two or three months are not that long a time to wait, as a prelude to such an important event in your life.'

'Sure, it is. Let me see him once at least so that I can explain all this to him.'

'I can't help you in that. I've given pitaji my word that we won't let you.'

'You can't even imagine how unfair it'd be to him,' Kanak said feebly. '...What will he think ... what's happened to me? ... Have I died or had a change of heart? He won't have any clue.'

'He should work it out if he has any sense. Pitaji probably gave him some translation work to do. When he brought it back after doing it, pitaji told him tactfully that he didn't want you two to have any relations other than those of brother and sister.'

'But I've pledged myself to him in another way.'

Nayyar said, 'Doesn't he know about that pledge? Then what does he know about you? That's what we want to see, whether he behaves like a gentleman in view of your having pledged yourself to him.'

'What'll I do if he gets depressed and loses heart?' Kanak began to cry.

'That means that you two really don't trust each other.' Nayyar asked, 'Do you know him so little after having spent so much time with him? Let's also see how much trust he has in you, and how strong is his commitment to you.'

'That's all right if he knew what was going on. That's why I want to explain all this to him.'

'What do you mean if he knew? We know how pitaji feels, how you feel. Let's find out how patient and trusting he is.'

'But what do we need this test for?'

'It's not a test for test's sake. It's to give us time to size him up, a way to judge his temperament and personality. Don't you see I'm sticking my neck out for you? Listen, I don't know how much you value him, but if you become a pariah and make him one too, that'll be creating a roadblock for your future, not making it very attractive.'

Two days later, just before Nayyar left for his office in the city, Kanak said to him, 'Jijaji, I'm ready to accept your conditions. If you don't want me to see him, let me write and explain everything to him. Then I'll do as you say.'

Nayyar refused to budge, 'I'll be risking the anger of the family if I agree to do that. I myself want to be sure that that man may not have the right personality or appearance, or even the money or social position, but at least he has some strength of character and commitment towards you.'

'Jijaji, don't make it three months.' Tears rolled down Kanak's cheeks.

'All right, two months. Two months are not enough, but we'll see. Sixty days from today. Give me your word that whether you're here or at Gwal Mandi, you'll make no effort to meet Puri or to write to him. Whatever I find out about him, I'll let you know. If something isn't clear, we'll both try to get at the truth.'

The Muslim League, in the first week of June, accepted the proposal to partition Punjab and Bengal into Hindu-majority and Muslim-majority areas. This demarcation of the areas of partition generated even more frenzied rioting and confrontations. Western Punjab had a Muslim majority, and more Hindus lived in the east, but many canal-irrigated regions of western Punjab had a predominance of Sikh farmers. In the eastern area, most workers and craftsmen in the industrial cities of Amritsar, Jalandhar and Ludhiana were Muslim. The League wanted large tracts of land to the east of Lahore to be included in Pakistan, and Congress and the Hindus wanted the boundary of Hindustan to run a long way to the west of Lahore. Lahore, almost in the centre of Punjab, was claimed by both sides.

The League and Congress accepted the British government's proposal that Hindu, Sikh and Muslim members of the Punjab Legislative Assembly could decide individually whether the people of their constituencies would choose Pakistan or Hindustan to reside in. The government also fixed a date, 20 June, for making these decisions public.

Barrister Jamal Mirza, a neighbour of Mahendra Nayyar and his family, was among the few Muslims who lived in Model Town. There was daily interaction between these neighbours, and neither had allowed the prevailing behaviour of Muslims and Hindus to dictate the character of their relationship. They also did not approve of the limitations of traditional restrictions on food or dress, and did not observe purdah. Their conversations were usually in English. They visited one another's houses and ate with each other without reservations or restrictions. The two men even went to the high court together, Mirza sometimes taking a ride with Nayyar, or Nayyar going in Mirza's car, particularly on days of rioting for the interests of safety. Mirza's younger sister was quite friendly with Kanak, whom she knew as a student at the Christian College. Both Nayyar and Mirza often had heated discussion as to where the line dividing the Punjab should run. Mirza was in favour of including even the most easterly districts of Ambala and Ferozepur in Pakistan. Punjab was one, he would argue, it should not be broken into pieces.

Nayyar would object, 'But in western Punjab, in the canal-irrigated areas of Montgomery, Lyalpur, Sargodha and Shaikhupura, Hindus and Sikhs make up 70 to 80 per cent of the population, and own most of the land in the bargain. Why should they stay in Pakistan? Should they cart off their land to Hindustan with them? Why can't Hindustan's border be placed there?'

'Who's to stop them from living in Pakistan?'

'Then what's the problem, if the Muslim-majority areas of Punjab remain in Hindustan?' There was a gradual, but marked falling-off in their daily conversations.

Kanak tried to concentrate on reading or writing, simply to pass the time. She would attempt to write a short story or play based on her own problem, or try her hand at writing an article, but did not succeed in having her imagination wipe out the ugly reality facing her. In frustration she just tore up and threw away whatever she had written. She did not feel like talking or lamenting her bad luck, either. It had become very hot in June, and people felt like taking a nap in the afternoon, at the expense of losing sleep at night.

The incidents of arson and killings in the city had greatly increased since the second half of May, but that had had very little effect on the affluent society of Model Town. Here the conflict between Hindus and Muslims and the issue of partition were purely verbal, although uttered in heated tones and mainly in English.

Nature too had been partial to this genteel colony of the affluent. Compared to the old city, it was cooler and breezier on the rooftops of Model Town at night. There were no tall buildings to prevent a breeze from blowing freely. The nights, whether moonlit or dark, were always pleasant, but for Kanak they were sheer torture. She would stare with sleepless eyes at the sky through her mosquito netting, and feel tormented by thoughts of Puri and the restrictions placed on her by her family. She could not drop off to sleep before midnight because of her unquiet mind, and because she had taken a siesta in the afternoon. She stayed downstairs and read aimlessly. The hot breeze of the first half of the night would turn cool and pleasant in the second half. It would remain cool for an hour after sunrise, lulling those sleeping on the rooftops into a deeper sleep.

Since Kanak fell asleep only late in the night, she slept until late into the morning too. A similar scene was played out on the rooftop of Mirza's house next door.

'Kanni! Kanni wake up! Come and look!' Kanta's loud call roused Kanak from her deep sleep. At once she smelled something burning. She got out of bed, pulling down the hem of her kameez.

Nayyar's mother was saying, '... I've been watching this for some time. I woke all of you just now when I began to feel scared.'

Nayyar stood there in his striped nightclothes, his eyes raised to the sky. A red storm seemed to be brewing over the city towards the north. Dark flakes of debris, like kites cut loose from their strings and floating free, were swirling high in the sky against a fiery backdrop.

'That's a terrible fire.' There was worry in Nayyar's voice. 'Difficult to say from this far where it might be.' He went downstairs.

Kanta picked up the still sleeping Nano from her bed. When she and Kanak went downstairs, Nayyar was on the telephone. They both stood next to him in curiosity and suspense. Nayyar's exclamations 'What! Oh! Really! Achcha! My God!' brought their hearts to their mouths in worry and anxiety. Nayyar hung up and said, 'The fire's burning in the bazaar inside the Shahalami Gate. It broke out around midnight. The flames can be seen from Gwal Mandi about a mile away, the air is filled with the heat given out by the flames, and there's a horrible stench of burning. The rooftops at Gwal Mandi are thick with half-burnt paper and cloth thrown up by the fire. There are rumours of shots being fired in the Shahalami area...'

Kanta's curiosity was satisfied. The fire was a mile away from her parents' home in Gwal Mandi. She set about her daily chores, but Kanak's heart began to sink. Bhola Pandhe's Gali was a long way inside the Shahalami Gate, but who could say?

'Hello, Nayyar!' Mirza called from his house. Begum Mirza's voice came too, 'Bahinji! Kanak!'

Kanak and Kanta walked with Nayyar towards the low boundary wall separating the two bungalows. Mirza said as they approached, 'Look at this! It's the beginning of the Apocalypse. Have your Hindustan and have your Pakistan! This is the end of the world. I called an uncle of Khadeeja in the old city. He lives in Chakki Gali, near Delhi Gate. The poor man was very distressed. He said that he could feel the heat beating out from the fire on his rooftop. He's afraid that the fire could spread in any direction. The idiot thought that Hindus were setting fire to the whole of Lahore.'

'The fire began in Shahalami. The Hindus will suffer the most there,' Nayyar said.

Khadeeja replied to Nayyar, 'Tauba, what savagery! No one sets fire to his own home.'

'I didn't like the scene I saw two days ago on the Mall Road,' said Mirza. 'You too must have seen the crowd gathered in front of the Assembly House. The Hindus shouting nara-e-Bajarangi! Muslims raising a shout of nara-e-Haideri! Tauba, tauba. If the police had not moved in, rivers of blood would have flowed. The tension of that situation came to a head last night.'

'But the curfew was imposed on the same day. It was in force last night too,' Nayyar expressed his doubts. 'Few people are allowed out during the curfew hours. Armed police were patrolling the bazaars. Who would have had the chance to set such a large-scale fire? Even if they began by themselves in one place, they couldn't have spread so quickly. There's a fire brigade outpost nearby in Rang Mahal.'

'Arrey bhai, with so much hatred in the hearts of both sets of people, there's bound to be destruction and killing. What else can you expect when Hindus and Muslims are bent on wiping one another out? You know what happened at the Assembly the other day. That's the root of this strife.'

Nayyar nodded his head in agreement.

'What else can happen?' Mirza switched to English. He could not carry on a discussion in Punjabi or Urdu. 'Admittedly, western Punjab has a

Muslim majority and the eastern regions have a Hindu majority, but there are vast areas in the east where village after village is Muslim. My village is near Jalandhar. All the villages for miles around are Muslim. Obviously, those people would prefer an Islamic way of life...'

'What about Lyalpur, Montgomery, Okada to the west? Those are all Hindu–Sikh villages,' Nayyar interrupted, to remind him.

'That's just what I mean,' Mirza replied. 'Just look at the warped thinking of the Hindu members of the Legislative Assembly from our western Punjab, and the Muslim MLAs from the east! Not a single Muslim MLA voted in favour of remaining in Hindustan! If these people aren't responsible for all this trouble, who is? Clearly, Jinnah will now be able to push forward his plan for shifting populations around. As far as I'm concerned, separating Hindus from Muslims and Muslims from Hindus and Sikhs, and uprooting people from the land of their forefathers is like attempting to separate one's flesh from one's bones.'

Neither Mirza nor Nayyar was happy about the antagonism between Hindus and Muslims. There was no quarrel between them; both wanted to encourage unity between the two communities, but they differed in their approaches to the question. Although their communities were at odds with each other, there own goodwill held their friendship together. That day, too, they rode together for safety's sake to the high court in Mirza's car.

By midday, Kanak was very restless. She wanted to telephone home for more news. The chances that her father would answer the telephone made her hold back. 'I'll tell pitaji that I want to speak with Kanchi,' she thought. 'But that little sneak will pass on to him what I ask her about, and he'll think that I'm concerned only on account of Puriji. So be it! Yes, I want to find out about Puriji.' Then she suddenly thought, 'Why not telephone Sarla Sharma's home near Shahalami?'

Sarla Sharma told her, 'The fire is still blazing in Shahalami, Pari Mahal, Papad Mandi, Machchi Hatta and Kanjar Phalan. It didn't spread towards Rang Mahal.' Bhola Pandhe's Gali was closer to Rang Mahal.

Kanak related all this to Kanta. The extent of the fire made both sisters anxious. That her husband had left and gone towards the city was increasing Kanta's worry. She called again towards noon to know whether the fire had spread beyond Shahalami.

Nayyar came home earlier than usual. He said, 'The fire that broke out at midnight has not been contained yet. Some parts of the Bajaj Hatta bazaar

too have burned down. All the fire engines in Lahore have been called in
to fight the blaze. The water supply of the area is not strong enough for
such a large number of engines. All the houses on the edge of the fire are
being demolished to keep it from spreading any further.

'I heard that a young Hindu man, angry at the blatant favouritism shown
by a Muslim magistrate called Cheema, had fired a shot at him. It's a well-
known fact that the officials are openly favouring the communities to which
they themselves belong. The young man was shot down on the spot at the
magistrate's order. Late at night, that same magistrate had the doors of
stores owned by Hindus broken down in his presence. Kerosene was poured
all around and the stores were set on fire. Hardly any shops are owned by
Muslims in those bazaars. Those who came to extinguish the fire were shot
dead for being out in the street during the hours of curfew.'

Nayyar told them, 'There are many rumours about how this fire
began, that it might be linked to the widespread panic among the Muslim
community after the Rajgarh incident. This could be the revenge brought
down upon the Hindus by some Muslim officials.'

The news made Kanak edgy, and she wanted to find out more. Nayyar
understood her anxiety. He made enquiries everywhere he could, and
told her that only the houses near the entrance to Bhola Pandhe's Gali and
Dhammi Gali had been demolished. The gali itself had not suffered any
fire damage.

Shahalami burned for three days before the fire could be put out. There
was peace in the city for the next six days, the kind of peace that settles
on a marketplace after two rival bulls have fought one another to a bloody
standstill. Kanak had gone to Gwal Mandi on Monday morning with Nayyar
to collect her clothing and books. Panditji asked about her health, about
Kanta and Nano, about the fear that seemed to have gripped the city after
the Shahalami fire, and then expressed his opinion that although the city
had apparently been quiet for the past week, he wasn't sure if it would
be possible to live and do business in Lahore. He might have to, he said,
move his press and publishing business to another city, maybe to Delhi,
Lucknow or Allahabad. After she spoke to her father, Kanak was forced
by her mother to drink a glass of buttermilk that she had just churned,
with a blob of butter floating on the surface. Everyone behaved as if there
had never been any quarrel or falling-out between Kanak and the family.

After she had spoken to everyone, Kanak picked up the issues of the Urdu daily newspaper and went upstairs to lie down. At Model Town, the only newspapers they subscribed to were the *Civil & Military Gazette* and the *Tribune*, both in English. The English newspapers reported the riots in brief and guarded terms, so as not to influence the public. Kanak saw the city news column in the Urdu newspaper, and read, 'High-handed treatment meted out to several young men arrested during the curfew when they had gone out to extinguish the fire burning near the Shahalami Gate. The police have yet to bring them before a magistrate. All the men were in the lock-up at the Old Anarkali police station. They had been denied their legal rights and were being subjected to unduly harsh treatment...' The newspaper also published the names of several men arrested at the site. Among them was Jaidev Puri.

Kanak's heart missed a beat. She sat up with a start. 'He's in police custody! The newspaper report says that he's being treated harshly. As it is, his mind must be in turmoil because of me. Shouldn't I go to comfort him? He's at the Old Anarkali police station. That's only ten minutes run by tonga. I don't care if anyone stops me! I'm going to go to him...' She sat in a daze for several minutes, staring at the floor.

She went to her father, and said to him in a normal but firm voice, 'Pitaji, I'm just going up to Suveera's. Her daughter is sick. I'd better go now, or it'll get too hot. I've got to go back to Model Town in the evening.'

'With such a terrible situation all around, beta? Haven't you heard about Doctor Shobha, the poor thing?' Panditji was clearly against her going out.

Kanak had heard nothing about Doctor Shobha.

Panditji said, 'Doctor Shobha Mongia, daughter of Doctor Raliaram Mongia, came to a horrible end. Doctor Raliaram used to run his medical practice in Bazaar Satthan. He purchased some land in Kila Gujjar Singh about twenty years ago, and built his dream house there, with attached clinic and dispensary. He moved into his new house in 1935. His daughter Shobha had taken her MBBS degree. A very bright and able girl. Father and daughter ran the medical practice together. Father Mongia was already well established. Shobha built up her obstetrics practice in about five years.

'Kila Gujjar Singh is a Muslim neighbourhood, but the buildings are owned by Hindus. Very few households are Hindu. After that incident in May, those few Hindus abandoned their houses and moved to localities near

Krishna Nagar and Gurudutt Bhawan. Doctor Raliaram was also advised that in the present situation it wasn't wise to stay in the neighbourhood. The doctor replied, "I'm not concerned with who's Hindu and who's Muslim. I'm only concerned about my clients. Whether Hindu or Muslim, my dharma is to attend to my patients. I have a hundred Muslim patients for every ten Hindus. Who'll look after them? How will I face my Maker?" The doctor refused to budge.

'The daughter was just like the father, kind-hearted and caring. Never refused to look at a patient, at any time, even at midnight. She used to joke: "How can one stop babies from coming? God alone decides their time of arrival, so how can humans do anything about it?" She practised moderation in everything, and always wore a white sari and a white coat over it. When Shahalami was burning, a Muslim man came to ask her for a home visit. The poor woman had just returned exhausted from another sick call. She hadn't had time even to take her coat off. They say, she told him: Come back in two hours. But the man who'd come for help was desperate. The patient was in very bad shape, he pleaded.

'Shobha handed her medical bag to the man. He had a tonga waiting. Fate played tricks; the family has their own car. Shobha too drove, and usually did her rounds by the car. But the father had taken the car elsewhere. Shobha got on the tonga. The man who had come to get her described later that the tonga had gone only about a hundred yards along the road towards the railway station when someone shouted, "That's a Hindu woman! Hindani! Grab her! Catch her!"

'The tonga driver goaded the horse to go faster. Someone threw a lathi between the horse's legs. The horse stumbled and fell. Four or five men came running up. One of them pulled Shobha out. The Muslim man who had come to take her and the Muslim tongawallah both cried for help, but none came. The goondas dragged Shobha into a gali.

'The man who had come to find Shobha went back to her house, distraught and crying. Shobha's younger brother telephoned the police. Doctor Raliaram was a highly regarded and important person. The authorities assured him that they'd search for her and they did their best too, but all their efforts went for nothing. Three days later, the doctor in despair abandoned everything, went to the railway station under police protection, and left the city.'

After hearing about the tragedy of Doctor Shobha from her father, Kanak still said, 'Pitaji, Suveera lives in Old Anarkali, near the police station. That area has never been involved in any riots.'

'Yes, that area's been free from rioting,' Panditji admitted. 'But, be patient. Tell Mahendra in the evening to go to Model Town along that route. It'll be safer in the car.'

'Pitaji, in the evening jijaji is really tired. Some days it's quite late before he's free.'

'Suveera's family has no telephone?'

'No, they don't have a telephone. And it's important that I go. I'll be back soon.' Kanak turned towards the door to leave.

'Wait, wait! I'll tell you what. Bhai Vidhichand!' Panditji turned towards Vidhichand, 'Go on your bicycle and get a tonga from the bazaar. Take care that you hire a Hindu tongawallah. I heard that Muslim tongawallahs sometimes are not all that trustworthy.'

He turned to face Kanak, 'You get into the tonga right here. Ask the tongawallah to wait when you get there.'

Kanak went into the living room to wait for the tonga.

Panditji called Kanak when the tonga arrived at the door, and said to Vidhichand in front of her, 'Bhai Vidhichand, go along with Kanni beti, down by the Old Anarkali police station. On your way back, stop at the Keval Book Depot and inquire about the cheque they were to send me in payment. Don't be too long, Kanni. Vidhichand has a lot of work to finish. Don't waste his time.'

Kanak ground her teeth in silent fury and got into the tonga. Vidhichand was a relative, but he sat in front with the driver, rather than next to his boss's daughter. The tonga was passing in front of the police station in Old Anarkali when Kanak gave the order, 'Stop here!'

Vidhichand was perplexed. Kanak got off the tonga without uttering a word and went into the police station. Vidhichand, uneasy and uncertain, had to follow her.

There was a room to the right. A man in uniform sat on a *takht* behind a low desk. His head bent, he was writing something in Urdu in a beige-coloured register. Kanak spoke to him in Urdu, 'I want to see Jaidev Puri.'

The man replied without raising his head, 'It'll cost you ten rupees.'

Kanak had some cash in her purse. She took out two fivers and held them out, 'Here.'

The constable raised his head and looked Kanak over, from head to foot, noticed her starched and ironed white dress, glanced at Vidhichand standing behind her like a servant, hesitated, gave her a respectful salaam and asked, 'Where have you come from?'

'From my home,' Kanak replied in English.

'From mimber saheb's place?' asked the constable in puzzlement, mispronouncing 'member'. 'Dhingra Saheb has telephoned.'

Not knowing what to say, Kanak said nothing. Without looking at the offered cash, the constable called, 'Chirag Deen!'

Another constable came into the room. The constable behind the desk said to him in Punjabi, 'Take bibiji to number four. She wants to speak to someone.'

Kanak went inside with the constable to a large courtyard. Vidhichand followed her like a pet dog. The constable took Kanak to a large room enclosed by an iron grille. There were several men inside. They all looked at Kanak. One of them came forward, stood close to the grille and grabbed the bars with his hands. The rest stayed back.

'How did you manage to get here?'

Kanak heard Puri's voice, but she could not recognize him immediately. His slim, short body seemed to have shrunk. His otherwise carefully shaven, pale-complexioned face had several days' growth of beard, and his hair was tousled. There was a stench of sweat. His white shirt and pajama trousers were so dirty that they appeared to be made of some dark coloured cloth, and had patches of stiff, dried sweat and grime. His face was streaked where the grime had rubbed off.

Kanak used all her strength to control herself. She said, 'I just found out, a little while ago from the newspaper report. What happened? What should we do?'

Mindful of the constable standing nearby, Puri kept his voice low and spoke in English, 'We've been shut up in this cage here like animals for the past six days. We were arrested and locked up without a warrant. We haven't been presented in any court. The law requires that we be sent to the jail lock-up. At least we would be able to get a breath of air there. I know the rules about jails and lock-ups. This is all illegal. Here the police can torture us, to make us confess to any crime. The police can harass our families and ask them for bribes for our release. We were arrested when we went to put out the fire. Seven others were shot dead. My father came here and I explained all this to him, but he's likely to listen to the advice of

his elder brother and Tara's future father-in-law Lala Sukhlal, and try to get
me out of here by bribing the police. That won't be right. We're all in this
together. If you speak to Mister Nayyar, he may submit an application in
the court about this.' Puri thought for a few moments, then said, 'Doctor
Pran Nath's influence could have been useful for getting us bail, but my
father said that his mansion has been burned down. There's no news about
where he might be.'

'I'll go and ask jijaji immediately. I've only just found out about all this.'
Kanak replied also in English. 'I tried to contact you, and sent you a letter,
but we weren't able to meet.'

That was all she could say for the moment.

Puri was talking cautiously, but Kanak was troubled by the unspoken
abuse, pain and plea for help in his voice. She bit her lip to control herself,
and looked through the bars of the cage into Puri's eyes, in order to convey
her own agony and helplessness. She turned her back to hide the tears
welling up in her eyes, and left the police station.

When she entered the living room at home, Pandit Girdharilal was
surprised to see his daughter come back so soon. He called out with great
relief, 'You're back already, Kanni beta. That's good. You did a wise thing.'
He had been right to send Vidhichand along, he was thinking.

'I'll be back in a minute,' said Kanak. She went straight upstairs, without
paying any attention to Kanchan, who was sitting and talking with their
neighbour Santosh. She almost collapsed on her bed. The sight of a suffering
and harassed Puri, gripping the bars of the cage, swam before her eyes.
The emotions rising in her heart began to seep out as tears. 'What good
will crying do?' she scolded herself, 'what I must do is something to help
him.' She could imagine how Vidhichand must be whispering about what
happened into the ear of her father. 'Let him,' she thought, 'I'll do what I
have to. Jijaji will come in the evening. But he can't bear any mention of
Puriji. I'll speak to him, nevertheless.'

'Kanni, come down. Pitaji's calling you.' Kanchan called after a while.
Kanak was prepared for that.

Panditji inquired sympathetically about everything, in detail. He did
not seem angry that Kanak had told a lie about where she was going, but
seemed only concerned with knowing the facts. What crimes were the
arrested men charged with? Had anybody applied for bail? Who would be
willing to put up the bail? Who was Doctor Pran Nath?

Kanak could not answer all the questions.

'Let's see what we can do!' Panditji muttered to himself, and turning to Vidhichand, said, 'There's a slip of paper attached to the telephone directory that has the number of the high court barristers' room. Ask them to get Mahendra Nayyar, the advocate. Say someone's calling from his home.'

He turned back to Kanak, 'When you read it in the newspaper, beta, you should've told me. Had I gone to see him, I'd have found out more. Achcha, you've been out in the sun. Go and rest.'

Kanak went back to her room and lay down, feeling unhappy that she had handed over to others the responsibility for helping Puri. She wanted to do it herself, to go quickly wherever she could, anywhere, to free Puri from that cage, but for the present she had done all that was within her powers. Another thought was surging in her mind. How big a heart her father had! All she did was to create problems for him. 'Has pitaji agreed to do what I want him to?'

In the evening, when she heard Nayyar return from the high court, she went downstairs without pausing to draw another breath. Nayyar ignored her, and went on with his explanations to Panditji, '... a defence committee of lawyers is working on the case. We're handling all riot cases without asking for any fee. The police are holding the arrested men for seven days on remand. The men will be sent to jail after that time. D.V. Sood says that bail applications for all the men have been filed.'

After telling Panditji this, Nayyar picked up a file cover from the table beside him, to show that he was ready to leave, and said, 'Achcha, I'm off. Have to prepare this case for tomorrow.' He turned and looked at Kanak, 'Are you staying or do you want to go? Got all your clothes?'

His tone of voice told Kanak that he was not very eager for her to come along, but he was the only person who could help Puri. 'I'll get them. I'm ready,' she replied.

Sensing Nayyar's silence as they drove to Model Town, Kanak ventured, 'Jijaji, you're so quiet. Are you angry with me?'

'No, nothing like that. I'm thinking of my case tomorrow. It's a bit complicated.' Nayyar did not answer her question.

Kanak said, 'Puriji's father and his sister's future father-in-law wanted to get him out by bribing the police, but he wouldn't let them. You couldn't have helped crying if you'd seen the state he was in, but he still refused to get out by illegal means.'

'Very well. Let's see what happens,' said Nayyar. He did not say anything further. Later in the evening, and the next morning too, they exchanged only a few words. Kanak got ready to go to Gwal Mandi so that she could keep abreast of any developments.

Nayyar said, 'I'm going that way. I've no objection to your coming along. But if a phone call can be made from the high court to Gwal Mandi, it can be made to Model Town too. However, its your call.'

'Why you're being so curt and offhand with me! What's the harm if I come along? I won't go out anyway,' she said as they drove to Gwal Mandi. Nayyar remained silent.

Kanak was waiting when Nayyar arrived in the evening. She had asked Kesari to keep tea ready. She looked at Nayyar affectionately as he came into the living room. He just nodded a namaste to her, glanced into the door to the office, and called, 'Pitaji, close down the office now. Why don't you call it a day?'

'I'm coming,' came Panditji's reply.

Nayyar took a chair next to Kanak. Kanak's eyes were dancing with desperate curiosity. Just to prolong the agony of her desperation, he asked, 'So, what have you been up to all day?'

'Nothing. Tell me, what happened?'

'About what?' he asked.

Kanak did not like this rebuff. Panditji came into the living room and said, 'Kanni, ask for tea to be served. My back stiffens up so much after sitting so long in the chair.' He moved his arms to stretch his body before sitting down and asked Nayyar, 'Yes, what happened? Today was their appearance in court.'

'Nothing,' Nayyar gave Kanak a sideways glance, and said nothing more.

'No bail was granted?' Panditji asked grimly. Kanak's heart was in her mouth.

'Uh-uh.'

'At least they must have been ordered to be transferred from the police station to the jail lock-up?' Panditji asked.

'Well, no.' Nayyar again kept silent for a moment. Then, as if feeling pity for Kanak, he said, 'I myself represented him, and asked Rai Bahadur to be present as well. For Rai Bahadur just to be there is unsettling for a magistrate of these lower courts. We said that there were no grounds for posting bail. So he was released without bail. Five other men were let off at the same time. Only three now remain in the lock-up.'

'You're a fine boy!' Panditji said in English and slapped himself on the knee as he congratulated Nayyar.

Kanak felt as if an iron vice gripping her heart had been loosened, and she could breathe freely. She shot an angry, pouting glance at her brother-in-law, as if to ask, 'Why did you have to make me suffer so much?'

Chapter 12

THE LAST CASE THE COURT HEARD WAS THAT OF PURI AND MEWA RAM. THE court sat for an extra half-hour, and Puri and Mewa Ram were released. Masterji, Ratan and Khushal Singh had been present in court since ten in the morning. Babu Govindram had had Ratan released four days earlier. The bail hearing for Bir Singh and others was postponed for three days. Puri had been arrested at the time of the Shahalami conflagration, when it was hazardous to pass through the fire-ridden bazaars of Bajaj Hatta and Machchi Hatta. Those arrested had been taken to the police station by way of Rang Mahal and Delhi Gate. The blaze had since subsided. Puri and the others returned to their homes through Shahalami.

The once bustling and vibrant bazaars of Shahalami had been burned to the ground. What remained were the ruins of two-, three- and four-storey houses, and vast mounds of garbage. A narrow path straggled between the rows of giant burnt-out pyres. To remove that debris would have been like digging up and carting away a mountain. Stumps of wooden beams, fallen steel girders, the remains of doors and frames, and charred planks were scattered around. From some still-standing smoke-blackened walls, broken balcony railings hung like skeletons or jutted out like the rib cages of giant animals. Bent and twisted water pipes and iron rods, as if they were the intestines of the burnt-out buildings, swung slowly in the wind. A terrible stench made one hold one's nose.

As Puri and Mewa Ram stepped into Bhola Pandhe's Gali, it rang with the cries of children playing in the lane, 'Jaddi bhappa and Mewa bhappa are back!'

When Bhagwanti heard the shout, she went down the stairs in such a hurry that she stumbled and almost fell. She screamed and burst into sobs as she clasped her grown-up son to her breast right on the chabutara. She had done the same when Puri had come back from prison two years before. Everyone in the gali came out of their homes to welcome the freed men. The sound of Kartaro crying loudly came from Khushal Singh's house. She had uttered a scream when she did not see Bir Singh return with Puri and Mewa Ram, and had begun to wail that her son had been left behind in the lock-up. 'The rich and resourceful can manipulate things. Why did they make a poor person's son accompany them at curfew time?'

Puri freed himself from his mother's embrace and said *pairipaina* to Meladei. Tara and Usha gave him a hug. Hari touched the feet of his elder brother. Tara said with pride, 'Our brave brother didn't care if he was sent to jail for the sake of his country and the truth. He spent two years in prison before this as well.'

When he saw Tara, Puri thought of Kanak coming to see him in the police cells, and of his own indignation with Kanak in the days before that.

He also noticed the faint lines of the scar on her forehead. It did not show much against her fair complexion, but the cross-like scar reminded him of the incident five weeks before, and the date of Tara's wedding three weeks hence. He turned his eyes away.

Before going up the stairs to his house, Puri went to Khushal Singh's place. He said to Kartaro, 'Masi, *pairipaina*,' and assured her that Bir Singh would be home soon.

The people of the gali did not want to let go of Puri. They made him sit with them and began to talk about the frontier between Pakistan and Hindustan that was to divide up Punjab. Everyone was certain that Hindustan would begin from the city of Lahore on the eastern bank of the Ravi River. The Radcliffe Commission had proclaimed that Sialkot in the north and Bahawalpur-Khairpur in the southwest would be part of the new Pakistan. If Lahore were to be included in the partition, the Commission would surely have mentioned this. Who could overlook the fact that 80 per cent of the real estate in Lahore was owned by Hindus.

Puri was told that after the Shahalami fire, Ghasita Ram and Panna Lal had locked up their houses and gone on pilgrimage to Mathura and Vrindavan. The gali people knew that the fire had scared them off, but not everyone had the means to leave like that.

Puri came upstairs for his dinner after Usha and his mother had called him several times. Tara served him as he sat down in the kitchen. His mother came and sat beside him. There were several kinds of vegetables in his thali. 'Are you trying to make up for the past two weeks in one go? So many things to eat in one meal?' Puri said to his mother. He found himself unable to speak directly to Tara.

'It's not so much,' his mother replied. 'Pushpa and Ratan's mother sent a dish each for you. Rampyari and Jeeva too brought something.'

'Have I become a guest in my own home just because I was away for a couple of days?' Puri showed his surprise, 'Neighbours usually do that when some guest arrives.'

'Kaka, if your neighbours don't help you out in your ups and downs, how could you live in the gali?' His mother said, and began to unload her anxieties onto her son, 'When you weren't here, you know we couldn't do anything. Hardly any time is left before the date of the wedding. Whatever else might happen in the city, the marriages that have been settled are being carried through. We must arrange for everything in the next two or three weeks.'

Puri did not look at Tara, but he knew she was silent, as girls were supposed to be when any talk of their marriage came up. She gave no sign of disagreement or dissatisfaction. A weight rolled off his mind, but left him with a feeling of sadness.

After dinner, Puri lay down on a charpoy on the rooftop. Masterji and the others on the roof, not wanting to disturb his rest, left him alone. The roof had been baking in the strong June sun, and its floor, the surrounding low walls and the corrugated tin roof over the *barsati* gave off waves of heat. But he did not feel the heat. After being locked up day and night for a week in that cage, Puri could enjoy the luxury of lying, even on a bare charpoy, in the open air under the faint moonlight. Only a few hours before he had been confined, and now! Wondering at the difference between his feelings of confinement and freedom, and relishing the pleasure of being at liberty, he could not sleep as thoughts crowded his mind and various images flashed through.

His thoughts did not dwell on community or social problems. Such ideas now seemed to him to be of little substance. His thinking and wishes seemed to have no influence upon a society composed of millions of others. Who knew what forces were at work in this human anthill, but it did not seem possible for an individual to make his way except in the direction the masses were going. Each member of this mass of people had his own worries; he had his own, Kanak had hers, and perhaps Tara too. His thoughts turned to Kanak.

His heart had been cleansed of all resentment against Kanak for having betrayed his trust. She had flown to his aid as soon as she knew about his troubles. There was no question of her loyalty to him, and he felt ashamed of having doubted her and of being angry with her. Nayyar had represented him in court along with Rai Bahadur. Has Kanak been able to handle the situation with her family? Otherwise, why would they have taken the trouble for me as they did? The week spent in that hellhole, this detestable ordeal was perhaps a necessary prelude to the beginning of my new life...he thought. Kanak had come to the police station and now he ought to go to her place to convey his thanks and express his gratitude for the help given by Panditji and Nayyar. Then he thought of the history book that he was translating ... had this disruption not occurred, the work would have been finished by now. Well, now he would work day and night, and try to finish what was left, and do his revision within three or four days, and hand it over to Ghaus Mohammed. Money was desperately needed in the house.

He began his work early next day. If someone came to congratulate him on his release from the lock-up, he'd get up and give the visitor a hug in welcome, talk with him for a short time and then return to his work. He meant to go to Gwal Mandi in the evening. For that, he needed clothes that were washed and ironed. Distressed by his arrest, the family could hardly have looked after his wardrobe in his absence. Puri had asked Usha in the morning to wash and iron his shirt and trousers.

He worked until five in the afternoon, then changed into fresh clothes and left for Gwal Mandi. To avoid looking at the horrible vista of the devastated bazaars, he went by the roundabout route of Vachchovali, Sootar Mandi and Lohari Gate, then took Hospital Road to Gwal Mandi. Nayyar's car was parked outside the entrance to Shaduram's Gali. The thought of Nayyar's presence at the moment of meeting Kanak dampened his enthusiasm. The door of the entrance to Panditji's office was closed. Puri was about to turn back, intending to return next day when Nayyar came through the door that opened into the living room.

Puri paused, finding relief in the possibility that Nayyar might be leaving. He smiled, said namaste, and began to offer his thanks.

Nayyar acknowledged with his customary reserve, then changed his expression to a smile of welcome, held out his hand and said, 'Come, come, Mister Puri.'

'I came to express my gratitude to Panditji and to you,' Puri said in English, using a phrase he had already thought up. 'It's fortunate that I met you.'

'There's no question of gratitude.' Nayyar held on to his hand and led him back into the living room. 'It was nothing to me. It was my duty. The lawyers' defence committee was formed for this very purpose. I am sorry that you had to suffer so much when you were only trying to help others.' Nayyar showed him to the sofa, and turning his face towards the aangan, called, 'Kesari, bring some tea.'

Puri had never seen Nayyar so polite and friendly.

'Which newspaper are you working for, these days?' Nayyar asked, sitting on the chair next to Puri.

Puri replied that he was not attached to any one newspaper, but was doing literary work as a freelancer.

Nayyar said, 'Wah, that's very good. You've freedom to do whatever you want. Isn't that what you wanted?'

'Yes, I'm quite happy about that.'

'Is Master Ramlubhaya your father?'

'Yes.'

'He'd mentioned Dr Pran Nath in connection with your bail. Is that the same Pran Nath, the university professor, who's also the advisor to the governor?'

'Yes,' Puri admitted, adding quickly so that it might not be taken as a boast of friendship with such an important person, 'Doctor saheb was a student of my father, and I was his student in turn. He's been very kind to me.'

'He's a decent and competent person, I know. He was one year senior to me at the Government College. Knew him then. Haven't had a chance to meet him in the past ten years or so. And who's this Lala Sukhlal?'

'Lala Sukhlal is a relative.'

'Your father, Masterji's brother or …?'

'No. A future relation. My sister's future father-in-law.'

'Oh, achcha. Sukhlal wields considerable influence in some circles. Your sister perhaps is Kanak's fellow student. She's finished her BA?'

'No. She deposited her fees for her exam in March. We thought that she'd sit for the exam and her wedding would take place afterwards. But the examinations were postponed.' From Nayyar's friendly tone and his inquiries, Puri could feel a change from his earlier attitude.

'Who is this tea for?' Kanchan's voice came from the aangan.

'Jijaji has asked for it,' the servant replied.

'Jijaji has gone out,' said Kanchan as she entered into the living room. Seeing that Nayyar was talking with Puri, she said namaste to Puri and asked, 'Shall I serve the tea for you people?' She poured tea into two cups.

'Kanchi, you're not having any?' Puri asked in a tone of familiarity.

'I've just had some with Pitaji,' she replied. She did not say anything else, but left after pouring the tea.

'There are problems everywhere because of the disturbances in the city. Will your sister's marriage be postponed until after her exams in September?' Nayyar asked, showing great concern.

'No, that won't be possible,' Puri said, grasping his knee in his clasped hands, 'The groom's parents don't want that.'

'Well, that's not a big problem,' Nayyar expressed his sympathy. 'She can appear for her exam after her wedding. The preparation for the exam will of course be disrupted. But marriage is a bigger exam than even the BA.' Nayyar laughed. 'It's become a problem to find suitable matches for educated girls. It's your good luck that your family found a good match for your sister. What's the name of Lala Sukhlal's son?'

'Somraj.'

'Somraj... er, is he a professional or is in civil service?'

'He's probably helping in the family business. I'm not quite in the know.' Puri found his own answer somewhat inadequate. He added quickly, 'The engagement was made in 1944 while I was in prison.'

'It's an arranged marriage then?'

Puri said uncomfortably, 'Yes, in a way arranged, but both parties were given a chance to see and get to know each other. I was in prison at the time.'

'That's good. If the boy and the girl are happy and the family is satisfied, what else is needed?' Nayyar said approvingly.

'You're right,' Puri breathed more easily now that the subject had ended.

Puri had finished his tea, and Nayyar had drunk only half of his. He began to pour more tea into Puri's cup.

Puri said politely, 'Have some yourself. You haven't finished yours yet.'

'I'll take some more shortly. You go ahead.' He filled Puri's cup.

Nayyar talked about various things to keep the conversation going, 'Why don't you write for the cinema? How much does a good journalist earn working freelance? Why don't you go to some hill station to have peace to write?' He seemed curious to know all about Puri.

Puri finished his second cup and asked, 'If Panditji is at home, I'd like to pay my respects to him and express my gratitude.'

'He's in, but he's not well. He just went to lie down. Don't stand on ceremony. I'll ask Kanchan to tell him later.'

Puri finally said what he had been gathering courage to say, 'I also wanted to thank Kanakji for her help.' He knew that Nayyar and Panditji had helped him at the request of Kanak. His guess was that the fact of her going to the police station would be known to them, so he said, 'She took the trouble to come to the police station.'

'Yes, you're right,' Nayyar agreed. 'The news that you were in the police lock-up was a matter of great concern to us. But she is not in at the moment. She's at Model Town. She comes here often, though.' Nayyar said reassuringly, 'I'll tell her too that you conveyed your thanks. I believe Panditji had some discussion with you about Kanak?' Nayyar stared hard into Puri's eyes.

Puri's face took on a serious expression. He looked away as he thought for a moment. Owing to the seriousness of the conversation, he chose his words carefully and replied in English, 'Yes, he did speak with me. But the reason for my coming here was that I felt it was my duty to fulfil an obligation. Kanak went to the police station because of her regard or sympathy for me.' He said more resolutely, 'You probably would have thought it ungrateful of me if I hadn't come here to express my gratitude. And in order to do that, I had to forget my feelings of dignity and self-respect to some extent.' Puri's face flushed with anger.

'My dear friend!' Nayyar gave a shrug of discomfiture at Puri's words, and placed his hand on the armrest of the sofa as he too explained in English, 'You misunderstood my intentions. May I say something, if you will allow me, as a friend to both you and Kanak? I won't want to overstep my boundary by offering advice to both of you.'

Puri was embarrassed, 'No, no, please do tell me.' He asked, 'Should I not have accepted her gesture of regard for me?'

'Of course! Why not?' Nayyar said in agreement.

'Panditji may not have interpreted the situation fully, and I too couldn't explain because I was so embarrassed.' He was speaking cautiously, 'I'm aware of the difference between her circumstances and mine. I don't think I ever overstepped that dividing line. In fact, I've never thought about marrying or starting a family without first having a firm financial footing.'

'Quite right. Marriage means that one takes on the responsibility of supporting one's wife,' Nayyar said, again showing his agreement.

'I'd reacted to her feelings out of regard for her, and out of respect for Panditji, and gave her my word for that reason. She knew about my strained situation right from the beginning. Now I find I'm in a strange bind.'

'I understand.' Nayyar rested his shoulders and head against the back of the chair as if to bear the weight of this understanding, and fingering his tie, said, 'I think I follow. Yours can be a difficult situation. I know that Kanak has rather romantic ideas of life, and was drawn to you because of your talent and her literary leanings. That girl doesn't hesitate or even think it necessary to hold back once an idea comes into her head. You do reciprocate her feelings?'

'Well... yes. Your guess is correct.'

'It's all quite natural,' Nayyar conceded. 'But you will agree that marriage means more than emotional compatibility. Marriage is not merely a relationship between two persons. It becomes, at least in our society, a relationship between two families. Don't mind my saying so, but I don't think it would be very pleasant to face the opposition of everyone in the other family or to be always at odds with them all your life. It's easy to see that Kanak is an attractive girl, and not only she but lots of other educated and impressionable girls would find you attractive. That's normal. No harm in calling a spade a spade. So many times in one's life one is attracted to someone, but one must also consider so many other factors before committing oneself for life. I hope you don't think I'm treading on your toes by saying such things?'

Puri shook his head, and said, 'Please go on.'

'Of course, if you'd spoken to me before reaching a decision—after all, we've been friends for close to one-and-a-half years—I'd have alerted you to the facts of the situation. Panditji may be a man of liberal outlook, he still has some other convictions too,' Nayyar said, weighing each word carefully. 'I personally am in favour of freedom for a man and a woman to marry whomsoever they wish, but at times one can face a dilemma. For example, let's assume that my sister's, or as is the case, your sister's marriage is being arranged. It was a matter of luck that the girl liked the boy, and that you too found him suitable for her, right?'

'Yes.'

'Had you thought,' Nayyar said with emphasis, 'the boy to be unsuitable, for any reason, you'd have told your sister so, and if you could manage it, stopped her from going ahead.'

'Well,' Puri entwined his fingers and cracked his knuckles, feeling that the lawyer had pushed him into a corner. Plucking up courage to give force to his words, he replied, 'I'd have discouraged her, but only to a certain point.'

'Sure, if she hadn't listened to you, you still wouldn't have acted against your better judgement. Would you have kept back all your support from her? Just think, if Kanak insisted on something like that, what price she'd have to pay to drop from her present circumstances?' Nayyar spoke with a grave resonance, a lawyer summing up his argument before a justice of the high court, 'My dear friend, you mentioned the issue of self-respect. Keeping that in mind, just think whether you are paying a similarly high price for the sake of this relationship?'

Every hair on Puri's body began to tingle with indignation. He could not speak for several moments. While addressing him as a friend, this lawyer had trapped him and pulled him down with his glib talk. He felt a deep sense of self-disgust. 'Why did I ever come to this house? The polished arrogance of the bourgeoisie!'

He got up and said, 'I've already told you that I've insisted on nothing up till now, and I don't intend to. Namaste!' He went out of the living room without a glance at Nayyar.

Kanak and Kanta had been anxiously waiting for Nayyar to come home. Kanta said reproachfully, 'What's kept you so late? You know how bad things are out there! I was half-dead with fear.'

'I was delayed at Gwal Mandi,' Nayyar replied.

Kanak said teasingly, 'Sure, when you have friends to chat with, why bother what happens to anybody else? We didn't even have tea while we were waiting for you.'

'Yes, I certainly was having a chat, but with someone else's friend,' Nayyar said to Kanak. 'I have a message for you too.'

'From whom?'

'From Puri.'

'Let's have tea first. My throat's parched,' said Kanta, and began walking towards the rattan chairs and table on the lawn, where the tea service was laid out.

Nano was playing with a huge ball on one side of the lawn. She held out her arms and called, 'Papa! Papa!'

'I had a cup with Puri. All right, I'll have another.'

Nayyar went to Nano. He threw her into the air and caught her, tickled her and swung her upside down in a circle. The child's ringlets and flounced frock billowed with the motion. She screamed with glee.

'That's enough, you spoiled little rascal!' Kanta lovingly scolded the child.

Nano had just learned to run. She would run with unsteady steps towards her parents who cooed in encouragement. She wanted to go on playing tag with her papa. Kanak impatiently watched Nano running with her chubby arms raised to Nayyar who was taking tiny steps backwards.

Nayyar came over and pulled up a chair near Kanak, across from Kanta. Kanak asked in a breathless voice heavy with curiosity, 'What did he have to say?'

Nayyar thought for a moment, sipping his tea, then said, 'He conveyed his thanks to you for going to meet him at the police station, and for your help.'

'And?'

He again sipped his tea before replying in a solemn tone, 'The rest of what he said wasn't very nice. At least, I didn't find it so.'

The glow in Kanak's eyes dimmed. She asked, 'What else?'

'That he thought that there never was any obligation to you, and that there's none now.'

Kanak's face darkened as she dropped her eyes. She said after a moment's thought, 'I don't believe you. Who's to say what he was thinking when he said that?'

'What context can there be other than your relationship with him?'

'You must have said something insulting to him. He prides himself on his dignity,' Kanak said with a little vexation.

'We were talking at your home. I'm not so lacking in politeness as to insult a guest. I simply asked him if both the families refused to go along with your decision, what price were you both willing to pay?'

'All right, I took the first step,' she said looking down, but turning towards Nayyar. 'Is it only a man who can take the initiative? Why not a woman?'

'It's strange for anyone to say what he did. Does that mean he really values you? It sounds as if you're running after him,' Kanta was displeased with Kanak's answer. 'Don't you have any self-respect?'

'Yes, a woman can certainly take the initiative, why shouldn't she?' Nayyar said in a conciliatory tone. 'But conceitedness is out of place for either a man or a woman. If you love someone, you can't put that person down. Why should anybody degrade that person in the eyes of other people?'

'But the fact is,' Kanak said biting her lip, 'it was he who made the first move.'

'Perhaps. It doesn't matter who acted first,' Nayyar said placidly. 'But even if you were the one to take the first step, like, for example, your sister who first showed romantic inclinations towards me ...'

'Liar!' Kanta, eyebrows raised in protest but with a smile on her lips, wagged a spoon to threaten Nayyar. Kanak could not see the humour.

'It's all right, if you don't want to admit it,' Nayyar too retained his serious demeanour, 'but still it was I who went to your father to ask for your hand. Who else could I have asked for it? Even if the woman takes the first step, it's still appropriate for the man to take the responsibility. A woman, because of some feeling of inferiority, takes pride in having herself asked for.'

'What airs you men put on!' Kanta interjected.

Nayyar pressed on, 'But if a man acts that way, it means that he must have an inferiority complex.'

'What kind of inferiority would he have?' Kanak asked, with a frown.

'I didn't say that he was inferior, but that he had an inferiority complex. Why did he say that there was no insistence from his side? It means that he doesn't consider himself fit to make an offer. He admitted that he was conscious of his difficult circumstances. That's why he never dared propose to you.'

'That's not true, but let it go. You're a lawyer, you can entangle him in your web of words, and make him say what you want. He's not devious and sly like you.'

'Am I devious and sly?' Nayyar asked.

'You are, indeed,' Kanak said with a laugh.

'And he's honest and truthful?' Nayyar remained serious.

'I fully believe he is,' Kanak said firmly.

'I have evidence to the contrary,' Nayyar said softly.

'What evidence?' Kanak challenged him.

Nayyar pondered for a moment before asking, 'The name of Puri's sister is Tara?'

'Yes. I know her. She's very brilliant, just like her brother. Very pretty too.'

'She was to sit for her BA exam this year?'

'Yes. So what?'

'Do you know she's getting married in July?'

'Oh... so?'

'Do you know to whom?'

'I don't know.'

'You're not on close terms with her?'

'Not very.'

Nayyar reflected a bit before asking, 'Do you remember, last year there was an altercation between a student and the invigilator at the university's Senate Hall? The matter didn't end there.'

'Yes. I do remember. When Professor Deen Mohammed was beaten up.'

'The name of that student was Somraj Sahni.'

'Probably. I don't remember.'

'Would you believe that an intelligent girl would agree to marry a man as disreputable as Somraj Sahni?'

'I don't know. I hope not... Why?'

Nayyar again thought a moment before replying, 'Puri's sister is being married to Somraj Sahni. I heard that the girl was against this marriage, but her brother and family overruled her objections.'

'This is the limit! He wants freedom just for himself. Marrying off his sister against her will!' Kanta said with disgust.

'That's not possible. I can't believe that,' Kanak protested.

Nayyar pushed back his chair and stood up. He pointed to the car parked in the driveway and said, 'Let's go to Bhola Pandhe's Gali right now. Everything will be cleared up then.'

'What'll be cleared up?' Kanak looked straight at him.

'You can find out for yourself whether or not Tara is being married in July to Somraj Sahni, who was caught cheating at an exam in the Senate Hall.'

'Wah, what kind of evidence is that? It could be Tara's wish too.'

'Your imagination has no limits,' Kanta said.

'You already did concede that a bright girl wouldn't agree to marry a man like Somraj,' Nayyar raised his index finger to remind Kanak.

'But it's not impossible. He may have some other saving graces.'

'What saving graces? Is he a great poet like Tagore, or a patriot who was a member of the Indian National Army?'

'How do I know? It's a question of one's tastes and likings.'

'I even heard that the girl was beaten up when she objected. That she was wounded on the head. Feeling defeated, she wound up saying nothing.'

'Impossible!' said Kanak and looked away. She then said, 'I'll ask Tara myself.'

'How would she have the courage to tell you the truth, now that she has accepted defeat?' Nayyar said. 'I had Puri confess it to my face.'

'What did he confess?' Kanak looked at Nayyar.

'Listen, I didn't tell Puri that I knew about the marriage. Somraj's father Sukhlal had come along with Puri's father to the court. Puri told me that Sukhlal was Tara's future father-in-law. I asked, what did her fiancé do? Is he a professional or is he employed somewhere? Is he a good match? Puri replied that Tara's fiancé was quite suitable, and was probably working with his father in the family business. He didn't know any more. The whole city knows about the Senate Hall affair, but Somraj's future brother-in-law, who's a journalist, doesn't know about it! Who would believe that?'

'How can that be possible?' Kanta said in disbelief. 'He's a first-class liar and faker.'

Kanak sat bolt upright in her chair, 'Listen, bahinji, don't start calling him names! I can't ...'

'Enough! Oho! No one's calling him names,' Nayyar intervened. 'I simply repeated to you what he said to me. What do you have to say about his pretending to be in the dark?'

'This all is legal doubletalk,' Kanak replied. 'He didn't confess that he was forcing his sister into that marriage.'

'How could he admit that?' Kanta said.

'Well, his not knowing about that Somraj affair certainly showed him up in his true colours,' Nayyar insisted.

Kanak got up and went inside the house. She lay down on her bed and covered her face with her aanchal.

Chapter 13

PURI HAD GONE TO KANAK'S HOUSE AS A COURTESY AFTER HIS RELEASE FROM the lock-up, but in return had received nothing but insults. That had upset him very much. He believed that Kanak was willing to do anything for him, to climb down from the reaches of her upper-middle-class status and stand by his side in the everyday life of the gali. But he could not forget or ignore the slight made by Nayyar.

So Puri began to reconsider: Would it be right for any self-respecting person to expect Kanak or any cultured, well-brought-up woman to live with him in his present situation without his losing his self-esteem? Why bring home flowers when one did not have a vase to put them in? There was no way he could silence Nayyar and Pandit Girdharilal without first getting rid of this stigma of unemployment and the chains of poverty. Unless he could bring Kanak home with due ceremony in his own motorcar, it would be a travesty to even think of asking her to come to him. And it would be perfectly justifiable for her family to insult him as they had done. He could not picture Kanak washing dishes or doing the laundry in the kitchen of his home in Bhola Pandhe's Gali wearing an old torn shalwar like his sisters, or only a petticoat and blouse like his mother. He convinced himself that it had been a mistake to feel attracted to Kanak before having a solid ground beneath his feet. Why ruin her life, and his own into the bargain?

Puri made a determined effort to control his thoughts, and set about finishing what was left of the history book. He completed the work and its revision in four days. He had decided to go and see Ghaus Mohammed at five that afternoon and deliver the finished work. He wrapped up the manuscript in a neat packet. He was sitting and talking with Khushal Singh on the chabutara in front of the house of the Woman of the Well. After his shop had been destroyed in the Shahalami fire, Khushal Singh had begun selling his wares from the chabutara nearest to the bazaar. Mukund Lal had set up his own shop on the chabutara of Bajaj Dewanchand.

Tikaram usually came back late from the office. That day he returned before 4 o'clock. Seeing his strained expression, Khushal Singh inquired, 'Babu, what's the matter? Why this long face?'

Tikaram worked at the Said Mittha bazaar branch of his insurance company. The mansion of Kammu Shah had been burned down last night, he said, as had been the office of the insurance company next door to it. There had been a number of knifings in that area, and several persons had been killed. All the employees of his branch had been summoned to the McLeod Road office and told that for the next month they would have to work in the record section at that office. They would be reassigned after the month, and go wherever the company told them.

While Tikaram was telling his story, Ratan arrived. Since all the business in the city had come to a standstill, there was little to do at his uncle's brokerage agency. Everyone knew that Babu Govindram had made money in wartime, and had built two houses in Krishna Nagar. He had continued to live in Bhola Pandhe's Gali for the high rents he earned from the other properties. Ratan could not care less if there was no work at the agency; he had other things to take care of.

The Radcliffe Commission had not yet announced where the boundary would run between Hindustan and Pakistan, to the south and east of Lahore. Lahore's status was still undetermined, but the district of Shaikhu Pura, across the river from Lahore, had been given to Pakistan. Scores of Hindu merchants, from towns and villages between Shaikhu Pura and Peshawar further to the north-west, were fleeing to the east. Camps for these seekers of refuge had been set up on the property of Rai Bahadur Badridas on Abbot Road, next to Ratan Talab outside Shahalami, in the Shiv temple of Melaram, in Gurudwara Shaheed Ganj near the fort, and in the neighbourhood of Gurudutt Bhawan. Ratan often went to one of these to help out. Mewa Ram and Bir Singh too, after he was released from the lock-up, went with him. These men also went to the railway station on behalf of the Hindu Defence Committee, to escort arriving Hindu travellers to their homes in the galis or to a refugee camp.

Birumal came back from his job at the post office just before five. He wanted to know the reason for the men of the gali to be huddled. Tikaram repeated the story of the burning of Kammu Shah's mansion and his office building.

Ratan breathed a silent curse, 'The Hindus are just not fighting back. What's to be done?' He cursed again, 'Muslim policemen are openly helping other Muslims. Between a hundred and a hundred-and-fifty displaced Hindus are arriving daily from the west ...'

Birumal butted in, 'Do you know what's being done to the Muslims in the east? Yaqub works in our section, he's from Bagwanpura. That bugger was crying. He lives in a two-room place. His father, his father-in-law and others fled from Kapoorthala and came to his house. His elder brother was murdered; his sister and sister-in-law were both kidnapped. There are now seventeen people in his two rooms. He was telling us that over two thousand people were crammed into the Bagwanpura Muslim camp. The stench is so bad that one can't breathe.'

Puri got up from where he was sitting next to Khushal Singh, and said, 'Achcha, I've to go. Just going up to Mori Gate.'

'What? You're out of your mind?' Tikaram stopped him. 'I've just told you how bad it was in that area. It's not safe to go there on your own today.'

'Bhai, I've got to go to get money someone owes me,' Puri explained.

'Let the money go to hell! No one goes there this evening!' Khushal Singh said decisively.

'What's your hurry? Wait it out for today. I'll go with you tomorrow morning around eight or nine,' Ratan volunteered.

'Not one but two people should go along to a place like that. Mori Gate is just beside Said Mittha,' someone else said.

Puri had to give up his idea of going to Mori Gate. The thought of taking bodyguards to meet a person like Ghaus Mohammed was not agreeable. Next day around nine in the morning, he went alone, with the manuscript tucked under his arm. He did not go by way of Machchi Hatta and Shahalami, but rather through Vachchovali, Sheesha Moti and Sootar Mandi towards Lohari Gate. Mostly Hindus lived in this area. By and large the shops were open, but the bazaars were not crowded. In the intersection near Sootar Mandi, he saw Masood, carrying a similar but slightly smaller package like his own.

'Hey bhai Puri!' Masood hailed him. 'I was horrified by the hellish sight Shahalami has become, I swear. Didn't have the nerve to face that, so I was going round to your place by this route.'

Masood's face looked haggard and drawn. His clothes, although seldom clean and tidy, now gave off a terrible stench of sweat. His usual black fur hat was missing too. Puri held out his hand, and asked, 'Is everything all right? What can I do for you? Tell me!'

'Everything's going to hell!' Masood said, letting out a deep sigh. 'You probably don't know. Poor Ghaus, may God grant him peace, has been killed.'

'What?' exclaimed Puri as the package almost fell from under his arm. He felt numbed with shock. His three months' hard work, his dreams, the sum of five hundred and fifty rupees, all disappeared in that split second.

'I was going to his place. The five hundred fifty he owed to me are gone too,' Puri blurted out, showing the package under his arm. He composed himself, and added, 'But what are five hundred? Even five hundred thousand are not worth someone's life.'

'Bhai, Ghaus was really a good human being,' Masood let out another sigh. 'There wasn't one speck of religious prejudice in him. He was martyred because of his Muslim-looking *sharai* beard. Who knows what further atrocities these riots will bring?'

'He was stabbed with a kirpan in front of the S.P.S.K. Hall,' Masood said. 'The attacker ran away leaving the dagger stuck in Ghaus's belly. When he fell, it pierced through to his back. I went just to meet him yesterday evening, and what I saw was his bier being carried out. My heart broke when I heard the whole story. Such a good-natured, outgoing person and not even ten persons could be found to mourn him. They took him to the cemetery in a police lorry. Only three people were allowed to attend his burial.'

Masood went on, 'You know how we all depended on him. He had asked me to prepare notes for the middle school exam. We settled for one hundred rupees. I have the agreement in his handwriting. The notes are ready,' Masood showed the package under his arm, 'anyone can check these and verify them. I don't have much money in hand and there are other problems too. I'll give the manuscript away for seventy-five. I was on my way to your place. You have a good reputation. You have contacts with all kinds of publishers. You also know Pandit Girdharilal of Naya Hind Publications ...'

'Don't even mention that scum. He's so devious,' Puri gave vent to his contempt.

Masood pressed on, 'You're a well-established writer. I consider you as my guru. Why don't you have a look at the manuscript? Maybe you'd like to have it published under your name. Whatever you offer me, I'll accept without haggling. You're a fellow writer.'

'No, no. Don't even say a thing like that,' Puri waved his hand in emphasis. 'I'll do what I can. Even if it gets published under my name, it would be wrong for me to accept your share of payment. All right, my friend, we'll go our separate ways now. I'll have to think about my manuscript too.'

Masood continued to pester him, 'I'm in dire need. Haven't paid my rent for the last four months. Promised to pay Dawood, my landlord, on the hope of being paid for this job. He'll throw my wife and children out into the street. You know my family, our women observe purdah. You keep this manuscript. If you can manage fifty right now, I'll even accept that.'

'Brother, I don't have any cash, even at my home. My own situation isn't very different.' His own problems flashed through Puri's mind. 'I'll let you know if I find some solution for you. I know where you live.'

Puri was trying to comfort Masood, but the thought of losing five hundred and fifty rupees, money for which he had worked so hard, was making him weak at the knees. 'Is this only my misfortune,' he thought, 'or the misfortune of Lahore, of Punjab, of the whole country? What'll be the outcome of all this? Why don't I speak to Girdharilal?' the thought came to him. He had an agreement for five hundred and fifty rupees signed by Ghaus Mohammed. Girdharilal would see with his own eyes that Puri could earn five hundred and fifty for just two months' work. He'd be doing a favour to Girdharilal. Pandit can reach some settlement with Professor Shah. 'You might have to fork out eight thousand now, but it'll be you who'll make twenty thousand later,' he'd tell Girdharilal. But his anger and hatred for that family did not allow him to pursue that idea.

Puri thought, instead of Girdharilal, why shouldn't he speak with someone at Dhanpat Rai & Sons, Educational Publishers? Any publisher would make money from a history textbook.

Surya Prakash, the owner of Dhanpat Rai & Sons, was a young man. He did not even make a show of grief upon hearing about the murder of Ghaus Mohammed. He said, 'A history textbook published by us has been prescribed for the past five years. Shah wanted to replace that by the one that Ghaus was going to publish. You want us to pay Shah to throw out our own publication? The Muslim members of the textbook committee help Muslim publishers. They've been replacing books put out by Hindu publishers with those of Muslim publishers. We'd offered Shah ten thousand rupees. Just look at his dishonesty and bias. Well, God sees everything. There used to be no Muslim publishers. Now they've taken over the trade. And not only this trade. They're taking over the whole country. We're winding up our business in Lahore, and have decided to keep just a branch office here, and move our presses and publishing business to Delhi. You Hindu writers are cutting off your own roots by writing books for Muslim publishers. These

Muslims take great care of their own brothers and their community. And we Hindus don't. All the Hindus want is money; it's always money first for them. Look at what they've come down to, who used to own the whole book business in Lahore.'

When Puri returned after hearing Surya Prakash's lecture on how to save the Hindu race, he felt as if the bars of an invisible cage were closing around him, imprisoning the spirit of the creative force in him. He lay down dejectedly on a charpoy. The manuscript of the history textbook, once worth five hundred and fifty rupees to him and eight thousand to Professor Shah, lay beside him. That fruit of several months' labour was not even worth a pile of blank paper now. It couldn't be used for anything except for wrapping up purchases in the grocer's shop.

Masood's face floated before his eyes. He recalled how Masood was willing to give up his manuscript for half the payment. Puri saw himself being driven to plead for a similar favour from someone. He had the ability to write brilliantly, but he didn't have the resources to get his work published. 'What choice is open to a poor person, other than working for others?' he thought in despair. He had no recourse other than to enter into slavery, and work for those who owned the resources. He could not fall asleep for a long time that night. The memory of how insultingly Nayyar and Girdharilal had treated him intensified his pain at being penniless and down on his luck.

Next day, swallowing his pride, Puri went to the offices of several periodicals. Each time he had to wait until the editor was free to see him, but he made light of this annoyance by laughing at it. He asked them what they wanted him to write, and accepted the assignments they gave him. *Sitara* asked him for a romantic short story. *Khatoon* extracted from him the promise of a story on some social problem with a moral, and then asked him to translate an article on birth control from the English. Within one week, Puri managed to rework one of his old short stories and write two articles on topics suggested to him, and earned twenty rupees. He got fifteen in cash and the promise of five more.

The magazines wanted short stories, and were ready to pay him fifteen rupees for one. There was a time when stories had come to Puri effortlessly, but under pressure to write and in his disturbed state of mind, he could not think of any, no matter how hard he tried. In desperation he thought of

reading some story in English and of rewriting it in Urdu, but after another
week he could not accomplish even that much.

With the possibility of Lahore going to Pakistan, many Hindus had begun
to talk of leaving the city. But the people of Bhola Pandhe's Gali, like those
from so many others, vowed that they would never leave the homeland of
their forefathers, that they would fight to the death for the right to stay
in Lahore. From the demarcation of the boundary between Pakistan and
Hindustan announced at the beginning of July, it seemed imminent that
Lahore would go to Pakistan. However, Hindus living in most galis of Lahore
and in the Bhola Pandhe's Gali too, continued to believe that Lahore would
not be given to Pakistan, as Hindus owned most of the city's real estate. They
were not going to give up their ancestral homes, no matter what happened.
Nobody would be able to throw them out of their homes.

After the Shahalami fire, Ghasita Ram and Panna Lal had had the doors
of their houses covered with iron sheets, locked them with huge padlocks
and had left on pilgrimage to Mathura and Vrindavan to attend festivals
held there in July and August. The people of the gali had looked down
on them, but by the middle of July these neighbours too had begun to
face an agonizing dilemma. The provincial government informed all its
employees that every individual had the right to choose whether to stay
and work in Hindustan or Pakistan and arrange a transfer accordingly. To
the average person, this meant that the government was unable to take on
the responsibility of protecting its Hindu employees in Pakistan, and its
Muslim employees in Hindustan. Who could ordinary citizens depend on
in such circumstances?

In Bhola Pandhe's Gali, the only government employees were Babu
Govindram, Doctor Prabhu Dayal, postal clerk Birumal, and Shaduram,
who worked at the secretariat. These men would sit at the chabutara of
Babu Govindram and discuss the situation late into the evening. Khushal
Singh and Masterji joined them. Babu Govindram wanted all of them to
stay in Lahore. Doctor Prabhu Dayal was in two minds. He was the only
person in the gali who had visited other parts of India. He would say, rather
sadly, 'One can live and survive, if necessary, anywhere in the world, but
the truth is, there's no city like Lahore.'

The mere thought of being posted to a different place frightened Birumal.
After he joined, he had worked for a few years in the Railway Mail Service.
For several months at the beginning of 1940, his posting was to Cuttack,

quite a distance to the south-east. He would say, 'Bhai, that country is totally different. They are also Hindus, but of a different sort. Their talk sounds like a pebble being shaken in a brass pot. The only clothes their women wear is around their waist. Bhai, their food is different, and so are their customs. They let boiled rice go stale before eating it. So many bugs that if the bedbugs didn't hold you down, the mosquitoes might carry you away. So what if the Muslims of Lahore have turned into our enemies? At least they're like us. Same language, same dress, their food too is almost the same. The only difference is that between a temple and a mosque.' He said, uttering a curse, 'It's been ten years since I went to any temple. How long can we remain enemies?'

Masterji's worries knew no bounds. All the necessary items had been collected for Tara's trousseau. The loan he had taken against his Provident Fund, and from his brother for their house in their ancestral village, had been used up in the preparations for the wedding, now only nine days away. If he considered moving to another city, all the money spent would have been wasted, and the things they had collected for the trousseau would be useless. Babu Ramjwaya had obtained for him on credit the wheat, ghee and other foodstuffs needed during the wedding celebration at prices below the going rate. How could he carry all that away with him?

Masterji talked about all this with Bhagwanti and his elder son. All his worries revolved around one point: Could the wedding take place in the present situation, with a curfew in force almost every day? This was the astrologically auspicious period for marriages. Marriages were being performed here and there in the city. He always came to the same conclusion: If a marriage could be celebrated in anybody else's house, it could happen at his too. It was all in the hands of God. Where would his family go away from Lahore? For the past twenty-seven years his life had been spent between his school and his home. Where else could he find work at his age? His heart sank whenever he thought over all this, and he would mutter, running his fingers through his hair, 'God, you are our only, you are our last hope ...'

Puri had lost all his attachment to Lahore. The city had been cruel to him in all manner of ways. Lahore had rejected him, he felt, and did not want him in her fold. Lahore favoured Kashish, who had unjustly fired him from his job; Lahore belonged to Kanak, who had stolen his heart; Lahore had taken sides with the stuck-up, conceited Nayyar and Girdharilal when they told him that he was socially inferior; Lahore had given its blessings to Ramjwaya, Govindram, Ghasita Ram, Panna Lal, Sukhlal and his son Somraj, who owned property in its territory; not to Puri who had nothing to call his own. Maybe he would have better luck in finding work in Delhi or the United Provinces. Maybe he could earn good money in Bombay, writing dialogue and scripts for films. But how could he ask his parents to ignore the wedding set for a week hence and move out of Lahore? If the wedding was postponed, all the money they had spent would go to waste and an unmarried daughter would become a millstone around their necks. A sister or daughter was nothing but a problem for the family. It would be possible to leave Lahore, he thought, only if he could first get away and arrange for a job and a place to live.

Marriages were indeed taking place, but they were lacklustre and brief affairs, even duller than the marriage of Ghasita Ram's daughter in June. There was a sense of panic all around. Families of the girls feared that if they left the city and moved away without going through with the marriage, who knew if they would ever meet the other family again? And these were hardly marriages as marriages used to be. A very small number of people from the groom's family, either together or one by one, would arrive at the bride's house. There was no question of holding the elaborate welcoming *mukut* ceremony, or of singing or playing music. The *phere* ceremony, of going around the fire seven times, was performed without any fanfare, and the bride was given away. The groom would make his way back to his gali sometimes on foot, or in a borrowed motorcar. The girl's trousseau and gifts would be taken quietly to the groom's house. Both Masterji and Ramjwaya were concerned whether Lala Sukhlal would agree to such a low-key and colourless marriage ceremony for his son.

Tara's parents did not have the courage to mention postponing the wedding, even for a short time. They had had a hard time suppressing the rumour of Tara's unwillingness to go through with the marriage. Lala Sukhlal and Somraj might interpret their request for a delay in unpredictable ways. Both Masterji and Babu Ramjwaya were compelled to go along with whatever Lala Sukhlal wished in this matter. It was better to be rid of the burden of the unmarried daughter, they would tell themselves, for she had to leave her family some day. Who was to know what the future held in store for her?

The rumour of Tara's opposition to the marriage had reached Lala Sukhlal's ears. Spluttering with anger, he had sworn at Babu Ramjwaya and Masterji hurling various degrees of abuse at them, and had threatened to have them beaten with shoes in front of all the people in the bazaar, 'What do I care for that pauper's daughter? There's no shortage of people offering us a dowry of fifty thousand rupees. Her family had knelt and put their pugarees at my feet, and begged me a hundred times to accept their offer of an engagement.'

Babu Ramjwaya and Masterji had to place their hat and pugaree at his feet, and swear a hundred times that the rumour was false. In spite of his bluster, Lala Sukhlal knew that the Senate Hall affair had cast a shadow on his son's reputation. The story of his son's engagement being cancelled because of that affair would certainly not have helped to ensure his engagement elsewhere.

Babu Ramjwaya and Masterji went to see Lala Sukhlal to get his orders and instructions about the marriage ceremony. Lala raised his voice a bit as he spoke, 'Arrey, we have no intention of causing any trouble for you people. We'll have to do what the times call for. We'll do what our dharma calls for, not put on some empty show. The scriptures tell us what our dharma, what our duty is. All those rituals and customs are not worth the effort in the present situation. I'll arrange for passes for the curfew. As I said, not more than eight or ten persons will go to your place, and we'll get the wedding over and done with. Your good name and ours amount to the same thing.'

On the evening of 23 July, when Masterji returned to the gali, his face showed the strain of a difficult situation. He loosened his jacket as he sat down on the chabutara. He let out a sigh, and said to Babu Govindram, 'Now you'll have to see the whole thing through. Lala Sukhlal wants the wedding to take place on Sunday.'

Dammo, Peeto and other children spread the news around the whole gali in seconds. Pushpa was showing her servant boy how to sauté the *guchchi* vegetable in a particular way, but she could not restrain herself when she heard the news and went straight to her window and called, 'Bahinji!'

She addressed both Bhagwanti and Meladei as bahinji. Sometimes when she meant to call one of them, the other would answer, or both would answer together. Puri and Ratan were both about her age. She felt awkward calling out their names loudly. Tara was an adult and Usha too was turning sixteen.

When Bhagwanti came to her window, Pushpa said, 'We'll carry out the ceremony of applying the haldi paste to the girl tomorrow.'

Kartaro spoke up from her window, 'Why not? Sure! Wednesday, Thursday, Friday and Saturday, only four days left before the wedding. We held that ceremony a month before my marriage.'

'Ma, bahinji says that she doesn't want to be bothered with the haldi.' Usha came and announced Tara's objection. There were only four days left before her elder sister's wedding, and she could not call her by her name in front of others.

'Wah!' Pushpa and Kartaro both protested. 'We're going to anoint her with the paste. She can wash it off later if she wants. And we won't let her change her clothes either. Otherwise how would she look beautiful on the day of the wedding?'

Bhagwanti said to her neighbours, 'Sisters, daughters, it's up to you to arrange everything. You don't have to ask me.'

Seeta called out from her doorway, 'Auntie, let's have singing at least for four days.'

'No more singing at anybody's place any more. This cursed curfew is on all the time,' Meladei said grouchily, to remind everyone.

'What's curfew got to do with it? We'll sing inside the house,' Seeta said.

Pushpa agreed with her, 'Yes, we'll be singing indoors. And since the twentieth, the curfew time is from eleven at night till four in the morning.'

Tikaram pointed out from the chabutara where he was sitting, 'Bhabhi, don't be foolish. What else does curfew mean? It's forbidden to sing or play any instrument or even make noise during curfew. Why invite trouble for such a small thing?'

Bir Singh called out from his doorway, 'It's only forbidden for us Hindus to sing!' He uttered an obscenity. 'The Muslim asses of Mochi Gate begin to bray their prayers at four in the morning, "Lord, call me to Medina." Nothing is forbidden for them. We'll have to pack them off to their Medina.'

'Bir Singh, my son,' Babu Govindram explained patiently. 'The curfew ends at four in the morning only because those wretches can eat well before beginning their Ramadan fast. And it begins again at eleven for their convenience. Bhai, these Muslim officials really have a lot of cheek.'

Meladei listening from the window above said, 'Whatever the reason, at least we get some relief.'

Masterji did not want her to have any doubt, 'Who cares about giving us relief? It is so for their own for religious reasons.'

'Well, there's no curfew during the day.' Pushpa suggested. 'We'll sing in the afternoon.'

Next morning Babu Govindram, the doctor, Birumal and Tikaram went off to their jobs, and Masterji to his tutoring. The schools all over the city had been closed for a month after the Shahalami fire. Ratan and Bir Singh returned to the gali from the railway station around ten after escorting the Hindus arriving from the west to the camps. Seeta called out to Ratan, 'Bhappaji, we'll sing in the afternoon. You and Puri bhai go and bring Sheelo bahin from Uchchi Gali.'

'Achcha,' said Ratan and went up the stairs to his house.

There was no one in the gali.

Bir Singh pursed his lips and looked threateningly at Seeta, 'Asking everyone but me, what have I done to invite your spite?'

Seeta stared back at him, shrugged her shoulders coquettishly and went back to her house.

After the incidents in Kila Gujjar Singh and Mazang, girls and women were not allowed to go out alone, even by way of the galis. Two men, instead of one, would escort them from now on. When Pushpa reminded Puri and Bir Singh again after eleven, they went off to bring Sheelo from her home.

When they retuned with Sheelo, Dammo called out loudly, 'A letter came for Jaddi bhappa.'

The postman knew everyone in the gali. Instead of coming back to deliver the registered letter, he had asked Tara to sign for the letter addressed to Jaidev Puri.

Hari explained to Puri, 'A letter arrived, under registered cover. Tara bahin signed for it.'

When Tara signed and accepted the registered letter for Puri, her mother said with curiosity, 'Girl, open the letter and read what's in it.'

According to her mother, a letter coming to the house was a letter for everyone in the family. Anyone could read it. Tara read the name of the sender, and said, 'No, baba, I won't open it. It's for my brother, let him open it. How can a letter addressed to one person be opened by anybody else?' Tara placed the letter on the top shelf of the cupboard. Her mother had never heard such a thing before, but she could not go against her educated son and daughter. She waited impatiently.

Puri came upstairs and asked Tara in English, 'What is it? A registered letter from whom?'

Their mother was listening. Tara answered in English, 'From Nainital. Mother wanted me to read it, but I didn't open it. The sender's name is K. Dutta, Vimal Villa. Could be from Kanak.' Her tone of voice suggested neither complicity in a secret, nor any kind of irony.

Tara reached into the cupboard and handed the letter to Puri. Every fibre in Puri's body throbbed with tension. He did not open the envelope in front of others, and went out to the veranda. There were several pages. As he unfolded the pages, he found two one-hundred-rupee notes tucked inside. He hid the notes in his fist as he read the letter.

In the six-page letter Kanak had put down the story of the constraints placed upon her in the past weeks. How, under pressure from Nayyar and her father, she had to promise them not to write or meet Puri for two months, how she could not hold back after learning about his being in the police lock-up. She had written:

'... We have decided to spend our lives together, and nothing can prevent that. The situation in UP is different from that in Punjab. There is very little communal strife here, the Congress is in power, and self-rule is almost a reality. Your talents will be appreciated, not in the climate of sectarian violence and enmity that is widespread in Punjab, but here in UP. These people appreciate talent, and patriotism as well. I spoke with one parliamentary secretary. It seems certain that we both will be able to get employment at a salary of two hundred rupees per month once we are in Lucknow. You will probably be offered even more. I have kept my promise to my family. Now I can expect my brother-in-law's support as well.

'If you don't come here, I'll have to come to Lahore. If you want me to come to you, reply immediately. However, I want us to end the torture and pangs of separation here in this cool climate, beside this lovely lake. Words cannot do justice to the natural beauty all around me. You can't imagine a lake surrounded by hills, even if I attempt to describe it. I have enclosed some money for your travel expenses and for staying in a hotel here. Even if you don't need it, don't be angry with me. The money belongs to you; you may tear up the bills and throw them away, but don't send it back. Wire me the time and day of your arrival. You'll be a stranger here. I'll meet you at the bus terminus.' Kanak also gave details of the route of the journey from Lahore. She asked him to reply by registered letter.

It had rained twice in the past week. Then the skies cleared, the sun shone brightly, and it became very humid. There were again thin clouds in the afternoon, and the air was perfectly still. The gali women felt very uncomfortable in the stifling heat when they held their singing party in the room in Bhagwanti's house, but what could they do?

Meladei invited all of them, 'Come, we'll sit on my side of the house.' She cleared her big room of the charpoys, and plugged in the table fan.

They began by singing seven wedding songs about a daughter asking her father to find her a suitable groom. Sheelo, Usha and Seeta sat in the centre with the dholak. According to the custom Tara, the shy bride-to-be, could not sit with the singers, but Sheelo had dragged her to the gathering. Tara had been fondly making baby clothes for Sheelo's son and Pushpa's daughter from leftover pieces of cloth bought for her trousseau. She sat quietly on one side, with her eyes on the garment as she put basting stitches in it. Relatives from her father's village could not come for the wedding. Women from other galis had not been able to join them either. That day Sheelo's mother had been unable to come as well. There were not many women, but the resonant voices of Sheelo and Seeta filled the room and made up for the small number present. One of them would launch into a new song even before the other could finish the one they had been singing. Usha and Pushpa were doing their best to keep up.

Masterji, fan in hand, was taking his siesta on a charpoy in the cool of the ground floor aangan. Puri sat in the veranda reading Kanak's letter over and over. After reading it for the umpteenth time, he thought, there were only four days to Tara's wedding. How could he leave before that? Tara knew who had written the letter, but she had not asked anything about it. She won't ask, but he'll have to tell the others something or other. He was so engrossed in reading that he did not notice that the women had gone over to Ratan's house, nor did he hear them sing.

Every sinew in Puri's body tingled with excitement and pleasure after he read the letter. He did not want to sit by himself. As he went downstairs, he heard the voices of Sheelo and Seeta now singing tappa songs filled with longing.

As Puri came out into the gali, Bir Singh was sitting with Ratan on the chabutara opposite him. Bir Singh said loudly, 'Look at Jaddi bhappa! He's been listening to the tappa upstairs. Didn't even invite us.'

Before Puri could reply, Masterji called him over to the aangan. He asked, 'What was in that letter that came from Nainital?'

Puri answered, 'I did some work for Pandit Girdharilal. The letter was from him. He's spoken about me to some parliamentary secretary in UP, and he's asked me to go there.'

'Very good! That's very good!' said Masterji, excitedly waving the fan over his body. 'The wedding's on the twenty-eighth. Tara will return here from her in-laws' on the morning of the thirtieth. You can leave on the thirty-first, at the latest on the first or the second. It's not wise to delay such things.'

When Puri returned to the gali, he heard Bir Singh calling repeatedly, 'Tayiji! Tayiji! Listen, please listen to me.'

Meladei looked down from her window, 'What is it? Speak up!'

'You asked Jaddi bhappa on the quiet to listen to the tappa. What crime have we committed? I too went to fetch Sheelo bahin,' Bir Singh complained. 'I too want to come up and listen.'

'Jaddi isn't anywhere upstairs, you idiot!' answered Meladei. 'If you boys want to come up, come on. Who's stopping you? You're not strangers. These are all your sisters here.'

Bir Singh pulled Ratan along, and asked Puri to come too. Hari, Vijay and Shyam followed them quickly upstairs. Seeing them crowd in, the women stopped singing. Seeta looked at Bir Singh with her furrowed brow, and complained loudly, 'What's the meaning of this rudeness? What's the meaning of boys barging into a girls' party? Leave us alone in peace.'

'Calm down, girl!' said Bir Singh with a hard glare. 'We have tayi's permission.'

'This ass dragged us all here,' Ratan slapped Bir Singh on the back. 'Don't be angry! We're leaving.'

Sheelo said quickly, 'Welcome, hearty welcomes, sohanyo, motianwalyo, baadshaho, you're most welcome.' In the relaxed atmosphere of the ceremony, she could speak freely.

Puri brought in a charpoy and all the males perched on it.

Pushpa said to Sheelo, 'Sing some more. Sing another tappa.'

Sheelo nodded her head. She continued to tap the beat gently with her fingers on the drum as she tried to recall the words of a tappa. Then she looked straight into the eyes of Ratan sitting opposite her, and sang out loudly, 'I sit in front of you and weep, but can't tell you of my pain…'

Puri had come up at Bir Singh's urging, but his mind was full of Kanak and her letter. The letter, like a strong gust of the south wind, had cleansed his heart of all feelings of disgust and anger against the female of the species.

The words sung in Sheelo's melodious and vibrant voice had jolted him out of his dreamy state of mind, as if they were addressed to him personally. As if Tara, after handing over Kanak's letter to him but not uttering a word about it to anyone else, was making one last proclamation of her readiness to suffer alone and silently ... 'I sit in front of you and weep, but can't tell you of my pain!'

Tara had gone to share her sorrows with Asad, he remembered. He recalled Asad's words, 'Tara's very upset... It's not all that unusual for someone other than a brother to understand the problems of a sister.' And Tara, splitting her scalp open by knocking it on the charpoy corner, then silently corroborating his explanation that she had fallen because she felt dizzy. Now she had stopped struggling, and was sitting quietly and letting others do to her as they pleased. She had given up the right to express her own mind. He saw himself, in his imagination, crushing his heart with both hands to suppress his feelings. The room had become very crowded, he felt, and he could not breathe. Sheelo sang out again in her pain-filled voice:

'Do not speak ill of my beloved. Punish me, if you want, by pulling on my braid ...'

Puri sat unmoving, his eyes fixed on the floor, as if he was listening intently to her song.

Ratan got up and said to Bir Singh, 'Come on! Let's go. Its time for us to start our duties at the railway station.'

Puri too went out with Ratan and Bir Singh. He had to write to Kanak and send the letter by registered mail.

Muslim families from the east and Hindus from the west were pouring into Lahore in search of asylum. To help these newcomers, the volunteers of the Muslim League, Congress, the Communist Party and the Hindu Mahasabha were given night curfew passes. As there had been several cases of Hindu and Muslim volunteers vanishing while they were out at night, these men usually returned to their homes by nine in the evening. If they were held up for any reason, they spent the night either at the railway station or at some refugee camp. Mewa Ram had to spend a night at the camp at Bawli Saheb. His parents spent that night without a wink of sleep.

One evening, when Ratan and Mewa Ram returned to the gali and Bir Singh did not, Khushal Singh, Kartaro and Peeto were all worried. They kept asking both of them repeatedly about Bir Singh. Both the men assured them, 'He must have stayed overnight at the railway station or at some camp. Don't worry. He'll turn up in the morning.'

It was still dark in the morning when the bugle signalling the end of curfew sounded. Kartaro came out and sat on her chabutara. After the sun began to shine brilliantly and Bir Singh did not show up, she and Peeto both began to weep and wail. Their neighbours tried to comfort them, 'Bir Singh is not a child. He'll be here soon.'

Although the gali people continued to comfort Khushal Singh and his wife, they too were getting uneasy when Bir Singh had failed to turn up even after nine. Ratan, Mewa Ram and Puri put on the armour under their shirts and tied pugarees around a *kulah* to protect their heads, and went off to look for their missing comrade. Doctor Prabhu Dayal and Babu Govindram were asked to telephone the police substation on the road where many medical doctors lived in Vachchovali, to inquire whether Bir Singh had been arrested for any reason.

Khushal Singh had no heart to set up his stall of papad–bariyan and freshly ground lentil paste on the chabutara of the Woman of the Well. He sat there quietly, his arms clasping his knees and his eyes fixed on the gate at the gali entrance. Masterji and Mukund Lal took turns sitting next to him and talking, to take his mind off his worries.

Sitting on their chabutara, Kartaro and Peeto cried incessantly. Occasionally one or the other would begin to wail. Birumal's mother sat with them for a while, asking them not to lose hope. When she left, Seeta's mother Purandei came to sit next to the crying women. Some woman or other would sit with them continuously. Kartaro and Peeto had not lit the fire in their kitchen.

Around half past eleven, Masterji went to Khushal Singh, took his arm and said, 'Come, sardar, have a bite to eat.' When Khushal Singh refused to budge, Hari brought a thali of food to where he was sitting. Meladei and Pushpa too sent to Khushal Singh a bowl of whatever they had cooked. Tikaram's wife took Peeto's hand and led her home, and Birumal's mother insisted that Kartaro come to her place and have something to eat.

Doctor Prabhu Dayal and Babu Govindram returned to the gali around half past one. Disappointment was writ large on their drawn faces. The doctor sat down on the chabutara to rest his legs without bothering that his trousers might get dirty. He said dejectedly, 'No one picks up the phone at the police station. We asked Lala Baisakhi Ram to come with us

to the office of the joint magistrate Khan Khurshaid Ali. He tried phoning
on our behalf. Khurshaid Ali is a very decent person. Not at all a religious
fanatic like some others. The good man was right when he explained why
it was so difficult to get any information. Between a thousand and twelve
hundred arrests are made in the city every day, he said. Many of these are
not reported. One should go to the police station personally and slip a fiver
or tenner to the desk clerk and ask there. That's the way to do it.'

Khushal Singh got to his feet, 'How many rupees do you need? Take
whatever I have. What do I need the money for!'

Masterji said, 'Listen, doctor. Come on, I'll take you to see Professor
Pran Nath. He's the advisor to the governor. Who'll fail to answer if he
telephones? His family mansion was burned down. The family's gone to
Lucknow. The professor is staying at the Savoy Hotel. He has his job, he
couldn't go off with them. A real gentleman. I was his tutor when he was
a boy. When Jaddi was arrested in '42, I went to him. He immediately
telephoned Khan Sahib Wali Mohammed and said that if the prisoner needed
someone to put up bail, he was ready to do so.'

Khushal Singh was willing to go and meet Nath, but Masterji told him to
wait and have patience. Masterji went with Mukund Lal to see Nath, taking
the Lohari Gate to go to Mall Road by way of Vachchovali and Sootar Mandi.
There was no time to have the invitations printed for Tara's marriage, but
he had to inform some guests who were close to the family. Masterji also
wanted to invite the professor to the wedding.

At about two, Rajrani, Sheelo and Kishori Lal arrived, escorted by two
men from their gali. Sheelo was so insistent that her mother had to find a
way to send her to Bhola Pandhe's Gali. And how could the mother not go
along herself? She had not been able to make it the previous day, but her
absence from that day's singing party would have forever been a cause for
complaint against her. They found the gali in a sombre and quiet mood.
Bhagwanti whispered the details into the ear of Sheelo's mother, who
then went and commiserated with Kartaro. There was no question now of
holding the singing party.

Puri, Ratan and Mewa Ram returned around four, having searched in
all possible areas. The gali neighbours were still telling Khushal Singh and
Kartaro not to lose heart. Some particularly fanatic Muslim officials, they
explained to Bir Singh's parents, arrested Sikh men under any flimsy pretext,
just to harass them. 'As soon as we've any knowledge of his whereabouts,

we'll get him out.' Every family in the gali was ready to put up bail for the missing man.

Sheelo and her mother stayed until five in the gali. Then Puri and Ratan escorted them back to their home.

Ratan and Mewa Ram took Puri, Tikaram and Birumal a little distance away from Khushal Singh. 'We've been saying for several days,' they said, 'that it wasn't safe for him to leave the gali. We ourselves were afraid to be with him. Only someone who knows us would have identified us as Hindus. There's no problem in identifying a Sikh.'

Puri said with frustration, 'Master Tara Singh has left Lahore, but not before waving his sword to threaten Muslims, turning every Sikh into an enemy of Muslims.'

Ratan said, keeping his voice low, 'We've left no place unsearched. Who knows if someone stabbed him and threw the body into the canal outside Chardewari or into a burning building? How would anyone know? We thought it safest to send him to help out at the camp in the mansion of Rai Bahadur Badridas. There are only a few houses belonging to Muslims in that direction, near Kila Gujjar Singh.'

Everyone was back in the gali by nine. There was still no sign of Bir Singh. Khushal Singh lay on his charpoy, listless and quiet. His pugaree loosened, then fell to the ground by his head. His long hair fanned out. Tears flowed continuously from his eyes, just like the stream trickling from a crack in a broken pot. Men from the gali came and sat with him one after the other.

Kartaro beat her breast and wailed. Peeto let out shrieks as she wept. It's a terrible thing to get the news of the death of a loved one. Kartaro was suffering the shock of the death of her strapping son by stages and degrees. Sometimes the grief hit her with full force, then lessened as someone held out hope of his being alive. Meladei, Purandei, Bhagwanti and Birumal's wife all came and sat beside her. They would mention several reasons why Bir Singh might not have returned home, and ask his mother not to mourn him by beating her breast, 'Hai, don't say such inauspicious things, sister. Your son may live a hundred years.' But the tone of their voices were not convincing.

Tara had received the pre-nuptial anointings, so it was not proper for her to go out of the house. She wanted to go and comfort Kartaro, but Bhagwanti objected, 'No balli, no. It's not fitting for you to go to her.' When

Meladei heard Tara's mother, she too joined in, 'No question of your going. It would be an ill omen.'

Tara persisted. Puri said when he heard her insist, 'How come it's an ill omen to go and comfort someone?' This was the first occasion he had said anything to support Tara for a long time. Tara went to see Kartaro for a few minutes, in spite of her mother's objections.

Next day Meladei, Purandei and Birumal's wife joined Kartaro in mourning for her son. Bhagwanti's daughter was getting married the next day, and it was not auspicious for her to sit and cry.

Kartaro's wailing had turned into cursing. She beat her breast vigorously and cursed Ratan, Puri and Mewa Ram that they had beguiled her innocent boy into going with them. She cursed their mothers, accusing them of doing away with her young son. She beat her breast and tore at her hair, praying to Waheguru that the women who had brought about the death of her son might lose their own sons, and that their families would die out childless.

For the mothers of Puri, Ratan and Mewa Ram her curse-laden mourning was intolerable. They could no longer sit with Kartaro.

Bhagwanti could not keep silent, 'What didn't we do to help her! Our boys risked their lives looking for her son. Maybe because this hag has such a black heart that God punished her.'

Puri and Tara both told their mother to keep her mouth shut. Masterji too scolded her, 'Careful! She's not in her right mind.'

The auspicious time for Tara's wedding was on Sunday evening, but until the day before, the gali was in deep mourning for Bir Singh. Khushal Singh collected his family's meagre belongings, and got ready to go back to the village in Doaba that he had left thirty years before. Kartaro was still beating her breast and cursing the whole gali. The women of the gali, wiping away their tears, walked with her in farewell to the end of the gali. Bhagwanti, Meladei and Mewa Ram's mother stayed behind. Ratan, Puri, Mewa Ram and Tikaram went with the family to the station to see them off.

In the early evening Puri, wearing only a vest and lungi because of the heat, was helping Tara's mother and Sheelo to pack Tara's trousseau in the tin trunks bought for the purpose. Masterji, his hand waving a fan, squatted close by, watching them. He was wearing only a lungi.

Ratan quickly came up the stairs. He said, 'Professor Pran Nath has come to see you. I'll bring him up.'

Masterji sprang up to standing position. Puri too dropped whatever he was doing. In deference to his status and to express his thanks for the help given by the professor, Masterji had personally invited him to his daughter's wedding. As a courtesy and out of politeness, he had invited his own headmaster too. But, so far, only a couple of Masterji's colleagues, teachers in the middle school grades like himself, had come and offered their help. He had not expected the headmaster or Professor Pran Nath to come and lend a hand in the preparation of the wedding.

Puri and Masterji both quickly donned their shirts. Puri called, 'Usha! Hari! Get a chair from Ratan's house.' He reached for his pajamas hanging on a peg and went to the veranda to change. Bhagwanti and Sheelo left the room.

As Nath entered the room, he joined his palms and said *pairipaina* to Masterji. Masterji was both flustered and deeply moved by the professor's graciousness. 'Namasteji, welcome! Bless you!' he mumbled several greetings in a row. Usha had brought the chair, but had got only one. Masterji asked the professor to take a seat.

'You take the chair,' replied Nath, and sitting down on a tin trunk next to the wall, said, 'Hope it doesn't break. I'm quite heavy. Right, where's Tara?'

Puri said namaste and stood beside him. Masterji said, rubbing his hands together, 'Professor saheb, it was very kind of you …'

'That's not right, Masterji,' Nath cut him short. 'Why do you address me as professor saheb? You know my name.'

Masterji was so moved that he was at a complete loss for words. He choked back his tears with an effort.

'Tell me where can I lend a hand in the preparations? I couldn't come earlier, was really swamped with work.'

Masterji could only join his palms in reply. No words came from his mouth.

Nath turned to Puri, 'So, what're you up to?'

Vijay brought another chair made of bent wire, and a metal seat. The professor got up from the trunk and sat on the chair. He described how all the members of his family had gone to Lucknow. The family owned a sugar mill in UP. Their mansion in Lahore had been burnt to the ground, but had been insured for 350,000 rupees.

Tara came and said namaste.

Nath got up from his chair.

Masterji and Puri said, 'Please remain seated.' Offering the chair to Tara Nath said, 'No, no. You take the chair. You're the heroine today,' he added in English.

'Doctor saheb, do please sit down. I've been sitting the whole day.' Tara said in embarrassment, but with a polite and friendly smile.

'No, no. Till today you were a girl, so it was a different matter. Tonight you shall be a lady.'

Tara hung her head in embarrassed silence.

'Come and sit down,' Nath said to her.

Tara was about to sit on the trunk, but the professor took the trunk and made her sit on the chair.

Masterji got up from his chair and said to the professor, 'I'll be back in a minute. You sit here.' Puri knew that his father was going to get something to offer the professor.

'You sit here,' Nath gestured for Puri to take the chair, and turning towards Tara, said, 'What's that on your forehead?'

Puri looked away. Tara ran her hand across her forehead, and said, 'It's nothing.'

'Was that scar always there?'

Tara looked down and nodded, 'Yes.'

'Didn't notice before,' Nath changed the subject. 'So, they've applied the bridal oils on you. You're smart, you are wearing dark-coloured clothes so it won't show.'

Tara replied, again looking down shyly, 'No, it's not that.'

Nath asked Puri in English, 'From which place will the groom's party be coming? What about that stupid boy she'd been engaged to?'

'Kakaji, come here,' Masterji called from inside the house.

'Coming,' said Puri, and left without answering Nath.

'Doctor saheb, you didn't go to any hill station this summer?' Tara asked.

'How can I? My family left, telling me to settle the insurance claim.' Nath talked about several other things, about how the city was being ruined. 'Who knows what will happen next?' he wondered.

Puri returned, a plate of mithai in one hand, the other holding a glass of water. Masterji was behind him. Puri asked the professor, as he came into the room, 'What have you decided, doctor saheb? You'll also have to make up your mind whether to stay in Pakistan or work in Hindustan.'

'Can't say. The university isn't being split up,' replied Nath. 'There's a suggestion of setting up another university in east Punjab. Madanmohan Singh's name has been suggested for the registrar's position. He'd definitely take it. As for the advisor's post, who knows who'll be appointed as the new governor of Punjab? He may or may not want me. Jenkins is scheming to keep Pakistan in the British dominion. I think the outcome of the talks should be known this week. Mountabatten will force some kind of decision.'

'The loss of your mansion must have cost your family millions. But that was God's will,' Masterji said sympathetically.

'It was insured, for three and half lakhs. Six months ago it was perhaps worth more.'

Masterji joined his palms in appeal and asked Nath to have some mithai.

'Wah, that's not as it should be. I've come to lend a hand at your daughter's wedding, not to sit and eat mithai. Don't treat me as a guest from the groom's party.' Nath looked at Puri, 'Tell me something I can usefully do.'

'There's not much left to do,' said Masterji. 'The times are such that we could hardly arrange anything. Otherwise, we would have put ourselves out more, and we'd certainly have asked you. I had thought of borrowing the cooking utensils for the feast and other stuff from your mansion. Now if we can somehow get through the phere ceremony, that'll be enough.'

Masterji again asked Nath to have some mithai. Nath ate a laddoo, and drank half a glass of water.

Nath reached into his pocket and handed Masterji a small square box, 'This is from me. Should've got Tara something more useful. Achcha,' he looked at Puri, 'a good fountain pen for you when you get married, okay?'

'Your blessing is all I need,' Puri said with his palms together.

Masterji accepted the proffered box, saying 'no, no' over and over and opened it. It held a pair of small, jewel-studded earrings. Masterji held out the case towards Nath, saying, 'No, bhai, no. Please don't lay such a load of gratitude on us.'

'How can you say that?' said Nath. 'It's my right. I'm as close to you as Puri.'

Masterji was again moved beyond words. Nath got up, said namaste respectfully to Masterji, and said to Tara in English, 'The best of luck to you. Have a happy, healthy and long married life. Hope to find you so happy at our next meeting that you don't recognize me.' He laughed and went downstairs, chuckling.

Tara stood silently, her head bowed in farewell and gratitude.

Tara's heart and mind were in turmoil. She wrapped her head in her dupatta and lay down. Behind her closed eyes, words in giant flaming letters appeared against a darkened sky, 'You like Asad? He's a good chap... Your father's elder brother has got you engaged to some stupid boy... My family thinks I'm attracted to you.'

Tara did not want to see those words, but they seemed to have been burned into her mind by a branding iron. She felt anger against herself rising in her heart. What's the meaning of such thoughts? These were past mistakes. Why did Professor Saheb have to turn up at this moment? She lay for about an hour struggling with her memories.

Six years ago, at the time of the first marriage of Somraj after he passed out of high school, Lala Sukhlal Sahni had hired the famous brass band of Bau, with all its twenty-five musicians in pugarees and colourful uniforms, to lead the bridal procession. He often mentioned the hiring of the band in his conversation. Now the times were different. This time he went, with only eight of his relatives in borrowed motorcars, to Bhola Pandhe's Gali for the marriage of his son.

Somraj was not wearing mukut, the ceremonial headgear in the shape of a crown with a small plume, and *sehra*, the wreath of flowers around his head. He had wrapped only a couple of garlands around his pink silk pugaree. The bride's family had not put up a loudspeaker to play music. Meladei, Sheelo, Pushpa, Usha and Seeta sang a few verses of conventional songs caricaturing the groom, but in voices that could not be heard outside the gali. Somraj's father took part in the ceremonies that welcomed the groom and his party, had dinner with the other guests, and went back home. Left behind were Somraj with his young nephew, who was acting as *sarbala*, the best man. Lala Sukhlal was to return in the morning to take the bride home.

The custom of *jaimal*, the traditional adorning of the groom with garlands as he enters the bride's home, was performed. Before the phere ceremony, the women of the gali took Somraj upstairs for the ritual of 'getting to know the groom'. Meladei had given her big room for this purpose. Sheelo was particularly troubled by the low-key activities of Tara's wedding in comparison to the air of noisy festivity and the large number of guests who had come to her own wedding three years before. Somraj looked stern without his wedding crown and the wreath of flowers covering his face, as if his heart was not in the marriage or some residue of Tara's reluctance to be married was still at the back of his mind. Sheelo tried to cheer him up and banish his misgivings by being playful and jovial.

On this sacred occasion of a marriage, Masterji had asked that the custom of indecent jokes and the singing of curses and abuse aimed at the groom not be observed. Sheelo still tried to bring in some humour to lighten the mood. She prompted Usha and Seeta to sing chants for Somraj:

'Jija, jija, lachi dey, nahin to sakki chachi dey (Brother-in-law, give us some cardamom, or else give us your aunt please).'

Somraj put his hand in the pocket of his jacket. Tara's sister, cousins and other girls, with Sheelo in the lead, held out their hands for the customary gift. Somraj pretended to take something out of his pocket, but when he opened his fist in front of them it was empty.

The sister-in-laws, shouted again with glee, *'Jija, jija, lachi dey...'* He again put his hand into his pocket, but the girls refused to believe that he had anything in his pocket, and continued to swear and scold him:

nahin to sakki chachi dey,
nahin to long-supari dey, (if not, give us cloves and betel-nut please),
nahin to bhain kunwari dey (if not, give us a maiden sister please).

Somraj again showed them his fist to quieten them.

Sheelo said cautiously, 'First open your hand, then we'll believe you.'

He opened his fist and showed cardamom, cloves and betel nut previously put in his pocket for this purpose. When Sheelo held out her hand, he pinched it instead of giving her anything.

The girls yelled with glee, and to pay him back for his trickery, began to chant other curses and abuse. They made him empty his pockets. Their shrieks of joy and laughter filled the whole floor.

Masterji had arranged for the proper ceremony of giving away the bride to be held in the aangan below. A priest chanted vedic mantras as the bride and groom performed havan. At the time, Sheelo and her group of girls were trying to steal and hide Somraj's shoes, and to sew the hem of his jacket to the cushion he was sitting on. Somraj would stealthily move his hand back and attempt to squeeze their fingers or pinch their hands to foil them.

After the havan was over, Sheelo asked the newlyweds to play some games meant to familiarize them with one another, and to dispel their shyness. A vessel filled with water mixed with milk was placed between the couple, a ring was thrown into it, and the first one to find it was declared the winner. During this and other games, Somraj continued to banter with the girls, making them laugh at his sallies.

All the customs and rituals were over by three in the morning. Meladei had laid out a bed in the big room in her house, and placed a table fan next to it on a bent-wire chair. Somraj was asked to rest there for what was left of the night.

Tara too was exhausted after sitting decorously for so long. Sheelo took her to the roof and both of them lay down together on a charpoy. Sheelo said, putting her arm around Tara's shoulders, 'See, how likeable he is. Such a good man! Now it's up to you.'

Tara, her eyes closed, was thinking, 'What's past is past. My future and my life are now with him. I'll do what I can, and try my best. It may not be that hard if I make the effort.'

Tara was made to have a bath in the morning, wear a new dress, and get ready for her send-off. Trunks with her trousseau were ready too, but only four could be fitted into the motorcars. The auspicious hour for her to depart from her home was at nine-thirty. Lala Sukhlal had said that he'd arrive at nine. He did so, with one of Somraj's sisters.

As Bhagwanti, Sheelo's mother, Meladei and others gali women led Tara downstairs, wearing clothes with gold and silver *gota* and her face veiled by a short *ghunghat*, all the laughter, teasing and merrymaking of last night turned into sobs and streams of tears. Tara too could not hold back her tears. Sheelo, Pushpa, Seeta and Birumal's wife began to sing in a hushed, tear-soaked voice:

'O father, I am still little.

My dolls are still lying in corners and alcoves of the house.

My days of playing with dolls are not yet over.

Why are you throwing me out?

I am being sent away.

My mother's blouse is soaked with tears, my father is crying rivers, brothers are crying, the whole world is crying.

Only my sisters-in-law are happy.'

The women of the gali, tears running down their faces, went with Tara to the gali gate. Puri, Masterji, Ratan, Babu Govindram, Babu Ramjwaya and Kishori Lal found themselves moist-eyed.

Before she got into the motorcar, all her relatives, some still crying, again embraced Tara and bid her farewell. Tara was trying to overcome her own pain of separation from her family and their bitter tears, in the hope of belonging to a new family. A daughter is born, only to be sent away like this some day.

On 30 July, as on every other day just before dawn, the cries of the newspaper sellers were heard near the gali entrance, 'Full liberty promised to Muslims in Hindustan, and to Hindus and Sikhs in Pakistan!' Copies of *Pairokaar*, *Chhatrapati* and *Siasat* were taken in by the gali people. Masterji and Puri went down to the gali.

Ratan read aloud from one newspaper: '15 August 1947 has been declared as the day for Hindustan's independence and for the formation of Pakistan. The executive committees of both the Muslim League and Congress have issued statements that the new governments will guarantee the safety of minority Muslims in Hindustan and minority Hindus and Sikhs in Pakistan. The minorities in both countries will have the same civil rights as the majority, as well as full freedom to practise their culture and religion. It has not yet been decided whether Lord Mountbatten will continue, for a period, as the joint chief administrative officer for both nations, or whether each nation will appoint its own governor general.'

Babu Govindram said contentedly, 'What, after all, was achieved by the supporters of Pakistan? In place of the Unionist ministry, now it will be a League ministry. If Hindus continue to live in Pakistan, then the Muslims will have to include some Hindu members in the ministry for their own selfish reasons. They used to rule over the whole of Punjab, now they'll have to be content with only half of it.'

Doctor Prabhu Dayal said, 'What's the problem if there is to be religious freedom and equal civil rights for all? If the Muslim League treats Hindus unkindly, won't it have to think about the millions of Muslims living in UP, Bengal and Bombay?'

Masterji was wearing only a lungi. He had no shirt on. He spoke as he held his *janeyu*, the sacred thread, taut in both hands, and rubbed it on his back to relieve the itch from a heat rash, 'Bhai, one should remain steadfast in his religious convictions. When Khilaji, Tugalak and Aurangzeb could not wipe out the religion of the Vedas, what chance can poor Jinnah and his Muslim League have?'

Babu Govindram said, letting out a sigh, 'Why, then, all this murder and destruction, when after all and in spite of everything, everyone will remain where they were?' They sat talking for over an hour.

Masterji said to Puri, 'Kaka, get ready early today. Go to Mulkraj for his motorcar. His car will have to be driven back to him after Tara returns from her in-laws' house. It's a great favour from that good fellow. These days, nobody has any consideration for their former tutors. What do you think?' he looked round the gathering for their approval.

'I'll leave soon,' answered Puri, as he quickly went through the rest of the *Pairokaar*.

Lala Sukhlal had agreed that the bride would stay at her in-laws' for a day and night, and then return to the home of her parents for about a week. Puri was to go and bring her to Bhola Pandhe's Gali.

Babu Govindram had something to add, 'There was no reason for Lala Sukhlal to hurry. He should have waited for a while, at least until things had quietened down. There was another auspicious period in two month's time. Tara's marriage could have been held properly then. Saheb, they have got pure gold. The girl is an incarnation of the goddess Lakshmi.'

All eyes turned towards the entrance to the gali. Babu Ramjwaya and his son Kishorilal could be seen walking in, silent and dishevelled. They were followed by Sheelo, her mother and Kishorilal's wife, all sobbing. The gali people watched them approach in puzzled silence.

They wiped away their tears as they talked. When they got the news of the incident at Banni Hata, Babu Ramjwaya's family had left for Bhola Pandhe's Gali just as they were. After midnight in the Said Mittha neighbourhood, a crowd of Muslims had attacked several houses in Banni Hata lane and set them on fire. Shots were fired by both sides. There was no trace of Tara or the sister of Somraj's father. The father of Madhodas, a neighbour, had not been able to escape either. Lala Sukhlal had received a bullet wound in the shoulder. Sukhlal's house, as well as houses on both sides and Madhodas's house across from his, had been gutted in the fire. The house behind Sukhlal's house, where the Muslim Khoja lived, had also been burned down.

Sheelo and her mother began to cry loudly as they stepped into the gali. Bhagwanti looked out of her window, and without being told anything, screamed as she slapped her hand to her forehead. Masterji too began crying loudly as he stood in the gali.

There was pandemonium in Bhola Pandhe's Gali. The family of Lala

Sukhlal had moved over to the house of Somraj's uncle in Mohalla Mohalyan. Babu Ramjwaya, Masterji, Rajrani, Bhagwanti, Puri, Sheelo and Kishorilal, despite their own grief, had to go to offer their condolences to Tara's in-laws.

In the evening, Puri, Ratan and Mewa Ram went to see the ruins of the burned-out houses in Banni Hata. Masterji's wish was that if any remains of his daughter could be found, they might be committed to the Ravi River, after performing the havan ceremony so that her soul would rest in peace.

Generations of moneylending families had lived in Banni Hata, carrying on the business of lending money against sureties of jewellery and similar valuables. The houses had old-style heavy carved doors and wooden beams in the ceilings. It was difficult to save anything, once a house caught fire. Armed police had cordoned off the smouldering ruins. Some police personnel seemed to be carrying out an investigation by sifting through the debris. The public was being kept away from the scene. This was done so that the onlookers might not carry off any precious metals that might be found. People whose houses had been destroyed watched helplessly from a distance, as policemen went through the remains of their possessions, cursing the police under their breath, '. . . These are the very people who allowed the fire to be set. How else could the goondas attack during curfewtime? Now they are stealing away our gold and silver before our very eyes.'

As Puri, Ratan and Mewa Ram came out of Banni Hata lane and into the Said Mittha bazaar, they heard a stranger comment sarcastically, '. . . Sukhlal used to boast so much about his power and influence. People say that the Muslims have abducted his daughter-in-law. He's saying that she died in the fire, just to save his face.'

Puri's steps faltered as he trembled with anger upon hearing such an insulting remark. Mewa Ram reached out, grabbed the stranger by his collar, and punched him hard in the face.

'Hey! Stop! What's going on! Look at these idiots! Fighting their own people. That's why the Hindus are unable to save themselves.' Several people intervened and separated the two. Mewa Ram and the unknown accuser continued to hurl abuses at each others' mothers and sisters, and shouting threats to break heads and spill blood. Puri and Ratan had to drag Mewa Ram away.

Chapter 14

PANDIT GIRDHARILAL HAD THOUGHT IT BEST TO SEND KANAK AWAY FROM Lahore for some time after Puri's release from the police lock-up. All civil cases at the Lahore High Court had been postponed indefinitely after the latest wave of rioting and killing. Nayyar had not been able to find any accommodation in the Mussourie Hills, and had to settle for a small bungalow-type cottage in the hill station of Nainital. Nayyar, Kanta, along with Nayyar's mother, Kanak and Kanchan went to Nainital.

Nainital was quite crowded. Although it was further to the east than Mussourie, it was teeming with well-off Punjabis and their families from western Punjab and Lahore. The main topic of conversation on all sides was the atrocities committed against Hindus in Punjab.

Two years previously, Nayyar had spent the high court summer recess in Nainital at the invitation of barrister Haksar of Allahabad, who also practised at Lahore. Nayyar was known in bridge-playing circles and several clubs of Nainital, and had become a member of the New Club soon after his arrival. He was addicted to bridge, and played it with care and skill. Unless his partner was totally incompetent, he mostly won his games. Kanta, Kanak and Kanchan would accompany him to the club as his guest relatives.

That evening, a large number of people wearing hand-spun khadi clothes and white, boat-shaped Gandhi caps had gathered at the club. A reception had been arranged in honour of Krishna Narayan Awasthi, the parliamentary secretary in the province's Ministry of Industry and Civil Supplies. Nayyar was told that besides being parliamentary secretary, Awasthi was an influential member of the Congress party in the United Provinces, as well as the secretary of the Congress Parliamentary Board.

The male members of the club usually favoured Western-style suits. Those who wore khadi clothes as a matter of principle wore Indian-style suits of fine woollen khadi. Nayyar and Kanak had never seen government officials wearing khadi suits in Lahore, and such a display of national sentiment in UP impressed both of them. Awasthi was wearing a kurta and dhoti of cotton khadi, a woollen Nehru jacket and a Gandhi cap. He also wore ordinary chappals, was of average height, slim built and dark complexion, and trickles of paan juice collected at the corners of his mouth. From the hair greying at his temples, his age appeared to be around forty. Everyone present was eager to speak to him and shake his hand. There were only half a dozen women from UP in the gathering, but among those from Punjab, the number of women equalled that of the men.

Nayyar's introduction to Awasthi was very brief, but he stepped forward when Kanak was presented to Awasthi, 'Kanak is the daughter of Punjab's veteran political leader Pandit Girdharilal. Panditji was an associate of Lala Lajpat Rai, Lala Hardayal and Sardar Ajit Singh. He was jailed during the 1911–14 freedom movement. Kanak is an MA and a very talented and fine writer. Many of her short stories and articles have been published.'

As Awasthi sat down to tea, he gave a special invitation to Kanak, 'Please join me.' Nayyar and Kanak sat with him at his table.

Nayyar and his family had been in Nainital for less than a week when his brother Rajendra arrived with their brother-in-law's mother, his two young children, and his adult sister. They told stories of several Hindu neighbourhoods in the town of Sargodha being ravaged, and of Hindu women kidnapped in broad daylight.

Mahendra and Rajendra searched everywhere in Nainital for a larger bungalow and also in the surrounding hills. Not a single house was vacant so they had to make do with the small bungalow in which no one could have a moment's solitude or quiet. In the presence of three boisterous children and two old women eager to prove their piety, there was hardly an occasion to sit and reflect, or have peace to read or write.

In the morning Nayyar's mother would chant from the *Japaji Saheb*, the holy book of the Sikhs, for a long time. Sometimes she would add *Sukhmani Saheb* to her intonations. If she was still not satisfied with such a display of devotion, she would recite prayers to Hanuman, the Ganga, or any other prayer that she knew. Not to be outdone, the mother of Nayyar's brother-in-law would first chant prayers to the figures of the various gods she had brought along in a small rattan box. Then she would don her silver-framed spectacles, and read aloud from a large-print copy of the *Bhagawat* scripture. Sometimes one old woman would preach the importance of dharma and indifference to worldly things to the other, and sometimes the second would explain a religious tenet sanctimoniously to the first. They both firmly believed that only their form of worship and prayer would save their families from the curse of God that had fallen on them.

Nayyar, Kanta and Kanak were bothered by this babble of religious precepts, but had to keep quiet. Nayyar would say, 'The Hindus don't want to leave any god unworshipped. After they've finished with their own, they don't mind worshipping the neighbours' gods too.'

Kanak's comment was, 'Despite having innumerable gods to protect them, the Hindus have to run around to save their lives.'

Nayyar would pretend to explain, 'No, the Hindus don't expect to be protected by their gods. It's rather the other way round, the Hindus feed and clothe them, carry them around, and protect them.'

Inside the bungalow the din of prayer and worship rose, and so did the clamour of children's voices. Outside, the Nainital rain seldom let up. It was not possible to while away the time by taking walks or reading on a bench beside the lake.

Nayyar spent most of his time at the club playing bridge. In the evenings, he would take a peg or two of whisky, and discuss the complexities of legal cases at the Lahore and Allahabad High Courts. Kanchan played carom at the club. She too was fond of bridge, and the players in the beginners' group sometimes asked her to join them. None of this interested Kanak. She had had enough of Nainital and the club after one week. She wanted to write something on the subject of family interference in the marriage of a daughter. But more than anything else, she wanted to sit and reflect: what next? Only four days remained of the period she had promised Nayyar to observe for not making any contact with Puri. All Nayyar had done during this time was to try to show Kanak that Puri was not fit for her. Kanak avoided Nayyar's company for that reason. She could not hear anything said against Puri. She was beginning to feel that she had been brought to Nainital to be a prisoner and her resolve in reaction had become even firmer, 'Let them do what *they* want. I'll do what *I* want.'

When there was some respite from the rain, Kanak left Vimal Villa. She would walk a distance towards Tallital or Mallital, find an unoccupied bench, and sit facing the lake. 'Maybe I should take a vow never to get married, as a show of protest,' she would think, 'and try to find some kind of a job.' Then she would remember the promise made to Puri as he held her hand, and her repeated assurances to him, and think of leaving her family. She was the cause of nothing but trouble to her family, and felt herself persecuted into the bargain. She must find a job, in view of Puri's financial situation, and even more in view of his fragile self-esteem.

There was no rain in the afternoon. Kanak was walking on the road
that skirted the lake looking for a vacant bench. The road was filled with
colourful saris, Punjabi-style women's shalwar suits, and smartly dressed
young men. She saw Awasthi coming from the opposite direction with two
other men. He said namaste to her first, and she responded politely. Awasthi
stepped away from his companions and asked her how she was doing.
Then he said, 'Come with your sister and brother-in-law and have tea at
my bungalow.' He gave her his address, and asked, 'When will you come?'

'I'll ask jijaji. Whenever he's free,' Kanak said with some hesitation.

'Tomorrow, or the day after, whenever you've got the time. Just
telephone to confirm.'

Nayyar was pleased at the invitation from the parliamentary secretary.
Kanak telephoned to fix a time. Nayyar, Kanta and Kanak dressed with
particular care when they went to Awasthi's bungalow. Awasthi was sitting
on a chaise longue in the veranda, surrounded by a small group. Nayyar and
Kanak felt awkward at having come at a time when he was busy. Awasthi
got up to welcome them and led them inside to the living room, leaving
the others to wait outside.

The tea was served without care or ceremony. The china was cheap,
chipped and cracked, and the stains of spilt tea and rings on the tablecloth
were evidence that no particular care was taken in serving tea. The three
of them exchanged glances of surprise. The fair-sized room did not lack
furniture, but negligence and sloppiness in housekeeping were evident
everywhere. Awasthi was making up for the deficiencies in the chinaware
and snacks with his effusive welcome. He inquired about the political past
of Kanak's father and his publishing business in Lahore, about Kanak's
literary efforts and her future plans in considerable detail. He told funny
stories. He talked about his experiences on tour with Govind Ballabh Pant
and Jawahar Lal Nehru, and many others.

No other member of Awasthi's family had joined them. After a while
Kanta asked with some hesitation, 'Won't Mrs Awasthi join us?'

Awasthi replied without embarrassment, 'She won't touch chinaware,
as she thinks it unclean. She's not fond of tea either. Women of our family
keep to their old-fashioned ways. They observe purdah too. If you'd like
to meet her, she's inside.'

When both Kanta and Kanak said 'Certainly! Of course!' Awasthi led
them through a curtain to another room inside the house. When they both

returned, Nayyar saw that they could barely speak as their cheeks were stuffed with paan.

Awasthi asked Kanta and Kanak, especially Kanak, 'You're an educated and enlightened young woman. You should help us in social work and contribute to our nation building. You have time to spare. You'll be in Nainital for the next couple of months. A certain Mrs K. Pant is doing good work here. You should meet her. She has established a Women's Arts Centre and other institutions in Nainital. She'll be here the day after tomorrow at nine in the morning. You should both come then.'

As Nayyar, Kanta and Kanak got up to leave, they were again offered paan. They each picked up one rolled leaf, but Awasthi laughingly pointed out that paan was invariably offered two pieces at a time, and it was polite to accept both at once. As they came out of Awasthi's bungalow and turned the corner onto the road, Kanta and Kanak went to side and spat out the paan. Four paans were enough for them for a whole month.

Kanta said with irritation, 'What strange people! They keep their women inside, in purdah, but like to socialize with other people's wives and daughters. I won't ever come here again.' She added in anger, 'Their wives are to stay indoors, and sit on their bed slicing betel nut to chew with their paan, and we're supposed to do social work! Did you know,' she said disapprovingly, 'that these UP women chew tobacco with their paan?'

Nayyar pacified her, 'Why get angry? Kanni is finding it difficult to while away her time here. No harm if she meets a few people. Nobody can force her to do anything against her will.'

As they reached the path beside the Grand Hotel that led to their cottage, Nayyar said, 'Let's go to the club. It's only seven o'clock. Why be confined to the house at this hour?'

'Jijaji, we have time. I wanted to have a talk with you,' said Kanak. 'There's never a chance with that crowd at home. I don't want you to lose your temper in front of the others, either.'

Kanta guessed what her sister wanted to talk about. She got edgy on such occasions, because Kanak was prone to making sharp comments in the heat of discussion. She said, 'I'll go and check on Nano. I'll send her out for a stroll. You people go on and talk about whatever you want on the way to the club. But don't be too late. Come home before eleven.' She began to climb up the hill to the bungalow.

Nayyar knew, but still asked, 'What do you want to talk about?'

'You made me promise to keep away from him for sixty days. Tomorrow is the sixtieth day,' Kanak said what she had been rehearsing in her mind.

'What's the point of this warning?' Nayyar asked after a moment's reflection.

'It's neither a warning nor a challenge,' Kanak said. 'The time for me to wait is over.' She added, 'I too have a mind and a heart of my own.'

'Can't you wait a bit longer? Do you want to get married immediately?' Nayyar asked.

'Immediately or not, whether I can wait or not, that's not the point. I must think of the anxiety and suspense that is tormenting him. Aren't you bothered at all that pitaji has not sent any letter? Wouldn't I be bothered?'

Both of them had reached the Capitol, where the road forked off to the club, but Kanak had not finished what she had to say. They turned around. Nayyar thought for a few moments before asking, 'I told you about Puri's treatment of his sister. Did you try to find out anything about that? I offered to take you to their gali.'

'Find out from whom? And what do I do then? I have to trust someone,' she replied. 'I have faith in him'

'You mean, I lied to you?'

'I can't believe him to be dishonest.'

They walked for a while in silence. Kanak spoke first, 'You told me that if I didn't change my mind you wouldn't go against me.'

Nayyar made an effort to speak without any emotion in his voice, 'Yes, I'll not put any obstacle in your way, but then I won't support or approve of your decision either. We'll just tell ourselves that we have no responsibility towards you. What else can we do?'

'Responsibility? Or keeping me shut up and dependent? Why should everybody go on feeling responsible for me?' Kanak was boiling inwardly, but she kept silent. They both walked in silence up to the post office and towards Mallital.

Nayyar said, 'I can't do anything to help you at the moment. I want to go to the club. I'm going back.' Kanak too turned around. When they reached the path leading to their cottage, Kanak went on, and Nayyar continued on his way to the club.

Kanak halted halfway along the path to the cottage. It was not yet dark, cloudy but not raining. 'What'll I do at the cottage?' she thought. She came back to the road and walked in the direction of the library, looking for an unoccupied bench facing the lake. 'Jijaji doesn't even want to talk about us! What'll I do?' she sat thinking. Puri's mental anguish, the promise she had made as he held her hand; what she had told him in Lawrence Garden... Just the two of them living as a couple in a small house, oblivious to everything around them, she in Puri's arms...She peered at her wristwatch; it was 8.30. She got up and went back to the cottage.

A light drizzle had begun to fall the next night, and had not stopped by half past eight in the morning. The weather did not encourage Kanak to go to Awasthi's house and meet Mrs Pant. She did not feel much inclined to discuss social work in her troubled state of mind, but neither did she want to sit quietly and feel imprisoned in the cottage.

Nayyar, Kanta and Kanchan did not seem willing to accompany Kanak as an escort to Awasthi's house. Kanak had seen a rickshaw carriage pulled by four persons for the first time in Nainital. The thought of riding in one, and seeing the coolies wheeze and gasp, especially on roads that climbed steeply, revolted her. She borrowed Kanta's raincoat, took a small umbrella and set out alone to Awasthi's bungalow.

Two persons, wearing khadi kurta-dhoti, the Gandhi cap and wrapped in shawls, were waiting in the veranda of Awasthi's bungalow. He was in his office. When the orderly told him about Kanak's arrival, he sent for her.

Awasthi did not get up when she entered, but just raised his eyes from a file before him and said, 'Come, have a seat.'

Kanak said namaste and took a chair across from his desk. Awasthi went on, 'I thought you mightn't come because of the rain. You Punjabi women are really brave, real go-getters. The women from our own community are good-for-nothing. Someone must always accompany them as if they were a piece of baggage. Let's get you some tea.' He thumped at the bell on his desk.

Remembering the tea served to her two days before, Kanak put her palms together and made an excuse, 'I've just had some with my breakfast. I'm not used to tea anyway. Don't send for it, please.'

'Yes, yes. You people like yogurt lassi.' He let out a loud guffaw, then became serious and added, 'Of course, lassi is very healthy. Achcha, have a paan.' Awasthi opened a book-sized paan-box and offered it to Kanak.

Kanak had to accept one.

Mrs Pant was late, probably because of the rain. Awasthi talked about other people from Punjab he had met in Delhi and Lucknow. He told Kanak, 'Some Punjabi women are hired for government jobs in our province. They're good workers.'

Kanak found an opening, 'I do want to help with the social work. I've worked with the Congress organization in the past, and at the time of the Quit India movement of 1942. If my family has to leave Lahore, I'd feel better if I had some kind of job elsewhere.'

'Wah, there's no shortage of jobs or employment for you. Capable young women like you can help so much in the building of our nation. Just now it's a patriotic thing to work for the government. The education department is being expanded. Then there's my own department. There are jobs everywhere. You should come to Lucknow. You'll definitely get some job. Just tell me what kind of work will suit you. No problem whatsoever.'

Awasthi pulled his feet up onto his chair and began to reminisce, 'I'm really fond of Punjab. I was at the Congress convention in Lahore in 1929. Punjabi girls are so full of life. Their behaviour is so uninhibited.' Some memory of that time brought a smile to his lips. 'I always remember those times. I became friendly with many Punjabi families at the time of the Tripuri and Ramgarh conventions. Once I sent them parcels of Lucknow's dussehri mangoes. Now the season's over, otherwise I'd have got some for you too. The real fun is in eating mangoes in a mango grove. I'll take you to one ...'

Awasthi's face took on a strange look, and his eyes were half-shut in a recollection of something. 'Perhaps his mouth is watering at the thought of juicy Lucknow mangoes,' Kanak thought.

After another hour's wait, Kanak spoke up, 'Mrs Pant probably won't come now because of the rain.'

'Yes, it seems unlikely. But don't worry,' Awasthi said to reassure her. 'I'll take you to her place some day. She comes here often. She's a member of the UP Legislative Assembly. Feel free to come here whenever you want.' As Kanak was leaving, Awasthi gave her the address of Mrs Pant's bungalow.

So now Kanak had Awasthi's promise of finding her a job. That took some load off her mind, and her thoughts were filled with plans for the future. In the hope of beginning her new life soon, she went to visit Mrs Pant in the afternoon of the third day after her meeting with Awasthi. Awasthi was there too, with another rather stout man with a huge paunch wearing khadi kurta-dhoti and cap, and a young woman in a khadi sari. Tea and freshly fried pakoras were on the table.

Awasthi introduced Kanak to Mrs Pant with great enthusiasm. The heavily built man too praised the courage and dedication of Punjabi women. The young woman began to describe how her school in Nainital had not received proper funding from the government. She asked Awasthi to help her. Munching on a pakora, Awasthi said to her dryly, 'Why do you worry? If funding is due according to the rules, you'll get it. You should first petition the director of the department. Wait for his reply before coming to me for help.' Despite his gruffness, the young woman's smile showed she felt obliged to him for his consideration.

The man and the young woman got up and bid respectful farewells to Awasthi. After they left, Awasthi repeated his praise of Kanak, and said to Mrs Pant that she could have Kanak help her in the work of the Women's Arts Centre.

Awasthi shook off his chappals, drew his feet up and sprawled on the big sofa chair. Kanak was sitting opposite him, occupying barely half of a similar chair. He said, 'You make up your own mind about moving to Lucknow. You'll surely get a job. I'm leaving for Lucknow on Sunday. You can come whenever you want. If you want, you can teach at some school. There are plenty of jobs, lots of them in the Public Relations Department. A salary of a hundred-and-fifty or two hundred rupees a month can easily be arranged. You can stay in Lucknow with Mrs Pant. What do you say, Mrs Pant?'

'Arrey, why not? My home is her home too,' Mrs Pant agreed.

Awasthi suddenly had an idea, 'Let's have a picnic, Mrs Pant, if the sky clears up the day after tomorrow as it did today. Have you seen the Naukuchia Lake?' He asked Kanak, turning to her.

Kanak admitted that she had never even heard of it.

Awasthi said, 'What's so great about Nainital? The really scenic places are some distance away. And what lovely views! Mrs Pant, you'll take care of the food. Same delicious chicken curry as last time.' He turned and looked at Kanak, 'You're not vegetarian, are you? Punjabis usually don't have such prejudices.'

Kanak admitted that she had no particular problem about eating meat.

Mrs Pant reminded Awasthi, 'You'll have to arrange for the motorcars.'

'Don't worry about that. How many motorcars?'

'Let's invite Shakuntala, and ask Verma too. What do you think? Maybe not, for it would get too crowded... You be at the bus station by nine o'clock,' Mrs Pant said to Kanak.

Kanak could not refuse. As she walked back home, she was thinking, 'What simple and well-meaning people! A bit unconventional, though. They still follow the Indian style of doing things. He's a parliamentary secretary, but not at all officious.' On reaching home she told Kanta and Nayyar about the promise of getting a job at a salary of two hundred rupees, and about the invitation to the picnic.

Both were silent for a while. Then Kanta asked, 'You'll go alone that far with them? There won't be anybody else. Awasthi's wife won't go along for sure.'

'What's your objection after all?' Kanak replied determinedly, 'Mrs Pant will be there. She's a member of the Legislative Assembly. Awasthi's no ordinary person either; he's a parliamentary secretary. Will all of you come with me too when I get the job?'

'It would be proper to ask pitaji about this first,' said Kanta.

'I didn't realize that I was a prisoner here,' Kanak replied angrily. 'I'm over twenty-one. Will I never be allowed to stand on my own two feet?'

Nayyar spoke up, 'Why do you think that everyone is against you? Why should we presume that pitaji would object? Take Kanchan along with you to the picnic. What's the problem if your sister goes with you? And two are better than one, in unfamiliar surroundings.'

When Kanak shared the bed with Kanchan that night, she lay on her side and thought for a long time, '...I can see a way out of this mess. I must take a bold step.' Her life in her father's household was over. The hope of finding a job had brought a complete change into her plans and thoughts. 'Tomorrow I'll send a letter to Puri and tell jijaji too. No one but I myself has the right to open any letter that comes for me. I'll ask him to reply by registered mail, and to write "personal" on the envelope.'

The invitation for the picnic depended on the weather remaining clear. Rain had begun to fall even before dawn, and it was still raining in the late morning. Kanak felt uneasy at not being able to go to the picnic, but she had no control over the weather. The rain did not let up, but began to fall harder. By ten, everyone in the family was waiting for the postman. They had written several letters to Lahore, but no reply had come from Panditji in the past two weeks. Around this hour, everybody's attention was focussed on the gate of the bungalow. Nayyar was reading *Readers' Digest,* sprawled on an easy chair in the veranda. Kanchan sat beside him, knitting a sweater for Nano. Kanak was lying on a bed inside, lost in thoughts about her future.

'There's the mail, jijaji,' Kanak heard Kanchan call, and came outside.

Kanchan was signing for the Express Delivery letter from the postman wrapped in his raincoat. 'It's from pitaji, for you,' said Kanchan and handed the envelope to Nayyar. Kanta too came out and the three sisters stood behind Nayyar.

Nayyar had read only a couple of lines when he exclaimed, 'Pitaji says that he received only one letter from us. He thinks that Muslim postmen are afraid to come to Gwal Mandi. He's asked us to send all letters by registered mail.' He began to read aloud.

From what Panditji had written, the situation in Lahore seemed very precarious: ...The printing press had been closed since 13 July. People were really alarmed after the announcement that government employees had the option to choose posting to Pakistan or Hindustan. Everyone was anxious to know to which nation Lahore was to be allotted. The Muslim machine operators, litho artists and binders working at the press did not have the courage to come to Gwal Mandi. Hindus had fortified the area with barricades against the threat of attacks from the Muslim neighbourhoods that surrounded Gwal Mandi. Old Fateh Mohammed, the printing-press operator, had probably been murdered. There was no question of any sale of textbooks as schools all over Punjab had been shut down. The weather was terrible; very little rain, but high, oppressive humidity. Scores of people were transferring their businesses to the east.

Panditji was feeling sorry that he had invested a lot of money two years before in new printing machines. To where could he now transport these machines and his stocks of printed books? People had lost faith in leaders and the government. The banks were no longer seen as a secure place for one's money. People were having their accounts transferred to branches of their banks outside Lahore, to Delhi or the United Provinces. They were emptying their safety deposit boxes of share certificates and securities, jewellery and other valuables. Panditji did not want to leave Lahore, but he had had his cash account transferred to the Delhi branch of his bank. The general feeling among Hindus was that they would remain, even if Lahore were to be included in Pakistan.

Panditji had advised Nayyar to think of getting his bank account temporarily transferred and to empty his safety deposit boxes. These could be replenished once things had quieted down. In the end, he had written that he too wanted to come to Nainital for a few days, but to leave Lahore

at this time would be unwise because it would be seen as running away in
the face of danger.

No one spoke after the letter reading ended. Kanta broke the silence,
'So what are we going to do?'

'Let's wait and see,' Nayyar said. 'The worst that might happen is that
Lahore would go to Pakistan. Do you think that over 100 million Muslims
living in India would fit into the area between Lahore and Peshawar? If
Muslims can live in Hindustan, so can Hindus in Lahore. Pakistan too
would need doctors, lawyers and engineers. And what can I take away from
Lahore—my house and family property?'

How could Kanta accept that her husband's interpretation was better
than that of her wise father? A woman considers her parents' wisdom as her
own. She said unhappily, 'Pitaji wrote this letter after assessing the situation
in Lahore. Are those people idiots who are getting out of the city? You'd
like us to end up starving and without a roof over our heads ...'

When Nayyar agreed to leave for Lahore that very evening, Kanta began
to complain, 'To hell with the property! When pitaji himself is thinking
of getting out of Lahore, how can I let you go back there? What matters
more to me—your life or the property? And what'll you be able do on
your own? You're all thumbs without my help!'

Rajendra volunteered, 'Why don't I go instead?' But that made sense
to no one. It was the elder brother who knew all the intricacies of the
paperwork of property and bank accounts. Kanak did not say anything; she
was preoccupied with her own problems. Her father's letter described how
circumstances had changed. Now the question was: Where would she go?
She did not want to be a burden on her father any longer. 'I'll settle down
in Lucknow,' she thought, but she first had to tell Puri about her decision
and ask for his approval. The whole day and that night too she wallowed in
indecision, weighing her options. Next morning at nine she told Nayyar
about her intention of writing to Puri. She wrote him a long letter, asking
him to come to Nainital. And if he couldn't or wouldn't come, she did not
forget to add, she would have to go back to Lahore to see him.

When Panditji arranged for Kanak and Kanchan to go to Nainital with
Nayyar, he had slipped three one hundred-rupee notes to Kanak and told
her quietly, 'Try to be as little a burden on Kanta as you can. Take care of
Kanchan's needs as well.' Panditji knew that his daughter was a bit of a
spendthrift. But in her state of emotional stress, Kanak had not needed

to use even one of the notes in Nainital. Puri's financial situation was no secret to her. Whenever she thought of his problems, she did not feel like spending money pointlessly. She enclosed two one-hundred-rupee notes in her letter. She went to the post office, and to make sure that it reached Puri, sent the letter by registered mail.

Since the reading of Panditji's letter, there was discussion in the family at least once or twice every day about the desirability and necessity of Nayyar going to Lahore and making some arrangement about his property. Nayyar was willing to go, but Kanta could not just ignore her father's warning. She could not let Nayyar walk into a place so full of danger and death. In the end, her argument was always that Nayyar would not be able to look after himself without her. Inwardly, she wanted Nayyar to realize the importance of her accompanying him.

Kanak had written to Puri on the twenty-first. There was no reply until the twenty-seventh. Anxiety and suspense began to gnaw her heart. Would she have to go to Lahore? Should she accompany her brother-in-law? When the subject of Nayyar going to Lahore came up again, and Kanta repeated her objections, Kanak asked, 'Should I go with him?'

'Achcha!' Nayyar said and looked at her very meaningfully.

Because of Kanak's determination and their mutual disagreement, she and Nayyar had been speaking very little to each other. The teasing and joking of the past had completely disappeared. In the agitation of fighting for her rights, Kanak had not felt this lack as much as Nayyar had. Six days before, she had told him about her intention to write to Puri, which for him had amounted to the breakdown of all polite exchanges and a declaration of war. He could not agree with her because of his high-mindedness and the stand he had taken. But that did not mean that he did not miss the warmth of a friendly relationship with her. He found this treatment to cure her disease even more unpleasant than the disease itself.

He took Kanak's offer to accompany him as her invitation to put an end to the bitterness between them, but for Kanak it was only a means to achieve what she wanted. To answer his meaningful 'achcha', she asked, 'Why?'

Nayyar dropped his pretence of seriousness, 'Will I be looking after my properties or standing guard over you?'

'Am I your property?' Kanak shot back. She thought he was harking back to the antagonism of their past disagreements.

'Look, it's not a matter of your being my property, but if someone in

Lahore wanted to whip you away like a piece of property, would he be frightened off if I just shouted at him?'

When Kanak found that she had misunderstood his meaning, her anger melted away and she too could not resist a joke in reply, 'That's all the confidence you have in your manliness? I agreed to go with you just to make sure you were properly dressed, like any other little boy, and keep your buttons sewn on. If you don't like that, very well!' She wiggled her thumb at him to show her defiance.

For the next two days they continued to banter and joke as in former times. Nayyar would say, 'Our ancestors said that the goddess of wealth was a woman whose name was Lakshmi. And Lakshmi means "property".' He would call out, 'Kanta, when do you want me to leave for Lahore? What's the danger now that I have a bodyguard?'

On the twenty-ninth Kanak was waiting for the postman, her eyes on the gate of the cottage. At 11 o'clock she went inside, lay down on her bed and pulled the blanket over her head to be alone with her disappointment. She had explained everything in her letter, and was thinking, it would be unfair if Puri continued to be angry with her.

'Kanak, listen,' she heard Nayyar's unhappy-sounding voice. What now? Kanak thought, he seemed normal only ten minutes ago.

'Yes?' she said, uncovering her face.

'Letter for you,' Nayyar said gravely in English. He laid the unopened registered letter beside her pillow, and went out without saying another word. The envelope was marked 'personal', and the word was underlined. He had obviously brought it to her to show that he knew about it.

Kanak was so happy and excited at receiving the letter that she did not care about Nayyar's displeasure. On the contrary, she was piqued, 'If he wants to be angry, let him. What harm am I causing anyone? Didn't he marry the woman he wanted? Didn't he write to her on the sly before their marriage? It was I who used to pass their letters, from one to the other! The question of the family's prestige has come up just because Puri doesn't have any money. Once we both find jobs in Lucknow and begin to earn salaries, everything will be fine. If he still doesn't want to talk to us, that's his problem. We can get along without his help.'

At midday on 30 July, the newspaper vendor brought the copies of the dailies that came from Delhi, Lahore and Lucknow. He handed a copy of the *Statesman* and the *Tribune* to Nayyar. Kanak came forward for the paper, but said nothing. Nayyar spoke up, 'Look, I've been saying all along that there'd be no reason why Hindus wouldn't be able to stay in Lahore. Look at these statements by the League and Congress—that the minorities in both countries will have the same civil rights as the majority, as well as full freedom to practise their culture and religion. Nainital is in Hindustan. What danger are the Muslims facing here?'

Kanak did not agree with him. She said, 'Jijaji, the situation is different in UP. The Congress is in power here. Congress was always against partition because it wanted to please the Muslims and have their support. Congress has never said that Hindus and Muslims were two different peoples.'

There was no immediate need, Nayyar decided, to go to Lahore. This fresh news was bound to be the main topic of discussion at the New Club. Nayyar reached there a little later than usual. As he walked into the club he met Pandey, a lawyer from Nainital, holding a whisky and soda. Pandey was a Congress supporter, but he often criticized its policies. He wore suits of khadi wool, but often took Gandhi to task. He called out to Nayyar in English, 'Nayyar, now you'll surely go back to Lahore. Jinnah has given his assurances.'

Nayyar had always been opposed to any transfers of population. He admitted, 'Of course we'll go back. Where else would we go?' He added, 'The Muslim League leaders are fearful of Hindu domination. Once they have a chance to form the government, that complex will vanish by itself. Then they'll stop feeling threatened.'

A Sikh in an expensive, well-tailored suit, his pomaded salt-and-pepper beard carefully groomed around his face, stood next to Pandey. He removed his whisky and soda from his lips, and raising his index finger and holding himself erect, said loudly in English, 'No, no. How can you say that? Jinnah's statement is nothing but empty words. Muslims have a deep-seated loathing of Hindus and Sikhs. Tell me, did the Muslim ministers in the interim cabinet in Punjab have any less rights than the Congress and Hindu ministers? But the Muslim League never let the ministry function. They created problems every step of the way.' His voice rose even higher, 'They don't want to cooperate, under any circumstances. All they want to do is to lord it over us. Gandhi himself eventually had to come round to the realistic ideas of Nehru and Patel.'

A local *pahari* man, wearing a long achkan jacket and tight, narrow pajama trousers, stepped forward. He said in support of Nayyar, 'But

Hindus and Muslims cannot forever remain in a state of war, ready to kill each other. Even after Hindustan and Pakistan are formed, they would have to live together in peace or the guns would start blazing on both sides. If Muslims remain in Hindustan, in principle, Hindus should be allowed to live in Pakistan. That would be politically necessary. Gandhiji has said the same thing.'

'What about Gandhi!' the Sikh interrupted him excitedly. 'Gandhi was against the partition to start with. He had said, "Partition over my dead body." He's had to eat his words, hasn't he? For you he's a god. Others think he's a devil. How can those who regard him only as a cunning old man believe what he says?'

Nayyar said without paying any notice to the Sikh's excitement, 'If the Congress and the League leaders have adopted a policy for any practical reasons, why should we doubt them?'

Pandey calmly took a couple of sips of his drink before replying, 'The League holds a different view. They treat Hindus and Muslims as two different nations. If they wanted to have peaceful coexistence, why would they have taken up that stand? And demanded a separate Pakistan?'

Nayyar said, 'But some of us don't consider them as two separate peoples. We want to prove that it's the nation and not the community that matters most. Punjab is my place of birth, and it's my motherland too.'

Pandey tilted his head back to show his disagreement with Nayyar, and replied, 'Don't be silly, Nayyar. Didn't the German Jews consider Germany as their motherland? Didn't Hitler get rid of them all? Listen! Pakistan will come into existence on 15 August.' His voice rose to a shout, 'Tell Gandhi to go to Pakistan after that, and try to change people's minds there!' Pandey waved his fist to emphasize his words, 'Jinnah is certain to forbid him going across the border into Pakistan, and if anyone enters his country in spite of his ban, then Jinnah's having him shot will be justified under international law. You may then repeat Gandhi's favourite chant *raghupati raghava rajaram* that God is compassionate as much as you want, but you'll have no grounds to take any military action.'

The Sikh said with apparent satisfaction, 'Yes, there you are.'

Nayyar straightened his back before arguing, 'International laws were drawn up by human beings. They don't offer an ideal solution to anything. The trial of Hitler's gang for their widespread acts of genocide has set new standards of international justice. I have faith in the goodness of human beings. Gandhiji would, I hope, be able to convince Jinnah of his good intentions.'

'Never! Never! Impossible!' the Sikh shouted.

Pandey lifted his hand as a gesture for the Sikh to listen, and asked Nayyar, 'Give me just one example where Gandhi was able to convince Jinnah of his good intentions.'

'It may be too early for me to reply,' Nayyar said with confidence. 'It was only after his death that Jesus Christ prevailed over his enemies.'

'Ho, ho!' Pandey roared with laughter. 'That, my friend, only happened one thousand years after Christ's death, and for who knows what social, political and religious reasons? The religion of Christ was spread by the might of the sword, not by turning the other cheek, that much you will concede. How many Christians today believe in turning the other cheek? How many times have the British offered their other cheek to us? But I do sympathize with your idealism.

'Oh, *aabkaar*!' Pandey turned towards the bar and called out to the barman, 'One large whisky for Nayyar sahib.'

'One for me too,' the Sikh said, and drained his glass in one gulp and handed it to the waiter.

Nayyar settled his feet and hips into a comfortable stance, and thrusting his hands into his pockets, said, 'Believe me, Pandey, all this quarrelling, violence and hatred won't last for long.'

A crowd had gathered around them. When it no longer seemed possible to have a one-to-one talk, they walked towards the bridge tables.

Kanak had written to Puri that she would make arrangements for his stay in Nainital. 'I'll put him up in a hotel,' she thought. A large number of visitors from Punjab had taken up long-term residence in hotels. At the club she had heard that most hotels were packed to full capacity. Indian hotels were packing in guests in addition to the places already filled, and were charging two and three times their usual rates, sometimes even more than the European hotels. European-style hotels were expensive, but they had neither increased their rates, nor did they admit more guests than their accommodation permitted. After Kanak received Puri's telegram indicating his arrival, she went to the post office and telephoned the Astoria Hotel to ask for a single room.

The answer was, 'Nothing available today. Nothing before tomorrow.'

'All right, please reserve it for tomorrow.'

The hotel stipulated that room would have to be vacated before 20 August.

Kanak accepted the condition and made a reservation in the name of J.D. Puri, saying that the guest would arrive by lunchtime the following day.

Any time that Kanak left the house, Rajendra would offer to go with her. Kanta's sister-in-law Swarna had never had such freedom to roam around in Sargodha. She too would get ready to accompany them. To avoid them, Kanak left the cottage early that day, long before the time when the bus from Kathgodam was due and sat waiting at the library, halfway to the bus terminus. Thick clouds had covered the sky like an impenetrable canopy since morning. The rain fell gently but steadily, slackened off for a while and then came back in a short downpour. One could see raincoats and umbrellas all around.

Kanak sometimes smiled inwardly at the two different faces of Nainital. When the skies were clear, streets teeming with tourists in colourful clothes looked like flowerbeds full of petunias and phlox. With pedestrians covered with raincoats and umbrellas during the rain, the same roadways looked as if they were full of mushrooms.

Kanak had an umbrella and Kanta's raincoat with her, but it would have been unpleasant to stand at the terminus in the rain. To keep Puri from feeling lost in an unfamiliar place, Kanak wanted to be at the terminus before his bus arrived. She wanted to see him the moment he stepped out of the bus from Kathgodam. She knew that the train reached the Kathgodam station at 10.30 in the morning. At twelve by her watch, wrapped in her raincoat and with umbrella held aloft, she left the library for Tallital.

The rain began to fall more heavily when she arrived at the terminus. She took shelter in the corner of a shed with a corrugated iron roof, next to the ticket counter. A thick cloud of smoke had gathered under the ceiling of the shed. A gaggle of *dotiyaal*s, coolies who carried heavy loads on their backs, sat hunched over a smoky fire, in rain-soaked woollen clothes. Seeing Kanak standing there, they moved away from her, to the other side of the fire.

The smoke made Kanak cough. The coolies looked at her fearfully, and tried to contain the fire by covering it with small stones. Whether they moved away from her in fear and tried to smother the fire because it was making a lady cough, or in obedience to some regulation, Kanak did not know. The coolies themselves were not aware of any such regulation, but their experience of life had taught them to be wary of the rich and the well dressed. Although the coolies had moved farther away from her and had tried to put out the fire, the thick smoke and the stench rising from their damp, unwashed and sweat-soaked clothes became unbearable for Kanak. She looked around and saw that others had taken shelter on the veranda of the post office. She walked over. The rain had stopped, except for some stray drops, and she hoped it would hold off for an hour, until Puri got to his hotel.

Kanak's legs were getting tired. A bus arrived. Coolies shouting and shoving each other in a race to reach the bus, surrounded it like flies swarming over a lump of *gur*. Kanak too went to look. The bus had come from Ranikhet, not Kathgodam. Kanak returned to the veranda. A bus arrived from Ramgarh, then another from Haldwani.

Finally the bus from Kathgodam came. The coolies again rushed at the bus and began to push and shove for the chance to carry the passengers' luggage. Kanak held her breath as she went forward. She tried to see through the milling crowd by standing on her toes and moving her head from side to side. Those arriving gradually moved aside to let the coolies remove the luggage from the interior and the roof of the bus. Kanak again returned to her spot, and stood with eyes on the road. A light drizzle had begun to fall.

Another Kathgodam bus arrived. The coolies attacked it as they had all the previous arrivals. Kanak could hear the driver of the bus, his assistant and the supervisor of coolies shouting at them to keep order. Her eyes were fixed on the door of the bus, inspecting every passenger that came out. She rushed forward. Puri, in a checked shirt and steel-grey trousers, was pushing the coolies aside in his attempt to get down. Kanak was impatient to reach him, but the crowd prevented her.

The surging crowd pushed Puri out, buffeted by the passengers and the coolies until he reached the edge of the crowd. He turned his head to look at the person who had grabbed his arm, and kept on looking, unable to speak. He took Kanak's hand into his own and pressed it lovingly, then let it go as he became aware of the other people around him.

Puri was reluctant to get into the coolie-powered rickshaw. He had never sat in a vehicle that was pulled by humans.

Kanak tried to explain, 'It's raining. You'll be soaked, and your luggage too.'

The coolies were pleading with their eyes against Puri's hesitation.

There was a gust of rain. Kanak took Puri back to the veranda. The rain overcame Puri's hesitation. The now happy coolies loaded up his luggage and brought the rickshaw as close to the veranda as possible. They both got in. Kanak said, 'Hotel Astoria'.

The coolies covered the rickshaw on all sides with tarpaulins. Kanak and Puri were enclosed inside, unable to see anything outside. Their eyes met in that box-like enclosure. The limits of this small space gave them unlimited freedom. They could not hear the plop-plop of raindrops on the tarpaulin, nor the splash-splash of the coolies' bare feet in the rivulets of rain on the tarmac, nor the ding-ding of the rickshaw bell.

The slowing of the rickshaw alerted Kanak, and she heard the coolies gasping for breath. She opened the tarpaulin just a crack and saw that the rickshaw was climbing the road to Mallital bazaar beside the hospital. It had gone past the path that led to Vimal Villa. The rickshaw had flown this far, she felt, or reached here in one giant leap. In those first moments of their meeting again, they were both lost in a silent exchange of love. Their lips were not free to utter a word. The rickshaw had covered the distance between the terminus and Mallital in one magic moment.

Kanak said, without removing herself from Puri's embrace, 'I'll get off at the next intersection and will take another rickshaw home. Your hotel is only a few steps away. The rickshaw will take you there. I'll be very late. Your room number is seven. Have a wash, eat some lunch and rest for a while. I'll come back around five or six. Then we'll talk.'

Staying at the best European hotel in Nainital was a totally new experience for Puri. So far, he had only heard and read about hotels. He was met at the reception by a smartly dressed man, who then handed him over to a bearer in a white uniform, who gave him a deep bow of salaam.

The bearer took Puri to his room where he stowed Puri's slim bedding roll on the lowest shelf of a big wardrobe. He asked for the key to Puri's small black tin trunk, took out his clothes and hung them on hangers in the wardrobe. Sitting on a chair, Puri watched him quietly.

After arranging Puri's clothes and shoes in the wardrobe, the bearer opened another door and asked, 'Will you have your bath, sir? Should I run the hot water?'

Puri nodded. When he went to the bathroom and saw three towels hanging there, he scratched his ear guessing at the separate uses for each of them.

The dining hall was large enough to hold a fair-sized meeting. Scores of tables were covered with snow-white cloths and surrounded by four slender chairs. China dishes and bowls whiter than the tablecloths, gleaming silverware, and fresh flowers in vases were elaborately arranged on the tables. Puri was a bit embarrassed and saddened by the thought that all this sparkling show was simply for the serving of a meal, afterwards to be cleaned again when the dishes were used and soiled. Food was Western style, served silently and efficiently by courteous waiters.

Puri's family was vegetarian in deference to Masterji's beliefs. Puri had tasted meat very seldom, and that too mainly as a protest against the family conventions. He was not familiar with the use of a knife and fork. Having a bath had given him an appetite. Sitting alone he did not eat much, but did not remain hungry either.

When he returned to his room and sat on the bed with its box-spring mattress, he was taken aback by its soft firmness. The touch was not unpleasant, something like caressing a young and unfamiliar woman. The feeling was new, but agreeable. Everything around him was spotless, gleaming, and clean smelling. Puri had travelled from the humid summer of Lahore, where one was always covered in sweat. He found Nainital not only cool, but almost a little cold. He lay down, pulling the top sheet and blanket over him. He had not slept much during his journey and felt tired, but he could not fall asleep immediately.

Puri opened his eyes and saw a smiling Kanak bent over his face. Her fingers were caressing his hair and eyes.

'Slept late?'

In the daze of his waking state and in the fading light filling the room, he could not understand whether it was sunset or sunrise. 'What time is it?' he asked, trying to pull away his hand to look at his watch.

'Quarter past six,' said Kanak. 'When I arrived the bearer told me that the sahib was sleeping. He had knocked three times, but you did not hear. He could not have come inside. They stop serving tea at six. Never mind; at least you've had some sleep.'

Puri was unable to take all this in. All this comfort and luxury, with no one to interrupt them, and Kanak sitting on the bed, leaning against him. She did not have to worry about being found out or being seen with him. Was he in Nainital, or in another world?

Kanak said, 'We have until half past eight. All the others have gone to the movies, jijaji is at the club.' Her tone changed, 'Not that I care. I have kept my word.' She quickly told him everything about her family's resistance and her promise to not meet or write to him for sixty days. She also described, in the same breath, the assurance given by the parliamentary secretary about getting a job paying two hundred rupees per month. 'I heard that Lucknow is quite a nice place, away from all this unrest,' she said,

Puri questioned her, 'He promised you a job. What about me? In your letter you said that I too would have a job.'

'If it can be arranged for me, it won't be a problem with yours. Writers are known everywhere. I'm sure he'd be familiar with your name. Your reputation probably precedes you.' She began to tell him how simple, straightforward and kind Awasthi was.

When they came out of the hotel, the sun was setting behind the mountains to the west. The overcast sky had cleared in the afternoon, and only some greyish-white clouds were still scudding overhead. Patches of clouds were swirling around the peaks of the hills covered with lush foliage and pine trees. The last rays of the dying sun had turned the velvety-green, craggy ridge of the mountain to the east into a ribbon of gold. People who had waited all day for the rain to stop were now crowding the bazaars. Kanak and Puri went through the bazaar to the road below the hospital and just above the maidan.

'Hey, there's the lake!' Puri's steps faltered, as he looked to his right.

'The rickshaw brought us along the road beside the lake. You couldn't see it because of the tarpaulins. Didn't you notice it when you got off the bus?'

'How could I? That crowd drove me crazy.' Puri continued to gaze in wonder.

Until now Kanak had talked of nothing but her own problems. She asked, 'Tara bahin's wedding went off well?'

Puri lowered his head. He said falteringly, 'As well as it could in the circumstances. The poor girl isn't alive any more.'

'What?' Kanak gasped with shock.

Puri briefly told her about the wedding taking place because of the insistence of Masterji, his uncle and Tara's in-laws, the attack on Banni Hata and how Tara could not be rescued from the fire. He blamed himself and his family, 'That was hardly the time to go through with the ceremony in Lahore. But parents are always in a hurry to get rid of the millstone of a daughter round their necks.'

'Was Tara unwilling to go through with the marriage?' Kanak asked, encouraged by Puri's frankness. 'Her fiancé had quite a bad reputation, I heard.'

'No. I was ... who told you that?' Puri asked, then said, 'Her engagement was arranged back in 1944. I was in prison at that time.'

'Tara did express some opposition, I was told,' Kanak said.

Puri thought for a moment before asking, 'Did your brother-in-law tell you that?'

'Yes, it was he,' Kanak admitted. She did not want to hide anything from Puri.

'Those galis are full of all sorts of gossip,' he said with irritation. 'Sukhlal had his detractors too. There were some whispers that theirs was a bad match. I don't mind admitting that I didn't greatly approve of her fiancé. But she'd already been engaged to him for three years. It had become a prestige issue for Sukhlal, my uncle, my father, for all of us. Unless Tara said so first, it didn't seem proper for me to make a fuss. Call it the timidity of a traditional Hindu girl or whatever, but she didn't object. How could I say anything in those circumstances?'

'Didn't they know each other well?' Kanak wanted to clarify matters.

'I'm not sure, but if something happened without my knowledge, or at the time when I was in prison, I couldn't have known about it.'

How could Kanak have any doubts about Puri after such a candid, simple and plausible explanation? 'Nayyar probably had made up the story to belittle Puri,' she told herself, 'and I believed him. Or maybe he coloured the truth a bit.' Her brother-in-law had been deceitful in his investigations, she decided. She did not ask anything further about Tara's tragedy.

They walked on the lakeside road up to Tallital. It was getting dark. On their way back, they sat on a bench for some time. Puri was captivated by the sight of the rolling waters of the lake in front of him, and by the twinkle of electric lights on the dark slopes of the surrounding hills.

'It would be a pity if a sensitive writer like you couldn't see such a sight. And how could I watch it alone? It was right to ask you to come, wasn't it?'

Puri took Kanak's hand in his in reply, and sat without speaking. While they were walking back, Kanak came face-to-face with some people she had met in Nainital. But she was indifferent, and walked boldly on with Puri, her head held high, a contented smile on her face. 'Who can stop us now! We have overcome all obstacles! Just like mountain travellers who go through clouds swirling in their path.' She said goodbye to Puri at the gate of his hotel.

When Puri returned to his room after dinner, he found that his bed had been made. The sheets had been straightened, and both pillows had been fluffed up. The top sheet and blanket had been arranged to form an open pocket, for pulling up smoothly. He had never seen anything like it. Rich people wore special nightclothes to bed, he remembered. He didn't have any, but not wearing fresh, clean clothes while in the room and in the bed seemed like an insult to the room and the bed. He took out a freshly ironed shirt and pajamas. Now, for the first time in his life he wore fresh, clean clothes to bed. His family and the people of his gali would have considered wearing such clothes inside the house, much less in bed, foolish and extravagant.

He lay on the bed. He switched off the decorative light hanging from the ceiling. Only the shaded bedside lamp remained alight. The figures on the pink shade were magnified in diffused forms on the walls, now also pink-tinted. He did not feel like reading, but he did not turn off the light, not wanting this lovely display of luxury to disappear from his sight. After his long struggle to bore his way through the stone wall of poverty with his bare hands, his heart was filled with the thrill of finding the path leading to the promised happiness and wealth. Jobs that would pay each of them two hundred rupees every month awaited him and Kanak in Lucknow! Four hundred a month ... a small bungalow ... clean, fresh clothes ... respect on all sides ... an uninhibited, smiling Kanak!

The excitement and hope of finally being within reach of happiness and wealth had driven away all thoughts of sleep. His mind, and body too, longed for Kanak. The picture was incomplete without her. Only a few hours before, when Kanak was in his arms, he had realized how absolute was his love for her. He tossed and turned restlessly for a long time before falling asleep with both pillows clutched between his arms.

If Nayyar, Kanta or Kanchan saw them together, Kanak had told Puri, they might complain even if they could not do anything about it. So why distress them unnecessarily? She waited for him at nine in morning in the park beside the secretariat, just above the hotel. They walked along the mountain road going towards Tallital, occasionally sitting down on a roadside boulder to rest and discuss their plans for a future, which had become more hopeful and promising after the assurances given by Awasthi.

The happiness and satisfaction that Puri had experienced in Nainital were beyond his most lurid fantasies. Kanak's willingness to surrender herself to him had overwhelmed him. Her love was not like a vessel full of water or even a well from which Puri could draw as much he wanted; it was, he felt, like the lake before him. He could swim in it, buoyed up by her love, but could never plumb its depth, no matter how hard he tried.

Puri was now eager to make this feeling of happiness and satisfaction permanent. He brought up with Kanak the subject of his going to Lucknow and launching his new career as soon as possible. Since Kanak had spoken with Awasthi, it would have been appropriate if she went to Lucknow with him. Kanak knew that too. She had made up her mind to begin their new life together, and she was not lacking in courage. Still, mindful of social and family norms, she felt a little hesitant about asking her sister and brother-in-law's permission to go to Lucknow, and left the decision until the next day.

Since coming to Nainital, Kanak would go out of the house whenever possible for an hour or two before, and also after, lunch because of the cramped conditions and her disagreements with the family. Kanta and Nayyar realized that. They also knew that she spent her time sitting and reading beside the lake or in the library. They were uneasy that this would raise a few eyebrows among their acquaintances, but they tolerated it because of the stress under which she was living. For the past few days, Kanak had been spending even more time away from the cottage. There was a noticeable change in her attitude and behaviour, and the explanation for the puzzle was not long in coming.

On 8 August at 3 o'clock in the afternoon, Kanak changed her sari and said to Kanta, who was sitting in the veranda, 'Bahinji, I'm going out for a while.'

'No, no, Kanni. We're invited for tea today at Mr Wadhwa's. Mrs Wadhwa asked especially for you and Kanchan,' Kanta said.

'How can I go there with you?' Kanak replied, then added a bit dejectedly. 'Had you asked me before now, I wouldn't have accepted Mrs Pant's invitation. She'd wait for me.'

'Have you told your jijaji?' Kanta asked.

'I've told you,' Kanak stepped out of the veranda before her sister could reply. Kanta sat fuming, 'What's meaning of such a reply?'

Kanak and Puri had walked quite a distance along the Bhowali Road deep in conversation. Around half past six they returned along the Lower Mall Road, and took the road beside Albert Hall which ran down to the lake. This road twists and turns to keep the gradient gentle. Kanak and Puri had taken the third turn when they heard the sound of loud laughter and looked in that direction. Kanak had no idea that the Wadhwas lived on that road. Her gaze met that of Kanta, Nayyar and Mrs Wadhwa standing with others near the gate to their bungalow.

'You couldn't come when we invited you, and here you are, gallivanting around,' Mrs Wadhwa called out to Kanak.

Kanak stopped as did Puri. Both were nervous, Kanak giving a sheepish smile as she thought up a reply.

Nayyar hailed Puri like an old friend, holding out his hand, 'Hullo, Puri. Your meeting at Mrs Pant's ended so soon? People like you find someone to discuss politics wherever you go.'

Without giving Puri a chance to reply, Nayyar began introducing him to Mr Wadhwa, 'You probably haven't met Mr Puri, but you must have heard his name. Arrey bhai, this is the well-known journalist and fiction writer Mr Puri.'

Mr Wadhwa replied in Punjabi, with a marked Peshawar accent, 'Why don't you come to the club, Puri sahib? That's the place to meet people.'

Nayyar replied on Puri's behalf, 'Arrey bhai, he doesn't have time to waste. Every second of his time is precious. All he needs is a pen, and then he's lost in his imagination.' By welcoming Puri enthusiastically, Nayyar had removed any possibility of Mr and Mrs Wadhwa being scandalized at seeing Kanak alone with a man.

Kanak and Puri had to walk back with Nayyar, Kanta and the others. Nayyar kept up a conversation with Puri, 'When did you arrive in Nainital? Saw you today for the first time. It's very difficult to a find a place to stay here. Where are you staying?'

When Nayyar was told that Puri was staying at the Astoria Hotel, he thought for a moment, then said with obvious surprise, 'That's a rather expensive place.'

Kanak was walking on Puri's other side. She pressed his hand to warn him not to say anything.

Nayyar suppressed his surprise, 'It must be comfortable and quiet there.' He was talking as if he and Puri were old friends.

When they reached the path on the Mall Road that went up to Vimal Villa, Kanta excused herself from going to the club to first go and check up on Nano. Before turning towards the Capitol, Nayyar invited everyone, especially Puri, to come to the club. At the club, Nayyar introduced Puri to everyone they met as the distinguished journalist and writer from Lahore, and asked, 'What will you have? Beer or whisky?'

Puri excused himself, 'Thanks, but I don't drink.'

'Have some coffee, then.'

Nayyar joined the players at the bridge table. Kanchan was asked by a group of amateur players to join them. Puri and Kanak watched people play carom for a while, then went and sat by a table piled with newspapers and periodicals and began flipping through magazines. Puri leaned over and whispered into Kanak's ear, 'Will we have to sit here forever?'

Puri and Kanak both felt uncomfortable at the club, and found the presence of others, their laughter and conversation meaningless and unbearable.

'I can't leave with you just now.'

Puri reminded Kanak, 'Make up your mind tonight or tomorrow morning about going to Lucknow. We're wasting our time here.' He found nothing appealing at the club. Around half past eight he got up to leave. Nayyar did not get up from his table, but shook his hand vigorously, said 'Goodnight, see you again,' and went back to his card game.

Nayyar and Kanak did not speak to each other at the club.

Next day, it became apparent from Nayyar's behaviour that he had not objected to Kanak going out with Puri the previous evening only to avoid unpleasant gossip. Kanak found him as distant and uncommunicative as before.

'I really don't care for his angry silence,' Kanak thought, but how could she tell her sister and Nayyar in that situation about her plans for going to Lucknow? They would have instantly guessed that she was going with Puri, but time was running out for her. Puri was growing impatient. They both had decided to begin their new life on 15 August, the day the country was going to gain its independence

Nayyar, awaiting the call to breakfast, was walking between the flowerbeds near the veranda, casually dressed in a cardigan and trousers. Kanak hovered nearby, looking for an opportunity to speak with him, but discouraged by his serious and unwelcoming expression. Kanta was combing Nano's hair, forming ringlets and tying them with ribbons. Kanak took the comb from her sister, and while tying the bows, she mentioned Awasthi's assurance of getting her a job, and asked for permission to go to Lucknow that evening or the following day.

Kanta too was annoyed after the incident of the previous evening. She gave a terse answer, 'Are you out of your mind? Do you want to go because you're afraid that it's costing pitaji and us too much to feed you the two chapattis that you eat? And how would you go alone that far, to a strange land?'

'I'll have to go wherever I can find a job. After all, women who want to be self-sufficient go to work somewhere or other. How do men manage? There are other working women who don't live with their families. Bahinji, what funny things you're saying! Why would pitaji object to this?' Kanak did not want to argue, so she said all this lightly.

Kanta did not want her in-laws' family to hear this exchange, and went to the veranda taking Nano with her. She spoke in a voice that Nayyar could hear, 'If you're so sure, write and ask pitaji. We won't interfere then.'

Nayyar saw that Kanta meant him to hear that remark, and walked over. Kanta went on, 'She wants to leave for Lucknow today. Says she wants to take up a job and become self-sufficient. I told her to write to pitaji and get his permission.'

'That's the right thing to do,' Nayyar agreed with his wife.

'It'll take so many days to get an answer from Lahore,' Kanak said. 'I want to leave today or tomorrow.'

'Do you have to leave on a certain day, or do you have an arrangement to go with somebody?' Nayyar asked.

'What's the problem if I do?' Kanak replied angrily.

'It becomes a problem when others, like us, find it a problem,' he replied. 'Why give people a chance to say unkind things? You should behave with some decorum until you're a married woman.'

'Didn't you two meet or want to meet before you got married?' Kanak thought her answer would silence him.

'Whatever we did, we did it in such a way as not to cause others to gossip,' Kanta said by way of a rebuke. 'We didn't go over the line as you two are doing.'

'What line have I crossed?' Kanak asked. 'What did I do that you didn't?'

Nayyar spoke in a soothing tone, 'There were others who put limits on our behaviour. We're doing the same with you. That's why you're angry with us. But it's for your own good.'

'You can well understand that it's natural for us to want to be together. Why are you weighing that against the conventions?' Kanak tried again to overcome his opposition, 'Think about your own past.'

'I do. But sometimes it becomes necessary to put limits on what's natural. That's civilized behaviour. Behaviour becomes conventional before people call it socially acceptable. Speed is a feature of a motorcar, but if the motorcar has no brakes, that attribute can become deadly.'

Kanak did not appreciate Nayyar's high-flown reasoning. In her irritation she retreated into herself. She sat down and wrote a letter to her father, and went to the post office to mail it. She went on to Puri's hotel and told him all that had happened. After much discussion, Puri had to decide to go alone to meet Awasthi in Lucknow. Kanak gave him the addresses of Awasthi and Mrs Pant, and all the other information that she had. She also wrote a letter to Awasthi for Puri to carry with him.

At 4 o'clock, Kanak took Puri to the terminus from which buses left for Kathgodam railway station.

Puri went to Lucknow, leaving Kanak in a fix. She was sure that he would write and ask her to join him as soon as he found a job. But what would she do if her father didn't reply before then? Would they be together on the day when the country achieved its independence? 'He might come to take me back,' she thought. She had mailed the letter to her father on the ninth. A reply by the twelfth was possible, but not certain. A letter from Puri should arrive by the thirteenth for sure. She wouldn't wait after the thirteenth, come what may. She would be in Lucknow.

Between the months of April and September, there were two mail deliveries per day in Nainital. At both times, Kanak waited with her eyes on the gate. More than her father's reply, she was anxious for a letter from Puri. She wanted to receive it herself from the postman. On the thirteenth the postman came around noon. Kanak was the first to go and collect the mail. It was an express delivery, addressed to Nayyar. Kanak recognized her father's handwriting before giving it to him.

Nayyar first read the letter to himself before reading it aloud. Panditji had received Kanak's letter on the morning of eleventh at 9 o'clock. He had written a reply immediately, and had it mailed at the General Post Office. In essence, he asked Kanak to wait. The assurance by the Muslim League and Congress to safeguard the rights of the minorities had had positive results, he wrote. The situation was comparatively peaceful. He welcomed Kanak's intention of becoming independent and working for the government in the newly independent country. But he also asked her to wait before going so far away, until he had a chance to make some inquiries of his own. He ended the letter by saying that if the transfer of power went on peacefully on the fifteenth, there was every likelihood that peace would prevail. He would reach Nainital by the eighteenth, and discuss all these matters with the family.

Kanak was piqued by what she saw as her father's old habit. He'll neither say yes, nor no. He would tie her up with an elastic leash; one could go a certain distance, but not too far. Kanak declared at once, without mincing her words, 'I've given my word to Awasthi. If I receive a letter from Lucknow any time now, I'll have to go there.'

Kanta was really annoyed, 'What new ways have you learned? Baba, we don't want to hold you back. Get married first, and then go. Then it's your problem.'

Nayyar also said to Kanta so that Kanak could hear, 'If you were going to ignore pitaji's advice, what was the point of asking him for it?'

Kanak remained steadfast in her resolve. She wouldn't be able to stay back, she knew, once Puri asked her to come. She began to say something in reply to Kanta. The newspaper-seller arrived at that very moment.

Nayyar was glancing at the first page as he listened to Kanak. He spoke up, 'Lord Mountbatten will arrive in Karachi tomorrow at 10 o'clock to hand over the administration to the government of Pakistan. At midnight on 14 August, Quaid-e-Azam Jinnah will be the new Governor General of Pakistan. India's Constituent Assembly, under the presidency of Dr Rajendra Prasad, will assume power in Delhi at midnight.'

He continued in the same breath, 'The train was stopped at the Lahore station because not a single person on it was found to be alive. It is estimated that over one thousand Hindu men, women and children were massacred at the Shahdara station. Then the train full of corpses was sent on to Lahore station. Afraid of the consequences of letting the train go further east, the railway authorities halted the train at Lahore. No information about the names and addresses of the murdered passengers was available.' The newspaper also carried reports of wide-ranging cases of arson in Lahore city, and of a mass exodus of Hindus from the city.

'Pitaji wrote the letter on the morning of the eleventh, and all hell broke loose in the afternoon!' Kanta's voice was quavering with fear. Everybody was quiet. Who could say what other disasters had occurred?

Kanak could not think of anything. Her mind was numbed by the cries of over one thousand men, women and children begging for their lives, and the thought of their being slaughtered with swords, spears and gunfire.

Chapter 15

LALA SUKHLAL, ALONG WITH A SISTER OF SOMRAJ, ESCORTED HIS SON'S BRIDE to her in-laws' house. Their motorcar halted at the entrance of the Banni Hata Gali. Somraj's mother and sisters came out to receive the bride, helped her to step down, her face veiled by the ghunghat, and led her to the doorway of the house. No brass band or fireworks celebrated the joyous occasion of her arrival as they had when the palanquin of Somraj's first bride had arrived on his doorstep, but his mother, happy at having a pretty daughter-in-law that she had hand-picked, carried out all the rituals for a new bride entering the house. A niece of Somraj, with a brass lota full of water on her outstretched palm, stood beside the entrance. As the new bride crossed the threshold into her new home, the mother-in-law poured a bowlful of mustard oil on both sides of the entrance.

Tara was made to sit in a room filled with the women of her in-laws' household. Her mother had dressed her in clothes of heavily embroidered silk. In the sultry heat of the July day, her body was bathed in perspiration. A portable electric fan was turning at one side of the room, but the draught it produced did not reach Tara through the circle of women.

The custom of unveiling the bride's face for the first time was performed. After being called several times, Lala Sukhlal came up, coughing, and sat in front of Tara. After her face was unveiled for him, he presented her with a gold necklace, gave her his blessing and got up. Next was her mother-in-law, and she too gave her a similar gold ornament and her blessing. Several women who were close relatives took part in the little ceremony, presenting her with a pair of earrings or a ring. Somraj's mother and sisters mentioned each woman's name and her relation to the family. Some women from the community and neighbours in the gali, according to their closeness to the family, dropped notes and coins of five, two, one or one-quarter rupees in Tara's lap.

They all commented happily, 'The bride is pretty and respectful,' and congratulated Tara's mother-in-law. Somraj's mother, in return, thanked them and wished happiness and prosperity to their families.

Amid the din of voices, some words of one of Somraj's sisters reached

Tara's ears, 'I don't say she isn't good-looking, but she's not as breathtakingly beautiful as we were led to believe.'

Another voice said, 'I heard that she's very proud of having finished her BA.'

The first voice answered, 'BA my foot! And she'd better keep her snootiness for her own parents' home!'

Tara had the first taste of what she'd be facing at her in-laws.

The mother-in-law called to one of her daughters, 'Maheshan, put out some clothes for your bhabhi. Let the poor thing have a bath. She's drenched in sweat.'

The mother-in-law spoke with obvious affection for the bride of her choice. The indifference in the sister-in-law's tone was equally obvious, 'I've to look after things in the kitchen. All these people have to eat. You'll blame me afterwards if nothing is done.'

The mother-in-law went and brought Tara a change of clothes, 'Come, daughter, take a bath.' She showed Tara the bathroom.

Although the wedding, given the state of unrest in the city, was performed without the usual elaborate ceremonial, nevertheless about twenty close friends and relatives had been invited for a feast. The whole house was filled with the savoury smells of cooking and spices, the clanging of pots and pans, and repeated calls to the guests to sit down for the meal.

After her bath, Tara had to wear another set of clothes of embroidered silk. When she returned to the room, her mother-in-law sent some food in a thali for her. What bride can feel like eating amidst the stress and tension of her first day in the new surroundings of her in-laws'? Tara was more thirsty than hungry. She took a glass of iced water, but there was no way she could avoid eating. She feared that a refusal to eat might be seen as an affectation. She somehow swallowed two puris. All the while she was conscious of the eyes of the girls and women around her watching how she broke off a piece of puri with her fingers, how she raised it to her lips, and how she drank from her glass. After she had finished eating, her mother-in-law asked the young girls sitting around her to give her some space to lie down and rest.

After dinner, around ten, one of the sisters-in-law asked Tara to follow her to a room on the third floor of the house and showed her to a bed. The room was brightly lit, and a dhurrie covered the floor. The blades of a ceiling fan spun overhead. Three large calendars hung on the walls. One showed Netaji Subhash Chandra Bose, in the uniform of the commander-in-chief of the Indian National Army, holding the national tricolour. In the second, Sita, standing beside Lord Ram in a forest, was pointing at a golden deer. The third was an advertisement for some soap; a young woman with ample bosom putting on a blouse with her arms raised and the corner of her aanchal held between her teeth. On the wall behind the headboard of the bed hung the photograph of some old man in a thick, old-fashioned frame.

A light drizzle had fallen in the evening, and a pleasant breeze blew in from the open windows. There were several large shelved recesses in the walls, mostly empty. On the top shelf of one were the statuettes of Ganesha and Lakshmi. Tara sat alone, looking around to observe and understand how the family lived. A carved, old-looking dressing table stood in one corner, probably bought from a junk dealer in the Neela Gumbad bazaar. Its mirror was cloudy and stained with age. The family had money, Tara could see, but lacked the taste and sophistication that she had seen in the homes of Zutshi, Narendra, Kanak and her other acquaintances.

The bed was under the fan, in the centre of the room. A sheet with an embroidered pattern adorned a soft mattress. A water-filled *surahi* and a glass on a three-legged stool beside the bed. Next to it, a covered tumbler of Muradabad brass, perhaps full of milk. Also, some green cardamom and pieces of *misri* candy on a plate.

The moment of her first meeting with her husband was very near, Tara knew. Tension tightened every fibre of her body. Pushpa and Sheelo had told her of their experiences in this encounter. Thinking of them, she felt embarrassed, nervous and a little afraid too. What was to follow, she knew, was natural and expected, but still ... A dupatta of fine red chiffon lay around her shoulders. Should she hide her face behind a ghunghat or not? she wondered. But wasn't that chiffon quite transparent? She'll cover her face now, she thought, and remove it if he asked, or remove it herself. She curled up at the foot of the bed, feeling very tired. She'd sit up, she thought, when she heard him coming.

Tara heard the door open and sat up, hunched over. She pulled the flimsy dupatta over her face and head, and looked out of the corner of her eye. Somraj was tall and slim. He looked handsome in a muslin kurta and cotton pajamas. He closed and latched the door. Tara felt her body shiver again, and she lowered her head.

Somraj walked to the bed. He stood quietly for a moment, as if thinking of the right words to say. Tara's ears awaited his words as eagerly as the oyster shell opens for raindrops.

'You're feeling shy?' Tara could feel the harshness in his voice. Her head drooped a little lower.

'You're acting shy now! You didn't act shy when gadding about bare-headed and taking part in processions on Mall Road and Anarkali?' Somraj spoke in an officious and nasty tone.

Tara held her breath, and let it out. She sat without moving.

Somraj asked, without waiting for her answer, 'You didn't want to marry into this family, right?'

Tara remained silent and unmoving.

'Who's your lover?' He said through gritted teeth.

Tara kept silent. Tears welled up behind her closed eyelids. She bit her lower lip.

Somraj waited for a few moments, then asked, 'You've been around, haven't you?'

Tears fell from her eyes.

Somraj pushed at her shoulder with his clenched fist, and asked, 'Why don't you say something? How many men have you slept with?'

Tara's head came up. She looked hard at Somraj with tear-filled eyes, and hissed at him, 'Shut up!' And hid her face in her hands.

He slapped the side of her face hard, left then right.

Tara removed her hands from her face, looked at him with angry eyes brimming with tears, and said quietly but firmly, 'Don't you dare hit me!'

Somraj lost control of his anger. He grabbed her plait, dragged her off the bed and threw her to the floor. He kicked her viciously, and hurled obscenities at her that Tara could never imagine a decent man uttering, 'You daughter of that starving schoolteacher, you dared refuse to marry me! You're proud of having passed your BA! I've had my way with dozens like you! I'll teach you a lesson! I'll have you raped by dogs and asses in front of everybody in the bazaar....' He kept his voice down.

Tara struggled with her legs and arms, as much as she could, to defend her body and her honour. She could not call out for help. Somraj was tall and strong. He used all his strength, but still could not completely overpower and dominate Tara and have the satisfaction of making her suffer for resisting and insulting him. Her refusal to surrender completely to him was the biggest insult of all.

Somraj lay down on the bed, angry at his inability to subdue her despite being her lord and master, exhausted by the struggle she had put up. He would take his revenge from this insolent female for the insult and rejection she had shown him, he was thinking. Where could she run away to escape from him? He'd break down her spirit, slowly and gradually, every last bit of it.

Tara lay curled up on the floor with her head in her arms, groaning and whimpering. Her body hurt everywhere from being punched and beaten. More than her body, it was her heart that ached. If only she could somehow die, she prayed. If this cruel, ruthless man goes out, she was thinking, she'd hang herself in her dupatta. 'He married me to treat me like this!' She hoped he might die, but even if he did, that would not be the end of her own sorrow and pain. The only escape for her was her own death.

All she wanted was to get up, open the door quietly, get out of the house and throw herself into the Ravi River. But there were many doors downstairs. She saw in her mind the main door through which she had entered the house. She did not even know how to reach the river from this house.

There was the sound of gunshots close to the house, followed by shouts, screams and the sound of running feet. Shouts and screams also came from downstairs, and from the house next door. Then there were more gunshots.

Somraj awoke with a start, leaped out of bed, undid the latch and left the room. Tara raised her head at the sound of his footsteps. With the door open, the shouts and screams of fear were louder. A Muslim mob has attacked, Tara thought. She sat for a few moments, then got up and went out of the room. On her right was a low wall, then the aangan below, and next to it stairs leading down. In front was the privy, enclosed by the usual one-brick wall. On the left was another wall with brick latticework, as high as her head, with the neighbour's house on the other side.

Tara put her foot into the latticework, hoisted herself up, and peered towards the other side. Seeing nobody on the neighbouring roof, she climbed over the wall. She tried to open a door to the staircase, but it was latched from inside. She looked over a wall to her right, and saw that the roof of the house adjacent was very low. She hesitated, then not caring if she died, climbed over this wall and hung by her hands on the other side before letting go. She landed with a loud thud. Hard on the noise of her fall came loud fearful calls, 'Who's there? Who is it?'

'*Oye* Sattar, what happened? Who's there?'

A few moments later, someone shone a flashlight on Tara. A clean-shaven young man, in a multicoloured lungi, an electric torch in one hand and a hockey stick in the other, stood looking down at her. People calling from houses all around could be heard, 'Who's there? What's happened? Everything all right, bhai?'

'Who're you?'

Tara said nothing.

'Where have you come from?'

Tara still said nothing. She was unable to speak or reply.

The young man went over and called into the aangan below, 'Chachaji, come up here.'

Then he said again to someone in the aangan, 'Looks like a Hindani. She jumped over from the roof of the house next door.'

A middle-aged man in a shirt and pajama came and stood beside the young man. Since he had no beard, it was difficult to know whether he was Hindu or Muslim.

'Who're you? Where did you come from?' he in turn asked.

When the questions were repeated, Tara replied, 'The house on the other side is on fire. The Muslims have attacked it. Guns are being fired. Please show me the way down to the gali.'

There were louder, more persistent calls from all around, 'Who's there? What's going on? Why doesn't somebody say what's happened?'

'This is a Muslim house. Have mercy on us, and go back where you came from,' The middle-aged man said harshly to Tara. Realizing that she could not go back the way she had come, he said to the young man, 'Take her to the stairs and let her out into the gali. Get rid of her quickly.'

'Come on! Hurry up!' The young man pointed the way with the flashlight.

Tara got up, followed the young man, and began to go down the stairs, limping. The middle-aged man was behind her. In the aangan below, a middle-aged woman and a young girl stood watching with fearful eyes. The young man hesitated for a moment before undoing the latch of the door leading to the gali. He turned round, and said, 'Chachaji, where would she go at this hour? The situation outside ... can't she spend the night here with ma or my sister?'

'No, no! No such thing!' The middle-aged man waggled his head emphatically. 'She's someone else's problem, don't make her ours. No, baba, no, I don't want to get involved in this trouble.'

The young man half-heartedly opened the door, and moved to one side to let Tara pass.

Tara stepped out and looked left and then right. Which way to go?

The young man saw her indecision, and said, 'It's a dead-end to the right. On the left is Kucha Lalmisir first, then the Bhati Gate.'

Tara turned left.

People in almost every house in the gali had woken up. A woman's voice, from behind the iron grille of a window, asked, 'Nadira's bhabo, who's there, what's happened?'

Someone replied from across the gali, 'Some young Hindani. Trying to escape by jumping over from the roof of a house on the Banni side. Some houses are on fire there, I heard.'

'Hai, baba, they are really bold. I'd have died with fright.'

'Shammo called over from her roof to say that there was rioting in Banni Hata.'

Tara kept walking quietly. They seemed to know about her even before she reached a spot in the gali. The lane turned, and she followed it.

She had not gone very far when she was pushed to the ground by what felt like a very heavy weight on her shoulders, and someone wrapped her chiffon dupatta tightly around her eyes and mouth. She was lifted off the ground. The gag was so tight that she had difficulty breathing. There was no way she could scream or call out for help. And who was there to call out to? Feeling helpless, she let herself be carried along, gasping for breath.

Tara felt herself being lowered to the ground. Then came the sound of someone thumping on a door.

A faint voice asked, 'Who's there?'

'It's me! Open up!' The person who had carried Tara demanded.

The person grabbed Tara's arm and she was dragged over the threshold into a house. The cloth muffling her eyes and mouth was removed. She found herself sitting in an aangan with a floor of beaten earth. A dim electric light shone from a room on her left.

'Who's this you've brought?' A woman said with surprise and disapproval. Her clothes were crumpled and dirty. She looked Muslim.

'Shut your trap!' The man ordered. He swore, trying to catch his breath after the exertion of carrying Tara. 'She's Hindu. Was trying to run away.'

'Get the bitch out of here!' The woman yelled. 'I don't want her here.'

'I told you to shut up!' He shouted and swore at her, and began pulling Tara by the arm towards the inner room.

The woman again howled in protest, 'No, no. I don't want this wretch here. You expect me to put up with a saut!'

The man again swore at her, and then cursed the Hindus en masse. He said, 'After I'm finished with her, I'll sell her for twenty-five rupees to Khalifa. Why would I want to keep her! Why are you making all this fuss?'

The woman continued to stand and shout in protest.

The man took Tara into the room and removed her gold bangles and necklace. When he tried to pull her earrings off, Tara removed them and handed them to him.

The woman came to the room and again screamed at the man to throw Tara out. The man placed the jewellery on a charpoy, and swearing obscenities at her, slapped the woman hard on the face twice. 'Quiet! I warned you.' He threatened her, 'If I hear so much as a squeak out of you, I'll tear you apart.'

The woman went back to the aangan and began to wail. The man sat on the charpoy. He lit a cigarette, drawing heavily on it. Sporadic gunshots could still be heard in the distance. Tara's legs were shaking. She sank to the ground and sat with her arms clasping her knees, her head resting on her hands. Her circumstances were so shocking and inconceivable that she was unable to think.

The man finished his cigarette and got up. He went to the aangan and drank some water from a clay pitcher. He lit another cigarette and lay down on the charpoy. He stubbed out the half-smoked cigarette on the brick floor, turned towards Tara and said, 'Come here, to the charpoy.'

He called several times. Tara did not move. He got up cursing her, grabbed her by the arm and pulled her towards the charpoy.

Tara tried to wrench her arm free and pleaded, 'No, no. I touch your feet and beg you. I'd sooner you cut my throat first.'

The man paid no attention to her begging and pleading.

Tara again tried to free her arm, shouting angrily, 'Go to hell! May your body rot! Don't you dare to touch me! Cut my throat first, kill me first!'

The man growled and grabbed her by the elbow. He put his arm under her knees, lifted her and threw her onto the charpoy. Tara's body was already hurt and aching from her struggle with Somraj. Her ankle and lower back had been injured when she jumped and fell on the roof. She was still dazed from the shock of being attacked and then gagged in the gali, but she fought back as hard as she could, all the time exclaiming, 'You may kill me, cut my throat if you want, but I won't give in to you.'

Nabbu's wife was sitting in the aangan, crying and swearing at Nabbu and the unknown Hindu woman that he had abducted and brought home, cursing them both that they might be bitten by a black snake, that their bodies might rot and become infested with maggots, and that they might burn in hell forever.

Nabbu was better at overpowering and defeating women than Somraj. Also, he was not afraid of this woman dying, or of her being injured or seriously hurt, or of his being shamed if she screamed. To end Tara's resistance, Nabbu ripped off her shalwar. Only a strip of cloth around the waist cord remained on Tara's body. Tara had still not given in and was continuing to resist. Annoyed by her resistance, Nabbu pulled Tara's arm behind her back and twisted it so hard that she screamed. Her body arched with pain and went limp as she fainted.

A roll of the kettledrums sliced through the silence of the dawn's early hours. With it came the sound of the sweet voices of Tajo tai and Badru:

> O camel rider, on your way to Mecca and Medina,
> Stop and turn your camel round.
> O camel rider, take us along.
> Your camel has bells around its neck.
> We're on our way to the shrine of the pir.

Tajo tai, along with Badru and Mehar who lived in the same house, sang out the prayers in the *asawari* style at four in the morning to alert other Muslims that the time to begin their fast was approaching. Khalid and Imtiyaz also had strong voices. They sang qawalis, sometimes before Tajo began and sometimes after she had finished from their rooftops, to play their part in the pious act of telling other Muslims to eat *sahari* and to smoke their hookahs before sunrise so as to prepare themselves to keep the fast until sundown.

Nabbu did not care what others thought of him, but he could not ignore what his neighbours felt when it came to religious observance, especially the ritual of fasting during Ramadan. He had to observe some religious routines to compensate for the sins of his everyday life. Among his neighbours, Mohammed Nabi, Fazal Deen, Tajo tai and Badrunissa, whom he addressed as bhabhi, maintained a strict watch over who observed the fast and who did not. For Nabbu it was easier to be a part of this group, to make sure that others remained steadfast in their observances than to perform his own religious duties. His responsibility was to check who came to fetch water on the sly from the communal water faucet. He was able to survive the rigours of keeping a daily fast only by keeping himself busy in such tasks.

The sweet-sounding voices of Tajo tai and Badru woke up Nabbu, but he could not forego the pleasure of lying late in bed. In a few minutes' time he heard Khalid and Imtiyaz singing the inspiring words of the qawali to the beat of handclaps:

'What do we need from God?
We'll take what we need from Mohammed ...'

Nabbu got up and, to shake off sleep, sat on the charpoy, with his feet on the floor. He mumbled the names of Allah the Holy and the Prophet, kissed his hands rolled into fists and then rubbed his eyes with the palms of his hands. He heard the sound of someone groaning. He got up, felt for the light switch, and turned on the light. He saw the woman lying next to the wall. She was still in the same supine position as when Nabbu had picked her up from the charpoy and thrown her down on the floor. Her pink silk kameez had rucked up around her stomach and torn scraps of shalwar attached to the cord still hung around her waist. Her wrists, tied together, were behind and under her back. Her hair was dishevelled and tangled, her eyes were closed, and groans came out of her open lips. Nabbu's wife was not in the room. 'That lowborn wretch must have spent the night in the aangan to show her disapproval,' he thought.

Sitting on the charpoy with his feet on the floor, he reached for matches and the pack of Star brand cigarettes that had fallen from the charpoy. He lit a cigarette and called out an order to his wife, 'Ari, listen. Get up! Do you hear me! Light the fire and make me some tea. I want to have tea before eating sahari.'

'Make tea! My foot! I'll be damned if I make you any tea!' His wife shrieked back from the aangan. She came into the room and continued to heap curses on him, 'It was you who brought that slut here! Drink her blood! Drink her piss! May she be the death of you! You son of a bitch, I'll be damned if I make tea for you! You ...'

Nabbu exhaled a long plume of smoke, then shouted some obscenities at his wife. 'You want me to grab your plait and beat you? You want your bones broken?' he threatened her, 'Make the tea, or else!'

His wife shot back even filthier curses at him.

Nabbu threw down his cigarette, got up and took a step threateningly towards her. His wife quickly reached into a corner for a long thick pestle used for pounding spices, held it in both hands and raised it over her head in self-defence.

It was pitch dark when Tara came to, with her head and body throbbing with pain. Her shoulders seemed to hurt most. Since her hands were tied behind her back, all she could do was draw up or extend her legs, and move her head. Moans came unconsciously from her open mouth, then they too ceased as her throat became bone dry. Nobody seemed to be around to hear her cries. In the dark, she could not be sure whether there was someone in the room, or she was all alone. She had been tied up and left to die, she felt, and so she would, eventually, suffering and thirsting for water.

She was awoken by the sound of shouts and screams, and opened her eyes. There was light in the room. Nabbu, swearing obscenities, rushed towards a woman standing in the room. The woman swung the pestle at his head. Nabbu stepped aside, then again went at her. When the woman swung at him again, he merely moved his head to one side. The pestle struck his shoulder. He threw the woman to the floor, grabbed the pestle from her hand, and dealt her several blows with it.

The woman screamed. She yelled at him that she hoped he might perish, and went on cursing him between her screams. Nabbu too shouted back obscenities at her as he punched and kicked her. Then he sat on the charpoy, gasping for breath.

Tara lay helpless and unmoving as she watched all this. The sound of qawalis drifted in. The woman was wailing, sobbing and bawling by turns. Nabbu sat on the charpoy, and swore at her, 'You dare to hit me! I'll break every bone in your body! I'll skin you alive. You don't want to make tea?

Fine. I'll go and have tea at Moosa's shop, but I won't give you a bite to eat. Whatever's left over, I'll throw to the dogs, but I won't give any to you.'

The bugle call announcing the end of curfew rent the air. Nabbu got up, collected the jewellery he had taken from Tara, and tucked it in a fold of the lungi at his waist. He went to a corner where an aluminium pot lay on top of a trunk made from an old kerosene can, took out some food left over from the night before, and went out. As soon as he stepped out, the whimpering and sobbing woman too got up with some difficulty and effort, and went to the aangan where she resumed her wailing with an occasional cry for help, 'O Tajo tai, he tried to kill me. Badru bhabhi, look how that butcher beat me up.' The woman seemed to be crying and, at the same time, telling her story to whoever was willing to listen.

Tara wondered what she should do. Only death could end her suffering and pain. She could try to hang herself by making a noose with her dupatta, but her hands were tied. Then she thought of something. She drew her legs up, and summoning up all her strength, turned to one side and came up to a kneeling position. She inched her body closer to the wall, and with the idea of killing herself, began to pound her head against it.

In the aangan, Rukkan was crying and complaining to Tajo tai, Badru and some other women how the previous night Nabbu had brought a saut to the house. She let out a shriek when she heard the sound of pounding coming from the room. '...Hai, that wretched thief is breaking open the lock to my box!' she yelled, and dashed inside.

She rushed back out, screaming, 'Hai, she seems to be possessed by some evil jinn! Come and see, she's calling up a jinn!'

Tajo, Badru and Mehar followed Rukkan into the room. They saw that a woman, naked from the waist down and with her hair flying, was pounding her head against the wall. Her hands were tied behind her back.

'Hai, she's trying to kill herself, she's committing suicide,' Badru said in alarm, and reached forward to grab her by the shoulders and pull her away from the wall. The woman fell sideways and lay there unconscious.

Rukkan again screamed, 'Hai, she's trying to kill herself so that her ghost may come and haunt this house.'

'Shut up!' Tajo shouted at her.

She untied the woman's hands, stretched her out on the floor and gently massaged her chest as she mumbled a prayer. Badru and Mehar began to

massage the soles of her feet and her legs. Rukkan was told to bring some
water and sprinkle it on the woman's face.

Tara felt a searing pain in her head. She tried to open her eyes, but could
not, because some water seeped in and made them smart. There was a
buzzing in her ears, as if bees were lodged inside. Her body felt stiff and
painful. She tried moving her head.

Seeing the hurt woman move, Badru put a hand behind her head, lifted
it slightly and put a dirty aluminium tumbler to her mouth. When Tara felt
the water on her lips, she drained the whole tumbler. Her eyes opened.
Feeling that her arms were untied, she tried to raise herself, and sat up
with some help from the women. She tried to pull down the hem of her
kameez. Mehar picked up Tara's dupatta lying nearby, and draped it over
her knees.

The women sat around Tara. The wife who had been beaten up, was
whining and cursing her tormentor as she showed various parts of her
body, 'May his hands drop off; may his body be infested with maggots! I
won't stay here with him any more. I'll go to my aunt's who lives in Chuna
Mandi. I spent all night crying in the aangan. Look,' she raised her shalwar
to show her bruised thigh, 'see how he beat me. I'm all full of bruises. I
came in just now when I heard the pounding. How do I know what he did
to her? That *mua* was saying that she'd run away from home. What can I do
if she has? I'll not put up with another wife, a saut in this house! You don't
know that bastard of a husband. Never mind a young woman, he can't even
leave a cow or a buffalo or a goat alone. If he wants to keep her, fine! I'm
moving to my aunt's. He pledged me a *meher* of two thousand rupees as
alimony. What do I care?'

Two other women arrived. One held a child on her shoulder; the other
had two onions and a knife in her hand. The first one exclaimed as she came
in, 'She's a Hindani!' and mouthed a curse that the genitals of all Hindu
women be consumed by the fires of hell. 'So what if one was raped! Those
shameless women deserve it!'

'Phitemunh, damn you! That's a terrible blasphemy! Say tauba, recant!'
Tajo tai said in rebuke. 'How'd you feel if a Hindu was to say that about
you? One woman should feel for another. God forbid that you fall into the
clutches of someone like him. Allah the Almighty has decreed that Hindu
and Muslim men should be different, but He has created all women alike.'

Badru said to Rukkan as she placed a wet cloth over Tara's injured head,

'Why are you so down on the life of this poor creature? She didn't come here of her own free will.'

Mehar stopped massaging Tara's feet and legs. She was sitting with her elbows on her knees, staring sadly and with pity at Tara's injuries. She said, letting out a sigh, 'Those dreadful men fight each other, but it's women they wreck in the process.'

Tajo said by way of explanation, 'Allah the Great made it men's duty that they should treat women kindly and protect them, because it is women who give men birth and nurse them ...'

'To hell with their kindness and protection!' Mehar said angrily. 'The shameless beasts degrade the very place they come out of. Whether a man is showing his love or his bad temper, he vents his feelings at the same spot. Look how the poor thing's been trampled all over and beaten, look how her limbs have been scraped! He almost broke her bones by thrashing her too,' she said, pointing at Rukkan. 'A man has the strength of an ox. Why wouldn't this poor creature want to commit suicide? What else can a helpless woman do but kill herself?' She gave a deep sigh of sadness.

The woman with the onions stood nearby, slicing and storing them into a fold of her dupatta. She said, 'Whether he has the strength of an ox or an elephant, I'd kill any bastard who did this to me. I'd slit his stomach, I'd bite through his jugular with my teeth!' She uttered an obscenity, 'I'd pull his balls out through his mouth.'

Mehar put her hands on her knees and pushed herself up, 'Wait, let me get her a glass of tea. Bano must have made some.'

'Tea later, first cover up her nakedness,' Tajo said.

'Rukkan, bring whatever old or used shalwar you have.'

'Hai, where do I have any old shalwar? I barely have enough clothes to cover my own body, as it is,' Rukkan pleaded. 'He's brought another woman into the house, and now you want me to dress her? Some kind of a friend you are giving me such advice!'

Both Tajo and Badru tried to calm her, 'What are you afraid of? No mullah has married her to him. How can he bring in another wife? Don't be afraid. Find something for her to cover her legs. Or, give her something now; we'll make it up to you later on. She can't stay naked. If one woman is shamed, all women are shamed.'

Rukkan went to get an old, patched-up shalwar from a peg. She gave it to Tara, who put it on while sitting up.

The neighbourhood rang with the azaan, the call to prayer. Tajo said to
Rukkan, 'I'm off for the namaz. Just keep an eye on her and see that she
doesn't try anything foolish. May Allah forgive these sinners; such behaviour
during the holy month of Ramadan. They murder, plunder, commit arson
and rape. Do you suppose they'll ever find forgiveness for those sins?'

Tajo, Badru and Mehar helped Tara to the charpoy. They went out for
the *farz*, the first prayer of the day, leaving Tara and Rukkan behind in the
room. Tara held her head in her hands, thinking, 'What have I been through?
Can't I just die? What hate do these women have for me that they didn't
let me kill myself.' She remembered something she had heard thousands
of times: Mere mortals may wish for whatever they wish, but everything
happens according to His will! 'What more does He wish for me? What
more punishment does He want to give me? Is this the penalty for the acts
of my past life? Or is it the result of refusing to marry Somraj? Or of my
wish to elope with Asad? But I *was* married to Somraj! What's next for me
to suffer, when I can't even die? Maybe I'll be sent to hell, to be tortured
there, to be burned alive, to be put in a vat of boiling oil, to be sawn in
two. Whatever it is, let it happen soon.'

The men of the neighbourhood learned from Tajo tai, Badru bhabhi,
Mehar and Laila that Nabbu had abducted a young Hindu woman, that
he had dishonoured her, and was keeping her until he could sell her off
to some lowlife. Tajo tai tried to put the fear of God into her neighbours,
'This is the holy month of Ramadan. Such sins are being committed in
our mohalla ...'

The men gathered to decide on the course of action.

A little after the namaz, Tajo returned to Tara's side with a glass of tea in
her hand. Women and girls from the mohalla would come to inspect and
stare at Tara. At Tajo's repeated insistence, Tara had a few sips of tea. Tajo
was continuously muttering some prayer or hymn. She'd tell Tara over and
again, 'Think of Allah, beti. He is our only hope in all our troubles. May
Allah have mercy upon you. May the Almighty be kind to you.'

When Nabbu returned home about an hour after sunrise, his neighbours
were waiting for him. Rebukes and reproaches were showered at him from
all sides. Men crowded onto the roofs that overlooked Nabbu's aangan, and
women, to keep purdah, spoke from behind the doors and windows of
their homes, 'How can you justify such sinful behaviour? You're known to
the police as a bad character, a real number ten, and even then you don't

desist. How long can we put up bail for you? You're giving our mohalla a
bad name!'

Nabbu was not intimidated by his neighbours' disapproval. 'What
business is this of yours? I've not done any bad to a Muslim woman. This
one's a Hindu. Aren't those people violating our women too? They set fire
to our homes, they explode bombs every day. The mullahs have issued the
fatwa for a jihad!'

Tajo held the status of tai or elder aunt to the children and the young
people of the mohalla, and of bebe, elder sister, to everyone else. She
could face up to anyone. She came forward and shouted in reprimand,
'Keep quiet, you vermin. To rape women is jihad? Everyone knows you're
a criminal. You utter blasphemies in the name of religion. Your tongue will
drop off in punishment.'

Nabbu sensed the mood and changed his tone, 'You can't say I kidnapped
her. She was running away, anyway.'

'If she was running away, what concern was that of yours? Who do you
think you are that you had to abduct her? You'll bring down shame on the
entire mohalla,' another voice shouted.

Nabbu gave in and said that he'd let the woman go.

Rukkan saw her chance to exact her revenge. She called out from behind
her door, 'He's lying. He was saying that he'd sell the woman to Khalifa for
twenty-five rupees.'

So what was to be done with the woman? Now nobody wanted to believe
Nabbu. If the woman was handed over to the police, they would charge
Nabbu. He was, after all, a Muslim. It was decided, after some deliberation,
that Hafizji should be informed, and his advice should be followed.

When Nabbu heard about Hafizji being told, he slipped out of the house,
taking Tara's jewellery with him.

In the Muslim neighbourhood around Bhati Gate, the name of Hafiz
Inayat Ali carried a lot of weight and influence. Hafizji had served in the
Government Intelligence Department for over thirty years, and had retired
from a senior position. He was addressed as Hafiz because he could recite
the whole of the Quran from memory. He had a good knowledge of Arabic,
and had worked, under an assumed name, for his British masters as a spy in
Arabia for several years. As a reward for his loyalty to the Crown, his elder
son had been given a good job in the Public Works Department, and his

younger son had been posted to Amritsar as a sub-inspector, after passing out from the Police Training School at Phillor.

After retiring on pension, Hafiz Inayat Ali found that his heart was filled with great remorse because, for the sake of earning a living, he had betrayed his brothers in religion. As atonement for his sins, he became a volunteer in the Jamayat-e-Islami organization, and began to devote all his time and effort to prove that Islam was a scientific religion, to convert the non-believers to Islam, and to make Muslims into observant and pious practitioners of their religion. People in the Muslim community, as well as Muslim officials, held him in high regard.

Around ten in the morning, an old woman escorted by two police constables came to Nabbu's house. She had come, the old woman said, to take the Hindu woman to the residence of Hafizji.

Tajo tai gave her assurance to Tara that she could go with the old woman without any fear. Hafizji was a respectable, God-fearing and well-meaning person, she said.

Tara refused to budge. She said, 'I won't move. I don't want to go anywhere. I want to remain here and die.'

Rukkan begged and pleaded with Tara, asking her to leave her home, but Tara refused to listen to her. 'If I can't be allowed to die here, why was I brought here? I didn't come here on my own. I'm already as good as dead. If you want to get rid of me, have me thrown into the river. Or, throw my body out once I stop breathing.'

Someone came to say that Hafizji himself was on his way. Badru got up and left. Tajo tai sent for her burka, and asked that a stool be brought over from next door. Rukkan became very flustered, and not knowing what to do, went out of the room. Tajo put on her burka and stood beside Tara.

Two constables in uniform entered the room, followed by Hafizji. He wore a Peshawari-style short turban tied around an embroidered *kulha* cap, a Turkish-style long coat and well-polished shoes. His shalwar, as stipulated by Shariah or Islamic law, stopped at his ankles so as not to become contaminated by the filth on the ground. He carried a walking stick. A carefully clipped beard adorned his well-fed face; his moustache too was clipped along the lips. He came and sat on the stool next to Tara's charpoy, just like a doctor at the bedside of a patient. Tara gave him one glance, and closed her eyes.

Hafizji told the constables to wait outside in the aangan. He put his stick down beside Tara's bed. His face took on a grave expression. He put his hollowed hands on his knees in a praying posture, closed his eyes and began to recite a silent prayer. When he finished, he blew his breath towards Tara. He said the prayer three times, each time blowing out his prayer-rich breath on Tara, and giving her a blessing, 'May all your troubles be over. May Allah bestow His mercy on you.'

Hafizji looked closely at Tara's wounded head. He addressed her as daughter, and explained the need for medical attention to her wounds. He said, 'Beti, come to my house. Let a doctor take care of your injuries. Then you'll be sent wherever you wish.'

Tara shook her head to indicate that she neither wanted to leave, nor to hear anything more.

Hafizji spoke with a little more feeling, 'Beti, you seem to come from a good family. You look intelligent too. I have daughters and sons, grandsons and granddaughters of my own. Have trust in His powers. Faith in Him helps persons in all their troubles. He looks after His flock, no one escapes His notice. The same Allah the Blessed One has sent me to help you and to be of service to you.'

Tara closed her eyes, and declined with a waggle of her head as before.

Hafizji tried again, with even more sympathy and affection, 'Beti, if you don't want to go back to your home, we can send you to any of your relatives or anywhere you say. If you don't want that, we'll take you to a hospital and you can stay there until your wounds heal. If that's not acceptable to you, stay at the home of this humble servant of God. There will be a mother and sisters to look after you. Beti, this place is not suitable for you. You can't get medical attention here. You can't be comfortable here.'

Despite his entreaties, Tara refused in a quiet voice, 'I just want to die where I am now. I'm already dead. If you don't want me to remain here, or if you really want to be kind to me, just have my body thrown into the river.'

Hafizji continued to speak patiently and soothingly, 'Beti, your speech shows that you're well-educated and cultured. Beti, be sensible. It was God's will that I come to help you. Otherwise how would I be here? Beti, what's the use of being stubborn? I've told you that you can't get medical attention here. Your remaining here is neither proper, nor can it be allowed. If you don't leave willingly, the police will make you leave. How can the police let you remain with the notorious badmaash who abducted you? He brought you here by force, and you couldn't do anything. In the same way you won't be able to do anything if the police want to take you away. It's trouble for you if you fall into the hands of the police. If you agree to come to my place, you can leave whenever you want, and go wherever you want. I'll have nothing to say about that. When I heard about you, I saw it as my duty to come to your aid; God sent me to help you. Meaning, it was ordered by God. Beti, you'll be in constant danger if you stay among these savages. Why invite danger knowingly?'

Tara thought for some time in silence. To fall into the clutches of the police was certainly not a comforting thought. She had never heard of anyone being treated fairly by the police. To her mind, the police represented nothing but brutal and cruel treatment. She agreed to go with Hafizji.

The house where Hafizji lived was not very large, but it housed only his immediate family. It was built in the style of other houses in Lahore of that period: a sitting room beside the entrance doorway to the house, then an open aangan with smaller rooms opening off it, and a bathroom. An iron grille acted as a roof over the aangan. From the aangan a staircase led to the upper floor, with a large room that overlooked the gali, two smaller rooms to left and right of the iron grille, and a kitchen.

Hafizji was happy that Ahmed Ali, his elder son, was reaping the benefit of his father's long record of government service, and had been appointed sub divisional officer in the Department of Canals. His current posting was in the district of Brar. Hafizji's second son Amjad Ali, the sub-inspector of police, was stationed at Amritsar.

The outgoing British administration had given its public servants and armed forces personnel the option of taking postings either in Hindustan or Pakistan. Amjad Ali had opted to go to Pakistan. It had already been announced that Amritsar would become a part of Hindustan. Hafizji waited, with a sense of uneasiness, for his son to come to Lahore on his new posting, but he also felt reassured by the thought that Amjad was an officer in the police force. Who could be more protected and safer than he? He also took comfort from the knowledge that either the British administration or the new government of Hindustan would see to it that his son returned safely to Pakistan.

Hafizji's three daughters were married. They were all, thanks be to Allah, blessed with children and living contented lives with their in-laws. Ahmed

Ali spent most of his time on official tours. His son Anwar was a college student. In view of her son's education, Ahmed Ali's wife Khursheed, along with her thirteen-year-old daughter Farzana and eight-year-old Qamaroo, lived with her father-in-law in Lahore. Her third child, Hajra, was a two-year-old toddler.

Members of Hafizji's household reflected the influence of his beliefs and values. His wife the begum, and her daughter-in-law gave a warm welcome to Tara in her suffering and injured condition. They gave her a hot bath, sent for medicine for her wounds and fever. Then they set up a charpoy for her upstairs, in the airy room that opened on to the gali.

Tara refused to eat anything, in spite of the well-intentioned appeals of Hafizji's begum and daughter-in-law. Hafizji tried to change her mind, sitting on a chair beside her charpoy, 'Beti, how will you get well if you continue to starve yourself like this? You're trying to kill yourself. Don't you have faith in Allah's mercy?'

Tara admitted, her eyes downcast, that her life was not worth living. Since the only wish she had was to die, what other recourse did she have but to keep up her fast until death?

Hafizji spoke to her lovingly, 'Beti, how can someone as educated and intelligent as yourself talk so foolishly? What sin are you trying to atone for by killing yourself? You are an innocent victim. The person who committed the crime should be punished for it. If the victim is punished instead of the offender, this would be an even greater crime. Tell me, if you starve yourself to death, what effect will that have on that badmaash Nabbu? It's we who are affected by your starving yourself. To blackmail people by the threat of starving oneself is the act of a stupid uneducated woman. Or Gandhi, who brought it in as a political manoeuvre. When he feels that he does not have a good argument, he tries to frighten others with the threat of starving himself to death. The British used to pay attention to him only because they saw him as their ally against the Muslim League.

'Beti, what you should do is to get your health back, and then help other right-minded people to rid this world of badness. Why think of the past? Why don't you think of the future? Why not have faith in Allah's mercy? If you kill yourself in our house, it would cause problems and difficulties for us, not for an evildoer like Nabbu.'

Tara had no answer to the simple logic of Hafizji. And how long could she go on being ungrateful to those who were helping her so selflessly? The thought of the problems that her death would create for Hafizji's family weakened her resolve. She forced herself to eat a little now and then.

Because of the unrest and the daily curfews, the delivery of milk from the countryside to the city had all but ceased. Still, the begum would force Tara to drink about three quarters of a glass of milk twice a day. The begum and Khursheed would often curse those opposing the formation of Pakistan. Except for Qamaroo and the toddler, everyone in the family was observing the Ramadan fasts. When the begum saved something from the sahari for the two girls to eat during the day, she kept a share for Tara too. The chapattis were cooked in the kitchen from wheat, as they were in Tara's home. The same kinds of vegetables were bought from the bazaar, but cooked in a way that made them taste differently from what Tara was used to. That was another reason for her reluctance to eat.

Tara began to recover in a few days' time. One day after the morning namaz of fazr, Hafizji had a chair put beside her charpoy, and began to read to her from the Quran. He would pause to explain the meaning and to elucidate some passages. He had especially selected passages where Allah was described as *wadahul mutwakkill*—most merciful, most compassionate, omniscient, omnipotent and supreme, and Mohammed as his last prophet. And passages that described those with faith in Allah and his prophet going to heaven, and warned that unbelievers would burn forever in the fires of hell. Hafizji would be droning away with his preaching, but Tara's thoughts would drift away to her own problems. For her, these sermons soon became as distasteful as being forced to eat a tasteless meal without having any appetite.

For the first few days, Khursheed and her mother-in-law talked to Tara about nothing but her injuries, about how she felt, and about her tastes in food. Feeling strong one day, Tara got up from the charpoy and sat on a chatai spread on the floor. Khursheed came and sat beside her, holding a dress for the toddler into which she was putting basting stitches. As Khursheed continued to sew, she began to ask Tara how she had fallen into the hands of that badmaash Nabbu. Tara told her briefly about the incident of the attack on the house of her in-laws, and how she had escaped by climbing over the wall onto the neighbour's roof.

Khursheed asked with friendly concern, 'Hai, there must have been your husband's mother and sisters, and other women in the house. Didn't you call out to them or your husband for help?'

Despite her reluctance and embarrassment to talk about it, but mindful of the kindness of Khursheed and the begum, Tara narrated, gradually and haltingly, how vengeful and cruel Somraj had been on their first night together. She could not avoid the mention of her own unwillingness to marry Somraj. There was no reason or point in mentioning the attraction between herself and Asad.

Both Khursheed and the begum bad-mouthed Tara's in-laws, and the inhuman treatment meted out to her by her husband, and then condemned the Hindu system that allowed such injustices and unfair treatment. They said, 'Such unfairness could never happen in our Muslim community. Before the nikah is performed among us, the mullah always asks the bride-to-be for her consent. If she says no, the ceremony can never go forward. In our Muslim community, the groom has to declare publicly and in accordance with the bride's social status, the amount of the bride's meher, the settlement due to her if he divorces her. This can go as high as eight or ten thousand rupees. If the man wants to leave the woman, he has to pay up. There couldn't be such cruelty among Muslims …'

Despite the misfortunes that she had suffered, Tara felt it was unfair to blame all Hindus for the unfortunate consequences of certain customs and traditions. She could not resist answering the women that the custom of asking the girl's consent, together with the rule that the wedding could take place only after she gave that consent, existed in the Hindu religion also. And that the problem was not in the theory, but in the practice. She also remembered Nabbu's treatment of Rukkan, but mentioning that now did not seem appropriate.

That evening Hafizji was still upstairs after ending his fast. Since the Shariah ruled that one avoid any type of smell or aroma that could excite appetite during the hours of the fast, the preparations for dinner began in the household of Hafazji only at sunset, after the ending of the fast. Waiting for dinner to be cooked, Hafizji sat in the open air on a charpoy that was set on the iron grille covering the aangan, smoking his hookah and chatting with his wife, daughter-in-law and the children of the family.

The begum brought up the topic of the contrasting status of women in Hindu and Muslin communities. Hafizji explained in great detail that the Hindu culture was primitive and barbarian. As in savage tribes, he said, the Hindus considered a woman to be family property, and the burning of a widow on the pyre of her husband to be a pious act. What other proof did one need of their barbarism? Unlike Hinduism, Islam gives both sons and daughters equal shares in the family inheritance. Both men and women have the right to ask for a divorce. A man may not have more than four wives at one time. The Hindus did not draw the line even at one thousand wives.

Tara listened, her eyes downcast. Wasn't it absurd that such sanctimonious claims of liberalism and equality with men were made by purdah-keeping families, and by women who had to hide behind a burka because they could not show their face to a man other than a close relative? But this was not the occasion for argument or a show of disagreement, nor was there any sense in doing so. Next morning, when Hafizji began to read to her from the Quran, she found it more annoying than usual. 'What difference does it make to me who's a Hindu and who's a Muslim?' she asked herself. She was not particularly religious or sectarian in her outlook, but still she found it unpleasant to hear her family's customs and traditions being criticized and maligned. All she wanted was to be left alone.

Since Tara spent most of her time lying on a charpoy, dhurrie or chatai, she had little else to do but think. And she had become tired of thinking. What was left to think about? How much longer could she think back on what had happened in the space of one night and the following day? All that did was to give her headaches. Whatever she thought was going to happen, never happened. What did happen was what she could have never have expected or imagined.

Even if she did not want to think about anything, her mind could not remain idle. Was all this written in her fate, she could not help but ask herself, and what more was left that could happen to her? At one time she had determined to kill herself when her brother had falsely accused her; now she was still alive after going through unspeakable humiliations. Why couldn't she hang herself with her dupatta at night, when everybody was asleep? But she wouldn't be able to die if that was not to be her destiny, no matter how hard she tried. She had put her faith in her brother, and he had failed her. If she had defied her family and continued to refuse to get married, would that shame have been harder to bear than her present fate? What could Somraj really do to harm her?

Tara felt grateful to the family that had been so kind and sympathetic to her. In this spirit of thankfulness she began to help Khursheed with some household chores. She asked Khursheed for the dress she was sewing for her munni, and finished it expertly, with a flower embroidered on the front.

She did not like to eat alone when everybody else was keeping the fast. When everyone ate the sahari before sunrise, she too ate something with them. She did not feel hungry at that time, but that saved her from staying hungry for the rest of the day. The family, including the girls, noticed and appreciated this consideration for their feelings.

Tara was living in comfort and safety with the family in their house, but the news she heard from outside was a source of worry and despair for her. Anwar was always reporting how victorious the supporters of Pakistan had been in the city, and how large numbers of Muslims were arriving from the east, and how Hindus were fleeing to the east. Whenever old Naseeban, the family's housemaid, returned from talking with the neighbours, she always spoke of incidents of arson and murder. When Kalu, the old latrine-cleaner came, he would sometimes excitedly speak of how the Hindus had abandoned the neighbourhood of Lohe ka Talab after most of it had been gutted by fire. At other times, he brought back rumours of Gwal Mandi and Old Anarkali being on fire and Hindus running away before the relentless march of the Pakistani juggernaut.

Hafizji had been told that Tara had studied up to the BA level. He gave her two books to read in the hope of setting her mind at ease. The books, published by Jamayat-e-Islami, were *The Life of God*, and *The Scientific Religion of Islam*. But Tara found them tedious reading, and full of important-sounding but meaningless words. The family was orthodox Muslim, but well meaning, she decided. How long could she continue to be a burden on them? But where else could she go? She would have to find a place somewhere. And where could she go but back to her parents? She had yielded to their wishes and agreed to get married. Now at least they would have to let her do as she wished.

A thought flashed through her mind: What if her own family thought that she had run away from her in-laws? There again would be the old question of their prestige! No, that life and those ties for her were now a thing of the past.

Her head would begin to spin in confusion. Another thought crossed her mind, perhaps the Communist Party comrades were still working to stop the Hindu–Muslim conflict and keep the situation peaceful. She was one of the thousands of victims, just like Dauloo mama, of the strife they were trying to prevent. 'What is an individual's life worth? And we are all just individuals.' She thought of Asad too, but that memory was not sweet, attractive or thrilling as before. She now disliked all men. She tried to blot out such thoughts, but they continued to haunt her, stealing away her sleep and bringing on headaches and muddle-headedness into the bargain.

Sometimes women neighbours came to visit Khursheed and the begum. Tara did not know any of them. She went to another room on such occasions, especially because she did not want to overhear any talk concerning herself. These visitors had rather loud voices. Once some words drifted to Tara's ears, 'She's from a good Khattri family, well-educated. A bit pale and weak, but looks just like any girl from a good respectable Muslim family. The boys these days like to marry a girl who's educated and knows English. Not a bad match for Amjad. Yes, let's fix her up with Amjad. Why not get the two married!'

Tara heard as she strained her ears, 'Wah, is she the only one left for my Amjad? We've been hearing of some very lucrative proposals for him.' Amjad's mother objected, 'We spent so much money and gave such huge dowries when we married off our three daughters. When it's our turn to receive a dowry, all you can suggest is a runaway Hindu widow?'

Tara was stung by the contemptuous tone of her words. But at the same time, she felt relieved that there was no hidden motive at work.

Tara addressed Hafizji as 'tayaji', his wife as 'maanji', and Khursheed as 'bhabhi'. One day in the course of conversation with Khursheed, she expressed her indebtedness to the family for their kindness and sympathy, and said, 'How long can I remain a burden on you? Have me sent to my parents. Let destiny decide what is to become of me.'

Khursheed had been asking Tara about her family and about the neighbourhood she lived in before her marriage. She conveyed Tara's wish to her in-laws.

Later that evening Hafizji was sitting as usual on a charpoy after ending his fast. He asked his wife and Tara to come and sit beside him on the chatai. He said, 'Beti, what's all this you've been saying to your bhabhi? How can you be a burden on us? If any of my daughters came to live here with me, would that be a burden on us? If you like, I'll make enquiries about Bhola Pandhe's Gali. But we all know that all the Hindus living in those mohallas have carted off their valuables and their belongings to cities to the east, because they did not want to remain in Pakistan. There are no Hindu families left in Shahalami, Bajaj Hatta or Machchi Hatta.'

He continued, 'The newspaper reports say that Quaid-e-Azam Jinnah said pointblank to Lord Mountbatten that after Pakistan comes into existence on 14 August, the British will have no jurisdiction over this country. Quaid-e-Azam himself will become the Governor General of Pakistan. And just look at those Hindu banias, they've decided that in Delhi, the Governor General of Hindustan will be Lord Mountbatten. You call that independence? Hindus don't know the meaning of independence, nor do they want to be independent. They just want to express their hostility to Muslims and their opposition to the creation of Pakistan. Hindus don't have what it takes to rule. Allah created Muslims to be rulers.'

Hafizji held out his hollowed hands in supplication and closed his eyes for a moment, mouthing a silent prayer. He held his clipped beard in one hand. When he spoke, his face had taken on a benign expression, 'The Hindus are heartless when it comes to the rights of their women. Hindu males are oversexed because they can't control their sex urges like civilized human beings. Our Islamic law stipulates four wives for a man at one time, but the Hindu religion imposes no such limit., 'The Hindus consider Krishna to be a god. They also call him jogiraj, the king of ascetics, and he consorted with sixteen thousand women at the same time. A Hindu woman can't remarry within her community after she becomes a widow. If a daughter, sister or wife from a Hindu family strays from the fold, even for one day, if she gets separated from her husband or father even for a short time, she is considered as having been tainted. She is treated like a *kulhar*, an earthenware cup, which is thrown away after just one person has used it.'

Next day, after the morning namaz, Hafizji repeated before Tara the promise of eternal peace in *bahishta*, heaven, to those who believed in Islam and in the wadahul mutwakkill Allah and his prophet, Hazarat Mohammed, and assured her that in the afternoon he'd try to get some news from Bajaj Hatta and Bhola Pandhe's Gali.

Eid-ul-fitr was now only a week away. The begum and Khursheed sat on the dhurrie, making new clothes for the festival on a sewing machine, with Tara helping them in their work. Khursheed said to her mother-in-law, 'This poor creature fasts everyday with us. If she accepted the true Faith, it'd be such a blessing to her.'

Tara felt that Khursheed had some hidden design behind her expression of sympathy, but she kept quiet.

In the evening, when Hafizji came upstairs to end his fast after the *magharib* prayer, he sent for Tara. He told her, with concern and anxiety that all Hindu families that lived between Rang Mahal and Shahalami had left, and their houses had been taken over by Muslim families coming from the east.

Tara, her eyes downcast, uttered a sigh, and remained silent.

Hafizji again mumbled a *dua* to Allah the All Merciful, and tried to convince her, 'Beti, we humans should have faith in Allah's will, and in the mercy of that *kadirmutwakkill*. Everything He does is for the good of us humans. He keeps track of the sun, the moon and the rest of creation. He does not neglect to take care of the beetle that lives inside a rock; so how can He forget you? No doubt He sent you here so that we might look after you. The holy *parawardigar*, Heavenly Provider, blessed us with three daughters, and we fulfilled our obligations to them. He has now brought you to shelter in our home. We humans are always ignorant of His ways. In His infinite mercy, He found a way to send you here so that you might have faith in *la ilaha ilillahu, muhammedur rasoolallah* and that we should acquire the *sawab* of causing you to come over to the true belief.'

The begum, Khursheed and her two daughters were sitting behind Tara. When Hafizji uttered the *kalmah pak* (There is no God but Allah, and Mohammed is the Prophet of God), they all kissed their fingers, touched them to their eyes, and said 'amen' in one voice.

Hafizji straightened his back, recited in a louder voice an *aayat*, verse, in Arabic from the Quran, and said, 'Those who do not have faith in Allah, the sole creator of this world, and in His prophet who brought His message to mankind, will burn eternally in the fires of *dozakh*. You,' he added, 'have been rescued from that punishment by the *rahim-karim*, Most Merciful God, and have been sent to us so that you may live in the lush gardens of heaven, beside running springs of milk and honey, and under the shade of date trees. You should be thankful for the mercy He has rained down upon you.'

Tara heard his sermon out, but said nothing. At night she lay thinking on her charpoy for a long time. It was now obvious that Hafizji and his family had been kind to her because they hoped to have the reward of converting her to Islam. That's why they had not let her starve to death. Tara did not want to change her religion. Although she had no place to go in the whole wide world, she still did not want others to treat her with pity and condescension. It was also clear to her that whether she had a place to go to or not, Hafizji would keep her in his house in the hope of some day converting her to Islam. What should she do?

After she had begun attending college, and especially after she became friendly with the members of the Student Federation, Tara had little interest in, or inclination towards the religious beliefs of Hinduism. She found the talk of hell and heaven and of various incarnations of deities, and the ritual of praying in temples or for the spirits of deceased relatives quite ridiculous, but the pressure to convert to Islam was equally abhorrent to her. She remembered Asad's words, one day when they were with Narendra Singh, Zubeida, Surendra and Hamid, '...Hinduism is not a religion or faith. It is a social culture and a way of life. It does not restrict itself to any one set of beliefs. You are a Hindu if you believe in God, but you can still call yourself a Hindu if you don't. You can believe in the god of your choice, a Supreme Being with a face or without any form, in one god or in a pantheon of gods. You may or may not believe in divine incarnations. You can either say that the brahman, world and illusion are one, or separate entities. You are free to believe whether you are reborn or not, and act accordingly. Islam does not allow you this kind of intellectual freedom, either you are a believer, or you're not. You can't deny the existence of God. If you do, you're a kafir, an infidel. And you can't believe in an Allah of your own choosing. There is only one Allah, *wahadul mutawakkill, wahadul shreik*, and you have to have belief in Him. And restraints don't end there. You have to believe that Allah had a final prophet, and that prophet was Hazarat Mohammed. And you can't use logic and science to question your belief, because at the time when the message of Allah was revealed to the Prophet, the science of today did not exist.'

So as not to be bothered by heat and hunger pangs during the days of fast, Hafizji liked to have a nap between 11.30 and 2.15, just before the time of the *zohar* namaz. On the eleventh, his nap was interrupted by a blast from the bugle announcing the beginning of the curfew. His first thought was that the kafirs had attacked during the holy period of Ramadan, and that Muslims observing the fast would be inconvenienced if the curfew continued beyond sunset. He also thought of going to his neighbour, the honorary magistrate Mian Nizamuddin Kasuri, and telephoning the police station to find out the reason for curfew beginning at this time, but decided to wait until after the prayer.

Hafizji returned home a few minutes after the muezzin had given the call for breaking the fast, seeming very nervous and agitated. The begum and Khursheed were awaiting his return, a plateful of dates at the ready. It was a custom in their house to end the fast by eating dates. This practice was *sunnat-ul-rasool*, because Hazarat Mohammed also used to end his fast by eating dates. It increased the sawab one earned from observing the fast.

Hafizji was so upset that he could hardly eat, but it would not have been propitious to refuse to eat at the stipulated hour. He bit a piece off one date, and said, 'May the wrath of Allah fall on these kafirs. Rioting and deceit is second nature to a kafir. The Hindu superintendent of police in Amritsar has made all Muslim police personnel surrender their arms under some trumped-up excuse, and ordered them to take off their uniforms. They were then given their discharge, and told to go to Pakistan. I have a sinking feeling. How could Amjad travel in safety without his arms and uniform? The situation is very delicate in Amritsar. It was the duty of the new administration to transport him and other Muslim officers safely to Lahore.'

When Amjad's mother and sister-in-law heard the news, neither could swallow the dates they were chewing. Tears flowed down their cheeks. They began to curse the kafirs for their atrocious and provocative actions.

Hafizji said, 'I also heard that an angry mob of Muslim police personnel rioted when they reached Lahore station. Who can blame them? There was ample reason for them to be upset. These two-faced Hindu Congress leaders declare in public that Muslims will have full freedom and civil rights in Hindustan, but the reality is just the opposite. It's clear what turn things will take in the future. These Hindus know nothing but deceit and fraud.'

The magharib prayer was over, but Hafizji did not rise, and continued to sit and say prayers for his son. The face of Amjad's mother when she got up after the prayer was streaked with tears. Khursheed too dabbed her eyes with the end of her dupatta. It was time to begin cooking food. The begum and Khursheed often gave Naseeban a hand so that the dinner would be ready sooner. Naseeban first chopped onions and garlic, and began to mix spices and grind them into a paste. The begum asked her to bring a knife and potatoes, but her eyes were filled with tears, and the vegetables lay untouched in front of her. Tara picked up the potatoes, and quietly began to cut them up.

Hafizji went back to Kasuri's house to telephone the police station for more news. Vilayat Ali, his other neighbour, had also found out about Amjad being in danger in Amritsar. Two women from that household had come to commiserate, and the begum and Khursheed were attending to them. Tara took over in the kitchen.

Hafizji returned after over two hours, more distressed than before. He said, 'I couldn't find out anything more. Many constables and officers from his section are back in Lahore. Some arrived by rail, others in buses. No news yet of Amjad. Only Allah can help us.'

Amjad's mother and Khursheed began to cry again. Hafizji told them to have faith in Allah, and to say a prayer for the safety of Amjad. He removed his turban, hung it on the corner post of the bed, and as a proof of his faith in Allah, lay down to rest for a while.

Qamaroo was hungry, and seeing Tara in the kitchen, asked her for food. Tara gave her a chapatti and some vegetables to eat. When Khursheed got up after saying her prayers, Tara said to her softly, 'Bhabhi, why don't you serve Farzana and tayaji?'

Khursheed asked her father-in-law to have something to eat.

'I'll wait for a while, beta. I'm not feeling up to it.'

Someone rattled the chain on their outside door. Since only Muslims lived around Teetarvali Gali where Hafizji's house was, there was no cause for alarm. But to be on the safe side, Hafizji told Naseeban to check who it was by looking out from the window before going downstairs to open the door.

'It could be that bhai has arrived,' said Tara, out of sympathy to the worried family.

'Amen! May your mouth be full of sugar and ghee, sister!' Khursheed said.

'Bless your heart! May you live forever! May Allah be kind to you!' The begum too gave Tara her blessing.

'Chachaji! Chachaji!' shouted Qamaroo, who had gone to the window with Naseeban. The child ran downstairs, yelling with excitement.

Hafizji sat up. The begum and Khursheed too stood up as if they had been given a new lease of life. The begum again gave Tara her blessing, 'Have a long life! May you prosper! You'll be rewarded for your good intentions. May Allah's mercy and His grace be with you.'

Hafizji said in approval of the begum's blessings as he walked to the stairs, 'She's a very fine girl. That's why Allah has sent her to you as a daughter.'

The begum and Khursheed followed him downstairs. Tara stayed upstairs.

They all returned upstairs after a few minutes. Amjad was wearing a grey linen suit, but no hat. He was clean-shaven except for a clipped butterfly moustache. Just by looking at his clothing no one could tell whether he was a Muslim or a Hindu. To Tara he appeared to be clean-cut and educated. She stayed out of his sight, in the kitchen.

Amjad sat on the bed as he began to talk. Tara could hear him in the kitchen, '... Khan Sahib Abdul Ghani asked me to stay behind. His wife and kids were with him in Amritsar. We had also detailed six Muslim constables for our protection. Khan Sahib has brought back all his stuff, except for the furniture. I too have managed to bring my clothes and all my other belongings. Most constables, poor fellows, could bring nothing back. That sly Hindu superintendent of police had called a unit of the Dogra military battalion. He ordered all Muslim constables to assemble on a parade, and ordered them to take off their uniforms. We engaged a bus for ourselves. Khan Sahib was carrying two shot guns and two pistols of his own.'

'What about your police-issue revolver?' Hafizji wanted to know.

'All the sub-inspectors were summoned to the main police station early in the morning. That day a Sikh military unit was there, with Tommy guns at the ready. That sly bastard asked the Muslim officers to come into his office one by one. Then he asked them to surrender their side arms and take off their belts, handed them their relieving certificates and sent them out through the other door.'

'Damn him! Curses be upon him! What depths of trickery! Tauba!'

Khursheed came into the kitchen to ask Tara to take some ghee and make paranthas for Amjad, and went back to listen to her brother-in-law's story. As she mixed ghee into the flour, Tara too could hear, '... Kaul surely was too smart for us in Amritsar. We weren't expecting him to move so quickly. I'm sure someone put him wise to our plans. That son-of-a-bitch Hasseb, he's very thick with Kaul. I'm sure it was he. The bastard will neither be happy in this world nor in the next. Ghani sahib was nervous for no reason. He asked us to wait, so that there'd be no cause for suspicion. Otherwise we wouldn't have left one kafir alive in Amritsar. Who can stop the police from doing what they want?' Tara, her head bent, heard all this as she kneaded the dough, and felt that she wanted to throw away the kneading tray.

'When did you arrive in the city? I telephoned Imamdeen several times at the police station.'

'We left Amritsar at half-past two. We got to the police lines here around four. You know Ghani Sahib, he tries to act like a pucca European. Nothing would do for him but a bungalow in the Civil Lines. We went all over the Civil Lines without result. Then we thought of Model Town. We went and broke open locks on two bungalows there. Ghani sahib occupied one, and the other was taken over by Sattar Sahib. I went back to the police lines to report my arrival. I didn't think it safe to move around in the city without a vehicle. It took a long time to find a jeep. Two constables came with me up to here.'

Khursheed served the men as they sat talking on the bed. Amjad broke off a piece of a parantha and said, 'Who's made these Hindu-style paranthas? Who's in the kitchen?' He had caught a glimpse of Tara.

'It's a Hindu girl. The poor thing was really in trouble. Since Allah the Merciful has sent her to us in His infinite wisdom, let's hope she converts to Islam. That act of piety should take place on the fifteenth.' Hafizji narrated Tara's story in brief to Amjad.

For the next two days, Hafizji explained to Tara the meaning of the true religion of Islam, and the salvation that would be hers if she embraced it with all her heart, and suggested that she convert to Islam.

Tara, her head bent, replied in a tone of entreaty, 'Tayaji, I'm deeply obliged to you and maanji, but I don't know what to do with my mind and thoughts. Neither my heart nor my mind allows me to become a convert. If the God of Islam or the God of the Hindus had me born into one faith, let me go on in the same path to the end of my days. I am always asking myself how I can change myself into anything other than what He made me. I will remember your kindness as long as I live. If you can do so, please be so kind as to send me to some one in the Hindu community. Or give me permission to leave, and I'll face up to whatever may happen.'

Hafizji did not lose his patience, 'Beti, the English education that you received in college has obviously affected your mental faculties. That kind of education makes a person vain and misleads him or her. Our human intelligence is limited. The laws of philosophy and the human sciences are ephemeral and transitory. But the laws and philosophy of the Quran are eternal and have never changed, nor will they ever change. The salvation of a soul lies in having faith in the Quran.'

Amjad Ali's duties as a sub-inspector had begun on the day after his arrival in Lahore. As he waited to be given charge of a police station, he continued to sleep at his home. On returning home on the evening of the thirteenth , he said that an official notification had been received that the city of Karachi would be the capital of Pakistan. Although Lord Mountbatten was to arrive in Karachi the following morning at 10 o'clock to preside over the investiture of Quaid-e-Azam as the Governor General of Pakistan, the new government would come into effect only after midnight on that day.

Amjad also told them that the inauguration of Pakistan as a new country would not be on the fifteenth, but on the eighteenth, on the propitious day of Eid-ul-Fitr. Quaid-e-Azam has issued an order that there were to be no celebrations during the day, or illuminations at night. The only ceremony to take place would be the unfurling of the new national flag of Pakistan. At the Eid prayers, a special dua would be said for the liberation of millions of Muslims forced to remain behind in Hindustan.

'That's right! That's appropriate!' Hafizji agreed enthusiastically, and said, 'Quaid-e-Azam is a devout Muslim. The flame of love for his religion and his community burns in his heart. What better evidence could there be of a man's religious and patriotic sentiments? Wah, wah!'

He continued to enthuse, 'That kafir Abdul Gaffar Khan, the Congress leader of the North-west Frontier, and his goondas used to poison the minds of people that Quaid-e-Azam did not follow the Shariah, that he did not wear a beard or dress in accordance with the Islamic law, that he was against women keeping purdah, that he didn't abstain in matters of eating and drinking, that his daughter had married a Parsee. Those North-west Frontier Congress-wallahs convinced a gullible Pathan to go to Bombay to assassinate Quaid-e-Azam. The door to Quaid-e-Azam's house was open. What did he have to fear? The Pathan walked straight in. And what did he see but Quaid-e-Azam, kneeling on his *jayenamaz*, prayer mat, deep in devotions, shaking his head and calling on the name of Allah in a trance of ecstasy.

'The Pathan stood watching, transfixed. Ten minutes passed, then half an hour; the Pathan's legs got tired from standing there, but Quaid-e-Azam did not come out of his trance. At last, Quaid-e-Azam began to say a dua to *wadahul-shareek khuda* and *rasool-i-khuda*, Peace be upon Him,' Hafizji stopped in the middle of the sentence so that he and others might kiss their fingers and touch their eyes at the mention of Allah and His Prophet, '... asking Him to help and show the right path to Quaid-e-Azam so that he might succeed in helping his people and his brothers in religion. When

Quaid-e-Azam got up from the jayenamaz, the Pathan threw away the dagger he was hiding under his clothes, fell at the feet of Quaid-e-Azam and began to cry and ask for forgiveness.

'Quaid-e-Azam lovingly embraced the man who had come to murder him, and said to the Pathan, "My brother in Islam, nothing can happen without the will of that *rab-al-alameen,* the Lord-God of the Creation. If Allah has told you to murder me for the sake of Islam and our Muslim brothers, you must carry out His command." Quaid-e-Azam bared his chest. "What greater blessing can there be than that my blood may be spilled for the sake of Islam and my Muslim brothers?" He has the fear of Allah in his heart. Gandhi doesn't even come close to him, by comparison. Everything Quaid-e-Azam says is for the good of Muslims. He understands that kafirs and momins, true believers, cannot coexist. His plan for the transfer of the two populations was absolutely right.'

Amjad said, 'At least two thousand Hindus have left the city since this morning. Probably the same number of Muslims have arrived from the east.'

Hafizji got up from the charpoy and said, 'I'll go and sleep. I have to get up for the *tahajjud* prayer at midnight.' He left.

Amjad gestured with his head in Tara's direction and said to his mother and bhabhi, 'What garbage have you been collecting in this house? Others are throwing the kafirs out of the country, but you've kept one in your own home.'

'Once she joins the *ummah,* the community of believers, she won't be a kafir any more. Your father, and we too, will reap that sawab. Doing something in the name of his religion is so important to your father. You know he's converted many kafirs—I know of at least nine—to Islam. On fifteenth of this month or on the auspicious day of Eid, his wish may well be realized,' Amjad's mother said to pacify him.

'Father's worry is always that jannat won't have enough people in it. If all the Hindus of Punjab converted to Islam and stayed on here, what good would that do for the poorer classes of Muslims?'

Tara had expressed her unwillingness to convert to Islam, but Hafizji did not give up hope. He marshalled all the spiritual resources at his disposal into another campaign of persuasion. To his ceremony of conferring the purifying breath after the first namaz of the day, he added similar ministrations after each prayer, by making Tara sit next to him as he chanted a mantra from the Quran to ward off the influence of the devil and evil spirits from her mind. He increased the number of duas he said each day to Allah the All-Holy that Tara might eventually see the light. For Tara, the feel of another's person's breath on her face was disgusting.

She was growing increasingly restive to get away from her place of confinement, but she did not want to fall again into wrong hands such as those of Nabbu. She hoped that by not antagonizing Hafizji she might some day be able to find a safe haven for herself. In some moments of extreme despair she even thought of quietly leaving their house, regardless of the danger. If she ever had to face a similar situation, she had decided, she'd fight to the death rather than allow herself to be abducted. She remembered how Rukkan had swung the pestle at Nabbu in self-defence. She also recalled what those women at Rukkan's house had said about doing to a man to ward off his attack.

The last day of Ramadan fell on 17 August. Hafizji had been in a jubilant mood since morning. The next day was not only the occasion for the Eid festival, but also for thanksgiving to Allah for creating Pakistan for Muslims. When he came home from saying the evening magharib prayer at the mosque, Hafizji asked Tara to come and sit beside him. He recited a dua that Allah might shower His kindness on her, and began speaking with Amjad's mother so that Tara too could listen.

'Our daughter Badru is about the same age as her, maybe even a few months younger. By the grace of Allah she has two children. And what lovely kids! It befits a young woman to be a mother. I have a couple of men in mind who have good jobs. But,' he pointed at Tara, 'the problem is that she's already married. In accordance with the Shariah law, a woman may not be married again as long as her lawfully wedded husband is alive. If she accepted Islam as her faith, her first marriage would be annulled automatically. How, otherwise, would a God-fearing Muslim agree to marry her?'

From what he said, it came out that he had already rescued three oppressed and persecuted Hindu women and given them a new and better lease on life by getting them married off to bright and able young Muslim men. One young woman had been well educated like Tara, and had left home after being ill-treated by her husband. Hafizji had her nikah performed with a Muslim who worked as a registry clerk under his elder son Ahmed Ali. Not only was she happy and content in her new life, but Allah had also blessed her with children.

Amjad's mother said, stroking Tara's shoulder affectionately, 'This poor young thing has none of those uncivilized kafir traits. In features and build she looks and behaves so much like our Badru. She's been eating with us whatever we eat. She has even kept thirteen Ramadan fasts with us. Allah had sent her to be here, she's almost like one of us now. And she's not a child; we should think of her own likes and dislikes. Show her some men from behind the purdah, and she'll select one herself.'

Hafizji said, 'Yes, why not? You're right. That can be arranged. But before that, it's necessary for her to accept the Faith and become a part of the ummah.'

Tara was sitting with downcast eyes. She said slowly, fingering the edge of her toenail, 'Tayaji, I have no such intention now, nor did I ever have. Whatever was destined for me, happened, and whatever Allah or Ishwar wanted, that too happened. There's nothing left for me to want. But if there's any other way I can please this Allah or Ishwar, I'm willing to take it.'

'Tut! Tut! Tut! You speak like that because you're under stress,' Hafizji stopped her from going on. 'Beti, it's all because of mental stress. It's wrong to go against the laws of nature. The law of God stipulates that a woman must marry. Allah has given woman the face of an angel, but the devil is always misleading her. That's why the Shariah stipulates that she should always remain in the custody of a male, of her father in childhood, of her husband when she becomes a woman, and of her sons when she is old ...'

Tara sat seething inwardly. When it comes to women, Islam is no less repressive than Hindu society, she was thinking.

Hafizji went on, 'For the protection of women, the Shariah says that if she is young and not pregnant, she must get married within four months and thirteen days of becoming a widow, or she may fall under the influence of Iblis, the devil. A marriage can take place in Islam only with the consent of a woman to the man of her choice. Whatever we do, will be befitting your education and personality, and with your consent.'

Her eyes still downcast, Tara said in a firm tone, 'No, tayaji. I have no such intention.'

Hafizji spoke as he got up, 'Beti, it's better not to make a decision on such matters when you're distressed. If you have faith in Allah and his Prophet, your heart and mind will be cleansed. Then your ideas will correct themselves.'

Amjad's mother added, 'Beti, such decisions aren't made in a hurry. Whatever we want to do, we only want to do for your good.'

When Khursheed heard that Tara was unwilling to accept Islam, she was infuriated. She remained quiet in deference to her father-in-law, but spoke up as soon as he was out of the room, 'These Hindu women get into the habit of roaming about in the bazaars and streets, just like an abandoned cow or a buffalo, without their heads and faces being covered. How can they observe purdah like us decent, respectable women? We are ashamed to take even a step out of the house without wearing a burka! May Allah's anger fall upon such shameless women! A woman has to have some sense of shame and decorum.'

Tara listened to her insulting remarks, but kept quiet. 'What can I say?' she thought, 'to anyone who can gloat over anything that is backward, coarse and repressive? How can I convince anyone so fanatic about her living conditions?'

Morning dawned on the holy day of Eid. Since they did not have to get up at daybreak to eat sahari before beginning their fast, the family of Hafizji woke up later than usual, after hearing the call for the fajr prayer. Hafizji had brought home an enormous national flag of Pakistan. The first thing he did in the morning was to go up to the roof and hoist it up a flagpole. Most houses of the neighbourhood had flags on their roofs. He called everyone, including Tara. Tara had seen green flags before, but never in such large numbers. And this new flag seemed a bit different from the usual flag of the Muslim League. And it also seemed to her that this flag had turned her Lahore and Punjab into another, unknown city and country. The faces of Hafizji's family were beaming with happiness, but Tara's heart was weighed down with worry and uncertainty. These flags were a reminder that she was away from her own people, a prisoner in a foreign land.

Everyone had a bath and wore new clothes especially made for the festival. Hafizji had asked that Tara too should be given a new set of clothes, but Khursheed ignored his suggestion. She voiced her objections to her mother-in-law, 'Only Muslims are supposed to wear new clothes for Eid. If she doesn't want to accept Islam, we have nothing to give her. As it is, the prices are so high that I could hardly manage a new set for everyone else.'

The whole family was in high spirits. Khursheed's youngest daughter looked like a butterfly in her colourful clothes. Preparations were being made to cook *zarda*, *sawainyan* and make tea flavoured with almonds and spices. Hafizji was still hoping to win Tara over. At his insistence, Khursheed took out for Tara, not without much grumbling, a set of her freshly laundered shalwar, kameez and dupatta.

When Hafizji saw Tara in clean clothes, he at once raised his hands in prayer reciting a dua that she might get salvation, and said to her affectionately, 'Beti, today is a blessed occasion. It's the holy Eid. This is the first day in the existence of a country of God. If you agree to profess your faith today by reciting *kailmah pak,* and join the ummah, your heavenly reward will be doubled.'

Tara replied very politely, her head bent in respect, 'Tayaji, I respect you more than my own father. I have no wish to mislead you. I'm telling you the truth, that I just can't bring myself round to changing my religion. I wouldn't have hesitated otherwise. You've seen that I have few other objections; I eat with you all. But, still if you insist I will agree, even though I will do so against what my heart and my mind tells me.'

Amjad's mother said, 'If you recite kalmah pak, the cloud of doubt hanging over your mind and heart will vanish by itself. You'll see the light, and you'll be at peace.'

Tara replied, 'If it's an order from you, I will. I'm ready to give it a try, if you ask me to. But please don't blame me if I don't change my mind.'

Amjad did not like Tara's answer. His brow wrinkled in annoyance at the irreverence being shown to kalmah. He could not stop himself from objecting, 'Reciting kalmah pak is not a matter of trial and error, or something to make fun of. Why should she recite it unless she believes in it?'

He got up and, to show his disapproval, went downstairs. Everyone was quiet. After a few moments, Hafizji also got up and followed Amjad downstairs. Khursheed now spoke up, 'Let this wretch go to the devil! God save us all, why disgrace the kalmah by having it uttered by some non-believer! What can anyone do if she's determined to go to hell!'

Tara got up, covered her face with her dupatta, and went out of the room.

Everyone except Hafizji was angry with Tara. No one spoke to her. She sat by herself without saying anything. Khursheed stopped asking her to come and join the family at mealtime. She would ask, rather reluctantly, one of her daughters to take a plateful of food to Tara.

As she sat alone and in silence, Tara became alert to any conversation going on in the house. She heard Amjad say as he ate his dinner, 'Let's get her off our backs. Why keep this problem at home when she doesn't want to accept the Faith? All the Hindus remaining in Lahore have been shut up into camps. I can have her sent there, if you say so. Then can fend for herself and be Hindustan's problem.'

Khursheed supported her brother-in-law, 'Wheat is selling for one and half seer a rupee. We should feed the family first. Who has enough to spare to feed a kafir?'

Hafizji tried to calm them, 'Be patient, everyone. To bring wayward unbelievers back to the path of Allah is a religious obligation and a meritorious action as well. Wait for ten or fifteen days. Remember, you are all Muslims. You should try to bring her round by your kindness and civility.'

Tara saw a ray of hope. 'Amjad is blunt by nature,' she thought. 'He is not mealy-mouthed like his parents, but blurts out whatever comes into his head. He doesn't like me, but he appears to be my only hope of getting out of here.'

Remembering what Amjad had said the previous night, Tara went to his mother in the morning and requested her help in finding the camp for Hindus.

The begum appeared to be shocked, 'Hai beti, what are you saying! What does a purdah-observing woman like me know about camps-shamps? Hardly any Hindus are left in the city. We all wanted you to accept the Faith, so that you could be happy in this world and also in the next. What can we do if you don't listen to us? You yourself ask the men about the camp.'

When Amjad returned home later, Tara gathered her courage and went to him. She addressed him respectfully as 'bhaiji', and told him that she wanted to be sent to a camp for Hindus.

Amajd answered without looking at her, 'Don't ask me about that.'

Tara did not know how else to deal with the agony of her imprisonment. None of these people were willing to take her to a Hindu camp. And if she went to look for one by herself, there was the fear of criminals like Nabbu.

'Is it not a sin to force me to accept Islam against my own judgement and wishes?' Tara asked herself. 'Somraj and Nabbu tortured, polluted and defiled my body. These people are bent upon destroying my soul. I was helpless on those occasions, but I didn't give in and did my best to resist and fight back. These people want me to accept their torture willingly, of my own wish, by breaking my spirit.'

What's the harm, she thought, if she just uttered the words of the kalmah, but did not believe in them? What would that do to her? She'd tell them that she was doing it under the condition that she wouldn't marry anyone. That might be one way to get out.

But she checked her thoughts. 'No, that wouldn't be right. In trying to deceive them, I myself might get caught. If I said yes to Islam, these people would begin to tighten their hold over me.'

Her head spun with confusion and indecision. Maybe she should just starve herself to death. She remembered her brother telling her what happened to people who went on hunger strikes in prison. But would these people care if she went on a hunger strike? Hafizji had already told her what he thought of someone threatening to go on a fast. What reason would these people have for feeling morally responsible if something happened to her? The British government was afraid of Gandhi's fasts because there would have been a public outcry if something happened to him. Fasting by someone matters only if his life has some value. 'Suppose I fasted and got so weak that I couldn't move, and these people pushed me out into the gali? I wouldn't even have the strength to get up and walk away. And if I fell into the hands of some criminal in that condition, how would I defend myself? Instead of freedom, all I would have is a shameful death. I'd lie unclaimed, with flies buzzing over my dead body.'

The family of Hafizji had another reason to celebrate the creation of Pakistan. Due to the shortage of police personnel after the Hindu officers left Lahore, Amjad was promoted to the grade of inspector, and was given the job of consolidating his department's resources. He continued to live at home.

On the evening of 22 August, Amjad said to his father when they were alone, 'There was a government order that if there were any Hindus left in Lahore, their whereabouts should be reported to the police, and to the Indian government's Liaison Officer in the city. The business of this girl has become more complicated. It wouldn't have mattered if she had converted to Islam, but as long as she's a Hindu, it would be a crime not to report her.'

Hafizji did not want to cause any problems for his newly promoted officer son. He said, 'It's her bad luck. How can we do anything against our own government's law? Do what you think proper.'

Next morning, before he left for his office, Amjad spoke to Tara without looking at her, 'It's proper that you go to the camp for Hindus. That's what you asked for. I'll send a vehicle and a couple of constables later in the day. They'll take you to a camp.'

What more could Tara ask for?

Chapter 16

AUGUST FOURTEENTH. PEOPLE HAD BEGUN TO DECORATE THEIR SHOPS AND houses since sunrise in Nainital. Men and women were walking around carrying flags with horizontal bands of ochre at the top, green at the bottom and white in between, and the emblem of a spoked wheel in the centre of the white band. Everyone wanted to have the national flag of an independent India flying from their shops and over their houses before midnight. Some had already raised it.

At many places in the bazaars, groups of people agog with excitement stood listening to the radio to know the news of the day. The bazaars were festooned in the colours of the flag and with garlands of flowers. Festive buntings and streamers also hung from thin poles driven into the ground at intervals along the roadways. Arches of bamboo were decorated with lush green leaves and swathes of the tricolour. The air was heavy with the smells of boiling ghee and hot syrup, of freshly fried jalebies. The scent of burning incense wafted through the air. The Boat House Club and the Capitol Theatre of Nainital, over which the Union Jack had floated at the time when Congress first formed the ministry in 1937, and even when the Congress protest movement was at its height, were now being draped with tricolour festoons.

Though the August air in Nainital was nippy many people were seen wearing clothes of white handspun cotton khadi. Those who had never worn a khadi garment in their lives also wore the boat-shaped white khadi cap with pride. The news of a train full of massacred Hindus in Punjab had dampened the spirits of Punjabi visitors, but they had put aside their grief and were participating with enthusiasm in an event that had no precedent in the history of the country.

A gargantuan banquet had been planned at the New Club for the night of the fourteenth. All members, with their families and guests, had been invited. The members had also been asked to contribute to the preparation of the banquet, and the families of the members had been asked to provide one dish apiece, in sufficiently large quantity, as a testimonial to their skills in cooking.

Kanta had been discussing with Nayyar's mother, his sister-in-law, Kanak and Kanchan about the dish that they could prepare for the banquet. Nayyar's sister Subhadra and her husband Ramprakash had also arrived in Nainital. The family first thought of making *dahi-bare*, fried lentil balls in yogurt, then *phirnee*, made with rice and sweetened milk. They also considered the Punjabi-style dish of spicy chickpeas. Pandey the lawyer made a strong case for chickpeas. But the Nayyar family was in two minds; people of every region had their own tastes and likings. It would have amounted to losing face if the people of UP, accustomed to a different style of food, did not appreciate the taste of Punjabi chickpeas. They settled for dahi-bare, Kanta had paid for eight seers of yogurt in advance, and put a quantity of lentils to soak in water overnight.

Phool Singh, the servant Nayyar had hired in Nainital, was a smart local man. He borrowed sets of mortar slabs and pestles from three neighbours. After breakfast, the women of the household took turns grinding the lentils into a paste. The taste and texture of the lentil balls depended on how well the paste was ground. Kanak also lent a hand, but her mind was elsewhere. Puri had not written to her from Lucknow. His future, and hers, rested on the success of his meeting with Awasthi.

Hadn't he been able to meet Awasthi yet? she kept wondering. He was, after all, in a new and unfamiliar city. If his letter arrived today, she'd still have to be in Lucknow on the morning of the fifteenth. She knew the time the evening train for Lucknow left from Kathgodam station. In her heart she knew that if he hadn't written, he'd come back for her. She'd wait for his letter or telegram until 11 o'clock, she had decided, then go to the post office and telephone the Astoria Hotel.

Kanak helped in making the lentil paste until half past ten. As she washed her hands, she said to Kanta, 'Bahinji, there's not much grinding left to be done. Phool Singh and the housemaid can do the rest, and Subhadra can supervise them. It's ten-thirty now, Nanda Sah must be waiting at the library. The frying of the lentil balls won't be finished before half past two at the earliest. I'm going out for a while.' She changed her sari and left the cottage.

When she telephoned the Astoria, the reply was, 'Mister Puri arrived not long ago. We will call him to the phone if you hold the line.'

Kanak's heart was stung by the disappointment in Puri's voice. He said, 'I'll tell you everything when I see you. Walk back towards the library. I'll meet you on the way. I'm leaving right now.'

When he reached Lucknow, Puri decided to follow Kanak's suggestion to go directly to Mrs Pant's rooms at the Councillors Residence on Abbot Road. She was in the bathroom, he was told. After waiting outside her door in the veranda for over an hour, he had to knock again on the door to remind her of his presence. A disembodied voice asked, 'Who's there?'

'My name is Jaidev Puri. I've come from Nainital, with a letter for you from Kanak,' he said in reply to the voice from some unseen source.

Mrs Pant, clad in a khadi sari, came to the door. Puri handed her Kanak's letter. She read the letter standing in the doorway, held it in her hand after folding it, and asked, 'Achcha, that young Punjabi woman in Nainital. What relation are you of hers?'

Puri was not ready for this question. 'A cousin,' he said.

'We don't know her very well. Probably Awasthiji has said something to her. When we next meet Awasthiji, we'll ask him. You come back some other time. Today we're busy with the Celebration Committee. All right?' she said, in a note of finality. She broke off the conversation without waiting for his reply, stepped back into the room, and was about to close the door.

In spite of his hurt feelings, he asked, 'How may I be able to meet Mr Awasthi?'

'Try at the secretariat!' She shut the door.

Puri rode around for nearly three hours in the tonga he had hired, looking for a place to stay. Finally he found a dharamshala, a rest house for travellers and pilgrims, near the railway station, but not before he had made an offering of a rupee to its Brahmin caretaker. The disgruntled tongawallah extracted from him enough money to equal a day's takings before letting him leave.

Three quarters of the enthusiasm that Puri had in his heart to work for the new national government was snuffed out by Mrs Pant's attitude. But it was to meet Awasthi that he had come to Lucknow. He shaved, changed his clothes, and reached the secretariat after the lunch break.

In spite of Mrs Pant's discouraging reception, Puri's spirits picked up when he arrived at the imposing, crescent-shaped building that housed the legislative assembly and the secretariat. The Union Jack was still flying just below the dome of the building, but all the limousines parked in the portico carried Congress flags on their hoods. Armed guards in uniform and police officers were smartly saluting people dressed in white khadi dhotis and white boat-shaped Gandhi caps. Puri went through the grand portico and entered the building, with no sense of awe, but with his head erect with pride and his mind full of the sense of becoming a citizen of an independent and sovereign nation.

On the second floor of the building, the door to an office in the outside veranda carried the nameplate of K.N. Awasthi, Parliamentary Secretary. Beside the door, a middle-aged peon was sitting on a low stool. A long achkan of red broadcloth, a cummerbund embroidered with golden thread and a brocaded band encircling a white turban bore testimony to the high office and status of Awasthi.

The peon tore a square of paper from a stack hanging on a cord beside the door, and passed it to Puri, 'Write down your name.'

Puri took out his fountain pen and wrote his name, adding 'From Nainital, with a letter from Miss Kanak Dutta' when two men arrived, talking to each other in loud voices. They were wearing khadi kurtas and caps, and holding the ends of their khadi dhotis in their hands. The peon got up, touched his hand to his forehead in salute, opened the door and stood aside to let them enter. The men went in without looking at the peon, who resumed his seat.

The peon accepted the paper that Puri held out to him, yawned, and gestured to Puri to wait on the bench next to him.

Puri did not like it that the other visitors had entered the office unchecked, while he was being made to sit and wait like some lowly employee. He remained standing. After some time, he looked at his watch, twenty minutes had passed. He shifted his weight to the other leg. Eventually he sat down on the bench. An electric bell outside the door sounded. The peon went in, came out with some papers in his hand, and walked along the veranda away from the door.

The peon returned in a few minutes, and sat down again on his stool with his back against the wall, as if the excursion had tired him out. He removed a cloth purse from his coat pocket, took out a small tin container from it, and then some dry leaf tobacco that he placed in the palm of his left hand. He extracted and added a dab of lime paste to the tobacco, and began rubbing the mixture with his right thumb. After about a minute of this, he gathered the mixture in his left hand, and smacked it with the palm of his right hand. Puri could not stop himself from sneezing. A cloud of fine tobacco dust had spread all around.

The peon looked sideways and smiled knowingly at this obviously inexperienced young man. Puri had never seen such a peculiar method of rubbing tobacco before chewing it. The peon deposited the mixture in his raised mouth, and used his tongue to push the wad under his lower lip. When each saw the other watching, they felt a sense of unspoken camaraderie. After a couple of minutes, the peon got up, peered out into the lawn below the veranda, and spurted a long stream of tobacco juice.

Puri became increasingly frustrated at being kept waiting.

The door to the office opened. The visitors and a third person, wearing similar clothes, came out and walked away. The peon, who had stood up when the door opened, again took his seat.

Puri felt himself obliged to ask, 'You didn't show him the chit with my name on it?'

The peon, raising his mouth to keep the tobacco juice in, replied in a voice distorted by mouthful, 'You saw for yourself. The sahib was in, now he's gone out.'

Puri found use of the word 'sahib' strange for the khadi-clad gentlemen.

The bell shrilled again. The peon went in. When he returned, he was carrying several file folders. He said to Puri, 'Sahib won't be back now.'

This news completely disheartened Puri. He managed to ask, 'What time does he get here in the morning?'

The peon waved his arm vaguely, 'Whenever sahib feels like it. He's the boss. He doesn't keep office hours like an Englishman, you see. You can come after ten, eleven, or maybe twelve.'

In his shrewdness, the doorkeeper noticed that his words seemed to cast a pall over Puri's expression. He remembered the way Puri had demanded that the slip with his name should be sent in, then his complaint that it hadn't been presented, and the disappointment when the sahib left without meeting him.

'Do you know the sahib well?' he asked Puri.

'Yes, I met him in Nainital. He asked me to come and see him here,' Puri quickly made up a story.

The peon seemed impressed. 'Then why don't you go and meet the sahib at his home in the morning? He'll have lots of time then. I'll tell him about you if you come there.' The peon continued to speak as he began walking slowly away, 'Babuji, I do my best to help everyone. A Sikh gentleman was here the other day. He was quite desperate too. I got all his work done. He tipped me five rupees.'

Puri arrived at Awasthi's residence on Park Road at nine the next morning. Several persons were waiting in the veranda, an orderly was seated to one side. Puri decided to claim precedence on the strength of his more respectable-looking clothes, and told the orderly to announce his arrival to Awasthi.

The orderly said, 'The sahib can't see you at the moment. He's having his daily massage.'

By Puri's good luck, the peon he had met the day before came out of a room. He saved Puri from losing face by giving him a salaam, and brought a chair for him to sit down. Puri again wrote his name on a piece of paper, and gave it to the peon, along with Kanak's letter.

The peon returned after a few minutes. He gave his assurance to Puri, 'I showed your paper to the sahib, and gave it to his personal assistant sahib. If you come to the secretariat at the same time as yesterday in the afternoon, you'll be able to meet the sahib.'

Kanak had told Puri how unassuming, friendly and accessible Awasthi had been with her. After being received with such indifference and disrespect by the same man, Puri did not feel at all like meeting him. But to come this far and return without a meeting seemed a very stupid thing to do. So he went to the secretariat at two o'clock in the afternoon. Awasthi was not in his office. After Puri had waited for over an hour, the peon suggested, 'The sahib is perhaps with the chief minister. All the sahibs are busy with organizing the Independence Day celebrations. He may come back here, but then he may not. Why don't you ask the personal assistant sahib?'

On the peon's recommendation, the PA condescended to see Puri.

The PA wore a jacket and trousers made from khadi, but he behaved in the true bureaucratic tradition. He asked in English, without raising his eyes, 'What can I do for you? Please have a seat.'

Puri explained, step-by-step, the story of Miss Kanak Dutta meeting Awasthi in Nainital, and about Awasthi's suggestion how she and others could help in the task of nation building.

The P.A. sahib listened to all this while reading a sheet of paper before him. He finally looked up into Puri's eyes, and asked, 'You mean that you want a job?'

'Yes, in a way … one can certainly be of help if one has a job,' Puri had to agree.

'And who might this Miss Kanak be? Never heard her name before. Is she a Congress leader or with the Congress party in Punjab? How does she know Awasthiji?'

After hearing that Kanak was a twenty-one year old MA student, the PA sahib asked with a wrinkled forehead, 'What relation are you to Miss Kanak Dutta?'

Puri hid his uneasiness as he answered, 'She's my cousin.'

A sarcastic smile came over the face of the PA sahib. He said in English, 'How many young girls like her, do you suppose, someone as busy as the parliamentary secretary would be able to remember meeting? Why didn't you bring Miss Kanak along to jog his memory?' He switched to Hindi, 'You Punjabis are really worth knowing, mister! You're real go-getters. Any means is all right for you as long as it gets the job done.'

Puri writhed with anger at the sarcasm, and said in English, 'What do you mean, sir?'

The PA too answered in English, 'I don't mean anything in particular. What I mean is that you people are really daring. Your women too can be very forward. They know how to say the right thing at the right time. Well, let's deal with the reason you're here. You've come from Punjab. How many Punjabis can we accommodate here? The Congress government already has the responsibility for making the newly born nation stand on its own two feet. How would the government cope if people like you want the government to assume the responsibility of providing jobs for you? Since you're a well-known writer, you should work to encourage a spirit of self-sufficiency among others, rather than look to the government for help, as you're doing. There are many newspapers in UP, and several in Lucknow. Look for a job with them.'

To save face, Puri had to say that he had come to Lucknow only because Awasthi had asked Kanak to tell him to do so. And that he didn't care for a job as much as he wanted to help the new government. He got up, said namaste, and left.

Puri had now begun to feel a certain bitterness and anger towards Lucknow; he wanted to get away from the city that very evening. In a city famous for its tradition of courteous behaviour and polite manners, he had received nothing but rudeness and insult. Lucknow, it seemed to him, had been cruel to him, as Lahore had been, only because he was poor. Nevertheless, since he had invested so much time and money in coming, he decided to stay another day and go round the offices of newspapers, to speak with journalists to find out about jobs.

The journalists he met wanted to know more about the situation in Lahore and Punjab rather than volunteering leads about jobs. The news of a train full of Hindus being massacred near Lahore, and of Hindus fleeing Punjab in large numbers had reached Lucknow. The journalists wanted to know whether the Hindus would give up Punjab, or were capable of offering resistance.

Puri tried to maintain a journalist's objectivity in his replies, but he could not remain completely detached from the issue of his own self-respect and the good name of Hindus from Punjab. From his knowledge of the political manoeuvring in Punjab, he tried to assure his listeners that the Muslim League, the Hindu Mahasabha, and some extremists on both sides of the conflict were playing into the hands of the British. Whatever might be the outcome, the Hindus of Punjab had never accepted defeat in the past, they would not now.

He also found out that the salaries of journalists at Hindi newspapers in Lucknow were lower than those in Lahore. Two journalists who could read Urdu spoke to him with more sympathy. They offered him tea and paan, and explained to him that in order to get hired, one must have a mentor on the board of directors.

Puri returned to Nainital and told all this to Kanak. He could not think of anything else to do but to return to Lahore. There he could hope to do something on the basis of his contacts and acquaintances.

Kanak and Puri were sitting on a bench by the lake, beside the library, anxious about their future. They had believed that carried on the woolly clouds of the promises made by Awasthi, they could reach the seventh heaven of substantial and steady income. That cloud had dissipated and disappeared at the first touch of the sunshine of reality. Puri no longer dreamed about riding on that cloud, but had not stopped hoping for the security of a regular income so as not to wither away in a desert of poverty. He resented Awasthi's two-facedness, and then Kanak's naiveté in trusting Awasthi.

After hearing Puri's story, Kanak felt equally downcast.

They heard loud noises behind them, and both turned around to look. A small jubilant crowd of local pahari people, with leaf cups of jalebies in their hands, was moving towards Mallital, singing, dancing, playing musical instruments, and whooping with joy.

It was not possible to talk any further in that clamour of music and cheering. Puri and Kanak silently watched the procession pass them by. All the people they had seen so far on the roads of Nainital, except the coolies that pulled rickshaws or carried heavy loads, were visitors and tourists. The pahari men they met at the club, the Pants, the Pandeys, the Joshis, the Bishts, the Sahs and the Rawats, except for the pahari-style hat, had worn the same clothes as the visitors from Lucknow, Delhi and Lahore. This crowd passing Puri and Kanak was of a different type.

All the dandies from the surrounding villages and hamlets, it seemed, had gathered in Nainital on the occasion of the Independence Day celebrations. They wore close-fitting black hats, like coconut halves, skullcaps, and black waistcoats decorated with two or three rows of stitching in white thread. Their tight, narrow trousers had been fastened over their shirts like riding breeches. Kohl and *surma* ringed their eyes, and their foreheads glistened with hair oil and perspiration. Instead of neckties, they had multi coloured scarves or cords knotted around their necks. Even on this overcast day many wore sunglasses as an adornment, and others carried flashlights in the full glare of noon. This group of pahari youths was rattling tambourines and singing.

Groups of young pahari women stood on the sides of the road, wearing dark red lehangas, black waistcoats and chaddars of various dark colours. Mindful of being in a city and from a sense of propriety, they had covered their heads and faces with the end of their chaddars. But to get a good view of the festivities and of the men singing and dancing, they were holding their head coverings with two fingers, just above their forehead. Their eyes were wide with wonder. For this festive occasion they had decked themselves out in heavy collars of silver, necklaces of silver beads of five, six and even seven strands, silver nose studs and nose rings, with brightly coloured bindis on their foreheads.

Kanak drew Puri's attention to the young women, 'Hai, look at them! How innocent and shy they look!' Perhaps she was thinking about the similarities and differences between herself and those women; women of the same country and of the same generation, but with such different circumstances and lifestyles.

The men sang jubilantly, with one hand over an ear in the pose of a
pahari singer:

> *Chilama ki peech*
> *Dui dandoo beech* …

Puri and Kanak listened and watched with fascination. They did not
understand the words, and the tune was as unfamiliar as was the rhythm
of the tambourines. Finding the road blocked, a pahari gentleman from
the lower-middle class, wearing a clean suit of heavy khaki cotton, stopped
beside their bench. He noticed the inconvenience caused to the tourists
by his fellow paharis. For the inhabitants of Nainital and other locals, all
visitors to the resort were presumably well-to-do. Anyone who could
afford the leisure to stay for a couple of months in a place as expensive as
Nainital, had to be well off.

To excuse the nuisance created by such country bumpkins before this
prosperous-looking young man and woman, the pahari man explained
with a laugh, '*Aaj ye shale bi mastia riye hain.* Even these oafs are enjoying
themselves today.'

'What are they singing about? What kind of song?' asked Puri.

'It's just a country song, a folk tune from the hills around here,' the
pahari tried to play down the singing before this well-dressed couple. 'At
one time, sahib, these people would never dare to sing and dance like this
on the Mall Road. It's all a matter of time, sahib. Once such country folk
and coolies couldn't even walk on the Mall Road.'

Puri was curious about the song. He again asked about its meaning, but
the pahari, afraid that he might himself be regarded as another yokel, did
not want to repeat the words of the song or explain what they meant.

The procession passed by, and the pahari man too said namaste, and
went on his way.

Puri and Kanak sunk back into their preoccupations, and went back to
discussing possible sources of income. After his return from Lucknow, Puri
had been feeling uneasy in the lap of luxury and comfort at the Astoria.
He did not feel at ease there, nor deserving of it. More than ever, he felt
that he had been able to stay there only because of Kanak's kindness and
consideration, which he might have to forego at any moment. He was
desperate to flee this trap of artificial luxury and return to Lahore, where

despite all his problems, he at least felt at home, among his own people, and where he could somehow earn a wage, no matter how little. Once again, any possibility for him and Kanak of being together in the future seemed as far beyond his reach as the dream of a one-legged person wanting to scale a mountain.

Kanak said to him resolutely, 'Whatever may happen, let's stay with each other today at the time of the declaration of independence.'

'What independence, and for whom?' Puri asked with frustration. 'Whose homes and families are being destroyed? Whose lives are being sacrificed? All these politicians know is how to take credit for something others have sacrificed their lives to achieve. Who do they think they are? At the time of the Quit India movement in '42, when Congress leaders and workers alike were being arrested indiscriminately, these very same people would telephone the police to come and arrest them in their homes so that they didn't have to fear being roughed up during their arrest. I too risked my life for the country's freedom. I too went to prison. All I get now are sermons about the importance of building the nation!'

'We don't owe them anything,' said Kanak. 'If anyone deserves to celebrate, it's people like you. You didn't go to prison for any reward. You and I are young and able. Why should we be dependent on anybody? We'll face whatever comes. But I'm going to confront Awasthi, some day soon. Listen to me! You've waited for so long, just wait for five days more. Pitaji has written that he'll arrive here on the eighteenth. We should go back to Lucknow together. I'll see what Awasthi has to say to me to my face.'

'Do you mean to say that I didn't know how to talk to them?' Puri said with annoyance.

'Hai, no such thing. I can never be as good as you. But I still want to remind Awasthi of the promise he made me,' Kanak said gently to soothe his injured pride.

Puri's anger boiled over. His belief was that if Kanak had accepted him as her husband, she no longer had any right to contradict him. He said, 'You mean to flirt with him and get me a job? I would spit on such a job.'

'What do you mean by flirting?' His words stung Kanak.

'If you choose to overlook what the PA meant, what can I do?'

Kanak thought for several moments before replying, 'Why did you take the PA's comment so much to heart? There are all types of people everywhere. Perhaps he reacted out of spite. Those bureaucrats are seldom helpful. It might have been different if you had met Awasthi. Maybe he was really busy at the time. We should go and meet Awasthi together.'

Puri was not to be placated.

Kanak said to him imploringly, 'Are you always going to push me away? Our future depends on our being together.'

When Kanak returned to Vimal Villa at one o'clock, she found Nayyar reclining on an easy chair, silent and grim, with his hands clasped behind his head. Kanak's first impression was that he was displeased with her having gone out. She went inside and saw that Kanta's eyes were watery and red from wiping away tears.

Kanchan told her quietly, 'Barrister Mirza sent an Express Delivery letter from Lahore. Some Muslim superintendent of police from Amritsar has broken open the locks of jijaji's house in Model Town and installed himself in it. All Hindus have fled the area. Mirza has written that he telephoned the police and registered a complaint against the illegal occupation of the bungalow, but the police will be unlikely to take any action on a complaint against themselves.'

Kanak soon heard about other contents of the letter. Muslim refugees coming from the east had occupied both houses belonging to Nayyar in Tilak Gali in the Old Anarkali area, as well as most other houses in that gali. Mirza's advice was that Nayyar should not return to Lahore for the moment, but should file a complaint from Nainital in the court of the Lahore District Commissioner against the illegal occupation of his property by persons unknown. And that Nayyar should send a letter appointing Mirza as his representative. Mirza had assured him that he would do whatever was within his power to protect Nayyar's property.

Nayyar's sister also had been crying. Kanta refused to eat any lunch; Kanak and Kanchan did not feel like eating either. Nayyar tried to eat a little to keep some semblance of self-control. Kanta's eyes would fill with tears time and again. She said, 'We were so dependent on the rents from our property. He seldom made more than four hundred rupees a month from his law practice.'

Tears flowed continuously from the eyes of Nayyar's mother. She would dab them away, and address some unseen deity by joining her hands in prayer, 'Wahe guruji, Parmeshwarji, we know whatever you wish will happen. Lord, you are the only one who can protect us.'

The mother-in-law of Nayyar's sister Subhadra sat beside her and reminded her how the Saviour had helped others in distress, 'He rescued the elephant from the jaws of the crocodile. He will save us too.'

Kanak was going to say some soothing words to her sister when they all heard the call, 'Telegram!'

In the families of Nayyar and Panditji, telegrams did not always mean bad news. Still, both Kanak and Kanta were stricken for a moment by a sense of foreboding: What fresh disaster now! Kanak quickly went outside and signed for the telegram.

The telegram was addressed to Nayyar. Kanak opened it, not out of idle curiosity, but because she too wanted to shoulder the burden of this calamity, if there was one.

It was from her father: 'Left Lahore on the twelfth and arrived safely here on thirteenth evening. Letter follows.'

Kanak cried out in surprise; the telegram had been sent from Delhi.

Just as a sense of danger makes animals and birds cluster together, much in the same way everyone in the family gathered around Kanak. She handed the telegram to Nayyar.

Apparently, Pandit Girdharilal had reached Delhi with his wife, having made the decision to leave Lahore immediately after the incidents of 11 August.

'The Gwal Mandi house is gone too. And the printing press ... all those stocks!' Kanta began to weep again, 'What'll become of us now?'

'What are you saying? He's reached Delhi safely along with your mother. Isn't that something to be happy about? He said he was sending a letter. Wait for it.' Nayyar said, as if he wanted everyone to control their feelings of grief.

But Kanta could not hide the emotions raging in her heart. She went to the bathroom, and began to sob loudly with her face covered with her aanchal. The others too turned their eyes aside and looked away, to hide their emotions.

There was all that lentil paste, ground and ready, Kanta remembered. How would the dish be cooked if she continued to cry?

Suppressing her sniffles and sobs, she got ready to fry the lentil balls. Her heart might be filled with sorrow, but she had given her word to provide the dish for the banquet at the club that very evening. That banquet had been arranged not for the sake of her family alone. Which Punjabi family had remained untouched by the plundering of their homeland? It was not proper to let one's personal problems get in the way of a celebration being held throughout the country. Of what importance was an individual's existence before that of a country? This was a celebration of their country gaining independence.

Phool Singh, a native of Nainital, was surprised to know that the bare were to be fried in ghee, and not in mustard oil was prevalent in that region. They all had been wiping away their tears in silence as if their lips had been sewn shut, but the surprise shown by their servant loosened their tongues and made them exchange a few words.

They all took turns, two women shaping the paste into balls and dropping them into boiling ghee, and another scooping the fried balls out with a slotted ladle and soaking them in a pot of water. The water was then squeezed out and the bare were put in containers filled with yogurt, and sprinkled with various types of ground masala. It was a quarter past six by the time this work was over. After spending more than two hours working over the stove, the women were all drenched in perspiration.

Everyone must be ready by seven, Nayyar had told them in advance. Mahendra's brother-in-law Ramprakash and Rajendra had dressed and left the cottage at six o'clock.

Kanak was aware that Puri would be waiting for her at seven, but she had to have a bath before that. Their cottage had only one bathroom, and they all needed hot water. This caused more delay. The women were also talking about which dresses to wear. Since they were going to an important event, they wanted to dress up as the occasion demanded. A woman's fine clothes and jewellery are kept for such festive occasions. Subhadra wanted to wear a shalwar suit with gold and silver zari, brocade, and Kanta had also chosen for herself a zari-embroidered sari. Kanta asked her sisters to wear dresses with some zari in it, as well as some jewellery. Her view was that since everyone at the club would be dressed for the occasion, her family should not fall behind! Whatever was meant to happen had happened, but they still had to think of their good name. Such a festive occasion was a once-in-a-lifetime event.

Kanak tried her best, but still could not get dressed and leave at the appointed time. Nayyar, in a dinner suit, stood waiting for them in the veranda, saying irritably over and over, 'It's half past seven! What's keeping you all?'

The shops on the Mall Road were decorated with lights as if it was the Diwali festival. The road too was well lit. The crowd milled about shoulder to shoulder, like the audience leaving a theatre. Hawkers stood in the middle of the roadway, crying their wares loudly. Groups of people singing and dancing blocked the road here and there. Kanak was looking carefully to spot Puri in the jostling crowd, but she reached the Capitol, without seeing him.

Kanak finally saw Puri, but Nayyar, walking just a few steps behind her, called out, 'Hullo Puri! Where did you get to all this time?' He held out his hand to Puri.

Nayyar held on to Puri's hand as he listened to Puri's reply. He asked, 'Did you accept an invitation from someone?'

'I don't understand. An invitation from whom, to do what?'

'You're our guest tonight for dinner at the club. Come along.'

Nayyar kept his hold on Puri's hand to make Puri walk beside him, and did not give Kanak a chance to get a word in edgeways. Kanak had begun to believe that Nayyar's politeness towards Puri was only because of his snobbish and condescending attitude, but she did like the idea of inviting Puri to the banquet, after his disappointed and frustrated return from Lucknow. Now that Puri was going with them as a family friend, she thought, she'd be able to talk to him without reservations.

The hum of the crowd spilling out on the street gave an indication of the size of the gathering inside the club. As they entered, many people came forward to shake Nayyar's hand. The Sikh transferred his whisky glass to his left hand, using his right to shake Nayyar's hand vigorously, then to embrace him as he complained, 'Yaar, late even on a day like this!'

Pandey approached them with long strides, unmindful of his drink slopping over. He pumped Nayyar's hand, then shook hands with everyone else including Puri, surveyed the scene with the proud gaze of a victorious commander, and declared in English, 'No political topics or discussion today. It's the day of our liberation from foreign oppression.'

The lights and bright decorations inside the club were dazzling. Many men wore white khadi clothes and Gandhi caps, but many others like the Sikh, Pandey and Nayyar were in evening suits. The women wore glittering saris and shalwar suits.

The number of guests far exceeded the 200 dining room chairs available. Small groups were beginning to form of people acquainted with each other, or from the same social circle. There were also separate groups of males, groups of business people and professionals, a mixed group of men and women, a group of women only. A good many had drinks in their hands. Some women sitting on one side of the room held small glasses with liqueurs of various colours.

Pandey took Nayyar by the arm and pointed, 'The bar is in that corner. It's eight o'clock now. Dinner is at nine. The inaugural session of the Constituent Assembly is to begin at eleven. The radio will broadcast a running commentary, and the speeches of the President and the Prime Minister.'

Pandey took a step towards Kanta, and asked, 'Bhabhi, what'll you have? Sherry, port, vermouth, crème de menthe, Cointreau?'

'No, no!' Kanta shook her head and her hand to decline the invitation.

'You, madam? You? And how about you, miss?' Pandey asked all the women. They all declined.

Nayyar was heading towards the bar with Ramprakash for a whisky. He stopped, and asked Puri, 'Come on, have one with us.'

Puri shook his head.

Nayyar insisted, 'This occasion won't ever come again.'

Puri begged to be excused.

Nayyar asked again, out of politeness, 'Half a peg?'

'No, Nayyar. Never force a person,' Pandey stopped Nayyar. 'Don't forget the rule about whisky. Never abuse whisky. Don't offer it to someone who can't appreciate it. And don't offer it to someone who can't hold it. We've only got forty-two bottles. And twelve bottles of rum. That's all. There are Punjabi tipplers here, like you and sardarji. He needs one bottle all to himself.'

On several large tables in two halls, a great variety of Indian and Western-style meat and vegetable dishes, kebabs, snacks, rice, pilafs and breads, and mithai and desserts were piled in mounds or arranged on salvers and bowls, and cooking pots. At nine, several prominent and well-known members of the club went around inviting the guests to help themselves at the buffet.

The guests surrounded the food-laden tables. They served themselves helpings of what they wanted on plates, and stood around talking and eating. A great many did not come to the buffet table, but hovered in corners busily talking with drinks in their hands. For Subhadra and Urmila, eating standing up was a totally new experience. Kanak and Kanchan showed them how to serve themselves. Kanak filled a plate for herself and one for Puri, and they both stood on one side of the room.

At quarter to eleven, no one was interested any longer in eating, and half the food piled on the tables remained untouched. Joshi, accompanied by Chawla, came up and complained, but with pride, 'People hardly ate anything. Not one dish was finished. We worked so hard for nothing! I told everybody that I would take the blame if even one dish fell short. A whole bucketful of ice cream is lying untouched, but sahib, there's not a drop of whisky or rum!' He wiggled his thumb in self-vindication. 'Visheshwar babu and Gairola are really angry. They couldn't find even a glass of liquor. But they arrived late and the guys had cleaned out the bar by then. What could I do?'

'Silence please! Silence please! Listen! Listen!'

The buzz of conversation in the halls died down. A radio announcer's voice, speaking in English, was heard:

'... The members of the Constituent Assembly have taken their seats. Dr Rajendra Prasad, President of the Assembly, is entering the hall. Dr Rajendra Prasad is wearing white khadi clothes.

'The visitors' galleries are filled with distinguished guests. Ambassadors and members of the diplomatic corps are sitting on both sides of the President's chair. The time is five minutes past eleven. Srimati Sucheta Kripalani and Srimati Nandita Kripalani will now sing Vande Mataram ...'

The sound of the national song being sung came over the radio. Those wearing suits and European-style clothes stood to attention. Many unfamiliar with this Western protocol, mainly those wearing khadi clothes, had no idea of how to show respect for the national song. They stood in a slouch, as if they were spectators at some sports event.

'... At this momentous time in our history, we are assuming power after years of long struggle ...'

'That's Dr Rajendra Prasad speaking,' someone said.

'In Hindi! In Hindi!' Several voices said, with surprise.

Nayyar had never been taught Hindi. He could not understand the meaning of what was said in formal Hindi. But to hear the President of the country speak in the language of the people was a wonderful feeling.

Dr Rajendra Prasad said, '... We thank Almighty God, who decides the fates of men and nations. We offer our gratitude to Mahatma Gandhi, the Father of the Nation, the Guru of the Nation, and our guide. We offer our gratitude also to all those who suffered and made sacrifices and contributed to the struggle for India's independence...'

Kanak nudged Puri's arm, as if to say, 'Listen, this is meant for you. Who can forget what you did for the country?' Her heart was filled with pride.

The crowd was in no mood to be silent and listen to speeches, nor did they want to have anything explained or spelled out to them. They all knew that in a few minutes' time, at the stroke of midnight, their country too would become a free and sovereign nation like the other nations of the world. The centuries-long ignominy of being enslaved would come to an end. That was enough for them. All they wanted to hear, and waited for, was the stroke of the midnight hour.

The radio was still broadcasting other speeches from the Assembly House in Delhi, but the club was filled again with the hum of conversation.

'Nehru! Panditji! Jawaharlalji! Pandit Nehru!' Several voices called and a hush fell upon the hall.

Pandit Nehru's voice said, 'Long years ago we made a tryst with destiny, and now the time has come when we shall redeem our pledge, not wholly or in full measure, but very substantially.... It is fitting that at this solemn moment we take the pledge of dedication to the service of India and her people, and to the still larger cause of humanity. This is no time for petty and destructive criticism, no time for ill will or blaming others. We have to build the noble mansion of a free India where all her children may dwell....'

But the crowd did not want to hear about pledges of dedication or about building any noble mansion. They did not care what price they had paid, or what ransom had been extracted from them, for this freedom. Nor were they worried about what they would get out of their liberty. Not to be free was a matter of national humiliation. All they wanted to hear was the stroke of twelve ring out.

The buzz of conversation rose again in the hall, drowning out the broadcast of Nehru's speech.

Musical chimes preceding the sound of a clock striking the hours was heard from the speaker, and then the chimes: Ding! Ding! Ding! Ding!

Kanak and Puri quietly held each other's hand. Through the echoes of the twelfth stroke reverberating on the radio, came the auspicious sound of blast of a conch shell. And then a loud call, 'Long live the Fifteenth of August!'

The crowd erupted en masse.

'Hurrah! Hurrah! Hurrah!

'Long live Mother India! Long live Mahatma Gandhi!'

Men and women leaped for joy. They hugged and slapped each other on the back. Most of the people in this crowd were from the upper-middle class, who either worked for, or had benefited from, the government, who had never been so bold as to rebel against the foreign oppressor or take part in the fight for freedom. But tonight, a feeling long suppressed in their inmost hearts, the desire to be free, had resurfaced in a burst of joy.

'A toast to independence! A toast to independence!'

Nayyar and Pandey turned around when they heard someone call.

Joshi was approaching them with a bottle of whisky in his hand. 'Yaar, I had hidden one bottle, to toast the nation's freedom!'

'Oh, you're a brick!' Pandey responded with unsuppressed glee.

From the radio came a broadcast describing the members of the Constituent Assembly being sworn in. The crowd inside the club had thinned out. Someone suggested, 'Let's go and look at the fireworks.'

On the esplanade in front of the club known as the Flat, groups of rickshaw coolies and dotiyals, in their ragged clothes but with white Gandhi caps on their heads, were dancing and singing to the beat of clapping hands:

Bairu pakey barah masa
Kafal paako chaita, meri chhaila...
Berries ripen all the year round
But, my lovely, the kafal fruit ripens only in the month of chaita...

Further down, near the bandstand at the lakeside, a group of people from the eastern United Provinces was singing the folk song *aalha* to the beat of a dholak.

A group of young Punjabi men was doing the bhangra dance, letting out whoops and cries by pressing their lips against the back of their hands and blowing, to imitate the call of a billy goat in heat.

Another group, in khadi clothes and Gandhi caps, was singing the national anthem. Some of them leaped into the air shouting, 'Long live Bhagat Singh! *Inqilabb zindabad*! Chandra Shekhar Azad zindabad! Long live revolution!'

Fireworks were being set off at several spots beside the lake. Their reflection in the lake turned the water into a sheet of red, then green and then gold that shimmered in the dark.

Pandey, the Sikh and Nayyar, their arms clasped, walked towards the lake. Behind them were Ramprakash, Subhadra, Swarna, Kanta, Kanchan, Kanak and Puri.

'Just look at these people bubbling over with happiness,' Nayyar said as he looked around.

The Sikh, his steps a bit wobbly, stopped to plant his feet and steady himself. Instead of his usual English, he spoke in a mixture of Punjabi and Hindi, 'Why shouldn't they be happy? And why shouldn't they show it? We're free, baadshaho! We are not animals any more, but humans. Who cares at what price freedom comes? ... No price is too great for freedom. I'd sacrifice my homeland for its sake.'

'That's right! This may not be the time to talk about the price,' Nayyar stood still as he spoke, 'but just today we got a letter from Lahore from our neighbour Mirza that each of my three houses have been illegally occupied. And today we also got a telegram that my father-in-law has had to abandon everything and flee to Delhi to save his life. Now we're without a roof over our heads, but we're free, we've been liberated!' He roared with laughter, 'And who cares?'

He sobered up, and turning towards Puri, said, 'Puri is the only one here who has spent time in jail in this fight for freedom. Bhai Puri, people such as you are the real heroes today, no matter who may have come into power.'

'It's true that it doesn't matter. I'm happy too,' Puri replied. 'I didn't expect any reward when I took part in the struggle.'

Pandey took a long pull at his cigarette, and flicked away the ash as he spoke, 'Reward! Why expect any rewards from independence? Isn't independence enough of a reward in itself?'

The Sikh said, 'We've got independence because of Netaji, but where is he today?'

'What did these people get from independence?' Nayyar gestured towards the group of coolies dancing, singing and clapping their hands, 'Tomorrow morning they'll go back to their back-breaking work, but still they can't help but feel some happiness.'

'Long live Netaji! Bhagat Singh zindabad! Long live revolution!' The group in khadi clothes, brandishing national flags and shouting slogans, passed Nayyar and others on their march around the Flat.

Joshi and Chawla came into view from the direction of the club. Joshi called out, 'The revolution has already happened! What more revolution do you want?'

'Yes, it's been a real revolution!' The Sikh, still attempting to stand steadily, said complacently, ' 'Twas indeed a revolution.'

'Was there a revolution?' Pandey pointedly asked Nayyar.

'Revolution?' Nayyar asked Puri in turn, 'Was it a revolution?'

'Revolution, well no… but to have got independence for the country was no less a victory,' Puri said by way of finding a placatory compromise for this group of drunks.

'Listen!' said Pandey, with hands on hips, as he struck a pose of great seriousness, 'We've got independence for our nation. All we need now is a revolution.'

The first thought that came to Puri when he woke up on the morning of 15 August was of going back to Lahore. He mulled over this for a long time. He had told his family and the people of the gali that he had been called to Nainital with an offer of a job. How would he be able to look them in the face now? He had been willing to sacrifice his life for the freedom of his country without even thinking of his future, but, he thought, '…An independent nation doesn't want to take the responsibility of finding me a job. Isn't that an act of ingratitude by my country? What bitter irony!' … But the country was not made up entirely of people like Awasthi and the others who only wanted to be government ministers. Not everyone could be a minister… 'What expectations did those coolies have last night when they danced and sang with joy? They were the citizens of an independent country, but just the same they must have strapped themselves back into their work of pulling rickshaws.' But how would he explain all this to his family and his neighbours?

On the previous afternoon Kanak had begged Puri to stay in Nainital for a few days longer, and to go back to Lucknow along with her to meet Awasthi once more, but he had refused to listen to her. Now the thought of returning to Lahore without success, and of the embarrassment of facing his family and his neighbours made him change his mind.

When he met Kanak in the afternoon, he told her that he was willing to stay in Nainital until the nineteenth, on the condition that Kanak would go to Lucknow with him on the evening of the twentieth. Kanak's father had written in his letter that he'd arrive in Nainital by the eighteenth. With that in mind, Kanak gave her word to Puri. She also let her intention of going to Lucknow be known to her family members at Vimal Villa, so that no doubt should remain in their minds, and sent her clothes to be laundered at urgent service rates and began to pack her suitcase.

Neither Nayyar nor Kanta said anything. Pitaji would arrive soon, they thought, and absolve them of all responsibility.

No Urdu or English-language newspapers published in Lahore were delivered to the cottage on 15, 16 or 17 August. The newspapers published in Delhi carried the news that trains had ceased to run between Lahore and Amritsar. The only mode of passenger transport was now in buses, escorted by the military. Such sketchy and incomplete reports were a cause of even more alarm in the hearts of Punjabis who had taken refuge in Nainital.

On 20 August, Puri read in a Delhi newspaper that he received late in the morning: In Lahore, the Pakistani military and police had herded all Hindus remaining in the galis and bazaars of Rang Mahal and Lohe ka Talab, and from Gwal Mandi and Old Anarkali, into a refugee camp set up in the buildings and the compound of D.A.V. College. There was also news about similar camps being set up in Gujranwala and Lyallpur, and about rioters and looters seizing Hindu women in these cities and marching them naked in procession through the bazaars.

Puri's heart skipped a beat. He read the reports over and over, and decided that he must return to Lahore at any cost. He could not stay where he was any longer, or under any circumstances. He quickly packed his bags. At half past twelve, he met Kanak at the library. She too was very worried. Her father had not reached Nainital as expected. A letter from him had arrived instead. Panditji and Kanak's mother were staying for the time being at a hotel in Delhi. The family of Vidhichand was in a refugee camp. Panditji was looking, continually and day after day, for other, more permanent accommodation, however modest or small. Hundreds of thousands of refugees had arrived in Delhi from Punjab. If he left for Nainital without first finding a house for the family, he feared, it would probably be even more difficult to find a place when he returned.

Puri told Kanak about the news he had read about Punjab, and about his decision to return to Lahore at once.

Kanak could not ask him to stay, in such a situation.

Chapter 17

AT BAREILLY STATION, PURI HAD TO CHANGE OVER FROM THE NARROW TO THE broad gauge railway and board a mail train going west. That train was very crowded. He had to fight and force his way into a compartment. Other passengers who got on at Bareilly were mostly Muslim men and burka-clad women, and those already aboard were also predominantly Muslim. A Hindu man sitting next to the window at the far end of the compartment shouted at a middle-aged Muslim attempting to squeeze in beside him, 'You want to sit in my lap? Take the next train.'

The Muslim replied that he too had the right to a place.

A Sikh man, stretched out comfortably despite the crowd, asked, 'Where do you want to go? To Pakistan?'

'Wherever. What's it got to do with you?'

The Hindu sitting beside the window moved aside and made space for Puri.

The Muslim man objected, calling this unfair.

'There's plenty of room for you in Pakistan.'

'That's your idea of manners? That's your sense of fairness?'

Another passenger, prosperous-looking from his dress, with a beard trimmed in the Islamic sharai style, was sitting with two women clad in burkas. He said to the Hindu in support of the middle-aged man, 'That's the problem with your attitude. There's so much hatred in your hearts and you blame Muslims for the partition.'

Puri felt embarrassed at accepting the seat he had taken. He stood up, 'Here, sir, you take this seat.'

The Hindu gave Puri a look of disgust, 'You're being kind to these people! You want us to treat them with respect? Didn't you know that no Hindu could even step on to the platform at Lahore railway station?'

'It's the feeling of hatred and enmity that is behind all this mayhem and rioting and bloodshed. Partition could have been accomplished peacefully and in a level-headed way. Just give each party its due,' the Muslim said.

Puri had given up his place, but could not help saying, '*Janab*, Muslims started up the hostility and confrontation when you asked for the division of the country on the basis of religion.'

The middle-aged Muslim agreed with Puri rather reluctantly, 'We're all God's children. Religion is simply man's connection with God. It's only a matter of faith and belief. To dispute territory on the basis of religion ...'

The prosperous-looking man interrupted him, 'Wah janab, how can you say that? Religion comes first. Religion makes us human beings. When Hindus and Muslims are two nations, have different points of view, when they differ in what they eat and how they live, when they won't intermarry, they logically should have separate spaces to live in as well.'

'Then get the hell out of here! And take all your people with you! Who's stopping you?' the Hindu shouted at him.

Another man said, in a sad voice, 'You don't want us here any more, that's why we're leaving. Otherwise we did live together, for generations.'

The Hindu again protested, 'Why should the Muslims stay here anyway? They got Pakistan for themselves, but they still want a piece of Hindustan. Pretty clever, eh?'

The Sikh said, 'We got rid of these people in Calcutta. There might be only a few left, under the protection of the army. They too are being moved to Dacca. That problem would have been solved if the army hadn't intervened.'

The Hindu said, 'The government is protecting these people here, otherwise they'd have learned the hard way. In Pakistan it's the government that's getting the Hindus killed.'

A Muslim passenger begged with joined palms, 'Bhai, our fate is in the hands of our leaders. Hindus or Muslims are both God's people. As long as we are in this compartment together, let's be quiet and keep the fear of Allah in our hearts.'

The middle-aged Muslim wriggled aside and made space for Puri.

The mail train halted only at major stations, and when it did, the people who wanted to come aboard were Muslims. As the compartment was already packed, the Muslim passengers inside the compartment told the newcomers to look for seats elsewhere. The man with the sharai beard, in consideration for other Muslim passengers, had the door to the compartment opened and let a few more in. This led to a row involving him, the Sikh and two Hindu passengers.

Some Muslim passengers were nervous that the train would take them only as far as Amritsar. A Hindu comforted them, 'The Pakistani government will take you beyond that point. If you can't depend on your own fellow Muslims in Pakistan, why did you want to have Pakistan at all?'

Puri expressed his anxiety to get back to Lahore to take care of his family. He might be able to take a bus, he was told, because there were perhaps buses going to Pakistan under military escort.

Travellers swarmed all over the train at Muradabad and Saharanpur stations. By now the crowd was so dense in Puri's compartment that even the Muslim passengers were loudly protesting against letting more Muslims in. The prosperous-looking Muslim too had fallen silent.

As it was delayed at every station, the train now was running hours behind schedule. There was no question of being able to sleep. Pressed on every side by closely packed bodies, none of the passengers could sit in comfort. Puri thought of reading something to pass the time, but it was impossible to reach his trunk. Also, there was not enough light for reading, the pressure of the crowd had dimmed the light too. There was not enough space even to stretch one's arms. Puri yawned continuously and kept looking at his watch. It was close to five in the morning. He had spent the night jammed among the passengers without a wink of sleep.

At Ambala station such a huge crowd rushed towards the train that everyone inside the compartment was alarmed. Nobody wanted to open the door, but two Hindu passengers had to get off. When the door was opened to let those two out, a few people on the platform forced their way in. So many people stood crushed in the tight space of the doorway that the door could not be shut. The air became so close that everyone found it difficult to breathe. The Muslims standing inside were now obstructing and pushing other Muslims to keep them out. All one could hear was the noise of screams, cries and sobs, wailing and shouts. Some were yelling to be let in, while others were crying out in pain at being trampled upon. Babies and small children were screaming out of fear, and from being shoved and jostled by the surge of the crowd.

The passengers left waiting on the platform were panicky and nervous, as if they would surely face death if they were not allowed to get in. From the thud of footsteps overhead, it was apparent that many had climbed onto the roof.

There were so many people inside the carriages and sitting on the roof that the engine was unable to pull the load. It strained, belched clouds of steam and chugged, but the wheels spun on the rails without moving forward. Every passenger blamed the others for this predicament.

A detachment of police constables, lathis and guns in hand, came on to the platform. The travellers on the roof cried out in protest and resisted, but the constables pulled and shooed them off. The engine again put out all its strength, and after much hissing and puffing and shooting out clouds of steam, was barely able to haul the train behind it. The doors of the compartment could not be closed from the crowd spillover, and many travellers were perched on the footboards and hanging from handrails outside the doors.

After the train began to move, the din quieted sufficiently for one to be able to talk in a loud voice. Two children were heard crying, one moaning and hiccupping pitifully. Someone asked in a weak, trembling voice, 'Does any kind soul have two mouthfuls of water for the baby?' Puri saw the man with the sharai beard handing a badna, the Muslim-style lota, to an old man.

Loud sobbing from a middle-aged woman drew everyone's attention. An old Muslim man sat next to her, his clothes splattered with blood. When he saw the passengers looking at him, he too began to weep and speak through his tears, 'Who knows what He wished for us? We abandoned everything we had, and left with our two young sons, the wife of one of them and our daughter. The Hindus and Sikhs of our village barred our way. Our sons tried to stop them when they tried to carry off our daughter and daughter-in-law. They were cut to pieces with machetes, and both women were taken away. This is our two-year old granddaughter.'

'Ah! Tut! Tut! *Lahaul!* Curses be upon them! Tauba!' Several voices expressed pain, sympathy and disgust.

Another Muslim man said, 'It's all the will of Allah. The true human being is the one who fears Him. About a dozen persons were murdered in our village also, and all Muslim homes were set on fire. But our neighbours, God bless that kind family, hid us first in their cowshed, and brought us to the station at night, hidden in their bullock cart.'

Another elderly man removed his turban to show a wound on his head, and prayed that the curse of Allah might fall upon those who had killed his brother.

Puri realized that the only two non-Muslims in the compartment were himself and the Sikh. After hearing his fellow passengers' stories, a fear was growing in Puri's heart. What if all the Muslims attacked him and the Sikh in revenge? But the expressions on the faces of the Muslims were not one of menace, but of fear and anxiety.

Two more women began to wail and wipe away their tears. The man sitting beside them sighed deeply as he told their heart-rending story to the passengers around him.

The train was moving at a very slow speed after leaving Ambala station. Barely able to breathe in the crush of bodies, Puri was desperate for the train to reach Amritsar. But when would it get there at this snail's pace? he wondered.

Puri had taken over the space vacated by the Hindu who got off at Ambala, and could now look out through the window. The speed of the mail train was quite slow, but it still did not stop at small stations, as usual. On all such stations, large crowds of Muslims, their meagre belongings tied up with jute cord, were waiting for trains to carry them away.

The morning was well advanced when the train halted at Sirhind station. The platform was deserted, except for soldiers standing on guard with fixed bayonets. An ominous stillness seemed to pervade every corner. There were piebald splotches of wet brown and black on the platform that appeared to be blood. On one side of the station, beside the fence, lay several corpses. From behind the station came the sound of distant shouts and cries. Only mail sacks were loaded and unloaded, and the train departed.

It had gone only a short distance past the signal post. Scattered houses could still be seen on the other side of the barbed wire stretched along the tracks. The wheels of the train ground to a halt with a metallic screech. The sound of gunshots came from close by, and of bullets hitting the side of the carriages. A group of people with swords, spears, machetes and guns in their hands, jumped over the barbed wire and charged at the train.

There were more gunshots, and the elderly man sitting beside Puri cried out in pain as a bloodstain formed on his shoulder.

Puri pulled away from the window.

Another man screamed, 'Hai, I've been hit!'

The compartment was filled with screams as panic spread through the passengers.

'Close the windows!' someone shrieked.

The attackers climbed on the running boards outside the carriages, swinging machetes at people near the door and hurling spears through the doors and windows. They pulled at those nearest the door and threw them down on the ground beside the track. Seeing the attackers advance, some of the persons packing the doorway shrank back. Three young men, two carrying swords and one holding a spear, came in. They struck at random at the passengers, and pushed them out of the compartment. They also threw out any luggage or bundles that they came across. Sporadic gunshots were still to be heard outside. A young woman screamed with terror and clung to her older woman companion. The man armed with a spear moved his weapon to his left hand, grabbed the young woman by the hair, dragged her towards the door and kicked her out. The spear rose, and came down on the mouth of the older women open in a scream, its blade piercing her gullet and coming out from behind. The man with the sharai beard knelt before one man brandishing a sword, pleading and begging for his life. The sword went through him just below the ribcage, and was pulled out. The women sitting next to the slain man collapsed in fear and rolled to the floor.

Nearly half the compartment had been emptied. No one had the courage to fight back. Puri's throat was dry with fear, and he felt as if he were about to pass out in a faint.

He heard the Sikh call out, 'Brothers, I am a Sikh and this man here is a brother Hindu.'

Puri too shouted, 'I'm a Hindu! I'm a Hindu!'

Several others voices said, 'Hindu! Hindu!'

There was a volley of rifle shots. The attackers began to jump out and run back towards the houses. On a dirt road beside the barbed wire, several jeeps were approaching. Soldiers carrying rifles jumped down form the jeeps.

No guns were firing now. In the ensuing silence, all one could hear was people crying and moaning with pain, and screaming for help.

Someone barked out an order, 'Everyone get back on. You have five minutes to board the train. The train will leave in five minutes.' The order was repeated several times.

Some of those thrown to the ground climbed back onto the train. A Muslim lying on the ground just below Puri's window held up his hand and pleaded, 'In the name of Allah!'

Puri went to the door, leaned out, grabbed his hand and hauled him. Two women, pulling their burkas together, climbed back into the compartment. The young woman also returned. She stood petrified when she saw the slashed head of her dead companion. A body lay barring the way just inside the door. The elderly man sitting beside Puri who had been hit by a bullet, lay moaning on the floor between the two benches. The children sat in stunned silence.

Puri's mouth was parched. Everything seemed to blur before his eyes. He went back to his seat. The soldiers were repeating the order for everyone to get back on the train. A few soldiers were helping the wounded climb back into the carriages. Puri heard someone moan loudly from the floor of his compartment. He saw the man with the sharai beard move his head and cry out again in pain. The Sikh put his arm under the wounded man and tried to lift him to a seat, but there was not enough space for him to lie down.

The train pulled out about an hour after the attack. Both sides of the track were strewn with trunks, bundles and the bodies of dead people.

The train reached Ludhiana station. Soldiers with bayonets at the ready stood guard on the platform, and also beside the train tracks. A group of officers stood in the middle of the platform. Another order was given out:

'Everyone should disembark within two minutes. There is a danger of attack ahead on this line. The train is being terminated here. No passengers may leave the station area. All passengers will be taken to the Muslim refugee camp for their protection.'

Some passengers got off with whatever was left of their luggage and bundles. The injured and their companions looked around in despair and bewilderment, undecided what to do. Puri could not see his trunk anywhere but there was no time to search for it. The Sikh too was in a fix. His luggage was too much for him to carry unaided.

Puri, his own bedding roll under an arm, went to one of the officers and said in English, 'I'm Hindu. I don't want to go to the Muslim refugee camp.'

The officer looked Puri over from head to toe, and rapping his cane against his trouser leg, asked, 'Your name?'

'Jaidev Puri.'

'Khattri! Where do you want to go?'

'I must get to Lahore.'

'What's your profession?' the officer wanted to know.

'Journalist.'

'Journalist?' The officer said with surprise. 'Don't you know about the situation in Lahore?'

'I had to go to Nainital three weeks ago. My family is in Lahore. I must go back to search for them.'

'Well, if you want to risk your life, it's your problem. You may leave.'

'There's another thing,' Puri said hesitantly. 'There are wounded and some women in my compartment who might need help.'

'It's possible. We'll check,' and the officer turned his attention to something else.

Ludhiana was a completely unknown city for Puri. Both in heart and mind, after the experiences of the past eighteen hours, he felt so exhausted and distressed that he did not want to do anything or search any further. He filled himself up with water from a tap, and collapsed with fatigue in the first place he could find in the station waiting room. He lay there for over two hours. Would he be able to reach Lahore? he wondered. He would have to search for his family in all possible places. Refugees from Lahore and other areas must have come to this city also. He should inquire at the refugee camps.

The railway station and the passenger waiting room stank like a latrine. Outside and around the station, every place that could possibly provide shelter from the sun and rain, and serve as a nook to sleep in was packed with Hindu refugees from the west. Puri walked around until midnight, and on the next day also to various reception centres set up in schools and other public buildings. He could not find anything about his family. A rumour was going round that the government had barred the flow of refugees pouring in from the west by closing down the train service and the roads between Amritsar and Ludhiana. That route was being kept open for the caravans of refugees going towards Pakistan. The routes open for Hindus coming from the west were through the barrage over the Sutlej river and via the town of Ferozepur. Puri heard many horrible tales of atrocities committed on Hindus in Lahore and western Punjab. That night he spent again in the waiting room, using his rolled-up bedding as a pillow.

On the morning of the third day, Puri boarded a train going to Ferozepur. This train was hardly crowded. The Moga District station appeared deserted. Blood was splattered all over the platform, and bodies lay strewn. Men with machetes and spears in their hands roamed around boldly. A man with a Sten gun slung over his shoulder peered into all the compartments, asking, 'Any chickens for sacrifice?'

The train took a long time to move out of Moga station. The engine blew its whistle several times indicating departure, but did not move. Puri had not eaten anything since the day before, and was famished. Through the picket fence he could see chapattis being cooked on tandoors on a street beside the station. But he did not dare to go even that far. If the train left while he was gone, who knew when the next train would leave?

Several Jats, wearing turbans and lungis, marched into the station. They held two young women by their arms, and were dragging them along. One woman had no dupatta covering her head, and her chintz kurta was torn at the right shoulder, exposing the pale pink skin of a firm young breast. The woman seemed terrified and in a daze. The other young woman was also in no fit state to arrange the blue cotton dupatta around her shoulders. Two men had bundles wrapped in red embroidered dupattas tucked under their arms.

The men herded the young women into Puri's compartment. In their hands they carried bloodstained spears and machetes. One was carrying a pistol. Tears streaked the faces of the women and they looked numb with fear. From their chintz shalwars with floral designs, the thick heavy silver ornaments around their necks and on their arms it was obvious that they came from a Muslim village. Their captors seemed to be quarrelling over something.

Puri was struck dumb by what he had seen, and it was some time before he could understand Punjabi spoken in an unfamiliar dialect. One man was cursing his companion in a loud voice, 'That hot young chick was the one to have. Didn't you see her tits? Damn it, just like a pair of fighting partridges with their beaks thrust out,' he made a conical shape with his fingers, 'and you idiot, damn you, you slit her throat!'

The object of this criticism looked at the others in the group for support before protesting, 'Wah, what rubbish you talk! She bit my arm. Here, see.' The man removed a rag tied round his wrist to reveal a bite mark, still oozing blood.

The accuser waved his hand in dismissal and said, 'Shame on you, and you call yourself a man! You sister-loving fool, you were scared of a woman? It takes skill to break these motherfuckers! You sister-loving idiot, if you'd asked me, I'd have handled that fucker in such a way that she'd have begged for mercy!'

Puri turned his face away.

He was forced to turn his face back towards them when his arm was yanked, 'Who are you? Pull down your pajama!' A spear was pointed at his stomach.

Puri trembled with fear.

'I'm a Hindu, a khattri.' His hands pulled down his trousers without unbuttoning them, and raised his shirtfront.

The man questioning him and his companions all burst into loud guffaws. Puri felt ashamed in front of the kidnapped women sitting with their heads bent. He turned away and pulled up his trousers.

'Where do you live? In Ferozepur town?' He was asked again.

'In Lahore,' Puri replied.

'Gave away your womenfolk to the Islamites, right?'

Puri had nothing to answer.

'*Abey*, why don't you answer?'

'I was in Nainital. I'm going back to Lahore.'

'Nainital? Where's that? In what country?'

'Beyond Delhi.'

'Past Delhi? In Hindustan?' They meant the United Provinces.

'Yes.'

'Going to Lahore? Isn't he brave!'

'He's a babu,' another man said.

The men stopped paying attention to Puri, and went back to talking with each other. They got off at the next station, taking the women along with them. Puri breathed more easily.

Other passengers in the compartment started to talk, 'What's going on in the world? Everyone has gone crazy. No one shows any decency or humanity any more. And where did all these weapons come from? Everyone seems to be carrying a pistol or a rifle.'

Puri felt angry, why hadn't these people spoken up before? But he too had remained silent. When weapons were needed to fight the British, he was thinking, no weapons were to be found. Now not only does everyone seem to have one, but the weapons need not be hidden from the police!

Gave away your women to the Islamites! The man's taunt gnawed at his mind. But what could he have said in reply?

All that he had read in the newspapers before leaving Nainital, and heard afterwards in Ludhiana from the refugees from west Punjab, about women being molested and raped and being paraded naked, all came back to him. His mind felt numb with despair. What had happened to human beings? Where did this lust to kill, maul and destroy come from? Poor Tara became a victim. What his mother must have faced, along with Usha, Toshi,

Pushpa, Ratan's mother and the other women of the gali? He remembered the stories about Hindu women, like Padmini of Chittorgarh, who chose to burn themselves alive rather than face humiliation. Was killing herself the only way a woman could escape torture and humiliation? Were such barbaric acts by men natural and excusable? There are some men who oppose such barbarism... There are those willing to risk their lives to fight such cruelties... I wasn't able do anything ... Everybody is powerless in times like these.

The image of that firm, young breast peeping out of the woman's torn kurta came back to his mind, with what the Jat had said about the attractive woman one of them had hacked to death. He was disturbed by the thought that a woman's beauty was always reprehensible to her. For, a man's desire was a dangerous thing. But what if a man did not desire her? ... Because of his physical superiority, he could still strip her of everything, and drive her off and desert her, like an animal, to fend for herself in some jungle.

And because he desires her, a man is willing to sacrifice and risk everything, even his life, for the sake of a woman. Is this what is called love? It is a man's part to bring his love to fruition. A woman is always at a man's mercy. A man is considered uncivilized if he assaults a woman and possesses her even if she does not want him. And he is civilized when he pleads for her love... The memory of being with Kanak in his room at the Astoria flooded his mind.

Puri sat at the window, thinking and looking out. The day so far had been cloudy and muggy. A light drizzle had begun to fall. A few drops fell on his face. What if there was no train for Lahore from Ferozepur? he wondered. Lahore was fifty miles away. On foot...?

The train reached Ferozepur. The station here was even more crowded than at Ludhiana. There was such a rush to enter the compartment that he could only alight with difficulty. The same train would return to Ludhiana, he thought. He took the overbridge that crossed the tracks. Every train heading east was teeming with frenzied people. Passengers were crowded onto the sloping roofs of the carriages. They had tied their luggage and bundles to the ends of their turbans and dhotis and slung them across the roof, sitting in the middle. The rain had begun to fall harder, but that did not seem to bother them.

There was no one Puri knew or could contact in Ferozepur city or the cantonment. He was heading towards the station waiting room, bedroll under his arm, when he heard an announcement, 'Brothers and sisters who have not had the prasad, please come to the langar. No need to feel embarrassed or shy about it.'

Just beside the overbridge, chapattis cooked in a tandoor were stacked in a column on a tarpaulin, with a huge pot next to it. Puri's hunger was reawakened. His steps turned automatically in that direction. Seeing him approach, a man poured a ladleful of thick daal over two chapattis, and handed them to Puri.

Puri accepted the chapattis. He knew it was a free public kitchen, intended for refugees, but he still took out a quarter-rupee coin and offered it to the man. The man pointed to a small box that had a padlock sealed with red wax, with a slot in the lid for depositing money. Puri slid the coin into it.

When he reached the waiting room, Puri looked everywhere and found that there were no vacant space large enough even to spread his thin bedroll. Scores of people had piled their belongings into small heaps, and were lying all around them. Puri tried to unroll his bedding over a strip of a space, but a man stopped him, 'Can't you see I've got women with me? Don't you have a mother or sisters?'

Puri quietly moved away.

At another spot, he saw an empty space perhaps a foot in width, and asked the people on both sides to move their beds a few inches. They replied, 'Not here. Go somewhere else.'

When Puri persisted, one man began to complain in a loud voice, 'We've had to run, leaving everything behind. And now this man wants us to give up even these few inches of floor space where we've stopped for a few moments to rest.'

Others tried to intervene, 'Bhai, all of us have had to flee the homes and lands of our ancestors, so why quarrel over a few feet of space? Who's going to live here forever? We're all together for a short time, just like boats on a river.' In spite of such comments, the man Puri had asked for a couple of feet refused to move aside and give up the space he had taken for his family.

Another family had not been able to find enough space to spread out their beds for the night, and were sitting nearby. A man from that family said angrily, 'Arey, this Sikandar here has declared it to be his kingdom.

No one can set foot in it. If he is so picky about the space he's taken over, why did he give up his home for Muslims?'

Puri lay down in the foot-wide space, using his rolled-up bed as a pillow. What's the world coming to? he reflected. 'All that I've been through this afternoon and evening. Some people call out to you to give you food and others won't even let you sit beside them. Cruel and kind... it takes all kinds to make a world.'

He got up at daybreak. A throng of women had collected outside the waiting room lavatory. The lavatories on the platform similarly had long lines. People carrying lotas full of water came towards the lavatories, but on seeing the queues stretching down the platform, went off towards the tracks away from the station, or crossed the fence and went into the surrounding fields. Puri too went into a field. If one looked towards the tracks receding into the distance or towards the fields, it appeared as if the landscape was dotted with sheep, with their heads down. On all sides, men and women, in their need to answer the calls of nature, squatted at short intervals with their heads lowered, ignoring others around them in the belief that no one could see them. The fresh coolness of the morning was made putrid by the presence of human waste.

The rays of the sun still touched the treetops. Puri left the station and resumed his search for news of his family in the camps for refugees fleeing Lahore and western Punjab. Under the railway overbridge and at every place that could provide any kind of cover, people who had lost their homes and who had nowhere else to go, were huddling in an attempt to brave the elements.

It was almost dark by the time he was through visiting the shelters set up in various schools and temples, by both the branches of the Arya Samaj organization, in the gurudwaras and in a couple of orphanages in the cantonment area. He found the bedding roll that he had to carry about quite bothersome, but where could he safely leave this sole possession? That night he stayed at the Hindu camp set up in the Islamia School near the tonga stand.

Next morning he went round the city centre. He checked at the Arya School, Ram Sukh College, Takht Singh School, Gobar Mandi, at all the gurudwaras and Arya Samaj camps, and was returning through the Sarrafa Bazaar when he saw somebody standing in front of a shop who looked like his friend Kalicharan Kaul. The young man, with several days' growth of beard, looked like any other Muslim or Hindu who had not shaved because he was still in mourning. The man's face looked haggard, with sunken cheeks. Maybe someone wearing clothes this dirty couldn't be Kaul, but the women sitting by the goldsmith's shop were definitely Kalicharan's middle-aged mother, his younger sister Kailash, and his wife with their infant son. Their faces were pale and drawn, and their clothes dirty and crumpled.

Puri called out, 'Kaul!'

The man looked at Puri when he heard the call. They stared at each other in suspense for a moment, then rushed forward and hugged one another.

Puri blurted out at once, 'Have you seen Masterji anywhere? Have you been to the DAV School camp?'

Kaul shook his head in answer to the first question, and nodded in reply to the second. Answering other questions by Puri, he explained how the people of his gali had escaped most of the violence up to the time they had to leave. The reason they had to leave was not their Muslim neighbours. On the morning of 17 August, a detachment of armed Baluchi soldiers came and ordered all Hindus to leave their houses. The Hindus were not given any time to collect their valuables, clothes or any other belonging. 'Get out in five minutes,' was the order, and they were told that there was no space for any luggage or parcels in the trucks waiting to ferry them away. The only jewellery that Kaul family was able to carry out was whatever the women were wearing at the time.

Kaul's mother broke into tears, 'I had gold ornaments worth sixty tolas in my box at home. Now I'm left with only these eight or ten tolas' worth that my daughter-in-law has on her, and the four gold bangles on Kailash's wrists.'

Kaul said, 'We had over a thousand rupees in cash in the house, but the soldiers didn't let us touch anything. All I could do was to put on my jacket that was hanging from a peg. It had 27 rupees and 3 annas in one pocket and all that was used up at the camp. No one was allowed outside the camp. Inside, wheat sold for one seer a rupee, milk one seer a rupee; and it was hardly milk, just milk diluted with water. It was awful there. As luck would have it, Mahajan had somehow managed to bring along four hundred rupees. He's smart, as you know.

'This morning we were loaded on to trucks by the Indian Army. Mahajan has been sent to Amritsar, we couldn't find any room beside him. Ten trucks were sent to Amritsar, ten came here. We were dumped here, without a paisa in our pockets.'

Kaul wiped his eyes on his sleeve, 'The baby's hungry. We need a cup of milk for him. When we tried to sell the bangles, we were offered 145 when they're worth twice that.'

'Let me give you something. I have twenty on me,' Puri offered, mentioning less than what he really had in his pocket. 'Take ten.'

'No,' Kaul grasped Puri's hand before he could pull out the money, 'What's the use? We'll need a lot more than that. We'll have to eat to stay alive. The only clothes we have are what we're wearing. Haven't had a wash for five days. I'll have to buy the women at least one dhoti each.'

Puri gave a shiver when he learned that Kaul's family had had nothing to eat. His experience of the past few days had taught him the meaning of real hunger. He held Kaul's arm and insisted, 'First get milk for the baby, and then you all should have some lassi. You can think about selling things off later.'

Kaul's mother was very reluctant to accept the offer of lassi, but relented after Puri insisted and Kaul also spoke to her. Puri took them to a shop selling milk and yogurt, and had lassis made up of half a seer of yogurt for each of them.

Puri went with Kaul to several jewellers. The bangles were weighed and examined each time, but the highest offer they got was for 150 rupees.

Kaul said in disgust, 'These are hard times, but our Hindu brothers want to have their pound of flesh. And they claim that they want to help their fellow Punjabis!'

Puri too was angry and frustrated at Kaul's situation. He said, 'I really don't understand this strange display of piety by our fellow Hindus. Many are providing food and shelter, and yesterday some of them were giving away clothes to refugees in the camps in the cantonment, but they also want to suck the last drop of our heart's blood. They want to have it both ways—to gain merit by feeding the hungry, and then exploit us by buying and selling to us without pity or scruple.'

Puri had been to all the camps in Ferozepur. He took Kaul's family to the camp at Har Bhagwan School, which he thought was a little better than the others. Before they parted, Kaul said, 'The Indian Army will not allow a Hindu on the road to Lahore. Either your family has already been sent to Amritsar, or will be sent to Amritsar or here in the next couple of days.

Go and look for them in Amritsar. I'll keep a watch here. If I find them, I'll let you know. But how would I get in touch?'

Puri said, 'You can write to me care of the postmaster at Amritsar General Post Office. I'll keep on checking in there.'

The main railway line from Ferozepur to Amritsar went through Kasoor Junction, on the opposite bank of the Sutlej river, which formed the frontier line with Pakistan. The rail service had been cancelled because of the repeated attacks and looting of the trains. The alternative train to reach Amritsar from Ferozepur ran on a branch line, via Lohiankhas and Jalandhar. Puri made up his mind to take that route to Amritsar.

The sun had risen when he arrived at Jalandhar station. A sea of people stretched as far as the eye could see. Hindu and Sikh refugees reaching Ferozepur had come mostly from the villages of western Punjab. In Jalandhar the refugees were predominantly shopkeepers and businessmen from the cities in the west.

A large improvised bazaar had sprung up on the maidan outside the station. Small pyramids of wheat and lentils were displayed for sale. At several places, masses of kitchen utensils and paraphernalia—tinplate and copper pots and pans, hookahs, spittoons and hand basins such as those found in Muslim homes, were being sold as scrap. Other peddlers had spread out used and new clothes for buyers to inspect. From the gaudy colours and the cheap brocade embroidery on cotton and silk, it was obvious that the clothes came from Muslim families.

Some people were selling small heaps of firewood of chopped or broken panels and the frames of doors and windows, charpoy frames, and the wheels and undercarriages of carts. Silver jewellery, of the kind worn by Muslim women, was also on sale.

A man was auctioning off fine clothes of silk and velvet, worn by Hindus, straight out of a luggage trunk. Two women sat silently next to him, their heads bowed.

Another man was inviting buyers to inspect his blanket.

Without paying attention to the bustle around, Puri went straight to the tent of the volunteer organization that housed the information office for the camp, carrying his bedding roll under his arm. When he did not get any news of his family there, he began making the rounds of other centres. He went to all camps run by the Arya Samaj, the camp at the D.A.V College that was quite a distance away, and to several gurudwaras. Horse carriages for hire were few and far between, and were charging exorbitant rates. He had only 23 rupees and 7 annas left from the money Kanak had given him. How could he spend any of it on hiring a carriage? This sum of money was his only hope of survival, and of the possibility of finding his family. There was no chance for him to earn anything by working. Who would be willing to talk about short stories and articles when all people could think of was finding whatever shelter they could, and of selling everything they owned to buy food?

After walking all day in the sun, his body felt sticky and itched from the sweat drying on his skin. His face was caked with a layer of dust and sweat. Swollen with blood, his feet had puffed up inside his shoes. To top it all, lugging the rolled-up bed around was extremely tiring for him.

The sun was setting when Puri arrived at the Islamia College refugee camp. He again met with disappointment regarding news of his parents, his sisters and his brother. He had no strength left to walk any more. When he left the station in the morning, he had felt the craving for a glass of cold lassi. And finding a 3-anna glass of lassi being sold for 6 annas had infuriated him. If robbing someone under the threat of assault with a knife was a crime, wasn't making someone empty out his pockets because he was hungry and thirsty also robbery?

Puri ate two chapattis and daal at a tandoor, and drank a lot of water. He thought of the elaborate breakfasts and meals he had been served with such style at the Astoria, and a smile crossed his lips over this irony of fate. He had been walking throughout the day carrying his rolled-up bedding. Every time he heard the calls of hawkers selling cold drinks of lassi or sherbet or fresh lemon *shikanjbeen*, he had suppressed his craving and looked around for tap water to quench his thirst. After the hunger, thirst and exhaustion of the day, it did not seem possible to go to another camp to continue his search, hauling his bedroll.

Puri saw that there were some unoccupied places in a side veranda of the Islamia College building. He walked up and saw that the desks and chairs used by students had been moved out of the classrooms and the luggage and beds of refugees now lay scattered inside. Women in dirty, bedraggled clothes, with sad grieving faces, were lying or sitting on charpoys and on the floor. The closed doors to several rooms displayed padlocks.

Many refugees had spread out their beds and piled their belongings in the veranda, which also had a room at either end. Puri saw a strip of unoccupied space in the corner on his right. He put his bedding next to the wall, leaving a passage for anyone wanting to go into the room, and sat down on it.

He was startled when he heard his name called. He looked to his left.

Inside a room nearby, Badhawa Mull Narang was sitting on a dhurrie spread out on the floor. He sat cross-legged, with his hands supporting him. Both spoke simultaneously when their eyes met.

Narang asked, 'Master Ramlubhaya is not with you?'

Puri's question was, 'Did you see my father anywhere?'

Puri asked again, 'Didn't you see him at any camp in Lahore?'

Behind Narang, with her back towards the door, lay Beyji, his wife. She too got up covering her head with a dupatta, and asked Puri when she recognized who he was, 'Kakaji, were you not in Lahore?'

Puri gave a very brief account of his going to Nainital, of his decision to return after reading about Punjab in newspapers, of the train being terminated at Ludhiana, and asked, 'How can I get some news of pitaji and others? Maybe they're still in Lahore, in some refugee camp. How can I get back to Lahore?'

Beyji and Narang both replied together, 'Wah kakaji, how can you go back to Lahore? It's like jumping into a raging fire. And who'd let you?'

Narang went on, 'We heard that all Hindus living in the mohallas of Rang Mahal, Bajaj Hatta and Machchi Hatta had fled by the fifteenth and sixteenth. The people living in Ram Gali left on the seventeenth. The Pakistani military people treated those families very callously. They were forced out of their houses, and their belongings were looted. Our area of Manso Gali was guarded by the Dogra Regiment. Every time the Muslims tried to attack, the soldiers fired at them.

'Bhai, we had no plan to leave Lahore. If Lahore were to be in Pakistan, we had decided, we would live in Pakistan. On the eighteenth when the Pakistani flags were unfurled from other houses, the people of our gali also hoisted green flags, thinking that if we had to remain there, whatever was the new flag of the country, we'd accept it.

'The Dogra soldiers told us in the afternoon that the Muslim officers wanted to clear the area of Hindus, who would be ordered to move to somewhere else. Baluchi soldiers were to replace them as our protectors. We had only four hours left. Actually, ever since the Ram Gali affair, we were afraid that we might have to leave at any moment. The women put on two of every garment with all their jewellery underneath; so that even if we weren't given any notice, they'd at least have an extra pair of clothes. The Baluchi soldiers hadn't let the inhabitants of Ram Gali take away a single thing.

'We quickly stuffed all our cash, valuables and a few clothes into suitcases. All the members of our family took a suitcase each and left the house. We couldn't carry any bedding, sheets, pillows or anything like that. We had two new quilts made last winter, with velvet covers. Your Beyji wanted to carry them, in case they were needed.

'I told her, "To hell with them! Our lives are at stake, and all you can think of is your quilts! If we have cash or gold with us, we can buy anything. Aren't we leaving behind our business worth many lakhs of rupees, carpets worth thousands, all this furniture, trunks and cupboards full of stuff?" All we could get out were these five suitcases. These dhurries, sheets, kitchen utensils, thalis, bowls, glasses and mattresses, all were bought here. Doesn't matter if we are without pillows. The only thing we brought with us was a lota and a tumbler for water.

'Everyone in our gali did just the same. Everyone of the four Hindu families was able to get out safely. We, six members of Ralia Ram's family, seven from Ushnak Mal's house, and everyone from Laddha Ram's. We hired a bus for ourselves. Had to pay three hundred rupees for it. We went to D.A.V. College, and joined the convoy under military escort. A different convoy had an escort of Baluchi soldiers, and may God send them to hell. There were eight buses in that convoy. When they reached Amritsar, the only people found alive were the drivers. The rest were dead... Bhai, we've been here for four days, and things are not working out. We are thinking about going on to Delhi.'

The concern for his own family deepened in Puri's heart. He again asked Narang about the possibility of joining a convoy going to Pakistan.

Beyji tried to dissuade him, 'Kakaji, don't lose hope like that. Do you suppose it's wise to jump knowingly into the jaws of death?'

Narang said, 'Do you suppose Masterji is still in Lahore? Even if he is, the government must have made some arrangement to get him out. What might happen is that he'd get here, and then worry about finding you somehow.'

Beyji said, 'Kakaji, the times are such that all we can do is to have faith in God. Just look at our family. What haven't we been through in the past six months?' Tears came to her eyes. Puri knew that she was referring to her daughter becoming a widow. 'When we see others in trouble, all I say is never mind what we may have suffered. May God show His mercy to others.' She wiped her eyes with the end of her dupatta.

Narang kept his voice low as he told Puri, 'That old Sikh couple with the infant, lying there quietly behind you, they were coming from Gujarat in the train. The train was attacked at Kamoki station. The poor man's young sons were murdered, his daughters-in-law were kidnapped. They killed his grandsons too, and took away his teenage granddaughter. All their boxes, bundles, bags filled with pots and pans, were snatched away. Just by luck, one infant grandson survived. These people would have been killed too, but for the Sikh guard regiment that arrived just in time. The soldiers put the couple back on a train. They're practically out of their minds with despair.'

Narang said, pointing to a man with a bandaged knee sitting with his back against the wall, 'See him? There are three of them. They fought back when their train was attacked, but the Pakistani police intervened and let their families be murdered. Eleven members of their two families were killed. Their women were raped in front of them. None of the women was let go. He suffered a broken knee. His two companions have gone to loot the Muslim houses in the villages around here. What else can they do? They need something to live on, now that they've nothing of their own left. And just look at our government, they're so unfair that they fire upon our people to save the Muslims.'

Narang continued, 'Well, our government is at least giving some protection to the refugees. The Pakistani government couldn't care less for any of their people. Our government is also trying to have the Muslim convoys reach Pakistan safely. But, bhai, neither side has been less cruel than the other. Very large numbers of Muslims have been massacred in the east as well. The road to Amritsar is strewn with dead bodies.'

Narang began a lecture on the virtues of patience, 'Go and shave. There's a communal water tap over there, have a bath. It's difficult to recognize you. Gives one a bad feeling, as if someone's in mourning. And in that beard, someone could take you for a Muslim and stick a knife in you.'

Puri replied that his trunk with his clothes and shaving kit had been lost.

Narang said, 'Why do you think you have no friends left? You can have Jaggi's safety razor.'

Beyji spoke to someone behind her back, 'Urmi dear, get up. Give kakaji your brother's shaving things. Get up now. How're you feeling? *Channa*, you'll feel worse if you keep on lying like this.'

A girl lying curled up, her face and head covered with a dupatta, put a hand on the floor to prop herself up and got to her feet. She went quietly to a corner and opened a suitcase.

Narang, sitting cross-legged as before, with one hand massaging his foot, said, 'Shave and have a bath at the tap. No one bothers about privacy here. There are no bathrooms. Women also bathe openly at the tap, but what can anyone do? You're a man.'

Beyji said to Urmila, '*Dhiye*, you go and have a bath too. Just look at you. Wash your hair. I'll hold a sheet around you to give you some privacy.'

Puri asked, 'Have Jagdish and Praveen gone out?'

'Yes. I have this bloody diabetes as you know. My insulin ran out. Only two injections left. Jagdish went to look for my medicine. Praveen was getting bored sitting around, he too went along.'

Puri glanced at Urmila. If he had seen her anywhere else, he would have never given her a second glance, much less recognized her. The golden-brown curls that spilled over her forehead, that refused to stay covered by her dupatta, now looked like strands of old rope. Her fair skin looked pale and lacklustre. Those eyes that had sparkled with youthful mischief, she had not raised even once to look at Puri. Her head lowered, she quietly took out the razor, shaving soap and brush from the suitcase.

Puri began to shave off his beard. Narang sat describing the dangers faced by people in his gali, '... even women were carrying pistols.'

Puri's thoughts had turned from his own problems to Urmila. What could have happened to her? That irrepressible spring of love had turned into a dirty puddle of tears!

He nicked himself under the nose.

After he had shaved, his face again began to look like that of someone people would recognize as Puri. He had a bath at the tap. He tied a bed sheet around his waist as a lungi, took off the trousers and shirt, and rinsed them to get rid of some of the sweat. He hung his clothes to dry in the veranda, spread out his bed, and lay down. He was feeling hungry, but fatigue brought on sleep.

It was quite dark when he awoke. One family had lit a hurricane lantern, and a candle glowed in another spot. The rest of the people lay or sat in the darkened veranda. The door to the room where the Narang family was staying was closed. Small cooking fires had been lit in the field in front of the veranda. In their dim glow Puri could see that bricks meant for the construction of an extension to the building had been used to build makeshift fireplaces. The delectable smell of chapattis cooking filled the air. The family with the candle sat with chapattis in their hands, having a meal.

Puri had had two chapattis around eight in the morning. He had been walking most of the day, and now he was feeling very hungry. He looked at his wristwatch. It was 9 o'clock.

The city bazaar was over a mile from Islamia College. What to do about food? He thought of going back to sleep, but the hunger pangs were getting harder to ignore. He knew he wouldn't be able to fall asleep. He got up, removed the sheet from around his waist, and put on his still damp shirt and trousers. He put back in his pocket the money that he had tucked in the waist of the lungi for safekeeping, and rolled up his bedding.

The grandson of the old Sikh couple from Kamoki was crying. They were both taking turns to cradle and rock him in their arms.

Puri said very politely to the old man, 'Sardarji, I haven't eaten since morning. I'm just going up to the bazaar. My bed is over here. Please keep an eye on it.'

'Don't worry, babu,' the old man said. 'May Waheguru help you, and help us all. He looks after everyone. I'll keep an eye on it.'

Puri turned right onto Jarnaili Road at the gate of the college, and began walking towards the bazaar. He had difficulty keeping on the road in the pitch dark. He could see some lights in the distance, and the glow of the city on the horizon. Those bright points of light made the darkness around Puri even denser. He had walked about a hundred yards when he heard, 'Babu, what time is it?'

Puri stopped and raised his wristwatch to his eyes to look at the time, but found he could not speak.

A vice-like grip tightened around his neck, and a knifepoint was touching his nose. He was stunned. He heard, 'Take off your watch! Don't make a sound!'

Puri was breathing hard. With his right hand he began removing the watch from his left wrist. The man held the knife next to Puri's face and pulled out the fountain pen from his shirt pocket with his other hand, patted his shirt pocket and then the pockets of his trousers. Along with 23 rupees 7 annas and 5 paisas, Puri also parted with the key to his lost trunk.

As he took off his watch, Puri had been able to steady himself. He gathered enough courage to say, 'I'm a Hindu... just like you.'

'Everyone's a Hindu here. I myself lost everything. And now I have to feed my family.'

What could Puri say? The man who had robbed him lifted a bicycle lying on the ground. He threatened Puri once more, 'Careful! Not a sound!' He got on the bicycle and began pedalling in the direction of the city.

Puri stood for a few moments in silence, and then turned back helplessly towards the college. He unrolled his bed again, and lay down in despair, holding his head between his hands. The mewling baby nearby, the pangs of hunger, the hurt and humiliation of being robbed, all drove sleep away. And he had no way of knowing how much of the night had passed and how much was left. No point now in thinking what he'd do the next day.

A clamour of voices woke him up. As he shook sleep away, the light of the morning sun shining into his eyes dazzled him. He shaded his eyes with his hand, as his ears picked out one voice:

'You're a weird one! The baby's been crying from hunger since yesterday, and you haven't said a word to anybody! If you did, who would be so stony-hearted as to let the baby go hungry while they had a feed themselves? Here, take these leftovers and feed him. And how long will you starve yourself? We have to go through what Waheguru wants us to. One can't quarrel with Parmeshwar. Your fate is no different from what has been suffered by hundreds of thousands of others. No use crying over it. The government has fixed a free daily ration of a quarter seer of wheat and one-sixteenth of a seer of lentils a head in all the camps. Go and collect yours, cook it and have a meal. Why feel ashamed? How long can you afford such feelings, my good man?'

There were several people speaking, but Puri still heard the old woman's sobbing voice, 'I've been telling him since yesterday that if it's the will of God, of Waheguru, what can he or I do to change it? What can I do when he refuses to listen?'

The old man said in a voice choked with tears, 'Am I a cripple, a beggar or a fakir? I'm a farmer, and have been all my life. My limbs are still strong. Never in my life have I eaten without setting aside the shares for a Brahmin, a *nai*, the poor and the fakirs, and before feeding ten others. Now you want me to go and beg for wheat? If you have become so shameless, go and get it yourself.'

As Puri sat up to shade his eyes from the bright sunlight, his head moved into the shadow. As he looked around, he understood the reason for the hubbub. While he was sleeping, more people had arrived and occupied the remaining places. He turned his head to look at the room where the Narang family was staying.

Narang was sitting, as usual, cross-legged on his dhurrie, smoking a cigarette. He had shaved and washed. Beyji was making paranthas over a makeshift fireplace beside the wall of the veranda. The appetizing smell of food fried in ghee spread all around. 'Namaste, Puri *bhraji*,' Praveen called out. He was eating a parantha in a small thali. Urmila was lying on one side, beside a wall, her face turned away.

Narang's eyes met Puri's. He flicked ash through the door into the veranda, in Puri's direction. He spoke softly so that only Puri could hear, 'Just look at the differences between these two different individuals, bhai. Hooray for the old-timer! He's a real Sikh. His young sons murdered, his womenfolk kidnapped, all his belongings looted, but he's not going to beg for a quarter of a seer of wheat. Then there are those who have turned begging into a fine art. They take advantage of their own and other people's misfortune. And they don't just beg honestly! They concoct such lies: They'd say with a sad expression, "We're from a well-off and respectable family. To beg we are ashamed, we feel like drowning ourselves in embarrassment. Our bullock cart is not far from here, just around the corner. There are ten of us, including women and children. We were robbed on the way here..."

'Another will say, "One of our two oxen was injured on the way here. Somehow it dragged the cart this far before collapsing. Please help us. Note down our address. Once we're back in our village, we'll send you back by money order whatever you give us." Others will tell you, "Whatever we managed to bring with us has been stolen in the camp..."'

Someone called loudly from the direction of the college gate, 'Hey Dhaniramma! Oye Mohan Singha! Hey, people, come quickly! Come and see the parade of Muslim women!'

Several people ran towards the gate.

How could Puri talk about the previous night's incident after hearing all this? The Narangs were the only people he knew in the whole camp. He felt dizzy and faint from hunger and frustration. He didn't know what to do next. Sitting on his backside wouldn't get him anywhere, but where could he go, and for what purpose? The first thing was to get his strength back by getting something into his stomach.

He bit his lip to control himself and suppress the pain in his heart, and stood up. The bedding that he had found so burdensome was now his only resource. The only way to get any money was to hawk the bedding in the bazaar next to the station. The blanket alone had cost him eighteen rupees, only a year before. There were also the dhurrie, two sheets, and a pillow.

Even if he got eight or ten rupees for it, Puri thought, how long would that money last him? But at this time, that was a considerable sum. Afterwards, he'd think of something, even do manual labour for a daily wage. Everyone wanted to work, but there was nobody to offer wages in exchange. Maybe he should go to Delhi, he thought. Several people had travelled on the train without a ticket, so why should he buy one?

He made a roll of his bedding, picked it up, and said to Narang, 'Achcha, namaste. I'm off.'

Narang flicked ash from his cigarette before replying, 'Going to the bazaar? Go ahead, but why carry this load with you? Leave it with us. One of us is always here.'

'No, it's not much of a load. I may go further.' Puri cut short their talk, and stepped down from the veranda. Another man from the veranda was leading the old women towards the centre for distribution of free rations.

Puri came out of the gate of the college and turned on to the same road he had taken the night before. The dense darkness had given way to shimmering sunlight. Now there was no cause for fear. Having had nothing to eat, he felt weak and had trouble walking. The sun felt searing and uncomfortable. Just down the Jarnaili Road, before the scattered houses began, he saw along the roadside small pyramids of wheat, piles of green and red chillies and other vegetables, and firewood heaped up for sale.

Puri had noticed that a number of men were clustered around something beside the wall of a house. He could hear snatches of several voices. A man standing in the centre was saying:

'Thirty-five! Thirty-five! Thirty-five rupees! ... Any more bids? ... Going for thirty-five! Thirty-five once, thirty-five twice. Any other bids before I accept this bid? ... Have a good look, folks! Come on! Sold to this bidder for thirty-five rupees!'

An auction was taking place, Puri decided. Why trudge another two miles to the station? he thought. Why not put his bedding up for auction here? He walked up. As he came closer, he heard the auctioneer's voice call more distinctly:

'All right, baadshaho! What am to I bid for this? Brand new, unused stuff! Check it over for yourself if you don't believe me!'

The crowd let out loud guffaws.

The auctioneer called out again, 'All right, let's have the first bid.'

Puri peered through the wall of people.

In the centre of the circle stood the auctioneer, forcing a young woman to stand upright by holding the plait of her hair. The woman was naked. The man thrust his knee into the small of her back and arched her body forward, so that the bidders could see all parts of the merchandise, and pulled her hands away from her tear-stained face. Her eyes were closed. The skin of her body where it had never been exposed to the sun was rosier than her face, and supple and translucent like the inner skin of a freshly peeled orange. Several young women sat slouching on the ground, their arms around their knees, their faces hidden in their hands. Their clothes lay beside them. Puri stepped back involuntarily.

An angry male voice rose above the noisy lewd laughter, 'What do you think you're doing? Have some shame! Think of what'll become of these poor women! If you dishonour them like this, what respectable person will want to take them in? It'd be better if you just twisted their necks and threw them away. How are you better than the *Musaltahs*—Muslims? What crime have they committed is not worse than what you're doing now.'

'That's right! He's right! The old man talks sense! Yes, have some shame!' Some voices said in support of the accuser.

Puri bit his lip to control himself as he went back to the road, his head bent, and began walking towards the station. He felt faint and sick with hunger, and stars swam before his eyes. How his blood had boiled in anger, he recalled, when he read the news that Hindu women were paraded naked. When both sides had proved their manliness by doing unmentionable things to women, how could either claim to be any less brutal? Why should they take second place in this contest to display inhumanity?

He remembered what the right-thinking man had said: If you dishonour them like this, what respectable person will take them in? The women's only crime was that they had been abused. Men can commit heinous and revolting acts, and women have to suffer the consequences! Women have to be both a target for his cruelty and his lust.

Puri spread out his dhurrie in the bazaar that had sprung up across from the station, arranged the blanket, sheets and pillow on it, and sat down. He did not know how to sell anything by crying his wares, as was necessary. He would say timidly to those who went past, 'Almost new stuff, bhai. Going cheap.'

People with their belongings perched on their heads, over their shoulders, or on their backs, came and went past him without paying any attention. The sun was getting hotter. Sometimes a person would reply before walking away, 'It's already a problem to carry around what we have.'

The afternoon was at its height. Puri pressed his hands on his temples to lessen a splitting headache. The pangs of hunger were becoming unbearable. No one had offered to buy his bedding; neither for eight, nor for five rupees, nor at any price. Spells of dizziness were making him sick.

'What's happening to me?' he gritted his teeth and scolded himself. 'What's become of me? I should be ashamed of myself. Is this any way to behave after going without food for only thirty-six hours? Why? I've been on hunger strike in prison for three days, for seventy-two hours. Over 200 fellowprisoners staged that strike along with me. What's wrong with me now? In prison they would tempt us with all kinds of food, and we never even looked at it. But what strength of conviction do I have now? That was a moral struggle, we wanted to defeat the enemy by the strength of our higher ideals! That was not when there was nothing to eat, like now.'

Pangs of hunger and a nagging, throbbing headache almost made him pass out. He needed an anna or two to buy some medicine for his headache. Images drifted through his delirious mind … he should join the crowd of lame, crippled and blind beggars hovering outside the station, and hold out his hand to beg, saying, 'Will some kind soul give this poor person a paisa or two for medicine? My head is bursting with pain.' And some kind person just might give him something to reap the reward of doing a meritorious act. A feeling of self-disgust overwhelmed him, 'What am I turning into?'

He could barely see because of the throbbing pain in his head, but he made a determined effort and rolled up his bedding. He lifted himself by pushing off the ground with one hand. With the bedding under his arm, he went in search of the distribution centre where free ration was being doled out.

The khadi-clad gentleman handing out bowlfuls of wheat and handfuls of lentils kept repeatedly asking the eager recipients standing in a queue to be patient. He also warned them, 'Brothers, don't be dishonest and unscrupulous by taking your share twice. Anyone doing that would be committing a sin, if any other brother or sister has to go empty-handed.'

Someone from the crowd said approvingly, 'Yes bhai, aren't we being punished enough already for the sins of our past life? Who knows what more suffering is to come upon us if we commit the sin of fraud here?'

'Be content with this free offering, bhai, be patient. This is the blessing of independence!' Another person used sarcasm to lighten the pain.

'What use is this independence,' someone else complained bitterly, 'when we have to beg for a bowl of wheat?'

'The Congresswallahs have gained power. Now they'll gain merit by doling out bowlfuls of wheat!' the jester said again, and roared with laughter.

Puri stood looking at the speakers as others behind him in the queue moved past him.

It was around five in the afternoon when Tara's alert ears picked up Hafizji's voice from the sitting room, 'Beta Qamaroo, listen!'

The sound of Qamaroo's heavy footsteps followed as she went downstairs. Then Tara heard Qamaroo coming back, her tread making the grating resonate as she walked over it to the veranda beside the kitchen, and spoke to her mother and grandmother. Qamaroo came over to Tara quickly and said as she tried to catch her breath, 'The police are waiting in the gali. They've come to take you to the camp.'

Tara rose at once, wrapping her dupatta around her head and shoulders. Khursheed and her mother-in-law had not risen to bid her farewell. Tara looked at them, made the gesture of namaste silently, and went downstairs.

Through the door to the sitting room she saw Hafizji sitting in an armchair. Tara salaamed him, lowering her eyes respectfully.

'May Allah be kind to you,' Hafizji gave his blessing in a sad voice, without getting up.

Tara moved aside the curtain hanging over the front door of the house. She saw a young man waiting for her in the gali. He was not in uniform, but had the air of a policeman. He wore a slightly dirty, silky shirt, a white shalwar, and a police-like khaki turban with its fringe shaped to form a fan. Like a police officer, he also carried a baton.

Seeing Tara the man asked, 'You're the one that has to go to the camp?'

Tara nodded.

'The transport is waiting,' the man pointed to the exit of the gali.

Tara did not find the look on the man's face very reassuring, but she had never heard of anybody, anywhere, being comforted by the sight of a policeman. Now that they had agreed, after her repeated demands, to release her from Hafizji's house, how could she express any unwillingness to leave?

A battered jeep was parked near the gali entrance, with another man sitting in one of the back seats, wearing a high fur hat. The ends of his moustache were curled up like the tail of a scorpion. He too wore a khaki police shirt, but without any insignia on the epaulets. In her nervousness Tara did not notice that fine detail. She was told to sit in the back, across from the man in the khaki shirt. The other man sat beside her.

After she took her seat, Tara noticed a shallow wicker basket on the floor. Four chickens, their feet tied with torn strips of cloth, lay on their sides in it. Their shiny black red-rimmed beady eyes were fixed on Tara, and their mute expression of helplessness and resignation pierced her heart like a knife. When they blinked, the opaque membrane over their eyes made them appear even more vulnerable. Her own pain and the humiliation of having her hands tied behind her back flashed past her mind.

The jeep went through the bazaar and reached the main road, where it picked up speed. Tara kept her head lowered, but she was looking out of the corner of her eyes. She was not quite sure what part of the city they were in. After going some way further she thought they were heading towards the bridge over the Ravi River.

Tara began to panic. Another trap! She gathered the courage to protest, 'I want to go to the D.A.V. College camp. This way goes to Ravi.'

'That camp is full,' the man sitting next to her said. 'We've been told to take you to the camp at Shahdara.'

A smile creased the face of the man with the fur hat sitting across from Tara. She did not like that look, but what could she do?

Baluch soldiers with fan-shaped crests on top of their khaki turbans, holding bayoneted rifles guarded a barrier on the road to the bridge. They motioned the jeep to stop. The man with the fur hat jumped out and walked over. He gave them a salaam, and exchanged a few words with them before the jeep was allowed to cross the bridge.

Tara had been to the tomb of Jehangir in Shahdara across the Ravi three times with her college friends. When the jeep kept on going past the tombs of Jehangir and Noorjehan, Tara again protested, 'We've passed Shahdara!'

'Shut up!' The man sitting across from her ordered gruffly.

Tara shivered. She knew she had again fallen into the hands of another Nabbu.

'Stop! I don't want to go with you!' She said as assertively as she could.

'Be quiet, you mother…' he growled at her, uttering an obscenity.

Tara realized that death was her only way of escape, and jerked her body around to throw herself out of the jeep. The man sitting next to her wrapped his arm around her and pulled her back.

Tara punched him in the face in an attempt to free herself. The man sitting across leaned forward and held her down by seizing her shoulders. The first man pushed her head down on his knees and leant his weight on her. She sank her teeth into his knee.

The man pulled hard at her plait to free his knee. Both men pushed her face and shoulders into the basket on top of the chickens, pressed her down with their knees, and dealt several sharp punches to her back.

Ever since the dreadful experiences of her wedding night, Tara's sleep had been fitful and troubled. At Hafizji's house she often had strange and terrifying nightmares about being dragged by the hands and feet, and about crying out for help while fighting to defend herself. Breaking out of sleep, she would lie in a cold sweat of terror.

When she opened her eyes, she saw the blurred outlines of an unfamiliar aangan around her. The skin on her face felt raw, her head spun and ached. She had again woken up after a nightmare, she felt. When she opened her eyes a little more, she saw three women who seemed to be fighting. One was completely naked, the second wore only a shalwar, and the third had on only a kameez that came to her knees. There were two other women wearing shalwar and kameez. None wore a dupatta. Tara shook her head to make sure she was not dreaming, and thought, 'Where am I?'

She propped herself on one arm and rose to a sitting position, drawing her knees up to her chest. For some time, she sat looking around with eyes blurred from a splitting headache. This was real and not a dream, she finally realized. The naked woman and the one in the kameez were fighting over something that apparently had to do with her. After listening to them, Tara vaguely understood that while she was unconscious, one of the women wanted to take some of her clothes.

The woman wearing the kameez challenged the naked woman, 'You thief! Now she's conscious, and sitting up. Let's see you take off her clothes now!'

The woman wearing only the shalwar spoke in defence of the naked woman, 'Who do you think you are! The village chief?' she said to the woman in the kameez, 'Why are you interfering? Are you a thanedaar?' The other two women also spoke up, but against the naked woman and the one with the shalwar.

The woman in the kameez came over to Tara. She put one hand on Tara's shoulder, and placing a can of water to her lips with the other, said, 'Drink some.'

Tara looked at it with distaste and turned her face away.

'Have some. It'll cool you down. Make you feel better.'

She had spoken to Tara tenderly, but her voice became harsh again when she replied to the woman in the shalwar, 'You were on the side of that thief! Just look at you! You wanted me to help you so that I too would become involved. Only you and I can feel some shame, but not her? What happened when she,' she pointed to the naked woman, 'took your kameez and put it on? How did you fight with her then! Why didn't you give your kameez to her? You tore the kameez to pieces. Neither she nor you could use it. Now you're supporting her! Have you no shame?'

Tara gradually pieced together the whole story that while she was unconscious, the naked woman wanted to steal Tara's kameez for herself. Banti, the kameez-wearing woman, prevented this. The naked woman had offered Banti Tara's shalwar, but she had refused to be a party to this dishonesty.

Tara gave Banti a look of gratitude.

The clothed women went and sat in the front of the room on the right of the aangan, and the naked and the half-naked women on the threshold of the room on the left. Banti remained beside Tara, urging her to take a few sips from the can. Tara's throat was parched, her tongue felt like a strip of dry leather, but she could not make herself swallow even a mouthful. The women continued to quarrel for a long time, and then sprawled out on the aangan floor and began to doze.

Tara sat for along time, her chin resting on her knees, assessing her new situation. It was clear that Amjad had removed her from Hafizji's house and sent her here. And that she would have to remain here for some time.

It was a brick house. A half-moon, shining brightly overhead among puffy clouds, was gradually setting towards the west. About a quarter of the aangan was still visible in the moonlight. The aangan floor was also made of bricks. In one corner was a handpump. Rooms on either side. The sleeping women, with their faces or the backs of their heads resting on the ground, looked like corpses, face down and face up. The sounds of their breathing and snoring were the only evidence of their being alive.

Tara sat slumped in the centre of the aangan, where she had come out of her faint, thinking, sometimes staring into the dark and sometimes with her eyes closed, about all that had happened to her and was still happening. Then, cramped by her position, she too rolled over and stretched out on the floor. The moonlight became a wedge at the bottom of the wall, and then disappeared. The sky was filled with stars. She would begin to drift off, and then be awakened by the bites of mosquitoes. Then she would detect an overpowering stench all around. Her dupatta, that she could have drawn over her to protect herself from mosquitoes and could have wrapped around her nose against the stench, was gone.

In her half-waking state, she sensed the stars beginning to dim. Darkness began to fade as dawn drew near. Soon she was able to make out various objects scattered around the aangan. In one corner, next to the drain outlet in the wall, lay the badly battered bottom half of a light-brown tin trunk. Its top lay a few feet away. Also the remains of two tin containers, lidless. Pieces of clay pottery and *maratbans*, glazed clay jars, ropes and torn chatais lay about. Two broken pieces of mirror glass glinted dully. As it got brighter, she could see grains of wheat, rice and lentils wedged among the bricks of the floor. Two rooms had no doors. Evidence of looting and destruction was everywhere.

Tara had still not moved. She was staring idly in the direction of the drain outlet and the bottom half of the trunk. Banti came into view carrying a can full of water. She turned her back towards Tara, and sat over the drain to relieve herself. Tara turned her face away in surprise and disgust.

Seeing Tara turn her face away, one of the women wearing shalwar-kameez said in the dialect of western Punjab, 'What else can one do? We can't get out of this aangan. The door to the stairs up to the roof is locked. What can we do? We're managing as best we can.'

Tara, her face turned away, said nothing.

'Satwant, pump up some water for me. Let me also scrub this can,' said Banti to the woman as she walked over to the handpump.

Satwant went over to the pump and worked its loose and rusty handle up and down. Clackety-clack! Clickety-clack! it screeched. Banti rubbed her hands on the brick floor, as if it was gravel, to scrub them clean, and tried to clean the can, as if it was a utensil, also by scraping it on the floor.

Unmindful of the other women, Banti took off her kameez and handed it to Satwant. Satwant worked the pump as Banti sat under the spout of water, rubbing and rinsing her body, and chanting:

Har-har gange, kashi vishwanath gange
Nahatya dhotyan gai balaa, dharati mata da tikka la

After her wash was over, she sprinkled some water on her kameez, mumbling:

Naha-dho main chadi chaubare
Utton mile mainu Krishna pyare

She went to a corner, sat down and began to say her prayers.

Even in her present circumstances Banti continued to observe her customary rituals as best she could. Whilst still saying her prayers, she came back and sat beside Tara, and said, 'Sister, you've been sitting in the same spot since yesterday evening. Haven't even had one sip of water. What good will it do to you if you don't eat or drink anything? Your suffering will increase, not lessen, if you get sick. You're not at home, so don't expect your family or relatives to feel bad and coax you if you don't eat or drink anything. What will happen is only what the Parmeshwar Maharaj wants to happen. Get up and have a wash, and drink some water. I'll fetch you some.'

Banti's kind voice brought tears to Tara's eyes. She replied slowly, through her parched tongue and lips, 'Bahinji, it's true that no one knows when sickness and death might come, but why doesn't death come to take me away! I've even given up trying to die. The only thing I want to do is die.'

'Bahina, dying or living is not in the hands of us humans,' Banti said. 'You think you're the only one that has suffered and endured? Sister, nobody came here in as good a condition as you. I can see the state you're in, and I too have been through it, and have seen others suffer. We human beings always feel our own pain to be the greatest. Just look at others! You were only kidnapped. The only damage you suffered is this slight bruising of your face. Those brutes probably didn't treat their own sisters and mothers that well. You've no idea what others have gone through, *na?*'

Banti sat with her chin propped on her knees as she spoke, 'Maybe it's no use saying it now, but let me tell you, when we heard that all the Hindus had fled from the neighbouring Dabboki village, we too got ready to leave. The Shaikhs living next to us told us to stay. They were the ones who brought all this suffering down on us. They never harmed us, that much is true. They always said that they'd help us. But God only knows what was in their hearts. The Pathans from the villages of Dabboki and Kachherian surrounded our joint home of five Hindu families in Chammoki village. We were thirty-six in all, counting all the men, women and children. There must have been five hundred of them, with swords, spears, hatchets and lathis in their hands. Baqar, of Dabboki, was their leader. What can I tell you, that scoundrel was one of our workers.

'Not only Baqar, sister, we used to help everyone and anyone in the villages around ours. What farmer or landowner didn't go to Hindus to borrow money? You know what they say, that they're not Muslims if they're not in debt! Hameedu, that scoundrel Baqar's father, was such a nice person. There never was any problem as long as he was alive. At the time of both harvests, he himself brought grain, raw cotton, a couple of seers of ghee, whatever he could give, as the interest on his loan. But not only him, they were all good to us. You know, be nice to people, and they'll be nice to you. When Shahji had to go to the railway station, Hameedu would bring his mare around the moment he found out. Shahji would ride his mare, and Hameedu would carry his bundle on his head up to the station. If we paid him a couple of annas, or a seer or two of grain, he accepted it gratefully. Never said a word of complaint. Used to say, 'I'm in debt to you for your generosity. If I'm ungrateful, how will I face Khuda on the Judgement Day?' And look at this Baqar, the same Hameedu's son. Just because he's learned how to read and write, it has turned his head. It's these city mullahs who went to villages and added fuel to the fire. And that scoundrel himself has been nothing but a thief and a robber since he grew up. He was the one leading them, the shameless creature.

'Pali Shah said to him, "Take whatever you want from our houses. Just spare us and our children's lives."

'They all assured us, "Give us all your weapons. Just take a few clothes, whatever jewellery the women are wearing, and enough cash to see you through wherever you want to go, and come to the well under the peepal tree. We'll escort you to the station. Sister, what else could we do? They had all those weapons, guns too.'

Satwant, covering her left eye with one hand, had come to sit next to them. She interrupted Banti, 'Bahina, the men of our village really fought back. The elder Sardarji in our family had a gun. Sodhi sahib is an army pensioner. He too had several guns. A crowd of thousands of Turks from the neighbouring villages followed our caravan for over ten miles. The sardars did not allow any one to come near. When we reached the railway station, the Muslim soldiers asked the men to surrender their guns, and allowed us to be attacked and robbed after we had boarded the train.' She broke into loud sobs.

As Satwant wiped tears from her right eye, Tara was able to see her left eye. It was covered with a white film, and bulging. Satwant was ashamed of her deformity even in this distress.

Banti resumed her story without taking any heed of Satwant's tears, 'When all the five families gathered at the well, the Pathans surrounded us. The Shaikhs of our village also had a change of heart. They too sided with the crowd. Two ruffians of our village, Anwar and Liakat, joined Baqar. 'Ya Ali! Allahu Akabar!' they began yelling.

'You can imagine!' Banti dabbed her eyes. 'With all that crowd around us.

'Baqar said, "All young women to one side."

'Chacha Pali Shah begged him with folded hands, "Let us go, beta. Remember the promise you made to us."

'Baqar lifted the hatchet in his hand and struck Pali Shah on the neck. Blood gushed out. Pali Shah was dead before he could utter a sound. All of us were trembling like a leaf.

'Baqar began to drag away my husband's youngest sister Kasho. She clung to me, and I put my arm around her. Liakat gave a shove to both of us, saying, "Let's take her too." I had my son Jaggi in my other arm. He got frightened and cried out. My mother-in-law took him from me....'

Satwant again interrupted, removing her hand from her eye, 'I took my Mihinder and hid behind the trunks in the train compartment. When those butchers found me and pulled me out, they snatched the boy from my arms and threw him to the ground...' Satwant beat her head with her hands and wailed, calling out the name of her son.

Banti continued, ignoring the wailing woman, 'Prodding and pushing our men with lathis and hatchet butts, they ordered, "Get away at once! Those who do not leave quietly, those who turn around even to look, will be cut to pieces." Everyone began walking away. Left behind were three young wives, and the three girls—Kasho, Satto and Phoola. They pulled children from the arms of the captives, and tossed them after the people who were leaving.

'We just stood there, trembling and crying, and watching them leave. As our families were disappearing from sight, Baqar said, "Keep the three girls separately. Consider them as the spoils of jihad. Any pious follower of the Faith, who wants to marry them, may take one.' He pulled at Satto's arm, 'This one's mine.'

'She wrenched her arm free. The well was close by. She jumped into it.

'Phoola too tried, but Anwar hit her with a lathi and she fell to the ground. You know, a girl is only a girl.' Banti wiped her tears with tips of her fingers, and flicked them off. 'Kasho and Phoola were crying and struggling as they were taken away. I prayed to Baqar with joined hands, "Brother, those are your sisters."

'Baqar cursed at me, "She thinks herself to be somebody. Let's take care of her." He hit me in the chest with the butt of his hatchet and I fell.

'Liakat too swore at me, "She thinks she's so high and mighty." I sometimes used to scold that badmaash. Whenever he came to our aangan to collect the laundry or to ask for some buttermilk, he would make lewd gestures at Satto. I not only told him off, but said to his mother too, "Don't send him to our place." Liakat was ripping my clothes off, so I pulled at his hair to ward him off. They all jumped on me. What can I say? I lashed out with my hands and feet, but what could a woman do to fight off such hefty men? Those bullies tied up my feet and hands, then tore off all my clothes. Can't tell you how they hurt me, in front of all that crowd, with hatchet handles and the ends of lathis. I just fainted.' Banti covered her eyes with her hands and sobbed loudly.

Satwant had again covered her bad eye with her hand. She said, 'Bahina, what woman was spared? Those animals didn't treat women as women. May they all die childless, and may nobody be left in their family to mourn them. It would've been better if they'd just slit our throats. No words can tell what we went through. Only for the last five days, since coming here, can I say that my body hasn't been abused.' She continued to cover her bad eye, as if the bitterest of all the sufferings visited upon her was the shame of having an ugly eye.

Banti used her palms to wipe the tears running down her cheeks, and said, 'When I came to again it was dark, around midnight. My hands and feet were still tied, and I was lying near the well. I kept on calling for water. I cried, I shouted, but no one answered. All around were the same neighbours who had been with us day and night, in happiness and in sorrow, in good times and bad. We used to spend all our time together, and did everything together except marry or eat with each other. How could they be so heartless?

'Kareemo came to draw water at daybreak. I begged her for a drink of water, but she filled her clay *ghara* pot and went away. Baqar's mother came quietly after some time, and threw this kameez on me. She'd brought some water with her in her lota. She lifted my head and poured some water into my mouth through the spout. I don't care if anyone thinks I lost my religion and faith. You can't lose it when you're not conscious. The poor woman also whispered into my ear, "Don't tell any one." My bonds were cutting into my flesh. I was crying and groaning constantly. Other women too came to fetch water, but not one even spared me a glance. Their hearts had turned to stone. They all used to come to our homes for festivities and for syapas, we always helped each other. And now such a change of heart!

'When the sun had risen, the man with the pointed moustache came, the same one who brought you here yesterday, he brings tandoori rotis for us too. The scoundrel brought nothing to eat yesterday. That other old slut didn't show up yesterday either. The same man arrived and untied my hands and feet. My circulation had been cut off, and I couldn't move them. And how could I cover myself? He grabbed my arm and pulled me up, but I couldn't stand on my feet. Satto was lying dead, with her clothes wet and covered in mud, next to the chabutara around the well. Her stomach was bloated. I began to crawl towards the well to escape that scoundrel. What else could anybody do, bahina? He pushed me to the ground and swore at me, saying, "All these Hindanis know is how to jump into the well." He growled at me to put on my kameez. I barely managed to, so he pushed my arms into it. I could hardly move my limbs. He was dragging me away, but I couldn't even keep steady on my feet. When I couldn't walk, he carried me for a while by hoisting me onto his shoulder, then got an ekka carriage and tossed me into it, and brought me here. I've been here since then.' Banti felt her stomach gingerly, 'My insides are hurt so badly I can't tell you. I'm hardly able to walk straight.' She started weeping again.

While Banti was talking, the rickety pump had been squeaking in the background. The woman wearing only a shalwar had taken it off and handed it to the woman in shalwar and kameez. While one pumped water, the other washed herself. While scrubbing her body the woman also chanted some prayer. After her bath, the shalwar-only woman too came and squatted near Tara, Banti and Satwant.

The woman in the shalwar said, 'Why should I tell any lies? The Muslims of our Noorcote village really helped us. Only three houses belonged to Hindus. When the Muslims from Siddhawali tried to provoke our villagers to attack us, those good people quietly brought us on ekkas to the Pamba station at night. Our train was attacked after it reached Kamoki station. What happened to the others, I have no idea. They pulled me out of the carriage. My ten-month-old son slipped from my lap. What became of him, no one knows.' she began to weep bitterly.

She said again after a few moments, through the tears streaming down her face, 'Who knows how many girls and women were kidnapped and taken away in ekkas? Who knows where they were taken? What they did to me, I lost count of that after ten or fifteen times. May God infest my attackers' bodies with worms. I didn't think I'd live, but I came through it somehow. And no one thought of giving me a mouthful of food. Who doesn't get hungry, bahina? I was dying of hunger and my breasts were aching with milk, and they kept abusing my body ...' she sobbed uncontrollably.

Satwant said to the woman wearing only a shalwar, 'Durga, help Amaro wash herself.'

'I told her, have a bath. "Not now," she said,' Durga suppressed her sobs as she replied. 'She has a fever.'

Satwant said with concern, 'Yes, it's better if she doesn't. Her body did feel hot. She's the daughter-in-law of the Sodhis from our village. Don't know what's been done to her. They took me away from the station. I saw her next two days ago when she was brought here. Hasn't said a word till now. Poor thing's had bad luck. Since she's come, we've had nothing to eat. Indeed she's unlucky. Comes from a poor farmer's family. The Sodhis married her only because of her good looks, but her luck didn't change. It was her five-month-old son those butchers at the station first threw on the ground and killed in front of us. I had hidden my Mihinder behind the boxes.'

Sunlight covered the top half of the wall on the left. Banti said again to Tara, 'Get up now. Come on, I'll work the pump for you. Have a bath. You're not the only one who's suffering.' She pointed to the sky, 'He who damned us to this hell, the same Almighty One will get us out. He answered Draupadi's call for help; He'll listen to ours too. His power is great. Have a wash and a mouthful to eat. I have half of a roti. Wonder when did you last have anything to eat? That scoundrel didn't get us anything to eat yesterday. Let's see if God sends us anything today or not. You have got any scraps left?' Banti said, looking at Satwant.

'Hai, I've nothing left. I saved half a roti, but I ate it last night,' replied Satwant.

'Go on, you liar!' Durga protested, 'I saw you taking three rotis from the pile. I know where you hid what was left over. Don't share if you don't want to.'

'You're a liar! I don't have anything,' Satwant retorted angrily.

'Anybody who hides food eats her own children,' Durga shouted angrily.

Ignoring their quarrel, Banti stood up, using Tara's shoulder as a prop, 'Come, have a wash.'

Three women had taken baths in the nude right in front of Tara. She felt shy about taking off her clothes, but prudishness at this time would have been an insult to the others.

Crouching down, she took off her shalwar shyly and put it on the ground. Banti took the shalwar and tucked it under her arm, saying, "You probably don't know it, but this caused the whole argument. That awful Lakkhi can't be trusted. When Durga was having a wash, she stole her kameez. It got ripped to pieces when they both fought over it. She was brought here totally naked. She neither talks to us, nor sits with us. Mostly stays inside the room. Always on the lookout to steal a garment when someone takes it off.'

Durga said, 'She seems to have a screw loose. She just lies there babbling, "I'm not the only one ... all of them, everyone!" Sometimes raves on, "I'm dead ... everyone's dead." Don't know what her village or town is. Talks like somebody from a city, from Gujranwala or Wazirabad area.'

Tara took off her kameez sitting under the pump. Her hesitation had attracted Satwant's attention. Pointing to Tara's brassiere, Satwant said, 'Hai, look at this city woman. Look, look how they tie up their bodies to shape them. Just like a nosebag over a calf's snout! These new fashions! How they push the tits up and thrust them forward. A curse on such women! They haven't a shred of shame or modesty in them!'

'Why are you turning up your nose? What's it to you what anybody wears or does? Everyone to his own customs,' Banti scolded her.

Tara, her head bent, kept silent.

After Tara had her bath, Banti broke a stale, dry tandoori roti in two and handed her a piece. Satwant came with two small pieces concealed in her hand. She gave them to Tara, and said, 'That's all I have, I swear by Waheguru. O Divine Protector, don't let us poor creatures starve.'

Tara did not feel like eating that dry, hard piece of bread. 'No, I'm not hungry,' she said, shaking her head.

'Why not hungry?' Banti reproached her lovingly. 'Eat up or you'll feel worse.'

'Isn't she picky! Does this city woman expect Waheguru to send paranthas made with ghee for her?' Satwant said sarcastically.

On Banti's insistence, Tara agreed, 'I'll eat a bit later.' She just took some water.

'The door chain is rattling,' Durga cried out in alarm. The women quickly moved inside the rooms. They waited for several minutes, but the door did not open.

Satwant said, 'She hears noises all the time. Who's likely to come in this blazing sunshine? The old slut always turns up with rotis in the late afternoon. That butcher brought food both times before midday.'

Banti said, 'When he brought me here, there were three other girls beside Lakkhi. Two days later, he came early one morning with two other men and took away those three. Only Maharajji knows what'll become of us. This *sirsara* cursed man is bound to sell us to someone.'

'Yes, what else? But if someone takes us in, at least it'll save us from being ruined and treated like garbage as before,' Satwant said gloomily.

Holding her head in her hands, Banti said, 'Who knows what Maharaj wanted to happen when He didn't let me die? He works in mysterious ways. He must have intended something else for me. Only He, who came out from the red-hot iron pillar to save Prahlad can save us too. If that brute sells me off to someone, I might decide to cut my throat with a sickle.' She sat quietly, clasping her head.

'The door chain *has* been opened,' it was Satwant's turn to cry out in alarm.

The thick, solid entrance door opened with a groan, then came the sound of it being shut again and a hoarse, rough voice said, 'Here I am, daughters! What could I do?'

An old woman walked into the view of those in the room. Her face was heavily wrinkled and she had henna-dyed hair. She carried on her head something bundled up in her dirty dupatta. She went on, 'He took the key from me two days ago and gave it back to me only today. I felt bad thinking that you girls would be starving.'

She placed the bundle on the floor. Opening it, she said, 'May Allah be kind to everyone and let no one go hungry. Today I had some salt added to the rotis.'

Satwant bent over the bundle. It had large, freshly made rotis baked in a tandoor. She picked up four.

The old woman rambled on, 'If it were up to me, I'd bring daal and vegetables for you all, but that heartless man doesn't want to pay for it. What do I have left now? Sometimes three, sometimes four girls used to stay with me. I used to feed them milk and ghee, *malai* and other good things. I'd do all that for you too if only I could.'

'Why did you take four? Are you the only one who's feeling hungry?' Banti asked Satwant.

'Yes, yes. Divide them equally, daughters. There are five of you, so I brought three for each. If these aren't enough, I'll bring a couple more. Who matters more, you or the bread? But what can I do? That bastard won't pay up,' the old women lamented.

'There are six of us,' Banti said to the old woman, and to Satwant, 'Divide them up equally among all of us.'

The old woman looked at Tara, 'Another one's arrived? May Allah protect her, *sadake*, welcome. But rotis are not more important than you girls,' she said. 'Tomorrow I'll bring three more.'

Banti said to Tara after the woman left, 'You're lucky. The rotis arrived just after you did.'

The brick floor had become quite hot by the noon hour. The women moved into the rooms that were still in the shade. They were chatting about various things when Satwant asked Tara, 'Bahin, have you any children?'

Tara shook her head.

'Haven't had any?'

'Hai, why? How many years since you got married?' Durga said in surprise.

Tara hesitated before answering, 'I'm not married.'

Satwant covered her left eye with her hand and looked distrustfully at Tara with her right, and asked, 'Hai, at your age? You city folk surely have such strange ways.'

'I was a college student,' Tara said, by way of explanation.

Durga held her fingers to her lips in amazement, and asked, 'What? You mean that big madrasa school?'

Tara nodded.

'So you learned English, Shastri Hindi, Farsi, all three lingos?' Durga asked.

When Tara said yes, the women stared at her with respect and some awe.

Durga began to repeat what she had already mentioned many times, that her baby girl had just cut her first two teeth. Tears began to flow down her cheeks as she described how the child had become sick from teething. She had not finished when Satwant began to tell how her son insisted on sitting on the horse with his father. That once he was injured when he fell off, and a lump had come up on his forehead. How she had to stay up several nights, holding him in her lap.

Banti too began to talk about her son, 'He was very fond of his grandmother, but always slept with me in my bed. I was always late, finishing the chores, cleaning up the kitchen, preparing milk for yogurt, but he would wait for me to put him to bed...'

She wiped her eyes, and continued, 'Maharajji gave me my first one a year and a quarter after my marriage, but took back that child after ten months. Maharaj did not show his mercy for the next five years. There was nothing wrong with me, but my mother-in-law was worried that someone in the family might have cast some evil spell. She took me to the Baba of Dipalpur. The Baba prophesied that I'd have a child within a year. And you know what? My Kewal was born after ten months.'

From talking about her son she went on to talk about her other misfortunes, 'When we heard about Hindus fleeing Dabboki, my mother-in-law put all our jewellery, mine and my sister-in-law's— the poor thing had died three years ago—in a brass *gagar*, all seventy tolas of gold, and buried it in the inside room of the house. We also had at least six or seven seers of silver ornaments, that our employees had left as collateral, locked up in heavy chests. The thugs must have stolen all that. Probably found the gold too! Who knows! Kewal's father and his elder brother had made a wad of a hundred and ten rupee banknotes, and a few of smaller value. Three thousand old silver coins, the ones with the Empress's face on them, those too were in those chests …'

It grew hotter in the afternoon. Durga yawned, and went to sleep in a side room. Amaro lay motionless as before, her eyes fixed on the ceiling. Banti and Satwant first lolled about on the floor then began to doze. Tara too stretched out. She closed her eyes, but could not sleep. The women's ramblings had kept her from thinking about her own situation. Now she began to give it serious thought. Her desire for freedom had brought her out of the frying pan into the fire. The captivity at Hafizji's now seemed like a safe haven, when compared to this hellish aangan. Now she didn't even know where she was.

The eyes of the trussed-up chickens lying in the wicker basket in the jeep flashed through Tara's mind. She and the five other women locked up were just like those birds, she felt. They could be done away with at any time, simply by twisting their necks, and served up to someone for their enjoyment. She remembered the tortures Banti, Satwant and Durga had gone through. Didn't these women realize the purpose behind their being imprisoned here? Were they willing to undergo even more humiliation and torture? God had forgotten about them, it seemed to Tara, but they hadn't forgotten Him. Human beings worried more about God than He did about them… Was there some way she could end her life? She had tried to kill herself by hammering her head against the wall, but all that happened was that she ended up by her knocking herself out. She lay for a long time wallowing in her thoughts.

When Tara opened her eyes, she saw the sunlight lingering on top of the eastern wall. The women had moved outside, now that the aangan was in the shade, and cooler.

Satwant pumped some water into the can, and sat down to eat a roti.

Banti called out to Tara, 'Bahin, just work this pump for me.' She sat under the spout and had a wash.

The twilight gave way to moonlight.

The women sat close together, and began telling their same old stories. As the night deepened, they lay about and drifted off to sleep. If any two awoke at the same time, they sat and talked to one another. Tara had passed the previous night in a semi-conscious state, but this night seemed much longer and harder to get through. She would lie down, then sit up, thoughts crowding and images flashing into her mind. She thought about her past life. She was born only to suffer. And why was she born into a poor family? Why couldn't she be content that her situation was her karma? Why did she want to escape from the circumstances into which she had been born? Why did she want to marry someone of her own choosing? Why couldn't she just spend her life like Sheelo, accepting its ups and downs?

And the night of her wedding! Being tortured by Nabbu! Hafizji's treacherous sympathy! What was the harm in converting to Islam? What did she gain by refusing Hafizji's offer? What did she gain by being a Hindu? How did that protect her? Despite what they had gone through, Banti, Durga and Satwant still clung to their Hindu beliefs.

And all this was past history. What about the future?

Tara spent the night between falling off into a slumber, and thinking hard with her head in her hands. At daybreak, the women began the routine of relieving themselves over the drain and then washing the excrement away with canfuls of water, of washing themselves and of pumping water for the others. What had made Tara turn her face away and had filled her with disgust the first morning, she was compelled to do herself. Banti had her bath and sat down to recite Krishna-lila. Satwant chanted the words of Japaji Saheb. Then all of them ate the remnants of the previous day's rotis, drinking water from the same can. Tara paced impatiently back and forth beside the eastern wall, then beside the western wall. She would sit for a while when her legs got tired.

The sunlight crawled across half the aangan. The women moved into the rooms. Tara had been pacing in front of the rooms on the east side.

The door chain outside the entrance door rattled. She too moved inside.

The door creaked open, and from the vestibule came the sound of the old women's sugary hoarse voice, 'Daughters, I've brought you rotis.'

Realizing who it was, Satwant, Durga and Banti came back into the aangan. They began dividing up the rotis. Tara stood watching them. She noticed the old woman looking at Durga with a peculiar yearning in her eyes.

Something from her childhood came back into Tara's mind. When her father would go out in the morning to buy vegetables, she went with him holding his finger. On seeing a choice lauki or some other particularly expensive vegetable, Masterji would eye it with yearning. The old slut's eyes held a similar look.

Turning her gaze to Tara, the old woman said, 'Hai, you look quite young. What village you come from?'

Tara turned her face away.

When she was leaving, the old woman stopped near Tara, 'Hai, I'll be damned! Look at those terrible bruises on your forehead, nose and cheeks! Hai, sadake, how I feel for you! I'll get you some ghee to smear over them.'

Tara responded again with disgust at this show of sympathy.

'Come, the rotis are still fresh and soft. Have some,' Banti called out to Tara.

The day was coming to an end. It was Tara's second day in that house, but it felt as if her imprisonment there had lasted for months. After sleeping off the afternoon, the women were back at their chatting, repeating the stories about their families. Tara had resumed her pacing the aangan, in front of the rooms. Banti called out to her to work the pump, and had a wash. Banti haemorrhaged because of her internal injuries, and her body frequently became soiled. She also had difficulty walking.

After her wash, Banti had gone to sit beside Satwant. She called Tara to come over, '*Kudiye*, why do you tire out your legs by marching up and down uselessly? Come and sit with us.'

Tara went and squatted down beside the two of them. She asked, 'Tell me, how long will this go on? How long are we to remain shut up here?'

'Listen to her! Do you think we're staying here as invited guests? It's the will of the true Protector, Waheguru. He'll rescue us, or whatever,' Satwant said, sighing deeply. 'Who knows where we are? What town, what village?

All you can hear is the cry of some vegetable-seller.' With one hand over her flawed eye, she wiped away her tears with the other.

Tara peered closely at Satwant. Although the bulging white of her eye, like the flesh of a peeled lychee, looked ugly, her face was pretty and her features sharp. Tara thought, was her disfigurement and her being tortured also the will of Waheguru?

Curious that Banti, Tara and Satwant were huddling and talking quietly, Durga came and joined them. In the absence of a kameez or blouse covering her body, she kept her arms crossed over her bare chest. Tara had noticed that her breasts, despite all that she had suffered, were firm and shapely like those of some marble statue in a museum. Her fair skin was tinged with pink, like a pomegranate flower, but her face was so pitted by smallpox that her features looked as if made of sponge. This too was God's will, Tara thought.

'It's scary to be shut up like this, sister, but what good does it do to be scared?' Banti let out her breath slowly as she tried to explain to Tara, 'The one who'll rescue us is Maharajji. When He so desires, He will appear out of a blue sky. He rescued Prahlad from the raging fire. This brute has caged us just like Noora the butcher used to tie up the goats he bought for slaughtering.'

'You're right, bahinji. God helps those who help themselves,' said Tara. 'Can't we think of some way of getting out of here?'

'How will we get out? The door's chained up. And where'll we go?' Banti asked.

'I'll tell you,' Tara leaned closer to her. 'When the old woman brings rotis next time, we will grab her. Then we can tie her up, and slip out.'

Satwant cut in, 'You talk like a mad woman. At least here in this aangan we're protected from the eyes of menfolk. Who knows what'll happen once we get out? It's like a mouse escaping from its hole right into the jaws of the cat. It seems like you don't know what men can do to you.'

'What do you know?' Durga said to Tara. 'Ask those women who've been raped by ten or fifteen at one time. They'll tell you. At least, we're all in one piece here. Who'd want to go out and get torn to pieces again?'

Banti said, touching her bare legs, 'How can I go out and face any man in this condition.' She pointed at Durga, 'Would she?' She waved her hand in the direction of the room where Lakkhi lay, 'Would she want to? If it was the dark of night, and just a matter of walking a few steps, it'd have been different. But if we bring down ruin and humiliation on ourselves, there'd be no one but ourselves to blame. As if anything more is needed for our ruin and humiliation. But Maharajji is my witness, it wasn't my fault. He's the one to forgive and rescue us.'

Banti touched her folded hands to her forehead and sighed before going on, 'Kewal's father asked us to leave for Amritsar before hell broke loose. But how could we? We hadn't yet paid for the actions of our past life? What can't happen if Maharajji wills it to happen? He might arrange for us to meet again. Mother Sitaji was held in captivity by Ravana, but was eventually reunited with Lord Ramji.'

'What are you saying?' Durga said. 'Who wants to accept a woman who has suffered such ruin, who has been taken away from her family? A woman once separated from her family and a fruit plucked from the tree cannot be put back as before.' She let out a deep sigh, as if expelling all hope from her heart.

'Who says I was separated from my family?' Banti was angry. 'Maharajji was my witness in whatever I went through. Whatever happened, happened in front of everybody. Did I leave my home of my own free will. They were coward enough to leave me behind, and I was taken away by force. Whatever happened, nobody could have prevented it. And now, who's to blame for all that?'

'If we have to die, let's die before we're sold off to some cruel heartless man, before we suffer more humiliation and dishonour. Let's get out when that old woman comes next time. Outside of here, won't we find even one well to jump into?' Tara said.

'It's not easy to die when you want, my dear. Didn't I try to jump into a well and kill myself? Do you think you can die unless Maharajji, unless Bhagwan wants you to? He's the one who decides. And who knows what He wants?' Banti badly wanted Tara to understand.

Durga too added, 'What bad karma is tormenting us? Who knows? But we'll come back in our next life as maggots in a sewer, if we kill ourselves. That much is sure.'

Tara had no answer.

The old woman's failure to turn up with the rotis in the afternoon disconcerted the women. Since she had been bringing them the rotis before noon for two days, and had promised to keep bringing them every day, the women did not keep food for the following day.

Tara, however, had not eaten up all of her ration of three rotis, and still had one left. When the old woman did not come until late in the afternoon, she shared the roti with Banti. The others had nothing to eat.

That annoyed Satwant and Durga, and they hurled some taunts at Tara and Banti.

Banti told Tara not to get angry, 'Never mind them, bahina. They're the kind who would throw a stone in a muddy puddle just to splash the passers-by and pick a fight with them.'

The afternoon wore on. Instead of talking about their children and families as they usually did, the women discussed only about the failure of the old woman to show up. Their eyes were riveted on the vestibule, and ears alert for the rattle at the door.

It grew dark, and still no sign of the old woman. The waiting women's faces fell. Tara was also feeing hungry, and the craving of the others for food added to her own pangs of hunger. Next morning, despite being hungry, the women went through their regular washing ritual. Banti, Satwant and Durga gave a little more time than usual to their praying and chanting. They told each other that the old woman or the moustached bastard would soon arrive with the rotis. When no one came until midday, they became even gloomier.

The sun was now beating down fiercely on the aangan. The brick floor radiated heat, but the women continued to sit on the doorsteps of the rooms rather than go inside. Despite being naked and racked by stomach cramps, Lakkhi too sat on the threshold with them, with her eyes fixed on the vestibule. They drank mouthfuls of water to ease their hunger pangs. A quarrel broke out between Satwant and Durga over drawing water from the pump. Durga cursed and swore at Satwant, saying that she always took more than her share of the rotis, and then ate them up all alone, that they all were suffering as a result of the sins of that baby-killer.

Tara had begun to feel a dull ache in her stomach from not having eaten. When her brother had accused her of plotting to elope with Asad, she remembered, she had hammered her forehead on the charpoy in anger and had eaten nothing for two days. She hadn't felt hungry at that time. To lessen her craving for food, she began arguing with herself: 'We feel hungry because we cannot suppress our craving for food. What if I didn't crave it in the first place?'

Tara's eyes travelled from Banti to Amaro, then back to Banti. Banti had not been saying much, and sat with her back to the wall, quietly chanting a prayer or reciting some hymn. Amaro, as usual, did not look at anyone, but stared blankly at the wall or the beams in the ceiling. Tara's eyes went to Lakkhi, who was moaning in pain from her stomach cramps. Banti would tell her to take a drink of water now and then. Lakkhi did not have enough strength left to be able to work the pump. She would take a few sips of water whenever Banti asked her.

At night Tara could not sleep for a long time because of hunger. They all were lying in the aangan. A light rain began to fall after midnight, and they all moved into the rooms. To ignore the hunger that had been reawakened by their interrupted sleep, they began to chat again. Satwant recalled how she mixed besan, onions and finely chopped spinach into the dough, and made crisp rotis in the tandoor. Durga's recollection was of the choori mixture made from ghee and gur. Banti thought that nothing tasted better than freshly baked chapattis and daal made from urad lentils. Tara also remembered the delectable smell of chapattis toasted over coals glowing in the stove.

Banti turned her face away to cut short the talk, and resumed her chanting. Satwant and Durga followed suit and began praying to their own guardian deity. One by one they all drifted off to sleep. Except Tara.

The day broke, but there was no break in the rain. Banti, Satwant and Durga had their bath despite the rain. On this day, their prayers, *jaap* intonations and chanting went on even longer.

The rain fell intermittently. The hours passed. Morning. Noon. Afternoon. The women continued to sit on the threshold of the rooms, their eyes and ears intent on the vestibule and the door beyond. The sun did not reappear, nor did the old woman with her bundle of rotis.

In the afternoon, it rained, on and off. The light from the cloudy sky dimmed, then faded into darkness, and with that faded the hopes of getting any food. It remained cloudy most of the night, forcing the women to remain inside the rooms. Sometimes one of them would say a few words to another. Banti, Satwant and Durga muttered prayers and chanted in fits and starts. Their voices were growing feeble.

They lay waiting drowsily for the dawn. Despite feeling weak, Banti, Satwant and Durga washed themselves and carried out their customary ritual of praying and chanting. God could become slack in his work, Tara felt, but not these women in their worship of Him. Despite being rejected by Him, they had no complaints against Him. Despite being ignored by Him, their devotion had not lessened. She felt angry with herself. These women might be simple-minded, but they at least had faith in something. She had nobody to rely on. It was so difficult to survive without someone's support, one really needed inner strength to be an atheist.

Bright, hot sunshine poured down out of a rain-washed sky. The sunshine intensified the women's pangs and made them more listless. Some reclined with their backs against a wall, others sat slumped over, on the floor. They all were silent. Banti's lips moved silently in some prayer.

Amaro seldom uttered a sound. Her mewling, tremulous voice rose, 'If this butcher wants to sell us off, why is he making us starve? It's better that he sell us, and so put an end to this torture. If there's more suffering in store for us, let's face up to that too. Some people tear your body to pieces, others starve you to death.'

Banti shook her head, deliriously mumbling, 'I won't be sold, no I won't! I won't leave this place. I'll die here, I'll die starving.'

No one else said anything

It was getting past noon. They heard the chain on the main door being unlocked and falling. Each woman craned her neck in anticipation, like fledglings raising their heads and opening their beaks when they see their mother bird returning to the nest. The door opened. The old woman, a bundle on her head, walked to the centre of the aangan. Durga, Satwant and Banti rushed towards her. Tara and Amaro remained sitting where they were.

The old woman opened her bundle of rotis. Tara was watching her, waiting to get her share. Satwant, Durga and Banti had again begun to bicker. Satwant and Durga had picked up two rotis each. Banti was asking them to divide the whole lot equally.

The old woman held her hand to her lips as she told them, 'Don't fight, daughters. What can I do? Sadake, rotis are not more important than you all. Do you suppose I want you all to starve? That rotten Gafoora doesn't give me any money. Gave me just a rupee, after three days, so I bought you eight rotis. What else could I do?'

After grabbing two each, Satwant and Durga sat together, stuffing their mouths with pieces of roti. Banti swore at them, and gave one roti each to Tara, Amaro and Lakkhi, keeping one for herself. As she was going back, the old woman again stopped beside Tara. She stared hard into Tara's face, and said, 'Hai, damn me, I forgot about ghee for you. Well, you look better.

Put some spit on your bruises just after you wake up in the morning.' She muttered under her breath, 'Why are you starving yourself to death? Come with me.'

Tara looked away without answering.

The women began to feel anxious the next day when the old woman did not come until midday. Satwant started a quarrel with Durga and Banti for no apparent reason. All three kept on grumbling and complaining for a long time. Durga sat weeping on one side. The old woman came late in the afternoon. The three squabbled again over the number of rotis, only five this time. Durga reached out and grabbed two before anyone else could. Satwant cursed Durga that she might eat her own children, and seized her by the hair. Durga clutched the rotis in one hand, gripped Satwant's kameez at the shoulder with the other, and tore it off. They scuffled, tearing at their hair, hitting out with their elbows and biting. Each hurled curses that the other might get raped, and her children perish. The rotis broke into pieces and fell to the ground.

The old woman held her hand over her mouth in an expression of despair and helplessness as she looked on.

Banti and Tara took the rest of the rotis. The old woman repeated her protestations of sympathy and concern for the women, 'Sadake, may all your misfortunes fall on me. *Kurban*, may I die to save you. These rotis are nothing compared to you. If I could do it, I'd treat young women like you like queens and massage you with ghee, feed you halwa and other fine food. But I can't help it when that rotten Gafoora gives me nothing. I had ten annas of my own, so I got you five rotis. That's all I could manage.'

Banti picked up the pieces from the floor and began dividing them equally. The old woman said quietly to Tara, 'Beti, may I die to save you! Listen, you're wasting away here for nothing. I tell you, that badmaash Gafoora is rotten to the core.'

Tara turned away in disgust.

The crumbs and pieces of roti gathered from the ground were mixed with dust and gravel. The women chewed them nevertheless, and swallowed them with some water.

Tara and Banti spoke together with Durga and Satwant, 'As it is, we just get crumbs and broken bits to eat. Why waste any by fighting over them? One life is as good as another. Our kismet has brought us all here. Let's not fight when the rotis come.'

Banti suggested, 'Tara's educated, and sensible. She'll divide the food equally in front of us all. Then each one can take her own share. It's stupid to fight and let it go to waste.'

Tara told the others what the old woman had said to her, and what she suspected, 'She's deliberately starving us so that some of us may agree to go away with her. The other day, she was trying to lure Durga. Today she tried her tricks on me.'

Banti confirmed Tara's suspicion, 'That's right. You and Durga are the youngest, and have pretty faces too. She's been eyeing you both.'

Satwant was piqued, 'Yes, those two are the heavenly beauties. They're the ones who are young and firm, and so are you. We're just old hags.'

Banti shouted back, 'You can pretend to be a virgin, for all I care. That old slut wants to take us to the city and turn us into whores. Sure, go along with her.'

'As if anything more was needed to make us whores,' Durga said gloomily.

Tara looked at her in silence.

Two days passed. The morning sun had not yet reached the aangan. Durga was in the middle of her bathing when the lock chain on the outer door rattled and fell. The old woman had never come this early. The women stared into the vestibule in alarm. The door was opening when they all ran into the rooms that still had doors, shut the doors and peered through the cracks. They saw the moustached Gafoor and two others dragging two girls by the arms. The men went back out, leaving the girls in the aangan.

The girls could not stand up. One slumped to the ground, the other sat hunched over. The outer door slammed shut. When they were certain that the men had left, Banti, Durga, Satwant and Tara went over to the girls. The girls wore no dupattas. Guessing from their wide-sleeved long-flowing kurtas, their lungis and hair done up in thin braids, Durga said in a hushed voice, 'Looks like they're from Maghiana or Baar.'

The hunched-over girl was quite slender, and looked to be about fifteen years old. The one who had slumped to the ground appeared to be perhaps twenty. The faces of both were covered in dust and streaked with tears and sweat. The one on the ground was moaning in pain, her head on her arm. Her lungi was soaked in blood. The younger girl had wrapped her arms round her head.

Banti squatted down between the two girls. She put her hand on the head of the younger, and asked, 'Kudiye, where're you from?'

Hearing her comforting voice, the girl broke into sobs.

Durga felt that by crying bitterly, the girl was making a big fuss of her own grief and suffering, and was belittling the pain suffered by other women. She said irritably, 'You think you're the only one who's been raped, eh? That others suffered nothing?' She began recounting her own story angrily, '...That's what they did to me, I don't know how many of them there were.'

In between her sobs, the girl told the women that they both were from Tobazar. Their family was travelling with a caravan of refugees. They were attacked by a mob, and a large number of people were killed. These two girls were carted off with a group of other women. She was barely able to speak because of her sobs and sniffles. The women, having suffered the same fate, guessed the rest.

Banti put her hand on the shoulder of the girl lying on the floor. 'Hai Ram, she's still bleeding. What relation is she to you?' she asked the younger girl.

'Sister-in-law.'

'Was she pregnant?'

'Yes,' the girl bent her head and nodded.

'Those brutes have caused a miscarriage,' Banti held her head between her hands in concern.

'You're a virgin. Go and sit away from us,' Banti said, looking at Tara, then asked Satwant and Durga. 'Come on, let's help her. Or else she'll die.'

As Satwant moved closer to the moaning girl she said, looking at Tara, 'Phew, a virgin! At her age! Just look at her! Still a virgin, you say? Those queer city women! You'd think they brought her here to be worshipped as the sacred virgin! As if those,' and she uttered an expletive, 'would leave any woman a virgin!'

Tara sat on one side, with her face turned away. Every hair on her body stood on end when she thought of the groaning woman covered in blood.

Banti said, 'It's always some woman who ends up as the target of their anger and cruelty. These shameless animals take out all their spite at the same spot. Even when they curse and swear, that's where they end up. The brutes first want to wallow in the very place they come out of, then foul it up. Their main complaint against a woman is that she gave them birth.'

Satwant too flared up, 'What's a woman to do? May Waheguru wipe
the earth clean of these shameless beasts. They have only one use for us
women. They fight and kill for it, and all their love and anger is pushed
into that one spot. They revel in it and enjoy it, and then try to destroy it.
Those,' and she again used an obscenity, 'are always crawling around after
it like mad maggots. We wouldn't go through such tortures if they didn't
treat us like animals.'

Murmuring in sympathy and fuming alternately, Banti, Durga and
Satwant used their simple knowledge and rustic methods to tend to the
bleeding girl. Soon it became difficult to sit in the aangan in the blazing
sun. Banti called to Tara and Amaro, and the five of them helped the new
arrivals Bisni and Kesaro to a room.

The sound of the main door opening again came just after noon. The
women looked in anticipation towards the vestibule, hoping to see the
old woman, but Gafoor, with his upturned moustache, came in. He was
carrying a large bundle. Seeing him approach, the women shrank back to
the far side of the room.

Gafoor called out sternly, 'Where is everybody?' He looked into the
rooms, counting the women.

The women's hearts had risen into their throats.

After counting them, he dumped the bundle on the floor, and without
opening it, said, 'These are rotis. Take them.' He went out.

Satwant got to the bundle before anyone else. She opened it, and said,
holding on to the rag in which the rotis were wrapped, 'I want this cloth.'

Durga cried in protest, 'Give it to me. I don't have a kameez. I'll have
it for a dupatta.' The two began to curse and swear at each other when
Satwant refused to give in. The rest of the women kept out of this senseless
squabble. Getting no support from anyone for this injustice, Durga began
to hurl curses all around.

The women were surprised and happy at getting such a large pile of
rotis. Tara counted them; twenty-five. She said, 'See! What did I tell you?
That crummy old woman was deliberately starving us so that one or other
of us would go away with her.'

They all ate to their hearts' content, and all felt some discomfort
afterwards. Lakkhi's condition worsened, caused by her recurring cramps.
She repeatedly had to go and sit over the drain. She moaned and groaned
continually, holding her stomach.

When the old woman came with the rotis just before noon the next day, she brought only twelve. Satwant could not hold back. She swore at her, 'You cheat us women in our suffering by taking away our share of food. Waheguru will punish you.'

At first the old woman played the innocent, then she too began to swear back at the women for accusing her of thievery, and then called them ungrateful for all the good she had done for them. She left in a huff. But when she returned the next day, she brought eighteen rotis, and the sugary tone was back in her voice.

Later in the day, when the sun was its fiercest and the aangan was giving off waves of heat, the outer door opened. The old woman had left after delivering the rotis, so the women quickly went indoors in alarm, and peeped out from behind the doors. Gafoor came into the aangan, wearing his high fur hat, a clean shirt and a new multicoloured lungi. From one shoulder hung a belt, with a holster attached to it. Two men followed him. One was middle-aged, with a henna-dyed beard, the other a young man, whose beard was neatly trimmed. This father and son appeared to be artisans of some kind, perhaps bricklayers or tinsmiths. Gafoora looked into the rooms. He stood in front where the women were huddling together, and called out to the men, 'Come on, have a look.'

The man and his son came forward hesitantly, and the three men entered the room. Only Lakkhi was lying alone, by herself in another room. The cowering women went and sat by the wall or in a corner, their heads lowered. The man and his son went around, giving them casual glances.

'Take a good look. Check them out by making them stand up,' Gafoor tried to encourage them.

The young man pointed at Durga.

Gafoor grabbed her plait, pulled her upright and raised her face.

The young man said nothing. He looked at Amaro.

Gafoor made Amaro stand up for him.

Amaro stared at the young man with wide, terrified eyes. Next came Bisni's turn. The young man looked away, dissatisfied, and asked, 'Don't you have any virgins?'

Gafoor surveyed the women, and pulled Kesaro up by grabbing her arm, 'Here's a virgin for you. One who hasn't had any kids, is a virgin. She's not even sixteen.'

The older man shook his head, 'She's all used up.' Kesaro slumped to the floor when Gafoor let go of her arm.

The older man gave Kesaro a hard look of appraisal, 'She's of no use now.' He turned back towards Durga, and said after a moment's reflection, 'This one can hardly be a virgin.'

'There's a virgin!' Durga said to protect herself, pointing at Tara. Tara had been sitting with her knees drawn up and her head tucked between her arms. She did not rise when her plait was pulled, but just allowed her head to be tilted.

She hissed angrily, 'Don't you dare touch me!' In her rage she had spoken in Hindi, instead of Punjabi.

'Oh! She speaks Farsi!' The young man took a step back.

'When you get into her, she'll forget all her Farsi!' Gafoor said to bolster up the young man's courage.

The older man said in rustic Punjabi, 'We don't need someone who can write petitions. We need a woman, not a clerk, for the boy.' He turned away his face to show his disapproval.

Gafoor, the father and the young man again looked the women over, then went out and stood talking in the aangan. The three came inside again, and Gafoor grabbed Durga's arm and began to drag her behind him. Durga screamed, thrashed around on the floor and tried to resist by digging in her heels, but Gafoor yanked her by the arm and pulled her out of the room.

The hearts of the terrified women were beating fiercely. They felt defenceless and unprotected. The noise of Durga's crying and screaming moved towards the vestibule. They heard the door being opened and closed. They sat in terrified silence for a while, and then burst into tears, 'Hai, what'll become of us? What'll they do to us? Who'll help us when they drag us away like that? Only God can help us.'

The old woman brought the rotis just before noon the next day. Noticing Durga's absence, she said, 'You see? He took her away. What did I tell you? That man, will sell you all. And such good girls.'

Each passing day made Tara feel as if she was sinking deeper into a bottomless pit of despair. 'Had I been alone, I surely would have attempted something,' she thought. She found it increasingly hard to get along with the others. 'These women were living in the hope that God would rescue them. They saw that He didn't do anything when Durga was taken away, but they do not lose faith in Him and continue to hope that He would still help them. And why do I sit idly by, and do nothing? God seems to be on the side of our torturer, that heartless scoundrel Gafoor and the old slut, rather than any of us.'

Her craving for food in addition to her imprisonment like some animal in a cage were eating away at her sense of dignity and self-esteem, she felt. In moments of acute despair she would wonder why she didn't accept the old slut's offer to get out of this prison, to be away from these stupid women. Outside, she might find some way to end her life. This fate was certainly worse than death. 'If the old woman repeats her offer today, maybe i'll agree,' she thought.

It was still early morning. The sky had turned cloudy before sunrise, making it difficult to guess the exact hour. Loud knocks on the outer door startled the women and made them look towards the entrance. The sound of the door chain clanging and then falling did not follow. The banging continued. The women ran inside the room. The old woman had never come this early. Gafoor, they guessed nervously. His arrival was always a cause for fear. Their ears were cocked for the sound of any movement. The uncertainty and the suspense added to their terror.

The clatter of hobnailed boots entering the aangan followed the sound of the door being flung open. Satwant and Banti were watching through a crack in the door. They stepped back apprehensively and looked at the women behind them, saying fearfully, 'Police! Sepoys!'

The women's hearts sank. In the course of their misfortunes they had usually suffered at the hands of policemen and soldiers. The abuse of their authority had been a cause of fear and threat for the women.

Someone gave an order from the aangan, 'Whoever is in the rooms, come outside. We're here to help you.'

Paralysed by their uncertainly and threat, the women huddled together in a corner. They all looked at Tara: What should we do?

Tara summoned her courage and stepped forward. She peered out from behind the door. She saw a police inspector in uniform, four constables, a few soldiers and an army officer. Also two respectably dressed young men; one in a white shirt and trousers, the other in a white shalwar trousers and kameez. With them was a young Hindu woman, in a shalwar and kameez of white khadi, her dupatta draped in the Hindu style around her shoulders. The woman's expression showed no trace of fear.

Tara spoke on behalf of the others, 'Bahinji, could you please come in?'

When the woman approached, Tara said, 'Please come in. Some of us don't have proper clothes. How can we come out in front of these men?'

The woman stepped into the room. She looked at the women huddling together, exchanged a few words with Tara and went out, asking her to wait.

She returned after several minutes, carrying a bundle of clothes. The women wrapped dupattas around their bodies. There was an extra shalwar for Banti. Even after covering themselves, the women hesitated to leave the room.

Tara, her head covered in a dupatta, stepped out, followed by the others with their faces veiled.

'You here?' Tara heard the words spoken in English. She looked up. Her body shook, and she felt as if she would collapse. Her head sank.

'I can't believe my eyes!' Asad was staring at Tara in open-eyed amazement.

Tara's head spun. She could not utter a word. A question from the woman who had come to their rescue saved her, 'How many of you are here?'

'There're now seven of us,' Tara replied, and led the woman into the next room as she described the precarious condition of Lakkhi.

The woman asked the constables to bring a stretcher, and some clothing and sheets. Lakkhi had been writhing in agony since the previous evening. She could neither lie down, nor sit up without feeling pain. She was still moaning, her body shaken by agonized spasms. Banti and Tara dressed her, wrapped her in sheets and put her on the stretcher. Although she could hardly remain still, Lakkhi tried not to moan and to control her pangs in front of the men by biting her lip and gripping the poles of the stretcher.

Two constables carried the stretcher out of the room. The woman and the police inspector checked all the other rooms. The inspector and constables went up to the roof, after breaking open the lock on the door that led to the stairs.

The woman said to Tara, 'We were told that ten or twelve women were locked up here.'

There were only seven at the moment, Tara assured her.

The constables went through the entrance first, with Lakkhi writhing in discomfort on the stretcher. The women followed.

Several constables, holding rifles, stood on guard outside the door. Tara now recognized that the man accompanying Asad was Zuber. He also stood with his mouth agape on seeing Tara, barely managing to stammer out a namaste. He too asked in surprise, 'How did you get here?'

Srimati Kaushalya Devi, a representative of the Indian government, had come to Shaikhupura in Pakistan with a guarantee of safe passage to rescue any Hindu women who had been kidnapped or taken away from their families.

A sub-inspector of the Pakistani police rode in a jeep with armed constables at the head of the convoy. Armed soldiers of the Indian Army followed in another jeep. Third in the convoy was a small bus, for bringing back the rescued women. An Indian Army truck, with a squad of armed soldiers, brought up the rear. An Indian soldier, carrying a sub-machine gun, sat beside the bus driver.

Kaushalya Devi and Zuber had got into the front of the bus. Asad asked Tara to come and sit with him in the back. After the rest of the women had taken seats, the stretcher carrying Lakkhi was placed in the aisle.

Their convoy was travelling through the looted and nearly deserted town of Shaikhupura, towards the Jarnaili Road. Asad said in English to Tara, seated beside him, 'I'm still not able to get over my surprise.'

Tara, her head lowered, made no reply.

Asad told her, 'Four days ago a young man from Shaikhupura came to the Communist Party office. He was too scared to give his name and address. He informed us that in the mohalla behind the bazaar mandi, ten or twelve women were locked up in the mansion of Udho Das. We asked the Indian liaison officer to take action. The Indian military cannot carry out any investigation without permission of the Pakistani government, and unless escorted by Pakistani police. It took four days to straighten that out, and nobody was aware that you were here all this time! How did this happen?'

Tara stared out of the window without replying. She was finding it hard to say anything, and what could she explain in one sentence? She felt like saying, 'I've nothing to say, I've nothing to tell you. I've sunk lower than the dust.' On the roadside, as far as her eyes could see, was the evidence of devastation and plunder: broken, upturned bullock carts, dead bodies, vultures and dogs fighting over the carcasses of oxen. A heavy, nauseating, choking stench hung in the air.

'I met Puri on the 31 July or maybe 1 August. He was very sad. I don't understand. Your people think that you could not escape the fire at the Banni Hata. They had no inkling of any other possibility,' Asad was speaking softly, as if talking to himself.

'All they wanted was to get me married off. For them I'm as good as dead. They got rid of the burden I was to them,' Tara told herself inwardly, but could not bring herself to say it out loud.

The convoy bringing back the women rescued from Udho Das's house crossed the bridge over the Ravi River and entered Lahore city. Tara recognized many familiar landmarks, but they all looked different now. Clouds covering the sky since daybreak came down as rain when the convoy had crossed the bridge. On both sides of the road, rain-dappled planks of stacked wood, clusters of bamboo poles and heaps of firewood in timber merchants' lots seemed also to be shedding tears in sympathy. The sky was weeping, the trees were crying, and rain streamed down the fronts of the houses like torrents of tears.

Tara, when she was little, had walked many times along this same road with Sheelo, Dhanno and Biddo, all wearing colourful dupattas and skipping ahead of her mother and other women from the gali as they all went for a dip in the river. There was no reason for fear at that time. Hindus and Muslims were not at each other's throat in those days.

Asad leaned towards Tara and said gently, 'Your family must have left Lahore. Puri said something about going to Nainital or UP in search of a job. Most Hindus have either left or been forced to leave. The rest are being moved out now. That's the government policy. Narendra Singh's family was stuck here in grave danger. We escorted them up to Amritsar. Pradyumna, Mahajan and others have gone too. How can we get in touch with Puri? Do you know his whereabouts?'

Tara shook her head.

'So what do you think now?'

Tara said nothing, just waved a hand to mean that she had no ideas.

The convoy came to a halt in front of the building between the D.A.V. College and the Tibba Farid police station.

'You won't be able to live in Lahore if you call yourself a Hindu,' Asad said hesitantly, leaning towards her.

Tara's head was bent. The days spent at Hafizji's house flashed through her mind.

To avoid looking at Asad and to give vent to the emotions rising in her heart, she looked up at the sky and let out a sigh.

The rain-drenched sacred sign of Om on the top of the building seemed to be weeping too, at having been abandoned by its devotees.

After Lakkhi's stretcher had been laid in the bus, no one had paid any attention to her moans. When the bus came to a stop, she was found dead.

Kaushalya Devi and Zuber got down from the bus. The rest of the women were waiting for the stretcher blocking their way to be removed.

Asad whispered in Tara's ear, 'Now's the time for you to decide your future for yourself.'

The Indian Army officer wanted the Pakistani police to accept responsibility for Lakkhi's body because she had died in Pakistan, before entering the Hindu camp, but the Pakistani police inspector refused to assume responsibility for a corpse after handing over a live Indian citizen to the representatives of the Indian government.

Crowds of refugees milled everywhere in the two-storey buildings of the D. A V. College, the high school, the student hostels, and in the adjacent courtyards and concourse spread out in an area as large as a small town, making the whole place buzz like a beehive. All the courtyards were filled with tents, large and small, and bivouacs, with high monsoon grass growing on the ground in between. The grass was trodden down, and strewn with excrement left by desperate people with no place to relieve themselves.

Asad walked fearlessly into this Hindu refugee camp with Tara. Kaushalya Devi considered him to be trustworthy and reliable. He said to Tara in English, 'You must be feeling very upset at the moment. Get some rest, and think things over. I'll come back in the evening, around five or six.' He left, after seeing the place Tara had found to stay.

Kaushalya Devi had put all the women liberated from Shaikhupura in rooms in the camp reserved for women who had been rescued. A young man came forward with a register. Kaushalya Devi began to supervise the registering of names and addresses of the new arrivals and details of their families. Since she already knew Tara's name, she asked for it to be recorded first and asked Tara about the rest of her family.

'Everyone in my family has left Lahore,' Tara replied.

'Their names and addresses?'

'There's no use now in giving that information.'

'Where would you like to go?'

'I don't know yet. I'll have to think about it.'

'How did you get to Shaikhupura?'

'They dumped me in a vehicle and took me there.'

'From where? Which gali or bazaar?'

'Don't know. Can't remember.'

Kaushalya Devi and the young man said irritably, 'At least give us the name and address of someone to whom we can send information about you.'

'I don't have anybody.'

Kaushalya Devi and the young man did not have any time to waste on gathering information about one single woman, so they began collecting details about the others. Kaushalya Devi arranged for each woman be given two handfuls of roasted grain and a lump of gur. Then she left, to arrange transport to take the women in her charge to Amritsar before nightfall.

Banti had attached herself to Tara, constantly pleading with her, 'Bahina, get me to Amritsar, and find out for me the whereabouts of my family. Only you can help me now. You're educated and clever. I'm just an illiterate country woman, who doesn't know how to talk to anyone.'

Tara was sitting on the veranda floor, her back against the wall, her cheek resting on her hand. 'What am I to do?' she thought. 'Don't know where my parents went, or if my brother is in UP? For them I'm dead, burnt to death, don't exist anywhere in this world.

'Asad had said he would come at five or six. Once I asked him to give me shelter, but today it was he who offered to shelter me. No, I can't trust any man now. Had he agreed then, it would have been different, and all this would not have happened. Who knows? And even if he'd agreed, that wouldn't have prevented the Hindu–Muslim conflict and kept Pakistan from being created. At least I wouldn't have fallen into the hands of Somraj, Nabbu, Hafizji and Gafoor.'

'You won't be able to live in Lahore if you call yourself a Hindu!' she remembered Asad's words. 'Neither he nor my brother believed in making a distinction between Hindus and Muslims. Narendra, Surendra, Zubeida, Pradyumna, Mahajan, none of them believed in it either. But did their disbelief make any difference?' The devastation and the heinous results of the belief of other people in making that distinction were all around her.

'Asad, whatever he is, good or bad, was born a Muslim, but he isn't like Gafoor, Nabbu, Hafizji and Amjad. He's their opposite, if anything. He and Zuber went to rescue Hindu women.

'But where can I go? I'm dead to my family. I'm someone who died in that fire. If I exist at all, I exist as a runaway from my in-laws' family! Should I go to Asad? Didn't I ask him to shelter me once before? But that was love. Love? Like the love between Sheelo and Ratan! Nonsense! I must keep away from the male animal!

'Who else do I know? And where? What shall I do? What shall I tell Asad when he comes at five?' Asad's gentle, sympathetic voice echoed in her ears. 'He's the only one I know, he's the only one who cares for me.'

'Get up, all of you! Let's go!' Tara heard Kaushalya Devi call, and looked to her left. Kaushalya Devi was covering the length of the veranda briskly in her short steps. She held one corner of her dupatta between her fingers, which made it billow behind her like the sail of a boat.

'Hurry up! Got transport to carry all of you. Otherwise you'll have to wait here for another three days. Who knows? I wonder how my own daughter's doing?'

Banti, Satwant, Durga, Amaro, Bisni and Kesaro began pulling their clothes around them. They all looked at Tara.

'Come on, hurry up!' Kaushalya Devi urged them once again, and snapped at Tara, who was making no attempt to rise, 'Get up!'

'Bahinji, let me stay here,' Tara said, with some hesitation.

'What?' Kaushalya Devi's brow became furrowed. 'Why? Who's here belonging to you?'

'There's someone I know.'

'You told us at first that that you had nobody. Now you say there's someone you know! What peculiar behaviour! Haven't you suffered enough so far that you want to play around? Just look at her!' She scolded Tara in a loud voice, 'Our responsibility is to get you out of Pakistan and back into Hindustan. After that you can play around as much as you like. Go quietly and get into the bus, or I'll have you thrown out of the camp. What cheek!'

'Bahinji, give me some time to think,' Tara pleaded.

'Think all you want after we reach Amritsar. Get a move on!'

Kaushalya Devi pulled Tara up by her arm, and herded them all towards the bus.

The military truck first went, with armed soldiers in steel helmets, then a station wagon carrying the women liberated from Shaikhupura. After the station wagon came five buses packed with Hindu families being sent to India for repatriation, then another military truck, and then five more buses, with two more military trucks at the tail end. A helmeted soldier, cradling an automatic weapon, rode alongside the driver of each bus. This convoy transporting the refugees headed towards Amritsar.

Kaushalya Devi had been on this road before, and she had seated Tara just behind the driver, next to the window, and had herself taken a seat on the aisle. The rest of the women sat in the seats behind them. Tara, her eyes closed, was giving her imagination a free rein, 'Asad would come at five or six. Whatever I hope for will never happen. I'll always be a cog in someone else's scheme of things. I'll always be the debris floating on the current of the river of destiny. Why can't I make a stand! That's why I haven't been able to put an end to my life.'

The bus braked suddenly and Tara woke with a start. She smelled a nauseating stench. On the side of the road lay scattered half-eaten corpses, some desiccated by the sun, others rotted by the rain. Vultures were perched on and near them, scavenging, jostling for space, and picking at the bodies. Broken and plundered trunks and boxes lay about. The charred remains of half-burnt buses were scattered here and there. Two skeletons of buses were still blocking the road. As the convoy of refugees went past these obstacles, the side wheels of the vehicles passed onto the unpaved shoulder of the road. The convoy jolted and rattled along very slowly.

Kaushalya Devi said in exasperation so that the Sikh driver could hear, 'Will this road ever be cleared? These buses have been here for the past nine days.'

'Bahinji, you've had nine days to see it,' the driver replied. 'I've had to look at it over and over for the past full month. The stench is sickening. These dead are Hindus, granted, but it'll be people in Pakistan who'll die if there's an outbreak of disease. The Pakistani government isn't bothered whether their citizens live or die. I heard, bahinji, that not a single Hindu from this caravan of refugees survived. Not less than two hundred persons must have been massacred. The thugs drove off the zenana as if they were a herd of goats, all bleating and crying.'

'May God give these people some sense,' Kaushalya Devi said with sorrow. After bypassing the bottleneck, the convoy again picked up speed.

Both sides of the road still bore the evidence of massacre, destruction and pillage. Tara closed her eyes to avoid the spectacle of the carnage.

Kaushalya Devi and the driver were conversing in loud voices, so as to be heard over the roar of the engine. Tara could hear them but paid no attention. Her mind was engrossed with thoughts about her future. She had suffered torture and humiliation that was worse than death. Where and how would she be able to find her parents, and her brothers and sisters? And when she did find them, what after that? Would she live with her family, and her brother after suffering so much because of them? She needed some kind of a roof over her head, but where would she find it?

The bus slowed down, then stopped. Tara was jolted out of her reverie. The driver looked out of the window to see what was ahead. He said in frustration, 'Oh, hell! How can we go forward now, bahinji? These people were in Atari yesterday. They've travelled only six miles in one day. They hardly have any stamina left to walk, anymore. These Muslims, I heard, are refugees from the districts of Jalandhar, Ludhiana and Ambala. At best, the bus can move only at a walking speed through this crowd. We won't be able to reach Amritsar before midnight.'

Someone barked an order from the military truck at the head of the convoy.

The soldiers jumped out of the trucks and stood guard on both sides of the station wagon and the buses, their weapons at the ready. The frightened passengers peered out with alarm. A huge column of men and women, walking with tottering, unsteady steps, was slowly converging on the convoy.

'Hai! Hai! They've come! They're here!' Amaro, Satwant and Bishi cried out in panic and terror.

'Be quiet! Calm down! Don't be frightened!' both Kaushalya Devi and the driver said to the women rather gruffly. 'They look half-dead themselves! How can they do anyone any harm? Don't you see how they're dragging along like dogs with broken backs?'

The phalanx of bedraggled, staggering refugees passed on either side of the station wagon in the convoy. Sweat and tears streaked their dust-covered faces, their backs were bent with exhaustion and with the strain of carrying their belongings, beards unkempt and dishevelled, close-fitting caps, shaven heads peeking from loose, dirty turbans coming unravelled, blue- and black-coloured clothes that were nothing but rags. They came in waves of small groups of ten or fifteen. An immense cloud of flies hovering over the heads of the refugees alighted on the convoy. The flies swarmed so thickly that one had to use both hands to ward them off, so as to avoid breathing them in. With them came the smell of death, a gagging, retching smell, as if their bodies continued to decay as they walked. The dust raised by their dragging feet made breathing even more difficult.

Every person in the column was carrying something. Frequently, a skinny dirty child was to be seen, weeping and whimpering, as it clung to the hip or was held in the arms of a woman, or was perched on the shoulders of a man. Stuffed gunny sacks, empty kerosene cans fashioned into containers, wrapped bundles and packages tied with ropes, and once in a while someone carrying on his head his sole belonging, a charpoy. Or a man and a woman balancing an upturned charpoy on their heads, piled with their meagre possessions and a dazed and shrivelled child or two.

A large number of the men carried in their hands their one and only symbol of comfort and relief: a clay hookah. Many women carried mud *chulha*s on their heads. Some carried as their only possession, a metal pot or a large tray. One woman laboured under a light stone *chakki* for grinding wheat. A few had a pair of hens or perhaps roosters, their feet tied. Some pulled along a goat or a sheep at the end of a rope. Another carried a newly born kid or lamb. Sometimes a gaunt scraggy dog, its stomach sticking to its ribcage, faithfully walked behind its master. The crowd was getting denser by the minute.

The vehicles of the convoy stood waiting. The driver, Kaushalya Devi, Tara and the women did not know what was more important—to use their hands to cover their noses against the stench or to wave them to drive away the flies.

When the army truck at the head of the convoy started its engine, the driver of the station wagon too switched on his ignition, saying uncertainly, 'Wonder if we'll be able to get on. Maybe the captain sahib has asked the soldiers to march ahead and clear the way.'

Flanked by the soldiers, the convoy began to move forward at a crawl. As the blade of a plough slices through the earth, leaving a furrow in its wake, so the convoy divided the caravan of Muslims as it moved ahead. The noise from the engines of the vehicles moving in low gear was deafening. The stench intensified, as did the swarming flies. The driver of the station wagon held the steering wheel with one hand, using the other to fight off the flies. Distracted from keeping his eyes on the road to avoid the oncoming crowd, he kept mumbling 'Waheguru, Waheguru' in exasperation, between bouts of spitting out the flies.

The passengers in the station wagon were also holding their noses with one hand, and waving the flies away with the other. The rescued women were mumbling God's name, visibly relieved that they were not a part of the caravan, but safe inside the vehicles.

The driver said in a loud voice as before, 'Here, look as much as you want, at these people going to the Promised Land of Pakistan. How has anyone benefited by uprooting people living in the same place for hundreds of years?'

'If they're not willing to live in Hindustan, let them leave and be with their own kind!' Kaushalya Devi said, from behind the hand covering her mouth.

'They're not willing?' the driver asked in surprise. 'What are you saying, bahinji! These poor people have been driven out by force, Hindus from one side just like Muslims from the other. But, bahinji, you've seen refugee caravans of Hindu refugees. Now see this one of Muslims. The Hindus were killed, they were looted, their women were kidnapped and violated, but those fleeing were mostly on some kind of carriage or pony trap, with villagers and farmers on bullock carts. The caravan of Hindus and Sikhs on horse carriages, camel carts and bullock carts that came across the Balloki barrage on the Sutlej River stretched back over fifty miles.

'The Hindus and Sikhs came loaded with trunks and cases, cash and gold, jewellery and security bonds. All that these people are carrying are clay hookahs, broken charpoys, chulhas, pots and pans, and maybe a chicken or two. That's all they had in their household. They can only take away with them what they owned, or what they attach any value to. What people say is quite true: If you're a "have" you're a Hindu. If you're a "have-not", you're a Muslim.'

Kaushalya Devi agreed with the driver in a tone of sadness, 'You're quite right, bhai. But all these people were once Hindus. This is the outcome of the Hindus' own bad actions from past lives. Who know what more punishment God has in store for them? *Hari om! Hari om!*'

'It's true, bahinji, that Muslims looted and plundered the houses of Hindus,' encouraged by Kaushalya Devi's reply, the driver went on. 'But Hindus have been looting and robbing the Muslims for centuries.

Otherwise, why would there be such a vast difference between the rich and poor, among people living in the same place? How come all the land and property of Punjab was taken over by the Hindus? The poor, in their anger and frustration, turned to Islam early on. This is another result of their age-old resentment. Bahinji, they're getting their revenge not only because their religion is different, but also because of their feelings of being badly treated.'

'Bhai, it depends on how you look at it,' Kaushalya Devi disagreed with the driver on this issue.

Tara was sitting with her eyes closed, one hand over her nose, driving the flies away with the other. When she tired of waving one hand, she changed over, and used the other to fight the flies. The drone of the engine in low gear made her head ring. A sorry fate for the people at whose hands she had suffered so much, she was thinking, the ones who had killed Hindus. But these did not look like murderers. Both Hindus and Muslims suffered and were killed. Were her heartless villainous torturers to be found among these people?

She opened her eyes when the vehicle again came to a stop. The sun was just above the treetops to her right, and its rays were shining directly into her eyes. As both her hands were busy keeping the flies off her face, she could not shade her eyes. The dust raised by the caravan was making everyone choke.

'Have we reached Wagha?' Kaushalya Devi wanted to know.

'Yes, bahinji. It took us an hour and a half to cover just four miles. Waheguru! Waheguru!' the driver replied. 'If Waheguru wills it, we might find the road ahead less busy. On the other side, the police makes some effort to keep the road cleared for traffic. This border checkpoint is on the Pakistan side.'

A few armed constables walked past the vehicles, peering into the windows. The convoy moved after about five minutes, and halted again after another two.

This was the border checkpoint on the soil of Hindustan.

When the convoy went forward again, the motors seemed to growl in protest against the constraint placed on their power as they moved slowly in low gear, cutting through the crowds. The sun dipped below the trees. Its rays, tuned pink by the dust cloud, seemed to be saying farewell.

Tara had closed her eyes again. Despite the deafening roar of the engines, the sound of empty kerosene tins being beaten like kettledrums fell on her ears. But she kept her eyes shut. Her mind was overwhelmed with sadness about leaving the land of her birth for another.

'*Dur* phitemunh! Damn you shameless people!'

Hearing the driver swear very loudly at someone, Tara opened her eyes. The women were looking to their right towards a group behaving like performers in some ludicrous circus act.

The women averted their eyes as cold shivers of fear ran up their spines.

One man, like an acrobat performing in the arena, was holding a pole upright. Others around him were beating empty kerosene tins like drums. A few others in the troupe, by pressing their lips against the back of their hands and blowing, were imitating the noise a he-goat makes when it meets a she-goat in heat. The body of a naked woman was fixed vertically to the top of the pole. Her legs were splayed, and wet with blood that shone in the rays of the dying sun. Her head and arms hung limp and lifeless.

A few naked women, hiding their faces in their hands were being marched in front of the man holding the pole. This group of men hurled profanities and filthy curses at the people walking in the caravan, yelling, 'Take them with you! Take your mothers and sisters with you to your Pakistan!'

'They rape the mothers and sisters of others. And those others, in turn, maim their womenfolk in revenge. Women are doomed either way!' Banti, sitting behind Tara, said with a sigh full of pain.

Satwant said angrily, 'The only crime women are guilty of is giving birth to them. Phitemunh to them! Damn you to hell a hundred, a thousand times! Men fight with other men and kill each other, but they don't strip one another naked and disgrace their bodies.'

'Damn them! Damn them!' The driver sitting in front of Tara kept on cursing and spitting out of the window in disgust at the drummers and others around them.

Kaushalya Devi said in distress, 'Why don't the army and the police stop these shameless people?'

'Who can stop them?' the driver replied. 'Who's thinking sanely any more? Who considers it to be their duty?'

'Show some decency, you shameless bunch!' The driver shouted at the revenge-crazed group of men, 'Don't cut off your noses to spite your faces.'

The sun disappeared below the horizon. At this sign of approaching night, the caravan heading towards Lahore left the road. The river of people split into two and flowed off the road, settling down and spreading out to the left and right. The convoy heading to Amritsar picked up speed. The women from Shaikhupura began to breathe more easily. Dusk was turning into night. Makeshift cooking fires were being kindled as far as the eye could see, on stretches of land beside the road. No end of the caravan was yet in sight along the road when the convoy turned off the Jarnaili Road on to a side road.

The buses and the station wagon carrying the refugees halted in front of a gate in the boundary wall of a large brightly lit compound, in which the tops of tents and bivouacs inside could be seen from the outside and the hum indicative of a large crowd could be heard.

'At last, sisters, we've arrived!' Kaushalya Devi said to the women by way of assurance. 'Get down! You've had to leave your homeland, but now you're in a new nation, to which you belong, and you're among your own people. Give thanks to God.'

Homeland and nation! Homeland! Nation! Her words echoed in Tara's ears.

Tara could not understand what Kaushalya Devi meant. She was willing to offer her thanks to Kaushalya Devi, but Kaushalya Devi wanted Tara and the other women to thank God for what they had been through, for having to leave their homes and native land. She kept silent. Those words kept echoing in her mind: homeland and nation.

The driver got down and was standing beside his vehicle. As Tara got out, his words fell on her ears.

'The people in that other caravan were going to their new country too, leaving behind their old homeland. The countries of human beings have been turned into nations by religion,' Tara heard him say in a loud voice.

'Those that God had created as one have been torn apart by the distrust of others, and all in the name of God.'

Part II

~

The Future of the Nation

Chapter 1

JAIDEV PURI WAS STANDING IN A QUEUE IN FRONT OF THE DEPOT distributing free ration to the refugees. There were three women and three men ahead of him, and the woman at the head of the queue was pleading with the supervisor of the depot:

'Bhai, there are four of us including two children. What will we do with this measly ration of one-and-a-half *pao* of flour and one-and-a-half *chhataank* of lentils? Give me at least a seer of flour.'

'Mai, you got the amount they've allocated for one person. Only those showing up in person get their share,' the man explained his helplessness.

A few spoke up in support of the woman.

Others supported the supervisor, 'We've all got more family. If some of us have five, there're others who have ten. What if someone claims ration for fake family members, and then sells it in the bazaar? It's only fair that the person making the claim should show up in person.'

Two of the men and a woman who were ahead of him, Puri saw, stood on one side holding their rations. The men put their portions of flour and lentils in the woman's dupatta. The older man said to the younger, 'You two go on ahead. I'll go get some firewood.'

Puri's bedroll was under his arm. He thought of taking the sheet from it to collect his ration. If he left his place to open his bedroll, he realized, he'd have to go back to the end of the queue.

He held on to his bedroll, and when his turn came, took the flour in the tail of his shirt and the lentils in the other end. He came out of the Mandi bazaar, and walked about in search of a dhaba, the makeshift eating place with a tandoor. He had hardly gone a hundred paces when he smelled chapattis being cooked, and then saw a dhaba. Soon he could hear the noise of hands flattening balls of dough into chapattis.

The cook—owner of the dhaba demanded one anna and his rations in exchange for cooked chapattis and daal.

Puri, desperate for food, asked for a smaller portion in lieu of money.

The cook continued to flatten a ball of dough as he ran his gaze over Puri, 'Don't you even have one anna? So you got the ration on dole?'

Puri had to admit the truth of this.

'I'll give you two chapattis and a helping of daal and vegetables.'

Puri handed over his ration to the cook, went inside the dhaba, and sat down to eat on a piece of jute matting spread on the ground.

He came out after his meal, washed his hands and rinsed his mouth with water from an empty oil drum to which a faucet had been attached. As he bent down to pick up his bedroll, the cook said to him:

'You're a strong young man; do you like taking free ration? Until you find something else to do, why don't you come and work here with me on a daily wage.'

'Yes, I'll do it,' replied Puri. He did not pick up his bedroll.

'The lad working here came down with fever. There's not much to do, anyway. Only cleaning up the utensils. You can eat all you want twice a day, and I'll give you four annas on top of that.'

'All right,' Puri agreed.

'Bravo!' the cook said approvingly. 'Get to work, young fellow. Collect all the thalis; get your own too. No shame in doing honest work, is there?'

Puri felt stronger after eating the meal. He rolled up his trousers over his knees, and his sleeves too, and got down on his haunches and began to scrape the metal thalis, in which meals were served, with a jute-fibre scrubber and a handful of ash from a can, and rinsed them out. His head still ached, but he ignored it. Customers drifted by in ones and twos for their meals.

In Lahore, Puri had always lived at his parents' home. There had not been many occasions to eat out at a dhaba. Only during the chaotic times of the Quit India movement of 1942, and in March and April of 1947, when he was helping his communist comrades to maintain communal peace in the city, and when the hectic pace of work gave him little time to return home for his meals, had he ever eaten at a dhaba.

But he knew how the dhaba worked. The chef, sitting next to the tandoor, shaped balls of dough into chapattis by flattening them between his palms and stuck them to the inside wall of the glowing tandoor. He then removed the cooked, steaming, speckled chapattis with a pair of iron spikes that jangled merrily. Several customers asked for chapattis spread with ghee, and for a dash of spiced ghee added to their daal. For such special orders, the cook would draw a measure of ghee from a container, heat it over the tandoor, add some chopped onions and spices, and pour it over the daal.

The cupful of daal would sizzle and sputter, and the aroma of hot ghee would rise and spread all around.

Puri's job, as the cook's helper, was to serve chapattis to the customers in a metal thali and daal in a bowl, with a serving of curried squash and a dab of spicy chutney. And a tumbler of water. Then he collected the empty thalis and sat down again on his haunches to scrub and rinse them. The throbbing in his head began to subside. 'If only I can spend the night here,' he was thinking, 'I'll make up my mind about tomorrow.'

The afternoon passed into evening. The bazaar was brightly lit. The cook switched on the light in his dhaba too. He joined his palms in the namaste gesture and bowed before the electric bulb, as if it represented Lakshmi, the goddess of wealth. More customers began to arrive. A man, wearing a khadi kurta–pajama and Gandhi cap, showed up. He asked the cook to send some food over to the house of one Soodji, who lived nearby. The dhaba owner again grumbled about his assistant not showing up.

The khadi-clad gentleman replied that Soodji's servant was also absent because of fever.

The dhaba owner first cursed and swore at malaria for making everyone sick, then called out to Puri who was scrubbing the thalis, 'Hey, it's only a few steps from here. Go with this babuji and have a look at the house where you've to deliver the thali of food.'

Puri followed the messenger about fifty paces into the bazaar when the man pointed to a flight of stairs, and went off on some further errand.

On his return, Puri saw the cook take some ghee from the container, and add a dab of it first to the dough as he shaped it between his palms, then some on the cooked paranthas. He added spiced ghee to a bowlful of daal, and also to a bowl of curried vegetables. The spoonful of chutney was neatly laid out on a leaf. Then he covered this platter with another thali. The thali was being prepared, Puri realized, for some one important.

The dhaba owner explained to Puri, 'Just deliver the thali. Say nothing about payment. If he asks, say it's eight annas. Watch your step, he's an important person.'

The flight of stairs was lit, apart from the glow of lights from the bazaar, by a light somewhere overhead on the landing. Puri went up, balancing the thali carefully. The stairs opened on to a small aangan. He called, 'Ji, I've brought food from the dhaba.'

Puri had spoken as if acting out the role of a servant on a stage, but it was no play-acting. His tone of voice and his manner had automatically changed to suit the work he was doing.

'Yes, yes, bring it in here,' someone answered.

Puri saw an open door to his left, and went towards it. The room beyond was brightly lit. He was taken aback to see the man sitting on a wooden takht, studying some papers in his hand. The platter of food almost fell from Puri's hands.

The man continued to peer at the papers, absent-mindedly stroking his closely cropped hair with the other hand. Without raising his eyes he ordered, 'Pull that little table over here and put the thali on it.'

Puri controlled himself. Emotions welling up from somewhere deep down in his heart choked his throat. He quietly placed the thali on the table, lifted and moved the table next to the takht. He wanted to go back without the man seeing him, but hesitated for a moment in indecision.

His eyes still on the papers, the man said, 'Bring some water in a lota for me to wash my hands.'

'Where's the lota?' Puri had to ask. His voice was hoarse and cracked.

'There, beside the water tap,' the man replied, looking up.

He stared intently at Puri's face. Drawing a short breath of surprise, he said, 'Puri! Jaidev! Arrey Puri bhai, what has happened?'

He grabbed Puri's arm and sat him beside himself on the takht.

Puri's head was bent. Controlling the tears gathering in his eyes and swallowing the lump in his throat, he said, 'Soodji, what can I tell you?'

A telephone lying in one corner of the takht rang. Sood reached over and picked up the handset.

Puri had a moment to regain his composure.

Sood reproached Puri like an elder brother, his speech peppered with his characteristic phrase 'what's-its-name'. 'How could you behave this way? Whatever happened, didn't you know that Sood lives in what's-its-name Jalandhar? It's not that the people of this city don't know Sood. You could've asked anyone, at what's-its-name the Sewa Samiti refugees centre, at the Congress party office, at any shop. Any tonga or tumtum carriage driver would have brought you here if you had just asked him.'

Touched by Sood's caring words and brotherly concern, Puri told him briefly how he had gone to Nainital and Lucknow at the beginning of August on the invitation of a parliamentary secretary of the UP government. That he was in Nainital on 15 August. There were few signs of trouble until 10 or 11 August, with the situation quieting down after the League and the Congress had reached an agreement about the Partition. He got news in Nainital on 19 August that all Hindus were being evacuated from within the walled city of old Lahore. He left immediately to help his family stranded in Lahore. There was no reason for Sood to misconstrue his words, or interpret his story in any other way. Puri also told him how he had lost his suitcase when the mob attacked the Muslims in the train, and how he had been robbed outside the refugee camp at Islamia College on the previous night. He made it obvious that he desperately wanted to get to Lahore, or look for his family in India, wherever they were.

Chandan the dhaba owner was worried. The young man he had hired earlier in the day had not come back after delivering the thali of food at Soodji's. He had been away for over two hours. Either he had gone off to some other address, Chandan suspected, or in his hunger could not resist the temptation to eat free paranthas, and had run away taking the two thalis and two bowls with him. The bedroll of the hired hand was still at the dhaba, but who knew what was in it, if there was anything in it at all. It was past 10 o'clock. When he did not return, Chandan went to Sood's house in search of him.

What he saw amazed Chandan. His hired help was sitting on the takht, next to the big leader and talking with him. Chandan said namaste respectfully, and squatted down on the threshold of the room.

Sood spoke angrily to Chandan, 'Why didn't you tell him about me or give him my address? He's my brother, lives in what's-its-name Lahore.'

Chandan touched the ground, and then touched his ears with his hands in a gesture of repentance, then joined his hands and pleaded, 'Maharaj-ji, how could I know that? Sarkarji, he said nothing to me, and he asked no questions.'

Sood said to Chandan, 'Achchha, go now and take this thali with you. Do you call this thing you sent me a chapatti? Cold and hard as bits of what's-its-name pottery. Aren't you ashamed that you've no consideration for what's-its-name your neighbours! Go, and get us two fresh thalis with proper food.'

The thali that Puri had brought still lay untouched. Chandan took it back. When he returned with hot fresh meals, he had Puri's bedroll under his arm. He again sat on the threshold, and whined with his palms joined:

'Sarkar, you're my saviour. Master, I have a permit for only three bags of flour. I have three children. The bazaar prices are sky-high. Flour is selling at thirty-five rupees a maund. Girdhari, Son Singh, Moola all have permits for five bags. Huzoor, this servant of yours should also get a permit for five bags.'

'Aarey Chandan, you're a real what's-its-name badmaash. I know all about you. You snake, you mix millet with the wheat flour at your dhaba,' Sood scolded the cook affectionately.

'Hare Ram! Hare Ram! What makes you say that, maharaj!'

'Three bags should be enough. You want to sell the flour in what's-its-name black market, I know.'

'Hare Ram! Hare Ram! Maharaj, if I sell so much as one seer in the black market, may the curse of spilling a cow's blood fall on me.'

'Isn't the inspector of this area what's-its-name Jameet Singh?'

'Yes, sir.'

'Come back tomorrow morning. Remind me when you come to give back the thalis. Get lost now, and stop bothering me.'

The bright sun of the fag end of the monsoon had blazed over the city all day. Around midnight the sky became overcast and it began to rain. The house servant was still running a fever. Sood started to pull a charpoy into the room from the back veranda.

Puri rushed towards him, saying, 'Wait! Wait! I'll do it.'

'I'll take care of it in a minute. You take rest.'

The telephone rang again.

Puri insisted, 'Answer the phone. Let me handle this.'

'Here, the phone rings all the time,' said Sood. He set the charpoy down in the place he had chosen, then answered the telephone.

Sood spread a sheet over a dhurrie on the charpoy for Puri. He himself took the takht. The light was switched off. Gusts of wind, carrying a fine rain came through the window that opened towards the bazaar. The ceiling fan turned slowly. Puri's body and mind enjoyed the moment with a feeling of utmost peace.

A heat rash had broken over Sood's body on account of his having to move around under the blazing sun all day long. The cool breeze soothed his skin. He lay in the darkened room, gently stroking his body where the rash and his old eczema itched most, and discussed serious matters with Puri:

'Now that it's time for the Congress to form a ministry in Punjab, these people want to keep everything in the controlling hands of their little clique, just like the old days. The high command has deputed two people to make decisions over what's-its-name everything. Those two want the members elected from our eastern districts to act as what's-its-name figureheads, but keep all the real power in their own hands. Let's see how they manage to run the government. I'm the one who understands these local areas, not the people who've just come from what's-its-name outside.'

Sood's voice became agitated as he described what he saw as a wrong done to him, 'You know, the Doctor is a past master of intrigue and infighting. He thinks of himself as what's-its-name the successor to Lala Lajpat Rai. You'd remember that we met at his place in December 1945. I told you about him even then. Now what's-its-name he thinks that he can lord over everyone.'

Puri remembered that he had gone with Dr Prabhu Dayal, his gali neighbour, to meet Dr Radhey Behari for a job at *Pairokaar*. There he had run into Sood. Puri and Sood were interned together at the Multan Camp jail. There were more than a thousand prisoners in that jail. Two groups had formed there, one owing allegiance to Pandit Devi Das and the other to Sood, partly because of the differing political viewpoints and divisiveness within the Punjab wing of the Congress, and partly because of personal friendships and old links. Pandit Devi Das represented the Congress stalwarts and those who had held ministerial positions in earlier governments, and regarded himself as the heir to the legacy of Lala Lajpat Rai. He had the backing of Dr Radhey Behari and, therefore, of the Congress high command. Sood and his group of radicals demanded recognition based on the grounds of active participation in the present rather than on the merits of somebody who had been a leader in the distant past.

Sood, being a lawyer, had been accorded the concession of the 'special class' in the jail, but he had refused this special treatment and lived with the other political prisoners. He had the backing of the socialist wing of the party. In jail, Puri had been one of the followers of Sood. Puri also remembered that Sood had not liked his going to Dr Radhey Behari for help, because Sood thought of Puri as a like-minded and trustworthy comrade.

Sood asked Puri to be active at the grass-roots level in the organization again, and use his skills to strengthen the left wing of the Congress. He confided to Puri what he suspected to be the Doctor's strategy: The Doctor knew that the Jalandhar district was Sood's stronghold. He wanted a member of his own group, Raizada Naubat Rai, to be the Congress candidate in the forthcoming elections for the Punjab Legislative Assembly. In return, Sood was offered the candidacy for the Central Assembly in New Delhi.

Vexed by the Doctor's subterfuge, Sood complained, 'I know his tactics. First, where can I put together the means to contest the election in that huge Central Assembly constituency? He probably wants to shunt me off to New Delhi, so as to keep all the power in the hands of his cronies, and to be able to strike a deal with Khizr. If I become a candidate, it'll only be for the Punjab Assembly. How can I be effective in Jalandhar as a member of the Central Assembly? A person can only have influence in his own backyard. If I have to be a useless politician, what's the point of being a member of anything?'

As an admission of his error in judgement, Puri told Sood what he had gone through. Alarmed by the riots and lawlessness spreading throughout Lahore, Puri said, he had written warnings as early as in March against the inflammatory speeches of Congress and Akali leaders. 'The Doctor is undoubtedly a communalist,' Puri said. 'He had me thrown out of my job at the newspaper. These people insist that if someone becomes their supporter, he should be prepared to call day night, and night day.'

Sood listened to Puri, grunting occasionally in a sleepy voice. The grunts gradually turned to snoring. His limbs relaxed, and soon he was in the deep sleep of exhaustion.

Puri agreed with Sood's views about the situation in Punjab after the Partition, and touched by Sood's kindness and concern, began to feel the same kinship with him as he had in the Multan Camp jail. He could not fall asleep for some time. He had come here as the dhaba owner's servant, to deliver a platter of food, and here he was sleeping peacefully under a fan. A soft breeze, cooled by rain, came through the window. He thought about the other refugees, how they must be suffering, those who had not found shelter indoors at the Islamia College camp? Where were the members of his family... huddling for shelter in some tiny, suffocating room, or under a tree, or out in the open without any shelter? 'My fate seems different from the rest of my family. But what can I do at the moment? I'll figure out something tomorrow. Maybe try my luck in Amritsar...'

The memory of being with Kanak, on the soft, springy bed in Nainital, came to his mind. Then the horrible sights and memories of the few past days... He tossed and turned for a while, before falling asleep.

Vishwa Nath Sood had studied law at Lahore. From his student days he had been an active participant in social protest movements, and public marches and demonstrations. He had no particular loyalty, either to the reformist Arya Samaji Hindus, or to the orthodox Hindu Sanatanis. He would be equally prepared to help in organizing a social function of the Muslim League. He did not draw back if his help was needed for a marriage function, or in the preparation of the funeral rites of a dead neighbour. Most of his time was spent as a worker for the Congress party. He had taken the vow to wear only homespun khadi cloth as early as in 1921. His natural inclination was towards social work and public life. After passing his law examinations, he had begun his practice as a junior lawyer.

In 1929, the British government had brought several revolutionaries to trial for taking part in armed insurgency and for the killing of Indians and Britons working for the government. The official Congress policy was the non-violent satyagraha movement and the drive towards independence by constitutional means only. Gandhiji and the Congress party had criticized the actions of the revolutionaries, but the public had shown great admiration for their sacrifice and courage. The revolutionaries' cry of 'inquilab zindabad' had echoed throughout the country. Defence committees were formed to aid the revolutionaries in the courts. People all over the country were helping in whatever way they could.

The veteran Congress leader and well-known lawyer Lala Ramnath had come out of retirement to join the defence team formed in Lahore in aid of the revolutionaries. Some young lawyers had come forward to help him, one of them being Vishwa Nath Sood. Newspapers carried glowing reports of this dedicated and hard-working legalist. The political career of young Sood was firmly established at that time. In the tumultuous and hectic days between 1931 and 1934, Sood was in the forefront of every Congress movement in Jalandhar district and in the Doaba region, and went to jail repeatedly as one of the leaders of the struggle.

The more the public admired Sood's selfless work, the less his family appreciated his dedication to the nationalist cause. His family owned a modest jewellery business and were financially secure. His elder brother, who did not finish his matriculation examination, joined their father in the family business. The second eldest also worked at the shop for some time after his matriculation, then set up a mill, and soon after, a hardware store. Sood's father bought two more houses beside the small house they owned. Sood's own life was dedicated to public service. Although he was a leader of the Congress and a lawyer, his family saw him as an encumbrance to them. The family had received several attractive marriage proposals for him after he had begun his law practice, with prospects of handsome dowries, but Sood did not break his vow to dedicate his life to the country.

After the death of their father, his brothers thought it prudent to divide the family property. All Sood got as his share was the old mill. Sood was a lawyer, but he did not object to this arbitrary division. He, of course, could not manage the mill, and hired it out. He had neither the time nor the inclination for marriage. He came to be known as the fakir vakil, a lawyer without possessions. In the 1946 assembly elections, when the Congress was reeling under the repressive measures of the British government, it was Sood's tireless work and his influence that won both the Hindu and the Muslim constituencies for the Congress, Sood himself taking the Hindu seat; and with his backing, the Congress candidate won the Muslim seat.

Sood's influence increased after his election to the assembly. He began to receive a monthly stipend of about three hundred rupees. The sole outward sign of this raise in his income was that he moved into a bigger, more comfortable room, with an attached kitchen, in the Mandi bazaar. Here he could receive a larger number of visitors. He also had a telephone installed. Instead of going for meals at some tandoor eatery, he hired a cook. He also got a few extra pairs of khadi kurtas and pajamas. He stopped washing his own clothes. Those in dire need could now ask him for a loan of twenty or twenty-five rupees. But his dress remained the same old kurta over pajama, or a dhoti, and the well-worn bicycle served him for transport.

The Congress had given Sood, as its representative, the task of handling the influx of refugees in the Jalandhar district. The responsibility of supervising the operation of the refugee camps and the distribution of free rations also rested on his shoulders. Government officials consulted him in almost every matter. The formation of a new ministry in East Punjab was in the offing. Ministerial appointments rested on many considerations such as recognition of the claims of the old-guard Congress leaders, recommendations from the Congress high command, and due attention to the influence of local Congress leaders. Sood carefully monitored each new development, and assessed its implications for his group.

The Congress high command had handed, even before 15 August, the responsibility of forming the new administration to Dr Radhey Behari, and to a leader of the Sikh community, and had declared that Dr Radhey Behari would be the new chief minister of Punjab. In spite of the strong support for his group's political ideals and policy within the Congress party organization and among the members of the assembly, Sood had not come forward with any proposals of nomination to the ministerial portfolios. But it was not possible to ignore his influence within the organization, and Sood spent most of his day touring the district to meet his followers and backers, and sometimes spending the night away from his home.

When Puri awoke, Sood had already taken his bath. He sat on the takht, changing into fresh clothes.

On seeing Puri awake, he said, 'You don't have to get up yet. You must be tired, and would like to make up for not sleeping well over the last few days. Sleep on if you wish.'

Puri got out of bed, and folded the sheet and the dhurrie.

Sudama, Sood's servant, brought from the bazaar two matthis, salted biscuits and some lassi. Using a piece of paper as a plate, he placed the matthis on a low table in front of Sood, and a glass of lassi. Sudama's face looked sallow from the fever. He said namaste to Puri after serving Sood his breakfast.

Sood said to Sudama, 'This is my brother. After he's had his wash, get him whatever he wants for breakfast. If I'm late coming home, give him his meal whenever he wants. Ask him what he wants and cook it for him. You understand?'

Sood bit off a piece of matthi as he said to Puri, 'The shaving kit is in the cupboard over there. And here is a pair of kurta-pajama. It should fit you, you're not that big. Poor people like me don't wear what's-its-name trousers. Sudama will get your laundry done.'

He was about the same height, or maybe just a bit taller than Puri, but had a heavier build.

Sood spoke as he chewed his mouthful, 'So, what're your plans now?'

'I'd like to go and look for my family ...'

Sood, his mouth still full of matthi, cut Puri short, 'Where will you look? Of course there's the chance of you running into them on what's-its-name street. You write the names and addresses of your father and his elder brother on a piece of what's-its-name paper. I'll telephone Sarban Singh at the main police station. He'd have someone go through the lists from all the camps.' Sood pointed to the rain-washed aangan, 'Why go out and get soaked in rain uselessly? Your face is drawn as if you were sick. Be patient. Just rest here today.'

'I'd like to go to Amritsar to look for my family.'

A motorcar horn sounded from the bazaar below the window. 'Arrey, they're here!' Sood muttered. He looked out of the window and waved his hand at someone to tell the driver to wait, and told Puri as he picked up his lassi, 'That'll be arranged. Some vehicle or other will be sent to Amritsar in a day or two, and you can get a ride there and back. It's not easy to get any other transport. And it's not possible to go by train.'

Two days later Puri was in a station wagon headed for Amritsar on some official business. The vehicle flew the tricolour flag of India, with the emblem of Ashoka's wheel. Two armed constables rode inside, and two other khadi-clad passengers carried handguns by virtue of their status as civil guards. The Grand Trunk Road was packed with vehicles and travellers of all kinds. An unending line of buses and trucks full of refugees fleeing Pakistan flowed towards Amritsar. Convoys of a different kind were heading towards Lahore: buses with armed escort vehicles, and a vast river of bedraggled Muslim refugees on foot, lugging their meagre belongings. The station wagon was forced to travel at a very slow speed. Broken-down bullock carts, tongas and various other types of horse carts, gutted buses and partially burned trucks, remnants of pillaged tin trunks and boxes, corpses scattered around and in heaps, and dismembered limbs could be seen on both sides of the highway.

The continuous passage of vehicles on the road had forced the slow-moving tide of refuges on to the tracts of land parallel to the road. A pall of dust, raised by the feet of the tired and weakened marchers, hovered overhead. Some of them pulled behind them equally exhausted skeletal cattle, goats or sheep.

A man in the convoy walked past pulling a mare by the reins. The seriously emaciated animal was clearly unfit for riding. As Puri watched, a Jat jumped out of a field alongside the column of refugees, snatched the reins from the owner, and calmly led the animal back into the field. No one from the thousands in the convoy protested; not one voice was raised, not one finger lifted. It was a sheer display of might being right. A cold shiver ran down Puri's spine. These were Muslims, the very same people that the Hindus pouring in from the west were fleeing from.

Puri had gone around various refugee camps in Jalandhar in the past two days, and had met several old acquaintances. His fellow prisoner in Multan Camp jail, Mehar Chand from the town of Pind Dadan Khan, refused to utter a word when he saw Puri. Every last bit of Mehar Chand's property had been looted, and every woman of his family had been abducted. Puri's blood boiled on hearing the atrocities suffered by the family and neighbours of Tek Singh from Sangla, another comrade from the days in Multan Camp jail. And it was not easy to listen to the blood-curdling accounts of Hukumat Rai, his classmate from the years Puri had spent studying for the intermediate exam. The eyes of Rudh Singh, another acquaintance, were bloodshot with anger. All he wanted was to go back westward, and die after killing as many as he could. And now, on his way to Amritsar, Puri was looking at dead and dismembered Muslims, at the naked, mutilated bodies of their women. He was seeing with his own eyes the endless line of marching corpses, Muslims too terrified and exhausted even to cry out in protest, the very people who had once been the rightful owners of the land from which they had been uprooted. An artificial boundary line had been drawn over the countryside, dividing into two countries the very soil to which the people were linked by family and history. The Hindus on the other side of that man-made line had suffered the same fate. Puri's skin crawled with fear when he thought of his family being ruined by the vagaries of the same fate as the people in front of his eyes.

The station wagon that had left Jalandhar at six that morning covered the distance of sixty miles to Amritsar in seven hours. Traffic bottlenecks in both directions had forced them to wait for over an hour to cross the bridge over the Vyas River. Amritsar was a much larger city than Jalandhar. Droves of disposssed people fleeing their homes in the west had settled like a swarm of locusts over every foot of the available space. One could not walk through a bazaar or down a street without having to push through surging crowds. Puri went to the poste restante at the General Post Office to inquire about any mail from Kali, whom he had met in Ferozepur, and left instructions that all letters meant for him should be forwarded to Sood's address in Jalandhar. He spent the rest of the day combing through the lists of refugees at camps set up at Khalsa College, Loha Garh, Darbar Sahib, Durgiayana, and in various schools and factories. There was no trace of his family. The station wagon left for Jalandhar at 11 o'clock at night. The traffic on the highway had thinned down at that hour, and they reached Jalandhar at two in the morning.

Next day, after thanking Sood for taking advantage of his generosity, he hinted that he now wanted to look for his people in Ambala and Ludhiana, if the possibility presented itself.

Sood replied, running his hand over his closely cropped hair as was his habit, 'An occasion for you to go there can easily be created. If you want, you can even go up to what's-its-name Delhi to look for your family. But does this haphazard running around, this hope of finding them purely by chance really make sense? Listen bhai, if you are banking only on luck you could just go down this what's-its-name stairway, and find your father standing in front of Ram Ditta Halwai's shop across the street. You should first try to guess where they might be, and look for them there.'

Sood continued, 'Wherever they are, they can survive if they have a bit of cash in hand. Does what's-its-name your father have some cash or valuables with him?'

Puri's voice trembled with emotion, 'That's my biggest worry. What savings could my family have put together? My father was a schoolteacher. I was unemployed for the last six months. We somehow managed my sister's wedding this July. We'd bought a lot of foodstuff like ghee, on credit, for the ceremony. The marriage was performed in a hurry; most of the stuff remained unused. That's all we had, but who could carry away all that? And who knows how they've been living and surviving till now? You know, I'm willing to do anything, but I feel so helpless in this mess that I can't think of how to go about it.'

Sood continued to run his hand reflectively over the top and sides of his head as he looked at some distant point outside the open window, and said, 'Bhai, your priority is to get yourself settled. First get your own place, so that what's-its-name your family can come and live with you.'

Puri answered excitedly, 'That's exactly what I had in mind, bhaiji. I'm willing to do whatever I can get, work as a clerk or even a peon, so that they and I can eat at least one good meal a day. At the moment, I don't even have a set of clothes to change into.'

His eyes still gazing beyond the window, Sood said in idiomatic Punjabi,

'Don't talk nonsense! Isn't this your what's-its-name home? If there's only one chapatti to eat, we'll share it; what's the problem? You're not exactly naked, are you? If you don't have what's-its-name trousers, you have kurta-pajama to wear. If it bothers you so much, get yourself a pair of trousers. But stop talking rubbish.'

'But, bhaiji ...' Puri began meekly, his voice full of gratitude.

Sood did not let him finish, 'I'd say you should settle yourself here in what's-its-name Jalandhar. We're old comrades, aren't we?' He looked into Puri's eyes for his answer.

'That's right, bhaiji. That's what I'd like too.'

'You used to work at that newspaper what's-its-name *Pairokaar*?' Sood began in a serious tone, looking at Puri, 'So you know how a printing press operates?'

'Sometimes I did go to where the paper was printed. And I did some proofreading. Whatever job's available, I'll be willing ...'

'Did *Pairokaar* have its own printing press?'

'Ji, no. It was printed at Nasiruddin's press.'

'What kind of presses were they?'

'A lithographic-cylinder machine.'

'In Lahore so large a press would naturally have been electrically operated. We've only got one treadle and one lithographic-cylinder. Can you handle all that?'

'I can do proofreading, keep account books, and do some supervising. If someone gave me a little guidance ...'

'That won't be a problem. Isaac, poor man, had to leave everything behind. He left the keys to his Kamaal Press in my custody. His treadle machine operator was Hindu. Still lives here. You can restart the printing press. No shortage of work. People wanting to have printing done sometimes have to run to Delhi. Some advance payment for work that you'll do can be arranged.'

Sood sent for a jeep from the Police Department for his round of inspection of refugee settlements. He and Puri went first to the Congress party's provincial headquarters. Next Sood went to the homes of two of his associates and had long discussions on the appointments to the posts of ministers. In the afternoon, he ordered the jeep to stop in the bazaar of Mai Heeran Gate, and led Puri on foot into a lane in Bahadurgarh mohalla. Over the narrow door to a small room hung a large signboard with the name Kamaal Press in English, Hindi and Farsi. Beside the board hung India's national flag, its colours faded by rain.

A man from the Kangra Hills sat in the doorway to the room, smoking a small coconut-shell hookah. The man hid the hookah behind the leaf of the door when he saw them approach, stood up, said pairipaina, I touch your feet, and bowed respectfully to Sood.

'How's it going, Raldu? No one bothered you again, did they?' Sood asked the hillman.

'The same man returned, boss. Came this morning too,' Raldu replied in a mixture of Punjabi and his hill dialect.

'He didn't create any trouble?'

'No, boss. Only said that you had told him that the press would be reopened. Said that he wanted to get a job in the press.'

Sood took out a large key from the pocket of his waistcoat and handed it to Raldu, 'Open the door.'

Raldu unlocked a door in the back wall. The door opened on to a small courtyard containing a modest two-storeyed red brick house. On the ground floor, next to the stairs to the first floor, was a small room. In this room was a plain desk, a couple of bent-wire chairs, and next to the wall, a sturdy-looking bench. In the adjoining larger room was the lithographic-cylinder machine and in one corner, a small treadle machine. A row of ink rollers stood against one wall. Reams of printing paper were stacked to the ceiling in two piles against another wall. A paper-cutting machine stood on a low dais near the third wall. The whole set-up looked well maintained and orderly, except for a layer of dust over everything, that showed that it had not been operated for some time.

Isaac Mohammed, the owner of Kamaal Press, was an amiable businessman. His father had set up the business, doing lithography on stone slabs and a hand-operated machine. The son joined the press after passing his matriculation examination. He got a second-hand treadle machine from Lahore, and installed an electric motor to run it. He had been able to buy a lithographic-cylinder printing machine just before the 1936 elections. His business was flourishing. Isaac's landlord Maula Baksh, who suffered from chronic asthma, owned three old rundown houses in the Bahadurgarh district. The rent from this property was his only income. Isaac occasionally helped his landlord by lending him money. In return for the loans Isaac first took possession of the room where his father had installed the hand-operated press, and eventually, of the rest of the house. In the courtyard of the old house Isaac put up a new building for his printing press, and living accommodations for his family above it on the first floor. The small room that opened on to the gali began to serve as the main entrance, to the printing press as well as to his home.

In the city of Jalandhar and for miles around, the population was predominantly Muslim, mostly tanners and curers of hides, and market gardeners. When the movement for the creation of Pakistan was at its height, Muslims living in the city and the countryside around it believed that Jalandhar would be a part of Pakistan. After the announcement in June 1947 that Jalandhar would go to India, large numbers of Muslims began fleeing to the west. Those who stayed behind were unnerved by the arrival of a vast number of Hindu refugees from the west in early August, but Isaac, like many of his mohalla neighbours, decided to remain in Jalandhar. Generations of his family had lived in the city, and, also, the fruit of his lifelong labour, his press, was in Jalandhar.

Isaac wanted nothing to do with the agitation for the establishment of Pakistan. He did jobs for both the Muslim League and the Congress party, and if he got the chance, took on work from the government. He gave five or ten rupees as a donation when the League volunteers came to his door, and the same to the Congress party workers when they showed up. Sood had not forgotten that Isaac had printed leaflets for the Congress at a particularly crucial time, thus becoming one of a group whom Sood trusted and favoured.

On 15 August 1947, the Muslims remaining in Bahadurgarh mohalla, on Isaac Mohammed's advice, hoisted the Indian national tricolour over their houses. These people were not willing to leave their homeland for the promised saltanat-e-ilahi, Kingdom of Allah. Hindus, especially refugees from the west, were not pleased with this outward show of love for India by the Muslims. How could they tolerate the presence of the community that had committed such terrible crimes on their Hindu brothers and had driven them from their homeland? The refugees needed houses to live in. Despite the efforts of the Congress, the communists and Sood himself, the neighbourhoods where Muslim families lived were repeatedly under attack. Twenty-seven inhabitants of Bahadurgarh had already been killed, and the first two houses in the terrace had been burned down. Sood had asked the deputy commissioner to post armed police at the entrance of the gali. Even such dangers had not persuaded Issac to flee the city.

On the morning of 23 August, a convoy of lorries led by military officers arrived at Bahadurgarh. All Muslims were ordered to gather any belonging they could carry, and board the lorries. The order was for them to be taken, for their safety, to the Muslim refugee camps.

Isaac's nervousness turned into extreme agitation. He asked for time, to be able to speak with Sood. The officer-in-charge refused to make any exception to his orders. Raldu had been working for Isaac for the past thirteen years, and lived in a small side room off the press. Isaac asked him to take a letter and the keys to the press to Sood. He said to Raldu, 'My boy, continue to stay here and keep watch. I'll be back in a month, or two or three at the most. You'll get your Rs 45 a month as usual.' He handed Raldu one month's salary in advance.

Addressing Sood as 'Respected Brother', Isaac had written about the good relations between the two of them and all the favours he had received because of Sood, and implored Sood to get him out of the refugee camp. And if that was not possible, to take into safekeeping the keys to the press. 'I'll be back, God willing; or else whatever fate may have in store for me.' He said he would then write to Sood to sell his press off and kindly send him the money. He also mentioned that both his rebuilt printing machines had cost eight thousand rupees between them, and there was a paper-cutting machine worth six hundred and stocks of paper worth eleven hundred rupees; that Raldu had been instructed to stay behind and keep an eye on the property. He requested Sood to be kind enough to continue to pay the man 45 rupees every month in his absence.

Isaac's note saddened Sood, but there was little he could do to help him. The situation was such that it would have been unwise to separate Isaac from his community and send him back. He asked Raldu to keep a careful watch over Isaac's property.

On 27 August—the evening Puri had carried the tray of food from Chandan's dhaba to Sood's house—Rikhiram, a refugee from West Punjab had come to see Sood late in the afternoon after talking with Raldu. He said to Sood, 'I had to abandon my own printing press, a treadle and a small litho machine, in Jhehlum. I have a large family. Many refugees have occupied abandoned shops in the bazaar and houses in the neighbourhood, after breaking open the padlocks. What else can one do? Justice demands that I should take over Isaac Mohammed's press. Raldu, that nobody from the hills, has occupied the press in your name. That's not fair.'

Anger furrowed Sood's brow as he spoke severely to Rikhiram, 'Who says that what's-its-name hillman has occupied the press? The press belongs to me and Raldu is my employee. That what's-its-name Isaac operated the press on contract. If he's gone that doesn't mean that anyone else can occupy the press. What right does anybody have over my press? Don't try anything foolish, I'm warning you. What's anyone got to do with my press being run or not?'

Refugees from the west living in the houses neighbouring Kamaal Press had told Rikhiram a different story. Sood telephoned Chaudhari Makkhan Singh in Mai Heeran Gate bazaar in Rikhiram's presence, 'Sardarji, your bazaar people are spreading rumours. I'll hold you responsible if any harm is done to Kamaal Press. Don't forget.'

Rikhiram joined his palms together and begged that he might be allowed to operate the press on lease. He was ready to pay any reasonable fees. He also assured Sood that he'd pay for repairs if any machine was damaged in operation.

Sood told him to come back some other time to discuss the matter.

Rikhiram came again when Puri went to Amritsar in search of his family. Sood said to him, 'Bhai, I won't lease the press. We'll run it ourselves.' Rikhiram then requested that he be hired in the press as an employee. He had owned a press, and knew how to manage everything in the shop, he assured Sood, and could do most technical work himself. He was earning three to four hundred rupees as profit every month from his treadle and small litho machine. Fate was cruel to him; he and his family had barely escaped alive when those bastards had set fire to his press and house.

Jaidev Puri had been waiting impatiently to find work for the past six months; now he had the opportunity to run a business. He had had little experience of working in a printing press, but he chose not to admit that. Rikhiram had begged to be given the press on a six-month lease, and was ready to sign a promissory note for one thousand rupees. Sood stipulated that six months' rent would have to be paid in advance, and that his brother would work as the manager. Rikhiram would have to pay the manager an extra Rs 150 per month. These conditions were acceptable to Rikhiram, but he had no money to put down in advance. He had to accept work as an employee of the press.

Refugees who had been employed in printing presses began arriving seeking work soon after the press was in operation. They had been making inquires with Raldu even when the press was closed. Within days of the opening, a clerk from the ration office arrived to place an order for two hundred fifty thousand ration cards.

Puri quietly watched Rikhiram handle the working of the press. How many sheets of a particular size of paper, how many pages could be printed at one time on the press, how many impressions in an hour, how much it would cost and what price to demand from the customer. Rikhiram knew all this by heart. Just by the sound of the printing machine, he could tell the operator, 'Nekram, look out, the driving-belt is loose. Oil the gears once more. Never ignore the machine; it is Lakshmi, the goddess of wealth for us!'

If Rikhiram saw that the text typeset by the compositor would not be enough and the machine might stand idle, he would lend a hand by composing a few lines himself. Or justify the text if the lines were not properly aligned. Or adjust the key that regulated the pressure of the cylinder if the impression was not right. Or shout at the men cleaning the lithograph slabs. He would lean closer to Puri and murmur, 'It's not easy to keep these people up to the scratch. I know every inch of the press operations. So just tell me what you want to get done. If Soodji keeps sending work our way like this, I can earn that six-month advance money in no time at all. Wish I had such profitable work back in Jhelum.'

Puri did not interfere in the way Rikhiram ran the press, but he also did not turn a blind eye to anything. He himself prepared the invoices, but with Rikhiram's advice. He reckoned up the jobs completed during the day. If the day's output was worth forty or fifty rupees, he would calculate the profit minus the cost. He would feel proud at how much his work would bring in. Concern for his family and the memory of Kanak would fade in the midst of all this hustle and bustle, and he would feel that all this effort would one day remove the obstacles that were keeping him away from them.

The Kamaal Press was busy doing printing work for the orders pouring in from the supply office, the ration office, and also for the Congress party office. The presses operated all day until midnight, and sometimes all night.

The floor above the office had two small rooms, the kitchen, a bathroom and a small aangan. Isaac's family had been able to carry away only their clothes, jewellery and a few kitchen utensils. They left behind a large bedstead, three charpoys, an old armchair, a rickety three-legged stool, an electric table fan that did not work, several tin trunks and other small items. The upper story was wired up with electrical outlets and had running water. Puri brought over his bedding from Sood's house. He moved everything into the side room except for the bedstead, which he used at night. He ate his meals at a dhaba in the bazaar.

While working at the *Pairokaar*, if Puri had to go to the printing press to make corrections to the final copy or carry out some errand, the awful din of the machines, the all-pervasive grime that soiled hands and clothes, and the smell of ink, cleaning fluid and rubber compound nauseated him. Now the bang, clang and clatter of the machines seemed stimulating and comforting, he did not mind if his hands or clothes got dirty. In fact an interruption stoppage in the rhythm of the machines gave him a feeling of loss.

Rikhiram had not bothered to negotiate his salary at the time of his employment. He had said, with a touch of bravado, 'Give me whatever seems proper after you've seen what I can do.'

The press had been operating for three weeks when Rikhiram mentioned to Puri how tight his financial situation was. He enquired what his salary would be, and requested an advance against it.

'Let me first consult Soodji,' said Puri. 'but before I do that, tell me how much you're asking?'

'You've been here watching, brother. You've seen that I can manage everything,' Rikhiram pleaded. 'We do 45, at times even 60 or 65 rupees worth of work every day. You can bring in more jobs, however many, and I'll get them done. I've a large family. I need at least 7 or 8 rupees a day, and may be more for sickness and such, God forbid! Back home, we lived fairly well, always fed our kids milk and lassi. Why'd I ask more? I know you won't offer me less than 250 a month.'

Puri knew Rikhiram was right, but still the sum seemed exorbitant. He said, 'I'll tell Bhaiji. Can't commit myself without asking him. He owns the press; so whatever he says goes.'

Puri conferred with Sood. Sood mulled over the output of the press, and

then telephoned two printing-press owners for advice. He sat and stared out
of the window, cracking his toes and moving his hand thoughtfully over his
closely cropped hair, and said, 'The government's decision is not to allow
the removal of any what's-its-name machinery to Pakistan. The Pakistan
government too has banned the export of machinery, but the press still
belongs to Isaac. You'll have to pay him some what's-its-name money. Don't
leave any cash at the press. I'll give you a letter of introduction; go and
deposit it in the bank tomorrow. Get what's-its-name a cheque book. It's a
lot less hassle when you pay by cheque. Understand? And his demand for Rs
250 is nonsense. What press will pay Rs 250? What'll the owner earn? The
investment for what's-its-name machines, rent, interest charges, all these
have to be taken into account. All he does is supervise; you've probably
picked up enough savvy by now. One hundred is quite enough. Give him
five or ten more if you think he's worth it, and useful. Not over 125, no
way. If he doesn't agree, tell him to buzz off. It's not a bloody charity.'

Puri said with some embarrassment. 'What about me? So far I've been a
burden on you. I've kept an account of whatever I spent on myself. I need
to get some clothes made, and there're all kinds of daily expenses.'

'Tell me what you want,' replied Sood.

'Whatever you say is fine with me.'

'Have you heard anything about your family?'

'I gave Delhi radio my address, care of you. If there's any news, it'll be
sent here.' The government radio services broadcast information about
families separated in the chaos of the massive exodus, from one country
to the other.

Puri usually ate at a dhaba close to the entrance to the gali of Bahadurgarh,
near Mai Heeran Gate. Next to it was the market square, where an amplifier
broadcast news bulletins with names, and the old and new addresses of
persons separated from their families. He listened carefully while he ate,
but he could not neglect his work and sit there all day listening. He had
mailed his family's old Lahore address and his new address to the radio
station. No reply had come, so far.

Sood pondered over his words, and then said, 'Your people are not here
yet; so take 125 or 150 for yourself. We'll settle up when they arrive.'

Puri was more than happy as he couldn't have hoped for more.

Rikhiram's face fell when he was offered only 100 rupees per month.
He said, 'Bhai, why such unfair treatment?'

Puri sympathized with Rikhiram's plight, but had to adopt a managerial attitude, 'My hands are tied. Those are my orders. I can recommend that you get a bit more, but Bhaiji's word will be final.'

When Rikhiram did not seem happy with 125 rupees per month, Puri repeated Sood's words sternly, 'What about you and the people that you hired back home? How much did you pay them?'

Rikhiram had inquired at several other presses. No one was willing to pay even that much. He bit his lip and kept quiet.

That evening, the press ran until 10 o'clock. Puri ate his meal at the dhaba, and lay down on the bedstead upstairs. September was coming to an end. The rains were late, and it had been showery since the day before. Every window in the room was open, letting in gusts of cool air. He did not feel like sleeping. He thought of writing a letter. He still remembered Kanak's address at Vimal Villa in Nainital, but then she might have moved to Delhi or some other town.

He had bought himself a fountain pen. One day when there was a break in the work, he had a fine letterhead printed on bond paper. On the left appeared 'J.D. Puri, Manager', on the right his address 'Kamaal Press, Mai Heeran Gate, Jalandhar'. Mentioning that his salary was Rs 200 per month did not seem an exaggeration. Kanak would be happy to read that. Didn't Sood say that he would reconsider the salary after his family arrived?

His imagination did not stop there. Sood's words came into his mind: The government has banned export of all machinery. Isaac won't be able to cart off his press to Pakistan. Puri even imagined that the press would be his after the money was paid. Should he tell Kanak so? What hadn't he gone through in the past two months? But now he was managing a printing press, anything was possible in the future. But wouldn't that be bravado ... reaching for a star! His owning the press depended on Sood, but there was no doubt about the 200 rupees monthly salary. Things were falling into place. It might be possible to find time to do some writing in the mornings or the evenings. He could certainly say to Kanak that the kind of life he had imagined for them was about to begin. Let it be in Jalandhar, if not Lucknow. If he did not have the prestige of a government position, at least he had the independence of being his own master. What'll Kanak think of this, what'll she say?

Rikhiram's distressed face after he was refused 250 rupees appeared before Puri's eyes. He had peremptorily rejected Rikhiram's demand.

But, then, every paisa had to be pinched in managing the press, and he had to get the most out of every paisa that had to be spent. His imagination would take off and he would slip into doing some quick mental arithmetic, calculating that the salaries for two press-machine operators and their helpers, a compositor, a calligraphist, Rikhiram and himself didn't add up to much above twenty rupees a day, or an average of about three rupees per head. The electricity bill and the cost of inks and the compound for rollers couldn't be more than another twenty rupees per day, when the work done could be costed at 60 or 70 rupees. Even if the overheads were thirty rupees per day, a large margin of profit remained for the owner. Suppose there were more than two machines! A press-machine operator's salary was twenty rupees per month. Imagine what the owner could save for himself after he had paid off the workers! He recalled the discussions on the surplus value of labour in the study circle run by the communists. His thoughts wandered … in factories that had eight, ten or twenty thousand workers, if the owners put away even half a rupee per worker per day … His head spun at the thought of such huge profit margins.

He shook his head to drive away such thoughts and got out of bed, switched on the light, and began composing a letter to Kanak. Memories of the past weeks interrupted his writing several times. He ended the letter when he heard the chimes in the distance striking one o'clock, and sealed the envelope to send to Nainital first thing next day by registered post. The desire to be close to Kanak made his blood race through his veins; it inflamed his mind. The gong sounded two o'clock before he fell asleep.

A large poster for the District Congress Committee was being printed on the litho-cylinder. This job, for 10,000 posters, had to be finished by evening. The treadle was doing tickets for a bus company. The lads working as helpers didn't have a free minute. Puri didn't want to interrupt the printing. He approved the final proofs for the next job for the treadle, and stepped out to go to the dhaba for a quick lunch. The sky had cleared after the previous night's rain, and the hot midday sun blazed relentlessly overhead.

Puri turned into the bazaar and stopped dead in his tracks. On his right Jagdish with an attaché case in hand was coming up to him, and Praveen balancing a trunk on his shoulder. Behind them walked Badhawa Mull Narang and Beyji, with Urmila in between. Narang too carried an attaché case and Beyji held a much larger one. Urmila was carrying the bedding rolled up in a dhurrie and tied with a dhoti or dupatta twisted into a rope. Their bodies were drenched in sweat. The weight of his burden was making the elder Narang gasp for breath. A mask of worry and gloom covered Beyji's face. Urmila looked exactly as Puri had seen her four weeks before on 26 August at the Islamia College camp: her head submissively bowed, a pale and sickly face, hair unkempt and tangled, like an eagle's nest.

Although Puri, when he had last seen her, was himself fraught with anxiety and in a desperate situation, memories of the Urmila he had previously known flared up in his mind: her extraordinary glowing complexion, her vivacity, her uninhibited, almost obscene longing for romance. In spite of his determination to remain aloof, he had all but succumbed to her charms. Beyji, decent person that she was, had dealt with that affair quietly and with tact. An intense awareness of that embarrassing and distasteful incident had kept him from accepting the invitation to Urmila's marriage, and visiting the family to congratulate them. But the news that Urmila had become a widow in March, just after the riots had begun to flare up, had really shaken him.

Stunned for the moment by this unexpected meeting, Puri addressed Jagdish and all the others together, 'Where're you all going? What's happened?'

Jagdish put the case he was carrying down on the road, and others did the same with their own loads. Urmila moved the roll from under one arm to the other. Beyji dabbed at her tears with the corner of her dupatta. Narang sat down heavily on the front boards of a nearby shop, struggling to catch his breath.

Jagdish said, 'Pitaji got very sick, and we couldn't go to Delhi. Yesterday afternoon, policemen came to the camp at Islamia College, with trucks. 'It's a Government order,' they announced. 'Everyone must vacate the building immediately. We were to be moved to another camp ...'

'Yes,' Puri cut in to say, 'the new secretariat will be coming up there in its place.'

'How would we know!' Jagdish said in an exasperated tone, 'The police loaded us into the trucks, and then dumped us in the grounds of an old mosque, seventeen miles out of town. The place was deserted. We spent the night without any food. A truck coming from the direction of Lohiyan charged us four rupees each for a ride up to an intersection some distance from here. We couldn't find any conveyance there. Now we don't even have a roof over our heads, or a place to unload our stuff. Father is in poor health. Thought we'd sit for a while in the waiting room at the railway station.'

'Come with me all of you, no need to wander around,' Puri said, taking Narang's attaché case in one hand and tucking Urmila's bed roll under his other arm. 'Come on.'

Puri brought the family back to the printing press. He summoned the two helper boys, told them to carry up the luggage, and led the family upstairs. He brought out the charpoys, and said, 'No shortage of space, the other room wasn't being used. That's the bathroom with running water, get washed. I'll send out for some food.'

When the food from the dhaba was delivered, Puri sat and ate with the family.

Puri opened up the second room, and got the boys to come up again and sweep and tidy it. He came upstairs several times to inquire if the family wanted anything. He intended to pay back the help and hospitality that the family had given him in the past. The feeling of being able to do so was overpowering.

In the evening, Jagdish went to the bazaar with Beyji to buy some groceries. Puri objected when he found out, 'You didn't have to trouble yourselves. You're my guests, you shouldn't have done this.'

'Kakaji, what's ours is yours too. May God give you lots more,' Beyji blessed him.

The evening meal was cooked in the kitchen. Puri ate with them, as one of the family, talking to each in turn.

He asked Beyji, Urmila and Praveen to take the large bedstead. He, Jagdish and the elder Narang slept on the charpoys. In the morning he went and got a seer of yogurt for them to make lassi.

Urmila's attitude of hopelessness, and grief-stricken apathy rankled him. He said to Beyji as if she were his mother, in Urmila's presence, 'What's wrong with Urmi? Who could change what fate had in store for her. That's no way to lead a life. She has to accept it and go on living, like the rest of us.'

Urmila sat quietly, staring fixedly at the floor under her feet. Beyji again dabbed her eyes with her dupatta, 'Kakaji, I've given up on her. Don't know what's wrong with her. Never says anything, nor listens to us. I've been after her since yesterday to change her clothes. No result.'

Puri insisted, 'No, that's not right. Get her to wash her hair. Just look at her. Whatever happens, you have to go on behaving and living your life like a human being.'

Puri sent out the electric fan that Isaac had abandoned for repairs. When he came upstairs for his lunch the next day, he brought along the repaired fan. Urmila lay on the chatai, her face to the wall. Puri said to Beyji, 'The heat must be bothering Urmi. Here's the fan. I got it repaired.' He switched on the fan and turned it towards Urmila.

Narang, Jagdish and Beyji sat and pondered over the state of affairs. After his three days' rest, the father said to Puri, 'Kakaji, Jagdish and I have decided to go to Delhi. If it's no trouble, can Praveen, his mother and Urmi remain here with you? Once we've settled in, we'll come back and get them.'

Narang and his son left for Delhi. Whenever they could, Beyji would sit with Puri and have long discussions. Her concern was mainly over the blows fate had dealt to Urmila, and what might come next. Calamity had ruined the whole country, but Urmila seemed to have suffered the worst of all. Beyji didn't say so in so many words, but her message was clear: her daughter's widowhood was a fate worse than death. What would be her future?

Urmila would sit near them, or some distance away, and listen to their talk. Bored with the repeated reviews of her problem, she would go and lie down in the next room, or take up some chore about the house.

Lowering her voice, Beyji said to Puri, 'I'd decided, no matter what people say, that I'd wait for six months and then enrol her into the women's or some other college. She's at the age when she can learn something and become self-supporting. Males are different, they all end up finding something or other to do. I worry for her. I want her to get some training, in the medical line if she can. What else is there for her? Whatever little I've saved, I want to spend, to give her a start in life. But for this upheaval I'd have had her signed up somewhere. We'll see what's possible once we're in Delhi.'

In the days when the Narang family had been living well, and in comfort, in Lahore, Beyji had little time or inclination to go to a temple or attend keertan-singing sessions. Living the good life, she would say, without causing suffering to others was the true form of devotion. A group of refugee women, distraught with grief and traumatized by violence, and eager to throw themselves at God's mercy, had been gathering near the press building, every morning and evening, to perform keertan in the hope of divine compassion. Beyji began attending these sessions to lighten her own grief. It was better to remember God, she said, than continually to remember one's misfortunes.

Puri, out of politeness, walked a few steps with her, to see Beyji off when she went to the bazaar for shopping or to the keertan meetings. During those few minutes together, she confided in him comments that she avoided in front of Urmila. 'What more can I say, kakaji. They say that when someone suffers a serious blow, their nature changes. But with the attitude that girl had, who knows if she'll ever be serious about studying? Her *lavan-phere* ceremony was performed; otherwise she's still a virgin. It'd be best to let a year or two pass, to let her heart become a bit lighter, and then find a suitable boy for her.'

Puri enthusiastically supported her view, 'Give her the chance to get some education. Then think of settling her down. It'd be best if you did both. But you must do something. She can't go on the way she is now.'

Urmila's mute indifference to herself in reaction to her tragic past seemed to Puri a cruel twist of fate. Her sorrow wrenched at his heart. Married only for two months, after spending two days with her in-laws her husband was murdered, how was she to blame for this cruel blow that fate had dealt her? Her misfortune was the result of other people's folly, of the war between two communities, for which others rather than the poor innocent were to be blamed. Puri and some like-minded and level-headed persons had tried, but had failed, to prevent the disastrous consequences of that confrontation. In her eyes, he must look as guilty as anyone, because of his helplessness to avert her misfortune.

In the depths of his heart, he felt guilty for another crime of omission. He had contributed to her misfortune by resisting her unquenchable, earthy desire for love, her lust for life as vibrant as an electric current. He was the one who had rejected her at the Murree hill resort, he had ignored her needs. He had let her suffer all the shame, the disrepute, the frustration and the blame for the incident. What would have happened if he had acted more boldly? An understanding mother like Beyji would surely have handled that situation diplomatically. Would Urmila have been able to avert her misfortune then?

Letters written in Urdu from Narang and Jagdish in Delhi arrived every fourth or fifth day, full of gratitude for Puri's kindness and with the request that he reassure Beyji, Urmila and Praveen. Delhi had hardly any accommodation available, and they were trying to make some permanent arrangements before sending for the family. Jagdish sometimes included a brief note meant for his mother, written in Hindi. Puri read his letters aloud to Beyji and Urmila, adding, 'Until some arrangement is made in Delhi, this is your home. Think of me as just the same as Jagdish or Praveen. And until I find something about my own people, you are my family. How can I let go of your affection and the comfort of your company?'

Eyes closed and palms joined, Beyji would pray to God to reunite Puri soon with his family, and assure him that she did in fact regard him in the same light as Jagdish.

Sitting in his office, Puri's ears echoed with the din and rattle of the press machines, and his head spun with the thought of Urmila upstairs, vulnerable, cursed by fate, a bud that had been shattered by a hailstorm before it had opened. An afterthought would be the memory of the letter he had written to Kanak at Nainital. How the tragedy of Urmila would sadden her.

Puri would go upstairs for lunch, after being summoned by Praveen, usually around midday. He would also go upstairs around 10 o'clock, and then again around three to look in on Urmila. He would call, even if Beyji or Praveen were present, 'Urmi, get me a glass of water.'

With downcast eyes, Urmila would silently bring him the water, and resume her position on the chatai with her back to the wall, or go quietly to sit somewhere else.

Puri thought that Urmila's all-consuming grief was the reason for her silence and her reluctance to speak to him. But there was a pinch of guilt too in his thinking: Didn't I cause her enough trouble at Murree? Why would she want to speak to me? Feeling ashamed of the wrong he had done, he now wanted to put things right.

Ignoring her silence and even the lack of any sign that she was paying attention, he would strike up some conversation in her presence with others about the problems and troubles people were facing after the Partition. He described Gandhiji's efforts to keep communal peace in Delhi. Or he talked about women who had not married, or had been widowed, but still had accomplished something for themselves by getting an education. After completing the Hindi Prabhakar certificate, he said, one could qualify for a university bachelor's degree and then a master's. And if some young woman passed the two-and-a-half year L.M.P. course, she could lead a respectable life as a medical practitioner.

Beyji, already deeply indebted to Puri for his generosity, didn't want to let him spend any more on the family. She said to him, 'Kakaji, what do men know about cooking and groceries! Stop bothering about it.' When she went for her keertan meeting in the mornings, either alone or with Praveen, she shopped for vegetables and other foodstuffs. When the need arose, she would get some in the evening too. She had not minded doing such jobs in Lahore when she had servants, and wasn't embarrassed to do them now.

When Puri saw her leaving, he would say, 'Why don't you take Urmi along? A walk would do her good, change her mood.' Urmila just shook her head in refusal if invited by her mother.

Puri had given Urmila some popular fiction to read. 'Have you read anything?' he would ask her. 'What did you read?'

He had not heard a reply to his letter to Kanak. What became of it, he often thought. Probably they had moved to another city, and the letter had to be redirected. Enough time had passed for some kind of response since the letter had been sent by registered post. Maybe Nayyar is behind all this. Not a nice person, and so vain about his wealth and status, and jealous in the bargain.

In the afternoon of the twelfth day, his letter came back. On it was inscribed in red ink: Left station.

Puri's heart sank. What else could he do to find her? He had lost his family, and now Kanak. His head buzzed. With eyes fixed unseeingly on the rafters overhead, he imagined: A vast flood has engulfed Lahore. The houses were coming down, crashing one by one. He had been absent on some business, and had returned to find the city inundated. Swift-moving streams were flowing through the bazaars, sweeping men and women along in its current. Hundreds of persons were being swept along into one immense swath of river. He had got hold of a floating beam and so was saved from drowning. He was searching for his family, but had found that they were gone. He saw Kanak, also holding on to a beam like himself. He called, but she did not hear. Next to her was Urmila, caught in a whirlpool, about to be pulled under. He was scared ... his hands touched and grabbed Urmila by the hair.

Puri shook his head and made an effort to concentrate on the papers in front of him. His thoughts drifted off again. If Kanak had had to move away, couldn't she leave instructions at the post office to forward her mail? She was not helpless and naive like Urmila; she was able to instruct others, to speak with clerks and officials. Didn't she want to hear from him? What more could he do now?

His hands capped the fountain pen on the desk and put it into his shirt pocket. Biting his lip to suppress the disappointment welling up in his heart, he went upstairs.

He sat on one of the charpoys, took a deep sigh and called out to Praveen to get a drink of water. His concern for Urmila's misery prevented him from asking her.

Nobody answered; neither Beyji, nor Praveen. Urmila, a dupatta wrapped around her head and shoulders and eyes downcast, brought a tumbler of water. She held it out to Puri.

'Beyji and Praveen not home?'

Urmila shook her head to say no.

He accepted the tumbler and put it under the charpoy. He said in a breathy voice, 'Urmi!' and took her wet hand into his. She pulled hers back.

'Urmi, don't you know me any more,' asked Puri, putting his arm around and pulling her closer as one tries to soothe a whimpering child.

Urmila did not say a word. She turned away and tried to wriggle free.

Puri held the hem of her kameez, and implored, 'Listen to me just this once ...'

Still silent, she yanked her shirtfront to free it from his grip. The cloth ripped. She scowled at him and kept an angry silence.

The ripping noise made him release his grip.

Flustered and embarrassed, Puri said, 'Urmi, I sympathize with your sorrow, but you have to keep a brave front, no matter what happens in life.'

Urmila stood silently, a little away from him.

Praveen's jubilant voice came from the foot of the stairs, 'Bhappaji, look what I got!'

Praveen had called out towards the office, presuming that Puri was there. Beyji was a few steps behind him. They both carried bags of groceries.

Puri reached under the charpoy to retrieve the tumbler. He was still agitated from Urmila's response to his emotional outburst, and Beyji was now back in the house. Who knows what she might tell her mother in revenge, he thought nervously. Tension dried his throat. He gulped water slowly.

Praveen called out again on reaching the top of the stairs and brandished freshly roasted corn-on-the-cob, 'Bhappaji, look at these!'

Puri found it difficult to share Praveen's excitement.

Beyji noticed Puri's serious expression, as he seemed to have difficulty in swallowing his drink of water. Urmila moved further away on hearing Beyji's footsteps, and stood against the wall.

Beyji's eyes travelled from Puri's face to Urmila, standing in front of him. Her kameez looked freshly torn.

Beyji's expression became solemn, at what she guessed had happened. She felt compelled to ask Urmila, 'Why is your kameez torn?'

'I was lying down, and it got snagged when I tried to get up.' Urmila's voice tailed off.

'*Hai*, it got so little wear, it was almost new.' Beyji wisely chose to limit her uneasiness to the tear in the kameez.

Puri did not accept the ear of corn offered by Praveen. Without meeting her eye, he told Beyji, 'Rikhiram makes such mistakes at times that it makes your head spin.' He got up and left.

Puri's gloomy expression at dinner made Beyji inquire politely the reason for his anxiety. Sighing deeply to indicate his inner feelings, he replied, 'I've had a letter from Delhi Radio that my message was broadcast twice, but got no reply from anyone in my family. These broadcasts reach most refugees. Why no answer? Who can tell?'

Beyji said kindly, 'God bless those radio people. They may broadcast it again. Kakaji, who knows where people uprooted by this cataclysmic upheaval might have landed? There must be places without radios.'

Puri breathed easily again. Urmila must have said nothing to her mother.

Saddened by his failure to contact Kanak and despite his own disappointment, Puri had tried to comfort Urmila by sharing her sorrow. His kindness had met with a rebuff. At Murree she had been the one eager to yield to him, and now she couldn't stand his touch! On top of his sorrow and pain this rejection wounded him really deeply.

What if Urmila had let out how her kameez was torn, Puri thought. 'Why should I be angry at her? The poor girl once invited me to share her unbridled love and passion; don't I owe something to her for that? I must help her forget her pain. I'm a man, I can handle my pain, I must wait and face up to whatever comes. The circumstances that have kept Kanni away from me have to be overcome. Urmila is stuck in limbo; the poor thing needs my help.'

In Beyji's presence, he spoke with Urmila as freely as usual, but anxiously awaited a chance to speak to her when they could be alone.

On the third day, Beyji and Praveen went to the keertan meeting in the morning. Puri went upstairs to Urmila and said in a voice trembling with emotion, 'Urmi!'

Urmila, looking down, motioned as if to ask 'what?'

'You're so annoyed with me that you won't even speak to me?'

She shook her head in denial.

'Listen!' Puri said, reaching for her hand.

She pulled her hand back, but remained sitting.

Without trying to hold her hand again, he sighed deeply and said tenderly, 'Listen Urmi, I know what you're going through. There can't be a greater pain, but it's one that can be made to go away. I mean, it's alright to grieve and wait for something to happen; but why mourn for ever,' he sighed even more deeply. 'And why think of something that can't come true? Why let yourself waste away, pining and grieving? You have your whole life in front of you, Urmi.'

Urmila inclined her head, but made no reply.

Puri put his hand on her shoulder as he got up, saying, 'Get hold of yourself, Urmi. Don't ruin your life like this. Be brave and look forward.'

Urmila had not shrunk away from his touch. Puri was relieved. He said nothing more, and went to the bathroom to have a wash.

Beyji had returned by the time he came back. Urmila was crying, he saw, and her mother was consoling her by patting her head. Puri kept quiet. When a short while later, he found Beyji alone as he was going downstairs, he asked quietly, 'What's the matter? Why was Urmi crying? Is she all right?'

Tears appeared in Beyji's eyes, 'She doesn't say anything. Kakaji, what else can she do but grieve!' She began to cry, 'Hadn't shed tears like that for some time. I asked repeatedly, but she didn't say a word.'

Puri took the newspaper along when he went up for lunch. He read aloud the news of Gandhiji's speech that India and Pakistan should have friendly and even brotherly relations. Both governments should invite back the refugees who had fled their homelands.

'He's a saint. What more can one want if that happens? God bless him! We had over two lakh rupees worth of stock in our godowns, we owned property. We just want to be able to live again like human beings.' Beyji prayed to God with joined hands.

Puri had addressed his remarks to Urmila, in hopes that she would reply, but she remained silent. When he next went up for his afternoon drink of water, he saw that she was again weeping in silence.

He looked at Beyji with questioning eyes, but got no answer. Calling her affectionately 'my dear', he asked Urmila the reason for her tears. When she did not reply, he went back downstairs without saying anything more.

Next morning Puri was waiting for Beyji to leave for her keertan gathering. He went upstairs as soon as she had stepped out. Taking Urmila's hand into his own, he asked gently, 'Why were you crying yesterday, Urmi?'

She tried to pull back her hand, but he did not let go. He said, '*Mere sir ki kasam,* swear on my life, that you'll tell me why you cried? You have to tell me.' As if his right to know was even greater than Beyji's.

Urmila burst into tears again.

Holding on to her hand, he put his arm around her shoulder, 'A good, brave sensible girl like you shouldn't cry like this. Take heart. Don't let on to anyone what I've been saying to you. Beyji told me that that the rite of lavan-phere was performed only in name, that you never stayed with your husband. As it is, you didn't even know him. You're still a virgin. Beyji wants to let some time pass before …'

Whenever he got the chance, Puri would put his arm around her, pull her close, and press his chin on her head, and kiss the parting in her tousled hair. Tears would well up in Urmila's eyes.

For about a week, Urmila could be seen weeping quietly once or twice during the day. Beyji's worry knew no end. Puri advised, 'She's definitely not feeling well. Take her to a doctor, or I'll have one come here.'

He had told Beyji to show her daughter to a doctor, but he knew that he himself was the cause of her tears, and was convinced that he alone could cure her. Her sorrow had hardened into a rock which the warmth of his affection and sympathy had melted, and it was now leaking out in her tears. He was healing the pain that wrenched at her heart, and this gave him comfort and satisfaction. Consoling Urmila by taking her into his arms and kissing her hair filled him with a feeling of contentment and generosity, but also made his nerves tingle with a pleasant titillation that brought back memories of Kanak. Clutching the short and slender Urmila to his heart was less demanding and gave him more satisfaction than holding the robustly healthy Kanak, who was as tall as himself, in his arms.

Urmila was not willing to consult a doctor, nor would she allow one to visit her. Her mother found this increasingly worrisome. Urmila would retort in irritation, 'Do you think I'm going to die? When did I cry? Did you see me cry?'

Her crying did die away, gradually, on its own. She also became more relaxed and less negligent of her appearance. She would sweep and clean the rooms or help in the kitchen without being told to do so. She began washing her own clothes, and her hair too.

Jagdish and his father had not been able to come back for the rest of the family, but their letters arrived regularly. Their business was beginning to take hold, because of their past contacts, but they had not been able to find any accommodation. Both were still staying with a business associate, content that at least the boy, his sister and his mother were living without discomfort in Jalandhar. Beyji too had written back to tell them that they should look after their health and establish themselves first.

Narang had realized how hard it was to find a house in Delhi, so he bought one that had been partially destroyed in Karol Bagh and began restoring it. Making it habitable was taking some time, and Beyji was waiting word of its renovation being complete.

Puri too had got news of his family. Amar Chand, the younger brother of Professor Pran Nath, had heard the mention of Jaidev Puri's name on the radio, and told Puri's father about it. Master Ramlubhaya had had no idea of Jaidev's whereabouts until then; he could have been still at Nainital or maybe had reached Lucknow. Masterji had been worried and distressed about not being able to contact Jaidev, but he believed that his son was safe, whether in Nainital or in Lucknow, and wrote to him immediately.

Jaidev's father explained everything in detail: Bhola Pandhe's Gali had been plundered and burnt down. Jaidev's family, along with the families of Tikaram and Birumal, had been moved to the Devsamaj Mandir refugee camp in Krishna Nagar. At that time, Professor Nath was still lodged at a hotel. Nath had told Masterji to take his family to the sugar mill owned by the professor's family at Sonwan in UP. And there they had all remained since then.

Arjun Lal Shah, the professor's father, had given shelter to Jaidev's family in recognition of Mastreji's service to the family of Seth Gopal Shah. Masterji had been given a job as a clerk at the mill's godown, and also acted as tutor to the children of the owner's family in his spare time. He was earning, by God's grace, about seventy rupees every month. They had a rent-free house in the mill compound, and free coal and firewood for their kitchen. Wheat, milk, ghee and such foodstuffs were relatively inexpensive in the countryside where they lived. But he had become anxious and distressed again after hearing news that Jaidev was in Jalandhar. He asked Puri to move at once to Sonwan. Jaidev's mother was anxious to see her eldest son.

Beyji congratulated Puri on getting the news of his family. She also encouraged him, 'You wouldn't know this, Kakaji, but parents' guts turn inside out in concern for their children. You must go and meet them.' Sood also gave his approval, 'Yes, go, and bring them back here with you.'

Puri did not want to neglect his duties for the sake of his family. Rikhiram was not showing the same zeal to supervise the press as he had done before his salary was decided. And Sood had been consulting Puri of late as a trusted friend in the process of outmanoeuvring his political opponents.

The *Chhatrapati* newspaper of Lahore was issuing a condensed daily edition in Jalandhar. At the suggestion of Sood, Puri occasionally wrote in it to explain the views of the left-wing Congress on the problems of refugees, and on the policies of the newly formed Congress government. The new government had appointed Sood as parliamentary secretary to win his support, but Sood and his group were not happy. They wanted Sood to have a seat in the council of ministers. Puri was busy in that campaign too.

In this life of relative comfort and ease, Puri had not forgotten the plight of other refugees. He had been appointed to several positions of trust connected with refugee settlement, and spent an hour or two every morning and evening at the office of the Sangh discharging his duties. The government scheme to distribute free clothing to the refugees operated under his supervision. He had also to keep his eye on another politician, Devi Das, who had been trying to wrest this responsibility out of his hands.

In addition to such weighty duties, Puri did not care to keep Praveen, Urmila and Beyji under his protection alone. Despite the presence of the ever-watchful Beyji, he constantly nursed the hopes of stealing a moment or two alone with Urmila. She was reverting to her old coquettish self, in fits of teasing and enticements. She whispered in his ear, 'Don't go.'

Puri sent his father a money order for one hundred rupees. He wrote to him in detail, giving a hint of his weighty problems, and asking the family not to put themselves out for money or anything else. He also wrote that he'd soon come to Sonwan to meet them all.

The rumble and clatter of machines in operation in his own press had never stopped Puri from concentrating on his work; it rather inspired him to work on. It was like music to his ears, and gave him a sense of power and achievement. Along with this feeling of accomplishment and zest for work existed, as a pleasant tension, the thought of Urmila upstairs. But this chain of thought, like a pleasant tune running through his head, would be broken by the jarring note of the memory of Kanak. In that state of confusion, a curtain would descend over his mind, paralysing him. A picture of Kanak's face, her eyes blazing and her expression stern, would appear on the curtain, and to one side, he would see the tiny face of Urmila, with her cute smile.

Puri knew that Kanak had some rights over him, but what about his own rights and responsibilities towards Urmila? If he owed something to Kanak, he also owed something to Urmila. Tall and independent, Kanak wanted to support him in his struggle, but Urmila needed to be held in his arms and supported by him.

The relief that Beyji had felt at Urmila shedding her stony indifference and behaving normally had turned into another worry for her. Urmila and Puri were becoming so obsessed with each other as to be oblivious to others around them.

One day Beyji could not help but scold her. Urmila shot back testily in reply, 'What are you cooking up now in your mind! If you can't stand to see me talking and laughing, just give me some rat poison.'

Beyji did not dare to grab Urmila by her plait and give her a couple of slaps as once she would have done. She was her daughter, but was now also a grown-up woman like herself. She shut her mouth, but made sure that Urmila got no chance to behave in a way that might call for rebuke. What could she say to Puri? His behaviour had been ostensibly beyond reproach. She thought of him as a good person, and she was under an obligation to him. The fault lay with her daughter. Urmila's natural inclinations, lying dormant under her despair, were reawakening. Beyji was reminded of

Urmila's flirtations at Murree that had caused her so much shame. How could she fault others when her own coin was tainted? She was at a loss as to how to handle the girl. She could not bear to see her daughter crying silently and wasting away in grief. But Urmila's now radiant and smiling face also caused her acute embarrassment. She would think, 'How will her father and brother feel when they see her in this state?' And she would tell herself, 'It's best if we can be rid of her by marrying her off somehow, and do so quietly, without further embarrassment. How would I face her father and brother? Spare them this humiliation, O God.'

In the first week of November, Puri had gone one evening to the office of the State Congress Committee, and from there to several meetings at different places, all through the night. He returned home at 9.30 the next morning. As he entered the house, Raldu told him that Beyji had sent for a tonga carriage at six in the morning, and gone to the railway station with Praveen and three suitcases. She had said that she was going to Delhi.

Puri knew that the train to Delhi left at 7.30 a.m. What could he do? He went upstairs and found Urmila lying on the chatai with her head shrouded in a dupatta. He called her name, and she broke into loud sobs. No explanation was needed, and nothing needed to be said. He sat beside her, and pulled her into an embrace. His hands wiped away her tears, and his lips pressed on hers to stifle her cries, 'Don't cry! Am I not here? Mere sir ki kasam, what is there to fear when we have each other?'

Urmila threw her arms around him, and burying her head in his chest, sobbed her heart out.

Chapter 2

WHEN PURI READ IN THE NEWSPAPERS IN NAINITAL THAT THE PAKISTAN government was evacuating Hindus from Lahore, he left immediately to be of help to his family. Kanak did not think it proper to stop him from leaving, even though it wrenched her heart.

From the day after his departure she had sunk into the deepest gloom at the thought of the danger he faced. Every nerve in her body ached for some news of him. In her anxiety she went through every newspaper available at the Library. The New Club was the place for news from Punjab. Many newly arriving Punjabis showed up there.

After the celebration dinner on 14 August, Puri had stayed in Nainital until the twentieth. Kanak had not felt like going to the Club during those evenings. To avoid being asked to accompany her family to the Club, she left the bungalow just before 6 o'clock every evening. But on the twenty-third, in her eagerness to get some news of Punjab, she offered to accompany Nayyar to the Club. At first, everything looked the same as the week before, but she soon noticed that the number of Punjabis had increased.

Some Punjabis played bridge, rummy, flush and other card games with the locals. Others sipped tea, coffee or a drink as they conversed with the other members. A group of them talked excitedly in the lounge. The newly arrived told breathtaking tales of escaping from the jaws of death. A young man just back from Rawalpindi and a mission to rescue the family of his in-laws was telling about his experience. It was not possible to travel by road or railway, so he had taken a flight from Amritsar. One could not go around safely in Rawalpindi without a police escort.

Others were talking about the vengeful attacks on Muslims in eastern Punjab. How all passengers in the Punjab Mail had been massacred near Ludhiana on 21 August, and similar attacks on trains to Pakistan in the cities of Ferozepur and Amritsar. Some tales of the atrocities were even more gruesome.

Kanak trembled at the thought of the hazards that Puri might have had to face. Losing their homes and property had left these Punjabis distraught with shock, embittered and desperate; they played the martyr, and pretended to

be better and from a higher class than the locals. They gambled recklessly
in card games to show that they did not care, and drank heavily. They all
claimed to have suffered losses of five, ten or twenty lakhs. Kanak had
seldom heard of anyone in Lahore being worth that much.

A young man wearing an ordinary, well-worn suit stood near Nayyar,
with an angry expression and an embittered look in his eyes. He was talking
loudly about his whole family being murdered, and about losing property
worth lakhs. Seated across from him on a sofa next to two women, Kanak
listened attentively. The danger and suffering the man had undergone tore
at her heart.

The man put his hand amiably on Nayyar's shoulder. 'Have a whiskey,'
he said, as if wanting to put aside his own pain and suffering.

Nayyar accepted his offer.

The man summoned the bearer and ordered whiskey. Glass in hand, he
resumed the story of his horrifying adventure. Nayyar and others listened
to him sympathetically.

The man looked at the people gathered round him as he told his story.
Kanak's eyes, like the others', were fixed at him. She did not like the way
he looked into her eyes if their gaze happened to meet. She averted her
eyes. Nayyar had barely taken a couple of swallows of his drink before the
man drained his glass. He asked Nayyar to have another.

'I still have mine. You go ahead,' Nayyar said.

The man called for another. He finished his second before Nayyar had
finished his first. The man insisted, 'You'll have to have another, to keep
me company.'

Nayyar swallowed his drink and agreed to have half a peg.

Third drink in hand, the man concluded his story and launched into a
bitter diatribe against the Indian government and the state of UP, '...Here
they are firing upon people attacking the Muslims.' He criticized Gandhiji
and Prime Minister Nehru. He drained his glass, put his arm affably around
Nayyar and offered him another drink for company's sake. Nayyar politely
refused, but the man ordered one more for himself.

The man's excessive show of familiarity offended Kanak. She had never
seen such vulgar consumption of alcohol in Lahore. Irritated by the man's
ogling glances, she turned her attention to others in the group. Most
Punjabis were vehement in their demand for the expulsion of all Muslims
from UP, Bombay, Madras, Bengal and other Indian provinces. '...Either

we Punjabi refugees should be allowed to expropriate properties, lands and businesses from Muslims, or we should be given a free hand to make up for the losses that we've suffered.'

One of them disagreed, 'That's unrealistic! There's such a thing as law and order. There are not many Muslims in India who own land and businesses.'

'Whatever! We should have the chance to make good what we have had taken from us. We sweated and worked hard for what we had,' another person replied angrily.

It was past 10.30. Kanak had made several signs to Nayyar that she wanted to leave. Nayyar held out his hand to the man who had been with him to say goodbye, 'I'll take my leave of you.'

'You're leaving? I too must be off. See you again. Please settle the bill, if you don't mind.'

Nayyar looked at the man with surprise, 'But...' The man cut him short. 'Baadshaho, what's wrong? We've lost lakhs of rupees and never whined. This is only 8 or 10 rupees.' He walked off towards the next room, his face tight.

Nayyar was taken aback. Sympathetic listeners to the man's story stood around him. He smiled and signed the bill.

Kanak fumed at Nayyar as they came out of the Club, 'What weird friends you have!'

'Friend? I saw him today for the first time. Wonder whose guest he was? What else could I do? People are turning into such goondas!'

A whole week passed without any letter from Puri. Kanak was confident that he would send some news, wherever and in whatever condition he might be. 'Don't you know how worried I'd be?' Vexed by the tormenting thoughts of what might have gone wrong, she would curse herself, 'Why did I let him leave? If he had to, I should have arranged for him to go by air. Or I could have gone with him. We would face the dangers together. And would have been together if...'

As a result of how she had been brought up to believe, and encouraged to think by her father, Kanak could not imagine any other differences between her own and a man's abilities, except physical strength. But from the accounts and stories she had recently heard and been told, it seemed that being a girl or a woman was the worst fate one could imagine.

Nayyar's hostility to her feelings for Puri was fresh in her mind, but Kanak still forced herself to ask for his help in finding out about Puri. Nayyar himself was distraught with worry on account of his own problems. He had come to Nainital with only two thousand rupees in his pocket. He usually made payments by bank cheques. He had written a cheque for the rent for their bungalow for July. All the shopkeepers with whom he had credit were paid by cheques at the month's end. On 8 or 9 August, he had written to his bank in Lahore to send a draft of one thousand rupees drawn on the Nainital branch of either the Allahabad Bank or the Imperial Bank. Neither had the letter, nor his telegram sent as a reminder, been answered.

His bank would send the draft once the storm had died down after 15 August, Nayyar had thought; it was only a matter of time. His worries knew no end when he heard, at the end of August, that an embargo had been imposed on the transfer of funds from one country to the other between Pakistan and India. The outlays spent on his own and his brother-in-law's family and on his two sisters-in-law were his responsibility. He regretted not following Panditji's advice to transfer his accounts to a bank in India, and not going back to Lahore to empty his safety deposit boxes of the family's jewellery and property deeds. What would he do for a living if he couldn't return to Lahore? He had little time or inclination to listen to Kanak's problems.

Kanta was in a daze too. To her, it seemed she was to blame for everything. She was the one who controlled the housekeeping budgets. Would she lose face before others? Would the family be brought to starvation? How could she ask her father for anything? He himself had barely managed to flee to Delhi, and had not been able to find proper accommodation in the three weeks he had been there. Nayyar had invited him to Nainital, but he had deferred, so as to avoid the embarrassment of being a burden.

Kanta could not pretend to be happy and carefree like Nayyar. She didn't want her brother-in-law's family and Nayyar's sister to know about their financial hardships, but she also had to cope with the dwindling funds. The amount of ghee used for cooking was drastically reduced. A single vegetable dish and daal replaced the two vegetable dishes, meat course and the daal on which they usually dined. She had her own daughter and three children of Nayyar's sisters to care for. Instead of four seers of milk per day, she began buying one-and-a-half seers. But her efforts to manage the household had the opposite effect. The pressure to make do with less money led to an explosive situation.

The mother of her brother-in-law looked on these austerity measures as a personal affront. Since her childhood, she had been in the habit of having a glass of milk before she went to bed, and a glass of fresh buttermilk on an empty stomach in the morning. Without such a diet, she suffered from dryness of skin, constipation, and dizziness. The mother-in-law remarked testily, 'If milk's become so dear, we'll get one-and-a-half seers separately for ourselves. We had two milch buffaloes in our backyard back home.'

Nayyar got a shock when he saw that his sister Subhadra ignored their financial difficulties and sided with her mother-in-law's unreasonable attitude. Her complaints were even more bizarre, '...When we first arrived, they bought mangoes and peaches every other day. Our children have become such a burden that they've stopped buying fruit. Now we're being asked to eat chapattis with only daal at both meals. All three sisters like to gad about. They stuff themselves at some restaurant every time they go out, but there's no money when we're concerned. Had we found a bungalow for our family, we wouldn't have had to face such humiliation. If we've become a liability, I'll cook whatever skimpy meals we eat on a separate brazier in the veranda.' She began to cry.

Ramprakash's sister Swarna could not overlook the injustice shown to her brother's family, and defended her sister-in-law, 'It's our misfortune that we have to depend on these people. We came to stay with our brother. Had this been his home and had we been treated like this, we wouldn't have accepted even a drink of water here. It must be fate conspiring against us that we've lost property worth lakhs, and now we have to look to others for our food. And just look at these women; the way they throw money about on fashion! They'd rather paint their faces than eat because their stomachs are rumbling.'

Subhadra's mother-in-law began to shed tears at being treated so shabbily by her daughter-in-law's family.

Nayyar's mother could not stop herself from making a sharp retort. Kanak and Kanchan were trying to pacify her when Subhadra and Swarna began shouting at them, 'You good-for-nothing creatures! What are you doing here? Neither do you have a place at your parents, nor will either of you ever get a man!'

The relaxed, sybaritic lifestyle at Vimal Villa degenerated into a battle

scene from the Mahabharata. Neighbours in the bungalows above, below
and to either side of Vimal Villa stood and peered out from their doors
and windows to see what was causing such a row. Nayyar's brother-in-law
Ramprakash slipped quietly out of the bungalow.

Stung by the abuse hurled at them, Kanak and Kanchan began packing
their bags. Nayyar called both to his room and said severely, 'Are you both
stupid? Is that the way to behave? That's all the help and sympathy you can
give me in the difficult situation I'm facing?' Both the sisters retired to a
corner, wiping their tears.

Nayyar also spoke angrily to Kanta, 'Have you gone mad? It was you
who invited them.'

Kanta broke into tears, 'Open my trunk and see for yourself. All there's
left is 625 rupees. I just want to make do with that until pitaji arrives. I can
blow it all in a week if that's what you want. Soon we'll be eating only dry
chapattis or half a meal, and what'll these people say then? If they want to
gargle with milk or must have the paranthas spread with ghee, it's better
that they move somewhere else. Why should they suffer because we're hard
up? I'd never ask these people for anything even if I was starving.'

Only two weeks before Subhadra was so fond of her bhabhi that Kanta
was reluctant to go to the bazaar with her. Subhadra kept her money tied
in a knot of the silk handkerchief that she carried, and if Kanta wanted
to buy something, Subhadra would begin to untie the knot. Kanta could
hardly prevent her from paying. She used to be happy only if she and Kanta
ate from the same thali.

Nayyar sat and took several deep breaths, thinking, 'My only crime is
that I don't have as much money as I used to have.'

After the frenzied melee of accusations and crying, Vimal Villa was quiet.
Only Nano and Subhadra's baby boy Dhammi, unaware of the tension, cried
out in play or called out to someone.

With a premonition of danger haunting her, and after the affectionate
scolding from Nayyar, Kanak's heart was cleansed of all resentment towards
her brother-in-law. Seeing Nayyar sitting alone and lost in thought, she
went and sat beside him. 'Jiai,' she said using the old endearment, 'what
are you thinking about?' She reminded him of the job promised by Awasthi,
the parliamentary secretary, and asked for Nayyar's permission to write to
him. He could be of some help, she said.

Nayyar was already peeved, he asked her directly, 'Is Puri in Lucknow?'

She met his gaze, and said, 'Jiai, I've never told you a lie. If I go away with him, I'll tell you beforehand. He left with the idea of going to Lahore. Today is the twenty-fourth day without any letter from him.' She turned her face away. Her eyes had filled with tears.

Nayyar kept silent in sympathy, then said in English, 'Forgive me, what objection can I have? Your father will be here soon. There's been no letter from him for a week; maybe it'll come today.'

Panditji's letter did not arrive, but another did, from Kakaram, Nayyar's clerk, who was now in Jalandhar. He had written to ask where Nayyar would want to resume his law practice. He recommended Jalandhar for this. It was expected that East Punjab's temporary capital would be moved from Simla to Jalandhar. A rumour was abroad that the high court might also be situated there. Kakaram was from the Mukerian tehsil in the district of Jalandhar. Since several of his relatives were tehsil officials, he might be able to help get legal work for Nayyar. Scores of houses and farm lands in the district had been occupied by refugees from Lahore, Gujranwala and Lyalpur.

Nayyar asked Kanta. She would have preferred settling in the same city as her father, but did not want to let this opportunity slip through her fingers. In the evening Nayyar wrote to Kakaram, accepting his advice. He told his clerk to search for some small house in an uncongested area, and said that he would soon write about his intentions.

On 16 September, Panditji did not arrive, but a telegram came from him in the evening that asked Nayyar to come at once with his family. Instead of asking when Nayyar might arrive, he explained in telegraphese how to reach his house: From railway station to Faiz Bazaar, Sir Syed Ahmed Road, at end of Silwali Gali turn into Durrani Gali, Naya Hind Press.

It had taken the telegram two days to reach Nainital. The delay in delivery and particularly the terseness of the message sounded ominous, and made everybody's imagination wander. Why couldn't Panditji come to the railway station? And had his printing press been moved to Delhi?

Fleeing Lahore to save their lives, Pandit Girdharilal and his wife had arrived in Delhi on 13 August. The population of the whole country, it seemed to him, simultaneously had fled to Delhi. He did not know the city very well, and had no intention of taking shelter in a refugee camp. The hotels were all filled to capacity. After searching in vain for some frustrating hours, a family from Multan staying at a newly constructed hotel in Faiz Bazaar agreed to rent him and his wife a corner of their room at five rupees per day.

Leaving his wife in the room to keep an eye on their belongings, Panditji would roam all day in search of a better dwelling place. The number of people who had moved to the city, in pursuit of lucrative business opportunities during the Second World War, was much larger than the housing available in Delhi and New Delhi could absorb. The rents in 1945 were 150 to 200 per cent more than those in 1939. To affluent families fleeing the towns and cities of western Punjab in March 1947, Delhi had seemed the safest and the closest destination. These rich refugees had been willing to pay any price for whatever accommodation they could get. Since 14 August the limitless flood of people ejected from Punjab had been pouring into the city. While the government of UP, as a precautionary measure, had banned the entry of refugees into the province, Delhi had thrown its gates wide open. But the city now did not have room even under its trees. And the new arrivals after the Partition, impervious to whether they had a roof over their heads, settled in any corner they could find.

Panditji had gone to see many of his old business acquaintances in the course of his search. He met Prof. N.C. Mathur too. He was welcomed with offerings of tea, mithai, lemonade and paan everywhere. Those he met offered every kind of help, except the assistance in finding a house. One or two even hinted with tongue in cheek, '...You Punjabis are having difficulty in getting houses? Those who're really desperate do succeed in finding one. Look in the vicinity of Paharganj, Sabzi Mandi, Pataudi House, Matia Mahal and Bairam Khan Road.'

After meeting with disappointment everywhere, Panditji found, after searching intensely and non-stop for eight days, one room on the third floor of a house behind the Golcha Theatre, on Sir Syed Ahmed Road. It was just a room with makeshift brick walls, and a roof of corrugated iron. But it had a door that could be locked. He and his middle-aged wife had to climb down to the aangan on the ground floor to use the water tap and the lavatory. It wasn't much of a home, but more like a place to cook and store their luggage, and take shelter when it rained. Now at least he could look for a proper house with a little more time and patience.

Panditji had made reconnaissance tours on foot of mohallas behind the Golcha theatre. Except for the building of Rajaram Agarwal, his landlord, most other houses had been built recently. The families living in Koocha

Chelan and Delhi Gate bazaar until 14 August had been predominantly Muslim, but recently these areas were being crammed with refugees from the west. A number of houses around Pataudi House and in Chitli Kabar bazaar and Tiraha Bairam Khan were still occupied by Muslims. The atmosphere was tense with the news that a big confrontation was in the making. Rumours were rife that Muslims had collected firearms and built barricades in bazaars close to Paharganj. But all Panditji saw were families of frightened Muslims, lugging their possessions leaving the mohallas, and Punjabi Hindus with their belongings on their heads and backs, moving in. Some Hindus were rumoured to have been killed. Panditji had seen, on two occasions, Punjabi refugees with swords, spears and machetes roaming lanes deep in the heart of the mohallas. Policemen standing or sitting at bazaar intersections and gali corners with fixed bayonets were unable to stop murders and occasional bomb throwing. As anyone could see, the 'transfer of population' was taking place. Property deals were also being made between those wanting to leave and those arriving from the west.

The tin roof became so hot in the afternoons that Panditji could barely sit under it. Compared to the kind of life he had led in the past three decades, the present times were like the days he had spent in jail thirty-five years before. But he had been a young man then, with the fire of patriotic self-sacrifice in his heart. At age fifty-eight, all he could do was grin and bear it.

The lanes and galis to the south of Delhi Gate still housed Muslims. Panditji had no qualms about living among Muslims. His first concern was for a place that was airy, had a water supply and a healthy environment; a place where he could begin a new printing press business, if it was not possible to bring his old presses from Lahore. And he was willing to pay a good price for it.

The Muslims remaining in the galis could be seen sitting huddled in the thresholds and doorsteps of their homes. Panditji, so as not to scare or alarm them, would address them as bhaijaan, dear brother, and inquire, 'Are their any empty houses in this gali?'

They would not answer, but stare with angry eyes and set faces. One looking particularly unhappy, sighed deeply and said, 'Bhaijaan, finish us off and throw us out, then all the houses will be empty. But when we go, we'll take a few of you with us. We have no place to go. We'll be buried here. We were born on this ground and we'll end up in this ground.'

A gentleman with a maulana-type beard walking past, wearing a khadi sherwani and a high Gandhi cap, stopped. The man who was speaking fell silent when he caught the maulana's eye. Seeing everyone salaam the gentleman, Panditji too greeted him with an adaab arz, and said, 'Why should you leave, bhaijaan? It's your home, stay here. If there's enough room next to you, let us stay too. We all belong to one people. One nation. It's our bad luck that we had to flee, leaving behind a house and printing press, the fruit of my life's work. But why complain? All we want is to go back to our homeland, but let it be how He wishes,' he finished, pointing to the sky.

Panditji was in his habitual Congress-supporter dress of khadi pugaree, khadi jacket buttoned up to the neck, and pajamas. The khadi-wearing Muslim replied for the others, 'Bhaijaan, such sectarian hatred is destroying the country and people. It's the duty of nationalists like you and me to stop this barbarian behaviour. Bapu has dedicated his whole life to this cause. I wish that Maulana Shaukat Ali and Mohammed Ali were alive, and that Dr Ansari was here. Alas, what horrible incidents in Calcutta. Those fanatics threw bricks and rocks at the house of Gandhiji's Muslim host. All panes of glass were smashed, and Bapu Gandhiji barely escaped, but just think how strong his belief is, if he has not given up. Only he, with God's blessing can save the country now.'

Panditji expressed his agreement. He requested the maulana to look for any vacant houses in the mohalla, and started to walk away.

'Sir, may I ask you for a favour?' he heard a voice say behind his back.

Panditji turned around and saw that the maulana had followed him. 'Please do tell me what it is, sir.'

'You're looking for a house, sir?' asked the maulana. 'A gentleman like you would want a nice, big place. Would you like to buy one? This Partition is permanent, believe me. Who knows if those leaving a house will ever return? Scores of Muslims go away every day. Even if the Partition is repealed, you would wind up with property in two cities. You should buy a property here.'

Panditji thought for a few moments, tapping the tip of his walking stick on the paved pathway. He said, 'Maulana, a property transaction is a matter of careful study and investigation. At the moment, my need is for a rented house. Well, bhaijaan, no harm in having a look, if it's no trouble.'

Panditji and the maulana walked a few steps down the gali. The gali branched off into another, a narrower one. At this point in the side gali was a small gate. Just below the civic number, was painted on the gate: Sultan Pasand Zarda Factory, Owner: Syed Abdul Samad, Durrani Gali, Delhi Gate Bazaar, Delhi. The maulana knocked on the gate and called loudly, 'Bijang! Bijang! Hey brother, Bijang!'

'Who's there?' someone growled back.

The maulana spoke soothingly, 'It's me, bhai Bijang, open up. Tell the women folk to observe purdah. I have someone with me.'

One half of the gate was cautiously opened. In the opening stood a gurkha, a khukri under his arm, barring the way.

As they entered, Panditji hesitated for a moment, and said, 'Bhaijaan, I hope I can trust you.'

'Have faith! I swear by Kalma Pak. Sir, the earth could not hide me if I lie,' the maulana replied reassuringly.

The doorway led to a small inner courtyard to the right. A patch of ground with some jasmine and henna bushes, then a brick pavement, and then the two floors of an old-fashioned house. The archways seemed to have been bricked up and fitted with doors. To the right were two small rooms opening up onto the aangan. The white, lime-based plaster on the walls was crumbling, revealing reddish lakhori bricks. The wall to the left was of bigger, modern bricks. A water faucet, and several mixing vats were sunk into the floor. A few clay and aluminium vessels, a couple of wicker chaise longues and two charpoys. The aangan smelled of scented tobacco.

The maulana requested Panditji to take a seat and asked whether he would prefer tea or sherbet.

Panditji begged to be excused. He began the conversation by referring to the unsettled state of the country.

The maulana said in agreement, 'What have things come to, quibla, respected sir, that we are short even of fresh betel leaves. It's become impossible to go fifty steps to the bazaar. As your honoured self can see, there's enough space for a mansion here. Around here it's as famous as Syed's Court. Our family has been in Delhi since the time of Emperor Shah Alam. All the land on the other side of that wall once belonged to our family. But it was just a matter of time. During the war, only a couple of years ago, the offer for this place was 50,000 rupees. Who knew at that time that doomsday was so close?' The maulana took a deep breath. 'That it was just a matter of time before we had to sell the ancestral property. You may measure it yourself with the chain, it's 2242 square feet. The land in the neighbourhood went for 7 to 8 rupees a square foot. It's built solid, you can see; unlike the buildings of New Delhi, that crumble away if you so much as breathe on them. It will take at least 300 years for this type of brick to crumble. Been like this since I was born; not even the slightest bit of decay. It's a matter of time. I'll settle for twenty thousand. The knife's at our throats, sir. What else can we do?'

A boy, about fifteen, had come and, after politely greeting Panditji, stood beside them. The maulana asked him, 'Sahibzade, bring the folder with the property documents. This gentleman has to convince himself that he's buying the property from its rightful owners.'

'No, no, bhaijaan, a gentleman's word is enough,' said Panditji, tapping the floor with his stick. He screwed his eyes up thoughtfully as he spoke, 'Bhaijaan, you're quite right, but we've had to leave all behind and live like nomads.' He took a deep breath, 'Sir, I do understand your problem. Forgive my saying so, but the house we left behind was worth one-and-a-half times the price you mention, built in modern style, for our own use, with full electricity supply and fans, running water, flush toilets. We had to lock it all up and leave. You must have heard about Lahore's Gwal Mandi, just like your Queen's Road or Kashmiri Gate. I've all the papers with me. You may have a look at them.'

The boy brought back an old-style folder made from black chintz and tied with a cord, and gave it to the maulana. He opened it and as he handed Panditji a sheaf of electricity bills, payment receipts for house and water taxes, lease deeds and rent receipts for two rooms, said, 'Your humble servant's name is Syed Abdul Samad.'

Panditji flipped through the documents as if they were unimportant, and handed them back. He said, 'Bhaijaan, my own situation is no different. We are, if not in the same boat, then in similar boats. Please take the trouble to come with me, or I can come back here with the documents for you to see. It's befitting for a cultured gentleman like yourself to go to Lahore. If you feel that an exchange of property would be acceptable, then we two brothers can help each other.'

Syed did not want to trade, but wanted the purchase price in cash and was willing to accept fifteen instead of twenty thousand, even a mere ten thousand. Panditji requested him to examine the documents of the Lahore property, and promised to bring the papers the following morning.

Next day, 4 September, was the festival of Janmastami. Panditji's wife, despite her poor health, wanted to keep the ritual fast. After some cajoling and argument, she agreed to take some fruit and milk. The Muslim fruit-shops in Faiz Bazaar and near Delhi Gate were nearly all gone. Some refugees had begun selling cucumbers, guavas, bananas and corn-on-the-cob from makeshift stalls and pushcarts. How could Panditji allow his wife to eat such indigestible fruit in her fragile state of health? He walked towards the bazaar at Fatehpuri looking for better fruits.

When he reached Fatehpuri, he saw that shops were being boarded up and shut down. The bazaar buzzed with the news that Muslim policemen had taken up arms and rebelled. Panditji turned around and went back. Frightened neighbours were saying that riots had broken out in the mohallas around Delhi Gate and Pataudi House. There was talk of Muslims firing rifles and machine guns from their rooftops, and there were sounds of gunfire too. The siren for curfew wailed. Within minutes, as Panditji watched, armed soldiers marched towards the area. How could Panditji go to Syed's house in such a situation? He joined the people sitting on platforms outside the Hindu shops that were still doing business, and sat there until evening. Sporadic gunfire continued all day. Passers-by would stop with further news. There was talk of a pitched battle in Paharganj, of heavy gunfire in bazaars barricaded by Muslims, and of Hindus who had cordoned off some Muslim mohallas and set them ablaze.

Sitting at Khoob Chand's shop close to the entrance to his gali, Panditji heard other rumours: The Garhwali soldiers had finished off all Muslims in Hauz Kazi, and all buildings up to Ajmeri Gate had been burnt down. A Muslim mob had attacked Hindus in Karol Bagh, but were all shot dead. Two thousand Muslims had been killed in Paharganj. Someone said that in many places soldiers and civil guards had fired on Hindus, sixteen Hindus ... no, twenty-four were killed. There was anger and resentment about firing on Hindus. People were openly cursing the Congress government and Pandit Nehru, 'If they allow Hindus to be killed in Delhi, where will we all go?'

On 6 September there was a stricter enforcement of the curfew. Even Hindus were restricted from moving in the bazaars. Military personnel supervised the removal of corpses from lanes deep in the mohallas. Panditji sat at Khoob Chand's shop. Next day people began to go out to buy groceries and other supplies. Panditji thought it unwise to go to Durrani Gali on that day also.

8 September. Panditji's little room under its tin roof was boiling in the sun by 10 o'clock. His wife was making chapattis and a vegetable dish on a portable stove. He could not bear either to remain sitting under the hot roof, or sit idly at Khoob Chand's shop. He went towards Syed's house. Soldiers with bayonets stood at bends in the galis. In Silwali Gali, where Panditji had first met the maulana, there were charpoys in front of many doorways. Refugee women were going through their bundles of clothes and tin trunks. Panditji was surprised; where did these people come from, during the curfew? At the very end of the gali, only a door on the left and two on the right had the trademark Muslim sackcloth curtains. Outside Syed's house in Durrani Gali, four armed soldiers sat on a small chabutara beside the gate.

Panditji knocked at the gate, 'Syed sahib! Bhai Bijang!'

The soldiers looked at Panditji. As he was alone and unarmed, they said nothing. Panditji again called out to Syed and Bijang.

'Who is it? Who are you?' A frightened voice replied from inside.

Panditji gave his name. The gate opened slightly. Panditji entered and greeted Syed. The sun was bright in the aangan. Leaving Panditji near the threshold, Syed fetched a low stool. He called Karim, his son, to bring a second stool.

As Syed picked up the stool Panditji protested in embarrassment, 'Tsk, tsk… what're you doing, Syed Sahib! I'll carry it myself … Isn't Bijang here? Please don't trouble yourself.'

Syed spoke despondently, 'What can I tell you? There's no flour in the house. We couldn't even get milk for the baby yesterday. Oh, what savagery! Bijang has just gone to the bazaar to get some groceries.'

Panditji expressed great sorrow at the madness spreading in the city, and the whole country, 'Syed Sahib, human beings have turned into animals. Exactly the same thing happened in Lahore. That procession on 11 August, with drawn swords, spears and machetes! Bhai sahib, at least here the government is punishing the rioters, and trying to maintain order. There the government itself confiscated their arms from Hindus, but the Muslims kept walking around with all kinds of weapons. The same sickness has reached here. Heavens above! What will our country come to?'

Syed said dejectedly, 'It's not fair that we should be made to pay for other people's crimes.'

'Certainly not, brother, of course not! This is savagery, madness.'

'What has religion to do with such behaviour? This is sheer beastliness. We have always been nationalists. For me, Panditji, Ram and Rahim are one and the same, but people here are bent upon bloody murder. They kill according to the faces they see; without seeing what's in the hearts. Good sir, what have you decided about the house?'

Panditji unbuttoned his jacket and took out some papers from an inside pocket. Syed looked through the documents. He agreed to an exchange of properties, but wanted five thousand rupees into the bargain. He said, 'Sir, I'm handing over my house to you. The godown there has a stock of tobacco worth al least one thousand rupees, plus the ingredients for making zarda and kiwam. Your house might be newer and better, but all you're offering are the documents and the key to the house. Who knows what we might find when we get to Lahore? Whether we can actually get possession of the house? Whom will we have to face and what problems may crop up?'

Panditji and Syed went into a long discussion. Panditji agreed to pay two thousand rupees in addition to the transfer of houses, but he also wanted a written guarantee that if he were ever to return to Lahore and live in his house, he'd be able to claim his house back without paying a penalty.

Syed put his hand on Panditji's knee and implored him to accompany him and his family to the railway station.

There was no question of registering their agreement in a law court. Panditji and Syed decided to write the terms of agreement on duplicate sets of papers and sign them. Bijang had come back from the bazaar while the transaction was going on. He was a witness to what was discussed and agreed.

Then he came up to them. Holding his belongings tied into a bundle and with his khukri hanging from his shoulder, he said in his Nepali dialect, 'First my wages.' Having served Syed loyally and diligently, he was unwilling to give up his hard-earned pay.

Syed reassured Bijang, 'Panditji is very kind and generous. He will retain you as the house guard.' Syed explained the necessity of a guard in the present situation, and Panditji agreed with him. Syed said to Bijang, 'We'll move out after Panditji has moved in. I'll pay you your salary and baksheesh too.'

Bijang put his bundle back in the doorway, but kept an eye on the proceedings.

Panditji brought along his wife and all their possessions before Syed vacated the house. Within a few hours of Syed's departure, he established a friendly relationship with Bijang as a fellow Hindu. Bijang's name now became Bajrang. Bajrang had done his duty by serving his Muslim employer, but had never eaten anything touched by those he served from fear of being religiously defiled. He too was happy to have a Brahmin as his new master. He willingly helped 'Ma Sahib' to clean and sweep the house. He brought bucketfuls of water from the faucet to wash the aangan and the two rooms, then got some joss sticks from the bazaar and lit them all around the house.

It had been a month since Panditji had any chance to relax in the open air. Sitting on a charpoy in the aangan, he talked with Bajrang, 'Thapa, how come a religious Hindu like yourself found a job with a beef-eating Muslim?'

For Bajrang there was no connection or conflict in his mind between his karma, his duty in this life, and his religious principles. He saw working for a living as his karma, and not eating anything touched by a Muslim as his dharma. Millions of Gurkhas, he said, who served in the armies of the beef-eating British and who gave their lives on the battlefield for their white masters, also went to paradise. While he was in the service of Syed, he too would have given his life to protect his master. That was in the line of duty. But he certainly would have welcomed the chance to kill other Muslims.

Maulvi Kasim Mohammed and Syed Abdul Samad wielded considerable influence among the habitants of Silwali Gali and Durrani Gali. Maulvi was a strong supporter of the Muslim League and Pakistan. He was convinced that once Pakistan was established, the power of the True Faith would soon take over Delhi and make it a part of Pakistan. He urged Muslims of neighbouring galis and mohallas to be ready to fight for their True Faith. Rioting after 15 August changed the situation in the city. Maulvi declared that living under kafirs was blasphemous, and left for Pakistan, along with several Muslim families.

Syed did not want to be seen in open conflict with Maulvi. He advised his wavering neighbours to have patience, and to act according to the circumstances. After Maulvi left, the poor and uneducated Muslims looked up to Syed. He was against Muslims fleeing Delhi. His advice was to wait a little longer, but also to be prepared to defend themselves as a group. Twenty-five years ago, when the Congress party and the Khilafat group launched their joint movement against the British, Syed had been

sympathetic to Congress. Mindful of the present situation, he again took
to wearing khadi clothes.

Muslim families remaining in Durrani Gali lost their courage when they
saw Syed's family slipping out, and began to leave en masse. 'It's better
that they go,' thought Panditji, 'why keep people around whose presence
might lead to trouble?'

Seeing Muslim families leave, a crowd of Punjabi refugees lugging
their belongings and with women and children in tow, rushed in. Their
number was far greater than the places available to house them. Scuffles
broke out and the gali rang with arguments and shouts of those wanting
to move in.

Worn out by the stress and fatigue of the past days, Panditji was lying
stretched out on a charpoy and ruminating about the future. Hearing noises
outside the gate of his house and Bajrang's threatening and challenging
voice, he got up to investigate. Bajrang had wedged himself between the
two leaves of the gate. Outside was a horde of men and women clamouring
to get in. Bajrang was growling at them to keep away.

Panditji called out from where he was, 'What is it? What's the matter?'
He tried to explain, 'Friends, this house is occupied. There are people living
here. Please look for a place somewhere else.'

The crowd insisted that there was an unoccupied courtyard inside,
that there was plenty of space. They wanted to come in and see for
themselves.

Panditji said, 'You can say what you like, but the house belongs to us.
We live here. Go somewhere else.'

A voice from the crowd shot back, 'I suppose the house belongs to your
father! The name on the gate is clearly a Muslim's. You can stay in one part.
We too need a place to live.'

He had bought the property, said Panditji. He offered to show them the
documents to prove it.

Those wanting to come in angrily retorted, 'You bought it! As if you got
hold of the treasure of King Qarun? We too have left behind houses that
we had bought and built ourselves. What if you claim to have bought the
whole of Delhi? Do you want us to die in the streets?'

Seeing that verbal arguments and pleadings were a waste of time, two
burly men from the crowd put their shoulders to one half of the gate, and
pushed hard. Bajrang nearly crashed into Panditji as he was flung back.

The crowd rushed in.

Loudly protesting their high-handedness, Panditji spread his arms to block the surging crowd. He was pushed back. The commotion had brought his wife out of the house and she stood behind him. She threw both her arms around his head protectively.

Bajrang took a step back and pulled out his khukri from its scabbard hanging on the wall. Yelling 'Har! Har!' he charged at the crowd.

The crowd backed precipitately away, screaming and falling over one another.

'Look out! Mind yourself!' Commanded one of the soldiers, pointing his rifle at Bajrang, 'Khabardar!'

The melee quieted down. The soldiers had not intervened till now, thinking it to be merely a row among Hindus.

The crowd demanded that the soldiers put Bajrang under arrest.

Panditji came forward to appeal to the soldiers against the high-handed attitude of the mob and to defend Bajrang.

A clamour of voices rose from the crowd, 'There's plenty of room inside. Why can't we take shelter in the house? How can we go on suffering the worst of the weather?'

To end the dispute, the soldiers inquired how many there were in Panditji's family.

Several refugees protested, 'These two old fogies have so much space when so many others have to live in the street.'

The soldiers sided with the crowd.

Panditji explained that he had a big family. The rest of the family was expected in a day or two. He again offered to show the title deeds for the house, then threatened to telephone Prime Minister Nehru.

The soldiers chose to remember their duty to keep order than mete out justice. They ordered the crowd to disperse.

Panditji's spectacles had been knocked off his face during the scuffle, his shirt was torn and he was out of breath. But he did not go inside to rest. He cleaned his glasses, and aided by his wife, immediately set to erasing the inscription on the gate with a lump of brick. He sent Bajrang to buy a stick of chalk, and wrote on the gate in Hindi and English: Naya Hind Press, Proprietor—Girdharilal Dutta. This house is fully occupied.

Utterly exhausted, he flopped down on the charpoy. He got up after half an hour and said to his wife, 'It's not over yet. People are bound to complain that only two people are living in such a big house. You keep the gate locked from the inside. I'll go and send a telegram to Nayyar in Nainital that they all should come here at once.' He patted Bajrang on the back and told him to remain watchful and be on guard.

The caravan of Mahendra Nayyar's family reached Delhi around noon. Their train was held back for six hours, to give way to two special trains carrying Muslim refugees to Pakistan. After spending eighteen hours in the packed and sweaty Inter-class compartment, they all looked weary and bedraggled. Anxiety for Panditji's health was gnawing at their hearts. No one was willing to believe that they had been summoned by telegram unless he had fallen seriously ill.

The family loaded their luggage onto two tongas at the railway station and set out towards Faiz Bazaar. Every passing moment of their first impression of Delhi filled them with apprehension and a feeling of depression. A sea of humanity stretched out on all sides; people without shelter, without a place of their own. Under the trees, on footpaths and by the roadside, in improvised shelters of reeds and straw, under tents and awnings. Or just out in the open. A premonition of what they might face made them forget the discomfort of their train journey.

At the first crossroads inside Faiz Bazaar, policemen diverted the traffic and made the tongas go through Daryaganj. The road ahead was jammed with people. They were told that Mahatma Gandhi had come to comfort the plight of Muslim families still living in Koocha Chelan, and express his compassion for them.

The Hindu tonga driver exploded with anger and cursed the Mahatma, 'He will end up getting all Hindus wiped out.'

Panditji had brought his charpoy into the doorway, and was sitting there, hugging his knees. He sprang to his feet when he saw the family arrive, 'Come on in! Kantu, Kanni, Kanchi ... my daughters!' His voice cracked with emotion as tears filled his eyes. He took Nano from Nayyar's arms and clasped her to his heart.

Nano screamed with alarm, then, recognizing her grandfather, hugged him back. Panditji's wife heard the noise and hurried out. She sobbed loudly as she embraced her daughters one after another. Panditji welcomed the others also with a hug, and politely escorted Kanta's mother-in-law inside.

Panditji was in ecstasy, 'Thank God! Thank Him! We are all together again. Now everything is all right.'

The relief that Nayyar, Kanta, Kanak and Kanchan had felt on finding Panditji in good health soon gave way to a silent concern, when they saw that the faces of Panditji and their mother had turned sallow like dry leaves, that they had lost weight and that the house was almost bare. They avoided looking at each other guiltily.

Panditji fussed over the rearrangement of rooms trying to show that nothing was wrong or had changed. A bed was set up for Nayyar's mother in one room. In another, they spread dhurries on the floor, unrolled quilts and mattresses that had been brought down from Nainital, and covered them with white sheets. The house had no electric fans. Patting Bajrang's back, Panditji said, 'Go, my lad, and get six hand fans.'

In late afternoon, after they had bathed and had a meal, the family lay down in the room on the mattress-covered floor. They waved the fans in their hands. Panditji lay face up in the centre, waving a fan over himself, feeling contented and happy, and repeating over and over again, 'A thousand thanks to Him! Everyone's here. We at least have a roof over our heads to protect us from rain, storm and sun. Just think what other people are going through. Babies dying of pneumonia, because they can't be sheltered from the rain. People living among the ruins of old buildings and in the shadow of walls. People who steal bricks from old graves to build walls and then cover the shanties with a straw roof. Tsk, tsk! Thanks be to God for giving us this place of rest.'

Next day brought a fresh round of worry when Nayyar broached the subject of going to Jalandhar to assess the prospects of beginning his law practice. Panditji agreed with Nayyar, but advised him, 'Son, wait here for a week or two. Send Kakaram your address here. Let Nano, Kanta and your mother stay here for the time being. First look for a house and an office for your law practice.'

Nayyar's messages to his bank in Lahore had gone unheeded. He went to the bank's head office in Chandni Chowk, only to find that neither had his account been credited with any money, nor had it been transferred to any branch in India.

Panditji would bring up the subject of starting some business or other. He had had to abandon his printing press in Lahore. Now he found that the governments of both countries had banned the export of any machinery.

Left behind in Lahore was a stock of books worth a hundred thousand rupees. Many booksellers of western Punjab had owed money to him. How could he hope payment of any old debts from those who had lost everything? It was not possible to start a new business even with the funds he had had the foresight to transfer to the Delhi branch of his bank. After sharing his concerns with the family, he would say with a deep sigh, 'We're still better off than millions of people left destitute. A thousand thanks to Him.'

Those were days of anxiety, of discomfort and inconvenience, and of an uncertain future, but it was also the first time Nayyar, Rajendra, Kanta, Kanak and Kanchan had come to this new and bustling city. They could not spend time quietly in the 'comfortable' place that Panditji had found, as they had been able to do in Lahore. They would go out in the late morning and spend several hours away from home. In the evenings they mostly went towards New Delhi. Camps for refugees had been set up in every available stretch of open space in Old Delhi and in the surrounding districts. The grand boulevards of New Delhi, Connaught Place and the government buildings had remained untouched by the flood of refugees. The invasion had rather enhanced the glamour and bustle of New Delhi. Streets were full of young Punjabi men and women wearing stylish and expensive dresses; as if they were there to show off their wealth and finery, or just to forget their misfortune by putting on a show of cheerful happiness.

Kanak's days in Delhi were full of gloom and despair. The constraints of space, the humid heat, and the house packed with people did not bother her. But she had still not got news of Puri and that constantly tugged at her heart and made her increasingly despondent: What if he had been left destitute and helpless by these cataclysmic, chaotic winds of change? Maybe he had been forced to seek refuge in some camp. How can anyone be found in this seething mass of millions of refugees? Had he been able to find his family? What could be the reason behind his inability to contact her? He knew her address at Nainital. If he had gone back to Nainital or had sent a message to her address, she would have to depend on Ramprakash to pass on any news. Before leaving Nainital, Nayyar had asked his brother-in-law to forward their mail immediately to Panditji's address his Delhi. How long would Subhadra and Ramprakash be able to stay in Nainital? There had been some talk about their moving to Ludhiana or Ambala. While roaming the streets or sitting forlornly beside the lake in Nainital, she would go back in memory over the time she had spent with Puri. She became withdrawn and pensive, hardly speaking to anyone.

Fearful of her husband going alone to Jalandhar, Kanta wanted to accompany him. Her mother-in-law, and her father and mother also, explained that she would only be an encumbrance. If the thought of her husband leaving her made her unhappy, this was considered natural, and she did not have to hide it. But how could Kanak reveal the real reason for her feeling downcast? Reading the newspapers end to end was the only way for her to hide her feelings. She read advertisements, legal notices and 'situations vacant' columns as well. If she saw some job advertised for a woman, she would read it carefully and wonder whether she should apply.

Panditji did feel for his daughters who had been brought up in comfort. He noticed Kanak's remote and absent looks, and the pervading mood of sadness all around. The monsoon season had ended, but a downpour fell in the early evening. It was not possible to go to New Delhi to escape the hours of tedium and the oppressive heat. His hand waving his fan, Panditji tried to divert everyone's attention and lighten the atmosphere by recounting a couple of anecdotes. Then he said, 'My daughters can face up to anything. They are like lion cubs. What could it be that they can't tackle? To live off one's family's property is to live the life of a leech. That's a parasite's life.' He roared with laughter at his own joke, took off his glasses and began to polish them with the end of his shirtfront.

After coming to Delhi, he had learned a new trick. If he wanted to avoid meeting someone's eye, he would begin to polish his glasses and screw up his eyes. He apparently thought that if he could not see others' faces, they would not notice the worried expression on his own.

Panditji picked up the thread of his thoughts, 'Mahendra, my son, I told you about it, remember? My first job was as a proofreader at Desraj's press for twenty rupees a month.' He again guffawed, as if wanting to tell his daughters to make light of every problem, 'Nobody was willing to hire anyone jailed for political reasons in those days. Desraj was a decent man. Even in that situation I found time to do some writing. The night-time was my own, I was young, and my spirits were high. I wrote light, romantic novels. *DreamWaves* was published by Makhzane Adab. I gave that publisher four novels in three years; *DreamWaves*, a novella about the life of Tipu Sultan, and translations of two English novels. My friend, who was willing to pay out royalties in those days? People wrote for fun, therefore the quality was better. Well, in lieu of royalties, I asked the publisher for 150 copies of each book. Those I traded with some booksellers for other titles, and opened a small shop in Sootar Mandi. Then I brought out the weekly *Des-Sandesh*, and got a second-hand printing press to turn it out. I was able to publish bit by bit about twenty books, school texts and notes that some friends of mine and I had written up. I then expanded the press, built the house, and what a comfortable house it was! I had thought that my daughters and sons-in-law would look after all that, but then this hour of doom sounded. It was all His doing,' he again roared with laughter, 'everything went to pieces.'

Still laughing, he took off his glasses and screwed up his eyes. His attempt to clean the lenses only smudged them. He went on, 'It was so well said by that poet ... what's his name, Kanni?... Yes, that's it, Momin! Momin said, listen Mahendra, you too Kanta,' he said, raising his finger, '"The gardener rues the bulbul's ruined nest, strewn by the storm along the ravaged ground..."'

Panditji shifted excitedly in his seat as he repeated the first half of the verse in a louder voice.

'Listen, Mahendra, "...But in the tree the bird, with swelling breast, rebuilds, and greets the dawn with joyful sound."Wah, wah! Beautifully said.'

Panditji's words, Kanak felt, were meant especially for her. She also knew that her father, despite his own great unhappiness, said such things to cheer up the family. He often did that to express his own burden of frustrations.

She prompted him to say more, 'The bulbul bemoans and laments over her misfortune. What else is there in poetry? Some poet may write poems about our misfortune, while others write stories about it.'

Panditji replied gravely, 'Beta, poetry and fiction have their own place, but why should we fall into despair and gloom?'

Nayyar sensed that Kanak's joke had missed its mark. A light drizzle was falling. Seeing his mother standing in the aangan and peering up at the grey sky, he said to her, 'Ma, what're you doing ... looking for God?'

'Yes, son, who else is there to look for at my age? He's the only one who cares,' she replied.

Kanchan leaned towards Nayyar, and dropping her voice so that her father could not hear, said, 'Ask her, who she looked at when she was young?'

'Really! Look, aren't you being just a bit too mischievous,' Nayyar said with a mock scowl.

'What did she say?' asked Panditji.

'Ma, Kanchi was saying ...' Nayyar raised his voice so that Panditji could hear.

Kanchan pinched the flesh on Nayyar's leg to make him stop. He rubbed the spot but went on teasingly, 'Ma, Kanchi was saying ...do you want me to tell her?'

His mother asked, 'What was she saying?'

Nayyar challenged Kanchan, 'Want me to tell?'

'Go ahead!' Kanchan threatened him with another pinch.

He stared at Kanchan mockingly as he spoke, 'Ma, she was saying, who did you ...? Should I tell ... ? Asking you to tell God that we're all fed up with this rain. He should stop it. Why is He making us suffer?'

His mother joined her hands in supplication to the sky and prayed, 'Divine Father, please stop now.'

'Bahinji, just look at how little these youngsters know,' Panditji spoke to Nayyar's mother in Punjabi. 'What do they know about how important this rain is for the wheat crop? Every act of God above brings some good to us humans.'

'You're right, bhaiji,' Nayyar's mother agreed, 'These children were born in cities and raised in cities. So what would they know about crops, How wheat is grown and so on?'

'If this rain is good for the crop, ask God to make it rain over where the wheat grows,' Kanak spoke up. 'Is He wasting all this water here in the city just to make us paddle about in mud? So that people get soaked and fall ill? Can't He see that wheat doesn't grow on top of our heads? When the gardener at our Model Town house watered the plants, did he soak us too? That gardener had more sense than God.'

'You're quite right, Ma,' Nayyar took his mother's side to tease his sisters-in-law, 'What do these girls know about growing wheat? They think that chapattis grow on one kind of tree in the countryside, and double-rotis on another kind. Listen...' he straightened his back as he launched into his joke, 'I once asked Kanni if she had seen the fields where wheat grew? She replied, "Yes. I went once to my uncle's place in the country. We were out in the open when a tiger charged at us fiercely. I was so scared that I climbed up a wheat tree" ... Aah!' Nayyar stopped in mid-sentence as he felt his back where Kanak had pinched him viciously.

'What is it? ... What's the matter?' Panditji wanted to know.

'Bedbugs, pitaji, and lots of them,' replied Nayyar, rubbing his back.

'Oh, aren't they all dead yet?' Panditji asked. 'Must be hiding in the crevices. I'll spray the furniture once again with DDT. Still have plenty left in the can.'

'Yes, they are really sneaky. They bite you when you least expect them,' Nayyar said, glancing at Kanak and Kanchan.

Nayyar and the two sisters continued to joke around till late at night, if only to prevent Panditji, Kanta or Nayyar's mother from moaning about their woes and the misfortunes.

The lights were turned off and the family went to bed. As there were more of them than the number of beds and charpoys, Kanak had to share a bed, either with Kanchan or Kanta or her mother. It was Kanak's eighth day in Delhi, and there was still no news of Puri. She felt relieved that in the darkness, no one could see her anxiety.

Thoughts continued to whirl in her mind: Pitaji says one should not be overcome by one's difficulties.... Is it really hard to live in poverty? Most people do; the people of the next gali are in an even worse situation than ours. So many cook their meals on the earth of the gali, do their laundry too; they even sleep in the galis. And we consider ourselves badly off! Had we always lived like this, pitaji wouldn't have thought of Puri as unsuitable. Who knows what he's going through? A ripple of sadness ran through her body. She must write to Ramprakash tomorrow and ask if there was a letter for her. He's such a lazy body; just the sort to forget to forward the letter if there was one.

Since her childhood Kanak had seriously nurtured the ambition to be a writer and a journalist. Her father had encouraged her. Puri had trained her for this work. She saw herself as his comrade and life companion in this field. If she didn't begin realizing that goal now, when would she do so? Who knew what fate had in store? If it came to living her life alone, she would live it in his memory, doing what he had taught her. Thoughts of a tough, lonely life were on her mind when she dropped off to sleep.

In Delhi, the daily routine of Panditji's family underwent a change. The daughters did not sleep till late in the morning. If they did, their mother would begin to do the housework quietly by herself. The sisters asked Panditji and Nayyar's mother to wake them up around six o'clock. That day, Kanchan, soon after she got up, began cleaning the kitchenware left overnight. Kanta sat at the faucet washing the family's clothes. Kanak wrapped her dupatta around her head and nose, and swept the rooms and the aangan with a broom.

They heard a noise outside. It sounded like Bajrang was keeping some one from coming through the gate.

Kanta called out to Kanak to investigate.

Kanak draped the dupatta around her shoulders and went to the gate. She came back with a slim Punjabi girl in tow. Newspapers were tucked under the girl's arm.

Regarding Kanta as the senior, the girl said to her, 'Bahinji, do you take newspapers? May I deliver the paper every morning?'

A bit surprised, Kanta paused in her work and said, 'Yes, sister, come, have a seat.'

The girl handed Kanta a newspaper, 'Don't ask anyone else to deliver. I shall come every day. No credit, though.'

Nayyar' mother had also come out, she said, 'Come, daughter, sit. Where are your people from? Who are your parents? Sit down for a moment.'

'Maaji, what's the point of asking me that? I'll deliver the paper.'

Panditji stepped forward to greet the girl and wish her success. He paid her for the newspaper.

The girl left. From her speech and dress, she seemed to be educated and from a middle-class family.

'Girls like us, our sisters, have to sell newspapers,' Kanta dabbed at her eyes with her dhoti's aanchal.

'What's the harm?' said Kanak, 'I will too, if the need arises.'

'Bravo! That's my lion-hearted daughter,' Panditji roared approvingly. 'These are the lion-hearted girls of Punjab. No one can kill the Punjabi people. They will survive! I saw with my own eyes people displaced in the Bengal famine, the earthquake victims of Bihar, those uprooted by the flood disasters in UP, all they did was to beg. But this is the real Punjabi spirit!' He took off his glasses and used the end of his shirtfront to wipe away his tears.

Everyone was silent. Kanta resumed her washing. Kanchan went back to doing the dishes. Kanak again wrapped the dupatta around her head and face, and picked up the broom. After some time she fetched her father a parantha and a glassful of lassi. When the two were alone, she said, 'Pitaji, I want to try to find a job here in some newspaper office.'

Panditji agreed, 'Yes, beta, why not!'

Gandhiji had left Calcutta with the mission of trying to restore calm in western Pakistan, but reports of the situation in Delhi made him hang his head in shame and pain. How could he accomplish anything in Pakistan unless peace first prevailed in India? He made a vow not to leave Delhi unless there was complete peace in the city, even if he had to sacrifice his life in the effort. The Congress government put the city under very strict military control. Orders were given to shoot rioters and troublemakers at sight. Army regiments from southern India were called in to replace soldiers from Garhwal and Sikh regiments. These new soldiers could not distinguish between the Hindu and Muslim inhabitants of northern India.

The majority of Muslims living in Delhi had been moved into evacuee camps. Those who did not want to leave Delhi had been funnelled into Urdu Bazaar, Ajmeri Gate and Hauz Kazi mohallas, and cordoned off by armed soldiers for their safety.

Girls and women from the families of Hindu refugees faced a different problem. Of necessity they had to go out to do their daily housekeeping chores. Since the new arrivals were strangers to one another, there were instances of inconsiderate behaviour and calling of remarks against women. Sometimes two groups of Hindu refugees complaining about the harassment and eve-teasing of their daughters and sisters clashed with each other. Panditji's daughters began going out only when escorted by Nayyar or his younger brother.

Kanak, Kanchan and Nayyar went out one morning to do some shopping and also for a breath of fresh air. As they stepped out, Kanak said to her brother-in-law, 'Jiai, you'll soon go off to Jalandhar. Help me today. I want to visit some newspaper offices. I'm totally unfamiliar with the bazaars and roads here.'

They discussed which newspapers they should go to. Besides several old well-established English, Hindi and Urdu newspapers, the Urdu dailies *Pairokaar* and *Sardar* had begun publishing from the city a month ago.

Nayyar said, 'If you're serious about taking up journalism as a profession, in my opinion you should begin at some English daily, even as an apprentice, for some months.'

'Why?'

Nayyar replied, 'I think that the atmosphere of an English newspaper office would be more to your liking and taste. Urdu newspapers don't seem to have high professional standards. It would not be appropriate for a woman to work there.'

Nayyar was speaking in English, so Kanak also protested in English, 'What nonsense!' She suspected that Nayyar was having a dig at Puri. 'I don't believe so. Neither do I have sufficient command of English, nor am I able to express myself well in English.' She began to argue, 'And how can we reach the masses through English?'

'I don't know about that. But it's the English papers that sell the most,' Nayyar tried to explain his reasoning.

'Excuse me,' said Kanak, 'but that's a rather servile attitude, a result of foreign domination. If you count the readers of all the newspapers published in the vernacular languages, the readers of English newspapers wouldn't amount to much. I'm more at home in my own language.'

'Do as you please,' Nayyar ended the conversation.

Nayyar and Kanak first went to the office of *Pairokaar*. Kanak was introduced to its editor Karam Chand Kashish as the daughter of Pandit Girdharilal, the nationalist leader of Lahore. Kashish was reminded that *Pairokaar* had already published an article by Kanak, and a short story written by her had appeared in its weekly magazine. Several other articles written by Kanak were also mentioned. She explained her wish to work at *Pairokaar*, and asked for the editor's help and advice.

Kashish was delighted to meet the daughter of an old acquaintance. He was full of praise for the promise that Kanak had shown as a writer, and gave his word that *Pairokaar* would welcome her contributions in future, as well as help her in getting recognition as a journalist. He seemed ready to do anything to help the daughter of someone as respectable as Panditji.

'But,' he placed his elbows on the desk, interlaced the fingers of both hands, and spoke in English as if sharing a secret, 'you're just like my own daughter. Believe me, and I'm telling you the truth, that a newspaper office is not a place fit for a respectable woman. I'd never advice the daughter of my esteemed friend to work in one. Would it be proper for a young woman to work surrounded by so many men? There's a lot of loose talk and indecent jokes in such places. Not fit for a girl from any respectable family. My advice would be to work at some school for girls, or do social work among women.'

Kashish thumped the desk with his hand, 'Tell you what! I have an idea.'

He snapped his fingers, 'Go to the camps and talk with refugee women. Listen to their stories and write them up with a little imagination. I'll myself edit the text to improve it. That's the work for someone with real talent. The staff of a newspaper mostly does routine work. We'll publish your articles regularly, I promise.'

When they were outside, Nayyar blurted out, 'Rogue! Felt like telling him so.'

Kanak agreed with her brother-in-law, 'You can't expect decent behaviour from people like him.'

Their meetings at two other, older newspapers were less than encouraging. One already had several apprentices; the other was disinclined to assume the burden of a new employee when they could not even accommodate their own trainees.

The premises of *Sardar* contained a motley assortment of printing press equipment. The presses stood on an unpaved floor under a temporary roof of tarpaulin and corrugated iron sheets. The office was in a room at the back of a veranda, with basic furniture of wood planks nailed together. A table fan placed on an upturned packing box in one corner turned at top speed. Stones and pieces of rusted metal served as paperweights on desks. A teleprinter stood ticking, next to a wall.

The owner–editor was not in. Sewa Ram Charkh, his deputy, was keeping an eye on everything. Nayyar spoke with him, then introduced Kanak and briefly mentioned her interest.

The businesslike Charkh did not seem happy at this interruption, even for the sake of a young woman. He did not ask Kanak and Nayyar to sit down. There were no extra chairs, or any extra room to put them. He listened to Nayyar with a pen in his hand, and then placed it in an inkwell. He spoke slowly, drawling his words, 'Yes, yes ! I understand, but if there was an opening we'd hire our former employees. On the staff of a newspaper, you work until late at night. For a woman.'

'Sahib has arrived,' a peon announced.

A youngish fit-looking man, wearing a dazzling white kurta, white churidar pajama trousers, a white well-ironed Gandhi cap with sharp creases, and sun glasses walked in. Everyone, including the middle-aged Charkh, left whatever they were doing and stoop up.

The sahib went through the cluttered room, picking his way carefully

through the maze of furniture. He looked at Kanak and Nayyar. His dark
glasses hid any expression in his eyes. Nayyar smilingly said namaste, and
asked in English, 'May I have a moment of your time?'

The sahib looked again at Kanak and stopped. He replied in English,
'Sure, sure! Please come upstairs with me to my office.'

Upstairs were two rooms on either side of a small aangan. In one, two
men sat working at a desk. Over the door to the second hung a cloth-lined
chick blind. Beside it was a name plate: S.P. Aseer, Editor–Director.

The peon ran ahead and raised the blind. Aseer stepped aside, to let
Kanak and Nayyar enter, 'Please!'

A dhurrie covered the floor. In one corner stood a modern office desk,
gleaming with polish, and three expensive-looking chairs. Four easy chairs
around a low, circular table occupied the other half.

Aseer held out some papers in his hand to the peon, 'Give these to the
manager.' Then he inquired the purpose of their visit. He had removed his
dark glasses. Smallish eyes above his fleshy cheeks had a sharp look. Kanak
thought him to be a serious person.

Nayyar went into a lengthy introduction of Panditji and Kanak, and
a brief one of himself. He smiled as he explained that Kanak wanted to
work at *Sardar*.

Aseer asked Kanak about her college education, and what work she had
done in Lahore. He said, 'You were probably also in the movement of '42
and '43? ... People like us were involved in everything.'

After a few moments of quiet reflection, he said in English, 'Newspaper
work has many sides: proofreading, copy-editing, columns, editorials.
The truth is that if you want to do just copy-editing, news selection and
translation, we may not have any vacancy. A number of experienced
journalists are already looking for that type of work. If you are really
interested and have talent—you're a fiction writer aren't you—your talent
would be wasted in such work. You wouldn't be able to do any serious work
if you get stuck in such drudgery. My father made me go through the mill
only as a learning experience. Remember, the real test of a journalist's
talent is not in the newspaper office, but in the field. The real skill is to
analyse the situation, to grasp its essence, its presentation; to create news,
to create opinion. If you want to do all that, you're welcome. All famous
journalists ... I mean people like Gunther, Fisher, Ehrenburg, Paula Hicks,
Iqbal ... which of these ever worked in a newspaper office? They wouldn't

be what they turned out to be if they'd been stuck at some office job...'

Aseer opened a tin of cigarettes and offered it to Kanak, 'Do you?'

'Thanks. I don't smoke.'

Aseer gave one to Nayyar and lit one himself.

'That's the kind of work I want to do. I need a break, and I need your help,' Kanak said.

He nodded as he drew on his cigarette, 'Sure, I'll help you. The time is right, new events and new problems every day. Gandhiji's in the city, so this is where the news is. A smart and respectable young woman such as yourself should be able to go anywhere. I'll give you one of our press passes. Write about your observations, and see if you can figure out anything. There's the refugee problem. In the early days your reports might need editing and rewriting. For that, I'll be here, and also Mr Charkh.'

On their way back from *Sardar*, Kanak felt buoyed by Aseer's response.

Nayyar was also supportive, 'You can do well if this man helps you and gives you a break.'

Kanak stopped to buy a *Writing for the Press* from a large bookshop at Kashmiri Gate. Panditji gave his own creative advice, 'Read through the "Around the Metropolis" and "Topics and Trends" columns in the newspaper.'

She and Panditji decided to attend Gandhiji's prayer meeting at Karol Bagh that evening. The Mahatma had been holding these meetings in a different part of the city every evening to promote tolerance, compassion and goodwill between communities. The broadcast of his prayers could be heard via amplifiers at different points all over the city. But Kanak wanted to have the Mahatma's darshan as well as to get some feeling of the spirit of the meeting.

Several Muslim women in burkas and Muslim men sat on one side at the open-air meeting place. Congress volunteers stood in a protective ring around them. Dhurries spread on the lawn provided seating space, but a large number of those present stood talking, or simply milled around. There were a few cries of protest, 'This prayer meeting is a mockery. Gandhi is doing this only to appease the Muslims.'

Gandhiji, his granddaughters and the rest of his party arrived in four motor cars. Many members of the audience rushed to touch his feet as soon as he stepped out. Congress volunteers holding hands formed a circle around Gandhiji to protect him from the crush of his admirers.

He was wearing just a loincloth. His head was slightly bent, his face sombre and sorrowful. He was the only one not fully dressed and stood out from everyone else. One did not have to enquire who he might be. He was not tall or fair or good looking, but his slim, wiry body and dark skin radiated a quiet dignity and a compelling presence.

Kanak felt a surge of respect for the man.

The volunteers barred others from approaching, but let the Muslim women approach him. The women wrapped their arms around his knees and broke into loud sobs. Tears fell from Gandhiji's eyes. He put his hands on their burka-covered heads and asked them to have faith in Ishwar–Allah. He would put his own life at stake to protect them, he promised.

One of the women wept as she held an infant up to Gandhiji. 'This baby's an orphan,' she said between her tears. 'Both his parents were murdered.'

Gandhiji clasped the infant to his heart and prayed to God to bless and protect him.

Gandhiji and his group then began the proceeding by singing hymns from the Bhagawad Gita. Then they chanted bani from the Guru Granth Sahib, and began to recite verses from the Quran.

'Stop! Gandhi murdabad! No reciting of the Quran. Down with Gandhi! We won't listen to anything from the Quran!' Chaos broke out. A crowd of angry rowdies were bent upon breaking up the assembly.

Many people sitting on dhurries called out, 'Be quiet! Silence! Shame, shame on you!'

Gandhiji lapsed into silence. A hush fell over the rest of his group, also.

The brazen hostility of the protesters pained Kanak. Panditji was also upset and disgusted, 'Tsk, tsk! What a shame!'

Gandhiji joined his hands and implored the crowd to listen to him quietly.

The angry and agitated crowd could not ignore Gandhiji's request, and the commotion gradually subsided.

'My brothers and sisters,' Gandhiji's pained, gentle but confident voice was heard to say, 'Only trust in God can give us succour in this time of strife and misery. Ishwar and Allah are one. What objection can there be in an appeal to Him through any form of religion...'

'We will certainly not listen to any reading from the Quran,' some voices from the crowd shouted back. 'These verses encouraged others to slaughter thousands of our brothers. Those who recite these verses raped our mothers and sisters. You preach the message of non-violence and compassion for all. By reciting these verses, you are reminding us of the infamy of the killing of our families and our children, how our mothers and sisters were dishonoured. You are reminding us of our shame and misery. We will not tolerate it at any price.' The suffering of the victims called for retribution in the shouts of the protestors. It was a scream of anger and agony.

The audience fell silent. Even those who had called out 'Shame! shame!' were quiet.

Kanak was in a state of inner confusion. Her mind was a whirling vortex of contradictory ideas of injustice, of revenge, of tolerance. Where was the solution... the answer? She fixed her eyes on Gandhiji in search of an answer.

Gandhiji spoke in a fearless voice, 'Some of my brothers find objections to my reciting verses from the Quran. I do not want to hurt their feelings. But if I cannot recite those verses in this meeting, I will not quote any other religious book either.'

'There's no need! You don't have to!' The protesters shouted back disdainfully.

'I humbly appeal to my Hindu and Sikh brothers and sisters in the name of human dignity,' Gandhiji spoke again when the shouting had subsided. 'All of our Muslim brothers and sisters remaining in Delhi are our responsibility, and of our Indian government. If one hair on their heads is harmed or they are threatened or endangered in any way, it will be like committing the most heinous crime, it will be a matter of utter shame for us...'

'Thousands of Hindus are being murdered every day in Pakistan! They are robbed naked and thrown out of that country. Don't you feel anything for them? Why don't you go there?' His opponents called defiantly.

Gandhiji again joined his hands solicitously and asked to be heard, 'My heart feels the same pain for my brothers and sisters killed in Pakistan and for those being asked to leave Pakistan. I want to go to Pakistan. I will pray with joined hands to the Qaid-e-Azam for peace and mercy. I will ask him that all killing and bloodshed should stop, and peace be restored. All Hindu brothers and sisters should be able to return to their homes and live in peace, but before that it is important that Muslims who have left come back to live here. As long as the lives of Muslims in Delhi and in India continue to be in danger, how can I face the Pakistan government and accuse them of murder and prejudice? How can I face them and ask them to restore peace? I am ready to stake my life for peace and order in both India and Pakistan.'

Afterwards, on the way home, Kanak fell into a moody silence. Panditji, his head bent, walked along pensively. After she had sulked for some time, Kanak blurted out, 'Calls for revenge won't put a stop to warlike feelings. Puriji said the same thing in his newspaper articles last March, and was thrown out of his job.' 'You're absolutely right, beti,' Panditji said.

Aseer was in his office in the late afternoon. He asked Kanak to have a seat in one of the easy chairs, after she handed him her report. He busily shuffled papers on his desk for some ten minutes, then rang for the peon. He ordered, 'Give these papers to the manager, these to the deputy editor.' Turning to Kanak, he counted the pages of her article and said, 'Four minutes.'

He rang again for the peon after he had finished reading. When the peon came, he said, 'Tea,' and came and sat facing Kanak.

'You have a really forceful style,' he said in English, 'but your viewpoint is off the mark. Politically, this is unsound. Such a point of view will be suicidal for Hindus. Gandhi has done considerable harm to us.'

Kanak thoughtfully rolled her scrap of handkerchief between her palms, choosing her words carefully so as not to offend Aseer, 'I took the human approach. I myself saw those women sobbing bitterly. Tears were streaming from Gandhiji's eyes…'

'Thousands of Hindus are living in conditions far worse than ever faced by those burka-clad women! Don't the Hindus need some place to live? Only yesterday, these same women and their brothers were clamouring for Pakistan. Doesn't Gandhi know that? He's preaching tolerance for the same Karol Bagh Muslims who fired upon Hindus with machine guns and Stens. Doctor Neelambar Joshi was murdered in the same Karol Bagh. Doesn't Gandhi have any regrets for Doctor Joshi? Neelambar Joshi, the greatest surgeon of Hindustan or Pakistan, among the four or five best in the world! Wasn't his murder a mockery of human values? And who murdered him? Not any stranger or outsider, but a Muslim doctor working at the same hospital. These are the values and compassion preached by Islam. Any faith that declares it a religious duty to wipe out all non-Muslims, a faith that called the killing of Shradanand and Lekhram, and Rajpal pious acts of faith, Gandhi wants us to be tolerant towards that same religious creed! These people have always been enemies of civilized human behaviour. Just visit any old Hindu temple and you'll see.'

'That all was in the past. I meant to say that we should leave behind those feelings of enmity. Not as Hindus or Muslims, but as human beings...'

Aseer raised his eyebrows, 'Are you a communist?'

'No, I'm not. What made you ask that?'

'That communist leader P.C. Joshi went to Gandhi a couple of days ago. Told him that they'll form Home Guard units to protect Muslims. These people first betrayed the cause in the '42 movement, then supported Jinnah, and now want to be Gandhi's militia.'

The peon brought tea and two cups in a tray.

Aseer took out a key from his pocket and tossed it to the peon. The peon took a packet of biscuits from a cupboard, and put it in front of them.

'Shall I pour tea for you?' Kanak said.

'That's your privilege. For yourself also.'

Aseer began in English as he waited for the tea to cool, 'Your style is more suited for fiction than for news reporting. Or is it just a young woman's ardour?' He smiled.

'Ji, I've published three short stories. Jai Puriji also liked them very much. He taught me how to write fiction.'

'Jai Puri...that *Pairokaar* chap? He was really a good writer. I know.'

'Is he here in Delhi?' Kanak asked nervously.

'Can't say. Must be with some newspaper, if he's alive.'

That hurt Kanak, but she said nothing.

As he sipped his tea, Aseer explained, 'Writing a short story is a different matter, you can take all kind of liberties. A newspaper aims to create public opinion. We'll publish your report, after some editing. Look for it in tomorrow's *Sardar*.'

Aseer called Harbans the peon. 'Take these sheets to Charkhji,' he ordered, 'and bring me a slip of paper and the pen from the desk.'

Aseer scribbled two lines on the paper and handed it to the peon along with Kanak's article. He took out a five-rupee note and gave it to the peon. 'And buy a tin of Gold Flake cigarettes.'

Aseer said as he finished his tea, 'You can also write about civic problems.

Plenty of scope in that for a smart and educated young lady like yourself. Focus on government news from official circles. I can get you some introductions. What do you think?'

'I'd be much obliged. Shall I make another cup for you?'

'Sure, and for yourself too.'

After pouring him the second cup, Kanak excused herself, 'One was enough for me.'

When Aseer had finished his second cup, Kanak said, 'I'll take leave of you. I've quite a distance to go, or I'll be late.'

'Where did your family find a house?'

'In a gali behind Faiz Bazaar.'

'I'll make up for delaying you. I've to go into New Delhi, so I'll give you a lift.'

'It'll be too much trouble for you.'

'Not at all. Your father used to own a printing press?'

'Yes, in Gwal Mandi. All that had to be left behind.'

'We did manage to bring ours here, but it wasn't easy. Had to bribe the police with a thousand rupees, otherwise we'd have lost machines worth thirty or forty thousand. Had to pay five thousand as a premium for this place, and then a rent of 500 per month. You can see how much space we've got. This is how our Hindu brothers lend a hand! Dam, rotten, scoundrels...'

The peon came back with the tin of cigarettes. Aseer turned the lid to cut it open. He pulled up one cigarette and held the tin out to Kanak, 'You take the first one. It's always the best.'

Kanak was annoyed as she had told him that she didn't smoke only three days before. She smiled politely before saying, 'Thanks. I don't smoke.'

'Really! Never! Not even after a cup of tea or to keep others company?' He lit his cigarette.

'No. Never tried one.'

'What's the harm in trying? I've often seen high society ladies smoke in public. It is quite accepted now. What changes the past couple of months have brought! All the old stigmas and etiquette have disappeared. New styles of living in a new world. The most urgent need is to get oneself settled in.'

'That's quite a tall order, though.'

'Harbans,' Aseer called again, 'ask the manager sahib to send me today's mail. I have to leave.'

Aseer checked through the typed letters for five minutes, signed them, and led Kanak downstairs.

Tonga carriages and motor vehicles jammed the road they were on. The footpaths could not contain all the pedestrians thronging the road. Time and again Kanak squirmed nervously in her seat in case the car would run over that man, or collide with that truck. Aseer drove with confidence, weaving his way through the traffic.

Kanak had to praise his skill, 'You drive like an expert. Marvellous! You change the gears so smoothly that one does not notice.'

'You drive?'

'No, no. We didn't own a car. I've learnt a bit in my sister's car, but I'm scared even if the road is empty.'

Aseer kept the conversation going. 'Give us Society News and Society Gossip-type stuff. I'll see that you get introduced around...' When he dropped her off in Faiz Bazaar, he again reminded her to keep on writing for *Sardar*.

The hopes that Kanak had felt at the time of her first meeting with Aseer had begun to wane after her experiences of the last few weeks. Five of her articles now had been published in *Sardar*. Most of her report on Gandhiji's prayer meeting in Karol Bagh was left intact. The conclusions, however, were completely rewritten. Her articles on the plight of refugees were published unchanged, but instead of her name, under the byline 'By our Special Correspondent'. She hoped that Aseer would keep his word and pay her for her writing.

She was also increasingly wary of Aseer's excessive familiarity. His continual offers of cigarettes despite her refusals, his hand on her waist to help her while going up or down a flight of stairs. Kanak found his touch revolting and distasteful, even slimy.

Kanak thought of herself as a bold and daring person. She did not care for convention. But when she went to the Chelmsford Club, she realized how limited her world had been. Since smoking and drinking formed a part of the normal evening's entertainment, why should there be different norms for their use for women and men? Wasn't it unsophisticated to shrink from the touch of a male hand and be unable to contort one's eyes and mouth in conversation? She had been thinking of herself as bold and capable in comparison with women whose world began and ended inside the boundaries of their houses and galis. She knew little about how those of higher social standing thought and behaved. She now felt inadequate in those circles. And the discussions at the club on the issues of religious tolerance, the right of Muslims to remain in India, and the problems of giving them equal status left her perplexed and undecided.

The tension at the club was almost palpable. The air rang with references to Kashmir, Baramula, Uri, Pattan. Sinha thumped the table with such force in his rage against Gandhiji that the glasses were almost knocked off. He was enraged because by stopping the Muslim evacuation from Delhi and other parts of the country, Gandhiji was only doing grievous harm to the country. He said, 'If our army hadn't stopped the Pakistani army's mechanized units at Baramula, Srinagar would certainly have fallen. Major Soni was saying that British officers were quite openly commanding the Pakistani army's raiders. What if Muslims in India indulge in sabotage now? The Muslims here are only waiting for the right moment.'

'Sabotage?' said Aseer. 'Not only sabotage. These Muslims had planned to stage a coup to take over Delhi. Stocks of army rifles, machine guns and hand grenades were discovered in their homes. Sardar Patel gave enough evidence to Gandhi, but he refuses to believe it. Patel is absolutely right when he asks how anyone can trust Muslims who have turned pro-India nationalists overnight.'

Mrs Baluja took a pull on her cigarette, and opened her darkly painted lips to show her pearly teeth and to let out the smoke. She raised her pencilled eyebrows, 'Yes, how dangerous, isn't it!' She placed her cigarette in the ashtray, next to Sinha's sending up a thread of smoke, and drained her glass of sherry.

Aseer called to a passing bearer, 'One more sherry.' He then asked the bearer to wait and said to Mrs Baluja, 'Or a small whiskey?'

'All right. I'll have one just to keep you company,' Mrs Baluja said with a laugh. 'Gandhi is bent upon getting us all killed. Did you hear about that incident in Connaught Place? Gandhi insisted that the government should rebuild the mosque after throwing the refugees out. It was Patel who took a tough stand, and got the matter hushed up. We can't depend on Gandhi.'

Sinha reached for his cigarette but picked up in his fingers Mrs Baluja's cigarette with marks of her red lipstick. Kanak was about to point that out when she saw the eyes of the two meet. A smile flickered over Mrs Baluja's lips. Kanak said nothing.

Aseer continued to vent his anger, 'At this moment, thousands of refugees are living in mosques and tombs, even in the ruins of forts swarming with bats and jackals. Some poor destitute had to break up tombs to get bricks to make some kind of a shelter. Gandhi wants to have all of them thrown out. Is it more important to save people's lives or to protect deserted and desolate mosques? Gandhi is on the side of fanatical Muslims, and doesn't think about saving Hindu lives.'

Mrs Baluja took a sip of her new drink, and Aseer and Sinha followed suit. She said, 'Patel saved us Hindus. Gandhi and Nehru would have got us killed.'

Aseer smiled and said sarcastically, 'His sympathies should all be on their side. After all, he was brought up in that culture.'

Sinha again blew up, 'The news about the aerial bombing of some eastern Bihar villages, where all the Muslim inhabitants were killed, has been suppressed. Hundreds of Hindus died there. I say,' Sinha again struck the table with his hand, 'let Gandhi go to eastern Bihar. I'll bet he won't return alive. The faith of a Muslim is such that he can never have nationalistic or patriotic feelings for India.' I myself have heard Hasrat Mohani declare at a public meeting in Kanpur ...'

'What did their Iqbal say?' Aseer cut him short, 'All Muslims are one nation, the world is ours! Do you suppose they'll ever let India be at peace?'

Their conversation depressed Kanak. How could anti-national feelings be tolerated? If the country is being threatened, national security cannot be compromised. How can anyone criticise the need to be alert to danger?

When they were leaving, Aseer added to what he had begun to say earlier when introducing Kanak, 'Kanakji wields a powerful pen. She's the daughter of an old and respected freedom fighter and a political personality of Punjab. Her family suffered great losses; they've had to leave their house and a large printing press behind. Her five or six articles, how many Kanakji? ...five articles have been published in *Sardar*. All were well received.'

'Certainly. We've got to help her,' agreed Sinha.

Pandit Girdharilal did not believe in doing anything that went against his principles, for the sake of his politics. For him, politics was a temporary business, principles were everlasting. He approved of the views of Gandhiji and Nehru. He would say, 'If India is to be a secular state, the policy of not discriminating between Hindus and Muslims, while not extending tolerance towards Muslims on the whole, is a contradiction in principle. One should not forgive traitors, but to brand someone a traitor on the basis of religion alone is morally wrong. Does history have no record of Hindu traitors? This poison of religious fanaticism will ruin this country. Bhai, the demand for a separate Sikh homeland has already been heard. What the future will bring, who knows? If one's religion becomes the basis of one's politics, Sikhs, Arya Samajis, Sanatanis, Jains all will ask for special rights. Bhai, in Punjab I even saw Arya Samajis and Sanatanis smashing each others heads.'

Kanak agreed with her father's opinion. If Puriji was here now, she thought, he could have written so well on this topic in some newspaper or other. Puri's memory insistently invaded Kanak's thinking. She had also received a reply to her letter to Awasthi in Lucknow. It came from Mrs Pant. Only a few lines, but full of optimism:

'... I replied to your first letter at your Nainital address. Probably you did not get it. If you come here, we'll do all we can. You can stay with me when you come.'

Kanak was worried: Ramprakash did not redirect any letters from Lucknow. If Puriji wrote, that letter too would not have been forwarded. Puriji must have given an address in his letter. Why would he write again when he didn't get any reply? In her eagerness, she quickly wrote a letter to the postmaster at Nainital, asking that any letter addressed to Vimal Villa might be forwarded c/o Naya Hind Press, Faiz Bazaar, Delhi.

As Kanak got the feeling that she had little chance to succeed in Delhi as a journalist because of her strong opinions, the letter from Lucknow kindled hope in her heart. She broached the subject of her going to Lucknow with her father. He agreed with her in principle, but still advised her to have patience and try her luck again in Delhi, 'Beti, what's a mere six weeks? Others might have to work as an apprentice for a year and a half before they get taken on. Life is a struggle.'

On 5 November 1947, the newspapers carried a statement by the chief minister of UP, 'Our state has no place for people who believe in the theory of Hindus and Muslims being two separate nations and two races. There is no question of anyone being asked to leave the state just because he or she happens to be Muslim, nor of anyone who refuses to consider himself or herself to be Indian being allowed to remain.'

The chief minister had also quoted a telegram received from the Pakistan government inquiring about the condition of Muslims in UP. The chief minister's reply was, 'Only the people of Uttar Pradesh and the Government of India, not any foreign country, has the right to demand an answer about any situation inside the state. Pakistan has attacked Kashmir. We will not entertain any questions from that country in these circumstances.'

A statement by Mister Lari, the deputy leader of the Muslim League, was also reported, 'The Muslim League under its leader Mister Mohammed Ali Jinnah has no right to legal existence in India.'

Panditji heartily approved of these declarations. He praised the people of UP as serious-minded. Kanak saw this as an opportunity to ask permission to go to Lucknow. Panditji replied, 'Beti, I have no objection, but we must give this matter a little more thought. Mahendra will arrive here from Jalandhar on Sunday. Let's ask his opinion too. What's the hurry?'

A delegation of Muslims from Bihar, UP and Delhi had gone to meet Gandhiji at Birla House, and to plead with him to stop the evacuation of Muslims to Pakistan. They wanted an assurance from the government that Muslims would be able to live in India without feeling threatened.

That evening, Gandhiji made a strong and emotional appeal during the broadcast of his prayer meeting at Birla House, '. . . Those Muslim brothers who have spurned sectarianism and who have pledged allegiance to patriotic Indian principles , who consider themselves to be a part of the Indian nation, and regard this country as their native land, to push them out of the bosom of their motherland would be a terrible crime.'

Disheartened by the restriction on expressing her opinions, and discouraged by the lack of payment for her work, Kanak had not written anything for over a week. But she was very keen to write in support of this appeal by Gandhiji, and to raise her voice against injustice. When her enthusiasm did not fall off after two days, she wrote a small article. If it was an injustice to force us out of our homeland, she reasoned, it is equally unjust to force out those Muslims who do not want to leave India. A policy of an eye for an eye, and a tooth for a tooth will only provoke further injustice. She felt confident that Aseer would publish this article out of respect for humanistic ideals and fair play.

She knew that Aseer kept to his office between three and six o'clock in the afternoon, and called on him. He started off by complaining about her not coming for so many days, then sent for tea. He made light conversation for a few more minutes before getting down to Kanak's article.

His face turned serious. 'Isn't the fact of people being forced to leave their homelands a result of the demand for the creation of Pakistan?' he asked.

'But the Muslims remaining in Delhi or in India were not responsible for throwing us out of Lahore. Those who believed in the Two Nations theory have already left. Why should these people who stayed behind be made to pay for the crimes of others?' Kanak answered his question with another.

'It's the Islamic doctrine that has created these feelings of hostility and prejudice against us. Those who are true believers in Islam have turned into our enemies. Is there another kind of Islam?' Aseer asked, leaving Kanak without any possible reply.

'No. The reasons for that enmity were economic,' Kanak replied.

'Let's get off this subject,' Aseer said, ending the conversation. 'Let's go to the club. You didn't return after that first visit.'

'I'm not in the mood. It also gets late.'

'Mister Sinha asked after you twice. He's the one who decides who'll write the pamphlets for the Information Department. It pays 200 to 250 rupees. If you want him to help you, you'll have to meet him.'

'Can't do it today,' she said, unable to contain her anger.

On her way home, as she turned at the corner of Silwali Gali, she saw a crowd of refugees in front of her house. She heard agitated voices and the frightened voice of her father.

Fear gripped her heart. Was their house again being assailed by a mob of the homeless looking for living space? How would she be able to pass through the crowd to get into the house?

As she drew near, she heard her father speak in a hoarse, high-pitched voice, '... I've a document in his own handwriting.'

Someone from the crowd spoke in Punjabi, 'Stop worrying! We'll see who dares to try to throw you out of your house.'

Another voice rose, uttering obscene curses, 'We'll cut him to pieces. This Gandhi will do us all in. First he made us lose everything, now he wants them to take over Delhi too. Just stop worrying.'

One of Panditji's neighbours spoke up, 'How can the police take any action in this business? They're siding with the Muslims, only at Gandhi's insistence. This isn't a criminal matter, it's a civil case. Let Syed file a complaint in the law court! We'll see what Gandhi can do then.'

Kanak felt relieved that people had gathered to help, not to threaten her father. The crowd made way for her.

Panditji was very upset. He explained that Syed had returned from Pakistan. He had come with his family and a police escort to claim back his house. 'He accuses us of defrauding him, and says that we have no house in Gwal Mandi. When I asked him to show the documents I had given him, he lied through his teeth that I had given him none. But I have those he gave me, in his own handwriting. Bajrang is my witness. That double-crossing Syed said that we broke the locks on his trunks and took out the papers. When I showed him his signature, he said that it was a forgery.' Panditji kept up his litany of frustration for a long time.

Kanak was also incensed and hurt by Syed's trickery.

The address delivered by Gandhiji at his prayer meetings and his statements were reported daily in the press. Panditji regarded Gandhiji's words as the conscience of the nation and the voice of reason, and read these accounts very carefully. He was astounded by something he saw in the newspaper on the morning of the third day.

Newspaper in hand, he called out to both Kanak and Kanchan, 'Look at this, beta. Read it out to me. That Syed is the ultimate liar and cheat.'

Kanchan began to read out loud. Kanak stopped in her chore of sweeping the rooms, and came out to listen. Gandhiji had issued a statement: 'Muslims who had left the country in fear were given assurance by the Indian government that they could come back and live in their homes. The government would guarantee the safety of their lives and property. Yesterday, a nationalist Muslim gentleman of Delhi, greatly distressed, came to me with the burka-clad women of his family. This veteran nationalist had fled his homeland in fear. After the assurances given by the Indian government, he returned to his motherland to live as a citizen of India. Yesterday, when he went back to his house in Durrani Gali, he found that it had been occupied by Hindu refugees from Lahore. Locks had been broken and the house was occupied in this good man's absence. The good citizen pleaded for justice and help at the Faiz Bazaar police station. When the police escorted him back to his house, a mob of Hindus prevented the police from carrying out their duty. It's a matter of shame for any government that its citizens are denied their legal rights, that they are denied protection for their lives and property. I make a strong appeal to the government to counter any opposition and interference in the restoration of law and order. To yield to mob violence is a matter of shame for the government. It's the duty of the administration that the house in Durrani Gali be restored to its rightful owner. The administration should not shrink from enforcing the strictest measures to preserve law and order, and from imposing justice.'

Already infuriated by Syed's duplicity, Panditji was now angry that Gandhiji had issued such a statement without listening to both sides in the dispute. He got ready to go to Birla House and show Gandhiji the property documents. Kanak and Kanchan said that they would accompany him. On his way to telephone Gandhiji's secretary to fix an appointment, Panditji told his neighbours in Durrani Gali and Silwali Gali about Syed's deviousness.

He telephoned Birla House three times in twenty-five minutes. The secretary was with Gandhiji, he was told, busy doing correspondence, and would be available after an hour. As Panditji was coming back with the intention of telephoning later, he found that Gandhiji's statement had also appeared in Hindi and Urdu newspapers. The editorial comments in these papers were critical of Gandhiji's statement and his lack of compassion for refugees.

By nine o'clock, curious refugees began to gather in Durrani Gali. By ten o' clock, their number swelled to over 200. Panditji's throat was dry as a result of explaining the situation to people. Kanak and Kanchan left whatever they were doing to attend to inquisitive women who came inside. This gathering of commiserating women unnerved their mother. The girls calmed her down. 'We'll explain the situation to Gandhiji,' they vowed. 'If the police intervene again, we'll sit in satyagraha here. We challenge the police to evict us from the house that we rightfully own!'

The excited crowd yelled threateningly, 'We'll see how Gandhi and Congress government remove a Hindu family from its house. If they remove one, they'll remove all. Who'll help us find a sanctuary?'

The size of the crowd and its anger had grown. Around eleven o' clock, Panditji wanted to go out to telephone Birla House again. He had to push through the crowd thronging the gali. He had gone only a few steps when he heard that a detachment of police carrying lathis and rifles was on its way. He returned home, his heart quickened with suspense.

Loud slogans and cries went up: The house won't be vacated! Down with Congress government! Gandhi murdabad!

Panditji's family was in a shock; what might transpire! Their hearts were beating wildly. They were ready to battle for their right! From the commotion and excitement it appeared that the crowd was getting bigger. They were mortified, but could not leave the house. Suddenly there was the crackle of gunfire.

Panditji fell back on the charpoy in the doorway, his head in his hands. His eyes filled with tears. 'There'll be bloodshed because of us! Let go, beta,' he said to Kanak and Kanchan standing next to him. 'Whatever is His wish. If we must suffer, we must. Let's go, let's get out of this place.'

Kanchan protested, 'Why, pitaji, where could we go?'

'There's no question of us going anywhere,' Kanak cut her sister short. 'We're fighting for truth and justice. Why should others die for us? Let me go out!' She hurried towards the gate, 'Please move aside! Let me pass!'

'Beta, beta! No!' Panditji called out as he followed her, 'Wait, you wait! Let me talk...'

Instead of letting her pass, the crowd yelled back, 'Get back inside! The house will not be given up even if a thousand of us die!'

They shouted louder than before, 'Congress government murdabad!' 'Down with Gandhi!' 'Down with Nehru!'

Panditji's heart had begun to pound. He called out, 'Did anybody get shot? Was anyone hurt?'

'We don't care! We're all ready to die! Gandhi and Nehru will be responsible for our deaths!' The crowd did not let him speak.

The shouting of slogans died down after half an hour, and the crowd thinned out. Some people had tried to take their lathis away from the policemen. The police had fired warning shots over their heads.

Panditji's guess was that the police withdrew from the scene for the time being, only because the situation had got out of control. Some action still might be taken in favour of Syed, he thought, at the insistence of Gandhiji. He sent a telegram to Nayyar to come at once in order to advise him. There were constantly new obstacles to his attempts to meet Gandhiji. So he wrote an account of the incident and mailed it to Gandhiji, attaching the property documents as proof.

Gandhiji's statement in support of Syed, besides the frightening incident at her own doorstep, had deeply upset and shocked Kanak. How she could explain this around to Aseer, she thought in embarrassment. It would be best for her, it seemed, if she kept quiet about her political ideals, and did something practical to earn a living. Lucknow could have provided such an opportunity, but her father had not agreed to her going there. Her brother-in-law would side with her father, she suspected. Her only hope now seemed to get some work through Sinha at the government department of information.

When Aseer reproached Kanak for having disappeared for so many days, she had to let out that the dispute in Durrani Gali was about her house.

'You see! Now at least you know the truth about nationalist Muslims!' said Aseer.

Kanak had come prepared to answer such sarcastic remarks. She replied, 'Which social class or community doesn't have some people like that? We bought our house legally, but the rest of the houses in our gali were taken over unlawfully.'

'If Gandhi couldn't stop Hindus being forced out of Punjab, what right has he to get their throats cut here? Is one nationalist Muslim more important than fifty thousand starving Hindus stranded at Bahawalpur? Look for yourself!' Aseer pushed that day's *Tribune* in front of her.

The report said: Fifty thousand Hindus were forcibly evacuated and sent to refugee camps in Bahawalpur. There they got only two chapattis to eat every other day. The supply of drinking water was woefully inadequate. Over one hundred have died of starvation.

Kanak made no reply. After a few moments of silence, she reminded Aseer, 'You mentioned something about going to meet Sinha sahib.'

'Oh yes. You've made me a bit of a laughing stock, like, as Sinha said, the best man who seemed keener on the marriage than the groom himself. He asked me several times about you. But you never showed up. Well, let's go today. I was going to see him anyway. It's six now; we'll leave by seven or quarter past seven. Here, read the newspapers until then.'

The sun had set, the street lights were on, but there was still some light outside. Aseer's car sliced through the congested traffic in Sadar Bazaar and reached the broad roads of New Delhi. He circled the Gol Dak Khana, and followed a hedge-lined narrow road to a small bungalow.

Aseer rang the bell. A servant peeped out, asked the visitor's name, and pulled his head back.

Kanak and Aseer sat in the veranda on light wicker chairs.

Sinha came out a few minutes later, buttoning his achkan. Seeing Kanak, he welcomed her, calling her visit a happy surprise.

'Sinha sahib, the achkan looks great on you,' Aseer flattered him.

'Bhai, what can you do? Everyone at the secretariat is having one made. As they say, the people of a kingdom emulate their king. If the prime minister likes the achkan, you have to have one.'

'It really suits you.... What do you think?' Aseer looked at Kanak.

'Yes, it sits very well on him,' Kanak had to admit.

'Hey Jheengur! Get us some tea,' Sinha turned his head and called out to the servant.

'No, no, no. Ask Kanakji, we've just had a cup. Have you had yours?' Aseer said.

After that Aseer and Sinha exchanged a few words in a hushed voice, '...You said... No, I haven't got it yet.' Kanak tried to ignore their whispered tête-à-tête.

'...It'll be done.'

'You want me to send my manager over tomorrow?'

'What's the need? I have written a note on the file. Yes, Kanakji, what have you to say for yourself? How the world goes with you? ... Splendid.'

Kanak found Sinha's accent a bit strange. She had first noticed it at the club. He spoke English like other people, but there was a lilt to his words when he spoke Hindi. He drawled the syllables at the end of his sentences.

Aseer mentioned the incident at Durrani Gali; how Kanak's family had barely escaped becoming the scapegoat in the controversy.

Kanak kept silent out of embarrassment.

Sinha said a few words against Gandhiji and then repeated his promise to help Kanak.

Aseer proposed, 'Do you want to look in at the club, or shall we go somewhere else.'

Sinha did not feel up to facing the club crowd.

They decided to go to Connaught Place. After Aseer parked the car Kanak followed him and Sinha into the veranda in front of the circle of shops, and up a broad staircase. She had been to that restaurant once before with Nayyar, Kanchan and Anil Kapoor. She was feeling a little hesitant. She would have dressed differently had she known that they would be going there.

The place was abuzz with voices. A band was playing Western music. Sinha wanted to sit away from the crowd. The bearer opened the door to a private booth. Kanak had to enter first. The wood-panelled booth had couches on both sides of the table, and a chair on the far side. She took the chair. Aseer sat on the couch on her left, and Sinha on the couch to her right.

'What shall I order?' Aseer asked.

'Whatever Kanakji wishes,' Sinha said.

'I don't particularly feel like anything. I've already had tea. Could I have some pineapple juice?'

'Wah, what's that? Have a gimlet. Gin with lime juice.'

Kanak expressed her reluctance. Aseer insisted, 'What's your objection! I'm asking you to try it just once. You'll be able to make your mind up only when you've tasted it. Leave it if you don't like it.'

Kanak did not like to hear herself criticized as prejudiced. She thought she would try the drink, but very carefully. Aseer and Sinha asked for whiskey. Kanak sipped her drink gingerly; it tasted bitter-sweet and sharp, unusual but not unpleasant. She had to admit it tasted good. She took two mouthfuls to get a better idea of its taste.

Aseer and Sinha were conferring together, and Sinha interrupted their conversation to ask Kanak in English, 'So, did you find it disagreeable?'

'No, it doesn't taste bad.'

'Then drink up. Let's have another round.'

'This is enough for me. You go ahead.'

Kanak finished her drink when they both insisted.

Despite her refusals, the bearer brought two more whiskeys and another gimlet on a tray. Kanak was feeling a slight buzz, and a strange, tingling sensation. After the first sip of her second drink, her eyelids grew heavy and she felt light-headed. Feeling that she had done something wrong, she decided not to drink any more.

Sinha again insisted, but she refused to take another sip.

'Why, do you feel any ill effects?' Sinha asked with a smile.

'I do feel a bit odd,' she replied laughingly, then thought, what was there to laugh about!

'Is it a bad feeling?'

'No,' she replied, then became serious.

'Then have some more. Just to please me,' Sinha said, touching her knee.

Kanak pulled back, saying she was sorry, but she didn't want any more.

'Just have a sip. How much more do I have to beg you?' Sinha's hand grasped her knee again.

The table shook as it was pushed back, knocking over Aseer's drink. Kanak rose suddenly, her forehead furrowed in anger, 'What is this? Let me out of here!'

'Nonsense! What's got into you?' Aseer glowered at Kanak.

Kanak bit her lip angrily, 'I want to leave! Let me out of here!' Her nostrils trembled.

Sinha and Aseer looked at each other. Aseer asked her to sit down and listen to him calmly.

Kanak refused to sit down.

Aseer got up to make way for her. He said to Sinha, 'I'll walk with her to the door.'

Kanak stepped into the downstairs veranda, which was lit with dazzlingly bright lights. People were milling around. She had never been to Connaught Place alone. She was angry at herself for her own lack of judgement. Tension and gin were making her head swim. She knew which buses passed through Faiz Bazaar, but did not know where the bus stop was in Connaught Place, and was in no fit state to ask anybody for information.

'Need a taxi?' A taxi driver whose fare had just got out and was paying him, asked Kanak.

Kanak breathed a sigh of relief. She climbed into the taxi. The driver slid into the traffic and asked, 'Where to?'

'Faiz Bazaar,' replied Kanak, thinking of another problem. She remembered that there were only ten annas in her handbag. What things have come to? she thought sadly. Ten or twenty rupees used to mean nothing to her. What could she do?

Kanak asked the driver to stop on Sir Syed Ahmed Road, beside the post office in Faiz Bazaar. He checked the meter and said, 'One rupee and two annas.'

'Bhai, I completely forgot. I've spent all the money in my purse. Wait here for two minutes, I'll bring you your fare,' she said helplessly.

'Wah, wah,' the driver replied in a loud voice, 'such a big handbag, and it's empty. You want me to wait here? Every minute costs me money. Why didn't you check your purse before getting into my taxi?'

'I'll pay for the time you wait. It's my fault, I admit.'

'You are trying to pull one on me? I'm from Delhi, too. I could wait here till morning, and you wouldn't come back,' he spoke louder than before.

'Come with me to my house if you don't trust me,' Kanak felt humiliated, but what else could she do?

The driver continued to shout. He directed his complaints to a shopkeeper nearby, 'Just see how these ladies carry on! They go about with handbags as big as a postman's sack, but don't have even eighteen annas in it. And she wanted to ride in a taxi!'

Naseeb Rai, another shopkeeper at the corner of the gali, came over to investigate. Kanak was petrified with embarrassment at the driver's rudeness. She tried to explain, 'I'm not saying I won't pay. I just forgot that I had no cash left in my purse. I'll go and get the money. I'll pay for the waiting time. If he doesn't trust me, he can come with me.'

Naseeb Rai scolded the driver, 'Watch your mouth, my good man.' He knew both Panditji and Kanak. 'Don't you see whom you're speaking to? Is that the way to speak to a lady? Take your fare and get lost. How much is it? Speak up.'

'Go home, daughter. There's no hurry to send back the money,' Naseeb Rai said reassuringly.

Kanak tried to pull herself together, so as not to upset her father, as she walked back home. The moment she reached the house, she said, 'Pitaji, give me some money. I got into a bit of a jam today.' 'Why, what happened, beti?' Panditji wanted to know.

'I got on the wrong bus at Tees Hazari, which took me to Sadar. The bus conductor told me to catch the bus for Connaught Place, and then take the bus to Faiz Bazaar. When I reached Connaught Place I found that I had no money left in my purse. Had to take a taxi. Borrowed money from the shopkeeper at the corner of the gali to pay the taxi. So give me eighteen annas. I want to pay him back.'

Panditji said by way of assurance, 'Must be Nasseb Rai. You relax, I'll pay him back tomorrow.'

Kanak did not want Naseeb Rai to tell her father about the taxi driver's impertinence. Taking Kanchan with her, she went back and gave the shopkeeper his money.

Nayyar arrived two days later. Although he had seen the documents for the sale and exchange of properties when he had come down from

Nainital, he and Panditji examined them again. Nayyar pointed out that the deed of sale had not been signed in the presence of any witnesses. Panditji explained the situation to two of his trusted neighbours, Jawahar Singh and Gur Dittan Mull. Both insisted on adding their signatures, and entered the date as 8 September 1947.

Kanak told Nayyar about her differences of opinion with the editor of *Sardar,* and said that she had no hope of finding work with a Delhi newspaper. She wanted to go to Lucknow to take advantage of the opportunity available there, she said.

Nayyar disagreed, 'Whatever your outlook, if you want to succeed in a profession, be faithful to its code. Do it as your obligation to your employer. Once we take on a client, whoever or whatever he might be, we put his interest first.'

'Yes, then you admit that you play the hypocrite, by being honest within your dishonesty. I can't condone any wrongdoing just for the sake of earning a living. That means I should steal if the need arises? There are others who give up their jobs for the sake of their principles.' She said, thinking of Puri.

'If you want to behave that way, be a Gandhi. Then people would accept your ideas just because of who you are. Don't you know that those who don't care for their job may find that their job doesn't care for them?' After matching Kanak's hard words with his own, Nayyar changed the subject, 'Well, whatever happened, I think if Aseer is willing to help you, you should take advantage of his offer.'

'Nothing is possible there. He's a despicable person. I don't want to see him ever again,' Kanak said, her head lowered, and described the events of that evening.

Nayyar thought that she was not blameless. 'Why did you accept the drink? I didn't expect that kind of behaviour from you. You yourself behaved appallingly.'

'How did I behave appallingly? Don't you drink yourself? You've told me many times that there's no harm in it if you have only a small one. You yourself have given drinks to Bahinji.'

'There's a time and place for everything. It depends where you are, and with whom.'

'Achcha, it was all my fault. Still I don't think I did anything improper. But I'll never work for Aseer.'

'What if something untoward happens in Lucknow?'

'Why should it happen? And if it does, can't I handle it as I did here in Delhi? Tell Pitaji to lock me up in some box.' She burst into tears.

Nayyar was forced to agree with her.

Chapter 3

A TEEMING MULTITUDE OF HARRIED HINDUS, DRIVEN OUT OF THEIR homeland, was winding its way towards East Punjab in search of refuge. They travelled in vehicles and on foot, escorted by Indian soldiers. One such convoy arrived at a refugee camp in Amritsar. The passengers began to unload whatever little they had been able to carry with them. At the head of the convoy was a truckload of armed soldiers, and just behind it, a station wagon with the women rescued from Shaikhupura. These women had nothing to unload; all they had were the clothes on their backs. Led by Kaushalya Devi, this group was the first to enter the camp through a gate in the boundary wall.

The brightly lit compound echoed with the sound of human voices. Tents and bivouacs dotted the yard around a central building. People walked around busily and purposefully. Kaushalya Devi, with her group of women in tow, was heading towards a veranda at the front of the building when they heard a woman keening.

Under the electric light in the veranda a young woman sat sobbing loudly, her head and face shrouded in a soiled, torn dupatta. Two other young women sat next to her in mournful silence; under their dupattas, their faces expressed dejection and pain. Their dirty ragged clothes and their black dupattas were in the Muslim style, but were worn in a way that revealed that they were Hindu.

Recognizing the silent women, Kaushalya Devi pointed at the one who was wailing, 'Isn't that Chinti?'

One woman nodded. Kaushalya Devi was surprised, and said, 'Hai, why? Didn't they find the address of her family at the Loha Garh camp?'

The woman who had answered sighed deeply, 'Her parents refused to take her back. We got her married off, they said, now she's her in-laws' problem. The parents are right,' she sighed again slowly, 'they had got rid of her as a burden.'

The women from Shaikhupura heard that. The woman's reply upset them so much that they felt the ground shift under their feet. They lowered their heads. This was their first experience of how people greeted returning lost ones in the new country.

Kaushalya Devi busied herself with rewrapping her dupatta as she turned away from the sobbing woman, and said to the ones in her group, 'Wait here, all of you.' She hurried to a tent across from the veranda.

She returned as quickly and asked the two women, 'Where has everybody gone?'

The women gave her no answer. Holding one corner of her dupatta between her fingers Kaushalya Devi went off again, brisk and businesslike, towards the right.

Men and women from the convoy, with children in their arms or on their shoulders, pulling along or carrying their belongings, began to enter through the gate. Their expensive-looking clothes were now crumpled and soiled. Exhausted middle-aged women, girls of tender age and soft-skinned young women came, hugging or holding sleeping or weeping children with one hand and balancing heavy bundles and baskets with the other. When they rested their burdens on the ground to catch their breath, they held on to them; they were precious even if heavy or troublesome.

'My brothers and sisters,' a white-bearded, middle-aged man wearing a white pugaree, white kurta and long white drawers stood near the gate and appealed with joined hands to those walking in. 'All of you my brothers, mothers and sisters should first check in at that tent over there. All of you will be given a space. Please go only to whatever place is allotted to you.'

'Come this way, come over here,' a burly man called out, as he walked into the tent.

'Please come in, in ones or twos,' a young man instructed from inside the tent. A crowd of men, women and children quickly formed in front of the tent.

The women from Shaikhupura were still waiting in the veranda. Bisni, unable to stay on her feet any longer, sat down first, followed by the others. Tara sat with her chin resting on her knee. She could not bear to look at the wailing woman. What she had heard echoed in her ears, '. . . her in-laws' problem. The parents got rid of her as a burden.' Had they all been brought here to face a similar fate?

As the crowd outside the tent grew bigger, a voice from the crowd suggested, 'Just one person from each family can give the names and the address. No need for others to clog up the place.'

Another voice said, 'Everyone's exhausted. Let's find a place to rest first, then we'll come and give all the information.'

Kaushalya Devi returned grumbling and sounding irritated. 'Come on everyone, follow me,' she told the women under her charge to go into the tent.

The white-bearded man now stood by the tent appealing with his hands together, 'The business of registration will go quicker if my brothers, mothers and sisters would just form a queue. Thanks be to Satguru, there's no need for anxiety.'

Unable to get through the jostling crowd, Kaushalya Devi spoke irritably to the man, 'Nattha Singhji, this is very unfair. No one was here when we arrived. The officials doing the registration were away. How long can I wait? I left my home yesterday morning. I too have a family. Left my daughter alone. We give up our time to help others; we shouldn't be pestered as a result.'

'All right, bahinji, don't be upset. No need to get upset.' Nattha Singh joined his hands in appeal before Kaushalya Devi, 'Go on and look after your family, your young ones. Don't worry, I'll get these sisters and daughters of mine registered. Did they get a drink of water, or anything to eat?'

When he heard they had not, Nattha Singh said in a tone of pity, 'Waheguru, Waheguru! Satnaam, satnaam! That should have been seen to first of all.'

Pointing to the women, Kaushalya Devi counted them aloud. Then she left.

Nattha Singh said to Chinti, who sat slumped against the wall, crying bitterly, 'Beti, have faith in Waheguru kartaar. You shouldn't bother about those bad-minded people in your family. They're paying for their sins, but still go on in their evil ways. Satnaam, satnaam! ... Come, my dears, let's have some prasad,' he said to the others.

The women did not feel like eating anything when they heard the reason for Chinti's lamentations. But they had eaten only two handfuls of roasted gram since the morning, and Nattha Singh's affectionate invitation stimulated their hunger. They got up and followed him.

The large yard at the back of the building was full of tents and a large canopied structure. Under the canopy, groups of women were making chapattis on stoves covered with large griddles. Two women kneaded dough as they bent over a large tray. Behind the stoves stood vats of daal. The women cooking food were not downcast, but full of sympathy, encouragement and energy. In one corner was a water tap, the ground around it wet and muddy. In another, a pile of used leaf plates and clay tumblers. Tara and her companions washed their hands and faces at the faucet and wiped them dry with their dupattas.

Tara and her group sat down on one of the runners of jute matting. A woman volunteer placed leaf plates and clay tumblers in front of them, as they were served with chapattis and daal. After a month of dry, stale chapattis, this food tasted like an exquisite meal to Tara. As she ate, Chinti's plaintive cry came back to her.

Nattha Singh came in and said with joined hands to the women cooking food, 'My dear sisters and daughters, your spirit of service is nothing less than saintly. I'm sorry to trouble you, but by the grace of Satguru maharaj two hundred and fifty more brothers and sisters have arrived. There might be about fifty extra mouths to feed. If all sisters and daughters knead dough from eight or ten seers of flour, we won't have to bother you again all night.'

'Oh!' exclaimed a young woman, her mouth widening as she gaped in surprise. Then she laughed. Another young woman began opening the sack of flour that lay next to the stove, and said, 'No problem, we'll handle it. We'll prepare the dough. This chance to serve people is our reward for good deeds in the past.'

Tara looked at her, then at her plate.

The woman making chapattis over the stove told the woman preparing to knead the dough to stop. She pointed at a large tray covered with a cloth, 'There's no need. The sisters from Khooh Sunarian have sent ten seers of dough. Let's use that first.'

There were only a handful of people waiting in line when Nattha Singh came back to the tent with the women from Shaikhupura. When their turn came, Nattha Singh asked with his hands together, 'Dear daughters and sisters, get your names and the addresses of your parents and in-laws registered. If anyone from your family has been at this camp, we'll be able to tell where they are now. We'll also try to inform them about you. Your addresses and whereabouts will be broadcast over the radio so that they know where to come to get you or where you might be sent on.'

The women with Tara looked at her in embarrassment at speaking the names of their husbands before strangers. They knew Tara could do this for them; she was a city girl, she could speak and understand English, Farsi and Hindi.

To get the Hindu women to give the names of their husbands or the men from their family was no easy matter. Tara faced the same problem that Kaushalya Devi had faced at the DAV College camp. Amar Kaur and Satwant Kaur knew about each other's family. Amaro mentioned the names of Satwant's husband and his father, and Satwant did the same for Amaro. With great reluctance Banti told the name of her husband and his elder brother. Bisni said shyly, 'He has the same name as that green-feathered bird, that chants gangaram and eats chooree.' Tara realized that her husband was called Tota Ram.

They asked Tara about her own family. She replied without meeting their eyes, 'I don't want anyone to know where I am. Just give me something to do, here or somewhere else. I'll be content with that.'

Those writing down the names spoke with each other in English, 'She probably heard that unfortunate women like her are neither accepted by their parents, nor by their in-laws.'

Tara lifted her eyes and looked at them. They guessed that she understood English. One young man spoke in English, so that she could hear, 'You can do as you wish. Yes, there are some heartless souls like that, but not everyone is that cruel. It's not your fault what you've been through. We've a lot of sympathy and respect for you. Give at least your name so that the head count tallies.'

Another man led them to a large room. Chinti and the other two women sat with their backs to one wall. The floor was covered with dhurrie. Moths circled the light bulb on the wall. As he was leaving, the young man said to Tara, 'You may switch off the light and shut the door. Turn the fan on if you feel hot.'

It was stuffy and hot in the room. Tara reached for the regulator on the wall and turned the fan on.

Bisni and Kesari were gaping at the light bulb. Hearing the fan rotate and feeling the breeze, they arched their heads and began to gape at the fan. They could hardly contain their amazement.

People passed by their open door in the veranda. 'Let's shut the door so that we can sleep undisturbed,' Banti suggested to Tara. When Tara agreed, she got up and bolted the door.

Shielded from the eyes of men, the women rolled up their dupattas, and using them as pillows, lay down on the dhurrie. Bisni's eyes were still fixed on the fan.

The moths circling the light were swept on to the women's bodies by the breeze from the fan. Tara found the bright light unnecessary and uncomfortable. She asked Banti and Satwant, 'Do we need the light? Shall I turn it off?'

'Yes, sister. Do if you know how to. We've no idea.'

Bisni was still staring at the fan. Without asking her, Tara switched off the light.

'Hai!' Bisni screamed in her Punjabi dialect of Jhang.

Tara's hand was still on the switch. She switched the light on. Bisni was both frightened and amazed.

Satwant said, 'She's from up-country. Never saw electric light before. We've been to the town several times, and we've seen it all.' She asked Bisni, 'Have you ever been on a train, sister?'

'Never rode on it,' replied Bisni, 'but saw it. Whenever we went to Bhakha from our village, we used to cross iron lines.'

Satwant spoke like a deep thinker, 'All this is a blessing of Maharaj-ji. Towns are full of His miracles. Flick with your finger, and water gushes out. Where we had our meal, water flowed non-stop from an iron rod.'

Tara smiled slowly. She worked the switch and explained, 'Don't be alarmed. The light goes off if you press it like this, and comes on if you press it again.'

She lay with her eyes closed in the darkened room, but could not sleep. Now was the time to think.

Next day, late in the morning, Banti said to Tara, 'My dear, let's go out and ask around by ourselves. May be we can find something about Jaggi's dad and the rest of the family.'

Banti's husband and his elder brother used to go to Amritsar to buy their stock of cloth once or twice every year. They dealt through an agent in the city. After her marriage, Banti had once gone to Amritsar with her husband and mother-in-law, to visit Durgiyana and the shrine of Darbar Sahib.

Tara thought that, just like Lahore, Amritsar too would have scores of schools for girls. She hoped to find work somewhere, even at a modest salary. She went to the tent to inquire about the address of some schools for girls.

A young man asked Tara why she wanted that information. He noticed the state of her clothes and her pale drawn face, and said sympathetically, 'Bahinji, all the schools have been closed to provide accommodation for the refugees. If you want to go anywhere in particular, I can come along to show you the way. My name is Dev. I am a student of the Dharm Samaj College.'

Dev got his bicycle and went out with Tara and Banti. As they came out of the gate, he called a tonga for the women. Banti was uneasy. She whispered into Tara's ear, 'Hai, but do we have enough money for this?'

'Never mind. Just get in,' Tara said.

From her experience of modern, educated people in Lahore, Tara knew that it was a woman's privilege to accept such gestures of help and courtesy. How could Banti, who spent all her life in a village, know that? Dev rode on his bicycle.

Dev and Tara took Banti to several camps in search of her family. Together they checked the records of people who had arrived as refugees and those who were still there. Dev felt sympathy for the women who had suffered through no fault of their own, and was willing to do anything he could to help them. He retained the tonga for them until the evening.

Dev did not speak about himself as the three of them went from one camp to another. All he talked was about the atrocities committed in Amritsar in spite of efforts to keep the situation peaceful. His young mind was so disgusted by the terrifying events he had witnessed that, to lighten his spirits, he could not keep himself from talking about it. He still could not tell the whole, shameful story, and just gave hints about how the news of atrocities and killings in West Punjab had made the blood of Hindus boil, and how, in their rage, they committed even worse crimes. It was women who suffered the most on both sides. He felt ashamed and guilty before all women for those acts of violence and humiliation, and to appease that feeling, he was willing to help any woman victim as best he could. He addressed Banti as 'mataji' and Tara as 'bahinji'. He invited them to his home for the evening meal.

Dev's father, Babu Santram, worked as a bank accountant. His mother, an educated woman, welcomed Tara and Banti like any other honoured guest. She neither paid any attention to the sorry state of their clothes, nor did she make any mention of the misfortune they had suffered.

Dev's mother told them, 'My son passed his F.A. exam in the first division. Now that his college is closed, he helps all day at the refugee camps.' She praised other students who were Dev's friends, 'Those dear boys are working really hard.'

Tara did not want to talk about herself, but it slipped out that she was going to sit for her BA final exam, and she too had been passing her exams in the first division.

Next morning, Dev came early, to take them to the camps that they had not yet visited. Banti had been wondering about where else to search for her husband and son. Among the sketchy details she could remember about her visit to Amritsar seven years before, was that they had stayed at a dharamshala. Her husband's agent had invited them for lunch in Guru Bazaar. It was a narrow and congested street, with the agent's office at the ground level and his residence above. She did not have even the slightest inkling of the name of the agent or his shop, except that her husband had been his client for many years.

Banti was sure that her husband and his elder brother must have come to Amritsar. The elder brother had mentioned going to Amritsar when they first suspected trouble from the Muslims in their village. And if they had come to the city, they must have gone to see the agent.

Dev took Tara and Banti from one end of Guru Bazaar to the other three times. Banti could not recognize anything. She had come here only once, seven years before, holding the hand of her mother-in-law as she walked behind her husband with downcast eyes and her face veiled by a foot-long ghunghat. How could she recognize anything now?

When Dev mentioned Banti's search for her husband's agent to his father, he too said in sympathy, 'How is that possible? There are hundreds of such agents, and thousands of traders visit them. It's like searching for one particular grain of rice in a warehouse full of rice.'

Dev had also told his fellow workers about Tara being a BA student. Two others came forward to help. Helping Tara meant helping Banti too. Dev and his two friends began making inquiries at each and every cloth agent in Guru Bazaar. After three day's search they found that the firm of Chetram-Pannalal supplied cloth to the shop of Gopaldas-Manohardas of Chimmoki village in Shaikhupura. Both the brothers had come to see the agent sometime in August, and said that they were planning to move to Ambala to begin a business. That's all Dev and his friends had learnt.

Banti now became anxious to go to Ambala in search of her son and husband.

The camp officials were full of sympathy for the women refugees. They were willing to do anything to help them. They traced the families of Satwant and Amaro to the Loha Garh camp, and found that the families had gone to Jagrawan. They sent news about Satwant and Amaro to their families, and were willing to house and feed the two women until they were reunited with their families. But they were not willing to risk giving shelter to a wayward young woman who refused to give information about her parents or her in-laws.

Dev's father and his mother understood Tara's mental state and her feelings. They knew that if a girl or a woman would be branded for life by society for crimes done to her by others, why—as an innocent victim—would she agree to give out information for which she might have to suffer? In Tara's refusal they sensed her fight against society's attempts to stifle her, her effort to keep her dignity and her desire to be independent. Their hearts went out to her.

Tara too found succour in the kindly attitude Dev's family showed towards her. Had they asked her, she would have agreed to stay with them and cook their food, clean their house and wash their clothes until she found another means of support. But Dev's family could not ask someone with her standards of education to work as a housemaid. Few Punjabi middle-class families hired cooks or maidservants. The wives, their wrists decked with rows of solid gold bangles, would do all household chores by themselves, then go out in fine and expensive clothes as respectable ladies. Then, perhaps, it was also unwise for Dev's family to put any further strain on their already overstretched budget.

Banti would hug Tara and tell her over and over, 'Come with me. You're like a younger sister to me. This illiterate simple woman, who can't even talk to anyone, depends on you. Maharaj made us sisters in time of sorrow; we should now always stay together. When I find my family, we'll both have a roof over our heads. If there's only one chapatti to eat, we'll share it; we already did. You know we helped each other in the worst of times.'

Tara agreed to go to Ambala with Banti. The only garments on their bodies that were not in rags were the thick dupattas they had been given at the time of their rescue from Keshoram's Haveli in Shaikhupura. More than poor, their clothes made them look like beggars. Dev's mother murmured apologetically for not being able to give them new clothes, and handed them two suits of her own salwar-kameez and dupatta. With the same apologetic air she put in each palm five rupees, and closing their fingers over it, said, 'What are five rupees worth these days, sisters? Keep them anyway. In time of need even a small sum may come in handy.'

Dev and his father had come to help Tara and Banti find a place in an east-bound train. The railway station was swarming with human beings for as far as the eye could see. The place buzzed like a beehive. People trod uncaringly on their fellow beings. An overpowering stench and chaos pervaded the concourse. Platforms were crammed full of passengers hoping to board the trains, with their luggage. Very few trains were in evidence. Trains coming from the east were specials carrying Muslims headed to Lahore. To forestall attacks by the agitated passengers, these trains sped past on tracks, remote from the platforms.

The trains that came from the west, under Indian military escort, were specials bringing Hindus. At the front and at the tail end of these trains were flatbed cars, with breastworks of sandbags. These specials too were allowed to go east without halting at Amritsar. The displaced, coming by road, were so densely packed in the station buildings that there was no place left for the disembarking passengers.

The commercial centre of Punjab had been turned into a frontier area between the two countries. Those who had been uprooted from their homes were desperate to go anywhere east or south; for them it was a matter of do or die.

The number of trains departing for the east was not even a tenth of what it used to be. Before the Partition, the engine drivers and firemen on the trains were mostly Muslims. The majority of them had gone to Pakistan, and were afraid to return to Punjab.

Tara and Banti, with Dev and Babu Santram, had reached the railway station early in the morning. A very long train made up of coaches and freight cars going east pulled up slowly to a platform. All the coaches and cars were so packed with refugees that no one else could enter them. How long these people had been inside the train no one knew. Scores of them were sitting on the roofs of the coaches, their luggage beside them. Scuffles and fights broke out when thousands of waiting men, women and children tried to force their way into the coaches or to get a foothold on the roofs. Dev and his father could do nothing. A male might have been hoisted to the roof to find a place, but not a woman.

Suddenly a loud call was heard. A young man with good lungs was speaking through a newspaper rolled into a megaphone, 'We are making a plea with joined hands to all males, young and old. We are all facing very difficult times, and should help each other in our trials. We should regard the mothers and sisters of others as our own mothers and sisters. We should regard the children and young ones of others as our own children. We plead with all you men with joined hands that all young and healthy males should take the uncomfortable places on the roof. Let the women and children and the sick have seats inside the compartments. Any healthy male who stays inside would be nothing but an unfeeling bastard!'

'Yes! That's right!' a tumult of shouts in support rose from all sides.

Some began to yell threateningly, 'Any man who stays inside is a mother——! Any healthy male sitting inside is a sister——!' Obscenities and abuses were hurled, but with good intentions.

Tara and Banti got the chance to squeeze into a compartment. Babu Santram and Dev apologized for not being able to help them further, and hoped that they would meet again. They wished the women luck, ask them not to forget to write, said namaste and left.

The September sun made the compartments boiling hot. Bodies of women packed together like sacks of flour were drenched with sweat. At one moment they would quarrel and yell at others for lack of space and, in the next, they would talk to the same person sympathetically. Every few minutes some man came around to offer a drink of water to all mothers, sisters and daughters. The water they drank broke out over their bodies in sweat. Vendors passed by the windows crying their wares, which were swarming with flies, straight from the cooking pot. Hand-held fans made from palm leaves that some young lads sold were in great demand. Passengers paid two annas for fans that had sold for two paisas only a few days before, but not without first cursing the seller profusely.

Tara felt that she was the only one silent in their compartment. Women, their hands working their fans, spoke loudly to be heard over the clamour of voices. Punjabi, their common language, seemed to give them a feeling of camaraderie. Tara understood very little of this hotchpotch of Multani, Derawali, Jhangi and other dialects of West Punjab. They talked mostly about unimaginable terrors and troubles. The loudest sound was of children bawling. Banti too praised Dev and his family for their kindness to the women sitting next to her, calling them angels on earth. Her listeners gave examples of acts of even greater kindness done by others to them, and of the help they themselves had imparted.

The women in the compartment became increasingly listless. At last, after several hours, the engine was attached. It growled and fumed about the heavy load it had to pull, let off steam in anger, and belched smoke in desperation and helplessness. Then it began to pull the train slowly and reluctantly. It picked up some speed, but not faster than a rickshaw, or a tonga pulled by an old tired horse. Some playful young men found this amusing. They began to play at jumping off the train and getting back on as the train moved slowly, the human tendency to find fun and play in every possible situation. Laughter was heard. Men sitting on the roof, their hands covering their ears, began singing tappas at the top of their voices, '...In Sawan the swings are on, but you are not there. I still think of you at the swings.'

Another voice rose in competition, 'Why do you hide from me? When you are in my heart, what good does it do if you are out of my sight?'

Tara felt a pang of memory at this. She remembered how Sheelo and Sita had sung tappas at the time of her marriage. And all that she had to suffer in the past two months. If life was like that, why talk of love? All that was airy-fairy nonsense!

The train went past several stations without stopping, then began to halt at only the bigger ones. At every stop, people came by with buckets of drinking water or lassi. Because of the tightly packed bodies, it was impossible to use the lavatories inside the compartments. Box cars had no lavatories. Whenever the stain stopped, men from the rooftops and women from the compartments got out and sat down in the open to relieve themselves. The only way to overcome shame and embarrassment was to close one's eyes. At some stations, the locals distributed salted chapattis, or daal and roti. At one station, the passengers were fed puris and vegetables; at another sweet halwa.

The people gathered on the stations to care for the suffering refugees did not let the train leave unless they had satisfied themselves that every passenger had been fed. The refugee passengers were in no hurry either. Very few knew or cared where they were going. They were not concerned about being late for anything. They were laughing at the fate that had failed to overpower them. They had already worried too much to worry any further.

Deep in that crowd, Banti was in a hurry. She was impatient and anxious to reach Ambala, but what could she say or do? The slow and erratic progress of the train infuriated her. The same train that was a metaphor for speed and swiftness, was crawling along with heavy load. It had taken twenty-four hours to reach Phillor. Banti did not know how far or where Ambala was. Tara, the educated and clever one, could not tell her either. At Banti's insistence, she inquired from some railway workers: How far was Ambala? When would the train reach there?

'Seventy-five miles from here,' she was told. 'Two to two-and-a-half hours by train at its regular speed, but who can call this a train? We may get there this evening, or maybe tomorrow morning, or even later. Nothing is certain.'

Trains symbolized a system of organization in India that worked like clockwork, that had been a bastion of strict procedure and discipline. Villagers could tell what time it was by seeing a train go past. Disorder had upset its well-regulated operation now. Tara and Banti spent their second day in the train as it chugged along sluggishly. Night fell, and the women, packed tightly into the coach, dozed and snored. There was no point in complaining to anyone for pressing up too closely. An infant who had been quite sick now appeared to be dying. The women made space for the infant's mother next to a window. It was well past midnight when the mother began to wail loudly, and others knew that the baby had died.

Everyone wanted to console the mother of the dead baby. Women clasped children to their chest and wiped their eyes on aanchals. For the next two hours the compartment rang with the heart-rending wailing of the grieving mother, of women crying in sympathy, and of children bawling. Gradually the others, except for the baby's mother, began to nod off and fall asleep. At the next stop, the father and uncle of the dead baby climbed down from the roof. The family mourned together for their lost one. Passengers from other compartments gathered to commiserate with and console the parents. A pick and a shovel were borrowed from the station office, and the baby was buried in a field about fifty yards from the tracks. The grieving parents were led back to the train. The train stood there for about two hours.

The morning of the third day dawned on the women in the suffocating compartment. A bright, hot sun rose over the horizon. For two hours, it shone into the eyes of tired and jaded women before rising above the level of windows. The train was inching along towards the platform of a station. On a signal cabin, Tara saw the sign: Ambala City. She roused Banti. They began to get ready to get off. Both had decided to go to a camp for refugees until they would find another shelter.

Only a few passengers got off at Ambala from the train that was headed to Kurukshetra. Tara and Banti, holding hands, their bundles under their arms, followed the flow of passengers towards the exit.

Banti was clinging to Tara's hand. Suddenly, without letting go, she pulled Tara to one side and called out, 'Sadhu! Oye Sadhu! O Sadhuramma!'

'Fresh roasted nuts! Come and buy my nuts like almonds! Only two paise each!' A small boy sang to advertise his merchandise. Banti rushed towards the boy vendor.

A boy of about nine, wearing a shirt and shorts, was selling paper cones filled with peanuts from a bag hanging from his shoulder.

He looked at the woman who called to him, and ran towards her and hugged her waist, 'Chachi! Chachi! Where have you been? When did you get here? Where's sister Satto?'

Banti held the boy in her arms and wept.

The boy asked over and over, 'Where were you, Chachi? You arrived just now? Where's sister Satto?'

Banti put her hand on the boy's chin, raised his face and kissed him on the forehead, 'My Jaggi is here, yes? Where are his bhaiyaa and his tayaa? Take me to them.'

'Uncle Gopal and Uncle Manohar went to Delhi. Uncle Manohar came back for a day. My lalla would know,' replied the boy and again asked, 'Where's my sister Satto?'

Banti ignored the question and said, 'Take me to your lalla and bebbe.'

The boy's face fell and tears came to his eyes, 'Ma died after we came here. She got really sick in the train. She was always crying for Satto. Severe stomach cramps would make her faint.' He dried his tears on his sleeve. 'Father is here at his shop at the crossroads in the bazaar. Let's go there.'

Holding Tara tightly with one hand and putting the other on the boy's shoulder, Banti went along, talking about his mother.

Sadhu took out two packets from his bag. Holding them out to Banti, he said, 'Here, auntie, have some peanuts. I get a rupee or a rupee and a quarter selling these here in front of the station.' There was a ring of pride in his voice. He had forgotten about his mother.

As they neared the crossroads, the boy ran ahead to announce the arrival of a friend from his village. His father, Boodha Mull, stepped out of his shop.

Banti had brought the news of the boy's sister Satto and now knew about the death of Sadhu's mother. She drew a ghunghat over her face and bewailed her grief.

Bhoodha Mull was from the Arora caste, Banti's caste was Khattri. Their clans were different. Custom forbade marriages between the two castes, but as their families lived in adjacent houses, Banti regarded him as an elder brother-in-law. To show him respect, she used to cover her head and face when he was around. Bhooda Mull too broke into loud sobs. To observe the ritual of grieving, Banti beat her breast, 'Hai, hai, Satto, you were so young! Where did you fly away to, my little bird?'

Bhoodha Mull's middle-aged widowed sister-in-law came out from the back of the shop with Sadhu's baby sister in her arms. She covered her face with a ghunghat, hugged Banti and began to weep and wail. She also hugged Tara, thinking her to be a relative of Banti. Tara had never had to participate in such grieving rituals before her marriage. Newly married women were also exempt from this custom, but how could she say anything? Tears came to her eyes also. She did not wail, but cried silently.

Refugee women living behind other shops came and sat around them to take part in the customary grieving. The shops of Muslim bakers, tinsmiths, ironmongers, cobblers and dairymen in this area before the Partition now belonged to Hindu haberdashers, dry goods grocers and mithai sellers.

When Bhoodha Mull's sister-in-law stopped to catch her breath after the first bout of wailing and grieving, Banti asked about her son.

The sister-in-law said, 'Gopaldas and Manohardas stayed here for about ten days, then left for Delhi with their mother and the child. Three days ago Manohardas came back for a day.'

The news of Satto's death had to be conveyed to her father by Banti, 'When the Muslims killed chacha Pali Shah near the well, and drove you all away by beating you with the butts of their machetes and spears, they began to manhandle the young women. That swine Baqar—may seven generations of his family be infested with worms—pulled at Satto's arm saying, 'This one's mine.' Satto wrenched her arm free and jumped into the well…'

The sister-in-law beat her breast and head with both hands and howled without hearing any more, 'Hai, hai! O my girl, born after so many offerings to the gods!' She wailed for a while, then unable to keep up such an energetic observance of grief for long, just wept in silence.

Banti told the rest of the women, 'The other girls and I ran towards the well, but those dogs tripped us with their lathis and dragged us away.' She wept as she spoke, to keep the sister-in-law company.

The neighbours, one by one, began to describe how they had suffered at the hands of the Muslims, and how some Hindus had taken revenge on the Muslims. One woman said mournfully, 'Whether a Hindni or Musalmani, the one who died without being violated and dishonoured was the luckiest. Sister, a woman can be trampled and trodden on by anyone. She is regarded as a cow or goat that can be taken over by anybody, who can be sacrificed just because she belongs to the enemy. What sins must we have committed in our past lives to be born as women?'

Banti gave several sighs in agreement. Tara listened in stony silence, as if she had turned into a statue.

The sister-in-law was weeping loudly. The neighbours sat with her for about an hour, then returned to their chores that had been left undone. The grieving family was not from their community, or even neighbours from their village, so they were not obliged to observe the custom of sitting and sharing their grief at the cost of their own household work.

Banti interrupted her lamentations to ask Bhoodha Mull about her son and husband.

Bhoodha Mull said, 'Manohardas seemed all right when he came three days ago. He came to get the medicine for your baby from a hakim in the Dari Wala Bazaar.'

'Is my darling baby all right?' Banti cried.

'No need to worry, bhabhi,' Bhooda Mull replied. 'You know, such a long journey, with a change of climate. Children get sick for the slightest of reasons. Your son's stomach got upset while he was here. We took him to a doctor, but that had little effect. Then we got the medicine from the hakim in the Dari Wala Bazaar. His medicines can work wonders. That medicine worked, so his uncle had come to get more. It was only a touch of indigestion, he told us. Nothing to worry about. They've found a house. Both brothers have begun doing their rounds as cloth merchants.'

Banti joined her hands and begged, 'No, tell me the truth. Swear on my head, what was wrong with my baby. He was cutting his teeth; children really suffer when they're teething.'

Bhoodha Mull assured her that Manohardas had said that it was nothing serious. '. . . The baby was in pain, but that soon passed. They're living in some mohalla, that used to be a Muslim area. Delhi is full of Hindus now. There are no Muslims left here, either.'

Before offering them a drink of water, Bhoodha Mull sent Sadhu to get some mithai from the shop nearby, and putting the leaf cup of sweetmeats in front of Banti, said, 'You shouldn't drink water on an empty stomach. This water's from an unfamiliar source, and might not agree with you. It's not water from our own village. That water was better than the milk from here.'

Banti was relieved after talking with the neighbour from her village, and knowing that her son and husband were both well. The feeling of relief also left her impatient to be back with her son and husband as soon as possible. With a neighbour's baby girl in her lap, as if the child was her own Jaggi, she and the sister-in-law sat for a while reminiscing about old times.

Boodha Mull wanted this neighbour from his village, who had been presumed dead, to stay with him for at least two days, but he also understood Banti's impatience to be with her family. He explained that the train situation was very bad. Manohardas had come by bus from Delhi, and taken another bus back. Banti and Tara were overwhelmed by the memory of their fifty hours in the jam-packed train. Bhoodha Mull took them to the depot from which buses left for Delhi.

Banti offered him five rupees, all the money that she had.

Without even looking at the proffered money, Bhoodha Mull said in a sad tone, 'Bhabhi, what if we are facing the worst of times? You are from my village, so you are like my sister, and your husband is like my brother. Can't I do this much for you?' He paid their fares and found them seats in the bus.

The bus that left Ambala with Tara and Banti in the morning reached Delhi just as the sun was setting. The neighbourhoods and streets that the bus had to pass through before reaching the terminus were so filled and packed with refugees that Tara could only look on in silent bewilderment. Those who could not find shelter indoors were camping under tarpaulins on footpaths and roofs.

Across the wide street from the bus terminus, in one corner of a park with an iron fence, were two small tents. Above them was a white banner with bold red lettering in Hindi, English, Punjabi and Urdu, announcing that this was the Refugee Information Office.

Many people were heading towards the tents, carrying their belongings. Tara and Banti followed. The office distributed the refugees according to the space available in the various camps around the city. One volunteer took a group of refugees to the camp just outside Kashmiri Gate.

Lights had come on by the time Tara and Banti reached the camp. An amplifier broadcast names and addresses of persons separated from their families. Tara gave the address of Banti's family at the registration desk, and registered herself as Banti's sister. They both were given cards to draw their rations. Newly arrived refugees were also offered cooked rotis or handfuls of roasted gram.

As Tara and Banti had no male guardian with them, they were sent to the hut reserved for women only. The hut was long and narrow, with walls made of reeds. The wide entrance had no doors or curtains. Outside, men and women made rotis over small cooking fires.

Beside the entrance to the hut for women, a youngish-looking woman sat with a grown-up girl, watching the people in other huts. As the woman asked Tara and Banti the name of their village and district, the sound of a child crying came from inside the hut.

The woman followed Tara and Banti inside the hut, explaining, 'We two are in this corner. In that corner is a woman from Sangroor, and her daughter-in-law. This chatai here belongs to an old woman from Gujranwala. On the chatai in the middle is a woman from Kamalia and her son. You two can spread your chatais here next to the entrance.'

Tara and Banti could not see anything for a few seconds as their eyes were still blinded by the bright lights outside. Then in the light filtering through the flimsy walls they saw some steel trunks and stacks of bundles, piled up at both ends of the hut. A young woman stood on one side, gently rocking her crying baby to sleep. In the middle lay an old woman, with her knees drawn up.

Banti unrolled chatais side by side for herself and Tara. The same woman said, 'There's a water tap outside. You can use my lota for washing your hands and face. Hai, you don't have any luggage or pots and pans. What's your caste? We're Sunars, goldsmiths.'

'Khattri,' replied Banti.

Another woman coming into the hut heard them, and said, 'We are Sarswat Brahmins. Use my lota if you like.'

Banti borrowed lotas from the first woman and from the one who had just come in.

Tara and Banti washed at the faucet. Banti spread a corner of her dupatta on the chatai and set down the rotis they had been given at the camp office, with some water in the lota. Other than a glass of lassi they both had had in Ambala, they had eaten nothing during the whole day. They began to eat the rotis.

The woman they had first met came up and sat beside them, saying, 'We listen to the radio all day in the hope that there might be some mention of my daughter's in-laws. Our names were announced yesterday, and again today, but there's no news of her in-laws, who had a jewellery business in Amnaabad. We're from Hafizabad. We just managed to escape, but so many were killed.'

She leaned towards Banti and pointing at the old woman, said, 'She's from Gujranwala. Everyone in her family was murdered, and her house was burnt down. They thought she was useless, so they let her go. She just lies there sorrowing, never says a word, or goes to get her rations. Eats if any one of us gets her rations and cooks for her.'

She pointed at the woman rocking her baby, 'Her husband was murdered, and they took away her sister-in-law. She has head wounds. Her three-year-old daughter and her mother-in-law are with her. That Brahmin woman who came in after you is a widow, with a four-year-old son. Her husband's family left them at the railway station, and went to Bombay. Sister, who wants to take somebody else's burden in these times?'

The women lay down to sleep, but mosquitoes attacking their feet, hands and faces did not let them fall asleep. Tara covered herself with her dupatta. After midnight a slight chill made them all curl up for greater warmth. As they were stirring from sleep in the morning, they heard someone singing bhajan in a loud voice next door.

Tara lay curled up with her eyes closed, thinking, 'In Bhola Pandhe's Gali, Khushal Singh used to pray to God every morning by singing assa di bar. His young son was murdered. My father used to mutter "God, you are our protector" all the time No one knows where our family is now. People's faith in God doesn't come from what they go through or what they hear other people have gone through. When they need to believe in something or other, their imagination finds them something to cling to.'

She heard Banti chanting a prayer and opened her eyes. Banti was sitting on her chatai. The Brahmin woman was going out, lota in hand. The woman said to Banti, 'Sister, keep your eyes peeled. Some people here steal anything they can lay their hands on if you're not looking.'

Seeing Tara stretch her limbs, Banti said, 'Maharaj-ji has been merciful to get us this far. Now He should reunite me with my Jaggi and my family. That little devil sleeps ever so lightly. When his grandmother used to get up early in the morning, he too got up with her. I would churn the yogurt

and take off a bowl of butter before he woke up. I would stuff some butter
into his mouth with my finger, and he'd go back to sleep. Then I fed the
buffaloes and milked them.'

Tara heard the note of hope and happiness in Banti's voice. She always
talked of her family, but today her voice reflected less despair and more
hope. Tara had no reason to look forward to meeting her own family. She
said, 'You're used to getting up early, sister. I can stay up until late at night,
but hate to get up so early.'

'You're city folk; you don't have to milk and feed your cattle.'

The Brahmin woman came back soon. She said to Tara and Banti, 'You
better go and do your business before there's a line-up. I even had a bath.'
She called out to the woman from the Sunar caste, 'Nihaldei, you too get
up and have a wash.'

An enclosure of chatais had been built around the faucet for the women
to wash themselves. Men washed in the open at another water tap, chanting
or intoning bhajans and prayers. By the time it was bright enough to turn
off the camp lights, Tara and Banti had had their bath. Banti returned to
chanting her prayer, Tara went back to her chatai.

Nihaldei's daughter Sukhdet, lota in hand, returned to the hut. She said,
'Hai, just look at those oafs. One says to another as I walked past, "That's
not fair. Girls watch us bathe, but they hide themselves behind the chatais
when they have their baths!"'

'May those bastards go to hell! May they become blind! Teasing girls like
that,' Nihaldei said crossly.

'Let them talk. Don't pay any attention to them,' the Brahmin woman
advised.

'Hai, all the clowns seem to have come to this camp,' Nihaldei said again.
'Always peering in as they pass by.'

Tara lifted her eyes to look at Nihaldei combing and arranging her hair
carefully before a mirror placed on top of her trunk.

'Hot chai…biscuits,' called a man with a brass tea urn as he went by
the hut. A few minutes later, another pedlar called out, 'Hot puris, halwa!'

Nihaldei bought four puris from the man. Sukhdet was now combing
her hair before the mirror. The three-year-old girl asked her grandmother
for halwa in a plaintive voice.

The old woman cursed the bothersome pedlar, hoping that all his family
might perish, and then cursed her granddaughter that she might die.

The Brahmin woman took up the child's plea, 'She's only small, and all children are always hungry in the morning. When my grandson wakes up, he calls for something to eat. I save half a roti for him. I buy a cup of tea for one anna, he dunks the roti in it and eats it. Who can get milk these days? Dear God!' She closed her eyes and joined her hands in silent prayer.

'When He meant us to lose all we had, why did He give us children? Now when the child is hungry, where can I dig up food from?' The old woman said with irritation. Tara gave her a sympathetic look.

Nihaldei spoke with her mouth full, 'This is all our karma. The wise ones said: Reap what you have sown.'

The grandmother ignored the remark and continued to clean her chatai of the clothes that the child had soiled during the night.

Over the loudspeakers they heard an announcement, 'This is All India Radio, Delhi. Today...'

The old woman said, 'Our name and address has been announced three times. So far we haven't heard anything from Dhammo's family. Who knows what God has destined for her?'

The radio at the house of Dr Prabhu Dayal across from Tara's home in Lahore used to broadcast bhajans or qawwalis in the morning. Now all it transmitted was news and the names and addresses of people displaced and separated from their families.

Tara asked the Brahmin woman, 'Where do you go to have your names broadcast over the radio? At the same place we registered when we came here yesterday evening?'

The woman said 'Yes' and Tara advised Banti, 'Sister, let's tell the radio people about your reaching here. Your family's in Delhi. If they find out from the radio that you're in Amritsar they'll run to that city to look for you.'

Nihaldei suggested, 'Use your card and draw your rations.' She complained, 'The damned authorities give out these rations for only a month, but give no spices or firewood. Do they want us to use our hands and feet for firewood? You spend four to six paisa every time for firewood. I buy my own salt, chillies and spices, and a bit of ghee from the bazaar. They used to hand out blankets. They even gave clothes to those who had none. We got nothing.'

The old woman could not help but say, 'They are doing a lot as things are. God is so merciful; He looks after everyone. How long can we depend on others? I'm waiting to get some news of Dhammo's family so that we don't have to rely on anyone else.'

Nihaldei took offence at this reply, 'Wah, we've left so much behind. We got neither a blanket, nor a single piece of clothing. I've been using my own money to buy spices and ghee. Who do you take us for? My family owned two houses ...'

Several volunteers stood around in the tent, but only one was writing down the information for the radio messages. One of the persons waiting suggested, 'Give us some paper. We'll write the details down ourselves.'

The person who was recording the details held out some slips of paper.

Tara took one slip, and said, 'If I could have a pencil...'

She was handed a pencil.

She wrote neatly and legibly, in good English, starting with, 'Please broadcast over the radio ...'

The man glanced at the paper as he took it from her, and asked, 'You used to teach at some school?'

'Yes, and I have a request,' she said in English.

'Please tell me what it is.'

'We were told in Ambala that our family was in Delhi. Can't remember exactly the name of the mohalla, but it was some "ganj".'

'Paharganj?'

'Ji, we were told that Muslims used to live there, but now Hindus have settled in.'

'That's right. It has to be Paharganj.'

'Could you please tell me how to get there?'

'You go across the bridge to Naya Bazaar, then take ... Tell you what. Go past the railway station. You'll see tonga drivers hailing fares for Paharganj. They'll charge you two annas per person.'

Banti did not have enough patience to draw, cook her rations and have a meal before going off in search of her son and husband. A pushcart vendor, waving a date palm branch as fan over a stack of cold puris, was touting his stuff as fresh and hot. Banti took Tara's hand and said, 'Remember how long it took us in Amritsar. Who knows how long it might take us to search here? We're strangers in this city, and it might be evening before we find anything. You have a couple of puris and a drink of water. If Maharaj shows

mercy and gets me together with my Jaggi and his father, that'll be the
end of our worries.'

Banti did not want to eat anything herself. If she stayed hungry and
suffering, she thought, God might be more inclined to listen to her prayers.
She wanted, with God's blessing, to have her son in her arms before having
anything to eat.

Tara refused to listen to her. She paid for eight puris, forced Banti to
eat four of them and had four herself. They had a drink of water from the
Brahmin woman's lota, and with their bundles under their arms, got ready
to leave.

Nihaldei asked, 'Where are you off to? When will you come back?'

Banti took this remark as they were leaving as a bad omen. Ignoring
Nihaldei, she muttered an aside, 'If Maharaj is good to us, why would we
return?'

Tara and Banti got down from the tonga at the tonga stand outside
Paharganj. Tara asked a middle-aged Sikh the way to Paharganj mohalla.

'Beti, this is all Paharganj. It's a very large mohalla; nearly a small town,'
replied the Sikh. 'Beti, who will be able to help you, everyone is newcomer
here. There are so many lanes and alleyways. Ask around and keep at it.
Waheguru will help you.'

Tara and Banti walked through a partially destroyed bazaar and turned
into a gali on their right. Several houses in a terrace were burnt out and
in ruins. The fallen debris had blocked the drains which had turned into
puddles of dirty water and filth. Tara and Banti, their noses covered with
their dupattas to block out the stench, picked their way gingerly through
the litter. Some refugees had taken shelter in the ruined houses.

If Banti caught sight of a woman in a doorway or threshold, she asked,
'Do two brothers from Chimmoki village in Shaikhupura district and their
mother live around here? They are in the bajaji, cloth-selling, business. An
old woman and a baby are with them.' Tara also asked any one she saw, even
men, 'Do you know anything about Manohardas and Gopaldas? Khatris
from Chimmoki?'

Most people shook their heads to say no in a preoccupied way. Some
would stop and ask, 'What's their line of work?'

'They go around selling cloth.'

'No, sister, don't know them. We're new here. Don't even know our own neighbours. There's nobody here from any time back to know about other people.'

So Tara and Banti would go and repeat their questions in another gali.

Banti was surprised. 'City folks are weird. In our village we knew about the people living in the villages around us. Here they don't seem to know even their neighbours.'

Tara said, 'You could ask any child in our Bhola Pandhe's Gali in Lahore about any of the people living there. These people are new to this place.'

It was past noon and they both were tired and plagued with a raging thirst. They cupped their hands and drank from a water faucet at the corner of two lanes. They needed to rest for some time. The house next to them was nothing but a burnt-out ruin. They sat on its broad chabutara.

Two women were sitting in the doorstep of the opposite house. A young woman was sewing patches on clothes that she took from a bundle. Tara and Banti had already spoken to them, and told them that they were looking for their families. The second, a middle-aged woman, asked Banti, 'Hai, a pair of defenceless women on your own, and you'll stay alone in this huge, burnt-out house? You really have guts!'

The woman spoke in the Derawali dialect of Punjab. For Tara, it was less comprehensible than the Hindi they spoke in Delhi.

Banti guessed at what she was trying to say, 'Why would just the two us live here alone? We're from the camp.'

The woman heard Banti speak in a dialect very different from her own. She asked, 'What district and village of Punjab are you from?'

'We're from Shaikhupura. This is my sister, she was a student in Lahore.'

The young woman tried to explain to Tara in her schoolgirl Hindi, 'This house is not fit to live in. Several others have looked it over and gone away. The shell of the house is barely holding out, and the roofs might cave in anytime. Some refugees from Multan stayed just one night here, then took off. Said that the house was haunted.'

Tara said, 'This is nothing, compared to the Shahalami bazaar in Lahore that was burnt to ashes.'

The young woman said, 'They say that eleven Muslim women were burnt to death in this house. The Hindus didn't even let them come out. The Muslims really put up a fight here. There was one young woman, nineteen or twenty years old. She stood on the roof alone and shot at the attackers. She kept on, even when men on the ground floor had surrendered. The

Hindus got to her only when her ammunition ran out. We were told that all her clothes were ripped off, they dragged her through the bazaar by her hair. They said that they'd let her go if she just said "Jai Hind". She refused. She was tough. They hacked her to pieces, but all she said was "Ya Ali! Pakistan zindabad!" The rest of the women were burnt alive.'

The second woman said, 'If they were Muslims, they would have taken the women away and raped them.'

Every hair on Tara's body stood on end. The burnt ruins of the house seemed to her to be a symbol of women not only suffering torture in the country, but in the whole world. Had fate brought her here only to see this? Not only herself, but countless other women had suffered at the hands of men. How long would women go on suffering in the same way? She heard Banti say, 'Sister, we saw what the Hindus did to women. I can't bring myself to speak about it. It was wrong, whoever did it. We women live only to be victims of men who are out to take vengeance in this world! Men might cut other men to pieces, but they don't humiliate them.'

The young woman said, 'Yes, it was a bad thing, whoever did it.'

The older woman said angrily, 'What do you know about what Muslims did to Hindu women? Why shouldn't Hindus do the same?'

The young woman fell silent, but Banti said sorrowfully, 'Let Hindus and Muslims give us rope to hang ourselves; then they can settle the score among themselves. God alone can make them answerable.'

'The Muslims must have caught both of you. You've lived among them, so that's why you are loyal to them. Why did you come here? You should've stayed back!'

The young woman hung her head in embarrassment. Tara and Banti could not bear to sit there any more. They got up and left.

In the afternoon, they both began their search in the left half of the bazaar. The lanes were narrower, and the houses smaller and poorly built in this part of the mohalla; the stench was overpowering. As before, they asked everybody they met in the gali and those sitting in their doorway.

Seeing the day come to an end, the women went inside to cook the evening meal. A few exhausted-looking men could be seen returning to their homes.

They continued to search in the lanes in the fading light of day. Their legs were weary, and they felt they would drop from fatigue. Their hope and patience were ebbing away. Finding no place to sit, they squatted on the gali pavement to rest their aching feet, carefully gathering their clothes so as not to touch anything. Their feet had swollen up from the day's walking.

Tara said, 'Let's go back. We can come back tomorrow.' Her throat was so dry that she could hardly speak. Banti's voice too had become feeble, but she did not want to give up exploring yet another lane, or turning into those that branched off to right or left.

The smoke from kitchen fires was adding to the darkness of the evening. Tara felt fear in the pit of her stomach. How would they find their way out of this maze in the dark? Who knew what dangers lay ahead? Why would they willingly throw themselves into the wolves, whether Hindu or Muslim?

She begged Banti to turn back. But Banti saw another lane and headed towards it. At the end of the lane there was still another.

'My baby!' Banti screamed suddenly, and rushed towards a small house. She snatched a frail-looking child from the arms of a middle-aged woman sitting on the threshold and clasped him to her heart, bursting out in loud sobs.

The child cried out in terror at being grabbed and pulled away.

The street lights came on and there was light in the lane.

As if the dark of sorrow had dispersed, the child recognized its mother, stopped crying and clung to her.

Such an outbreak of joy at this long-awaited reunion left Tara perspiring profusely. Her knees buckled and she sat down on the gali pavement. It took her a few moments to collect herself. She took a breath of relief, feeling as if all her weariness had been washed in the sweat pouring from her body.

Banti's eyes were on the child's face, as her hands ran over his head and back, 'Hai, how thin he has become! All skin and bones, what happened to you, my baby!' she began to weep.

Attracted by the loud crying of Banti and the child, several women from the neighbouring houses gathered around them. They guessed that the child's mother, who had been separated from him, had come back. Their eyes and lips opened wide in amazement, they asked:

'Hai, how did she get separated from her child? Where was she, all this time?'

'How could she live without her little baby?'

'Hai, she must have a heart of stone!'

One woman spoke up loudly to tell the others, 'They told us that the child's mother had fallen sick and died on her way here.'

Banti was engrossed in kissing her child and fondling him. Tara explained that the Muslims had locked several girls and women in a big house near the mandi in Shaikhupura. After their rescue by the Indian government, she and Banti had searched through several camps and eventually arrived here.

'Ah yes, her story is the same as Manso's from that neighbour's family. She too managed to get here after being abandoned.'

'But did they take her back! How could they?'

Banti's mother-in-law came up quietly, took the child away, and stepped inside the house.

Banti was following them when the mother-in-law shouted at her angrily, 'Stop! Go away! Don't come in here!'

'Why! This is my home, where else should I go?' she pleaded and bent down to place her head at the mother-in-law's feet.

'Go away, I told you. Of what use you are to us!' she kicked Banti's head aside with her foot.

Banti was stunned. She held on to the door jamb to steady herself, and then sank to the floor, with her hands to her head.

Tara felt her knees giving way. To keep herself from falling, she sat on her haunches beside Banti.

A few more men and women from houses in the lane came and stood around Tara and Banti. Arguments broke out over whether the daughter-in-law should be allowed to enter the house.

The woman who had mentioned the child's mother being dead, protested again loudly, 'How can they take her back into the house? The daughter-in-law of that family from Chukri had come back, just like her. Do you suppose the Muslims would have left them undefiled? They broke down the doors of homes and raped the women they found inside. Would have let these two go untouched? Just imagine!'

Tara felt choked by the anger and frustration rising inside her. She somehow managed to say to Banti's mother-in-law, 'Maaji, how is she to blame? She didn't stay behind on her own free will. You were cowards, and left her behind. She came back at once to you, without thinking of anything else. For the past nine days she has been looking for you.'

A young man spoke up in support of Tara, 'She's right. You're the guilty ones. Aren't you ashamed of yourselves, you were spineless enough to leave her behind! You're the biggest sinners, you shameless people. The child's mother has the first right over him, not that old woman!'

Another voice said, 'Hundreds of Muslims must have ravaged ... She's been dishonoured!'

Holding out his arms towards his mother, the child was screaming and weeping.

'The child wants to go to his mother! It's her child, why can't she have her own child!' someone pleaded.

'How is he her child? He belongs to the father.'

'Don't ask me! I don't know anything!' the mother-in-law held tightly on to the child. 'My sons will decide when they return.' She shut the door.

The crowd continued to stand and argue about Banti's right to her own child and the mother-in-law's reaction. Everyone talked, but no one listened. They spoke in different accents and in different dialects of Punjabi. Tara's head was spinning. She didn't know what to do. Surrounded by the crowd, she and Banti sat on the ground helplessly like criminals, their elbows on their knees and heads between their hands.

'They've come! They're back! They're both here!'

The clamour of voices quieted. There was the sound of hobnailed shoes and of the steelyard measure tapping on the gali pavement. Tara and Banti looked in the direction of the noise. Two men, each carrying a bundle of bolts of cloth over one shoulder and a steelyard measure in their hand, were approaching.

Banti covered her face with her aanchal and began to weep.

Several voices from the crowd, speaking simultaneously, told Manohardas and Gopaldas what had happened, along with their own opinion and the story of Manso who, just like Banti, had come back to her family. The brothers listened in silence. Gopaldas knocked at the door with the end of his steelyard. The door opened. Gopaldas quickly stepped inside to evade the crowd. He stuck his head out and said, 'She was among Muslims for two months. How can we take her back?'

The mother-in-law stood wedged in the half-open door, waiting for Manohardas to enter.

'You go in,' Manohardas told his mother and took her place in the half-open doorway. Pointing to the sky with his yard measure, he spoke in a plaintive voice to Banti and the crowd, 'Whatever was His wish. We were driven away from our homes and faced ruin. Thousands suffered the same fate. It all was His doing.'

Tara used all her strength to cry, 'Have some fear of God! Was it her fault in any way?'

'But was it our fault? We lost our home, and we lost our daughter-in-law. It was all His will. Why did you bring her here?'

Manohardas was about to shut the door when the same young man angrily pushed at the door, and stammered in protest, 'Have you no sh-sh-shame! If you're not to blame, who is? If you were so bothered about your r-r-religion, you should have died p-p-protecting her. You b-b-betrayed that innocent woman...'

'If some one grabs you and stuffs shit in your mouth, will you cut off your head?' a young woman shouted in fury, her hand pointing accusingly.

'Who are you to meddle in other people's affairs? What have you got to do with this? Go away!' Manohardas slammed the door shut.

Tara was at a loss what to do. Her head reeled. What was happening in front of her? What was she to do?

'I'll kill myself here!' Banti screamed.

She had struck her head against the front door sill.

Tara went numb with shock. The people watching them were stunned too. Banti hit her head on the door sill and shouted, 'I'm going to kill myself here.'

Five, ten, twenty times she struck the door sill with her head. Her voice became faint but she continued to beat her head down.

A woman standing nearby screamed.

Another woman cried out and ran away.

A man cursed loudly at Banti's husband and his family.

In the light of the street lamp, Tara saw Banti's face, bruised and running blood, rising and falling, rising and falling. She suddenly realized that Banti was trying to kill herself!

She pulled Banti up and held her head against her knees as hard as she could.

An enraged Banti pushed Tara away. Tara fell backwards.

Banti struck her head twice more as a man tried unsuccessfully to grab Banti by the shoulders.

Tara got up and tried again to pull her back. Banti fell backwards lifeless. Her mouth was open, and her face was covered in blood.

Tara put Banti's head in her lap and covered it with her dupatta. Her own body was shaking violently. She closed her eyes as she felt her strength draining away. Some voices from the crowd muttered angrily in disgust about the treatment meted out to Banti.

A few came forward to help. Tara felt she was going to faint. She bit her lip and shook her head to remain conscious, and wiped Banti's face with her dupatta as she leaned over her face.

Tara opened her eyes and saw three women and four men standing over her

'This one's still alive,' she heard. She saw Banti's body lying beside her knees, as flies buzzed over her blood-covered face. Next to her on the gali pavement was a bolt of brand-new red cloth.

Tara's head throbbed with pain. She opened and closed her eyes several times then, in a flash of clarity, realized that Banti was dead.

'Just look at these shameless people! Getting a red shroud for her, because she has a husband who's still alive!' a woman said in anger and disgust.

'She became a sati for her husband,' another woman said.

'Became a sati even when her husband is alive,' said the third.

Tara sat in a daze. She did not have enough strength to cry.

'Come, you can wash your hands and face at our house,' one of the women said, putting a consoling hand on Tara's shoulder.

Tara shook her head in refusal.

Sunlight had covered one half of the gali. Tara sat unmoving and watched. A bier was being made for Banti. Gopaldas and Manohardas worked in silence, aided by two other men. Some women carried Banti's body into the house to give it a ritual washing.

The body, shrouded in the red cloth, was placed on the bier with due ceremony. Gopaldas, Manohardas and two others lifted the bier and put its poles over their shoulders.

The gali echoed with the chant of a bier being carried out : *Ram-nam satt hai! Gopal-nam satt hai! Har ka nam satt hai!*

Tara wept inconsolably. Her only friend and companion was now lost to her.

A young woman came up to Tara, laid her hand gently on her shoulder, and said, 'Come with me, sister. Have a wash, and drink some water.'

'I want to go back to the camp,' said Tara. She wanted to run away from this place.

The young woman and another young man supported Tara as they walked her to the tonga rank. They both cursed their fellow Hindus for such callous behaviour, in the face of their so-called claims of kindness and compassion for others, 'Whatever we Hindus suffered was not enough to teach us a lesson. Such unfeeling and cruel people have no place on this earth; may they vanish without trace.'

Tara, barely conscious, her eyes half-open, got on to a tonga going from Paharganj to the railway station. In front of the station building, some other tongawallahs were touting for fares: 'Two annas per person up to Kashmiri Gate.' Tara had no strength left to walk. She sat in one of those tongas.

When she arrived at the camp, the residents were crowding round the water taps for their bath, and filling up their water containers. Some of them, with towels and angauccha on their shoulders and chewing on twigs of the neem tree to clean their teeth, strolled on the path between the rows of huts, waiting for the crowd to thin out. Tara, her eyes downcast, went straight to her hut. She did not notice that those she passed stared at her with curious, questioning eyes. A throbbing headache blurred her vision.

In a corner of the hut sat Sukhdet, peering into the mirror perched on her trunk. In another corner Dhammo, facing the wall, was breastfeeding her baby girl. Upon hearing Tara come in, they turned to look at her. Tara did not return their gaze. A woman she had not seen before was sitting on her chatai. Tara lay down on Banti's chatai, and using her arm to pillow her head, closed her eyes.

In the haze of confusion caused by her throbbing headache, she heard faint voices near her head. Then in a distinct voice, 'Where did you go?'

Tara opened her eyes and saw Nihaldei standing over her. Nihaldei's hands were smeared with the dough she had been kneading, and she held them away from her clothes. Dhammo's mother-in-law, her head between her hands, was squatting beside Tara's chatai, and staring at her with anxiety and curiosity. Dhammo's eyes, with the child at her breast, were upon her. Sukhdet also stood close by. Tara saw that everyone was looking at her inquisitively.

'Where did you go? Where did you spend the night?' Nihaldei asked again, in a loud harsh voice.

Tara did not feel up to giving any explanation. She let out a long sigh, covered her face and head with her dupatta, and defiantly turned on her side.

'Her salwar was covered with blood when she came in. Look...you can see for yourselves. I was shocked and thought, what happened to her? She tried to hide the state of her clothes and threw herself down quickly,' Sukhdet stated loudly.

Not getting any reply irritated Nihaldei. She spoke in a voice louder than the girl's, 'Yes, and just imagine what they were up to. One of them didn't even come back. Wonder what they were doing all night? Just look what they've been through.'

'What's that to us? They'll pay for it, whatever they've done,' said Prasanno, the Brahmin woman.

'May Maharaj damn them to the deepest hell,' said Dhammo's mother-in-law. 'If I could help it, we wouldn't stay here another moment. I'm just waiting for news of my daughter-in-law's family so that I can get out of this place. I can't bear to see such things. Why doesn't God call me to Him?'

'They went out to have fun! Maybe they met some really tough characters,' Sukhdet said in a giggly voice.

Dammo's mother-in-law raised her voice to outdo Nihaldei and Sukhdet, 'That's why they eat puris and halwa every morning! Poor women like us get to eat dry chapattis. You call this a camp? It's nothing but a den of vice. May all these sluts go to hell! How can we stay here any longer? I have to think of my young daughter-in-law.'

'Let's go and complain to the camp officials! Let's ask then if this is really a camp! I too have a young daughter. We don't want these women here! The camp's turning into a brothel! Come, let's tell them.' They all babbled on, except the old woman from Gujranwala, who lay curled up on her chatai.

Tara understood their allegations. This was yet another humiliation for someone who had already fallen into a bottomless well of misfortune; one who was sinking deeper and deeper, but who had no strength left to save herself by speaking up. Rather, she felt like someone against whose rotting, lifeless body hateful accusations were being hurled by her tormentors; one for whom the only escape now was in her corpse to be thrown into a raging fire or into a deep, fast-flowing river.

As she lay surrounded by jeering women, her head and face covered by her dupatta, she thought grimly that she'd soon be an outcast. They would grab by her plait and drag her away, ripping off her clothes. She was the object of their anger and hatred because she had fallen victim to her torturers, and they were angry because she had fought back, because she resisted being abused by Somraj and Nabbu.

In her imagination she saw that they had torn the clothes off another girl, and were dragging her through the bazaar, the same girl who had fired shots at the crowd attacking her. They were hacking her body to pieces, because she refused to say 'Jai Hind' but said 'Pakistan Zindabad' instead. The girl continued to yell defiantly, 'You can't put me down, do whatever you want with my dead body. I didn't bend my head to you. If I die, it's not because I lost, but because your brutality won.' Tara imagined that she also desperately wanted to grab a gun, or a sword, so that she too could fight to her last breath. Then she wouldn't feel any pain either, even if they cut her body to pieces.

The women surrounding Tara jabbered on. She did not understand their words, but she knew that God was being invoked to punish her. She thought in a daze, 'God neither listens to them, nor does He listen to me.'

In her half-conscious state, she began to imagine that God was commanding her to appear before Him for punishment. She was being dragged before Him, and His face kept on changing in the same way as close-ups of different actors change on a cinema screen. God had a lush, black curly beard, a well-trimmed moustache, and a red fez on His head, His radiant face now flushed with anger! Holding a lota with a spout, He was standing beside a namaz prayer rug. Sometimes God appeared to have a clean-shaven face, just like a young boy's, with mischievous eyes and a flute to his smiling lips. But God in all His guises ignored her and looked the other way.

'Hey, listen! You, bibi,' one of God's angels ordered her. 'Get up! Can't you hear?'

'Her name is Tara,' Sukhdet said quickly.

'O Tara bibi!'

It was not a dream, Tara realized. Someone was calling her name. She had to remove her dupatta and open her eyes. She recognized the face with its long, grey moustache and tiny gold rings in its ears. The camp peon was standing over her.

After their arrival, Bhajan Lal, the peon, had brought Tara and Banti to the hut reserved for women. Tara had seen him again at the registration tent.

'Get up! You've to report to the camp office,' he said to Tara.

Next to him stood Nihaldei, looking as if it was her orders the peon was giving, while the other women looked on.

'I'm not feeling well right now. I'll come later,' Tara said. She had a throbbing headache, and didn't want to lose face in front of other women.

'You've to come when they tell you! She talks as if she were a begum! Get up! You think this is your father's house!' Bhajan Lal spoke in a thick Jat accent.

'Yes, why don't you get up?' Nihaldei waved her hand before Tara's face to emphasize the peon's command, 'You were all right when you were gadding about the city all night!'

Tara closed her eyes and grit her teeth. She used her hands to push herself up to a sitting position, then to stand, and followed the peon out. As she stepped out of the hut she heard someone say, 'Why do they allow such shameless hussies in the camp! Let them go to some whorehouse.'

For a horrifying moment Tara thought she would be thrown aside like useless rubbish, and that end now faced her. Her mind dulled by blinding headache, she tried to imagine what they might do to get rid of her! Why go to the camp office to meet further humiliation? The bridge over railway tracks was not far away; she could always jump in front of an oncoming train.

'Get in!' Tara raised her eyes. Bhajan Lal had pulled aside the tent fly.

Inside the tent were Vimalji and the young men who worked under him, but another woman was sitting in Vimalji's chair behind the desk. She had a smooth, light brown complexion, her hair arranged in a bun in modern style, and a slender but full figure. She wore a well-tailored sleeveless blouse, a white voile sari, and inconspicuous make-up.

'Is this the woman?' the woman asked Vimalji in English.

Vimalji nodded his head. He looked at Tara and said, 'This is Doctor Shyama, vice-president of the Refugee Relief Committee.'

Vimalji had spoken in English, to indicate to the woman that Tara understood English, adding, 'Taraji was a teacher in Punjab.'

Doctor Shyama got up from her chair, and took a step towards a curtain that divided the tent. She said to Tara in English, 'Please come in. We'll talk inside,' as she drew aside the curtain.

Shyama sat beside Tara on a takht and asked her in a soft, gentle voice, 'Did anyone harass you? Any physical problems? Are you hurt?'

'No, nothing. I have a terrible headache.'

Shyama checked Tara's pulse, felt her forehead, and said, 'No physical problems. Well, your elder sister also went out with you. Where is she? Did she stay behind?'

Shyama's tone and her gentle behaviour brought tears to Tara's eyes.

Unable to say anything, she cried softly. When she attempted to speak, no words came out from her dry throat and mouth.

Shyama guessed her condition. She got up quickly, pulled the curtain aside and asked for a tumbler of water. Tara finished the tumbler in one draught. As she wiped away her tears she described the previous evening's incident, haltingly and in a low voice.

When Tara had finished, Shyama said, 'Better change these clothes. Do you have any others?'

Tara asked, 'Could you please find me some kind of work? I'm willing to do anything. After what I've been through with those women, I don't want to go back to the hut.'

'Don't let those foul-mouthed wretches bother you,' Shyama said reassuringly. 'I don't know many people in the school management committees, but I'll try to find out. You can help with the running of the camp and the registration work till then. Just wait here and I'll get some medicine for your headache,' Shyama went out to the other half of the tent.

Shayma explained something to Vimalji and others in a low voice. Their voices were muffled, but Tara knew that they were talking about her, and about how she could be helped.

Bhajan called after a few minutes, 'Bibiji, may I come in?'

He came in with a clay cup full of hot milk and three small packets of medicine. He put everything on a chair next to the takht, and said politely, in the tone of one willing to help, 'I'll get you some water.'

He brought some water for Tara to wash her face and hands.

Shyama came in and said, 'Have one dose of the medicine now with milk, and rest. If the headache persists, take another after three hours.'

When Tara went back to the other side of the tent after a while, Shyama was still there. She advised Tara, 'Go back to your hut and just ignore those women. I'll certainly do something about you, and I'll see you again. Try to take things easy for a while.'

Tara went back to the hut reluctantly. A cacophony of quarrelling voices was coming from the hut. She could hear Nihaldei, Sukhdet and Dhammo's mother-in-law speaking very loudly. She went inside with some nervousness. Puzzled by their verbal duel, she went and lay down without looking at anyone.

Nihaldei and Sukhdet stood in the corner they were occupying. Facing them stood Dhammo's mother-in-law, a few steps ahead of her corner.

They were like two competitors facing off in an arena. In a furious tirade of abuse they blamed the other for telling lies and for making false accusations against Tara, as well as for having brought down reprimands by the camp authorities.

Prasanno came and sat beside Tara, 'Sister, when did you come back? I wasn't here when you returned. I was washing clothes at the water tap. I've just found out what happened. They told lies about you. Now let them face the consequence. It's good that they got shouted at. Now they don't know what to do.'

The slanging match had attracted women from other huts. Tara squirmed with embarrassment at their questions. Even if her accusers had been proven wrong, it still reminded her of her humiliation. The neighbours returned to their huts, but not before satisfying their curiosity, and advising the quarrelling women to keep peace and live together in harmony.

The confrontation ended with both sides deciding to ignore the existence of their opponent. Silence prevailed in the hut in the afternoon, with everyone dozing off on their chatais.

'Bibi Taradeviji,' Bhajan's heavily accented voice was heard from the doorway of the hut. 'Doctor memsahib has sent clothes for you. Please come and take them.'

As Tara was slow in getting up, Prasanno went to the entrance and said, 'Give the clothes to me. I'll hand them to her.'

'No, no, mai,' Bhajan refused. 'I'll hand them myself. I'll only give them to the person I've been told to deliver to.'

Bhajan came inside. He had a bundle under his arm and a slip of paper in his hand.

By now the women were wide awake. They got up to examine the bundle Bhajan had brought. Prasanno said to Tara, 'Sister, just check that what it says on the chit is in there.'

'How do I know what's in it and what's not! I swear by the Ganga if I even so much as opened it. Go ahead, open it and look,' Bhajan proclaimed his innocence.

What he had brought was wrapped in a blanket. Prasanno unrolled it on Tara's chatai. The blanket was not new, but of good quality and little used. There was one bed sheet. A few more clothes were rolled in a white towel. Prasanno undid those too. It had two cotton saris, one sky-blue and the other with a checked pattern. Two half-sleeved blouses, two petticoats.

Everything was washed and ironed, and had the smell of a well-kept, prosperous home. There was also a bar of Sunlight soap.

The women's eyes widened in amazement. Nihaldei came over and began examining the quality of the cloth.

When Bhajan left, Nihaldei said, 'These dhotis have been worn, but they're still in good condition. The material is fine, and good quality.'

Sukhdet also came to look at the blouses and the petticoats. Dhammo and her mother-in-law watched from their corner.

Prasanno said to Tara, 'Come on, get up now, sister. Have a bath and change your clothes. Don't worry about the clothes you were wearing; I'll wash those when I do the other laundry. What difference would a few more clothes make? There's plenty of soap.' Nihaldei made the same offer to Tara.

'I'll be back in a little while,' said Tara, getting up.

'Hai, that place's filthy. Your feet are unshod. Here, use my slippers, take my lota too. I always say whoever wants it is welcome to use it,' Nihaldei said in a friendly tone.

Tara had her bath in the enclosure reserved for women. After her bath and a change of clothes, she looked like a different person. Sukhdet lent Tara her own comb and mirror. Tara saw herself in a mirror for the first time in two months; a strange-looking, sallow, sickly face stared back at her. She spread the blanket on the chatai and lay down. She thought of Banti, and tears rolled down her cheeks.

Next morning, after she had washed, Tara didn't feel like lying idly in the hut. She went to the camp office to see if she could be of any help. The office, buzzing with voices, fell silent when a respectable-looking woman walked in.

Vimalji said in welcome, 'Come on, come in, Tara bahinji.'

The two junior volunteers offered their chairs to Tara.

Their sudden silence embarrassed Tara. She said, 'The Doctor sahiba told me yesterday that...' she slipped into Punjabi in the middle of speaking Hindi, and completed the sentence in English, 'I came to ask you if I could offer any help.'

Vimalji replied as he cleaned his ear with a matchstick, 'Bahinji, the real work is to collect groceries, clothes and money from the people of this city, and get aid from the government. That is being done by Khanna Saheb, Mahashayji, Prasadji, Doctor Shyama, Mrs Agarwal and Dayavantiji. Only those who have the right contacts can do that kind of work. Our job is to distribute whatever aid we receive. We might get ten or twenty requests for help or assistance, or someone wanting to have his name broadcast over the radio might show up. There's another, rather tedious job. The deputy commissioner has asked all camps for a copy of the list of their residents. Each camp will forward that information to the Kingsway Camp. Our list is one hundred and thirteen pages long. You can help copy that.'

Tara agreed.

'Do you need a pen?'

Tara said yes, and Vimalji removed a fountain pen from the pocket of his waistcoat and handed it to Tara.

All those present were men. 'Can I sit and work on the other side?' Tara asked Vimalji.

'Yes, sure.'

Tara went to the other half of the tent. As soon as she was out of sight, everyone began to laugh, as if her presence had inhibited their laughter. Were they laughing at her, Tara wondered. She heard someone speak in a low voice:

'Vimalji's smart; did you see how quickly he gave his pen!'

'He certainly is. And you just sat on your hands,' said another voice.

'He's got style. See how he asked: Do you need a pen?'

'Bhai, she's a modern girl. Speaks fluent English. Vimalji's having a gala time surrounded by those good-looking girls.'

Tara felt bad. Are these people here to help others, she thought angrily, or to joke at their misfortunes? 'Oh, let them blabber on; why should I care about what they say. Didn't my college friends do the same? Amrita, Surendra, Krishna, Sheelo too, what rot they talked.'

Next morning, the conversation at the camp office was of a different sort, and in different voices. Some Urdu-speaking Punjabi was venting his anger at the way Hindus had been fired on, to protect Muslims, 'These leaders are betraying us; they're sacrificing Hindus for the sake of Muslims. The Pakistan government cares for its people. All this is Gandhi's doing. He wants to be regarded as a saint by the Muslims, so he encourages them every day in his radio broadcast.'

Tara concentrated on her work, trying to ignore such comments. She had difficulty in reading one or two names, but did not feel up to asking anyone from that noisy group.

The tone of conversation changed again after a while. Some Delhiwallah was speaking jokingly with a Punjabi, 'Of course, Punjabis are big-hearted. They want to live well, even if they have to borrow money to do it. Look at any Punjabi woman, she'll be in silk and satin, decked in gold jewellery. We lost everything, they'll tell you, all that was left are these clothes we're wearing. Get us a card for free rations, give us some blankets, find us a house, find us a job. Listen, if they're so badly off, what about their clothes and jewellery?'

A Punjabi replied in a loud, heated voice, '*Saala*, you'd have been dead by now if you had to face what we went through. That's the Punjabi spirit, don't you realize. You've hardly ever seen bad times. If there are floods in your country, your people can be found begging all over Punjab. Have you ever seen a Punjabi beg? We've been facing plunder and invasions from centuries back.'

'Wah, what brave people! Haven't you fled and come here? Hey, if this isn't begging, what is it? What's a card for free rations, eh?'

'You call this begging, saale? Motherfucker, we gave our lives for the sake of your independence,' the Punjabi roared in anger.

Tara heard furniture pushed around violently. It seemed that a scuffle would break out, when a voice said, 'Arrey, what's this! What now! Listen, argue all you want but keep your fists down.'

'You use your tongue, I use my fists!'

'Oh really! What a gentleman!'

'I'll stuff your gentlemanly style up yours.'

There was the sound of the furniture being rearranged. The threat of a brawl seemed to have been averted. Tara was hurt by the aspersions being cast about ration cards.

'Arrey, you don't know the secret of silk and satin clothes?' another Punjabi voice tried, making peace, 'Bhaijaan, we all have a couple of sets of good clothes for special occasions. Who would wear the old ordinary things when fleeing, and leave behind their good expensive clothes? What they wear is what they brought with them, they just don't have any other clothes. They might own a piece or two of jewellery, so they wear them because they still don't have homes to keep them safe. And how long can anyone get free rations? These few pieces of jewellery would come in handy when one has to settle in. You might say that we've survived because we ate good food, and lived off the fat of the land.'

'Achcha bhai, let it go,' Vimalji intervened to restore calm. 'We'll regard you as a political refugee. We're doing for you what we can, and we'll do even more if we can.'

Tara had filled eight sheets of foolscap paper. She had the copied names and addresses of nearly three hundred families. From the quiet on the other side of the tent, it appeared that everyone had gone. She thought it a good time for her to leave.

She found only Vimalji and Bhajan in the office.

She put the originals and the copies in front of Vimalji and said, 'Bhai sahib, I'll be back in the afternoon.' She hesitated a bit, then said, 'I'll finish this work. If you could help me by telling me the names of some schools. You have got your hands full looking after so many.'

'Yes, yes.' Vimalji acknowledged, 'I've already inquired at some schools, and have left messages at other institutions to tell me if there's any vacancy or if they need some help. So many well-educated women are looking for work. You people have lots of guts, but it's a case of first come first served. It's always good to go and inquire in person.'

Vimalji wrote down the addresses of several schools for girls for Tara.

Prasanno said to Tara that if she gave her ration card, and a few paisas for firewood, then she'd cook for her. Tara understood Prasanno's situation. Her husband's elder brother had abandoned Prasanno and her son at the Delhi railway station without leaving her any money, and had gone on to Bombay. She had been forced to earn some money on her own. She washed clothes for the families of some well-off refugees at the rate of one anna for ten pieces of clothing. Soap was supplied by the family. She earned three to four annas per day. Refugees at the camp were allowed free ration only for one month, and she had now been at the camp for twenty-two days.

Nihaldei cut in and said to Tara, 'Why should you pay anything for firewood? If you're cooking for two persons, it's just the same for three. I'll get the rations for you, sister, and cook for you. What are you worried about?' She said to Tara so that Prasanno could hear, 'She has neither a pot nor a pan of her own, and borrows kitchen stuff from us or from Dhammo.'

Tara wanted to help Prasanno, but did not want to get on the wrong side of the belligerent Nihaldei either. She gave her ration card to Nihaldei. When she returned to the hut, she found only Dhammo with her mother-in-law and Rikkho, the young woman who was the last arrival. The old woman from Gujranwala seldom got up from her chatai. Nihaldei had told Dhammo where she had put Tara's share of lunch.

In only two days' time the women in the hut had discovered that Tara could sit at the table with the men in the camp's office, that she was educated, and from a decent family, and that people listened to her. On the third day, Prasanno asked Tara to get her a blanket for her four-year-old son. The woman owned nothing but a change of clothes. It got chilly after midnight. Tara replied, 'Take my blanket at night for the child. I need only the sheet to cover myself.'

Dhammo's mother-in-law found time to speak with Tara when no one was around, 'Beti, the camp officials told us that we've been here for a month now. They're going to send us far away, to some camp called something like kung. We heard that the camp was in the middle of a jungle. No free rations there. How would I manage with two babies and my young daughter-in-law? Someone said that widows were being allotted houses. Please get us one. We'll earn something by cleaning house and cooking for other families.' She stopped when she saw Nihaldei come in.

Tara had her daal and roti, spread out her blanket and lay down. Thoughts about her future raced through her mind: Why not inquire at some school rather than go back to copying lists at the camp office? What would she have done if Banti was still alive? Six days had passed since her death. Whenever Tara was alone, the horrible incident of Banti's death would pass before her eyes. The more Tara tried to forget Banti, the more she came to her mind. She had spent only about a month with Banti, but it seemed as if they had been together all their lives.

Only two months and five days before Tara had entered her in-laws' house as a new bride. She left her husband's house barefoot. Since her childhood in the gali, and up to the time of the incident at Banni Hata, she had never stepped out of her house without some kind of footwear.

She held felt some discomfort while roaming the lanes of Amritsar and Paharganj without any footwear, but never felt shame or embarrassment. Now that Shyama had sent her clothes that a respectable woman might wear, she felt awkward and self-conscious about her unshod feet. It was not difficult to walk on the smooth camp ground, but she still felt ill at ease. She also felt uneasy at going out in the crumpled dhoti that she wore in the hut, but, at the same time, did not want to wear the other dhoti.

She would wear the other dhoti when she went to some school for girls, she thought, but it would look ridiculous going barefoot. What impression would that make on others? The five rupees that Banti had received as a gift from Dev's mother, she had given to Tara, and had asked Tara to keep the money safe by tying it in a corner of her dupatta when they went in search of Banti's family in Paharganj. Those five and her remaining four rupees were now Tara's total capital. She had hidden this money in her brassiere for a time of special need or unexpected expense, but now she needed to spend some of it to buy some kind of footwear.

Nihaldei seemed to know most about what was available around the camp, and in the city of Delhi. Tara asked her, 'Sister, where could I get an inexpensive pair of slippers around here?'

'Anywhere! As many as you want. Thousands of shops around here,' Nihaldei replied, waving her arm in a gesture that meant the world beyond the hut. 'This is no village or empty countryside.' She was eager to escort Tara to the bazaar.

They had come through the gate of the camp and were on their way to Kashmiri Gate when Nihaldei said irritably, 'Just look at these bums. The moment a girl steps out of the camp, they begin to follow and bother her.'

Tara was disconcerted. Without raising her eyes, she glanced sideways and saw that a young man had accosted Nihaldei and was speaking to her.

'Want a room or some place to live? I know of a good place,' Tara heard the man say.

'Get away, you bum! What's it to you? We don't need your help,' Nihaldei scolded the boy in her broken Hindi.

'You wanna sell any jewellery, any clothes, any other stuff? I can take you to the right place,' the man persisted.

'Get away from us, and may you leave your wife a widow! Beat it! Stop bothering us. We know where to go,' Nihaldei said angrily, with a wave of her hand to fend him off, and to discourage him from following them.

'Hey! What's up with you?' asked the man cheekily.

Tara watched him out of the corner of her eye. His dirty clothes, oil-slicked hair and insolent, toothy grin gave her a feeling of revulsion.

When they reached Kashmiri Gate, Nihaldei said, 'The bloody shopkeepers here charge double the price. The market of Chandni Chowk is just across that bridge. There are hundreds of shops there.'

Tara cheered up on knowing that Chandni Chowk was not far away. She said, 'I was told that Dariba Mohalla is nearby, and Chawri Bazaar too. There are some girls' schools. After we get the chappals, would you take me there?'

'No problem! That's no bother! Why are you so scared, sister?' Nihaldei reassured her. 'If you just ask for directions, you can even get as far as Bukhara.'

The shopkeeper wanted six rupees for a pair of chappals. Nihaldei bargained and haggled with him, and brought the price down to three and a half rupees. In Lahore, the shopkeepers might have quoted four rupees for some article, and then accepted three and a half for it, but demanding six rupees and then selling it for nearly half the price made Tara feel that she had come to a city of crooks.

Nihaldei had no hesitation in asking passers-by in the street about schools for girls, and led Tara through the galis and alleys of Katra Neel and Dariba. These galis were narrow and winding just like those in Lahore, but lacking in the active buzz of groups of women sitting and chatting on their doorsteps. Any men that they came upon stared at them in surprise. If they passed local women dressed in chadars over their saris or dhotis, the women shrank back as if afraid of being defiled. They also heard disparaging comments, 'These are refugees! They are really brazen!'

Tara met helpful people at two schools. 'Send a written application to the management committee if you want a job,' she was told. They also gave her the names and addresses of the secretaries of the committees.

At other schools the reception was less than cordial. 'Heaven knows where this crowd come from. A couple show up every day. No one knows where they live, or where they're from. And they want to be teachers! I've been teaching here for eight years. Who knows if they even know how to teach?'

Tara was bone-tired. Such cold and indifferent responses plunged her into the depths of despair. She realized that she would not find a job without some sort of a letter of recommendation. In Lahore, her brother had similarly been unable to find a job without a recommendation. She nervously watched the crowds filling the bazaar of Chandni Chowk. Strange men bumped into her intentionally, others leered at her. A few called remarks at her. As if she had asked for all this just because she had dared to come to a bazaar without a male to protect her. Nihaldei could not stop herself from shouting back taunts. This bothered Tara. She had gone with Banti to so many places in Amritsar and in Paharganj, and nothing like this had happened to them. If it happened, Banti would merely have ignored it. Tara wanted to get back to the camp.

Nihaldei proposed, 'This bazaar is known for its chaat. Come, let's eat some.' Tara refused, but Nihaldei paid no attention.

Tara was helpless, as she could not go back alone. At the chaat stall, she stood uncomfortably behind Nihaldei, her head bent. She refused to eat anything. The way the chaat seller wiped the leaves on the dhoti covering his thighs before using the leaves as plates for serving chaat, and the way he spoke with an unpleasant smirk on his face, irked Tara, but there was little she could do. Nihaldei grumbled that the spices and chillies in the chaat burned her mouth, but had four servings of it, nevertheless.

Dusk fell while they were still at the chaat seller. Nihaldei seemed in no hurry to return to the camp. She strolled through the bazaar, enjoying the scene, chatting away with Tara. She had seen and heard a lot in her three weeks at the camp, and had a lot of gossip to tell about its residents. A girl from section six, Nihaldei said, had got involved with a boy. The girl's parents were unwilling at first, but then took the boy and the girl to a gurudwara and got them married.

Nihaldei went on about another girl who was about Tara's age. The camp officials were always pampering her. She was often invited to go to the camp office. Nihaldei said, 'I knew what she was up to the moment I laid eyes on her. She disappeared just after a week. Someone must have lured her away. Sister, I'm always on tenterhooks thinking of Sukhdet. Who knew her husband would do that to her? She just stayed for a couple of days at her in-laws', then came to visit us. Her husband never turned up, to take her back to his home. That was two years ago. That girl is still so naïve.'

Tara and Nihaldei returned to the hut. Prasanno was having her meal and also feeding her son. Rikkho was talking with Dhammo. Sukhdet was nowhere to be seen.

Nihaldei asked Prasanno anxiously, 'Where's Sukhdet?'

'How would I know?' Prasanno replied as she chewed a mouthful of food.

'She was in section five, with that boy ...' Prasanno's son spoke up.

'None of your business! Shut your mouth! Eat!' Prasanno hushed him up. 'What do I know? I took back the washing that I did for a woman in section three around sunset. Sukhdet wasn't here when I got back. I borrowed the tray to knead my dough, and went to cook it over Dhammo's cooking fire. Came back only a few minutes ago. Ask anyone.'

'We know nothing either!' Dhammo's mother-in-law said. 'She comes and goes as she pleases. Ask her anything and you only get a rude reply.'

'So what? She's probably chatting with some neighbour. You make mountains out of molehills if I ask you about anything,' Nihaldei shouted at the old woman. 'Nobody can stand it, the way you go on and on!'

Just then Sukhdet entered the hut, hiding something under her dupatta.

'Where were you?' Nihaldei asked threateningly.

'Hai, I haven't been anywhere. I was right here all the time. Just went out two minutes ago to see Bholi in section two.'

'I asked you to do the cooking, and you've been gadding about as if everything depended on you. Who knows what type of people live in the camp? I'll break your legs if I ever find you away from the hut.'

'I was just going to knead the dough when Bholi asked me to come over.'

'Hai, stop lying or we all will be struck by lightning!' The old woman said, raising her arm towards the sky. 'What barefaced lies! Like mother like daughter! You were away since the sun was about a bamboo high. Your mother was asking us about you. We're damned if we tell her, and damned if we don't.'

'You're a liar, so was your father, and your husband whose death you caused. What has all this got to do with you, anyway? Am I some kind of servant of yours?' Sukhdet cursed the old woman.

'Ma, this has nothing to do with us! Why do you stick your nose in?' Dhammo said to her mother-in-law. 'It's her daughter; she can do whatever she wants with her. It's her problem, not ours.'

Dhammo's mother-in-law, Sukhdet and Nihaldei all shouted at each other. Prasanno and Rikkho tried to pacify them. Tara too tried to make peace. When things quietened down a bit, Nihaldei went outside to cook her meal, taking Sukhdet with her.

Tara had given her rations to Nihaldei. She ought to go and help in the cooking, she thought. Why should she act like the queen bee and wait for others to dance attendance on her! She took off the new dhoti she had worn when going out and folded it carefully, changed into the old one before going outside. As she turned the corner, she saw Nihaldei cursing and flailing Sukhdet on the head with a piece of firewood.

Tara turned around quietly, and went back to the hut. She lay down tired on the chatai. How long can I live like this? she wondered. She wished she had Banti with her. The gory incident of Banti's death again swam before her eyes. The fate of a woman depended on the kindness and goodwill of men. She must find a job, any job!

Tara tried to help out as much as she could at the camp office to lighten her load of obligation at accepting free rations. Next morning she was at the camp office at eight in the morning to begin her copying work. There was nobody but Bhajan in the office at that time. She went back at half past eight. Vimalji had commented upon her diligence, and Tara was glad of his approval and sympathy. The need to get a recommendation from some local personage was at the back of her mind. Doctor Shyama had seemed to be a kind and sympathetic sort of person, but she had not returned to the camp. Tara asked for some writing paper from Vimalji, and wrote letters of application to the secretaries of school committees whose names she had been given. She requested Vimalji to have these sent to the addresses. Then she put in extra effort and copied twenty-one pages of her lists by the evening.

She was on her way to the camp office at 8.30 next morning when she came upon Vimalji in the passage between the rows of huts. He was introducing a khadi-clad man to the camp inhabitants. Although the stranger was of slighter build and considerably shorter than Vimalji, he appeared to be someone important from the way he carried himself.

Vimalji praised Tara's biddable manner and diligence as he introduced her to the man, then said, 'Prasadji is one of the vice-presidents of the Relief Committee, and the Congress Party's ...'

Even missing out on Prasadji's full introduction, Tara realized the weight and influence he carried in his person.

Prasadji thrust his hands in the pockets of his roomy kurta as if in the pockets of trousers, and straightened his back, pulling his body up to its full height. He looked Tara over, from head to toe, and asked, 'How long have you been here?' In the next breath, he said to another person coming towards him, 'Hello, have you settled in? No more problems?'

He asked Tara again as he walked towards the next hut, 'You're helping us by making copies of the registers, I gather?'

Before Tara could reply, he turned to other refugees in the hut and began asking after them. He said, 'You're guests of ours. Your difficulties are our difficulties. It matters to us that you have problems. We have assumed the responsibility of administering a large country and now we have to care for millions of our displaced brothers and sisters. But a solution has to be found to this situation.'

As Prasadji moved towards the next hut, he asked again, 'Did you teach at some school or college in Lahore?'

'Ji, I...'

Prasadji called to another person, 'Hello, what did the deputy commissioner do in your case? I spoke to him about it.'

A thirteen- or fourteen-year-old girl said namaste to him. Prasadji patted her cheek. The girl stepped back shyly. Prasadji patted her on the back.

'So, you...' Prasadji picked up the threads of his conversation with Tara, but broke off to address two well-dressed women, 'You are well?' Prasadji seemed to make no distinction between rich and poor.

Tara left Prasadji to continue commiserating with others, and headed to the office tent. She was sitting in wait for Vimalji to come back and give her pen and paper.

Vimalji raised the tent flap for Prasadji.

'Oh, there you are! I've been looking for you outside,' Prasadji said to Tara.

Vimalji repeated his appreciation of the help Tara had given, and said that she was looking for a job.

'She's a graduate. Why would she have any difficulty in that? Sure, she'll get a job. Come with me, I'll arrange for you to meet some people.'

A grateful Tara got ready to go with him.

A motor car was waiting beside the office. Prasadji opened the rear door for Tara. She had not had many occasions to ride in cars as grand as this. She felt a little conscious of her crumpled, shabby dhoti as she sat in one corner of the back seat. Prasadji got in and slid closer to Tara to be able to talk with her. He ordered the driver, 'Take us to Jaganji in Sabzi Mandi.'

As the car began to move, he edged even closer. He asked, 'So, tell me, if you have any problem, if you need anything. Don't hesitate to ask me. I'm a simple, straightforward person. I don't get much free time from all this Congress work and refugee business.'

'Thanks. I don't need anything at the moment.'

'You used to live in Lahore. That's a very progressive city. I used to visit it often.'

'Ji.'

'You want a job at a school. That can be fixed. Some educated girls have

also found jobs as stenographers. That work pays well. One can learn to
type quite quickly. I got one girl hired as a private secretary.'

'Ji, whatever work I get is fine with me.'

'No difficulty at all. Trust me. Stop worrying. It's my job to worry on
your account.' He smiled slowly, 'Punjabi women are quite adventurous.
Many Punjabi girls have done well in the cinema industry.'

Tara did not find his smile and his remarks suitable in keeping with his
important position. She did not say 'yes', but in order to be polite, made
a show of smiling back.

Prasadji said, 'I'll put in a word for you at the Indraprastha College. The
woman who's the principal is a friend of mine. There are also many other
possibilities. No shortage of work for those who want it. Don't feel depressed.'

'Ji, I have every confidence in what you say.'

Prasadji's talk ranged over many topics. The car passed through tree-lined
streets of bungalows, and came to a halt before a big house in a bazaar.
Prasadji asked Tara to wait for a couple of minutes, and went inside.

He returned twenty minutes later. The driver said the moment he saw
Prasadji, 'I've been told to bring the car back by 11.30 by bade sahib. He
has to go Shahdara.'

'Never mind. I'll explain things to him,' Prasadji replied, straightening
his cap as he looked into the rear-view mirror over the dashboard.

'It's not so simple, sahib! Bade sahib will give me hell,' the driver said,
rather disrespectfully.

'Well, then drop us off at Connaught Place. I'll get a taxi later,' Prasadji
said irritably. Moving a little closer to Tara, he said, 'So, tell me more. It
must be hard to pass the time alone at the camp.'

'Ji?' Tara was unsure of his meaning.

'There's Nari Kala Mandir. It's a large and well-run institution. They've
a school, and give arts and crafts courses.' He also mentioned some other
organizations.

The car was now on a smooth, broad road bordering a large, well-
maintained garden. A row of splendid buildings, just like those on the Mall
Road in Lahore, flanked the road. The Mall Road was a place in Lahore
for ordinary, middle-class people just to promenade and do some window
shopping. Only the rich and the city's elite could afford to shop there.
Tara felt embarrassed at going to visit a school situated in such elegant
surroundings in her crumpled, drab dhoti.

'Where should I let you off?' asked the driver.

'Right here.'

The driver stopped the car in front of one of the buildings in a large circular plaza, and Prasadji and Tara got out. The driver left immediately, without waiting for further instructions.

Seeing the grand building with its columns and broad veranda, Tara had imagined it to be a part of a major college or institution. As she stepped into the veranda, she saw shops with huge windows and glass-panelled doors. Tara thought to herself, why had she been brought here?'

Prasadji was giving a running commentary, 'How do you like this place? This is Connaught Place, the centre of New Delhi; just like the Mall Road in your Lahore. It really comes alive in the evening. You can hardly walk because there are so many people. I'll bring you here some evenings. Come, let's have a cup of coffee. I'm sure you like coffee.'

'Ji, I don't particularly feel like it at the moment.'

But Prasadji did not seem to notice Tara's reluctance, guided her through the revolving door of a restaurant, and followed her inside.

Heavy curtains on the windows blocked out the daylight, and muted lighting gave the restaurant interior an aura of mystery. Prasadji led Tara to a corner sofa. He removed his Gandhi cap, and placed it on the arm of the sofa. The restaurant was nearly deserted. A young couple sat close together on another corner sofa, and a man alone at one table.

'What would you like to have with your coffee?' asked Prasadji as a bearer approached.

'Ji, nothing at this time.'

'Have something. I didn't have any breakfast,' said Prasadji. 'Had to go to Indraprastha and Kingsway Camp early in the morning. There's so much work that sometimes I get no time to eat. What do you think of this place? Lahore used to have quite a few fancy restaurants.'

'Ji, this is very nice,' replied Tara. She had not been to a fashionable restaurant more than four or five times. The Blue Nile, where they were, appeared to be more intimate and better appointed than the Standard Restaurant of Lahore.

Prasadji ordered a plate of vegetable sandwiches.

Tara had had nothing to eat since morning, but she had already declined the offer of food. She was hungry, but just didn't feel like eating. She felt a bit peeved about being brought to a restaurant on the pretext of going to some school in search of a job. When Prasadji kept insisting, she had two pastries and a sandwich. These whetted her appetite, but she did not accept anything more.

Prasadji tried again to console her, 'Why are you so glum? You should be more cheerful.' He reassured her that she had nothing to worry about. Tara was feeling uncomfortable with his toothy smile and the way he gazed into her eyes, but she was also careful not to alienate him. 'He's the vice-president of the camp, and holds some position in the Congress Party…' Keeping her eyes downcast, she repeated 'ji, ji' and made an effort to smile.

As they came out of the restaurant, she realized that the car that had brought her here was gone. How would she get back to her camp in this unfamiliar city? From the driver's remarks she guessed that the car had been borrowed. She wanted to go back, but Prasadji continued to walk unconcernedly, talking about Connaught Place. Many young hawkers had laid out small displays of their ware at the base of the tall columns in the veranda. Some sold items of haberdashery; others had bindis and similar adornments for women, or candies and toffees. They were all boys like Sadhu Ram from Banti's village, Tara noticed. Everything was allowed to boys, but not to girls like her.

Prasadji turned suddenly into a large store selling clothes. Tara could not stand alone outside and wait, so she followed him inside. Without looking at any of the salesmen, Prasadji walked towards a man sitting on a desk at the back of the store. Hearing his name called, the man got up and came forward. Prasadji placed his hand on the man's shoulder and whispered something. The man glanced at Tara. Both of them went to one of the shelves, and selected a sari with a floral pattern. The sari was packed in a bag and handed to Prasadji. Tara did not see him pay for it. He and Tara came out of the store.

As he was walking along the veranda, Prasadji held out the bag to Tara, 'Have a look, and tell me what you think.'

Tara took the bag and, without removing the sari, examined the part that she could see at the top of the bag. 'It's nice, very pretty. I don't know much about clothes.'

'How much do you suppose it cost?'

'I can't guess,' she held out the bag to give it back to Prasadji.

'This is for you.'

'No, I won't accept it. I have plenty of clothes,' Tara said in a firm tone of voice.

'Wah, how can you do that? I got it for you.' Prasadji refused to take the sari back.

Several times Tara tried to give him back the sari, repeating in a quiet voice that she did not need it, and that she nevertheless appreciated his efforts to help her, but Prasadji refused to listen. Tara was helpless. How could she create a scene in the middle of the bazaar? She muttered 'Thanks' and kept the bag.

Prasadji turned into a doorway in the veranda that led to a lane. He said, 'Come, let me show you my office.'

Beside a staircase was a signboard with the name of some agency. Tara did not have time to read the name. Upstairs, a man sat working at a desk in a room that had been partitioned in two. There were three or four empty chairs. The man stood up on seeing Prasadji.

Prasadji, his hands searching for something in the pockets of his kurta, asked the man a few questions in a low voice, then turned to Tara and said, 'Come along, come inside.' He turned back to the man and said, 'Bring me today's mail.'

On the other side of the partition was a takht, with a mattress covered with a bedspread. And two armchairs. On a shelf were a surahi, earthen water pot, an electric hot plate, and a few other items that a single person might use from time to time.

The secluded half of the room made Tara uneasy. She said, 'I'll sit on the other side. Finish up your work, and I'll take my leave of you.'

Prasadji took out a key and opened a cupboard. Rummaging through it, he said, 'No, no. You relax here. I'll work on the other side. Make yourself at home and stretch out on the takht.' He turned on the ceiling fan, and went back to the other half of the room.

Tara took a chair. She was angry at herself for coming to this unfamiliar place with a rogue in her eagerness to have a job. She shuddered at the memory of an incident from her past. Here she might have to contend with a human being, not an animal, but still it had been foolish to come to this place. 'The need for a job is really ....'

She heard Prasadji speak to his assistant angrily. Then the sound of the handset of a telephone being lifted, and Prasadji voice, 'Jairamji ki, Bhaiyaa sahib.' From what Tara overheard, she understood that Prasadji was asking to borrow someone's car.

Tara was sitting sideways in the armchair. For several minutes no sound came from the other half of the room. It was pleasant to sit under the slowly turning fan. She closed her eyes, and her thoughts drifted back to the events of the past two months. She had been drowned in the ocean of mischance, sunk to its deepest depths, and had still survived. Now her feet had touched the ground. The thought of what might happen next made her throat tighten. 'Where are my father, mother, brothers and sisters? Probably in some camp. They'll all be safe if they somehow made it to UP. Bhai was to go to Nainital after my wedding. Wonder what became of bhai's friendship with Kanak? Anyway, I've come this far, and now I'll find a foothold somehow. Doctor Shyama didn't come back to the camp. Vimalji and Shyma are the only two decent ones in that lot. This Prasad is a nasty character. Why is he taking so much time? What will the women at the hut think?'

She heard the ticking of a clock and looked towards the sound. A small timepiece on the shelf showed seven minutes past one.

She again closed her eyes, and shifted her position to rest her back. 'I'll wait only until a quarter past one,' she was thinking. 'I'll find my way back somehow. A tonga will cost eight or twelve annas; at the most a rupee.' She thought of Banti... then of Dev in Amritsar and his family....

Tara felt someone touch her hair. She opened her eyes and straightened up with a start.

Prasadji was sitting on the arm of the chair, smiling as he caressed Tara's hair. 'You've slept in the chair, and not on the takht?' he said, caressing Tara's cheek.

Tara pushed his hand aside and stood up, 'I want to leave. I have to finish my work at the camp.'

'Arrey, what's the hurry? The car'll be here in another fifteen or twenty minutes. Sit down.'

'Ji, no. I'd like to go. I don't want to trouble you any more. Just tell me how to get back.'

Tara refused to sit down. Prasadji walked downstairs with her, explaining on the way, 'From the Odeon cinema there, you can find transport to any part of the city. It's two annas up to the Fountain. From there, another six paisa or two annas to Kashmiri Gate and the Law Courts. I'll come to the camp sometime. Just don't worry.'

A tonga was hailing fares near the Odeon cinema. Prasadji told Tara to sit in it. Three seats were already taken. When she was seated, he put the bag with the sari in her lap.

After the tonga had begun to move along an unfamiliar road with its load of strangers, Tara breathed a sigh of relief for having slipped through the fingers of a rogue. The tonga went at a brisk clip on the smooth, metalled road in the bright sunshine of October.

As Tara walked to the hut, she was conscious of the bag with the sari in her hand. She had not been able find a chance to throw it away. And what purpose would be served by throwing it away? Before entering the hut, she concealed the bag under the aanchal of her sari.

Prasanno had spread out the washing on the electric cable strung between bamboo poles, and was keeping watch so that no one would walk away with the clothes. She called out when she saw Tara, 'Bahina, you were away a long time. Nihaldei and her daughter went out after eating lunch. They left your share in that covered pot over there.'

Tara hid the bag under her clothes wrapped in the blanket. She asked Prasanno for her lota, and washed her hands and face. Then she took out her lunch out from Nihaldei's corner, ate it, and went over to the camp office.

Tara managed to keep the bag away from the eyes of the women during the evening and night. In the morning, after she had washed, she took the blanket back from Prasanno and was rolling it around her clothes when Nihaldei's eyes fell on the bag.

'What did you buy?' Nihaldei was full of curiosity.

'Oh, it's nothing.'

Nihaldei could not resist. She quickly reached for the bag, and took out the sari. 'It's brand new. How did you pay for this?'

'Let it go. It's nothing.'

'Hai, what's the harm in telling us how much it cost? Do you suppose we'll pinch it?'

How could Tara say that she paid ten or twelve rupees for the sari when she had already told the women that she only had very little money?

Nihaldei was piqued when Tara did not reply. She threw down the sari on Tara's chatai, 'If you didn't buy it then who gave it to you?'

'Who could give me that?' Tara tried to retrieve the situation, 'The same people as are giving everything else. The camp people. Who else?'

Such unfair and partial treatment by the camp officials infuriated Nihaldei, 'Are the camp people your family? They send you these blankets, saris, sheets and soap, and make so many excuses when we ask for a couple of handfuls of flour.'

Dhammo's mother-in-law joined in, 'Yes, it's true. We've been here for almost a month now. I never saw the camp people give anybody such expensive clothes. Without some good reason no one gives anything to anybody, nor does anyone accept.'

Tara said irritably, 'Why do you keep picking on me? You too can go and ask them. I didn't beg for anything. Don't I work all day at the office copying out lists from the register?'

Prasanno was dunking pieces of last night's chapatti in the cup of tea that she bought for one anna, and feeding it to her son. She said in support of Tara, 'Yes, she's right. Feeling jealous of someone's good luck does no good. She helps out at their office. Anyone who works hard, who's got some brains, gets a reward. Good-for-nothings like us get what we deserve. Why should we envy someone's good fortune?'

Nihaldei was furious, 'Arrey, she might be a mem or princess to her family. What a great beauty, what a houri she is! Don't I know about these camp people! Heaven knows what she does with them in that tent! And all we're good for is to cook her meals and feed her.'

Prasanno protested, 'That is a load of rubbish! You, a mother and daughter gobble up your own rations and hers too, and then accuse her like this. I saw you sell extra flour to Kamalo for four annas!'

Nihaldei shouted curses at Prasanno, and took out Tara's ration card and tossed it away. When she told Prasanno to go and get herself and her houri friend fixed up at the camp office and how to have it done, Tara had to close her ears in embarrassment.

Prasanno was not the one to be cowed by the woman's aggressive attitude. She yelled back, calling Nihaldei a low-caste, 'Who do you think you are? I'll pull your tongue out!' She accused Sukhdet of debauchery, and tried to grab Nihaldei by her hair.

Sukhdet, surprisingly, had so far stayed out of the squabble. She raised her finger and warned, 'I said nothing to nobody. Don't drag me into this, or else!' She shouted at her mother, 'What's it to you what she does? Why do you interfere?'

Nihaldei screamed at her daughter, 'You can put up with their abuse if you like! Do you think I'm scared of them?'

Tara picked up her ration card, and was about to set out for the camp office. Prasanno held out her hand, 'Listen, bahin, give me your card. You are not cut out for this type of work.'

Nihaldei blew up at Tara. 'Go and tattle on us to your boyfriends at the office,' she bellowed. 'I know you'd have us thrown out of the camp if you only could. Let's see what you can do. I'll call a meeting of all camp people to decide this matter. Why are sluts like you allowed in this camp? I'll ask them. Just you come back and I'll cut off your hair.'

It was well past the noon hour. Tara heard someone say in the other half of the tent, 'It's two o'clock. I'm going out for lunch.'

Tara had been feeling hungry for some time, but the thought of the pugnacious Nihaldei was holding her back. Then she thought, how long would she be able to live in fear like this? Complaining to the officials meant more humiliation, and everyone in the camp would hear about it. She'd have to go back sooner or later. What would she do in the evening?

The situation had taken another turn, she found, when she returned to the hut. Nihaldei was not in her corner. Prasanno, Dhammo and her mother-in-law, and Rikkho were talking agitatedly. Only the old woman from Gujranwala lay curled up on her chatai.

Prasanno immediately told Tara that there had been no sign of Sukhdet since morning. Nihaldei had looked everywhere in the camp for her. They all knew that Sukhdet used to meet on the sly a boy from Jadanwala in section five. One day, the boy's sister-in-law had come over to the hut and threatened Nihaldei that they would get Sukhdet's legs broken if she even came near their hut.

There was still no trace of Sukhdet when Tara returned in the afternoon. Nihaldei came and sat beside Tara. Her eyes were puffed up from crying, 'You yourself saw it. My daughter was so simple and naïve. That boy from the Arora family from Jadanwala was after her life. He must have lured away my innocent girl. Should we ask the camp officials for help? My girl will be ruined. Who else can I ask but you, bahin?'

Dhammo's mother-in-law said to no one in particular, 'No matter what you do, this thing will bring you shame and scandal. She was a young woman, not a girl. Her husband had left her. Whoever sweet-talked her, she would go to him. The young give in to their impulses. If the insects that live on grass and muck, and four-footed cattle can't control their urges, how can she, who was brought up on grain and ghee? She needed a man. How could staying with her mother satisfy her? The Arora family says that she was the one who lured away their boy. A twenty-year-old man is still a boy. Such things don't happen without the consent of the female....' The old woman was settling old scores with Nihaldei.

There was a big hullabaloo around eight in the evening. The boy's family came to the hut to accuse Nihaldei of helping her daughter to elope with their innocent son. The boy had stolen three hundred and fifty rupees from his brother's trunk.

No camp official was in the office at that hour.

The representatives of camp residents held a meeting and warned the two families, 'All we know is that the girl and boy are equally to blame. Why didn't the girl's mother keep a tighter rein on her? She used to wander around the camp like a motherless calf. We all have daughters and sons. We don't approve of such scandals. Don't make trouble here. Go and report the matter to the police if you want. If you cause a ruckus here, we'll throw you and your stuff out of the camp.'

Gloom prevailed in the hut for two days. Sukhdet was not found; and who was there to go and look for her? The women talked in whispers or behind Nihaldei's back. Tara had worries of her own and tried to lose herself in the work of copying the lists. She had done all 113 pages, but new names were added each day, and there were twenty more pages.

Tara returned to the hut for lunch. The women were still discussing Sukhdet's disappearance. Dhammo's mother-in-law was saying, 'That girl was bound to do something like that. Attractive single women have no problem in finding someone. There's no shortage of men willing to take them in. It's different for those who have children, or old hags like us.' Tara did not like her comments. She looked at Rikkho.

Rikkho was about to say something in protest, but kept quiet when she heard a commotion outside the hut. There were loud shouts, 'Hey you! Come here! Over there.' The women rushed to the entrance of the hut and peered out.

They saw two men wearing suits and hats, and some police officers. Several constables were going around busily between the rows of huts. The women were scared. The police had come to investigate Sukhdet's disappearance, they thought grimly. Who knew what the police might do to them?

A group of men and women appeared, and began to sweep the ground with brooms. Vimalji and Prasadji, with some other men, were seen approaching rapidly. One of them ordered the washing hanging on the electric cable to be removed at once. Two constables came and inquired how many people were in Tara's hut. They withdrew after being told that the hut was for women only.

A thorough checking of the huts and the residents seemed to be going on. Tara did not go to the camp office. Another group of camp officials moved in and out of the row of huts.

Doctor Shyama came into Tara's hut with another woman. They both wore sunglasses, their bodies and clothes carried the fragrance of different perfumes. They looked distinct and of a very different status from the women of the hut who wore crumpled, old and dirty clothes.

Shyama saw Tara and spoke to her in English, 'Hello, how are you? No more problems, I hope? I was in the camp office on Wednesday. Vimalji said that Prasadji had taken you to the Indraprastha College. Any luck there?'

'Ji, nothing came of it,' Tara replied meekly in English. 'Please find me some work, any type of work. I am also ready to work as a nurse.'

Shyama said to her companion, 'Tara is a graduate, from a good family. Mrs Agarwal, you should do something for her.'

Mrs Agarwal was of stout build, and a rather dark complexion. Sweat had made tiny furrows in the layer of talcum powder covering her fleshy neck. She took off her sunglasses as she adjusted the heavy kundan pendant of her gold necklace, and looked at Tara closely, 'I'll think about it. Is her English fluent?'

'Tara is a graduate,' Shayma interrupted Mrs Agarwal, and continued in English, 'She has really been through a great deal. She's a courageous and responsible young woman.'

Mrs Agarwal nodded as she looked into Tara's eyes, 'Achcha, I'll speak to her later.'

Shyama said to everyone, 'Listen, the Prime Minister is coming to inspect the camp. All of you have to arrange and store your belongings neatly. Change clothes if you have any others. If anyone of you has any complaints to make, you can tell me or Mrs Agarwal here. We'll explain things properly on your behalf. Or you can tell Tara, and she'll convey it to us.' Shyama and Mrs Agarwal left to visit other huts.

In their hut only Tara fully understood the reason for the feverish activity in the camp. She explained to others, 'Pandit Jawaharlal Nehru, the Prime Minister, the highest vizier of the country, is coming to the camp.' She felt a tremor of excitement. She had never seen Pandit Nehru, and now she would be able to see him up close. He and Mahatma Gandhi were the two biggest leaders of the country. Intrigued by the hectic activity in the camp, the women stood in the doorway and watched the goings on curiously.

Prasadji, Vimalji and one of the men dressed in hat and suit came and stood at some distance from Tara's hut. The man asked in a loud voice, 'Does anyone here have any problems?'

'There's only one water tap for so many people,' said a voice.

'Water tap? All right, we'll put in another.'

'The deputy commissioner sahib says that he will have another faucet installed by tomorrow,' Vimalji reassured them.

Prasadji added, 'You are our own people. We try to serve you as best as we can. If you have any problems or complaints, you can tell me or to Vimalji. You know that we come and meet with you everyday. Pandit Nehru has only ten minutes to visit this place, but we are always here as his representatives. Panditji will pass along the pathway between the huts. You should all stand outside your huts to have his darshan. Do not block the pathways. After that Panditji will address you all for five minutes. At that time, you can assemble in front of the camp office tent. Panditji likes discipline. He does not like unruliness. When Panditji goes by your hut, stand the children in front of you. Panditji loves children.'

Prasadji came inside the hut for women and repeated his remarks. How many children were in the hut? he asked. Prasanno's four-year-old son and Dhammo's three-year-old daughter were presented to him.

Prasadji beamed with delight, 'Wah! What lovely children! But why do you keep your children so dirty? Wash their faces, change them into clean clothes. Go on! Hurry up!'

Dhammo's mother-in-law nervously took the girl away. Prasanno had no other clothes for her son. He was wearing just a kurta, and no underwear. She whispered into Tara's ear. Tara told Vimalji. After a few minutes of frenzied action, Prasanno was given a white kurta, two sizes too large, and a pair of underpants for her son. Prasanno happily washed her son's face and dressed him in his new clothes.

The camp residents were told to stand in orderly rows in front of their huts, to keep silent, and not to break ranks. All the young children wearing clean clothes were made to stand in front. Prasadji instructed the children, 'Beta, when I come with other people, you have to say "Long live Nehruji", "Chacha Nehru zindabad!"'

'Hush, hush!...Quiet, keep quiet!...He's coming!'

The camp residents looked expectantly towards the camp office, and the neat rows became bent and buckled as they eagerly craned their necks to have a better view. A hush fell over everyone. Tara's heart pounded at the importance of the occasion. She stood inconspicuously near the entrance to the hut. Prasanno's son and Dhammo's daughter stood in the front row, their hands joined in namaste.

A small group came from the direction of the camp office. Walking ahead of everyone were Prasadji and a middle-aged man with a young man's gait, smartly dressed in an achkan, churidar pajama and a Gandhi cap. A half-opened rose was stuck in the second buttonhole of the achkan. Prasadji was walking on tiptoe with his face raised, in order to be able to speak to the man. Behind them walked the deputy commissioner, police officers, Dr Shyama, Mrs Agarwal and a few others.

When the group reached in front of Tara's hut, Prasadji said, 'In this hut are the unfortunate women separated from their families.'

The Prime Minister slowed down. He leaned forward, patted the children on their heads, and asked the people in his entourage, 'Do children get milk?'

His aides and the camp officials looked at one another. Prasadji and the deputy commissioner replied in unison, 'Yes, sir.'

At the end of that row of huts, the Prime Minister turned towards the next row. An old man joined his hands and called out, 'Maharaj-ji, may you rule forever. You evicted us from our brick houses and brought us here. Give us at least some simple rooms somewhere to live. If you can't do that, why are you throwing us out of this place?'

The prime minister stopped and pulled at a button of his achkan.

Prasadji and the deputy commissioner explained something to him in a low voice.

The Prime Minister said, trying not to show his irritation, 'That's the
system, the rule for refugee camps. Every place has some kind of rules.
We can't go on supporting you for the rest of your life.'

The old man opened his mouth to add something. Others in the group
gestured to him to keep silent, and muttered to him in an undertone.

Over a hundred residents had gathered near the camp office. Prasadji's
voice came over the amplifier, 'Our most venerated Prime Minister,
brothers and sisters! It is our good fortune that the prince of all our hearts,
the pride of the nation, our leader and Prime Minister Jawaharlalji Nehru
has spared some of his invaluable time to agree to come and visit us here.
Nehruji is not only the jewel of our nation, he is among the finest jewels of
the whole world. Our country depends on him alone and on Gandhiji…'

'What's this nonsense…' the Prime Minister's voice interrupted.

He pushed Prasadji away from the microphone. Prasadji flashed a toothy
grin, and said, 'Now our most respected prime minister will say a few
words.'

The Prime Minister began, as he pulled at one of the buttons on his
achkan, 'Brothers and sisters of the camp!'

Tara felt a ripple of excitement through her body. This was the voice of
the man at the helm of the ship of state!

'Everyone, including me, knows that you have undergone terrible
sufferings. That is why I've come here to meet you and see the conditions
you are living in. Our country has gone through certain political changes,
that have had some good and some bad results. You all know this much, that
if we accept the good results, we cannot avoid the bad results. These results
are before you, you all are witness to them, but the Congress party or the
government cannot be held entirely responsible for them. Although we may
be responsible to some extent, and… and we do accept that. We consider it
our duty to help you in your difficulties, and are doing our utmost. Tell us
your problems and complaints. Who else will you tell your troubles to? The
government and the camp officials will listen to your difficulties, and will
do everything possible to help you. But you must also remember that just
like your small camp here, we have established several much larger camps
in Delhi. There are hundreds of such camps all over the country. A heavy
burden rests on our shoulders and a heavy responsibility too. You should
also not think only about your personal problems and situations. These are
very important times. Our nation and the whole world are going through

very trying times. All of us, every citizen in the country has certain grave obligations. We should not lose sight of them. We should not be narrow-minded and think only of our own personal problems. Jai Hind!'

'Jai Hind!' Prasadji shouted the slogan after him.

'Jai Hind!' The gathering responded with one voice.

'Long live Pandit Nehru!'

The crowd repeated the call.

The Prime Minister's speech, Tara realized, was over. What she heard had not inspired her. She was hoping to be overwhelmed by the words of the nation's steersman, the prince of world leaders who had captured the heart of the nation.

The crowd dispersed in a few moments.

The women in Tara's hut gathered around her and asked, 'What did the grand vizier have to say?'

Tara did not know what to tell them, and simply repeated the words of the prime minister.

'Tara, listen!'

She turned around and saw Shyama and Mrs Agarwal standing in the doorway. Tara smoothed her sari and went over to them.

'Mrs Agarwal wants to know if you can teach small children, and look after them?' asked Shyama.

'Ji, sure. I'd be able to do that quite well. I've done that kind of work. I used to tutor the children at the mansion of Raibahadur Gopal Shah in Lahore.'

'Achcha, take whatever you have with you. Go with Mrs Agarwal. You'll put up at her place.'

Tara went to her chatai to get her roll of bedding.

Chapter 4

AN IMPOSING, TWO-STOREY MANSION. A BIG CAR WAITING IN THE PORTICO. A groomed driveway of red earth curving through lush, green lawns, and well-tended flowerbeds and hedges. Servants in uniform, of white kurta and dhoti, or pajama. Tara's room was at the back of the mansion. The directions given by Mrs Agarwal accentuated the intimidating aura of her employer's status in Tara's mind.

'You see, all sorts of influential people, government officials and political leaders come to this house. Be careful always to dress properly. What sort of wardrobe do you have?'

She had three dhotis, Tara said. And that she would take care to dress as befitted the importance of her employer.

She waited in her room for instructions. A maidservant brought a small bundle of laundered and ironed clothes. She salaamed Tara with a smile, showing teeth blackened from chewing paan and tobacco, and said, 'Miss sahib, you must be the new governess for Puttan and Lalli.'

Tara welcomed this opportunity to know something about the family by being friendly to the maid. She smiled back, 'Yes.'

The maid said enthusiastically, 'Miss Edward sahib used to work here. She wore a skirt. She found job at a school. A foreigner Miss sahib works as the governess at Chausia sahib's house. You are our own desi Miss sahib. The mistress has sent some of her own clothes for you.'

Tara was keeping careful watch to learn how things were done in the household. She changed into a white dhoti, combed her hair in front of the mirror of a small dressing table in the room, and sat down in a chair so as not to crumple her sari. She reflected on how she would go about her duties carefully and conscientiously.

The maid came back after half an hour, and said, 'Sahib and madam will see you in the drawing room.'

Mr Agarwal sat on a corner sofa, in a white shirt and trousers, and smoking a cigarette. Mrs Agarwal sat on another sofa to his right. Tara entered the room with her hands joined in namaste. Sahib was about to rise from his chair, then thought otherwise, and pointing to a sofa across from him, said, 'Please have a seat.'

He asked, 'With whom did you work in Lahore?'

'Ji, I used to tutor the children at Rai Bahadur Gopal Shah's mansion. Professor Pran Nath was quite satisfied with my tutoring work.'

'I knew the rai bahadur. Who is this Professor Nath?' Mr Agarwal asked, wrinkling his forehead.

'Ji, Doctor Pran Nath was the economic advisor to the governor of Punjab, and a professor at the university. He was the grandson of the rai bahadur.'

The wrinkles disappeared from sahib's forehead. He paused to draw on his cigarette, 'How many children?'

'Three. A three-and-a-half-year-old girl, one four-and-a-half, and one five-year-old boy. They were nieces and nephews of the professor. I followed the Montessori method to tutor them.'

'Hmm... You lived with them?'

'Ji, no. I lived with my family. I was preparing for the university exam.'

'Well, we'll give you accommodation here as well. You'll have your meals with the children, and to start with we'll pay you seventy-five rupees per month. Is that all right with you?'

'Whatever you offer is fine with me,' Tara replied, and added, 'I'll think of Mrs Agarwal as an elder sister or mother.'

'Why, you must be around twenty-two or twenty-three,' Madam cut in.

'Ji, that's right,' Tara said, and realized that Madam didn't want to be considered as old enough to be her mother.

The sound of a child's playful giggle came from outside the room. Mrs Agarwal asked Shivni, the maid, to bring the children in. A four-year-old girl wearing a frock and a six-year-old boy in shirt and shorts, wriggling in embarrassment, came in. Another, older boy looked in and scampered off.

'Come back here, Bhupi bhaiyaa. Mummy's calling you.' Shivni's pleading had no effect.

'She's your new Miss. Her name is Tara,' Madam said to the children.

Tara smilingly held out her arms towards the children. The boy shrank away from her touch, and began to play with burnt matchsticks in an ashtray on a side table. The girl hid her face shyly in her mother's lap.

Madam tried cajoling the children into talking to Tara, 'Puttan, Lalli! She's Miss Tara, the same as your former governess Miss Edwards. She'll take care of you, and teach you many things. She knows lots of ways to have fun.'

'Yes, child. I know lots of fun things. Come to me,' Tara said affectionately to them.

The boy again turned his face away shyly, and remained where he was. Lalli shook her head and said, 'She's not a Miss. She's aunty.'

'Oh dear! How sweet!' Tara said cheerfully. Tara used to make fun of the accent and ways of speech of her convent-school-educated friends. Now she spoke like them.

'Hai, why isn't she a Miss?' Madam asked.

'She's not a Miss, she's an aunt,' the girl again shook her head and insisted.

'A Miss wears a skirt,' Puttan spoke up.

'Wonderful! How intelligent!' Tara's praise of the children had a good effect on both parents.

Madam put her arm affectionately around her daughter and said, 'Darling, recite that poem for Miss Tara.'

Lalli buried her face again in her mother's lap. Madam promised her rewards of lollipop and ice cream. Her brother also encouraged her.

Lalli stood like a little doll.

'Chubby cheeks,' she put her fingers to her dusky cheeks.

'Rosy lips,' she moved a finger to her lips.

'Dimpled chin,' she touched her non-existent chin, them hid her face again in her mother's lap.

After some prompting from Puttan, she said touching her short, bobbed hair, 'Curly hair.'

'Very fair,' she recited, pointing to her face.

'Eyes blue,' she fluttered eyelids over dark eyes.

'Mother's pet, is that you!' Puttan finished the poem for her.

'Very good! How lovely! Very sweet!' Tara patted the children on their backs to win them over.

Mrs Agarwal explained a few ground rules to Tara, and left the rest for her to pick up herself. Tara moulded herself carefully into the lifestyle of the AA villa. Madam desperately wanted her children to speak English always and to learn the social etiquette of the British. She found it frustrating not to be able to speak English fluently at the club and at social gatherings. She had noticed that although the country had become independent, it was only those people who could not speak English who spoke Hindi. She wanted her daughter to be able to recite and act out nursery rhymes in English. Her nine-year-old son Bhupi was in the second standard, and Dolly, the eldest daughter was in the sixth. Bhupi and Dolly did not consider themselves to be children, but it was Tara's responsibility to decide on their daily diet, and to look after the laundering and ironing of their clothes.

As instructed by Mrs Agarwal, Tara told the children to come to the dining room at 7.30. Bhupi arrived a little after the others. Tara tried to pat him affectionately on the head, but he hunched his shoulders and pulled in his neck like a turtle. He sat at some distance from the other two at the dining table.

Dolly did not come for dinner, but sent a message through Shivni, 'I don't have dinner so early.' But she could not suppress her curiosity about the new governess, and hovered near the dining room as Tara and the children were coming out. Dolly wore salwar and kameez with her dupatta of some gauze-like material, twisted like a rope, thrown casually over her shoulders.

Dolly put her hands on her hips and pushed her shoulders back to show Tara that she was not a child. Then she said in English in a bossy tone, 'You're to work as governess to these children? They're really spoilt!' She asked, 'You have a BA? Can you speak English fluently?'

'I try to get by,' Tara said with a smile. 'If you wish, I'll speak to you only in English. You would prefer that. Am I right?'

Next day, just after the noon hour, Dolly asked Tara, 'Do you go to watch English movies?'

'I haven't been to one in quite a while. I'm new to this city.'

'They're showing *Nolly's First Experience* at the Regal. Tickets are not sold to anybody under eighteen. Will you go with me?' She said, with a touch of pleading.

'Let me think about it, dear,' Tara replied after a moment's consideration. She was now in the habit of weighing up every answer carefully.

Besides the people Tara had been introduced to, there was also the children's grandmother. Like Tara, she lived in a room at the back of the house. The grandmother was devoutly Hindu, and the decadent goings-on in the rest of the house disgusted her. The kitchen was her area of influence. She sat on a moodha of reed and jute in the scullery to make sure that the cook, Shivni and the other servants washed their hands regularly. She inquired about everyone's caste. On her second morning with the family, Tara had greeted her with 'Maaji, pranaam,' which pleased the old woman immensely.

There was another member of the family, someone who appeared to be a university student, and who had deliberately ignored Tara on her first evening. Lalli and Puttan had called out on seeing him, 'Bhaiyyaji has arrived.' The servants treated him with respect.

Tara again saw him in the veranda next day as she ushered the children to the dining room for lunch. She said namaste to him, and lowered her eyes before he could respond. In the evening Tara was with Lalli and Puttan as they played badminton on the lawn, when she heard the roar of a motorbike and looked towards the noise. The young man on the motorbike waved at her. Tara waved back. She had learned by that time that Nottan— Narottam bhaiyya—was the eldest son of the family, and had had his education in England. The grandmother had told Tara that Dolly and Narottam were the children of Mr Agarwal's first wife. Tara and Narottam had had no occasion to speak to each other beyond exchanging namastes.

Tara had been hired at the AA villa as a governess for the children, but she was asked to undertake several other tasks before her first week was over. The children left for their convent schools at seven in the morning, and returned at half past one. This young woman would sit around idly until then, thought the mistress of the house, but she was being paid for the whole day. She had not failed to notice that Tara could manage and supervise others quite efficiently.

Mrs Agarwal had given Tara two of her blouses, and Tara asked her permission to use the sewing machine to alter the blouses to her own measurements. Madam realized that Tara was quite clever with needlework as well.

Mrs Agarwal now had ample time to do social work. When she went out, she would ask Tara to answer the telephone, 'These servants don't know how to take messages.' Sometimes she would ask Tara to mend some garments from her own wardrobe. Tara soon began to relax and feel comfortable in her new lifestyle. She had enough spare time to read two English and one Hindi newspaper. She was not dissatisfied with the present arrangement. She did not want to begin worrying again about her future, but the thought of what she would do with her life would cross her mind now and then. It might be possible to pass her BA exam, and find a job to become self-supporting.

Mr Agarwal's office was in Connaught Place, on the second floor, and he kept another, smaller office at his residence. What madam had said about the different types of people who came to visit, Tara found, was quite correct. The guests were welcomed according to their social standing and importance. Some were asked to wait on the wicker chairs in the veranda, while others were ushered into the drawing room. Some special friends and intimates, who came in the evenings, were entertained by Mr Agarwal in a drawing room upstairs. Shivni and Jugal, the cook, were kept especially busy at such times. Madam did not mind meeting or mingling with the visitors. If some special or distinguished visitor arrived, she quickly went to her room to change her sari, touch up her face and comb her hair. Tara soon sensed that Madam did not like her mingling with the guests.

One afternoon, Tara was playing with Puttan and Lalli in the veranda to the right of the main entrance to keep them amused when the family's second car drove into the portico. Prasadji stepped out, and seeing Tara, came towards her. Tara said namaste to him.

'Arrey, you're here?' Prasadji exclaimed. Then he expressed approval, 'Very good! Very nice! I had spoken about you at the Nari Kala Mandir, but what you've found is certainly better. We'll be meeting one another here. Where's Mrs Agarwal? Isn't she ready yet?'

Prasadji looked at his wrist watch. They were going to Mahatma Gandhi's prayer meeting at Birla House. He patted Puttan's cheek, 'Where's mummy? Go quickly and get her.'

Puttan ran inside.

Prasadji stood ogling at Tara as he spoke, 'This is really nice. You look so much better since you came here. No one can look a picture of health as you Punjabis. Good food also makes a difference.'

Madam came out, straightening her khadi sari, 'I've been waiting so long. I sent the car to fetch you at four.'

Prasadji bid Tara an abrupt farewell, 'See you again,' as he and Mrs Agarwal went to the waiting car.

Lalli screamed as she got up to run after her mother.

Tara quickly gathered the child in her arms. Lalli whined in protest, and flailed her legs to break free. She was not dressed to go out. And what was the point in taking her to the Mahatma's prayer meeting?

'Miss will give you a lollipop. Miss Tara, you give Lalli a big lollipop,' madam said as the car drove away. There was no lollipop in the house for the child, and that created a problem for Tara. Tara sometimes took care of her young brother and sisters in Lahore, and if they misbehaved, she felt compelled to give them a slap or box their ears. But at the AA villa, that, of course, was out of question.

At the villa, the furniture, ornaments and collection of various objects d'art and knick-knacks in both drawing rooms and the main dining room were in keeping with modern fashionable taste. Mrs Agarwal wanted to be seen as a thoroughly modern woman, but she lacked the training and the patience to acquire a discriminating eye. Her children were rather spoiled. The children had found that they could get away with anything by being stubborn, and by throwing a temper tantrum. Madam would first say no to them, then try to distract them with bribes of candies, and then threaten to shut them up in a cellar full of rats or give them away to the man who came with the dancing bear. In the end, she would curse them and yield to their demands. Shivni spoiled the children even more by praising them for their self-willed attitude in front of their mother.

Tara's work of supervising the children was made even more difficult. Out of loyalty to her employer and as a conscientious tutor, she did not consider it right to bribe the children or to make empty promises. She considered this an unsophisticated approach, and did not want to set a bad example by lying to them. The governess before her had left behind some books on education and the rearing of children. Tara went through them. But she realized that if she followed the scientific method and taught the children according to proper techniques, this might bring her into a conflict with her employers. She would fret inwardly: How do I bring to line in a few days children spoilt over years? In order not to appear a failure before madam, she sometimes had to resort to unscientific and unsound teaching techniques.

At 7.30 in the morning, Puttan and Lalli left in the bus of their convent school, and Bhupi and Dolly in another school bus. Sahib and madam would still be in their bedroom upstairs at that time. They usually came down for breakfast at 8.30. Tara sat in a wicker chair in the veranda glancing through the morning newspapers. She looked up when she heard the sound of footsteps. Narottam, a dressing gown over his striped nightwear, was coming towards her.

Tara rose from the chair, said namaste, and held out the dailies to him.

'No, no. I'm sorry if I disturbed you. There's no hurry. You finish with them first,' Narottam said courteously.

'Thank you, sir. I'll read them later. You can have them,' Tara said out of deference to the chotey sahib.

'No, no. Please continue,' Narottam pointed to the dew drops shining on the grass. 'Just look at the dew. The weather has changed, but the sun is still hot during the day. You go on reading; I can read the papers later.' He smiled and nodded at her, turned around and went back.

Their first conversation had amounted to only a few words, but Tara already knew a lot more about him from his mother.

Mrs Agarwal had given Tara some blouses that were not altogether to her liking as their tailoring was defective. Tara had altered them to her size, but felt a little uncomfortable wearing blouses cut high according to the fashion. She had never before worn anything so stylish. She had seen Dr Shyama and many other women in Delhi wearing similar blouses. When madam saw how expertly Tara had altered the blouses, she said, praising Tara's skill, 'Those damned tailors charge five rupees for each blouse, and ruin the cloth in the bargain. I feel so uneasy when they take my measurements. I have so many blouses that I don't wear.' She got the blouses out, and put them on to show to Tara how badly and loosely they fitted.

Mrs Agarwal had put on weight around her waist. Tara pointed out that blouses were badly cut, and offered to sew her a new blouse.

Mrs Agarwal immediately asked Shivni to get a piece of cloth from her trunk. As she sat with Tara, discussing various styles of blouses, she began to express her disgust at the new fashions the young girls were following.

Dolly had bought a pair of jeans the day before, imitating her neighbour Mukta Sapri, and had gone to Mukta's house to play badminton wearing them. Mrs Agarwal complained, 'What's this fad for jeans! If she were a child, it would be another matter. Such tight-fitting clothes don't look good on grown-up girls. Hips, thighs and calves all stand out in them.'

Tara agreed, 'Yes, such styles are not very proper.' But thought to herself about the complaints madam had made about her own blouses not fitting well.

Mrs Agarwal grumbled on, 'If I say anything, the girl sulks, and if I don't, my husband scolds me for not being strict enough. Even if I care for and treat those two a thousand times better than my own children, the two of them will always regard me as their wicked stepmother.' She raised the subject of Narottam, 'I swear by the children I gave birth to if ever I made the slightest bias against either of them, but they never regard me as their mother. Fifty thousand rupees went on paying for his engineering studies in England. But he's holding out for a government job. Engineers in our office get paid a thousand a month, and he wants to settle for something that pays only five to six hundred!'

Such an introduction to Narottam made Tara think of him as someone eccentric, and rather conceited and arrogant, but she did not give it any further thought. She had no desire to get involved in the squabbles of her employer's family.

The grandmother thought of Tara as a decent person, and more so when she heard that she was a vegetarian. The old woman remembered her first daughter-in-law with affection and was critical of the second, 'That poor dear never stepped out of this house. The menfolk could eat anything they wanted, but she never allowed onions and garlic into her kitchen. The kitchen for meat dishes was kept totally separate. This one sits and eats with all kinds of men, doesn't observe purdah, and has no sense of decency. She's hardly ever at home. When Narottam's grandfather had built this mansion, he named it "Agarwal Ashram". These people have renamed it in the Christian style, something like "a a". What kind of name is "a a"? But what difference does it make to me; my life is nearly finished. They can do whatever they like.'

After Narottan returned to his room, and while he was shaving, he remembered that his first impression of Tara was that mummy had found a refugee as an inexpensive replacement for her children's tutor. He had not been sure if she would measure up. Now he found her to be cultured and well-spoken.

That same evening he was going through the hallway towards the staircase to his room. Puttan and Lalli saw him and called out, 'Bhaiyyaji's back.'

Narottam slowed down on seeing Tara in the dining room with the children. He asked, 'May I join you?'

'Please do,' Tara said politely.

Narottam put the two magazines he was holding down on the dining table. He took a chair, and said, 'You're very punctual. You turn up for dinner every evening at the exact time. I feel rather hungry today. Didn't have any tea in the afternoon. If it doesn't disturb you, I'll have my dinner with all of you.'

'Of course. Please join us. Would you like me to bring you something?'

Shivni was serving Tara and the children. Narottam asked her, 'What's for dinner?'

'Huzoor, Jugal hasn't prepared the regular dinner. It's what he made for the children, just soup, vegetables, daal.' Shivni said apologetically.

'Bring me whatever's ready.' Narottam picked up the magazines and turning towards Tara said, 'Do you read the *Literary Digest?* Here's the latest issue.'

'Haven't had a chance to see it for several months. My brother used to get it often. I like it, but I find that the articles in it are a bit biased. Maybe that's because I'm not very knowledgeable,' Tara said hesitatingly, as if she was being too forward.

'You're quite right. I totally agree with you. But they're well-written pieces, that's why I get it.'

'Ji. Those anecdotes at the end of the articles can be really amusing.'

'Absolutely. They're excellent, but even those aren't free of bias. Well, you can keep this issue for now. I have *Life* magazine to read. There's a good piece in it on Mexican Indians.'

Tara was using knife and fork to eat dinner with the children. She had to get up in the middle of what Narottam was saying to adjust the napkin tied around Lalli's neck.

Jugal brought Narottam's dinner in a thali.

'Excuse me, but I'll just use my fingers for eating,' Narottam apologized to Tara in a well-mannered way.

'Of course,' Tara thought Narottam's apology was directed at her use of knife and fork. 'You're not a child. That rule is only for the children.'

'As I well know.' He tried to make amends for his remark, 'Mummy's great ambition is that her children learn European ways. I was in England for five years, and I like using a knife and fork, but that depends on the type of food. It feels like a punishment to eat Indian food with a knife and fork. What do you think?'

'You're right.'

After that Tara and Narottam began to talk to each other if they happened to meet. Tara did not find him, as madam had said, to be conceited or arrogant, but more like a young man well-behaved for his age.

In the second week of November, life began to take on a faster rhythm at the villa. The annual convention of the All-India Congress Committee was to he held in Delhi. Prasadji promised Mr Agarwal that he would be one of the five vice-presidents of the Welcoming Committee, and extracted a cheque for one thousand rupees from him as a donation. Since the takeover of the government by the Congress, Mr Agarwal and other big businessmen of Delhi had become increasingly interested in the affairs of the party.

Prasadji asked Mr Agarwal to provide hospitality to two leaders of the

Congress party. A reception was also to be held for over one hundred delegates at the AA villa.

Madam pulled Tara into this whirlwind of activities at her house. Tutoring the children was put on hold. It was a matter of some relief that Narottam, to maintain the family's prestige, was also lending a hand.

There were two motor cars at the villa. One was used by Mr Agarwal, the other was for madam as she went around with Prasadji to make various arrangements. She had no time to shop for things needed at home. She called at sahib's office, and asked for one more car to be put at her disposal. She then dictated to Tara a list of things to buy, and gave her some cash. Tara had been wearing the same clothes that Madam had given her, and those now looked quite shabby. Madam gave Tara an extra fifty rupees to buy whatever clothes she wanted for herself, and told Narottam, 'Go with Tara. She doesn't know much about the best places to shop. Advise her on what kind of linen to buy.'

Narottam agreed to accompany Tara on her shopping trip.

Since her arrival at the villa, Tara had been to Connaught Place twice. Once Dolly had taken her along for shopping, and in the previous week madam had asked Tara to accompany her when she went to buy woollens for the children.

When they reached Connaught Place, Narottam asked, 'So, what do you have to buy?'

Tara said, 'Bahinji's list includes table covers, towels, bed sheets, dried fruits and a few other things. I want to get some white voile for dhotis for myself, and some wool, if possible.'

Narottam took Tara to a large cloth store. She asked to be shown some voile, and when she found a quality that she liked, she asked for some white lawn cloth for petticoats and white poplin for blouses. She mentally calculated the length of material she needed, and inquired its price. It came to more than she could afford, so she asked to be shown some less expensive voile. She did not like the quality, but told the sales assistant to cut a length for her.

'No. Cut some from the bolt you showed us first,' Narottam said to the assistant.

Tara protested, 'No, I want the second one.'

Narottam motioned to her to keep quiet, and asked the assistant for the more expensive voile. Tara did not say anything for fear of creating a scene.

When they were shown the tablecloths, towels and bed sheets, Tara wanted to check that the material carried the seal of genuine khadi.

'The seal of genuine khadi can be found only on cloth sold at the Gandhi Bhandar cloth store,' she was told.

'The Gandhi Bhandar wants to keep the monopoly and profits from khadi to themselves. That's what the East India Company did,' Narottam said jokingly.

The sales staff smiled to show that they understood the joke. Narottam picked up the packets of Tara's purchases, and said, 'Let's go to the Gandhi Bhandar.'

As they came out of the store, Tara complained, 'Why did you do that! I only had fifty rupees for myself. I had to use some of bahinji's money.'

'The voile that you picked out was of inferior quality. I've enough money. You don't have to worry.'

'Wah, why should you pay for my clothes?'

Narottam looked at Tara with mock surprise, 'Are you a disciple of Gandhi?'

'Why? What do you mean?

'Don't you get it? You'll be rewarded with a cup of coffee if you find the answer to this riddle. Whenever I come to Connaught Place, I have coffee at the Blue Nile. Let's go there.' Narottam was making fun, just like Tara's friends from the Student Federation in Lahore.

There were many other restaurants in Connaught Place, but by sheer chance Narottam had invited Tara to the Blue Nile. She had been once before to the same restaurant with Prasadji, at about the same time of day. Tara remembered her desperate need to find a job. That day also, a sari had been forced upon her. By coincidence, Tara was wearing the same sari today. She sighed inwardly at the painful memory. Today instead of feeling desperate, she was laughing and joking.

Tara said in the same spirit of fun, 'I didn't solve the riddle, so I shouldn't accept your coffee.'

'Well, you have to accept it because you couldn't solve it.'

'First tell me the riddle.'

'It's simply that you believe in non-cooperation.'

'Non-cooperation? With whom?'

'Well, you used the money that I had on me. Tomorrow if I'm short, I'll naturally ask you.'

'That means it's a loan,' Tara said.

'With interest, if you insist.'

Tara said with a smile, 'I don't ask for any interest, but I'll accept a commission for safekeeping.'

'Well, your insistence on genuine khadi showed that you believe in Gandhi's philosophy. But what if mummy doesn't like this genuine khadi?'

'She's the one who asked for it.'

'Really?' Narottam's eyebrows went up in surprise, 'Is that so? She actually asked for it just to show off in front of the Congress leaders. Do you know what she used to do during the war? I was in the UK then. I came home for two months, and saw that mummy used to go to the Knitting Club.'

'Which club?'

'The Knitting Club, a club for knitting woollens. They used to get together to knit sweaters, socks and suchlike as a show of their support and admiration for the soldiers at the front. Or you might say, to show their loyalty to the British. It was a nice hoax. The vicerene would invite wealthy society ladies once a week, sometimes to the bungalow of the chief secretary, sometimes to Government House to knit for the soldiers for about an hour. The Club had a session at Chausia Sahib's bungalow, so mummy had to organize a party at her own house. About thirty to thirty-five ladies showed up. The party must have cost her between a hundred fifty to two hundred rupees. How much they could have knitted in one hour, you can well imagine.

'Then we had Latif, our Muslim bearer. He's gone to Pakistan. He would give wool to some poor woman and pay her a rupee or a rupee and a half to knit a sweater. Mummy then passed it on to the Club. Now it's the turn of genuine khadi. Of course, when mummy goes to Gandhiji's prayer meeting, she puts on a khadi sari.'

After going to the Gandhi Bhandar, Narottam said to the driver, 'Take us to the dried fruit store.'

'Huzoor, memsahib asked me to take you to the Khari Bawli bazaar for dried fruits. Here they charge double the price,' the driver replied.

'Well, now. She didn't tell you to go to Kabul or Kandahar? It would be even cheaper there,' Narottam glanced at Tara.

'Let's do as bahinji said,' Tara suggested.

'As you wish. What can I say?' Narottam shrugged his shoulders in resignation.

The car drove towards Khari Bawli by way of Ajmeri Gate. On the left, alongside the fenced-in railway tracks, were row after row of refugees under shelters made of reeds and straw.

'You see that?' Narottam asked Tara. 'The Congress government bangs the drum for Gandhiji's ideals, but never listens to what he says. Gandhiji said that if the refugees couldn't find shelter, they should be housed at the Viceregal Palace and in the bungalows of the government ministers. Lord Mountbatten agreed, either out of compassion or for diplomatic reasons, but the leaders of the Congress party refused to oblige.'

The car was crawling through the Khari Bawli bazaar because of the heavy traffic of handcarts, trucks and tramcars, and the crowds of pedestrians. The air was thick with the pungent smell of spices. Tara could not stop herself from sneezing, 'I'm sorry.' Narottam sneezed even louder, 'I'm sorry, too.'

'What are these queues for?' Narottam asked the driver.

'Huzoor, for sugar rations, from the government shop. Huzoor, in the morning the queue is sometimes half a mile long.'

Narottam said to Tara, 'If there's such a shortage of sugar, why don't they forbid the use of sugar for non-essential use? Just one mithai shop uses up in one day so much sugar as might do for a whole mohalla. And only those people can afford mithai who are already overloaded with carbohydrates. Sugar substitutes could be used in restaurants. The price of sugar would automatically fall. The opposition to price control is only to protect arbitrary price fixing and profiteering.'

'But Gandhiji is against price control,' Tara said.

'Why should he be? If there was no control of prices in England during the war, the people would have starved to death. Price control means controlled distribution of commodities. Why should anyone object to that? There's no restriction on selling below the price fixed by the government. This question might come up during this convention of the Congress party, that's why daddy is so worried. There's a sugar shortage, and daddy's hoarding sugar stocks worth seven lacks. How could I follow him into that type of business? I'll take on a real job somewhere; even if the salary is only five hundred a month. You know that petrol rationing is in force these days. The Congress party has asked daddy for two cars with petrol for the duration of their convention. Don't they care where the petrol will come from? When they had petrol rationing in England, the prime minister used to walk to Houses of Parliament.'

13 January 1948. Newspapers and radio reported: Gandhiji had gone on a fast unto death. The whole country held its breath in suspense. Delhi was at the centre of this suspense and tension.

The bloodshed and rioting between Hindus and Muslims had not stopped in spite of Gandhiji's constant pleas for communal harmony. Delegations of Muslims from UP and Delhi came to tell Gandhiji about the atrocities committed against their communities. News reports from Bahawalpur, Lyalpur and Jhelum in West Punjab told of hundreds of thousands of Hindus living in miserable conditions, of thousands dying of starvation. Indian and Pakistani troops battled in Kashmir.

Under the terms of the division of assets and liabilities announced by the British for the undivided country at the time of Partition, Pakistan was to be paid 550 million rupees towards the second instalment of arrears due to it. Pakistan had attacked Kashmir, a part of the territory of India. There had been no declaration of war, but the two countries were fighting pitched battles. The Government of India declared that unless Pakistan withdrew its armies from Kashmir, their share of the joint assets would not be handed over.

Gandhiji was of the view that Pakistan should be given its share, as a gesture of goodwill, without imposing any conditions whatsoever. As the government wanted to use the arrears as political leverage to keep Pakistan from attacking its territory, the Indian Cabinet found Gandhiji's proposal unrealistic, and rejected it.

Gandhiji saw that his appeals and efforts for tolerance and compassion were not being heeded, and decided to sacrifice his life for his cause.

The previous day, 12 January, was a Monday. Gandhiji observed silence every Monday. On the days of his silence, his messages were read out at his evening prayer meetings by his personal assistant Pyarelal, or by Pyarelal's sister. At the 12 January prayer meeting an announcement was made on behalf of Gandhiji that he would begin his fast at noon the next day. Gandhiji would end his fast only after complete cessation of communal violence in India, particularly in Delhi; otherwise, it would end only in his death. No reasons for his fast, or conditions for ending it, were specified, except that communal violence should cease and Hindus and Muslims begin to live together amicably.

The main point of discussion in the newspapers and in the public was the propriety of withholding Pakistan's arrears. But Gandhiji's appeals and statements mentioned only restoration of communal peace and harmony. He was constantly appealing to the government to ensure the safety of Muslims, and asking that Muslim families who had fled Delhi in fear of their lives might come back to the city and live without fear. He had also asked the government to have the Muslim houses and mosques occupied by Hindus vacated and returned to their rightful owners. It soon became apparent that most Hindus, especially those driven out of West Pakistan and East Bengal, saw Gandhiji's statements and appeals not only as appeasement of the Muslims, but also as detrimental to Hindus. These Hindus were boiling with anger at the thought that Gandhiji was on the side of Pakistan and of the Muslims at a time when Pakistan had invaded Indian territory.

At the AA villa, the telephone had been ringing continuously all morning on 13 January. A large number of people arrived before noon. Heated discussions were held in the drawing room. Tea was prepared and served frequently to the guests. Mrs Agarwal had found that Tara could always be trusted with the responsibility of looking after the guests.

At the time of the convention, when Congress leaders had stayed at the villa, and during the preparations for the reception held for them, Tara had had many occasions to meet and discuss the arrangements being made with Mr Agarwal. Since then, he would ask after her every time they met, and would remind her to tell him or Mrs Agarwal if she faced a problem, or needed anything. Sometimes he had questions about the children. Tara had sensed that madam always intervened on such occasions. Mrs Agarwal would say, 'I look after her as anyone would for their employee. If she needs anything, she should tell me herself. Just look at her coat; is it any worse than mine?'

There was a story behind Tara's winter coat. She had knitted a cardigan for herself in November. Madam had admired the design and her knitting skill, and said, 'Hai, you knit really well. Make one also for me. Choose the wool yourself.'

Tara would continue to knit as she read the newspaper or tutored the children. Narottam complained, 'You knit for everyone. What crime have I committed that you don't knit something for me?'

'Get me some wool, and I'll knit something for you that you won't forget. What'll I get as my reward?'

'Very well. Let's settle that before I get the wool.'

'Whatever you think is proper. But let that go for the time being. I'll knit for you anyway. I'll get the wool, too.'

Tara knitted Narottam a pullover in thick steel-grey wool, in a cable pattern picked out in deep red. Madam could not take her eyes off it. She suggested that Tara knit a similar pullover for Bhupi. Tara had to slow down her knitting speed.

The weather had turned very cold in December. Around the middle of that month, Mrs Agarwal had given Tara an extra seventy-five rupees, and said, 'Get yourself a woollen shawl or something warm.'

Tara bought a dark brown shawl for twenty rupees. Her cardigan and that shawl were the only clothes she had to keep her warm in the Delhi winter. If she took the children out in the cold biting wind that blew after a winter shower, or if Dolly, wearing a long winter coat, dragged her out somewhere, Tara would shiver with cold in her light clothes.

One evening Mrs Agarwal was going out, taking Tara with her. Mrs Agarwal wore her winter coat and Tara was wrapped up in her shawl. They met Mr Agarwal and Narottam, both wearing overcoats, in the veranda.

'Miss Tara, why are you not wearing a coat? It's very cold today,' Narottam said. Then asked again, 'Mummy, doesn't she have a coat? It's really cold out there.'

Tara did not like his comment. She bent her head and looked away.

'Yes, it is,' Mr Agarwal said. 'Why don't you get her a coat?'

'Why don't you buy her one yourself?' Mrs Agarwal said, trying to suppress her annoyance. Her reply was aimed at Narottam.

Narottam was seething inwardly at the taunt thrown at him by his stepmother. Next morning Tara had just sat down in the veranda with the newspaper when Narottam arrived, 'When would you like to go to get your coat?'

'I don't want any. I don't feel the cold that much. I won't accept it.'

'Daddy had asked you to. Won't you do as he says?'

'But I don't need one. I never felt the need for one. As things are, I find myself under a heavy debt of obligation.'

'What obligation?' Narottam protested. 'Miss Edwards's salary was a hundred rupees a month. Everyone needs a winter coat. You have to get one today.' He went away without waiting for any reply.

At 10.30, madam was dictating a letter to Tara in English.

Narottam came in, dressed to go out, and said, 'Yesterday daddy said to get Miss Tara a winter coat. I am going in the direction of the shops. I can get her one now.'

'Bahinji, I really don't feel that cold. I've never worn a winter coat,' Tara pleaded.

'Daddy saw her shivering with cold yesterday. That's why he asked,' Narottam said to his mother.

'Did I tell her not to get one?' Mrs Agarwal said. 'Why don't you go with him since he's inviting you?'

'Bahinji, I...'

'I don't like these useless affectations,' Mrs Agarwal said irritably. 'Why am I being dragged into this?'

Tara, her head bowed, went with Narottam.

Narottam drove. Tara's eyes were red with anger as she sat biting her lip.

'Why are you so quiet?' Narottam asked.

Tara blew up, 'I'm under some curse. Just because I'm an employee, you all think you can insult me whenever you want.'

Narottam said nothing, but he had not expected Tara to be so upset over such a small matter. He said in English, after a pause, 'I'm sorry if my lack of discretion caused you so much hurt. Believe me, I don't feel any less respect for your dignity than I would for Dolly. You may fault me for my indiscretion, but don't have any second thoughts about my motives.'

Tara got a new winter coat. In deference to her employer, she showed it first to madam. Narottam had removed the price tag, but that did not fool Mrs Agarwal. Suppressing her resentment, she said, 'Very nice. It's good quality, expensive material. This style is in fashion. Ratnara wore the same when she came to the club the other day.' Once Tara left, she could not help but mutter, 'Father and son are both dazzled by her.' The comment reached Tara's ear.

From that day on, if madam saw Tara without her coat on a day that was cold, she did not forget to nag Tara about it.

Tara had noticed a growing resentment in madam's attitude. She had been told that madam also had harboured similar grudges against the previous governess. Miss Edwards, if she had, for any reason, spoke with Mr Agarwal rather than Mrs Agarwal, and even gossiped and joked with him. Madam kept a careful watch over Tara, but had not found any fault with her conduct. That did not stop her from remarking acidly, 'God only knows where we find such women. Who can trust these unprincipled baggages.

They're always on the lookout for a chance to snare a man.'

Narottam also managed to find some excuse for talking with Tara. Nothing that Narottam ever did or said to her had been out of place, but Tara, mindful of her position as an employee of the family, had to tell him, 'You say you treat me as Dolly's elder sister, but do you know what they say about me?' She repeated to him the scurrilous comment and the tone in which she was described. Her experience had convinced her of Narottam's decency, he would not betray her trust.

He said, 'Mummy will go on saying things like that no matter what you do. Whom has she not suspected of having ulterior motives? She's just not able to think otherwise. She didn't trust even her younger sister. Aunty Sumitra used to live with us. The same mistrust and suspicion made mummy send her to the hostel at the Lady Harding School. Don't think any more about it. Why be afraid if you're not guilty.' He refused to change his behaviour towards Tara.

Tara sat sulking. She had been with the family now only for three months, and things seemed to be already turning sour. 'There's no place for me anywhere. I'm all alone. Banti was right. It's one's misfortune to be born a woman. I wouldn't mind working at some school for even half the pay I get here.'

The political crisis created by Gandhiji's fast was the topic of discussion in the drawing room at the AA villa. Visitors arrived shivering in the cold, damp air of January, but their faces and voices were full of the heat of excitement. Mr Agarwal was asked to take up the cause of safeguarding the interests of the Hindus. He did not go to his office. There were repeated demands to send tea in for the visitors. How could Madam miss out on such animated and important discussions? She would pop her head out of the drawing room and say, 'Tara, have two cups of tea sent in. Tara, do this... do that...'

Tara had set up a makeshift arrangement for making tea in the room next to the drawing room. She sent cups of tea and snacks through Jugal, or through Nundlall, the chauffeur. Stray remarks and bits of conversation in impassioned voices fell upon her ears:

'That would be suicidal for the Hindus. The mullahs are poisoning the atmosphere.'

'Why would Sardar Patel agree? He'd never agree to that!'

Tara heard madam's voice, 'Nundlall! Tell Tara to send in a few more cups of tea.'

'Let Gandhi die! What do we care if he's opposed to an even-handed settlement. The Cabinet has reached a decision. Should the Cabinet go back on its decision just because of him? What about the credibility of the government?'

'It was in yesterday's news that the Pakistanis massacred every single one of the two thousand passengers on a train. And he wants to make a present to them of 550 million rupees?'

'Mukherjee won't give in. Let's all go to him.'

'Will Gandhi have our demolished temples rebuilt? Rai Sahib, you must join up with us.'

'There must be a demonstration by the refugees. We'll make the city of Delhi tremble. What can a handful of Congress people do to stop us?'

The whole day was filled with such excited talk. Tara also felt that Gandhiji's fast was detrimental to the Hindus, that it was meant to protect the Muslims. What she had heard made her think: It would be suicidal for the Hindus to accept Gandhiji's demands. People did not trust Pandit Nehru and Maulana Azad, but surely Sardar Patel, Shyama Prasad Mukherjee and Sardar Baldev Singh won't let such excesses happen. Why was Gandhiji doing this? What might happen next?

Narottam had also been present in the drawing room. When they met in the afternoon, she looked at him inquiringly.

'The situation is very tense. Gandhiji's fast is a denial of the decision of the Cabinet. It's against the nation's interest, and favours Pakistan. The masses support the Cabinet's position.' Narottam's voice was tense with anxiety.

Tara said, 'If Gandhiji wanted to fast to prevent something, he should have done it to prevent the partition of the country. Why do it after the worst has happened?'

On 14 January at 11.30 in the morning, Jugal relayed a message to Tara, 'You are wanted in the drawing room. Prasadji has come.'

'Where's bahinji?'

'She's also there.'

Tara adjusted her dhoti around her shoulders, and nervously went to the drawing room. She found that Mr Agarwal and Narottam were also there.

Mr Agarwal said, as Tara entered, 'Come over here and have a seat.'

Prasadji looked very grave. He continued with what he was saying,

'Everyone from the Council of Ministers has reached Birla House. The Cabinet is holding a meeting on the lawn, near Gandhiji's bed. As representatives of Delhi's citizens, you all should go to Gandhiji and give him your word that there will be complete peace in the city.'

'But there was a demonstration yesterday with people shouting slogans 'Let Gandhi die', and chanting that they won't allow the transfer of assets to Pakistan, and so on,' Mrs Agarwal said in a worried tone.

'Sardar Patel has taken care of all those troublemakers by imposing Section 144 that forbids public gatherings. The government cannot tolerate disorder. The army is patrolling the streets. Pandit Nehru and Sardar Patel want the representatives of the citizens to reassure Gandhiji that peace and goodwill will prevail. Rai Sahib, you have to get involved now. You should take the lead at this moment. You should be among the representatives of the Hindus.'

Mr Agarwal sat thinking, cracking the joints of his fingers.

Prasadji turned towards Mrs Agarwal, 'Pandit Nehru and Sardar Patel also said...'

'But the Cabinet's decision was different...' Mr Agarwal said with concern.

'I'm telling you that Pandit Nehru and Sardar Patel have asked for this show of support,' Prasadji cut in. 'The Cabinet's final decision can wait.'

'Section 144 and army patrols. Do you suppose Gandhiji would have approved of this? This amounts to peace by sword and guns! This goes against the whole spirit of his fast. If peace has to be maintained by the use of force, what's the use of his fast?' Narottam asked

'You don't understand. It's an international crisis. Gandhiji is India's soul,' Prasadji said heatedly. 'Administering the country is one thing, Gandhiji's wish is another. We all can't be like him. The government and Gandhiji have the same end in mind.'

Prasadji turned to Mrs Agarwal, 'Well, bahinji. You, Dayavantiji, Begum Kazmi and Mrs Chausia will lead the women's delegation to Birla House. Tara bahin, you must come along too.'

'What'll she do there? We need someone here at home.'

'What are you saying, bahinji?' Prasadji cut Mrs Agarwal short. 'It's a question of Gandhiji's life, it's a question of Asia's prestige. Her presence is very important; it will create a great impression. The refugees are the ones opposing Gandhiji. The more refugee women come along, the better.'

'All right! Take her along. You go with her,' Mr Agarwal cracked another joint as he looked at Tara.

'She doesn't have any khadi clothes…'

'That doesn't matter. Not only the Congress party members, but all kinds of people should go to Gandhiji.'

Mrs Agarwal's big car, carrying her, Tara and Mrs Dayavanti Jeevan Singh was approaching Birla House when their way was blocked by a procession marching in the same direction. The marchers carried placards with boldly painted slogans: Blood for blood! Let Gandhi die! Gandhi is a traitor! India belongs to us! Kashmir belongs to us!'

'Hai, what's this?' Mrs Agarwal asked apprehensively.

'Pandit Nehru! Nehruji!' exclaimed Dayavantiji.

Two police motorcycle outriders coming in from the opposite direction braked to a stop. A motor car flying the Indian flag also stopped behind them. Two outriders bringing up the rear moved forward and stopped on either side of the car.

A policeman signalled Mrs Agarwal's car to stop on the left-hand side of the road.

The marchers still shouted, 'Down with Gandhi! Let Gandhi die! Gandhi is a traitor!'

Pandit Nehru got out of the car. He walked fearlessly towards the protesters. Several police officers quickly surrounded him on all sides.

Nehru challenged the crowd, 'Who wants Gandhi to die?'

The crowd shouted back, 'Gandhi is a traitor! Let Gandhi die!'

Nehru took two steps forward, 'Whoever wants Gandhi to die, let him kill me first! Come forward whoever has the guts!'

The crowd fell silent.

Nehru repeated his challenge, 'Step forward whoever has the guts!'

The crowd stood in a stunned silence.

Nehru scolded the crowd, 'You should all be ashamed of yourselves! You're saying such absurd things about a person sacrificing his life for you, who has put his life at stake for you. Gandhiji is the soul of this nation, he's the heart of this nation. If he dies, you and I and the whole country will die. What will the world think of us then?'

The crowd remained speechless.

Pandit Nehru asked the police officers, 'Why are these people gathered here? Why is the road blocked?' He got back into his car.

'Please disperse! Don't block the road!' came the order. The motorcycles roared and the car drove off with its police escort.

Tara, Mrs Agarwal and Dayavantiji watched with bated breath. Everything had happened within the space of one minute.

Tara breathed a sigh of relief as their car began to move again.

'What shameless people,' said Mrs Agarwal.

A constant stream of motor cars arrived at Birla House. Police constables directed the cars to be parked on both sides of the road in orderly rows, taking care that the road was not blocked. The police kept the whole area under surveillance. Visitors were checked at the entrance before being allowed to pass in.

A group of women and Prasadji were waiting in the veranda. A deathly hush pervaded the house. People walked on tiptoes and spoke in whispers.

'You're all late! Hurry up!' said Prasadji.

Congress volunteers stood on guard all around, but Prasadji motioned to them, and a way was made for the delegation of women to come through.

Gandhiji sat slumped against a large cushion on the bed, a pashmina shawl around his shoulders. Two mullahs with long flowing beards sat beside him, drying their tears.

Gandhiji's eyes were closed and his face was sombre. The women said namaste and sat down. Tara could hear her pulse pounding in that heart-wrenching silence.

Gandhiji opened his eyes. He joined his hands in greeting to the women. He said to the mullahs, 'You yourselves have admitted that you gave me an exaggerated picture of the situation. I suspected as much when I heard your overblown account. I didn't say anything at the time because you were all in a dangerous position. I hope you've learned a lesson on what exaggeration can lead to. I have faith only in Allah. He will show us the way.'

Gandhiji looked at the group of women. Dayavantiji was sitting closest to him. She assured Gandhiji on behalf of the women of Delhi that they have taken vows to end communal violence and to restore peace. Gandhiji should accept their plea to end his fast, or the country would be orphaned at this critical hour of its birth.

Gandhiji expressed his faith in the promises of the women. He said, 'My fast is meant to awaken a sprit of compassion and a sense of duty in the hearts of the people. I feel sorry and ashamed that it was women who suffered the most in both parts of the country. My fast is a protest against those atrocities, to do penance for them. When I am convinced that the people's hearts are purged of hatred, I will not refuse what you are asking me to do. Please have trust in God. Pray to Him to give guidance to the people of our country.'

The sound of loud calls and the chanting of slogans came from the direction of the road outside.

'Blood for blood! Let Gandhi die!'

'Gandhi is a traitor to this country!'

'Throw the Muslims out! Kashmir is ours!'

'We won't allow any payment to Pakistan!'

The women trembled at the thought of the violent mob reaching the gates of Birla House.

'Who are these people?' Gandhiji asked in a low voice.

'Bapu, some people are making noise on the road outside,' a girl standing beside Gandhiji replied. 'Bapu, pay no attention to them.'

'What are they saying?' Gandhiji asked.

'Bapu, they are saying, "Let Gandhi die",' said the girl.

Gandhiji closed his eyes for a moment, then asked, 'How many are there?'

'Bapu, not many. Just a few, creating a disturbance. They'll soon go away.'

'Ram! Ram! Ram!' Gandhiji again closed his eyes.

Two women sitting close by began to chant *ramdhun* in a low voice.

Tears rolled down the women's cheeks. Tara was seated at the very back of the room. The incidents at Lahore, what she had been through, and the atrocities she had witnessed flashed before her eyes. This great soul was sacrificing his life in protest at the savagery of the whole nation, to atone for their sins. He's truly the soul of the nation! She herself, her brother and so many in Lahore had tried to prevent the madness from spreading. They had never imagined that enmity between neighbours would lead to such a horrible end. She herself was one of its victims. But she was willing to forgive and forget all that if it would save the life of this great soul, and bring success to his mission.

Tara and Narottam reached for the newspapers the moment they were delivered. Every headline was about Gandhiji's condition and his efforts for peace and communal unity. In the legislative assembly of West Pakistan,

Sir Feroze Khan Noon, Nawab Daultana and Khan of Mamdot had paid homage to his mission, and called him the greatest man in the world after the Prophets.

On the morning of 16 January, newspapers reported that the Indian government had reversed its earlier decision, and had announced that it would immediately release the arrears of payments to Pakistan. The government, in a lengthy press statement, justified the Cabinet's earlier decision, and explained the new decision as a gesture of faith and goodwill in support of Gandhiji's creed of non-violence.

The newspapers carried a statement by Gandhiji that the reversal of the decision by the Cabinet should not be taken as a sign of instability in the new administration after the transfer of power or an act of surrender, but rather as a magnanimous and far-sighted action. Gandhiji expressed hope that the Cabinet's gesture would help find an amicable solution to the Kashmir problem. He also gave assurance that if Delhi's Hindus, Sikhs and Muslims signed a joint declaration to renounce violence and end communal strife, he would end his fast.

The Maharaja of Patiala arrived in Delhi, and called upon all Sikhs to save Gandhiji's life by ensuring an end to violence and strife. The Nawab of Malerkotla came to Delhi to meet with prominent Muslim clerics and leaders, and the high commissioner of Pakistan advised the Muslims in India to stop living in fear and to do everything they could to maintain peace. The leaders of the Hindu Mahasabha and of the Rashtriya Swayamsewak Sangh made appeals against any action that might jeopardize hopes of Gandhiji ending his fast. Pandit Nehru gave many public addresses.

A storm of peace efforts broke over Delhi. Processions of refugees and citizens of Delhi marched in every part of the city, chanting slogans and calling for peace.

A rumour was heard that Lord Mountbatten, Pandit Nehru and the well-known journalist Arthur Moore also had started to fast in support of Gandhiji.

Thousands of people in the city of Delhi began a fast as a symbol of their prayers for the success of Gandhiji's mission. Before the Partition, the Sabzi Mandi was a predominantly Muslim area. Hardly any Muslims lived there now. The Hindu refugees living in Sabzi Mandi invited one hundred and fifty Muslims from various parts of the city to a communal banquet.

A delegation of one hundred Muslim women wearing burkas went to Birla House to meet Gandhiji, and pleaded with him to break his fast without any delay. They told Gandhiji that all of them had been fasting for the past three days in sympathy with his cause.

Gandhiji said to the women, 'According to the tenets of Islam, a woman does not cover her face before her father, son, brother or close relatives. If you regard me as your father and brother, why do you veil your face before me?'

The hundred women as one raised their veils and uncovered their faces.

Gandhiji assured them he would end his fast as soon as he was convinced that the poison of communal hatred had disappeared, and all women were safe in the city. They should keep their faith in Allah the All-merciful, and pray that he might succeed in his purpose.

All possible measures had been taken to ensure communal harmony. The people, the government, and the local administration were doing their best to convince Gandhiji that no effort had been spared to end the violence.

In view of the gravity of the situation, Mr Agarwal had spent all afternoon visiting prominent citizens to get them to sign the Peace Petition. In the evening, a meeting was organized by Delhi's chief commissioner and the deputy commissioner at the request of Dr Rajendra Prasad, the minister for food and president of the Constituent Assembly. Mr Agarwal was among the one hundred and thirty representatives from all religious communities who attended this meeting of the Communal Harmony Committee. The Committee unanimously decided that it would agree to any conditions dictated by Gandhiji for ending his fast. A team of doctors examining Gandhiji issued a statement in late afternoon that described his condition as critical. The hearts of the citizens of Delhi rose in their throats. By the evening, two hundred thousand citizens of Delhi had signed the Peace Petition.

On 18 January, Mr Agarwal left at eight in the morning to attend a meeting of the Communal Harmony Committee at Government House. Everyone was at tenterhooks as to what might happen next. The Indian government's decision to hand over the arrears to Pakistan had agitated Narottam at first. But now he too had become withdrawn and pensive, in view of the threat to Gandhiji's life. He found it difficult to concentrate on anything. He wanted to speak with Tara to lighten his heart, but madam, to ease her own tension, had kept Tara engaged in one task or another.

Mr Agarwal returned at a quarter past one. From the window of his room, Narottam saw the car enter the driveway, and raced downstairs. Madam also rushed out to meet her husband.

'Gandhiji broke his fast. He sipped some orange juice,' Mr Agarwal said to Narottam. He looked at his wife, 'Fix me some lunch quickly. I've been away from my work for three days. Also, I've some important business with Mr Rawat. Nottan dear, please telephone and find out if Rawat Sahib has gone home for lunch.'

Dayavantiji telephoned at 3.30 to ask Mrs Agarwal to come to her house immediately. Madam had been co-opted as a member of the Women's Peace Committee.

Tara was returning with Lalli and Puttan from a walk to India Gate, and as they entered the veranda, the telephone rang. She went to the drawing room to answer it, with Lalli holding on to her finger. Lalli saw a clock, its mechanism visible under a glass dome, on a shelf full of curios next to the telephone table and wanted to play with it.

Tara knew from her experience that if Lalli had asked her mother for something like that, she would have at first threatened to have the child locked in a room that was infested with rats, then would have asked Shivni to take the child away from the drawing room. It was also possible that madam, after calling her daughter a pest and cursing that she may die, would have handed her the clock to shut her up. Had the clock been broken, madam would have hidden it somewhere away from sahib's eyes.

Lalli had learnt that if she behaved petulantly, and threw a tantrum she could get away with anything.

Tara had seen that while she attempted to instil some discipline in the children, others were constantly spoiling and cosseting them. She just could not let Lalli have the clock just to indulge her, and if it broke in the process it would have amounted to dereliction of responsibility entrusted to her. Tara had already asked Shivni to serve the food in the dinning room, but Lalli continued to scream and roll on the ground in a fit of obstinacy. The child wanted to play with the clock, not eat dinner.

Just then madam arrived. She had heard Lalli's screams at the gate. She said tiresomely, 'We spend on that woman one hundred and fifty rupees per month, and I come back to the house to find it in a mess. If she can't handle the children, what good is she for us! What happened to Lalli? Has she been hurt?'

Shivni was also in the veranda, she replied, 'Nothing like that, huzoor. She wanted to play with that clock from the drawing room.'

'Why didn't someone give it to her for a while?'

'Sahib had telephoned. He...' Tara tried to convey the message.

'Sahib's message can wait. Here I return dog tired, and find the house sounding like a fish market. I never get a moment's peace. Is your duty to look after the children or to worry about the phone?'

'Bahinji, she'll calm down in a moment. That clock...'

'What did sahib say?'

'Sahib is bringing along Mr Rawat, Mr and Mrs Surya, and a few others. He asked me to tell you that they'll be home by eight and they will use the upstairs drawing room.'

Madam's tone changed. 'That's another bother! If that was the matter you should have telephoned me at Dayavantiji's. It's going to be eight. Shivni, see if the driver has left. Call him here.'

Madam complained irritably until the driver came, 'Why don't these spongers do all that at their own homes. They come to us for their debauchery. I have to dish out hundred and a quarter rupees each time to entertain them. These freeloaders get three-three, four-four thousand per month as salaries, but make others pay for their liquor.' Whenever madam was angry plebeian cadences crept into her accent and language.

She said to the driver, 'Arrey Nundlall, you know that place, from where Latif got all that stuff. Arrey, the same, all that stuff...fish, kebabs, chicken!' She held out two ten-rupee notes, 'Ask Jugal for some containers to carry it back. Careful that you don't take anything from grandma's kitchen.' The driver said, 'Huzoor, I don't touch those things. Latif used to get all that. Send someone with me, I'll show them where to buy.'

Madam sent Jugal away with the driver. She looked to Tara, 'None of them has any sense. If they break a glass or drop a bottle, I'll have to answer with my life. Each glass is worth five rupees. Latif knew how to handle everything.'

Madam picked a key from a bunch, and pleaded, 'Tara, please set the tables in the upstairs drawing room. Shivni, you go with her. Shivni has done this before. Take out the proper glasses for drinking. The table covers are in the same cupboard. Just make sure they're all clean. Polish the glasses again. They must be arriving. Should have given me some more notice. He flies into a temper if everything is not ready. I'll just wash my face and change this damned khadi sari. It's been chafing my skin. Just look how I'm covered with dust.'

'Bahinji, let me first see to the children's dinner, then I'll manage everything,' Tara said. Lalli was still crying and struggling in Shivni's arms.

'Give her a good slap on her face. Go and dump the brat in her grandma's room. She'll find some other servant to give her dinner.' Madam ordered Shivni, 'Tara's busy now. You also go upstairs with her.'

Tara took the key and went to the upstairs drawing room. A cabinet was full of an assortment of multicoloured bottles in different shapes and sizes, with horses and dogs and cats on the labels. Realizing it was liquor, she looked at them in revulsion. She had been told since she was a child that there was nothing as evil as this. Her gali neighbours frowned at the mere mention of it. Her brother was broad-minded, he made concessions to eating meat but he too drew the line at drinking liquor. Dewanchand or Birumal sometimes sneaked a drink, but if the neighbours found out, they all spat at them contemptuously. On special occasions, such as Holi or Baisakhi festivals, it would be smuggled into the house of Tara's uncle Ramjwaya. Sheelo never failed to inform her cousin of such scandalous goings on. Tara thought to herself, about what she had been reduced to doing. Is this what they meant by tutoring the children, being their governess? She was being treated just like a housemaid!

Shivni had lent a hand to Latif in the past in discharging this delicate and responsible duty. She explained enthusiastically to Tara, 'Side tables are for ashtrays, and glasses are placed here on both sides of the sofa, and on the right side of the chairs. The long-stemmed glasses here on the serving table. Those with handles are for beer, but they are used only in hot weather. Miss sahib, place a few tiny ones also. If any memsahibs are present, they first take the coloured stuff, later everything. Madam does not like any, but she takes one too and sits there sipping it. The coloured stuff is called bhine, the ones with dogs and horses is bhiskey. I peep through the window sometimes. Let me get a few soda bottles from the cold storage, and then you tell me if anything else is needed.'

Tara had not finished arranging the room when she heard footsteps and voices coming up the stairs. A woman's voice said something, and Mr Agarwal laughed heartily.

Tara wanted to slip out of the room before the guests entered. Had she gone into the front veranda or to the one that led to Narottam's room, she would have had to return again through the drawing room. The back entrance to Narottam's room was always kept locked.

'Please!' Tara heard and turned around. Mr Agarwal had raised the curtain over the door to let a woman enter. Tara lowered her eyes and stood quietly next to a wall.

'Oh, you Tara!' Dr Shyama held Tara's arm and made her sit next to her on a sofa. She looked at Tara all over. Three other men and a woman came into the room.

'I'm so delighted to see you again. Hai, how lovely you look. You are happy here?' Shyama asked.

'Ji, I'm very happy. It's all because of you.' Shayma's questions discomfited Tara, particularly in the presence of Mr Agarwal and others.

'Miss Tara, the governess of our children.' Mr Agarwal introduced her to the others. He asked Tara, 'Is Mrs not back yet?'

'Ji. She's back. She should be here any minute. I'll go and tell her.' Tara said rising from the sofa.

'She'll come herself. Don't hurry her.' Shyama grabbed her arm again. 'Very brave young lady. She's from Lahore. What can I say to you all about her; her personality speaks for her.'

Tara blushed with embarrassment. Shyama introduced her to the others, 'Meet Mrs Surya.'

'Very pleased to meet you,' Mrs Surya held out her hand and Tara shook it.

'Mr Rawat, secretary, ministry of home.'

'Pleased to see you, sir.' Unable to meet Rawat's stare, she lowered her eyes.

'Mr Dey, deputy secretary, public works.'

'Glad to meet you, sir.'

'Mr Surya, secretary, ministry of health.'

'Very glad to have met you, sir,' Tara joined her hands and said namaste to all of them.

'Hullo!' Mrs Agarwal came in, in a new chiffon sari, her face freshly made up, as if she was appearing on stage. 'Excuse me,' she said in English, and switched to Hindi, 'I didn't know you all had come. I just went to speak with mother in her room.'

'Your absence was not noticed,' said Rawat. 'Your representative was here.'

Tara got up again, 'I'll take my leave of you. Hope to see you all again some time.'

'Wah, why are you leaving? Please sit with us,' Rawat said.

'Yes, please give us the pleasure of your company,' both Dey and Surya added their voice to Rawat's.

'Excuse me, but I have to look after the children,' Tara said politely.

'She's our children's governess,' Mrs Agarwal interjected.

'Doesn't matter,' Rawat hunched his shoulders and spread out his hands as if intimidated, 'I have faced governors many times. Never had a reason to fear them. Miss Tara won't be offended if we behave ourselves. Am I right, Miss Tara?'

'Well said, sir.'

'Very fine, sir.'

'Very nice,' said Dey, Surya and Shyama together.

Tara smiled in acknowledgement. Rawat must be a highly placed official or an important person, she thought.

'She hasn't had time to change her clothes,' Mrs Agarwal tried to come to her help.

Sahib looked sharply at his wife to shut her up, and said, 'Please join us, Miss Tara. There's no shortage of help downstairs.'

Rawat again said, looking at her, 'It's a different matter if Miss Tara is not happy with her dress. It might be casual, but it suits her very well. The art of good dressing is that it all appears effortless.'

Dey and Surya again heartily approved, 'Sure! You're perfectly right, sir.'

Tara sat down shyly next to Shyama.

'Listen,' Rawat said leaning forward, 'You all are educated, Urdu–Farsi knowing pen-pushers. Mrs Surya, you know Sanskrit, you have an MA in Sanskrit.'

'Our Tara is also an MA,' Mrs Agarwal said proudly.

'In Sanskrit?' Rawat looked at Tara.

'Ji, no. My subject was economics...'

Before she could correct Mrs Agarwal, Rawat interrupted her to ask Mrs Surya, 'Yes, Mrs Surya, do you remember what Dushyant said when he first saw Shakuntala: *iyamadhik manogya valkalenapi tanvi.*'

'How nice. You have a wonderful memory,' Mrs Surya expressed her amazement.

'I'll translate it, with Miss Tara's permission.'

'Ji, of course. With pleasure.'

'Well, it means that slim and graceful women, wearing clothes of bark, has entered my heart. So, do clothes really matter?'

'Wah, wah! That's great!' The room filled with laughter at Rawat's remark.

Dey said admiringly, 'You have such a heavy administrative responsibility on your shoulders, but you still find time to read classics.'

Tara blushed and bowed her head. Shyama whispered consolingly into her ear in English, 'This is all innocent fun, don't be embarrassed.'

'Well, ladies first,' said Mr Agarwal. 'What would you like to have?' he asked Mrs Surya.

'Nothing special, perhaps a sherry.'

Mr Agarwal took out a bottle from the cabinet, filled a sherry glass and put it on the table next to Mrs Surya. He looked at madam, 'Where's soda water?'

Tara saw Shivni standing outside near the curtain with a tray in her hand. 'Its here,' she said, and got the tray and put it on the serving table.

'You?' Mr Agarwal asked Shyama.

'Give me a sherry, or port, if you have.'

'Of course.' Mr Agarwal put a glass of port next to Shyama, and said, 'Dey sahib, don't you agree that Latif was so well trained. We had no problem as long as he was with us. He knew how to serve drinks in the proper way, he had been Sir John Shuster's bearer.'

'That's right. Hindus don't have the trained servility of Muslims,' said Dey. 'Leave aside peons from the Thakur caste, even if your servant is a low-caste, he will mind cleaning a tumbler from which you drank water. What to say of a Pathan or a Shaikh, even if your Muslim servant is a Syed, he will double up if he sees dirt on your shoe, use his shirt tail to wipe it, and will thank *you* and salaam into the bargain. That's why the British preferred Muslims as servants.'

Mr Agarwal agreed, 'You are absolutely right. These people have black hearts. When the Punjabi refugees were angry, they went and protested against Gandhiji, but when the mullahs had some tough times they were willing to accept Gandhi as their father. These are the very people who until yesterday wanted to turn Delhi into Pakistan ... What'll you have, Miss Tara,' he asked in the same breath.

'Ji, nothing.' Tara rose from the sofa, 'You please sit. Tell me how I can help?'

'No, no. It's perfectly alright,' Sahib motioned her to remain seated. 'Have something, it's very light.'

'Ji, no. You'll have to excuse me. I've never taken it.' Her voice was polite, but firm.

'Leave her alone. She's fine,' Shyama said.

'But let me help you.'

'All right, you serve us. What do you say, Rawat sahib?'

'Sure. It'll be double the pleasure if that's no trouble to her.'

Tara asked madam, 'For you?'

'Give a spot of sherry.'

Tara read the label, and filled a glass as sahib had done.

'Which whiskey will you prefer?' Mr Agarwal asked Rawat.

'Hague, never vague.'

Sahib got the bottle for Tara and pointed to one of the glasses. He began to open a soda bottle.

Tara began to pour whiskey into the glass.

Madam corrected her, 'Put the glass in front of him and ask "say when".'

Sahib again looked sharply at madam to silence her.

Tara blushed at her ignorance, and went to Rawat with the bottle in one hand and a glass in the other.

'May I help?' Rawat sprang to his feet, and taking the bottle from Tara, poured some liquid into the glass, and said, 'This is one peg. Don't give Dey and Surya more than this at one time. They might take advantage of your simplicity. They are real oafs.'

'Thank you, sir. I'll be careful,' Tara tried to hide her awkwardness. She was a little bewildered by what these responsible, mature people were doing. She had heard that alcohol made people fall to the ground in a drunken stupor. Will the same happen here? None of them seemed concerned about that.

The need to attend to the guests made her concentrate to the task at hand. A strange, heady, bitter-sweet smell came from the drinks. She asked Dey, Surya and Mr Agarwal their choice, and served them Hague and Black & White. Sahib filled the glasses with soda water.

Surya smiled and lifted his glass, 'Sir, who do we toast to? To thank God that Gandhiji ended his fast?'

'Oh, yes, yes,' Mr Agarwal said. 'The situation was really critical. You should have seen Pandit Nehru. It seemed that he too had gone on a fast.'

'My sense of duty to the government and to my country obliges me to say that in my opinion this fast will have grave and far-reaching repercussions,' Rawat said with a solemn voice. Everyone too became solemn. 'But the events were not under our control. It would certainly have been disastrous to let Gandhiji die. Rescinding its decision can have a very detrimental effect on a government's credibility. But subjugating a nation to an individual's wishes will definitely have serious consequences.'

Rawat smiled to lighten the mood, 'Why don't we drink this toast to welcome the evening's guest of honour, our new friend Miss Tara?'

'Oh, fine. Very good.' The room echoed with approval.

Tara's face flushed. Instead of feeling uneasy, she felt that she had gone back to her college days, and her friends and classmates were having fun at a picnic at Jahangir's Tomb or in the Shalimar Gardens. There was no reason to fear or suspect anyone's actions.

'And to Tara's future!' Shyama said, looking pointedly at Rawat.

'Yes, of course. Whatever I can do.'

'Sir, you can do everything,' said Surya.

'It's Agarwal's responsibility more than mine,' Rawat looked at sahib.

'Of course, sir,' sahib admitted. 'I have a great regard for Miss Tara.'

Shyama began to praise Punjabi refugees for their efforts for communal harmony inspite of their own problems, and how their resentment of Gandhiji was changed by his fast. Mrs Agarwal also gave several examples of the refugees' goodwill.

Sahib saw that Rawat's glass was empty, and got up to go to the cabinet. Tara also rose to her feet, 'I'll serve him.'

'You remember, Hague for Rawat Sahib?' he asked.

'Yes.'

Sahib opened an engraved box and offered cigarettes and cigars to the guests. Madam said to Tara, 'Offer Rawat Sahib cashew nuts.'

Tara went around with a plateful of nuts.

Rawat took out a pipe and pouch of tobacco, and as he filled his pipe, he replied to Shyama, 'Yes, no doubt their hearts have been changed, but not their minds. This was Gandhiji's third fast unto death for the cause of Hindu–Muslim unity. Emotions might overrule rational thought for a while, but it does not remove the cause of enmity. As the secretary of Home Affairs

I know that there's been little change in people's attitude and thinking. Some people became even bitterer under this type of moral pressure. There were others who marched in processions and shouted slogans that Gandhi was a traitor, and to let Gandhi die.'

'Yes, indeed, I saw it with my own eyes,' said Mrs Agarwal. 'They were shouting outside Birla House, and we could hear them inside. Gandhi was pained to hear about the protestors. I too felt awful.'

'Gandhiji heard them?' Dey was full of curiosity. 'What did he say?'

'He asked, "How many are there? What are they saying?"... There were only a handful of them.'

'What would he have done if there was a large crowd?' asked Dey.

'Doesn't matter how many,' Shyama said. 'Do you suppose Gandhi would have been cowed? He only listens to the voice of his conscience.'

'I admit that Gandhiji would not have broken the vow he made,' Rawat took charge of the discussion, 'but did those slogan shouters have a change of heart? Certainly not! They were muzzled by the administration.'

'Yes, Pandit Nehru really gave it to the people in the procession. I saw it with my own eyes,' Mrs Agarwal said in support of Rawat.

'Well, neither Patel had a change of heart. He simply had to cave in. After the government's statement about paying the arrears was released on the fifteenth, he left for his home town in Kathiawar the very next morning. It is feared that he might resign.'

'There was rumour about Patel withholding the payment until Pakistan recalled its troops from Kashmir,' Surya said.

'That rumour was based on fact,' Dey said, biting the end of a cigar.

'Absolutely correct,' Rawat stopped putting a match to his pipe bowl, and said agitatedly, 'Not only Patel, but the whole Cabinet was against it, and had made its decision public. But Gandhiji's fast browbeat Nehru and Rajendra Babu. Then the others too gave in. Patel was all alone in his stand.'

Rawat took a sip of his fresh drink, 'I say this on the basis of my twenty-four-year experience in administration. The government has suffered a serious blow to its credibility in matters relating to Pakistan and to its ability to administer the country by allowing the Cabinet to rescind its decision.'

'Yes, sir, that certainly was a blunder,' Dey agreed. 'The government's press release clearly stated that withholding the arrears was lawful and morally justified in view of Pakistan's invasion of Indian territory. Gandhiji first accepted it as India's legal and moral right to withhold the payment, then, strangely and inexplicably, chose to oppose the Cabinet's decision to assert that right. I am surprised that Gandhiji did not oppose India sending its troops to defend Kashmir. And why did he oppose withholding the payment when its specific purpose was to put pressure on Pakistan to desist from its acts of invasion? Let's suppose for a moment that he goes on fast to recall Indian troops from Kashmir. What then?'

'I can tell you the secret behind it,' Rawat said. 'Gandhiji asked Mountbatten about this. Mountbatten replied that if India decides to withhold the arrears due to Pakistan, this will be the first dishonourable act on the part of India. Gandhiji went on to declare that the arrears should not be withheld.'

'But wouldn't the Hindus and India both suffer because of this decision?' sahib asked.

'The Hindus will suffer miserably,' madam sided with her husband. 'Those poor Hindus who found shelter in mosques, they will now be driven out in this cold weather and rain. Tara, how many mosques did Gandhiji mention in his list of conditions?'

'Ji, one hundred and seventeen.'

'But the result and overall impact of Gandhiji's fast was laudable,' Shyama said. 'At least we got rid of the feelings of enmity and violence.'

'Gandhiji put more emphasis on magnanimity and compassion than on legal niceties of what was right and moral,' Surya agreed with Shyama. 'If disputes can be resolved with goodwill, why bother with legalities. Don't human considerations reign supreme?'

Rawat again leaned forward to speak, 'Nobody would have found fault with that approach if it did generate goodwill. Then it certainly would have been a victory for India.'

'It was indeed a victory for India.' Shyama waved the cigarette held between two fingers, 'It had a good influence on all of Pakistan.'

'What is the proof of that influence?' Rawat asked.

'Wah, there were so many statements in West Pakistan's legislative assembly. Can't think of the names now...'

'Ji, Sir Feroze Khan Noon, Nawab Daultana, Raja Gaznafar Ali Khan gave statements,' Tara named the people, and added, 'the chief minister, Khan of Mamdot, said that they would leave no stone unturned to save Gandhiji's life.'

'Zahid Hussain, the high commissioner for Pakistan, was also present at

Birla House,' Mr Agarwal said. 'Whatever you want to know about news reports, you can ask Miss Tara. She reads two newspapers everyday end to end.'

'Why won't she read them? She has time, has leisure. She can do what she wants,' madam could not resist saying.

'So in your view these statements are ample proof of the impact of Gandhiji's fast?' Rawat continued on the same track.

'Yes, why not? Why should we think otherwise?' Shyama replied with a question.

'Well, I too read all those statements very carefully. In my opinion what the Pakistani leaders said had a smug undertone of being vindicated by Gandhiji. You'll agree that the sum of 550 million rupees is something tangible, more than a statement or mere words. What tangible steps the Pakistan government has taken to create an atmosphere of goodwill, I ask you. Have they made the announcement to recall their troops from Kashmir, or admitted that they will not intervene in the matter of Kashmir? Let me tell you something else. Gandhiji ended his fast at forty-five after twelve. Zahid Hussain was then at Birla House, correct?' Rawat asked Mr Agarwal.

'Sure he was. He too joined his hands and asked Gandhiji to end his fast. He also gave his assurance to do his best to maintain communal peace and harmony.' Mr Agarwal's voice was tinged with pride at having been present at Birla House.

'That's right. Well, Gandhiji has already received a blow to his confidence.' Rawat took two puffs of his pipe, and continued, 'At three o'clock , Gandhiji sent Pyarelal to Zahid Hussain's place to ask if the Pakistan government would now have no objection to Gandhiji visiting to West Pakistan? And would he be welcome there? You know the answer he got?'

'What, what? Tell us?' they all wanted to know.

'The high commissioner for Pakistan replied: "No, not so soon. Let me first consult with Lahore." Believe me, he won't get the permission, much less an invitation.' Rawat drained his glass and continued puffing his pipe, as if nothing more needed to be said.

Sahib signalled Tara to serve another round of drinks. Tara was about to refill Shyama's glass with sherry when she said, 'Bhai, I had enough of this sweet stuff.' She glanced at Rawat and Mr Agarwal, 'If the men do not see it as a challenge, give me a small whiskey.'

'Bravo! Bravo! Sure!' They applauded.

Shayma looked at Rawat and said, 'But what an example Gandhiji presented before all. Just consider its international implications.'

'Yes, it's a great historical event,' Dey said.

'This is a historical blunder!' Rawat sat up straight, and said, 'The government's historical weakness. Just examine this event from a pragmatic point of view. Gandhiji is a great man, I admit. Everyone wants to emulate a great man. If people are unhappy with any government decision, they will just go on a fast. Some even might sacrifice their lives doing so.'

'Wah, keeping a fast is no joke. One needs spiritual strength to be able to sustain such hardship,' Shyama protested.

Rawat shook his head in disagreement, 'I do not think that one needs any amount of spiritual strength or resources to keep a fast. This is a matter of firm resolve and willpower. There are those who kept fasts longer than Gandhiji. What was the name of that Irishman yes, Maxwini, was it?'

'Sir!...I'm so sorry. Excuse me!' Dey apologized for interrupting his senior official.

'No, no. Go ahead,' Rawat said.

'Sir, you will remember that I was an undersecretary in UP's Jail Department. I can't recall the name...but several terrorists or you may say young revolutionaries were in jail at that time. The government refused to accord them the status of political prisoners and B Class facilities. Some of them fasted for fifty, sixty and one for even over one hundred days.'

'What are you saying?' Shyama said in amazement. 'Fasting for fifty, sixty and one hundred days? Who can survive that long?'

'Sure. This was reported by the jail authorities, not their supporters. They were remarkable people. I was in charge of their case. Confidential reports were sent from the jail. They would survive only on water for three to four weeks, without any food. Just on water, without any added salt or soda or lemon juice. No admirers surrounded them, or people who encouraged them or who sympathized with their cause. They were physically and mentally tortured to make them break their fast. They were weighed regularly. Some lost thirty, forty even fifty pounds. Some would refuse to drink even water so as to lose more weight and cause trouble for the government. The government of course could not let them die. They were fed forcibly. That process is very dangerous and painful. They were tied down and fed by a rubber tube pushed through their noses...'

Mrs Agarwal shivered visibly.

Dey continued, 'Just think, how weak someone would be after fasting for twenty or thirty days. If the tube was inserted through their mouths, they tried to bite it off. So the tube was pushed through their noses, and they were fed milk and vitamins that way. One of them died because milk was accidentally pumped into his lungs. After feeding them milk they were left to starve so that they would feel hungry and ask for food themselves. But they did not give up their fast. Those who refused to drink water were given water forcibly. Amazing people. They relented only after their conditions were met.'

The room seemed muted and hushed after Dey ended his horrifying tale. Shyama had put her cigarette on the ashtray. She was so shocked that she forgot to pick it up. She said to Dey, 'Those revolutionaries also had a spiritual strength. We all have a profound respect for Bhagat Singh. When did I say that he lacked such strengths or resources, but it is beyond common people.'

'Listen,' Rawat raised his hand, 'Gandhiji called those revolutionaries as people who believed in violence. According to Gandhiji, such people did not have any spiritual strength. Which means that there would be no difference between theirs and Gandhiji's fast if they did have the spiritual strength. In view of what just happened, the government decided to concede to Gandhiji's terms. Let's suppose for a moment that instead of silencing the refugees, someone provoked them and one thousand refugees went and surrounded Birla House and declared that they were going on a fast against any payments to Pakistan? Or what happens if Gandhiji, in pursuance of his creed of non-violence, decided to go on a fast to recall Indian troops from Kashmir?'

'Please, don't say any such thing,' Shyama joined her hands and begged.

Tara was also carried away by the logic behind some of the arguments. She looked at Rawat and said hesitantly, 'Excuse me, but may I ask you something?'

'Sure.'

'In your view the success of Gandhiji's fast against a decision of the government can encourage others to follow his example to similarly protest other decisions of the government. And that would create problems for the administration.'

'Definitely. That's what I think,' Rawat conceded. 'The working classes, peasants, students, employees—any of them can begin a fast in support of their demands.'

'Ji, that is possible,' Tara said. 'But is it not better for the government itself that such protests are by peaceful means of fasting, than by bombs, guns, swords and rioting? The fasting method at least won't involve violence and strife, and will have the possibility for exchange of views and for reason to prevail.'

'Yes, that is true,' Shyama said enthusiastically.

Rawat looked at Tara for a moment, then said, 'Miss Tara, it's a waste of your talent to ask you to be just a children's governess. You should either become Gandhiji's private secretary, or join the editorial department of some newspaper.'

'Sir, I hardly know anything. I'm good for nothing.' Tara said modestly.

'But I shall give you an answer.' Rawat said, 'Tell me, can you call fasting a logical argument? Gandhiji is truly a mahatma, but a lot of charlatans hide behind the guise of mahatmas. One mahatma begets one thousand fraudulent clones. But revolutionaries like Bhagat Singh cannot be emulated by sham and hypocrisy; one must be prepared to risk their lives.'

'Sir, you're perfectly right,' Dey said enthusiastically.

Mr Agarwal got up to offer another drink to Rawat, but he covered his glass with his hand in a gesture of 'no'.

'We have dinner, then?' Sahib asked.

'I'll have it served in one minute,' Mrs Agarwal said, getting up. 'Tara, come with me.'

Madam was having the table laid in the dinning room with the help of Tara, Shivni and Jugal. She did not want to touch anything that had meat in it, and asked Tara to arrange it on the table. Tara too found the smell of meat unpleasant. She tried to avoid touching the meat courses.

At the table, both Rawat and Dey asked about Narottam.

Jugal said that chotey sahib had his dinner, and went to see a movie. Tara also had to join them at the insistence of Rawat and Shyama. Rawat and Dey brought up the topic of Narottam.

Mr Agarwal said that Narottam was more interested in taking up a job than joining the family business.

Dey said, 'If he wants to do a job, the Tatas pay quite well. But he seems more interested in doing some meaningful work than just a good salary. The boy is somewhat of an idealist.'

Mr Agarwal said, 'Yes, that's true.'

Tara was intrigued. Shyama, Mrs Surya and others were eating with obvious relish the food that had smelled so disagreeable to her. Only she and madam were not eating those dishes.

After dinner, sahib and madam were walking the guests to their cars waiting in the portico to see them off. Shayma trailed behind, holding Tara's arm and telling her, 'I'd like to see you more often, okay. Mrs Agarwal was saying that you have plenty of spare time. Take some interest in social work. Who else will do it if not you...'

'Miss Tara!'

Tara turned her head. The rear door to Rawat's car was open, and he stood beside it, his hand extended. He shook hands with her, and said, 'Goodnight. You must come along with Mr and Mrs Agarwal.'

After shaking hands with him, Tara also joined her hands and said namaste in her habitual manner.

Tara was usually free after putting the children to bed at nine. She would read a magazine or a book in her room until 10.30 or eleven before going to bed. It was past eleven thirty, but she was not sleepy. She lay on her bed, and opened a magazine, but her thoughts were on the behaviour and manners of the respectable people she had met, people who had done all that without any feeling of guilt, shame or fear that was considered so evil by the common folk. Neither were they ashamed to drink, nor did they talk nonsense or fall down in a drunken stupor. These were of a different type; they discussed politics and social problems. Maybe those acts were not so evil for them, that it was a crime only when one was poor and without means.

'Mrs Agarwal did not like my sitting with them upstairs. But what could I do; I was trapped. She was not happy with my taking part in the discussion. I just couldn't hold my tongue.'

It was 19 January. Things were getting back to normal after the disarray and chaos of the past six days. Tara had sent the children off to their schools, and was on her way to get the newspapers. She was feeling a bit piqued. Madam had made some nasty comments earlier in the morning. One of Lalli's exercise books could not be found. Tara and Shivni searched for it, but in the end Lalli had to go to school without it. Madam, when she found out, said, 'She has no time to care for the children. If one can get by with wagging her tongue, why should one work. All she knows is to talk with people.'

Tara was hurt. She always prepared the school bags before putting the children to bed, but she got no time to do that the previous evening. They got her involved in all sorts of things, she thought irritably. 'All that is not part of my duties. Now I have to listen to taunts. I am her employee, she pays me, so why won't she want the satisfaction of belittling me.' She was not at fault, Tara decided. It was a cold morning. She stood in the rays of sun near the stairs, and began looking at the newspapers.

'Good morning!'

She recognized Narottam's voice and looked up. Still perturbed by madam's comment, she could not smile, just returned his greeting.

Narottam dug his hands in the pockets of his woolen dressing gown and asked, 'How are you?'

'Okay.'

'Did these people bother you last evening?'

'What do you mean?' Tara asked, her brow furrowed.

'They made you sit with them against your wish and maybe forced you to have a drink.' Narottam's voice was full of anger against his father.

'Who says so?' Tara said to protest the allegation of her harassment, 'They invited me to join them, sahib also asked me, so I stayed back. There was no question of any force.'

'They did not force you?' Anger dissipated from Narottam's voice.

'What do you mean by forcing me? To do what? They asked me to sit with them, especially Dr Shyama and sahib, and I did. They had drinks, I did not. That's all to it.'

'Hmm. I misunderstood the whole thing, that's why I felt bad. Grandmother was saying that you did not seem to be that kind of person, they must have forced a drink on her. Forgive me, don't mind my asking.'

Tara had a good feeling because of Narottam's anger for her concern. She said, 'What you heard was rubbish. They did have drinks, but talked very sensibly. Why didn't you show up? Rawat Sahib told many interesting facts about Gandhiji's fast. He asked about you at dinner.'

'Yes, I returned at nine. Didn't want to intrude upon them. I had already made a plan to see a movie with a friend. Why was mummy shooting her mouth this morning?'

'Let that go. She's always has some comment to make.'

'This work and this family's atmosphere is not suited for you.'

'Hmm.'

'Rawat can get you a good government job if he wants. He's the home secretary. He has guts. Do not misunderstand me, but he's supposed to have a roving eye.'

'How can I ask him? What'd sahib and madam think?'

'Wait for the chance. Daddy also sucks up to him and Surya for his own work. Tell Dr Shyama to put in a word. Was Mr Dey there?'

'Why do you ask?'

'He has to be there if Dr Shyama had come.'

'You're naughty.'

'Everything goes. Daddy had told me that Rawat wanted to see me. I'll have to go to meet him. I might talk about you if I get the chance.'

'You're so good.'

'Good and naughty at the same time?' Narottam said, raising his eyebrows.

'As the occasion calls.'

'Why don't you explain?'

'What's the fun if I have to explain?'

Rawat had asked Narottam to come on Tuesday, 20 January at 5.30. Narottam played billiards quite well. They will have a couple of games at the Chelmsford Club, Rawat had said. Narottam telephoned Rawat's bungalow exactly at 5.30 to inquire if sahib had come home. His orderly informed him that sahib has just arrived.

As Narottam was leaving, Tara also came out with Lalli and Puttan to take them to India Gate for a walk. Seeing her, Narottam said, 'I'm going to meet Rawat. Will see if I can remind him about your job. Today is a good day, because he seldom comes back from the secretariat before seven or 7.30. When the ministers are working all night, how can the secretaries rest? Maybe he got off early for some reason. I'll be back by eight.'

When Tara brought the children back at seven, Mrs Agarwal was talking with some one on the telephone. Madam said the moment she hung up, 'These Punjabis may go to hell. What do these evil people want? Someone threw a hand grenade at Gandhiji.'

Tara just stared at her. Madam said angrily, 'Some Punjabi threw a hand grenade at Mahatmaji's prayer meeting. The explosion blew apart a wall, but not a hair was damaged on Gandhiji's body. Who can harm him when God is protecting him?'

Narottam returned at 8.30. He told sahib the whole story as they sat on the dinning table. Tara listened from behind an open door. Narottam said that when he reached Rawat's bungalow, he was told that Rawat had gone back to his office soon after his arrival at home. Narottam went on to the club, and it was there he learned that the explosion took place at the time of the evening prayer meeting. The grenade fell about 75 feet away from where Gandhiji was sitting. The damage was mainly to a section of a wall with some latticework. There were reportedly three culprits; two managed to escape but one was caught. His name was Madanlal Pahwa, a Punjabi from the North-West Frontier region. Gandhiji was not at all perturbed, he only laughed at people running around frenetically.

The next day's newspaper carried extensive reports and photographs: Madanlal Pahwa had been evicted from a mosque in Delhi where he had been living. The police suspected a wide-ranging conspiracy behind the act, but was not ready to disclose the facts.

That evening's conversation at AA had a different tone: the refugees have indeed been treated unfairly.

The whirlwind of peace efforts gradually quieted once their objective, to get the Mahatma to end his fast, was accomplished. People went back to their daily grind of life. A stream of hawkers came to the AA throughout the day. They carried on their shoulders and backs bolts of cloth, and dhurries, blankets and bedspreads; women with an assortment of baskets made of reeds and palm leaves, young boys with sewing paraphernalia, lace and hair ribbons, books, magazines and fountain pen ink; others bearing face powders and creams, and shoes and chappals. They were mostly Punjabi refugees.

Mrs Agarwal, out of idle curiosity, would glance through their wares, then say, 'Arrey, this is all counterfeit stuff. I was taken in two times. They're all frauds.'

Tara would look at the refugees and think of her family. Considering evrything, she had never lived so well as she was doing now. On 22 January, madam again gave her seventy-five rupees as salary. She still had thirty-five left over from the last month. She said hesitatingly, 'Bahinji, I don't need more at the moment. Deduct the price of coat from this if you want.'

'Wah, do you suppose that coat cost only seventy-five? Don't pretend to be that innocent. Dolly's coat cost one hundred and ten. How would I know how much yours was for; no one told me anything.'

Tara thought that she'd pay Narottam back, and won't hear a no from
him. She knew that the coat was for ninety-six rupees.

Narottam protested as if he was hurt, 'Why do you make this distinction
between your money and mine. I never think twice about asking you when I
need money. Didn't I take three and a half rupees from you to buy cigarettes
that day in Connaught Place?'

'I'll deduct that much from the ninety-six.'

'Not acceptable. I didn't say I was borrowing. The coat was bought
because daddy had asked. You speak to him about it.' He refused to talk
about the money any more.

One thought worried Tara: that her parents, and brothers and sisters
might be still at some camp. 'Mother was so affectionate, but simple.
Pitaji was so good-hearted, but the yoke of poverty broke his back. How
they were coping, who knows. They sent me away just to get rid of their
burden, so that others may not think badly of them.' Tara felt that she was
ready to forgive her parents, but not her elder brother. 'He claimed to be
progressive and a liberal. He did not care for caste differences when it came
to his marriage. But he betrayed my trust.'

Another thought struck her: She could, if she wanted, find out about
her family by giving her address on the radio, or by some other means. Or
she could find out about Seth Gopal Shah's family. Sahib knew about the
Shahs, he might be able to trace them. But she won't go and live with her
family. She had one hundred rupees, she would send the money to help
them. 'Who knows where my in-laws' family is? The house was set ablaze,
but they must have been rescued. What if my parents felt obliged to send
me back to live with the in-laws?' Her mind weighed down by such dark
thoughts. Tara quailed at the possibility, she took a deep breath, and told
her self that there was no point in worrying about this.

On 30 January, madam had to go with Lalli and Puttan at five to the birthday
party of Shuchi, the youngest daughter of their neighbour Duggal Sahib. On
Saturday 31 January, Rawat had asked Mr and Mrs Agarwal and Narottam
to dinner at the Chelmsford Club, and had specially invited Tara.

Tara said to Narottam, 'I have never been to a club. I'm a little nervous.
The strap of my chappal is broken. The children are going to Duggal Sahib's.
Let's go to Connaught Place. I want to get a pair of sandals.'

When they reached Connaught Place at quarter past five, Narottam said,

'Treat me first to a coffee at the Blue Nile. Then we'll look for your sandals.'

They had not finished their coffee when a buzz of excitement filled the restaurant. People began getting up from their tables.

'What's going on?' Narottam asked with surprise.

The restaurant's manager approached them, 'Excuse me, but we have to close. Gandhiji was assassinated at Birla House.'

Tara and Narottam were numb with disbelief. They left their coffee, and came out of the restaurant. Shopkeepers were pulling down the shutters and closing their stores. Groups of people stood around talking. Lorries full of armed policemen appeared on the streets. Tara and Narottam returned quickly to AA to listen to the news on the radio.

Instead of going to his room upstairs, Narottam switched on the radio in the drawing room and tuned to Delhi shortwave. Someone was reciting the Bhagavad Gita in a doleful voice. A news bulletin was broadcast shortly after:

This evening at fifteen minutes past five, when the Father of the Nation Mahatma Gandhi was heading towards his prayer meeting, a Hindu young man killed him by firing three shots from a pistol. Mahatmaji died when the bullets hit him. He uttered the words Ram! Ram! as he breathed his last. A young graduate student of the Lady Hardinge Medical College was present at the meeting place when shots were fired. The young woman immediately attended to Gandhiji. Dr Bhargava and Dr Jeevraj Mehta reached the spot in a few minutes and examined him. Gandhiji's body was lifeless. India's Governor General Lord Mountbatten, Prime Minister Jawaharlal Nehru, Home Minister Sardar Vallabh Bhai Patel, Dr Rajendra Prasad, Maulana Abul Kalam Azad have arrived at Birla House.

The government had made an appeal to the people that they should desist from going to Birla House. Large crowds would aggravate the problem of traffic congestion. Further news would be broadcast again shortly.

Mrs Agarwal had heard the news at Duggal Sahib's. She returned quickly leaving the children behind. She changed into a khadi sari. She was ready to go to Birla House, but had heard nothing from Mr Agarwal. Hawkers on bicycles with newspaper specials began to arrive soon after.

Tara saw to the children's dinner, but ate nothing herself.

Mr Agarwal arrived at 7.45. Mrs Agarwal broke into tears on seeing him. Mr Agarwal left immediately for Birla Hose with her.

A news bulletin at eight next morning gave details of the arrangements made for Gandhiji's last journey.

As a sign of mourning for the Father of the Nation and in his honour, the national flag would fly at half mast on all government buildings. The government has ordered that all offices and bazaars would remain closed for three days. Gandhiji's body would be placed at 11.12 in an open balcony of Birla House for ten minutes for his last glimpse. His funeral procession would begin at 11.30 from Birla House. His cremation and last rites would be performed at Rajghat on the bank of the Yamuna River.

The Father of the Nation would be given a state funeral, with full national honours. The commander-in-chief of Indian army would make arrangements for the funeral procession. All branches of Indian armed forces and mounted soldiers would participate. Public was again reminded to stay away from the roads leading to Birla House. The route of the funeral cortege was described and people were asked to leave enough space for the cavalcade vehicle carrying the body and the soldiers to pass. Arrangements had been made so that everyone along the route would be able to pay his last respects to Gandhiji.

Mrs Agarwal listened attentively to the broadcast. She said to Tara that she and sahib would go to Birla House at nine, and from there to Rajghat. The funeral procession was likely to be enormous, and would make its way down Rajpath and India Gate. She asked Tara to take the children to the house of Vohra Sahib so that they could watch the procession from its roof, and said that she'd telephone Vohra Sahib. She had sent Nundlall earlier in the morning to get some garlands. She instructed Shivni to have some paranthas made for her to take along, because she and sahib would not come home for lunch.

Mournful music was continually being played on the radio. There were readings from the Bhagavad Gita, the Koran, the Bible, the Granth Sahib and the Zend-Avesta at regular intervals, and news about the route and about Gandhiji's final rites were also broadcast.

The cortege was scheduled to reach India Gate at half past twelve. Narottam and Tara, with the children and Narottam's grandmother, arrived at the Vohra residence on the intersection of Akbar Road near India Gate at 12.15. Shivni, with Lalli in her arms, had also come along.

Over one hundred people from the neighbourhood gathered on the roof of the Vohra residence. To the left and right of India Gate, as far as the eye could see, heads of densely packed men and women lining the boulevard looked like a surging black river. Groups of onlookers could be seen on the roof of every house around India Gate. People were perched on branches of trees, hung precariously from telephone and electric poles, and clung to every possible place where a bird or monkey could have perched.

The detachment of riders approached first. Their lances, with white pennants attached, were tilted forward as a sign of mourning. Following them were row after row of soldiers, their guns pointed downwards. Behind them came four rows of fifty soldiers each, pulling a large weapons carrier with ropes attached to the bumpers. Gandhiji's body, covered with flowers and rose petals, lay on a raised platform, only his face showed.

Mrs Vohra was watching the cortege through binoculars. She gave a detailed description to others, '... Gandhiji's son is sitting beside the body, and Sardar Patel is sitting near the feet of the body. Nehruji, Maulana Azad, Baldev Singh and Rajendra Babu are standing on the platform.' Mrs Vohra lent the binocular to Narottam for a few minutes, and he let Tara use them for about thirty seconds. When Tara raised the binoculars to her eyes, she could clearly see the ashen faces of the leaders.

Bringing up the rear were thousands of marching soldiers. Behind them an unbroken stream of motor cars, four abreast, stretching for miles.

'This ostentatious display of kingly grandeur and might is not in keeping with the ideals and beliefs of Gandhiji,' a voice was heard from nearby.

Tara and Narottam turned around and saw that a young man wearing a khadi kurta and dhoti had uttered the words. His face had a contemptuous expression. Ignoring people staring at him with surprise, the young man continued, 'Gandhiji, a servant of the downtrodden masses, who wanted to live in a colony of the untouchable bhangis, who opposed violent means and military might, would have never approved of such a display. He didn't even like to be kept as a prisoner in Agha Khan's palace. He thought the money spent on guarding him was an act of cruelty on the people of the country. Gandhiji preached to the government ministers to move out of their palatial bungalows and into huts. These people put him in a palace as soon as his voice was silenced.'

Narottam said what Tara had in mind, 'This is merely an expression of our feelings, a show of reverence for him. The government is showing respect to him on behalf of the country's people.'

The young man said, 'According to Gandhiji's beliefs, this wouldn't be a show of respect, but a mockery of his principles. He'd have expected humility and compassion from a government that claims to follow his ideals, not a display of might and grandeur. The government is showing its power in his name. Gandhiji belonged to the poor and the oppressed, and this government of the rich has taken him away from those people.'

Some people turned exasperatedly away from the young man. Tara and Narottam listened in silence. The young man continued, addressing his words to them:

'It's been always like this. The saintly, when they are alive, belong to the poor. The rich expropriate them after their death. The Buddha begged for alms for his sustenance. After he achieved nirvana, kings became his messengers and representatives. The same happened to Christ, and that's what is being done to this saint. Tomorrow these people will build a memorial to commemorate him, and bury his principles under its foundation. They build stupa shrines over the relic of a tooth of the Buddha, and in the name of spreading the Buddha's philosophy of renunciation of the material world, invade other lands with vast armies to expand their empires. Just like the Buddha and Christ, they will not follow Gandhi's ideals, but turn him into an avatar for worship.'

Mr and Mrs Agarwal returned to AA after six. Sahib was sombre and quiet, madam was constantly drying her tears. Some of their neighbours had gathered in the drawing room to hear about Gandhiji's last rites. Tara stood in one corner.

Mrs Agarwal said, '...There were maunds of sandal wood, vats of ghee, huge piles of coconuts. Mountbatten Sahib, Lady Edwina and their daughters sat on the ground with Pandit Nehru and Sardar Patel. We were just behind them...'

She waited until the tears choking her throat cleared, then continued, 'God resided in Mahatmaji's heart. He had a premonition of his last day in earth. Everyone was saying at Birla House that he had declared seven days ago that "if my prayers are heard, I will not die on a bed. I'll die from a bomb or a bullet."

'Yesterday morning a journalist asked him, "Are you going to Sewagram on the first of February?"

'He asked, "Who says so?"

'When the journalist replied that it was in the newspapers, he said, "Yes, the news is that Gandhi is going to Sewagram on February the first,

but let's see which Gandhi goes there." He asked not to send the telegram
about his arrival, and said, "Why spend money unnecessarily."

'He knew about what was going to happen and was laughing as he walked
to the prayer meeting. Someone told him that two men had come to meet
him from Kathiawar. He said, "Enough for now. I'll meet them if I come
back from the prayer." He knew he won't come back. That was the end of
his earthly existence.' She broke into sobs.

Mr Agarwal wiped his tears with a handkerchief. Others also dabbed
at their tears.

'Arrey bhai, he was an avatar of god,' a voice said.

Many sighed deeply in agreement.

Chapter 5

WHEN ONE FALLS INTO THE PIT OF POVERTY, THE LACK OF OPPORTUNITIES become a wall that keeps him imprisoned. He is at his wit's end trying to find a way out of that prison. But if any chance comes his way and becomes the ladder which he can climb and peer over the rim of the pit, he finds himself on the edge of freedom and success, and begins to see paths towards achieving his ambitions.

Nine or ten months before, Puri could only dream to earn four hundred rupees per month or become the chief editor of some newspaper. Saying it aloud would have meant inviting ridicule. His belief in his own capabilities did make him aspire such success, but he knew that he would have to wait for several years to achieve it. Only Kanak had given him hopes of succeeding; she even considered him capable of working miracles. Puri's imagination would soar to the zenith thinking of the confidence and trust she had in him.

Before the division of the country, Puri had attempted to climb the steep mountain of his ambition, but his foot had slipped. By resigning his sub-editor's job at *Pairokaar*, he had got stuck in the mire of unemployment. He was struggling to save himself from being swallowed up in that swamp when the political earthquake of Partition rocked the country and sent shock waves throughout the land. Great imposing institutions were shattered and fell to ground, and in their place appeared vast expanses of swampy wasteland. The mire in which Puri was trapped was engulfed by a surging flood. The force of its current swept Puri out, but only towards more disaster. In the middle of that powerful stream he felt his feet touch something solid, and he found himself perched on a submerged rock. As the waters receded, Puri realized that he was in fact on the roof of a fair-sized, well-built house. There was no one to challenge his right over the building; there was no one to question if the building belonged to him.

For the past four months, Puri had been sweating blood to make a success of Kamaal Press. Sood's influence was proving a boon, and both government and private business continued to pour in. Having amassed a capital of three thousand rupees made his blood race with a thrill of excitement. His thoughts would turn to the possibility of using this capital to publish, with Sood's blessing, a weekly periodical sympathetic to Sood's ideology. Puri had been given an indirect hint to that effect.

The newly developing opportunities fired his imagination.

Muslim officers predominated in the Punjab police before the Partition, but virtually all Muslim officers from East Punjab had opted for Pakistan. The number of Hindu police officers arriving from the west was much below the requirement, and the need for policing and administrative duties was growing every day. To meet this shortage, the Government of Punjab had created new posts of district and deputy commanders that were equivalent to superintendent and deputy superintendent of police, and began appointing trustworthy people to these positions of responsibility. In addition to the their status and administrative powers, these posts also carried salaries of 400 rupees per month for the senior and 200 for the junior appointments. It would not have been difficult for Puri to get appointed to one of these jobs with the help of Sood.

Puri broached the subject hesitantly with Sood by saying that if his salary was a burden on the press, he would like to apply, with Sood's approval, for the rank of district commander.

His suggestion did not please Sood, 'The job of a superintendent of police is to carry out the government's orders, it carries little political weight. He who gives the orders and decides the policy is of far greater importance. Someone who owns a printing press has considerable political clout. Would it be wise to surrender that to another person? And why do you see yourself as a burden to the press? How much do you suppose Issac made from the press? Even if he turns up to claim his business back, all he can demand is its selling price. These old, worn-out machines can't be more than half or one-third of their original value.'

Sood's reply gave Puri the hope of turning his dream into reality.

The means of printing his weekly were already in Puri's hands. Even if Soodji remained the owner of the newspaper, he'd be the editor-in-chief. The anticipation would send his pulse racing. Giving up the chance of a job that could pay 400 rupees a month made him feel proud of himself. Regardless of the situation under foreign rule, what would a superintendent of police amount to in comparison with the chief editor of a newspaper in a free country? He thought up a name for the weekly: *Nazir*, the spectator, one to express the feelings and problems of the public, as the faithful representative of the people.

It was bitterly cold in the last week of January. Puri shook off the attraction of the warmth of Urmila snuggling up to him, and got out of bed. The bone-chilling, icy wind and fog did not deter him. He reached Sood's residence in Mandi Bazaar at six, before daybreak.

Sood had been appointed the parliamentary secretary, but this had had little effect on his daily routine or lifestyle. The number of people coming to see him had increased several-fold. Early morning was the only time one was sure to find him at home and to have a private conversation with him. Puri was known to be Sood's friend and confidant. Sood's private secretary or his old servant Sudama could not stop Puri from going into Sood's bedroom.

Sood stirred and stretched his limbs wearily to shake off the last residue of the previous day's tiredness. He opened his eyes and saw Puri quietly sitting in a chair.

'So early? What's the matter?' Sood asked.

Puri prefaced his answer by stressing the need for a weekly paper. He was willing, he said, to take on the responsibility of publishing such a weekly if he could hire an assistant editor at one hundred rupees per month. *Chhatrapati* newspaper was not in opposition to Sood, but its editorial policy was to support the faction of the Congress party holding ministerial responsibilities. It also held a virtual monopoly on government advertisements. Puri had eighteen hundred rupees in the bank. Payments of two thousand three hundred were due from the district courts, the ration office and the municipal board. He explained how his weekly could survive for three months even without any advertising revenue. Once it was well established, they could turn it into a daily newspaper.

Sood calculated the revenues from advertisements and from the sale of the weekly. He asked questions about the problems that might arise if there were no advertisements or if the agencies distributing the paper did not pay their bills. He thought quietly for a little, running his hand over his closely cropped hair, and then told Puri that he would recommend Puri's application for the government-allotted quota of newsprint to publish the weekly.

Reassured, Puri was about to leave when Sood gestured for him to wait. Sood said, 'I haven't seen you for several days. When did you call your wife? You didn't even mention that you had got married.'

'Ji, I did not,' Puri blurted out in the confusion of being taken off guard.

He had not prepared himself to answer any questions of that kind.

'Who's that girl staying at your place?' Sood asked, knitting his brow.

Puri answered cautiously, in view of Sood's question and the tone of his voice, 'She's the daughter of Badhawa Mullji Narang, of Lahore's Manso Gali. He was very distressed at not finding some shelter for his family. I had asked them to come and stay with me. My father was a friend of Narangji, and a tutor of his son Jagdish. I've also tutored Urmila for some time.'

Puri rambled on in reply to the unexpected question and to explain the situation to Sood that Narangji and Jagdish had gone to Delhi in search of a house leaving Urmila, her mother and younger brother behind.

'So, what's-its-name, the girl's mother and brother are also staying with you?'

'Her mother was here. She left only a couple of days ago with her son. Jagdish had written that their father was not well,' Puri said.

'Then the mother went off, leaving her grown-up daughter alone with you! That's scandalous!' Sood said with an edge in his voice.

'Ji, I had given them one room. Urmila is staying in that room.'

'How can she live on her own? How could the mother just go away leaving her what's-its-name grown-up daughter behind? There's something fishy!'

Puri was caught in the web of his own explanations. To hide his nervousness, he said gravely in English, 'That poor thing is really unfortunate. She became a widow in March, when the riots were just beginning. She was married for only two months.'

'Then have the parents abandoned their widowed daughter?'

'Ji, I don't think so.'

'Then you've taken what's-its-name her over, have you?' Sood's voice became even harsher, 'Have you no concern for your reputation?'

'Bhai sahib, how can you say anything like that?'

'How can I say anything like that!' Sood rebuked him sharply. 'Even if that girl is what's-its-name a widow, that doesn't excuse her staying with you away from her parents. What relation do you have with her? You must have been friendly with her before. What'll people say? So far everyone's under the impression that she's your wife. That's what I was told, that you had called your wife here. You live with her, you're seen together, and she doesn't dress like what's-its-name a widow. Why doesn't she go back to her parents? I'm saying this because someone asked me about it.'

'Bhai sahib, people will say anything. The truth is that she had a difference of opinion with her parents.'

'Difference of opinion? Is she what's-its-name a communist? Is she well educated?'

'No.'

'What else does difference of opinion mean?'

'Ji, she wants to get some more education. She wants to be self-supporting.'

'And her parents weren't willing to let her study?'

'Something like that.'

'What have you got to do with this? How are you involved? Are you attracted to her?'

'No, nothing like that.'

'Are you engaged to anyone, or want to marry someone?'

'Ji, there was some talk, but nothing came of it. That fizzled out because of the Partition,' Puri said, to convince himself of the honesty of his intentions towards Urmila.

'Whom did your family talk to about your marriage? Must have been some people in Lahore. Where are they now?'

'Nothing was decided,' Puri said to make himself look better in the eyes of Sood. 'Pandit Girdharilal talked with me casually about it a couple of times. I had just resigned from *Pairokaar*. Everything was so uncertain; what could I say?'

'Which Pandit Girdharilal? The one who took part in the freedom movement, who owned the Naya Hind Publications?'

'Ji, yes, but no decision was made. Now I'm in no hurry. Let my family come here first.'

'You're a stupid ass. You say you couldn't find anything about what's-its-name Pandit Girdharilal? That's not likely. Did you try?'

'They were all in Nainital. I wrote a letter at their Nainital address at the end of September. It wasn't answered.'

'Who stays put in the hills at the end of September? They must be the ones who called you to Nainital. Didn't you like his daughter?'

'Bhaiji, it was nothing like that, and I was not quite myself at that time.'

'Let's forget all that nonsense. You write to this one's parents to take her away. If they don't, we'll have her packed off to the Vanita Ashram or some other hostel for women. Such rumours are not good for people in the political arena. People will jump at any chance to sling mud at you, and you give them reason to do so.'

Puri's mind was reeling as he went back to the press. He had prepared himself to talk about a different matter, and when Sood brought up the subject of Urmila all he had to offer was a lame excuse. How could he throw Urmila out? Send her where? But what would he tell Kanak? He and Kanak were as good as married, even if there was no legal ceremony.

A worrying thought niggled at the back of his mind. It was a blunder to get involved with Urmila, but the circumstances overpowered him. Kanak, whatever she meant to him, was away from him now. Urmila was near, and she was totally dependent on him. He thought, he would wait for a while and hedge his bets, and try to salvage the situation. He could not leave Urmila in the lurch. But what would he say to Kanak if she came? Two wives…what a web he was caught in.

Puri's problem was further complicated by the letters that his father had written to him recently. In his first letter, Masterji had been quite contented, with God's grace and blessing, in his present situation, but Puri's mother was very anxious to be with her son. Puri had got his salary increased to two hundred rupees per month so as to be able to help his family, and had been regularly sending fifty rupees every month to his father. Soon Masterji's letters began to speak more of problems than of contentment. So far he had been tutoring his younger son Hardev at home, and the boy would lose a year if he did not present himself for the examination. The school nearest to their home was in the city of Basti. Hardev had to be sent to a boarding school to continue his studies.

Usha, his second daughter, had passed her matriculation exam in Lahore. She wanted to go to college. She had already lost a year. What else could they do for a sixteen-year-old girl except let her continue her studies? The family had few acquaintances in Sonwan and, therefore, could not think of finding a suitable match for her. Masterji wanted to come to Jalandhar to give his son and daughter proper schooling.

Puri's concern, if his family came to Jalandhar, was Urmila. Masterji could take over Rikhiram's job, but where would he hide Urmila? He had been making excuses to his father that he had not found a house, and that he was still living with a friend. That it was not easy to find a dwelling, and once he did find one, he would ask them to come, or would come himself to bring them back to Jalandhar. He also asked that his brother should be sent to the boarding school in Basti.

Puri had pinned all his hopes on the possibility of getting the newsprint quota for the weekly by the end of February. He would sit, with his elbows on the desk and chin cupped in his hand, in the midst of the clatter of machines and revel in the thoughts of how to make his weekly more eye-catching and influential—just as a would-be mother about to deliver her first child ruminates about the child in her womb.

Puri had every confidence in his own ability and competence as a writer. He knew that he could, by using his imagination, create plausible characters and situations as vehicles for his own ideas and opinions. He could invent, for his readers, something that never happened. He could, with pen and paper, invoke feelings and moods. He could describe any happening or incident in such as way as to make it believable. Being able to do so gave him a sense of satisfaction, and a confidence in his own prowess. Manipulating words and phrases, of which he had an inexhaustible supply, was for him merely child's play.

He had gone to the district court to register the publication of *Nazir*. As he came out of the office of the press clerk, he saw Mahendra Nayyar on the veranda.

Nayyar called out cheerily, 'Hello!' and warmly shook Puri's hand.

Puri was taken aback at meeting a relative of Kanak. He smiled weakly, and asked, 'How long have you been here? You've begun to practise here? How's the business?'

'Bhai, it'll naturally take a while to establish myself at a new place.'

'Panditji is also here?' Puri asked nervously. It would have been wrong not to ask. His pulse quickened at the thought of having his fears confirmed.

'No, he is in Delhi. He hasn't yet begun the printing business, but his house has the signboard of Naya Hind Press. It is in Durrani Gali, near the Delhi Gate Bazaar.' Nayyar gave the address without being asked.

To hide his nervousness, Puri said in a preoccupied way, 'I came here to file the application for the publication of a weekly magazine. There are also some problems about getting the quota of newsprint. I'm all alone, and have to manage the printing press as well. I am looking for an assistant.'

'Congratulations! That's great. You found something to suit your temperament and talents. Where do you live? Have you found a place?

Let's meet again. If you give me your address I'll come and visit you,' Nayyar said amiably.

'No. I haven't found any place yet. I spend the night at the press office, or sometimes go over to Soodji's house. Have you bought a house? How's your practice coming along?'

'I've sort of a place to live. I started only four months ago. I am new here. It all depends on one's contacts and the people one knows.'

'I'll take you some day to meet Vishwa Nath Sood, the parliamentary secretary,' said Puri. 'This weekly is being brought out with his help.'

'Sure. Thanks. At present I am applying for bail on behalf of the boys arrested for being members of the RSS. Soodji may not approve of that.'

'I'm surprised that you are sympathetic to the RSS. The khadi jacket that you have on gives a different impression.'

'This jacket! That's interesting. I didn't take along my legal attire to Nainital. We couldn't get back to Lahore and had to get this one. Who has the cash for a vicuna jacket now?'

'But are you sympathetic to the RSS? Especially after Gandhiji's assassination?'

Nayyar laughed, 'Puri, I am surprised to hear that. When you were arrested at the time of the Shahalami arson, had you gone there to set fire to anything? You know very well that one can be arrested for no good reason. Every member of the RSS could not have been involved in the plot to assassinate Gandhiji. And Godse also has the right to a fair trial.'

'Well, you are trying to establish yourself as a lawyer. The supporters of the Hindu Mahasabha would certainly look kindly upon you after what you are doing,' Puri said sarcastically, to settle an old score.

Nayyar stared hard into Puri's eyes, 'Thank you for your kind suggestion. Somebody who's not afraid to get on the wrong side of the government will not beg for sympathy from the Mahasabha people.'

Puri's expression grew serious.

'Well, see you again.' Nayyar walked off without shaking hands.

As Puri sat in a tonga on his way back from the district court, his thoughts went back to the news about Kanak. 'Would Nayyar write to Delhi about meeting me? Why should he? He must be happy that I have lost contact with her. Even if he did write to Kanak's father, that old devil probably would not tell his daughter.' His mind remained preoccupied with Kanak until he reached the printing press.

Puri knew that besides being the editor and the manager of the weekly, he might have to write most of the articles himself for the first few issues. He wanted to have good, solid material for the first four issues. He desperately felt the need for an assistant, someone who was like-minded and carried the same flame in his heart—someone committed to journalism, with enthusiasm to match, who would intuitively know what Puri was thinking and put it flawlessly into language. And they would between them turn the weekly into a vibrant voice that would touch the hearts of people. Kanak shared his dream, but she was not with him when the time had come to turn the dream into reality. Had she been there, they would have worked as one and achieved great new heights. Kanak's dream was to have a small house of their own, both of them at their desks, writing and creating. Now Urmila had taken Kanak's place. How had it happened? But it had happened, and that was a fact.

And how long could Puri's memory of his feelings for Kanak and of her capabilities compete against the overwhelming presence of Urmila. Her large eyes shinning with invitation, the glowing complexion, the golden hair, the naturally pink lips that looked like rose petals. To hold her in his arms, to clasp her to his chest, to incline his head to kiss her lips, all this made Puri feel like a man. Sometimes Kanak's face would float into this procession of images. Puri would be filled with a smug self-satisfaction at having had two women surrender to him in succession. In his mind he would compare both of them. Kanak as tall as he was. Kanak marching shoulder to shoulder alongside him. Kanak able to discuss and analyse social issues and politics. And Urmila just burying her face in his chest and leaving herself open to his wishes. Kanak was a comrade and companion, Urmila an adoring lover and a devoted, unquestioning follower.

Puri had bungled his explanation of Urmila's presence in his home. It was necessary to retrieve the situation and give it some appearance of respectability. He had to keep secret his liaison with her, and go through the pretence of getting her accepted as his wife. He could, with Sood's help, get Urmila admitted into some college, Puri thought. She could stay, just to satisfy Sood, with another family for some time. Then he would have a proper marriage for everyone to see, and bring her home. Masterji would also be happy if things were done in that way. Nayyar had told him the address of Kanak's father, but it was best not to act on it.

Puri began to write the text for a poster to advertise the launch of *Nazir*.

His plan was to have the posters displayed in all the big towns between Jalandhar and Delhi. Any fears about the success of *Nazir* would have meant doubts about his own capabilities and worth. Such doubts never crossed his mind. Carried away by heady ambition, Puri imagined: The weekly would be advertised widely. People would see his name as the editor, and talk about him. His body trembled with excitement and the fountain pen almost slipped out of his fingers. Could Kanak, with her interest in current affairs and the habit of keeping up with contemporary literature, fail to come across *Nazir*? He put the pen on the desk, took a deep breath and rested his head between his hands. What should he do? What might happen?

Puri began to daydream that Kanak had come, crying and claiming her right over Puri inspite of Urmila's presence. She pleaded as tears streamed from her eyes, 'But you had accepted me as your wife before Urmila came to live with you.'

After wallowing in self-disgust and loathing, Puri decided that this was no time for silly sentimentalism. 'Did Kanak ever make any effort to find me? I was separated from my family, destitute, hungry, and forced to beg so that I could eat. She faced no danger and had the means of contacting me. I'll tell her: It was you who forgot me. What did you do to find me?'

He thought of another argument in self-defence, 'Would someone as liberal and adventurous as Kanak be still waiting for me? As long as I was in the picture, she tried hard to get me. She won that game. In her need for sensation and thrill, she must be after another adventure. She's not the kind that dedicates herself to one man and sits around and mopes all her life.'

He picked up his pen again and began to write, as the publisher of the weekly, a blurb to promote it, using superlatives that had been applied by others to his work. It claimed how an experienced and distinguished writer like Jai Puri could contribute to the success of *Nazir*. The advertisement was meant to attract people's attention to a new publication, which had such a celebrated personality as the editor. He gave the text he had penned to the calligraphist, instructing him to write the banner headline in a bold, ornamental script for a poster in the size of 18 x 22 inches.

The poster campaign was barely a week old when three unemployed young men, with a literary bent and desirous of a chance to prove their talent and industry, showed up to meet the famous writer and future editor of *Nazir*. Some erstwhile journalists, from newspapers and magazines that had closed down in Lahore and with more experience than Puri himself,

also came seeking employment. Puri was in no hurry to choose his assistant.
He wanted to take his time to examine the writings of the young aspirants,
and then make his selection. He was interviewing one such candidate in
his office when a middle-aged man entered and called out in a tremulous
voice, 'Kakaji! Jaidev!'

Puri stood up and said, 'Pairipaina.' He squeezed out from between the
chair and the desk and bent forward to touch the feet of his father's elder
brother. He offered Babu Ramjwaya a chair, and standing beside him, asked,
'When did you arrive? I thought of going to Hoshiarpur to meet you after
I got my father's letter, but couldn't manage. There's no one here but me.
Just couldn't get away.'

Puri told the applicant for the assistant editor's job to come back another
time, and inquired after his aunt, and his cousins Kishor Chand and Sheelo.

Babu Ramjwaya's appearance had shocked him. It was the same
man whom Puri could not dare to contradict even if he said something
unreasonable, whose wishes even his father could not oppose. Instead of
his customary turban of fine, starched muslin, his uncle was wearing an
ordinary old black cap. His moustache had turned completely white, and
the glow of a rich diet had vanished from his complexion, which now
looked sallow and pasty. Instead of a tailored wool jacket, he wore the blue
uniform issued by the railway. If Masterji had not written in his last letter
about his elder brother, Puri would have had difficulty in recognizing his
taya in his baggy trousers, with an old cloth sack in his hand.

After Masterji had found his son's address through the radio, he had been
diligently searching for his relatives and friends. The information centre
for refugees who had worked for the railways was in Ambala. Masterji
had written to his elder brother care of the Ambala centre. Three months
later a reply came from his brother that after spending a month and a half
at some refugee camp, he was now posted to Hoshiarpur railway station.
Masterji wrote to his son that Babu Ramjwaya was facing a difficult time,
and as Hoshiarpur was quite close to Jalandhar, Puri must go and visit his
taya. They wanted him to solve every problem immediately, Puri thought
to himself in irritation. How could Masterji know about the dilemmas and
tribulations his son faced?

It was four in the afternoon, but Puri asked Babu Ramjwaya, 'Should I
get lunch for you?'

'No, son. I ate before leaving home.'

Puri summoned the lad working as assistant on the treadle machine. He took him outside, gave him a rupee, and asked him to get half a seer of hot milk, and some snacks.

Babu Ramjwaya had learnt from his brother's letter that Jaidev had found a job that paid one hundred and fifty rupees per month. He congratulated Jaidev, and continued in the same breath, 'Son, we have been ruined. We owned two three-storeyed houses in Lahore, and now all of us have to live in one room. We couldn't bring anything away with us. We had fifty-seven tolas of gold ornaments, but had we brought that along the police would have taken it.' He said in a whisper, 'We buried it in one of the houses. Let's hope God allows us go back some day. Kishor Chand has no job. You are the only dependable one, who's gainfully employed. We all have to look to you for help, beta. What are a hundred and twenty rupees a month in these expensive times? We got more than one-and-a-half times as much in rent in Lahore. Kishor Chand made about a hundred to a hundred and fifty each month. I was in the parcel office at the Lahore station. That had a few moneymaking sidelines. And as you know, we got our rations cheap from the village.'

Puri was talking with his taya when Rikhiram came to ask, 'Bhaiji, it's five o'clock. Do you want us to stop, or should the cylinder machine continue to operate. About three thousand impressions remain.'

'Bhai, do whatever is necessary. Check also the work marked out for tomorrow's schedule,' Puri spoke like the manager of the press.

'Kakaji, won't you be going home?' Babu Ramjwaya looked at his old wristwatch. 'Where are you living? Your father just gave the address of this press. I had to inquire at a few places to find you.'

Puri did not answer him immediately. He looked around to see if any one was close enough to hear. He picked up a red pencil from the desk and grasping it tightly, said, 'Tayaji, it's so hard to find any place. I've looked everywhere. I want to bring father and mother here. Hari and Usha can't get proper schooling where they are. I sometimes go over to Soodji's place, or spend the night at the Congress office, or on the bench right here.'

Puri was in the middle of his explanation when Rikhiram came back. Puri stopped and asked, 'Yes, what is it?'

'The job on the treadle is finished. The litho-cylinder can run up to eight o'clock. Are you staying on? May I go now if I am not needed?'

Puri generously gave him permission to leave.

Babu Ramjwaya felt his lower back and said, 'Beta, can I lie down for an hour on this bench? My train is at eight. My back is really hurting. I caught a chill, and it's been bothering me ever since. None of us have enough warm clothes. Back home there were stacks of blankets and quilts, but now we have to shiver in the cold.'

'I'll get a charpoy for you,' Puri called Raldu to bring his charpoy.

Puri moved the furniture back to make room for the charpoy. He noticed the surprise on Raldu's face. Rikhiram too had noticed the charpoy as he put on his jacket before leaving. Puri just averted his gaze. He thought that he would explain later that he did not want to invite a casual acquaintance to stay at his home.

Seeing Babu Ramjwaya in that miserable condition filled Puri's heart with remorse. As much as he wanted to lavish his uncle with hospitality, who had always thought of him as good-for-nothing, he had to suppress the urge to take his taya upstairs and show how well he had done for himself. For, how could he explain Urmila living alone with him?

Babu Ramjwaya rubbed his back as he lay on the charpoy describing the losses he had suffered and his present financial worries. Puri's taya had never acknowledged having so much wealth. Puri told his own life story of past few months, 'In the beginning I was worried about finding work. Now I spend my time worrying about a place to live. One can't find even a house in ruins unoccupied in this city. As soon as I find something, I'll come to Hoshairapur and bring you and the rest of the family here. You all can live with me for some time. Whatever my resources and means may be, we'll manage somehow.' As he sat talking with his taya, the thought of Urmila coming downstairs unannounced was making his heart pound.

At seven, he took his taya to the railway station to see him off.

On his way back, Puri hung his head in shame for not letting his taya stay with him. He was disgusted with himself for having to hide his behaviour from others. The realization that he had stooped so low was in itself an admission of his poorness of spirit.

Puri had become well known in the city and had built up a large circle of friends in the past five months, but he did not dare to invite anyone to his home. Soon he was going to be the respected chief editor of a weekly paper. How shameful was the hollow reality of his life! He would have to change this situation; he must make Urmila his wife and a respectable woman. But he would first have to explain the situation to Urmila, and ask her not to worry and to have patience. Tender feelings for her filled his heart.

Puri had to stop at the Congress party office for about an hour on his way home. He found Urmila knitting a second sweater for him, as she waited for him with the dinner ready. She complained, 'Hai, where did you go? Why didn't you come upstairs for a cup of tea or milk? What kept you so long?'

'What can I tell you. An acquaintance turned up at the office at the last moment. I walked with him up to the railway station discussing some matter. I also had something to attend to at the Congress office.'

They both ate from the same thali. Urmila had not been out for several days, and wanted to go out for a while after the dinner. Puri took her on an outing every second or third day. He felt proud when she accompanied him dressed in her showy, colourful clothes. He had begun to avoid going out with her, feeling guilty. He made the excuse of being tired, and lay down.

Urmila smiled affectionately and said, 'Sadake, may all your troubles be mine, what am I here for?' Lovingly she began to massage Puri's legs and feet.

A thought crossed Puri's mind: Would Kanak have done the same? Would her nature permit her to do so?

Urmila began to tease and flirt with him. Several times she asked him, 'You are very quiet. Hai, are you really that tired? Tell me the truth, is anything bothering you?'

Puri could not tell her what was in his heart. To put her mind at rest, he began to make love to her, and then fell asleep.

A refugee next door to Puri's had got some buffaloes and begun a milk-selling business. He delivered milk at six in the morning by jangling the chain lock outside the front entrance. Urmila would remain under the quilt because of the cold and because she was not fully dressed. Puri would get up and take the delivery. He was used to getting up early. He would switch on the light, get back into the bed and work on the first issues of *Nazir*. As no housework needed to be done that early in the morning, Urmila would snuggle up to Puri, and stay in bed until 7.30.

That day too Puri had got the milk. He closed the door without bolting it, but did not turn on the light to begin work, and got back into bed. He put his arm around Urmila, and spoke into her ear, 'Listen!'

Urmila hugged him back, 'Go back to sleep. It's so cold.'

'I want to tell you something.'

'What.'

'Let's get married.'

'What more has to be done for us to be married?' Urmila clung to him.

'Not that. I mean, let's tell everyone. Let's have a civil marriage in the court, or at the Arya Samaj office.' Puri explained to her what a civil marriage was. 'A court marriage means that the husband is punished if he desserts or deceives his wife.'

Urmila hugged him even tighter to show her love, 'Be quiet, what's more important than love and trust. May I drop down dead if I ever doubt you.'

'It's not a question of doubt, but we must be careful of what others say. Why not make it public, and live together openly without fear.'

'What's the fear now? I live openly with you, go out with you. Don't people see that?'

'But that doesn't mean we are married. They'll want to know when the marriage took place and who was there?'

'Who doesn't know that it was my parents who left me here with you as their son-in-law.'

'I don't mean that. There's Soodji, and others who know me from Lahore. When I came here first, I told them that I wasn't married. They'd expect me to get married properly. What's the harm if we do? I want you to be able to be seen with me in public.'

'Hai, you want me to be a laughing stock.' She leaned against his chest, and thrust her face closer to his as she explained, 'The bridal procession will start from this house, which is the same house as the bride's house. You will take me away as a bride from here, and bring me to my new home back here? That's stupid! Had you ever been married, you'd have known how these things are done. All you had to do was to sweet-talk a simple girl like me into it.' Urmila lightly slapped his cheek playfully, and kissed him.

Puri said, 'It won't be like that. I'll make arrangement for you to stay for a while with someone else. Once we are married, I'll bring you back here.'

'You don't know anything about anything. You are good at only one thing,' she said nuzzling his nose, her eyes shinning with laughter. 'You want to marry me six weeks from now. What will I say to people when they begin to laugh at me after six months? I won't do any such stupid thing.' She broke into laughter.

'Laugh at you... why?'

'You're crazy! As I said, all you know is how do one thing, and talk sweet.'

'Is that so? How late are you?' Puri asked anxiously as he caught her meaning.

'I'll know for sure in five or six days. But why rake up the past? We can say we got married in Lahore, that's all. Actually, it was two-and-a-half years ago.' She said, looking into his eyes. 'Didn't we have something going at Murree, when you slapped me? You're really bad. Then too it was me you got a thrashing. You always cause me trouble, and are doing the same again. I won't talk to you.' She buried her face in his chest.

There was the sound of knocking at the front door. Someone called out.

'Who the hell has come at this hour?' Urmila asked irritably.

The door creaked open and a woman came into the outer room. She then peered into the bedroom.

Urmila dived under the quilt. Puri had to straighten his clothes and quickly get out of the bed.

He looked at the visitor, recognized the face, and caught his breath in surprise.

Chapter 6

A FEW MONTHS EARLIER, IN THE SECOND WEEK OF NOVEMBER 1947, KANAK GOT
out at Lucknow railway station, feeling both nervous and cautious in a new
and unfamiliar city. She immediately noticed a difference in the behaviour
and the manner of speech of the people. The scene outside the station was
as she had seen before, with refugees crowding every space in between
the flower beds in front of the building. The tide of the dispossessed had
reached as far as 300 miles from Delhi. In a sense she too was one of them,
searching for a new life for herself. She had Mrs Pant's address. She hired
a tonga outside the station building to go to the Councillors' Residence.

Mrs Pant welcomed her warmly. She said, 'You must be tired after the
night-long journey. Rest for a while if you want. Or have a wash and a bite
to eat, and be ready by half past ten. Come with me to the Council House.
You can meet Awasthiji there. I'll also show you the Assembly in session.'

Kanak sat in the visitor's gallery overlooking the imposing, circular hall
of the Legislative Assembly, with a roomy upholstered chair and a desk for
every member. The Council of Ministers and the Speaker of the House
were seated in the centre. Most members wore immaculate white clothes
and Gandhi caps. For about twenty minutes Kanak sat overwhelmed by
the sobre, serious and awe-inspiring ambience of the hall. She tried to
listen to the proceedings. A member spoke standing behind his desk, 'A
newspaper report says that a building material that could replace cement
has been invented in Kanpur. What is the government doing to encourage
this development?'

Someone from those seated in the centre replied to the member's
question.

Maybe Mrs Pant will also speak, thought Kanak. How would she look,
addressing the House? She looks so ordinary and simple, but if she can
speak here, she must be very competent.

Her eyes searched and found Mrs Pant, who was sitting on a bench
meant for two members, with another woman of about her own age. They
both leaned towards each other and seemed engrossed in some private
conversation rather than the proceedings of the House. The head of the

member behind them nodded as he dozed off. The feeling of awe in Kanak's mind began to wear off.

She again tried to pay attention to the House proceedings. She knew nothing about the subject under discussion. A man standing beside the ministerial bench was reading something in English from a sheaf of foolscap. Similar papers lay on the desks of all the members. Some members were themselves reading the sheets. Others leant forward or sat with their elbows on the desk or looking away with head resting on one hand, apparently listening attentively to the speaker; or perhaps thinking about something else. Many members left the hall one by one. Mrs Pant and the other woman also got up and left. The proceedings continued as before.

Mrs Pant beckoned to Kanak from the entrance to the gallery. As Kanak went to her, she said, 'Let's go and meet Awasthiji.'

The door to Awasthi's office was closed. A fat peon sitting outside got up and respectfully opened the door for Mrs Pant.

In that spacious office, behind a large and heavy desk sat Awasthi, with his knees drawn up, talking with a portly man dressed in an achkan and Gandhi cap. Awasthi invited Mrs Pant, 'Come in, come in.'

Seeing Kanak behind Mrs Pant, he repeated his welcome in a heartier voice, 'Come in, Kanakji, when did you arrive?' nodding to them to take chairs at the desk. After inquiring from Kanak about Delhi, he said, 'There was a lot of disturbance in Delhi. Overcrowding by refugees created so much disorder. It must have quieted down now that Gandhiji's there.'

'Yes, it has quieted down. It was worse before we arrived in Delhi.'

Awasthi gave a glowing introduction to Kanak about the man in the achkan, 'He's from your region of Punjab. He owns several businesses in Kanpur.'

The door to the office opened again and two khadi-clad men came in, were given an effusive welcome by Awasthi and invited to join the group.

As the men were taking chairs, Awasthi said, 'So Sharmaji, didn't Lari say that day that they would create another Pakistan here?'

The man with Sharma spoke up, 'Arey bhai, that leader of the League party made such an idiotic demand. He hits the roof whenever the proceedings of the Assembly are in Hindi. Arey bhai, you speak a little more Farsi and we speak a little more Sanskrit, but we both use the language of the man in the street. His stupidity has been made plain. If you claim to believe in democracy, you should be ready to accept the majority opinion.'

Sharma said, 'They hate any mention of Hindi because they're Muslims. They say, a Muslim's language is Urdu. Let them bloody well show me one bloody Muslim who can speak or read Urdu in my village or the five villages of Kurbjawar. Arey, if you have changed your religion this doesn't mean that you've disowned your ancestors and their language. Everyone speaks Awadhi, Bundeli and Bhojpuri in the countryside. The whole problem is confined to cities. All because of the insistence on being regarded as distinct from the Hindus. When things go against them, they go and cry to Gandhiji that they are Indians, that India is their motherland. But the language of India is not theirs.'

'Well,' said Awasthi, 'this fellow is threatening to create Pakistan here. We must keep an eye on him.'

Sharma agreed, 'Not only that. Before they left, they threatened to return like the invader Mohammed Ghouri, and take over our province.'

Awasthi's paan-stained lips widened in a smile, 'Sharmaji, the paans you sent this time were really good. Excellent.' He searched under the files piled up on the desk, and took out his paan box. He opened it and offered it to Mrs Pant, 'Help yourself and ask Kanakji too.'

Awasthi looked at Sharma and his companion, 'Mrs Pant's guest Kanakji is from Punjab. She's the daughter of Pandit Girdharilal, the veteran Congress leader and a comrade of Lala Lajpat Rai. She has her MA and is very talented.'

Kanak did a silent namaste to Sharma and his friend.

Mrs Pant deposited two paans in her cheek, and said appreciatively, 'Very nice. Very evenly made.' Awasthi motioned to her to offer the box to Sharma.

Sharma accepted the box, raised it to his forehead to express his thanks, and placing it on the desk, said, 'Bhaiyyaji, get us some chai-wai. Paan-wan can come later. I'm not used to having paan. Can't have more than five or six in a day.'

Awasthi rang the bell to summon the peon.

'Listen,' Awasthi looked around to count those present, and said, 'Ask them to send six cups of tea and samosas.'

Awasthi picked up the paan box and offered it to the Punjabi businessman, 'You have some, Chawla sahib.'

Chawla was extracting one paan from the box when Awasthi commented, 'Sahib, you must have two, we take two at a time. Actually, Punjabis can't appreciate paan. What do you say, Kanakji?' He turned towards her, 'How many do you have in a day? You must like paan.'

Kanak remembered that it was not considered proper for unmarried women in Punjab to have paan except on special or ceremonial occasions. She answered, 'Ji, I'm not used to paan. I have it only once in a while.'

'Once in a while?' Awasthi broke into loud laughter. 'My daily ration is fifty paans.'

Kanak looked at him with amazement.

Sharma's friend spoke up as Awasthi paused to have his dose of paan, 'Bhaiyyaji, the lorry permit for Thakur Giridhar Singh...'

Paan in cheek, Awasthi said as if he had remembered something, 'Arey, I completely forgot.' Rummaging through the files, he came up with a small silver box, opened it and offered it to Mrs Pant, 'Here, have some chewing tobacco.'

'I was about to ask you for some,' Mrs Pant said over her mouthful of paan.

'Munavvar sent it. Just try it. Be careful about how much you take, it's strong.'

Mrs Pant took out a pinch on her palm, put it into her mouth and held out the silver box to Kanak. Kanak politely joined her hands, thanked her and said no.

Sharma's friend took the box, tilted it over his palm to take as many grains as he wanted, and passed the box to Chawla.

Chawla also excused himself.

'You don't have tobacco with your paan?' Awasthi said with a mixture of surprise and sympathy at this lack of sophistication, 'How can one enjoy paan without tobacco? You chew paan or just chew the cud like cattle? Paan without tobacco is like doing it to woman with no tits.'

Sharma and his friend slapped each other's hand and responded with a loud guffaw, 'Wah, wah! Well said, bhaiyyaji! A million rupee remark!' Sharma's friend laughed so much that he forgot all about the lorry permit.

Kanak lowered her gaze, opened her purse and began searching for something as if she hadn't heard.

'You sometimes say such embarrassing things!' Mrs Pant said with a strained laugh. The remark made Kanak feel uncomfortable and insulted, but she suppressed her anger. 'Is this what I came here for? But pitaji and jijaji had said: Be careful. Lucknow people are very polite and observe the rules of etiquette.'

Sharma animatedly began to describe how Khalikuzzman left Lucknow and his property had been confiscated by the deputy commissioner.

The peon returned with a man in tow carrying tea and samosas on a large tray. The peon pulled out a small table for the tray. Mrs Pant served samosas on plates to everyone and poured tea.

Sharma's friend found the opportunity to make his pitch, 'Yes, bhaiyyaji, did anything happen to that poor Thakur Giridhar Singh's application for a permit for a lorry? If he's put out it'll cause us problem in the District Board election. The file has been held up for the past two months. You get it approved by Guptaji, and I'll see to the rest.'

Kanak did not feel like having tea or samosa, but to avoid having to speak in such company, she just forced the tea and a samosa down. Awasthi and the others were loudly discussing some matter.

There was another round of paan after tea.

The sound of a bell ringing came from outside.

'Is a division for a vote taking place in the Assembly, or is there a lack of quorum?' Awasthi, paan in hand, asked Sharma and his friend. His expression became serious. 'This is not right. Some people should remain in the chamber. Let's go.'

The awe that Kanak had felt in being at the legislature and the centre of government was all but over.

'Achcha, you all go to the Assembly, I've to go somewhere else,' said Mrs Pant.

Kanak said namaste to everybody and left with Mrs Pant.

When they reached the main road outside the Council House, Mrs Pant pointed to the left and said, 'We came from this direction? You know the way back. Here's the key. Go and have some rest.'

'Is there a post office close by? I want to inform my father that I reached Lucknow.'

'There is the General Post Office, on our right. The Burlington Hotel across from our house also has postal and telegraph facilities. You can ask Chhedilal, the guard, to get postage stamps, or send a telegram for you.'

Sitting alone in Mrs Pant's room in the Residence, Kanak was thinking, 'Was it wise to come here? What Puriji had said about these people was quite correct. I could go back today to Delhi, but that would mean losing face with pitaji because of my insistence on coming here. What vulgar and contemptible attitudes these people have! Those who take women as only sexual objects, how could they have any respect for them. Mrs Pant should have objected to that remark rather than laugh at it, what kind of a person can she be!' Kanak remembered hearing obscene remarks and name calling by the riff-raff on the streets of Lahore, but these were the elite of Lucknow, respected and well regarded.

Gloomy thoughts about being alone in this unfamiliar city were on her mind, 'Puriji went back from here feeling disappointed and insulted. Why did I ever trust these people and come here? But what could have I achieved by staying in Delhi? Aseer and Sinha were no better than these people.'

She took a deep breath and thought, 'A woman is truly helpless without a man to protect her. Puriji is my only support, the bedrock of my existence, but how do I find him? And what have I done so far except wait to hear from him? I dithered over contacting him only because of my respect for pitaji. I can have a message broadcast for him on the radio, but what contact address will I give? Nothing is certain here. Will we ever be together again? I am not able to earn a living in spite of all the education I've had.' Kanak remembered the young woman selling newspapers in Delhi, who was younger than herself.

It was necessary to inform Panditji that she had reached her destination safely. 'What should I write to him? Nothing that would increase his worry for me. It's better to send a telegram, saying only that I had arrived. Now that I'm here, I should have patience and see what comes next.'

Kanak nodded off to sleep in the armchair. The sun had set when she woke up. Mrs Pant was not back. Kanak freshened up. What to do now, she thought. She looked around the room for something to read, but there were neither any newspapers nor books. Some foolscap sheets lay on a small table. She picked them up and saw that they were about the assembly proceedings. She read a few of them idly. Finding those dull, she took out *Path of Success* from several books that she had brought with her. Panditji had given it to her for advice and guidance.

She began to read the chapter 'Why Should People Help You?' The author's advice was: You will meet some like-minded and friendly people in your everyday life, and others whom you may find unhelpful. It would be wiser to be pleasant and agreeable to those you do not like. It would be useful to have the goodwill of people rather than their ill will and hostility. Showing your eagerness will make you appear weak. People usually prefer to help those who appear resourceful and become their friends than to help someone who appears helpless.

Kanak used her finger to mark the page, closed the book and thought: Is it wise to behave in a devious and dishonest way?

Mrs Pant returned at eight. She and Kanak had dinner at the Residence's cafeteria. After dinner, Mrs Pant again went to visit someone. Kanak resumed her reading. Mrs Pant came back at ten.

Next morning as she was leaving for the Council House, Mrs Pant took out some papers from her bag and muttered irritably, 'These secretariat people are such bungling idiots. They've given me the forms in English. Today's the last date. My reimbursement will be held up for no good reason.

'Can you write English?' she asked Kanak. When Kanak said 'yes', she said, 'Fill these up for me, will you. I'll sign. Or my travel allowance will be held up. These people are such a nuisance.'

Kanak began to fill up the claim form for a round trip to Mrs Pant's hometown at the time of the Dussehra festival. She was thinking, 'So many speeches in the Assembly were in English. Could Mrs Pant follow what was said?'

Mrs Pant said as she was leaving, 'You saw the Assembly House yesterday. You'll get bored sitting there again. I've to go there to record my attendance. Awasthiji will be in the Assembly till one. You can come later if you want to meet him. You know the way. Leave the key with Chhedilal. I'll also speak with Awasthiji about you.'

In spite of her eagerness for finding work, Kanak had no desire to go to Awasthi's office. She wondered: Couldn't she do something else without asking someone like Awasthi for help? There must be newspapers in Lucknow. Or she could look for a job at some school. It was preferable to find work as a nurse in Lucknow than to go back and be a strain on her father's finances.

She took out *The Innocent Sin*, a novel that she had brought with her. As she read, she found herself inadvertently comparing her own situation with Orissa, a character in the book. Another day passed. She had nothing else to do but worry. Sitting idle was making her uneasy. She had been here for only two days, she thought to comfort herself. The sun had set. She turned on the light and went back to her reading.

There was a knock on the door, 'May I come in?'

Kanak went to the door and peered out. It was Awasthi.

'Please come in,' Kanak said, opening the door. 'Have a seat.'

'Where's Mrs Pant? Not back yet?' he asked.

Kanak offered Awasthi the armchair, took an ordinary chair herself and sat at some distance.

'You didn't come back yesterday, nor did you come today. I thought I'd look you up on my way back from the secretariat.'

'I thought I'd be interrupting your important work. And since you had asked me to come, you'd remember the reason for my calling on you.'

'Of course, I remember. Do you have any problems here?'

'Ji, no. I'm quite comfortable.'

'Don't hesitate to tell me. Be frank. If you're not comfortable, another place can be found for you,' Awasthi said, as if giving her a chance to change her mind.

'Ji, no. I've no problem here.'

'I mean if you're used to a different food, then feel free to tell Mrs Pant. Consider this your home.'

'Ji, I've no problem or inconvenience here.'

Awasthi asked about her parents, where they were living in Delhi, and advised, 'It'll be better for you all in Lucknow than in Delhi. Ask all your family to come here.'

Kanak told him about her father buying the house in Durrani Gali, and described the incident with Syed.

Awasthi expressed his sympathy, 'Gandhiji talks in terms of ideals, but it's different in practice.' He asked, 'What type of job would you like to have?'

Kanak replied that she was willing to do any work, but she would prefer a government job to teaching in a girls' school or at a women's institution.

'That's the right attitude,' he smiled slowly at her answer. 'It'll be done, believe me. And don't despair. Yes, if you need anything, if you're short of cash, don't worry. Treat us like your family.'

'Ji, no. I have enough.'

'If you're short of money, I'll send you some,' he smiled a little more widely.

'Ji, no. I don't need any.'

'I'll be angry if you stand on ceremony,' Awasthi said, closing his eyes. His lips stretched so wide that red paan juice leaked at the corners.

'Ji, I'll let you know if I need anything,' Kanak said, suppressing her disgust.

'Achchha, I'll go now.'

Kanak stood up politely to see him out.

'Arey, sit, sit. You mustn't get up. Ladies do not get up.' He laughed loudly and remained seated. 'How's the food in the mess here?'

'It is quite good.'

'I don't suppose you'll get meat dishes here. You're used to eating meat, have some delivered from outside.'

'I'm used to vegetarian food. Our family didn't mind eating meat, though.'

'Achchha, I'll go now,' he again said with a smile. Kanak stood up again.

'No, don't get up. I've missed Mrs Pant. She didn't say when she'd be back?'

'She came back quite late last night.'

Kanak remained standing. Awasthi got up, 'Come and see me again. I'll let you know.' He paused, and said, 'Don't trouble yourself; I'll come to give you the news myself. But don't worry about anything.'

He smiled and seemed ready to leave but hesitated. He put his hand on Kanak's shoulder as if to reassure her. Kanak detested his touch. She felt no hesitation at shaking hands with a man, but Awasthi's touch did not seem that innocent. After he had gone, she smiled to herself and thought scornfully: The only thing Congress party people have learnt from Gandhiji is to feel free to paw any girl or woman. Every one of them thinks he is the Father of the Nation.

Thoughts continued to swirl in her mind when she went to bed after dinner. She was determined to become self-supporting. So many days had passed and she had not been able to do anything about her resolve to search for Puri. A radio broadcast was her only resource. How long would she go on living with the fear that her father would hear the broadcast of her message to Puri? Still, it was not possible without reaching a decision to continue in Lucknow. The memory of those evenings spent with Puri in Nainital's Astoria Hotel made her tingle with warmth and yearning. Her body ached for his touch, and tears flowed from her eyes. She was not the type to sit around moping, but in her loneliness, she wrapped her head in the sheet and cried her heart out.

A week passed without any news of a job for her. She had written to her father that she was staying with a member of the UPs Legislative Assembly, Mrs Pant, and that there was some hope of finding work soon with the help of Awasthi, the parliamentary secretary. But when she wrote to her sister and brother-in-law in Jalandhar, it was not with as much conviction, 'Nothing is certain so far, but I must be patient. It is natural that this will take some time.' As if she wanted to draw comfort from her own words.

Kanak was finding it increasingly dreary and monotonous to while away the hours sitting in Mrs Pant's room and waiting for news from Awasthi. Seeing her bored and listless one evening, Mrs Pant offered to take her to Hazaratganj for a cup of coffee. Thakur Murli Dhar Singh, another MLA living in the residence, came along.

Thakur cut a rather imposing figure. His khadi kurta and cashmere vest fitted snugly over his broad shoulders and rotund belly. When he found out about Kanak's search for a job, he assured her that he could definitely get her appointed as a schoolteacher in Sitapur at one hundred and fifty rupees per month.

She did not immediately agree to go to yet another unknown city. She thanked him and said, 'Awasthiji is already trying for me. If that doesn't work out, I'll certainly ask you.'

Awasthi showed up again the next evening. Mrs Pant was there and she sent for tea. While they all were having tea, Mrs Pant said that she had some urgent work with one Shastriji, finished her tea and left.

Awasthi talked to Kanak as if an emotional intimacy existed between them, 'You came here because of the promise I made to you, so have confidence in me. Don't be shy with me.' He smiled, put his hand under the shawl around his shoulders, and took out five ten-rupee notes from an inside pocket. He took Kanak's hand, and putting the money into it, said, 'You're short of money. Why didn't you ask me?'

Kanak pulled back her hand. Her face turned serious, 'I'm not short of cash. I want to be self-supporting. I'll ask my father for money if I need any.' She told Awasthi about the promise made by Thakur to get her a job in Sitapur, and added, 'If you want I can ask Thakur Sahib.'

Awasthi stared at her for a moment. He put the money back in his pocket and said in a serious tone, 'Well, that's all right. I came to tell you to write an application to the director of the Information Department for a job as a journalist, and give it to me tomorrow. Don't forget to mention your publications. No need to be depressed.' He did not stay much longer, and before he left, he reminded Kanak not to lose confidence in him.

There was no chance of Mrs Pant returning early. Kanak was feeling hungry, so she went to the dinning hall. There was no one there. She had not finished her dinner when Thakur peered in. He came into the room, saying how happy he was to see Kanak again, and sat next to her. He summoned Bechu, the mess servant. 'Go, boy, and bring half a pao of rabari from that shop on the corner,' he said, tossing an eight-anna coin onto the table.

Thakur offered the leaf cup full of sweet milk pudding to Kanak. She shook her head and declined, but Thakur persisted, ignoring her reply as if he had a right to insist.

Kanak always paid for her meals herself. She took out a two-rupee note from her purse and put it on the table. Thakur told Bechu not to accept the money from her, but charge it to his account. Kanak asked Bechu to bring back her change.

Thakur picked up the note and tried to put it back into Kanak's purse.

Girija Bhabhi, another MLA, came into the room. 'What's this? What's the problem here?' she asked.

Thakur shrank away, then laughed sheepishly, 'Look at her, bhabhiji, she's our guest. Isn't her insistence on paying for her meal herself contrary to our Lucknow etiquette?'

'I want to pay for my own meals. One can be a guest only for a day or two,' Kanak put the money back on the table.

'She's so mule-headed, bhabhiji, and unreasonable,' Thakur said, grinning apologetically, and left quickly.

'I'll take the change later,' Kanak said to Bechu, and began walking away.

'Hey, girl, hold on, sit down for a minute,' Girija Bhabhi said sharply in precise Urdu, in a voice slightly softened by the folds of fat around her throat

Girija Bhabhi had the kind of figure that overflowed a chair, a very fair complexion, and a bearing that commanded everyone's respect. Most people addressed her as bhabhi—sister-in-law; some called her 'mummy'. She was a veteran Congress party worker, and came from a well-known and distinguished family.

Kanak sat down next to her.

'I've noticed you around here for several days. You're staying with that woman from Nainital, what's-her-name, Mrs Pant? What do you do? Are you a Punjabi refugee?' Bhabhi asked, her fair, fleshy brow furrowed.

Feeling a little nervous, Kanak hastily spoke about herself, describing how she had met Awasthi and Mrs Pant, and why she had come to Lucknow, adding in a worried voice, 'I've been here for eight days. Only yesterday I was told to submit an application for a job, which I did.'

'If they really wanted to offer you a job, they should have asked you to send your application by mail, rather than ask a young woman to leave her family and come here,' Bhabhi's raised eyebrows deepened the furrows on her forehead.

Such a negative observation upset Kanak.

Bhabhi continued, 'Beti, be cautious with these kind of people. Be on your guard, understand. It seems that you were brought up in a liberal-minded family. These people are small-minded, they keep their womenfolk in purdah, and jump at any chance to flirt with anybody's daughters and sisters. Watch out, your reputation is in your own hands. If you see anything fishy, go home at once, or come and tell me. I'll find you a decent family to stay with. Listen, mention my name to Awasthi. Ask him to tell me about the vacancy for which he sent in your application, and who's dealing with it.'

After a wait of three weeks, Kanak got a call for an interview from the director of the Information Department. The director's peon ushered Kanak into an anteroom where two young men were sitting and talking. Both stood up to welcome her. One was of a slim build, wore glasses that were a bit large for his swarthy face, and was dressed in a dark-brown achkan and a Gandhi cap. The other, taller and well built, wore khaki, military-style bush shirt and trousers. He was clean-shaven, his tanned face had a peculiar inexplicable cast, and a penetrating gaze.

'Bahinji, have you also come for the interview?' The achkan-clad man asked as Kanak took a chair.

'Yes,' Kanak replied.

'For a Hindi or Urdu language position?'

'I'm more fluent in Urdu. But I know Hindi also.'

'Then you applied for the Urdu post?' he asked with a smile, showing his paan-stained teeth.

Kanak nodded in agreement.

The man stood up, and pulling his achkan straight, said, 'Your humble servant Shiv Prasad Tewari, "Alok". I'm a freelance journalist, and also write poetry. I am often invited to poetic gatherings. Mr Gill is from Punjab.'

The other man remained silent and merely gave a civil nod to acknowledge Kanak's namaste.

Alok looked at his wristwatch and asked the peon with a large tilak painted on his forehead, 'What do you think, pandit? The sahib should arrive by eleven?'

'He's usually here by eleven or 11.30,' the peon replied, moving a wad of chewing tobacco to the other cheek.

'Shuklaji hasn't arrived?'

When the peon nodded in affirmation, Alok said, 'I'll look in on Shuklaji for two minutes. Call me when the sahib arrives.' He went out when the peon agreed.

Kanak sat staring at the blank wall, hands around her purse.

'You used to live in Lahore?'

'Yes,' Kanak replied, turning to face the other man.

'I seem to remember seeing you there at the time of the '42 movement.'

'You were in Lahore too?'

'I was with *Sitara*. Is your family in Lucknow too?'

'My parents and sister are in Delhi. I came here alone.'

'You were probably in the Student Congress. Was your father in service or a businessman?'

'My father owned the Naya Hind Press and publication house.'

'Your father is Pandit Girdharilalji?' The man's eyes opened a little wider.

'Yes.'

The man went silent, fixing his gaze on the floor. Kanak turned her eyes away. She would have liked for this sobre-looking man to talk about Lahore to pass the time.

Kanak heard him say 'Excuse me,' and looked back at him. 'You came from Delhi hoping to get this job?'

Kanak nodded, and asked, 'Do you live in Lucknow?'

He raised his eyes to answer her, 'Yes,' and asked hesitantly, 'Is Panditji in trouble?'

'Everyone's in the same boat now. We had to leave behind the printing press, our house, and everything else. The house we found in Delhi is more like a ruin.'

When he spoke again after a few moments' silence, Kanak saw that he was again looking at the floor, 'I've come for the job of a Urdu journalist, but I'm working as a proofreader for an English daily.'

They both fell silent looking away.

'Doesn't Panditji know any Congress people here?' He asked after some thought.

'Hardly anyone,' Kanak replied.

Alok returned walking briskly, 'The director sahib has arrived in his office.'

'Have you brought any references?' the man asked Kanak.

'Awasthiji, the parliamentary secretary, recommended me,' Kanak confessed.

'Then it's a sure thing,' Alok interjected. 'Let's see who's summoned to appear first before the court,' he said, and laughed at his own joke. 'Let's all wait for the interviews to be over, then go and a have coffee at the Coffee House.'

The peon went into the office when a bell rang, and returned to announce, 'P.S. Gill shaab.'

Gill replied without getting up, 'I don't want to appear for the interview.'

Kanak looked at him with surprise, and took a deep breath.

The peon went into the office, returned and called out, 'Miss Kanak Duttaji.'

After Kanak's return and before he was summoned, Alok said, 'Both of you please wait for me. We're going to be colleagues. I'll also be out in a few minutes.'

Gill asked Kanak after Alok went in, 'Your interview went well?'

'Can't say now. Will know in a couple of days. You should have gone in for the interview.'

'I already have a job.'

'But you came for the interview.'

'Yes, the pay was better here. I thought there wouldn't be any other applicant for the Urdu position. The liaison officer had said so.'

'The director asked me if I had worked with any newspaper and if I had done translations. What could I say? I just told him that I have no practical experience, but I have confidence that I can do the job. But in your case you had experience to qualify for this job.'

By being frank Kanak wanted to show that she appreciated Gill's kindness, but his gesture still might not guarantee her getting the job.

'No, no. It's not that.' Gill waved aside her thanks before looking at her, and said, 'I wouldn't have been hired because I had no recommendation.

Except two lines scribbled by the *Herald*'s editor. The liaison officer had advised me to come with a good recommendation. But from whom? I came only because I thought I would be the only candidate.'

They waited in silence for Alok. A thought crossed Kanak's mind, and she said to Gill, 'Excuse me.'

'Yes.' He looked at her.

'You worked at *Sitara*? Probably you knew Jai Puriji?'

'Sure, I did.' he stopped when Alok returned.

'My job is all settled.' Alok seemed very pleased. 'I knew it. They themselves invited me to appear here. Let's go.'

As they were leaving, the peon came and salaamed. Alok gave him a rupee as baksheesh.

When they came out of the secretariat, Alok took his position in the middle to be able to talk to each of them. He began a detailed account of the director's questions and the answers he had given. His report, longer than the interview itself, did not end till they reached the Coffee House. He was in really high spirits. Alok inquired about the questions Kanak had been asked, and gave his opinion on how she should have answered them.

Kanak's spirits sank on being told that she had not answered properly.

Alok asked Gill, 'You were the editor of the paper in Lahore?'

'The owner was the editor, but I did all the work. It was a weekly.'

'But you do copy-editing in English at the *Herald*?' Alok said with surprise.

'I can do that too. Now I'm working as a proofreader.'

'Proofreader? How much do they pay you?'

'Not much.'

'Do tell.'

'Eighty rupees.'

Kanak looked at Gill.

'This job would have paid you three times as much,' Alok said. 'Your appointment was certain. It could be a bad move for you to miss the interview.'

Now Kanak could not look at Gill. Alok advised Gill in a serious tone that he should try again next time there was a vacancy for a journalist in the Information Department. And since he would be working there, Alok assured Gill, he would definitely try to help Gill.

Over coffee, Alok advised Kanak to be more fluent in Hindi, 'Now, as you know, Hindi will be the national language. Who would care for Urdu or English?' He assured Kanak that he would help her get her writings published in Hindi journals, and asked, 'Do you write any poetry?'

Kanak said no. Alok began to recite a poem of his own 'The Sound of Change' and followed it by 'The Stranger'. Kanak and Gill had no occasion to say anything. Their eyes met twice. She's was dying to ask about Puri.

After the coffee, Alok offered to take Kanak by rickshaw to the Councillors Residence, but Kanak declined. He left, saying that he hoped to see Kanak at the office.

The Residence was on Gill's way to his destination in Udayganj. Kanak broached the subject as they began walking towards it, 'You said you knew Puriji?'

'Yes, quite well. Is Puri in Delhi? Is he at some newspaper?'

'I don't know. There's no news of him. He was neither with *Sardar*, nor with *Pairokaar*.' Kanak's enthusiasm began to wane.

'He wouldn't be at *Pairokaar*,' Gill said. 'Kashish treated him vary badly. I spoke in his support in that meeting of journalists.'

'Puriji was in Nainital on the nineteenth of August. There has been no news of him since then'

'I think he must be somewhere in UP. In Allahabad or Agra. He knows Hindi quite well.'

'He went from Nainital to help his family in Lahore on the nineteenth of August.'

'Nineteenth of August was a bad day. We were at Lala Moosa Camp then. It looked like as if we would all be killed there, but somehow we survived. One can never see the future.'

On their first meeting, as they walked in the winter sun surrounded by strangers, they felt a closeness because of their connection with Lahore, and Puri. And this gave Kanak an excuse to talk to him about Puri. She could not talk about Puri with her family without embarrassment, but with Gill she felt no hesitation. She had begun to have a feeling of trust and respect for Gill's kind and generous heart.

Kanak asked, 'Can you use your address to send a message for broadcast over the radio?'

Gill said, 'Sure, but how many people really get to listen to the radio? Puri would hear the message only if he is at some camp. The place I'm staying at belonged to a Muslim who had fled from the city. I haven't listened to the radio even once in two months. But, surely there's no harm in having the message broadcast.'

Kanak picked up the thread of the conversation, 'Puriji helped me in my studies for quite some time. I wanted to sit for the Hindi Prabhakar exam. My father offered to pay him, but he refused. He encouraged me to write, and showed me how to improve. Pitaji really liked his short stories and wanted to publish a collection of them, but this political upheaval made that impossible. Puriji got two of my short stories published in the weekend edition of *Pairokaar*. Several articles were left unfinished. None of the contemporary writers can match his brilliance. We'd invited him to Nainital, that's why I'm all the more worried.'

Gill agreed with Kanak, 'Puri is a very good writer. I found his imagination really inspiring. I've known him for several years. He was two years junior to me. He was at Dayal Singh College, I was at Christian College. In '40 and '41 we met often at literary gatherings. We were together in the Quit India movement. Our meetings became less frequent because of our differences about the war in '42, but this year in May he came to *Sitara* several times.'

Gill and Kanak reached the gate of the Councillors Residence. Gill slowed down and put his hands in his pockets, like someone who stops to think.

'Do you have to go? Aren't you enjoying the sunshine?' Kanak asked.

'I'm in no hurry. You want to walk more? The Station Road is just ahead.'

They walked up the slope. Kanak said, 'Are you a member of the Communist Party?'

'No. Not any more. I used to work in the editorial section of *Quami Jung* in '43 and '44.'

'You probably knew Narendra, Asad, Pradyumna and others. Puriji was helping them to maintain peace in March, April and May of this year. Were you also with him then?'

'I'd left the Party by the end of '45.'

'Why? Didn't the Party support the demand for Pakistan?' Kanak asked, surprised.

'I was expelled from the Party.'

'Why? For what reason?' Kanak pressed harder.

'It's a long story,' Gill paused, then added hastily. 'Because I cut off my hair. My parents were Sikhs. I too had uncut hair until 1945.'

Kanak scrutinized Gill's face. He looked sober and friendly. She thought,

'How would he look with a turban, his face covered with a beard?' His short, crisp hair and clean-shaven face gave a feeling of confidence and trust. To forcibly stick a turban and a bushy beard on such a face, she felt, would have been such an injustice. She felt a surge of sympathy for him.

She could not help asking, 'It should be a personal choice if one wants to cut his hair or shave his face. Why could it be a reason for the Party to expel someone? Narendra Singh and his sister Surendra were hardly orthodox.'

'I know that communists are not superstitious or intolerant; they shouldn't be. Many Sikh members in the Party didn't believe in keeping their hair long. But the Punjab branch of the Party made it a rule that Sikh members must not cut their hair because this might antagonize people.'

Kanak said in agreement, 'That would amount to deception, making people act contrary to their beliefs. That's not fair.'

Gill agreed with Kanak but defended the Party, 'It wasn't deception, but more like political discipline for practical reasons.'

'You did well to get rid of your hair! I wonder how you'd have looked if you still wore it long.' Feeing self-conscious, she added quickly, 'Well, you didn't follow the rule for the sake of your private belief. It was a matter of principle. You did right.'

'Yes, maybe...' He walked along the footpath, his eyes on the ground. He did not finish his sentence, and seemed lost in thought. Kanak asked to break the silence, 'Does a person's own freedom and beliefs have no value?'

'I don't know,' he muttered, as if his thoughts were still elsewhere. 'I lost the Party, I lost myself, I lost my family and I lost everything.'

'What happened?' Kanak asked gently.

Gill walked a few steps in silence, then said, still looking down, 'My uncle disowned me when I cut my hair. My father had died when I was little. My mother died before I sat for my matriculation exam. I was raised by my uncle who also paid for my schooling. He was an overseer in the Canal Department. He was very upset and wrote to me to say that I should never show my face if I had really mutilated my hair. When I was in Rawalpindi studying at the college, I fell in love with a girl. Her father was a lawyer. We were attracted to each other even before I grew a beard. We had decided to get married when we were still young.

'Saraswati was afraid that her father wouldn't agree to our marriage because of my shaky finances. She also knew that I had no income, that I was devoting all my time to Party work. So she finished her BA in Rawalpindi, and came to Lahore to train as a teacher. She wanted to begin earning some money so that we could get married. In Lahore we also had the chance to meet and talk to each other. She disliked long hair and bearded faces. When I met her in Rawalpindi in '45, she said, "I'll do anything for you, but can't you get rid of this nuisance on your face?" I didn't believe in keeping my hair untrimmed either. I asked permission from the Party when I returned to Lahore. They refused. I reasoned, "Why should I agree to something I didn't believe in?" The Party said that it would set a wrong example, and still refused. I found that hard to accept. I got rid of my long hair and beard.'

Kanak said, giving a quick upward glance, 'It would have been self-deception, going against one's beliefs just to please other people.'

Gill replied, 'No, the Party thought of it as self-discipline necessary to be in line with the masses.'

Gill's voice seemed to come from far away as he walked with his eyes downcast. He spoke again after a few moments, 'The training college for women in Lahore was closed in May after the riots. Saraswati had to go back to Rawalpindi. In the middle of August came the news of intense rioting in Rawalpindi. I left at once to help Saraswati and her family. It was chaos everywhere. It took me three days to reach Rawalpindi. By that time her house and the whole neighbourhood was burnt down. Not a single one of her family survived. I also had to take refuge in a camp. I met a Sikh carpenter there and his family, and came here with them in the first week of October. I at least got the proofreader's job. Out there are thousands looking for work. You yourself saw that. Panditji was quite well off in Lahore. Why did you have to look for a job?'

Kanak listened without uttering a word. Lost in their conversation they reached the Aishbagh bridge past the railway station. The sun sliding towards the horizon shone into their eyes. They turned around in silence. Her mind searched for some way to break his painful silence as her heart went out to him. Gill stopped in front of the gate to the Councillors Residence.

'Miss Dutta, forgive me,' Gill said in English, taking a deep breath. 'I got carried away and lost track of time.'

'Won't you come again? I feel so lonely. I know hardly anyone here,' Kanak said earnestly.

'I take this road going to my work. If you need any help let me know. I stay at the office even in my free time. There's nowhere else to go. Our telephone number is 893.'

'Do come around if you have time. I'm in room seventeen. What time do you get back?'

'I get off at an awkward time, 2.30 or three in the morning. May I come tomorrow after midday?'

'Sure. I really enjoyed the walk today. I was so fed up with having nothing to do.'

Next day Kanak opened the door to Mrs Pant's room and sat behind the bamboo curtain, reading the newspaper, then a book as she waited for Gill, and thinking absent-mindedly, 'Such a nice man, and what he had to go through.'

Girija Bhabhi came by after her lunch around two o'clock, cleaning her teeth with a toothpick. She invited Kanak to her room to ask about the job interview. She lay down, asked Kanak to sit beside her on the bed and began to talk. Lahore had a sizeable Kashmiri community, and many of Bhabhi's relatives lived there. Bhabhi was very fond of the city. Kanak could not get away for nearly an hour.

Gill had not arrived by sunset. The room seemed to close in around her as she waited for him. She decided not to wait any longer, went to the front veranda to call his number, and asked for Gill.

Gill said, 'I went to room seventeen between 2.15 and 2.30. The door was shut. I'll come tomorrow at the same time.'

Kanak was dismayed. Her thoughts returned many times to their conversation.

She waited impatiently the next day, as if waiting for someone from her family or an old acquaintance. She wore a suit of salwar-kameez and dupatta instead of a sari, in order to be able to walk more comfortably.

Gill said, 'The other day your speech indicated that you were a Punjabi, but in a sari you looked a bit foreign to me, and older. Today you look more natural.'

Kanak gave a satisfied smile.

That day they walked in front of the Council House and past the bazaar of Hazaratganj, through the lawns and parks beyond, crossed the bridge over the Gomati River and went up to Faizabad Road. It was pleasant to walk under the winter sun on wide, deserted, tree-lined roads. Kanak spoke of her days in Delhi, the incident at Durrani Gali, Syed's complaint to Gandhiji and the intervention by the police.

Gill spoke briefly about his journey on foot from Rawalpindi to Ferozepur.

Wanting to be frank with Gill, she told him about Aseer, the managing editor of *Sardar*, and Sinha, her stupidity of accepting the drink, and how she resisted their advances. She felt greatly relieved after opening her heart to Gill.

To fill a pause in the conversation, Kanak asked, 'How did you meet Saraswati?'

Gill told her everything in great detail.

On the way back, Gill was still deep in his story as they crossed Hazaratganj. On reaching the Coffee House, Kanak said, 'We must have a coffee.'

As they sat over their coffee cups, Kanak remembered, 'What a blessing that bore Alok is not with us.'

Gill failed to turn up the next day. After waiting until sunset, she telephoned anxiously.

Gill said that the proofreader on the afternoon shift was sick, and he had to fill in for him.

Gill could not come for the next two days either. Kanak felt lonely and even more miserable than she had the week before. Mrs Pant said when she returned that evening, 'Give me some mithai, here's to celebrate your letter of appointment. You have to join tomorrow.'

Kanak's heart brimmed with joy. With the dearness allowance added, her salary was going to be 235 rupees per month. She thought of telephoning Gill at once and telling him, 'You stood aside to let me have this job, but will I be up to it? I've so much to learn.'

Kanak got back from her first day in the office after being there from 10 to 5. She had not done any real work, but spent most of her time sitting at a desk receiving training. She felt tired and entitled to some rest; so she lay down and covered herself with a shawl. The short winter day was fading into dusk. Feeling lazy and to give her eyes some rest, she did not turn on the light. She thought she would overcome her fatigue before telling Gill about her first day on the job.

'Is Pant in?' She heard Awasthi's voice from outside. She straightened her sari and got up. Wrapping her shawl around her shoulders, she went to the door, 'Please come in.'

Awasthi entered with a laugh, 'What are you doing? Thought I'll come and congratulate you.'

Kanak said shyly, 'It was all due to your kindness. You deserve the credit. I thought I'd go and thank you tomorrow during the lunch break.'

'Come and sit down. You have nothing to thank me for,' he said, sitting on an armchair between the two beds. 'You're right. It was my responsibility and you were so unsure of yourself. Come sit here, why don't you.'

Kanak was about to switch on the light.

'Arey, let it be. You're not going to do any embroidery, are you? My eyes are tired after pouring over those files all day. Let me rest them a bit. Sit down.'

Kanak sat primly on the edge of the bed near the armchair. 'Would you like me to send for tea?' she asked.

'Arey, who wants tea.'

'I'd like to have a cup.'

'You can have it later. What's the rush?'

Kanak was sitting with her legs together, and her clasped hands around her knees. Awasthi took one of her hands into his, and said with a smile, 'Are you happy now?'

She pulled back her hand, and wrapping her shawl tightly around her shoulders, said, 'Thanks. You really helped me.' Her tone became serious, and she moved away a little.

'Are you thanking me or throwing stones at me? Let me congratulate you properly. Come here.' Awasthi's paan-stained lips spread in a peculiar smile. He tried to grab Kanak's elbow.

Kanak got up from the bed and moved towards the door. She said, her brow creased in anger, 'What are you doing? Speak out whatever you want to say.' She switched the light on.

'What do I have to say? That's a fine way to show your thanks and gratitude!'

'If that's what you think, I don't want this job. I can go back to Delhi.'

The bamboo curtain covering the door was raised. 'What's going on?' asked Mrs Pant as she entered, then exclaimed in delight, 'Aha, Awasthiji! When did you come?'

She looked at Awasthi, then at Kanak. 'Why, what is it?' she asked with curiosity mixed with surprise, her eyes again going from one to the other.

Awasthi, his face grim, sat in the armchair without moving. He gave Kanak a hard stare, 'What do you mean by this? Who do you think you are?'

'What has happened?' Mrs Pant asked uneasily.

'Whatever we do for her, she's never satisfied,' Awasthi said from the chair, his eyes hard and glaring.

'What happened,' Mrs Pant asked again.

'Ask her,' said Awasthi as he went out into the veranda.

'Why don't you say something? What happened?'

'I don't like all this,' Kanak replied, her eyes downcast.

'If you don't like it then take your things and get out! What is it that you don't like?' Mrs Pant asked in a harsh voice.

Kanak's body and mind burned with rage. She flashed a piercing look at Mrs Pant. Then bowed her head and biting her lip, stood silently. She felt like walking out then and there, but where could she go?

Mrs Pant admonished her again, 'Why don't you speak up? What is it that you don't like? Didn't we do everything we could for you? If you're used to such fancy living, why don't you find a place in the hotel across the street?'

'No, bahinji, that's not the reason. I'm much obliged to you as it is,' Kanak said meekly.

'What is it then? What else do you want?'

'I don't like being pawed,' Kanak tried to explain that her anger was not directed at Mrs Pant.

'Oh sure! Aren't you the last of the touch-me-not maidens! It was you who was chasing Awasthiji. You used to go after him in Nainital, now you're here from Delhi. Aren't you ashamed of smearing his reputation? Everybody knows about his status and high position,' keeping her voice low, Mrs Pant accused Kanak of improper behaviour.

Kanak, her head still bent, said quietly, 'Bahinji, you weren't here. What can I tell you? Believe what you please. Where can I go at this time of night? I'll leave tomorrow.'

'Don't do me any favours. Do whatever you like.' Mrs Pant continued to mutter disdainfully as she changed into an ordinary sari. 'So it's come to this! You do someone a favour and they snap back at you. Doing a good turn earns you a bad name.'

Mrs Pant went out of the room. Walking towards the dinning hall she called out in her normal tone, 'Arey Bechu, be kind enough to serve me a couple of chapattis.'

Kanak stood motionless, wrapped in thought for several minutes. Then she went out resolutely, shut the door without locking it, and went towards

Girija Bhabhi's suite. She tapped gently at her door with her finger. Bhabhi asked in a growl, 'What is it? Who's it at this hour?'

Kanak pushed the door open, went in and said, 'It's me, mummy.'

Girija Bhabhi had a suite of two rooms. She lay on her bed in the inner room, reading the morning newspaper in the light of a bedside lamp. She held the paper at arm's length.

'What are you doing here at this hour of the night?' Bhabhi asked removing her reading glasses. Her tone changed when she saw Kanak's expression, 'What's happened? Come here.' She moved aside to make room for Kanak.

Kanak could not speak for a while as she sat on the bed. Bhabhi put her hand consolingly on her back and asked, 'Why, was that mua Thakur bothering you?'

Kanak bit her lip to choke back her tears, and briefly told about Awasthi's behaviour and Mrs Pant's harsh words. Then she said, 'Mummy, where can I go at this time of night? I'll go back to Delhi tomorrow. I don't care to have such a job.'

'Hah, just look at this stupid girl!' Bhabhi scolded her affectionately in her typical throaty voice. 'This so-called job was not a charitable gift from what's-his-name Awasthi! You are now a government employee, entitled to your salary. Is this what you mean by your so-called resolve to stand on your own two feet? Listen, if you cry I'll give you a slap. What can that bastard do to harm you? If he dares, I'll go straight to the CM. Such scoundrels give the Congress party a bad name. When these no-goods had nothing and were jailed for taking part in political movements, they were fine. Reaching public positions has gone to their heads. Common decency is too rich a dish for curs like them to stomach. And if that creature from Nainital bothers you again, tell her to speak to your mummy. Such an uncultured, stupid female. Are the likes of her worthy of being members of the assembly? Don't worry, I'll make some arrangement for you. I had my suspicions since I first saw you with her.'

Feeling no appetite, Kanak didn't even think of dinner. Rage over the indignity meted out to her was making her feel hot even under a single blanket. Feeling light-headed, she dozed off thinking, 'The fear of being humiliated makes a woman so vulnerable. Men can treat other men like slaves, profit from their labour, take away their money and demand bribes from them, but women they only want to humiliate.' She cried quietly,

thinking of Puri, 'Where are you? Have you forgotten me? Didn't you hear
my radio message? What else can I do? I can't go back to being a burden
on my father. What if Gill and not Mrs Pant had come at that moment?'
Kanak saw in her imagination Gill punching Awasthi in the face. 'Gill is so
nice, but why do I always need a male to defend my honour? Why can't I
defend myself? Mummy was right, what harm could Awasthi do? It was he
who got snubbed. I can belong to no one but Puriji. Where is he? There's
no point in losing heart. Look at Gill. What he has not been through. Maybe
I'll see him tomorrow.

Girija Bhabhi made arrangements for Kanak to stay with a respectable
Kayastha family on Cantonment Road near the Councillors Residence.
Munshi Shankar Saran was a retired school headmaster, who had rented
out half of his house to supplement his pension. He had married off his
three daughters, but the eldest became a widow and came back with her
six-year-old daughter to live with her parents. She had managed to pass the
teachers training exam after her husband's death, and was now teaching
at a girls' school.

Munshiji rented out Kanak a room in his half of the house. A charpoy
fitted into one end of the room without leaving any space at the head or
foot. A small cupboard was built into the wall. Between the door and the bed
was just enough space to fit another bed. Munshiji put a cheap rattan chair
and a low three-legged stool in this empty space so that the room could be
considered 'furnished'. With a window overlooking the street and another
on the adjoining wall, the room could be said to be 'cross-ventilated'. Out
of his respect for Girija Bhabhi, Munshiji had accepted Kanak as a paying
guest at 75 rupees per month.

As Kanak had to change her residence in a hurry, she could not tell Gill
about it immediately. Girija Bhabhi had been very supportive, but Gill
was of her own age and from Lahore. He was someone she could speak
to freely to her heart's content. A couple of days later she telephoned Gill
after work, to tell him about her new address.

She changed from sari to salwar-kameez upon reaching home. The street
lights were on. She looked onto the street through her window, and seeing
Gill approach, quickly left the house. Their eyes lit up upon seeing each other.

'I thought that you had forgotten about me,' she said, pretending to
pout, giving him an accusing look.

'Wah, every time I came this way, I passed in front of room seventeen of the Councillors Residence. How would I know that you changed your address? I asked Mrs Pant yesterday when I saw her. She replied brusquely, just like a UP-wallah, "What do I know? She's left this place."' Gill added, 'I'd have been worried if you hadn't phoned me.'

Their eyes met again. Kanak's heart filled with satisfaction that there was someone who cared for her, someone she could lean on.

'What's this? You're not wearing anything warm.' she said with concern. She had a shawl wrapped around her shoulders. She had left her heavy woollens in Delhi, and had brought along only a shawl and a cardigan when coming to Lucknow in November.

'It's not that cold yet,' Gill tried to make light of her remark.

'It's chilly today. I'll knit you a sweater. I used to knit one every year for my brother-in-law. Do you know all the trouble I've had to face here?'

Kanak told him about Awasthi's misbehaviour, Mrs Pant's reaction, and how Girija Bhabhi had come to her aid. Then she poured her heart out and talked about Puri coming to Lucknow in search of work and what he had to go through in the city. This led her to tell Gill about her love for Puri and her father's opposition to their friendship. She said, 'If I could find him, I wouldn't care about this job. We both wanted to do something literary together.'

'You should be able to find out about him,' Gill said in a rather strained voice. 'But I'll be very lonely if you go away. We've known each other only for a few days, but Kanak, after meeting you I feel that all is not lost. You'll go away, and you'll forget me.'

He spoke tenderly, calling her by her name. Kanak felt a thrill of joy.

'Why do you say that?' Kanak said, looking into his eyes, 'That'll never happen. I've never trusted anyone so readily, didn't hide anything from you. I don't know why. That's the truth.'

She looked again into his eyes, and dropping her gaze, said, 'I had a high regard for my jijaji, more than I could have had for a brother, but I've never confided so much even to him. I don't know why I took to you. Why would I loose contact with you. We will keep in touch. And who knows what may happen, what fate may have in store for me?' She bowed her head sadly.

Gill tried to reassure her, 'Don't lose heart. We'll find Puri. I'll do all I can.'

Kanak's job at the department of information was to read through Urdu
newspapers and prepare a summary news bulletin. The work was not
difficult, but it was not very interesting either. She was the only female
amongst the office staff. The director sat in a separate office. The other
journalists spent a good deal of time idly chatting, and going out to have
paan and a smoke. Kanak had ample time to do her own reading. Once in
a while she would be given a government statement in English to translate
into Urdu. All this was preferable to spending time in the company of
Munshiji's middle-aged wife, and his eldest daughter who behaved like
another middle-aged woman.

Her office duties ended at five. That week Gill was working on the 4
p.m. to 2 a.m. shift. Twice he had taken time off between seven and eight
to come and meet her. They went for a walk on the road along Chattar
Manzil. She no longer felt lonely after meeting Gill, and evenings held the
promise of going for a walk with him.

The Christmas holiday fell on a Friday. Kanak took Saturday off to be able
to go to Delhi to get her winter bedding and the rest of her warm clothing.
She had been living away from her family only for one-and-a-half months,
but it seemed like ages. She wanted to reassure her parents about her
well-being, and also wanted to meet them to bolster up her own courage.
She wrote to her brother-in-law inviting him to come to Delhi for two
days, and to bring Kanta and Nano along so that she could meet them too.

It had turned quite cold in Lucknow. Fog filled the air in the mornings
and evenings. Kanak wanted to knit a sweater for Gill before going to Delhi.
She went with him to the bazaar in Aminabad to buy wool. A crowd had
gathered near the shop. The refugees had set up makeshift displays on the
footpaths in front of the regular shops. This led to some kind of quarrel
everyday. The established shopkeepers felt that they had welcomed and
helped their suffering Hindu refugee brothers, but now the same refugees
were stealing their business. The refugees in turn argued vehemently that
they had nowhere else to go.

Pandit Girdharilal had his daughter sit beside him as he told her how proud
and happy he was at her achievments. He continued in the same vein, 'Beta,
you are a very brave and sensible person. A job is only a means, not an
end in life. You should also look after the other aspects of life. Everything
has its proper time. Life should follow a natural pattern. You're all alone

there. If you were here, we could talk to our acquaintances and friends and arrange something nice for you. You can make sensible decisions, so nothing would be done without your consent. Now you should think about settling down in life.'

Kanak took the hint and replied, 'Pitaji, what need is there to begin searching with that idea in mind? I'm quite happy. I was thinking that once I'm settled down properly, once I find a decent house, you, mother and Kanchi should come and stay with me. Lucknow is so much quieter compared to Delhi.'

Kanak had to go back to Lucknow on Sunday evening. On Sunday morning Panditji said, remembering Puri, 'Bhai, there's been no news of Jaidev Puri. You people should at least make some effort to trace him. He's a very capable and talented young man. He has a personality. He must be with some newspaper or doing literary work, I think. A person like that can't remain unknown, but we must try to find out about him. That's our duty. Once he is located, we should keep up correspondence with him. I always admired him. He wrote wonderful stories. I was thinking, what if one of his stories was made into a film.'

Kanak took heart at her father's words. This was an indication of her father's acceptance of her wishes. Panditji had made no reference to Puri before this. She surmised, 'It's possible that he might be in the film line. He had considered it.'

'Then he'll become known very quickly. We've got information about most of our acquaintances little by little. I thought of having a message broadcast for him on the radio, but he's not the type who'd remain unnoticed for long. He's a brilliant young man. We're sure to hear about him if not today, then very soon. A short story by him or some other writing is bound to appear somewhere or other sooner or later.'

When Kanak reached Lucknow railway station at 8.30 in the morning, Gill was there to meet her. He hired a rickshaw and dropped her at her lodging. Kanak had to get ready and go to the office, so there was little time for them to talk. She told him that he must come and meet her in the evening. She was impatient to tell Gill about her father's change of heart.

In the evening when they went for a walk, she told Gill about her stay in Delhi.

Gill replied in English, 'That's good. Not only has an obstacle been removed from your path, but a weight has been lifted from your heart. You must be feeling relieved. For me there's no one else but you. If you're happy, I'm happy too.'

Kanak was silent for a few moments, then she replied also in English, 'Do you think what I feel for you is any less intense? Who else do I have but you, you tell me?'

They walked leisurely and companionably talking about the uncertainties of life, feelings of loneliness and the emotional and practical limitations of love in the absence of somebody one could trust and confide in, somebody really close to one's heart. They reached the railway station. The neighbourhood was full of the noise of refugees seeking shelter on the pavements. Both of them were so engrossed in talking about their dreams and sharing their views that the presence of others around them was intolerable. They walked for quite a distance on the lonely, dark road going to Raebareilly before turning around.

Going for walks gave them both great pleasure. Not being able to do so upset them. On New Year's Day, Kanak left her lodging just after noon, and they both sat and talked in sun-dappled shade of trees in the Botanical Garden. Kanak was often curious about Saraswati, and Gill held nothing back from her. Listening to him Kanak got lost in her own thoughts. Gill being so ready to do anything for the sake of his love seemed so beautiful and attractive to her. Sometimes they would look into each others eyes, lower their gaze and sit in silence. They were content just to be together.

Away from her family and all alone in Lucknow, Kanak had begun to experience her independence. Not to be beholden to anyone gave her a sense of pride and dignity. Her father was not going to interfere with her attempt to decide her future. She was completely free; bound by nothing but her own discretion. And she had a trusted friend like Gill, in whom she had unlimited confidence and with whom she shared all her secrets; who, she knew, would not abandon her in times of stress and difficulty.

This fond feeling between them and a sense of mutual trust and confidence brought them so close that there was no need for any formality. They fulfilled each other's natural need for companionship. Gill could show his disapproval to Kanak without any qualms. He would affectionately call her 'Kiki' or sometimes just 'Kee', and Kanak would feel a surge of attraction towards him. She had a pet name for him: Gillu. He would give her a playful pinch just to see her reaction, and she would have to grasp his hand to stop him. As she trusted him, his playfulness did not annoy her.

That week Gill was on the 8 p.m. to 4 a.m. shift. When Kanak met him on the Saturday evening, she had something in mind that she had been meaning to tell him. Pressing against his arm as they walked along Station Road, she said, 'I want to say something. Don't say no.'

'What is it?'

'Promise me that you'll agree in advance. The thing is that Puriji once refused when I asked him for something in the same words. I felt very insulted. Even the slightest formality in close relationships bothers me very much. I couldn't say no to anything you ask me.'

'Do you have to drag Puri into every discussion between you and me?' Gill sounded annoyed.

'Why does it upset you? In spite of my memories of him, I get the same satisfaction in your company. Who else do I have? Don't you miss Saraswati?'

'The truth is that I don't any more. I loved her for four years, while she was still alive. Didn't put my friends and family before her. If I had to, I'd certainly have laid down my life for her, but I'm alive and she's dead. Up to now I felt dead too, but everything has changed. Why did you make me feel that I was still alive? For me you're the one, but for you it's still only Puri,' Gill replied in a hurt voice.

Kanak's head was bent. Taking Gill's hand in hers to console him, she tried to explain, 'Gillu, can you forget someone you've loved?'

'Love is the only real thing in life. It doesn't exist only in your imagination and thoughts.' He asserted, thinking of Kanak's reply as a reproach.

'No, Gillu, don't be angry. I asked only so that I could understand you.' She clasped his hand tightly, as if not wanting to let him go. 'Tell me, is it really possible to forget someone you've been in love with? For me the wish to love and to be loved is entirely natural, and to let go of that desire seems unthinkable.'

'What do you mean by letting go?' Gill said irritably. 'You tell me, if a wound begins to close, shouldn't you let it heal? Should you go on pining over your loss and your pain? If it's so wrong to seek the fulfilment of love, why don't you push away someone who is in search of it?'

Kanak pulled at his hand lovingly to pacify him. She said, 'Listen. It's true that I can't forget him, but haven't I been fair in revealing my affection? There's no contradiction between my feelings and my bevaviour.' She held his hand tightly in both of hers, as if she wanted to convince him of her sincerity. Had they not been walking outside, she would have taken him in her arms to reassure him. Her soft, warm tone was meant to show him that her affection had given her the right to give him a close hug.

In her heart she believed that she could put her trust in Gill and abandon herself to her feelings for him. He was like a pet lion and she could even playfully put her head between his opened jaws, in full confidence that he would not hurt her or take advantage of her. She thought that she could play innocent and flirt with him, and then stop him just by raising her hand.

Gill's anger did not subside, 'Achchha, let's change the subject.' He tried to pull his hand away.

'No, I won't let you stay angry.' She did not let go of his hand.

'First you push me away, then you pull me back!' Gill seemed even more annoyed.

'Gillu, do I really push you away?' Her eyes brimmed with tears.

'You don't want to admit that you're doing it, but you do hurt me. Why do you pretend to be so innocent? That's why I ask you to leave me alone. You've had enough of love. You just want to see me suffer, and you do that by stopping me from getting close to you.'

'Gillu, how have I made you suffer, what pain did I ever cause you?'

'If you don't want to understand, forget it.'

'Gillu, only the thought of what is right... You know very well. What else can I say...'

'That's just what I mean. You draw too fine a line between right and wrong for me to see it. I want to stay away rather than be pushed away.'

'I touch your feet and beg you. Do not torture me like this.'

'Why should you feel tortured? The one who feels tormented is I because I cannot tear myself away and find myself rejected when you give me the cold shoulder.'

'Achchha, enough of your anger. It's up to you.'

'Well, let it go. Forgive me. I'm sorry for what I said.'

'You're saying the same thing over and over again.'

'What do you mean?'

'Don't put the blame on me. It's up to you now. I've nothing more to say.'

'You're cross with me?'

'Why should I be? It's you who are upset. I'm tired, I can't walk any further.'

Walking rather slowly, they had reached the Charbagh railway station. Gill hailed a rickshaw.

Sitting in the rickshaw, with her mind and her body in turmoil, Kanak felt drained. She rested her head on Gill's shoulder. Gill had his arm around her. The rickshaw was travelling along Station Road. Kanak bit at Gill's arm as a punishment for making her cry. She had never before allowed him to kiss her.

Mindful of the rickshaw driver, Gill said in English in a low voice, 'Jodh Singh and his family will go to his brother-in-law's house tomorrow morning for the Akhand Paath chanting ceremony. They won't be back before evening. The other people in the gali don't bother with us Punjabi refugees. It's a small house. I'll hang a dhurrie on the wall as a signal. At this time I'll show you where the gali begins.'

Kanak listened quietly, her side pressed to his.

'You come to the door and call for Kartaro or rattle the chain lock.'

Gill showed Kanak the way to his gali in Udayganj, and then hired another rickshaw to drop her near her home. Noticing that Kanak had not said a word, he asked, 'Kee, tell me the truth, you're not cross?'

'Get away, you idiot,' she replied, smiling warmly.

They squeezed each other's hand before getting out of the rickshaw. Kanak agreed to be at his house between 10.30 and eleven.

Gill had been waiting anxiously, since ten in the morning for a call at the outside door or for the lock chain to rattle. He had left the door unlatched. He paced around the small aangan restlessly, unmindful of the cold. The chain rattled and he rushed to the door, and opening it, said, 'Come in.'

'No,' said Kanak, and paused to catch her breath.

Gill was shocked to see Kanak's eyes blood-shot, and her face thin and bloodless. A part of her shawl covered her unkempt hair. The rickshaw that brought her waited nearby.

'I came so that you shouldn't hang on waiting for me. Please forgive me. We'll talk when you come in the evening.' She paused for breath after each sentence, then turned back to leave.

Overwrought and at a loss, Gill went in the evening to Cantonment Road to meet Kanak. She came out when she saw him from her window, dressed in her usual style and seemed outwardly composed, although her face looked pale and haggard.

As they turned on to Abbot Road, Gill asked, 'You don't look well. Do you want to walk? Shall we go and sit somewhere or take a rickshaw?'

'I'll walk. I'm fine,' Kanak replied, her head bent. 'Forgive me for my behaviour.' She spoke haltingly, 'I deceived you. Not only do I love Puriji, but we've been like husband and wife. I don't know what came over me yesterday. I was swept away by my feelings for you, and in one moment of delirium I tried to make you mine too. That would have meant deceiving you both. I did something dreadful, but at least I saved myself from actually doing something wrong. I blame myself and I'm so ashamed. I didn't sleep all night. I just cried by myself. I'm so sorry.'

A feeling of self-loathing and shame overwhelmed Gill. He said in a guilty tone, 'I'm the one to blame. I thought that the nightmare of Partition had wiped out the past and that I had found you in place of Saraswati and we could be husband and wife. It was me who caused you to act that way.'

'No, no. It didn't happen that way. It was my fault. I perhaps made too much of my feelings for you, and in the end we both had to pay for it. I knew it wasn't the right thing to do, but I was drawn to it unconsciously.'

Both were trying to analyse their motives and behaviour in an attempt to take on the blame of this uncomfortable episode. They tried to examine it objectively and as something that had happened in the past. Kanak said, 'The truth is that I encouraged it. I tried to hide and hold back my feelings so as not to give in to them. You've made me face up to that. The memory of Puriji helped me. It's different for you. You don't have to answer to anyone. It was me who hid from the truth.'

Kanak's voice was strained with pain, 'I won't be able to stop loving you. What had to happen did happen. I've caused you much pain. Forgive me if you can, give me your support as you have done up to now. Otherwise I'll have to accept that I lost you because of my recklessness. I'll never forget you. Your love for me was so selfless. I can't stop loving you, nor can I leave him. I'll accept the consequences of my mistake.'

She felt so drained that she had to take a rickshaw to get back home.

Kanak's behaviour now took on a seriousness that reflected the heaviness of her heart. Confused by the turmoil of her feelings and thoughts, she was drowned in a numb listlessness. Days and events slid by. Her face showed her worry and distress. Munshiji, his wife and their daughter advised her to consult a homeopath that they knew. They would wonder: Was the young woman affected so much by Gandhiji's death? Or had she got some bad news of her family? Her office colleagues were puzzled that someone who had been so spontaneous, outgoing and sociable had become so withdrawn. Now when she smiled, it looked forced and a pale imitation of her former good humour.

After a week she seemed to recover and return to her old self. She and Gill met only three times in the next two weeks. There was a forced seriousness to their conversation, as if each was guilty and ashamed in the presence of the other. There was no mention of the unpleasant affair.

Kanak got a letter from her father every Friday. Nayyar was too busy to write. When she wrote to Kanta, her sister wrote back rather briefly and that too after a week or so. She had no hired help, and seemed to be strained out from looking after her house even if it was small. She would ask Kanak to keep writing even if she did not always reply. When Kanak returned from her office in the second week of February, Munshiji's wife handed her a thick envelope that had come in the mail. The weight of the envelope made Kanak look at the handwriting—it was from her brother-in-law.

She opened the door to her room, sat on the bed and eagerly ripped open the envelope. Nayyar's letter was in English. There was also a large sheet of paper that had been folded several times. Kanak read the letter first.

After a few lines of news of the family, Nayyar had written, 'Perhaps you have already received Puri's letter. If not, I am giving you some unexpected news. I ran into him at the law court about a week ago.'

Every fibre in Kanak's body became tense with excitement. She gripped the letter tightly and devoured its contents, 'It was good to see Puri! I had no idea that he was in Jalandhar too. I was excited to meet him, but I can't say why he showed no joy or enthusiasm at meeting me after such a long time. When I told him that I had settled in Jalandhar, he expressed no desire to meet me again. He asked about Panditji. I told him that he was in Delhi, and gave him the address. Maybe he meant to inquire after you. He didn't mention you, so I didn't bring it up either. It's possible that you might have got his letter care of pitaji, otherwise this poster will explain everything. It could be that he was so abrupt because he has so much on his mind. That's all for now. I'm up to my neck in the struggle to make a living. Hope the work you're doing is to your taste. Nano remembers you and can now say in complete but broken sentences that her aunt has gone to Lucknow. Tell me all about yourself in detail. Love from Nano and your sister.'

She raced through the letter, read it again from beginning to end, and then unfolded the poster. It announced the publication of *Nazir* with Puri as the editor. The first issue was to be published on 1 March . The address was: Jai Puri, Chief Editor *Nazir*, Kamaal Press, Mohalla Bahadurgarh, Mai Heeran Gate, Jalandhar.

Kanak read the advertisement over and the letter once again with particular care. She did not like what Nayyar had written, 'Jijaji is so prejudiced and sees something wrong or cynical in everything about Puriji.' She again went over the poster and the part of the letter about Puri, and decided, 'Jijaji can think what he wants.' She repeated to herself several times, 'Jai Puri, Chief Editor.' The echo of those words was so satisfying to her.

A sense of impatience overcame her: What should she do? Her thoughts seemed inadequate and the room too small to contain her feelings. She lay down on the bed to compose herself, and closed her eyes. In her imagination she saw Puri in various situations. The office of the periodical, a printing press... a very busy Puri.

Luckily Munshiji's granddaughter called and distracted her, 'Aunty, come and have your meal.' Dinner time in Munshiji's home was around six. Going in to dinner helped Kanak to collect herself. The thought crossed her mind that she might have told Gill if they were meeting later that evening, but he was on the night shift. She lay down on her bed again to reflect. She spent the night waking up and falling back to sleep, and thinking things over.

By morning she had made up her mind. It was Sunday. At eight o'clock she took a rickshaw and went to Gill's house. He was surprised to see her so early. She asked him to step out into the gali, and showed him the poster that Nayyar had sent, but not the letter with the negative comments about Puri. She simply gave a summary of what Nayyar had written.

Gill congratulated her, and said he too was happy to get the news.

'It turned out well because of your good nature and support,' she said, moved by his kindness.

Kanak wanted to leave that very day for Jalandhar by the Punjab Mail that left Lucknow in the early afternoon. Her father had apparently withdrawn his objection, but how could she ask his permission to go to see Puri before they were married? Her father himself would have written to Puri after getting the news, but the business of writing letters and then Puri's coming to Lucknow could have easily taken up a couple of weeks. Puri also had the burden of launching the weekly. Waiting that long while counting every second would tax her patience to the limit, Kanak felt. The thought of surprising Puri by arriving at his home unannounced gave her a thrill of excitement. If she could just for once satisfy her longing and talk to him about their future together, she would have all the patience in the world. Let the agony of six months' separation come to an end.

Gill agreed with her after a few moments' thought, 'I'll see you off. On Monday morning I'll also hand in your application for leave. You've been working only for two months. Don't ask for a long leave of absence. Send me a telegram from there about your plans.'

The Punjab Mail, crossing hundreds of miles of fog-blanketed plains of the United Provinces and Punjab overnight, reached Jalandhar at dawn. Mist swirled about the city roads in the freezing cold. Kanak had wrapped a shawl over her long coat. She had only hand luggage. She hired a tonga and after inquiring the way several times, found the gali in Mohalla Bahadurgarh with the house that had the signboard of Kamaal Press.

The door below the signboard was closed. Acrid, oily smoke smelling of burning paper and cloth seeped out from between the cracks of the door. Kanak knocked. A growl came from inside, 'Who's there?' The door opened and a man, hunched up because of the cold, peered out. The servant fell silent on seeing a lady standing by the tonga.

Raldu did not know whether the woman bundled up in a coat and shawl was Urmila's mother or someone else. A well-dressed lady had come in a tonga and was asking for his master. Must be someone from the family, he thought. Without any question he opened the door that led to the inner courtyard and took Kanak's luggage from the tonga.

Raldu climbed the stairs carrying Kanak's blanket and bag ahead of her, but moved aside upon reaching the landing to let her go first. The door was shut, and Kanak called, 'Please open the door.' She kept her voice low, not to show her excitement. Her heart rejoiced at the thought that her words would reach Puri's ears.

She had climbed up the stairs without pausing and now leaned against the door to catch her breath.

'Who's there?' She heard Puri reply as the unlatched door opened from the pressure of her hand.

She went into the room. It was light enough for her to see. The door to a room on her left was open and she saw Puri pushing the quilt aside and getting out of the bed.

A flash of excitement ran through her body like an electric current. She wanted to jump into Puri's arms when behind him the light-complexioned face of a girl peeped out from under the covers—eyes wide with surprise, hair tousled and the bindi on her forehead smudged.

The face disappeared again shyly under the quilt.

Puri did not respond with any eagerness, he was far too surprised.

Raldu put down the bag and the folded blanket on top of it, and went back downstairs.

The electric feeling suddenly drained out of Kanak's body. She felt limp and her knees gave way.

'You?' Puri exclaimed in amazement, taking a step forward. The words seemed to be forced from his lips. He looked at her aghast.

Kanak's head swam and she covered her eyes with her hands.

Puri collected himself. He held her arm and moving her away out of sight of the bed, asked, 'Have you just arrived? You've come from Delhi?'

Kanak squatted down on her haunches as her knees buckled under her. Such an end to her long search for Puri and this reward for all her struggles left her completely at a loss. Her head was reeling, her breath short.

Puri closed the door between the rooms. He helped her to her feet and led her to the doorway where he unrolled a chatai and helped her sit on it. Taking her into his arms, he murmured into her ear, 'Kanni!'

Kanak began to weep.

Puri said quietly, 'Kanni! Listen, Kanni! Listen to me.'

Her face buried in her hands on her knees, she broke into loud sobs. The intensity of her crying prevented her from hearing what Puri said or uttering a word of her own. Through her tears she could still see the girl's pretty face, her dishevelled hair, her smudged bindi, and another wave of tears would sweep over her.

Holding Kanak in his arms, Puri pleaded and even begged her by touching her feet to be heard. It took a while for Kanak to calm down enough to listen to him.

She took her hands from her face. Her eyes were swollen and red, and still filled with tears. 'What does all this mean?' she asked.

'I'll explain everything. I never hid anything from you. Give me a chance. You began to cry the moment you walked in, without even asking for an explanation.' His voice trembled and his lips quivered. To hold back his tears, he turned away his head.

Taking his hand in hers, she asked, 'What is it, tell me.'

Biting his lip to show his effort to hide his agitation, Puri asked, 'Why should you start crying without even asking me for an explanation?'

'After what I saw for myself?'

'You should have at least heard me out,' he said in a strained voice. 'You don't realize what I've been through.'

'Tell me,' Kanak's tone was softer.

Puri fell silent for a few moments, then making an effort to swallow the lump in his throat, replied, 'There's more to it than you saw at first glance. You've no idea of the life-and-death situations I've been thorough. You simply can't imagine the nightmarish feeling of being at the mercy of chance. You don't know how many times I've stared in the face of death, how helpless I was and I still am.'

Kanak sat with her chin resting on her knee, her eyes fixed on his face. Avoiding her piercing stare, Puri tried to collect his thoughts as he slowly began, 'Let me explain what brought me to this situation. When fate deals you a bad blow it knocks you senseless, without knowing where to find help or whom to turn to for help. Your reactions surprise you when you recover from the shock, but that leaves you even more helpless. Now, Kanni, only you can save me.'

He stopped to draw his breath. Kanak asked, with a stony glare, 'Who is she? How did all this happen?'

'Kanni, have I ever hidden anything from you? I've always told you everything.'

'What did you tell me? When?'

'I've told you about that incident at Murree, about the girl whose tutor I was there.'

Kanak recalled that two years before, when they had begun sharing their secrets to show their trust in each other, Puri had told her about an incident with Urmila at Murree, and how he was not attracted to just any girl, that physical beauty alone did not appeal to him.

'How did she get here?' Kanak wanted to know.

'That was her fate!' He replied, with a deep sigh. 'The very same reason that brought me here. What I've been through makes me doubt sometimes whether I'm really alive. What a horrible nightmare this Partition has turned out to be! The train I took after leaving Nainital was attacked just before reaching Ludhiana. It was full of Muslim passengers who had got on at Saharanpur and Ambala. Mobs bent on murder and bloody revenge didn't want to leave a single one of them alive. Many spears and knives were thrown.' He saw Kanak shiver, and continued, 'but I was at the end of the compartment and a human wall of bodies saved me. The spears hurled by the attackers hit those on top of me and that saved my life. It wasn't easy to crawl out from under the dead bodies. When it was over I could hardly believe I was still alive and that I hadn't gone mad.'

Kanak shivered again, and took hold of his arm. Puri continued his tale of being robbed at dagger point on a dark road, his feeling faint with hunger and the futile attempt to sell his bedding, about washing dishes at the dhaba in return for a meal.

Tears welled in Kanak's eyes. Puri went on speaking in a choked voice, lost in his recollections.

'Puri bhaiji!' Someone called from the stairway.

Puri got up quickly and went to the landing.

Rikhiram stood halfway up the staircase. He knew about Urmila living upstairs, and Raldu had told him that another woman guest had come, so he tactfully called without coming up all the way.

Seeing him still dressed in his pyjamas, Rikhiram asked, 'Bhaiji, are you well?' Usually Puri was in the office before the arrival of the workers at the press. By his presence he ensured that the staff arrived punctually, and began work without wasting time.

'It's all right. I've just got a headache. Tell the treadle operator to print the work ordered by Charan Singh. The litho-cylinder can finish printing the court job. I'll be down in a few minutes.'

Puri went back inside. He leaned down and spoke in a quiet voice, 'You've been travelling all night in this cold. A cup of tea?'

Kanak held his arm and made him sit down again, 'That can wait. How did she get here?'

'I haven't told you yet how I got to this house.'

'Still, tell me, where did you meet her?'

'It's a long and tragic story,' he said in a pain-filled voice. 'Her family had come to Jalandhar as refugees. This poor soul had been widowed in Lahore. Her father had lost everything. They were really in a bad way. Her father's heart was giving him trouble. Her mother also was in a sorry state. Her young brother was with them as well. One day I went to their refugee camp and found that the family had left abandoning her. She had tried to hang herself with her dupatta, but had fainted before she could kill herself. Both of us were going mad with the blows that fate had dealt us out. She tried again and again to commit suicide. Taking care of her took my mind off my own troubles, otherwise I might have done something to myself. I couldn't treat her with the contempt and disgust I had formerly felt for her. I had to hold her in my arms so that she wouldn't attempt to kill herself again while I was asleep. I had to make her believe that she wasn't alone, abandoned with nowhere to turn. Right or wrong, just to help her out of her suffering I had to tell her that I loved her. I talked to her, even slept with her. I tried everything… it was a question of life or death. Even with my confused state of mind, I never saw her as my wife or of her replacing you. Call it infidelity if you want, but from the moment she got better all I intended was to make her capable enough of taking care of herself and then sending her on her way. As things were I just couldn't write to you immediately after meeting Nayyar.'

Kanak, her head bent, listened in a stony silence.

'Wait a minute, I feel a bit faint. Let me get us some tea.' Puri opened the door to the bedroom so that the lock chain would not rattle, and went in.

Urmila was standing with her ear against the other leaf of the door. She had changed out of her nightwear and her dupatta was wrapped tightly around her shoulders. Her forehead still showed the smudged bindi and her face was white as a sheet. Puri knew that she had been listening to him and Kanak.

Puri was unnerved. He held Urmila's arm and led her from the door to the other side of the room, and whispered, 'I'll explain everything to you. Don't get upset.'

She let herself be pulled away, but did not look at him.

'Did you make tea?' Puri asked.

She stood in silence.

Puri looked into the kitchen. The stove had not been lit. He remembered that the milk delivered that morning had not been boiled. He put one hand on her shoulder and raising her chin with the other, said imploringly, 'Don't you worry. Trust me. Don't panic and make things worse. This is your home. Treat her politely just like a guest.'

Urmila went into the kitchen without looking at him.

Puri went down the stairs and called the boy who worked as help on the treadle.

He gave the boy a rupee and told him to get a loaf of bread, butter and some snacks from the halwai shop.

Then he went back up and sat beside Kanak on the chatai, 'Kanni, seeing the situation here must have hurt you, but I'm glad you're here. I'll need your help in working out this situation. I've already told you about her tragic and hopeless situation. I've already asked Soodji to make some arrangement for her to stay with a decent family and send her to school. But before that she must be treated in such a way so as not to be reminded of her earlier misfortunes.'

Kanak sat without saying anything, her eyes downcast. Puri told her about meeting Sood when working at the dhaba, and about Sood's invitation to manage the press. In between he implored Kanak, 'She's going to bring tea. Please ask her to sit with us.' He continued, 'I wrote to you at your Nainital address at the first chance I got. When no reply came, I wrote again. When I got no answer the second time, I sent a letter by registered mail.'

He got up and took out an envelope from a cupboard, and presented it to Kanak as a proof of what he said, 'I was really desperate when this was returned. Then one day I ran into Nayyar in the court. He told me about your father staying near Delhi Gate, but did not give me the full address. Because of my past experience of his rudeness I did not inquire anything further.'

'What did jijaji say to you?' Kanak was asking when there was a noise behind them and Puri turned to look. Urmila had pushed forward a thali with tea on it, but had remained behind the door.

'Come in, come in here,' Puri took the thali and said to Urmila.

Kanak could not say anything, but just turned her eyes away.

Puri put the thali on the chatai, then went inside and talked Urmila into sitting with them. Both women sat with their heads down not looking at each other. Puri offered bread and snacks to both. He brought another cup and poured tea.

Kanak and Urmila still sat in silence. Perhaps Kanak was seeing again in her mind's eye the sight she had witnessed on entering the house and Urmila's ears were ringing with the conversation she had overheard. Puri repeated several times without looking at either of them or using either's name, 'Do eat something, have this, drink your tea. It'll get cold.'

He put a piece of sweet *barfi* in his mouth, but in his state of mind felt that he was chewing on a lump of clay. Kanak ate nothing, just sipped at her tea. Urmila sat motionless.

Puri could not think of anything to do or say. He was guilty in the eyes of both of them. By the time he finished his tea, an idea had formed in his mind: 'Even if these two can't stand each other, they should at least behave themselves. Why are they being so difficult? If they hold any grudge against me, they should take it out on me.'

He remembered hearing that his grandfather had two wives. 'Why should this seem so terrible? Men often had two wives, and many still do. These two should at least stop behaving badly.'

Footsteps sounded on the stairs and they heard, 'Arey Puri, how're you? What's the matter?'

Puri gave a start, and jumped to his feet. He was heading towards the landing when they heard, 'Are you still in bed?'

The unlatched door opened to a push from outside. Sood came in and what he saw stopped him in his tracks.

Behind Puri sat two young women on the chatai, their heads lowered, and looking upset. This sight so embarrassed Sood that he turned back and went downstairs without saying a word. Puri had begun to follow him when Sood called, 'Puri, come downstairs.'

Puri found Sood and his peon Jagannath standing at the foot of the stairs. Sood's face was flushed with anger. He asked the peon to go outside and sit in the waiting tonga, and led Puri into the office. He closed both doors to the room, and said, 'What are you up to? You'll blacken your name, and mine too. You pretend to be what's-its-name sick, but are enjoying yourself with two different women. If such a thing doesn't make you sick, what will? I told you to get married to what's-her-name the first one, or to send her back to her family. And now I find that you've got two of them!' Sood's tone became severe, 'Who do you think you are anyway? Some prince or raja that you need what's-its-name a harem for yourself?'

'Bhaiji, listen to me please. It's not my fault. The other one arrived just now. What could I do?' Puri tried to explain.

Sood cut him short, 'Not your fault? You were sitting with them as if you were all married. And you have the cheek to lie to me!'

'Bhaiji, go up and see for yourself. Raldu brought up her bag and blanket, that stuff is still laying beside the door. She didn't warn me about her coming.'

'How is it that a girl can show up without any warning? Have you been up to these shady games before coming here? You think such behaviour will brighten up what's-its-name the Congress image?'

'Why do you think that, bhaiji! She is Kanak, daughter of Pandit Girdharilal. She saw the poster for the weekly, and came here.'

'You told me that nothing had been what's-its-name arranged between you and her. You lie about everything.' His anger rose a notch. 'If nothing was arranged, why did she come here? Why don't you admit that you had what's-its-name deserted her and were trying to catch another one? Is that any way to behave, luring girls from decent respectable families? If you want to do that, pack your bags and get out of here!'

'Bhaiji, at least listen to my explanation.'

'What explanation? Haven't I seen enough with my own eyes?'

'You told me to send Urmila away. Since then I've been trying to find some place for her...'

'Why didn't you ask me?' Sood cut in. When Puri did not reply, he added accusingly, 'You thought I couldn't figure it out? Are you trying to fool me? Why are you playing about with what's-his-name Girdharilal's daughter? You want to have two at one time?'

'Bhaiji, I don't want anything. If there's any proof that I called Kanak here, you can have me shot. Her brother-in-law Mahendra Nayyar is an advocate in Jalandhar. She might have come to visit her sister and dropped in to see me.'

'She came with her what's-its-name baggage and bedding here to meet her sister?' Sood retorted angrily, 'Why did you ask for my help if you wanted to behave like this? Why did you apply for the secretaryship of what's-its-name the ward committee? You'll drag your name, mine and the good name of the Congress party through the mud. How can you continue to be the editor of a weekly paper?'

How could Puri admit to himself that he was caught up in a web of his own making? He saw himself as the victim of circumstances. In response to Sood's accusations, he wanted to shout back: 'I don't give a damn about you, nor do I care about the press and the paper.' But he couldn't. The accusations levelled against him were being taken as true. Feeling helpless he kept quiet, and Sood also remained silent.

'Bhaiji,' Puri said in a pleading voice. 'A set of coincidences is making me look guilty.'

Obviously angry and concerned, Sood took off his Gandhi cap and ran his fingers through his hair as he stood thinking. Then he pushed his hands into the pockets of his *bandi* jacket and looking at the wall, said, 'Come on, let's go back upstairs. This matter has to be cleared up.'

Sood was climbing the stairs ahead of Puri, but stopped halfway. Remembering that there were women upstairs, he said to Puri, 'You go first.'

In the room, Kanak was sitting alone on the chatai.

'Bhai Soodji is the parliamentary secretary,' Puri said to Kanak.

In response to Kanak's namaste, Sood asked, 'You're the daughter of Pandit Girdharilal of Gwal Mandi?'

Kanak nodded in confirmation.

'Where is Panditji now?'

'In Delhi.'

'You came here with his permission?'

Kanak resented the question, but she replied, 'I was in Lucknow. I came from there.'

'Why did you come without telling him? That was not right.'

'What is that to you!' she lifted her eyes and showed her annoyance at his questioning.

'Yes, this does concern me.' Anger was making Sood stutter again, 'You aren't married yet.'

Kanak hung her head in response to this outrageous insult. Without looking at Sood she replied in English, 'What has all this got to do with you anyway?'

'I've told you that it does concern me. Panditji is an old and respected member of what's-its-name the Congress party. I am concerned about his reputation. Puri is like m-my what's-its-name brother. I'm bothered about his image being smeared. If what's-his-name Panditji wants the pair of you to get married, you're a part of my problem too.'

The way Sood silenced Kanak by stating his authority over her made Kanak feel that her brother-in-law Nayyar had appeared in a more belligerent avatar. She sank her head even lower and had difficulty in breathing. She wanted to look at Puri for support.

'Bhaiji,' Puri said boldly, 'I used to visit her house in Lahore and she also came to our place.'

Kanak gave a sigh of relief.

Sood rebuked Puri, 'Did Panditji allow you to be alone together before getting married? Don't be silly. Why don't the two of you just get married?

Panditji wants it and you both want it. Why are you both bent on blackening his name and mine?'

Puri said nothing.

Kanak covered her eyes with her aanchal to hide her tears. She could not bear to deal with such a situation in front of a person like Sood. If her brother-in-law had rebuked her in this way, she would have replied, 'All right, just get us married off!' But what to say to a stranger asserting rights over her?

Pointing to Kanak in tears, Sood said to Puri, 'This won't serve any purpose. I'll write to what's-his-name Panditji today to arrange your marriage without delay and stop all this nonsense. Also she can't stay here. Let her go off to her sister's. You can go and what's-its-name visit her there.'

Sood crossed his arms over his chest and let out an angry hiss to show that his decision was final and irrevocable. Turning to Puri he asked quietly, 'Where's the other one?'

Moving like a puppet, Puri went towards the aangan to check. Urmila was sitting absolutely motionless in the aangan, her back to the wall and her head on knees clasped between her arms. Puri stood looking at her for a few moments. He could not bring himself to ask her to face Sood in such a state. He went back inside, and pointed to the door to the aangan.

Sood stood uncertainly, then went out into the aangan. He stopped in front of the motionless figure seated against the wall and spoke in a serious tone, 'You don't really want to get married, y-y-you want to be independent, so what's the point in staying here?'

Without waiting for her reply, he continued, 'You should learn some skill. Go to the Normal School, train as a nurse or get some kind of a job. If you want to go to college or take some kind of training, your expenses will be taken care of. There's no sense in your remaining here.'

Urmila, head on her knees, seemed too stunned to reply.

Sood asked, 'You want to get to the Normal School or the nursing school?'

Urmila still remained silent and motionless.

Sood thought for a moment, then said, 'Achchha, the nurse from the hospital will come to get you.' He walked towards the stairs, and Puri followed him.

Puri saw Sood off at the main entrance to the press. Sood got into the tonga waiting in the gali without saying a word, and the tonga drove off.

Puri did not have the courage to face Kanak and Urmila together. He sat downstairs in the office and thought about what he could do next. He felt trapped and could see no way out. Where could Urmila go? She was in no way to blame. How could he let her down? But he could not let Kanak down either. He was equally guilty in the eyes of both.

Rikhiram came and asked him something. Without knowing what he was asked, Puri blew up, 'Am I supposed to do everything here? Don't I have to get the weekly ready?' He pulled himself together, and his voice took on a tone of authority, 'Should I attend to Soodji or listen to you? You had your own press once. Can't you make decisions for yourself?'

Rikhiram replied politely to this rebuke, 'I'm doing what I can, but it also makes sense to check things with the boss.'

Resentment rose in Puri's heart. Sood's sly manipulation was demoralizing. Why should he put up with it? 'Why should Soodji interfere in my affairs? I alone am responsible for my actions. I am prepared to deal with it and face the consequences, even at the cost of my life. What had happened in those abnormal circumstances could not be judged according to regular standards. It would take unusual considerations to find solutions. I myself will have to bear the consequences, not someone else. I simply cannot send away either woman. The problem concerns the three of us, no one else should interfere. But where would I be without Soodji's goodwill? The house and the press belong to me only through his generosity. The three of us just cannot leave the house and be out on the street.' The storm of protest in his mind subsided.

Puri realized that Urmila had been the victim of great misfortune, which he was unable to ward off. The unbearable agony of his helplessness made him want to tear out his heart with his own hands. He had nothing to offer as a solution. What, then, was the point of facing Kanak and Urmila again?

In that fit of impotent anger and frustration he felt caught in the trap of the press, the house and *Nazir*. How could he break through the strong invisible mesh that entangled him? How could he have got into all this trouble without the bait of a press and a house? Wouldn't a job as a helper and dishwasher at Chandan's dhaba have been better than this humiliation?

The clatter of machinery stopped and he realized that it was one o'clock. Noticing that he had forgotten to wind up his watch that morning, his fingers absent mindedly wound it up. He still could not muster the courage to go upstairs to his apartment.

The work resumed after the lunch break. His eyes went to his watch. Half an hour had gone by. He asked the peon for a drink of water.

There was a rattling at the lock chain at the main entrance to the press. The peon went to check and came back with a middle-aged woman who looked like a servant. The woman handed Puri an envelope addressed to him. It was a letter from the civil hospital. On Sood's order, the hospital ayah had come to get Urmila.

Puri felt he was being turned into an unfeeling machine, that he was being forced to do something wrong. He sat idle for a few moments more.

The ayah reminded Puri, 'Babu, call the girl. The ambulance is waiting in the gali. The driver will be upset.'

Puri summoned all his strength to get up. 'I'll call her,' he replied, and went upstairs.

Since Sood had left after pronouncing his decision, Urmila had remained sitting against the wall in stunned silence. After a few minutes the realization dawned on her, 'They're throwing me out! Where will I go? What refuge do I have in this world?' Tears ran down her cheeks. She felt like screaming and crying, but how could she let that saut, that other woman, hear her wailing? She calmed down, and with her head bent, wept in silence. Her ears were alert for any sound of footsteps. If 'he' came, she would clasp his feet in her hands and beg, 'Don't throw me out into the street. I'll do anything you say, I'll stay in some corner and keep out of your way. Or give me some poison and kill me, but don't make me leave.'

But when nobody came, the suspense made her ever more miserable. Her tears had dried up. The sun climbed up and was now overhead, leaving a yard-wide strip of shade at the base of the wall against which her back rested. She had not moved from her spot. Then she heard footsteps. At last, it was Puri. She rose quickly. Puri's eyes were red too.

'The woman from the hospital is here to take you with her. Don't worry. I'll come and explain everything to you. Take some clothes. The ayah's waiting downstairs.' Puri spoke almost in a whisper.

She bit her lip to choke back her tears, and begged him with her palms joined, 'Don't make me leave. I...'

'Don't be upset. Just go now,' Puri said in the same tone of voice, and quickly went back downstairs. He found it hard to stop himself from crying.

Urmila held her head in her hands and leaned against the wall for support.

Then she sat down again. After a while she heard someone call her name from the stairwell. It was a woman's voice.

Clenching her teeth, she forced herself to get up. Without bothering to hide the noise, she threw open her tin trunk, and took out a salwar-kameez suit and a dupatta. She knew that the other woman was sitting on the chatai in the next room. To avoid looking at her, Urmila walked past with her eyes averted. The ayah was waiting on the landing. Urmila followed her down, holding on to the side on the stairwell for support.

Puri was waiting in the doorway of the press. As Urmila went past him with her head bent, he held out his closed hand and said, 'Take this, you might need it.'

Urmila ignored his extended fist.

Puri stood in the doorway and watched Urmila walk behind the ayah as they went through the gali towards the bazaar. The driver opened the door of the van and the ayah helped Urmila climb in, and then got in herself. The driver shut the door.

Unable to hold back his tears, Puri went towards the lavatory at the back of the press. He returned fifteen minutes later, washed his face and hands at the water faucet, and sat down in the office. A few minutes later he slowly went upstairs.

When he had gone before to get Urmila, Kanak had been asleep covered with her blanket, her face towards the wall, and he had gone through the room without making any noise. Now he called, 'Kanni, are you asleep?'

Kanak sat up, 'I fell asleep after you left. Hadn't slept last night. Oh, its three o'clock. Where have you been?'

'Kanni, you went to sleep without eating anything. I've been occupied with a few things. I had to make some arrangement for that poor girl.'

'Has she left?' Kanak asked with some relief.

'I'd talked to Soodji about her. She hasn't passed even her matric exam. She wanted to train as a nurse, but until she becomes self-supporting, I have to do my duty by her.'

Ignoring Puri's mention of his duty, Kanak said, 'This brother of yours, Soodji, has a strange way of talking. How is it his business if I stay here?' Her cheeks became crimson with embarrassment. To hide her shyness, she shot him a reproachful look, and laid her head against his shoulder. She said, looking into his eyes, 'Did I come all this way only to be put through this?'

Taking her in his arms, Puri said, 'Even pitaji would agree with Soodji's arrangements.'

'Who does this Soodji of yours think he is anyway? When I went to Delhi in December, pitaji brought up this subject himself. He wants us to get married soon,' Kanak said a little smugly, and nuzzled his chest.

She asked about the launch of *Nazir*, and then told Puri the story of how she had got her job and how Awasthi had mistreated her. 'You didn't send for me, but I've arrived at the right moment to help you.'

Kanak thought it prudent to spend that night at her sister's. She had Nayyar's address from his letter. Puri took her to the address in Mandi Bazaar. He didn't want to go in uninvited, but changed his mind after Kanak's insistence and in consideration of his future relationship with her family.

Nayyar and Kanta realized that Kanak had come to Jalandhar after getting the news from Nayyar's letter, and thought that Puri had known in advance about her arrival and must have collected her at the railway station. No doubts remained in their minds about the purpose of her coming. They still asked affectionately, 'Couldn't you have informed us also about your arrival?'

Kanak sidestepped the question by saying, 'Didn't my sudden appearance please you even more?' Pretending to be busy playing with Nano, she quickly changed the subject.

Nayyar's family had to make do with limited living space. Their house, although not very old, consisted of two rooms opening on to a small aangan, a bathroom, a tiny kitchen and an even smaller bunker for storing coal. The room overlooking the bazaar served also as a living room, with just an ordinary desk and three kitchen chairs and a small takht pushed against the wall. At night a charpoy was put in the room for Nayyar's mother to sleep on. Nayyar chatted with Kanak until after nine, and then turned to the study of his next day's court cases. Kanak had to share a bed with her sister. Kanak could not help remembering the style and comfort in which Nayyar had lived in his Model Town bungalow in Lahore, but there was no point in mentioning it now.

After Sood had taken the matter of Puri and Kanak into his hands, he had wanted to resolve it quickly as he did everything else. He asked Puri for Nayyar's address, and invited him to a meeting. The letter Kanta and Nayyar wrote to Panditji made no reference of any misconduct, and merely asked Panditji to give his blessings to Kanak for a happy and successful married life.

Puri decided to consider his actions as indiscretions committed in a state of mental confusion caused by the turmoil in his life. In order to go on with his life in a straightforward and honest way, he saw it as his duty to accept responsibility for his past mistakes.

On his way back home after seeing Kanak off on the train to Delhi, he stopped by at the civil hospital.

Urmila came out on being told she had a visitor. Seeing Puri, she bowed her head and stood in silence.

Puri again told her not to worry and that he would help her in every way. He asked if she needed anything.

Urmila did not look back at him. She turned to go back, without saying a word.

Puri went back three days later, but was told that Urmila had been sent to Ludhiana to train as a nurse.

Chapter 7

SEVERAL UNEXPECTED PROBLEMS, IN THE AFTERMATH OF THE DEATH OF Gandhiji, had kept Home Secretary Rawat very busy. Overburdened by the demands of his position, he had little time for himself, much less to think about fulfilling his promise to Tara. One evening, exhausted by a day's work at the office and needing a change of scene, he went to the club. When he met Mr Agarwal there, Rawat was reminded that he had neglected to invite the Agarwals to dinner.

The inclusion of Tara in the invitation displeased Mrs Agarwal. Her misgivings about hiring Tara were proving well founded. 'Rawat, Dey, sahib, Narottam, they can't seem to tear their eyes away from Tara. How Shyama had taken Tara's arm and made her sit beside her! She's always encouraging Tara unnecessarily. And Rawat chatted with Tara as if he had known her for years. Doesn't he realize that Tara is the same age as his own daughter!'

For the dinner at the club, Mrs Agarwal had worn a Benarasi sari with real gold and silver embroidery, and her *navaratna* jewellery. No one paid any attention to her expensive outfit. Tara had gone in a simple white voile sari with a wide black border, a black blouse, and two thick black glass bangles. Mrs Agarwal was put out at being ignored in front of her employee. She thought, 'What do men care about fine jewellery and silk? All they fancy is young woman, a new one everyday.'

Madam had taken care to give Tara as little opportunity as possible of coming into contact with her husband or men who came to the house as visitors. She had had bad experiences with Miss Edwards, and with her own widowed younger sister, but young women, it seemed to her, just couldn't resist the chance of parading before men. Narottam had been hovering around Tara from the moment he laid eyes on her. Since the evening of the party in the upstairs drawing room, sahib too had begun to pay a lot of attention to Tara. His hair was turning grey, but his old habit seemed to be dying hard. He'd send for Tara for such trivial tasks as finding the newspaper. Filled with resentment towards Tara, Mrs Agarwal did not feel like speaking with her, but as the mistress of the house she could not always avoid it. Her irritation would often make her scold Tara.

The feeing of contentment and of having found a refuge at AA gradually disappeared from Tara's mind. Which woman cannot sense the jealousy eating away at another woman's heart, and the feelings that men harbour towards her own self? She knew that she was a mere employee, and as such could not ignore others in the family. She was well aware of the reasons for madam's resentment, however overblown, and found them embarrassing. She felt madam was taking advantage of her helplessness. Even the slightest attention from sahib bothered Tara. The kindness shown by Rawat gave her heart, but she had reservations about his sympathy too.

Tara's application for a government job had been submitted. Narottam drafted the application, had it typed up, and got Tara to sign it. The application stated that Tara was an MA student. She was uneasy about stating such an untruth, but Narottam insisted, 'Both mummy and daddy told everyone that you're studying for MA Rawat said the same thing when he telephoned the director of the Rehabilitation Department to recommend you. You want them all to be proven liars? You'll be hired first as a temporary employee. If someone demands a proof, we'll deal with it later.'

Narottam filled Tara in about Rawat, 'He's forceful and good at heart, but people say women are his weakness. His wife's dead, his son's a deputy collector in Bihar. There's nobody else in the family except his elder sister and the boss-lady, his daughter Neelam.' Neelam was a student of Miranda College, and had failed once in her BA exam. Rawat wanted to marry her off before his retirement and, for that reason, was particularly warm-hearted towards Narottam. Mr Agarwal was willing to be broad-minded about Rawat being from a different caste, and turn down offers of a substantial dowry from other families. However, Narottam was unwilling to marry anyone as vain as Neelam.

Tara's tribulations increased in March 1948. Mrs Agarwal's manner was becoming increasingly brusque, and the assurance that Tara felt by Narottam's presence in the house had ended. Although it was Tara who was seeking a job, it was Narottam who received an offer. Despite the disapproval of mummy and daddy, he accepted the position of works manager (under training) at the Shaadpur Ordnance Factory. He left on his motorcycle for the factory at seven in the morning, and did not return before 6.30 in the evening.

One evening Mrs Agarwal was away from home. Tara was with the children at their dinner when sahib came home. He first inquired about madam from a servant, then sent for Tara. He said, 'I'm going to the club. Do come along. Rawat Sahib was asking after you.'

Tara did want to remind Rawat about her application for the job, but she said, 'Bahinji's not home. Without her permission...'

'Arey, you come along. Change your sari if you like. I'm waiting,' he commanded.

Rawat was in the Billiard Room. Mr Agarwal and Tara went in. Rawat saw them, and gestured to them to wait, and continued his play.

After the round was over Rawat escorted his guests to the lounge. Mr Agarwal promptly ordered two whiskeys and a pineapple juice for Tara. Rawat broached the subject himself, 'Did you hear from the director of rehabilitation?'

Tara gave Rawat a forlorn look, and shook her head, 'Ji, no.'

'What?' Rawat exclaimed and summoned the butler. He lighted his pipe and giving the butler a telephone number, said, 'Call this number and let me know.'

The butler came back shortly to inform him that the call had gone through. Rawat, pipe in mouth, went to the telephone,

When he returned, he questioned Tara, 'Why didn't you go to meet Mittal, I mean, the director of rehabilitation?'

'Ji, I know nothing about it. When was I called?'

'You silly girl,' Rawat said, chewing on the stem of his pipe. 'He's been waiting for you to fill the vacancy. He says that he had someone call your place.'

'Ji, I don't understand.' Tara said apologetically.

Rawat feigned anger at Mr Agarwal, 'Why, *lala*, what's up? You don't want to let the girl slip through your fingers?'

'Sir, how could I be so bold,' Mr Agarwal laughed. 'How could I compete with you?'

Tara did not appreciate being the butt of a joke, but to humour Rawat she lifted her eyes to him and smiled shyly.

'Look at her!' Mr Agarwal spoke up. 'She blushes only when you're around. She doesn't even smile for me.'

Tara gave him a weak smile also, just to restore the balance.

Rawat raised his finger in warning, 'Miss Tara has to meet the director of rehabilitation day after tomorrow at eleven. Don't forget!'

'Sure. The car will drop her there at quarter to eleven.'

When Rawat finished his drink, Mr Agarwal said, 'Have another. Or would you like me to order dinner?'

'No, no. No dinner,' Rawat said to Mr Agarwal. 'Have you ever eaten *ghurarh*— mountain deer? Chandola sent some from Ranikhet. Have dinner at my place.'

Tara wanted to go back to AA, but could not refuse Rawat's invitation.

On reaching the drawing room in his home, Rawat summoned a bearer. 'Serve dinner,' he said, nodding at Tara and Mr Agarwal, 'Two guests. Bring us whiskey and soda for now.'

Rawat and Mr Agarwal sipped their drinks as they waited for the dinner to be served. Tara picked up a photo album and was browsing through it when the curtain over the door to the next room swayed gently. From a strip of a sari visible under the curtain she knew that someone had peeped in.

It was 10.15 when Mr Agarwal and Tara reached home. Madam came out of the drawing room, but said nothing. In anger her large fleshy face looked even more puffy. Mr Agarwal went to his room upstairs. Tara was going towards her room at the back when she heard madam's stern voice, 'Come here!' She returned to the drawing room.

'Where have you been?' Madam demanded.

'Sahib took me to the club. Rawat Sahib had asked for me.'

'Did you come here to work or to have a good time? Who gave you permission to go there?'

'I told sahib that I should get your permission, but sahib said...'

'Why bring sahib into this? Are you here to work for me or become a saut? Do you think I'm blind? If you feed milk to a snake a thousand times, it'll still bite you.' Madam continued to abuse her in a harsh voice. Tara stood with her head bowed.

Jugal came and said quietly to madam, 'Sahib's calling you.'

'All right. I'm coming,' madam replied sharply, and continued to shout at Tara. 'You're not needed anymore. Go back to the camp tomorrow.'

'What's going on?' Mr Agarwal came into the room.

Tara turned immediately to leave. As she was going out she heard sahib shouting angrily. She quickly went to her room and closed the door.

Seething with anger and humiliation, she spent the night in a state of panic 'Why can't I die if a peaceful life is not my destiny.'

The children were woken at 6 a.m. Tara would have a wash, change her clothes and be ready before that time. That morning she had not slept a wink, but got dressed as usual after looking at the small timepiece in her room. Instead of going over to the children's bedroom, she sat and waited. She had been told to go back to the camp, and she did not want to stay a moment longer. She did not want to have to face anyone after being treated rudely the previous night. She decided not to go back to the camp, but find out Shyama's address and go to her. She had 175 rupees of her own, enough to rent a room somewhere. Tomorrow was her interview with the director, and she had every hope of getting that job.

Shivni called her name from outside the door, then came in, holding Lalli's school uniform. She said, 'Bibiji, what's wrong? Are you not well? Can Lalli wear the same tunic again, or should I get out a fresh one ready?' Shivni spoke in a normal voice, as if nothing had happened.

'Let her wear the same one.'

'Will you come, or do you want me to give the the kids their breakfast? Do you want me to bring you some tea?'

Shivni's manner conveyed no hint of disapproval, thought Tara. She replied, 'I'm coming.'

Narottam was having his breakfast when Tara shepherded the children into the dinning room. He had been having his breakfast regularly at 6.30 in order to leave early, sometimes even before the children arrived. He asked Tara in English, 'What was all that hullabaloo last night?'

'Nothing.'

'There was a row between mummy and daddy. I could hear it in my room.'

'How would I know?'

'Mummy hit the roof when she found that daddy took you to the club. She questioned everyone. They went at it hot and heavy last night and I suspect mummy ended up in tears. Quite a messy situation.'

Tara had to explain. She said, 'I'm leaving today.'

'How can you leave? Where will you go? You'll have to make some arrangement before that.'

'So I should let myself be humiliated? Or get thrown out?'

'Who can humiliate you and who'll throw you out? Going to the club was no crime. Daddy took you, it was his responsibility.'

'Mrs Agarwal has ordered me to leave this house.'

'She talks nonsense at times. If you must leave, it can be only after proper arrangements are made.'

'What if she comes and orders me away again?'

Narottam was silent for a moment, then said, 'I'll stay. I won't go to the factory. I'll telephone.'

Tara insisted, 'No, go to work.'

Narottam ignored her protest and dialled 281, his factory's number.

Mr Agarwal was in the drawing room with two visitors who had come at 8 a.m. He ate his breakfast at 8.30, and sent for Tara before leaving for the office.

Tara stood with her head bowed. Sahib asked in English, 'Is anything troubling you?' Then added, 'You don't have to worry about anything.'

On hearing that sahib had sent for Tara, Narottam stayed within earshot. Sahib said when he saw Narottam, 'You didn't go to the factory today?'

'I couldn't. My motorcycle's spark plug is giving trouble. I've informed the factory.'

'Why don't you get a small car for yourself? Okay, you're free today. Miss Tara has to go to her job tomorrow. If she needs clothes or anything, you take care of it. Give the bill to me, understand?'

Madam hadn't come out of her room. The household chores were done as usual, only the sound of madam's voice was missing. When maaji inquired about her daughter-in-law, Shivni said, 'She has a headache.'

Spending the night being angry left Tara tense and edgy. She sat with the children for lunch, but could not eat. After sending the children off to their rooms for a siesta, she asked Shivni, 'Would you know where sleeping pills or the headache medicines are kept? Bring me some. Give me a cup of tea, or just hot water with it. I'm going to lie down.'

Shivni brought her tea and the medicine. She sat down on the floor next to Tara's bed, and said kindly, 'Do you want me to rub your head with oil or massage your temples?'

Tara said no, but Shivni remained sitting near her. She muttered under her breath, 'Madam didn't eat anything. She's sulking. She got a real dressing down last night. She talks far too much. Gets a good thrashing when she does that. She asks for it. The same thing happened when her sister was here. She's from the bania caste, not from any sahib or officer-type family. Families of upper-class people don't behave the same way as we do being poor, low-caste people, where a woman can't speak or joke with men. She herself is always sucking up to her guests. I've seen thousands of women and wives from upper-class families. I've spent my life in their service. I'm not saying this only to please you, but, bibiji, I've never seen anyone as sensible and even-tempered as you are. Everyone praises you.'

'I want to sleep. You also get some rest too.' Tara turned her back to the maid.

Shivni left, but Tara could not sleep. She was thinking: Is it a curse to be born as a woman? Is that all there is to being a woman? Such a rich *sethani*, mistress of a mansion with so many servants, a mother, who owns jewellery worth a fortune, has high social status and prestige, but her husband can still beat her whenever he wants. The incident on her wedding night came back to her mind. A woman is at the mercy of menfolk all her life.

At 10 o'clock next morning Shivni came to tell Tara that Laxman, the chauffer, was ready with the car. Tara had sent the children off to their schools. Madam had stayed upstairs again for the second day. Tara's mind was made up. She did not care what madam thought, but still sent a message to her through Shivni, went herself to the kitchen to tell the grandmother that she was going for her interview, and left.

How long could Mrs Agarwal keep on sulking on an empty stomach? To carry on this way was to prolong her own suffering and humiliation. She came downstairs in the morning of the third day, but kept to the kitchen area and away from the drawing and dining rooms. Tara as usual had seen the children off to school. She had to reach the P Block in the Central Secretariat. She had found that she could catch a bus from near India Gate to get there. As she left home at 9.15, she rather reluctantly went to madam to tell her where she was going. Madam was sitting on a low stool, stuffing some eggplants with a spicy paste.

Her head bowed, Tara said, 'I'm going to work.'

Shivni had already given madam every scrap of news.

'Did you tell Laxman to be ready with the car?'

'I'll catch the bus. I know the way. I'll be going there everyday,' Tara replied without looking up.

'Just look at her behaviour!' Madam said sharply. 'Will it be proper for a young woman from a decent family to travel alone in a bus.'

'Tell me, has she found a job in a government office?' the grandmother asked in her typical Delhi accent.

'Whatever I said to her was for her own good,' madam said. 'It's up to her now.'

'She looked like a well-balanced one to me,' the grandmother said. 'How would a young woman feel among all those men? Won't she be nervous?'

Tara left and walked towards the bus stop.

After taking her job, Tara stayed on at the mansion for thirteen more days. Nothing was available for a rent that she could afford. There was no vacancy at the Working Women's Hostel. If Narottam found out about a room or a shared accommodation, he would take Tara there on a Sunday. It was prudent to find a place suitable for a young woman. Narottam would tell her, 'What's the hurry, you're not in the middle of some desert.'

Mrs Agarwal would ask, 'What problem does she have here! If she rents some place, she'll need a servant, or face the hassle of cooking her own meals. Here she has us if she needs anything. Who'd help her if she's all by herself? I always considered her as a younger sister. If I criticized her that too was out of concern for her, for her own good.'

Mrs Agarwal actually did not want Tara to leave. Tara still took care of the children in the morning, which was the time they needed attention. Madam was not obliged to pay for Tara's help, and could reap no benefit from having another empty room. More leftovers were thrown out than the meagre meals Tara ate.

In his search for a suitable place for Tara, Narottam remembered Miss Mercy Sorel, the nurse. Eight months before, when Puttan had become seriously ill, two nurses attended to him round the clock on twelve-hour shifts. One of them, Mercy, appeared to Narottam to be a wise, good soul. She had a phone in her flat that she shared with another nurse. That Mercy was the girlfriend of Comrade Niranjan Chaddha formed another link between her and Narottam. When Narottam was studying at Delhi's European School sixteen years before, Niranjan had been a teacher there. Mercy had been on Narottam's mind after the news of the arrest of several Communist Party members in the second week of March 1948. He contacted Mercy.

Mercy Sorel had been living in a newly built area of Daryaganj for two-and-a-half years. Beside a small sitting room next to the landing, the first-floor flat had two more rooms, a kitchen, a bathroom and a veranda. Mercy was her baptismal name, Sorel her family name, but everyone called her Lila.

Silva, her roommate who was also a private nurse, got married and went away to Mysore. Mercy continued to pay the old rent of forty rupees a month. There was no shortage of people willing to share, but she did not want to rent out her spare room to some family. What if she came home in the morning after a night shift, and couldn't get to sleep during the day? She could not share the apartment with a single male either.

Mercy agreed to rent out a room to Tara on the recommendation of Narottam, but not before laying down her own conditions: Tara would not put up any relatives or friends in her room. She would not cook meals on a stove in her room or in the veranda. If she wanted to share all expenses for her room, two meals, breakfast, tea and the maid's service, she'd have to pay one hundred rupees per month. If she wanted to have her meals out, she'd pay only thirty-five rupees for rent and electricity. If she used the telephone, she'd pay for that. The rent would have to be paid in advance, by the first week of the month. What better arrangement could Tara hope for? Paying one hundred a month sounded like being a spendthrift, but what did she need to save for? She accepted.

Lila Mercy Sorel, in her late twenties, had a glowing, dark complexion. With sharp features and large eyes her face looked striking, like something sculpted in bronze. She was the same height as Tara, with very long hair and the nurse's belted uniform accentuated the narrow waist of her shapely figure. She had been a nursing sister at the Irwin Hospital, but had quit when passed over for promotion. She had maintained her contacts there, and got calls to work in the private ward. She charged fifteen rupees for working the day shift, and eighteen for the night. Her good relations with doctors ensured that she was seldom without work. She had been living in Delhi for five years. Having lived in Lucknow, she could converse in Hindi, with only minor lapses of grammar and a sprinkling of English which she spoke fluently because of her schooling. She was fond of reading novels and magazines, but had little interest in newspapers. With Tara she was rather formal for the first few days, addressing her as Miss Tara. Once she got to know her, she began calling her Tara. Then she said, 'Why do you have to be so correct and call me "Sister"? Everyone in my family calls me Lila.'

Tara took a liking to her. Mercy was rather outspoken and forward because of her European upbringing, but guileless.

Tara had to invent a cover story for herself, not wanting to be reminded of the bitter and harrowing experiences of the past year. She did not want

to advertise the humiliations and tortures she had suffered, or be the object
of pity from some and hatred from others. She made up a story of having
been brought up by her sister. After finishing her MA, she had been working
as tutor–governess, her sister and brother-in-law fled Lahore and went to
Bombay, then she found a job in Delhi.

Mercy said consolingly, 'You're hardly an old lady. Being twenty or
twenty-one is not considered old. Now that you found a government job,
you'll also find a good husband. Lots of chances of that in Delhi. I know
many people here. I'll introduce you to a few when I get time. I usually
get to know the families of my patients. As you know only the well-to-do
can afford to hire me. With the taxi fare included, they usually have to lay
out as much as eighteen or twenty rupees per day.'

In the first week of May, yet another veil was lifted from between Tara
and Mercy. Tara had returned from her office at quarter to six. Mercy was
on a day shift. Tara had developed a taste for tea at the Double A. Chimmo
the maid laid out the tea things for her in the sitting room. Tara poured
herself a cup of tea after freshening up and changing her sari. The door bell
sounded in the way Mercy rang: one long and one short, just like a dash
and a dot. Chimmo was busy in the kitchen. Tara went downstairs to open
the door thinking it was Mercy.

The door opened to reveal a young man. He asked with some hesitation,
'Sister Mercy's not in?'

'She should be back in fifteen or twenty minutes,' Tara replied, assuming
the man to be an acquaintance of Mercy. His voice sounded familiar.

She offered the man a seat in the sitting room, and asked, 'Can I pour
you some tea?'

He replied affably, 'Please do. When did you come here?'

Tara looked at him closely, 'Bhai Hira Singh? How come! You're now
Hira Lal. I thought I recognized the voice.'

'You're living in Delhi now? Have you joined MA? Puri's in Jalandhar.
He's publishing some newsweekly.'

'I've found a job,' Tara quickly collected herself, as if she knew about
her brother.

'That's good. You look so grown up, may be because of the sari you're
wearing. Are you teaching at some school?'

'No. I'm with the Rehabilitation Department. What are you up to here
in Delhi?'

'The same old thing.'

'What d'you mean? Are Narendra and Pradyumna bhai here too?'

'Don't you read the newspapers?'

'There wasn't anything about you in the newspaper. Maybe I missed it,' Tara said lightly.

'Didn't you read about the arrests? Narendra Singh was arrested in Ambala. Pradyumna's gone underground. Comrades are being arrested everywhere after the last party congress. Bebe Zubeida had arrived here from Lahore in early February. She's married Pradyumna and become an Indian citizen. She'll definitely come and see you when she hears about you.'

'Of course. I'd like to meet her too. I'll go myself. Well, your reward for being an absconder is that you had to cut your hair short.' Finding the door at the bottom of the stairs unlocked, Mercy came up. She was surprised to see Tara and Hira Lal talking to each other like old acquaintances. Hira Lal took an envelope out of his pocket and handing it to Mercy, said, 'She knows my past identity. She used to attend the Study Circle in Lahore and was a great help to us. Her brother was also in the peace movement.'

Mercy took the envelope. She called out to the maid as she headed to her room, 'Chimmo, get me a cup of tea also and something to eat.'

When Mercy returned to the sitting room, her face was washed and her hair combed. Hira Lal was deep in discussion with Tara, '... a bourgeois democratic revolution has little chance in our country. The political power is not in the hands of the feudalists or the zamindars, landowners; it's in the hands of the capitalists. Our task is to capture political power with the help of the landless peasantry and the working class.'

'How would you capture political power?' Tara wanted to know. 'The masses neither understand your ideology, nor your programme. Only two people in our gali understood what communism stood for; my brother and Dr Prabhu Dayal. They both didn't agree with your party. Our office assistant Darbari Lal says that under communism only those get to eat who have blisters on their hands. I also heard people talking at the club who thought that communism means widespread looting and anarchy. Why would they sympathize with you?'

'We have to fight that kind of ignorance,' Lal said.

'And you people have launched the revolution before removing that ignorance. Will you teach communist ideology to the masses after you have seized power? But the masses won't let you take over power. They are the very people for whose good you want to introduce communism. They'll support Gandhiji's successors in preference to you. People understood the struggle against the British, they'd never understand rising against their own government. You should have adopted the rational approach. How long did the Congress take to take the pulse of the masses? You want to accomplish everything in one fell swoop. Your party has been declared illegal in Madras and Bengal. What could you do to stop that from happening here?'

'So we should just let the Tatas and the Birlas take over?' Mercy said.

'You mean that we should just wait for the right time and let the capitalists strengthen their grip?' Lal asked.

Tara relied, 'Does the good of the people rest with you or the capitalists? Until this January your party kept calling Gandhiji the Father of the Nation, and proclaiming that everyone should strengthen Nehru's hand. Today Nehru has become the agent of capitalism. Won't the masses be confused?'

'Nehru surely is a lackey of the capitalists,' Mercy said.

'Achcha, I'll give you our party's programme to read. Then we'll talk.'

Mercy laid down thirty rupees in bank notes on the table. Lal put the money in his pocket, and looking at Tara, said, 'Now you have a job. Why don't you help us? It's a critical time for the party.'

'I don't have faith in your programme. I might contribute as a personal donation.'

'You must help the party. Give at least twenty rupees every month. That's not much for you,' Mercy pleaded.

'I'll give something today, but can't promise anything for the future. I don't agree with the party line.'

'Working for the government made you change your attitude quickly enough,' Lal teased her.

'What kind of argument is that? I'm willing to listen and be convinced.'

Mercy scolded Lal, 'She's willing to help you, and you're being nasty! Do you want me to give something on your behalf?' She asked Tara.

'No, I'll get the money.' Tara took out twenty rupees and gave it to Lal.

Chimmo, an empty bucket in her hand, was coming down the stairs after sprinkling water to cool the roof. Tara went up to lie in the open air. The news of the marriage of Zubeida and Pradyumna brought back memories of Lahore and of Asad. 'Zubeida has come to Delhi. If what I had wanted had come true then I'd have been in Lahore or somewhere in West Pakistan now. What a life that would have been. Could I even dream of what has happened to me?' She thought about the days spent with the family of Hafiz Inayat Ali. She had found that life intolerable. 'Does that mean that whatever has happened was for the better,' she wondered.

The air became cooler after sunset. Darkness was falling, but the stars were still not visible. Her unseeing gaze fixed on the sky, she sank back into her memories. 'Had I been able to go with Asad, I'd have been his wife, just as Zubeida is Pradyumna's wife. Asad never believed that Hindus and Muslims were two different peoples, still I'd have been in a Muslim home in Pakistan. Zubeida too will live among Hindus. Would I have agreed to stay back in Pakistan for Asad's sake? At that time I could have, but not now.' Tara turned on her side. There was no point in wallowing in memories.

She turned again and saw Mercy at the top of the stairs. Although there was another charpoy, Mercy chose to sit on Tara's. She was worried: Comrades were being arrested. How long could they carry on like this? Gradually she divulged the cause of her anxiety, and many of her secrets: In 1944 Niranjan Lal Chaddha had gone into hospital for two months with a broken shoulder, and Mercy had met him there. Their friendship grew, and they fell in love. Chaddha was very intelligent, and high-minded. He was imprisoned for three years in 1942 for participating in revolutionary activities. He lost his job at the European School, and survived by acting as a private tutor. He was an important leader of the Communist Party. Mercy and Chaddha had planned a civil marriage in April, but he had to go into hiding in March. He had written to Mercy that he'd try to contact her.

On the third day after meeting Hira Lal, Mercy was still at home when Tara was leaving for the office. Showing that she now had complete trust in Tara, she confided to her that she was waiting for a message to go to see Chaddha.

That afternoon, Tara came back from her office to find Zubeida in her sitting room. They warmly hugged each other. Overcome by tears and emotions, neither could speak for a few moments.

Zubeida told Tara where Mercy had gone, and said, 'I was amazed when Hira told me about you. I saw you last year, perhaps in early April. I don't think I met Puri bhai after May that year. It was in September, may be 28 or 29, when Asad came to me. He was distraught. He wanted me to make some arrangement for you. In the evening we both went to the DAV College camp to get you, but you were gone. How did you get to Shaikhupura?'

Tara was silent for a moment, lost in thought. Zubeida knew about her past, which she wanted to keep secret. Although she and Asad had been very careful to hide their friendship, Zubeida was among two or three people who had inside knowledge of their feelings for one another.

Tara willingly described the traumatic circumstances on the night of her wedding, and the story of her escape after the house had been set on fire. In the end, she just said, 'I haven't told any of this to anyone here, nor do I want to. They all think of me as unmarried.'

Zubeida agreed with her, 'You are unmarried! Who'd call that affair a marriage? I am glad that I didn't say anything to Hira about you. I might have told Mercy, but we didn't get a moment alone. No need to tell her now.'

Remembering Somraj's behaviour at the university's Senate Hall, Zubeida criticized Puri's insensitivity to Tara's feelings 'Was Puri bhai out of his mind?'

She told a long story about herself without Tara's asking: Just to please her husband's family she had changed her name to Jamuna. For a while they both lived in his family's house. If he noticed the family treating his wife badly, he'd threaten to leave. Since his going underground, the in-laws had made life miserable for Zubeida. The police constantly watched her in the hope that her husband might come to visit her. She finally moved into the Working Women's Hostel. Several people sympathetic to the communists were trying to find her a job; she was also trying on her own. She had asked Miss Sewabhai to plead her case before the prime minister.

Mercy returned after half past nine, but Zubeida could not wait that long. From her manner Mercy seemed to like Zubeida very much. Tara had noticed that either Mercy liked someone wholeheartedly, or could not tolerate him or her at all. She apparently knew about Zubeida's mistreatment at her in-laws; as an Indian Christian she herself had suffered from Hindu narrow-mindedness. Her anger boiled over in sympathy for Zubeida, 'No one in the world is more self-righteous and intolerant than Hindus! Why are they so insufferably sanctimonious? They have been held down and conquered for thousands of years, but they still consider themselves the holiest of the holy. Other religions have some redeeming qualities, these people have only the arrogance of their holiness. Who can be more self-righteous than those who regard other people as untouchable!'

Tara usually got back home from the office at about quarter to six. If Mercy was home, they would have tea and a little chat lounging in their chairs. Sometimes they would send old Chimmo to wash clothes to get her out of the way, and cook Punjabi or Madrasi food and gossip some more. Tara seldom went out in the evening. Narottam showed up on Saturday evenings or on Sundays. If Mercy had guests, she sometimes went out with them, or entertained them at home for a couple of hours. On such occasions, Tara stayed in her room and read, laughter and conversation trickling from the living room. Sometimes Mercy would invite her to join the guests, mostly people she had met in course of her work. If the visitor happened to be a doctor, Mercy took special care and was particularly attentive in her hospitality. Such visitors had to be treated well, Mercy would later explain, for they were the ones who got her jobs. If they were not kept happy, they would criticize her at every step and make it hard for her to be hired as a nurse.

Mercy often complained about the unfair practices and rackets that went on at the hospitals, 'State hospitals were nests of private practice for doctors. Doctors' salaries were about four hundred rupees a month, but they could make another fifteen hundred by seeing patients privately. One could not be admitted to a hospital if one did not first pay a doctor for consultation. A surgeon in Lucknow did the most horrible thing at his private clinic.' Her eyes widened with fear she said, 'He opened up a sixteen-year-old boy's stomach for an operation, then half way through said to the boy's father, pay me another thousand rupees for me to stitch his stomach back up. You'll find it hard to believe, but I know both the doctor and the patient. These doctors are nothing but butchers, they squeeze money out of you by threatening that they'd let you die. They won't even touch someone unable to pay a fee. Who could stoop to something so low! I have to depend on them for my living. As long as you flatter them it's fine, but you cross them and there's no work for you.'

On the third or fourth day on her job, Tara could not believe her eyes when she came across a young woman, who was as surprised on seeing her and called out, 'Tara bahinji!'

Tara was now sure that it was Sita, daughter of Purandei, her neighbour from Bhola Pandhe's Gali. They jumped into each other's arms. Unable to believe her eyes, Sita just stared at Tara's face for a few moments. Tara too looked at Sita with some surprise. How much Sita had changed in the past nine months! She was dressed and made up like a married woman. Her face was powdered and rouged, kohl on the rims of her eyes, lips painted, bindi on her forehead and hair done fashionably in ringlets. Her kameez fitted snugly and made her bosom thrust out in a way that made Tara look away in embarrassment. What a dramatic change comes over Punjabi refugee girls once they arrive in Delhi, Tara thought. They seem to lose all sense of decency and modesty.

'You're looking very nice. Where's your mother? What're you doing here?' Tara broke the silence.

'Where have you been all this time?' Sita asked.

'At first I tutored some children in Delhi. Now I am working at this office.'

'I didn't mean that. Everyone in the gali thought something happened to you when that Muslim mob set fire to your in-laws' house in Banni Hata. We were told that you were never found, perhaps you didn't survive.'

'As you can see, here I am,' Tara answered.

'Yes, but what happened? Your mother, Masterji, Puri bhappa and Usha cried their eyes out and we all cried with them. We all thought that you were... Sheelo and Pushpa cried the most.'

Sita described in a few sentences how the people of the gali were evacuated to the Dev Samaj Camp. Some former pupil of Masterji, who looked like an official, took Tara's family away. 'They are probably somewhere in Hindustan—maybe UP.'

Tara stood lost in her memories, then said, 'I'm late, and have got to get to my desk. I'll see you again at one o'clock, during my lunch break.'

'I work in this office too, Bahinji. A few minutes won't matter.'

It was the first time Tara had met someone from her past life. The joy she felt turned quickly to anxiety. Sita had said that Tara's family and neighbours thought that she was no longer alive. Asad had told her the same thing after her rescue from the house in Shaikhupura. For a moment the feeling of being thought of as dead made her feel depressed, then she thought, 'Maybe it's better for my family that I am dead. They've washed their hands off me. Why should I become a cause of worry for them again?' She had given her name as Miss Tara Puri when applying for her job, in the same way her brother used Jai Puri as his pen name. 'Sita is in the same office. She didn't even finish her matric exam, but still found the job as a clerk. She knows about my marriage. In Lahore her mother could hardly make ends meet. Here Sita's dress, her jewellery and make-up are very obvious.'

Tara thought up a story by the time of the lunch break. She told Sita, 'The women at my in-laws had taken me to a room on the top floor. I wasn't well that day. Downstairs the wedding feast was still going on when the Muslim mob attacked and set fire to the place. Everyone was trying to save himself, no one thought of me. The stairs were already in flames, I couldn't go down. I climbed over a wall and jumped on to the roof of the house next door. I fell and sprained my ankle, but managed to limp down to the gali. A kind Muslim man showed me the house of a Hindu. By morning my ankle had swollen up and I had a fever. That good soul asked me many times if he could take me somewhere. All I said that I had nowhere to go, and that nobody was looking for me. They could, if they wanted, just throw me into the river. I lived with that family for about two weeks, then went with them first to Amritsar, then to Ambala. Eventually we came to Delhi. I've been working since I arrived here.'

There were few occasions for Tara and Sita to meet at the office. Tara's position was three grades higher, and in a different section, and she seldom left her room during the lunch break.

Tara had no reason to socialize either; she had few acquaintances in the city. Mercy did sometimes drag her to the bazaar. The tide of refugees covered the city like a swarm of locusts. On the pavements of Chandni Chowk, in Daryaganj and Connaught Place, all one saw were Punjabi hawkers and peddlers. A shanty town had sprung up on the maidan in front of the Red Fort. Pointing to those structures Mercy would say, 'That's a whole new bazaar. People looking for bargains would rather go there than to Chandni Chowk.'

Tara took a bus from Daryaganj to her office. On her way back she often saw a curious sight near Connaught Place, a food cart built on a bicycle. A wire basket fixed to the handlebars held a pot of curried chickpeas and disks of *bhatura* bread. From the crossbar hung bags with other supplies. The bicycle was parked on its stand. A folding table over the rear wheel was fitted with a small brazier and a griddle. The owner—cook would take plates and spoons from the bags to serve chickpeas and bread warmed over the brazier to clients standing around the table. His six- or seven-year-old son would take out tumblers form a bucket hanging from the handlebars, and serve water from a municipal water tap. The boy would also wash the dishes at the same tap. After serving the clients on one corner, the mobile restaurant would move to the next. Tara always felt proud at the sight; what could be a better answer, she thought, to the accusation that the refugees were freeloaders.

As Tara was given more responsibilities at the office, she began staying late to finish her work. Shivnath Misra, the office superintendent, was rather old-school in his approach to running the office. His Indian-style jacket remained buttoned up to the neck and his round Kristi cap sat firmly on his head as long as he was at his desk. He did not chew paan while in the office, and the peon was not sent to get his lunch. After his first appointment as an upper division clerk thirteen years before, he had risen to his present position by dint of hard work. When the director sahib appointed Tara as Misra's assistant, he gave him the hint that she had come with the home secretary's recommendation.

Being burdened with a twenty-one-year-old novice with an MA did not please Misra very much. How could she be expected to do any useful work? Several refugee girls like her had already found employment in the office. The doubts he had about giving Tara any work to do soon vanished, and he began sending more files to her desk.

At the beginning of June, Misra summoned Tara to complete the formalities of her appointment. Since she had been an MA student in Lahore and had done some social work in Delhi, she was considered to have graduated MA according to a government notification. Misra also formally asked her, 'Are you a member of any political party? Do you have any sympathy or connection with the Communist Party or the RSS? Any person who does is not eligible for government service.'

'No, sir,' Tara replied without hesitation. After the news of general strikes in Kanpur, Calcutta and Bombay, she did not want to have anything to do with people who created trouble for no reason.

In June 1948 the refugee portfolio was transferred to a different government minister. Mohanlal Saxena, the new minister, wanted to pursue the policy of settling the refugees. Now the emphasis was not only on feeding and clothing them and providing medical services, but also to make them self-reliant. Small loans were given to the refugees for starting a business. In September the minister had a decree issued that all camps would be shut down in six months' time, and the refugees would not receive free shelter and rations after that. In view of the major problems of food shortages and unemployment facing the country, the minister could not afford to spare one million rupees per day for the upkeep of the camps.

There were several complaints against the refugees: That many of them had begun some business and were earning a decent income, but continued to draw free rations. They were accused of abusing the benevolence of the government, and of being unwilling to earn their own support. Also, in order to afford expensive clothes and food, they were reluctant to give up free rations and shelter. As if the partition of the country had given them some right to act as permanent non-paying guests! The refugees were offered land and accommodation in Okhla and Neelokheri, but nobody wanted to leave Delhi. How long could their countrymen go on tightening their belts in order to give handouts worth a million rupees each day? Such comments hurt Tara; she was also a refugee. She had never imagined that she would earn a salary of Rs 275 per month. She was willing to accept half that amount, she told herself. She did not need more than that.

Tara's office was given several additional projects: allotment of plots of land to the refugees for building houses, incentives and funding for starting small businesses. In order to remain within the ministerial requirements to cut expenses, no new employees were hired and the work load was redistributed among the existing staff. On the recommendation of the office superintendent, the assistant director sahib deputed Tara to dispose off the applications for loans and grants for self-help schemes for women. She was given a separate office and a peon in attendance.

She was deep in studying a file one day when she heard 'huzoor' and raised her eyes. The peon of Sitole, the assistant director, salaamed and said, 'The sahib has sent this old woman to see you.' He moved aside to let the woman enter.

The old woman stood with her palms joined, wrapped in a dirty old dupatta. The sight of her ragged salwar-kameez, her gaunt deeply lined face and tear-filled eyes pierced Tara's heart. She recognized the face and gasped, 'Biddo's grandma!'

The refugee woman from Sangaroor, her daughter-in-law and grandchildren had been in Tara's hut at the Kashmiri Gate camp. The poor soul was nothing but skin and bones. Tara pushed back her chair, went round and put her hand on the old woman's arm.

Recognizing Tara's voice, the old woman knelt and put her forehead on Tara's feet and began to cry. Tears came to Tara's eyes. She raised the old woman and guided her to a chair.

The old woman resisted, pleading, 'No, no, *dhiye*, daughter! I've never sat on such a thing.' On being pushed into the chair, she sat with her knees drawn up. Tara listened to her story perched on the desk, with her hand on the woman's shoulder.

The refugee camp at Kashmiri Gate was closed in December. Since then the old woman had been living, with her daughter-in-law and grandchildren, in one room of a crumbling house in a lane next to the outer wall of Mori Gate. Several other families lived there too, one to each room. Both women earned a small living by grinding spices or cleaning lentils at a bania's shop. Their joint income would be fourteen annas, sometimes even eighteen annas a day. On some days they earned nothing. All their gold ornaments had been sold off.

She had applied for a sewing machine, she told Tara, on the eighth day of the third month of the year. On the twenty-second day of the fourth month, she had paid five rupees to an inspector. Now Sumitra, her neighbour, says that she would receive the machine after paying ten more.

The old woman swore by Maharaj-ji that she had no more money. If she was not given the machine, at least her five rupees should be returned. Her granddaughter was sick. The doctor's advice was to feed her milk and oranges. As long as she had some gold to sell, she bought medicine and food. Where could she get all that now? Sumitra had been allotted another sewing machine, and a grant of 200 rupees. Her husband made and sold *vilayati*-style ink for fountainpens. Nobody paid any attention to poor people like herself, Khemi mai.

Tara bit her lip and sighed. She had been in charge of the distribution of sewing machines for the past two months. Seventy-two machines had been distributed so far. Someone living in Daryaganj had also complained to her about irregularities in distribution. She thought for a minute. Since she knew the correct procedure for dealing with complaints, she summoned Padam Singh, a clerk, and ordered, 'Thakur Sahib, write down this poor woman's statement and take her thumb print as signature. Get two other clerks to sign as witnesses.' She told Khemi mai to come back after her statement was recorded.

Khemi mai returned and bending to touch Tara's feet again, pleaded, 'Please get me my sewing machine. My daughter-in-law knows how to work it. I swear by Maharaj-ji that we'll pay back every month as much as we can. I'll also pay interest,'

Pushing two folded ten-rupee notes into her palm, Tara said, 'First get your granddaughter treated. Get her everything that the doctor has ordered. Come back if you need any help. I hope you'll have your machine by the first week of next month.'

Khemi mai put her arms around Tara and broke into sobs, 'Beti, why has Maharaj-ji done this to me so that I have to depend on charity. In His mercy He will rid us of this shame. I won't die before I pay back your loan. I've suffered enough in this life, but let me free myself for the next.'

Tara prepared a case file with Khemi mai's complaint against inspector Bhanu Dutt and forwarded it to the office superintendent, who launched an inquiry and asked for a list of those given sewing machines. He told Tara to go in the office jeep, with senior inspector Indranath, to investigate whether the people on the list had actually received machines, and to verify their addresses.

Tara and the inspector visited eleven people. At three places they were told about Bhanu Dutt demanding a bribe of twenty rupees. The names of two recipients were fictitious.

The assistant director ordered that Bhanu Dutt be suspended from his position, and recommended to the director that he be dismissed.

This caused a great hullabaloo in the office. Bhanu Dutt was a khadi-wearing member of the Congress party and had been jailed for taking part in the satyagraha movement. He pleaded against this so-called injustice in the cabals of influential Congress leaders. He tried to persuade the clerks of upper and lower grades to go on strike. But many in the office knew the facts, and the strike fizzled out.

Bhanu Dutt announced that he would go on a fast to protest against such unfairness. He spread out a black blanket in a veranda of the office, and clad in white khadi kurta-pajama and Gandhi cap, lay down on it. He wrote out a statement, and showed the paper to people who came by to ask questions. The gist of his statement was:

Assistant Superintendent Miss Tara Puri had fabricated an accusation of accepting bribe against him. The basis for her charge was that contrary to her wishes, he had failed to recommend the allotment of a sewing machine to her aunt Khemi. Miss Tara Puri was paid a salary of three hundred rupees per month. Why did she not help her aunt? Miss Tara Puri had close relations with the senior officers of the department. She drank alcohol in the club with the officers, and danced with them. All her behaviour, whether proper or improper, was condoned.

In her report on Bhanu Dutt's case, Tara had already mentioned, with proof from the register of the receiving clerk, the fact that Khemi mai's application had been submitted before her appointment to the department. She had nothing more to add in her defence.

Mr Mittal, the director of the Department of Rehabilitation, received several calls from influential Congress party leaders to settle the matter quietly. Sensing the direction the wind was blowing, he just expressed his inability, 'The case file has gone to the secretary of the ministry. I'll have to abide by his decision.'

It was the fourth day of Bhanu Dutt's fast. Tara received a telephone call from the director asking her to come to his office immediately for a few minutes. In the director's room she saw somebody who looked like a young Pathan, beardless and with shoulder length hair. The visitor wore a khadi kurta with a neatly folded dupatta slung on the shoulder. Mittal sahib made a polite introduction, 'Miss Tara Puri. She works in the section for the resettlement of refugee women. She will explain the situation to you.' Nodding towards the visitor, he said, 'You know Miss Manjula Sewabhai, of course? She's an advisor and consultant to our department. Please have a seat, Miss Puri.'

Turning to Miss Sewabhai, he said, 'Miss Tara Puri herself conducted the inquiry with a senior inspector.'

'What inquiry!' Miss Sewabhai cut short the director and said to Tara in English, 'I know everything. If the administration applies pressure, these poor people can be made to confess to anything. Many people have told me about the incident. Bhanu Dutt is a veteran Congresswalah, he went to jail for Congress. He's now being called dishonest. Why are you after that poor man? Isn't your own salary enough for you that you want to get your hands on the sewing machines!'

The director was taken aback by Miss Sewabhai's unexpected outburst. What could he say to such an influential, well-regarded woman?

Miss Sewabhai again threatened Tara, 'Who're you to get him dismissed? I'll telephone the Prime Minster and get you fired! You'll have to apologize to Bhanu Dutt.'

Tara straightened her back and rose to her feet, 'Madam, I'm an employee of this department. Whatever you have to say to me, say it through the director of the department.' She turned towards the director, 'Sir, may I leave?'

Mr Mittal said, 'I'm sorry. Miss Puri. You may go, for the moment.'

The director telephoned her again ten minutes later, 'I'm really sorry for the unpleasantness, Miss Puri. Your reaction was perfectly justified. Would you please come to my office for a minute?'

He asked her to sit beside him as he explained, 'I'd called you because I thought that two women could discuss the problem amicably. But this woman is out of her mind. She's a favourite with the Prime Minister and pokes her nose into everything. I'll report to the secretary of the ministry, but you should also drop a word in Mr Rawat's ear.'

Tara was burning with anger. Seeing her sulk, Mercy asked, 'What's the matter?'

Tara told the whole story, and said, 'I feel like resigning from my job.'

Mercy calmed her down, 'Don't do that. These Congress party people behave irresponsibly in everything. They're always turning up at the hospital with chits from some minister or member of Parliament. They get themselves admitted even when they only have a cold, so that they don't have to pay anything for the treatment. And poor sick people can't find a place. When the doctors see their superiors breaking rules, they too look for ways to make money on the side.'

At 7.30 Tara telephoned Narottam that it was urgent for her to see Rawat. She thought it prudent to meet Rawat with Narottam present.

Narottam came over around 9 p.m. He said, 'Rawat's gone to Simla. He'll return on Monday.' He agreed with Tara after hearing about the incident, 'Your self-respect comes first. What did that tiresome woman mean by showing up at your office? And even if she did, the director himself should have dealt with her. The director probably wanted to shift the responsibility to you.'

Tara said, 'The director admitted that the PM indulges her. Everyone's scared of her. Who knows what she might tell him.'

Bhanu Dutt ended his fast on the persuasion of Miss Sewabhai. The office was buzzing with the rumour that Miss Sewabhai had reported Tara's unjust and rude behaviour to the PM. Since Tara was still on probation, everyone expected her to be dismissed in punishment.

The news of the Bhanu Dutt incident had reached Dr Shyama, who telephoned Tara, 'Miss Sewabhai is a bit hot-tempered, but good at heart. I'll speak to her. You also go and meet her, everything will be all right.'

Tara did not agree to that. She had made up her mind to quit the job. With enough savings she was confident of finding a job at some school or college and was not willing to put up with such humiliation.

Narottam came on Tuesday evening to escort Tara to the club. When they saw Rawat standing surrounded by a circle of people, they stood to one side waiting for an opportunity to speak to him.

Rawat saw them and came over. Putting his arm around Tara's shoulder as if she was his daughter or a younger sister, he exclaimed, 'Well done, you brave girl! You rightly shut up that obnoxious woman! I heard the whole story. Mittal had nothing but praise for you. That woman went straight to the Prime Minister as if she intended to eat you alive! And just look at the Prime Minister's lack of sense. He had his PA telephone Saxena sahib.

'The call from the Prime Minister's office infuriated Saxena. The poor minister had been waiting for a week to discuss policy with the PM. But the PM had time for Miss Sewabhai, and not for the minister. He wrote a private memo to the PM saying that "It was improper for Miss Sewabhai to interfere in the working of my department. If there was any need, she should have spoken to me. Inspector Bhanu Dutt's case was dealt following correct and fair procedure. The matter will be explained to the PM whenever he has time.'

Narottam said jokingly, 'And she was all set to quit her job.'

'Silly girl!' Rawat chided Tara. 'Girls will always be girls. Why did you feel insulted? The real insult was to the government. If you want to be a civil servant, remember to leave your ego at home. You're a representative of the President of India. If the minister had reinstated that dishonest inspector for some policy reasons, you still would have got a commendation from the director in your service record for your diligence and capability. We wouldn't have thrown you to the dogs.'

The section assistant had filed an unfavourable report on Sita's work performance saying that she was not carrying out the responsibilities of the assistant dispatcher properly. And she was often late for work. And, therefore, she should be dismissed after one month's notice. There had been reports of her flirtatious behaviour, and two clerks had had a scuffle over her.

Superintendent Misra did not want a refugee girl to lose her livelihood; if she had to work, her family must be facing hard times. Four other refugee girls employed in the office were good, conscientious workers, who did not while away the time smoking and gossiping like their male colleagues. Misra thought that Sita could do better if only she paid a little more attention to her work, but did not know how to tell this to the girl. He explained to Tara that if she could get Sita to mend her ways, the girl might avoid being fired. He telephoned the section assistant to ask Sita to meet Tara.

Tara was very busy when Sita came to see her. Thinking of their past acquaintance Tara chided her her in Punjabi, '*Muree*, why don't you visit me at home. Well, today I don't have a moment free. You know where Daryaganj is? Come to my place. We'll have dinner together.' Tara gave her the directions, then jotted the address down on a slip of paper.

Sita accepted, but failed to turn up. She came the next evening at 8 p.m., wearing an expensive-looking long coat. Tara complained lightly, 'Why didn't you come yesterday?'

'Bahinji, I went to a movie yesterday.'

Tara looked at her quietly, and said after a brief pause, 'You spend so much on your clothes and go to movies, how can you afford all this?'

'I'm not so concerned with saving money as you are. You get a good salary, but just look at your clothes. You dress like an old maid,' Sita said jokingly.

Tara also replied affectionately, 'Even if you don't save, how do you get along on a hundred rupees a month? Is your mother still working?'

Sita bowed her head and nodded, 'I've told mother so many times there is the need, but she doesn't listen.'

'You have so many salwar-kameez suits! Hai, what lovely earrings! How much did they cost?'

'It's a present,' Sita said with affected nonchalance, and smiled slyly.

'So where does the money come from?'

'Everything's possible,' Sita said offhandedly. 'When God wants you to have money, you find it in every nook and cranny.'

'Did you come across some gold buried in your house that the Muslims had left behind? You're really lucky,' Tara ventured. There had been rumours of refugees finding hidden money and jewellery. People would say: It's all His doing. Some loose everything, others find treasures.

'No such luck! There's no shortage of money in Delhi. Whoever wants money, gets money. It's not like Lahore!' Sita said with the same boastful self-confidence.

Tara kept quiet for a few moments, then took Sita's hand and made her sit beside her on the sofa. Tara asked, 'Doesn't your mother object to your spending money?'

'You think I ask mother for money?'

Tara was shocked: How rude and disrespectful Sita had become! She felt like telling her to go away. But Misra had asked her to put some sense into Sita's head. Tara remembered that Sita used to flirt slyly with Bir Singh and Mewa Ram, her neighbours in the gali back in Lahore. Now she had no fear of losing her good name. 'What'll become of this girl!' she thought.

Concealing her dislike, Tara said, 'You know that there's a complaint against you? Misraji said to me that perhaps you don't want the job anymore.'

'That damned good-for-nothing is after my life.'

'But why is he against you?'

'He thinks I'm his slave.'

'What do you mean by "his slave"? He received a complaint that you don't do your office work properly.'

'I do the best I can, as well as I can.'

'What'll you do if you are sacked?'

'Wah, what do I care? I'll find another job. I've had offers of one hundred fifty per month. I'll also be able to learn typing.'

'Why would someone pay a hundred and fifty?'

'Why not? The offer was made.'

'If that's so, why don't you find a job for Vedi and Satya?'

'Like hell. Have they ever looked at themselves in a mirror?'

Tara said in an earnest voice, 'Sita, such attitude isn't right. What have you got yourself into! Have you no shame?'

'What have I done? Can't I have a little fun?'

'You call that having fun?' Tara scolded her as if such was her right. 'Accepting presents from others, having fun at their expense?'

'What's that to you?' Sita shot back. 'Why are you jealous if I have some fun. Did I ask you for anything?'

Tara was incensed, but controlled herself in order to pacify Sita, 'Why would I be jealous, sister. Whatever I said was because I consider you my young sister, like Usha. You have the right to come to me if you need anything, but who are these people willing to lavish presents on you?'

Sita stood up angrily, 'What about those who got you the job with three hundred rupees salary? First look under your own bed before finding fault with others. Why did you run away from your in-laws? We are not in your office where you can bully me. We all get what's in our fate. I've no shortage of job offers,' she shouted as she stormed out.

Tara was appalled. All she had in return for showing concern was rudeness. Offering advice could have created problems for herself, she realized, 'Let that stupid girl learn her lesson. What should I care! She made accusations against me. Other people probably must be gossiping about me too. But whatever Sita did, isn't it true that a woman is always judged by absolute moral standards? Some women tremble with fear at any approach by men, when others lead them on or lure them into their snares!'

To dispel her annoyance, she picked up the half-finished sweater she had been knitting for Mercy, but could not continue. Had Mercy been home, she would have chatted with her. But she was on a night shift. Tara had her dinner, slipped under her quilt and tried to sleep to forget the incident. Sleep came after a long time. When she woke the next morning, and for several days, the words of Sita were on her mind.

Tara had built up a reputation in the office for her efficiency and sound judgement. She also liked her work. Mercy was increasingly fond of her. Sometimes she would loosen Tara's hair tied in a simple bun, and rearrange it in some new style. When they went out together to the bazaar, Mercy would ignore Tara's resistance and put lipstick on her mouth. Tara would wipe her lips clean, but some colour would remain and Mercy would be even more pleased, 'Hai, it looks so natural.' She bought a light shade of lipstick for Tara.

Tara would laugh and say, 'What's the use of all this silliness?' But bitter-sweet memories filled her heart. The women living in the gali had begun to praise her for her good looks before she was even fifteen. For this reason her mother and taayi had built hopes of finding her a rich husband; for this reason also Somraj had agreed to marry her after laying eyes on her only once. Asad used to say that when she smiled and looked at someone shyly, her face reflected the goodness of her heart. And she would look at him, beaming with pride and happiness. But she did not want to remember all that now. What was the point?

February 1949 had begun. The winds of spring were stripping off the old leaves from the trees to make way for new buds. Whirling eddies of dried leaves rose and settled back on the wide clean streets of Delhi. On its way out, the dying winter made its presence felt by an occasional nip in the air. Exclaiming 'It's no longer cold', young women discarded the heavy, loose coats that hid the curves of their bodies, and stored them away until the next cold season. The chilly air gave them gooseflesh, but they seemed not to care.

Those working as temporary employees in the Department of Rehabilitation were getting goose pimples for another reason. The minister had decided to implement his decision to close down Kingsway Camp with its 40,000 occupants and all other camps in the country with their one million residents on 31 March. The minister again gave assurances to those in the camps that the administration would provide help for those seeking employment, offer plots of land or dwellings for them to resettle, and loans for starting new businesses. He confirmed that no one would be entitled to free rations and that all inhabitants should make living arrangements outside the camps before the closing date.

Refugees who had found employment with the Department of Rehabilitation feared that the closure of the camps implied the end for their department. Where would they go, what would they do? Soon the one million camp inhabitants in the country were united with other refugees in a show of public protest against the minister's decision. The individual state governments were apprehensive that they would have to assume the burden of looking after the refugees living in camps in their states once the Central government gave up its responsibility. They feared that these destitute, hungry and desperate people might create law and order problems. The state governments also came out in favour of postponing the decision to abolish the camps.

Several delegations met with the Prime Minister to appeal against the camp closures. The office of the Department of Rehabilitation was abuzz with discussions and rumours about how the situation would turn out

Tara had also heard people debating on the same topic at the club. A businessman–contractor was arguing with Rawat, who was against the suggestion to continue spending one million rupees each day to feed and house the refugees. Rawat said, 'Where's this million coming from? This is undermining our government's schemes for improving irrigation, education and health services. Is it wise to spend a million each day to feed those who do nothing but twiddle their thumbs? I'm for spending two hundred million to train unemployed refugees and make them productive. That will benefit the country in the future. It was a mistake to give out free rations even for this long. Some of the refugees have been in the camps for over a year. What do they do all day? I've heard that some spend their whole day at the movies, others gamble. Some operate small businesses, but live in the camp because they've become used to getting free meals. Isn't it ridiculous that our peasants and farmers who grow food have to exist on three or four annas a day, and we continue to spend one rupee every day on these freeloaders.'

Rawat's reasoning made sense to Tara. She was willing to work to carry out the minister's orders, even if it meant losing her 300 rupees per month. This outlook had displeased several temporary employees at her office. In spite of being warned six months before about the forthcoming closure of the camps, few people had paid heed in hopes that the date for closing would be postponed. Many Congress leaders supported the refugees and Miss Sewabhai was also working to have the minister's decision overturned. Large numbers of camp inhabitants staged protest marches in the first week of March, but the minister refused to reverse his decision.

A woman social worker at one of the camps, who was also a Congress veteran, went on hunger strike to protest the minister's decision. Her demands were that the hundreds of people employed as camp staff and those who worked at the Department of Rehabilitation should be re-employed before the shutting down. Her hunger strike gave new impetus to the agitation against the minister. Street marches were organized and demonstratuons were held at refugee camps and all over the capital. Slogans calling for the minister's dismissal were voiced.

It was rumoured throughout the department that the prime minister was unhappy with the minister's intransigence, and had asked him to reconsider his decision on humanitarian grounds. The minister suspected involvement of camp employees in instigating the hunger strike and the protest demonstrations. He ordered the director of the department to serve notice on the camp commandant that unless an end was put to the strike and the demonstrations in seven days' time, all employees would be dismissed and the camp administration would be handed over to the army. The long-term plan of action would be announced in due course.

A group of office clerks suggested that a petition supporting the fasting woman's demands signed by all temporary and refugee employees of the department should be presented to the minister. They came to Tara to ask for her signature, but when she refused, an argument ensued.

Tara said, 'Since this department and the camp had been created only to deal with the problem of refugees, these arrangements could not be expected to be permanent. If the creation of the camps and the department has not been a solution to the problem, it is only fair that the administration finds another answer. I certainly can't oppose the demand for closing down the department only to save my skin. I also disagree with someone else going on a hunger strike to save my job.'

Tara's logic encouraged several clerks already uneasy about putting their names on the appeal to refuse to sign the petition. This angered others who accused her of sowing disunity among the employees. One of them, Haveli Ram, threatened to denounce Tara in slogans that she was a puppet of the director and senior officers. Narendra Chawla, another clerk, had a hard time restraining him. Narendra believed that if the employees reasoned with Tara she might be persuaded to change her mind.

Three days later, Narendra showed Tara a copy of *Nazir* that had an article with forceful and stirring arguments against the closure of the camps. Tara had not studied Urdu in school, but had learnt it from her father and could read the script only in print form. She found the style of writing very impressive and there was something familiar about it. Even though she did not agree with the views expressed, she read the whole article. A chill went down her spine when she saw the writer's name at the end: Jai Puri.

Tara sat stunned for a few moments. She remembered Hira Singh telling her that Puri was publishing some newspaper from Jalandhar. She turned to the last page to see the name of the publisher. It was 'Managing Editor: Jai Puri, Editor: Kanak Puri, Mai Heeran Gate, Jalandhar.'

She felt faint with memories crowding into her mind. The incident of going to Kanak's house in Gwal Mandi with her brother's message came back to her. How her brother had exploded with anger when he saw her and Asad coming out of the restaurant. The argument between them in the tonga and her knocking her head on the charpoy after he accused her, all that flashed before her eyes on the page of the weekly. Then she remembered, her brother had planned to go to Nainital just after her wedding.

She thought that the news that she had been burnt to death at the Banni

Hata house must have taken a weight off her brother's mind. He then probably went to Nainital and married Kanak. The family would not have objected to that. How upset her mother had been at hearing that Kanak was a Brahmin. But brother had progressive ideas; he would not have cared for such disagreements. She folded the pages of the weekly and put it aside.

With bitter memories tearing at her heart, Tara found it hard to concentrate on her work. It was nearing four o'clock. Sitting with her elbows on the desk, she idly drew circles on a sheet of paper with a blue pencil and scored them over. She raised her head on hearing a noise, and saw that Narendra had come in with a file in his hand.

Tara held out *Nazir* to him.

A strange smile flickered on his lips as he spoke, 'Bahinji, it's good that we did not send our petition. The camp commandant has had the fast ended unconditionally.'

Chapter 8

PANDIT GIRDHARILAL HAD GIVEN HIS CONSENT FOR PURI AND KANAK TO have a civil marriage. Puri sent for his parents, his younger brother and two sisters before going to Delhi for the ceremony. His two-room apartment over the press office would be overcrowded, but he decided to sacrifice comfort for the sake of accommodating his family. He was candid with Kanak about all his family having lived in one room in Lahore.

Puri's association with Sood was increasingly drawing him into the Congress party organization. He gave up his shirt and trousers for a simpler dress of a khadi kurta and pajama. Kanak made sure that he changed into a fresh outfit every day. If needed, she washed and ironed his clothes herself.

Over the entrance to the office, the signboard of *Nazir* was fixed next to that of the press. An extra desk was put in the office. Puri himself wrote the editorials, opinion pieces and the two columns of the satirical 'Haat Bazaar Mein'—What I Heard in the Bazaar. The galloping inflation, nepotism and underhand corruption common in the British Raj had not disappeared, but as most people felt, seemed to have grown even more in the first months of the Congress party rule. Those who had suffered in silence and fear under foreign masters were now refusing to take things lying down. Their anger was becoming more vocal and they were openly critical of the government, 'It was better to be governed by the British than by our own people. Now everyone flouts the law and accepts bribes with impunity.' Gandhiji, when he was alive, often used to warn the new government not to indulge in 'pomp and show and extravagance' and used to remind the Congress to stay true to its ideals and the commitment to the people. That voice was now silent. Puri would write biting satires on such themes.

With the launch of *Nazir*, Puri found little time to supervise the press. Since time hung heavy on Masterji's hands, Puri put his father in charge of the accounts. Kanak's responsibility was to translate from English selected news and articles from other newspapers. Puri would also ask her to look out for certain articles in *Harijan* that carried Gandhiji's warnings to the Congress government, and in *Crossroads*, the Communist Party organ, that criticized the government policies favouring capitalists and big industrialists.

Kanak would rewrite these for *Nazir* to reflect the viewpoint of ordinary people. After several days of back-breaking work, they both readied enough material for one issue of the weekly.

During her two-month-long stint as a government journalist in Lucknow, Kanak had often felt guilty about accepting a monthly salary of 250 rupees for sitting idle. Now in Jalandhar she was putting in a hard day's work for which she would receive no payment. The last pages of *Nazir* came off the press on Thursday night. On Friday morning she read the new issue end to end. The elation and satisfaction that she felt was her reward. She had a deep sense of fulfilment that her life was worthwhile and had a purpose.

Puri's mother Bhagwanti thought highly of her new daughter-in-law who, like her bright and clever son, could sit at a desk and work in an office. Mindful of the fact that Kanak came from an affluent and highly regarded family, the mother-in-law also deferred to her. But Kanak was not her ideal of a daughter-in-law. Even after becoming the mother of two children, Bhagwanti had never unveiled her face in the presence of her father-in-law. She thought: How can a daughter-in-law dare to open her mouth and jabber away to her husband in the presence of her in-laws? Who would respect or value such a woman?

Kanak did not draw down a ghunghat to cover her face in the presence of her father-in-law and audaciously addressed him as 'pitaji'. As a token of her respect, she sometimes remembered to cover her head with the corner of her sari or dupatta when he was around. There were few occasions for Bhagwanti to discuss the household or the kitchen chores with her daughter-in-law, and little else that she could talk about with Kanak. Once in a while she would reminisce, with tears in her eyes, about Usha's elder sister, 'Tara also had studied up to BA level. It was in my poor daughter's fate to die on her first night at her in-laws.'

Puri's mother had not been able to satisfy her ambition of seeing her son as a bridegroom, riding a mare at the head of his bridal procession, with *sehra*—the wreath of flowers—around his head. She had had to hand out the congratulatory shagun and other customary gifts in the marriage of the son of Masterji's elder brother and other relatives. Now when it was the time for herself to receive shagun in return, the daughter-in-law arrived quietly, just like a visiting friend or a relative. In Bhagwanti's mind, the responsibility for her being deprived of shagun lay on Kanak.

Because of Panditji's financial situation and other constraints, Kanak's send-off from her parents' home in Delhi had been a brief and simple affair. Her bridal reception at her in-laws' had been equally modest. Women from the families of Sardar Mehar Singh and Lala Kripa Ram of Mai Heeran Gate, and a few from the families that had settled in her gali had come to welcome her and offer the congratulatory shagun. Such an austere event had not satisfied Usha, and to brighten up the occasion, she had invited over four girls of her age from the gali. Kripa Ram's daughter had brought the dholak. The girls had sat Kanak in their midst, and had sung tappas until midnight. One of them had lamented about her sweetheart:

You have spread thorns in my way.
Those buttons in your shirt are fortunate
that they are next to your heart.

Another had taken up the male part:

When I return from the office,
I'll take off the shirt
and put you next to my heart.

On Puri's advice Usha had enrolled in a college. Bhagwanti was a little annoyed with her daughter who, of late, had begun to idolize her daughter-in-law. Usha refused to oil her hair and styled it in two loosely woven plaits, and her dupatta seldom stayed over her head. She imitated her sister-in-law's manner in everything. She preferred tea to milk or lassi. It was fine for boys to behave like this, but Puri's mother did not approve of girls drinking tea.

On her return from college, Usha would read some book or newspaper, or go and sit with her bhabhi in the office among a crowd of men. Bhagwanti did not say anything to the daughter-in-law, but nagged at Usha when Kanak was not listening, 'Is that any way to behave? Girls should behave like girls. You don't want to end up as a pen-pusher in some office, do you?' She wanted her daughter to be married off soon. She could see the result of girls getting too much education.

Kanak had achieved her heart's desire after much struggle and persistence. She was content to be working and blissful in togetherness; for her this was a honeymoon. Most of her day was spent in the office. She often worked until midnight, after Puri had gone to bed. Translating news and features, selecting opinion pieces from other publications for *Nazir*, and proofreading was not quite the kind of literary work that she had dreamt about or the kind of work that was dear to her heart. She would remember: Aseer had rightly said that newspaper work was mostly routine. But not minding the daily grind, she conscientiously burnt the midnight oil.

Since the nights were hot and humid in the apartment, charpoys were laid out for Puri and Kanak to sleep on the roof in the open air. Exhausted by the heat and hard work, Kanak would go to the roof and put her arms around Puri deep in sleep in the cool air. She felt reluctant about disturbing the sleep of her equally exhausted husband, but her tired mind would not allow her to fall asleep. Sometimes she could not suppress a surge of desire, if she was his, he was hers too. Inspite of herself, she would wake him. Later she would feel guilty because of Puri's annoyance.

One morning in July Kanak felt nauseous and her face looked pallid. Puri checked her pulse, felt her forehead and said to his mother, 'Give her a few drops of the Amritdhara medicine, or should we call a doctor?'

His mother ostentatiously ignored his suggestion, 'It's nothing. She'll be all right.' She did not appreciate her son's undue concern for his wife. She knew what was ailing the daughter-in-law. She thought to herself, 'Must he pamper her so much?'

Kanak felt better by midday. She called out to Puri, and as he sat beside her, said shyly, 'Maaji is probably suspecting something. Maybe she's right.'

Puri looked worried and surprised. He said after a moment's thought, 'If that is so, let's ask Mrs Channana from the hospital to examine you. The medical advice is to be particularly careful in such condition.' He added as an afterthought, 'If it's true, you'll be confined to the house. You won't be able to help with *Nazir*.'

Despite Kanak's shyness, Puri took her to see Mrs Channana the next day.

Mrs Channana knew Puri as the editor of *Nazir*. On being told that Kanak was helping in the editing of the weekly, the doctor welcomed her warmly. After examining Kanak, the doctor chided her affectionately, 'Haven't you been foolish! Married only for four months, and got this millstone around your neck. You should have enjoyed yourself for at least a year. This was going to happen anyway. Puriji tells me that you write very well, and are very good at editing. This would be the end of your editorship. Will you sit in the office with the baby clinging to your breast like a monkey? If you feel unwell in the first week of pregnancy, how will you do your editing later? A professional woman must tread with care. I was married off when I was in the third year of medical school. I took every precaution, but still slipped. The delivery was due around the time of the final exam and I'd have lost a whole year. You know how much a year of medical school costs! And then to be the butt of jokes. Think again, it won't be so hard at this stage.'

When Puri was invited to a public function or social event, he liked to take Kanak along. He thought that being accompanied by an educated and cultured wife gave him an elevated status and importance in the eyes of society. Kanak's help was also needed for editing *Nazir*, and hiring an assistant would have meant parting with another 125 rupees or so every month. He was also in no hurry to be elevated to the rank of father. Kanak could imagine the thrill of having a lovely, cuddly baby in her lap, but disliked the idea of failing to be a companion and help to her husband in his work.

The mother-in-law sulked in silence after Kanak had recovered completely. She quietly begged forgiveness from God for the sinful ways of the new generation. Now if she saw Usha spending too much time with Kanak, she would reprimand her, 'Don't you have anything else to do? Won't you ever learn how to run a house, or will you stay a layabout all your life?'

Sood had not said anything to Puri about the salary he could draw for himself or for Kanak. But there was a tacit understanding that the press and the weekly belonged to Puri. What could he pay himself for something that was his own? Although in three months' time *Nazir* had become popular with its readers and had built a reputation for itself, it had attracted very few advertisements. The profit earned through the printing press was Puri's main income.

He had been too busy to scout out business for the press. He left that responsibility to Rikhiram, and raised his salary by twenty-five rupees a month to keep him happy. Masterji continued to keep the account ledgers besides keeping an eye on the petty cashbox and the general working of the press. His habit of not overlooking even the slightest irregularity and of accounting for the last paisa often led to arguments between him and Rikhiram. He never failed to object to Rikhiram slipping a couple of annas to the clerk at the railway parcel office or half a rupee to the peon at the law court to grease their palms.

Rikhiram would say, 'Everyone does it.'

Masterji would reply, 'A bribe is a bribe. Whether of one paisa or of a thousand rupees.'

Puri would keep quiet. Both Masterji and Rikhiram would take his silence for approval.

One evening the press had to work overtime. Rikhiram separated out the reams of paper for the District Board printing job at four forms per sheet, and left. That stock ran out at 7.30 and the machine operator sent a message to ask whether he should stop work. Masterji came downstairs and found that only twenty reams had been used, and five apparently remained. He told the machine operator to print the remaining five.

Next morning, Rikhiram complained that Masterji had wasted five reams of paper. Masterji tried to correct him, 'The job order was for 50,000 forms. Do the sum yourself. You had given paper for only 40,000. Were the five extra reams needed or not?'

Rikhiram shouted at Masterji in front of the workers, 'You think you're the only one who can count? Why do you meddle in things you don't understand? Paper worth sixty-five rupees got wasted because of you. Should I now give the clerks at the Board office their cut out of my own pocket?'

Masterji did not know much about the printing business, but he was not so naïve as not to suspect what Rikhiram was up to. Evidently, he was planning to deliver 40,000 printed forms but charge for 50,000, and save five reams of paper in the bargain. There would have been an overcharge Rs 80 in the invoice. Masterji found this unacceptable. He knew about shady deals in government departments and had some inkling of what his elder brother Ramjwaya had been doing, but for him dishonesty was still a sin—now more than ever, when his fellow countrymen where masters of their own destiny. His family's benefactor Sood was the parliamentary secretary in that government. To defraud one's own people!

Puri often voiced his disapproval of bribing and other corrupt practices in *Nazir*. Masterji felt proud that his clever son was fighting for justice and truth—the very son, who once gave up a job for the sake of his principles. So he complained to his son about Rikhiram's lack of scruples and how he had humiliated him in front of the staff. Puri told him to keep quiet about it.

Masterji had great regard for his son's abilities, and thought him as more intelligent and gifted than himself. But he could not keep silent; it was a question of his own self-respect and dignity. He asked in front of everyone, 'What do you write in your weekly? Didn't you write that the government's money is the public money? And if some people are sent to jail for petty crimes such as thieving, those who steal from the government and the people should be hanged?'

Puri was stung by the force of his father's accusation. Being chastened in front of the family felt particularly humiliating. The press and the weekly belonged to him, and were the basis for his high standing in the community. He replied brusquely, 'Stop bothering yourself if you don't like all this business. Stay out of the office and take it easy at home.'

Her husband's defiance of Masterji upset Kanak very much. Wrapped up in her work, she sometimes did forget to cover her head in Masterji's presence, but she always spoke to him respectfully. If Masterji wanted something done, not only did she do it herself, but happily and out of a sense of duty. She thought that Masterji's criticism was justified. Perhaps he should not have said that in front of everyone, but he was after all the father of the family. Still she kept her own counsel.

At dinner that day Masterji said he did not feel like eating. Puri brought himself to apologize for his harsh words by explaining, 'I am also sickened by such underhand dealings, but if we don't go along with the accountant at the Board office, he'd find someone else to do the printing. Or he would niggle over the bill in a way that it'd be over a year before we get paid. I can't root out every bad thing that has been instilled into our people's blood over the centuries. If we're born in an atmosphere of evil, we'll have to breathe some of it in. We have to root it out gradually. The weekly has hardly any advertising revenue. The income from the press can at least allow us to raise our voice to protest corruption and injustice. If the weekly was making a profit, why would I tolerate such shameful practices? How can I close the press down just like that!'

Kanak filled a thali with food, and took it to Masterji. She sat beside him, bowed her head, and said respectfully, 'Pitaji, you're absolutely right. Please forgive what has happened just this once. He won't allow such things to happen again.'

Masterji gave her an ashirvad of good wishes, and replied, 'Beti, I've worked hard all my life. We were poor but I always tried to be honest and upright. How can I swallow a fly knowingly? God keep you well and give you good sense. Whatever is His wish! Oh God, Thou art our protector.' His voice choked and he broke off.

As a result of Masterji's refusal to eat, Kanak's mother-in-law was also unwilling to have dinner. Puri and Kanak usually ate together from the same thali. Usha arranged a thali for them, and took it to their room. On being told by Usha that dinner was waiting, Kanak muttered, 'Tell him to go ahead. I don't feel like having anything.'

Puri called Kanak, and said angrily, 'Why is everyone ganging up on me and spitting in my face? If I put up with all this only for my own sake, do away with me!'

Her eyes filled with tears, Kanak quietly swallowed some half-chewed food.

Kanak addressed Puri as 'ji' when they were in the office or in the presence of the family. She also called him 'ji' when they were alone, but in a different tone of voice. When they were lying on their charpoys on the roof at night, she took his hand in hers and said, 'Ji, I know such incidents upset you. We must do something about it. Other publications have plenty of advertisements.'

Puri replied, 'Who has the time! The refugees don't leave me a moment's peace. Look, you yourself are seldom free before ten or eleven at night. We must have someone else to help us out in the office.'

Nazir had added to Puri's status and influence, but it had also made him increasingly busy. He became secretary of the Ward Congress Committee. At the Refugee Association other people were still trying to usurp his authority. In the elections of the association in May of that year, he had been elected as the secretary. In the hope of enlisting the support of *Nazir* and of Puri, the Municipal Primary School Teachers Association elected Masterji as their president.

Masterji had become detached from the affairs of the press after the rebuff he had received. He was finding it difficult to remain idle. Regardless of his son's high social standing and the respect shown to him because of his son, he wanted to earn his own living. But how could Puri live with the idea of his father doing a job that paid a mere seventy or eighty rupees per month? When Masterji refused to change his mind, Puri had another idea. He invoked Sood's influence to have a coal depot allotted to Masterji. Now his father could have an income of his own of around three hundred rupees per month.

The plot of land for the coal depot was across the railway tracks in

Basti Nigar Khan, about two miles from the Kamaal Press, and came with a small, two-roomed house. Masterji decided to move into the house on the depot for the sake of convenience. Puri's mother had another reason for moving. Although Kanak was always polite and courteous towards her, the mother-in-law was increasingly worried about Kanak's bad influence on her daughter.

The space in which Puri had lived alone or with Urmila for several months now held a large family. He had stoically put up with the inconvenience. Still he and Kanak did not let his parents leave for several days. Eventually one morning Puri's parents went to their new home, with their younger son Hari, and the two youngest daughters.

As long as Puri's mother was with them, there was no question of hiring a servant or a cook. But one was needed after she left. Could Kanak now spend time in the *Nazir* office as well as devote herself to the housework? Puri told her that until a servant was found, she should order their meals from the dhaba, and send someone from the press to bring them.

Kanak took a break from work at 11.30 that morning and went upstairs. In the past weeks she had also felt cramped for space, especially when it rained. Now the rooms seemed empty and so much bigger, and the sun streaming in more dazzling. She chopped up whatever vegetables she found in the kitchen, lit the stove, put the vegetables on to cook, and began to knead the dough. Her mother had done the cooking in their home in Lahore, but two servants had always been in attendance. If the daughters were called to the kitchen, it was only to teach them a special recipe. Although she might never have learned or received training in the art of cooking, a woman is always confident about being able to cook in the same way as fish are confident of being able to swim.

When Puri heard her call and went upstairs, the smell of something frying in ghee was coming from the kitchen. He found Kanak sitting in front of the stove in the afternoon heat and making paranthas. Her face was flushed crimson like a tomato and beads of perspiration broke out on her forehead and flowed down her temples onto her cheeks.

She smiled at him, 'It's very hot here. I'll give you lunch in a thali and you can eat it in the room.'

A memory flashed through Puri's mind. In winter Urmila sometimes called him to the kitchen and served him there as she cooked. He suppressed the memory and chided Kanak tenderly, 'You overdo things. I asked you to send someone from the press to the dhaba for food. Why did you trouble yourself by cooking?'

'Why, don't you want to eat what I've cooked,' Kanak's eyes shone with love.

'Dish out some food for yourself also.'

'There's only one more parantha left to make. Let me finish.'

Puri stood mesmerized, his hand on the door frame, looking at her. The last parantha was cooked and transferred to the thali. Kanak doused the stove and began to put away the utensils for kneading and rolling the dough. Puri carried the food-filled thali to the room.

He was back shortly into the kitchen, 'Come, Kanni. What're you doing now?' He could not bear to tear himself away from her even for a few seconds.

'Hai, look at me! I'm all covered with sweat,' Kanak said, pointing to her clothes. 'Let me pour two lota-fulls of water over my head to have a quick wash and change into a fresh dhoti.'

'You look lovely just as you are!' He grabbed Kanak as she headed towards the bathroom, her face all flushed and her body drenched in sweat, took her into his arms, and began ardently to kiss her on the lips, forehead, chin and cheeks. Kanak, her heart filled with pride at this show of affection, said in a coaxing voice, '*Chhee*, you bad boy! Just look how sweaty I am!' She put her arms around Puri's neck.

The empty apartment that had taken on a forlorn look after the departure of the in-laws was now filled with the cooing and moans of fervent love-making. Puri and Kanak now had the opportunity to lose themselves in a frenzy of passion.

Kanak did not mind cooking and washing, making beds and doing laundry, and sweeping and dusting the house for Puri. Then, in addition, she edited and proofread the weekly. She had been brought up in luxury and spent the hot summer months in the cool of hill resorts, yet the hot weather of Punjab in the months of July and August did not seem to bother her.

However, one thing did eat away at her and it was Puri's testiness, especially when basking in the afterglow of their love-making. She had experienced this first just three weeks into their marriage. She felt crushed and depressed by such unkind and offhand behaviour in those moments of languorous ecstasy.

After bringing Kanak home as his bride, Puri had behaved politely and carefully towards her in the presence of his family, as if she deserved more respect than himself. His mother was not pleased with the daughter-in-law being cosseted in this way. But hardly two months had passed before Puri's behaviour began to worsen, particularly when he was tired, agitated or piqued for some reason. Such lapses hurt Kanak's feelings badly, but she tried to overlook or forget them. She was ecstatic for some days after Puri's parents and the rest of the family had moved to Basti Nigar Khan, now that she and Puri could lose themselves in unrestrained passion. She had hoped that by offering herself, heart and soul, to her beloved she would be able to improve the situation. Nevertheless, the result of this freedom from the need for restraint, ample time to give in to their impulses, and of Kanak's selfless love was not quite as expected. Kanak sensed a fading of Puri's love and desire for her. What once had driven him to bouts of passionate love-making now seemed to leave him cold. His desire for sex seemed to be dissipating. If sometimes he did give in to a burst of passion, it seemed to fill him with a sense of contrition.

Kanak gave serious thought to the situation and came to the conclusion that her husband was tired and overburdened with the responsibilities he had taken on, and that she was adding to his problems and worries. She felt regretful and ashamed of herself, and resolved to control her feelings. Then, after some time, Puri's ardour would return. Kanak would feel some satisfaction, but Puri would soon go back to feeling peevish, detached and filled with self-disgust. Kanak would be overcome by shame and curse herself, 'Are my urges so strong?' She could not help feeling insulted.

The policy of *Nazir* was to support the ideology of Gandhiji and of the left wing of the Congress party. Except for Puri and Kanak, none of the employees of the weekly or of Kamaal Press had any sympathy for the Congress. Manmohan Siddhu, the weekly's new manager, had turned his back on the Congress like the majority of Punjabis. He believed that the Congress had surrendered to the demand for the partition of the country, and was responsible for the tragic results and the salughter of Hindus. The ban on the Rashtriya Swayamsewak Sangh as an illegal organization had also angered Siddhu. Rikhiram and the cylinder-machine operator were against the Congress because, in their opinion, it was not sufficiently anti-Muslim. But as they all worked for Puri or for the *Nazir* weekly, they had to do whatever they were told. Puri also found it tiresome. With like-minded staff, he thought, they could work more smoothly and in a more congenial atmosphere.

Siddhu had been hired at a monthly salary of 125 rupees before Masterji left for his new home. He had worked as the assistant manager at the *Kesari* weekly in Lahore, and had proved his worth by increasing *Nazir*'s circulation and roping in several advertisers. Kanak remained the only person in the editorial department. Puri was spending more time than before in his social engagements. When Kanak began to feel unwell again in November, Puri realized that it would not be possible as before for her to spend ten to twelve hours a day in the office. It would not be advisable.

Bhupendra 'Raks' had worked in the editorial department of the *Chhatrapati* newspaper in Lahore. He also wrote short stories and satirical pieces. He had offered to *Nazir* without payment two short stories, and a satirical article on the Communist Party's new line. In December Puri hired him as the assistant editor, but soon became dissatisfied with his performance. Raks's attitude was strictly businesslike, and mercenary. He had a good command over Urdu and a thorough knowledge of the workings of a newspaper office, but he was in it for the money and not somebody who could be trusted with major responsibilities.

Kanak continued to work in the office as much as she could until April 1949 and then into May, but she was hardly in a condition to sit in the office. Raks was not prepared to do even half the work that Kanak did in her condition. Puri's need was for an associate who could replace Kanak and also share some his own burden.

Kanak and Puri had sent the news of their marriage to Gill and copies of *Nazir* were regularly sent to his address. In their letter to Gill they had written: 'You are an experienced journalist. We both are looking forward to your help by way of advice and suggestion.' Gill had honoured their request by sending in four articles over the past year to *Nazir*.

Kanak had told Puri about meeting Gill in Lucknow, and about Gill's generous nature and the understanding that had developed between them. As a proof of her devotion to Puri, she had even confessed, 'Had I not lost my heart to you, I'd have surrendered to Gill. But you thief, you had already stolen my heart away. You kept your hold over me so that even when I was hundreds of miles away and there was no hope of seeing or meeting you again, your attraction kept a grip on me.' She gave him an accusing look,

'You played fast and loose here but made me stay faithful to you.'

Shame-faced, Puri replied, 'Kanni, why do you want to remind me of my pain and desperation?'

'Never mind my joking. Whom else can I joke with if not you?' She made up for her comment by showing her love for him.

Whenever the subject of the need for an assistant editor came up, Puri would always think of Gill, and mention this to Siddhu and Kanak. Siddhu would say, 'If Gill joined us, there would be nothing like it. In Lahore, he was the mainstay of *Sitara* weekly.'

Puri also thought the same, but was reluctant to invite him for two reasons.

In the past, Puri deferred to Gill as his senior in journalism, and had asked for Gill's support in protesting his dismissal from *Pairokaar*.

Gill's salary as a proofreader in Lucknow was under a hundred rupees per month, and Puri was willing to pay him 150. But would he agree to work under Puri, even for a higher salary? Puri was paying himself a monthly 250 rupees, which covered salaries for both himself and Kanak. Gill had no family. As a socialist and a comrade he should have agreed to an offer of 125. Had he worked as a 'whole-timer' for the party, he would have been paid only Rs 40 per month.

The other concern Puri had imagined was that Gill might begin to slip the Communist Party line into Puri's weekly. Gill had been expelled from the Party, but nobody could trust these Communists! Even after a break-off from the party, from experience Puri knew the saying 'once a communist, always a communist'. Puri had no intention of making a change in his name as the Managing Editor, and of Kanak as the Editor. Would Gill agree to leave his name out of the editorial board?'

For a beginner in a new business, experience is the best teacher. Experience had taught Puri that the secret of successfully managing and editing a weekly paper was not limited to the ability to write well. A foot soldier's forte lies in his skilful use of arms, but a general seldom picks up a weapon. As a general's ability is shown in leading his troops, a skilled editor knows how to marshal the talent of good writers. Instead of slogging away all day in writing an effective article, he knows how to use what others have written, on the right occasion and in the appropriate context. Puri's resentment at his former editor Kashish began to subside, and turn against people like Raks who prided themselves in doing as little work as possible.

Instead of writing to Gill himself, Puri asked Kanak to do it. After requesting Gill's help for old time's sake, she explained the situation in plain words:

'How can we ever hope to pay you what you deserve? But if Puriji and I can get by on the little we draw, we hope you can also do the same. You already know the weekly's editorial policy. You may not fully agree with it, but that's no reason for you to deny us your support. And without your name appearing on the editorial board, how could you be held responsible for its policy? Not only do we need your cooperation, but being a part of the team might mean something to you.'

Gill came to Jalandhar.

The office of the weekly had been in a single room upstairs, but now the space was inadequate. Also Puri and Kanak found little peace or privacy with the press below and the office next door. As luck would have it, a small house in the Vikrampur mohalla got vacant when its occupant, a government officer, was transferred to Simla. Puri had the house allotted in his name. A living space had to be found for Gill. By breaking down the brick stove in the kitchen upstairs at the press, enough space was created to fit in a charpoy, with a few feet to spare. Gill moved in.

Rikhiram had been running the press almost single-handedly. The printing of the weekly and outside jobs kept the press so busy that he often asked Puri to buy another treadle machine. On his suggestion Puri had already added Hindi and Punjabi Gurumukhi type fonts. In undivided Punjab the practice had been to print all government notices and documents in Urdu and English only, but now the Sikhs were demanding that government documents should be available in Gurumukhi also, and lately the Hindus had asked Hindi to be given an equal status. There was no shortage of work and new presses were being set up all over.

Gill took the responsibility for the publication of *Nazir*. Now Puri's presence was not required even when Kanak could not come to the office. Puri had many other commitments to keep him occupied. If he came to the press, he seldom stayed more than a couple of hours. Gill sometimes also wrote the editorial. Things had begun to move smoothly when calamity struck.

Puri was in the office of the paper one day when the chowkidar called out to him to come downstairs, 'Bauji, come quickly. A clerk from the law court and a policeman are here.'

It's probably some urgent printing job, Puri thought.

Rikhiram had been absent for three days. He had neither asked for leave, nor sent any explanation for his absence. Everyone at the press presumed him to be sick. Since no other employee could handle such an emergency, Puri had to go downstairs.

Puri felt the earth shift beneath his feet when he heard the reason for the court official's visit. The bailiff had come to collect Rs 13,130 from Kamaal Press, and intended to repossess the press property in case the money was not paid.

Nonplussed and at a loss, Puri called Gill over. On examining the court order they realized that the court had issued a decree against Rikhiram, the manager of the Kamaal Press, that unless the sum of Rs 13,130 due to the moneylender Achharu Ram was paid, the press property would be seized. Neither Puri nor any of the staff had a clue about the indebtedness of the press.

Leaving Gill with the bailiff, Puri went to the bazaar to telephone Sood from Sardar Mehar Singh's office. Sood was equally taken aback by the bailiff's visit. He asked Mehar Singh to join with Lala Kripa Ram in using their influence to help Puri out, and to stand surety if necessary until Sood could fully investigate the case.

Puri explained to Mehar Singh and Kripa Ram that Rikhiram was not really the manager, but only an employee of the press and, therefore, had no authority to take out a loan. Also there was no record of a loan negotiated with Achharu Ram.

Mehar Singh and Kripa Ram knew a little about the workings of the law courts. Their conjecture was that Rikhiram had perpetrated some kind of fraud. The court had accepted as evidence that Rikhiram was in fact the manager and a representative of the press, and had issued writ in favour of Achharu Ram. Puri now had to file an appeal in the court, but that would have to come later. The press must immediately be saved from being seized.

Out of his regard for Sood, Mehar Singh agreed to be the custodian of Kamaal Press. It took the whole day to compile a list of all the property of the press. One copy was given to Achharu Ram, the other kept by the bailiff.

Puri and Gill went to Adda Hoshiarpur mohalla to search for Rikhiram. It was a while before they found his house in a gali. They could hear the sound of a treadle printing machine some distance away. They were told that Rikhiram had brought in the machine some days previously.

Rikhiram confronted Puri with blatant hostility, 'Do whatever you want! Did you get the press from your father? I've as much right to this press as you. I had to give up a printing business of my own in Jhellum. What did *you* know about running a press? You got the press by licking the arses of Congress politicians, and now you've come to threaten me! The press should be mine, not yours. I've earned you a fortune in the last eighteen months and made a rich man out of a beggar. What have you done to show me your gratitude? And you have the gall to accuse me of stealing from you! Pay up thirteen thousand one hundred thirty rupees first, then look me in the face. I'll see you in court.'

Later that evening Puri, Kanak and Gill went to see Nayyar. He and Kanta listened sympathetically to what had happened, but had many questions: How could the court accept Rikhiram as the manager or an authorized agent of the Kamaal Press? How could Achharu Ram advance him, an employee, such a large sum in the name of the press? Why had the court issued such a decree?

Puri explained that Rikhiram had received a number of summonses to appear before the law court. On several occasions he had asked for a leave of absence for half a day or the whole day to attend court hearings. Rikhiram had pretended that there had been a brawl in his mohalla, and that he had to appear as a witness to the incident.

In September 1947 Rikhiram had gone to Sood to ask his permission to reopen the Kamaal Press apparently abandoned by Isaac Mohammed, and had been told that the press belonged to Sood. In order to earn a living he was forced to take a job at the press.

In May 1948 Isaac Mohammed had returned to Jalandhar from Pakistan under a special travel permit. He had hoped that with Sood's help, he might be able to get a reasonable price for the property he had entrusted to Sood's care.

Isaac had a tragic story to tell. He had been resettled in Sakkhar, in the Sindh province of Pakistan. The Sindhi language was incomprehensible to him, and the city was full of Urdu-speaking Muslims who had fled from the United Provinces and Bihar. These Muslims considered refugees from Punjab as uncouth and made fun of Punjabi and Sindhi speakers. They also thought that a person was not a true Muslim if he could not speak Urdu.

The Hindus and Sikhs forced to leave the cities now in Pakistan had been mostly shopkeepers, tradesmen and professionals. Muslims who had gone to Pakistan from India were mainly artisans and office workers. What could such people know about keeping shops or practising trades? As a means of subsistence Isaac had been allotted the shop of a Hindu herbs and spice dealer. But the goods in stock were completely unfamiliar to him. His children ate up some of the almonds, raisins and other dried nuts and fruits; he disposed off the rest at whatever price he could get. The stock might have been worth thousands, but for him it was worthless. What could he know about medicinal herbs, or the difference between dry pomegranate seeds and dry cumin seeds? He had sold half a gunny sack of black peppercorns for three rupees a seer. In Jalandhar he found that the rate was thirty to forty rupees a seer. The poor man tore at his hair in frustration. One customer would ask for *banafsha*, another for *neelofar*, and the third for *gazawan*; for him they were all the same. Sometimes his mother was able to identify some herb used as medicine. Old-timers knew about such things. Any gunny sack he undid or any box he opened brought on a fit of sneezing. And then there was the constant fear of selling something poisonous instead of a medicinal herb. It would have been another matter if he had been selling wheat, lentils or millet. Whenever a customer came, he would say, 'Listen bhai, if you can find what you're looking for here, please take it.'

Isaac spoke to his former neighbour, the watchmaker Haji Imamdin of Mai Heeran Gate, who had also been sent to Sakkhar. Imamdin had been allotted a liquor store formerly owned by a Hindu. Haji, as a devout Muslim, could not even handle anything alcoholic. Government officials would drop in and walk out with a bottle without paying. Or some moneyed connoisseurs would pick out a bottle worth fifty rupees, and drop a ten-rupee note at the cash counter on their way out. The store was emptied out and he got little or nothing in return. Imamdin had gone to Lahore to get the tools needed for his profession, but could not afford to buy them. The going price was five times the standard. The poor man was forced to go without eating even though it was not yet the month of Ramazan.

Puri had welcomed Isaac back warmly, had installed him upstairs at the press and had treated him hospitably with paranthas and lassi. Isaac was happy to see that his press was operating well. He was entitled to search for and retrieve any gold or silver or jewellery that might have been buried in the house. But no refugee from India had the right to dispose off their abandoned property. Sood, of course, would not have allowed any illegal transactions.

Rikhiram had told the tale of his own woes to Issac, and said that it was perhaps his fate that he had to abandon his own press in Jhellum. Sood had instructed Puri to buy out Issac by paying him 2000 rupees, and for that purpose, had also arranged for Puri to take out a loan of 1000 rupees from Lala Kripa Ram.

Issac had gone back a disappointed man, but Rikhiram, with a feeling of revenge in his heart, had hatched a plot with Achharu Ram the moneylender. He had a free hand at the press. He surreptitiously used the rubber stamp 'For Kamaal Press, Manager' on several sheets of official letterhead, signed as manager promissory notes totalling Rs 12,000 at 6 per cent interest, backdating them at short time intervals, and took for himself Rs 3,000 cash from Achharu Ram.

Nayyar said that Rikhiram probably had told Achharu Ram that the press was being run in partnership between him and Puri, and that he would attest before the court that he had taken out the loans. The court would then issue a decree. He had probably also told the moneylender that Puri would never be able to repay Rs 12,000, and that he and Achharu Ram would become joint owners of the press and earn at least of seven to eight hundred per month. The press machines alone were worth at least Rs 15,000. In case the press was auctioned, Achharu Ram would be able to buy it by paying a maximum of seven to eight thousand extra for a property worth over Rs 15,000. And that Achharu Ram had probably thought that even if Puri managed to prove his 50 per cent ownership, Achharu Ram would still be legally entitled to the other 50 per cent of the press.

Puri, Kanak and Gill were flabbergasted. Kanak said with disbelief, 'How's that possible? How could the court issue such an order?'

Nayyar replied, 'Why couldn't the court do that! The promissory notes were submitted as documented proof that money was loaned. The borrower admitted to having taken up the loan. It's a civil right to claim back any money owed to him and the legal system helps him do that.'

'But shouldn't the court have verified who the owner of the press really was?' Puri asked.

'The court had issued its summons in the name of Rikhiram, the manager of the press, and he had accepted the summons. He had appeared in the court in the name of the press and had declared under oath its legal obligation. No one had raised any objection before the court. The promissory notes had been on the letterhead of the press, rubber-stamped and apparently signed by the manager. What other judgment could the court have given?' Nayyar replied.

'The court judgment is miscarriage of justice,' Kanak began to condemn the legal and the judicial system. 'Everyone knows Puriji. The judge should have called him to court to explain who Rikhiram really was, what kind of person he was, how long he had been with the press, and in what capacity? The court could have made some inquiries as to who's the real owner of the press.'

'Kanni, you sometimes talk like an idiot!' Nayyar rebuked her. 'The law courts are objective and impartial to individual identities or allegations. The law says that if the judge personally knows any of the parties involved or has any prior knowledge of the case, he must disbar himself from hearing the case and transfer the case to another court.'

'But why?' Kanak said with surprise, 'How could a judge dispense justice without knowing all the facts?'

'So that lawyers get the chance to stretch the truth by their arguments!' Gill spoke up.

Nayyar tried to explain, 'According to jurisprudence, a bias for or against an individual might occur if the judge knows the persons or has a prior acquaintance with the facts.'

'Why appoint those as judges who are prone to prejudice?' Gill asked. 'The legal system in an industrial–capitalist society operates like an automatic dispenser. Whoever controls the machine controls the system.'

Wishing to put an end to the discussion, Nayyar said to Puri, 'Well, for the present you can only save your press by having access to the very same legal system. Do you want to save your press or not?'

'You yourself have said that Achharu Ram probably handed over only around three thousand rupees to Rikhiram,' Puri reminded Nayyar.

Gill added, 'If so, wouldn't the promissory notes be considered invalid or a fraud.'

'Bhai, Achharu Ram may not have parted with even a half a paisa, but those promissory notes are still valid evidence. The truth is one thing, what's on the promissory notes is something else. How can the notes be considered invalid when the signatory acknowledges having signed them?' Nayyar explained.

'Even if no money actually changed hands?' Kanak asked angrily.

'Isn't it fraud to sign a receipt for money without really receiving it?' Gill added to Kanak's question.

'Rikhiram may not have received any cash.' Nayyar slapped the tabletop to add emphasis to his answer, 'But those promissory notes are legally admissible evidence.'

'That means the law gives one the opportunity to commit fraud.' Gill said.

'A promissory note only means that the signatory admits accepting a repayable loan,' Nayyar interrupted him to explain.

'Then the wording should have been altered accordingly.'

Puri asked, 'Why did nobody question whether Rikhiram has the signing power?'

'Anybody and everybody has the right to sign a promissory note. And the law allows anybody to borrow or to lend money. You may say that your press is not bound by the promissory notes fraudulently signed by Rikhiram.'

'Let's say so,' Kanak agreed.

'It should have been the concern of Achharu Ram to check that out, but he was conspiring with Rikhiram anyway. The notes are on the official letterhead and with the rubber stamp of the press, and that's proof enough for the court that Rikhiram was a representative of the press. The task of the court was now to confirm the right of Achharu Ram to issue a loan and to help him recover it.'

'A capitalist government always takes the side of the loan giver. It doesn't give a damn for the unfortunate borrower. There's always a bias in favour of the banias,' Gill said.

'What makes you say that, comrade?' Nayyar said to Gill, 'When the zemindars had a powerful lobby in Punjab, didn't they have that law passed for the transfer of farmland? It stipulated that any repossessed farmland seized from a bankrupt could not be bought by a bania or a moneylender, but only by another farmer.'

'That's true,' Gill agreed. 'The laws always favour those who make them up or are able to influence their application.'

'Are you dreaming about some perfect law that would be fair at all times and in all cases?' Nayyar said sarcastically.

'Well, how would it be if we presented proof that the press never received the loan?' Puri asked.

'How would you do that? Are the promissory notes proof enough or not?' Nayyar cut Puri short, then added, 'What you'll have to prove is that Rikhiram had no right to sign the notes as the manager of the press.'

'But we received no money. Why would we have taken out a loan when the press did not need one? And how did we spend all that money?'

'Once again you are talking absolute nonsense. The court is not concerned with the fact whether the press got the money or not. There *is* evidence that the loan was made. The judge cannot know what is true or false, but can only make his decision on the basis of the evidence before him. The judge cannot ignore evidence even if it misrepresented the truth.'

'Doesn't common sense count for anything?' Kanak and Gill spoke together. 'It would mean that the law can be used to harass somebody by making up false evidence.'

'Yes, that's quite possible. The interpretation of the law is not a matter of common sense, but of specialized knowledge. If the only thing necessary in a law court was common sense, why would we need lawyers? Well, the first thing you should do is report to the police that Rikhiram fraudulently used your letterhead and the rubber stamp. The court order can be rescinded on these grounds alone. You will have to prove that Rikhiram in fact was neither the manager of the press nor authorized to represent you.'

There was no end to Puri's problems at this time. Nayyar acted as his counsel without charging any money, otherwise he would have had to pay several hundred rupees in legal fees alone. But there was still the inconvenience of appearing before the court. Achharu Ram engaged a lawyer in defence of Rikhiram.

Puri presented in the court as evidence the letter from Issac Mohammed entrusting Kamaal Press to Sood. Sood had to testify as to appointing Puri the manager of the press. The stubs from the bank cheque books were presented in support of his testimony. The defence lawyer requested the court to take cognizance of Rikhiram's signature as the manager on the receipt books and on the attendance register of the press. The hearings continued for a long time.

Puri and Kanak were exasperated to observe the legal wrangling and
to see how lawyers, by legal hair-splitting, could make the dispensation of
justice such a long and vexatious process. The law could be interpreted,
they found, to suit either the plaintiff or the defendant. If both the parties
were resourceful and had the funds, they could afford to hire legal aces who
were expert in litigious minutiae. Even if they knew the facts, the litigants
were bound by the court's judgment because it had the legal machinery
behind it to enforce the decision.

The court finally delivered its verdict in December 1949. The Kamaal
Press was cleared of the responsibility for paying back the loan allegedly
taken out by Rikhiram, but Puri was still not free of the annoyance of more
court appearances. Rikhiram was now being tried for the criminal offence
of fraudulent use of the press letterhead and rubber stamp.

Nayyar advised Puri to stay out of the criminal case. His recommendation
was to let the police prosecute Rikhiram, and to avoid getting himself
involved so as to not to waste time in what could be a further score of
court appearances. The defence lawyer would drag Puri's name through
the mud during the cross-examination. And there would be no profit to
the police in sending Rikhiram to jail. If anything, the police could only
hope to benefit by receiving something under the table, editing the charge
sheet favourably and letting Rikhiram off lightly.

Rikhiram was finally acquitted on the grounds of 'insufficient evidence'.
In the end, Puri had something to show for all his troubles. After the court
case was over, Sood had the press officially allotted in his name to avoid
any future problems.

Chapter 9

THE FEELING OF PANIC AND CONFUSION BEDEVILLING THE EMPLOYEES OF THE Department of Rehabilitation proved to be unfounded. The government support for the refugee camps was officially withdrawn on 31 March 1948, but the department staff continued to work as before. Although free rations were no longer distributed, refugees continued to occupy some of the camps. The majority of the occupants of the Kingsway Camp had been running various kinds of small businesses for some time. Now those who had been inactive so far also somehow scraped together enough resources to make some kind of a living. Long-time residents of Delhi were now seeing trades and professions never previously practised there. Makeshift shops would be set up even on relatively unfrequented roads. Refugees with handcarts offering to iron clothes on the spot appeared in the alleys. One did not even have to leave the house to pay bills for electricity, telephone or water. The refugees would take the bill, make the payment and bring back the receipt. The charge for being saved the trouble was only two annas. Shoppers now received their purchases in home-made paper bags. Those who had fled from Punjab now objected to the label *sharanarthi*—resourceless. They, instead, wanted to be known as *purusharthi*—resourceful.

At the Department of Rehabilitation the workload had increased rather than lessened. The minister had refused to allow the hiring of additional staff because, in his opinion, two employees less were better than one too many. The department had now been allotted the task of approving small business loans, and of investigating refugee claims for land and property that had been abandoned in what was now Pakistan. Tara had been given the responsibility of checking the claim applications.

She was going through the claims file when one applicant's name Mohanlal Tandon with father's name as Motilal Tandon of Sheeshamoti Gali, Lahore, caught her attention. It brought back memories of Sheelo—of their childhood together, of Sheelo's mischievous and ebullient nature, of friendly quarrels with her and of a cousin who had kept no secrets from Tara. Sheelo's affair with Ratan and its consequence flashed through Tara's mind. The address on the application form was: House No. 1315, Shakti Nagar, Sabzi Mandi, Delhi, and it stated that Mohanlal was now working as a clerk in the Education Division of the Central Secretariat. Tara could find out the exact location of his office and contact him, but she decided to meet Sheelo first.

For office workers forced to sit on hard chairs from ten to five, six days a week, the greatest pleasure on a Sunday is the luxury of stretching out on charpoys for an afternoon siesta. It was the last Sunday of June. Taking this day to be its last opportunity to prove its might, the loo was blowing with all its fury over the roads, the tarmac surface of which had softened in the heat of the sun. The loo also reached into the remote recesses of the bazaars, and into the surrounding mazes of narrow winding lanes and alleys. The shopkeepers, not expecting any customers at this hour in the heat, napped behind hessian curtains lowered over their storefronts. Taxis, tongas and rickshaws were parked in any available shady spot, with their drivers dozing off in wait for the heat and the loo to subside. The only sound to break this lull was the Punjabi-accented cries of purusharthis selling blocks of ice, sherbets and ice cream. Even the loo was unable to wither away their spirit of enterprise.

The force of the loo was felt even more in the new, sparsely built areas of Daryaganj. Mercy had had thick hessian curtains over her windows and in the veranda since the beginning of May, but the air circulated by ceiling fans in her rooms remained hot. Old Chimmo was sleeping in the kitchen after wetting the floor to keep it cool. Mercy had taken up regular work on weekdays from 8 a.m. to 1 p.m. at the clinic of Dr Ayyar. She was in deep sleep. Tara lay on her bed; what came to her was not sleep, but memories of Sheelo.

She forced herself to kill time until four o'clock. Then unable to wait any longer, got up and changed her sari. She went to the kitchen to ask Chimmo to lock the door at the bottom of the stairs behind her. Chimmo asked her not to go out in the heat and the loo, but Tara ignored her advice, and left.

On reaching Shakti Nagar the taxi driver asked Tara where to drop her. The locality was only partially built up. On one side of the main road was a row of newly constructed, two-storeyed houses; shanties and straw-covered huts filled the other side. The rays of the sinking sun lit up the fronts of the houses with dazzling brightness.

Tara gave the address to the driver. The driver checked out the house numbers as he drove slowly. He called out to some children playing with spinning tops nearby to ask for the house of Mohanlal Tandon from Lahore.

Three children came over, and eagerly pointed to where Mohanlal lived. They led Tara through the veranda and the aangan to the back of the house.

The scene that met her eyes reminded her of Punjab. The shady backyard of the house held several charpoys and chatai mats. Groups of two or three women sat together, each with some piece of work in her hand, and talked in loud voices. Laundry hung on clothes lines. A few feet away was a gathering of men seated on two charpoys facing one another and chatting as they passed around the stem of a hookah. The women sat with their backs to the men in a show of propriety. At the rear of the house were several garages with their doors wide open. Charpoys and other household furnishings piled inside indicated that these also had been turned into living quarters.

Some women raised their heads to look at the visitor.

The children escorting Tara announced, 'She's come to visit Bau Mohanlal!' They showed Tara to one of the rooms, calling out, 'Ghullu's mum! Chaachi! Someone's here to see Ghullu's mum.'

The door to the room was ajar. Tara went in. A woman lay on a large charpoy, her face covered with her dupatta. She got up on hearing the call. A baby was asleep, draped in cotton netting, beside the woman.

The woman on the charpoy was Sheelo. How much she had changed! Ashen-faced, with dark circles under her eyes and tangles of unkempt hair... but undoubtedly Sheelo. She just stared at Tara with sleep-filled eyes.

'Sheelo!' Tara called out, and rushed to her. She held Sheelo tightly in her arms and put her cheek against hers as tears flowed from her eyes.

Sheelo tried to push Tara away so as to be able to look at her face, and stared in disbelief, 'Tara! You are Tara!' as if she was unsure of what she was seeing.

Wrapping her arms around Sheelo, Tara buried her tear-stained face in her breast. Sheelo once again lifted Tara's face as if to confirm the reality of what she had seen, hugged her tightly and wailed, 'Hai, my cousin! They said you had been burned to death. May those be damned who said you had died! My cousin...'

Sheelo had cried out so loud that the baby woke with a start and burst out crying. Tara freed herself from Sheelo's embrace, and took the child in her arms, 'Hai, sadake—may all your misfortunes fall on me! Don't you cry now.' Sheelo again put her arms around Tara as if not wanting to let her go.

Hearing Sheelo's wail, several women came and peered into the room curiously. Guessing that some lost family member had turned up, one said to another, 'Two separated sister have met. May Rabba bring together also those who haven't found their loved ones.'

It took Sheelo some time to gather herself. She took Tara's face in both her hands, and asked, 'Muree, Where have you been? What happened to you? So you must have got out alive?'

Tara nodded in reply to her last question, and asked, 'Where's Mohanji?'

Sheelo said as if she had not heard, 'Were you in Jalandhar? Where did you come from today?'

'I've been here in Delhi?'

'Is jijaji also here?'

Tara bowed her head and gestured to indicate that she did not know. To avoid further questions from Sheelo, she began to inquire about Sheelo's family, and about their journey from Lahore to Delhi.

'Those who died were the lucky ones! As thousands of us accepted our fates and went wherever God sent us, we did the same and ended up here in Delhi,' Sheelo said briefly, and repeated her question.

Tara replied, her head bowed, 'Don't ask me anymore about all that. Maybe I did die in the fire, or maybe it was all a terrible nightmare. I don't remember anything except that when I woke up I was in some refugee camp in Delhi. Then I found a job with a rich family here. Now I am in government service.'

Ghullu had moved from Tara's lap to his mother's. Tara again took him in her arms to hide the pain arising in her heart. She rubbed his nose with hers, gazed into his eyes, and cooed, 'Baby mine, don't you want to come to your aunty!'

Tara's show of affection won the child over. Sheelo, chin on her knee, was sitting quietly. Then, wiping her tears, she began to reply slowly to Tara's questions.

'We were at the DAV College Camp in Lahore, two families crammed in one small room. It was so hot and muggy. Ghullu became sick. You couldn't get anything at that place. One seer of wheat cost a rupee, so did milk. My husband refused to buy milk, you know how he is. Ratan had refused to speak to me until now, but that did not stop him from looking for me. Your family was at the Dev Samaj Camp. One day he came, looked at Ghullu and asked, "What's wrong with him?"

'I began to cry, "He hasn't had any milk. We are starving and I have no money to buy anything." He forced me to accept fifty rupees. I gave the money to my husband and said, first of all get some milk for the child. When we went to Ferozepur, he tracked us down there too. Ghullu was having diarrhoea and cramps. I asked and asked my husband to get a doctor, but neither he nor his parents would listen to me. When he came, I was in tears, and begged him to save my baby. He got the chief medical officer to examine Ghullu, and paid the doctor out of his own pocket. That was the beginning of the problem. My husband and his mother began to swear at me and ask what connection he had with me.

'Then we moved to the refugee camp in Kurukshetra. He used to come there also every couple of weeks to check up on me, and that created more problems. How could I tell him not to come! My father-in-law was offered a job in Simla, my husband got a job in Delhi. Ratan comes here also at least once every month. He lives in some mohalla in Delhi called Karol Bagh…' Sheelo put her forehead on her knees and started to sob.

Tara made Sheelo swear that she would tell the truth, and asked, 'Anything else troubling you?'

Seeing his mother sob, Ghullu also began to cry. Tara pressed the child to her heart to soothe him.

Sheelo dried her eyes and called out through the door, 'Suman! Come here for a second, dear.'

A girl of about nine came running. Sheelo kissed her cheek and said, 'Look after Ghullu for me. Here's one anna. Buy some mithai and you both share it.'

Speaking fondly to Ghullu, Suman took him away.

Sheelo broke down and wept, then said, 'Last month my mother-in-law and her daughter were visiting. Ratan showed up one day when they had gone to the bazaar. He had brought two tins of baby food, a few oranges and pomegranates, and some lengths of cloth. He had brought such stuff before and my husband had not objected, so I accepted the things. My sister-in-law kicked up a great fuss when she found out. She said, "Why is that fellow so concerned about Ghullu? How come Ghullu resembles him so much!" From that day on my husband became suspicious and asks me every day, "Did you have something going with that fellow? Tell me the truth, whose child is Ghullu really?" I said, "If you doubt me, just kill me." One day he told me, "If you're a faithful wife, a sati, you'll stick your hand in the fire to prove your loyalty."The next day, "Put your hand on my head and swear that you'll become a widow if you're not telling the truth."What should I do, do tell me. He left in a huff this morning and hasn't come back yet.'

Sheelo said after both sat quietly for some time, 'I'm paying for my sins. Sometimes I feel like setting myself and Ghullu on fire so that this suffering might end. I can't stand this anymore.' She began to cry again.

'Don't talk rubbish,' Tara said sternly as she put her hand over Sheelo's mouth. 'I'll take you away with me if he's so harsh to you. I'll rent a place just for the two of us.' She explained to Sheelo her living arrangement with Mercy.

Sheelo's eyes brimmed with tears, 'I don't know. I just wish that I and my baby were both dead, but then I think of Ratan, and of what he might do!'

'Why don't you just go and live with him?'

'Are you mad? How can I! I'll blacken my name and the family's name!' Sheelo slapped her forehead despondently, 'I'm tied to this no-good man because I too walked around the fire seven times with him. I've never said so till now, but I really never desired him. It's my dharma to live with him because I'm married to him. Since he's begun to act like this, even his touch feels repulsive. And this good-for-nothing can't live without me. He fights with me, yells at me, makes me cry, but doesn't leave me alone. If I push him away, he becomes even more abusive. What can I do now?' She began to cry again.

Tara sighed deeply, and said, 'You have to find some way to get out of this mess.'

'Only my death can put an end to it.'

Tara said, 'Listen, don't do anything foolish.' She wrote down her address and Mercy's telephone number and gave them to Sheelo, then added her own office telephone number. She asked for Ratan's address in Karol Bagh. When she offered Sheelo some money, Sheelo refused, 'If he sees the notes he'll think that Ratan had come. I'll be in trouble again.'

Tara said, to reassure her, 'Achcha, I'll leave now. I'll come again next Sunday. Call Ghullu. I'd like to kiss him before I go.'

'Hai, you mean you'll leave without eating anything in my place?'

Tara said after a moment's thought, 'All right. Let's get something. What'd you like?'

'Wah, you think I don't remember?' Sheelo said with a smile. 'You loved *moongra* and *chhole-kulche* from Ramditta's shop. Remember how we both used to run and get it from him in the Machchi Hatta bazaar? I'll ask one of our neighbours' kids. All those things from Lahore are also available here.'

Sheelo went out, and Tara used the opportunity to look around the room. All of Sheelo's possessions were in that one room. Bricks were placed under the legs of the large charpoy to raise its height. There was another, smaller charpoy under it, and beneath that, two steel trunks. Clothes hung from pegs on the walls, and were slung over a line. In a corner were empty kerosene oil canisters for storing wheat and lentils, and on top of them, some wilted vegetables. A few pots and pans were stacked to one side of the large charpoy. A wall shelf showed two tins of baby food, and several containers of spices and other kitchen items. In another corner was a brazier made by lining the inside of an old bucket with clay, apparently unused since the morning.

After a while a young boy brought some food in leaf cups and wrapped in newspapers, with a chunk of ice. Sheelo made ice water in a lota. She served the food on a thali that she took from the stack of utensils, and put it in front of Tara on the charpoy. She sat beside Tara and invited her fondly, 'Have something. The chickpeas are still hot.'

'You also have something. I said yes only because you couldn't have eaten since this morning. I wasn't really hungry.'

'You know I couldn't eat until my husband had eaten first. Who knows if he has or hasn't?'

'You deserve a good slap in the face! You stupid idiot!' Tara was infuriated, 'To hell with your *sanskaras* and conventions! He torments you so much, you are repulsed by him, and yet you're willing to go hungry because of him! Why should you give a damn?'

'But he's my husband. This is my fate!' Sheelo took a deep breath, and bowed her head.

'If you won't eat neither will I!'

'You know how it is. I can't eat anything.' Tears welled into Sheelo's eyes.

Tara left without eating, fuming at Sheelo's attitude.

Tara received another letter from Narottam on her return from the office next day on Monday afternoon. Reading it after the previous day's events put her in a better frame of mind. Narottam had been transferred first to the Kanpur Ordnance Factory as works manager, then to Calcutta where he had been for the past three months as the assistant deputy director. His letters, a page and a half long, arrived regularly, with news of his activities and amusing anecdotes. Tara would write back, 'Don't invent all these stories and don't keep writing that you miss me. Poor Neelam is on tenterhooks waiting for you. I hope you have not lost your heart to some Bengali lass. Don't do anything foolish, or else! But I have every confidence that you are being a good boy. A real good boy.

'You must have met new people in Calcutta. There you can go to cinemas, clubs and theatres. I had only two friends, you and Mercy, and you went away. I will make you answer for it when you come back. So don't just pretend that you miss me.

'Anyway, how can I complain if you have to be in Calcutta because of your job? What else can I write, but we shall have a real good chat when you are here. The pressure of work keeps me busy in the office, but Sundays become boring without you. Well, everything seems boring these days.'

In his most recent letter Narottam had written, 'I owe you a lot for what has happened in my life. I have been posted to New Delhi as the liaison officer with the Ministry of Defence. Look, you made a wish and I got the transfer. Why did you not make that wish earlier?

'I will reach Delhi on Friday. I am longing to hear what you have to say when we meet face-to-face, or perhaps you will just smile as usual and say nothing. And if you speak, will it be what I am waiting to hear. Because if you don't say it I will have to say it. But I am not sure I would be able to do it properly. I am just an ordinary person who knows only how to deal with clumsy ungainly things such as machines, not with fine and subtle points of language like you.

'I feel as if I am already in the train that will take me to you and the train has taken wings…'

Narottam showed up on Friday evening. Mercy was at home, and she and Tara warmly welcomed him. He stayed for about two hours, but spoke very little and mostly smiled. With thoughts of Sheelo tugging at her heart, Tara was not very talkative either. When he was leaving Tara said, 'You wrote that you had so much to talk about, but you've hardly said a word. We are meeting after five months. Now you must come every day.'

Mercy was at home again when Narottam came the next evening. This time also he did not say much, but had a faraway look, as if all his new responsibilities were weighing on his mind.

Mercy said lightly, 'What's the matter. Why're you both so quiet? Tara is angry that you left her alone and went away to Calcutta. You have to make it up to her.'

Narottam asked as he was leaving, 'Tomorrow's Sunday. If it's convenient, I'll come around ten o'clock.' He knew that Mercy had to go to work for an emergency.

Tara had decided to go and see Sheelo, but she agreed, 'Have lunch here.' She could go to Shakti Nagar after midday, she told herself.

Tara had once made paranthas stuffed with potatoes for Narottam, which he had greatly relished. On Sunday morning she told Chimmo to get together the ingredients for the same dish. Mercy said as she was leaving for the clinic, 'I'll be back before lunch. Wait for me.'

Narottam arrived at 10.15. Tara was in the kitchen, dressing lady's finger for another spicy dish. Although working in the kitchen had left some stains of turmeric on her dhoti, she decided not to change into a clean one. She had put a few mangoes in ice water intending to serve them as desert after lunch. Now she asked Narottam to have a seat, sliced a mango and putting the plate in front of him, said, 'Taste this. I'll be back in a minute. Just want to make sure that Chimmo doesn't mess up the okras.'

Narottam had not touched the mango when she returned. When Tara insisted, he ate one slice and wiped his hands on his handkerchief. He had not said a word.

'Why're you so quiet? Thinking of Neelam? Have been to see her yet?' Tara asked with a smile. When he made no reply, she felt awkward and kept silent.

'Do you really think that I'm a useless good-for-nothing?' he asked.

'I've had no reason to change my mind,' Tara replied, pursing her lips, then frowned and added, 'You seem to have developed a taste for flattery now that you're a high official. Do you want me to butter you up to your face?'

'No, I don't want you to sing my praises at all. I don't think I deserve it. Perhaps everyone finds me insufferable. Anyway, nobody can be aware of his shortcomings.'

'Well, what do you want then,' she asked, without looking at him. She felt an urge to laugh at his seriousness and the effort to suppress it caused her face to flush

'Promise me that you'll listen to what I have to say.'

'I'll do my best,' Tara tried to keep a straight face.

'You've known me for some time, and quite well.'

'I think so,' Tara said earnestly.

'Please tell me any faults that you may have seen in me,' he asked gravely.

Tara bowed her head, thinking, 'What's wrong with him today!'

'Why don't you say something?'

'There's one fault you have,' she pretended to be solemn, her eyes on the floor.

'What?'

'You ask silly questions just to annoy me.'

'I had no intention of annoying you. When have I annoyed you deliberately?'

'Don't be an idiot? Would I keep asking you back if you were really annoying me?' she avoided eye contact to keep up her pretence,

Narottam said nothing.

Rising to her feet Tara said, 'I'll be back in a minute. I just want to check again on Chimmo. She's so clumsy.'

Tara had a suspicion that the young man had something bothering him. Deciding to drop the pretences, she said as she returned from the kitchen, 'Why, what happened? Did Neelam find anything wrong with you?' Thinking she might have asked too much, she blushed.

Narottam's face also became flushed. Clearing his throat and leaning forward, he said in English, 'That Neelam business has turned into a problem. Rawat said something to daddy about announcing our engagement. You know how I really feel about her.'

Without looking at him, she asked, 'How *do* you feel about her?'

'You know very well that I don't want to marry her. But to tell a father that I don't like his daughter can be a bit hurtful.'

Tara said sympathetically, her gaze still averted, 'You'll have to tell the truth sometime or other.'

'That hurtfulness can be avoided if I own up to another truth,' Narottam's tone became even more sombre.

'Which truth?' Tara asked in a confiding tone as if to show her willingness to share a secret.

'I need your permission before I admit anything.'

'Do you suppose I want to add to your problems by keeping you from confessing the truth? Why wouldn't I give you my permission?'

'I've a great regard for Neelam, but in all honesty I must confess that

I've made up my mind... to declare my love for you.' Narottam had to summon all his courage to utter these words.

Tara felt as if a live electric wire had touched her. She sighed deeply, got up and went towards the kitchen, but instead went to her bedroom through the veranda. She lay down on her bed as if completely exhausted. Her mind was in turmoil, 'What's got into this young man?' Then she realized, he must be sitting all alone. She got up, washed her face, and poured some water into her hair to cool her head. She combed her hair and changed into a fresh dhoti. She had a drink of water, then sat and thought for a while. Then she went back into the living room, sat in the chair beside Narottam, and said in English, 'Nottan, have you lost your mind? Why would you say a thing like that? What have we been to each other? Don't you remember that once you had said I was like an elder sister to you and Dolly?'

'I'm sorry,' Narottam said, looking flustered. After a moment's silence, he added, 'If what I said has pained you or has offended you, I take back my words for now and forever.'

'Nottan, it's not a question of feeling offended. I'm really honoured by your affection for me, but that's all. Don't talk like a child. I'm very fond of you, but what you have in mind is neither possible, nor acceptable or proper. The only people I have in this world are you, Mercy and an unfortunate cousin of mine. That is why I always want to stay fond of you. You should have at least considered the difference in our ages. You're still only a boy. After what I've been through the hands of men, I'll fear and hate them all my life. I've been able to feel some fondness and respect for you because I didn't see you just as another man, but more as a brother. I still want to go on feeling that way. You're really a good young man. Just forget this foolishness of yours and I'll forget this incident.'

His head lowered, Narottam said, 'I'm really sorry. Forgive me, I think I'd like to go now.'

'Let's forget what's just happened. You neither need to feel bad nor ask for forgiveness. But don't go yet. Mercy said she'd be back for lunch. If you're willing to forget everything, why can't you stay?'

'My dear sister, I will forget it. And I'll always stand by your side, but I'm not quite myself at the moment. I won't be able to face Mercy in this condition. I'll come again.'

Tara let him go.

When Mercy came back she found the plate of sliced mango on the table swarming with flies. Yelling at Chimmo in a mixture of Hindi and English, she sent the plate flying, and it broke, 'She wants us to die from cholera! This wretch has no *sharam*. The angel of death is dragging her towards her fate, and she wants us to go with her.'

Lying on the bed in her room, Tara heard Mercy shout, then Chimmo's explanation, 'Chhoti bibi had cut up the mango. Why blame me?'

'Did both of them eat lunch?'

'Nobody ate. The sahib left.'

Before Tara could get up Mercy came into her room, 'Why did Narottam leave? I tried to get back *jaldi*...' Her anger had calmed down after smashing the plate.

'He said he had to be somewhere at one o'clock.'

'We'll eat if you're very *bhookhi*, otherwise I'll have a quick wash. I'm all sweaty.'

They sat across from each other at the table for lunch. Mercy kept staring at Tara, then said, 'Why, what's wrong?' She reached out to feel the pulse on Tara's wrist, 'How do you feel? Did you two have a quarrel while I was out?'

'No! What ideas you do get into your head! You were out in the loo, maybe the heat has affected your mind.'

Tara was forcing herself to eat. Since they had their meals together every day, Mercy noticed that Tara was only pecking at her food.

'So, my little one, are you trying to fool me,' Mercy laughed as she rolled a parantha around a stuffed okra and a whole green chilli, 'My dear girl, I know how to treat romantic as well as physical disorders. The truth is written all over your face.'

'Take care of your own heart and body,' Tara replied, keeping her eyes on her plate.

'I've been expecting something since the day before yesterday. You both were so quiet, unable to speak to each other.' Mercy took another bite at her rolled-up parantha and gave a meaningful smile, 'I know the truth. He must have proposed. You, my little one, must have been thrilled to bits, but you've had to pretend to be shy and embarrassed.'

'Didi, please talk sense,' Tara said irritably. 'Think of his age, and mine. He's like a younger brother to me.'

'Hai, just look at you grandma!' Mercy raised her eyebrows in surprise, 'How old are you? Twenty?'

'Why not say twelve? I'll soon be twenty-two.'

'And he's what … eighteen?'

'He claims to be twenty-four. He's so childish, just like a boy. Well, I've no plans to get married.'

'Achcha, if he did propose, it's to your own advantage because he'll stay young longer. If you don't catch him now you'll be sorry later. Yours is the right age to get married, otherwise you'll be too old like me…'

'Don't talk nonsense, didi,' Tara again said angrily. 'You marry him.'

'How many men can I marry? I wish my old boy was back. Well, Tara, I'm warning you that you'll be sorry. We have a saying: If a man proposes to a girl when she's young, she frowns and demands, "What are you?" When she grows older, she asks the man, "Who are you?" When she's past her prime, she screams in desperation, "Where are you? Where are you?"'

'Didi, please, don't you have anything else to talk about?'

'Won't you ever get married?'

'No, I won't.'

'You've grown up to be such an old maid without ever falling in love, or is it that you haven't wanted to. Don't you have a heart and body?'

'When did I say that I don't? Love is something else. Don't I love you?'

'What difference will that make? That Punjabi nursing sister Kanta says, "If a eunuch sleeps with another eunuch, nobody gets anything."'

'Please stop. Isn't there anything else in the world besides sex?'

'Don't you need sex? Or are you not normal?'

'You might say so. I don't need all that.'

'Then we must have you medically examined.'

'Didi, should I get up and leave you?'

'Hm.'

Mercy finished eating, drank some water and reaching for a plate of freshly cut mango, said in English, 'Listen Tara, you're in denial. You're trying to fool yourself. A difference of two or three years in age is acceptable. In your heart you feel attracted to him. You've been silent since the day his letter arrived. You're afraid to let yourself go.'

'No, didi, it's not really like that. You've misunderstood the whole thing,' Tara said in a serious tone. 'I didn't tell you about her before, but I have a cousin. Her husband is tormenting her for no reason. She has a two-year-old baby boy. I've been worrying about her. What if that stupid husband of hers throws her out? She doesn't even have enough education to stand on

her own two feet.' Tara covered her eyes with her aanchal. Sheelo's face
had swum before her eyes.

Mercy ate in silence for a while. She said as she got up, 'It's a different
matter if you want her to stay here for a couple of days. But as I've told
you in the beginning, I can't have more than one person here, and you
know how children are.'

Tara had laid down to rest, but she dozed off. It was 5.30 when she woke
up. She wanted to go to Shakti Nagar, but did not have the strength. Another
time, she thought.

The thought of Sheelo was constantly on her mind. Tara decided not
to take seriously what Narottam had said; she felt that she did not have
to worry about him. But what would become of that poor Sheelo? If her
husband was tormenting her, why did she not tell him, even swear if she
had to, that the baby was his? What's the harm in saying so, just to calm
him down? Perhaps that stupid girl thinks that if she swore by putting her
hand on his head, it might kill him. She couldn't bear him to touch her, but
was willing to go hungry unless he had eaten first. Who else but a Hindu
woman could be so servile and completely ignorant! What if Mohanlal
did throw her out? Should I look for a larger accommodation? I should be
able to get something for sixty or eighty rupees per month. We'll both live
together. It's my destiny that I end up always with abused women. First it
was Banti, now Sheelo. A man can throw out a woman whenever he wants!

The thought passed her mind: Why not find Ratan and discuss the
problem with him? Memories came back to her of her own girlhood. How
Ratan used to tease her, and how she had quarrelled with him! She liked
him, but his teasing put her off. And how disgusted she had felt when she
saw him kissing Sheelo! She had been angry with him, but was envious of
Sheelo. Then there had been Asad! And now this Narottam episode! Tara
had no objection to falling in love, but was relieved that she had not got
into trouble like Sheelo. Love created such problems! 'Should I ask Ratan
to take responsibility for Sheelo? But hadn't he already asked Sheelo to
elope with him! He'll surely agree to take her in now. And who is there
in this unfamiliar city to object? My past dislike of him was foolish. He's
not such a bad person. But I'll have to ask Sheelo first. Maybe her husband
will straighten himself out after a few days of complaining, but that idiot

Sheelo says that she can't stand him. She's as stubborn as a mule. I hope she doesn't do anything foolish to herself.'

Mercy had a high-quality radio in her apartment, but neither of them ever listened to it. Some Punjabi refugees had moved into the apartment across the gali. Their radio played at full volume and was seldom switched off. Either the whole family was hard of hearing, or they wanted the whole gali to profit from their radio. On Monday morning Tara was having something to eat before going to the office when a classical song came over the radio in a female voice:

Aye ri aalee, pia bin
Mohe kala na parat, sakhi, ghari pala chhin
Aye ri aalee, pia bin
Jabse piya pardes gaban kino
Ratiyan katat monsaun taare gin gin...

Sister o'mine, without my darling
I know no peace every hour every minute every heartbeat
Sister o'mine,
Ever since he's gone away
My nights are spent counting the stars...

Tara let her thoughts wander: The singer might be feeling some longing for her beloved at the moment, but she would only learn her lesson after she's suffered at his hands. Banti and Sheelo and Mrs Agarwal, had all been treated badly by their husbands! Which woman in my gali in Lahore was not cowed into submission by her spouse! Mercy wants to be with her lover, but she too will only learn from experience. Poor Sheelo.

Tara was going downstairs on her way to the office on Thursday when the telephone rang. Mercy was at the clinic. The telephone rang mostly for Mercy; for Tara only once in a fortnight. If Mercy was out, Tara would take a message and leave it for her.

She went back up and answered the telephone. 'Please get me Tara bahinji,' said a young boy's voice, in a Punjabi accent. 'Ghullu's mum, Sheelo chachi, has asked Tara to come to her immediately.'

Tara wanted to know who was calling, and what the matter was, but the caller hung up.

It struck Tara that Sheelo must be facing some drastic situation. What should she do? It was just after nine o'clock and, therefore, too early to call her office to report her absence; even the peons would not have arrived at that hour. But she had to respond to Sheelo's call for help.

Tara took a taxi to Sheelo's place. She was in such a hurry that she got out and went into the building without paying her fare. Suman was keeping an eye on Ghullu outside the room. Sheelo lay on the charpoy under a sheet. Tara called out to her as she sat on the charpoy, and pulled the sheet away from Sheelo's face.

Sheelo's sallow face was the same colour of the yellow crepe kameez she had on. Her hair was matted, her eyes dry and bloodshot. Without getting up she put her arms around Tara and her head in Tara's lap. She neither said a word, nor shed a tear.

Tara kissed her, and then asked, 'What's happened?'

Tara had to ask several times before Sheelo replied in a faint voice, 'Take Ghullu away with you.'

When Sheelo refused to answer any more questions, Tara said firmly, 'I won't do any such thing unless you tell me what happened. If you won't speak, I'll sit here in silence too.'

Sheelo finally said, 'Just do what I've asked you, nothing else.'

'Why should I take him away? I won't unless you explain first.'

Sheelo said, 'I finally owned up last night. I was fed up and had no strength left in me. I told my husband, "Yes, Ratan is Ghullu's father. Now kill me and my baby if you want." This morning he said that he didn't want me here anymore. He took all my jewellery, then told me to go back to my parents. He said that he'd put me on a train when he returned from the office. I've nowhere to go. You just take Ghullu away.'

Tara fell quiet on hearing this. From Sheelo's dull look she had guessed what was on her mind. There was no point in asking any more questions. She sat thinking, with her head in hands and Sheelo's head in her lap.

The taxi driver peered in and asked, 'Bibiji, you want the taxi to wait?'

Tara pulled herself together and answered, 'I'm coming.' To Sheelo she said, 'I'll be back in half an hour. Wait here for me.'

Tara got into the taxi and told the driver to take her to Karol Bagh. The address she had was incomplete; all it said was: House number 3, Naai

Wali Gali. She had never been to Karol Bagh before. She was not sure of finding Ratan at home. And how would she explain to his parents why she had to talk to him?

On reaching Karol Bagh the driver parked the taxi near some newly built houses as he inquired about the address.

Tara suddenly called out, 'Ratan bhappa!'

Ratan heard the call, turned around and came over. He leaned into the window of the taxi and stared with blank astonishment.

'Sheelo's going to kill herself,' Tara blurted out, ignoring his shocked expression.

Ratan's lips opened to pronounce Tara's name but instead he asked the question, 'What? ...What's happened?'

'When did you see her last?'

'It's been several days.'

'Come with me. I'll explain,' she said moving aside to make space for him in the back seat. The taxi drove back towards Shakti Nagar.

Tara said bluntly, 'Sheelo has told everything to Mohanlal and he's asked her to leave his house. She's all set to commit suicide. She called me to take Ghullu away.'

Ratan listened with a dazed expression, 'What should I do, please tell me.'

'I can keep her with me for a couple of days. Can't you arrange anything?'

'I'll do something.'

'What will your parents say?' Tara gave him a worried look.

'They've gone to Dehra Dun. My aunt has passed away. They'll be back on Monday.'

'Will she be able to stay with you?'

'Why not! And yes, where have you been all this time?'

'Never mind about me. I'll tell you everything later. Think of Sheelo first of all.'

Outside Sheelo's room Tara called Suman and took Ghullu up. Holding Sheelo by the arm, Tara led her out of the room and into the taxi. Then she padlocked the door, handed the key to Suman and said, 'Give this to Mohanlal. Sheelo is going to her mother's.'

Narottam telephoned Tara on Saturday evening and spoke as if nothing had happened, 'Charlie Chaplin's *Modern Times* is being screened on Sunday

morning. Invite Mercy and the three of us can go. I'll come around 8.30
and have breakfast at your place. We'll have lunch in Connaught Place.
Will that suit you?'

A weight was lifted from Tara's heart. She accepted.

When she left the apartment with Narottam and Mercy on Sunday
morning, Tara saw Ratan waiting for her in the gali. She stepped aside so
as to speak to him alone.

Ratan had rented a place in a lane off Pachkuian Road and had moved
Sheelo and the baby there in the evening of Saturday before his parents'
return. He had come to take Tara to his new home. Seeing Tara's dilemma,
he said, 'It's all right. I'll come back around three o'clock or sometime in
the late afternoon to take you there.'

Tara took a careful note of Ratan's new address, and told him that she
would go there on her own from Connaught Place.

While she watched a very entertaining, insightful and topical film and
had lunch at the Palace, Tara in her heart was eager to be with Sheelo.

Ratan had explained that near a tailor's shop on Pachkuian Road and
down an alley past three houses she would see, next to a flight of stairs,
the name Ratan on the door of a garage.

She located the garage and was about to knock on the door when she
heard the familiar sound of Ratan's voice inside, 'Aha ji! Aha!'

Tara pushed gently and the unlocked door opened a little to show Ratan,
his back to the door, sitting cross-legged on a chatai on the floor. One of his
arms was around Sheelo sitting on of one of his knees, and he was holding
Ghullu on the other knee as he rocked the child, 'Aha ji *sadda tabbar*! What
a nice family we are!'

Tara was about to step back in embarrassment but the sound of the
door opening made both Ratan and Sheelo turn around. Sheelo began to
get up but Ratan, not caring about Tara's presence, did not let go of her.
Sheelo simply covered her face shyly. Ghullu was gurgling happily, 'O! O!'

Ratan said, 'Tara, just look at my family!' Tara's heart brimmed with
affection as tears filled her eyes. She scolded Ratan affectionately, 'What're
you doing, Ratan bhappa! Why're you bothering this poor girl?'

His arm still around Sheelo, he said to Tara, 'Why call me brother? Call
me brother-in-law!'

'Never, *chandrya*—you lunatic! Sheelo's younger than I am. I'm going to call you by your name. It's you who should address me as bahinji.' Tara sat on the chatai and took Ghullu in her arms.

A quick look showed her that this place was not much different from Sheelo's one room dwelling in Shakti Nagar. A charpoy by the wall, clothes hung from pegs and slung over a line. A shelf built into the wall held two aluminium pots, a couple of thalis and some mangoes. However, Ratan and Sheelo looked happy and contended.

Since Tara found it inconvenient to carry the bulky office dossiers home to work on them, she stayed on in the office and seldom reached home before half past six. The winter days being short, it would be dark by then. Mercy had seemed rather preoccupied for the last few days and was mostly out of the house. Chaddha would usually come to her apartment quietly every few weeks or would send her a message for a secret rendezvous. Mercy had not heard from him for several weeks now. To ease her mind Mercy would go visit her friends and acquaintances to forget her worries in small talk. Or she would go to the cinema.

A light rain was falling that afternoon, and it had become quite cold. Tara returned from the office and called, 'Chimmo aunty, I'm nearly frozen. Make me a hot cup of tea and bring it to my room.'

She hung up her rain-drenched coat and crawled under the quilt on her bed. Chimmo was serving tea with a plate of *chirwa*—flattened rice fried with peanuts—on her bedside table when the doorbell rang. Tara was a little annoyed. If it was Narottam or Mathur, she thought, she'd have to receive them in the living room. She was wrapping a shawl around her shoulders when a young woman stepped into the living room. Tara was a little surprised to see her; it was Sita.

Tara called from the bedroom, 'Sita, come in. What brings you here today? Come on in, it's cold. Your coat must be soaked, take it off. Here's a shawl. Come, the tea's hot.' She was talking to Sita in Punjabi, but broke into Hindi to summon Chimmo, 'Chimmo aunty, please bring another cup.' Slipping back under the quilt, she moved to the far side of the bed to make room for Sita.

Sita was wearing the same coat as last year and was looking decidedly worried and crestfallen. Her devil-may-care attitude had also disappeared. When she removed her coat to hang it up, Tara saw that her clothing was not as showy or fashionable as before.

Sita covered herself with the shawl and sat on one side of the bed, keeping her feet on the floor as the cuffs of her salwar were splattered with mud.

'Have a cup of tea first. This chirwa is really hot, but you know how these darned Madrasis like Mercy eat a lot of chillies,' Tara said, her mouth burning from the spicy mixture.

'Go ahead. I don't feel like it.'

'Not even a cup of tea? At least taste the chirwa.'

'No. bahinji. I had something to eat not long ago and don't feel like anything now.'

In spite of Tara's insistence, Sita refused to try even a mouthful.

Hanging her head, Sita said, 'Bahinji, I've left my job and I'm in a bit of a mess.'

'Why, what's happened?'

'Bahinji, those people who offered me the new job turned out to be frauds. I quit when they failed to pay me for two months. I'm looking for another job. I desperately need to borrow 150 rupees. It's an emergency. I'll pay you back very soon.' Sita kept her head bent.

Tara thought for a few moments before replying, 'I'm sure you'll pay me back, but what kind of a job are you looking for, and where?'

'Whatever I can get. That's why I've come to you. Can you please help me?'

'How can I help? I already tried to put some sense into your head. Misraji was willing to give you a second chance, but you refused to listen. You replied as if you were without a care in the world. And you had money to throw about with both hands.'

'Bahinji, maybe I was really stupid then, but I'm not like that now.'

The doorbell rang again. Chimmo recognized the familiar ring, and went downstairs to open the door.

'Are you in bed?' Mercy called as she went into Tara's room, panting from climbing the stairs.

'Yes, didi, it's freezing cold today,' Tara said, moving over again so that Mercy could join them on the bed. 'This is Sita, a neighbour of mine from Lahore. She lives in Sadar Bazar. She's just like my little sister.'

Mercy's coat was not wet, so she sat on the bed without taking it off. She stared hard at Sita who seemed to be squirming nervously.

'Didn't you come to Dr Ayyar's clinic?' Mercy asked, mixing her grammatical genders as she usually did when she tried to speak in Hindi.

Sita still sat with her head sagging.

'Didn't you learn from your first mistake?' Mercy asked in a harsh tone. 'Don't you have any concern for your own health even if your husband doesn't care? Or are you like some animal? The doctor didn't charge you the full fees the first time thinking that you were hard up. You refused to take precautions. This time you'll have to learn your lesson the hard way and pay up one hundred rupees.'

Tara looked at Mercy and then at Sita.

'Tara, I'll have some tea too,' Mercy said, and called out to Chimmo to bring another cup and to put some hot water in the bathroom so that she could have a quick wash. 'I'll be back in a minute.'

Sita broke into tears. In a low voice, Tara said disdainfully, 'So that's why you wanted to borrow the money. Shame on you! Get out!'

Joining her palms, Sita pleaded, 'Bahinji, help me this one time. I touch your feet. I won't do this again.'

'How do I know that you won't?' Tara said, sickened by what she had heard. 'Did anyone force you to do it the first time? Is that what you meant by having fun? You can go to the devil for all I care. Where're your friends now who were so ready to spend money on you?' Touching Tara's knees, Sita said plaintively, 'Bahinji, I'm at your feet. I'll pay you even if I have to earn the money by washing dishes. Or else I'll take some poison.' Sita stuffed a corner of her dupatta into her mouth to suppress the sound of her sobs, but her back shook from a spasm of crying.

The thought came to Tara, 'What'll Mercy think of me for saying that Sita was just like my sister!' She said contemptuously to Sita, 'She'll be back soon. Get the hell out of here before that.' Sita was going towards the staircase on her way out when, overcome by a fresh storm of tears, she stopped and stood with her head against the wall.

Mercy was talking with Chimmo in the kitchen. Tara got out of bed, went up to Sita and said scornfully, 'Will you leave now or bring me more shame.' Inspite of her anger, her eyes were brimming.

Sita raised her puffy and reddened eyes and pleaded, joining her palms again, 'Bahinji, please...'

Tara gave in, 'All right, come back tomorrow.'

Mercy, with her coat off and a shawl around her shoulders, came into the living room with her tea. She sat in an armchair and asked in English, 'Your friend has left?'

'Yes.'

'What does her husband do?' Mercy asked, taking a sip of her tea.

'What do I know?'

'You said she was just like a sister from your gali. She must have come here to borrow the money for the clinic.'

'I'd rather not talk about her!'

Mercy took a few more sips before saying, 'You're angry that she's decided to have an abortion?'

'Is that something to be happy about?'

'Who would want an abortion for the fun of it? If she's wants one, it must be because she's forced to it by the circumstances. Would she be able to look after the child if she doesn't go through with the abortion?'

'Never in a million years!' Tara exclaimed angrily.

'Well, I suppose if she could, she would never have asked for an abortion,' Mercy said, taking another sip. 'She's really naïve. Had she been a bit more cautious, it might have cost her a rupee or two. Now she'll have to pay a full hundred. And if she doesn't, she's stuck with it for the rest of her life. If you like I can speak to Ayyar on her behalf. I'll give up ten rupees as my cut of the fees.'

'What do you mean?'

'You know I've been working with Ayyar at her clinic. I take ten per cent. The nurse she had got married and went away to Trichur. Ayyar offered me a wage of Rs 350 per month, but I didn't accept. Now I make between fifteen and twenty every day, just for working from eight till one o'clock. Now and then there's nothing, but sometimes forty or fifty rupees in a day. One day it came to a hundred. Ayyar is a bit money-minded and can size up her patients' ability to pay at a glance. Not a paisa less than 250 rupees from the unmarried ones and widows. There was that case of an eighteen-year-old unmarried daughter of a rich seth. Ayyar demanded a thousand, and the father paid up without uttering a word. If it's some working woman who earns only 100 or so a month, Ayaar might settle for 40 or 50. But she's an absolute expert. I had assisted in many difficult cases when I was at the Dufferin Hospital, but she has a technique all her own. But that wily woman keeps it secret. Her procedure takes barely ten minutes and there's very little pain.' Mercy began to demonstrate the process by using her hands.

'Please! Don't go on!' Tara turned her head away in distaste.

'Why, what's wrong? It's a standard medical technique. Just like any other operation. It frees a woman of something unwanted and unwelcome. Arrey, it's always the woman who pays the price. Anyone can face this problem. Perhaps, even you some day.'

'Please don't talk rot. The very thought fills me with horror,' Tara said angrily.

'What an idiot you are!' Mercy refused to back down. 'Is it nonsense to help someone out if they are sick? As Ayyar says, abortion is just another surgical procedure, and she's quite right.'

'Don't compare it to treating an illness. It's committing a crime.'

The doorbell rang again.

'Chimmo, see who's there,' Mercy called, and continued passionately, 'Ayyar is right when she says it's just like any another disorder. All physical disorders are due to a lack of care and restraint. Anything that causes a physical or mental pain is a disorder.'

There was the sound of footsteps briskly coming upstairs, and then a male voice asked, 'May I come in?' Mathur entered, saying, 'This seems like a heated discussion, Mercy didi. What's it about?'

It embarrassed Tara even more that a male had intruded into the conversation.

'This one's totally opposed to abortion,' Mercy said bluntly in English. 'I was explaining to her that anyone who uses precaution and restraint can avoid such a disorder. And those who don't or can't, have to seek medical help. What's disgusting or improper in saying so?'

Mathur avoided meeting their eyes. So did Tara, but Mercy ran on without embarrassment, 'Who nowadays wants to be blessed with four or five children? And who can afford to provide healthy food and proper education for all of them? And if people can't, the life in a family with many children will become just a hell on earth. Is an unwanted pregnancy or a child for them not a problem that will plague them all their lives?'

Mathur replied to Mercy in good English without looking at her, 'It's a matter of personal choice for a family, in accordance with their circumstances and way of thinking. Of course, it can become a national problem for a country that is overcrowded and has a large low-income population.'

Tara said nothing but Mercy pressed on, 'Why, there are thousands of young men and women like you who don't want to get married. Don't they have or will they never have a need for a physical relationship?'

Mathur now looked at Mercy as he replied, 'Those who don't want the responsibility of marriage and family should make some sacrifice and abstain from sex.'

'Such talk about sacrifice is meaningless,' Mercy said intensely. 'With or without marriage, everyone has sexual needs. It's a natural urge, a physical necessity. What should people do who have no chance to get married? I know from personal experience that girls in the nursing profession or in the teaching line or those working in offices, all want to get married. Either the parents of such girls can't arrange husbands for them, or they themselves can't find someone equal to their status. But they have bodies and sexual needs. If they suppress their natural urges, they end up suffering from some illnesses or other. And if they make one slip, then normal life is over for them.'

Mathur kept his eyes on Mercy's face as he answered, 'Mercy didi, sex may play its part in human love, but we shouldn't allow wild and uncontrollable physical desires to dominate the relationship.'

Mercy seemed really annoyed, 'What is love really between a man and a woman? Love is just another glorified name for sex.'

Feeling increasingly uncomfortable, Tara changed the subject by asking, 'Mathur bhai, what's happened of your situation?'

Mathur had been a lecturer at a college in Delhi. In the 1930s he had been sent to prison for three years for his involvement in the revolutionary movement for India's independence. Such a history precluded any possibility of his joining the civil service, and his temperament would not have allowed him to work under some British bureaucrat in any case. His family contacts had landed him a well-paying job in a large private company. He was capable and efficient, and after ten years service was earning over Rs 900 per month with allowances. Mathur had again felt the urge to serve his country after India became independent. The new government had changed the name of the Indian Civil Service (ICS) to the Indian Administrative Service (IAS). Competent individuals with experience and nationalist views were being recruited directly into positions of responsibility. Mathur was willing to accept a salary lower than the one he was receiving in return for working for the national government.

Mathur and Niranjan Chaddha had once been associates and comrades-in-arms in the nationalist moment. They had drifted apart because of differing political viewpoints, but Mathur still held Chaddha in high esteem because of his integrity. Mathur also respected Mercy for her principles and because of her willingness to court danger for Chaddha. He often repeated, with great seriousness, his own personal maxim: 'The character of a man is greater than his politics.' Although Mercy was quite able to look after herself, Mathur visited her once or twice a month to offer the services of a friend and well-wisher.

Mercy had described Mathur to Tara as a fine and reliable person, although a chronic bachelor and a great help to the mothers, sisters and wives of all his friends. She had also added jokingly, 'No woman can have any reason to fear him.'

Mathur said in answer to Tara's question, 'I gave indisputable proof to the Prime Minister that the IAS is riddled with nepotism. Those who have qualified in the first division are being passed over in favour of others with only a third division results.'

'What did the PM say?' Tara asked.

'What could he say? His only reply was, "Those who pass in the first division and come out at the top are mostly communists. How can such people be allowed into the IAS?"'

Mercy was pleased, 'Communists don't have to depend on scraps thrown to them. The PM should admit that communists can also be suitable candidates.'

'But you're not a communist?' Tara asked Mathur.

'No. I told the PM, "Neither do I believe in communism, nor have I ever been a member of the Communist Party." He replied, "I don't know what to say. Perhaps there's something against you in your background report."

'I spoke plainly, "How can the background reports submitted by the CID and the bureaucrats be taken to be unbiased? Didn't those hirelings of the British Imperial Indian army, those Brit-lovers, brand the former members of the INA as traitors? And didn't the police and the bureaucrats, the former lackeys of the British, say that those who had participated in the revolutionary movement were not suitable for government service?" The PM just kept quiet, what could he answer?'

Mathur continued hotly, 'Acharya Kriplani is completely justified in asking under what circumstances did the country have its revolution? And what became of the political ideals of Gandhiji? The slogans in praise of

Gandhiji have begun to ring a bit hollow just two years after his death. The administration is now in the hands of a clique of former ICS officials, who have no idea of serving the people, but only of keeping their cushy jobs. They don't believe in democracy, but only in bureaucracy. The legal system hasn't changed and neither the police raj. Not only is it still possible to jail somebody without trial, but under the Defence of India Act the police have more powers than ever before and have become a law unto themselves. Even if a high court acquits people, the police arrest them again on a new charge. Such things make one want to hang his head in shame. The British government never censured Bhagat Singh's statement at his trial for bombing the Assembly, but the present government has suspended the statements of Gandhi's assassin Godse. Does that mean that they can't reply to Godse's accusations? Is it true democracy to gag someone unjustly? Kripalaniji is dead right when he says that revolution means a change of rulers. When did that revolution happen, I ask you?'

Tara said, 'The changeover may not have been far-reaching enough, but it was certainly a major change that it is now the rule of our own people rather than of a foreign power. The machinery of administration and the administrators themselves can only carry out the government's policies, and those who decide the policies are certainly different people.'

Mercy jumped in, 'What's all this talk about change? Things are worse than before. The capitalist class feels encouraged that power is in the hands of the party that survives mainly on their donations. And now the government has taken away even the right to strike from the poor working class. Price controls have been removed to allow the capitalists to earn even greater profit so that they can fill the Congress party coffers. What have people got from the so-called independence? The price of wheat and cloth is higher now than in war time. If there're shortages of wheat and cloth, why can't the government give everyone an equal share? Why do they give the capitalists a free hand to raise prices as much as they want?'

Tara lay down on her bed and switched off the light. The thoughts crowding her mind were not about the many injustices of the political situation, but rather about Sita and of anger and outrage at her recent loose behaviour. 'The little fool should be made to realize the seriousness of her behaviour. But how? And why only take it out on her and not those who took advantage of her? Mercy is right when she complains that nobody punishes those who adulterate foodstuff for profit and make people sick, and black marketeers who let others die of starvation by raising the price of grain. But it's the victims like Sita who are condemned as wrongdoers and treated like social outcasts.'

Her thoughts wandered, 'Who would give her a job when in a few months time her condition as an unmarried mother-to-be becomes evident? Who will accept her as a wife if she didn't go through with the treatment? The idiot says that she'll pay me back by washing dishes. But where would she get the money to pay for the delivery? And what if she died in child birth? Who would employ her, an unmarried mother, as a servant? No Hindu family would contaminate themselves by accepting water touched by her.' Yet another thought came to her, 'Wouldn't everyone cast me out if they knew what I had been through?' Her body trembled involuntarily. In her imagination she saw Sita as a pariah, hungry and crying, with a baby in her arms, without the father of the baby at her side.

Tara felt a surge of anger at the unknown father of Sita's child, and a twinge of compassion for Sita. Suddenly her body shuddered again as she thought: What if something unfortunate had happened as a result of what she herself had undergone? She and Sita in a way were sisters in misfortune. However, she had been bound and gagged as a prisoner, and Sita had participated without coercion. She tossed restlessly in bed for a long time before falling asleep.

The next day Tara first expressed her disgust at Sita's folly, then explained to Mercy that she could not leave Sita in the lurch without helping her.

When Sita returned that evening, Tara spoke to her sternly, 'The Devil take you for your hankering to have some so-called fun. After what you did I felt like never wanting to see you again. I'll help you only if first of all you swear to behave in future properly and with some decency. What's happened to those who promised you the monthly Rs 150? And what qualifications have you when you couldn't even work as a low-grade dispatcher clerk. Take six months' training and pick up something useful. Learn Hindi typing and shorthand. I'll pay the fees for the courses. If you don't agree to do that, get out now. My friend Mercy will take care of your problem and we'll both foot the bill, but I won't give a single paisa to you. I'll give your mother fifty rupees every month for both of you, but I don't promise to do it forever. If I see or hear about even the slightest misbehaviour on your part, you and your mother will be on your own and I couldn't care less.'

Mathur had been very impressed with Tara's cheerful nature and intelligence, and had become rather fond of her. Tara had turned twenty-two, which was a good age for marriage even for an educated woman like her. To Mathur it seemed unfortunate that she might never find a husband because there was nobody to find a possible suitor for her or to arrange a dowry. Tara was in government service and her salary of 300 rupees per month amounted to a dowry in itself. However, even without this additional benefit, Mathur felt that her winsome personality was enough to make any respectable and well-to-do man feel fortunate in having her as a wife.

Mathur had a variety of contacts in the community. He would sometimes bring his married sister over to meet Tara and Mercy, or invited them to his sister's where other guests would also be present. He would introduce Tara to the company, and dutifully give detailed information later about some of them to her. One such person was Nityanand Tewari, a former student of Mathur with a PhD in history from the Delhi University and now working there as a lecturer. Tewari had been visiting Tara and Mercy for some time, either alone or with Mathur. He knew that Tara was fond of reading and often brought her a book or two. Tara too found Tewari's personality and his conversation pleasing. Mathur often praised Tewari in the absence of the latter, and would explain how Tewari had achieved his success solely by dint of dogged determination and hard work. Tewari had recently accepted a higher position at Aligarh University, sixty miles from Delhi. When Tewari sometimes came all the way to visit her on a Sunday, Tara could not but feel uncomfortable.

Mathur felt some embarrassment broaching the subject of Tara's attitude to her own prospect of marriage, but frequently told her in great detail some of the matches arranged through his counsel and effort. And how the couples thus united were living happily together. Confident of his own power of judgement and his ability to assess character and personality, he told Tara about four eligible bachelors of acceptable nature and family background, between the ages of twenty-five and forty who were earning anything from 400 to 2000 rupees per month. Whenever he found a chance to speak to Mercy alone, he would invariably inquire, 'Did you sound Tara out? What are her ideas?'

Tara felt secure in the conviction that Mathur was an upright gentleman and her well-wisher, but was sometimes fed up with the repeated suggestions of marriage prospects. She complained to Mercy, 'Didi, why don't you talk

Mathur out of this matchmaking? And why is he so concerned about fixing me up? Why do people think that an unmarried woman is a loose woman and that she must be pegged down? That a man must become her master?'

Chapter 10

AT THE TIME OF THE REFUGEE ASSOCIATION ELECTIONS IN 1948, JAIDEV PURI had come across Somraj Sahni, who was canvassing for Puri's rival Prem Nath Gulati. Puri had learnt that Somraj's family was also in Jalandhar and that his father Sukhlal had passed away in the beginning of the year.

One of the businesses run by Lala Sukhlal Sahni in Lahore had been the transport of goods between East and West Punjab by the two trucks that he owned. After a Muslim mob had attacked and burnt down his house, he had fled Lahore with his family and arrived in Jalandhar two weeks before the Partition came into effect. Jalandhar had been evacuated by its Muslim population. Sukhlal had taken over a very large house in Basti Nigar Khan that had been abandoned by a family of Baigs, and had resumed his transport business, extending the service as far as Ambala. His customers were willing to pay any price in view of the impending chaos. In four months' time he had been able to send Somraj to Delhi to buy another truck.

In Lahore Lala Sukhlal had been a part of Hindu Mahasabha, but he was also a supporter of Dr Radhey Behari and a member of his inner circle. Sukhlal had continued his association with the doctor in Jalandhar, and had sided with the anti-Sood camp in the factional in-fighting of the Congress party in Punjab. The struggle among the warring sections within the party vying for power and control had left its mark on the Refugee Association. Puri was in the Sood camp and Somraj was campaigning for Gulati, a candidate from the doctor's group.

Puri had never harboured friendly feelings for Somraj. On the other hand, he had felt bitter that no attempt had been made to save his sister from the fire at Banni Hata. Now that his sister was presumed dead, he felt no obligation to show any deference to his brother-in-law. He felt that his social status was now elevated enough for him to refuse to be patronized by anybody. Therefore, if he met Somraj, he did not treat him in any special way except for a brief, business-like 'hello' and 'how are you'.

When Masterji learned of the death of his daughter Tara, he counselled Puri, 'Even if God granted only a short life to your sister, that does not mean that a connection formed in accordance with His will can be broken.

We can't just ignore our relationship with the Sahni family. They are living their karma, we should observe our duty too.' Masterji, his wife, Puri and Kanak went to offer their condolences to the Sahni family.

When the two families met, the ritual to mourn Lala Sukhlal could not be observed properly and according to the old traditions of Lahore. Social mores and customs had changed in just a few months following the change in circumstances of the Punjabi people. As Masterji, Puri and also Somraj were of the opinion that the practice of the traditional elaborate grieving was unnecessary, the women of both families had to be content with a brief ceremony of mourning. Masterji expressed his regret at the delay in learning about the death of Sukhlal because of the turmoil of the times. He also paid tribute to the kindliness and the benevolent character of Sukhlal.

Puri was not only the editor of *Nazir* and the secretary of the Refugee Association, but was also seen as the right-hand man of Sood, the leader of the dominant group within the Congress. Somraj had become particularly friendly and respectful towards Puri. He had related a long story about the attack on his family's Banni Hata residence and how the fire had gutted it. His eyes frequently filling with tears, he would assure Puri that no effort had been spared to rescue Tara. Showing burn scars on his arms and lower legs, he said, 'It must all have been in the way God intended it. We had no interest left in the house or the property once she was gone, so we decided to abandon everything and leave the city.'

When Masterji had moved to the house in Basti Nigar Khan, Somraj had begun to help him in many ways. The supply of coal to his house, only a few hundred yards away, came from Masterji's depot. One of Somraj's trucks ferried shipments of coal from the railway station dump to the depot. He introduced several regular customers to Masterji and arranged for the slack to be sold to some furnace-burning businesses and kilns.

The women of both families gradually began to visit each other. If Somraj's family needed a fresh supply of coal, his mother or sister or one of the nieces came to leave a message with the family of Masterji. The visiting women usually stayed for short chats. Familiarity leads to a sharing of secrets, especially among women. Since they have to depend on one another in times of crisis, they were always impatient to share the reasons for their problems.

Somraj's elder sister Maheshan had been living with her parents after she became a widow. When she or Somraj's mother came to visit, they

would sit beside Tara's mother and open their hearts as they dried their
eyes on their aanchal, 'We searched so hard before we brought home a
bride who was pretty as the moon for our Somraj. She was such an angel,
a devi. She foresaw the disaster that was coming upon us, so she left this
world before suffering any disgrace. It must be God's plan that we have
to be outcasts in our own home,' and they would begin to tell a story of
their own misfortunes.

Kundanlal, the elder brother of Lala Sukhlal, had owned a jewellery store
in Gujranwala in western Punjab, and the income from his store had
allowed him to buy two houses besides the one in which he himself lived.
After his death the business suffered under the management of his eldest
son, Kartaram. Dataram, Kartaram's younger brother, was an employee in
the post office department. Both families were barely making ends meet.

Kartaram was obese, with flabby folds of flesh and layers of fat over
his neck area, making his neck-less face appear directly attached to his
shoulders. This deformity had reduced his voice to a barely audible whisper.
Everything frightened him. His wife Shanti was his direct opposite—
slender, flamboyant and sharp-tongued. When the family was fleeing
Gujranwala, Kartaram had tripped and broken his ankle at the railway
station. Dataram somehow managed to bring his mother, his own wife and
family and his injured brother and his wife to Jalandhar.

Lala Sukhlal had given shelter to his widowed sister-in-law and the rest of
the family. After two-and-a-half months Dataram had been posted to Karnal.
When he took his wife and daughter there, his mother also went with him.
Kartaram and Shanti had remained behind in Jalandhar. Kartaram's ankle
had healed imperfectly and the doctor now wanted to reset it. Kartaram
did not have the courage to face the pain, and was willing to walk with a
limp for the rest of his life rather than undergo the surgery.

During that time Prem Nath Gulati was the secretary of the Refugee
Association. Somraj sought his assistance in getting an abandoned shop in
the Sarrafa Bazaar allotted in the name of his cousin, and Kartaram took
over the empty store. From Gujranwala he had brought silver and gold to
the value of Rs 10,000 and another Rs 3,000 in bank notes. Shanti had
made him hand it all over to Somraj for safekeeping. When Kartaram asked
for his gold and cash, Somraj would say, 'It's in the bank as collateral for
a loan. I'll pay you interest on it.' Shanti would taunt her husband, 'As if

your new business is doing so well that you want the money returned so that you can throw it down the drain with the rest?'

Inarticulate with rage, Kartaram would mumble incoherently.

Encouraged by Bhagwanti's expressions of commiseration, Somraj's mother or sister would sit on the charpoy beside her and, head in hands, say, 'We've become beggars in our own home, worse than slaves. Where could we go and do away with ourselves to escape from this shameful treatment. Shanti has taken over everything as if it belonged to her husband, and orders us around as the mistress of the household. We have to depend on the scraps thrown to us. Butter and ghee are considered too good for the likes of us. She's taken over the control of her husband's money and bosses him around. Such shameful behaviour!'

Next time, they would add to the story, 'That witch has fed Somraj some magic potion. Or she knows a mantra that keeps him under her thumb. He simply refuses to listen to us. A pandit charged us two rupees for doing a puja that was supposed to bring Somraj back to his senses, but nothing happened. Then we gave a rupee and a quarter and a lock of hair from that witch's comb to a *naai* to prepare a counter charm, but that didn't work either. This kind of magic was known only to the Muslim fakirs. They would have driven an iron nail into the threshold and, in a flash, everything would have been alright. But all of them have gone to Pakistan.'

Maheshan said, covering her mouth with her hand to hide her embarrassment, 'And that good-for-nothing mass of blubber feels no shame. A real man would have cut such a woman to pieces with a machete. She has put her poor husband's charpoy down in the aangan below, and she herself sleeps in the upper storey. Everybody knows that, but neither she nor Somraj shows any shame or embarrassment. Nobody would have dared to behave like that in Lahore. That witch had a daughter born to her after marriage, but the baby died within six months. Since then she's been barren. Such a barefaced hussy!'

Bhagwanti flew into a fury on hearing this. She still saw Somraj as her idealized son-in-law, to whom puja should be offered all his life. To her, Tara's claim on Somraj's home was still valid, and she found it unbearable that some khasamkhani—man-eating—slut should assert her claim over what was her daughter's by right. She would not have minded if Somraj had remarried; men were expected to do that. Bhagwanti had invited Shanti to her own home and had given her the usual presents on festive occasions because she was a member of Somraj's family. However, she was not willing to close her eyes to immoral and scandalous behaviour in the home of her dead daughter's in-laws.

Bhagwanti went to the Kamaal Press to complain to her son, who now had acquired a social stature equal to anyone's. Somraj also deferred to him. Why Puri couldn't persuade Somraj to behave himself, she wondered.

Puri's explanation to his mother was, 'Why should we get involved in such a mess? Everyone knows that Somraj is a crook and a goonda. I said so before Tara's marriage but nobody paid any attention. Why should we bother about him when my sister is no longer alive? I try and keep him at arm's length. He's no good, no matter how you look at him. Let him stew in his own juice. People like him form the clique of hangers-on around Dr Radhey Behari. The truth will be out and Somraj will get what he deserves. Don't we have enough problems of our own? Pitaji and you insist on treating this goonda like a relative when he's no such thing. Let's not disturb that wasp's nest when there's nothing to be gained.'

Kanak agreed with Puri about the uselessness of keeping up the tradition of meaningless family connections. She also disliked the prospect of involvement in other people's problems. Yet, something niggled at the back of her mind. She had already heard from her brother-in-law about Somraj being an undesirable character. Puri had told Kanak that he was opposed to Tara's marriage, but it was Tara herself who had wanted to go ahead. Kanak found it distressing that a bright good-looking girl like Tara had fallen for a crook, and had felt very sad in Nainital when Puri had told her about Tara's death. She thought, 'Had Tara been alive, she and I would have been good friends.'

A year had passed since Puri's first meeting with Somraj and his family. In the government there had been a Cabinet reshuffle, and Sood had been inducted into the council of ministers. The capital of Punjab was still at Simla, and Sood spent most of his time there. Puri acted as his representative in Jalandhar. There had been frequent occasions for Puri and Somraj to meet each other. Somraj would come to the *Nazir* office to advise as to who could be called to testify as a witness in the case against Rikhiram, or pay a social visit to Puri at his home. He was willing to help in any way possible, even offering to have the treadle machine carted off from Rikhiram's home to the Kamaal Press. He had also offered to get Rikhiram beaten up in the bazaar for defrauding Puri, but Puri had turned down those proposals.

Somraj treated Kanak with an irritating overfamiliarity, as the wife of his brother-in-law. When he found nothing else to say, he would begin to pay her compliments for being so capable and hard-working. He had presented to Kanak's newborn baby girl the congratulatory silver bowl and baby rattle. Kanak quietly stored them away. The mere sight of Somraj brought back memories of Tara and her heart would fill with bitterness.

One day in December 1949, Phirkoo the peon at the Kamaal Press brought up the afternoon mail. Kanak began to sort out Puri's personal mail from the letters for *Nazir*. Once in a while there would be a letter from her father. In the delivery there was an envelope mailed from Delhi and marked 'personal' in one corner. Puri was not in the office. Kanak was curious, so she opened it.

The contents of the letter left her feeling stunned, so she read it a second time. It was from Babu Govindram of Karol Bagh, Delhi. Addressing Puri affectionately as *azeez*, he had written how pleased he was at finding out Puri's address. He sent his affectionate greetings to Masterji and Puri's mother. He remembered their living side by side for thirty years in the two halves of the same house, facing their problems together and sharing their joys. There were a few lines about how much he looked forward to meeting Masterji again and to receiving a letter from him, and about certain things that he wanted to discuss at the time of their meeting.

Govindram also had words of praise for *Nazir*, and of regret for not having noticed earlier the name of the editor. He congratulated Puri on having lived up to everyone's expectations, and then gave the sensational news, 'You must have already exchanged letters with dear beti Tara. It was such a wonderful surprise to see her alive and healthy when she visited our house two days ago. She told us how no one could reach her because the staircase was already in flames when her in-laws' house was on fire. She escaped by climbing over a wall and jumping on to the roof of the house next door. She hurt her ankle, but some kind Muslim family guided her to a Hindu home. It was her karma that she met such helpful people. She had come to Delhi with the same Hindu family. Tara is just like a devi, such an angel. It was as if that she had gone to paradise, and returned as her old self. Still the same smiling face, the same cheerful nature, and brimming over with the same feelings of affection. You must be happy, Jaidev, to learn that she is now holding a responsible position in the Department of Rehabilitation at a salary of Rs 350 per month.'

Unable to control her elation, Kanak called out excitedly, 'Gillji!' She had addressed him as Gillji when Gill had first come to Jalandhar, and had continued to do so in order to show her respect for him. Sometimes she would also call him *bhraji*, elder brother.

'Incredible news! Tara is alive!'

'Who's she?' asked Gill.

'Don't you know Tara, my sister-in-law? She used to participate sometimes in the peace marches organized by the communists before Partition.'

Gill shook his head.

'Hai, she's a very sweet-natured girl and brilliant. In all her exams she was always in the top division.' Kanak leaned closer to Gill and said in a low voice, 'She's the one who was married to this crook Somraj. A Muslim mob had set fire to her in-laws' house on her first night in it. Her family thought that she and an old aunt could not possibly have escaped and must have died in the fire.' Kanak read out the whole letter breathlessly. 'Although we had very few chances to meet, I'm very fond of her. I myself will go and bring her here for a visit.'

Gill said he was happy to hear all this and offered his congratulations.

Kanak waited impatiently for Puri, but he did not come to the office that afternoon. Bhagwanti had been staying at her son's house since the birth of her granddaughter to help take care of the infant. Every day Kanak used to go home to take lunch and breastfeed her daughter, and would return by 5 o'clock to feed her. On that day Kanak found it hard to suppress her excitement and not tell her mother-in-law so that she herself could break the news to Puri. Puri returned home around nine in the evening. As soon as she saw him, Kanak said in a jubilant voice, 'Promise to give me some mithai before I give you this letter with some very good news.'

Noticing Kanak so bubbling with excitement, Puri's mother called out, 'Why, what is it?'

Puri stood silent after reading the letter, running his fingers through his hair reflectively.

Kanak spoke up, 'Her address is in the letter. Write to her to come and meet us immediately. Hai, I wish I could fly and bring her here.'

Puri's mother came into the room and asked again, 'What's going on?'

'We'll have to think this over,' Puri said to Kanak in English, letting out a deep sigh. 'First of all we should write and ask her to explain her circumstances.'

'What circumstances?' Kanak asked in English. 'Why can't she come to Jalandhar to meet us and her parents?'

'Don't you realize the situation Somraj has created? And that he's the one who has the first claim on Tara as her husband.'

'That bastard will have to break off with Shanti. It's high time anyway that someone put an end to it.'

'We certainly don't know the whole story about Tara. Something doesn't ring true here. How's it possible that she never saw or heard about *Nazir*? It wouldn't have been difficult for her to find out our address. And it's not she but someone else who wrote to us. Perhaps she'll refuse to come here. After all she wasn't very happy in her marriage.'

Kanak said, frowning, 'But you told me that she was attracted to Somraj?'

Puri replied, 'Maybe there was a brief adolescent infatuation at first, but she soon got over it. There was another man, a Muslim, you might know him—that communist Asad. She was under his spell. That was the time when everything was upside down. She was also emotionally rather unstable. Her marriage had been arranged while I was in prison. It was a matter of protecting the family's good name.'

Hearing her son and the daughter-in-law talk in English, Puri's mother again asked, 'Why don't you tell me what's happened?'

'Yes, yes, in a minute,' Puri gestured with his hand for her to wait.

Kanak felt confused. She remembered what Nayyar had told her about Tara being against the marriage. The agony of being married against one's wishes! She found it difficult to believe that the person standing before her was the same Puri she had known. She asked incredulously, 'Did Tara not agree to this marriage?'

'At first she did, but then she changed her mind. What could I do in such a situation?' The image of seeing blood trickle down Tara's forehead flashed through Puri's mind.

'That's strange. Everybody talks so highly of her. The letter also...'

'What does anybody really know about her,' Puri bristled at her reply.

Kanak answered back, 'Well, let her come and give us the facts herself. She can also meet with her family.'

'Do you expect us to make fools of ourselves?' Puri asked angrily. 'If Tara comes here, my mother will have a fit about that other woman. Somraj's sister and mother will have hysterics too. Somraj would want to know why Tara had kept silent for so long. And if he said that he can't accept her since she had stayed away voluntarily—and that's only too true—she will become a problem for us.'

'You seem to be on Somraj's side,' Kanak said in protest.

Puri's mother muttered in vexation, 'What's this about Somraj? What is the world coming to when you have to conceal things from your parents! As if we're not fit to be told whatever is on your mind. The damned *angraize* have gone away but have left their damned *angraizee* language behind.'

'There's no reason for you to get so excited.' Puri lied to his mother in reply, 'Somraj wants to file nomination papers for the District Board elections. What do you know about it? What should I tell you?'

Seeing Kanak turn silently away in protest, Puri said, 'Careful, don't say anything about this to my mother, pitaji or anybody else. People can't keep their mouths shut. Let me think this over a bit. I'll certainly do whatever I can to help Tara. I'll write to her myself.'

Kanak was silent. She remembered: Her whole family had opposed her wish to marry Puri. Nayyar did not approve of Puri either, and had accused him of selfishness and duplicity. She had vehemently denied the accusation then. It seemed now that there had been some truth in the accusation. In Nainital Puri had chosen not to mention Tara's unwillingness to marry Somraj. 'If she had been unwilling, how could she have been forced into the marriage? What if Nayyar had accused me of having an adolescent crush on Puriji?'

Kanak felt so bitter that she did not want to eat dinner. This angered Puri even more. Kanak said nothing except that she had a headache, and went to bed. Her heart was still heavy the next morning and she kept to herself.

Later, at the *Nazir* office, Gill tried to tease her, 'Did both of you as husband and wife finish off all the mithai to celebrate the news about Puri's sister? Where's my share?'

'Let's forget it,' Kanak could barely hold back her tears.

'Why?' Gill said, looking at her. 'What's the matter?'

'I can't explain. He seemed rather upset about the news. Don't utter a word to pitaji or anybody else about that letter, not even to Puriji.'

'But what's the matter?'

'Puriji told me not to,' Kanak looked at Gill pleadingly, and bent her head.

From that day on, Kanak did not say a word about Tara, either to Puri or to anybody else. Strange thoughts weighed on her mind. She felt as if it was herself and not Tara who had been maligned and treated callously. Linked to this feeling was the memory of the incidents of her father-in-law distancing himself from the press, and troublesome business of the court case against Rikhiram. Duplicity everywhere. 'Puriji's temperament and personality has a peculiar side to it,' she thought, and a feeling of sadness came over her. In the days that followed, if Puri wanted to be close to her or share a moment of joy with her, Kanak pretended to be busy with her baby daughter.

Puri also resented Kanak's undue sentimentality and her obstinate refusal to side with him against Tara. At first he made no attempt to placate Kanak and the atmosphere in the house continued to be strained. After about three weeks he broached the subject again, 'You've said that I was being unfair to Tara, but she hasn't even answered my letter. Draw your own conclusions.'

'Would you like me to write to her?' Kanak asked.

'You mean you don't believe me' Puri said, nettled again by her question.

'I didn't say that, but what objection can you have if I did so?'

For the last few days Kanak had been answering Puri back instead of keeping quiet out of consideration for her love for him. Her attitude had strained their relations in the past, and did so again. Kanak remained in a huff for a couple of days.

Irritated by the tension between her son and daughter-in-law, Bhagwanti said pointedly, 'Both of you should look after your home now. I have to go and take care of your father and others. This is the result of giving up old customs and of accepting newfangled notions about choosing your own wife! If a husband indulges his wife in everything, why would she even listen to him? If she's allowed to sit next to him on a chair, she's bound to get uppity. The tradition in our family was that a woman never sat on a charpoy or *peerha* seat in the presence of men.'

When Puri came to the *Nazir* office, Kanak spoke to him normally to keep up appearances. They would begin talking to one another, but with some effort.

The mother-in-law had little sympathy for the daughter-in-law. Bhagwanti thought that her son had married the spoiled daughter of a well-to-do family, and was now afraid of his wife. Kanak found little time to visit her sister, and Kanta in turn had few occasions to come and see her. Kanak was also nervous that she might inadvertently let drop some unkind remark about her husband if her sister asked after Puri. The only people from whom she could expect kindness were her father-in-law and Gill. Masterji was away in Basti Nigar Khan, but she saw Gill almost every day. Gill had guessed at the tension between her and Puri despite Kanak's efforts to hide it, but he was careful not to show his knowledge. He always found some other topic to talk about. Kanak also felt much better after a light-hearted discussion and after sharing a laugh with Gill and Raks.

The process of designating new voting constituencies was in progress in East Punjab as the result of the influx of vast numbers of people uprooted from the west. The Sikhs and the Akali Dal, despite the fact that the Sikhs were only a minority in the total population, were trying to have the boundaries of the constituencies drawn up so as to favour the Sikh candidates. In their efforts to dominate the party and the formation of the new Council of Ministers, both factions of the Congress were competing to woo the Sikh members of the Assembly and various Sikh community organizations in order to ensure their support. The Sikhs were coming up with a new demand every day. The factional rivalries and political manoeuvrings within the party were constantly on Puri's mind. At home, Kanak had become increasingly distant. He felt that there was no place of refuge in his life. His public life was an uphill struggle, and at home he found no peace or solace to help him forget his worries.

Puri decided to speak with Kanak. His voice was choked with emotion and his eyes brimming with tears, 'What has become of us and our life together for which we both worked so long and hard? If you reject me and my love, neither my family nor the newspaper, nor political power has any meaning for me. I don't know why you always misunderstand me. Tara is also my sister. Let's forget what she may have done in a fit of adolescent emotion. She's already been through a lot. If she had wanted to meet us, she would have answered my letter immediately. Pitaji and mother will insist that she goes back to Somraj if they find out about her. How can I ask her to come here, and then throw her into the clutches of a brute like Somraj? The people and the law will be on Somraj's side. If my poor sister wants to live her life in peace, we should let her do just that. Don't you see what I mean? You really did not have to ask my permission before writing to her. I'd prefer that you went to Delhi and met her yourself. Only then will you realize what the truth is. I feel humbled by your kindness and generosity towards her. You're so big-hearted...' His words trailed off and halted.

Before Partition, Jalandhar had been a rather unimportant town of 50,000 or 60,000 people. In the three years following the partition its population had exploded to over 300,000. The Hindu traders and shopkeepers driven out of the cities and towns of West Punjab knew only one way of earning a living, and so the ground floors of the houses in city lanes were quickly converted into shops and the narrow streets had been turned into bazaars. The shortage of accommodation was getting worse every day.

To ease the housing shortage for the middle-class families, the administration began to build, about a mile outside the city, an estate of bungalow-type houses called the ModelTown. Newly constructed dwellings priced between fifteen to twenty thousand rupees and plots of land at a lower price were sold by public auction to help the refugees. The bids were accepted in the form of a yearly payment of a percentage of the total cost of the property. No family was permitted to buy more than one plot or bungalow. At first many houses and plots were bought by people who paid the full price on purchase. Then the down payment decreased to 75 per cent, then from 50 to 40 to 20 and finally as low as 10 per cent.

One morning Somraj showed up early at Puri's house in Vikrampura. He usually came at this hour if he had some news to give or wanted some advice, habitually chewing on a neem twig to clean his teeth. Kanak had very little liking for Somraj, and hated the sight of anyone cleaning his teeth.

Somraj called out to Kanak as soon as he arrived, 'Bhabhiji, I've something to tell you.'

He said when he saw her, 'You must speak with Puri bhappa. You're paying five hundred rupees in rent every year for this house. The houses in ModelTown are going for a yearly instalment of 10 per cent of the full price. One-and-a-half or two thousand a year is not a big amount, and the house becomes your property. It's an open, airy area, go and see for yourself. The layout of each house is such that one half of it can be rented out.'

This was the first thing Somraj had ever said that Kanak liked. She had been feeling uncomfortable in the cramped rooms and narrow stairways of their house, which was wedged between a row of dwellings, with more houses across the gali. She had been brought up in a spacious house. After her sister's marriage, Kanak had liked going to Kanta's house in Model

Town in Lahore, and the images of its lawns and flower beds came back to her mind. 'Jaya would be so happy and healthy in such a place.'

'Bhraji, a roomier place would be so much nicer. Who wouldn't want that, but how would we manage two thousand every year? As is it we just get by every month.'

Puri chimed in with Kanak, 'We can't take on the responsibility of paying back such a large sum for the next fifteen years. We should wait until we can really afford the house. There'd hardly be over five thousand rupees in the bank accounts of the press and *Nazir*. I've just finished paying back Kriparam his one thousand rupees. I need cash for paper supplies and for hundreds of other expenses. To take a loan of twenty thousand...' Puri said, arching his eyebrows. Owing to his being raised in underprivileged circumstances, the mere thought of a large debt was making him nervous.

Somraj's reply to Puri's hesitations was, 'Why do you think that way? You do have to take a loan but the house becomes your property in the end.'

'No, it won't. Until we've paid off the loan the house will belong to the government. Also, what about the interest payments?...'

'Why think of the interest? Won't you save the rent? Each house has two identical halves. If you rent out one, half the loan will be paid off by the rental income. Remember, the value of the property will appreciate by 50 per cent after only two or three years.'

'Namaste, Puri bhappaji,' said a visitor named Suraj Prakash as he joined them.

When Suraj Prakash learned the topic of conversation, he said, spreading his fleshy palm in front of Somraj's face, 'Yaar, who are you trying to explain these details to about money and property! Our friend here is the writer–artist type. What would he know of such worldly affairs? All he wants is a simple meal twice a day. A cup of tea will do if there's nothing to eat. People like him are driven by their imagination. Every time they put their pens to paper, they create gems. Other people may earn thousands of rupees by publishing what they write, but a man like him does not care. You haven't yet figured out the true Puri bhappa. He has no attachments, just like a fakir. It's you who must take care of him.'

Suraj Prakash raised his voice, 'We're not telling him to earn the fortune, but one certainly needs a roof over one's head. He's married, has a baby daughter.' He said, edging forward excitedly, 'Look, I've bought a three-kanal, 1,500 square yards plot in Model Town. I'll have a house of my own design built on it later, but Puri bhappa should not let slip past him this opportunity of buying a house.'

'But he doesn't agree...' Somraj said.

'Don't listen to him! You apply for a B-type bungalow at 10 per cent for him, and leave the rest of the deal to me!' Suraj Prakash slapped his chest with his hand as he said 'me'.

'No, no. I don't want to buy anything on credit.' Puri waved his hand to emphasize his point. 'When I have the money, I'll buy the house or the land.'

'How can you say that, Puri bhappa?' Suraj Prakash said in surprise. 'You may have the money later, but the house or land may not be available by then. What's the risk? You won't lose money because it'll remain safe in the form of your property, and that'll soon appreciate by 25 or 50 per cent. Didn't that happen in the case of Krishna Nagar and Model Town in Lahore? People bought land at fifty rupees a *marla* and resold it at three to four hundred a marla. Genda Shah made a fortune that way.'

'No, no. That's not my point. I don't want anything on credit.' Puri repeated his objection.

'Listen!' Suraj Prakash waived his hand in front of Puri's face, 'I've bought land so I can't buy a house as well.' He looked at Somraj, 'Let Puri bhappa give you the first down payment of three thousand rupees and you apply on his behalf. I know he'll be uneasy paying the necessary bribes.' He slapped his chest again with his hand, 'And leave the rest to me. If he wants I will lend him the three thousand. Where's the question of buying on credit? I only stand to profit from this deal. The rent from the house will pay off the interest on the loan.'

Kanak could barely contain her enthusiasm for moving to a bungalow from the congestion of the gali. However Puri wanted to weigh up every aspect of the proposal. He could not agree to Suraj Prakash's offer just like that. He also was a little wary of Suraj Prakash because of a past experience.

Puri had first met Suraj Prakash in Lahore. This was the time when Ghaus Mohammad, the owner of the Adayara Munavvar Publishing Company, had asked Puri to ghostwrite a history textbook for a professor. Since by the time the textbook was ready, Ghaus Mohammed had become the victim of sectarian riots, Puri had offered the manuscript to Suraj Prakash, who not only had refused to publish the textbook, but treated Puri rather disrespectfully.

Suraj Prakash had taken up his textbook publishing business again in Jalandhar. At the time of the elections for the Refugee Association in 1949 he had come out openly in support of the editor of *Nazir* and Sood's trusted lieutenant. When Puri had expressed his gratitude for Suraj Prakash's backing, he had affably waved aside Puri's thanks, saying that he was only supporting an honest person fighting for a good cause. Although Puri had been greeting Suraj Prakash with a casual namaste on the odd occasion of their meeting, he had never mentioned the subject of their encounter in Lahore.

In November 1949 Sood had had Puri appointed as a member of the committee for the selection of textbooks for the high school curriculum. Suraj Prakash had come to visit Puri one evening in February of the next year, but Puri had not been at home and had suspected the textbook publisher of having some ulterior motive for his visit. Puri knew about the underhand dealings in the selection of textbooks. In his own high-minded view he was opposed against any corrupt practice in the field of education, which he saw as a betrayal and disservice to the country. He was particularly sensitive to the responsibility that had been conferred on him.

When Suraj Prakash had returned the next evening, it turned out that he had come only to give Puri news about the clandestine activities of the Rashtriya Swayamsewak Sangh. The subject of his personal business interest had not arisen. He talked mostly about Puri's column 'Haat Bazaar Main' or some other literary subject. He related several amusing anecdotes and revealed the political shenanigans of Puri's rivals in the Congress. He appeared to be, for all practical purposes, simply a supporter of Puri's views and an admirer of his writing. Puri had written several articles in *Nazir* in favour of the demand that Hindi be made one of the official languages of Punjab. Although Suraj Prakash scarcely knew Hindi, he supported the cause.

Under the British Raj, Urdu written in Arabic script had been imposed on Punjab as the official language of the administration and as the medium of education and learning. Knowledge of Urdu thus became essential for finding a government job and necessary for literary pursuits. The Hindus, Muslims and Sikhs of Punjab conversed in many dialects of Punjabi in their homes and in social situations, but used Urdu only in education and official business. Although Urdu had served as the language and the script for their literary creations, neither Hindus nor Sikhs had accepted it as the first language in their culture. With the newly acquired right of self-determination after Partition, neither group was willing to tolerate the continued dominance of Urdu.

The supporters of Hindi and Punjabi argued intensely in public as to which language should replace Urdu. At the root of their disagreement was the natural preference for one's own first language as well as the fear of irreversible dominance by the favoured community. Master Tara Singh, who had once pulled out his sword and challenged the Muslim League supporters to make demands for a Pakistan, had voiced along with his co-religionists their claim for a separate homeland for the Sikhs. The Hindus regarded this as an unreasonable demand by a minority group. The Hindus continued to speak Punjabi and argue in Punjabi against what they regarded as the unwarranted imposition of Punjabi. A compromise proposal to grant equal official status to both Hindi and Punjabi was opposed by both factions as each saw it as the victory for the opposite side. Suraj Prakash like Puri was against giving equal status to both languages. He would say, 'I stand to profit if the prescribed textbooks are published in both languages, but one should not always think of only making money. One must also consider what is good for the country and the people.' Puri felt relieved that Suraj Prakash had no selfish axe to grind, but was simply being friendly.

Behind Puri's reluctance to invest in a house in Model Town was the desire in his heart to be able to live in a place befitting his new position and status. His objections were defeated by Kanak's enthusiasm for a bigger and more spacious residence and in March 1951 they moved into their new house in Model Town. Although the house had two identical halves, with a kitchen and bathroom in each section, Puri felt that renting out the other half would be neither convenient nor appropriate to his advanced social position. A separate room was needed to receive visitors, another for Puri's office. Kanak wanted a room of her own. She put a bed for Puri in his office, and took the room next to the bathroom for herself and for Jaya's cot. Usha was sitting for her BA exam that year. As there was no electricity yet in the Basti Nigar Khan house, she pleaded with her mother to let her stay at Puri's house. Kanak used the second kitchen as a bedroom for Heeran, Jaya's ayah.

Puri had been apprehensive that the move to Model Town would make it difficult for them to live within their budget. In the first place there was the cost of commuting to the city and to their office. Kanak could not come home for lunch as before. They also had to go to a bazaar in the city for the simplest of needs. As Heeran alone could not look after the baby and the house, they had to employ another servant. Puri had been drawing 250 rupees every month for himself from the press account, now he added to it another 125 as salary for Kanak. With the thought of the yearly payment of 2500 rupees for the house constantly niggling at his mind, any extra money spent became a sore point with him. Puri thought that Kanak was to blame for the extra expenses, '...She was the one who so much wanted to live in Model Town! Isn't it a wife's responsibility to manage the household expenses?'

At Basti Nigar Khan, even with Puri's mother keeping a dairy buffalo, the household expenses had been less than 250 rupees per month for a family of five. Masterji and Bhagwanti had been more than content with their situation. The mother-in-law would occasionally remark in Kanak's hearing, 'If the wife spends her time sitting in a chair in the office, who would take care of the household?' Irked by such taunts and Puri's persistent irritability, Kanak would sometimes burst out, 'All right. I'm not clever enough. You can manage the house yourself.' She would remember how Gill was living on his 150 rupees per month, and envy him his tranquil life. What was the point of having creature comforts and a good salary if the chase after the mirage of an easy life was making them so unhappy? There was no longer any semblance of the dreams they had dreamt together of devoting themselves to art and literature. Puri had written not even one short story in the past three years. Kanak had begun one, but had not had the time to finish it. When she tried to discuss this case of writer's block with Puri, he just shrugged it off, 'Let's first get settled down. There'll be time for writing later.' If Kanak wanted to read something out aloud to Puri or to suggest to him that he should see a particularly fine piece of writing, she would find him preoccupied and unable to clear his mind of other problems.

Suraj Prakash confided in Puri that he had to get his textbooks printed in Delhi, Allahabad and Aligarh because of a problem with the printing presses in Jalandhar. Nine of his publications had been prescribed as texts for courses taught in the middle school, Matric, Intermediate and BA levels. He also published booklets of notes and guides to textbooks. Hem Raj of Vidya Sadan was his long-time business rival. Whenever Suraj Prakash engaged a press to print his textbooks, Hem Raj offered higher rates of payments to have his own books printed by the same press. Consequently, the textbooks ordered by Suraj Prakash would be delayed and reached the market after those issued by his competitors.

Suraj Prakash had a business proposition for Puri: Puri could install a letterpress cylinder and print all textbooks for Suraj Prakash. Otherwise Suraj Prakash would have to invest in his own press. Printing the textbooks would have been worth about 15,000 rupees every year, more than sufficient to buy a second-hand letterpress. Suraj Prakash was even willing to advance that sum to Puri against the cost of having his textbooks printed in the future.

Puri had in any case been thinking of adding a letterpress machine to his establishment. With Hindi and Gurumukhi replacing Urdu as the official state languages, there was less and less work for the litho cylinder. Not to move ahead with the times, Puri realized, would be suicidal, and accepted the offer of Suraj Prakash.

By the beginning of 1951, the chief minister of Punjab had found himself powerless to administer the state because of the factions of moderates and hardliners battling in the Punjab Legislative Assembly and the disagreements within the Cabinet. The next state elections were not due for another ten months. The governor of Punjab, following directives from the Central government, postponed the formation of a new Cabinet and took charge of the administration himself.

In Punjab, as everywhere else in the country, people were feeling embittered and disillusioned by the blatant nepotism, high-handedness and widespread corruption in the post-independence state governments. Those who had been given the title of 'Rai Bahadur' under the Raj for toadying to the British and former civil servants and hangers-on of the British government now sported crisp white Gandhi caps as members of the Congress party. Funds for the party were no longer raised in the form of the membership fee of a quarter of a rupee or by issuing receipts for one rupee donation to the party coffers. Now the contributions came from industrialists and big companies as cheques for thousands and hundreds of thousands of rupees. Congress party members, who had held jobs with salaries of a 100 or 125 rupees per month only four years before, had now begun to draw ten times more as members of some government committee or by virtue of being related to some government minister.

The sons of ministers, who had failed to pass even the easy high school exam, were dissatisfied with their salaries of over one thousand rupees as heads of nondescript government departments. Any position below that of managing director of a company was deemed unthinkable for the son-in-law of a minister.

The capitalist class, who saw making huge profits as their dharma, were hopeful of recovering their outlays by making generous donations to the Congress party. Reports of scandals involving big industrial companies and elected representatives and rumours of a nexus between the two were circulating widely. Disgusted by such exposés, the public had begun to despise any member of the Legislative Assembly (MLA) as *mailay*—tainted. No other political organization was strong enough or well enough organized to challenge the supremacy of the Congress party. The two potential rivals of the Congress, the Rashtriya Swayamsewak Sangh and the Communist Party of India, had broken out into open revolt against the government thus giving it a legal excuse to suppress them. Resigned to the fact that the Congress would win the forthcoming general election, people would say, 'Let the Congress continue in power. It has been bleeding us dry for the last five years. It will soon have its fill. If another party comes into power it will first suck our blood as much as the Congress has done, and still not be satisfied.'

In an atmosphere of such hostility towards the Congress party and distrust of its leaders, there were a few exceptions. In case of Sood there was neither any suspicion of dishonestly making money, nor any rumours of acquiring property by graft. Even Sood's many detractors conceded that he had no craving for the traditional lures of *zar-joru-zamin*, gold, women and land. Hundreds of people had profited through their association with Sood, hundreds more were hopeful of doing similarly. They were his rank-and-file supporters, whose dedication and loyalty were beyond question. His grip on the Punjab Parliamentary Board was firm, and now that his ministerial duties were temporarily removed from his shoulders, he had ample time and opportunity to strategize for the coming elections. Since his own election to the House was almost a certainty, the packing of the legislative assembly with as many of his candidates as possible had become his main concern.

Sood imposed that Puri should stand as a Congress candidate in the elections. Puri discussed the subject first with Kanak, and then again with her in Gill's presence. Both of them were lukewarm about the idea of

Puri's candidacy. *Nazir* had generally been critical of the previous Congress administration and particularly of its self-seeking members of that legislative assembly. The weekly's editorial policy had been to emphasize Gandhiji's ruling laid down during his last days that instead of winning elections to form the government, Congress workers should remember their own grass roots and serve the people of India. Neither Gill nor Kanak could approve of a volte-face in Puri's thinking by contesting the election as a candidate for the Assembly. Kanak's enthusiasm for Puri's candidacy had dampened after she had observed the sad reality of the Congress administration in Punjab and the truly contemptible nature of its members in Lucknow.

Puri's argument was that it would be ridiculous to allow burglars to enter one's house and then stand outside and call for help. The appropriate course of action, therefore, was to get elected to the House and strengthen Sood's hand rather than to oppose the government openly like the communists had unsuccessfully tried to do. Also, as an MLA, one could use democratic and constitutional means to ensure that the Congress remained true to the socialistic policies adopted at the party's plenary session in Karachi in 1931. In Puri's view it was imperative to check the growing pro-feudal and pro-capitalist influence on the Congress government platform. Besides, it would amount to national suicide to allow the responsibility of representing the people fall into the hands of vested interests. Masterji, Nayyar, Somraj and many others agreed with Puri. Pandit Girdharilal had written a letter to lend his support to Puri's idea. Kanak could do nothing but hold her tongue.

Puri wanted to make full use of *Nazir* in order to boost the election campaign for Sood and himself. Rather than be accused of self-promotion, he thought it prudent to name Kanak as managing editor instead of himself, and to appoint Gill as the editor of the weekly.

Gill had decided to honour his pledge of friendship to Puri. He thought up a creative way to combine his own views with Puri's expectation, and introduced in *Nazir* a forum for discussion and debate on the responsibilities of a citizen in a democratic society. In his editorials he would forcefully argue that any indifference to the governmental policies and the legislative process should be considered burying one's head in sand and neglect of civic duty. He would also urge the public to consider their options carefully before finally casting their vote in the coming elections. At the same time he would warn the readers of *Nazir* to be objective rather than emotional and vote for the Congress candidates with progressive ideas and policies rather than for a motley collection of political parties in disarray. He would remind the public that the Congress was a representative of the majority of Indians, and if the public remained watchful, the Congress would live up to people's expectations and fulfil its promises.

Puri was greatly impressed with and appreciative of Gill's writing skills. He would miss Gill if the latter did not come to visit ModelTown in the evening.

One day in June that year when Kanak arrived at the *Nazir* office at ten in the morning, she found Gill speaking respectfully and kindly to an old, sickly-looking man. He introduced him to Kanak.

Comrade Daulatram Azad was released from prison two months ago. Since then whenever he found a job at some workshop or factory, a CID plainclothesman hovered around to keep an eye on him. Who would have wanted to hire a marked man and alienate the police? The poor soul lacked the wherewithal to start any business or trade.

Azad had studied only up to Urdu Middle School. He had been working as a lathe operator in Rawalpindi in 1930 when he joined *Atishichakkar*, an underground group that sought to free India from the British by armed insurgency, and had begun to make casings for small explosive devices for the group. He was among the suspects arrested after bombs had been exploded at several places in Punjab.

Azad was convicted for armed conspiracy and given a seven-year prison sentence. In prison he had come in close contact with some university-educated left-wing intellectuals, who had completely transformed his ideas of how India could be freed from foreign rule. Instead of sporadic individual attempts to fight the British, Azad had begun to dream of fomenting a people's revolution that would create a proletarian state. By the time he was released, his younger brother had taken on the responsibility of supporting the family. Azad had joined the Communist Party and had begun to organize workers on the 'party wage' of twenty-five rupees per month. He had been thrown into jail a second time in 1940 after the Communist Party had declared its opposition to the imperialist war in Europe. He had been released in 1942 with other communist inmates when the party line was changed in support of the war, and had gone back to organizing the working classes. He was arrested again and sent to prison a third time in 1948 when the Communist Party called for open revolt against the Congress government.

The communists interned during 1948 and 1949 were acting according to the party dictate of 'struggle from outside and struggle inside the jail'. They staged protest demonstrations in defiance of the jail regulations. They provoked the prison officers by shouting 'Down with Congress imperialism! Down with the capitalist government! Down with the Congress party government! Give us jobs and bread, or hand over your power. Just one more push and out with this rotten government! All power to the rule of the workers!' How could the prison officers, now loyal to the Congress government, tolerate such open defiance? Those, who had beaten up people shouting slogans such as 'Down with British imperialists' during the British Raj, now had to stifle slogans and chants opposing the Congress government. Azad and other communists like him, hardened from serving prison terms under the British rule, knew how to counter repressive and authoritarian measures under the Congress raj by calling the prison officers such names as 'government dogs' and 'prison mongrels'!

The Congress government, in accordance with its avowed faith in non-violence and popular democracy, had introduced many revisions in correctional regulations. Under the British Raj, the meals for the inmates had been chapattis made of wheat mixed with coarse grain flour, and daal served in thalis and bowls made of tin. Under Congress rules the chapattis began to be made of wheat and the food was served in thalis and bowls of brass, and an occasional lump of sweet gur. Instead of knee-length shorts, the inmates were issued ankle-length pyjama trousers. But the shackles and truncheons wielded by the warders had remained the same, as had the cells for solitary confinement. Police intervention in the jail affairs had increased, and the prisoner's legal rights were fewer.

Under the British Raj, Azad had been housed in the B-Class jail barracks meant for political prisoners. His rations had included bread, butter, meat and milk, and he had been allowed to borrow books from the prison library. When he had been released from the Deoli Camp after serving the two-and-a-half-year prison term for armed conspiracy, he had gained 10 pounds.

The Congress party that had once believed in facing bullets and baton charges with bowed heads and peaceful resistance when fighting the British had now adopted a different policy for communists who believed in violence. Since the government had proof that the communists were preparing for armed insurgency, the question of their legal and democratic rights and treating them with any leniency did not arise. Azad and other communist prisoners were made to wear, for weeks at a stretch, two-foot-long shackles that kept their feet apart, and were beaten with truncheons and dragged along the ground inside the jail even when they tried to make a peaceful protest, in the Congress party's own satyagraha style. Locked up in solitary confinement, they went on hunger strikes for weeks on end, and were fed milk forcibly through rubber tubes inserted in their nostrils. After suffering torture and humiliation for months, they were to learn one day through newspapers that the party had once again changed its line and they had been ordered to work among the masses after their release.

During the upheaval caused by sectarian riots in Rawalpindi, Azad's younger brother had been murdered and his wife had gone missing without a trace. Azad had been barely able to escape with his aged mother, and his nephew and niece. The following year he had ended up again in jail. On being released, he had learned that his fourteen-year-old nephew was working for eight annas per day at a roadside cycle repair shop in Ambala Cantonment whose owner continually slapped the boy around. His mother, Azad discovered, had found work as a maid for a khadi-wearing lawyer, and his nine-year-old niece was taking care of the lawyer's baby boy, in return for free meals and a total of fifteen rupees per month for both.

The Communist Party, Azad found, had been weakened considerably after its abortive attempt at the people's revolution. Only a small number of 'important' comrades had been chosen to work for a party wage, and he was not among them. Besides, he now wanted to take care of his aged mother and send his nephew and niece to school. He knew how to work a lathe, but who would give him a job with the CID shadowing him. For a while he drove a cycle rickshaw, but his weak lungs could not take the strain and he soon developed a cough and began to spit blood-spotted phlegm.

Gill had got his first introduction to Marxist literature through Azad in Rawalpindi while studying for his Matric exam. When Gill entered university, Azad would join him and other politically minded young men and quietly listen as they discussed Marxist ideology. Gill's expulsion from the party for disobeying the dictate against Sikh men cutting their long hair had infuriated Azad. Gill had continued to treat Azad with respect and later on, when working at the *Sitara* weekly, had occasionally helped Azad with money. Azad had come to Jalandhar after seeing Gill's name as the editor of *Nazir*.

Azad's heart-rending story deeply moved Kanak. She vented her anger on the Communist Party policy that had caused Azad so much suffering, 'What's wrong with the party, it changes its policy so often. First it opposed the war, and then the same war became the People's War. In 1948 it was total revolution, in '50 it became the bourgeois democratic revolution. No consideration for how many lives such dithering may have ruined.'

'And what has your Congress been up to? What about Gandhiji?' Azad replied to Kanak's show of sympathy by glaring at her. 'At the time of his non-cooperation movement and civil disobedience he made thousands of students leave their studies, made thousands of others give up their government jobs, millions suffered police beatings and went to jail, and then your Bapu felt that he had committed "a Himalayan blunder" and called off the movement. He told everyone to make bonfires of foreign-made cloth, and then told them to stop doing it. He went on his Dandi march to break the salt law, and then gave it up. He launched his jungle Satyagraha, and asked farmers not to pay land revenue, and let that also peter out. He called for a boycott of the legislative councils, and then accepted the existence of the same councils. He called for a boycott of the Round Table Conference, then went and took part in it. At first he renounced the boycott of the war, and then himself denounced it. He opposed the partition of India, then accepted it. There are hundreds of instances of Gandhi and the Congress changing their policies at the slightest excuse. Don't you try to lecture me! I've been fighting for the country's freedom since before you were even born. The Congress has changed its final goal so often. Sometimes it wanted dominion status, then full freedom under the Empire, then complete independence, then a republic, then the Ramrajya, then capitalism, then socialism. Our party has always had one single objective: dictatorship of the proletariat! We only changed our tactics. You congresswallahs dare to preach to us? First go and look at yourself in the mirror!'

Azad began to cough and wheeze heavily. Gill tried to pacify him by saying 'It's all right! That's enough!' but Azad kept up his tirade between bouts of a hacking cough.

Kanak's face fell at Azad's rebukes, but she managed to reply, 'Respected brother, the Congress and Gandhiji cannot be blamed for their mistakes. Gandhiji did what God asked him to do, but the communists claim to be guided by rational considerations only.'

Azad reflected for a few moments with his mouth open, then clapped his hands and burst into laughter, 'Arrey, she's very quick, really a sharp young woman!'

Gill and Kanak told Azad to bring his family to Jalandhar, and gave assurances that they would be looked after.

Puri also expressed sympathy for Azad, 'He has suffered because of his political beliefs. We really don't require another employee, but let's try and accommodate him at the press. I don't think I'll be able to pay him more than forty or forty-five rupees per month.'

Gill pleaded for Azad, 'They are a family of four. Even the most ordinary accommodation will not be available for less than ten or fifteen rupees monthly. He'll need money also for his medical treatment. You've helped out so many people. Soodji has been very generous with assisting his supporters get official permits for buying and selling certain items. Visheshwar Dayal and Khem Singh got permits for five tons of tin. Soodji may not be a government minister for the moment, but he still is very influential. The government officials also know how powerful he is and that in six months from now he'll be back in the new council of ministers. Get poor Azad a quota for at least one ton of some commodity. That way he won't be a strain on you.'

Puri thought for a while, then said, 'I could speak to someone, but Azad is a member of the Communist Party.'

'Is he not a political sufferer? Are Communist Party members not political sufferers?' Kanak cut in.

'He indeed is a communist, but he's old and sick,' Gill said, to cool tempers. 'He went to jail for revolutionary activities and also as a conscientious objector. The Communist Party is no longer illegal. The government should treat all political parties impartially.'

'Yes, that's true. Well, let me see what can be done,' Puri conceded. 'Perhaps all the permits have not yet been issued. Soodji also wanted political sufferers to get a small quota of permits.'

Puri spoke with some people and had Azad's name included in a list of those who were to receive quotas for tin sheets. Gill was relieved that Azad now would be able to set up a small business, or lacking the necessary investment, could resell, as some others had done, his quota to another businessman and have a monthly income of 125 or 150 rupees. Delays continued to plague the quota allotment process. Sood had asked the district supply officer to consult with him before issuing the new quotas, but was himself often absent, being in Delhi or Ambala or Simla.

In November Sood ordered the list to be redrafted. Azad's name was dropped for Shankar Lal Mathani who got a quota for three tons of tin sheets.

Puri explained his helplessness to Kanak, 'I tried my best but Soodji got the list altered. What could I do?'

Kanak blew up, 'But you gave your word. Gillji has been supporting Azad for the past five months. Doesn't Soodji realize what he did was unfair? Azad is a political sufferer, what has Mathani done for the country?'

'You don't understand, so don't just shoot your mouth off.' Puri snapped back at her in English. 'Mathani has a lot of influence in the Sindhi community. Azad can always be helped some other time.'

'Shame on this election of yours, and on such lying politicians!' Kanak blurted out, then realized that she had said too much and regretted her outburst.

'What do you mean?' Puri said with rage in his eyes. 'Who do you think you are? I'm not your puppet!'

Kanak covered her face with her aanchal and went to the back veranda. Jaya screamed and burst into tears, but Puri continued to rant and rave for some time.

The rainy season was coming to an end. The deadline for the selection of textbooks prescribed in the state curriculum of Punjab was not far off. Suraj Prakash continued to drop in for a chat in the evenings. Kanak did not join in the conversations, nor did Puri discuss the matter with her, but Kanak knew that the textbooks were being revised and new ones introduced to bring about a change in the educational system. Suraj Prakash stood to gain from publishing and selling the textbooks and Puri from printing them in his press. A letterpress cylinder recently added to the Kamaal Press had been operating in day and night shifts in an improvised shed under a corrugated iron roof in the courtyard of the press. Puri also seemed relieved at the lightening of his financial worries. He had complained, on several occasions, about the ever-increasing difficulty in commuting to the office and about the time wasted in travelling to his social engagements, and had even wondered aloud, 'If a small second-hand car could be found.' Kanak had thought, 'That's not a bad idea.'

Himmat Rai, a retired accountant, lived in the bungalow next to Puri. Himmat Rai's son Jivat Rai, a sub-inspector in the Coaching and Goods division in the Railways, was posted to Amritsar. God had blessed him generously with two sons and four daughters after just ten years of marriage. Since there was an acute housing shortage in Amritsar, Jivat Rai's family was staying with his father.

Himmat Rai was often exasperated at the cost of his grandchildren's schooling, 'In my time, all we used until the primary school was a *takhti* wooden tablet and a slate for writing. We never bought the text and exercise books that are now required, until Matric. In my days, the eighth grade students had four, at the most five, textbooks. Now there's no end to the subjects and the textbooks on the syllabus. The school bags have become bulky as a lawyer's briefcase on his way to the law courts. And the children are neither taught nor do they learn anything at the school. Every day one of the kids needs a new textbook or an exercise book. How can poor people afford all this? Is this a way to spread education or to make it more difficult?'

Kanak knew that the state of her father's finances was not very solid. Five textbooks published by him had been on the school curriculum before Partition, but the booksellers had failed to make payments due to him from the past. He had brought a used treadle printing machine after coming to Delhi, and in the following two years had managed to bring out only two rather inconsequential publications. Puri had made a special effort to have them prescribed as texts, but the textbook selection committee had eventually removed them from the list because of their poor availability.

Pandit Girdharilal was still struggling to re-establish himself as a textbook publisher. It was no longer possible to earn a respectable income by publishing literary books that sold at a trade discount of 33 per cent, and sometimes even more. Therefore, returns were too low, as Panditji had found, even if 500 copies of a literary work sold in a year. It was increasingly difficult to get a book prescribed as a text unless the publisher was able to advance royalties to the writers who had contacts to push the particular book onto the state school curriculum.

Panditji had written to Kanak that he had laboriously compiled a useful and interesting book on civic duties meant for teenagers, and was doing his best to present it before the next meeting of the textbook committee. Kanak had given the letter to Puri.

The day of the meeting arrived. The thought that Puri might forget about her father's book was constantly worrying Kanak, but the bitter memory of the Azad incident was still fresh in her mind. The fear of embarrassment and of losing face before Gill had made her blurt out harsh words, and she could not bear the thought of it happening again. 'Who knows what assurances Puriji has given to other people? Would he again take my recommendations seriously?'

The families of Nayyar and Puri were finding less and less time to visit each other. Kanak's mother had sent the customary presents for both her daughters to Kanta on the occasion of the Karwa chauth festival, and Kanak's share had to reach her before the day of the festival. Kanta's servant was down with fever; therefore, she herself had to bring the presents over to Kanak. Nayyar came along for a visit. The incident of Azad's quota was less than a week old and the relations between Kanak and Puri were still strained. Kanak was careful to conceal the signs of the quarrel with her husband, especially from her brother-in-law, but Nayyar could guess something was amiss. He looked meaningfully into Kanak's eyes, but acted as if he had not noticed anything.

Kanak had had a close and trusting relationship with her brother-in-law and some feeling of confidence in him that had once given her the courage to admit her love for Puri to Nayyar and ask for his support. She felt that she could die of embarrassment that her love for the same person was now causing her to feel ashamed to look Nayyar in the eye and having him feel sorry for her.

After Kanta and Nayyar left, Kanak sat brooding, 'What has come over both of us? We no longer talk of love.' But if she did feel a romantic urge lately, it subsided when she looked at Puri. She would remember how violently Puri had reacted with irritation, anger and self-disgust after their tender and intimate moments, and how he had talked about Urmila and boasted of his sexual prowess, and such memories would weigh her down with sadness.

Kanak reasoned with herself, 'If it's in his nature to behave that way, I can still love him. We are husband and wife, just like my sister and Nayyar.'

The next day was Karwa chauth, observed by married women all over the country as a fast day in the belief that they would have the same husband in the next life. Kanak did not believe in the ritual, but still observed the fast. She could not get up before sunrise to eat *saragi* to sustain her, yet decided to go without food all day, the thought of her argument with her husband deepening her sadness. She thought of what Panditji had written in his letter, and realized that she was reluctant to ask her husband to help her father in his need. 'Is this the beginning of a rift between us? What's happening to our marriage?'

She reproached herself, 'Can this rift between us be my fault? If it's in his nature to behave in a certain way, he can't help it.' She resolved that she would not let her own nature get the better of her, that she would suppress her ego. All day she remained quiet and lost in her thoughts.

At the office, not eating anything or drinking water all day made her feel dizzy around five o'clock, so she had a cup of tea. She rang the bell to summon the peon and asked him to call a rickshaw for her.

Gill asked, 'What's the matter? You're very quiet. Feeling well?'

'I'm on a fast and haven't eaten anything. I feel rather weak. I just need some rest,' she tried to smile as she replied.

On reaching home Kanak could spend only a little time with Jaya before going to her room to lie down. She lay quietly, thinking about what had been on her mind all day and strengthening her resolve. It was growing dark, but Puri had not yet returned. She was beginning to nod off when Heeran came into the room and asked, 'Beti, how are you? Want me to switch on the light?'

Kanak said, 'I'm all right. Yes, switch on the light.' She looked at her wristwatch—it was seven o'clock. She asked Heeran to switch off the light again and drifted in and out of sleep as she waited for Puri.

'Come, beti, and look at the moon.'

Kanak had observed the fast in the past because it had been a custom in her family, but had seldom bothered to perform the rituals such as looking at the moon. Yet she got up and went to the veranda.

Heeran held a small lighted clay lamp and a flat sieve, and had put down a *patra*, the low wooden seat. Kanak had seen her mother perform the ritual, and had repeated it herself three years before when her mother-in-law was staying with her. Heeran had made all the preparations for the ceremony in the previous two years and Kanak had gone through the motions just to please her.

She stood on the patra, and took the lamp and the sieve from Heeran. She placed the lamp inside the sieve and raised it to look at the moon through it.

Heeran began to recite the Karwa mantra, 'After adorning myself in sixteen different ways, I stand on this patra on my roof and make the offering...'

Kanak listened quietly but attentively to Heeran, with a good feeling in her heart. She made a silent wish for the long life and well-being of her husband.

Puri called out to the servant as he entered the house, 'Chaila, give me dinner.'

Kanak got up when she heard Puri enter. She took out a fresh towel, went to the back veranda where Puri was sitting at the dining table, and said, 'Here, take this and wash your hands and face. I'll bring the thali of food to your room.'

Puri said, 'What's the matter with my face and hands? They're all right.'

'Hai, the streets are so dusty. Besides, going around one gets covered in sweat,' Kanak said tenderly. 'Chaila will bring you some water. I'll get the food.'

Kanak brought food up in one thali for both of them. As they ate, what she wanted to say to him was on the tip of her tongue, but Puri was preoccupied with his own thoughts about the forthcoming elections, 'The Congress will have to give at least forty seats to the Sikhs. The candidates of the Akali Dal will naturally be all Sikhs. There's no chance for the Hindu candidates in the areas where the Sikhs are in the majority. That means that the Sikhs will also be in the majority in the Assembly. It can't be helped, even if they are only 33 per cent of the population.'

After dinner, Kanak herself brought water for Puri to wash his hands, handed him the towel, and followed him to his room. As Puri lay down on his charpoy, she sat on its edge and came straight to the point, 'Pitaji had written a letter about his new book, you remember?'

'Hmm,' Puri said, deep in thought. 'It might be more difficult this time around. Well, I'll speak to Jodh Singh about it. These people want bribes for even the smallest of favours.'

'Ask them to read the book,' said Kanak.

'Who reads the book!'

'But you have to do this for pitaji,' Kanak said with pleading eyes.

'Why not,' said Puri, entwining his fingers with Kanak's.

Unpleasant memories filled her with dread, but she did not want the evening to turn sour. She said with a smile, 'I want to sleep. I was on a fast, *na*, and I'm feeling a little dizzy.'

'What fast?' asked Puri, reaching for her.

866   *Yashpal*

'Wah, don't you know? I observe only one, the Karwa chauth.'

'That's superstitious nonsense,' he said, clasping her head to his chest.

Kanak took a deep breath, and closed her eyes. Pulling herself away at this moment would not have been a tactful thing to do. She did want a bit of romance, but...

Chapter 11

TARA HAD BEGUN TO HAVE A SENSE OF EMOTIONAL STABILITY AFTER HER TWO years with the department of rehabilitation. Sita, whom she had taken under her wing, had been training rather diligently to become a Hindi stenographer.

Ratan and Sheelo had at first lived together for five months in a by-lane off Pachkuian Road. Ratan had declared to his parents that either he would move back to their house with Sheelo, or stay separately. After five months of silence, Babu Govindram had finally yielded. Ratan's mother had personally gone to Ratan's rented room and had very affectionately brought Sheelo home as her daughter-in-law. She had said nothing about Sheelo's arrival to her neighbours, and who was there to ask! One Sunday after he had moved back, Ratan had come to take Tara to his parents' home. They had been very keen to meet her.

On that day when Tara had stayed with the family till late evening, Ratan had inquired about Puri, Masterji and chachi, Tara's mother. Tara had simply said that her brother was the editor of *Nazir* in Jalandhar, and the rest of the family must also be fine.

Ratan had been too preoccupied with scratching out a living in Delhi to look at any newspaper. On knowing about Puri and others, he had excitedly told Tara about his plan to write to Puri and also about visiting him in Jalandhar.

Tara had replied in so many words that there was no need to meet anybody or to write to anyone about her. Sheelo had sensed what was on Tara's mind, and had convinced Ratan and also her mother-in-law not to dig too much into her past. No need was felt to warn Babu Govindram.

Babu Govindram had applied for a government loan, on the basis of claims allowed for land and property that had been abandoned in West Pakistan, as compensation for his family home in Hafizabad and the two houses he had owned in Krishna Nagar in Lahore. He was an old hand at dealing with bureaucratic machinery, and knew all kinds of ways to get a job done at government offices. Ratan had informed his father that Tara was with the department that dealt with the claims, and that he should not worry too much about the loan. Tara had indeed got the work done in next to no time. Babu Govindram, who did not expect to have the process completed so quickly even after spending an extra Rs 200, was brimming with affection and gratitude for Tara and wanted to do something to help her. He had asked Ratan for Puri's address, and had told Ratan later that if a reply came to the letter he had written, he might visit Masterji and Bhagwanti in Jalandhar.

Ratan had guessed that his father must have written something about Tara. He decided to wait and see, without alarming her.

A few days later two envelopes mailed from Jalandhar were delivered at Babu Govindram's address, one for him, the other for Tara care of him.

On his return home on the day of delivery, Ratan saw the envelope addressed to Tara. He went to Daryaganj the same evening and handing the envelope to Tara, said defensively, 'I didn't think it proper to tell anything about you to babuji. He couldn't contain his eagerness and wrote to Puri bhappa. He wrote back that Masterji, your mother, Usha and Hari were all fine and hale and hearty. Puri bhappa is now married.'

Tara listened to Ratan with her eyes lowered. She opened the envelope after he left. In a long, affectionate letter, Puri reassured Tara that he would personally come to Delhi to know her story. He expressed surprise that Tara had not been able to get in touch with her family through radio messages or other means of contact. He assumed that Tara had not noticed *Nazir* because she had little practice of reading Urdu. He wanted her address so that he could keep in touch with her through letters. He also wrote that Kanak was now Tara's sister-in-law, that Masterji's coal depot was doing well, that the family's finances were beginning to look up and that Tara should not hesitate to ask him if she needed money. After all this was the news of Somraj's disgraceful behaviour, that he was living with his sister-in-law. Puri gave assurance that Somraj had not been told about her. Since Somraj lived close to Masterji's home, Tara's mother and father too were kept in dark about her so that he may not learn about her through them. Tara could write to Puri how she wanted it handled, and her wishes will be respected. Puri closed the letter by repeating the assurance that he would soon come to Delhi to meet her.

Tara was lost in thought after reading the letter. There was no one with whom she could share it. Her past life flashed through her mind, her life in the gali in Lahore, her reluctance to marrying Somraj, her brother's attitude, her first night with her husband … terrible, hellish experiences. Now she was on her own, not dependent on anybody. She didn't want to lose her independence. 'I have nothing to do with Somraj, he can do what he wants. It's good too that pitaji and mother were not told.'

Even though it was disquieting, she read the letter again three times in the next three days. She thought about what to write in her reply, whether she should reply at all. On the third day, when the panic in her mind and her distress subsided a little, she began to wonder if there was more to the letter than met her eye. Puri had asked to be told in advance if she wanted to come to Jalandhar rather than that he wanted her to come! Somraj and others had not been told about her! Puri would do what she would tell him to do!

She thought, 'He would be inconvenienced if I arrived without notice. If I do not reply, everything would remain as it is. Why should I blow into a dying fire to rekindle it, and get ashes blown in my face for nothing?' She did not feel the need to ask her brother for anything. It was better to leave the letter unanswered, she decided.

The storm raging in Tara's mind gradually dissipated. She knew that in future she will have to be independent and self-reliant. The rumours surfaced again that the government intended to phase out the Department of Rehabilitation once the task of settling and helping the refugees was accomplished. Tara's friends and well-wishers like Narottam, Rawat and Dr Shyama encouraged her to apply for the Public Service Commission. In keeping with the Prime Minister's progressive views, a special provision had been made to induct qualified women into government jobs. In May of 1950 Tara was selected for the Central Secretariat Services.

Tara's new appointment as an undersecretary was to the post of the director of the Women Welfare Centres. She was now entitled to government accommodation. But, the number of officers and clerks in the new government had grown like wild grass in the rainy season, and officers appointed before Tara or transferred to Delhi from other cities had been waiting to be allotted houses. There had been an increment in Tara's salary and she had begun to receive a conveyance allowance of Rs 50 per month. A peon was put at her disposal. She could now easily afford to live by herself, but renting a whole dwelling just for one person seemed excessive. She also would have had to hire servants, and what she had heard about men hired as help behaving more and more discourteously and sometimes improperly had frightened her. She was quite content to continue to live and share expenses with Mercy as a paying guest. Very conscious of the fact that people would notice her new social status, the only change she had allowed in her dress was changing into a crisp white sari every day that had been washed and starched by a dhobi. She had also begun to feel uneasy about waiting for the bus in a queue, and mostly took a taxi.

On learning about her conveyance allowance, Mercy and others advised Tara, 'Gazetted officers like you are eligible for automobile loans. It would be convenient for you and befitting your position if you get a small car.' Mathur and Narottam offered to assist her in the selection and purchase of a car.

Tara replied a little sheepishly, 'You must be pulling my leg! I will be responsible for organizations that help and aid women who earn as little as 12 annas and one rupee a day, and you want me to go to inspect them on a motor car?'

'Forget such romantic idealism,' Narottam replied, with Mercy and Mathur listening. 'You are a representative of the government and of the President of India. The President resides in a huge palace. He is not embarrassed by the sight of shanty towns or of the homeless sleeping on footpaths. People like us are government servants, who symbolize the power and the prestige of the administration. If you want to be a bleeding-heart liberal, better join the movement of Vinoba Bhave or become a member of the Communist Party and carry on the struggle on the party wage.'

Her inability to answer such an argument did not make Tara change her mind about owning a car, but an unexpected combination of circumstances arose three months later.

In July of that year Chaddha came out of hiding after more than two years. The room he had been living in a lane behind Shradanand Bazaar before going underground was repossessed and rented out during his absence by his landlord to another person at twice the rent.

On getting Chaddha back after such a long separation, Mercy did not want him to be out of her sight even for a few hours. She made an audacious decision and asked him to move in with her, then applied for a court marriage. She could barely contain her happiness and thrill. Her lips were constantly spread in a smile, her large eyes shone with delight. The surge of blood in her veins made her smooth, bronze complexion glow. Bubbling with excitement, she chirped all day.

Mathur's visits became more frequent, and other comrades often showed up to meet Chaddha. Long discussions ensued; the topic generally the same: a criticism of the Communist Party line by some, and its defence by others. They discussed P.C. Joshi's policy of 'strengthening Nehru's hands', the call given by B.T. Ranadive for socialist revolution, and engaged in passionate polemics of the bourgeois democratic revolution, role of the working classes in a democratic revolution, the danger of bourgeois monopoly, and the people's democratic revolution.

These discussions bored Tara. Chaddha was for the policy of eliminating feudalism and the capitalist hegemony with the help of national bourgeoisie. His primary concern was agrarian reforms, the ending of zamindar's rights over agricultural property and the nationalization of heavy industry. In his view, the abolition of the 'privy purses' of the former royals by the Congress was a step towards democracy.

Mathur and Tewari supported the socialist agenda of the Communist Party, but strongly objected to the current party line. They did not consider the Communist Party of India to be an independent entity, but only an arm of the international communist movement. They were critical that the CPI did not decide its policies in accordance with India's needs, but to conform to the strategy of international communist movement.

'What's wrong with that?' Chaddha would ask. 'An end to a capitalist and exploitive system in any country would be conducive to democracy. How can such progressive international cooperation be against the national interest of any country? Does the Congress government accept international aid to solve the food crisis in the country, or not? Has your government not taken the Kashmir problem to the court of international opinion? Did the government not seek help and loans from the USA, Britain and also from the Soviet Union to develop the nation's industry?'

'That's what I meant,' Mathur said. 'The USA and Britain are helping us to only keep us dependent on them. You must remember that they help us only in the production of consumer goods, not in establishing heavy industries or in setting up production of weapons of defence. The Soviet Union is also mainly concerned about increasing its influence.'

'That is because the capitalist nations have an imperialist agenda,' Chaddha said by way of a warning. 'You should learn from the example of the Soviets helping China and Korea.'

Tara jumped in support of Chaddha, 'The Congress government has been forced to postpone its declared goal of nationalization of industries to appease the USA and Britain. Why doesn't the Congress carry out the resolution adopted at its Karachi convention twenty years ago?'

'The government has sold out to the capitalists,' Mercy said in disgust.

'No, no,' Mathur attempted to correct everyone, 'CPI does not give importance to our national situation, but to the dictates of the international communist movement. When they realized that it was possible for the communists to come to power in China, saw socialist states being formed in the Eastern Europe, heard of attempts at revolutions in eastern Burma and Indonesia, they became ready to launch the socialist revolution in India also.'

Moving to the edge of his chair, Narottam said, 'Sir,'——he still called Chaddha 'sir' out of an old habit——'the comrades were all set to install the dictatorship of the proletariat in India. There is an old comrade acquaintance of mine,' he said turning to Tara, 'you know him too. The same comrade who used to come to AA to sell party literature to me. I met him again in Connaught Place last year when I returned from Calcutta. He had copies of his new short story collection on him. He gave me one, and said, "I wrote these in a new style. Give me your opinion when you have read them."'

'That comrade really writes well,' Tara recalled. 'I have read one of his story collections.'

'That's true, but listen to this. The comrade came again to the AA after about a fortnight. I had read his new work. I said with some reservation, "Bhai, I didn't like the stories of your new collection as much as the last one."

'The comrade blew up at me, "Why would you like them? You want bourgeois trash and sex. Progressive literature is not your cup of tea. That is your class nature."

'I tried to explain, "But that's not true. I liked your first collection."

'He said, "You liked the earlier one because then it was still not the time to say things plainly. Now I have clinched the issues from a working-class point of view."

'I made another attempt to explain to him, "But progressive literature can also be good fiction. I enjoy reading Gorky, Mykovsky, Fast, Hemingway and Alexi Tolstoy." I also mentioned a couple of Hindi and Urdu writers.

'The comrade continued to rage, "I don't buy your explanation. My previous writing was just bourgeois frippery. The time for all that is long past. The decisive moment is here. It's your class nature. You can't escape it now." The comrade got up angrily to leave.

'I asked, "I won't be able to escape what?"

'The comrade made a fist and warned me, "Those who are not with us are against us! Whatever happens at the time of revolution, what happened in France, in Russia, in eastern Europe, will also happen here!"'

Mathur cut in, 'He didn't threaten to hang you from the electricity pole?'

'He could have,' Chaddha said smilingly. 'Who doesn't threaten when excited? What is your Congress government doing in Telengana?'

'Your party is responsible for what's happening in Telengana. You challenged government with arms, it replied with arms.'

Narottam raised his hand to ask everyone to listen, 'I said worriedly, "Dear brother comrade, I have always supported you. I support Marxism also. I buy party literature, I have also contributed money to the party."

'The comrade sneered at me, "Lip sympathy means nothing. What does it matter if you give away a few rupees? You can throw away twenty without a thought when playing bridge or flash. The test of theory is in practice."

'I pleaded, "Comrade, how can I be against you? Won't you have any consideration for an old friend?"

'The comrade turned his back to me and said, "Can't promise you!"'

Mathur and Tara burst into laughter.

'Get lost, you big mouth! You are a true bourgeois!' Mercy scolded Narottam. She did not appreciate joke about communists.

'You find childish people everywhere,' Chaddha again conceded with a smile.

'It's not only about being childish. Your party always gets instructions from outside India for all its decisions and activities. It's a well-known fact that your party radically changed its policy at the Calcutta Congress on the basis of an editorial in the Cominform newspaper *For a Lasting Peace, For a People's Democracy*. You can't deny this.'

'There's no need to deny it,' Chaddha replied. 'What's wrong if the party decided to form its policy to go with the international progressive outlook? If at any time the comrades in this country cannot apply Marxist principles to the situation, why can't they take inspiration from the example of other more experienced people? Where's the problem? The Congress government also invites experts and consultants from foreign countries.' He knocked on the table with his finger, 'Countries struggling to be free of imperialist oppression will naturally want to form a united front with countries against imperialist aggression.'

'No, no. National interest has never been your party's first concern,' Mathur protested. He again began to analyse the events of 1942 to support his contention.

Tara had heard all this many times. She got up to go to her room.

'Arrey, sit. Where're you going?' Mercy asked her to stay.

Lost in a feeling of deep contentment, Mercy at times suspected that Tara might be feeling ignored, and would become even more affectionate and caring towards her. She wanted Tara to joke with Chaddha and tease him as if she was her younger sister, so that there would be some joviality around the house. Tara also enjoyed light-hearted and amusing banter, but only to the extent that her background and upbringing allowed.

Previously Mercy would sometimes have a meal without waiting for Tara, but to give Tara a sense of belonging, she and Chaddha would now wait for her to join them. Mercy also wanted Tara to keep her company in the living room until Chaddha wanted to retire. Not wanting Tara to feel any distance from her, sometimes she would behave unabashedly in Tara's presence. She would take Chaddha's hand into hers or rest her head against his shoulder. If Tara turned her face away or got up to leave, Mercy would insist that she stay put.

Tara at times felt uncomfortable in the presence of the amorous couple. During her childhood and the part of her life spent in the gali, she had seen a different kind of behaviour between husbands and wives and members of a family. Love had been a totally personal and private affair in the world of the gali. Etiquette dictated that newly-married couples did not speak to each other intimately in the presence of others. Tara did not think such restrictions were necessary or acceptable. 'Mercy is a modern woman. She has had a different upbringing, has a different notion of propriety. Why should she have to pretend to be shy? She and Chaddha are a couple, they can behave as they want, but why do they have to be so overly demonstrative!' If she felt out of place and went to her bedroom, leaving them to be alone, the sounds of a man and woman talking and laughing together filled her with a strange feeling of restlessness.

Tara had been working assiduously to expand the scope of Women Welfare Centres, and to make them into a success. She came back home from office completely exhausted, and found no relief from the constant presence of visitors and the babble of a crowded living room. She had spent the last two-and-a-half years in that flat in peace, and had become used to the solitude of her room. And when there were no sounds of heated discussion, she had to witness the spectacle of Mercy's courtship. She would feel fed up and want to run away to some place else.

After the standard of living she had become used to and her new position, it was not possible for her, she felt, to live in a cheap rental somewhere. The wait for the government subsidized housing was as long as before. The thought of moving to the Working Women's Hostel again came to her mind. There had been all kinds of unsavoury rumours about the hostel. Even if she did not care for the rumours, a room could not be made available just because she wanted to move in. Sometime ago there was a vacancy, but at that time Tara was quite content living where she was. She asked two clerks at her office to lend a hand in finding an accommodation. She knew that even a modest dwelling of two rooms with a bathroom would not cost less than Rs 60 a month. And she would need someone to do the cooking and the housekeeping. She found it preposterous that a person would be needed full-time to cook and look just after her needs, and that person would have to be paid a salary, fed meals and given a place to stay! Two years ago she would never have considered hiring help and would have preferred to do the chores herself on her return from office, but now it seemed necessary. Why was it so, she asked herself? The answer was that she needed peace of mind to do her job well. The thought of spending close to Rs 250 a month only on herself was anathema to her, but she found she could not escape the reality of her social status in the eyes of others and their high opinion of her. The burden of the monthly stipend to Sita was still on her. Faced with a dilemma, she decided not to let her heart rule her head, and to put up with the inconvenience at Mercy's place.

It would not have been right to stop helping Sita, who had been lately behaving herself. She had trained hard to become a proficient typist. Mathur often found her typing work that earned her Rs 15 to 20 per job. Her mother brought home unfinished socks from a hosiery factory and by finishing toes and heels of the socks, both got an extra rupee per day. They were paying Rs 12 every month for their small dark one-room accommodation.

In the first week of October, Mr Batra, the deputy secretary, sent for Tara and asked her, 'Do you have any connection with the Communist Party?'

'Ji, no,' Tara answered. The question took her by surprise. She had been investigated for her political views a second time at the time of her appointment as an undersecretary. Why the question again? She gave Mr Batra an inquiring look.

Mr Batra asked again, 'Do communists visit your house? Do they hold meetings there?'

What she had heard about Special Establishment Police flashed through Tara's mind. By now she had learned to speak with tact and diplomacy within government circles. It was well known that Sardar Patel and Rajaji had declared communists to be 'Enemy Number One'. The government did not consider officials with partisan feelings for the Communist Party as trustworthy.

Tara said, 'How can anybody visit my house? I don't own a house. Since I was alone in Delhi and was afraid to live all by myself, I became a paying guest of nursing sister Mercy Sorrel. She had her own flat, but lived alone. She got married to one Mr Chaddha in August this year. They have many visitors. If there are any communists among them, I don't know. As it is, it causes me much inconvenience.'

Mr Batra nodded his head to show that he understood, 'A confidential inquiry about you has been ordered. I think you should not continue to live as a paying guest. Do you own a car? No? Well, you should, considering your position and need. I know this is your personal business, but take it as advice from a well-wisher. Well, I have noted down your answer, but it'd be better if you found another place soon. Any inquiry about you will not look good in your service roll. I'll report that you're searching for another place to stay. Do you know that your service record so far has been excellent? Did you try for government housing?'

'I was told that there was no chance. How could I get a residential accommodation with so many waiting for one?'

'That's correct, but ladies can be given priority. I'll make a recommendation. The government can also rent an accommodation for you. Well, all this will take time, maybe another six months. But you must move to another house soon. Even if you have to pay a high rent, it'll be in your own interest.'

Despite her closeness with Mercy, Tara had been thinking of moving to another place to get away from the increasingly inconvenient circumstances, yet she did not like being pressurized into doing so. She knew that under the regulations, government employees could not be a member of any political party. In principle there was nothing wrong in the rule that the people in administration should not have any bias towards or prejudices against any political party, but it was different in practice because sympathy for the Congress was considered as a show of loyalty rather than affiliation to a political party.

Tara could not bring herself to tell Mercy about the pressure to change her place of residence. For her to admit it was demeaning. She brooded over her dilemma, 'The President, the Prime Minister, the Cabinet ministers, they all are members of the Congress party. Even if they are not in the executive, in matters of government policy they tilt the scales in the Congress party's favour. Isn't such partisanship an indication of the dictatorial tendencies in the Congress government? What else does this bullying others into buying *hundi*s mean?' Hundi, literally a bill or invoice, was something like a bond or certificate that could be used to buy khadi cloth. Gandhi used to ask public to buy it so that the money could go to help khadi weavers. The Congress government tried it for a while as a proof of its faith in Gandhi's philosophy.

From two weeks before Gandhiji's birthday on 2 October, government employees were being encouraged to buy khadi hundis. They were told about senior officials who had bought hundis worth Rs 100 or Rs 200. Batra had got one for Rs 150. Word had quietly spread that each employee was expected to buy hundis worth 10 per cent of the salary. Tara also bought, rather reluctantly, a hundi for Rs 100.

A couple of clerks in Tara's section, encouraged by her approachable attitude, said, 'We don't mind buying the hundis, but we don't care for khadi. We don't believe in khadi, and it costs more than other cloth. But if you say, we'd buy it nevertheless.'

Tara replied, 'What belief has got to do with it? Buy it and use it for what you want. You are under no compulsion to wear khadi.'

All the staff bought hundis of small denominations, but not without grumbling under their breaths. Tara's section assitant, Ram Swaroop Bhutt, was over ten years older than she was. He could not bring himself to call her madam, so he always addressed Tara as huzoor. One day when he brought a file to her office, he stood respectfully before her desk and began to gossip about various clerks, 'Such and such was saying, "Gandhi Ashram and khadi has always been political symbols. Why do we have to wear khadi?" Such and such said that the seven annas out of a rupee that the khadi weavers will get as a subsidy will be extracted by the government from the public. That means that they pay the tax so that those wanting to wear khadi can get it cheap. Why were they being compelled to buy the hundis? Such and such said, "We are told that government employees should not participate in the PWA (Progressive Writers' Association) and the IPTA (Indian People's Theatre Association) because those are communist organizations, but we are told to buy khadi. We are made to pay to keep the Gandhi Bhandaar out of the red. If Nehru is so fond of working at the spinning wheel, he can sit at the Rajghat all day and do so, but why force it on us?"'

The clerks' grumbling reminded Tara of her own reaction to the official pressure to make her move to another dwelling, when she had thought in exasperation, 'Should I resign over such a minor issue? But I'll be making that sacrifice for what great ideal? I am working only so that I can survive. And so is everyone else.'

As a result of hectic efforts of Mathur, Ratan and two of her staff clerks, Tara found a residential accommodation. It was about the same size as Mercy's flat, but the rent was Rs 80 per month. Tara realized that she would now need a woman to do the cooking and to look after the house when she would be at work. Had Tara not been a woman, she would have had no problem finding a servant. Tara could not ask her peon to stay at the flat, for he was alone as his family lived away from Delhi. Peons at government offices liked working for superiors who could provide them with living quarters. They would do cooking for the boss and clean his house in return for free accommodation and meals, and get baksheesh for buying tobacco in the bargain. On the first rung of the career ladder, women had become clerks and officers, but not peons.

Tara called Sita to her new flat and told her plainly, 'I had to rent a new place and I am facing unexpected expenses. I don't think I'd be able to help you with money as before. I'll give you and your mother one room here. Your mother can keep the house. Whatever simple meals I will eat, you will also eat.' Many stories of scandalous acts by displaced women and adventurer refugees were doing the rounds. Tara preferred this arrangement to taking the risk of trusting some stranger. What better deal could Sita and Purandei think of?

For the first few days Tara had her hands full organizing her new place.

The covered veranda next to the first-floor landing, she thought, could do as a sitting room for receiving guests. One room she turned into her bedroom; the other, slightly larger, she gave to Sita and her mother. There was another veranda at the back with the kitchen on one end. An old, heavy and ugly-looking dining table discarded by her landlord lay there. Tara covered it with a sheet of oilskin.

Behind the flat, just across the gali, was a row of small, dilapidated houses. What was until 1947 a poor Muslim neighbourhood was now inhabited by lower-middle-class Punjabi refugees. Tara and Sita were sitting in the back veranda eating lunch on Sunday when some men and women from the row of houses began to talk loudly:

'Just look at those! Behaving like a *mem*!'

'They look like mem!'

'Wah, to me they appear to be Punjabi women!'

Two men sitting on the charpoy and eating from one thali, swore and said, 'Aren't they some show-offs! Having their meal sitting at a table!'

Tara and Sita picked up their thalis and went inside. Purandei came out of the kitchen and began to shout back, 'We can do what we want in our own house! What's to you! Aren't you sitting on a charpoy and eating like a *mlechchha*—an unclean Muslim! There isn't a girl as fine as my niece in the whole world. She's a government official, an under-*sektari*. All she has to do is phone, and police will come and teach you a lesson!'

Sita sat alone for dinner in the veranda, and no one uttered a word. Tara joined her the next day.

Tara had more free time in her new flat. Among her few visitors was Mathur, who came around every Wednesday or Thursday at six o'clock. He had taken on the role of Tara's elder brother and guardian. He would bring some fruits tied in his handkerchief, or some mithai or savoury *dal-moth* mixture.

Narottam always came by in the last week of the month to escort Tara to the club. In between if he read a good book, he would bring it for Tara. He came also to lighten his heart by talking to Tara if some comment made by his mother was troubling him. The issue of his engagement with Neelam was over, for which he had even more praise for Rawat than he previously did. Rawat had dropped the idea after sensing Narottam's reluctance without bearing any ill will and had found another boy for his daughter.

Tara's assistant Bhutt and Khushi Ram Mehta, an upper grade clerk, also stopped by her house to see if she needed help. Tara would smile inwardly when Bhutt addressed her bahinji or mataji when he spoke with her at her home, but she was careful not to show it. Bhutt made sure to tell Tara about the latest gossip and report to her hearsays he had heard at the office. It was he who had told Tara that two clerks on her staff, Mahadeo and Bishwas, took a cut from the purchases made for the welfare centres. Since he could not provide any evidence in support of his accusation, Tara was unable to take any action.

Mehta had been particularly helpful in finding the accommodation for Tara. He had been living on Pachkuian Road in a similar flat for the last five years, but paid a monthly rent of Rs 45 at the old rate. As his monthly salary with allowances came to only Rs 220, he had to sublet one room. He paid a courtesy call every Sunday morning with his one-and-a-half-year-old daughter Guddi, prompting her to join her hands in greeting one and all, 'Say *jai* to your aunt! Say jai to the junior aunt! Say jai to maaji!'

Mehta often said to Purandei, 'Maaji, let me know if there's anything I can do.' After Tara had moved in, he had also been helpful in buying kitchen utensils and groceries. His uncle had opened a grocery store in Paharganj bazaar, where packages of cleaned and picked lentils, spices and other similar items were sold. The business had flourished. Mehta bought groceries for Tara from that shop.

Ratan and Sheelo came around one day with Ghullu. Tara decided to ignore the disapproving look on the faces of Purandei and Sita, and treated Sheelo and Ratan with more care and affection than she normally would. When everyone sat down for a meal, Tara held Ghullu in her lap and made it a point to eat from one thali with the couple. Sita and Purandei quietly lowered their raised eyebrows.

Tara could see that Sheelo was pregnant. Although Karol Bagh was not far from her flat, she advised Sheelo, 'The roads are not in a good condition around your area. I'd rather visit you than have you come all the way here.'

One evening Narottam turned up, and just after him, Mathur. Noticing a cardboard box in Mathur's hand, Narottam asked, 'Have you got pastries in there? My timing was good! I'll also have some.'

'Not pastries, bhai, look!' Mathur handed the colourful box to Narottam. It carried the tag: Devi Chand, of Said Mittha, Lahore. In the box were burfi sweets.

'That's great!' Narottam said. 'Punjabi refugees have knocked some sense into the heads of Delhites, otherwise mithai used to be sold here in leaf cups from which flies rose in a swarm.' He leaned forward excitedly in his chair, 'My uncle came from Bhiwani to Delhi for a visit after several years. He felt nostalgic about eating chaat in Delhi, so I took him to Chandni Chowk for some. We were served chaat in plates, with a spoon. My uncle is orthodox Hindu, he thinks china or glassware is unclean. He said, a bit uncomfortably, "Bhai, I don't want foreign-style chaat. Give me some on a leaf plate. Unless you can lick your finger after you have wiped the plate, you have not had chaat. All my life I have eaten chaat and puris in leaf plates, and drank water from clay tumblers. I'm too old to learn anything new." The poor soul was completely nonplussed by what he saw in the city. He said, "Everything's gone topsy-turvy in Delhi. It's so much more crowded, crawling with people." He kept on turning his eyes away from the sight of brassieres strung for display in stores.'

Tara looked away self-consciously.

Narottam begged her pardon, and continued, 'That's the logic of market economy. The more a thing sells, the more it is advertised. In Europe you see rows of stocking advertisements showing only women's legs. For them the beauty of women lies in her legs...'

He said, looking at Tara, 'If didi promises to forgive me, I'd like to say something.'

'Yes, go ahead,' Tara promised.

'Here the boys and layabouts say to one another: Let's go do some girl-watching to pass the time. In Europe the expression is: Let's do some leg-watching to pass the time.'

'Quiet, you shameless person!' Tara chided him, trying not to smile.

Mathur broached a different subject, 'The Punjabis have nearly run long-time Delhites out of business. They are such fierce competitors. Most of the business is now in their hands. Not only have the refugees settled in the districts of Lajpat Nagar and Karol Bagh, they are all over Chandni Chowk. Delhites are slowly awakening and have begun to learn from the Punjabis. Until now they used to take it easy and open their businesses sometime after ten o'clock.'

Mehta's wife and his sister came up the stairs and into the room. The sister was gorgeously dressed and carried Guddi in her arms. When she saw Tara, Guddi held out her hands and said, 'Bua, jai!'

The child also wore an expensive frock, her hair was styled in ringlets tied with a ribbon. Tara folded Guddi in her arms, gave her a kiss and put a piece of burfi in her mouth. Narottam and Mathur both said that the child looked pretty.

The guests explained the purpose of their visit without sitting down, 'Tomorrow on the festival of Basant we are holding Guddi's naming ceremony. Mehtaji has already asked you, but we thought we'd come by to remind you. We have invited a pundit, but Mehtaji said that the name will be selected by you.'

'You came all the way for such a small thing! I surely will come.'

The visitors left.

'Have you made many friends in the neighbourhood?' Narottam asked.

'One was the wife of Mehta, a clerk in my office, the other was his sister. Decent people.'

'Clerk?' Mathur said in surprise. 'They were dressed and talked as if they came from the family of a New Delhi contractor, businessman, or some Rs 2000-a-month official. The people of UP and Delhi did not have the custom of dressing up. Nobody would have recognized those as belonging to a middle-class family.'

'Why should they be recognized as one? Why should you be concerned how much property or cash they have? And why should they accept that they are poor?' Tara asked. 'Do they not have the right to dress as they want?'

Narottam said to Mathur, 'Professor sahib, clothes do not belie one's economic status.'

'What does? How can you tell?' Mathur asked.

'The nails and the heels always give away. A working person cannot have soft hands and feet of an idle person. You are bound to see some rough and cracked skin.'

'You've been really looking close, Nottan. What've you been up to, you oaf?' Tara asked. 'Do you like hands and feet of idle persons?'

'I regard idle people as parasitic. I hate long painted nails.' Narottam said. 'I also wondered how people who dress like this can manage to do so.'

'They are fond of good clothes and they like to spend on them. They don't go begging to buy them,' Tara said.

'Assuming that they don't, how *do* they manage on so little? Delhites seem to have also caught this disease.' Mathur said worriedly.

'They do manage, somehow,' Tara said. 'It's also a matter of finding ways to manage. Go and watch from the veranda in the back. Notice the sorry state of the dwellings, and compare the clothes of young men and women going in and out of the front doors. They wash their clothes carefully, and if there is no iron in the house, they pay the ironing man with his handcart to iron the clothes. In my office you can judge from one's dress who's from Punjab, who is from UP or Bihar or Bengal. Punjabis seem to assert that they are as good as you are. How much they earn or how well off they are is none of your business. They don't want to admit that they are going through a difficult time.'

'But why this difference in temperament between Punjabis and people from other provinces of India? What could be the reason?' Narottam posed a serious question.

Mathur knitted his brow as he ventured a guess, 'It could be that the Punjabis did not have to face the same subjugation by the British after the Mutiny as did the people of UP and Bihar. The Punjabis were also given preference for recruitment into the police and the armed forces. I do not believe it is because of the climatic reasons.'

Mathur and Narottam continued to discuss the changes brought to Delhi by the Punjabi refugees.

On the day of the Basant festival, Tara went to Mehta's flat with Sita. About forty people were present, including half a dozen clerks from Tara's office. There were several people older than Tara, but it was she who was given most attention and respect. Feeling awkward, she sat among a group of women and tried to behave as if she was no different from others.

The ceremony was performed according to the Vedic rites. The air was thick with the scent of oblations in the *havan kund*, sacrificial fire, and everyone chanted Vedic mantras. After the fire ceremony was over, Mehta, his palms together, prayed to Tara, 'My mataji requests that you give a name to the baby.'

Being given such honour and responsibility was making Tara break into a sweat. She replied, just to go along, 'Any name that mataji takes to bless the child would be auspicious. Mataji, please say a name.'

The officiating priest said, 'Deviji, with your permission, the baby's grandmother and her parents would like to name the child after you. So that she may be as capable, upright and successful as you are.'

'That's right! That's true!' Many men and women nodded their assent.

Tara bowed her head. Her ears rang, as if a heavy brass vessel had crashed down to the floor and its reverberations were filling her mind. She thought to herself, 'No! No one should have to go through what I had.' With an effort she pulled herself together, gulping the lump in her throat as she managed to say softly, 'May she be happy! May she keep well!'

The priest recited a mantra and made the augury that the baby may be as talented and famous as the intelligent, capable and courageous lady who has selected the name for her, and may shine in her life like dhruva the Pole Star.

'This is as it should be! So be it!' A hum rose from the gathering.

Guddi was placed in Tara's lap to receive her blessings. She bit her lip to choke back her tears, and clasped the child to her heart.

After the rites, Mehta first offered a laddu to Tara, then began to hand out bags of prasad to the guests.

The priest launched into an Arya Samaji bhajan befitting the occasion:

'Come let us all sing a song in His praise...'

And all others joined in.

Tara sat with her head bent. In her mind's eye she saw a similar incident five years ago, the naming ceremony of her friend Surendra's nephew was done according to the Sikh custom, instead of the havan ceremony, a Sikh priest had recited from the Granth Sahib. That day also the child, a boy, was named Tara Singh. Asad had whispered into her ear that she now had a namesake.

Tara found it difficult to stay any longer in the company of people. As soon as the bhajan singing was over, she pressed a congratulatory five-rupee bill into the child's tiny fist, and begged off early from the party. Some girls and young women were going to play the dholak drum and sing tappas to the beat. Sita wanted to join them. Mehta offered to escort Tara back to her flat, but Tara declined, and left alone.

On reaching home she lay in her bed, thinking. Memories of Lahore kept returning to her mind. That day the prasad was not in the form of laddus, but as ghee-drenched halwa that could only be accepted reverently with one's hands. How embarrassed Asad was because he did not have a handkerchief on him to clean his hands. She and Asad had walked from Gwal Mandi to her gali. That was the first time they had talked so frankly with each other. How their friendship had grown, how far in the future she had planned, what confidence it had given her! 'Maybe I was gullible but he also had given me an assurance. Then he let me down, or did he? He had reasons of his own. He certainly wasn't selfish. He had tried to help me again, but only after I had been ruined. Had his pipe dream worked out, where would I have been today? In what situation? Would I have been able to live with it? Maybe whatever happened, happened for the better. Was I supposed to end up like this by some strange quirk of fate. Was I destined to become a victim of the country's partition or was it the country's destiny to be partitioned?' Whenever she thought of Asad, she was overwhelmed by such memories. Then she would tell herself, 'Let bygones be bygones. I am good as I am. Why do I have to admit that my sense of self has been destroyed?'

Tara was woken from a light sleep when Sita called out to her. Purandei said with affectionate concern, 'Hai, you've had nothing to eat. Come, girls, I'll serve you both.'

While they were eating, Sita said, 'Bahinji, you left, but everyone was talking about you. Some woman said, "Hai, how lovely she is. Such a virtuous-looking face. Does not look more than twenty-two or twenty-three, but has attained such a high position. Very sober and sensible. Behaves so much like an elderly and wise lady."'

'Stop jabbering! As if I am not old!' Tara interrupted her.

'Ashes and dust on to heads of those who say so! Those who call you that are old and old are the daughters and daughters-in-law in their family! Certainly not you!' Purandei came to Tara's defence.

Deputy Secretary Batra rang Tara to tell her, 'There are many queries about the report you prepared for the Planning Commission. The Commission has also asked for all kinds of details and explanations. I am forwarding their letter to you. I suggest that you find the answers to the queries and go personally to their office. I'll inform Dr Nath. All right?'

Dr Nath was the economic advisor to the industries section of the Planning Commission. His office was in the Commission's new edifice on Mansingh Road. Tara laboured over a new report that included answers to all the questions for three days. At 3 p.m. on the day of the appointment given by Dr Nath, she went to meet him with her peon carrying the files.

Dr Nath's peon stood up on seeing a lady arrive, with her own peon in tow. He presented Tara with a chit of paper to jot down her name. Tara wrote: Undersecretary for Small Scale Industries, Women's Section—Tara Puri.

The peon went in, returned and raised the curtain over the door for Tara to enter.

Dr Nath sat with his elbows on a large desk, listening to his stenographer read a letter that had been typed up. A ceiling fan turned leisurely in the pleasant warmth of early November. Without looking at Tara, he said in English as the stenographer read on, 'Please wait for a minute. Have a seat.'

Tara sat down on the left side and looked at Dr Nath, her eyes widening at seeing Professor Dr Pran Nath! Scars from childhood on one temple and cheek when boiling water was poured over him to kill him! Tara could hear her heart pound. Her fingers went involuntarily to her lips. Then she sat straight and arranged her aanchal to collect herself.

When the stenographer finished reading, Dr Nath signed the letter and turned to face Tara. He stared at her for a few moments with unbelieving eyes, then looked at the chit on the desk. His face lit up. He took a deep breath before speaking, but no words came out. Then leaning forward, his eyes bright with excitement, he said in a more assured tone in English, 'You are Tara!' He looked again at the chit, 'Tara Puri! You wrote your name. I can't be dreaming. I cannot make a mistake in recognizing Tara.'

A storm of memories of the past five years was raging in Tara's mind. To calm the emotions churning in her heart, she sat silently, her eyes downcast.

Dr Nath held out his hand, 'Don't you recognize me?'

She shook Dr Nath's hand to confirm his guess, then pulled it back and entwined her fingers in an effort to steady herself.

Leaning further and with his eyes resting on her, Nath spoke from the heart, 'What an absurd rumour, but Masterji himself told me, he was in tears. He was so distraught when he came to see me at the hotel. He said that you were on the top floor of your in-laws' house, and could not be saved. Was all that nonsense?'

Nath broke off and Tara heard the loud clack of a typewriter from the next room. Memories were exploding in the fire of her own mind.

All the pains and memories in Tara's heart were awakened, ready to spill out into the open. She wanted to cry out loud. What Nath had not done for her? The problem of lack of fee at the time of her joining BA had been resolved with his help. Her secret, for which she had injured herself to save her face before her brother, and later had thought of killing herself, Nath had known about that and had been sympathetic to her. He had not betrayed her confidence when that secret had become a cause for shame for her. But at the moment it was necessary to collect herself and not cry in front of a person she held in such high regard. She was no longer the same dewy-eyed girl, but a gown-up person and a government official.... Her head was spinning. She just sat silent and unmoving, her fingers entwined, her teeth clenched. The clacking of typewriter became louder.

Nath put his elbow on the desk. Leaning towards Tara, he picked up a round glass paperweight, made it spin like a top as he slowly recounted past incidents, 'Masterji went to Sonwan. I remained in Lahore until the end of August. Such scenes of devastation, of people wreaking havoc! I was afraid that if I went out of the hotel, some Muslim bearer might recognize me and stick a knife into me. Inside the hotel it was safe because nearly all the guests were Europeans. Sitting idle in my room I used to think how simply incredible the theory of Hindus and Muslims being two peoples and two nations had once seemed, but then what was happening before my very eyes! Things don't happen just because we passionately believe in something. If we Hindus saw those who were demanding Pakistan as our enemies, how could we force them to stay with us? If we, I mean collectively and as a community, have been considering a people as untouchable and unclean, wouldn't it be deception to begin acknowledging them now as a part of us. Whatever might have been the historical reason for such behaviour, we have to pay the price for it now. The seed of partitioning the country as Hindustan and Pakistan was not sown by the British by allotting Hindus and Muslims proportional representation in government jobs on sectarian lines or by creating separate electorates for different communities. It was sown on the day when we Hindus began discriminating against the Muslims by calling them mlechchha. A Hindu may be subjugated and exploited by other Hindus branding him as untouchable because he sees himself as a part of the same religion. The Muslims have no such religious obligation, so why should they tolerate the insult of being considered untouchable? The device that we Hindus had used to protect our hegemony, the results of that ploy have come back to haunt us. What an irony!'

Nath took a deep breath. He closed his eyes for a moment, and perhaps realizing that Tara was sitting tongue-tied, opened his eyes but looked at the paperweight that his fingers had been twirling, 'When I was at Simla I wrote to Masterji at Sonwan. He wrote back, but I could not write again. I spent six months in Simla doing nothing. People were playing all kinds of politics to get appointed at the University of Punjab. Government of Punjab sent me to the Centre. The Centre packed me off to Bengal.

'Bengal's Chief Minster Ghosh wanted to develop the province in keeping with Gandhiji's ideals. I thought I could be of use to him, but his ideas were at cross purposes with the interests of a lobby of politicians who were powerful in Bengal. They engineered Ghosh's ouster. The new chief minister thought that as Ghosh's man I had no place in his scheme of things. So for the past one year I have been here, helping to launch the First Five Year Plan.'

Tara sat silent and motionless as before, her fingers entwined.

Nath spun the paperweight a little harder, and asked, 'Is Masterji here in Delhi? Is Puri also here?'

'Jalandhar...' Tara said, swallowing hard. Her throat was dry.

'You're here with your in-laws?' Nath asked.

Tara shook her head.

'Achcha, you're here because of your job. You are holding a good position. You must have been selected through the Public Service Commission.'

Tara nodded.

'Memories of Lahore came back when I saw you. You used to come to the house to tutor Kikka, Gulli and Bholi. The chaos of those days! The last time I went to your home, your hands were painted with henna and the bridal oils had been applied to you. You were looking so young. Now you look so serious, a lady in white.'

Tara raised her eyes. She gave a thin, wan smile.

'Your in-laws, your husband,' Nath smiled and asked, 'where are they?'

Tara again bowed her head.

Nath kept silent. After a few moments thought, he asked again, 'What is Puri doing in Jalandhar?'

'Newspaper...'

'Which newspaper?'

'*Nazir*.'

'*Nazir*? Must be in Urdu. Never saw a copy. Doing well?'

Tara nodded.

Nath said, 'You've hardly said a word. Tell me about yourself. You know I'd like to know about you.'

'Some other...' Tara said, again swallowing hard.

Nath briefly stared at Tara, then turning his gaze away, said, 'It's all right.' The typewriter click-clacked: All right ... all right ... all right!

Nath kept his eyes averted to spare Tara further embarrassment. His

fingers continued to twirl the paperweight. Then looking at his watch he
said, 'It's half past four. I won't be able to do any work now. I'm so happy
meeting you that I won't be able to concentrate.'

Overcome by a feeling of gratefulness, Tara bowed her head with a
smile on her lips.

'Come tomorrow by 10.30 or eleven, and we'll work. Will you be able
to? It won't be inconvenient?'

'No, no inconvenience at all,' Tara assured him.

Reaching to ring for the peon, Nath asked, 'Would you like some tea.'

'If you want.'

Nath asked, 'You have to go back to your office from here?'

'Not really.'

'Why don't we have tea somewhere else. We'll be able to talk. We are
meeting after…must be over four years. Feels as if the world has been
turned upside down in between.'

Tara lowered her eyes and nodded.

Nath selected some files from his desk and rang for his peon. When the
peon came, he ordered, 'Take these files to my place. Take the bus today.
I'll be back by seven or eight. And give back these files of memsahib to
her peon.'

It was Nath who did the talking as he drove, 'The house I found is quite
far, beyond the Flag Staff, on Alipore Road. It's about twelve miles to my
office and back.'

Nath took Tara to the Royal to avoid the crowd in Connaught Place. She
must also say something, Tara thought at the restaurant. She related the
story of the Bhaudutt incident.

Nath dropped Tara at her flat at 7 p.m.

Tara said, 'Please come up for a few minutes.'

'Not today. Another time.'

In the new flat, Purandei lived as Tara's bua, aunt, and Sita as her cousin.
Purendei's black coarse-silk lehanga had faded and worn out, and she
wanted to get a new one. The traditional respectable dress for middle-class
married women in Lahore and Amritsar, whether well-to-do or from lower
levels, had been black lehanga, but Punjabi refugee women in Delhi, even
older ones, had switched to wearing saris and dhotis. Tara and Sita advised

Purandei, 'Why are you so hung up on that depressive-looking garment. Follow others' example and start wearing a dhoti over a petticoat, or get a tailor to make you a salwar.'

Along with her lehanga, Purandei also gave up her thick cotton chaddar coloured with ashes dissolved in water. She was now mindful of wearing clothes in keeping with Tara's high social status. In February of that year Sita was hired, through Tara's efforts, as a Hindi stenographer in the Department of Information at a monthly salary of Rs 125 including allowances.

Sita bought some new clothes on getting her first salary. Tara's influence could be seen in her choice of clothes. Instead of satin and crepe in gaudy colours, she chose poplins in pastel shades and broadcloth. She also got two inexpensive, flower-patterned saris. She wanted to buy some dhotis for her mother.

Purandei protested affectionately, 'How can you even utter such a thing? May Maharaj-ji save me from committing the sin of accepting money that my daughter has earned. I didn't use your salary even when the times were tough. All I wish is that some day I may properly send you off to your in-laws. That's all I want.'

Purandei could not keep to herself the news of her daughter becoming a government employee at such a good salary. She proudly complained to her neighbours Gurandei and Tayee, 'I was so shocked when my daughter offered to buy me clothes.'

When Tara found out, she thought, 'Bua didn't complain when I got her new clothes, but she can't accept Sita's money because she gave birth to her. Or maybe, it's just a ruse to save her daughter's money.' That called to her mind the rumours going around about Purandei in her gali in Lahore, the neighbours calling Purandei shameless, accusations of secret goings-on between her and Ghasita Ram and of her accepting packets of mithai on the sly from him, that her indiscretions were sure to ruin her daughter too. 'Was doing that not immoral?' Tara thought. 'Is it really a sin to accept money from one's daughter? Or a sin is only something for which one is afraid to be criticized.'

In the flat next to Tara lived Duli Chand Talwar, a real estate agent from Old Anarkali, Lahore, who had done quite well after coming to Delhi. He had purchased, soon after his arrival, several tracts of agriculture and some barren land on Mathura Road at four annas a square yard. He had begun to resell pieces of that land after marking it as residential plots. Now in 1950–1 the plots were being sold for Rs 8 to 10 a square yard. He owned two buildings with flats and shops in Kamala Nagar that brought him about Rs 1400 per month in rent. He also owned a Buick, but lived in a rented flat at Rs 125 per month. He had married off his two daughters. One of his two sons was helping him run the real estate business. He was about fifty years old, and had a florid complexion. Everyone in the neighbourhood called him Lalaji or Tayaji and his wife, by extension, Tayee.

Exercising her right as a neighbour, Tayee had become Tara's self-appointed guardian. As there was a servant and a daughter-in-law to take care of her own household, she had plenty of time to keep an eye on her neighbours and offer them advice. Purandei had no male in the family except two young women of marriageable age, therefore Tayee took it upon herself to worry over them. She'd drop in to chat about the riff-raff moving into the neighbourhood, and in between, would inquire quietly about plans for marrying off Tara and Sita.

At the time Purandei had come to live with her, Tara had strictly instructed her not to talk to anyone about her family, about her marriage and about the incident of her in-laws' house burning down.

Tayee seemed rather taken up with worrying over Tara, and showed it by praising her often. She would say, 'There's no hurry about the younger one. A twenty-year woman is not considered too old for marriage now. I married my younger one when she was twenty, after she had done her BA. But sister, it becomes tough to find a match for a girl who has had too much education. I should know, for the trouble I had in finding a match for my younger one. Your elder one is a BA–MA officer, you'd have to find a match who is higher than a BA–MA. If she's 800–900 rupees a month officer, you'll have to match her with an officer who earns at least Rs 1000 or more. It's no joke to marry off your daughter. And she's holding such a high position, but is docile like a dairy cow and so polite. Addresses everyone by using "ji". When she talks, it feels as if flowers not words are falling out of her mouth. She'll need someone who's just right for her.'

Tayee would begin to talk about her nephew, 'My brother's younger son is an officer in the Forest Department. His salary is only a thousand a month, but by God's grace, he manages to make a lot more over and above. He has an official car, half-a-dozen minders. The older is in the Railways. His salary isn't that much, only five hundred a month, but he too has plenty of extra income. The younger one has an eight-year-old boy, studying at some English boarding school in Dehradun. His wife, poor soul, died of a heart attack at the time of her second delivery. The dear boy is hardly old, just around thirty-five. He had no shortage of marriage proposals, but says that he wants a match who is well-educated and intelligent. He has a position, you know. High officials, the deputy commissioner, magistrates often stay as house guests. Such a nice family.'

Tayee would repeat all this in the presence of Tara. She was waiting for some kind of signal from Purandei.

Sita had been behaving herself under the influence of Tara, and after her own bitter experience. Tara had noticed that the young woman, after living for some time under self-imposed constraints, had lately been acting a bit restless. She had learned songs she heard over the radio, particularly sad songs and those about love. She had a good voice and sometimes sang to herself in Hindi:

'...It's like watching someone's youth turn to ashes...'

Or in Punjabi:

'Long, and oh so dark, my sweetheart

Are the nights away from you...'

Purandei let Sita serve tea or sherbet to Mathur, Narottam and other male guests, but frowned upon her daughter sitting with them in the living room. To her mind it was different with Tara, who held a responsible position and was more matured, but Sita in her eyes was still naïve. Purandei of course forgot that Sita worked alongside young men in her office all day. Tara could not help but observe that Sita seldom came into the room when Mathur, Chaddha and others came by, but always passed through the room when Narottam was present. Sometime she would find an excuse to linger, adjusting and readjusting her dupatta or aanchal. Tara also detected Narottam's eyes following Sita. She had not expected such behaviour from Narottam, but could not ignore what she saw.

Tara immediately spoke with Narottam, 'Nottan, what's going on? Come clean if you have any intentions towards her.'

'Didi, how could you say that?'

'Then why are you leading her on?'

'What if a woman challenges you to flirt?' Narottam said to avoid being cornered.

Tara felt deeply hurt.

'What if your dallying gets her into trouble?'

'No such thing. I don't intend to go that far.'

'For you it might be innocent fun. What if she thought you were serious about her? She isn't all that sophisticated, just a simple girl from the back lanes of the city. She actually wants someone to settle down with.'

'Achcha, no more of this,' Narottam said.

'Anyway, Nottan, what's all this I've been hearing about you?' Tara decided to have her say after broaching the subject. 'I don't approve of it.'

'What?'

'About your acting like a *bhanvara,* bumblebee. A new girlfriend everyday. It was Lavang Vyas two or three months ago. Then it was Rekha. Then Meena. Now it's Deva.'

'Deva? How can you, didi? She is Dolly's teacher at the Miranda College, much older than I am. Have you ever met her? She's the serious, academic type, no chance of any misunderstanding there.'

'All right, may be not her. But is it proper to give hopes to others, have a good time and then drop them? Aren't you afraid of getting a bad reputation?'

'Didi, I never gave anybody any hopes. I don't chase anyone. They want to get me in the catch-me game, and I slip out.' Narottam said with a smile, 'It's not me who's being a bhanvara. It's just that there are butterflies all around me.'

'Nonsense!' Tara said with a frown. She knew she could scold Narottam for his own good. 'Who do you think you are?'

'I know who I am. I have no illusions about me, that's why I am not fooled. They are just a bunch of leeches who want to cadge off others. They are looking for a fat catch, and I don't want to be their prey.'

'Isn't it egotistical of you to think that those women are so completely besotted with you that they can't see how badly you treat them, and you can discard them when you want.'

'None of them is besotted with me; all they want is to flirt.' Narottam moved to the edge of his chair, 'They are the ones who are willing to take a gamble. And no risk is too big for them. I don't want to gamble, so I just let go of them.'

'If this is not being egotistical, what is?'

Narottam said with great seriousness, 'Didi, you call me an egoist! Show me one from all these who'd want to be my partner or companion for life. All they want is someone to feed them all their lives. These women don't see the person, just how much money he has, and compete fiercely for one who has money. To love someone and to take advantage of someone are not one and the same thing. Name me one who'd be willing to stand beside me and face the challenges and struggles of life? Suppose I am in Chaddha's position tomorrow. Will any one of these be willing to make sacrifices as Mercy has done? People say bad things about Dr Shyama, but I think that woman has moral courage. She does not deceive anyone to take advantage of him...'

Tara took a deep breath, and sat silently, her chin resting on her fist. 'This boy is fighting his own demons,' she was thinking.

About two months after Guddi's naming ceremony, her mother Saroj broached a subject rather hesitatingly with Tara. The younger uncle of her husband had owned a big cloth store in Okada, Punjab. When he came to Delhi as a refugee, he did not have enough money to open another store. Therefore he opened a small store to sell buckets, trunks and small stoves made of iron and steel. Soon he began to manufacture tin boxes and containers by hand, then bought a machine to do the job. That business was now earning him over Rs 1000 per month. Since his son, who had done his BA, did not want a job that paid only Rs 150 or 200 per month, he had joined the family business. Mehta's aunt had come to the naming ceremony. When she had found out that Sita was a Brahmin, she had asked Saroj to convey the message of a marriage alliance to Tara.

Saroj said that Mehta's uncle did not care if the son got a large dowry or expensive presents, but the bride must be pretty and without any physical defects. The son had been married only a year before partition. His wife had gone to her parents' home for her first childbirth, and everyone in her family had been murdered in the riots. Saroj also made clear that the uncle considered his twenty-six-year-old son to be unmarried in a way.

Tara passed on the message to Purandei. Purandei was very excited, but did not want to be seen accepting the proposal right away. Covering her mouth with her hand, she raised an objection, 'The boy was married once. How can he be called unmarried?'

What could Tara say to her? She kept quiet, and gave no reply to Saroj. Although Mehta came by every Sunday with Guddi to ask if he could be of any help, he also did not bring up the subject when Tara did not. One Sunday after Mehta had left, Purandei asked Tara in a hushed tone, 'His family did not give any answer about the boy?'

Tara was surprised, 'Bua, it was you who said that the boy could not be called unmarried. They kept quiet when they got no response from you.'

'Hai, may I die! When did I mean to say that? All I meant was that you do as you think proper.'

'When Mehta comes next time, I'll ask him to send Saroj over. You speak to her yourself.'

'Beti, what could an uneducated stupid woman like me say in this matter?' Purandei asserted her confidence in Tara, 'It's all in your hands, you know what to do. This good deed will be done by you. You arrange this, and I'll go bath in the Ganga. What more can I say? You are Sita's elder sister, you are also her brother. I didn't mean anything particular. If the boy has no children, he's like unmarried. Men are like that. A man and a horse are as good as new once they have had a bath.'

'Why don't you ask Sita what she thinks about a marriage partner?'

'Hai, who asks such things of daughters?' Purandei said, obviously surprised. 'What does the poor girl know? It's not same with you, you are older and wiser. You tell them to show the boy to you. I'll come along if you want, but don't whisper a word to anyone. People cannot bear seeing good things happening to anyone, you know.' Purandei knew that her neighbour Gurandei was also searching for a match for her younger daughter.

Tara said nothing. She thought, 'I may not be all that wise, but I am doing matchmaking just like an older person.'

When Saroj came by one day, Purandei said to her in a roundabout way, 'My husband's elder brother lives in Amritsar, my brother and his wife are in Ajnala. Let me also consult them. Such big decisions are not taken in a hurry. I don't know about the custom in villages and small towns, but in Lahore and Amritsar one did not say "yes" or "no" right away. There's a way how such things are done. The women from the boy's family went for months to help out at the girl's home before they were given an answer.'

Saroj and Mehta's sister-in-law paid several visits to spend some time with Purnadei. They seemed to agree on most matters, except that the boy's family wanted him to see the girl before setting the wedding date. How could Purandei say no, for such practices had become the custom in Lahore and Amritsar also? She finally agreed to take a dressed Sita to the temple of Hanuman on a Tuesday afternoon, and that Saroj will point out Sita to the boy from a distance. Purandei did not want her innocent girl to see the boy.

Thinking it was useless to argue with Purandei, Tara decided to ask Sita about her choice of marriage partner. Sita said shyly, 'Bahinji, I don't know. Whatever you decide is right for me.'

Sita had not been told anything about the search of a groom for her, but she had known everything from the first day itself.

Tara said to tease her, 'Don't accuse me later that we pushed you into the marriage blindfolded. I heard someone say that your groom has a very dark, pockmarked complexion and perhaps a squint.'

'Well, it is still all right if you approve of him,' Sita bowed her head, trying to suppress a smile. She had had a good look at the boy on the way to the temple.

'If you're too shy to have a look at him, you don't have to.'

'What's there to be shy of? Everyone likes to have a look these days. Sometimes they even get to talk to each other,' Sita said, keeping her head down.

'Go away, you wretch! Moments ago you didn't care. Now you want to talk to him.'

Sita bashfully covered her face with her dupatta.

Mehta's uncle Pundit Bulaki Ram did not want to delay the wedding for long. Mehta and Saroj came to visit and to reassure Purandei, 'We are as much from the boy's family as from the girl's family. Who wants to show off! We are all in the same boat, trying to resettle ourselves after losing everything. The sooner this good deed is done, the better. You won't have to bother about anything. We'll help you do everything.'

Purandei had a letter written to her brother-in-law in Amritsar. The brother-in-law's family had broken off relations with her sixteen years ago, and had no intention of participating and, therefore, sharing the cost of her daughter's wedding. Purandei's brother and his wife came from Ajnala, as did her own sister from Jagaraon, for the occasion. It did not enthuse Tara, rather it meant guests crowded into her flat for several days and an extra expense of several hundred rupees. She was doing it as a duty. Mathur had taken over the charge of organizing the ceremony, and came by every day to offer his advice.

When Narottam was told of Sita's wedding by Tara, he called her over and asked, 'Congratulations! What would you like as a present?'

Sita dropped her head shyly.

Tara said to help her, 'Achcha, we'll think of a good present for you.'

When she had invited Mercy and Chaddha, how could Tara not invite Mr and Mrs Nath?

After her chance encounter with Nath at his office at the Planning Commission, Tara had gone back to meet him the next day. Before leaving for her own office around 1.30 p.m., she had invited Nath to lunch at her place on Sunday.

On the following Friday and Saturday she spent over Rs 60 in redecorating her living room. She did everything with great care, as if preparing for a festive occasion. She changed the curtains over her door and windows, and got matching covers for the settee and the table.

The floor of the aangan of Nath's mansion in Lahore had been bricked over, leaving no space for house or flower plants. Nath had kept a few potted crotons in a veranda in his wing, and some bougainvillea creepers that grew in tubs on the roof nearby. In his study he had two small potted palms with lush fronds. He had told Tara the names of several plants he had, and Tara remembered how very fond he was of narcissus flowers. Tara bought a small Chinese palm and a colourful coleus from a nursery, and brass pots, to keep them in, from an emporium.

When Nath arrived he asked, 'You live here all alone?'

'A neighbour from my gali in Lahore and her daughter stay with me.'

'When did you come here from Jalandhar?'

'I never went there,' Tara said, bowing her head.

'How did you find your in-laws after the fire incident?'

Tara remained silent, her head bent.

Nath complimented Tara on her small but clean and well-appointed flat. He said, 'I have so much space in my bungalow and it's a shame to let it go to waste. My bibi doesn't have such good taste.'

'What?' Tara's eyes widened in amazement. 'Why didn't you bring your wife along with you? Why didn't you tell me? Why haven't you introduced me to her?'

'Hmm!' Nath said, pursing his lips.

'When did you get married?' Tara wanted to know.

Nath looked away and said, 'It's useless to plant a garden at my place. I am leaving for Simla in the beginning of May. Last year also I was there until the middle of September. The plants either wither away in my absence or the stray cattle eat them up.'

'I'll come to your place next Sunday to meet bhabhiji.'

'Want me to send her here?'

'How can that be?'

'Why?'

'First I must visit her and then you can bring her here.'

'Do we really need such formality?'

Tara said nothing in reply. 'He is such a distinguished person,' she was thinking. 'If I continue to insist he would think I was being undeservedly familiar.' She did not mention the subject again.

Nath began to talk in a friendly and caring way. He told Tara about the death of his father Devi Lal in Sonwan in 1948. Then he reminded Tara, 'I'd once told you about the problems about inheriting family property. Whatever we got as the insurance claim for our Lahore property, my brothers invested it all in starting a second sugar mill. Now they have formed a limited company in which I am a sleeping partner. As working partners each of them draw a thousand every month. The company will remain a loss-making business to save taxes. They will continue to draw their salaries, I'll continue to share the losses. The value of my share will gradually dissipate.'

Tara tried to make conversation by relating some incidents about the spoiled children at the AA mansion.

Nath's brushing aside her eagerness to meet Mrs Nath by calling it an unnecessary formality had upset Tara. She thought, perhaps Nath did not like her reticence to answer the question about her in-laws. 'But what could I say? Nath did not approve of Somraj in the first place.' She remembered Nath's words. 'Your father's elder brother has gotten you engaged to some oaf.' Tara's thoughts kept on returning to what Nath had said about her feelings for Asad even after knowing about her engagement. She wondered if such a broad-minded person would mind such a triviality.

Tara's memories of Asad had been jogged a few months ago by the news she had read about the arrest of several communist leaders following the uncovering of an extensive political conspiracy in Pakistan. Asad had been among those arrested. 'He is still working for the party,' Tara had thought.

'He could not stand by me because of his unswerving loyalty to the party. 'What if I had stayed behind and waited for him in the DAV College camp? Would that have been such a mistake? Would Kaushalya Devi and the camp officials have let me go with him? Social pressures make an individual so helpless! The society that we live in sometimes leaves us in limbo, at other times comes to our rescue, but always remains cold and unfeeling.'

Tara again saw Asad's name in the newspaper in the second week of May: Mrs Zohra Asad had applied to put up bail for her husband, and that he had been released. Asad and Zohra had been married only two weeks before his arrest. Zohra's round face swam before Tara's eyes. Her complexion like red wheat, her crinkly hair. Zohra was a medical student. All Tara thought on reading the news was, 'Achcha, Asad married Zohra. The poor man got arrested soon after his wedding. Well, it's good that he's been released. India and Pakistan have not only become two separate countries, but two different worlds.'

Nath had told Tara about his going to Simla in the beginning of May, but had left without leaving his address there. That meant Tara's meeting Mrs Nath would be delayed until August end or September. Nath had telephoned Tara on his return from Simla to ask after her and to tell her that he was back.

Sita's wedding was to take place during a period of auspicious days at the end of September. Tara began to telephone all her friends to invite them. She rang Nath's bungalow at eight o'clock in the morning hoping to be able to speak to his wife. The voice that answered was of the old peon.

Tara said, 'This is Tara Puri speaking. Call Mrs Nath or sahib to the telephone.'

'I'll tell sahib,' the peon said hesitantly.

Tara was alarmed: Why the hesitation?

'It's you Tara?' Nath said cheerfully. 'How are you getting on? I was thinking about calling you or dropping by.'

'You'll have to come by,' Tara said, pretending to be angry. 'Sita is getting married. You must bring bhabhiji.'

'Um,' said Nath, after some hesitation.

'You must,' Tara insisted.

'Achcha.'

'Not achcha, but you have to.'

'All right.'

Purandei had seldom had any material possessions. Her husband had been alive when their one-year-old firstborn had died. Sita was only an infant at the time her mother had become a widow at age twenty-one. She had somehow managed to pay for Sita's education up to high school. Then came Partition, and she had to leave Lahore.

In spite of living in poverty for years, Purandei had retained some residue of her middle-class values. Her daughter was going to be married and her husband's elder brother had turned his back on her! She groped around in her steel trunk and, came out with bits of cash that had amounted to Rs 650 to the present day. The two gold bangles that she had on her wrists for the past twenty-five years had whittled down to the thickness of a wire. She sold them off, but it did not suffice. Her eyes would often fill with tears. She pleaded to Tara with her hands joined, 'Beti, I haven't kept a paisa even for my *kafan*. Now its up to you to arrange your sister's wedding. God will bless you for this.'

Tayee-to-all-neighbourhood was also keeping a watchful eye on preparations for the wedding. The truth about Purandei's finances and her relationship with Tara had not remained hidden from her, and that had made her affection for Tara well up even more copiously. Tara had to obey Tayee's command to get for herself four gold bangles.

On the day of the wedding, when Tayee noticed Purandei's wrists without bangles, she said sternly, 'Are you out of your mind? It'd be a bad omen to do the marriage rites and give away the bride with your wrists bare.'

When Tara offered two of her bangles to Purandei, Tayee reproached her too, 'Beti, what's wrong with all of you. You did not hesitate to spend money on every other thing. Think of your own senior position and reputation? Is that the way to behave like a government official? Do you want to bring shame to all Punjabis? It'd be such a disgrace if you greeted the groom's procession without suitable ornaments.'

Tayee brought a pair of gold bracelets and a gold chain of her own, and borrowed four gold bangles from a neighbour for Tara and Purandei to wear.

Tara had thought that she would have to spend around six hundred rupees, but it had already cost her Rs 850. Although Mathur was careful to spend only on essentials, a new expense cropped up every day. Tara was helpless in the face of social expectations and the customs that had to be observed. In spite of everything, there had to be a show of joy and of festive spirit. The consolation for her was that rationing was being enforced in the city, and nobody could have more than twenty-five guests at a feast. Tara was not willing to disobey the rule.

Mehta was alert to ensure that Tara did not experience any difficulty. He and his uncle, who lived in Paharganj, were also looking after the arrangements at the bride's home. In the pre-partition days one would hire a *halwai* who would prepare the food over a makeshift stove in or near the family's house. That was not the practice any more because a neighbourhood halwai promised to deliver all that was needed at a reasonable price. The arrangements to welcome the bridal procession and for the wedding feast were made in the way such things were usually done by the middle-class families living in galis and by-lanes in a city.

The row of flats on Pachkuian Road had shops on the street level. Evening was the time for business. To block the entrance to the shops or the alley would have meant picking a quarrel with the shop owners. Tara's flat was in the corner and its entrance in the back lane. A small area in the back lane was enclosed with shoulder-high walls of fabric attached to poles driven in the ground to welcome the guests and the bridal procession. The canopy of the mandap was festooned with green mango leaves and paper buntings. Strings of electric bulbs hanging in the enclosed area were lit before dusk fell. The enclosure was lined with chairs and electric pedestal fans. Two tubs were filled with bottles of soda and chunks of ice. All this was the barest possible arrangement.

Mehta did not forget to arrange for a gramophone and loudspeaker to play music to give the event a festive air. Half an hour before the expected arrival of the groom's party, popular songs of the day began to blare from the loudspeaker to announce that a wedding was taking place.

Soon after dusk came the sound of the brass band leading the groom's procession. Purandei's brother and his wife, her sister and a group of neighbours acting as hosts came forward to welcome the procession. Tara too had to wear a red sari suitable for the occasion. Mercy, a red bindi adorning her glowing dark-complexioned face just below the sindoor-filled centre parting, looked resplendent in a pink sari. A garland of *bela* flowers was wrapped around her hair tied in a bun. Chaddha, Mathur and his sister, Narottam and Miss Deva stood alongside Tara. Guests from the girl's side do not attend the wedding just for the fun of it, but to offer help and assistance. Several clerks from Tara's office, the section assistant and the elderly superintendent were present, without waiting to be invited, to lend a hand.

The brass band was playing *boliyan* from Punjabi folk songs. In the middle of the procession was the groom riding a mare, with a mukut in the shape of a crown and a sehra, wreath of flowers, around his head. Four men carrying big Petromax lamps on their heads walked alongside the groom to show up his fine clothes and adornments. Just ahead of the groom's mare was a group of Punjabi young men, arms stretched and hips twisting, clapping in time to the music and shouting 'hokka! hokka!'. They were dancing the bhangra and singing boliyan in which the last word of the first line or the rhyming pattern determined the second half of the couplet:

'He went away and worked hard for twelve years, and brought back what?Dried fruits and nuts!
'Hearts of old maids yearn for their long gone youth.'

And

'He went away and worked hard for twelve years, and brought back what? Silver!
'Hey, boys, choose whoever you want, there goes a carriage full of girls.'

A number of married and unmarried women from the neighbourhood were waiting at the first floor windows in the gali to sing in welcome to the procession. The 'girls' answered the 'boys' in unison:

'He went away and worked hard for twelve years, and brought back what? Silver!
'Hey, girls, choose whoever you want, there goes a carriage full of boys.'

A handful of women were in the procession. Their expensive saris with zari borders and richly embroidered salwar-kameez suits, and the quantities and sizes of gold ornaments they wore came as a surprise to Mathur, Chaddha, Narottam and Miss Deva.

Chaddha said, 'Can anyone guess that only five years ago these people were refugees, some of them seeking shelter under trees?'

A friend of Mehta standing nearby said, 'Bhai sahib, when the boy's family arrived in the city four years ago, they did not have enough cash even to start a bajaji business. They survived for four months by selling kulfi ice candy. The women of the family made kulfi at home, and father and son sold it in bazaars. Now they must be worth fifty to sixty thousand.'

Tara said, 'It's not a Lahore custom to dance bhangra in groom's procession. Only villagers did that at country fairs. Many refugees came from the countryside and the North-West frontier. A whole new Punjabi culture has developed in Delhi.'

After the customary welcome and the ritual of jaimal, the traditional adorning of the groom with garlands, girls and young women of the gali took the groom upstairs to Tara's flat. The guests were served refreshments in the enclosure. Tara remained standing near the entrance, eyes fixed on the road. She had asked Nath to come by half past eight so that he may not get bored. Dinner was going to be served to her friends in a separate room in her flat.

Tara stepped forward when she saw Nath's car. He had come alone. Seeing her red sari and gold bangles, Nath said cheerfully, 'You yourself are looking like a bride. Really, you are looking very pretty.'

Tara changed the subject to hide her embarrassment, 'Where's bhabhiji?'

Nath said, 'You didn't have to wait long for me?'

'Why didn't you bring bhabhiji along?' Tara persisted.

'Just drop it,' said Nath, as if he did not like the topic.

Tara was again suspicious, 'Do they not get along?'

Upstairs she introduced Nath to other guests, 'Professor Dr Pran Nath, economic advisor to the Planning Commission.'

Everyone welcomed Nath. Chaddha sat next to Nath and began to discuss, 'The government is planning to increase the food output by agricultural reforms, but how could all farmland be properly cultivated without an equitable distribution of land? What about landless peasantry? What's the point of increasing the food output if the people don't have the cash to buy it?'

The hint of bad feelings between Nath and his wife had upset Tara, and it continued to niggle her. Nath was wearing an open-collar shirt without a jacket, his shirt sleeves were rolled up and creases from folding the ironed but well-worn shirt could be seen. Tara noticed that the collar was beginning to fray.

Tara thought, 'His wife does not take care of his clothes! Perhaps they don't talk to each other. I've never seen them together. Doctor sahib is such a kind and understanding person, why did he ever marry such a woman? Perhaps Mrs Nath is fond of gadding like Mrs Agarwal, perhaps she is quarrelsome like Mrs De. Who knows Sita won't turn out to be like one of them after six month's of married life?'

The discussion on the government policy bored Mercy. She asked Tara, 'Will Sita continue to work or will she quit her job?'

'It'd be better if she continued,' Mathur gave his opinion. 'If she quits, all the money spent on her training will go waste.'

'I don't want her to quit, but she perhaps will.'

'That's such a national wastage,' Nath said. 'Mostly girls from relatively well-off families get the opportunity to go for higher education, and they generally quit after they are married. The money spent on their education by the country goes to waste. Only those girls who make a pledge to work for a certain number of years should be allowed into medical and vocational training colleges.'

'Girls study up to BA or MA level so as to improve their prospects for marriage,' Narottam added.

'I seldom heard them discuss politics or literature. All they talk about is fashion, films and festivals,' said Mathur.

'How would literature help anyone in cleaning the kitchen and doing the laundry?' Mercy asked.

'Quotations from Shakespeare and Byron could surely come in handy when writing a letter to one's spouse,' Nath added.

The wisecrack was probably aimed at his wife, Tara guessed. She had mostly kept out of the conversation. She already had her hands full managing the event, and did not have Sita to help her.

The bride and the groom left for her in-law's house early the next morning. On returning from the office, Tara felt that the apartment had taken a forlorn look. Purandei also looked a little sad, but clearly relieved that such a heavy burden was off her shoulders. She made sure to sit next to Tara and to thank her, 'Beti, everything went well with Maharaj-ji's blessings and your determination. I will thank Maharaj-ji all my life that He relieved me of such a heavy responsibility. From now on, you are my daughter.'

An odd thought came into Tara's mind, 'Had I been her daughter she'd also have been worried about relieving my burden.' But she said nothing to Purandei, and began to inquire about returning the things that had been loaned by the neighbours.

Two days later, as the custom dictated, Purandei went to bring Sita back for a brief stay. Had she not, Sita's in-laws would have taken this lapse from the custom as a lack of concern for her daughter. Sita arrived before Tara had returned home from the office, and they embraced each other. Back in Lahore, Tara had hardly ever exchanged a word with Sita. In Delhi she had helped Sita despite her disgust for the girl's dissolute way of life. But a bond had developed between them after living under the same roof for the past ten months, just as between two bullocks put in the same pen.

Tara looked intently at Sita. A change seemed to have come over the girl in the past two days. She was acting more grown-up and self-confident, and as someone on the same level as Tara.

Tara asked in a conspiratorial tone, 'Tell me, were you scared?'

Sita replied, smiling bashfully, 'Hai, I was really scared.'

'How about his family?'

'Very nice people.'

'Will you be all right now?'

'Why not? Only the first day is scary.'

'How did he treat you?'

'Not badly,' Sita replied offhandedly, as if to imply 'what's there to share with you on this subject.'

Tara smiled at Sita to indicate that she felt happy for her, but the smug and boastful look in Sita's eyes seemed like arrogance. She thought, 'Sita seems happy. She has found what she longed for—a husband and a shelter. Could she have fallen in love in just a couple of days?' Then thought to herself, 'What else is love? Isn't love the fulfilment of whatever one wants and desires? Isn't love also a need and a hunger, or the desire to satisfy that hunger and need?'

She chided herself for denigrating Sita, 'When I was taken to that room on the third floor, what was I waiting for? I had no feelings of hatred or hostility at that moment. Rather I waited and hoped for love. It was his abominable behaviour that filled me with fear and loathing.'

In her mind's eye she saw herself as a wife doing household chores, minding her children and in such situations. The images continued to go round and round before her eyes.

She recalled Mercy's words, 'Are you abnormal?'

She said to herself angrily, 'No, I don't want that kind of normality. I am fine as I am.'

On Saturday, Tara returned from her office at 1.30 p.m. to find that Sita's mother-in-law and another woman had come to escort the bride back. Sita had wrapped a few of her things in a bundle, and was waiting to say goodbye to Tara. When she left an hour later, Sita hugged Tara lovingly, and Tara hugged her back. Purandei, aanchal over eyes, was crying quietly and tears came to Tara's eyes. She and Purandei went down to the gali to see Sita off. As the taxi drove away, Tara again felt a pang of loneliness.

Mercy had barely had an opportunity to talk to Tara during the excited melee on the evening of the wedding. Just before leaving she had said to Tara, 'I have something important to tell you. Either drop by my place or ring me. I can also come to your place some evening.'

Tara had thought, 'She probably wants to ask me for a contribution for the party. Why else would she want to talk to me alone?' Feeling the need to lighten her mood by talking to someone, she rang Mercy.

Mercy said, 'This is not a good time. I have company. Come to lunch tomorrow.'

Tara again sat forlornly. Purandei's presence or absence in the house meant little to her. 'Wish Narottam or Mathur would come so that I can have company.' She thought of going to visit Sheelo, then thought better of it, 'I can enjoy my own company.' She lay down on her bed without changing her clothes. Her mind began to cast up memories of her past. A couplet she had heard from her brother came to her mind. She hummed pensively:

The bulbul bird is born to lament, the moth to immolate itself
The fate I got that was the worst of all.

Then she scolded herself, 'What's wrong with you? What reason do *you* have to mope about? None!'

She forced herself to read a copy of a report submitted by the Planning Commission that Nath had given her. 'I must know what's happening in the country,' she told herself. Purandei, with nothing left to worry over and time on her hands, had gone to the hosiery factory to get more socks to work on. Tara had read nearly fifty pages of the report when Purandei retuned around 6 p.m.

On her way back from the factory, Purandei had stopped by Sadar Bazaar to meet some of her former neighbours. She had walked over five miles, and looked tired. She had hardly had any respite after the grind of her daughter's wedding. She continued to sit and chat idly to rest her feet.

Tara put the report aside, got up and said to Purandei, 'Bua, you must be very tired. Stretch out a bit. I'll make the dinner.'

'No, no. Why should you? I'm still alive. I'll do it.'

'No, let me do the cooking today. It's been months. I just want to see if I haven't forgotten everything.'

'Go away, *kamali*, you crazy girl!' Purandei said affectionately. 'A woman never forgets how to cook. She is born to cook and feed others.'

When Tara ignored her and went into the kitchen, Purandei sat down on the threshold and began to explain where things were stored.

Tayi dropped in, curious as ever to find out what Purandei had given to Sita in her trousseau. On seeing Tara doing the cooking, she said appreciatively, 'A woman looks good only in kitchen and at her in-laws' house. You should think about settling her too,' she said, then began to badger Purandei. 'We'll have to find someone who's just right for her. We must marry her into a family like my brother's.'

'Maharaj-ji has already helped us so much, He will take care of the rest,' Purandei said to end the topic. She knew that such talk irritated Tara.

Sunday. Tara was at Mercy's place at 1 p.m. Mercy asked Chimmo to serve lunch.

Tara did not see Chaddha in the flat. She said, 'What's the hurry. Let's wait for jijaji.'

'He's gone to Lucknow. I asked you to come so that we could talk alone. What have you decided about Tewari?' Mercy came straight to the point.

'Decide what?' The question took Tara by surprise.

'Don't you know?'

'I know Tewariji. Nityanand Tewari, from Aligarh.'

'Didn't Mathur say anything about Tewari's intention about you?'

'I'd said even then that I had no such intention.'

'You had said that you had no intention at that time. You didn't say that you didn't like him.'

'Who am I to find a fault in him? He's a good person, but I've no desire to tie the knot,' Tara said with some irritation.

'Wah, Mathur says that you had told him that Tewari was a very nice man. Someone who acts high and mighty like you isn't going to say "yes" outright any way. You are twenty-four. Mathur is fond of you as he's of Tewari. Tewari was his student, right. He's been promoted to a Reader. Yes, his salary isn't as much as yours. But money isn't everything.'

'Mathur bhai is demonstrating a loss of his mental faculties,' Tara said in English. 'What he couldn't do for himself, he wants it for others. He's so obsessed with matchmaking, why doesn't he find a match for himself?'

'He's a sanyasi both in practice and in thinking. He's over forty-three. What's the point in him getting married now?'

'So he tries to please himself by arranging marriages?'

'What's wrong in that? You know he has great regard for you. He worries for you as if you were his own daughter.'

'I do not respect him any less. I would have called him "uncle" if his hair were grey.'

Chimmo served lunch. She had forgotten that Tara could not tolerate food with lots of chillies. Tara ate, although chillies made her eyes water and she felt as if her tongue was on fire.

'Do you know that Mathur said that Tewari had rejected several good proposals. He is completely devoted to you.'

'Nonsense.'

'Not nonsense. He worships your photograph.'

'Don't you exaggerate!'

'I swear by you. Mathur told me.'

'How did he get my photograph?'

'Mathur asked me for one.'

'That photo had both of us in it. Must be worshipping you.'

'I cut it into half and gave yours.'

'You did me a great favour. Should I thank you for it?' Tara was really annoyed.

'What disfavour did I do? Do you mind if someone values you and desires you?'

'What should I do with this kind of desiring? There's another one, who probably dreams about me. He makes way for me, parts the curtain for me as if I were a soap bubble that would burst if something touched me.'

'Why does that irritate you?'

'Why shouldn't it? Why is everyone bothered about me when I haven't given any such indication? Do they want to give me a bad name?'

'Will you ever like anyone?'

'Why such a concern about that?'

'Why shouldn't I be concerned?'

'Neither am I looking for someone to support me, nor am I desperate for it like Sita.'

'Mathur thinks that Tewari's age, his physique, his education and background makes him just the right person for you.'

'What made him decide that it does? I have never felt anything for Tewari, never thought about him in that way. He shouldn't wait for me.'

'Whom do you have in mind?'

'I'll let you know when I find someone.'

'Hmm,' Mercy said, looking intently at Tara.

'When will jijaji return?'

'He has many places to visit. First Lucknow, then Patna, from there on to Calcutta. He'll be away for two weeks. Why, what's the matter?'

'He had said that when he comes back, he'd like to meet Dr Nath. Doctor sahib told me that his house was over a mile from the nearest bus stop. I'll invite him over when jijaji is back.' Tara changed the subject. 'Didi, I can't seem to find a good car for myself. They want a lot of money for a small car. I think I should get a Ford. Doctor sahib gave the same advice. I don't drive around all day so I don't have to worry about the cost of petrol.'

'You seem to be besotted with Doctor. Always talking about him. He hasn't captured your heart, has he?'

'Don't talk rubbish, didi,' Tara said angrily, straightening her back.

'I am talking rubbish? Haven't I noticed? You always want to be next to him, swooning over him.'

'You can't compare me to him! Have you no regard for his position!' Tara said, face flushing with anger.

'Since when have you become such a toady? And what about his position? Is he some kind of God on earth? He is a man, you are a young woman. But why are you blushing?' Pleased with herself, Mercy said, wiggling her thumb before Tara, 'I've got you!'

'Have you no consideration for his being married. He has a wife.'

'Wife?' Mercy said with surprise. 'She was not with him that evening.'

'They probably had a falling out. I have never seen them together,' Tara said ominously.

'Could that be because of you? The same problem as with De's marriage?'

'Didi, you are the limit,' Tara said in a reproaching tone. 'I have never even met Mrs Nath.'

'She might have seen you both together, and became suspicious.'

Angry tears filled Tara's eyes, 'Didi, I'll never come here again if you go on like that. You have no idea how indebted we are to Doctor sahib. He helped my father, he helped my brother, he helped me. I respect him more than I respect my elder brother. He was like our saviour. We can never forget what he did for us.'

Mercy kept quiet. Tara was also quiet for several minutes, then said abruptly, 'I am leaving.'

'Stay a while.'

'No, let me go.'

Mercy was silent as she accompanied Tara downstairs, then hugged her and kissed her on the cheek before seeing her off.

Tara felt her anger drain away.

Chaddha returned to Delhi after a month. Very eager to meet Nath, he asked Tara to organize a meeting. Nath arrived at Tara's flat at 4 p.m. on Sunday. Tara went downstairs when she heard Nath toot his horn, and took him to Mercy's place in Daryaganj.

The only people present besides Mercy were Chaddha and Mathur. Chaddha and Nath had a long discussion. Mercy did not participate in deference to Nath, leaving the chore of hospitality to her 'younger' sister Tara. Mathur and Tara also kept out of the conversation.

Mrs Agarwal had not broken off her relations with Tara. She telephoned Tara from time to time, especially when she wanted new blouses made for herself, and would send her car to get Tara. She would say, 'It's no use asking the *mara* tailor. The stupid guy takes every kind of measurements, but still can't give a good fitting.' She always invited Tara on the birthday celebrations of her children.

Puttan's birthday party was in the second week of November. Tara came back from the office, had her tea, changed her sari, and reached AA a little behind other guests. It was an informal, homely affair, and the presence of scores of women and children set the room abuzz. The guests had formed three groups: children on one side, women on another, and a mixed gathering of women and men on the third. Several Gandhi caps were visible. By now Tara had begun to recognize the Congress party members. Several of them had come to her office to get some work done or to plead someone's case.

Prasadji complained, as if he had a right to do so, 'Taraji is seldom seen, like the Eid moon. She's now a big government official. Why would she want to meet ordinary folks like us?'

'How can you say that, bhai sahib! You are the raja's kinfolk,' Tara replied.

Mr Agarwal roared with laughter, and others joined in, 'Wah! Wah! Well said! The raja's kinfolk! Well said!'

Tara gave her congratulations to Mr and Mrs Agarwal.

Sarafji and Gopi Babu said Jai Hind to Tara. Mrs Agarwal said, putting her arm around Tara's shoulder, 'However big an official she may become, she'd always be like a younger sister to me.'

From bits of talk that she heard, Tara realized that the conversation was about the elections. Delhi was buzzing with news of the elections for the legislative assemblies and the Parliament only two months away: Who will be the candidates? Who will run on the Congress ticket? Who was most likely to win?

Tara, a present for Puttan in the folds of her aanchal, went towards the children's corner to give him a kiss. When she came back she saw Prasadji and Gopi Babu talking to Mrs Agarwal. Tara hesitated, but Mrs Agarwal said pointing at her, 'Ask her! Tara knows everything. Tara has seen her in the club so many times having drinks with De and Rawat Sahib.'

Gopi Babu said, his mouth full of paan and rubbing his eyes, 'Arey, she has such a bad reputation, a woman with such a low character. I've known her for ages. When she used to live at Kashmiri Gate, she had an affair with Dr Jafri. He used to refer all the Muslim cases to her. Samarth, the agent of Malcolm Hayes, was always shacked up at her place. Now she has De in her clutches.'

Prasadji thrust his hands in his kurta pockets to push back his thin shoulders to make them look bigger. He said, straightening his back, 'I have all the information about her. Singh and Mahashay are encouraging her. I won't let her be a candidate and give the Congress a bad name. She has a bad character.'

Narottam was standing nearby. He pursed his lips on hearing this, and moved away.

The mudslinging was aimed at Dr Shyama. Tara knew that Shyama belonged to a faction in the Congress that opposed Prasadji and Mrs Agarwal.

Mrs Agarwal added, 'She openly drinks at the club, smokes, gambles at cards, eats eggs, fish, meat, just like some Christian. What is it that she doesn't do? Neither does she have anyone to keep a check on her, nor does she have any consideration for anyone. Ask poor Mrs De whose family she has ruined. Now she is going around meeting the members of the election board and begging for the Congress ticket. Also went to meet Dutt.'

Prasadji said challengingly, 'How will Dutt help her? And who does this Shyama think herself to be? I brought her into the Congress party, I helped her establish her practice, and now she dares to defy me! My own cat snapping at me! I introduced her to all the important people she knows. I'll turn her practice to ashes. Does she think that she's the only lady doctor left in the city? There's Miss Griffith, there are Barodkar, Mrs Charan, Singhal. She can do all the free cases she wants in the *bhangi* slums! That kind of popularity means nothing. I'll make it impossible for her to live in Delhi!'

Tara called out to Lalli and went towards her. After exchanging a few words with her, she went to greet Dolly. Dolly first pretended to sulk, then complained in the mixed Hindi–English of a convent school student, 'I wished you the moment you came in. But the way you ignored me! I felt like never speaking to you again.'

Tara swore that she was telling the truth that she did not see Dolly and that she herself was looking for her. Dolly was appeased and began to admire Tara's sari, 'Hai, you are looking so sweet!' She rolled her eyes, 'You look dazzling!'

Tara walked over to commiserate with Maaji, then stood talking with Narottam. She was waiting for some guests to leave, for her own early departure would have certainly been noticed by Mrs Agarwal. Sarafji, Prasadji and Gopi Babu had left. Narottam had promised to drop her home.

Mrs Agarwal again said to Tara, 'What do I care? I don't give a hoot about the stipend for the MLAs. All these people pestered me into becoming a candidate. I would win even if I were to run as an independent. She won't be allowed to run on the Congress ticket and, on top of that, will have to face embarrassment. Try and tell her what's good for her. She listens to you.'

Tara did not like to hear unkind things about Shyama. She was grateful to Shyama for her help. Shyama always treated her with affection when they met. Mercy was generally disdainful of the Congress party members, but Shyama was among the handful that she called 'unselfish' and 'honest'. 'Shyama is the true doctor,' Mercy would say. 'She's not greedy for money. Anybody can call her any time of the day or night. If the patient is really poor, she gives them a couple of rupees out of her own pocket for medicines and milk.' But Mercy too had heard rumours about Shyama's romantic liaisons. She had also told Tara that De's wife, who went around disparaging Shyama, had no spotless reputation. As a private nurse, Mercy often heard rumours about the scandalous liaisons of the upper-class society.

Tara returned home, but the gossip about Shyama was on her mind. She herself had seen Shyama smoking and drinking quite openly at dinners, but her heart refused to hold it against the doctor. Mrs Agarwal took a small drink now and then, Tara thought, but after a little pretence. She allowed herself to be persuaded to accept a drink, and then criticized others for doing the same behind their backs. Shyama took a drink freely, and did not criticize others for doing it. 'Some people loathe food cooked with onions. Mrs Agarwal also thought eating meat was worse than drinking.'

A thought came to Tara's mind, 'Could the quarrel between Mr and Mrs Nath have happened because of me? Mercy had said so. Perhaps someone spread rumours about Shyama. Perhaps Mrs De did so, in a fit of jealousy. But Shayma is not at all a bad person, she's so kind. I want nothing to do with election politics or with their squabbling. Why are they ganging up against that poor soul?'

Tara had not met Shyama for a long time. The last they had seen each other was at Shyama's bungalow about a year ago. Tara decided, on next Sunday, that she would rather go and visit Shyama than spend the day alone.

Shyama lived quite far, on Rajpur Road. When Tara prudently telephoned her bungalow before going over, Shyama asked, 'Why, what's the matter? Are you feeling well? You don't have to be shy. Want me to come and examine you this afternoon?'

Tara tried to reassure her, 'Bahinji, I just wanted to see you. It's been a while since we met.'

'Then come over. You are more than welcome. Come at four. We are playing bridge. You join us.'

'Bahinji, I never learned to play bridge. I'll come around seven.'

'Do you play flash?'

'No, bahinji. Only if I must.'

Shyama insisted, 'Doesn't matter if you don't play. Come early and have tea here.'

Tara reached Shyama's place at seven. Chairs and tables were set out in the veranda, but the place was empty.

Shyama's gardener and maid explained, 'Someone came around two o'clock and took her to see a patient. She hasn't returned. Guest mems and sahibs came but went back.'

Tara had paid off the taxi before speaking to the gardener. She was asking the gardener to get her a taxi when Shyama arrived, driving her small car. She said to Tara, 'Hai, you have been waiting all along and were now going back?'

Shyama escorted Tara inside as she inquired about her. She looked tired. When they sat on the sofa, she leant her head back wearily, 'It was such an abnormal case. Anyway, both the mother and the baby are safe. It's been such a long time since I saw you. You thought of me at last. You don't have free time now that you are such a big official.'

'Don't say that, bahinji,' Tara said politely.

'No, no. I said it without meaning anything. You're very sweet. I don't know why I felt there was a bond between us when I first saw you,' Shyama said, putting her hand on Tara's shoulder. 'Remember?'

'How can I not remember? It's been a long time since I saw you last. I've been thinking about you,' Tara said, her heart melting.

Shyama hugged her briefly, then said, 'Want some tea?'

'I had some before I came, but I will give you company.'

'Bindo,' Shyama called out. 'Get us some tea.' She said to Tara, 'Wait a minute. Let me freshen up. I am really very tired.'

After a short while Tara heard Shyama call from behind the curtain over the door to the next room, 'Why don't you come here?'

Shyama was wearing a dressing gown. She asked Tara to take the sofa next to the bed. 'Tara, don't mind. I'm really exhausted,' she said lying down on the bed on her side, facing Tara.

The maid brought tea. Tara pulled the tray towards her and began to pour. Shyama asked, 'Tell me, how do you spend your time?'

'Nothing special. Divide my time between office and home. I had gone to AA this Thursday. It was Puttan's birthday. You didn't come.'

'It's better to keep those people at a distance,' Shyama said, sipping her tea.

'What's going on, bahinji?' Tara said to start the conversation.

'What do you mean?' Shayma asked gravely. Then said, 'I'll have another cup.'

Taking a sip from her second cup, she said, 'I'm sick and tired of these people and the Congress. If I let all that go, it's only my patients' cases and loneliness for me. I had thought that today I would play bridge for three or four hours and that will provide some diversion. And I had to go and attend to the darned case.'

She fell silent, leaving her tea unfinished and gazing at the wall.

'What's the matter? You look worried,' Tara ventured.

'What is there except worry,' Shyama gave a deep sigh.

'What's this argument about who'll be the Congress candidate?' Tara asked.

'The problem is that three seats are reserved for women candidates. Mrs Agarwal wants to contest on the Congress ticket. Prasad is backing her. Some people have proposed my name, which started all the trouble. They don't want Mrs Agarwal, and they have a point. What did Mrs Agarwal do before 1947? She used to toady to the wives of angraize secretaries. She's a complete dolt, and what will she do in the assembly? She's paid some people to back her. But why bring up the question of men and women candidates? Why not send those to the assembly who understand politics, finance and the working of administration. Mahashayji is having my name dragged through the mud by insisting on my candidacy.'

Tara said after remaining quiet for a few moments, 'Why do you give them the chance to talk such rot about you?'

'What do you mean?'

'Bahinji, please don't take this as backbiting, but I feel bad when someone bad mouths you. I really have a great regard for you.'

'Who was saying what?'

'The same person, Mrs Agarwal. Nobody believes her, but it hurts to hear such slanderous comments. She was telling those Congresswallahs whatnot about you in connection with Mrs De.'

Shyama turned and lay on her back. She closed her eyes.

Tara too remained quiet. Silence fell in the room. When Tara looked at Shayma she saw that Shayma was pressing her temples with her fingers.

'You have a headache? Want me your massage your temples?'

'Un-huh.'

Tara sat on the bed and began to massage Shyama's temples. After about two minutes Shyama said, 'That's enough.'

'It's all right. Let me. My fingers are not yet tired.'

'I don't have a headache. I am just tense.'

'Why, what is it?' Tara asked, putting her hand on Shyama's forehead.

'Come, sit next to me,' Shyama said, making space for Tara.

'What's the matter, didi? You look upset.'

'I don't know what to do with my life. Maybe it's my fault that I did not get married. Maybe women who stay closeted in their homes are better than we are. The grind of household work, worrying about their children probably keeps their mind free of any thoughts. Their bellies are full, their sexual needs are met, but I couldn't live like one of them. If a woman has to be kept bound and gagged, why let her express her individuality and assert her independence? If I had a husband, I'm sure he'd feel compelled to beat me to death. Perhaps I would have changed and turned into a mute animal who never strains at the leash, one who comes back and stands mooing in front of the house even after it had been shooed away.'

Shyama fell silent. Tara was quiet too, deep in thought.

Shyama again said, 'I am already thirty-three. Should I marry now? Whom should I marry, some boy of twenty-four or twenty-five? Which eligible male waits for marriage until he's thirty-five or forty? Should I steal another woman's husband? Once men could forcibly carry off the women they desired. But times have changed. Had I wanted to steal somebody's husband, it wouldn't have been impossible to do so. But neither have I ever thought of it, nor do I want to do it. What's De's wife afraid of? She thinks that I'll take away the horse that pulls the cart of her household, but I'll not do so. If I spend half an hour or an hour in his company, what do I rob her of? He's her man, lives with her. He's the breadwinner, provides her with a roof over her head, and she bullies him in return. She is what she is because of his position. Without him she'd be left a destitute. If I exchange a few words with him once in a while, will it rob the family in a way that they will starve? Or should I just pair up with anyone who comes by as if I were a cow or a sheep? Every male I could want to be with is already burdened with family responsibilities.'

Tara felt as if Shyama was talking about something repugnant, like a disease. She said, sighing deeply, 'Didi, why let it bother us? Can't one live without it?'

'How can one live without it?' Shayma said ruefully. 'Is it not self-torture to suppress and deny one's natural urges? What is natural for the married is also natural for the unmarried. One does try to restrain oneself. Then something happens while you believe that you are trying to restrain yourself, trying to live without it.' Shyama, hand supporting her temple, fell silent.

Tara offered her opinion, 'Can't love also imply self-restraint?'

Shyama heaved a sigh, and said, 'Is yearning for something love? Doesn't love mean a deep sense of fulfilment that makes life worthwhile? Maybe it's only desires of the flesh, but what else is our heart, our brain. If you cut up my body you won't find thoughts of love stored in my heart or brain. The desire and thought of love are expressed in the form of physical attraction.'

Shayma again let out a despairing sigh, 'At times I thought of seeking an answer by losing myself in some spiritual pursuit, but my heart wasn't in it. How could I force myself into developing a belief in something? Some can, and do. There are women who believe that witchcraft can help them have a child, and are willing to risk their lives for it. Can you or I believe in such things?'

Tara said after a moment's thought, 'Didi, we have to observe the rules of the society we live in. We may feel hungry, but we have to be able to learn to control our hunger.'

'First experience hunger for a few days, then talk about it,' Shyama said, looking into Tara's eyes.

'I have remained hungry for up to three days, and have eaten barely anything for days on several occasions, didi. I have seen people fight over scraps of food. And others who did not. One's dignity and self-respect means something, for which one may sacrifice one's life.'

Shyama listened wide-eyed as Tara briefly described the incident of her confinement in the house in Shaikhupura. She remained quiet for some time after Tara finished, then asked, 'Are you willing to believe that it was your karma?'

'How can I? Why should I believe that God made others commit sins so that I could have my bad karma? I had to tolerate it because there was nothing I could do to prevent it. There's a limit to what one can do.'

Shyama said after a few moments' silence, 'I really tried hard to keep away. But De got very upset.'

Tara said, after some thought, 'But, didi, they have three children. What'll happen to them?'

'What threat do they face? It's that wretch who's creating the scare. What have I taken away from her, let her tell me. She's eaten up with jealousy, she resents that her husband has a few moments of happiness. Pride of possession, what else? And jealousy! All she does is live off her husband's money and grumble about everything. De's mother still manages the house. They have a cook, an ayah. It was that wretched woman that first began doing hanky-panky with other men. De felt too ashamed to admit it to anyone. He stopped talking to that wretch. Once he had even thought of committing suicide by swallowing poison. There was a time when a man could cut off the head of a woman like her to save his honour. Nowadays all a man can do is hang his head in shame. She goes around trying to paint him as a demon. He swallows his anger and disgust, and keeps quiet. One day he was so distressed as to think that he'd close all the doors to the bungalow and set it afire so that they may all perish.'

Tara did not know what to say. She was lost in thought. 'There is no end to pain and misfortune one may have to suffer. Some suffer physically, others suffer emotionally. My own misfortune, Banti's misery, problems faced by Biddo's grandmother and Mrs Agarwal, and by De, Sheelo and Shyama. When there is no other problem, it's the unfulfilled desire to love and to be loved. Of all mistakes in the world, marital incompatibility is the worst. Was I spared that fate? But at what price? Had that rock been around my neck, only death could have saved me.

Shyama dropped Tara back at her flat after 10 p.m.

Purandei opened the door when Tara rattled the lock chain. Her face took on a serious expression, as if she had swallowed what was on the tip of her tongue.

Tara ignored her, 'Anyone can think what he or she wants. I am responsible for myself.'

The whirlwind of excitement created by the forthcoming general elections had thrown the city of Delhi into disorder. Candidates from all political parties had come to the flats on Panchkuian Road to ask for votes and a chance to be able to serve the country. Walls, doorways and even vehicles had been plastered with the posters of some party or other. Slogans, hailing one party or denouncing another, had been painted on walls. Some people, out of mischief, had painted messages on the backs of stray bulls that roamed in the streets. Boys were encouraged to tear up posters of rival parties, or to alter a slogan, by touching up with paint, into obscene graffiti. Children would, for the reward of two pieces of candy, first shout slogans for one and then for the rival party. Propriety and decorum were being ignored in the fervour to do good for the country and the people.

Tara was happy that Shyama had declined to be a Congress candidate and that Mrs Agarwal had not been given the Congress ticket. The Congress election campaign was the biggest and the most elaborate. The opposition parties that had entered the fray looked like a bunch of rams surrounding a huge elephant and fighting each other to be able to take on the elephant. The government officials knew that the Congress will form the next government. They were supporting the Congress with resigned servility.

Chaddha, Mercy and Mathur were in the thick of the chaos of elections. They too knew that despite an inefficient and corrupt administration, the Congress would win. The communists and the socialists denounced the Congress as the party of capitalists, and were calling for a government on the pattern of a workers' state. They also criticized the Congress for enlisting the help of the administrative machinery in its election campaign.

The opposition had demanded that there should be a caretaker government on the British pattern during the elections, and the administration should be in the hands of a non-partisan executive. The Congress government had rejected such a demand. The bitterest rivalry was between the communists and the socialists. They knew that by dividing the anti-Congress vote they both would lose, but had been unable to form a joint front.

Tara and Narottam had largely been spared the frenzied activity of electioneering. Being government officials, they were not expected to participate in the election campaign. All processions, speeches and use of loudspeakers had to stop twenty-four hours before the polling day in accordance with the rules. In the sudden silence after days of raucous campaigning and harrowing din, Tara felt as if the city had been deserted by its inhabitants.

These were the first general elections in independent India. Polling day was a public holiday, and Narottam did not have to go to work. He had little interest in any single political party's fortunes, but he was curious about the outcome, as one is in the result of a horse race. Harsukh Ram, his neighbour, had bet him fifty rupees that the candidate for the Jana Sangh party would win. Mr Agarwal's friend Rai Navin Chandra was contesting as an independent against a Congress candidate. Narottam drove to some polling stations in the western part of the city, and found the scene rather interesting. Every political party had set up a camp near a polling station, and workers from different parties were vying with each other to present the arriving voters with slips of paper showing their identification number from the electoral rolls. Party volunteers were particularly polite and courteous towards the voters. Arrangement had been made in the tents of some independent candidates for the voters to partake of refreshments and paan.

Narottam spotted Miss Deva on the footpath of a bazaar near the Kashmiri Gate, and offered her a lift in his car. She was on her way to Faiz Bazaar. After waiting for the bus in a queue for some time, she had tried to get a taxi, but all taxis had been hired by one political party or another for their own use. Taxis had also been hired in advance to deny their use by a rival political party.

Deva, who was really peeved, said, 'Do the police not know that it is unlawful to offer transportation to voters?'

Narottam replied with a laugh, 'Is it lawful to offer refreshments to the voters?'

After giving Deva a ride to Faiz Bazaar, Narottam drove on to his home in New Delhi. Later is the day, he thought, 'This carnival atmosphere in the city is only for a day. One never knows if it will happen again or not in five years' time? Why not go around one more time?' Then he remembered that Tara had been appointed the supervising officer at the polling station in Sabzi Mandi. 'I should go and check up on her. What would the poor soul do if she can't find a taxi to get back home? I could give her a lift.'

Narottam found Tara in the midst of a messy situation at her polling station. A short while ago, a crowd of agitated people had surrounded the desk where she sat. A man with the badge with an emblem of a clay lamp, the symbol of Jana Sangh, had accused another man wearing an emblem of a pair of oxen, representing the Congress, with offering money in exchange of ballot papers. Several Jana Sangh workers had surrounded the alleged culprit, and had demanded that he should be immediately searched. The man thus charged had refused to be searched.

Tara had referred the matter to the police.

The Jana Sangh workers had insisted that the search should be carried out in their presence.

Tara's reply had been, 'My responsibility and duty is not to search the accused, but to hand him over to the police. I cannot do anything more than that.'

The police had taken the suspect to the police station to conduct a search on him.

The Jana Sangh workers were now accusing Tara of favouritism, and that the police of the Congress raj was not likely to find any incriminating evidence on the accused.

A jeep of the Election Department was standing by to take Tara to her home, but she decided to go in Narottam's car. Narottam asked her what the matter was.

'Let's first get out of here. I'll explain when we reach home,' Tara said tiredly.

Narottam drove by Sadar Bazaar to be able to check upon Chaddha who was at a polling station in that area.

Chaddha was with a man called Brij Behari, an associate of Prasadji, with whom Narottam had a nodding acquaintance. He had to offer both a ride.

The polling was over. There was no point in getting worked up any more over canvassing for votes. The soldiers in the battle for votes could now relax, and have a friendly conversation. Brij Behari was accusing Chaddha that the communists were encouraging caste prejudices and a certain partisanship by telling voters from the lower castes not to cast their vote for the Brahmin candidates.

Chaddha tried to lay the responsibility entirely at his door, 'You are accusing communists for encouraging caste bigotry when your own chief ministers of Congress government preach sectarian fanaticism in their election rallies. In a public meeting in Lucknow, the chief minister of UP said that the atheists are not afraid to commit a sin. How did belief in God become synonymous with the Congress party and nationalism? The Congress party workers say in election rallies that all women would be regarded as public property under a communist government.'

Narottam interrupted him, 'Comrade, you are just having a good gossip!'

'I myself heard it said.'

'Does that mean that these people are either ignorant or plain frauds?' Narottam asked.

'All is fair in love and election,' Brij Behari said, enjoying Chaddha's frustration. 'Comrade, you could not take even one punch from me. How would you compete with the mighty Congress? You want to know how a propaganda campaign can perform a miracle at the time of elections? Let me tell you about an incident from the 1937 elections, when the first Congress ministry was formed. At that time the Congress candidate who was an ordinary woman defeated the well-known public figure C.Y. Chintamani, the editor of the *Leader* newspaper.'

'It made history!' Chaddha said, touching his ear. 'That was a classic.'

'Why, what happened?' Narottam was curious.

'Yes, please tell us,' Tara also said.

'Arey bhai, Chintamani was a well-known Indian liberal, who decided to take on the Congress. He had been the editor of the only national English daily published from Allahabad for the past twenty years. His opponent, the Congress candidate was a Rajput woman, and the constituency was in the rural area near Agra. Our country, as you know, has only 10 per cent literacy, and very few of these know English. Who could read English in the countryside and who would have known about the editor of an English newspaper, C.Y. Chintamani? The Congress fellows told the voters, "Listen, bhai! Would you vote for the daughter of a Rajput or for *bai* Chintamani, the prostitute from Allahabad?" Who would have voted for a bai? The Congress candidate won. Chintamani went and whined before Gandhiji.'

'This shows the typical modus operandi of those who control the mass media. This is an example of the freedom of speech under a capitalist democracy and of the non-violence preached by the Congress,' Chaddha quipped.

'That's the limit. What did Gandhiji say?' Narottam asked.

'Gandhiji was very sad, but what could he do?'

'No, what I wanted to ask was if Gandhiji went on fast to oppose the result and to force the Congress candidate to resign?'

'As I said, all is fair in love and war, and elections are war. This was none of Gandhiji's business.'

Narottam stopped the car below Tara's flat. Tara had to say out of politeness, 'Come upstairs. You are all very tired. A cup of tea.'

Chaddha accepted. Narottam also had no objection. Brij Behari decided to join them.

Narottam asked Tara, 'So, what was the problem about buying and selling ballot papers at your polling station? They put a mark on your hand and you can't go again into the polling booth.'

Brij Behari chuckled. Chaddha said, to save Tara the explanation, 'What if you don't drop the ballot paper into the box and bring it back with you and then sell it to me? I can go later into the polling booth, where no one watches me, and can stuff one hundred ballots into the box.'

'My God!' Narottam said, sighing deeply at the thought. 'They use such devices to get elected so that they may compete for the chance to serve the country and the people? If so, think about what they won't stoop to once they get to the assembly and the Parliament? Is this any way to elect a democratic government? A dictatorship would be better than this.'

'How would we get a dictator?' Tara asked. 'Now if we want a dictator, we'll have to elect one. You mean we give away the right and the opportunity to remove the wrong person should we elect one?'

'What do you mean by dictatorship?' Chaddha asked. 'Is it not the dictatorship of the Congress at present? All governments act more or less dictatorially. The power and rights of any government can be constrained only by that government's volition and commitment to do so. What else would you call these anti-strike laws? Declaring the RSS to be an unlawful organization, the mass arrest of communists, detaining someone on mere suspicion and preventive detention? What else is the government order not to give jobs to communists? What would you call dismissing five thousand workers from your ordnance factory C on the suspicion of being communists? What else is dictatorship? The question is: What is the class outlook of the government? The dictatorship is of thieves or of the proletariat!'

Narottam noticed that Tara was tired and getting bored. He stood up and said, 'Bhai, it's late, I'd better leave. Come, I'll drop you both at Connaught Place.'

The storm of activity surrounding the elections subsided gradually as did the turmoil caused in Tara's mind by what Shyama had said. She began to have the same feeling of sympathy for Shyama as one has for a sick family member. She would think, 'If Mrs De can cause such trouble for De, and if what Mercy said has some truth in it, why can't Mrs Nath do the same? What rot has set in the life of Doctor sahib! Feelings of mistrust and bitterness can arise between a couple just on the basis of doubt and suspicion, but those doubts and suspicions can also be dispelled.'

Tara would imagine, 'What would Mrs Nath be like? Like Mrs De? Mrs De has some reason to complain, what reason could Mrs Nath have? Perhaps she did see me with Doctor sahib.' Tara was appalled by the thought. She decided, 'If she suspects something, she must not do so any more. But there has to be an occasion to do so.'

She had made up her mind to somehow meet Mrs Nath, 'I'd clarify my position at that time.' Nath had ignored her request to meet bhabhiji. Although she wanted to telephone him and to meet him, she decided against it.

Narottam had taken Tara to the club on the last Saturday of March. When Tara came back home at nine, Purandei told her, 'The same doctor had come.'

Tara at once rang Nath's house. The familiar voice of the old peon answered, 'I am sahib's chaprasi. Which sahib is calling?'

'This is Tara Puri speaking. Give the phone to bibiji.'

'Which bibiji? This is the bungalow of the sahib from Planning.'

'I know. Call memsahib to the phone.'

'Huzoor, I don't understand. Should I get sahib on the phone?' the peon muttered. Then came Nath's voice, 'Hello!'

Tara apologized for not being home and suggested, 'May I come to your bungalow tomorrow?'

'Have you got the car? And have you learned to drive?'

'Not yet. Narottam said that the one I had in mind was not the right choice. I'll come by taxi.'

'Hmm. It's very far. You don't know the area. I'll come by tomorrow afternoon.'

Tara reminded Nath, 'Achcha, listen, you have to bring bhabhiji along. You haven't introduced me to her yet. I'll not accept any excuses. You must bring her.'

'All right. I'll come tomorrow by four.'

'Don't forget to bring bhabhiji.'

'All right. I'll try.'

'Not only try. I'll be waiting for her.'

'All right.'

Tara made preparations with great enthusiasm to receive Nath. That evening and the next day also she thought carefully about explaining everything in a way to clear the air. Her father's high regard for Nath, about her own working as a tutor at the mansion. 'I've known Doctor sahib since I was this small.'

Nath arrived alone.

When Tara expressed her disappointment at not seeing bhabhiji with him, Nath smiled cryptically, 'All right, next time.'

Her attempts to meet bhabhiji would be in vain, decided Tara. Nath did not want her to meet his wife. 'But what can I do? Being insistent wouldn't be good manners,' she thought. 'Their relations may have become so bad that Doctor sahib finds it beneath his dignity even to talk about it. Perhaps he's given up all hope. Maybe he was hurried into marrying her, and now can't stand her. If so, he made a blunder. But how could he?'

The storm of excitement caused by the elections was finally over. The castles in the air built by some people about the downfall of the Congress government were blown away like wisps of mist. Congress ministries were formed in all the states of India. In Parliament, thirty out of the 500 MPs were communists and socialists. The Communist Party of India was no longer banned. Communists and socialists had also been elected to the state assemblies. The Congress had a decisive majority in all state assemblies, but the number of people who were critical of its policies had vastly increased. After a few weeks, everything reverted to normal. The future of the five year plan, and the efforts to ensure its success were frequent topics of conversation in the government circles. Tara had been transferred to the ministry of trade and commerce.

Narottam rang Tara one evening, 'Daddy would like to meet Dr Nath. He has old business relations with Nath's family firm Gopal Shah & Sons. Daddy wanted to know if it would be better to invite Nath for dinner or for tea. If Nath takes drink-*wink*, dinner would be better. You are also invited.'

Tara had no idea about Nath taking drink-wink. Perhaps he does, she thought, after spending so much time in England. She told Narottam, 'If you want me to come, make it tea.'

Narottam said, 'Sister Mercy had mentioned Mrs Nath. It would be proper to invite her too.'

'Yes, certainly,' Tara agreed.

The invitation from Mr Agarwal was for Sunday evening. Tara could not suppress her glee as she thought, 'That's good. Now Doctor sahib will have to bring his wife. Let me meet her once. I'll take care of the rest.'

Tara arrived at AA on Sunday before Nath. As soon as he saw her, Narottam grumbled, 'What made Sister and you imagine the existence of Mrs Nath?'

'What do you mean imagine?'

'Daddy said to Dr Nath on telephone, "Do bring Mrs Nath along." The doctor was taken by surprise. He replied, "There's no Mrs Nath. I am not married."'

Tara was nonplussed. Hiding her confusion behind a smile, she said, 'You yourself had said that Sister had mentioned something about Mrs Nath.' But thought to herself, 'I must find out what's going on. Doctor sahib did say "my bibi doesn't have such good taste". He had also promised to introduce me to her. This is turning out to be a mystery.'

Mr Agarwal welcomed Nath amiably. He brought up the subject of his old relations with Nath's family business, and that he had met Nath's father Devi Lal Shah in Lahore. He told Nath that he had bought stocks of sugar this year also from Sonwan and Gadari mills. Mr Agarwal had many questions about new business opportunities in private and public sectors under the five-year plan.

Mrs Agarwal jumped in the conversation with a word of praise for Tara, 'She's such a fine girl. She's like my younger sister. She loves our children. She stayed with us for six months. The children got very attached to her and listened only to her. When she told us that she had been the children's governess in your family, we thought, "Who could be a better candidate?"'

'Children's governess?' Nath said in a tone of surprise. 'She has been the governor of many mother centres.'

Mr and Mrs Agarwal laughed heartily at Nath's comment. Encouraged by her remark being turned into a joke, Mrs Agarwal continued, 'But I'll say a thousand times that she is not at all snobbish like a government official. She was in such a miserable condition when I first met her at the camp.'

Tara quickly looked at Nath, but his eyes were elsewhere, as if he was willing himself not to look at her. He absently took out a cigarette case from his pocket and held it open for Mr Agarwal.

Mr Agarwal slid a tin of 555 towards Nath, 'Here, the cigarettes were right in front of you.'

'You go ahead. I'm used to Capstan,' Nath's thoughts were somewhere else.

Mrs Agarwal prattled on, 'I said to Rawat Sahib that she's such a talented girl.'

As Nath got up to take leave of the hosts, he asked Tara, 'You'll stay behind or can I drop you at your place?'

Tara also took leave of Mrs And Mr Agarwal.

As the car reached the road, Nath said, 'What a comic situation you put me into! Who is Mrs Nath? Who else have you told about this?'

'You're bad. I won't speak with you,' Tara blurted out. Despite the feeling of having said something rude, she added, 'You have fooled me for so long.'

'It was I who was made a fool of. You got even with me. But how did you believe it without having any doubts about it? You're quite sharp otherwise.'

'Didn't you say to me that "my *bibi* doesn't have such good taste" and that you'll introduce me to bhabhiji?'

'Arey, I meant old Bhoop Singh, my peon. Kothari calls him my bibi. The servant I had stole some stuff and ran away. Bhoop Singh said that he'd cook for me and clean the house. He now lives at my place.'

'But when I practically implored you that I wanted to meet bhabhiji, why didn't you explain,' Tara protested.

'It was pointless for you to ask. I would have told you myself. What haven't I shared with you. You really imagined things.'

Tara had no anger left in her. The joy in her heart made her feel as if she was floating. She said, 'Should you make a fool of someone just because that person trusts you?' She looked at Nath for answer. The car was not on ground, it was airborne!

'It was I who was the butt of the joke. And what was that Mrs Agarwal said? Why were you in the camp?'

'She was right.'

'In the camp? Not with your own family or with your in-laws? Why?'

'I have no sasural.'

'What do you mean?'

They had reached Tara's flat. She said, 'I'll tell you when we are home.'

Chapter 12

THOUGH PURI AND NAYYAR HAD BECOME AMIABLE TOWARDS EACH OTHER during the court case against Rikhiram, Puri found it increasingly hard at times to maintain their relationship. He could not help but smell haughtiness in Nayyar's attitude, and that feeling brought up bitter memories from the time before Partition.

Puri had a love–hate relationship with Nayyar. He had been able to get Kanak despite Nayyar's opposition, and had been the winner in that contest between the two of them. The court case against Rikhiram had happened just when Puri had been ready to forgive Nayyar in the victor's pride, and he had again found himself under Nayyar's obligation, even having to flatter him. This niggled Puri. He would console himself, 'It's not such a big deal. Kanta is elder to Kanak, and Nayyar is my senior in age because of that relationship. It was his duty to help me and Kanak.' Still, he wanted to do something more for Nayyar to level the score.

It was January of 1950. Puri arrived at Nayyar's house early in the morning on a Sunday. Since Nayyar did not have to go to the court and it was very cold, he was still in bed sipping tea to fully rouse himself. In a gesture of closeness, Puri sat on the bed.

Kanta asked, 'How's Babli? Was she up? What was Kanak doing? You came so early in this cold. What's the matter?'

Puri explained that he was on his way to Sood's house and that it was best to go early in the morning if one wanted to be alone with Sood. He looked at Nayyar and said, 'Jijaji, the government is going to hire two more lawyers in the Majana case. Trilok Chand Bagga is also trying to get hired. I had spoken with Soodji about you. How about going with me to meet Soodji? Personal contact makes a lot of difference.'

'I've never visited Sood for any reason until now,' Nayyar said, pulling the quilt up to his shoulders. 'It'd seem as flattery to go and see him about the hiring. Anyway, what's my claim? Bagga has been a Congresswallah for the past two years.'

'You don't bother about that,' Puri said to assure him.

'Thanks for thinking of me, but, my friend, such flattery is beyond me,' Nayyar said.

Kanta said in support of Puri as she handed him a cup of tea, 'What's flattery in this? Don't you go to meet your other clients?'

Puri could not help feeling piqued. He wanted to get up and leave without drinking his tea, but he controlled his anger. For a few minutes he pretended to play with Nano to hide his feelings, then said jokingly to Nayyar, 'I disturbed your sleep by arriving so early in the morning. Treat it as intermission. Now you can have a matinee session.'

Kanta asked Puri to stay a little longer, but he refused, and left.

On his return home, Puri vented his irritation on Kanak, 'Nayyar acts so high and mighty, as if the minister should have gone to him to beg him to take up the case, or as if I would have not given him his share of the fee. You had said that the family was facing tough times. He's reduced to appearing in the court for a fee of ten or twenty rupees, but is snooty as ever. In Lahore he used to flaunt his family's wealth, but that was hardly any achievement.'

Kanak said to placate him, 'That's in his nature. Don't let that bother you.'

Nayyar had, indeed, been facing financial difficulties after the Partition. Although he had received the jewellery and bonds from his bank locker and his and Rajendra's claims for Rs 60,000 each had also been approved, living in the cramped Mandi Bazaar accommodation had become increasingly difficult. He had purchased in an auction, in lieu of his claim, a plot of land in the New Area near the courthouse. People buying land on the basis of claims would bid three, even four times the market price. There was little hope of receiving cash from the government in payment for their claims. They thought it to be a deal if they could get four annas worth out of a rupee. Nayyar too had bought the land after bidding Rs 90,000 for a plot worth Rs 30,000.

Puri and Nayyar's other friends were against his buying the land at an inflated price, but Nayyar was desperate for a house of his own. He had sold off virtually everything he owned to build the house, and when he ran short of cash, had taken a loan with the plot of land as a collateral, on which he had to pay interest. His law practice, by local standards, was not doing badly and he managed to make around six hundred a month. But in Lahore only the rental income had been about 400 rupees per month, and he had not mended his ways after coming to Jalandhar. Puri wanted the satisfaction of doing something to help Nayyar, but felt that Nayyar would rather suffer a loss than take help or advice from him.

Any indication of bad blood between Puri and Nayyar became a cause of worry for Kanak, Kanta and the rest of the family.

Usha had not been able to continue her studies at Sonwan. After the family had moved to Jalandhar, Puri had got her admitted in the second year of the Intermediate course so that she would not lose a year at school. That had been done without much problem as the rules had been relaxed due to disorder that followed the Partition, but Usha had to put an extra effort to prepare for the exam and Puri had to hire a tutor for her. Having jumped a year had left its mark. In BA, Usha had to work hard again to keep up with the rest of the class. As Masterji's house in Basti Nigar Khan had no electricity, Usha had moved to her brother's house in Vikrampura to be able to study at night. Just before her exam, Rajendra Nayyar, now a lieutenant in the army came to Jalandhar on three week's leave. Rajendra was acquainted with Kanak, and at times came to meet his sister-in-law's sister.

Rajendra had passed his BA exam in 1946. He was interested in everything but studies. Since he had barely managed to pass in the third division, he could not muster the courage to join MA. He had hoped to start some business with the help from family contacts or get a decent job. He could also depend on income from the family property. The Partition, however, changed the situation.

After the Partition, for six months Rajendra had made every effort to find work that would earn him a reasonable income. His brother had been trying to establish his law practice in Jalandhar and had much to worry about his own finances. How could Rajendra borrow money from him to start any business? In early 1948 he applied for a commission in the army. He was a healthy, smart and sharp young man, he got through.

Rajendra threw himself wholeheartedly in army training. He had matured a great deal after he was commissioned as a second lieutenant in 1950. Kanak found him to be more agreeable than before, and did not mind his chatting with Usha.

Usha, who was nearing twenty, was not any less beautiful than her sister. Her features may not have been as chiselled, but she was vivacious and cheeky. Since she had been spared the constant scrutiny of gali neighbours when growing up, her behaviour was not as cautious and timid as her sister's. At the time of their third meeting, Usha had reciprocated the message in the eyes of Rajendra. Kanak also had guessed the chemistry between them.

Kanak said to Puri, 'They like each other. What better match could there be for Usha? Mother and pitaji are unlikely to have any objection.'

Puri had no objection either, but he said, 'It's not a good thing for them to meet so often. Let Rajendra speak first with his brother and bhabhi. You don't say anything. You know Nayyar's nature. He'll think that we are currying favour since his brother will soon be promoted to captain. Let them broach the subject. The wedding can take place in summer once Usha is through with her exams.'

Kanak could have spoken to Kanta just as to Nayyar, but did not mention the subject even to her sister because Puri had asked her not to. She did not want to undermine Puri's feeling of self-respect by being the first to broach the subject. Four months later, Rajendra was back in Jalandhar, this time on a leave for six weeks. He had seldom come to Jalandhar in the past years. He was posted at Bareilly Cantonment, and usually spent his leave at Nainital or Mussourie. But this year he had come to Jalandhar even in summer. He showed up every evening at Kanak's house in Model Town. Usha was on preparatory leave before her exams.

Rajendra now liked to speak mostly in English, and had a different attitude. He would tell Kanak and Puri without dilly-dallying, 'We'll go and catch a movie.' Or 'Bhabhiji has invited Usha for tea.'

Usha could hardly study in such circumstances. Her eyes and the look on her face belied any interest in the course books. Her face would fall if Kanak did not give her permission to go out. Kanak would then have to say, 'Achcha, don't be late.'

A thought ran through Kanak's mind, 'I had to go to meet Puri secretly only a few years previously. How bold the new generation has become. Why should I not let them go out together?' But she would also tell Usha and Rajendra casually, 'There'll be plenty of time for movies and for going out after exams. Let her first get over with that.'

Puri would fume at Usha's outings and say to Kanak, 'People in the city know us. It's not proper for them to go around openly like this. If Rajendra is so impatient, why doesn't he get married and have the problem over and done with. And if his family is interested, why don't they approach us? The boy's family doesn't have to worry about their reputation. It's we, the girl's family, who have to worry about getting a bad name.'

Kanak was surprised to hear that, 'Why do you say that?'

Puri was annoyed, 'You begin to argue about everything without looking at the implications.'

Just then a visitor named Gyaniji called Puri's name. Kanak had to remain quiet, but that evening she did not allow Usha to go out with Rajendra.

It was the fifth week of Rajendra's stay in Jalandhar and hardly a day had gone by when he had not come to see Usha. Next time Rajendra came, Kanak called him to come to the veranda to speak to him.

'What are your intentions?' Kanak asked. 'Is it proper for you two to go out so often?'

'Do you have any objection? Yes, we want to get married,' Rajendra replied without hesitation.

Kanak said, suppressing her smile, 'Dear boy, if you want to marry her, you should go about doing it properly. Have you spoken with jijaji and bahinji?'

'What objection could they have? It's I who will decide. My brother did say, "Usha has said yes. If her family agrees, so much the better." I have full confidence that a person as nice as you would be glad to see others happy.'

'Do you learn to use weapons in the army or wag your tongue?' Kanak chided. 'Bahinji did not say anything to me about this.'

'What was the point in doing so?' Rajendra said. 'We can't get married for a while. When I go back I will apply for the permission to get married. It could take three to four months. I won't be entitled for leave of absence before April or May of next year. What's the use of a short leave for a couple of days? We would like to go to Kashmir for our honeymoon.' He smiled.

Kanak said, 'Next year is fine, but there should be some basis for you two to go on seeing each other. If you have taken a decision, why not get engaged.'

'Why do we need that formality?' Rajendra said. 'We'll have the wedding as soon as it is convenient.'

'Engagement is also a part of marriage. What's your objection to it? You'll remain aware of your responsibility.'

'I have no objection if you want it that way,' Rajendra said, raising his finger. 'But then you or bhai sahib should not say that it is not right for Usha to meet her fiancé before the wedding. People with old ideas do not think that to be proper. Now we can go on meeting as friends.'

'Achcha, we won't object, but the engagement must be announced. And you have to tell this to bahinji today, or I won't let you see Usha.'

'I'll definitely tell her tonight, but bahinji, this evening…'

'Un-uh,' Kanak shook her head.

'Bahinji, please!' Rajendra joined his hands and pleaded. 'You are so good.'

'Get lost! Don't be late,' Kanak said, hoping Puri would not notice them going out together.

In the evening of the third day when Kanta came to visit Kanak, the sisters sat alone together. Kanak said, 'Bahinji, it'd be wonderful to have this relationship, but if you had such an idea you should have given me some hint.'

Kanta said apologetically, 'I don't have to tell you that your jijaji also approves of this match with Usha. The important thing is that if Rajendra is happy, we are happy. I asked your jijaji if I should speak to Kanni or Puri. You know how blunt he can be. He said, "Don't be the first to broach the subject. We are facing difficult times, and Puri has become a man of high status. What if he pooh-poohed the idea? Maybe he is trying to fix up his sister with the son of some minister or big industrialist. Let the boy and the girl decide themselves." What could I do?'

Kanak said crossly, 'Bahinji, it's not fair. Why should jijaji say such things about Puriji? He has such deep respect for jijaji.'

Kanta agreed, 'You're right. I said the same to your jiajji to his face, but didn't tell you till now thinking that you'd mind. Well, let's forget it.'

Kanak did not let on what Puri had said to her. 'What's the use,' she thought. 'Hope the bad blood between them won't last.' But she felt hurt that she was not able to criticize her husband as frankly as her sister had criticized hers. She knew the reason was Puri's inferiority complex.

Rajendra and Usha got engaged before he went back after his leave. After the ceremony, Puri and Nayyar hugged each other like close relatives.

Puri returned from Simla after the first session of the assembly was over. Nayyar and Kanta came to Model Town in the evening to meet him and to discuss the wedding plans. Rajendra had written that he had been granted leave from the third week of June, and that the wedding should take place by the end of June. Kanak wanted to show off the lawn and the flowers that she had planted in the garden of the bungalow. It was the beginning of May. She had chairs placed for them to sit in the lawn owing to the heat.

Nayyar thought that Puri's behaviour had changed in the past two months. He seemed preoccupied with his own thoughts, and would look away momentarily before speaking. Nayyar was fond of Simla, and wanted to know about the city,

Puri said, looking away, 'Jijaji, the courts will remain closed in August. If you wish you can stay in my government quarter when you go to Simla.'

'Why don't you go to Simla?' Kanta asked Kanak.

'How can I drop *Nazir* and leave? Couldn't even go to Delhi for a couple of days.'

Kanak had not finished when Nayyar said to Puri, 'No, thank you. You mean I go to Simla for the sake of free accommodation? I will pay the rent if I go.'

Puri kept silent.

Kanak bowed her head, then got up and went inside the house.

Kanta went after her and saw that Kanak, aanchal over face, was crying. When Kanta tried to soothe her, Kanak said wiping her eyes, 'These two will soon be close relatives, and look how they behave with each other!'

Kanak did not want to come outdoors, but Kanta insisted and dragged her to the lawn. They found Nayyar trying to make jokes to make up for his silly remark, and Puri smiling with his face turned away and acting as if nothing had happened.

Kanta began to shout at Nayyar, 'Sometimes you really cross the limit! Is that any way to behave? What a response to a gesture of goodwill! Is this how one behaves with one's relatives?'

Nayyar said in a serious tone, 'I'm really sorry for what I said. But, Puri, I didn't mean it as an insult to your goodwill. It was my frustration at not being able to go. Achcha, I ask you both to forgive me.'

'Jijaji, it's all right. I was really not that upset.' Kanak's anger melted away.

Although the unpleasantness apparently ended, it later surfaced again and became a serious bone of contention for Puri and Kanak.

By giving Kanak examples from Nayyar's past behaviour, Puri wanted Kanak to admit that Nayyar was a malicious person and had an inferiority complex. Kanak refused to concede since Nayyar had apologized to both of them. This angered Puri and he said resentfully, 'You'd rather believe him than me. What could be the reason behind such bias towards him? Have any of your dormant feelings for him been rekindled so that you have to control yourself in my presence?'

Kanak looked at Puri with reddened eyes full of tears, and asked in a firm voice, 'What do you mean?'

'I am,' Puri said, trying to reply convincingly, and began to explain what he had said in psychological terms that had no bearing on their conversation.

Yet the scene between Puri and Nayyar had a positive outcome. Nayyar decided that since Puri was going to be a close relative, he would get rid of his old antagonism towards Puri. Nayyar's behaviour at the time of wedding of Usha and Rajendra was in keeping with his decision.

But there was another disagreement between Kanak and Puri at the time of the wedding. When the bridal turmeric paste was applied to Usha and the singing of auspicious songs began, Puri's mother shed a few tears for Tara.

Kanak said to Puri, 'What could be a better time to invite your sister?'

Puri said, scolding her for a foolish suggestion, 'Why do you want to cause a lot of trouble for everyone? Don't you remember that I wrote and asked her to come here, and she did not even reply? She refused to come when the time was right. Don't you know that Somraj now has two kids from his bhabhi. Why do you want to make life difficult for him, for Tara and for the whole family?'

In the last week of September, Kanta's boy servant brought to the Kamaal Press a letter from Kanchan in Delhi that was meant for both her older sisters. There was also a note from Kanta that she was going to Delhi for two days after getting the news that her mother was not well, and asking Kanak if she wanted to go too?

Kanak could not be away from Jalandhar at that time. Puri was in Simla for the assembly session, and was not due back for several days. The house could not be left under Heeran's care alone. Her mother-in-law in Basti Nigar Khan had been running a fever, and Kanak was expected to regularly visit her. She could hardly go to see her mother while her mother-in-law was unwell!

Kanak stopped by Kanta's house on her way home from office. She said, 'When Puri returns we both will definitely go to see mother. Otherwise I alone will reach Delhi next week Thursday evening. Send me a telegram about her condition.'

Puri returned to Jalandhar in the first week of October, but was too busy to find time to go to Delhi. In the meantime Kanta returned from Delhi and reassured Kanak about their mother's condition. Puri also said that he may be free to go to Delhi after a week.

Next week, on Thursday morning, Puri was going for his bath when the telephone rang. Kanak answered, and said to Puri, 'Listen, it's Gill calling from the office. Your cousin Kishor Chand has come from Hoshiarpur, and is inquiring about Tara and Sheelo. Your cousin is on the phone now, you talk to him.'

Puri's face took on a serious expression as he listened to the person on the other end. He said, 'Ask Raldu from the press to bring you here. It'd be better to discuss all that when you're here.'

Puri sat down in a chair in his sleepwear of lungi and vest made from khadi, his right fist under his chin to support what was weighing heavily on his mind. He said, as if thinking aloud, 'Don't know what more problems this girl will bring upon us.'

'What did you say? Who?' Kanak asked concernedly.

'Tara, who else?' he said, removing his hand from under his chin and taking a deep breath. 'Kishor Chand said that Sheelo's husband Mohanlal told him that Tara took Sheelo away from her husband's house pretending to send Sheelo to her parents' home. Sheelo never reached Hoshiarpur. Nobody knows where she is.'

'When, how did Tara take her?'

'We'll find out when Kishor Chand arrives,' Puri said, looking into the space beyond the window. 'Sheelo already had a son before the Partition. Where could she go? How did Tara meet her? What more trouble has Tara created now for us?' He went to have his bath before Kishor Chand's arrival.

Kanak had never met Kishor Chand. Hers had been a court marriage in Delhi. Babu Ramjwaya had been peeved at not being consulted about the marriage arrangement, and for not being included in the wedding party. Even though that had saved him the expenses of the customary present of cash and clothes to the bride. He did not give up his grudge even at the time of Usha's wedding. Masterji had gone to Hoshiarpur to personally invite his elder brother, but Babu Ramjwaya did not relent and, thus, once again avoided the responsibility of sharing the expense of a girl's marriage in the family. Puri reminded Kanak of that incident, and said irritably, 'Those people had taken offence and had broken off relations with us. Why are they now dumping their problem on my head?'

Kishor Chand was very upset about Sheelo's disappearance. There had been no letter from Sheelo and Mohanlal for the past three years, or any reply to the letters sent to them. A letter had arrived ten days previously from Mohanlal's father Jaikishan demanding an explanation for not receiving any news about Sheelo returning to her husband. If Sheelo was not sent back immediately, he had threatened, they will arrange a second marriage for Mohanlal, and will not have any more responsibility towards Sheelo.

The letter from his daughter's father-in-law had come as a complete surprise to Ramjwaya. Where had his daughter been all this time? He had sent Kishor Chand immediately to Delhi to find out.

Kishor Chand's questions had made Mohanlal bristle with rage. He had said: He did not reply to the letters because Sheelo never wrote to him during the three years she has been away. She often insisted and kicked up a fuss about going to her patent's home, but he could not get any leave. Finally he decided to send her by the train on a Sunday morning, and told her to inform her parents to receive her at the station. When he returned from his office on Friday, he found the doors to his room padlocked. The neighbours gave him the key, and told him that Sheelo's cousin came and took away Sheelo and her son in a taxi. The cousin said that Sheelo was going to her parents.

Kishor Chand had refused to believe that the cousin could be Tara. Mohanlal had explained: Tara had not died in the fire at her in-laws. She had come to meet Sheelo several days before taking her away. Tara had told Sheelo that she worked in some government office, and had found Sheelo's address in Shakti Nagar from the claim application submitted by Mohanlal. Sheelo's leaving on the sly had galled Mohanlal so much that he neither had wanted to write to her parents, nor had tried to contact Tara. He did not think it worth the trouble to go after a woman who had shown such insolence! He had thought that eventually Sheelo would be sorry and beg for his forgiveness, and he would take her back. He was not a bit concerned about her, and it was not he, but his father who had sent the letter to Hoshiarpur.

Mohanlal had been so mad at everyone in Sheelo's family for her uppity behaviour that he had not even invited Kishor Chand to stay for the night. Kishor Chand had thought that it'd be useless to question him about Tara. As there was no time to write to Jalandhar and wait for an answer, he had taken the night train to Jalandhar.

Puri, his chin resting on his fist, listened considerately to Kishor Chand. He was at a loss to explain the mystery. After some thought Puri said, 'Tara didn't come here. We'll have to inquire at Delhi. You've been travelling all night. First have a bath, and drink some tea or lassi. Then we'll decide what to do next.'

Kishor Chand said with surprise, 'Why didn't Tara come here? She must have written something about all this.'

Puri shook his head.

'What kind of behaviour is that?' Kishor Chand said disgustedly. 'Neither at her parents' home, nor with her in-laws! And ruining other marriages on top of that.'

Puri looked away and kept silent.

Puri maintained a serious demeanour while talking with Kishor Chand, but when he went to have his bath, Puri said worriedly to Kanak, 'I just can't understand what Tara is up to? Why is she bent on taking revenge? Why did she mislead a married woman who has a child into ruining her own life? We'll be in an awkward position if tayaji came here and created a scene. Tara is bent upon giving us a bad name. What can anyone do now when Sheelo's been away from her husband for three years? She was always a bit of a flirt.'

'Bent on revenge!' Kanak was shocked. 'What did you say? What revenge? What do you mean?' she asked.

'Nothing. It's just that I've so much on my mind,' Puri said, jerking his head.

Kishor Chand was very agitated. He returned to the living room after pouring a few lotas of water over his head, his dhoti folded and wrapped around his waist, and continued to dry himself with a towel. Kanak avoided looking at him, but Kishor Chand did not seem to notice. To him such behaviour was customary and everyday in galis and mohallas. Kanak got up and went to the veranda at the back. She called out from there, 'Please come. Tea and lassi are ready.'

Kishor Chand came to have lassi without bothering to put on a shirt. He said to Puri, 'Let's go to Delhi together to solve the problem Tara's created. Why did she take Sheelo away from her husband's home without our permission? Will she take care of Sheelo and her child all their life if Mohanlal were to remarry? Let's leave today.'

'I'll go with you,' Puri agreed. 'But what does Mohanlal have to say about this? Why was he silent for three years?'

Kishor Chand said irritably, 'He was so angry that he refused to talk about it.'

'Well, then, why didn't Sheelo write to her parents about it? She could have let you know if her husband was harassing her.'

'How do I know? Tara had met her and Sheelo probably had confided in her. They must have cooked up a plan together. Tara is older than she is. Sheelo was always running to your house to ask her advice for the smallest reason.'

'Not that much older. Only about six month's difference between them,' Puri said.

'Well, she's older. They were close to each other. Sheelo must have confided in her. Tara dumped her husband and her own parents so that she could have fun. Must have told Sheelo to do the same.'

Kanak did not appreciate Kishor Chand's comment. She looked at Puri.

Puri protested, 'What do you mean? Tara is highly educated, and that has allowed her to be appointed to a respectable position in a government office.'

'What's such respect worth if she's not with her husband?' Kishor Chand cut him short. 'She and you can live and behave as you want, but why did Tara lead Sheelo astray?'

'What do you mean astray? Sheelo's not a baby,' Puri's tone became serious.

'Mohanlal may be upset, but Sheelo could also have had some reason to be angry. She couldn't have left her husband just because Tara asked her to do so,' Kanak said to her husband, but it was meant for Kishor Chand.

Puri motioned her to keep quiet, 'Yes, Sheelo should have written to her parents if there was a problem. She had studied enough to be able to write.' He tried a different track, 'We can't know the whole story unless we go to Delhi and find out for ourselves. We'll leave tonight.'

'Masterji does not live here? Where're chachi, Usha, Hari?' Kishor Chand asked.

'Hari left for his college just before you arrived. Pitaji and mother have gone to Sonwan for a few days. Pitaji misses Sonwan a lot. Change your clothes. Want me to give you something to change into?' Puri wanted Kishor Chand to put on his shirt.

'I have clothes.' Kishor Chand scratched his hairy chest and continued to sit.

Kanak got up from the table. Puri and Kishor Chand went on discussing various aspects of the problem. Kanak used to leave for office by 9.30 a.m. If Puri was home, they left together. Kanak would give Jaya a wash and change her clothes before leaving. She served a meal to Puri and Kishor Chand, but ate in the kitchen.

Puri explained to Kishor Chand, 'It's no use if we reach Delhi in the evening or at night. If we take the night train we'll arrive in Delhi just after sunrise. You must be tired after travelling all night. The bed is ready for you. Rest for a while. I have returned from Simla after several days and must take care of some business at the weekly office and the press. I'll be back by afternoon.'

Delay at home had made them miss the bus, so Puri and Kanak had to hire a tonga to their office. Puri had been reserved and unemotional with Kishor Chand. His frustration now boiled over. He said in English so that the tonga driver would not understand, 'All this is going to create quite a scandal. Can't this idiot understand that if Sheelo has been in hiding for three years she must have left her husband, or she would have gone back to her parents. She can run away or go to hell for I care, but why did Tara meddle in this affair. That's why this man is bullying us. We're not responsible for Tara. I'm only concerned about my reputation.'

'Tara couldn't have taken away Sheelo against her will,' Kanak said in agreement.

'He says what'll become of Sheelo if Mohanlal marries another woman. Mohanlal already must have tried to marry again during this time. For people like Mohanlal a wife is nothing more than a servant who's only to be kept fed and clothed. When he failed elsewhere, he probably thought that he would try to get back the one he could push around. Sheelo's an adult. What can we do if she doesn't want to go back to him? It's strange that they both kept silent for three years. But what reason Tara had to get involved in this?'

'Tara had our address. You also wrote to her. She did not care to answer us, but went to Sheelo on her own. She also met Babu Govindram's family. What could be the reason?' Kanak said with suspicion.

'What do I know?' Puri replied. 'Maybe she didn't want to face me.'

'Why? You said she wanted revenge. Why so?'

'I had caught her meeting secretly with Asad, so she's probably harbouring some sort of resentment against me. When I had asked her what she was up to, she had bashed her head to appear innocent.' Puri continued, 'I also wrote about Somraj in the letter to her. She hasn't answered, so you can draw your own conclusion. Why should we pick a quarrel with Somraj for nothing?'

Kanak kept silent. Her own secret meetings with Puri, her being found out with him in Nainital by Nayyar and Kanta went through her mind. She felt grateful for Nayyar's gentlemanly behaviour. She thought of the letter Babu Govindram had sent from Delhi: 'Tara beti is like a devi.' Jijaji did tell me that Tara was married off against her wish.

After they reached the office and before she could start to work, Puri called Kanak to one side and explained, 'It won't be appropriate for me to go to Delhi. You wanted to go and meet your mother, so why don't you go? You can find Tara's address from Govindram. I don't know what Tara has in mind. She seemed quite happy at the time of her wedding and even during the months before that, but now she's clammed up after being told about her in-laws. My appearing at her doorstep may scare her, there may be a scene. Govindram and Ratan are in touch with her. Go with them to her place. And tell Hari not be too friendly with Kishor Chand. There's no need to mention all this to pitaji for now. Do as you think proper when you have assessed the situation in Delhi. Give Sheelo's address to Kishor Chand. Don't take on any other responsibility. There's no need to give Tara's or Govindram's address to Kishor Chand.'

The weekly went to press on Thursdays, so it was the busiest day for Kanak, but she could not help thinking, 'He does not want to go to Delhi. He still feels so much anger towards Tara. And Tara is nothing if not a mystery. Either she is showered with praise or severely condemned. Hope I don't get into some mess. If that appears to be likely, I won't get involved.'

Puri said to Kishor Chand in the evening, 'Something unexpected has turned up. I won't be able to leave for two days. Since it's a family matter, it'd be easier for Kanak to talk to women. You can stay at Kanak's parents.'

Kanak and Kishor Chand reached Delhi early in the morning. It was 10.30 before Kanak finished talking with her parents, had a wash and got dressed, and was ready to go to Karol Bagh with Kanchan. She had asked Kanchan to telephone her college for a day's leave. Kanak told Kishor Chand to wait for her to come back or, if he felt like it, to go for a walk in some bazaar for a while. Although Jaya had come to her maternal grandparents after a year and a half, she remembered meeting them. She sat in their lap, delighted them by giving kisses and hugs, but began to wail when she saw her mother leave. She had to be taken along. Kanak told her mother that she had to visit several people and not to worry if she was late in returning home.

The taxi dropped Kanak and Kanchan at Karol Bagh. Kanak had difficulty in recognizing the district where she had come five years ago with her father to attend Gandhiji's prayer meeting. The area that had been sparsely built with one or two-storeyed houses was now buzzing with activity. The bazaar was not crowded at this hour, but the stores were chock-a-block with goods. Fruit vendors, with oranges and bananas piled up high in handcarts parked under the shade of a tree or in the shadow of tall buildings, were shouting in competition with one another. The scene was reminiscent of the bazaar outside Lohari Gate or the Anarkali square in Lahore. Punjabi women, with some piece of work in their hands, sat on charpoys placed on the shady side in galis. Smoke rose from a couple of tandoors, and the thump of laundry being beaten with a bat could be heard. Some women, sleeves rolled up and salwars raised up to knees, were walking up and down trying to avoid male gazes.

The address Kanak had was from Babu Govindram's letter of three years ago: Number Three, Nai Wali Gali. Govindram was not at Number Three anymore, but the nine-year-old daughter of the family living there accompanied Kanak and pointed out Govindram Khanna's new dwelling on top of a row of shops in the bazaar. Fixed to a door in the gali behind the shops was a small letterbox with 'Govindram & Sons' inscribed on it in Urdu and English, and next to it, the button for a buzzer.

A girl of about fifteen opened the door to the stairs to the first floor. Kanak said, 'I've come from Jalandhar. I am Tara bahin's bhabhi.'

The girl's eyes opened wide. She moved aside to make way, then unable to contain her excitement, turned around and leapt up the stairs.

Kanak and Kanchan were half way up when they heard her yelling, '*Jhhai*, mom, bhabhi has come from Jalandhar. The wife of Puri bhappa has come.'

Meladei, smoothing out her aanchal, came to the door at the top of the stairs. She gave aashirwad to Kanak and Kanchan. She showed them to a takht covered with a duree and khes, and asked, 'Where's your luggage?'

Kanak said, 'We've no luggage. I'm staying at my parent's home.'

Meladei said complainingly, 'Wah, if that is home then this is also your home. You always stay there. This time you should've come here.' Turning her face, she called out towards the next room, 'Channa beti, come here. Your bhabhi's come.'

Her daughter-in-law came and shyly said namaste.

'She's you elder brother's wife. Do pairipaina,' Meladei said in a voice choking with affection. The young woman bent down to touch Kanak's feet.

Kanak pulled back her feet, and holding the woman's hand, made her sit beside her on the takht. Jaya was hugged and kissed. She had to say namaste to everyone.

Meladei said, 'My daughter, you've been out in hot sun. First tell me, what'll you have? Orange juice, lassi, lassi with *peras* or lemonade? Have whatever you like. Don't be formal. You are Bhagwanti's daughter-in-law, so you are also mine.'

'Maaji, we ate something less than an hour ago. Don't feel like anything right now. It's like home, we'll ask ourselves,' Kanak and Kanchan both said.

Meladei said, shaking her head, 'I won't have any of that. For me there's no difference between you and Dammo, Tara, Usha or Channa. You can have something to eat after an hour or hour and a half, but have something to drink.'

Meladei began to ask after Kanak's in-laws, Jaidev, Hari, Usha and others. How happy she had been, she said, to know about Puri becoming a 'member', and about Usha's marriage, adding as if to complain, 'Hai, you people didn't even inform us about Usha's wedding. It's all the result of Masterji's hard work and of doing his dharma.' She said good things about Puri for his intelligence, sincerity and principles, and how decent he had been to them. Then she mentioned Tara, and began to praise her to the skies, 'She's like a devi, she's the personification of peace and generosity. Who hasn't been helped by her? May God give a daughter or a daughter-in-law like her to everyone. That poor Brahmin woman Purandei, our neighbour from Bhola Pandhe's Gali, was really badly off, with a twenty-year-old daughter to care for and nobody to help her. Only Tara arranged vocational training for the girl, got her a government job, and then spent her own money on the girl's wedding. Where can one find such big-hearted person? And what she hasn't done to help us. We always sing her praise and give her many aashirwad. May God give her a life of a hundred years, may she become the lord officer of the highest rank.'

'I'd like to meet Tara bahin. Where does she live?'

'You mean her flat on Panchkuian Road?' Meladei said. 'She moved into that place two years ago. You haven't been to Delhi lately?'

Around 1 p.m., a five-year-old boy wearing a convent school uniform arrived. Meladei wiped the sweat off his forehead with her aanchal, then said, 'Ghullu, do pairipaina to your mami.'

He was a good-looking child. Kanak pulled him into her lap. Her mind was busy working what the relations of bhabhi and mami could mean.

Govindram had gone to Meerut on business, and was expected back late in the evening. Ratan came home for lunch. On being introduced to Kanak, he respectfully addressed her as bhabhi, and touched her feet. He sat down next to Kanak, and began to complain about not being invited to Puri's wedding. He asked the same questions about the family in Jalandhar that Meladei had asked.

Meladei broke in, 'First share with us whatever plain and simple lunch there is, then you may chat till the evening.'

Meladei stopped insisting only after Kanak and Kanchan swore many times that they had no appetite. The daughter-in-law filled three platters with grapes, bananas and oranges, and put it before them. Ratan asked his thali to be sent where they all sat. As long as he was eating his lunch, Meladei kept on asking Kanak and Kanchan to have some fruit. If they said no, she'd complain lovingly, 'My daughters, even though we live in Delhi, we are pukka Punjabis when it comes to eating, but you live in Punjab and hardy eat anything! What has happened to you?'

After Ratan finished his lunch, Kanak asked him to give them Tara's address or to accompany them to her place.

'I won't let you go out in the blazing sun with the child. I can't do that. She's so sleepy. Relax here for some time, even if our place is small. Have your dinner early, then go,' Meladei said decisively.

Ratan agreed with his mother, 'Tara bahin would be in her office at this hour. She's seldom back before 5.15 or 5.30. You rest here, we have hardly talked. We'll leave at five o'clock. I'll take you there.'

Ratan's baby daughter Munni was sleeping in a cot draped in mosquito netting. Dammo fixed another bed for Munni and Jaya, laid them in it and covered them with mosquito netting. Meladei asked for a charpoy to be brought into the room for her. So as not to disturb the sleeping children, the rest spread out mattresses in the other room and sat on them.

Channa took out two fresh dhotis from a steel trunk for Kanak and

Kanchan to change into so that their saris won't get crushed. Ratan began to describe recent happenings in Tara's life: Her sharing a flat with Mercy in Daryaganj, the Bhanu Dutt affair, the problems at her office after the camps had been closed down, Tara's promotion to the post of undersecretary, and how hard she worked and how even the secretary of the department thought twice before changing the remarks she made on case files. There was rampant corruption in government offices. The clerks in Tara's office sometimes accepted bribes without her knowledge, but she could not be bribed even with a million rupees to change even one letter in her remarks on case files.

Ratan went on, 'We'd have been ruined if Tara had not helped by arranging a loan of Rs 16,000. We had all but used up all our money in buying a 134 square yard plot of land where we have a row of shops now. Then we took a loan against the land and bought another plot of 100 square yards. One had to have the guts of a Punjabi to pay 125 per cent of the actual price, half in cash and the rest on deferred payments at 12 per cent interest. The locals used to laugh at us. Bhabhi, when the foundation for these three shops was laid, we hardly had Rs 2,000 in cash. Then people began to offer advance payment for renting the shops. We decided on a rent of Rs 700 for the three. My father refused to accept even one paisa less than a premium of Rs 10,000 for the shop in the middle, and Rs 15,000 for ones on both sides of it. People had to pay up. We got the shops built in three months, sometimes working at night by gaslights. Last year we built these rooms on the first floor, and rented out half of it at Rs 125 per month. It's not a bad deal for us to pay 12 per cent interest on the loan. When we build the second floor, a rent of Rs 150 per month is almost certain. I used to work with Gajendar Singh at one anna in a rupee as my share of the profit. I was forced to. This year I bought my own truck in instalments. Gajendar joined his hands and begged me to join him. I said to him, "All right, we'll work together but you'll have to give me three annas in a rupee…"'

Ratan noticed Kanak not taking any interest in his business talk. Kanchan also had said 'excuse me' and turned her face twice and yawned. Ratan added a few final words, 'Bhabhi, it's not money that matters. It was Tara who saved Channa's life. I was able to have my own family only because of her kindness. Otherwise I had vowed never to marry.'

Channa got up shyly and left the room.

Kanak gave Ratan a questioning look.

Ratan smiled, 'You didn't recognize her? Channa is Tara's cousin Sheelo. She'd have committed suicide if Tara had not reached in time.'

His words gave Kanak goose pimples.

Ratan went on, 'Now I'm related to you in more than one way. You're my double bhabhi.'

Kanak was unable to say anything, so she just smiled.

Ratan got to his feet, 'Bhabhiji, I've to go out for a while. You take a nap. I'll be back by five and take you to Tara bahin. I'll also ring her from the shop below.'

Kanak could hardly take a nap. She was puzzled by Tara's labyrinthine story. Kishor Chand's anger and Puri's worry! But when she came to Sheelo's home she found her so happy! How would she now bring up what Mohanlal and Kishor Chand were asking?

Sheelo came and asked Kanak, 'Bhabhiji, would you like some *shikanjbin* lemonade?'

'No, no.' Kanak held her hand and ask her to sit. She asked, 'I'm so happy about you. Tell me, what happened?'

Sheelo cast her eyes down and kept silent. When Kanak repeated her question, she said, 'Tara will tell you everything.'

Ratan came back just before five o'clock. The hospitality started all over again. Pakoras and kulfi-faluda were ordered from the bazaar. Kanak was used to having a cup of tea at this time, but how could she make a special demand in the midst of such lavish treatment?

Jaya's dress was soiled from eating kulfi. Kanchan had brought a change of clothes for her in a bag. Jaya's clothes were changed and her hair combed.

A minor crisis arose as Kanak got ready to leave. Meladei wanted to gift Kanak ten rupees and a sari. Kanak's protest and embarrassment were completely ignored.

Kanak tried to slip five-rupee bills into the hands of Ghullu and Munni. Sheelo was stopping Kanak from doing so, but at the same time, handing Jaya some money. After a bit of argument, money changed hands.

When they made their way downstairs, Kanak saw that the bazaar asleep during the noon hours had awakened. Shops were packed with customers and it was difficult to walk even a few steps on the road without bumping into another person. People of Lahore had been fond of good clothes, but in Delhi they seemed to want to flaunt their clothes. Kanak felt as if she had come to Delhi not from the city of Jalandhar, but from some village.

Ratan knew that Tara did not want to have anything to do with her family. She had not been very thrilled when Ratan had given her Puri's letter. He had telephoned Tara at her office to ask her permission to bring Kanak over to her home. He had also told her about Kanak arriving at his home, about how warmly she had spoken to Channa, and how well she had taken to Ghullu and Munni. And that Kanak wanted to meet her very much. Tara had said 'yes'.

Mrs Agarwal had invited Tara to her home that evening. Tara thought that she would telephone and offer her regrets. Several possible scenarios came to her mind, 'What could be the reason behind Kanak wanting to meet me? But why should I have any fears? I have nothing more to do with Somraj. He's living with his bhabhi, and he can for all I care. If there is a message concerning him, it'd be best to give a clear answer now.'

Tara said to Purandei on reaching home, 'My bhabhi has come from Jalandhar. She'll be here around six o'clock. I'll have tea with her. Ask Parsu to get some fruit and mithai.'

Purandei's heartbeat quickened on hearing the news. Tara's bhabhi was like a daughter-in-law to her. She had heard that Tara's elder brother Jaddi had become a newspaper's sahib and a 'mimber', that his wife has had English education and was from a well-off family. Parsu was still a greenhorn. Just three days previously he'd broken the lid of the teapot, and Purandei had to use a *katori* in its place. She could borrow a teapot from tayee. And tayee had to be told and consulted. This was the daughter-in-law's first visit to the house. What should be given as the customary gift for seeing her face for the first time?

Purandei had little opportunity lately to observe such customs. The traditional way was to put in the daughter-in-law's aanchal the present of one rupee and a quarter, seven pairs of dried dates and a dried coconut, but that practice was now outdated. The present-day custom was to present her with five or even ten rupees. It was best to consult tayee. How could she keep such important news to herself without sharing it with a neighbour? She also had to inform the Mehta family to come and meet the daughter-in-law, or they were bound to complain later.

Kanak and Tara were meeting after five-and-a-half years. Kanak hugged Tara warmly, and Tara responded kindly and courteously, but what won Tara's heart was the way Kanak's eyes lit up on meeting her. She felt as if she had been reunited with an old and dear friend. Tara then embraced

Kanchan, and touching Kanchan's chin with her fingers, said, 'Hai, you have grown up. You are looking so pretty. You live in Delhi, na?'

Jaya was clinging to her mother's knees and Tara had to coax the child into her lap. Jaya did not easily make friends with Tara, not until she had been pampered for some time.

Tara and Kanak had been young women when they had met last. When they met again, both had matured and their bodies had filled out. Kanak had put on a bit of weight compared to Tara. She could not take her eyes off Tara's face. She thought that Tara had a quiet dignity about her, and looked beautiful and more attractive than before.

When Kanak had gone to Bhola Pandhe's Gali, Tara had been studying for her exam wearing an old pair of crushed salwar-kameez. Her hair had not been properly combed. Today, on her return from office Tara had changed into a fresh white voile sari. Her hair, parted in the centre, was tied in a bun at the back of her head. Gold studs, each with a single black stone, suited her fair-complexioned face very well. She did not wear a necklace. On one wrist was a small stainless-steel watch with a black strap, and on the other, one heavy gold bangle.

It was still warm on the October evening. The ceiling fan rotated slowly. Kanak sat on the sofa with her arm around Tara, and put her head on Tara's shoulder without saying anything. Then, noticing Ratan who was sitting opposite them, she checked her emotions, 'Never got the time to find out your address whenever I came to Delhi, but I had always wanted to.'

Tara asked after pitaji, mother, bhai, Hari, Usha and Toshi.

Purandei, clad in a fresh dhoti, came into the room to give aashirwad to the daughter-in-law. Tara introduced her, 'My buaji.'

Ratan said, 'I suppose bhabhiji will be here for two hours. I'll come back and take her to Faiz Bazaar.'

Kanak and Tara told him not to bother.

Kanak had so much to ask and tell, but did not know where to begin. She started, 'We came to Delhi from Nainital in September 1947...'

Parsu put fruit and mithai on the table. Purandei brought tea, and said, 'You both'll have dinner here,' and went back without waiting for Kanak or Kanchan to reply.

Tara leaned forward to pour tea. Kanchan said, rising to her feet, 'You both talk. I'll make tea.'

A voice was heard from the direction of the stairs, 'May I come in?'

'Yes, yes. Do come in,' Tara said, without getting up.

'You're not yet ready ...' Narottam said as he entered the room, but halted in mid-sentence when he saw two women guests.

Tara introduced Kanak and Kanchan to Narottam, 'He's my brother.' She asked him, 'You're coming from the *kothi?*'

'No, I was at Kapur's. Mummy said that you were coming over, so I took this route. Thought I'll get a chance to drive your car.'

'I had rung mummy.'

'I didn't know. Achcha, I'll take leave of you.'

'Do sit down. Have some tea.'

Narottam said to Kanak, 'Didi told me that you were a very good writer. It was a pleasure to meet you. You come to Delhi often?' He gave Kanchan a quick glance.

Kanak continued the conversation with Tara, 'Office work keeps you busy?'

'Very busy! Sorry to barge in,' Narottam said, looking around the room, 'See, the files were also brought home.'

'I've become used to it.' Tara said. 'It's routine. When it has to be done, what's the point of putting it off or finding it a chore?'

Narottam finished his cup, shifted in his seat, and looked at his wristwatch. Tara asked, 'You have to go somewhere?'

'I don't have to go anywhere, but I'll be intruding if I stay.'

'Do intrude then,' Kanak said. She realized that Narottam and Tara were close friends.

'If you are not busy, then stay. You can drive us. The rush at this hour makes me nervous.'

'It'll be my pleasure. I love driving.'

Kanak apologized to Narottam for giving him the trouble.

'You are also my bhabhi now,' Narottam said.

'Of course,' Kanak admitted.

Tara asked Kanak about Rajendra and Usha.

Narottam exchanged a few words with Jaya. Then leaning towards Kanchan, said, 'Our elders are busy with each other. Can we talk?'

'Sure.'

'You also like to write?'

'No question of like to. I never could. I was a student of chemistry.'

'Did you like chemistry?'

'Had to study it for the purpose of exams. What I like is music.'

'Very few girls study chemistry. Now that you've done your MSc, what are your plans?'

'I am teaching chemistry to girl students.'

'Teaching is a good profession. You didn't sit for the entrance test for medical colleges?'

'I did. My marks were not high enough. Only nine girls were selected from Delhi, I was the tenth.'

'Oh, hard luck. You didn't try again?'

'Didn't have the time. Would have wasted one whole year. Medical studies last five to six years. I wanted to be self-supporting.'

'Was there any particular hurry?' Narottam said, choosing his words carefully.

'Our financial circumstances were such after we came here from Lahore.' Kanchan's answer touched Narottam's heart.

Tayee called out to Purandei from the stairs. She had come to meet Tara's bhabhi.

Purandei came to the sitting room with tayee.

Narottam rose briskly to his feet. Bending close to Kanchan's ear, he whispered, 'Please tell didi that I'll be back in about an hour.'

Tayee expressed great pleasure in meeting Kanak. After some casual conversation, tayee began to praise Tara for her kindness and generosity. Then, as an aside, said to Kanak, 'Try and fix Tara up now that you are here. It's not right to let her grow old. Who won't welcome such a girl into their family? She is like the goddess Lakshmi. She'll be a real blessing to any family.'

Tara felt uneasy with such praise in front of Kanak. She said to Kanchan, 'Come. I'll give you a tour of the house. Do you want to freshen up?'

Before she left, tayee called out to Tara from the living room, 'You and your bhabhi have dinner at my place tomorrow.'

After tayee was gone, Purandei began to tell Kanak that tayee was very fond of Tara, and had suggested her nephew many times as a prospective match for her. Purandei also said some very complimentary things about tayee's nephew, the forest officer. Tara said irritably, 'Would you please let us talk with each other.'

Purandei said, asserting her right, 'Hai, let me say what I want to. I have to tell all this to the family's daughter-in-law. Who else will do so if I don't?'

Kanak understood that everyone took Tara to be unmarried, so she also kept quiet about it.

When Mehta's wife, his sister and another neighbour Gurandei came to meet her, they also treated Kanak with affection and respect. Kanak knew that it was all because of Tara. She had found out about Tara's situation and about other people's opinion of her without asking a single question. She felt relieved that she had not formed any opinion about her husband's sister despite his disparagement, but she also had had no chance so far to discuss the matter that was the reason for her visit.

Narottam came back just as Mehta's wife and others were leaving. Kanak could not talk about Kishor Chand in front of him. It was nearing eight o'clock. She was supposed to give some answer to her husband's cousin waiting for her return.

Kanak looked at Narottam and said hesitantly, 'If you permit I and bahin will have a word in private.'

Tara took Kanak to her bedroom. They sat down on the bed facing each other. Kanak explained why Sheelo's parents were worried, and about Kishor Chand's visit to find out about Tara and Sheelo.

Tara said after a few moments, 'What did I do for which Sheelo's family is hassling me? Mohanlal had thrown Sheelo out of his home. The reason for which he had done so is now twice as much.'

Tara told Kanak about Sheelo's relationship with Ratan in Lahore. She said, 'I agree what Sheelo had done was wrong, but that wrong has now been set right. If her family wants her go on living in shame, if they think that their good name lies in hiding a mistake that has been corrected, it's their problem. I had no hand in any of this. I just told Ratan about Sheelo's situation.'

Kanak stared at the floor in silence. Then asked, giving Tara a quick look, 'You know that Somraj is also in Jalandhar?'

'I have nothing to do with him.' Tara said, eyes downcast.

Placing her hand on Tara's shoulder, Kanak asked, 'I had heard that you did not want to marry him.'

Tara nodded.

'But why did you agree to this marriage against your will?'

Tara said after a brief silence, 'What had to happen, has happened. What can I say now?'

'Were you forced into the marriage? Didn't your brother give you any support?' Kanak asked with surprise.

'My brother let me down. It was also my fault. I didn't have the courage, I just gave in.'

'How did your brother let you down?'

'Bhai was against my marriage to that man. Then he lost his job and couldn't find another. He didn't get paid for some work he had done for others. All this made him buckle under pressure from the elders. What else can I say?'

'I can't understand why you agreed if you didn't want it.' Kanak expressed her surprise.

'Lack of courage! I didn't have the courage to fight the circumstances alone. I thought: Others would think badly of me. Marriages were arranged like that, and I was no exception. So that it won't bring shame on my parents.'

Kanak was lost in thought for a few moments. Then she asked, 'You were not with your husband even for one night?'

'Could we drop that subject? Let's talk about something else.'

Kanak was overcome with sympathy for Tara. She kept silent.

'I don't feel like leaving you and going back.'

'You don't have to. It's your home.'

'I know, but I haven't told my mother. My parents will worry. Won't you ever come to Jalandhar to meet your brother?'

'Why didn't he come here?'

Kanak gave no reply. After a brief pause, she said, 'Achcha, I'll go now. I'll definitely meet you next time I am in Delhi.'

'I'll come along to drop you.'

'No, not tonight. Kishor Chand is waiting for me. He can be a difficult person. I'll feel bad if he said something unpleasant to you.'

'You and Kanchan come tomorrow at noon. We'll have lunch together. It's Saturday, I'll be back by quarter to one.'

Tara said to Narottam, 'If you are free tomorrow, bring her and Kanchan here. I will serve you potato-stuffed paranthas.'

'Sure.'

Kanak objected, 'Why should we trouble him? Taxis are available around the corner from our gali.'

'Don't bother about troubling him,' Tara said, asserting her right over Narottam.

'Why do you want to deprive me of paranthas! I'll get to eat them after six months only because of you,' Narottam appealed to Kanak.

Tara took Jaya in her arms and gave her a kiss, 'Tomorrow I'll take proper care of you.'

Narottam went to drop Kanak and Kanchan in Tara's car.

Kanak returned home quite late. Kihsore Chand was put out for having to wait so long. As soon as he saw Kanak, he asked, 'What did you find?'

Kanak did not want to burden her parents with her husband's problems. She replied, 'I'll tell you in the morning,' and went and sat with her mother. She thought out an answer during the night, and said briefly to Kishor Chand in the morning:

Mohanlal had thrown Sheelo out of his home. If he wants to marry again, he may. Sheelo won't go back to him. She now is the mother of two children. Tara had nothing to do with this matter.

Kishor Chand demanded angrily to personally meet with Tara and Sheelo.

Kanak refused to help and told him in so many words.

Kishor Chand was so angered by Kanak's attitude and her explanation that he packed his bags and left for the railway station.

Kishor Chand went straight to Hoshiarpur from Jalandhar station on his return from Delhi. Kanak's reply had made his blood boil, but the journey had given him the time to weigh up the pros and cons of the matter. His anger had gradually subsided. He thought, 'What is the point of hanging family's dirty laundry in public? Telling people about the matter will only bring even more shame on the family. Sheelo's dead for us. Mohanlal can do what he wants. He's not our relative any more.'

Kanak told Puri everything in detail on reaching Jalandhar on Monday morning. Her voice dripped with affection as she repeated the praise and tributes to Tara that she had heard from everyone. She asked, 'Why are you so angry with her?'

Puri still had in his mind the letter from Babu Govindram, '*Hoon*, so that's what he meant by sharing our problems and joys.' He said irritably,

'That's some example of neighbourly behaviour and friendship. Like they say, even a thief spares seven neighbours when robbing a house. Ratan and Govindram didn't have even as much concern for our reputation!' 'What do you mean? I don't understand,' Kanak protested.

'What is it you don't understand?' Puri felt that Kanak just wanted to quibble.

'Sheelo is now Ratan's wife and has a right to live with him. Ratan's parents treat her just like a daughter-in-law. I don't see any betrayal of friendship in this.'

'Was she not Mohanlal's wife? Ask Kishor Chand and his parents about the humiliation they felt. If this scandal gets known in Jalandhar it won't do any good for our reputation,' Puri said harshly.

'But now we know the truth. Why blame Tara for anything? Sheelo had made a mistake and it was her good fortune that it was rectified. Why should she be made to live in shame all her life? I think Sheelo's heart won't ever accept Mohanlal as her husband, no matter how much her family may punish her for it.'

Puri was peeved, 'You mean if one finds it shameful to live with some person, one can have relations with another person?'

'What are you taunting me about?' Kanak said, looking hard at Puri.

'What else are you saying?'

'Do you want me to agree that we should tie Sheelo up and send her to Mohanlal?'

Puri could not tolerate being left speechless. He said irritably, 'I don't want anything to do with that family. All I said was why did Tara have to get involved in this? But what is it that you are praising and trying to prove?'

Kanak took a deep breath, and said, 'She's your sister, but I'll say that her heart is much bigger than yours!'

Puri blew out his breath angrily. To keep himself under control, he began to walk out of the room. As he reached near the door, he turned around and unable to control his anger any longer, said, 'I see that you yourself are all heart after you met another big-hearted person. I don't think I'd be able to put up with someone with such a big heart. Maybe you should find for yourself someone with a heart big enough.'

Kanak could not go to the office. Puri went out at eleven o'clock without saying anything to her. Kanak did not know if he had eaten or not. She had had nothing to eat, just drank water several times. She kept her face averted from Chaila and Heeran. She felt disgusted if anyone saw tears in her eyes. The thought came to her mind over and over, 'What happened? What wrong things did I say? Should I just bash my head as atonement for my crime?'

Puri and Kanak did not speak to each other the next day. Kanak did not take tea to Puri's room in the morning, and had hers alone. Heeran and Chaila both talked in hushed tones. Seeing everyone quiet and tense made Jaya nervous and she did not want to leave Heeran's side. She would snivel, ready to break in tears. Heeran would pray to God to give her the child's troubles, and try to divert Jaya's attention and keep her away from her mother and father. Kanak found the tension very humiliating, and went to the kitchen resolved to do something about it. She asked Chaila several questions, gave him instructions, then took Jaya in her arms and sat with the child. She gave Jaya her bath, changed her clothes, combed her hair and tied them with ribbons, all the while fussing over her and talking with her. At nine o' clock she called out to Chaila so that Puri could hear, 'Get food ready for both of us. I'll have my bath and be out shortly.'

She asked Chaila after her bath, 'You didn't tell babuji to come for his meal?'

Chaila returned from Puri's room and said, 'He's working. He'll eat at 10.30.'

The message was clear: First repent and grovel.

Kanak was furious. She had her meal and left for the office.

'You came back from Delhi today?' Gill asked.

'No, I came yesterday. I was very tired. Couldn't sleep in the train.'

Gill looked at Kanak and kept silent. She knew that her explanation was not very convincing.

Puri did not come to the office all day. Kanak worked till afternoon, talking with Gill and Raks in her usual manner. Raks left at 5.30. Kanak gave no sign that she wanted to leave.

'Will you stay for some time?' Gill looked at her and asked.

'I did not do any work yesterday. Let me work for another hour.'

'Don't bother about that. You can call it a day if you have to take care of the house. I'll order tea if you are staying, but you don't like tea from the bazaar.' Kanak did not like tea made with milk that was kept boiling all day.

'Get some. I'll have it today.'

'You can go. What's pending will be taken care of. Come, I'll walk you to the bus stand,' Gill rose, pushing back his chair.

'I wanted to work for another hour.'

'Let's go.'

Walking beside her in the gali, Gill asked her, 'Trouble at home?'

'What do you mean? Who said so?'

'I know.' Gill did not let her off. 'You haven't really understood your husband,' he said in a serious tone in English. 'Puri isn't any more the lumpen proletariat of his pre-Partition days. He now thinks like a petty bourgeois. He doesn't see lack of opportunities and anomalies of the system around him. He doesn't feel the need for change and for redefining what is right and what is wrong. He has taken his roots in the city. Any notions of change and disorder make him nervous. You point out these inner conflicts and make him ill-tempered. Why are you ruining your family life?'

Gill's meaning was clear. Kanak knew that Puri had discussed the matter with Gill and had perhaps accused her of being wilful. Was it right for him to do so?

Gill had become so close to both Kanak and Puri that at times it was difficult to hide from him the quarrels and arguments they had at home. Nevertheless, Kanak had never complained to him about the differences between her and Puri. She thought it was unfair of Puri to tell Gill a different version of events in order to vent his frustration and to seek Gill's sympathy. Unable to suppress her annoyance, she said, 'You tell me, how can one live all the time by hiding the reality and by deceiving oneself? Should I just continue to put up with deception? Was it for this that I faced the resentment of my family?' Her eyes brimmed with tears. Since Gill had come to know so much about her, she decided, that he should be told exactly the way it had happened. She did not take the bus from the G. T. Road. As they walked towards Model Town, Kanak opened her heart to Gill.

Gill said understandingly, 'You fell in love and got married, now you must see it through.'

'What haven't I done to fulfil my commitment, you tell me. When was I not ready to make compromises? Where did I go wrong or behave selfishly?'

'I explained how Puri doesn't see the need for redefining what is right and what is wrong. Yes, five years ago he would have thought along the same lines as you.'

'Five years ago?' Kanak said sceptically. 'Do you know what he did to Tara five years ago?' She told him about Tara's marriage. Then, her frustration boiling over, she said, 'Jijaji had found about it at that time. He had also told me, but then I just couldn't hear anything against him.'

'What did you see in him after all? It was by reading his short stories…' Gill had to bite his tongue.

Tears blinded Kanak for a moment. Inspite of being in a public place, she covered her eyes with her aanchal. She quickly collected herself, dried her eyes and removed the aanchal. Luckily, nobody was walking towards her on that side of the road. She walked about twenty-five steps without uttering a word, then asked Gill, 'He spoke to you about us. Why can't you explain to him my point of view?'

'If I said anything that supported you against him, it won't be possible for me to work here any longer.'

'What do you mean?' Kanak asked.

'Puri will never tolerate that I oppose him and support you. If I keep quiet after hearing him out, he takes it as sympathy for him. If I support you he'd see it as me meddling in his personal affairs. He would suspect that I am brainwashing you, and that you are simply echoing my opinions. That'll make him even angrier with you. How would I be able to remain here?' In the course of their talk Kanak and Gill had arrived at the bungalow. If Jaya had seen her mother, she would have jumped into her arms and would not have let her talk to anyone other than her. Kanak and Gill had sat in the veranda to finish their conversation.

The veranda had turned pink from the rays of the dying sun. Gill's words made Kanak look at him. The rays lit her face and he could see deep into her eyes through her dilated pupils. As if her heart had risen to her eyes. Kanak's chest heaved with a deep sigh. She got up and went indoors.

After the bitterness of the past two days, Gill's words had overwhelmed Kanak and she had run away from Gill. Who else would she be able to rely on? 'Babli,' she called.

Jaya came running and wrapped herself around Kanak's knees. She wanted to see inside her mother's purse. Kanak often carried toffees and red and blue pencils for Jaya in it. Jaya burbled on, 'Mummy, a fly fell into my milk. Amma Heeran took it out like that and threw it away. Mummy, Chaila sat me on Shera and I rode it like a horse. Mummy, want me to show you how to write a-aa-e…'

Jaya made a drawing about the size of her head on the white wall with a blue pencil.

'Hai, Babli! My jewel, don't write on the wall!' But the lines on the wall looked lovely to her. Heeran had washed Jaya's face and changed her clothes. Kanak, to face the turmoil in her heart, began to comb her hair again and tie a different ribbon.

Gill was sitting in the living room. Kanak called out to him from where she was, 'Tea will be ready shortly. Would you like to have some water?'

Puri had not returned when Kanak came out of her room, there was no news when he would. Gill had had the chairs put in the lawn. Jaya was sitting on the arm of his chair deep in a serious discussion about the lemondrop tree. How tall is the tree? Did it have any leaves? Were children allowed to climb the tree?

Kanak had been able to collect herself after freshening up and changing her sari. She began to pour tea and—without looking at Gill—said, 'If he takes you as a trusted friend, why can't he accept you as my friend?'

'No husband with accept that. He would want to monopolize his wife.'

'What do you mean by monopolize? I agree that the wife should stay within limits, I abide by those limits. You know that very well.' Cover of darkness made it possible for Kanak to continue, 'Husband has his rights, but I don't believe that implies that the wife can't be friends with any other person or can't rely on a friend for emotional support. I don't like doing things on the sly.'

They heard the sound of a jeep approaching. Kanak said in the same breath, 'He's arrived.' The jeep came to a halt at the bungalow's gate.

Puri seemed to be talking to the jeep's driver. In the few seconds before his arrival, Gill advised Kanak in a hushed voice, 'Well, there's no need to take risks just to be a show-off.'

Gill said to Puri, 'We've been waiting for you for an hour.'

Puri began to explain the reason for his being late. Kanak was stirring sugar in tea that she had poured for herself. She gave the same cup to Puri. A third cup was already in the tray.

'Thanks!' Puri said. He was exhausted. Receiving a cup of tea immediately after his arrival pleased him very much.

Gill said, looking at Kanak but meaning to address them both, 'What's the long face for! Talk to each other properly.'

Puri thought that Gill's words were in his support.

'When did I not do so? Whoever wants to vent his anger, takes it out on me,' Kanak said, in a grumbling tone.

Puri felt that presence of Gill was the right time to tell Kanak about his mounting worries and expenses after his election to the legislative assembly and the ensuing responsibilities, and why he found rickshaws and tongas to be inadequate means of transportation. He said that Somraj had advised him to buy a second-hand car and that he had baulked at the idea in view of the bigger expenses, but it had become increasingly difficult for him to do without a car.

'How will the car lighten your workload?' Gill asked. 'I'll at least save time, bhai. I feel uncomfortable about borrowing some vehicle ever so often from Suraj Prakash and from the owners of the Doaba Mills. It'll also be convenient for Kanak to go to the office and the press by car.'

'I think,' Gill said, taking a deep breath, 'that it certainly will be more comfortable and you will be spared the inconvenience of travelling through wind-blown dusty roads, but your workload won't be lightened. Rather you will have to worry about earning more to meet the car's expenses.'

Puri and Gill had a philosophical discussion about a person's basic needs, whether he should cut his coat according to his cloth, and the meaning of real happiness.

Kanak sat thinking that after a long time Puri was talking about something other than the problems at the office or political intrigues within the Congress.

Puri and Kanak did not talk any further on the subject of Tara and Sheelo, but Kanak and Gill discussed and analysed the topic at length, particularly the role of Tara. After meeting Tara personally and knowing the opinion of so many about her, Kanak was convinced that Tara was unselfish and honest, and had borne the brunt of disparagement without rancour. It was natural that some criticism of Puri came up in their discussion.

Puri had been elected to the assembly from the eastern district of Mukerian. Very few among the voting public could have recognized his face or had heard his name before the elections. The old inhabitants of the area and the Hindu and Sikh refugees from the west who had settled on agricultural land that had once belonged to Muslims had voted for the Congress party. They had given their vote not to Puri, but to the picture of a pair of oxen, the election symbol of the Congress. The average peasant thought: The Congress and the Muslim League had divided the British Raj between them, and eastern Punjab and the rest of India had gone to the Congress. The Congress was now the raja, and in future crop levies and taxes will have to be paid to the Congress government instead of the British government. Farmers displaced from western Punjab could retain farmland that they had occupied in the eastern part only with the approval of the Congress government. Those who had not yet been allotted land, could only hope to receive land from the Congress government's beneficence.

In theory the Congress party and the Congress government were two separate entities, but the colours of their flags were identical. The fine difference between the emblems of the chakra, wheel, and the charkha, spinning wheel, became clear only when the flags were unfurled. According to the government decree, the administration was to remain neutral during the election. The government had begun to publicize, just before the elections, its plan to spend hundreds of millions of rupees to remove unemployment, to build a network of irrigation canals to help peasants and farmers and boost the agricultural sector, and dams to provide cheap electricity for the benefit of the people. The public had learned to express its dissatisfaction with the British by voting for the Congress party. How could the peasants now ignore the mighty Congress and vote for a motley assortment of political parties? A vote for Puri was seen as a vote for the Congress.

Sood was travelling from Simla to preside over the annual function of a school in Amritsar. The school had been unable to procure adequate financial aid from the government. With their eye on the prospect of increased aid, the management of the school had set the date for the function to suit Sood. The real purpose of Sood's visit to Amritsar was to meet with the Sikh leaders. Puri had gone to the railway station in the morning after a cup of tea. He had said that he might have to go to Amritsar.

Jaya was riding her tricycle in the veranda, pretending it to be a train, letting out shrieks of delight. Kanak was ironing Jaya's frilly voile frock with an electric iron in her bedroom. Heeran had not learnt to use the iron even after working two-and-a-half years for Kanak. She could lovingly massage Jaya with ghee or butter, and rub oil in the child's ear and nose. She could comb and arrange Jaya's hair in a plait, but puffing them and forming ringlets and tying them with ribbons in a bow was beyond her.

Suddenly Shera barked menacingly and Jaya screamed.

'What happened, Munni?' Kanak was startled. Jaya has fallen off the tricycle, she thought. She put aside the iron and ran to the veranda.

Shera was barking to stop some people from coming into the bungalow. Jaya was screaming out in terror. Kanak took Jaya in her arms and called Shera back.

A very tall Sikh jat, with a woman and three children in tow, walked into the veranda. The well-built jat carried in one hand a lathi taller than he was, his other hand held a bundle of two or three kitchen pots tied in a torn sheet and slung over his shoulder. It was a bitterly cold morning, but he wore no kurta but a dirty, knee-length underpants. Locks of hair stuck out of a tattered dirty turban wrapped around his head like a rope, and his copious beard and moustache were matted and grimy. The children's noses were runny from the cold. The woman wore shabby and patched salwar-kameez and dupatta, and held in her arms a baby girl about the same age as Jaya. The baby's nose was also runny and she was wrapped in a ragged piece of khes. A six-year-old boy wore knee-lenght underpants and a ragged cotton vest, and the little hairs on his arms were standing up because of the cold. An older boy wore a torn kurta, and his hair was tied in a knot with a piece of cloth.

The man's eyes were bloodshot but dry. He looked at Kanak and said, 'I want to see Puri Babu.'

Kanak was scared. There was no man in the house except Chaila. Hari had left for college an hour ago. She said, 'He does lives here, but he has gone to Amritsar. He will return by this evening.'

'Sit down,' the man ordered the woman and the children. 'If he doesn't return this evening, he'll come back tomorrow. He'll come back some time. He hasn't been to the Congress party office since yesterday morning. We can't search all over the city for him.'

The woman looked exhausted. She sat down in the veranda, her back against the wall. The man and the children also sat down.

Jaya had buried her head fearfully in her mother's bosom and was looking at the visitors out of the corner of her eye. Kanak tried to soothe her and handed her to Heeran.

Once in a while visitors from Puri's constituency came to meet him and to ask him to look into some complaint or application they had made. Puri would offer them tea or lassi, and his commiseration. Perhaps the Sikh had come for a similar reason, Kanak thought.

Kanak returned to the veranda and asked the woman, 'What is your business?'

The woman gave no reply.

The man replied, 'I came here after writing to the tehsildar, the deputy commissioner, the Congress committee, to everybody. Puri is the member from our area. I got no answer to the two letters I wrote to him. We'll leave this place only when something is decided about our case. If we have to die from cold and hunger, we'll do it right here. If Puri doesn't help us, he'll have to cart our five bodies to the cremation grounds to burn them. Or he'll have to answer Rabb wahe-guru.'

'What letter?' asked Kanak.

'What letter?' the man said, flying into a fury. 'You people enjoy the benefits of membership snuggling down in your warm quilts, eating halwa made from *kun*, drinking milk and lassi. When would you have the time to read our letters? Puri Babu talked through big loudhailers to get our vote, he promised us the moon before the elections. He said that the Congress government will give land to every family, that we'll be given loans to buy ploughs and oxen, that water will flow from tube wells run by electric power. All he did was to give us a rough deal by taking away the 12 *ghuma*, each ghuma a 4,000 sq. yds, land that we were allotted, and giving it to his cronies in parcels of a hundred or two hundred sq. yds each. Either give us back our land, or we'll die from hunger and cold right here at your doorstep. And we'll come back to haunt you even after death.'

Kanak had no knowledge of the problems arising out of temporary and permanent allotment of agricultural lands. All she knew was that after the Partition it had been the time to plant the rabi crop, and the administration, thinking that unplanted agricultural land would exacerbate the food shortages, had allowed the refugee farmers from western Punjab to cultivate land vacated by the Muslim farmers. Now the farmers were being allotted land permanently on the basis of the land and property left behind in western Punjab. Those who were landless before the Partition were going to remain landless after the Partition.

Kanak felt compassion for the distraught Sikh, and sympathy for his anger. Jaya was wearing a wool dress that Kanak had knitted last year. She changed Jaya into one that she had knitted recently, and gave the old dress to the Sikh's baby daughter. She sat down with them in the veranda to listen to their woes.

Bela Singh was from the Sialkot district in western Punjab. In 1947 he had taken over a plot of 12 ghuma agricultural land and a water well, the property of a Muslim family that had fled to Pakistan.

Bela Singh had been a tenant farmer in his village Naroha. Since he could not produce ownership papers for the land that he had cultivated in the district now in Pakistan, a court order for his eviction from the land was issued in 1950. His land was allotted to Dasauda Singh, who had been able to prove his ownership of 1.5 *murabba*, 150,000 sq. yds canal-fed land in western Punjab.

Bela Singh had participated in the political movements launched by the Akali Dal and the Congress, and having campaigned for the Congress during the elections, knew little about politics. He was not willing to be a mere farm labourer after having been owner farmer for three years. He appealed against the eviction order. His court case had had several hearings till 1952. His appeal was turned down after the elections were over. Dasauda Singh came with the bailiff and police constables, and occupied Bela Singh's land.

Kanak had to go to the office. Raks had a cold and cough, and had been absent from the office for the past three days. Gill was all alone in the office. Just before she sat down to have her meal, Kanak said to Bela Singh's wife, 'Puriji won't be back before the evening. You people get something to eat in the bazaar. Come back in the evening. This is Puriji's home, he'll return here. Why should your family stay hungry?'

Bela Singh took umbrage at her suggestion, 'We're not going anywhere. We'll eat or drink only after we get our land back. Babu may come back this evening, or tomorrow, or the day after, or he may not come back at all. Where would we live without our land and how would we survive? We want our land or we'll starve ourselves to death. We'll wait for his return.'

'You don't have to go out if you don't want to,' Kanak said. 'I'll give you some wheat and lentils, and wood for fuel. You can make a stove out of some bricks and cook for yourself. The children are hungry. I'll send you some chapattis for them.'

Kanak brought about ten chapattis, some cooked daal and vegetables and gave to the woman. She repeated her offer of wheat and lentils.

Bela Singh said, shaking his head, 'No. We're much obliged to you, but it's enough that you gave food for the children. We'll eat only after our problem is solved.'

Since Jaya had begun to go to the day nursery, Kanak used to drop Jaya at the school on her way to the office, and Chaila used to bring Jaya home at 1.30 p.m. on a bicycle, with her sitting in a basket attached to the handlebars. When Kanak was about to leave at 10 a.m. with Jaya, Heeran said nervously, 'These people are sitting in the veranda. I'm afraid of being alone.' Heeran had witnessed the killing of her family and the looting of their house. She had been hit in the head with a *farsa*. Sikh soldiers had found her whimpering and barely conscious. She had spent four months in a hospital. Even the slightest tension gave her palpitations. Sometimes she would scream in her dreams and fall into a dead faint. Kanak could not just tell her to keep quiet. Kanak said, 'Don't' be afraid. Chaila knows how to use the telephone. I've also asked our neighbour Himmat Rai to keep an eye on the situation. Hari'll be back soon.'

Kanak had to tell about Bela Singh when she explained to Gill the reason for her being late. They both knew that what had happened in Bela Singh's case was perfectly legal. But legal considerations aside, the question remained: What about the landless? There could be no two opinions that every individual had a right to earn his living. Gill and Kanak criticized the newly enacted law as they discussed the problem. Kanak wanted to write an article in *Nazir* and pose the question: Should only those who had owned land in the past be allotted land in the present situation? Couldn't there be another, equitable method of the distribution of the agricultural land?

Gill advised her against doing so. He said that any criticism of the government will rankle with Puri. He reminded her of the time when Puri had objected to Kanak writing an article in support of the strike by patwaris. He said that there was no point in her starting another quarrel with Puri. Kanak had to keep a lid on her criticism. She said nothing to Gill, but thought to herself, 'Puriji and I now disagree over the slightest of reasons. He has changed so much!'

When she was leaving for home, Kanak requested Gill, 'If he didn't return today for any reason, it will be a hassle for me. Please come to the bungalow with me.'

When Kanak and Gill turned the corner near the bungalow, they saw a crowd of onlookers gathered on the road outside the boundary wall, which annoyed Kanak. On entering the gate they saw Puri standing in the veranda. Beside Puri was Hardev, a *balisht*, space between the tips of the thumb and the little finger, taller than Puri. The young man stood, arms akimbo and hands rolled into fists, waiting for a signal to grab the peasant by the scruff of his neck and throw him out of the bungalow. Dust and sweat caked Puri's face, and his black pashmina weskit was covered with a fine layer of dust. Puri's briefcase was in his hands, showing that he had just arrived. Puri was speaking patiently and sympathetically to Bela Singh, who was sitting with his back against the wall, 'My brother, law is the same for everyone. I can't change the law. If your complaint is that you didn't receive justice, appeal to the law court. I'll definitely help you if you follow the rules, but threats won't work with me.'

Bela Singh bellowed at Puri, 'Can't you see that I have no money to buy clothes to cover our bodies and fill our bellies, and you are telling me to go to court! I know you. It's your government that makes laws, and it's the government that decides court cases. I'd have thought of myself as a good-for-nothing, someone who was not fit to live and would have jumped in a well with my family if Dasauda Singh had taken away my land on his own. But it was your police that threw me out of my land, so now your police should give me another land or you give it to me. You uprooted me from Naroha, so I found shelter in Mundari. And now I've been thrown out of there. If we have to die from hunger and cold, we'll do it here before your eyes so that you can have peace of mind.'

Puri turned his back to put an end the conversation, and said, 'It was the police that threw you out, so go and stage your protest at their doorstep.'

'Why did you come to ask us for vote?' Bela Singh again bellowed. 'I've petitioned everyone. How do I know who's police, who's the deputy, what's session, and who's the lord vizier? You asked for my vote promising me that you'll get me justice.'

Puri went into the sitting room. Kanak and Gill followed him. Gill closed the door behind him.

Kanak asked Puri, 'You are tired, must also be hungry. What'd you like to have?'

Puri was tired, but had eaten lunch. He asked for a cup of tea, and began to tell Gill about the discussions in Amritsar on the question of Hindi and Punjabi languages. Kanak went to the back veranda to check on Jaya.

Bela Singh continued his satyagraha in the front veranda. His baby daughter would begin to cry after every few minutes. Kanak had tea served in the back veranda. Jaya had already had her milk, but insisted on having tea with her parents. Kanak seated her on a chair beside her. On hearing the baby cry from the other veranda, Jaya repeated to her mother what she had heard from Amma, 'Mummy, the children that cry are bad.'

Kanak said that it was so.

Gill asked Jaya, 'Babli, if I drink your tea, will you cry?' Jaya widened her eyes, shook her curly hair and said uncertainly, 'I won't give you my tea.'

Puri encouraged his daughter, 'Babli, give your tea to uncle. Say, you can have mine, I'll get some more for myself.'

When Jaya did not agree to part with her tea, Gill said, pretending to reach for her katori, 'I'm going to take it.'

Jaya shouted, 'No!' She looked at him angrily and raised her chubby arm to hit him.

Suppressing her smile, Kanak said as if shocked, 'Hai, Babli! One does not hit uncle. One gives *laddi*, kisses to uncle.'

'Is she any the less than Bela Singh? She's ready to fight for her tea,' Gill said to Puri. 'She'll also learn to talk tactfully when she becomes an MLA.'

Kanak smiled. She liked that comment on Puri.

'Hoon!' Puri turned his head and looked at Gill, 'Comrades will always support violence.'

'That's true,' Kanak gave her support also to Puri.

'Why, isn't it violence to take away Jaya's tea?' Gill asked. Since Kanak and Puri had laughed once at the joke, it fell flat.

The sound of the baby crying could be heard again.

Kanak said, 'It'd have been better if the size of every farmer's family and their needs were taken into account at the time of the allocation of land to the big farmers. Those who got none are bound to want some.'

'What if a farmer's family has grown?' Gill asked with a smile, then said in a serious tone, 'Bhai, the same system should apply to agricultural land as it is applied to all other means of production. When people have no resources to do business or trade, they can find work in mills and factories, or do clerical work in offices. In the same way, those who own no arable land should be able to find work as farm labours. Or else, all means of production should be nationalized...'

Puri interrupted Gill to make an important point, 'How can Punjab disobey the law as it is applied in the rest of the country. The Constitution says that government cannot interfere in private ownership of property and the freedom to do business.'

'Does the Constitution not promise everyone the opportunity to earn a livelihood in a welfare state? It also mentions nationalization of means of production for the benefit of the people. It is reasonable, to a certain extent, to allow people to continue to own private property, but the evacuee property has been declared to be national property before its reallocation began. If somebody had been a big landowner in western Punjab, why should that person be allowed to claim a share of the national property bigger than others? Instead of reallocating the land, the people should have been given a chance to do collective farming on it.' Kanak replied to Puri and Gill.

'How can you say that?' Puri cut her short. 'How can half the country have the freedom to do business and the other half be subject to the nationalization of means of production? Those who had to abandon large properties and agricultural lands in the west...'

'Is it the government's responsibility to keep the first half rich?' Kanak also cut Puri short. 'Then why did the government say that its policy was nationalization of resources and means of production?'

'Nationalization! Nationalization! What would you achieve by parroting the word like the communists?' Puri said irritably. 'The first important thing is to increase the production, not to let the established means of production go to ruin. What would the nationalization of poverty and hunger accomplish?'

The sound of Bela Singh speaking loudly came again. Hari came to tell Puri that a visitor named Amar Singh had come to meet him.

Puri got up and went to the front veranda. Bela Singh was telling his story to Amar Singh in a voice that the people gathered outside the boundary wall could also hear. He continued to declare his unfair treatment to the onlookers even when Amar Singh had stepped into the living room.

For the next two hours Puri tried to ignore Bela Singh's presence, but how long could he tolerate someone blatantly denouncing him in his own house and making him an object of ridicule! Puri said to Kanak, 'Go to his wife and explain to her that they must leave our house. If they agree, give them something to eat. But get them out of here. How long can we go on being prisoners in our own home?'

Kanak's attempt to cajole Bela Singh's wife bore no fruit. He agreed to take some more food for his children, but the couple refused to end their hunger strike and leave the bungalow.

Puri issued a final warning to Bela Singh in stern voice, 'It's not satyagraha to stage a sit-down in someone's home. It's a crime to enter someone's home unlawfully. If you and your family leave immediately, I'll try to help you get some land in Ram Nagar or Saboot Garh. If you are not out in ten minutes, I'll call the police to throw you out.'

'Who do you think you are? Our fate is not in your hands, but in the hands of Waheguru. You can do what you want! I was beaten up with lathis by the British government police. I'd like to have a taste of lathis of your Congress police. You just sit and enjoy yourself, and leave us to our fate.'

Puri waited not for ten, but for thirty minutes, while he made conversation. 'Things are getting tough everyday. The public thinks that independence has given them the right to create disorder. The other day, a man claiming to be a writer threw himself in front of the President's motorcade. He had a bundle of papers under his arm. He appealed to the President that he had gone to prison for the sake of the country's freedom, and was now devoting time in the service of literature, but his family was starving ...

'The President is a pussycat, really. He told the chief minister to do something for the man. Now the same writer, who can't write even one sentence correctly, wants his book to be included in the syllabus. What an extraordinary way to ask for charity! If you refuse them, you risk being unpopular with them. The public expects so much in return of giving a vote to you. They just want you to give in to their every demand. The government has lost all prestige.'

Puri telephoned the police station and explained the situation to the station officer. A police lorry arrived shortly afterwards. Bela Singh lay down like a martyr to the cause of satyagraha, and began to shout, 'Vande mataram! Inquilab Zindabad! Satsiri akaal!' A crowd of curious onlookers quickly gathered again outside the boundary wall.

The policemen threatened Bela Singh with lathis and offered to explain to him the real meaning of serving the cause of satyagraha.

Kanak was watching from inside. She stood near the door and pleaded in English with the police inspector, 'Please do not handle them roughly. Just take them away.'

Bela Singh's wife and the baby in her lap burst out crying when two constables grabbed the Sikh by his shoulders and feet. As the constables carried the man to the lorry, he shouted, 'People, look! Look at the height of cruelty! I was on hunger strike to get justice! They are taking me to jail.'

Bela Singh's wife was terrified. She had no clue where the police might take her husband. Holding her daughter in her arms and crying, she led her two sons into the lorry. Bela Singh was still shouting slogans when the lorry drove off.

Puri had gone to Simla to attend the meeting of the Transport Advisory Committee. He saw the latest issue of *Nazir* there. He was very upset when he read the editorial. From the language and the style he knew that the editorial on the topic of nationalization and allocation of evacuee properties had been written by Kanak. 'She should have consulted me before writing on this subject,' Puri thought. In the past such wilful behaviour by Kanak had caused him problems. He was also angry with Gill for not vetting the editorial.

There were people around Sood who were jealous of the patronage that Puri enjoyed and who were not averse to backbiting. When Puri went to meet Sood, he took Puri to task for his carelessness, 'What's going on? Is this how what's-its-name *Nazir* intends to help me?'

Sood had no time to read the editorial. He was told the gist of what was in it. In order to keep his self-respect, Puri tried to answer diplomatically, 'Bhaiji, the editorial does not criticize the government or any action of the administration. It simply presents another viewpoint about the policy regarding the allocation of arable land.'

Sood kept exceedingly busy. He had no time for splitting linguistic hairs or for going into details. He was constantly surrounded by sycophants and yes-men. How could he tolerate one of his protégés or subordinates talking back to him?

Sood chastized Puri, 'You can't fool me! The purpose of what's-its-name weekly is to make fun of me? You say it was nothing important. If it wasn't, how come others noticed it? If you keep on like this, I'll have what's-its-name weekly closed and the press locked up. I don't want any of this.'

Puri felt dizzy with anger. He remembered how he had once refused to put up with Kashish's threats and his insulting behaviour in a similar situation in Lahore, and had not cared about losing his only source of livelihood. But it wasn't a one-hundred-rupee job that was at stake now. Even when there was no reason to fear that Sood's displeasure could destroy him in one fell swoop and he was not willing to allow anybody to browbeat him into submission, he was being held back by his roots that had spread far and wide.

Puri decided not to let his heart rule his head. 'I call Soodji "bhaiji",' he thought. 'It's unreasonable of me to feel insulted by his criticism. It was nothing but mischief-making by those who tattle to him on me.'

The squabble between Puri and Kanak over Tara–Sheelo affair had ended. It was peace in the house, but the feeling of closeness, the spontaneity and the giving in to sudden impulses of their first months together was not there. In the light of their past quarrels, Puri took Kanak's editorial as a blatant act of disobedience. He thought: She has regard for no one.

On his way back from Simla, Puri was full of angry feelings for Kanak. Whenever he was annoyed with Kanak for her stubborn attitude and her coldness towards him, the memory of Urmila's adoring behaviour comforted his bruised ego. Urmila may have been away from him, but she was still infatuated with him even after having suffered from his hands.

It had become quite easy for Puri to meet Urmila after his election to the assembly. She had finished her training a year ago, and had been posted as a staff nurse at a Simla hospital. As there was no other way to contact her, Puri had gone to meet her at the hospital and had spoken to her for a few minutes in the hospital veranda. Puri had told her that she could come to see him without fear in the MLA quarters.

Puri had met Urmila several times during the next five years. When she had visited him for the first time in his quarter, he had told her, in a voice choked with tears, about his unbroken love for her and his feeling of helplessness. He had talked about the promise he had made to her at the time to their brief meeting in Ludhiana, and had reassured her that although he now had a wife at home, his heart was still with Urmila. That although he was unfortunately already engaged to Kanak in Lahore, he had never wanted to marry anyone but Urmila after being with her in Jalandhar. As the house and the press had belonged to Sood, he had to keep quiet at that time, but he had decided to try to find a solution. Puri had reminded her, 'That's why I told you not to worry when you were leaving. I couldn't find you when I went back to the hospital the next day. I was told that you had gone to Amritsar. I searched for you in Amritsar, but I was out of luck. It was only after eight months that I found out about your posting in Ludhiana. How abrupt you were with me when we met in Ludhiana, but I still couldn't forget you and went to meet you again.'

What Puri had said was not true, but it was from his heart. Every nerve in his body had been taut from a longing for Urmila. In Urmila's bright brown eyes, he had seen the reflection of his own feelings.

She had come to meet him at 6.30 p.m. They had been alone in the room, with curtains over the door and the windows. She had sat in a chair next to him. When Puri had tried to take her hand into his, she had pulled her hand free and shifted positions to be away from him.

To soften her up Puri had reminded her, 'Don't you remember how we were,' he had paused, taken a deep breath and had said, 'pulled away from each other's arms.'

Urmila had looked away and remained still.

Puri had not wanted to take any risks. He did not have the courage to close the door. But he could also not tolerate Urmila moving away from him. He would have felt better if she had said, 'Hai, someone might come!'

'Want me to close the door?' he had asked, to arouse her.

Urmila had shaken her bowed head.

'How can anyone forget that agony?' Puri's voice had become soft and sentimental. 'You know, poetry was born out of pangs of agony. Valmiki, world's first poet, cried, "Oh! Ill-fated Hunter, by which reason you have killed one male bird of the couple ..."'

Urmila neither knew Sanskrit, nor anything about the fable of the birth of poetry. Puri had explained to her the meaning of the shloka and the story of the pair of mating sarus, cranes oblivious of the surroundings, and had said, 'We were in the same situation. What we suffered, that painful memory will never go away...'

Urmila had kept a stony expression, and had risen to her feet.

Before she had left and when they had been outside on the road where there was no danger in being alone with Puri, she had told him, her head bowed, 'You threw me out! If you have got balls, throw out that witch now. I'm ready to come back. I don't care for this nursing-*vursing*. But first we'll get married. Then I'll see how that Sood of yours can shout at me!'

Puri had come across Urmila again in a shop on Mall Road before he had gone back to Jalandhar. Urmila, always fond of flashy clothes, had been dressed up as usual, with the kohl lining her eyes fashionably drawn beyond the side corners of her eyes. As she had exchanged namaste with Puri, she had introduced her companion as Dr Mongia, and had said that they were both out shopping.

In accordance with the government rules, Puri was entitled to a travelling allowance equivalent to three times the first class railway fare. There were some MLAs who, despite such a generous allowance, saved money by travelling in second or third class. Many members of the legislative assemblies considered such practices a blow to the prestige of the assembly and the government. In their opinion, an MLA should receive the fare for the class of actual travel. Puri was of the same opinion. After receiving such complaints frequently, the UP government had decided that the MLAs in that state will receive an allowance of three times the railway fare irrespective of the class in which they travel, thus endorsing the unscrupulous behaviour of the MLAs. Puri had written in his column 'Haat Bazaar Mein' in Nazir: If such is the state of the morals of the people responsible for framing laws, how ethical and right would those laws be and of what importance could ethical considerations be for such people?

Puri could travel in comfort, sleeping overnight, since he always travelled in the first class. Usually he left Simla in the afternoon and reached Jalandhar at four in the morning. If he got delayed for some reason, he changed trains at Ambala and reached Jalandhar at 6 or 7 a.m.

Puri had the whole berth to himself, but the problems in his mind did not let him sleep for a very long time. There would be a quarrel about Kanak's editorial in *Nazir*, he knew, but he could not also keep quiet about it. Every time he had a problem with Kanak, Urmila would come to his imagination. But during his most recent stay in Simla he could not even have the satisfaction of seeing Urmila.

When Puri had gone to Simla last September to attend the meeting of the Education Committee, he had met Urmila. Urmila had told him how uncomfortable she had been in Simla in winter, and how the past winters had been hard on her. She had wanted to be posted to Amritsar, and had applied for a transfer. Puri had put in a word with the director of the Department of Health on her behalf and she had been transferred to Amritsar.

Puri woke up before the Kalka–Amritsar Express reached Jalandhar. He knew that the jeep from the Doaba Mills would be waiting at the station to receive him, but his longing for Urmila dragged him to Amritsar.

Puri left his suitcase and holdall in the waiting room of the Amritsar station, and reached the Civil Hospital just before 8 a.m. The hospital wards were being cleaned. Without disclosing who he was, Puri asked a ward boy, 'Staff Nurse Miss Urmila is on duty, or would she be in her quarter?'

The middle-aged ward boy thought for a moment, then asked, 'The same Urmila Miss who got married to Dr Mongia Sahib?'

The words slipped out of Puri's mouth, 'Got married?'

'Yes, they were married last week. She just went to Dr Mongia Sahib's quarter. She was on the night shift in the surgical ward.'

Puri swallowed hard and said, 'She must have gone to sleep if she was on the night shift. Achcha, I'll come some other time.'

Puri was shocked to the marrow. His heart filled with bitterness as he thought, 'Such deception! The same Mongia, with whom she had gone shopping. That's why she was so decked up! That's why she got herself transferred to Amritsar! I had advised her to go to Ambala, but she lied to me that it'll be better for her in Amritsar because two of her batch-mates were already posted there. She had told me that she wanted to get married to me! Woman, thy name is frailty! He who trusts you is a fool! I made a fool of myself! What was the need for all this deception?'

Puri took a rickshaw home. Only Shera came forward to greet him. The empty house echoed with the sound of laundry being beaten with a bat. Chaila was in the kitchen, clattering the pots as he cleaned them, singing a film song on the top of his voice. Puri told him to unload his luggage from the rickshaw. His own voice sounded rather meek to him. He thought, 'Is this my home or a transit camp?' He knew that Kanak would have waited for him, at the most, until 7.30.

Heeran and Chaila quickly got to looking after their master. Chaila had somewhat learnt the correct way of doing things, but Heeran, even after working three years for the family, had not learnt to make tea properly. Heeran had no one else in the world but Kanak and Puri. Kanak could trust her with the keys to various cupboards in the house. But Heeran did not trust Chaila, and kept the keys tied to the waist cord of her salwar.

Puri had a bath, and waited to be served a meal. He was angry and bitter: How hard he worked, how many responsibilities he had taken on, so many successes and so much praise he had earned, some people were even envious of him, but he did not amount to much in his own home! It seemed that everyone was involved in this web of deceit. This was the result of his generous and unsuspecting nature. Urmila's words echoed in his ears. He thought of her tempting, irresistible body which was now a poisonous snake that he should have crushed, but that had escaped and slithered away into the grass. Trust a woman! She wants nothing but gratification, and deception is her only weapon.

Chaila brought food for Puri in a thali. Puri had not eaten anything that day, and was hungry. He began to eat absent-mindedly, going over Urmila's deception in his mind, 'She had such a strong sex drive. Would she have stayed all this time without sex? Never! She turned out to be a deceiver! I was lucky to have escaped from her clutches.'

He did not feel like going out. He thought of the sleep he had missed, and lay down. To drive the thoughts of Urmila out of his mind, he began to think, 'I'll have to speak to Kanak. What if she is too stubborn to admit that she was wrong?' If Gill or Raks had done something similar, he would have fired them, but Kanak's name appeared as the editor–manager of *Nazir*. To avoid any inconvenience during his absence from Jalandhar, Puri had changed all bank accounts to operate under Kanak's signature in March before going to attend the session of the assembly. But it was still he who owned the weekly and the press.

Puri used to temper his feeling of Kanak's antipathy towards him by overlaying it with the memory of how Urmila used to dote on him. Now when that remedy had slipped out of his hands, Kanak's antagonism became increasingly intolerable for him. In his mind he went through the history of his affair with Kanak, 'Her family's bitter opposition! I was penniless and without a job! Would anyone believe that she came to meet me in the police lock up? She invited me to Nainital. She came to Jalandhar without caring for the good job she had in Lucknow. She found me in that compromising situation. She saw a snake with her own eyes, but believed me when I told her it was a rope. She put up with so much, trusted me so much, and accepted my right over her.' A feeling of gratitude for Kanak swept over Puri. Then another thought crossed his mind, 'That was because of my handling of the situation. I really managed it well. But this bitterness between us, where did it come from? She does not find me desirable anymore. Is this a loving relation between a husband and wife, is this how married people live? How did this happen?'

Puri thought with intense concentration, 'The reason is her wilful attitude, her conceit. She used to be so full of love and unrestrained passion for me, used to wake me up if I was asleep. She's not like that any more. Perhaps she has exhausted all her passion. Perhaps her womanliness has been suppressed because she works like a man. Why does she have to involve herself so much with *Nazir* and the press? Can I call this place my home? What hasn't she done for the business? Few could have been more devoted than she had been. I must stop the situation from deteriorating.'

It was 2.30 when he woke up, feeling better after a nap. What was on his mind before falling asleep came back to him: He had to defuse the situation. He continued to lie down for some time. When he could not stand doing nothing, he got up and telephoned Kanak at the office.

Kanak said with surprise, 'Which train did you take? I had called the railway station at eight o'clock to inquire. None of the trains was running late.'

'Thanks,' Puri said with gratefulness. 'I woke up after the train reached Amritsar. Arrived here at 10.30 from there.'

'You should have telephoned me. Did my not being at home cause you any difficulty?'

'You would have come all the way from the office. It's you who'd have been inconvenienced.'

'Why are you talking so formally?'

'No, no. I had no inconvenience. Took a nap after lunch. Now I am going to visit Gyaniji in Vikrampura. I may come to the office, but don't wait for me after five o'clock. Tell Gill to come over.'

Kanak and Gill left for home after waiting for Puri till 5.15. Puri reached home about ten minutes after they did. During their casual conversation, Puri explained that the Transport Advisory Committee had recommended running state-owned buses on more routes in Punjab, which, in his view, was a pragmatic approach to the nationalization of the transport system. He explained that the privately owned buses would have to provide better service in order to compete with other carriers, and that would generate revenue for the government. The private carriers would be phased out. Then he brought up the topic of the editorial in *Nazir*.

Puri began by accepting the responsibility for an editorial published in the weekly. He said, 'There's nothing objectionable in that editorial. It's only an emotional take on the economic condition of the society and the country. There's no conflict with the fundamental policy of the Congress, and Pandit Nehru has the same point of view in the matter. But someone has filled Soodji's ears against the editorial. Soodji's behaviour has become very mechanical. All he thinks about is the affairs of the Congress Working Committee, who could be in the council of ministers, and about the next elections. He has nothing to do with ideological issues any more. He doesn't want to hear a dissenting voice. I'm in a quandary. I can't say to him that the weekly is none of his business because I have always considered him my elder brother.

'There's no question of being intimidated by Soodji, or by anyone else. You both know how I gave up my job for the sake of my principles when I was even worse off. Of course, I can't be disrespectful to Soodji. He may be sharp-tongued, but he's a good person at heart. I don't see anyone as unselfish as he is in the whole Congress party. Without me at his side, self-serving people will have him in the palm of their hand. He's surrounded by yes-men as it is, and his supporters have given him a swollen head. All newspapers want to get on the right side of the government for the sake of advertisements. We sometimes do raise our voice in *Nazir* against the government, but what'll we do if others connived to destabilize our weekly? We should try and avoid, at least for some time, getting on the wrong side of such people. If we don't remain active on the progressive front, these yes-men will bring ruin on the entire party. Both of you manage the weekly. All I can say now is that if we want to achieve something solid, we should avoid radical opinions or sensationalism just to attract more readers as others are doing. We should rather aim at fostering a deep and insightful outlook in the public.'

Puri spoke without looking at Kanak or Gill. His tone bespoke the responsibility that rested on his shoulders, and a feeling of dejection and frustration. Kanak thought: Perhaps he is a little weary after being away for so many days. She remembered the way Puri had spoken to her on the telephone. She thought, 'Soodji and other people must have complained about my editorial. Why doesn't he come out with what's bothering him. Perhaps he'll tell me later.'

'There was no criticism of the government policy in the editorial. It simply expressed another point of view,' Gill said in support of Puri.

Puri did not reply, but continued to sit, as if exhausted.

Kanak asked Jaya to sing a song she had learnt at the nursery:

'Chhun karti aye chidiya
Daal ka dana layee chidia...'

Kanak urged her daughter on, 'Bravo! Sing the whole song for your papa.' Jaya sang eagerly, but Puri sat silently, without paying her any attention.

Seeing Puri rather uncommunicative, Gill got up and left. After spending the day at the office, Kanak always had something to attend to when she got back. Around 8.30 Chaila informed that dinner was ready. Kanak called out to Puri as she went towards the dinning table, 'Come and have dinner. It's on the table.'

'Have it sent to me here.'

Kanak peered into Puri's room and asked, 'Why, what's the matter?'

'All right, I'm coming.' Puri said, getting out of his bed.

Puri said little during the dinner. Kanak tried to begin a conversation, 'Simla must be very cold and deserted at this time of the year.'

Puri just grunted in reply.

After dinner, Kanak asked Heeran to move Jaya, who had gone to sleep in Kanak's bed, to her crib. Then she gave her instructions for making yogurt. Before going to her own bedroom, she went into Puri's room to check if his bed had been made.

Puri's bed was ready, but he was sitting in an easy chair, with a blanket around him and hand cupping his chin.

Kanak said, 'Don't feel like working? Go to bed if you are tired. Would you like to drink some milk?'

'Thank you,' Puri replied, without looking at her.

'What's the matter?' Kanak asked. 'You were so formal on the telephone earlier today.'

'What's formal in this? If you do me a favour, I must thank you.' Puri said politely, as if overcome by a feeling of gratitude.

'What do you mean by doing a favour? Every woman does these things in her home. There's no need to give thanks for such small things.'

Puri sat silently.

'What's behind your anger?' Kanak asked without sitting down. 'That editorial?'

'Forget that. I already said what I had to say.'

'Then what?'

'You don't have to take so much trouble for me.'

'You don't want me to do all this for you any more?'

'I didn't mean that. I'm already so obliged to you.'

'There's no need to feel obliged. Let it continue as it had in the past. What's the need to feel obliged today?' Kanak turned around to go.

'I'll tell you if you sit down for a minute.'

Kanak sat on the edge of Puri's bedstead.

Puri said in a choked voice, 'You gave me the right to expect all this from you because we were husband and wife.'

'What else we are now?'

'Hear me out. We had to face many obstacles and problems because we wanted to get married, but are we living like a married couple?'

'How else are we living?'

'You know the natural urge of life, the relationship between husband and wife, we don't have it any more. Doesn't that mean a breakdown of a relationship? Isn't it unnatural to live together like this?'

Kanak lowered her head and looked into space beyond the open door. She said after a brief pause, 'One child is enough for me. I'd be happy if I took good care of her.'

'You mean that the relationship between couples is only for the purpose of having children, or that it inevitably ends in having children. Were we attracted to each other only so that we could have a child?'

'Well, I can't help if I don't want to have that kind of relationship. I'm sorry,' Kanak said, her head bowed.

Puri asked, 'Is it unreasonable or abnormal for me to have such a need?'

Kanak was silent.

'At least give me some reply. Have I said anything wrong?'

'I didn't say that, but it's not possible for me to do anything about it,' Kanak said without raising her head.

'Will you have any objection if my need became so compelling that I have to fulfil it somewhere else?'

'Do as you wish. There's no need to discuss such things with me,' Kanak rose to her feet.

'And I should continue to suffer if I consider cheating on you as wrong?'

'I'm very sorry.' Kanak said, and went out of his room.

Whenever husband and wife clammed up after a quarrel, Chaila and Heeran also became glum and Jaya too became morose. Kanak thought such an atmosphere to be a bad influence on the child, and she would force herself to act in a way as if nothing had happened.

Next morning, she herself brought Puri his morning cup of tea, hoping to put an end to the disgraceful show. Puri did not speak to her. Kanak put his bath things in the bathroom, took out his clothes. She sat at the table when he ate, but he did not say a word. After he had finished he asked

Chaila to get him a rickshaw, and left alone for the city. Kanak too went to office at her regular time.

It was the same on the morning after next. That day Puri came to the office at 3 p.m., looking very busy and serious. He went straight into the press manager's room and sat there checking the accounts for quite some time. Then he came to the editorial section. Ignoring Kanak, he asked Gill about the matter for the next issue of the weekly, and read all of it. He discussed a few office matters. Then he stood up, gave Kanak a sudden smile and said, 'How long will you stay? I'll go to Adarsh Nagar before going home.' He looked at Gill, 'Will you come over to Model Town? Do come.'

Puri had done something he had never done before—insulted Kanak by ignoring her in presence of others. This was his punishment for Kanak for not remaining subservient as a wife. In the past he had kept their differences hidden from others. Anger was boiling up in Kanak. She could neither write a word, nor read what was in front of her. She could not think of an excuse to go away from the office. She said after ten minutes, 'I have to go to my sister's place for some important work. I'll finish off the rest of the work tomorrow.'

Kanak returned home, told Heeran that she had a headache, and went to bed. Jaya wanted to cling to her mother whom she had not seen since morning. Kanak, in a foul mood after the insult she had received, wanted to keep away from her daughter. She called Chaila over and said, 'Your work can wait. Take Babli out for a stroll up to the roundabout.'

Chaila carried off the child who was wailing in protest.

Heeran came with some ghee in a katori, 'Let me massage your head with this.'

'Let it go, mausi. Stop bugging me,' Kanak covered her face with her aanchal.

'Hai, crazy girl, you've burned your brain out by drinking all those cups of *lal* tea. You use your brain all day, so what else will you get if not a headache!'

Heeran continued to stand with ghee in her hand. She said after a few moments, 'No, *puttar*, one does not cry over such matters. You are smart enough to know how to flatter and win him over. What else can a woman do? You are a good person. God forbid, he never hit you even with so much as a flower. Mine used to break my bones. Men are bound to get angry.' Kanak listened quietly from under her aanchal.

Heeran went away dejectedly and got busy in other chores.

After about an hour, Gill's voice came from the veranda, 'Babli!' Then he called, 'Chaila!'

Heeran came and said to Kanak, 'Babli's taya has come.' Heeran had been addressing Gill by that name.

'I don't know if I can get up. I've a headache,' Kanak said irritably.

'No, puttar. Get up. That's a good girl,' Heeran said lovingly.

'Achcha, ask him to sit.'

Kanak had to get up. She combed her hair, changed her sari. She knew her eyes would betray her mental state, but could do nothing about it.

'Puri's not back yet?' Gill asked.

Kanak shook her head and took a chair next to him.

'So?'

Kanak was silent.

'Why don't you say something?' Gill said. Kanak kept a stony silence, as if stopping herself from saying anything.

'Don't want to talk about it?' Gill asked sympathetically.

Kanak took a deep breath, and said, 'Impossible!'

'What is impossible? It's not possible to tell me?'

Kanak sat staring at the floor. She took another deep breath, then said, 'To go on living here.'

Gill said, arching his eyebrows, 'Kanni, you are being stupid.' He continued gently in English, 'You must be more tolerant. I have explained it to you so many times.'

'What more should I tolerate? Am I a prostitute?' Kanak spitted out the words, then covered her face in embarrassment. She went back to her room and fell on the bed. She wept for several minutes, trying to muffle the sound of her sobs. A feeling of shame filled her, and she thought, 'What have I said!' Then she corrected herself, 'But I was right. Must I put up with all this shit just to be able to live in his house, to be considered his wife? What else does a prostitute do but that! Am I not an individual? I won't ever accept his demands, tolerate his behaviour. I don't want to live only as his wife.'

She heard Puri's voice from near her bed, 'Kanni, come outside. Gill's waiting.'

Kanak remained still.

Puri said irritably, 'Can't you behave yourself at least in front of others?'

'No, I can't. How did you behave at the office?' Kanak snapped back in a choked but angry voice from under her aanchal.

Puri went back, and said to Gill, 'Kanni's not feeling well. She often gets these terrible headaches. It could be her blood pressure. I'll consult a doctor.'

'Yes, she looked very tired during the day. You must consult a doctor,' Gill said sympathetically.

Chapter 13

In the last week of April, on the way back from the kothi of Agarwals, Tara had replied to Nath's question by saying that she had no sasural. Her answer had taken Nath by surprise, and he had wanted her to explain why. It had not been easy for Tara to describe the few hours she had spent at her in-laws, and what had happened to her after that. Tara had said briefly and haltingly in English, her head bowed, 'He found out that I didn't want to marry him, and seemed to be harbouring a grudge against me. He knew that I was alone and helpless, and he tried to take revenge by humiliating me. I resisted and he became violent. Shortly after that a Muslim mob attacked the house and set it on fire. I managed to escape by jumping on the roof of the house next door.' The truth about what had happened to her had come out of her lips for the first time, but she felt much lighter after doing so, just like a boil when lanced gives relief after the initial pain.

Nath did not ask any question. He did not say anything to express his surprise or to show his sympathy. Sitting still, he listened to her with his eyes half-closed. Several times Tara bit her lip and fell silent. Even then Nath kept his gaze turned away.

When she finished, Nath said, 'I'm really disappointed in Puri.' Then asked, 'How did you reach the camp?'

Tara had never told anyone about the humiliation and degradation that she had suffered. Although people would have sympathized with her for a while, she would have also demeaned herself in their eyes forever. She did not want that to happen. She had invented a story about her past, but she could not tell a lie to Nath. Her head still bowed, she answered him in five sentences, 'A goonda abducted me from the gali. A retired Muslim gentleman got me out of his clutches. I had to leave the second place because I refused to convert to Islam. Then some Muslim goondas locked up me and some Hindu women in a house. The Indian Army rescued us and took us to a camp.' Tara did not care what Nath would think of her. She just could not tell him a lie.

Nath spoke only one sentence, 'Tara, you are really brave and very courageous.' His voice was full of affection and admiration.

Nath's words lightened Tara's mood, 'Doctor sahib, does your wife, I mean our bhabhiji, cook well?'

'Barely manages to. He's no chef. He can make everyday stuff like daal, vegetables and chapattis. There's always some yogurt when he brings my lunch in the tiffin carrier.'

'Why so, Doctor sahib? Get someone who knows how to cook. You should have proper meals.'

'Yes, I do need one, but where to find one? What if he robs me? Actually I had hired a duffer. Although his name was Bhola he was anything but simple. Stole everything except the clothes I was wearing. Also four hundred rupees in cash.'

'Doctor sahib, didn't you lock your stuff?' Tara asked with concern.

'I did, but he was the one who laid out clothes for me. He was good at his job. He could sew buttons, get the cloths ironed, could manage everything. Sometime I forgot to take back the keys from him. Perhaps that was too great a temptation for him.' Nath made light of his loss.

'Doctor sahib, had you given him enough, he would not have stolen from you,' Tara said in reply to Nath's joke

'You take me to be that generous?'

Tara asked, 'Is bhabhiji able to manage the house?'

'He's old. Can't even thread a needle.'

'Then how can he be of help to you?'

'He doesn't want to let go of me. By living in my house he saves rent, his food expenses also. Probably eats better at my place. I give him fifteen or twenty rupees every month. It won't be right to ask him to leave. His son's in school, appearing for his Intermediate exam. Poor soul borrowed fifty rupees from me to send to his son.'

'Then keep a help for bhabhiji. Doesn't one keep a servant to help the wife? Bhabhiji will keep an eye on the servant,' Tara said with a smile.

'Yes, that's possible. You're right,' Nath agreed, as if it was something he should have thought of himself.

Nath's straightforwardness touched Tara's heart. She asked, 'Doctor sahib, would you like me to get you a servant?'

'Why, are you running some agency?'

'Something like an agency, Doctor sahib,' Tara said, laughing. 'It seems that my peon Durga Pande is trying to find some job in Delhi for every boy from his home district. Parsu was sent by him. He also found servants for two neighbours.'

'Then you must get me one.'

Tara inquired about the bus route and the bus stop near Nath's bungalow.

'Doctor sahib, would you like some dinner? It's 8.30.'

'I was waiting for you to ask me.'

'Give me a minute,' Tara said, getting up. She went to the kitchen to see what Purandei had cooked. The food was rather simple. She thought, 'Why didn't I ask him earlier?' She sent out Parsu to get a couple of dishes from a nearby restaurant, and something from the halwai. The dough was ready. Purandei always made fresh, hot chapattis for her. Tara asked her to make some paranthas.

Tara brought food for Nath in a thali.

Nath asked, 'How about you?'

'You go ahead. I'll have some later.'

When Nath insisted, Tara got a thali for herself.

Nath said looking at her thali, 'You're serving me restaurant food. You did the same on the night of Sita's wedding.'

Tara's thali had two katoris and Nath's had four.

Tara nearly died of embarrassment. Had she known he'd notice, she'd have taken a small portion for herself.

She offered a sort of apology, 'Doctor sahib, I forgot to check if there was enough for all of us. Achcha, I'll cook for you one day. How about this Sunday?'

'Not this Sunday. I'm off to Patna for a week. We'll fix a date when I return.' Ignoring Tara's 'no, no,' Nath gave her half a share from his katoris.

Tara let the next Sunday pass. Narottam was also away from Delhi and, she thought, that she'll invite him too when calling Nath over for dinner the Sunday after. On Tuesday Tara was in her office when Durga Pande came to her, showed her the slip of paper with Nath's address on it, and said, 'Huzoor mataji, I had obeyed your order to send a servant to the bungalow of the sahib. Huzoor, the sahib has gone to Simla. Now whenever huzoor orders me to.'

Tara thought irritably, 'Why didn't Doctor sahib tell me? He had said that he'd call me on returning from Patna. At least he could have given me his address in Simla. Now he won't be back before September.' Then she told herself, 'But who am I to complain and get angry? One should be happy with what one gets without asking.' She remembered Mrs Agarwal's words, 'A lemon becomes bitter if squeezed too much.' She thought, 'Doctor sahib is surely an old friend, but when I have borne in silence the loss of my parents and my brother, why should I have any claims on him.'

Tara sometimes felt pangs of regret, 'Is there someone I can call my own?' Then she would think, 'Shyama, Narottam, Mercy, Mathur ... I can call them as my own. Then there is Rawat Sahib and Doctor sahib.' But was there anyone with whom she could quarrel, for whose well-being she could worry?

The object of Tara's worry and concern for the past three months had been her car. She had at first felt embarrassed at the suggestions to get a second-hand small car for herself, but a car had become a necessity after her promotion to the position of undersecretary.

After examining and rejecting several cars during the past year, she could no longer resist the urge to buy a brand-new sedan. The car had cost Tara all her savings and she had to take out a loan against her salary to pay for it. Shining like a black gem, with strips of chromium all around and seats upholstered in red velvet corduroy, the car had become the focal point of her life. In the beginning she had hired a chauffeur so that the car won't get scratched or dented, but it was Narottam who had been teaching her to drive and to look after her car. Tara had also bought two manuals on maintaining and driving a car.

The car had brought a new sense of excitement into Tara's life. Hardly two months had passed before she could recognize various noises that the car made. When she touched the starter button, the engine responded with a faint raspy sound. When she nudged the accelerator with her foot, the car growled louder, as if it was alive and responding to her touch. At Tara's command it could go swift as wind, with her ensconced in its lap, in sun or in rain. All its power was under Tara's control. She sat in its lap, but loved it like a baby. When she parked the car in an unfamiliar area, she was always concerned that some kid might scratch its paint, or some careless driver might dent its body. It was like a powerful but silent partner that shared her sad secrets. If she was lonely she went for a thirty- or forty-mile-long drive, and felt the thrill of the speed. When the speedometer needle went past 60 mph, she praised herself by saying 'Bravo!', and gently told the car, 'That's enough!'

When Narottam had been posted in Calcutta, he used to write to Tara every two weeks. Tara also used to get letters from Tewari in Aligarh. At first she had answered two of his letters. Tewari eventually stopped writing when his letters went unanswered. Tara seldom received any other mail. Everyone she knew in her new life was in Delhi. In July a letter came to her home address from Miss Deva. She had met Deva through Narottam and they had become good friends. Deva had got a good job in Lucknow and had moved to that city. Her letter was about her new job, and included a bill of lading for a parcel of mangoes she had sent for Tara.

A couple of days later a telegram came for Tara at her office. Tara was astonished: 'Who would send a telegram? Why?' She thought of her parents and her brother. Maybe...

The telegram read: 'Could not meet you before leaving. Give news about your well-being. Pran Nath.'

He had included his address in Simla.

Tara was overjoyed and thrilled to pieces. Her heart was filled with serenity and contentment, as if there was someone whose kindness and good wishes would protect her forever from every problem and danger. Her eyes saw the telegram's message in English written on every file on her desk. She wanted to reply immediately to the telegram, but decided to take her time and write a long and detailed reply.

She stayed up late at night to write the letter to Nath. She complained about his going away without informing her, and not showing up after accepting her dinner invitation. So many other things. She filled up eight pages, but felt she hadn't said what she wanted to say. 'This is pretty inane,' she thought. 'The purpose of writing to him should not be to bother him with silly details. I'll just send a telegram in reply.' It was eleven o'clock. She picked up the phone and sent an express telegram: 'Many thanks for your kindness. Am perfectly happy and well. Letter follows. Tara.'

Despite tingling with excitement, she wrote the letter with care, leaving out unnecessary details. She knew that Nath's knowledge of Hindi was rudimentary, but what she wanted to say could not be said in English. She took care to write legibly, printing the letters:

Most Respected Doctor Sahib,

I received your telegram as a token of your boundless good wishes and blessings for me. How can I ever thank you for it? You have very kindly never expected such formalities from me. Many years ago when I was seeking admission in college, you had advised that I should learn to be financially independent. Under your kind and generous guidance I have managed to become capable of earning enough so as to stand on my two feet.

I am quite well due to your good wishes and blessings, and free from worries at present. I used to feel that the circumstances had left me all by myself. That complaint was removed on the day I met you in Delhi. I felt that I had met my guardian angel. My family has always been recipient of your kindness. I have continued to be a recipient of the same. How can I thank you for something that I regard as my right to receive from you.

Whenever Narottam and I meet, he remembers you respectfully. So do Chaddha, Mercy didi and Mathur bhai. When they say nice things about you, I feel good at heart because I know that you have favoured me most with your kindness and generosity. I know your time is important. You have been entrusted with the responsibility of drawing the Plan to solve our country's problems or with doing what is needed most by our country. How useful you are for the country and society. I feel that I have become self-supporting, but have not been useful for the society! I hope you will guide me also in future.

You will probably return after two months, but I feel overwhelmed with your kindness even when you are far away. That feeling is always close to my heart.

I hope to receive your blessings as I've done in the past and which I consider to be rightfully mine.

Your student,
Tara

Tara's guess was that in a week or so she would receive a reply from Nath. She began waiting for his letter after a week had passed. When no reply came for two weeks, she wanted to remind him, but thought, 'What's the point of reminding him if he's not in Simla or is very busy. I can't ask him to explain himself when he's been so kind to me.'

When no letter came from Nath until the third week of August, she tried to comfort herself, 'Perhaps all he wanted was to find out whether I was unwell or was facing any problem. He got the answer. That's fine with me. What did I write that was so important that he had to write back?'

Towards the end of September Tara got a telephone call from Nath that he was back and would come over that afternoon around six o'clock.

Nath came carrying a bundle wrapped in a towel. He held it out to Tara and said, 'Here, this is for you.'

The aroma of apples filled the room. Tara's heart was filled with joy and gratitude, and she was overcome by Nath's concern for her. She took the bundle, held it reverently next to her heart and asked in mock anger, 'Why didn't you reply to my letter?'

'You didn't ask me anything so what I could say in reply? And such chaste Hindi! It was almost Sanskrit. I had difficulty figuring it out even with a dictionary. Felt as if I was reading a homily on the importance of devotion. By the grace of God and His help, I'll learn Hindi. It's going to be the official language. You'll have to tutor me.'

Tara did not mind the friendly reproach from Nath. It crossed her mind, 'Perhaps I wrote too much about my expectations and I may have come across a bit too assertive.'

The *mundan* ceremony of Mercy's son Ashok was on the first Sunday of June 1953.

Marcy had asked a Hindu pundit to perform the rites of havan and pooja. After the havan ceremony, Ashok's black, silky-soft curly hair was cut and his head was shaved with a straight razor.

Heera Lal didn't let go of the chance to have a friendly quibble with Mercy. He said, 'Bhabhi, what a shame! After marrying a Hindu you also have turned into a Hindu. Have you lost your senses? You've made his pretty face look like an earthen pot.'

Mercy said, flashing her eyes at Heera Lal, 'How have I turned into a Hindu? How could I let the boy stay hirsute when his uncle had cut his hair?'

The pundit could not help but preach, 'Hair from mother's womb are contaminated and bad for the health of the baby. They make the baby hot-tempered. All Aryan practices have a scientific...'

Mercy could not stand the pundit's lecture. She said, 'The ritual of mundan is performed nowhere in the world except India. You mean the brains of rest of the world are heated up. I didn't have a mundan. Do you think I'm hot-headed?'

'Maybe a little bit,' Narottam said quietly.

Mercy gave Narottam a look, but continued, 'The boy had an itchy scalp, his head needed to be shaved.'

The pundit joined in enthusiastically, 'That's the scientific explanation. The Aryans had…'

Narottam barged in, 'Didi, instead of burning a pao of ghee in the fire as offering, you could have used it to make paranthas.'

Mercy blew up, 'Doesn't your government spend millions on the Republic Day celebrations! And you mind my using up just a little ghee for my son? How could I shave such a lovely head of hair without any ritual?'

The moment he heard the words 'government' and 'republic day', Mathur spoke up, 'PM has a fetish for grandiose ideas.'

That was the start of a political discussion.

Tara took Ashok in her arms, and said as she took off his shirt, 'The custom is that after the child's hair is cut, he wears new clothes sent by his nani, maternal grandmother. Instead of nani Ashok will wear clothes given by his *masi*, aunt.' She had brought along a romper suit as a present. She changed the boy's clothes and sat him again in her lap.

'Listen everybody!' Mercy said to attract the gathering's attention, and then pointed to Tara, 'What do you think? An empty lap looks better or one with a child in it?'

Tara turned crimson with embarrassment. 'Didi, you…!' she said, pretending to leave with the child. 'All right, I'm going and taking Ashok with me.'

The guests began to leave after refreshments were served around ten o'clock. Mercy asked Tara and Narottam to stay on for lunch.

Tara said to Narottam, 'What's the point of sitting here and listening to the comrades' discussion for the next three hours! Since I have come this far, let's go and visit Kanchan.' When Kanak had come to visit Tara in November, Tara had gone to drop her off in order to see the location of her father's house. She explained to Mercy that she was going to visit someone in Faiz Bazaar, and will be back in an hour.

Tara and Narottam made their way downstairs and walked to the car. Narottam turned the ignition on, then said abruptly, 'Didi, this may not be a good time to visit Kanchan.'

Narottam's reluctance to visit Kanchan surprised Tara, 'Why, what's the matter?'

'Let me first get out of here.' He seemed distracted as they drove off.

'What is it?' Tara again asked.

'Kanak bhabhi is at her parent's home.'

'When did she come?'

'About a month ago.'

'*Hain!* No one told me.'

'I didn't know either.'

'When did you find out?'

'I had gone yesterday evening to their home. Bhabhi didn't say much, seemed a bit quiet. Panditji was also very quiet. Everyone was speaking in hushed tones. When Kanchan came with me to the spot where I was parked to see me off, she told me that bhabhi had been in Delhi for the past month. Kanchan didn't mention anything when she had come to visit you that Sunday.'

'Yes, she didn't. I'm surprised.'

'What surprised me most was that bhabhi was here all along and even you didn't know. When I asked Kanchan if bhabhi had met you, she just shook her head. How long will she stay here? I asked. Kanchan said that she'll tell me later.'

Narottam did not take the Golcha turn, but drove on towards Delhi Gate. Tara said worriedly, 'We should find out why she's been here so long.'

Tara and Narottam went for coffee at the Blue Nile in Connaught Place. Narottam said, 'I went there only yesterday. Will it be proper to again so soon?'

'Find some excuse.'

'What sort of excuse?'

'You can't find an excuse? Buy two seers of mangoes. Say Miss Deva had sent a parcel from Lucknow for me, and I wanted to give some to Kanchan.'

'Write a note with that message. I'll go either today or tomorrow.'

'Don't pretend to be so innocent. Who did you ask for advice when you were courting Kanchan?'

'Didi, that is different.'

'Listen, go tomorrow. Say that you had told me about Kanak being in Delhi, and that I had said that I'd go to see her. You must tell me about your visit. You can ring me, if you want.'

After they returned to Mercy's flat, Tara wrote a note, 'Narottam tells me that Kanak is in Delhi. Please telephone me and let me know when she is going back. I'd like to meet her.'

Narottam said when he came Monday evening, 'Kanak bhabhi didn't say anything about going back. Panditji had gone out, her mother was in the kitchen. We sat in the aangan. She said that she was looking for work in Delhi, and that a monthly salary of 150 or 200 rupees would be fine. Something is wrong. She also said that she'd go to your place to meet you.'

Tara remained preoccupied with the thought that something untoward may have happened in Jalandhar.

Kanak came to Tara's flat unaccompanied by Jaya or Kanchan at 8.30 in the morning on Sunday. Tara had washed her hair and was drying them sitting under the ceiling fan. They hugged each other warmly.

'You didn't bring Munni along?'

'It'd be very hot and sunny when I go back, that's why.'

'You came after such a long time. If you hadn't said that you'd come, I'd have gone to meet you.'

'I hardly do anything at home. You return home tired from the office.'

Both fell silent, thinking of what was coming next. Tara began to inquire after the family in Jalandhar. Once that was done, they again sat silently. Finally Tara asked, 'Narottam said that you were looking for a job here?'

Kanak bowed her head and nodded.

'But why? You liked managing the weekly.'

'I can't live in Jalandhar any more.' Kanak said gravely, looking at the floor.

'What happened? Did my mother say anything to you? Bhabhi, you know her...' Tara said, putting her arm gently round Kanak's shoulder and ready to share a confidence with her.

'No, it's not that,' Kanak said, cutting her short.

'Then?'

'It's not possible for me to live in Jalandhar. He's what he is by nature and I know my big failing is that I can't be a compliant wife. Everyone gives him so much respect. But I can't. Maybe I am punishing myself for it, but I can't live with him. I feel we just aren't compatible. Problems began six months after our marriage. I put up with it for five years, but can't do that any more. If my decision sets the tongues wagging, so be it. I don't know what to do?' Kanak covered her face with her aanchal.

Tara was puzzled, but at the same time she could see that Kanak was deeply distressed. She hugged Kanak, and said, 'Come, let's go to the bedroom.'

Kanak wept for ten minutes. It was hot in the room, but Tara kept her arms around Kanak. When Kanak felt a little better, she briefly told Tara about her marital problems at Tara's behest. She also described what Puri had said about Tara and their quarrel over Sheelo. In the end she said, 'Our natures and temperaments are just not compatible. I tried to put up with him as long as I could for the sake of appearance. But not any more...'

Tara had no reason to fear her brother, but she was still hurt to know how he felt about her. Now there was no hope for her to reunite with her family. Rather, she felt for Kanak, who was fighting for her independence and the right to exist as an individual. Tara was thinking, 'How could Kanak turn herself into an uncomplaining slave? If this is what marriage means, it's better to remain unmarried. First impressions can be so deceptive!' She shared her thoughts with Kanak.

Tears again filled Kanak's eyes. She said, 'Pitaji, jijaji and others were so much against my friendship with him.' She described her arguments with Nayyar about Puri, and the lies that Puri had told her about Tara. She made no bones about what she had given up for Puri's sake, and said, 'In spite of doing all that for him, this is what it has come to now. If I could suppress my feelings that easily, could be that quiet and compliant, our marriage wouldn't have taken place at all in the face of my family's objections.'

Tara simply said to her, 'I don't see it as your fault. Earlier, you did what you honestly thought was right, and I can't blame you for the present situation.'

Kanak had told her father, 'I don't want to go back to Jalandhar for some time. I feel like staying in Delhi. Ma is not keeping well. Kanchan has her teaching job. I want to spend time with ma. It doesn't really matter if I'm not in Jalandhar. Managing the weekly does not take more than two persons. I'd like to take some time off and get some rest.'

Although Kanak had not said in so many words, Panditji had guessed that his daughter and son-in-law now had a strained relationship. He was worried that the situation might drag on. His worry increased when he found out about Kanak looking for a job in Delhi, and realized that the divisions between the two were deeper than he thought. He knew his daughter's temperament, and the difficulties that her obstinacy might create.

Panditji wrote a letter to Puri, 'Kanni is my daughter, and you are my son. You are not two separate souls for me, but one and the same, because I cannot imagine the disconnect between your life and well-being, and hers.

Both of you should live in harmony because your fates are tied together. Your understanding and experience of life is deeper than hers. Because your share of responsibility is greater than hers, Kanak should defer to you. We shall do our best to counsel her, but first and foremost it is your right and obligation to counsel and win her over. You are her guiding light and mentor, and she a part of your life. Therefore it's your responsibility to enlighten her when she errs or is at fault. Her lapses of judgement will also have a bearing on you. It will be your magnanimity to come here and offer to take her back with you.'

Puri came to Delhi immediately after he got Panditji's letter, in the hope that Kanak will listen to her father and agree to go back with him to Jalandhar. Panditji explained the situation to Puri when they were alone together, 'Barkhurdar, I do not know the reason and the circumstances. And I don't need to know them,' he laughed, crinkling his eyes. 'You both are adults, not kids.' He lowered his voice, 'I think that Kanak has been deeply wounded, and only you can redeem the situation. She is looking for a job here. I'm sure that beti Tara must have been in touch with her bhabhi. Tara is a good and kind person. I came to know from Kanchi that Tara, in sympathy with Kanak, was helping her find a job. Tara beti wants to help Kanak like she helps everyone, but the help that Kanak really needs would be to persuade her to return to Jalandhar.' Such praise of Tara incensed Puri, 'She's helping Kanak find a job! So that Kanak won't have to go back to Jalandhar. She's always tried to harm us and hurt us. She ruined Mohanlal's family, now she wants to do the same to me. I'll never ever have anything to do with her!'

When he was alone with Kanak, Puri reminded her about how she had pledged her love to him and the sacrifices she had made for him. With tears in his eyes he made every possible promise to her, even begged her by touching her feet. When she did not relent, Puri vented his frustration by vilifying Tara, 'You're under the spell of that snake of a woman, who has ruined so many lives! She's a misanthrope. What she likes best is to ruin others' families.'

Puri went back from Delhi unsuccessful. There was no question of his meeting Tara.

Before coming back home empty-handed, Puri had concealed for over a month the fact of Kanak going to Delhi with Jaya, keeping even Masterji and his mother in the dark about it. Heeran was limited in what she could do in the house, and it was often inconvenient not to have another woman to supervise her. Puri had to ask his mother to come and live with him in Model Town. He had explained that Kanak had gone to Delhi because of her mother's illness, and might stay there for a month or two. Kanta or Nayyar were not told anything. He had hoped that Kanak would eventually return, and the news of his wife leaving him will remain hidden and not cause a scandal.

Puri, who had always been jealous of Nayyar's hold over Kanak, was now forced by circumstances to ask for Nayyar's help. His hope was that if Kanak listened to Nayyar and agreed to return to Jalandhar, he won't lose face with anyone except Nayyar. As Kanta and Nayyar were now related to him twice over, it would also be in their interest to keep his situation secret. Puri decided to share his problem with Nayyar and Kanta.

'Her wilfulness and arrogance makes her exaggerate even the most trivial matters. She's been living in Delhi for over a month now. How could it have been possible for me not to say even a word about running the press and the weekly? Because when I did, it was for her good and for our mutual benefit. What do I stand to gain from the business? She has our finances in her hands and the house is also in her name. I've always given her more importance than me. Still, if you both say so, from now on I won't interfere at all. As it is, I get little time to spare after attending the assembly, doing the Congress party work and sitting on all those committees. If I ever intervened in anything, it was only because I couldn't bear to see the fruit of my hard work going to the dogs.'

Nayyar replied with appropriate solemnity as he gently rubbed his eye with a finger, 'It's matter of concern and I'm sorry about it. I'm also surprised that simple disagreements between you two were blown rather out of proportion.'

Puri reassured him, 'What other reason could there be? If there was, let her tell you both about it. If I'm not aware of a fault of mine, she can tell me about it.' His face took on a meek and helpless expression.

Nayyar said by way of reassurance, 'She must have done this after throwing a tantrum, believe me. Who else does she have in this world but you? Have faith, because she had put you in one side of the scales and the rest of the world in the other, and the scales tipped in your favour.'

Puri wanted that Nayyar and Kanta, for the sake of family honour, should go to Delhi and bring Kanak back with them. Kanta gave Puri assurance that they will do whatever was necessary and possible. If they must go to Delhi to bring her sister back, they will. But the news of her leaving must remain secret.

Nayyar later told Kanta bluntly, 'Our intervention won't get any result. They are by nature two very different people. Kanak could have put up with him out of a feeling of respect and admiration, but this man doesn't have that kind of personality. They had met when she was young and impulsive, and had been attracted to him. She had refused to listen to anyone because of her loyalty to him, her own self-respect and for the freedom to choose her lover. They had hardly got any time to know and understand each other. Our disapproval of their meetings had aggravated the situation. How many times do you suppose they could have met before they got married? If they met behind our backs, they were either overtaken by excitement, or were gung-ho to fight the injustice of our opposition. Such emotions don't last. I think they'll continue to argue and quarrel for the rest of their lives.'

Nayyar could not find time; therefore Kanta went alone to Delhi. Kanak being a burden on her already financially strained father was constantly on Kanta's mind. Her father had not written even one word about Kanak either to her or to Nayyar. He evidently had been deeply hurt, and wanted to keep his pain to himself. He apparently thought that even Nayyar's rational approach and analytical skills won't be able to save the family honour in this instance. Her mother had no say in the matter, and her father seemed completely at a loss on how to talk to Kanak about it.

Kanak was fed up with explaining her decision to her father in a roundabout way and to Puri in a straightforward manner. Now Kanta had arrived in Delhi to persuade her to go back.

Kanta asked Kanak about the main reason for disagreement between her and Puri. Kanak did not want to go deep into the reasons for her decision, and tried to sidestep the question by saying, 'Nothing in particular. It's just how I feel.'

In an attempt to probe further, Kanta repeated what Puri had said, and asked, 'What did he do after all that caused you so much anger?'

Kanak had to present her side of the argument. The difference between the two versions surprised Kanta. In order to find a way to patch up their differences, she said, 'I agree with you, but the issues that trouble you are obviously not important for him. If you don't want him meddling in the way you run the press and the weekly, he won't. You should stop bothering with the press and the weekly, if you ask me. Take care of your home. I always found your house suffering from neglect and looking like some transit camp. Let *Nazir* go to hell!'

'I was able to spend five years in Jalandhar only because I was involved with *Nazir*. Otherwise it would have been difficult even to pass two years,' Kanak said.

'What an odd thing to say! I think that you should get rid of the things that cause problems between you two. Don't interfere in matters where he wants to be the boss. Just take care of your home, make it look like a home. Don't I live like that, like a mother and a housewife?'

'Duty of the wife and rights of the husband are the main problem,' finding herself cornered Kanak blurted out.

'What did you say?' Kanta asked anxiously.

'What more can I say?' Kanak said, bowing her head.

'Didn't you get married to him? Aren't you his wife?' Kanta said, trying to suppress her anger and surprise.

'I am. So what should I do, kill myself for him?' Kanak could hardly contain her fury.

Kanta asked after a brief pause, 'Why did you say what you just said?'

Kanak had to explain what had slipped out of her mouth. 'If I married him that does not mean that I am a prostitute or his mistress or a bought slave who has no individual existence,' she said furiously.

Kanta was lost in thought. To understand Kanak better, she asked, 'What's the problem? You have only one daughter. She's four.'

Kanak said shaking her head, 'But why should anyone bother me if I don't want it? Or why should anyone think that its' his right to pester me?'

Kanta said sceptically, 'Why do you call it a bother?' Then in a sympathetic tone, 'Do you have a problem? Have you consulted any specialist?'

Kanak had to explain, 'I have no problem. If there's anything wrong, it's with him, maybe his mind, maybe his body.'

She could not but continue, 'I eventually give in when he puts pressure on me, but I always regret it. It's a strange situation. He begins to act weirdly. Becomes angry and gets depressed for no reason. In frustration he has said that Urmila was like this and this, but you are like that and that. Sometimes pulls his hair out. He swore at me, insulted me so much.'

Kanak's tear-filled eyes became red with anger. She continued, 'After a while he again feels it necessary to exert a husband's right. I can't stand all this, I just can't.'

Kanta bent her head, and sat thinking with chin resting on hand. She said in a voice full of sympathy and concern, 'Why do you want to go away from your home? Stay in your home. You don't have to agree to all that.'

'I've been trying that for five years, from before Jaya was born. He refused to listen to me and insisted on having the husband and wife relationship. He even threatened me that he would have liaisons if I didn't agree. I said, "You don't have to tell me." Still he doesn't leave me alone.'

Kanta asked after some thought, 'Does he have any sexual or physical problem?'

'I don't know. I don't want to know.'

'Well, you don't have to put up with all that, but Kanni, you must go back. You will malign your name if you leave the home like that. What will people say?'

'I said that I tried to ignore it for five years. Should I let him humiliate me in the fear of what others will say? I don't want to tolerate it any more.'

What could Kanta say in reply? After a few moments she asked, 'Who's this Urmila?'

Kanak recounted what she had seen after coming to Jalandhar the first time.

Kanta, with finger on cheek, listened wide-eyed to Kanak. She chastized Kanak, 'Damn you, you knowingly swallowed the fly. And you thought you were so smart and wanted to be your own woman. Couldn't you see what he was up to?'

Tears flowed down Kanak's face. She bit her lip and sighed, 'He cried and gave every kind of excuse. I have only myself to blame. I just couldn't mistrust him at that time.'

Kanta returned to Jalandhar unsuccessful in her mission and told Nayyar all that had happened.

After he knew the facts surrounding the mystery of Kanak's flight from her home, Nayyar said, 'I had noticed that their natures were completely different, and had thought that although Kanak had been adamant to have her way, she'd spend all her life quarrelling and arguing with him. Thousands of couples end up in the same situation. Subhadra used to be in the same boat, but she realized the necessity of changing her attitude according to her circumstances. I didn't know that the situation was this hopeless between Kanak and Puri. It's possible that Puri's unfulfilled desire for Urmila has influenced his mind in a way that he feels a deep resentment towards the person who separated him from Urmila. Puri first takes revenge on Kanak, then hates himself for doing so. It could be that Kanak has a more vigorous sex drive than Puri, and he feels threatened and disgusted with himself when he can't keep up with her. He loathes himself even more when he tries to overcome that self-disgust. Their natures were apparently very different from each other right from the beginning. I don't wish them to spend their lives quarrelling, but in all likelihood they will continue to be unable to tolerate each other.'

'What do you mean?' Kanta asked in a worried tone.

'That Kanak and Puri cannot live in a state of mutual hatred. Hatred causes pain and suffering. It's only natural for anyone to want to relieve pain and suffering. A scandal caused by Puri forming a liaison with someone or deciding to live again with Urmila won't be as serious as one caused by Kanak becoming entangled with someone.'

'What nonsense! One can't say such things about one's sister or daughter.'

'I am saying this because I've always had a soft spot for Kanak.'

'She's had nothing but bad luck. You still shouldn't say such things about her.'

'What if she's family? She has a human body. Whatever is natural for us, is natural for her. It'd have been okay for us to have sympathy and feel sad for her if she could be meek and remain subservient to Puri. But she's a bold and determined person. She has taken bold decisions twice, and she is not going to hold back if something else came to her mind. I am concerned how we will react in that situation? Are we always going to be against her?'

Kanta took a deep breath and kept silent.

If Narottam insisted, Tara went occasionally to the club with him, but of late his interest in the club had waned. Kanchan and Narottam had been seeing each other, and Kanchan came to Tara's house frequently to meet him. Tara did not mind their meetings for they went about it quite decently; she rather felt good about it.

For over three weeks, Tara had spent all her free time to help Kanak find a job. She didn't have time even to think about going to the club.

Narottam said to Tara on the last Saturday in July, 'Kapur has asked me several times to invite you to the club.'

Tara asked in British-style Hindi, 'What does major want?'

Tara had met Major Kapur a couple of times at the club. Kapur habitually spoke in English. When he had to speak to the servants and bearers in Hindi, he had the same mannerism and pronunciation as the British. His behaviour was always very correct. He had, in Tara's words, geometrical manners.

Narottam said, 'Kapur's sister Mrs Khanna and Col. Khanna know you. They would like to meet you at the club.'

Nath had introduced Tara to Col. and Mrs Khanna at the annual dinner of the Punjabi Association to celebrate the Baisakhi festival. She had met them again once at the club, and at another time at the house of Mr Agarwal.

When Tara went to the club to meet the Khannas, Mrs Khanna asked Tara join in playing tombola. As luck would have it Tara won the Snowball. Since Tara was not a member, Narottam had paid for the two-rupee ticket for himself and Tara, and Tara was playing on his card. Narottam was careful that Tara did not miss marking a number on her card. Tara's card won the Rs 164 jackpot. Narottam offered the money to Tara.

Tara pulled back her hand, 'But it was your card.'

'I'll deduct two rupees for my card.' Narottam removed Rs 2 and dropped the rest in Tara's lap.

Tara was gathering the money from the folds of her sari when Mrs Khanna said, 'Miss Tara should treat us to dinner.'

'Why should Miss Tara do that? She's our guest,' Kapur objected.

'That is between her and Narottam. We must celebrate her winning such a large snowball,' Mrs Khanna insisted.

Narottam tried to wriggle out, 'What's in it for me?'

Tara was putting the cash in her purse. She took it out and placed it on the table.

'You are in a tight corner!' Mrs Khanna teased Narottam.

'Oaff! You always get me into difficulty,' Narottam said testily to Tara. 'Achcha, we'll go for dinner,' he agreed.

'No!' Kapur said, shaking his head, 'Give the money back. Taraji's card won the jackpot, you still must pay for the dinner. Etiquette dictates it.'

'But I was playing on Narottam's card,' Tara said.

'If a guest wins a prize, standard practice and etiquette dictate that it should go to the guest. He should also return the two rupees to you,' Kapur insisted.

'Now you are really trapped,' Mrs Khanna again teased Narottam.

'Listen, Miss Tara is my guest at the club. She'll stand us dinner at the Palace,' Narottam said, trying again to escape responsibility.

'That's right,' Tara said in agreement.

'How can we allow that? A gentleman does not take the prize away from a guest.' Kapur glowered at Narottam accusingly.

'What's to you? It's between us sister and brother,' Narottam said, and looked at Tara, 'Right?'

'Yes, that's right,' Tara agreed.

Kapur was miffed at his defeat. 'This saala is a true bania,' he said, snappishly.

'Just look at his cheek!' Narottam complained to Tara. She smiled and blushed.

Mrs Khanna glowed with happiness.

Kapur apologized in English politely, with a pained expression on his face, 'Miss Tara, I am extremely sorry. I apologize for saying something inappropriate. But how can you consider him as your brother! He's a rascal, don't you think?'

Tara said smilingly, 'A brother is a brother.'

'What have you got to say for yourself?' Narottam challenged Kapur.

Tara took Narottam, Kapur, Col. and Mrs Khanna to the Palace. The dinner ended at 11.15. Tara was not totally unfamiliar with the style and cost of expensive restaurants, yet the amount of the bill surprised her. The drinks for three men and the two women cost Rs 52, and the dinner for five was Rs 44. Tara placed six notes of Rs 10 and ten notes of Rs 5 in the plate with the bill.

Narottam whispered in Tara's ear, 'Leave the change as tip.'

Rs 110 out of 164 were used up in one dinner.

Before they said goodbye, Col. and Mrs Khanna made Tara promise that she will have lunch at their place next Sunday. Kapur or Narottam was to give her a ride to their bungalow in the cantonment.

For Tara, Rs 110 was not a trifling sum, but she had no qualms about spending the money. She did not give any importance to the Rs 54 remaining in her purse either. Yet she could not help thinking what Rs 110 were worth to an average person. The monthly salary of a low-level government clerk was not much more than the amount splurged on a dinner for just five persons. And Rs 14 left as tip! If the waiter had just one such customer every day, he would earn more than the starting monthly salary of a doctor in a government job.

What an anomaly of the social system! Thought Tara, while riding back with Narottam. She had recognized Mr Saran in what seemed to be a party in another section of the restaurant. Saran had been selected for the administrative service in the same batch as Tara, and they both had been posted to the ministry of industries. Saran had flashed a smile of greeting at Tara.

Tara couldn't help asking Narottam, 'How can government officers afford to party like this in expensive restaurants on monthly salaries of 1,000 or 1,500 rupees?'

'Who spends from their pocket?' Narottam replied. 'Industrialists and mill owners bear the cost. If they can get some permit after spending five hundred rupees, to them it's like paying the cab fare to their office. They consider it the cost of doing business. No one can splurge on money earned honestly and fairly.'

When Tara went to the Khannas on the second Sunday in August, Mrs Khanaa did not let her go back with Narottam. She asked Tara to stay for the afternoon tea. It began to rain in the afternoon. Since the Khannas were going to stay home because of the rain, Major Kapur gave Tara a ride to her home in his brother-in-law's car. As Kapur drove, he regaled Tara with stories of how it poured with rain in Assam, in Hindi spoken with an English accent.

The macadam surface of the road was wet and slippery. Near the turn to Pachkuian Road were two tongas, one following the other. The horse on the tonga in front tripped, making the tonga lurch and tip over. Some women were riding in the front tonga. Men riding in the other tonga were helping the women, and three young men passing by on bicycles had stopped to help right the tonga in spite of the light rain.

Kapur slowed the car when he saw the road obstructed. A crowd had gathered in the middle of the road, leaving very little space for the car to pass. Kapur expressed his annoyance at those obstructing the road in a low voice. Twice he honked briefly in warning, then driving carefully and slowly, tried to squeeze the car through a gap between the road and the left-side footpath. In spite of his being cautious, the fender of his car brushed against the wheel of a bicycle lying flat on the road, nudging it forward.

'I'm so...' Kapur had not finished the sentence when the men helping to right the tonga charged at the car. The bicycle resting on the spindle of the paddle had been pushed forward a few inches. Two young men blocked the car's path and the third picked up the bicycle and examined it. It was not damaged but the young man came to the car window, ready to fight, 'Are you blind? Can't you see?'

Other young men joined the first in shouting at Kapur.

Tara noticed that Kapur's face was flushed with anger. She was also annoyed and nervous. Kapur replied in an angry but controlled tone in his British-style Hindi, 'Didn't you see the car? Why did you block the road? Didn't you hear me honk twice at you?'

'You son-of-a-horn!' One of the men surrounding the car stepped forward and threatened him.

Slowly, Kapur released his breath through clenched teeth and glared at the man without saying a word. It was obvious that the belligerent crowd was bent upon insulting him. Ignoring their shouting, he turned on the ignition. Tara could see that he was feeling humiliated, specially the ignominy of humiliation before a young woman.

Kapur drove the car up to the entrance of the gali behind the shops. Tara could step on to the chabutara at the bottom of the stairs leading to her flat, but in crossing that foot-wide space some raindrops could have fallen on her.

Kapur implored her to remain seated. He went upstairs and got an umbrella from Parsu. Standing in the rain he opened the umbrella over the foot-wide space. Tara felt awkward in being helped like a baby or an invalid, but there was little she could do.

'Please come up for a while,' Tara asked courteously and to show her sympathy for the impudence of the young men.

'You're probably tired,' Kapur replied. 'If it does not inconvenience you.'

'No, do come up. It's you who did the driving and you who must be tired.'

Kapur took a deep breath as he sat on a chair, 'Don't you think that those people were intentionally disrespectful?'

'They were certainly impertinent. But you behaved with great restraint. I was really scared.'

'This is the result of us gaining independence!' Kapur said, trying to stay calm. 'People think that independence means indiscipline and the right to openly flout the law.'

'One must not overlook indiscipline, disorder and incivility.' Tara tried to make him feel better. 'Would you like some tea?'

'No, thank you. We had tea only a short time ago. You go ahead if you want. I'll take your leave now. I will come again sometime for the pleasure of your company.'

Kapur left. Tara found it pleasant under the ceiling fan with a cooling breeze coming through the window. Stretched out on a small sofa, she was thinking, 'The behaviour of those men was certainly uncalled for, but what about Kapur's attitude? Why people with cars think that pedestrians and bicyclists are always hostile towards them?' She had spent twenty-four years of her life without a car. She could not agree with Mrs Agarwal that people walked on roads only to be a nuisance to the car owners. From her childhood she had seen cars speeding past in a cloud of dust and the drivers carelessly splashing the pedestrians with mud and nonchalantly driving off. That those who used tongas or rode bicycles were unable to do anything after being hit or injured by cars. Either the car owners did not realize how pedestrians felt or those without cars were not ready to suffer forever in silence. After feeling intimidated by the car owners for a long time, the pedestrians were refusing to take it lying down. 'If Kapur had only said, "Please move your bicycle just a bit…"'

Tara remembered when Mrs Agarwal had heard about her buying a car; she had rung her to complain, 'Congratulations! Won't you show us your new car? That would please me so much.' Tara felt awkward going to Mrs Agarwal's house in her own car, but not going after her invitation could have been taken as a slight by her. Her chauffer Kripal Singh drove when she went to AA.

Mrs Chausia and Mrs Bhandari were visiting Mrs Agarwal. They all admired Tara's car. After inquiring about its price, everyone began to complain about the high-handed manner of the police and the hostility of the pedestrians towards car owners. Mrs Bhandari said, 'It's good that you have a chauffeur. Now it's so dangerous to drive yourself. The public is ready to pick a fight for the smallest of reasons. They will rough the car driver up even if the pedestrian or the bicyclist was at fault. If a chauffeur is driving they might let him go unharmed, but they never relent if the owner is at the steering. They are always ready to brawl, or at least curse and abuse. What the times have come to!'

Tara thought, 'If a chauffeur is driving they might let him go unharmed, but they never relent if the owner is at the steering! Why did she say that? Isn't that the viewpoint of a particular class? Well, I'll try to steer clear of such situations.'

Major Kapur had said that he'd come again someday for a visit. He telephoned Tara on a Saturday, 'I'd like to come over in the afternoon if it is convenient for you.' It was convenient for her, so Kapur said that he'd come at 5.30.

Tara was fond of sewing her own clothes. Clothes made by a tailor never satisfied her. She had stopped wearing salwar-kameez combinations. Although buying a sewing machine only for making a blouse or other such clothing once in a while seemed wasteful, she still could not resist. She had also got the attachments for embroidery along with the machine, and had embroidered a few tablecloths. She could sew, if she wanted to, something for Mercy's son, Sheelo's daughter and for Mehta's daughter 'little Tara'.

Buying the sewing machine became a headache for her. Every month Mehta's wife or his sister borrowed the machine for a week. If Tara lent her machine to them, she could not refuse her Punjabi neighbours. One saving grace was that only Punjabis borrowed her machine. Those from UP, Bengal and Maharashtra had no such habit. If she wanted to use the machine after it was returned, she had to first spend half an hour in cleaning it.

She rested for a while after returning from the office on Saturday. Then she oiled and cleaned the machine and began to sew a blouse. She had not finished working when the timepiece on a short stool nearby showed 5.25. She should get dressed, Tara thought, for Kapur will soon be here. She called Parsu and asked him to get some snacks from the bazaar. She wanted to finish hemming the blouse's shoulder.

A low, solemn voice came from the direction of the living room, 'May I come in?'

Tara again glanced at the timepiece. It was not even thirty seconds past 5.30. Tara felt that Kapur had arrived on time like the mail train. Parsu had just left for the bazaar. She felt acutely embarrassed, but had to arrange her aanchal and receive the guest a bit awkwardly. She could meet Narottam, Chaddha, Mathur or Mehta dressed casually, but Kapur's behaviour was always very formal.

Kapur took a chair after Tara sat down. To alleviate her embarrassment,

Tara said, 'Please don't mind. I was so engrossed with some household chores that I didn't realize it was 5.30.'

'Maybe my watch is a bit fast. I hope I'm not early.' Kapur politely took all the blame.

'It is past 5.30, actually. I was busy sewing. I'm all covered with dust. Hope you won't mind the untidiness,' Tara said with a smile.

'Oh, no, no! No such thing,' Kapur tried to reassure her. 'Natural behaviour, if you permit me to say, can be the best indicator of one's true self.'

'It's very kind of you to say so,' Tara replied formally, with a polite smile.

Kapur said, pointing to the copy of the *Literary Digest* on a side table, 'Do you read this regularly?'

'Not regularly. Only when Narottam gives me a copy.'

Kapur picked up the magazine and unfurling the pages, said, 'I haven't read this issue yet, but I usually do read it. I really like it.'

'Me too. It often has short but interesting articles if you want a bit of light reading.'

Kapur raised his eyebrows, thought for a moment and concurred, 'That's exactly what I meant.'

After some chit-chat Tara asked, 'You'll have a cup of tea, *na?*'

'I had some before I came. Please don't trouble yourself. Of course, I'll give you company if you are having tea.'

Over tea, Kapur again talked about literary matters. He mentioned books by Shaw, Maupassant, Maugham and Sartre. He praised Sartre's depth and insight, wanted to know what Tara thought of him. He asked her permission to light a cigarette during the serious discussion.

Tara had read only one novel of Sartre. She praised it, then said, 'I felt that instead of trying to find a way to solve his conflicts and dilemmas, he believed that his salvation lay in plunging himself heroically into the core of his vortex of despair. Forgive me for not expressing myself well. I'm not at all well read.'

'No, no. You did a very good analysis of his thinking.' Kapur said in praise. 'You're able to appreciate the soul of literature. Narottam is very impressed with your understanding of literature.'

'Don't talk of him! He loves to exaggerate. He himself is a good person, so he praises everyone else.'

'No, no. Literature runs in your family. Narottam told me that your brother is a well-known writer, a weekly's editor and an MLA. Your family is a cradle of art and culture.'

'My brother is certainly a well-known writer. My bhabhi is also a good writer, but I don't have much knowledge of literature. I was a student of economics.'

Kapur moved from discussing literature to a discussion of films. He said, after a slight hesitation, 'If you have no other engagements and it's not inconvenient for you, let's go to see the 6.30 show of *Madame Bovary*.'

'No, no inconvenience and it is a wonderful idea, but I am expecting a friend later this evening.'

At 6.45, Kapur apologized profusely for staying for such a long time. He told Tara that he was living in the Officers' Mess. After saying goodbye politely and expressing the hope of having the pleasure of meeting Tara at the club or at his sister's house, or being permitted to visit her again, he left.

Kapur was a handsome and strapping fellow. Tara liked his company, but she also found it stressful to respond correctly to his all too polite behaviour.

Tara had just returned from the office when the telephone rang.

'Is Taraji at home?' the caller asked.

'Namaste, Mrs Khanna. I am speaking.'

'I'm going to be informal and call you Tara. I'm older than you. You can call me Nimmi didi if you wish.'

'Sure, didi.'

'I'm going to Connaught Place for shopping. You had really spoiled Raja the other day. Since then he has been asking repeatedly for Tara Aunty. Can't forget you and wants to meet you again. Can we come over by seven o'clock?'

'Do come, didi, I'll be waiting.'

Mrs Khanna came with her son Rajeshwar. Tara welcomed them warmly and lavished the boy with hospitality. Raja was engrossed in his new mechanical merry-go-round, but Mrs Khanna spoke to Tara very amiably. When the guests were leaving, Tara said out of politeness, 'Do you have to go? Have dinner with me, whatever simple and plain dinner there is.'

Mrs Khanna said, 'You're alone here. Why don't you come along and have dinner with us? I'll have you dropped back by ten.'

'Some other time, didi.' said Tara. Mrs Khanna then invited her with such genuine affection to accompany them on a picnic to Okhla next Sunday that Tara could not refuse.

On Saturday, 1 October, Tara came back from her office, had some tea, and lay down to rest and read the morning newspaper. She got up when the clock showed 6.15. She said to Purandei, 'Bua, I'm going to stay with Mrs Khanna in the cantonment, and will return tomorrow morning. Don't bother cooking for me. Make whatever you want for dinner.'

Mrs Khanna was to pick her up at seven o'clock. She had pleaded to Tara, 'Stay overnight. I'll be all alone. You're off tomorrow.'

Col. Khanna had gone to Lucknow for four days, but Kapur was expected to join them for dinner. Tara was a little uneasy at the thought of staying overnight at another place, but she liked to walk in between the flower beds and sit in the cool of the lawns around Mrs Khanna's bungalow. 'What's the difference,' she thought, 'here I'll be with bua, there with Nimmi didi.' She began to quickly pack a dhoti for nightdress and a change of clothes in an overnight case.

The telephone rang. Tara answered, 'Hello.'

It was Nath at the other end. Tara felt a thrill of joy.

Nath asked, 'How are you? I returned the day before. I'm leaving my office now. Will you be home?'

'Ji, yes,' slipped out of her mouth. She thought, 'I hope Nimmi didi doesn't arrive immediately.'

Although Tara knew that Nath sent for a cup of tea between four and five from the office canteen, she gave instructions to put water for tea on the boil. Nath arrived in ten minutes. He again carried in his hands a bundle wrapped in tablecloth, its size and shape showing the contents to be two or two-and-a-half seers of apples. He looked in better health after spending time at a hill town.

Tara accepted the bundle and sat down cradling it in her arms.

Nath asked, 'How have you been?'

'Absolutely fine. Narottam told me several times that Mr Agarwal was asking about you. Your brother had come from Sonwan and had stayed with Mr Agarwal.'

'Which brother? Brij Kishor or Radha Krishna?'

Tara had no idea. She complained, 'This time you didn't write even once!'

'Hmm. And you?'

'Doctor sahib, what was there to write about? I'd have wasted your time for nothing.'

'Aren't you bright!'

Tara felt shy and kept quiet. Then went to get tea.

After asking about Mercy, Chaddha and Mathur, Nath said, 'This was the best time to be in Simla, but too cold for Doctor Solis. We also needed to talk to the minister.' Tara knew that Nath's office was working on the Second Five Year Plan.

Tara heard Mrs Khanna toot her horn, and looked out of the window. She said to Nath, 'Excuse me for a minute,' and went downstairs.

Tara said to Mrs Khanna, 'Didi, please come up for five minutes. Doctor sahib is with me. We'll leave shortly.'

On reaching upstairs Tara said, 'I was a student of Doctor sahib in Lahore. My older brother was also his student.'

Nath rose to welcome Mrs Khanna. He said in Punjabi, 'She was my student in name only. It was her father who first taught me to write the alphabet on a *patti*. He was my guru. I know her whole family.'

Mrs Khanna complained, 'We never meet except at the Punjabi Association dinner.' She said to Nath that he must visit her house in the cantonment.

Nath realized that Mrs Khanna had come to collect Tara. He said after a few minutes, 'I'll take leave of you. Hope to see you again.'

Apprehensive about the gossiping nature of women from the galis, Tara had pointedly told Purandei and Sita not to disclose how the report that she had perished in the fire at her in-laws had reached Bhola Pandhe's Gali. And that she ever had a husband or a sasural. Purandei had hidden that secret like a woman hides her nakedness. Purandei had interpreted Tara's instruction as that when the time comes, Tara would get married and go to her sasural. In Purandei's mind every woman had to have a sasural. Therefore she was excited about tayee's proposal of her nephew's marriage with Tara.

Tara had not liked the talk about tayee's nephew in the first place. When her Kanak bhabhi had come to visit just for two hours and Purandei and tayee had brought up the subject, Tara had been annoyed. Although Kanak had been more sympathetic and affectionate towards her than she had expected, Tara still had been embarrassed by such talk before Kanak. 'Why are these people spreading such rumours when I have no intention of getting married,' she thought.

That night, Tara called Purandei to her bedroom after Kanak had left and told her quietly but firmly, 'Bua, have you lost your mind? You were talking all that rubbish before my bhabhi. She knows everything about me. She'll think that I'm on the lookout for another husband and sasural.'

Purandei replied in a whisper, 'Ashes and dust on to heads of your sasural people. Who can call you married? We don't have anything to do with your sasural family anymore. God didn't want you to live there, that's why the god of fire appeared in their cursed house and saved you. What happened to them and where they are, who knows. You, of course, will have another sasural soon.'

'Bua, why are you after my life? Why do you feel that you have to get rid of me? I am warning you that you must not talk to anyone about my marriage. Tell that also to tayee.'

When Purandei tried to enlist Sheelo's support in this matter, she said, 'Wah bua, have you gone crazy! How can we say yes when neither we know the man, nor have we ever seen him. Tara will get married when she wants and where she wants.'

Purandei reassured her that tayee was willing to invite her nephew for a couple of days.

Sheelo objected even more vehemently, 'Wah, you could only find a widower for my sister! Is he a prince or what? My sister's salary is over one thousand and she has her own car. That clerk in the Forest Department gets at the most 700 if not 600. What if he makes extra money by taking bribes? Tara won't marry anyone who takes bribes. Then he has a seven- or eight-year-old son. No matter how much you love and care for someone else's child, a stepmother remains a stepmother. One can never do enough for a child born out of someone else's belly.'

Purandei understood that Tara won't marry a widower. Tayee asked again after a few days, 'Any letter or news from Tara's bhabhi? How are things at Jalandhar?'

Purandei replied, dropping her voice, 'You know there's no shortage of marriage proposals for her. Her parents tried to fix her marriage many times, but what can they do if she doesn't listen? This girl has given up all thoughts of marriage.'

Tayee's visits to Tara's flat became less frequent. When she came, she did not bring up the subject. Tara had just breathed a sigh of relief that the matter was over when another problem cropped up. The portents of the second problems were felt about three months ago, but she thought she had handled the situation well. The storm clouds on the horizon had appeared to have blown away.

It was bitterly cold. The fog was so dense even at 8.30 in the morning that the sky seemed overcast. Tara had taken a bath with cold water as was her habit, and was sitting wrapped in a blanket reading an article from the magazine section of the two-day-old Sunday paper when the phone rang. That irritated her because she didn't want to remove her arm from the blanket to answer it. Who could this be? There was little possibility that a senior officer would call so early in the morning to discuss some official matter. It could be Ratan or Mathur. Mathur always called Tara in the morning if he wanted to come over in the evening. He had not visited her for several days.

Her irritation turned into joy on hearing Nath's voice. 'Namaste, Doctor sahib.'

'Why does everyone take me to be your guardian?'

Tara's heart filled with pride. 'I think they are right,' she said.

'They are right? Well, will you be home this evening?'

When Tara replied yes, Nath said he'd explain what he meant in the evening.

Tara was curious: What problem could be that pressing? Could anyone have said something bad against her to Nath? She tried to guess, 'Mrs Agarwal must have complained to Doctor sahib that I had appointed Shyama to the Women Welfare Committee.' Narottam had told Tara that Mr Agarwal was building a friendly relationship with Nath through his contact and business dealings with Nath's brothers. Nath had been invited to the lunch that Mr Agarwal had given for the minister of industry.

Nath said to Tara, 'You consider me your guardian, and now some others have asked me to play the role of your guardian in a matter concerning your marriage. Tell me, how can anyone take a decision about the marriage of someone with your intellect and high standing?'

Tara was silent, her eyes downcast.

Nath said in a voice full of laughter, 'Achcha, if you're too shy to answer that, at least tell me what answer I should give to Mrs Khanna?'

Tara blushed with embarrassment. She said slowly in a quiet voice, eyes still downcast 'At present there is no question of that happening. When the time comes you'll give me the right advice.' She could barely raise her eyes and look at Nath.

'There is no question?' Nath said with surprise. 'Col. Khanna had invited me for lunch on Sunday. Seems that Mrs Khanna thinks that you like her brother. Kapur must have said that he likes you, that's why she was so enthusiastic. I met Kapur for the first time that day.'

Tara denied the allegation, 'No, Doctor sahib, it's not true. Her impression that I do is totally unfounded.'

'You think it to be unfounded. They have taken for granted that you'd agree. I said that it's you who'll decide about your marriage. If you and Kapur have decided something, it's all right.' Nath went on, 'What surprised me was that outwardly they are very modern in their outlook, but orthodox and conservative at heart. Mrs Khanna said, "It's fine if the boy and the girl like each other, but a love marriage won't be a good idea. If they start loving each other before marriage, what'll they do after they get married? Marriages should be arranged by the family." Mrs Khanna is really fond of you.'

Nath raised his eyebrows to express surprise, 'They like you very much, but don't think it proper to broach the subject of marriage with you. I am your family's well-wisher and trusted friend. I have met the boy. The boy and the girl agree to the marriage. Therefore I should write to Masterji that you two make a good match. I expressed my inability to do that. I said, "I don't interfere in these matters even in my own family. Besides, I don't have Masterji's address. I'll have to get it from Tara. Why don't you ask her for the address?" I also said, "Of course, if Tara was willing and Masterji didn't agree, and Tara asked me to speak with Masterji, probably I will."'

Nath seemed lost in thought as he lit a cigarette. He did not say a word till he had smoked half the cigarette, as if he was in his own house and there was no need to make polite conversation. He finally said without looking at Tara, 'Kapur, by temperament, appears to be a serious person. I think he's a decent sort of a chap. Perhaps after knowing him for some time...'

'Doctor sahib, I've met him several times,' Tara said in English. 'His behaviour is very mechanical. He seems to have a superiority complex that he is from the upper class. It'd have been better if he had left the country with the British.'

Nath nodded to indicate that he understood what she meant.

Encouraged by Nath's empathy for her, Tara opened her heart to him, 'Doctor sahib, the Khannas have a peculiar lifestyle. I have twice stayed overnight at their place. Everyone gets up late after sunrise, but the servants begin doing household chores much before that. The husband is in a hurry to report for duty. The orderly readies his uniform. Memsahib has her breakfast at 7.30. It's the ayah's responsibility to look after the children. When sahib leaves for his office after breakfast, memsahib gets dressed, puts on some make-up and goes to the neighbour's house to play mah-jong. Then has her lunch. After that it's siesta time. Tea is taken at four. Then either she has some visitor or she goes to visit someone. All they talk about is their promotions and transfers, or about furniture, shikar and films. In the evening they go to the club. Don't they get fed up of such monotony?'

Tara went on, 'The other day Narottam began discussing the student movement in UP at the colonel's house. He said that the University of Lucknow was an autonomous body, and the governor's interference in the affairs of the students union was illegal.

'The colonel cut him short, "Excuse me, but we are not concerned with politics. We stay away from discussing that subject."

'Narottam asked, "What subjects do you talk about?"

'The colonel said, "We talk about everything but the army's rule is that we cannot discuss religion, politics and women."' Tara began to laugh, 'Narottam asked, "What's left to talk about?"'

Nath nodded in approval, and said, 'What do women do in most families? The same work that servants do in well-to-do families!'

'No, Doctor sahib. Why do you say that? I observe the women who are now my neighbours and since my childhood I had watched women who were my neighbours in the gali. Women don't only do chores, they are the homemakers. It's not possible to run a family without their contribution. I think their work is productive labour.'

Nath lit another cigarette. He again nodded his agreement, and asked, 'Don't you ever want or wish for a family life?'

Tara said after a brief silence, eyes cast down, 'I don't see myself in either of these roles.'

'What do you think your role is?' Nath asked.

'Never thought about it.'

'Why? It's natural to think about it, unless there is a reason for not doing so.' Nath said in a frank and sympathetic voice as someone who was speaking to Tara in her own interest.

'One's way of thinking changes according to one's circumstances.' Tara did not look at Nath.

'What do you mean by circumstances?'

'What had to happen has happened.' She bent her head a little more.

'That's nonsense. That was an isolated incident. It's not rational to blame yourself for a crime committed by somebody else or because you were a victim of circumstance. Forget all that and have a positive attitude so that you have greater fulfilment and satisfaction in your life.' Nath said as if preaching to her.

'I think I'm happy in my present state.'

Nath thought for a moment, drawing on his cigarette, then asked in an even tone, 'Any news of Asad?'

Tara shook her head, then said as she remembered, 'Yes, I had read in the newspaper two years ago about his arrest by the police in Lahore. His wife had applied for his bail.' She too spoke in an even voice.

'Yes, yes. I remember.' Nath again lapsed into silence.

Tara felt a huge surge of relief for handling a difficult question well. She suddenly broke into a smile.

'Why, what is it?' Nath asked.

'No, nothing,' she said bashfully.

'What did you want to say?' Nath leaned back in his chair and asked with eyes half shut, as if he wanted her to go on.

'Why don't you think about the same thing?' She said shyly, and then realized that she had spoken to Nath as if he was her age.

'Me?' Nath replied with a question. 'I think I told you. At the time when my bhabhis had made it impossible for you to tutor the children… Didn't I tell you?'

Tara shook her head, 'No. Told me about what?'

'The story of my circumstances. That old dispute about inheritance of the property. How my bhabhis plotted to make sure that I didn't get married. You know all that. My father wanted the same thing, but he kept quiet about it. My grandfather had died by the time I returned from England. I fell in love with someone, a teacher at the Lahore Convent School. We decided to have a civil marriage. This was around 1944 or 1945. I told her about the dispute in my family. She insisted that I should claim my share of inheritance. We had long heated arguments. She had a strange personality. She could be very generous and unselfish, and at the same time very cold-hearted. We had an intimate relationship, but she said that she'd marry me only if I promised to claim my part of the family property. One day the situation worsened to the extent that she called me a coward and a wimp and whatnot! I lost my temper and said to her rather angrily, "Do you want to marry me or my property?" She also said some nasty things, "You are afraid to fight for what is rightfully yours! You are afraid to stand up to injustice. You are not man enough!" I thanked my lucky stars we did not get married. I don't know what I would have done if she had behaved like that after marriage.'

After a brief silence, Tara smiled.

'What?' Nath asked.

'Doctor sahib, that was just an unfortunate incident. Why blame yourself for something that was not your fault...' Tara could not finish the sentence because she was caught up in laughter.

Nath too began to laugh, 'I am not pining away in her memory. But imagine my difficult situation if the woman I marry wants to bring up the same question, which is quite possible. You want me to again get myself into a mess?'

'You could meet someone who is like-minded.'

'Yes, that's not impossible, but I'll soon be forty.'

'That can't be true,' Tara said. 'You don't look more than thirty-five or thirty-six.'

'Well, it means that I first look for someone who's around thirty-one or thirty-two and interested in getting married. Then fall in love with her or try to win her heart.'

'I can introduce you to someone,' Tara said, thinking of Doctor Shyama.

'That settles it. I try to find someone for you and you search for me. When you didn't approve the one I chose for you, why would I approve anyone you select for me?'

'But you never chose anyone for me.'

Mrs Khanna came to see Tara only a couple of days later. She tried to inquire about the address of Tara's parents and brother in a roundabout way.

Tara was ready with an answer. She said, 'Bahinji, I've already made up my mind about this matter. My family's finances are a bit tight. I'm responsible for the education of my brother and sisters.'

Mrs Khanna said with surprise, 'But your brother is an MLA in Punjab, and the editor of a weekly.'

'Bahinji, so what? He was elected on a Congress ticket and he has little time left from politics. My bhabhi also works in the weekly. I have a younger brother and two sisters. My brother will pay part of the expenses, and I'll have to pay the rest. I haven't yet paid back the car loan. You know about the expenses these days.'

Mrs Khanna did not give up hope. Before leaving she said, 'Well, there's no hurry. Don't think this was the only reason I came to see you. You're like my younger sister. When will you visit us next?'

Tara was relieved that the rumour about her and Kapur did not go round.

Tara was annoyed with Narottam. He was the one behind her friendship with the Khannas. She asked him when he came next to her flat, 'What's this mess you all created for nothing?'

Narottam assured her that he had played no part in the matter. 'Mummy had said nice things about you to Mrs Khanna. The Khannas had indeed asked me about your family and parents. Now that you mention it, let me tell you the whole story. Kapur had made me promise that I won't tell anyone. I was waiting for you to say something about him. Kapur treats me as his friend, but he did something that disgusted me. I didn't want you two to be very friendly.'

'But it was you who introduced us.'

'I didn't know all this about him at first. I came to know the whole story only two months ago.'

'You can tell me about it now.'

'It all came out after Kapur made me take a vow of silence. He was having an affair with someone for the past eighteen months. He was really attracted to that girl, even gave her a ring. I know it because I loaned him money for the ring, which he returned. He used to call her "my bhabhi". After he met you his whole attitude changed. I asked him what was going on. First he made me swear that I'll keep his secret, and then told me that he had been mistaken about that girl and had changed his mind about marrying her. His reason was that if a girl could sleep with him before marriage, how could he be sure about her morals? He said that marriage was not a matter one should take lightly.'

Tara sat stunned, barely breathing.

Narottam said disdainfully, 'I told him at his face, "That was a very mean thing to do. That was outright deceit. You are more responsible than her for this depravity. She slept with you because she trusted you, because she saw you as her husband. You betrayed her trust."

'Kapur replied blatantly, "I regret my failing and accept what I did was folly. I am willing to pay the price for my mistake. But I can't marry a girl whom I know is easy. I don't mind fooling around a bit before marriage, but we should not compromise the sanctity of marriage. The basis of family should be the purest of motives and morally correct behaviour. This girl must be an easy prey for anyone, otherwise why would she sleep with me before we got married? She should have exercised self-restraint if she was at all virtuous."

'What he said next really alarmed me. He said that he did not approve of such loose behaviour and now hated girls who behaved in that manner. That he has finally decided that either he will marry you or won't get married at all. You are the only girl he's ever met whom he considers to be chaste and upright and for whom he has any respect.'

Tara sat stunned and still as before.

'I asked him if he'd proposed to you. If he'd said "yes" I'd have warned you no matter what. He said that he would never stoop so low again. That love before marriage was immoral. That marriages should be arranged by families. I gave him no reply. It would have made no difference to him. But since then I don't want to look at his face. Have you ever seen me with him or with the Khannas in the past couple of months? I was carefully watching his behaviour towards you and if he tells you about his intention.'

Tara made up her mind to stay away from Kapur. She had emerged unscathed from this rigmarole, but what Narottam told her distressed her very much. She remained silent. Narottam also sat without uttering a word. Neither she nor he felt like saying anything more.

That night and the next day Tara was in a sad mood. She thought, 'I was at the centre of this nonsense which became quite a serious affair. It could have turned into a scandal. If a man loves a woman, it creates problems for her. If a woman falls in love with a man that again gives her a bad name. No matter if it's the fault of a man or a woman, it's she who has to suffer the consequence. The onus is always on her to prove her innocence. Not long ago, a besotted hero would have simply carted off the woman who was the object of his affection. What does that foolish man thinks himself to be?'

Tara was deep in her inward turmoil. Mehta's wife Saroj came in the evening with little Tara holding on to her finger. The mother had got the girl to rehearse what she was going to say on arrival. She joined her tiny, chubby palms with fingers spread and said, 'Buaji, *matte!*'

Tara clasped the girl to her breast, 'It's my Gaggi? Where had you been all this time?'

Saroj removed a katori from under her aanchal.

'Why do you take such trouble,' Tara said when she saw the katori.

'It's nothing. My *jeth*, husband's elder brother, came yesterday. He's posted at Karnal station. He brought some *sarson ka saag*. Nice plump shoots. Peeling and cleaning them is always a chore. You don't have the time to do it. I had put the greens on the stove to cook in the morning. Thought I'll bring you a katori-ful. It's from Punjab. I'll give it to bua.'

'You sit here with me,' Tara said and called Parsu to take the katori to the kitchen.

Saroj began to complain about her neighbours who were from UP and Bihar. 'They are so unfriendly, bahinji. We have been neighbours for almost four years, but not even once have they bothered to speak to us. I had cooked whole *urad* lentils soon after they had moved in. Poor me, I offered them a katori-ful. The kayastha woman said, "Bahinji, we don't eat anything cooked by others." I told her that we also were Hindus. She replied, "All the same, we follow our own customs."'

'Why bother if they don't eat what somebody else has cooked. It's their problem!' Tara said irritably. 'But they are still better than Punjabi neighbours. They at least don't poke their nose into what doesn't concern them. Punjabi neighbours will not be content until they find out about all the relatives on your mother's and father's side. They will even keep track of how much cumin and coriander you have in the spice box in your kitchen.'

Gaggi was trying to wriggle out of Tara's arms. She knew where biscuits and fruits were kept in Tara's flat, and she was free to take what she wanted. Tara guessed what the child wanted, so she patted her fondly on the back and let her go, 'Go you pest, go to bua.'

Tara asked after Saroj's family. Saroj saw it as a signal to talk about her troubles. A serious problem had arisen about the marriage of Mehta's sister Kunt. Mehta's mother and older brother, who lived in Karnal, wanted to marry Kunt off to a boy they had found after a great deal of search. Kunt was unwilling to marry the boy. Mehta's mother and brother were angry that he and his wife had brainwashed the girl. They had accused the couple of conniving to grab Kunt's salary.

Saroj swore that she was telling the truth, 'Bahinji, it's inauspicious to tell a lie at the time when day and night meet. May God punish us if we ever took a paisa from Kunt's salary. May He forgive me for saying that it's we who spend money on her. You well know that wheat is now two seers for a rupee. Only we know how we are making do with Rs 225 every month. On top of that we are stuck with the responsibility for an unmarried young woman. She buys whatever clothes she likes and deposits the rest at the post office. We want her to go to her sasural not tomorrow but today. Her education has loosened her tongue. She says, "Tara bahinji didn't get married. I'll do the same." I told her that she won't become Tara bahinji even in her next four births.'

'Why do you talk such nonsense! Perhaps she doesn't like the boy. So find her another,' Tara interrupted Saroj to stop her prattle.

Little Tara came in with two tangerines that Purandei gave her. The tangerines were too big for her hands, so she held them against her chest.

'Come here, Gaggi, I'll peel them for you,' Tara said lovingly to the child.

'Hai, muree, how'll you eat all that! No, bahinji, don't give her so much. She just had something to eat before we left home,' Saroj said, grateful for Tara's affection for her daughter.

'It's all right. Tangerines are mostly water,' Tara pulled little Tara into her lap. She listened to Saroj as she fed the tangerine sections one by one to the child.

'Bahinji, today's girls are not the same as girls of our generation who used to run away shyly the moment there was any talk of their marriage. Now they talk frankly about who they want to marry. Some say that they would get married only if it made life easy for them. Bahinji, how can people like us pay a dowry of twenty-five or fifty thousand rupees for marrying our daughters into families where they can have an easy life? Whenever you find a suitable boy from a well-off family, one demands a motor car in dowry, another wants a house.' Saroj lowered her voice, 'Bahinji, now it's best if the girls themselves find someone to marry. His only crime is that he doesn't want to force his sister into marriage. Kunt plainly asks why she should ruin her life by getting married to someone who can't make her happy. What can we do if she's so obstinate?'

Saroj covered her lips with one hand to show her embarrassment, 'That Karamdei from Barbatan says, "We had to leave behind everything our family owned. We have five daughters. How can we arrange dowries for all of them? I have told my girls that all we will do is educate them. If they can find grooms for themselves, we will marry them, otherwise whatever God wills for them."'

Saroj finally said, 'Kunt is off on the day of the Lohri festival and Sunday. We have to sew many clothes. I'd like to borrow the sewing machine for two days if it's not inconvenient for you.'

Tara said, 'Parsu has gone out. He will bring the machine to your place when he returns.'

Tara sank back into her mental turmoil after Saroj left, 'It's not fair for Kunt's mother and brother to be angry with her because she doesn't want a millstone around her neck for life. They are afraid of being criticized for not doing their duty towards Kunt. I was in the same situation. Why should the girls, who are boldly trying to earn a living, leave their fate in the hands of others? I see girls working for a living everywhere I go in Delhi. It'd have been extraordinary for me to think of finding a job for myself before the Partition, but now I see it happening in everyday life. Saroj said that it's high time girls found husbands for themselves. Parents of thousands of young women perhaps want the same thing. Only six years previously most people would have turned a deaf ear to such ideas. Just as some inmates of a jail are killed but many others are freed when the walls of their prison tumble down in an earthquake, in the same way the Partition caused a great deal of destruction but also shook loose and destroyed attitudes and conventions that had become so entrenched in the minds of people over the years. Thousands lost their lives, thousands of others were ruined and were never able to recover from the blow, but the Punjabis have risen from the ashes with a grit never shown before by them.

Tara thought of Kanak, 'The poor thing fought with her family to marry the man she wanted. She stood with him shoulder to shoulder and shared his responsibilities. Why should she have accepted a traditional subservient role?' Her thoughts turned to Kanchan, 'It'd be good if she gets married to Narottam. She's so worried about her father. Her father is very kind-hearted. His health seems to have deteriorated lately. He used to live in such comfort in Lahore. Narottam talks about Kanchan hesitatingly and softly as if she might come to some harm if he took her name in a loud voice. His parents will certainly be upset because Kanchan's family is not well off, but they are not equal in stature to Panditji.'

Tara had always felt awkward acknowledging her lack of interest in her brother's affairs. When she had gone to visit Kanchan, Panditji had talked to her affectionately about Puri and had said many good things about him. She had just nodded, as if she had heard such things about her brother many times.

Next morning Kunt came to Tara's flat. On seeing her Tara said, 'Hai, I forgot yesterday.' She called Parsu and told him to take the sewing machine over to Saroj's house. 'Come, sit down for a minute,' she said to Kunt. 'Tell me, what caused all this fuss at your home?'

Kunt was about five years younger than Tara, and called Tara 'bahinji' in deference to her position among the neighbours. She caught Tara's drift and said shyly, 'Nothing, bahinji. There's no fuss of any kind.'

'But there is. Your mother has matched you up with a nice boy. Why are you refusing to get married to him?'

'Ji, my mother has no idea what I want,' Kunt replied. 'My elder brother is no better. The boy gets a monthly salary of Rs 75, perhaps a hundred with allowances. He has a big family. They have a dairy buffalo, but no servant in the house.'

'Won't you ever get married?'

'Bahinji, what'll I get from getting married into a family like this and spend my life cooking and cleaning up after the buffalo?'

'You want someone who earns five or seven hundred every month, has a car and servants?'

'Bahinji, one should be able to live in comfort after marriage,' Kunt said, with a bashful smile.

'*Mari*, what will you do?'

'What all other unmarried women are doing.' Kunt bowed her head to hide her embarrassment.

Tara said seriously, 'You get a salary from the school where you work. If you get married to someone earning 150 or 200, won't you both have enough to live in comfort?'

'Yes, bahinji, if there's someone like that,' Kunt agreed. 'Bahinji, my friend Geeta works at the post office. She got married to a clerk in her office. Geeta's salary is 125, her husband earns 175. They live fairly well. They have breakfast at home, eat out in the evening, and have time left for fun. They pool their salaries to manage the house. Bahinji, many couples are doing the same. On Sundays when Geeta cooks at home, her husband does the dishes,' Kunt said, giggling.

Tara was listening attentively. She said, 'Just as they do in *vilayet*—Britain.'

'Bahinji, what's wrong with that. I like it that way.'

After Kunt left, Tara went back to thinking, 'How circumstances change everything! How much girls like Kunt have changed in the past five or six years!'

Chapter 14

THOUSANDS OF GIRLS AND WOMEN WERE SEARCHING FOR JOBS IN DELHI, BUT only those with connections had been able to find one. How could Kanak, who had just come to live in the city, get a job immediately? After working and keeping busy for the past five years, idly sitting around was beginning to try her patience. Tara consulted Miss Saxena, the deputy secretary of the Department of Social Development, and found out about the vacancy for a temporary women welfare inspector at the Community Development Centre in Aliganj, twenty-seven miles from Delhi. Miss Saxena's advice was that if Kanak was willing to face the hassle of living in a village for a few months, that experience will make her eligible for selection for a better paying and permanent position at one of the training centres in the city. Kanak agreed to take up the job.

Jaya was four years old and had to be enrolled in a kindergarten, Montessori or convent school. She had been going to nursery in Jalandhar. If Kanak were to leave the child in Delhi for the sake of schooling, how many responsibilities could Kanchan take on? Kanchan left home early in the day for her college that was far from home. Kanak's mother was mostly bedridden. Kanak took Jaya along to Aliganj.

Kanak was provided with living quarters and a woman helper in Aliganj. Her duties included visiting several places during the day, and the woman helper was to escort her on those visits. There was no one to leave Jaya with, so Kanak had to take her along even if seeing unfamiliar people wearing strange dresses frightened her city-bred daughter. How could she leave Jaya behind to play with half-naked, dirty, emaciated and bloated-bellied village children? There was the fear of catching some disease from everything one touched and the air one breathed. Kanak had to go to some shockingly unclean and germ-infested parts of the village, but the entire place was like that and Kanak was being paid to look after people living in those conditions. To keep Jaya away from villagers and their children was like treating them with disgust. But to let Jaya mingle with them was to push her in the jaws of disease.

This was Kanak's first encounter with the so-called serene and unaffected ambience of villages. Her family had been well off and lived in a modern city, in a house that had electric light and fans, a modern bathroom and other essential facilities. She could only dream of such luxuries in Aliganj. To stay in that village was like a severe punishment. But her conscience told her: If 90 per cent of the country's population could live in similar conditions, why couldn't she? It was her duty to do something more for the country than just make a living. Wasn't it an anomaly to sit under the fan in the weekly's office, have tea or sip ice water, and pen articles demanding progress and advancement for the masses living in the villages without any knowledge of the reality of their lives?

Kanak was willing to put up with the discomfort and the unclean surroundings of the village just to be away from Puri and from laying herself open to ridicule and also out of a sense of duty, but she did not want Jaya to live in those unhygienic conditions or to neglect the child's education. There were excellent elementary schools in Delhi, but hardly any arrangement for modern education within a 150-mile radius of Delhi, before the cities of Lucknow, Ambala and Dehradun. It was as if good schooling and healthy living conditions were the prerogative of the children of the elite or of government officials residing in Delhi. The British masters had set up schools for their own convenience, without giving any thought to the needs of the masses. The same old system had continued to prevail. It was deemed appropriate to have air conditioning in the government buildings and to have roadside flowerbeds in Delhi, Lucknow and other capital cities, but to neglect even the basic sanitation or toilet facilities in villages. Delhi claimed to be concerned about the development, welfare and security of the same villages, and yet to live high on the hog!

Kanak was faced with the dilemma of choosing between giving proper care to her daughter and working for a living and helping the country. She thought, 'Unless the country has a network of crèches where children receive proper education and meals in clean and healthy surroundings while their mothers are at work, how can a woman who is also a mother earn a living? Should I campaign for better and widespread day care centres, or work to support myself?'

Kanak saw village women, babies in their arms, doing back-breaking work in severe conditions to scrape a living, and working in the fields as they suckled their babies. She saw them gathering cow dung with one hand while clasping a child to their bodies with the other, and carrying an earthenware pitcher filled with water balanced on their heads and a child in their arms. If a child urinated or defecated on the beaten-earth floors of their huts, the mother ignored it and continued to do whatever she was doing for some time before cleaning up the mess. Flies would cover the faeces and then settle on the lips and eyes of the child and on food, but the mother would only take care of the child after finishing the work in hand.

Kanak would think: How could the villagers live in such abominable surroundings? She could also see that those conditions did not bother the populace. They were born in the midst of excreta and urine and disease-spreading germs. Such conditions were natural for them and they had perhaps become immune to the germs. Kanak's job was to teach them the benefits of cleanliness and hygiene, and to tell them about cottage industries so that they may improve their economic conditions. But she was hesitant to lecture them in view of their poverty and lack of resources.

Kalavati, a village woman who had lived in Delhi for some time, said, alluding to Kanak's helper, 'Bahinji, we all like tidy homes and clean clothes. I'd keep things clean if I had a helper like you do.'

Kanak found it very hard to sleep even under a mosquito net in August. She would spray the rooms with Flit several times during the night to protect Jaya from mosquitoes. She was a government official, therefore all shallow ditches had been filled up and wild growth had been cleared up around her house. The small supply of the phenyl solution and the DDT powder given for the villagers was used up to disinfect the officials' houses, but did not save them from swarms of mosquitoes. Kanak would think angrily, 'Delhi is full of green vegetation but one can sleep in the open without a mosquito net. If there are no mosquitoes in the city, why it can't be the same in the villages? Because the country's President and Prime Minister lived in New Delhi and it was the face that India presented to the world!'

Kanak was concerned about Jaya's health and future, and had decided to leave Jaya with her parents in Delhi in September. She had asked Kanchan to enrol the child in a convent school or in some other good school. Her plan was to go to Delhi every Saturday evening and take the bus back to Aliganj on Monday morning.

Around noon on Saturday, Kanak had notified the centre's manager that she wanted to go to Delhi later in the afternoon and return on Monday morning. The director had sent back his verbal approval. When Kanak did the same next weekend, she was summoned before the manager.

Varma, the manager, said gruffly, 'You cannot be absent from your job and go to Delhi on holiday every weekend.'

Kanak replied, 'I don't go on holiday. I go to visit my daughter. Tomorrow is Sunday. It won't affect my work.'

The manager motioned her to be quiet, 'I have to observe the rules. Sundays are for having a rest, not to leave the place. You're not being asked to work on Sunday. The government job is for twenty-four hours and thirty days a month. You may not leave your place of work without permission, and you may not go away every weekend.'

There had been a face-off between Kanak and Varma soon after her arrival. All officers at the centre were city dwellers, staying in the village for the sake of their jobs. They found the village dull and boring. They had no pastime other than playing cards or gossiping with each other. The mail reached Bombay, Calcutta and places a thousand mile away from Delhi the next day, but it took up to four days to reach Aliganj.

Varma and other officials lived alone, without their families. Varma had been heartened when a modern, good-looking woman who went without covering her head and was not bashful, came to work in the village. But Kanak concerned herself only with her job and did not meet anyone after work. She did not want to socialize. In the beginning she had accepted two invitations for tea and a game of cards, but had made excuses for not attending after that. Varma did not appreciate such snobbery from his subordinates. He decided to exercise his authority and power.

Kanak began to take casual leave in accordance with rules to go to Delhi. She could not be away every weekend, so she went every two weeks. Varma would find some excuse to harass her. He would ask her to visit places that were eight or ten miles away from the centre, but would not provide her with the office Jeep, requisitioning the vehicle for his own use. Kanak would file a written complaint and ask it to be forwarded to the director of the department. She was constantly torn between her self-respect and the necessity of a job.

Kanak had come to know about the mutual attraction between Narottam and Kanchan, and about Panditji's hearty approval. Panditji wanted this to happen soon, while he was still around, but Kanchan kept on postponing it. When Kanak had gone to Delhi during the Dussehra holidays, she had stayed for one night with Tara. Tara knew that Kanchan was not willing to leave her father alone to care for her sick mother after her wedding. Narottam had promised Kanchan that he could easily get himself transferred to another ordnance factory as works manager, where he would be entitled to a bungalow. Then Panditji and her mother could stay with Kanchan. But Kanchan was reluctant to suggest this to her father.

Kanak also did not approve of Narottam's idea. Solution to the problem lay on her shoulders, she felt. Her job at Aliganj seemed to be the only obstacle to Kanchan's marriage. She was unhappy in her job, and felt embarrassed for having taken Tara's help to get it. Kanak had also realized that her father was in no condition to run the press business. His health was not bad for someone who had crossed sixty, except his failing eyesight.

The Government of Punjab had put the printing and sale of textbooks up to class 8 under state control. The government got the books published and set quotas for booksellers. The printing presses stayed in business, the only people to suffer were publishers like Panditji who did not do retail business. Two slim volumes written by Panditji had been approved as textbooks. An annual income of three to four thousand rupees was now lost, and the remaining stock became worthless. Panditji had to let go the help he had hired.

By the end of July, Gill had left *Nazir* and had come to Delhi. Heera Lal, Sarola and Ajay used to write to him, 'Your *Nazir* has become a complete dud. Come over to Delhi if you want to work only to make a living. If you have fair writing skills and are not obligated to write only on particular topics, you won't starve in Delhi.'

Gill had Pandit Girdharilal's address, and sometimes paid him a visit. He also kept in touch with Kanak through letters. When Kanak would come to be with Jaya, he would come to meet her. Panditji found Gill to be a serious and mature young man. He asked Gill, when Kanak was not present, about Puri's behaviour and attitude towards Kanak. Gill told Panditji about Puri's social position in Jalandhar, his association with Sood, Suraj Prakash and Somraj, his disagreements with Masterji and Kanak over Kamaal Press, whatever Puri had told him about Tara, and then Kanak's version of the story. He also told Panditji that Puri had made no attempt to reunite Tara with Somraj because of the fear of an altercation between him and Somraj, and that the scandal might sully his reputation.

'I know Tara beti. She's a decent person,' Panditji said. He thought for a while, head in hands. He heaved a deep sigh. He took off his glasses and polished them with his kurta tail. 'Barkhurdar, a man proves his mettle by surviving the circumstances. What is fate? Our circumstances are our fate. When we remain steadfast in adverse circumstances and do not surrender, we come out the winner. If we surrender, we are left with no conscience, which is even worse. We all have to die eventually.' He let out a loud laugh. 'My dear, in a system full of deception and fraud, one is punished for not going along with the system. If one wants to live honestly, one must learn to live with the problems and suffering such a life will bring. Suffering is the test of honesty.'

Panditji lowered his gaze to the floor, his head resting on one hand to support the burden that lay on his mind. He closed and opened his other fist, as if weighing up his own thoughts. He finally said, 'Barkhurdar, Kanak herself chose the path of suffering. She had wanted to follow her own judgement and conscience. She should now pay the price for doing so. It was her privilege to marry the man of her choice. It's now her obligation to live with her choice and to set her husband right. She shouldn't give up just like that. That's what all her well-wishers should tell her.'

Gill had a hard time for a month trying to establish himself as a freelance journalist in Delhi. He had put up with Ajay while searching for work. He found out about many weeklies and monthlies in Delhi not sold in the market. The embassy of some country would buy 1,500 or 2,000 copies of the magazine at cover price. The rest were sent free to government offices and libraries for publicity. Some journalists had found novel ways of making a living. If they wrote an article on a specified issue or subject and got it published, by spending five or ten rupees out of their pocket, in a small-town newspaper or magazine, they could get Rs 100 as reward from the information department of the embassy of some countries. Ready-made blocks of photographs were available for such articles. The periodical that published such articles could also get advertisements at attractive/good prices.

Veteran journalists would joke: The newspapers in this country had been first published to bolster the nationalist movement. At the time of the foreign rule, editors had constantly faced the threat of imprisonment and of the paper being shut down. The life of a journalist and writer used to be a *tapasya*, hard work and little reward. After the country's independence that profession had turned into a business.

Gill's first job was to write weekly columns on two topics for a newspaper at Rs 20 per week. Next was a 'Weekly Diary' in the Urdu daily *Sardar*. After some time he got the job of translating an embassy's information bulletin into Urdu and Punjabi. Once he was sure of earning Rs 300 to 350 per month, he rented a room in Ram Nagar at Rs 60 per month. He was hardly better off than before because of high cost of living in Delhi, but there was the thrill of being close to the centre of political activity in the country and in touch with the international scene.

When Kanak had come to meet Jaya at the time of the *Vijayadashami* festival, Gill had encouraged her to move to Delhi. 'Are you attracted to some ideal for which you want to suffer the discomfort of village life? All those employed at the centre want is to draw their salary and idle away the hours. They don't think about the ethics of what they are doing, they have no principles. If you do things differently, you won't fit in. They will try to cause trouble for you. Your salary is barely adequate for your living expenses there and Babli's school fee here. New Delhi has become an arena for international power contest and ideological confrontation. It's the propaganda battleground for both superpowers. Both sides need cannons—I mean journalists—to fire salvoes of propaganda. Money is being spent like water. There are those who can be bought and there are we, who want to make an honest buck. There won't be any shortage of work for you. I know the ropes. Come and live in Delhi if you want to help your father.'

Kanak went back to Aliganj and handed in her notice, effective after a month. Three weeks later she got a telegram that her mother had died following a stroke. Kanak packed her bags and left for Delhi.

Chapter 15

TARA CAREFULLY READ EVERYTHING ABOUT THE PLANNING COMMISSION published in the newspapers. The First Five Year Plan, which dealt mainly with the agricultural sector, was in its third year. The Second Five Year Plan was to focus on the industrial sector. At the Avadi convention of the All India Congress Committee, Pandit Nehru had announced that to maximize the growth of the country's economy and to develop its industries, the government will follow the path of 'socialistic pattern of society'. Pandit Nehru was the president of the Congress party and the prime minister in the Congress government. His statement could not be ignored since it represented the policy of the government as well as of the ruling party. In the context of his statement, the new plan meant nationalization of heavy industries and development of the public sector. The announcement of the new policy caused exhilaration in some sections of the productive sectors and anxiety in others. Some people were not ready to believe that such a drastic change would take place.

The responsibility and importance of Dr Solis, the chief economic advisor to the Planning Commission, and Dr Nath, the economic advisor to the ministry of industries had suddenly increased. Those feeling threatened by the announcement of 'socialistic pattern of society' were anxious to know the views of Dr Solis and Dr Nath, and to give them—what they considered—the right advice. The number of people wanting to meet Nath and to invite him for lunch and dinner had also grown. Chaddha and his fellow communists, the communists MPs as well as other MPs were eager to present their points of view to Nath. These people would either invite Nath, or would go to his bungalow.

Gill had come again in contact with the communists after moving to Delhi, especially with liberal communists like Chaddha. Gill knew Chaddha from the time of the Communist Party's wartime agitation. Gill was associated with an important, anti-nationalization weekly of Delhi. He had a good understanding of that weekly's viewpoint. He had been a student of Nath. When Chaddha went to see Nath, he often took Gill along. Nath's bungalow was beyond Alipur Road, about three-fourths of a mile from the nearest bust stop. On Chaddha's request, Tara would take him and Gill in her car to meet Nath. Her car had become a free taxi for the comrades.

When the comrades came to visit, Nath put his cigarette tin on the table in front of them. He always asked if anyone wanted to drink water and had tea served. Tara met bhabhi—peon Bhoop Singh—for the first time at Nath's bungalow. Some time ago she had asked Durga Pande to send a servant for Nath. She was puzzled at not seeing any other servant at the bungalow.

Bhoop Singh did not wear his peon's uniform or his white turban with the brocaded band at the bungalow. On his head was a tight fitting, flat black cap. He had been wearing his home-washed shirt for several days. He wore the pyjama, half of an old uniform, waist-cord tied over his shirt, britches-like, in the Kumauni style. He hadn't shaved for a couple of days, and had a long, salt-n-pepper moustache. He was over fifty-five years old, but still agile. Having served British sahibs, he greeted the guests by bending low from the waist as if doing salaam, but said 'Jai Hind'.

The first time Chaddha went to Nath's bungalow, he took the whole group along: Gill, Mercy, Mathur and Tara. Nath asked Bhoop Singh to serve tea. Bhoop Singh went to an inner room and came back with tea leaves and a silver-plated tea pot, which he placed on the centre table. Next time he returned with the sugar pot in one hand, and in the other, a bottle of milk just out of the fridge. Two minutes later he brought five cups, six saucers and six spoons in a tray. It took him a little longer to return the third time, carefully holding in one hand an electric kettle emitting steam, and in the other, two pieces of cardboard. He put the cardboard on the table and on top of it, the kettle.

Nath was listening attentively to Mathur. Looking at the kettle, he asked, 'What kind of tea do you all like? Strong or light?'

Mercy said, 'I'll make tea.'

Tara was thinking, 'Perhaps the peon did not know how much tea to use, therefore Nath himself was making tea. One cup probably broke. The old man has brought all the china in the house. Had Mercy found such dirty cups and teapot at her flat, she would have harangued Chimmo to death.

Mercy poured some boiling water into the pot, and handed it to Bhoop Singh standing close by. Bhoop Singh took the pot and looked at Mercy, waiting for her to give the order.

Nath noticed the peon standing still. He took the pot from Bhoop Singh, poured the water into the cups to warm them, and said to Bhoop Sigh, 'Throw away the water.'

Bhoop Singh carried the cups out. Nath smiled at Tara and Mercy. 'If you continue to visit, he'll learn a few things.'

In this break in the serious discussion, Tara asked, 'Doctor sahib, Durga Pande had sent a servant to your bungalow. Did that man show up?'

Nath replied in English, 'This man does not let anyone else work here. He himself had hired a servant for me, but had a quarrel with the man after accusing him of theft. He didn't trust the boy you had sent either. He used to measure out everything that was to be cooked. When they had an argument, I had to take the peon's side and let the boy go.'

Tara smiled. 'He is the *malkin*, mistress, of the house.'

'He exemplifies feudal loyalty.' Nath noticed that one cup was short. He said, 'You all go ahead. I'll have a cup later.'

Mercy insisted on having her tea later.

Tara asked, pointing to the condensation on the bottle of cold milk, 'I'd rather have some water cold as this.'

'Water.' Nath looked at Bhoop Singh.

Bhoop Singh brought a bottle of water from the fridge and a glass, and put them on the table.

Nath remembered, 'Bhoop Singh, we have biscuits. Why don't you serve some?'

When Bhoop Singh went back to get the biscuits, Tara asked, 'Doctor sahib, I'll ask Pande to find someone smarter than him for you.'

'What's the use? He won't let anyone else work here.'

'Don't send someone as smart,' Mathur barged in and said to Tara, 'as the one that was sent to my place.'

'Why, what happened?' Tara asked. They all looked at Mathur.

'What can I say?' Mathur said, glancing sidelong at Tara, 'She's found servants for everyone. Unluckily, I had also asked her to get me one. Last week, when I returned home, I saw a young man wearing shirt and trousers sitting in a chair in the veranda. I asked him: Whom do you want to meet?

'"I'd like to see Mathur Sahib," he replied.

'"I am Mathur. What do you want?"

'The young man replied: "Are you looking for a servant? Durga Pande, Miss Tara Puri's peon, has sent me."

'For a moment I was completely taken aback, but tried to gather my wits: "But I need someone to clean the house and cook."

"'Ji, I'll manage everything," said the young man sitting in a chair.

'His reply didn't convince me. I asked: "How will you work as a servant? You wear trousers, you sit in a chair in front of me."

'The young man replied: "I am sitting in chair now. Once you hire me, I won't sit in a chair when you're around.""

Mathur's story brought a smile to everyone's lips.

'He said the right thing,' Mercy said. 'Did you hire him?'

'Things have changed. We'll have to change with the times,' Nath gave a warning.

'I agree.' Mathur said. 'But this new thing took me by surprise. I might have hired him. I went inside the house and my mother asked who had come to meet me. When I told her, she was furious with the young man.'

'Poor chap got punished for thinking that he also was a human being,' Gill said.

Bhoop Singh brought a tin of biscuits. Then brought a plate when he was told to get one.

Nath said, 'You all have come here for the first time. I have no snacks to offer you. Tara, why didn't you bring some along?'

'Doctor sahib, it is fine,' Tara said quickly. Mercy endorsed her.

Chaddha leaned towards Nath and began, 'The fear of inflation is absolutely misplaced. If people get more money as wages, they will spend it to buy products that are at present imported. The production of cloth and other consumer items is not higher than the demand for them. Such a policy will take the pressure off the agricultural land, and improve the standard of living. The economy will be able to sustain the growth to a great extent by using its own resources. Why should we spend Rs 50,000 on importing bulldozers? Why not use that money to provide work for 50 landless peasants?'

Tara was listening to Chaddha. Mercy listened for some time, then whispered into Tara's ear, 'Come, let's have a tour of the house.' She looked at Nath for permission.

'Want me to show you around?' Nath was about to get up.

'You carry on,' Mercy said, putting her hand on Nath's shoulder to stop him. 'We'll see it ourselves.'

Next to the living room was Nath's study—office with a large desk and several chairs around it. Two shelves were stacked with files, government reports and books. Files and papers were piled also on the desk. The walls were bereft of any pictures or calendars. On close inspection, a fine layer of dust could be seen on the white-washed walls. Next to it was Nath's bedroom. The bed was covered with a bedspread, its colours faded from repeated washings. Dirty laundry was piled up inside a cupboard with glass panes. A fridge stuttered and hummed in one corner. Mercy opened the fridge to inspect it. There was a smell of milk turned sour. Half a loaf of bread, a tablet of butter and some yogurt in an earthen *kulhar*. Two bottles of soda water, half a bottle of whisky, and two bottles of beer.

'All household needs are in the fridge. The old man keeps the house in a mess,' Mercy said in English, mindful of Bhoop Singh standing behind them. The room had an attached bathroom. Marcy could not help peering inside. She muttered a dissatisfied 'huh'.

They went towards the three rooms across the hallway from the living room. Bhoop Singh tagged along, keeping an eye on them. The doors to the rooms were shut. Mercy turned around and asked, 'Are these rooms kept closed?'

'Yes, huzoor, furniture and bedsteads are stored there,' Bhoop Singh replied petulantly. He had not liked their meddling.

Mercy asked, 'Where's the kitchen?'

Bhoop Singh pointed towards the back veranda.

Mercy and Tara walked towards the kitchen. Bhoop Singh went ahead, unchained the door and turned the light on. The stove was waist-high, European style. Two clean aluminium pots, a few others which had not been washed. Some charcoal was piled up beside the stove.

Most of the almirahs and storage racks were empty. Three bundles lay on one side; out of one some wheat had spilled on the floor, some lentil seeds from the second. One half of a *lauki*, gourd, had turned brown.

Mercy and Tara peered into the pantry. A couple of plates and a well-scrubbed, gleaming thali were stacked against the wall. Tara said quietly into Mercy's ear, 'This must be the malkin's.'

Mercy asked her in English, 'When will you take charge of all this?'

Bhoop Singh was within earshot. Tara protested, without sounding irritated, 'Didi, you are out of your mind. You can at least hold your tongue.'

'Hmm,' Mercy said, nodding vaguely. They walked around the bungalow and went towards a grassless lawn in the front.

Tara had felt like a fool after repeatedly insisting to meet Nath's wife.

Memories of that incident still brought a smile to her lips. When Tara had told about it to Mercy, she had expressed surprise at Tara's naïvety.

Tara had said in her defence, 'Didi, I got a surprise and I asked him when did he get married? But he led me on. Why shouldn't I have believed him?' After that the subject of Nath's marriage never came up.

Mercy replied to Tara's rebuke after Bhoop Singh left them alone, 'What's wrong with my mind? Can't I see? He's very fond of you and, you are head over heels in love with him. Why don't you come out with what's in your heart?'

Tara protested, 'Don't you know the meaning of having respect for someone? I told you everything, that he's my brother's guru, and my guru. He always helped us when my family was in difficulty. He's one of the most distinguished scholars in the country. Not only I, but everyone treats him with respect. I respect him more than I respect my own father. Aren't you ashamed of saying such things?'

'Stop making excuses!' Mercy refused to believe Tara. 'You won't marry someone whom you don't respect or whom you hate, will you? Even if the poor soul has proposed to you, you must have turned up your nose.'

'What gave you that idea?'

'What I've seen and what everyone notices. He likes you.'

'As a matter of fact, he used to like me even eight years ago.' Tara tried to reason to shut Mercy up and thought at once, 'What did I just say? Now she'll talk more nonsense.'

'O, ho!' said Mercy after Tara set her own trap.

Tara kept quiet and pretended to be angry, but the thought crossed her mind, 'What would others be thinking about me? What if some baseless rumour went around? Mercy's worried about me, but I wonder what nonsensical things she might have said to Chaddha and Mathur. Her concern is likely to become a problem for me. It's better to have a frank talk with her.'

On the way back, Chaddha and Mathur got off near Red Fort; they had something to do in Chandni Chowk. Tara drove Mercy to her flat. Since both were alone together, Tara said in a serious tone, 'Didi, it's the last time I am going to tell you something.'

Mercy indicated 'what' by raising her eyebrows.

'Neither will you think about my marriage, nor will you utter another word to anyone about it. Promise me.'

'But why shouldn't I think about it and why shouldn't I talk about it?'

'I've told you hundreds of times that I don't want to get married, that I won't, I won't.' Tara's eyes were moist.

Mercy put her arm around Tara's, 'At least tell me why? You want to keep it secret from me?'

Brushing off her tears, Tara said, 'What should I tell you why! Any reason is as good as the next. It could be my mental or physical state, it could be my nature. All I can say is that I don't want to get married.' She covered her face with her aanchal and burst into tears.

Mercy pressed Tara's head to her shoulder and promised, 'I won't do it again if you mind it so much.'

Next time Tara took Chaddha and Gill to meet Nath on a Sunday afternoon, Kanak instead of Mercy went with them. The comrades had been using Tara's car as a free taxi. Since she did not let anyone but Narottam drive her car, she drove herself.

Tara had taken some snacks and biscuits along. It was very hot. Nath asked Bhoop Singh to bring water for the guests.

'I'll get it,' Tara said, getting up.

As Bhoop Singh watched, she washed the glasses with soap. She asked for a fresh towel, and wiped the glasses dry. She put the glasses on a tray, and told Bhoop Singh to take it to the living room. She herself carried a bottle of squash and two bottles of cold water from the fridge.

Nath noticed the glasses and the bottle of squash, and said, 'Thanks.'

Gill and Chaddha had brought newspaper clippings for Nath with statistics on the achievements of China and other socialist countries in industrial development. Chaddha had some typed notes which he elucidated for half an hour. Tara joined in whenever there was any reference to recent criticisms of the Plan in the newspapers. They discussed several other topics. Around five o'clock, Nath asked, stopping in the middle of stretching his arms, 'You will all like some tea perhaps?'

'Sure,' Chaddha replied.

Tara again got up from her chair. Today she had no fear of Mercy making stupid comments. Tea was served properly, with biscuits and snacks in plates.

Nath again thanked Tara affectionately.

'Did you notice, Doctor sahib,' Chaddha said, 'the touch of a dextrous person?'

'Uh-huh,' Nath nodded.

'Doctor sahib, Leela often complains that you don't think about arranging

this girl's marriage,' Chaddha said, then looked at Kanak. 'Leela says that
both guardians of the girl are very careless.'

'Excuse me. Have I become a millstone around somebody's neck?' Tara
did not like the joke in front of Nath.

'What he meant was when will you make someone very happy?' Kanak
said.

Nath took a sip of tea, and said, 'She will arrange her own marriage.
There is no dearth of her admirers. If she finds someone, we will get her
married to him. Why don't we arrange a *swayamvar* for her?'

'Certainly not, Doctor sahib,' Kanak said. 'I am warning you that men
will fight for the opportunity to ask her hand in marriage. But if you didn't
approve of somebody I won't let him come near her.'

Tara had held the position of undersecretary for the past three years, and
had been with the department that gave grants for expansion of industries
for eighteen months. She did not find her job difficult, though she felt that
she was doing more work than was due to her so that the work in her office
may not lag behind. She had been eager to learn after her appointment
as a senior grade clerk in 1948. She had enthusiastically prepared for her
selection for the Public Service Commission in 1950. That enthusiasm
was now missing.

Her employment with the government was permanent and secure. The
performance of her official duties had been excellent in the first few years.
Now it was not easy to give an adverse remark on her service record. Any
senior officer making such a remark would have had to justify it. Official
rules and regulations safeguarded her job and entitled her to an annual salary
increment of Rs 50. Being specially diligent or efficient in her work would
not have made much difference, for her promotion was based on seniority
and which she would have received when her turn came. The office life and
work was same every day, with nothing to relieve the monotony. There was
no reward for being innovative and imaginative, or for showing initiative.
Job security and lack of opportunities for advancement by improving one's
performance made government officials lazy, apathetic and arrogant. All
Tara had to do was to work according to the rules. If there was a reason
for her to feel thrill and joy, it was outside the realm of her office. But an
incident blew a storm of stress and strain in Tara's dull and routine office life.

Tara did not leave her office during the lunch break. She had tea sent to her room. She would sit quietly for ten or fifteen minutes, or glance through the newspaper. That day after lunch her assistant handed her the telephone and said, 'Deputy Secretary Mr Chari.'

Chari said, 'Miss Puri, I am sending Mr Sahni to you. The PA of the minister of industries has put in a word for him. It's about a loan for a cooperative. He'll give you his application for the loan. Get his work done today, if possible.'

Tara said at once, 'Sir, all the monies have been allotted as loans.'

'Well, see if there's some possibility. I've not disposed off all the cases. The PA of the minister of industries had rung,' Chari said, emphasizing the last sentence.

Tara was rather annoyed. She had already dealt with the applications, approving after careful screening and investigation only those cases that were eligible and deserving, and rejecting several. Whose application would she now reject, and why?

The deputy secretary's peon pushed open the door to Tara's office, and held it open for the person behind him. The well-built man was clothed in white kurta, Nehru jacket and white Gandhi cap. When Tara saw him, her eyes widened with incredulity and she bowed her head.

Somraj Sahni was in Delhi with a letter of recommendation addressed to the minister of industries from Sood, the omnipotent government minister of Punjab. He knew that usually it took months to get a decision on applications and inquiries sent by mail. The only way to get an answer quickly was to meet personally with the government officials. The minister had given instructions to his PA about Somraj. The PA had telephoned the deputy secretary of the concerned department. The deputy secretary had reassured Somraj, and had asked his peon to escort the person sent by the minister to the office of the undersecretary.

Somraj had followed the peon to the undersecretary's office with such confidence that he had not bothered to look at the nameplate on the office door. He had made no mistake in recognizing Tara and the sight of her sitting behind the desk had surprised and unnerved him.

Tara gritted her teeth and kept her gaze fixed on her desk. She remembered that she was a government official and brought herself under control. She motioned Somraj to take a chair, and held out her hand for his application.

She took the papers from him and held them in front of her face to read them. What she saw was not the words on the pages, but the events of seven years ago. Her mouth was dry; she swallowed several times and again made an effort to pull herself together, then began to read the application for the loan.

Somraj had applied for loan as a political sufferer in the war for the country's freedom.

Lies! Fraud! Flames of anger leapt up in Tara's mind, but with the application was a testimonial on the letterhead of the State Congress Committee with the committee's rubber stamp, saying that Somraj Sahni had been incarcerated for two years as a political prisoner.

Tara went through the application to see if the requisite report from the department's inspector was attached. It was not. She knew that this was an attempt to circumvent the long and complicated procedure for dealing with loan applications by pulling a few strings.

Behind the veil of paper sheets, Tara collected herself enough in the next ten minutes to again become the firm and dispassionate government official. She said in a steady voice from behind the veil, 'The reply will be sent by mail.'

To be a supplicant before Tara sitting magisterially in the officer's chair was excruciatingly uncomfortable for Somraj, as if he was sitting on a bed of spikes. He got up as soon as he heard Tara's reply, and stormed out of the room without saying a word. He went away without meeting anyone else in the office.

Somraj was an old hand at getting things done at government offices. He was not so naïve as to believe that his application could still be approved. He knew that if a minor clerk, leave aside the undersecretary, raised an objection about a lapse in procedural rules, even an official of the highest rank cannot ignore it. To cry before anyone about his failure was to invite humiliation on himself. He swallowed his anger and did nothing.

It was not very difficult for Tara to save herself the trouble of dealing with Somraj's application. She could have ordered an inquiry into the case, or put the file aside for future consideration. The deputy secretary had given the order, 'Get his work done today, if possible', verbally and not in writing. His meaning was clear: Get this done somehow. She had to give him an answer.

For about forty minutes Tara browsed through the files on her desk while thinking anxiously about the answer she could give. There was no hitch in approving Somraj's application. All she had to do was to reject an application that had been approved, and sanction a loan of Rs 25,000 to Somraj. No one would have raised an objection to the application being submitted late or about the missing inquiry. All she had to do was just obey order from above, but she could not bring herself to do it. Her heart rebelled. This was fraud, a lie, an outright deceit.

But how could she write what she felt in her remark on the application! How could she tell the deputy secretary over the telephone what she thought! She did not know if Somraj had pulled any strings. To accept the certificate from the State Congress Committee as true and to carry out the order of her senior officer would have been the correct procedure. Her responsibility ended there. But, then, to approve Somraj's application would mean depriving someone eligible for his rightful claim. A number of similar incidents, she knew, took place every day in the secretariat. What would she accomplish by putting obstacles in the way of Somraj? Since she had not deliberately upset the apple cart so far, she had acquired a reputation as a strict officer, rather than a good officer.

Her heart protested. She would be writing the first remark, and will be responsible for the fraud carried out by following the correct procedure. 'I won't do this.'

Tara made up her mind and rang Mr Chari, 'Sir, I see many problems with this case. I am sending the file back to you. Whatever instructions you write on it will be carried out.'

Mr Chari banged the receiver down without saying anything. Even if the minister's PA had called, how could he write a remark approving the application without first receiving a note from the undersecretary? He could only endorse the undersecretary's decision, not cut his hands off by himself taking the decision.

Tara could not help feeling worried and nervous after incurring her senior official's wrath. She needed to share her worry and anger with someone. Without disclosing who the applicant was, she mentioned the incident to Narottam and also vented her frustration before Prabha Saxena. Both reassured her, 'You don't worry about these sycophantic crooks. It's the fault of ministers who encourage these people! What harm can he do to you? If he writes an adverse remark in your report, you can challenge it. At the most, he can have you transferred to another ministry. He cannot ruin your record.'

Tara remembered the trouble she had with Bhanu Dutt soon after she had
begun to work for the government. At that time Tara could depend on Home
Secretary Rawat for support to fight any injustice. Rawat had retired and
was now with the Public Service Commission. But she was still not scared;
her feet were firmly planted in the civil service.

When the sudden appearance of Somraj had upset her, Tara had tried to
clear her mind of worries by discussing the matter with her friends. What
she could not share with anyone was the deeply buried pain and terrible
memories that the sight of him had dug up. Thinking of the past would
make her head reel.

'Who ruined my life? That animal Somraj or that goonda who had
abducted me? I fell into that butcher's hands only because Somraj had been
so cruel to me. Could I have lived with Somraj? Is this what thousands
of women were fated to suffer? What was the crime for which we were
punished?' Images of the brutalized Muslim women seen on the road to
Amritsar flashed in her memory. That memory gave her gooseflesh. 'Was
it necessary to have to live through the ordeal of crossing the Vaitarni, the
mythological river between the material world and Paradise? And what
Paradise did I find after going through that ordeal? My life is like a leaf
blowing in the wind, no one knows what will happen next. Maybe I should
end the life.'

Tara was transferred to the ministry of information as a result of the
incident of the loan application. Although not a demotion, in a way it was
her defeat and the victory of deceit, which left her deeply wounded.

Chapter 16

TWO YEARS HAD PASSED SINCE KANAK HAD LEFT JALANDHAR.

Kanta had gone to Delhi to try to change Kanak's mind about returning to Jalandhar, but had been unsuccessful in her mission. Puri had come to meet Kanta on her return, but what could she tell him except, 'Bhai, I tried to convince her as much as I could, but if she gets it into her head to say no, she doesn't budge. Don't you know that?'

But Puri did not give up. He wrote Kanak several letters, but she didn't reply. He began to write almost every month to Panditji in a literary style, addressing him courteously as *mohtarim*, respected sir. He would write about his involvement in the assembly, in various committees, his public responsibilities and the hectic schedule at *Nazir*. He would express his concern about Jaya's and Kanak's health, 'How does Jaya look now? What does she talk about? I haven't seen her for so long. Would you be kind enough to send me her recent photograph? Does she remember her papa or not? You can imagine the state of the household. Without the mistress of the house.'

Panditji's worry increased as time went by. He had comforted himself with the thought that the salve of time may eventually heal all hurts, but that hope had gradually dissipated. Kanchan and Narottam were married in May 1954, and they moved to Kanpur. Kanak began writing for several newspapers and was able to establish herself as a journalist in Delhi. She got regular assignments from a fortnightly. She taught Hindi three times a week at an embassy and earned something on the side by doing English to Hindi translations. She was able to make Rs 250–300 a month, sometimes a little more, but only after working very hard. She insisted on contracting out the Naya Hind Press at Rs 200 per month.

Panditji adopted new ways. He gave up tea, milk, meat and fruits, and just wanted to eat chapattis without the usual smearing of ghee, and boiled vegetables. When Kanak objected, he said, 'Beta, it's good for health to avoid eating certain things at my age. They cause a problem if I can't digest them.' Half-sleeved kurta and loose regular pajama trousers replaced his customary dress of long achkan coat, churidar pajama and turban. He felt the turban to be an unnecessary burden. He wanted to do his own laundry.

Kanak said irritably, 'Pitaji, why do you want to do that?'

Panditji patiently explained, 'Beta, I get some exercise this way. Since I lie on the bed the whole day, I don't get hungry enough to eat even two chapattis. One must have appetite so that one can eat.' He wanted to give up eating dinner for the sake of his health, but abandoned the idea when Kanak too refused to eat.

Jaya became Panditji's only concern and delight. He would speak to her as if he was her age. He would teach her to speak English, make her learn spelling and practise multiplication tables. He would tell her stories. He was always ready to give her a bath, but could not comb her hair properly.

Gill came sometimes. Panditji liked to discuss the poetry of Iqbal, Ghalib and the Sufi shayars with him. When they talked about the current situation, Panditji always concluded by saying: A person can stay on the right path only when he's selfless. Every generation has a role to play and obligations to meet in the march for social progress. The wish to take responsibility for the future and to form attachments with the present is of no use.

While discussing political or social issues, Panditji would begin to talk about life and death. He would then recite couplets about the inevitability of death:

The prison of life and the bondage of grief—in essence both are one.
Before death, how would a man find release from grief?

In the end he would say, 'Barkhurdar, our body is a machine made of blood and flesh. When the machine is in motion, energy is produced which is our consciousness. One day the machine is bound to wear off. The worn-off machine will run erratically. Why mourn that? The lust for life is a matter of fun. Life is a play, isn't it? A show must end sometime. Once the show is over no one stays behind. In the same way, our soul leaves the body just like that, without notice.'

He would roar with laughter.

The bier is on the shoulders, the soul in heaven
The foot soldier has left the mounted one miles behind.

Gill would listen to Panditji totally engrossed, nodding appreciatively, as if listening to these philosophical clichés for the first time. He would think: The discussion about the cycle of birth and death and about soul has been the biggest pastime of the people of this country and the tradition has become the national pastime.

Kanak, sitting with them or busy with some chore nearby, would heave a deep sigh on hearing such talk. She didn't like these discussions. She would think, 'Pitaji is gradually cutting himself off from everything. If what will be will be, why worry about it.'

Panditji wanted to be free from all worries. He had no reason to worry about Kanta and Kanchan, but his worry for Kanak did not leave him alone even for a second. He had always regarded his second daughter as an extraordinary person. She had constantly caused him extraordinary problems. By causing her father more troubles, she had received more attention from him, just as parents worry more for a son or daughter who is sick or is in difficulty. Whenever Puri's letter came, he'd show it to Kanak and say, 'Let me know when you reply to him. I'll also write him a note that you can enclose with your letter.' Kanak would remain silent.

Panditji's letters to Puri were always full of reassurance and sympathy for him. He would worry for days that preceded the writing of his reply, thinking, 'What'll become of this girl? It's fortunate that so far Puri's been patient and tolerant, but there's a limit to everything. My daughter is ruining her future. It's been three years she has broken off her relations, and there's no sign that she'll change her mind. Is her hurt so deep that even time cannot heal it? My life's almost over. What'll happen if Puri took his frustration out by doing something rash?' Panditji had been preaching to Kanak the virtues of peace, tolerance and forgiveness for the past few months. Kanak had listened to him in silence. She behaved as though she had forgotten that she and Puri were a married couple. Her attitude had kept Panditji from discussing the matter with her.

Puri again wrote in October. There was an obvious tone of frustration on his part. He ended the letter by saying, 'Pitaji, advise me what I should do in this matter? Don't you agree that I've shown enough patience and understanding? Don't I need to live in my home with my family? If I am being punished, what was my crime?' Puri had evidently reached the end of his patience. The undertone of the letter sent Panditji to the depths of despair.

Kanak had just come back from work in the evening when Panditji called out to her. 'Beta, there's a letter from Puri. Let me know when you reply, I'll also add a few lines,' he said, handing her the letter. Panditji later found the same letter tucked in *Deewan-e-Ghalib* under his pillow. Kanak had said nothing about replying to the letter. Panditji had only one option left: to call Kanta from Jalandhar, and make one last effort to convince Kanak.

Panditji wrote twice to Kanta urging her to come to Delhi for two days for an unexplained urgent matter. Kanta wrote to Kanak asking her the reason for being called to Delhi. Kanak wrote back, 'I don't know the reason. Pitaji keeps his worries to himself, but he is definitely worried. What can I say? He's asked you to come here, I haven't met you for two years, so you must, must come. Bring Nano and Dheeru along.'

Kanta came to Delhi. After Kanak had left for work, Panditji showed Puri's letter to Kanta and voiced concern, 'Beta, we can't blame Puri for his growing impatience. Three years have gone by. We should try to make Kanni understand the situation. Even if Puri had treated her shoddily, which mistake in this world can't be forgiven? We should not sacrifice our life on account of past mistakes. Life is above and beyond such petty considerations. Beta, you've been like a mother to Kanni, you should try to explain to her that she's in error.'

Kanta, her head bowed, thought for a while sitting across from her father on another charpoy. She did not want to prevaricate any more. Her father was wasting away worrying for Kanak. He had called her from Jalandhar to discuss the problem that had been nagging at him. Who else but she could present Kanak's side of the story? And whom else could her father talk to about his worry but her? She could not just stand and watch him waste away. She had realized that Kanak will not return to Jalandhar. It wouldn't have been fair to compel her to go back. As the eldest of Panditji's children and mother of two of her own she had a responsibility towards her family.

After examining her nails intently for a few seconds, Kanta said, 'Pitaji, it's not Kanni's fault.'

Although her head was bowed, Kanta could feel Panditji looking at her anxiously. How could such a brief explanation serve as an answer to his worry! It was necessary to give an explanation. In order to be neutral, she said in English, 'They are having marital difficulties.' Her explanation only deepened the mystery.

She made another effort, 'Puri by nature is a very nervous person. Nayyar had consulted a specialist. The doctor thought that Puri has psychopathic personality. He just won't leave poor Kanak in peace. He gets perverse satisfaction from tormenting her.'

Once the difficult part was over, Kanta added with emphasis, 'He's a good writer. He's also a politician, knows how to talk, but he has no concern for morality. When Kanni first arrived at his house in Jalandhar, he was living with some refugee girl.'

'Didn't Kanni find out?'

'How could she not find out? But she was in her defiant mood. She didn't want to renege on the promise she had made to him. It seems that Puri is still obsessed with the same refugee girl.'

Kanta kept her head bowed. She heard her father sigh. She knew that he had understood.

Since Kanta was at home, Kanak came back from work at 3 p.m. thinking that her sister may want to go to the bazaar or to visit someone. She had said many good things about Tara to Kanta. 'If my sister wants to meet Tara, I'll take her there. Three of us can go to the bazaar or to the cinema.'

When Kanak did not find Kanta in her bedroom, she peered into Panditji's room. Her father was sitting motionless on his bed. Kanta, her head bowed, was sitting on a charpoy. Kanak stepped back quietly.

When Kanta returned to her room, Kanak asked, 'What's the matter? Why is pitaji so upset?'

Kanta told Kanak about her talk with Panditji.

Kanak slapped her own forehead dejectedly, and said, 'Why did you trouble him with all these problems? Can't you see his health has deteriorated because he worries so much?'

'His main worry is sending you back to Jalandhar. He's called me here to convince you. If I hadn't told him he'd have sulked thinking that you were being stubborn for no reason. Now it's over and done with.'

'What is over?' Kanak's eyes brimmed with tears. 'I'm fated to cause problems for everyone.' She clutched her forehead and lay down on the charpoy.

Jaya came in, calling 'mummy, mummy!' She pulled at her mother's aanchal to tell that her frock had become wet while she was giving her doll a bath.

Kanak did not remove the aanchal from her face. Kanta lifted Jaya up tenderly and went to another room.

At five o'clock Kanta called, 'Kanni, get up. I have to buy some clothes for Nano and Dheeru. Also some material for Nayyar's trousers.'

Kanak got up, washed her face and changed into a fresh sari. She thought,

'Jaya will insist on going out with us. I should change her frock and comb her hair. She must be in piatji's room.' The child liked being with her grandfather.

Kanak saw that Panditji was lying on the bed, eyes closed and arm pillowing his head. Jaya had got some pieces of coloured paper from the printing press, and was calling him over and over to show the paper. It was hard for Panditji to open his eyes, and he kept saying 'Yes, beta! Yes, beta!' without opening his eyes. Kanak went back quietly.

Kanta wanted to buy a present for Jaya. She asked, 'You're not taking Jaya along?'

'Let her stay home, bahinji. If she's home, she'll be a distraction for pitaji. Otherwise…'

Kanak and Kanta crossed the aangan quietly so that Jaya may not hear, and went out.

Kanta went back to Jalandhar after two days. Kanak kept a close watch on Panditji. It killed her to see that she was the cause of all his worry and pain. Panditji did his best to hide his worry and behave in a normal way, but didn't always succeed. He would sit on a reed chair, *Deewan-e-Ghalib* or *Musaddas-e-Hali* or the large-print edition of Gita in hand. Kanak would look sideways at him and find that he would be brooding, book in lap and temple resting on his hand. Kanak knew that he was worrying over her misfortune.

After about a week Panditji began to behave like his normal self. In the evening he would again tell Jaya stories and help her memorize the multiplication tables. One day Kanak heard him tell Jaya the legend of Guru Govind Singh's two sons. It was a long story, with all the details such as how some pitiless persons had bricked up the two brave boys in, beginning at their feet. When the brick wall had reached the boys' necks, they were told that their lives would be saved if they agreed to renounce their religion. But those brave boys rejected the offer without fear and were bricked in. They died, but their name and the story of their adherence to the dharma lives on.

Kanak, exhausted after the day's work, was lying on a charpoy waiting for dinner. A Punjabi widow living in Durrani Gali had been employed to mind the kitchen in the morning and evening. Kanak could hear her father tell the story to Jaya who lay beside him. A thought ran through Kanak's mind. Would the sectarian violence between different religions ever end?

Sectarian conflict had claimed the lives of Hakeekat Rai and Guru Govind Singh's sons, had forced her family and her neighbours in the gali to leave Lahore and become destitute. All this because of the belief in a god whom no one has ever seen! The attempt to listen to her father was interrupting her train of thought. But what was the use of thinking such thoughts?

Kanak remembered that in her own childhood she also used to listen to her father tell stories. She heard Jaya who was completely engrossed in the story ask Panditji, 'Both boys died? Then what happened?'

Panditji replied, 'Beta, children who practise their dharma and do good deeds, who are not afraid to tell the truth, they are brave children. Such children never die.'

Jaya again asked, 'They don't die even when their throats are cut?'

Kanak found her daughter's simple question very endearing. Jaya asked one question after another. She remembered that her father used to say, 'Kanni, you used to ask so many questions when you were young. Always liked to split hairs.'

Kanak pricked up her ears to hear her father's reply.

Panditji said, 'Yes, beta. Those who are not afraid to do good deeds, they never die.'

Kanak looked at her daughter. Jaya was holding her foot with her hands. She asked again, 'They never die? Even when all others are dead?'

Panditji replied, 'Yes, beta. They never die. Others see the example of their good actions and bravery, and become brave themselves. They learn to practise dharma and do good deeds.'

Jaya asked, 'What's dharma?'

Panditji elucidated the concept of dharma, 'A child who is fearless, who obeys his elders, doesn't grab things that doesn't belong to him, who's not greedy, who doesn't eat unhealthy food, who keeps himself clean and doesn't hurt others, that child is brave and one who practises dharma. You'll also practise your dharma and become brave.'

'Is mummy also brave?' Jaya asked.

Her daughter's question gave Kanak a thrill. She held her lower lip between her teeth as she waited for her father to answer.

Panditji said ardently, 'Your mummy is very brave. She practises her dharma. She's not afraid to do a good deed. She doesn't deceive anybody. My beti, you'll also be like her.'

Kanak let out a sigh, and thought, 'I hardly did any good deeds. I wish

my daughter does.' But her mood was lightened; her father was not angry
with her. 'If pitaji feels I haven't shamed him, I don't care what anyone
else feels.'

Panditji liked to have dinner by eight o'clock. He had been following the
regimen of walking a mile after dinner. Since he had trouble in walking
through the galis after dark, he had calculated that making seventy rounds
of the aangan added up to 1 mile 36 yards. After dinner, Kanak would walk
round the aangan with him. During the walk father and daughter discussed
a lot of subjects: argument in favour of Kashmir becoming a part of India,
achievements and failures of the present government, the ethics of India
not joining any military treaty, India's contribution to international peace,
Jaya's studies and her health, letters from Kanchan and Narottam, Second
Five Year Plan's chances of success, and other social, moral and sometimes
philosophical topics. Some of the subjects had been discussed over and
over again and Kanak had come to know her father's views and opinions
on those subjects well.

A month after Kanta's return to Jalandhar, Kanak had discerned a change
in Panditji's views and in his way of thinking—the like of which would
have befitted him three or four decades ago. There were some precepts
that he kept repeating:

It is important that someone should have the courage to believe that
moral judgements are a matter of common sense and reason rather
than of tradition and convention. Instead of putting blind trust in
traditions and conventions, we should rely upon common sense and
reason when making a moral judgement.

For the fulfilment of one's life, a right action is the one which
is appropriate according to the circumstances. Actions done in
accordance with the circumstances give the sense of fulfilment that
makes life worthwhile. No definition of social and moral behaviour is
correct for all times. There is no eternal definition of correct social
and moral behaviour.

A person gets what is in his karma. This does not mean that our
fate is decided by our deeds of past life about which we know nothing,
but that our lives are determined by the way we change our existing
circumstances.

It's always the right time to make an effort for the betterment of one's life.

The notions of right and wrong depend on our knowledge and experience. Our conscience should be the grounds for correcting our mistakes.

Good or bad deeds are transitory, therefore, should not control our lives. Knowledge gained through experience is important for life. It is the life force that engenders subsequent actions and karma.

A person can make amends for his or her past mistakes if it is done conscientiously and with proper guiding principles and intention.

Our knowledge and understanding of the world changes with time.

If our present knowledge and ideas are to form the basis of studying the society of fifty years ago, we must also realize that the present society is the outcome of lessons learned in the past and the misconceptions dispelled since then about scientific ideas—laws, medical science, agriculture and technology, and social and individual responsibilities.

Such discussions for the sake of it bored Kanak. At times she would think that her father was perhaps nostalgic about the comfortable life he had led, or maybe senility was creeping in as he grew older and weaker? She would listen quietly, thinking 'whatever it might be, it has taken some load off his mind'.

One evening while they were going round the aangan, Panditji said something rather nonchalantly. Giving a simple reply to him made Kanak break out into a sweat even in the mild cold of February. She found it difficult to continue their walk after she had replied to him. She went and lay on her bed.

Next morning, Kanak was desperate to tell Gill what her father had said, but decided to exercise self-restraint. It was not possible not to tell him, but what would be the result if she did? Would she be able to handle the situation? Her head seemed to fly off her shoulders. At work she found it hard to concentrate. Three times she reached for the telephone to ask Gill to meet her in the evening, but pulled her hand back each time. She was uncertain about what might happen when they meet. Would she be able to dam the flood of emotions? That year the Yamuna had inundated vast areas. She saw the scenes of flood in her mind's eye. The thought of what might happen kept her in the throes of self-restraint and did not let her fall asleep. Finally, she thought of a way out of her dilemma, 'I'll first ask him to give his word that he'd respect my wish.' Then she fell asleep.

Kanak's feelings of concern and anxiety were not without reason. Gill had showed great self-restraint during his four years at Jalandhar, and had behaved as if there had been no attraction or secret between them. He had behaved like Kanak's elder 'brother', who knew all the weaknesses and secrets of his 'sister' or friend, and had her welfare at his heart. He always took Puri's side if he got into an argument with Kanak, because it was in Kanak's interest for Gill not to antagonize Puri. He did not shirk from telling the truth if he thought it to be in Kanak's interest. Kanak too was aware of her responsibility to do what was good for Gill; who else was there but Kanak to look after him? In her attempt to care for Gill, Kanak had once upset Gill.

When Nayyar used to live in Mandi Bazaar, the house across the gali from his had been bought by Dr Bedi. Nayyar and Bedi had recognized each other the moment they had come face to face, even though they were meeting again after more than ten years. They both had been fond of tennis in their student days, and had played on rival teams a couple of times in the Wrangley tennis tournament. In Lahore Bedi was a student in the medical college and Nayyar at the law college. They hugged each other warmly on meeting again in Jalandhar.

Only the width of the gali separated the families of Nayyar and Anoop Singh Bedi. The families very often visited each other. Even Nayyar, who rarely paid a visit to anyone, went and socialized once in a while at Bedi's house. If Nano or Dheeru so much as sneezed, Kanta would consult Bedi bhraji. Bedi's wife Basant Kaur was very welcoming. But Kanta was really enamoured with Basant Kaur's sister Amaro, Amar Kaur.

Amar Kaur was extraordinarily beautiful, like a character born out of some artist's imagination. Below her jaw line was a birthmark, as if a talisman had been painted there to ward off the evil eye. She had an equally genial nature. She spoke very little, and when she did, it was in a voice that was sweet and shy at the same time. Kanak had been fascinated by Amar Kaur after meeting her only twice at Bedi's house. When she had heard Amaro's tragic story, she had been stunned.

Anoop Singh Bedi's brother Ishar Singh Bedi was also a doctor. He had begun his practice, like his brother, in Montgomery in south-eastern Punjab. He married Amar Kaur just a year before the Partition. He had bought a shop in Chaura Bazaar to use for his practice. Six months before the Partition, he and Amar Kaur had moved into the rooms above the shop which was at the gali's corner. The neighbourhood was predominantly Muslim, except a few Hindu families.

When tension began to grow in their city, Anoop Singh asked his brother to move in with him in Sai ki Gali. Since all houses belonged to Hindus and Sikhs, it was safer for everyone in Anoop Singh's gali. However, Ishar Singh said that if even one family moved out of his own gali, all other Hindu families will lose confidence and the Muslims will gain the upper hand. He borrowed a shotgun and some cartridges from his brother.

When Ishar Singh brought the gun, Amar Kaur took an interest in it. Ishar Singh asked, 'What'd you know about a gun? Have you ever seen one before?' Amar Kaur replied that her grandfather, a retired subedar, owned a shotgun and was very fond of hunting. There were several ponds that skirted around their farmland where ducks used to land. Whenever her grandfather went for a walk in the morning or the evening, he took his gun along. If any of his granddaughters or grandsons were around, he took them along too. Amar Kaur's grandfather had made her shoot at ducks several times. Her shoulder would hurt for a couple of days every time she fired the gun.

In the evening of 19 August, news reached Sai ki Gali that Hindu families living in Chaura Bazaar had been attacked. The Muslim police could not be trusted to rescue them. About fifty men from Sai ki Gali, carrying arms, went to help the beleaguered Hindus. The carnage was nearly over when they arrived. The Muslim mob ran away when they saw the armed Hindus. Amar Kaur was found lying unconscious near a second-floor window, a shotgun in hand and clothes drenched with blood. Her baby daughter had been killed by a bullet. Her husband had been shot several times.

Anoop Singh said, 'How many times could the poor girl fire? She probably fired three or four times before the recoil from the gun dislocated her shoulder. A shotgun pellet had struck her on the upper arm, another had wounded her jaw. They carried her in an unconscious state to Anoop Singh's house. She and Anoop Singh's family lived for a month in a refugee camp, and then came to Jalandhar. Amar Kaur's life was saved only because she was with a doctor.

Basant Kaur said, 'Amaro was fit as a fiddle and good-natured, but after the death of her husband and baby daughter and the wounds she had received, she remained shell-shocked for about two years. Then she must have thought that she could not spend the rest of her life in a vegetative state. She had already passed the matric exam. She asked her jeth, to enrol her into some training course. Dr Anoop Singh agreed; he thought that this might give Amaro a new lease of life.'

Amar Kaur completed the training course at the Health School. When Dheeru was born in 1951, she stayed with Kanta for a while and cared for her. Kanta and Kanak took her to their heart and began to call her Amaro. Nayyar, Puri and Gill also sympathized with her. 'A character born out of an artist's imagination' was what Puri had said about her. When Kanak extolled Amaro's beauty before Gill, he agreed that one should feel fortunate in being able to see a young woman like her.

Amaro tried not to be a burden on her relations, and they on their part did not think of her as one. They felt compassion for her, and thought: Let bygones be bygones. Why should a girl on the threshold of becoming a woman spend her life cursed with loneliness? If she agrees, we'll marry her off. They did not express their intention in so many words, but often dropped hints about it. Doctor Bedi invited Gill over every now and again. Others had also noticed that Amaro liked Gill. Kanak and Kanta had sensed that Puri was jealous of Gill on that account.

Basant Kaur whispered in Kanta's ear. Kanta consulted Nayyar, then discussed 'the secret' with Kanak and Puri. Kanak was confident that she could get Gill to agree.

Kanak wanted Gill to be married, from the bottom of her heart. She thought that by helping to arrange his marriage she would be able to make up for the injustice she had meted out to him. And once he was married, she would stop feeling self-conscious in his company.

Gill replied, 'Don't talk nonsense. I've no intention of getting married.'

Every time Kanak found the opportunity, she tried to convince Gill, 'You yourself said that one should feel fortunate in being able to see a young woman like her. Who can be a better match for you than she? Once she's with you, her personality would blossom out. She has such a lovely nature.'

'Does that mean I should marry her just because she's a fine girl? What an odd thing to say. I've never thought about her in that way.'

Kanak pressed him, 'I can't imagine a better couple. It'd be a sight for sore eyes.'

Kanak's repeated insistence annoyed Gill, 'Why are you matching me up with her? Am I some kind of stud? If so, I'll never go to Bedi's house.'

That episode was forgotten. In Jalandhar, Gill had spoken to Kanak umpteenth times when they were alone, but he never even once had made any attempt to touch her or to allude to the secret between them. Kanak had realized that Gill was not particularly enamoured of Puri, and if it hadn't been for her, he wouldn't have stayed behind in Jalandhar. She felt a stab of sadness. She had received a number of letters from Gill telling her that Delhi was full of opportunities, which had given her a sense of gratitude and a glow of pride. She knew that he was her friend and a man of his word, that he had great self-restraint and a will of iron, and her heart was filled with tender feelings for him.

The first time Kanak had met Gill in Delhi was when she had been posted at Aliganj and had come to Delhi to leave Jaya with her parents. Gill knew about Puri and Kanta coming to Delhi, and about their going back unsuccessful after failing to persuade Kanak to return to Jalandhar. At that time Gill had taken her to Rajghat to be able to speak to her in peace and quiet. After hearing her story, he had asked, 'Is your decision final?'

'Absolutely final.'

Gill had said, 'We cannot do things at our will or just because we believe that they can be done. It's possible that family considerations and social pressures may make you think again about your decision.'

'I've done all the thinking I could. It's possible that I might just kill myself.'

'It could happen that you will feel a sense of guilt or self-disgust in the aftermath of your decision.'

'I don't see why. I admit that I had made a mistake. Or maybe even committed a crime. I simply want to forget about it. Instead of suffering forever for having made the mistake, I'm willing to be punished for it once and for all.'

After that conversation, every time Kanak came to Delhi from Aliganj, she would meet Gill. They would go for long walks. There was always so much to say. In Jalandhar, Gill's behaviour towards Kanak had always been proper. His behaviour changed with the new setting.

Kanak was faced with a painful situation. She had to control her own feelings before she could ask Gill to have control over his. And to be able to gain a control over herself, she had to negate what every fibre in her body and her every breath wanted.

Gill said irritably, 'You still run away from me? Why can't we be husband and wife? You don't want me the way I didn't want Amaro.'

Kanak, in the throes of hiding her feelings, retorted, 'You can be angry with me all you want. If you don't want to see me, don't. But don't you realize my situation? What would you gain if you make me feel like some criminal and humiliate me? If I get too disgusted with myself, I'll just drown myself in the Yamuna. But what'd people think of you? Doctor sahib, Chaddha bhai, Tara—they all have a high opinion of you. You want to shame both yourself and me before them?'

Kanak could not hold back her tears. Gill, whom everyone thought to be so serious, kind and sensible, lost his self-control and became so defenceless when he was with her. His vulnerability made Kanak feel helpless, and his anger at her made her cry on the quiet. But that crying gave her a thrill of satisfaction, which was the heart of the problem. The only solution Kanak could think of was not to be alone with him.

Kanak telephoned Gill and asked him to meet her at six o'clock in the Coffee House which she knew would be crowded at that time. Before Gill arrived, Mittal, a government journalist who knew both of them, joined Kanak at her table. Then came Mrs Raina, who was doing research on the theatre of India under a fellowship from a foreign government. These people showed no sign of leaving when they saw Gill arrive.

Kanak regretted the place she had chosen to meet Gill. How could they talk in peace in the Coffee House? On her table a discussion had begun about the Prime Minister's activities. Does he spend any time working in his office? Every day the newspapers carry a statement given by him at some social event, every other day he lays down some foundation stone or inaugurates something—an art exhibition or a children's function or a newly built bridge. Whether a conference on travel trade or a seminar on some philosophical problem, the Prime Minister seems ever willing to inaugurate it. There was no end to his travels, his official tours and the speeches he gave. Four to five hundred people were involved every time he undertook a journey. Was there any accounting for such gratuitous spending? The Prime Minister frequently preaches that one should work, not just give speeches, but the example he sets is of giving a speech every day.

Kanak did not find the opportunity to talk to Gill. They came out of the
Coffee House and walked through Connaught Place. It was 7.30 and dusk
was falling. Kanak wanted to get back home by eight o'clock. As soon as
they left the crowded street and began to walk on Barakhamba Road, Kanak
said, 'I've something special to tell you. But first give me your word that
you will do what I ask you.'

'Have I ever refused to do anything that you asked me?'

'Still, I want you word. It's something special.'

'What promise do you want me to make?'

'First promise you'll do what I say, and then I'll tell you.'

'What's that important?'

'Something is.'

'Something very special?'

'Yes, very.'

'Is it right to put me under such constraint?'

'Trust me. I won't do anything ...'

'Don't you trust me?'

'I do. That's why I want you to promise me.'

'All right. I promise.'

'Pitaji got another letter from Puri wanting to know how long he must
wait and asking us to set a time limit for a decision. He also wrote that
we should not blame him if he lost his patience and decided to take some
drastic action. Pitaji said if a relationship has ceased to have a meaning or
basis, there was no point in continuing it. That if a relationship existed
only on paper, it'd be right to end it. He asked for my opinion and I said
I agreed with him. Pitaji said that he'd write to jijaji to speak to Puri that
this relationship may be ended legally and without bitterness and hassle.'

'Divorce?'

'What else?'

'Pitaji suggested that himself?'

'That's what I said.'

'Was I wrong when I suggested the same thing last year?'

'How could I be the one to say it?'

Gill and Kanak were near the taxi stand at the Mandi House roundabout.
Gill raised his hand and called, 'Taxi!'

'Hai, why?' Kanak protested. 'We'll talk while we walk,'

'We'll talk in the taxi.'

When the taxi was on the road, Gill put his arm around Kanak and said in an assured tone, 'You'll have to give me a kiss to celebrate this occasion.'

Inspite of feeling muddled, Kanak reacted according to a decision made earlier and pushed Gill's arm away. She said hastily, 'Listen! You had promised to listen to me.'

'What?' Gill said in a hurt tone.

Tears seeped out in the corners of Kanak's closed eyes. 'Please excuse me.' She said biting her lip, 'Don't touch me until this matter is decided. Just behave as you did in Jalandhar.'

Gill was silent.

Kanak implored him, 'Gillu, everything depends on you now. You can control yourself. I trust you more than I trust myself. I touch your feet and beg you to help me. Only six more months.'

Gill remained silent.

'Gillu, please don't be cross with me,' Kanak pleaded with a catch in her voice.

'All right,' said Gill.

Chapter 17

THE GENERAL ELECTIONS FOR THE PARLIAMENT AND THE STATE LEGISLATURES were to be held in the beginning of 1957. The Congress government wanted to launch the Second Five Year Plan in 1956, a year before the elections so as to win the support of the public.

Politicians are prone to short-sightedness, particularly when assessing the future. People are somewhat like the elephant in the fable of blind men, except that people as a whole are much bigger than an elephant. Politicians come into contact with one small section of people and represent a wide body of people. The same was true about the Second Five Year Plan.

The Prime Minister of the Congress government—who was also the president of the Congress party—and the political leaders who supported his policies were hopeful of winning the trust and approval of the people by carrying out the Plan for the country's industrial development by nationalizing the resources to give a boost to the public sector. Several other influential Congress leaders feared that the implementation of the Plan through the public sector would antagonize a very large section of the public. The Prime Minister tried to reassure everyone, through public information campaigns, that the aim of the Congress government's socialistic policy was not to bring about socialism as practised in the West, but to protect the private sector and free enterprise from the evils of the socialist totalitarianism. The leading newspapers of the country were under the control of big capitalists and most of them had declared the policy announced by the government as detrimental to the national interest.

A minor incident happened in the midst of the suspense about the Plan. In 1947 the British had transferred the power to the Congress government. At that time the Flag Staff House, a palace-like edifice serving as the residence of the commander-in-chief of the British imperialist armed forces, was designated as the living quarters of the Prime Minister of the Congress government.

The Prime Minister saw himself as a representative of the country's poor. He considered living in the palace-like edifice an uncalled for ostentation. He wanted the residence of India's Prime Minister to be 'simple and ordinary' like the residence of Britain's prime minister.

The Central Public Works Department estimated that the construction of a 'simple and ordinary' residence suitable for the Prime Minister would cost four lakhs of rupees. The huge cost of the residence upset the Prime Minister. He said that he could have a house of that size built for a lakh or a lakh and a quarter. He gave up the idea of a new residence, and in order to save money, agreed to live in the palace-like residence. The opponents of industrial development in the public sector had been using the incident as an argument in their favour.

The Prime Minister and those responsible for drafting the Plan were not ready to accept that the incident was a proof that the development of large-scale and heavy industry in the public sector was bound to fail due to the inefficiency of the public sector. They thought the incident was rather an example of the crooked and dishonest administration they had inherited from the British government.

The news added fuel to the debate among the public about bribery and corruption. Tara's neighbours and her friends knew that she was against taking bribes and that they could freely discuss and criticize the widespread practice of offering bribes to corrupt officials throughout the country. Tara was aware that such topics were not discussed with officials who accepted bribes, and that she was not regarded as a 'good' official both in government and business circles because of her intransigent attitude. Some business people were always on the lookout for the opportunity to slip Rs 500 or 1000 to some government official and reap the rewards. If there was an outcry about bribe-taking and corruption, it was only on the surface. Both givers and takers of bribes profited in this culture of corruption; what suffered harm was the credibility of the government and the public good. The worldly-wise lost no sleep over this state of affair; for them it was somebody else's problem.

Ratan offered bribes to officials and also cursed those who took bribes. Tara didn't like that. Ratan would frankly tell her, 'I can't operate my truck unless I pay the traffic police 500 rupees per truck every year and one rupee per month for every intersection the truck passes through. Otherwise the truck will be stopped for speeding or for overloading, or just to check the papers. All they have to do is to signal by hand. If I have to go to the police station, the whole day is wasted and I suffer a loss of forty or fifty rupees. Then the truck owner will have to appear in court repeatedly to answer the charges. Who can afford to take such losses? We cough up the money because we can't help it. What's unfair in that?'

Tara had no sympathy for Ratan. She would say, 'Of course it's unfair. You park trucks in crowded bazaars, block the road needlessly and hassle everyone. You overload trucks and that causes accidents. Your fellow truck owners use footpaths for loading and unloading goods as if the footpath belonged to them. I have seen with my own eyes people trip and fall over and get hurt because of blocked footpaths. Have you no concern for them?'

Mathur was increasingly dissatisfied with the administration's laxity and its policies. He would say, 'People who do not take advantage of their position and opportunity to exploit the situation are exceptions. The public can see police constables, office peons and clerks taking bribes. I'd like to ask who in the government, from the very top to the very bottom, is not exploiting the system to their advantage? If people take bribes, they do it for the sake of their children and family. Name me one person in the government whose children and family are not profited by his job. Government employees and officials will only follow the example of their superiors. There are rules and regulations against government officials accepting gifts and freebies. The officials are not so stupid that they can't find a loophole in the law. It's the little people who suffer most from ever-increasing taxes and galloping inflation. The government reports show increase in productivity, but it's the prices that go up instead. I don't see any benefit of all this planning, except hundreds of millions of rupees of public money finding its way into the coffers of big capitalists and the pockets of government officials. Go and have a look around the Bhakra Nangal hydroelectric project. Cement purchased by the state for building the dam has been used to build private houses up to a 50–60 mile radius of the dam. The cement factories make a killing, the contractors clean up and the government officials line their pockets, the real loser is the taxpayer. Sand is supplied in the name of cement. The cost is estimated at one rupee for something that would cost four annas, and three-fourths of the allotted funds is skimmed off by racketeers. Who stands to lose when dams built with sand instead of cement will begin to crumble? Neither the contractors nor the government engineers will come forward to accept the responsibility.'

Narottam had been transferred to the Seetalpur Ordnance Factory as works manager. He came to meet Tara whenever he was in Delhi. He was constantly perturbed by the attempts to hide bad management and inefficiency in the factory. He was beginning to realize that the refusal to join his father's business so as to earn an honest living was nothing but chasing a mirage. Once, during the discussion on the sad state of affairs, he said, 'Who can be called an honest person? Are the MLAs who make laws honest? Do you suppose that they spend twenty or twenty-five thousand rupees out of their pockets to contest elections only because they want to serve the country? My uncle tells a story about the MLA representing his village. The MLA had spent time in prison for taking part in the nationalist movement, no doubt about it. He owned fourteen bighas of land and a small, dilapidated family house. He applied for and got a government loan from Lucknow for installing a cooperative tube well or you can say that the District Congress Committee got him the loan. He took another loan for Rs 5,000 from my uncle against his agricultural land. Then he contested the state assembly elections on Congress ticket, and won. In the next three years and a half, he built two new brick houses, and now owns sixty bighas of land. Whatever the *thanedar*, the local police chief is paid in bribes, the MLA takes 50 per cent of it. He operates as a self-appointed agent to get any work done in the government offices. He occasionally sends a message to my uncle, 'Lala, send a can of desi ghee to my house.' My uncle dare not ask for payment, so he consoles himself by saying *jai ramji* to the MLA and hopes that in troubled times the MLA may prove useful to him.'

Such grumblings about the system irritated Tara, but she could see that the space around the shops below her flat was in a state of chaos. Owners of the furniture store and the restaurant had encroached on the footpath in front of their shops. The owner of the general store had put two display cases outside the shop for a better 'show' of goods. The traffic police constables turned a blind eye to the encroachments upon receiving bribes of two or four rupees. The encroachments caused inconvenience to the residents of the flats. Talwar Sahib and Tara had problem in parking their vehicles. Everyone grumbled, but no one spoke out loud—why should one pick a quarrel with the neighbours? Tara too felt irritated, but kept quiet. She thought, 'When the public is not prepared to raise their voice in protest, what can the government do?'

Tara told Mercy what she thought one day when Mercy began to complain about a lack of civic sense. Mercy snapped back, 'Sure, why would you find fault with the government. You've changed your tune since you became a government official.'

Gill was also present. He had a different viewpoint, 'People lacking the courage to raise their voice against corruption and disorder is certainly not an indicator of good governance and respect for the rule of law.'

Tara did not reply to Mercy, but said to Gill, 'And whose fault it is if the public quietly accepts political corruption and profiteering so that they may also have the opportunity to take advantage of the system?'

Nath was well acquainted with the workings of market economy, free trade and the private sector. He knew that in the private sector, industrialists and businessmen inflated the cost of production and management to show a lower margin of profit in order to save on income tax. In his view there was no reason that industrial production in the public sector could not be profitable and successful and that it should be able to provide investment for economic growth.

In Lahore, Kalicharan Kaul had been among the students who held Nath in high regard. He had continued to meet Nath in Delhi. Although Kaul had an MA degree, he had not tried to find a job in Lahore and had lived off the rental income from his family property. After the Partition he had been forced to look for work. He had been selected for the IAS in 1948, and was posted in the Department of Income Tax. While working for the government, he had passed the exam to qualify as a chartered auditor. After a while he had left his job, opened his own office and had begun to work as a tax lawyer and consultant. His past experience as an official of the Department of Income Tax had proven to be very useful. He now had another accountant and five clerks on the staff. His job was to audit and verify business accounts, and the accounts verified by him as a licensed auditor were legally accepted to be correct.

Kaul was particularly enthusiastic about exposing the weaknesses of arguments against nationalization and state ownership of large industries. Without caring about what others thought, he would say, 'Why would some rich industrialist pay me three or four thousand rupees if I didn't save three or four lakhs for him? My profession is lawful and I have a licence to practise it.' He would name names, 'This person has hired several retired income tax commissioners as consultants and pays each one of them over 35,000 rupees per year. Imagine how much tax he must be saving if he can afford to pay three or four lakh every year to accountants to cook his books. All this is done lawfully and with bravado. Such underhand practices won't be possible in the state-owned industries.'

Mathur or Gill would answer even in the presence of Nath, 'Then the public sector officials who regulate and control the industrial production will be prone to accepting kickbacks.'

'How could they possibly accept kickbacks?' Kaul would protest. 'If the officials have to account for their wealth and if there are no ways they can use their ill-gotten gains, how would they hide their unlawfully earned money? If you work at a sweet maker's shop, how many sweets can you eat on the sly?'

Gill said, 'You are dreaming of a system based on socialism. The ministers of the Congress government are trying to reassure the public that their policy of a socialistic pattern of society will save the country from socialist totalitarianism.'

'They can say what they want. Public ownership and nationalization of industries is a must if we want to increase industrial output by using our country's assets and resources. Otherwise, all plans are bound to fail.'

After listening to such discussions Tara would think, 'Why can't people have faith in the future? Why do they think that everything is doomed to failure right from the start?'

Dr Solis and Nath, more than anyone else, realized that the policy of industrial production under the public sector would be more advantageous to the country. But their personal views and beliefs were not enough and a definite working plan and detailed data were needed to convince the government circles that such a policy was feasible. Nath's section was working to prepare the plan and to collect the data. His office had not shifted to the hills in the summer that year because his staff had to work closely with other government departments. Moreover, the Prime Minister did not approve of the British custom of moving government offices and officials to the hills in summer.

Chaddha thought that the data researched and collected by him to show the efficacy of the public sector was more reliable. He had promised to give Nath all that data by the evening of 15 July. Chaddha had enlisted the help of many of his friends in compiling the data. Tara had also been asked because she was good at maths. She had worked until midnight several times sitting under the fan in muggy weather. She had also promised to drive Chaddha and his comrades to meet Nath on the fifteenth. On that evening, Chaddha went with Narottam and Tara took Gill and Kanak with her. Nath was not home when they reached his place, but arrived after an hour.

Nath apologized for his absence from home, 'I was stuck in an awkward situation.'

The Prime Minister had performed the inauguration ceremony of the Indian Anthropological Society that afternoon. Dr Solis was a member of the organizing committee, and had invited Nath to the function.

Nath was peeved, 'Now hear this. When the president of the Welcome Committee invited the Prime Minister to inaugurate the council, he referred to him as "our scientist Prime Minister". The Prime Minister spoke for over an hour on the problems of population growth and food shortage. As is his habit, he said everything three times. It was difficult to swallow what he said. Why did he speak on a subject if he did not know anything about it?

'When Dr Solis was asked to speak, he could not help but say, "It would be a bit rash to formulate government policy on the basis of the views expressed by the Prime Minister on population growth and food production. His ideas lend a fresh perspective to the subject, but are not based on scientific theories."

'The Prime Minister said heatedly, "You all have become such specialists in your area that you only think mechanically. You should be broad-minded about scientific ideas and have a pragmatic approach to the problems."'

Chaddha was listening attentively, temple resting on his hand. He blinked once, and asked, 'What was it that the Prime Minister wanted to say? He shouldn't have agreed to inaugurate a symposium on a scientific topic.'

'It's others who ask him to do so,' Tara said.

Gill joined in, 'People invite him to such events because they know that the Prime Minister feels flattered.' Turning towards Nath, he said, 'Doctor sahib, does the Prime Minister really think himself to be a scientist? Didn't he object to his being called a "scientist"?'

Tara spoke up before Nath could, 'An honorary doctor of science degree was conferred on the Prime Minister by the University of Delhi. How is he to blame?'

'Does the Prime Minster not know that he is not a scientist but a politician?' Kanak said. 'To accept such a degree is to encourage sycophantic behaviour.'

'You blind the Prime Minister with flattery and he would believe anything you tell him,' Gill said. 'When I was living in Lucknow, if the sweeper did not show up in the morning or if the gali's open drains and gutters were not cleaned, we'd know that the Prime Minister was visiting. All the cleaning personnel would be put to cleaning the roads in welcome of the Prime Minister. The Prime Minister should see the roads clean at the expense of ordinary people enduring the stench of blocked drains. The mantra of the bureaucracy is: Keep your superior happy.'

Kanak said, 'The government officials are only concerned with filing their reports and keeping the files complete. If the public sector worked along these lines, then?'

Chaddha expressed his concern, 'Without union representation in organizational decision making ...'

'One second,' Nath gestured to indicate that he wanted to say something. He had not been able to get a word in edgeways. He called Bhoop Singh over and told him to bring tea, and said, 'I'd have been delayed even more had I stayed there for tea.'

'I'll see to tea,' Tara said, and went inside with Bhoop Singh.

While Tara boiled water in the electric kettle and helped Bhoop Singh to make tea, she could hear Narottam speaking in an agitated voice in the living room. She knew that he was talking about the Seetalpur factory. Narottam was in Delhi on leave, and had already told Tara about an incident that was troubling him. He often quarrelled with Chaddha on the subject of the high-handedness of labour unions, and wanted to discuss the subject with Nath. Narottam had the belief that allowing union representatives to to be a part of the factory management would be very detrimental to the national interest.

When Tara came back with Bhoop Singh carrying tea, Narottam was saying, 'I wrote a note to the superintendent that for making a groove in a sprocket, it wasn't necessary to score it twice. The superintendent already knew that. If the two-score method was dropped, the daily wage would have been cut by one hour. The union gave notice to strike. The superintendent lost his nerve. He was afraid that he'd be criticized for the way he handled the crisis. He asked me to write in my report that the lathes at our factory were older than the lathes at the Babora factory and did not work as precisely. Therefore, the second score was needed. I didn't agree to that. The superintendent put off the order to cut the daily wage, and wrote to the director general a confidential note about the looming strike. The director general "suggested" over the phone that a strike should be avoided at all costs. Why wasn't it made clear to him that workers oppose every measure to reduce the wages in order to cut the cost. The workers would never settle for eight workers doing the work of ten.'

'No one wants to be unemployed,' Gill cut in. 'The workers should have a guarantee that they'd be given some other job.'

'They have the guarantee, but they don't want to be transferred to any other factory. They always put their convenience first. They goof up at work half the time. The supervisor is afraid to object. If he does, he gets a thrashing. Any disciplinary action against a worker means strike! The management knows that government won't stand behind them in case of workers going on strike. A strike bursts the bubble of popularity of the government, so the management has to cover up the affair and report that everything is well under control. They are only interested in drawing their salaries, and their only concern is keeping their superiors happy. To me it feels like cheating the factory and I've failed the people and the country. I don't want any more of this.'

'That indeed amounts to defrauding the country. Why don't you inform the newspapers about it?' Kanak asked.

'Don't even think of doing like that,' Narottam warned. 'It's an official secret. But it shows that be it the the workers or the bureaucracy or the minister—nobody cares about the country. The workers want to do the least possible amount of work but receive as much wage as possible. The bureaucrats report to the ministry that all's well so that they can retain their jobs. The ministers have to contest the next election and therefore can't afford to antagonize the public.'

Chaddha gave a detailed explanation that the workers have a negative attitude because they feel oppressed by a ruthless management. Only employee representation on management boards and their participation in decision making can result in workers having a responsible attitude.

Narottam was not willing to put his trust in workers and kept on repeating, 'That is never going to work .'

'What is it that you want? Should labour unions be abolished?' Nath interrupted him.

'That can't be done in a democracy. The only course is dictatorship,' Narottam said in a firm voice.

'You want the Prime Minister to be a dictator?'

'At the moment he's the only trustworthy person. He's the only one who can save the country from regressing.'

'And what if he's surrounded by those who suck up to him and blind him with flattery?'

'Isn't he already?'

Tara had looked at her watch several times. The discussion bored her. She had heard all this not once but hundreds of times before. Endless discussion, no solution. She waited for the chance, then said, 'Doctor sahib, may we take your leave?'

Tara had been unable to comprehend why she had to suffer so helplessly, so she had explained it to herself as a sardonic twist of fate. The sense of achievement and deep contentment she had felt during the past seven years had given her a new self-confidence. She had become sure of herself and her ability to handle different situations, but then something happened that left her feeling powerless before circumstances. Purandei had become ill after she got drenched in rain and had caught a cold last August on her way back from the Hanuman temple on the Queens's Road. Her condition had deteriorated steadily.

Problem and worry does not come alone but in multiples. The same happened with Tara.

On a Sunday afternoon in May, Khem Singh, the domestic servant of Tara's neighbour Talwar came to see her with Parsu, and sat down on the floor before Tara, his palms joined respectfully. He said, 'Sarkar, I have a request.'

Khem Singh made a request on behalf of domestic servants of the neighbourhood, 'Huzoor, you're the only big government official here. Huzoor, only you can do us justice. We can only appeal to you. Who else will listen to us? Huzoor, the servants in the houses of government officials in New Delhi get four hours time off every day. They also get one evening free every week. In the embassies servants are off duty on Sundays. The employees in the restaurant below have afternoons free. Sarkar, we are human beings, we can have chores of our own. Huzoor, we should be given some rest time.'

Tara realized the serious implications of Khem Singh's request and his apparently polite demand for his rights. 'Today he was asking politely;

after a few days he and others will threaten to go on strike.' In Delhi the behaviour of domestic servants towards their employers was changing. The white-collar middle class felt uneasy about the servants' attitude and demands for higher wages. Tara was paying a greenhorn like Parsu Rs 18 every month, meals and clothing. Parsu might have been a little dense, but he well understood that he had been a domestic servant longer than Khem Singh. Therefore, if Khem Singh got twenty rupees per month, so should he. Parsu also knew that there was no dearth of job opportunities in Delhi, and that he'd probably get more money in a new job. Sure, he was quite happy working for Tara bibiji. He felt obliged to her for spending money on his treatment when he had fallen sick, but how long could he go on suffering a loss of two rupees every month?

Although Tara had never hired a servant for herself before 1952, she was aware of the change in servants' attitudes. She knew that Mercy had hired Chimmo at twelve rupees per month and free meals. The servants in the houses of Dr Prabhu Dayal, Ghaista Ram and Dewanchand, her neighbours in Lahore, had been paid monthly salaries of eight or ten, at the most twelve rupees. Those servants used to work, without a squeak of complaint, from before their masters woke up in the morning until after their masters had gone to bed. The question of domestic servants receiving luxuries such as time off and a day's weekly leave never arose.

Tara also knew the reason for the change in their attitude. Nath had twice hired servants at Rs 25 and 30 per month, but both proved to be unsatisfactory. Bhoop Singh would get irritated with them and grumble, 'These low-born have been spoiled rotten. They used to come to the plains from their homes in the hills to look for work, or starve. These days they have no shortage of work in the hills. Government offices are opening everywhere. If not offices, some road is being built here or there. They can easily earn Rs 1.25 or 1.50 daily. Now those who come here are just good-for-nothings who want to get paid without working for it. On top of that they steal from their employers. Bite the hand that feeds them. Shameless bums.'

Tara thought, 'Khem Singh came to plead with me probably because I had got him the job through Durga Pande. Still, he has no business speaking to me on behalf of Parsu or asking me to tell my neighbours how they should treat their servants!' Tara knew very well how her neighbours would feel about this matter.

Tara said to Khem Singh, 'If Parsu wants to say anything, he can do it himself. Why are you pleading his case? If you have any complaints, tell Talwar Sahib about it.'

Inspite of Tara's curtness, Khem Singh said politely, 'Huzoor, Parsu is a bit simple. He asked me to talk to you bibiji.'

'No, you don't worry about Parsu. And don't bother to speak for him. If you have any problem, speak with Talwar Sahib or tayeeji. I've nothing to do with all this. And what's troubling Parsu? I leave for office at ten o'clock. He is free between twelve and five o'clock. He either sleeps all day or goofs around. You think I don't know?'

Khem Singh did not go away. He said with an ingratiating smile, 'Sarkar, how can anyone have difficulty at your place. Huzoor, you treat your servants like your children, but, sarkar, we are on duty all day. Huzoor, sometimes a person needs time for chores of his own.'

'If Parsu needs time off he can tell me. You may go.' Tara ended the conversation.

A couple of days later Parsu said hesitantly to Tara, his eyes downcast and fingers entwined as he scratched the heel of one foot with the toe of the other, 'Bibiji, all servants get a break until five in the afternoon. Buaji does not give me any time off.'

Tara did not want this conversation to drag on, so she said shortly, 'Don't talk rubbish. What do you do in the afternoons?'

'Bibiji, I had gone out for a while and buaji shouted at me.'

Tara said angrily, 'You've come to me to tell on buaji! Don't you know she doesn't keep well? Sometimes she even shouts at me. She's like our mother, treats you like her son. Didn't your mother ever shout at you? Don't be stupid.'

Tara said to Purandei, 'Give this *moya* some free time in the afternoon. We have to move with the times. He's at least trustworthy, hasn't stolen anything from us so far. If he quits it'll be a hassle for you.'

Purandei denied Parsu's allegations in a loud voice, 'He sleeps like a crocodile all afternoon. I send him to the bazaar to buy two annas worth of stuff and he returns in two hours. Disappears whenever he wants without telling me. I won't bother with him any more. He can goof around all he wants.'

Tara said sternly to Parsu, 'Behave yourself if you want to work here. Don't hassle buaji. Don't go out without telling her. If you have some

work of your own, you may go out between one and five o'clock, but
come back on time.'

Not even a week had gone by when tayee and Gurandei came to complain
to Tara, 'What harm have we done to you that you've caused this trouble
for us. Everybody's servant says that you've ordered that all servants will
get hours off every day.'

Tara protested, 'That is not correct. I didn't give any such assurance. I
have nothing to do with other people's servants, nor do I want to.' But her
explanation had no effect.

Both boy servants working at tayee's house as well as Gurandei's servant
Murli began to disappear between one and four o'clock. When questioned,
the servants would say simply, 'The secretary memsahib gives Parsu the
afternoon off. Servants get time off everywhere. We also want an afternoon
break.' The neighbourhood servants would get together in afternoons and
play cards or gamble with cowry shells for chips.

Tayee was annoyed with Tara and began to denigrate her, 'Why'd she
worry about her servant? Her household hardly needs any attention. She
throws her old bua some crumbs from her table and uses her like a slave.
Peons from office work at her home. She's happy when something bad
happens to others.'

Gurandei said harshly, 'If she says she didn't encourage Murli to ask for
time off, I'll call him here and let's see her deny that before him. Then I'll
deal with him.'

Tara was reluctant to defend herself or settle the matter in a meeting
with the servants. That would have meant her arguing and quarrelling with
the servants before her neighbours.

Gurandei stood on the first-floor landing and began to speak in a voice
that other neighbours could hear, 'If she wants to act snooty because of
her car and her government job, she can do it in her own house. We don't
live on handouts from her so she can't intimidate us. Why didn't she get
married until now? Wants no husband or children to worry over, but is
jealous of other's children and family. That's why she has so much money
but is still cursed by God to remain unmarried.'

Most of Tara's neighbours stopped talking with her for inciting their
servants to ask for a break in the afternoon.

Tara was beginning to regret her decision not to move to a new residence.
In 1953 she could have been allocated a newly built, four-room government

accommodation on Ferozeshah Road. To show their neighbourly concern at that time, the families living in her gali had asked Tara not to leave. Tara had been in two minds whether she'd be able to manage a bigger flat and the ensuing lifestyle. The rent would have been deducted in proportion to her salary. She would have needed to employ another servant. In the end it would have cost her an extra 100 rupees every month. Mr Siddhu, a deputy secretary in the ministry of finance, had implored her to please let him have that flat and she had continued to stay where she was. She was now sorry she hadn't moved at that time. She would have lived among cultured, well-behaved people, removed from the messy situation she now faced. She had also considered living in the Working Women's Hostel like Miss Haldar, but had given up the idea because it would have meant chucking Purandei out.

Tara felt there was no one who could give her succour. Sometimes Saroj came and told her what Tara's neighbours were talking about her, and then pour out all her troubles and problems of her family. That kind of talk was no consolation to Tara. It rather depressed her and made her feel she was on her own.

There were only a handful of people whom Tara could visit or who would come over to her flat. She now found Chaddha's endless political discussions and his constant criticism of government at Mercy's home dreary and repetitive. Tara was not prepared to accept that the government so far had not done anything or that everything could be accomplished in one day. Sheelo was more concerned than Mercy about getting Tara married. Convinced that Tara had not been able to forget Asad, she would begin to talk about him with a solemn face in a confidential tone. Tara had told her not to talk about Asad, but Sheelo couldn't help commiserate and say to Tara, 'So what if he's married to someone else?'

Going to visit Kanchan meant having to put up with the always grumpy Mrs Agarwal. Mrs Agarwal was sure that Tara had connived to get Narottam married beneath his station. If she went to see Dr Shyama, she would offer to take Tara to the club or some bridge party or would begin her litany of complaints against Mrs De.

When Tara got bored with the rest of her friends and fed up with being alone with Purandei at home, she would go to visit Prabha Saxena in the evening.

Prabha Saxena was now a deputy secretary in the ministry of education. She was known in the secretariat for her administrative ability and air of quiet authority, and her quickness of mind and objectivity. Tara, because of her closeness to Prabha, had come to learn her inner thoughts and details of her personal life over time. Just as Rawat had been Tara's mentor, Prabha too had taken care of Tara and stood by her. Rawat, not one to mince words, had noticed Prabha's fondness for Tara and had joked one day in the club by parodying a Sanskrit shloka, 'Tara's comeliness arouses masculine feelings in Miss Saxena.'

Tara was probably the only person Prabha could open her heart to. At times, to lighten her own mood, Prabha would tell Tara about her past affairs. Tara thought her stories were another version of Dr Shyama's tales. She knew Prabha didn't get married for the sake of her career in the civil service, but lately she had become increasingly disillusioned with her success and the recognition. Now when Prabha was close to retirement, worries about the future were constantly on her mind. She would take a deep breath and say, 'Girl, don't you make the same mistake as I did. Look at my life. I'll leave whatever possessions and money I have to some nephew or niece, but that won't make them my flesh and blood. I've done all I could do in this life and from now on its downhill for me. When I think back over the past years I feel as if I wasted my chances to fulfil my womanhood. Nothing in the world matters more than having the sense of satisfaction that comes from caring for a child you gave birth to. No one asserted his right over me or called me his own, I never had a tiff with anyone or cried for anyone, never cooked for anyone and waited for anyone to come home.'

Tara felt an unease listening to Prabha's musings. It brought a frightening picture of her past life to her mind, she was standing alone surrounded by a ghostly silence in a desolate place, and she wanted to scream, 'One has to live the life one is fated to live. It can't be helped if one has a lonely life. Am I also not alone! It's natural for us to have desires and wishes, but what's the point of feeling sorry for oneself if they remain unfulfilled.' Tara felt something clutch at her heart whenever she had such thoughts.

The weather was continually unpleasant in September. Either it rained, making it difficult to go out because of the mud in the streets or the air was so still that it felt hot and closed and very inconvenient. It was hard to spend all day reading, especially reading without any purpose. Whom could Tara pay a visit to? She didn't want to listen once again to same discussion on the same subjects, but if she stayed home alone, all her worries and problems would niggle at her mind. One way of taking her mind off her troubles was to go for a long drive, or to busy herself in doing trivial, everyday things. At times she'd put on make-up and dress up in fine clothes. Looking pretty gave her a good feeling. Then she'd go and spend some time among people in a bazaar. She'd buy an expensive sari or something similar to reassure herself, 'I feel contented. I can do anything I want. What more can I want from life?' Spending money made her feel good about herself.

Dressing well also had its problems. She would invite stares from people, or remarks would be called out at her. When the Punjabi owner of the furniture store would see her dressed nicely, he would pass a double entendre to the shop owner next door, 'Would you like some Black and White?'

The second shop owner would say, 'Bhai, who can afford that kind of high class stuff. I just look and get my fix.'

Tara understood what they meant. She often wore clothes that were black and white, and her car was also black and white. In Connaught Place, she would hear behind her back, 'Hey, that same *maal* is here.' Tara would feel like laughing rather than get angry at such Romeos, but would grit her teeth to hide her smile. It was better not to give anybody ideas.

That evening she was again alone at home. She got dressed in an expensive white georgette sari. She had thought of going into a movie theatre without checking out what was playing. Then she had a better idea. She would go to Karol Bagh and get Sheelo's children, and Jaya from Faiz Bazaar, and treat them to ice cream. She loved to play with children and buy toys for them. As she combed her hair and tied them carefully into a bun, she mulled over whether to go first to Karol Bagh or to Faiz Bazaar. She was adding a hundred rupee note to the cash in her purse when she heard someone knock at the door to her flat.

'Who could come at this time?' Tara thought irritably as she called out to Parsu to check. Despite feeling lonely, she did not want any one visitor to spoil her planned evening of fun.

'Doctor *shaab*,' Parsu came back and reported.

It was Nath. Tara's irritation was washed away. She went quickly to the living room. Nath was switching on the ceiling fan.

Tara was surprised to see Nath wearing a light grey woollen shirt and grey wool trousers in the muggy heat. He was drenched with perspiration.

'Is Doctor sahib feeling well,' she thought anxiously. She had never seen him wear anything but white trousers and a white bush-shirt in the summer.

'You are going out?' Nath asked.

'No, no. Please sit. I thought I'd go out because I was bored. Might have gone towards your bungalow. Why are you wearing these woollens?'

'How can I explain it,' Nath said, taking a chair. 'Bhoop Singh has created quite a problem for me. I don't know whether he used to take my clothes to a laundry or had them laundered by a dhobi. He didn't leave behind any laundry receipt. Yesterday and the day before I found shirts and trousers in an almirah. I thought he may have put some clothes in storage. I checked this morning and found none. I ordered four cotton trousers at a shop in the morning on my way to the office. The man promised to have them ready by four o'clock, but they were not ready even at seven. I'll have to go back at eight. I bought two ready-made bush-shirts. Bhoop Singh didn't come to the office. I don't know where he is.'

'Where could he go?' Tara asked with concern.

'You don't know?' Nath asked. 'Didn't you read the newspaper? Don't you know about the Class IV government employees' movement?'

'Yes, I read about it in the newspaper, but Bhoop Singh was living at your bungalow of his own free will,' Tara said with surprise. 'He could've told you in advance if he didn't want to live there any more. You should've telephoned me that you had no servant.'

The Central Secretariat Peon Union had passed a resolution: Peons are government employees. They will not work at any official's residence. It's not a part of their job to clean house, wash motor car, take official's children to school or for walk, bring lunch from the official's home to the office, fetch them tea, cigarettes or paan, or pour them a glass of water from the surahi. Such work is demeaning to them. Their job is to do officially assigned work: dust the office, fill up the surahi in the sahib's office, and carry the files or messages from one place to another. Making peons do domestic servants' work is to debase them and is against regulations. The Union can cite the pertinent articles and rules in the official manual in support of their demand.

The officials were affronted by the attitude of peons. They agreed on peons not cleaning the car, but deemed that the refusal to get lunch from home or tea from the canteen or to pour a glass of water as impertinent behaviour. Tara had the same opinion. She had never asked her peon to work at her home, but now and then sent him to bring her tea or asked him to draw a glass of water from the surahi placed on a low three-legged stool in her office. For such chores her peon would get the customary baksheesh of two rupees at Diwali, Dussehra and Holi festivals. Last year Durga Pande had put his palms together and pleaded with her for a loan of thirty rupees to buy medicine for his wife. That loan was still unpaid.

On the day Tara had read the news, she had rung the bell at three o'clock to call Durga Pande to her office to make clear her stand on this issue. Without looking at him she had ordered, 'Ask the canteen waiter to bring tea.' She had not asked him as usual to get her tea.

Tara had rung again after ten minutes to remind the peon, 'Go to the canteen and remind the waiter to bring tea.'

Durga Pande had pleaded with his palms together, 'Huzoor mataji, please don't blame me. Huzoor, I have never objected even to cleaning the shoes of officer sahibs. Huzoor, why put on airs if I have to do a job. Recently some people who can read English have been recruited and they have begun to quote all kinds of rules and regulations. Mataji, will it taint my caste if I got your tea? It's always been my job. But if I do that now, these young hotheads will spit on me, they'll insult me.'

Tara's anger subsided. She thought, what made a person act so meekly? What was wrong if a person resisted attempts to make him act so? She remembered what Sita used to say about the senior dispatcher in her office. She had heard similar complaints from a couple of girls who worked in other offices. It does not take long for a person to give in to the circumstances.

Nath explained that Bhoop Singh had argued with his union representatives that staying at Nath's bungalow was his own decision and that he was capable of deciding for himself what was good or bad for him. He didn't want anyone to intervene on his behalf. Besides he'd soon stop working because he was going to retire in seven months' time. He said he'd rather give up his job than stop serving a kind and generous boss like Nath.

Two days previously Nath had found a crowd milling around the entrance to his bungalow on reaching home at 6.30 in the afternoon. About thirty peons had gathered outside the gate and Bhoop Singh had been standing defiantly in the veranda.

Nath had asked nervously, 'What's the matter?'

Bhoop Sigh's defiance had irked the union representatives. After the secretariat had closed, Basant Lal, a militant union official, had gone with union members to Nath's bungalow.

A young peon had come forward boldly and explained, 'Sir, we won't do anything that will disturb the peace. We'll stay outside the bungalow. If some peon goes against our union's decision and continues to work at the home of his boss, we'll try to convince him to stop doing that. It's a prestige issue for our class.'

'That's all right. I don't want any peon to work in my home against the decision of the union,' Nath had replied.

The same peon had said, 'Excuse me, sir. Then why does Bhoop Singh stay overnight at the bungalow? We know that he cooks and washes the dishes and does other work.' Nath had conceded, 'Bhoop Singh is not under any pressure to work here. He's been doing so of his own free will, for his own benefit. If the union has any objection, he should stop.' Nath looked at Bhoop Singh and said, 'I don't want you to work here against your union's decision.'

Bhoop Singh had taken a deep breath and had looked at Nath aghast. He had turned and had gone to his room at the rear of the bungalow. He had returned in a few minutes with his steel trunk and bedding. He had put the bunch of house keys in front of Nath. He said a namaste without looking at Nath and had gone out of the bungalow without saying a word. The union workers had followed him, shouting, 'Inquilab zindabad!'

Gill had telephoned Nath at 9.30 in the evening from the Coffee House in Connaught Place. After inquiring about the incident at the bungalow, he had said that a journalist friend had told him that the news about the incident at Nath's bungalow would be published in the next day's edition of newspapers along with the union secretary's statement praising Nath.

Nath had very politely requested, 'Gill, please don't let this news get published. I can do without such fame.'

Gill had reassured him laughingly, 'I thought so, that's why I told you.'

Nath told Tara how impotent he had felt that he could not help his peon, 'I am very sorry for treating Bhoop Singh the way I did. I thought about it all night. How could I ask him to go against the union? The union's decision was justified and within the law. There are historical reasons why the union members have made it into an emotional and confrontational issue, but they are not fundamentally wrong.'

'Where do you eat your meals?' Tara asked worriedly.

'That's not a big problem,' Nath said, waving his hand in a dismissive gesture. 'You can get something to eat anywhere in Delhi. The problem is that my place hasn't been swept or dusted for three days. There's no place to seat a guest. Ask your peon or your servant to quickly get some help for me.'

Tara pursed her lips and said, pretending to be angry, 'Why didn't you telephone before and tell me about it?'

'Listen, did Puri come to see you?' Nath asked.

Tara was caught unawares by Nath's question. Unable to say anything, she only shook her head.

Nath gazed out of the window for a moment before speaking, 'The Advisory Committee met for the last time before the details of the Plan were officially announced. There were lunches and dinners everyday at some place or another for the Committee members. Vishwa Nath Sood from Punjab is also on the Committee. In his opinion, the time is not yet ripe to invest in the public sector. Sood spoke very little at the Committee meetings. Today at lunch he said that he wanted to speak with me at my residence. How could I have invited him with the state my place is in? I thought it'd better to go and see him where he was staying. He's at Chausia's. I came to your place from there. Puri was also with Sood. Didn't he have your address? But Kanak…well, whatever.' He lapsed into silence.

Tara said nothing, just looked away.

Nath shifted in his chair, 'What an odd bunch of people! And the way he keeps on talking despite his stutter… I mean Sood. Puri was just acting as his yes-man. I guess Sood must have discussed with Puri what they'll say to me. People dislike and criticize the way bureaucrats behave, but Sood's style is totally dictatorial. He acts just like some American boss running his business empire. He refused to listen to me and just rambled on between stuttering and saying "what's-its-name"! What's the logic of his argument? What kind of behaviour is that? Very strange man indeed.'

Tara gave Nath a questioning look.

Nath said, 'Sood said even with the promise of rapid industrial growth under the proposed Plan, who could be certain that it would be implemented? The need of the hour is a strong and effective Central government that could implement the Plan. The Plan looks good on paper, but what if some reactionary government got elected next time and cancelled the Plan calling it impractical and unrealistic? As it is, the

Congress party will lose the trust and the support of the most important section of the electorate if the Plan is put in operation before the elections. The majority of the electorate will take that simply as grounds for bringing in communism. The future of the Plan would be in danger if the Congress failed to come back in power. The decision to implement the Plan at this time will amount to political suicide for the Congress.

'Puri argued in support of Sood, "Vast amounts of capital that could be used for investment will disappear in an atmosphere of uncertainty about the future of the economy. Any totalitarian leanings in the government's policy will dry up the aid from the countries of the West. It'd be wiser to have a politically pragmatic perspective rather than force a policy based only on economic principles."

'Sood said to me by way of warning, "The first and foremost aim of any government plan should be to strengthen the hands of the Congress government."

'I said to Sood, "The Plan is not dependent on the outcome of the forthcoming elections. It's the politicians who can best predict political future. We formulated the Plan within the parameters laid down by the government. The Plan is about increasing industrial production under the public sector by using our national resources, something that cannot be done in a free-market economy and private sector in the present undeveloped state of our country. That I think is the present policy of the Congress government. The framework for the Plan was provided by the Prime Minister and the Cabinet. They were briefed from time to time on the broad outline of the Plan."

'Sood got angry and began to stutter, "The Prime Minister likes to build castles in the air. He meets with huge crowds of people at one time. But those people are of no use to us. Let him try to collect donations to the election fund from the crowds. He won't get even one thousand rupees from a crowd of one lakh people. The expenditure will be one crore for each state in the next elections. Will the Prime Minister be able to arrange those funds? It's all right to talk of socialistic patterns, but we must take into consideration its implications. He will give the Plan his blessings and then have nothing to do with it. How can the rest of us accept something that is unrealistic because we all will be responsible for the political fallout? You keep this in mind."

'Sood went on to talk about other things and said something rather odd. I was surprised as well as saddened because I think he did it on Puri's suggestion. Sood said, "You are an economics scholar. Your subject area involves study and research. You're wasting your time here, your rightful place is at the National Research Institute. You'll get a higher salary and have ample time and facility for research. After a year or two, the opportunity to become the vice chancellor of any university in Punjab may come your way." Sood was willing to make a promise to me.'

After a brief silence Tara took a deep breath, and said, 'There seems to be a web of intrigue and deception. I'm always scared what these people might do.'

Nath again said, 'Puri's attitude surprised me. When he stepped outside to see me off, he spoke with the same old familiarity, but was very businesslike in Sood's presence. I thought he might come to see you. But if he meant to, he should have come by now. They are going back to Punjab by the night train.'

'Doctor sahib, would you like me to serve dinner?' Tara said to change the subject.

'I'll have dinner, but let me first get my trousers from Connaught Place. The shops close at eight o'clock. I'll be back in ten minutes.' He went downstairs, leaving his briefcase and the bundle of clothes on a side table.

Tara went to the kitchen. Purandei said in a weak voice from where she lay on a charpoy, 'Doctor sahib's come? Let me get up and make a couple of chapattis for him.'

'No, bua. You don't have to get up. I'll manage. He'll be back in a while.'

Tara checked up on what Parsu had cooked and saw that chapattis had not been made. She said to Parsu, 'I'll cook the chapattis. You get one pao rabari and a bowl of meat from the downstairs restaurant. Then have your dinner and be ready to go with Doctor sahib to his bungalow.'

When they were having dinner, Nath again brought up the subject of Puri, 'I've met Kanak only a couple of times. I don't know the whole story, but I found her to be honest and straightforward. Something that Puri did or said must have hurt her deeply.'

Tara agreed with him, 'She's a brave and decent person. Her family was against her marriage to bhai, but she insisted on getting married at great personal sacrifice when he was so hard up. I guess something happened between them that distressed her very much. She had told me many things.'

Nath was about to pick up his briefcase and the bundle when Tara stopped him, 'Doctor sahib, take Parsu along with you. He will work at your place until we find another servant for you. He can cook a bit.'

Nath protested, 'What're you saying? How will you manage without him! Bua's sick. Tell your peon to find someone for me. Will you eat out every day? This is crazy.'

'No. Doctor sahib,' Tara said firmly. 'I've told Parsu to go with you. Bua's much better now.' She called Parsu over and handed Nath's things to him.

Since Parsu was away, Purandei took her bath in the morning and was going towards the kitchen holding on to doors and wall for support when Tara stopped her, 'No, you don't go into the kitchen. I've cooked khichari for both of us.'

Tara had gone into the kitchen after several days. She found that Parsu had not cleaned the kitchen properly. She thought, 'Men are not interested in keeping the house clean, they always try to get away with doing as little as possible. Wonder how things are at Doctor sahib's bungalow? How will Parsu manage alone? I'll leave work after lunch and go there to check on him and explain what's to be done.'

She left her office at three o'clock for Nath's bungalow. The gate of the bungalow was shut. She honked her horn twice. When no one came to open the gate, she knew Parsu must be sleeping. She got out, opened the gate and drove in. Parsu had closed all the doors without locking them and was sleeping in the living room on a durrie under the ceiling fan.

Tara checked every room. Parsu had done some hasty dusting, but the rooms still needed rigorous cleaning.

Tara woke up Parsu and got him going by pointing to what he had neglected to clean. She asked him to get the duster and the broom, and tightly wrapped and tucked in her aanchal so that it won't get in the way. She told Parsu to move the durries in the living room and found a layer of dust underneath. She got him to clean the cobwebs from the corners near the ceiling and wipe the walls down. She asked him to bring bucketfuls of water and wash the floor. Parsu said several times, 'Bibiji, please stop. Let me do it.'

Tara said, 'I'm showing you how to clean a house.'

While the living room floor was drying, she asked Parsu to start on Nath's office, and clean and tidy the kitchen after that. She wanted to finish the cleaning before Nath's return. She looked into the bathroom, and saw a couple of used towels and a bunch of dirty underwear lying on one side. There was no laundry soap. Tara sent Parsu to buy a box of detergent.

Tara went into the bedroom and saw that Nath had made an effort to straighten the bed sheets and cover them with a bedspread. The sheets were all crumpled, as was the khes and the durrie. When she bent down to move a small carpet that lay next to the bed, she saw a pile of discarded clothes under the bed. She pulled them out and found four trousers and four shirts. She gathered the clothes in her arms to put them in the almirah. She had touched a man's clothes after years.

Tara felt a strange sensation. She could smell the sharp smell of a man's perspiration on the clothes, but did not want to let go of the clothes. The smell was agreeable. 'These are Doctor sahib's clothes,' she thought. She touched them to her forehead reverently, and kept holding on to them. Then feeling embarrassed she thought, 'Hai, what stupid behaviour!'

It was nearing 5.15 when Tara finished tidying up. Parsu had not come back with the detergent, which worried her. She wanted to finish the rest of the work and leave before Nath came back. Her clothes and hair were full of dust. She did not want to face Nath in that condition.

Parsu came back at 5.30. Tara was nervous that Nath would be back before long. She placed a bucket under the water tap in the bathroom, added a large dose of detergent, and dumped the towels and the underwear into it. She said to Parsu, 'The sunshine will last only for a short time. I'll wash the clothes and you run and spread them out on the wall to dry. Take care that no one walks away with the clothes.'

Parsu spread the clothes out to dry, and was on his way back for the next lot when he heard Nath's voice, 'Paras Ram. Open the gate.'

Nath's car was at the bungalow's gate. Parsu ran to open the latch.

As he drove in, Nath noticed the clothes drying on the wall and commended Parsu, 'Wah, you're a hard-working young man. You did the laundry. Where did you get the soap from?'

'Huzoor, bibiji is doing the laundry. She bought the soap.'

Nath saw Tara's car in the portico. He parked behind her, and went inside quickly. He called, 'Tara, listen! What are you doing?'

Tara was in the bathroom. She had removed her sari and hung it on a peg so that it won't get wet. She was in her blouse and petticoat, wringing out the remaining laundry when she heard Nath calling. She felt that she'd die of shame and the clothes fell from her hands.

Nath called several times. Tara tried to quickly wrap her sari, but her hands were limp and clumsy.

Nath irritably asked over and over for her to come out. Tara opened the door when she was fully clothed.

Nath was standing in front of the door, brow furrowed in anger.

Tara turned her back shyly, and stood holding on to the frame of the bathroom door.

'What are you doing?'

Tara stood silently.

'I'm very sorry. Achcha, come away from the door,' Nath said in a gentler voice.

Tara did not look at him. She said with her head bowed, 'I won't speak to you.'

'What was the need to do all this?'

Tara continued standing with her back turned, scratching the doorframe with her nail.

'You come here!'

'I won't speak to you,' she said, feigning anger.

'At times you do things to an excess. Come here.'

'I don't want to speak to you.'

'Why?'

'Because you didn't telephone me!'

'But why did you do all this?'

Again silence.

At a loss what to do, Nath grabbed her elbow and pulled her away from the bathroom door.

Tara could not keep her footing when pulled by a strong and healthy man. She tried to hold herself back, but stumbled and fell into Nath's arms.

Never before in her life had Tara endured such emotional turmoil and anguish. In the past painful and traumatic things had happened when she was in a state of shock and was barely conscious. But the turmoil and agony she was undergoing now was happening when she was very much alive and her mental faculties sharp.

The tragedy that had struck the country and divided it into two parts was all but over, but the trauma she had suffered during that calamitous event had left a indelible mark on her. 'Whatever I suffered was in my fate, but how can I knowingly ruin someone else's life!' Sometimes she felt as if she was going through hell, at other times, seventh heaven. Both hell and heaven seemed to be pulling her in opposite directions and break her into pieces. And she wished that her body would break into thousands of pieces, and those pieces would blow away like dead leaves in a wind storm, and become dust under Nath's feet.

What Nath had said next was not totally unexpected, but on hearing his words she had merely bowed her head.

Nath, with much awkwardness and hesitation, had proposed to her, 'You had said that when the time comes, you'll let me decide whom you will marry. If you don't find me too old for you, would you agree to marry me?'

Later, when Nath was at her place they had sat facing each other, silent like two statues. Feeling awkward in the silence between them, he had asked tenderly, 'Won't you say anything?'

She had broken down and wept bitterly, then had gone to her bedroom to control herself. In trying to suppress her tears and to be able to answer Nath, she had not realized how much time had passed. Finally she had steadied her nerves and had come out of her room, only to find that Nath had left. She looked out of the window and saw that the lights had come out in the streets and in other houses.

Tara was mortified when she realized her impoliteness. She thought that she should telephone Nath immediately and ask for his forgiveness. The moment her hand touched the telephone, her eyes filled with tears. Afraid that she would not be able to talk coherently, she pulled back her hand.

At 10.30 she shut the doors of her living room with a firm resolve and dialled Nath's number. She clenched her lip between her teeth when tears again flowed down her face.

She said 'It's me, Tara' and had a hiccup, but managed to blurt out in the same breath, 'Forgive me, I am in no condition to marry anyone.'

Tara did not want to continue, but Nath quickly asked, 'What do you mean? Why do you say that?'

'I'm telling the truth. I am in an unfit condition. Please forgive me.' Although Tara tried to hide it, Nath knew she had been crying.

'Put the receiver down for now. We'll talk when I come to see you tomorrow.'

Tara went back to bed, covered her face with her aanchal, and wept. She wanted life to drain out of her body in the same way as the tears flowing out of her eyes.

Purandei was alarmed, 'What is wrong with this girl? Must be suffering from something very painful.' Tara didn't want to eat anything. When Purandei came again and again to ask her how she felt, Tara began to get increasingly irritated and shut the door to her bedroom.

The next day Tara was feeling so miserable that she had to take the day off. Her thoughts were continually in turmoil: What would she tell Doctor sahib? The only way to answer him was to be open and forthright.

Nath rang at eight o'clock on Sunday morning. He said tenderly in a voice filled with concern, 'Tara, can I come over if it's convenient for you? I am very anxious to hear you say yes.'

'Doctor sahib, mine won't be the right place to have a talk,' Tara replied in a clear and calm voice. 'I'll come to your place by nine or 9.30.'

Seven years ago, Tara used to think often about committing suicide. She would also condemn herself for the thought, 'Why should I kill myself like a coward. I won't be afraid to die when the time comes.' On her way to Nath's bungalow, she told herself, 'The time has come.' She tried to remain calm and in control.

Nath was shocked to see Tara. The constant smile on her lips was missing. Her face was devoid of any colour; she looked like a wax statue, like someone walking in her sleep.

Instead of sitting in the living room Nath took Tara to his office, sat her down, and took a chair next to her. Tara sat with her elbow on the armrest, chin cupped in her hand and eyes downcast.

He gave her time to settle down, then asked softly, 'What did you mean by saying you were unfit for marriage? Tell me now.'

Tara replied, eyes downcast, 'I have a disease.' She had prepared herself to say those words.

'What do you mean by disease? What disease?' Nath asked, two deep wrinkles forming at the bridge of his nose.

Tara continued to sit as before. She said without hesitation, 'I had told you about it. I've never lied to you, never hid anything from you.'

'What did you tell me?' Nath asked with a note of surprise.

'I had told you,' Tara said, swallowing hard, 'how I escaped the fire at my in-laws' house in Banni Hata,' she swallowed again, 'and a goonda abducted me from the gali.'

Nath was lost in thought. He took a deep breath, 'Is that possible? So many years have passed since then. How did you think of it now?'

Tara's head was bowed. She said haltingly, with a determined effort, 'I sometimes feel a slight irritation.'

'If it was so, why didn't you take medicine?'

'When I was living with Mercy in 1948, I didn't know what it was. I tried to explain to her, but she refused to believe me, "It's not possible. A virgin can't have that kind of infection. You must be mistaken." Everyone thought I was still a virgin. How could I explain my problem, how could I ask for its treatment and face humiliation and shame? Mercy had also said that such infections could remain dormant for years until they flare up one day. I had decided that I'd kill myself than face all that shame and humiliation.'

Tara had resolutely done what she had decided to do. She wanted to get up and leave, but her legs failed her. Whatever determination and courage she had been able to muster, she had used it up.

Nath stared silently at the floor. After a brief pause, he raised his eyes, looked at Tara and said with conviction, 'All right. A virgin cannot catch a certain disease, cannot ask for the treatment for that disease, but I have the right and an obligation to have my wife treated for any disease. Mrs Nath will get the medical treatment for...'

Tara's body trembled and her elbow slipped from the armrest.

Nath got up and put his arm round Tara's shoulder to steady her. She had hid her face in her aanchal. Nath's touch made her shiver uncontrollably.

Nath, thinking his touch had bothered Tara, removed his hand. After a moment's thought, he said with the same conviction, 'You won't ever have to live with me if you don't want to, but you will be Mrs Nath until you are completely cured. If you feel uneasy about getting treatment here in Delhi, it can be arranged for you to be treated in Bombay. If you don't want it there, I can take you to England or to Vienna. From this moment onwards, you are Mrs Nath. You had accepted me as your guardian, and this is the order of your guardian. We can have a court marriage or a traditional wedding next week or whenever you want.'

Nath sat down and was deep in thought for several minutes. Tara had not removed the aanchal from her face.

Nath asked, 'Is there anything you want to say?'

Tara rose to her feet and crumpled to the floor near Nath's feet. He stood up to help her. She wrapped her arms around Nath's knees, pressed her face to his legs and broke into sobs.

Chapter 18

AFTER SEVERAL DAYS' DELIBERATION, PANDIT GIRDHARILAL AGAIN WROTE A letter to Mahendra Nayyar in March 1956 about the complexities of Kanak's marital problems. Panditji summarized what Puri had written in his last letter, and conceded, 'Barkhurdar, Puri so far has been very patient, but it seems unlikely that Kanak would ever return to Jalandhar. Therefore, he cannot be faulted if he wants to go his own way. Kanak also does not want to stand in his way. We should accept what Puri wants as the will of God and agree to let them legally end their marriage. Since that is the only way out of the problem, it must be done with the utmost goodwill. Son, who else but you can carry out a responsibility as grave as this!'

Nayyar was sorry to see his father-in-law tormented by Kanak's problems to add to the hard times he had been facing since the Partition. Kanta had already told him about the reasons behind her sister's marital troubles. He also knew that Kanta had felt compelled to give her father a hint of the acrimony between Puri and Kanak. He came to the conclusion that Panditji had failed to convince Kanak to change her mind. Nayyar realized that Kanak could not be bound hand and foot and packed off against her will to Jalandhar, and that an annoyed Puri may have threatened to file for divorce. Panditji was feeling harassed and wanted this long and messy business to end, and Nayyar could guess how traumatic the whole affair was for Panditji.

Nayyar was concerned and he wrote back, 'If something cannot be helped, we must accept it as a vagary of fate, yet I'd like to consider different aspects of the problem and to meet Puri one more time. He at present is in Chandigarh to attend the session of the assembly. I shall speak to him after his return and write to you.'

Several conjectures formed in Nayyar's mind about Kanak's marital breakdown. He realized that Kanak would probably never return to Jalandhar and that Puri could not afford to ignore the possibility of his divorce and his second marriage causing a scandal. He had some inkling of the cowardly side of Puri's personality. At times Nayyar thought, 'Perhaps that girl, Urmila, suited Puri so well that he became obsessed with her and cannot forget her. Either he wants her back with him, or thinks of her in reaction to the disgust shown by Kanak at his boorish behaviour. In such a situation Puri may refuse to listen to reason. But what is the harm in sounding him out once?'

Nayyar was also angry with Kanak. She had seen Puri's duplicity with her own eyes, but still had agreed to get married to him. That was definitely foolish of her! Why did Puri agree at that time to throw Urmila out? Both Kanak and Puri are at fault and they should accept that they will have to learn to live with the consequences. How would they face people when the word gets out about the break-up of their marriage? A scandal will not only damage their reputation, it will bring shame on their families and relatives. One must learn to tolerate an incurable and lifelong disease.

Nayyar telephoned Puri on his return, 'Do you keep very busy? We should meet every once in a while. I got another letter from pitaji. I'd like to see you this evening or whenever it's convenient for you.'

When Puri was told about the letter from Delhi, he was genial and polite, 'Jijaji, I returned only four days ago. There was a huge backlog of work. You have a busy schedule, so I thought that I'll look you up and also get a bite to eat at your place. You know well how little furniture I have. The house looks as if it is haunted by ghosts.'

Nayyar's sympathetic attitude encouraged Puri to talk about himself frankly, 'Jijaji, how can I even think about getting a divorce. The stress of politics and public life can age a man in advance of his years. People begin to gossip if you so much as burp or sneeze. I'll lose face if the word got out that my wife does not live with me. I don't have to hide from you that malicious gossip about her blackens my name first. You know more than me that she can be stubborn, but I am ready to give in to her if I must. She knows that our house is in her name. I also have told her that I won't interfere any more in anything, and that we should maintain our prestige and reputation in the eyes of society.'

'My impression of Puri was correct,' Nayyar thought as he mulled over the reasons for Kanak's estrangement from Puri, and the best way to resolve their differences. 'How would she be able to live with Puri unless a solution to their problem was found?' Nayyar and Puri were of the same age group, their wives were sisters and they could frankly discuss even confidential matters. Avoiding Puri's eyes, Nayyar said in English, 'It sometimes becomes difficult to live with sexual incompatibility.'

Puri's face turned crimson with embarrassment when he caught the drift of what Nayyar had said. He too protested in English, 'I don't quite understand. We have a daughter. There would have been more children if we hadn't taken precautions.'

'No, no. I meant something else,' Nayyar said to reassure him. 'I was talking in general about the probable causes. You know people talk about such personal matters in a roundabout way. May be Kanta was guessing or it was only her imagination.' He continued dispassionately without looking at Puri, 'It's a psychological fact that some women for whatever reasons develop a fear of sex. They look normal and healthy, but they lack the sex drive. For them sexual intercourse becomes intolerable.'

Puri quietly waited for Nayyar to finish.

'Such reluctant and uncooperative behaviour from a wife would feel terribly unfair to any normal, healthy husband,' Nayyar continued, 'but what can the wife do if she's not her normal self, or if she's sick or in rather poor health. What I mean is that the husband should make some concessions on account of the wife's condition.'

Nayyar waited for Puri's reply. He had to twist facts in order to make Kanak and Puri reach a compromise.

Puri took a deep breath, 'Jijaji, I'm willing to leave it up to you to decide. I won't say no to anything you tell me to do. You know I've never considered her to be a chattel or a servant. Don't you already know my views on these matters? I've always left everything in her hands. I'm willing to suppress my feelings if that will make her feel better. I'll never ask her to go against her wishes. She should come and take charge of her house. I'm worried about my daughter more than anything else.' Puri's eyes filled with tears.

'You know, her absence from our home gets noticed more than my being away from home. I haven't told anyone here that she's doing a job in Delhi. All I say is that she's in Delhi for the sake of Jaya's education and because of her father's illness. That our main place of residence is Delhi and this house in Jalandhar is meant only as a stopover. I'll be spending most of my time away from home. The elections will be held in the beginning of 1957 and I won't have a moment free. You do what you think is right. I leave the decision to your discretion.'

What more could Nayyar expect from Puri? He was satisfied that he had found a way to resolve the problem. He felt sorry for both Kanak and Puri, but there was nothing else he could do.

Puri came several times to Nayyar's house. He would linger after dinner and discuss many things. He told Nayyar, 'Soodji has the fate of the Congress candidates for the next election in his hands. He's the Congress Parliamentary Board's head honcho. The Akali Dal has made an electoral pact with the Congress. The communists do not really matter. The Jana Sangh appeals mainly to small business owners and shopkeepers and that too only in the cities. The influential Jana Sangh leaders have lent their support to Soodji. The capitalists and big industrialist are nervous about the implications of the new Plan, but who else can they depend on if not the Congress? Even a scarecrow will get elected if Soodji told the public that it was a Congress candidate. The main question is who'll get the Congress ticket? To widen its sphere of influence, the Congress will also allow some independents to contest on the Congress ticket.'

Nayyar said in agreement, 'Yes, that's right. The Congress must widen its base.'

Although Nayyar had a different opinion, there was no point in arguing with Puri on this subject. That very morning he had overheard the ground-floor tenants complain about the present administration: Wheat was selling for two seers a rupee. One could get it at three rupees a seer from the control shop, but it was out of stock there. Nayyar knew that the owners of the control shops sold their quota of wheat in the black market, but nobody could bring them to book. Sood had asked all shops that received the government quota to make a donation of one thousand rupees to the Congress election fund. The shop owners had to cover their loss. What was the point of giving the Congress one thousand rupees if one could not make a profit of five thousand rupees? In Nayyar's view, the excesses and corrupt practices of a ring of people who had benefitted from their contacts with Sood had alienated the ordinary people.

Nayyar wrote to Pandit Girdharilal at the end of May to put Panditji's mind at rest, 'Probably Puri wrote to you in a fit of temper. I had a long talk with him. He's very conscious of his social status and afraid of what people would say that he won't do anything that would give him a bad name. He's willing to make any living arrangement which would be acceptable to Kanak. In view of Jaya's future and his social prestige, he has even agreed that Kanak may live alone in the house here.' In Nayyar's and also in Kanta's opinion it was proper for Kanak to live in her house in Jalandhar.

On reading Nayyar's letter, for two days Panditji sat hand on forehead or circled around the aangan brooding over Kanak's future. On the third day, when Kanak returned home, he said to her, 'Beta, there's a letter from Nayyar and Kanta between the pages of *Deewan-e-Ghalib*. You also read it.'

Kanak had brought some cantaloupes for Jaya. Jaya was clinging to her mother. Kanak fed her two cantaloupes and finding her body drenched in sweat, wanted to have a quick wash. But she could not suppress her curiosity and first read the letter. What she read made her sit down and catch her breath. She sat quietly for a few moments, and then had a wash. After dinner she could not bring herself to circle around the aangan with Panditji, and went to lie on her bed.

Panditji had seen Kanak read the letter. Next morning when she was going to work, he asked, 'Beta, have you read Kanta's letter? Where did you keep it? I'll reply to her letter today.'

Kanak dropped her eyes and said, 'Jijaji is wasting his time. I'll never go back to Jalandhar.'

What Panditji wrote in his second letter took Nayyar by surprise. He was piqued that Panditji didn't clarify his position in his first letter. He found himself in a quandary because his talk with Puri was based on a different premise.

Panditji had written, '*Chiranjeev*, may he have a long life, Puri has a lot of patience and that is praiseworthy, but he had previously agreed that the relationship between him and Kanak had become devoid of meaning and substance. It would now be sheer hypocrisy to pretend otherwise. You can deceive others, but you can't deceive yourself. It seems unlikely that the two would be able to bear each other and live together. Puri is willing to curb his feelings and make compromises in order to meet his obligations or for the sake of his prestige, but such an arrangement would be a complete sham and not amount to much. If life has gone out of a relationship, if feelings have died, the carcass of that relationship will rot and the putrid stench will permeate the lives of their families. To cover up or hide that stink will be harmful for one and all. What Puri had felt earlier about ending the meaningless relationship was spontaneous and exact. That is also what Kanak wants. In my view if they had made a mistake earlier by getting married, their mistake may be forgotten and something should be done to relieve their unremitting mental strain.'

Nayyar couldn't help notice the words 'That is also what Kanak wants.'

He said irritably to Kanta, 'If pitaji had made his position clear, I would have kept quiet and not talk over Kanni's problem with Puri. If anyone needs to be brought around, it's her. But what's the point if pitaji is in agreement with her!'

Before Nayyar could vent his spleen on his wife for her sister and father's vacillation, Kanta used a housewife's common sense to give a different explanation, 'Kanak can never behave sensibly. First she shamed the family by insisting on getting married to someone for stupid reasons, and now she wants to divorce him. I don't know what's wrong with pitaji. Maybe he's consumed by pity for his unlucky daughter. He wants her to live in peace, but how would she if that's not her fate? Will she get married again? What explanation will we give to Masterji, how will we show our face to him? Pitaji doesn't think about all this, all he cares for is Kanni. She's always been so cheeky! I'll write and ask her to come here, and have a talk with her. Why is she making a nuisance of herself?'

What more could Nayyar say? He stroked his eyebrows in a thoughtful silence, then said, 'Kanta, say what you want, but I have respect for your old man. What he's saying is fair and just. We're worried about losing face, but he has his daughter's best interests at heart. He was a revolutionary in his younger days, but his ideas are still revolutionary. Whenever you choose justice over self-interest and fear, it's the beginning of revolution. You cannot fight for justice and fairness without first being selfless and fearless.'

Her father's praise pleased Kanta, but she could not bring herself to support the rather impractical suggestion he had made. She shot back, 'So you want them to get a divorce? That's how you want to start revolution?'

'Well, what I can do and what I'll do depend on how much courage I have of my convictions,' Nayyar replied fingering his eyebrows. 'But one can have the right idea in head.'

Kanak was not at all enthusiastic about going to Jalandhar, even if it meant going only to her sister's home there. She didn't want to show her face or meet anyone in that city. Although it was difficult to take time off from her busy schedule in Delhi, she couldn't refuse when her sister and jija asked her to come to Jalandhar. Alienating them would have caused another problem for her. Kanak explained her predicament to Gill.

Gill said, 'Nayyar is a lawyer. He will think of arguments to support whatever he wants to say to you. The divorce law is a complicated business.

It'd be better if Puri started divorce proceedings.' Until now Gill took comfort from the fact that Puri wanted to divorce Kanak, but now there was a cause for concern. Kanak was going to Jalandhar to decide on her next move.

Since Kanak didn't know the exact date of her travel, she'd written to Kanta that she'd try to reach Jalandhar by the next Sunday. She could foresee having hectic discussions with her sister and jija, and had decided to leave Jaya behind despite Kanta's repeated asking to bring her along; besides, Panditji will worry and brood even more in Jaya's absence.

When Kanak got off the train at Jalandhar station, the June sun was dazzlingly bright. Kanak kept her eyes downcast as she came out of the railway station to avoid meeting anyone she knew, and took a rickshaw to Nayyar's house near the law courts. As fate would have it, someone called, 'Bibiji, namaste,' when the rickshaw was going past the intersection of Chahar Bagh.

It was Chaila. He got off his bicycle when he saw Kanak, with a beaming smile on his face. Then he got back on and began to cycle next to the rickshaw as he explained that Puri had asked him to take a letter to Mehraji's house. He was surprised that Babli was not with her mother, to which Kanak had no answer.

When Kanak's rickshaw took the road to Nayyar's house, Chaila warned the driver, 'Where're you going? Go to Model Town. '

Kanak had to explain, 'I'll go first to my sister's house.'

Chaila thought that Kanak had brought something for Kanta from Delhi, and that she would go to her own home after meeting her sister. He pedalled rapidly towards Model Town to give the news to Puri.

Kanak was meeting her jija, Nano and Dheeru after two years. She hugged and kissed the children, had a light-hearted banter with Nayyar and filled her sister in on news about Jaya and pitaji. The excitement of Kanak's arrival was not yet over when the telephone rang. Nano ran into an inner room to answer it. She called out to her daddy.

Nayyar returned after answering the phone with a worried expression on his face, 'How did Puri come to know that you were here?'

'I met that idiot Chaila on the way.'

'Really? That means the approach I had in mind to talk to him has gone completely haywire. Puri asked why he was not told about your coming here. I had to say that you had not told us either, and that you had arrived this morning.'

'I don't want to talk to him,' Kanak said, eyes downcast.

'But who am I to tell him that he can't meet his wife or he can't talk with her. You don't understand the legal implications of saying that. He's coming to see you right now.'

'You should've asked me first.'

'How's that possible? How could I tell him that I'll have to take his wife's permission?'

Kanta, standing close by, said, 'It'd have been better if we'd first discussed the matter among ourselves.'

'That's what I'd planned,' Nayyar admitted, 'but how could I say no to him? He'd have thought that I was being difficult.' He turned towards Kanak, 'Listen, Kanni, we both would like to ask you not to spoil everything.'

'What do you mean by spoil? Everything's been decided. Pitaji already wrote to you about that.'

Nayyar tried to soothe her, 'Yes, pitaji did write about that, but Puri does not want to divorce you. He'll think that pitaji and we are pushing you to divorce him. You should broach the subject yourself. Ask him to give reasons for his decision, and tell him yours. He should at least have some chance to have his say. You decide once you've heard his side of the story. He'll probably arrive in a few minutes. He's got a car. Whatever other shortcomings Puri might have, he really loves you. It's also the question of Jaya's future. Talk to him with restraint, don't shoo him away. Kanni, we both request you that whatever you want to say to him, say it politely.'

'Kanni, we want a compromise ...' Kanta was saying when they heard footsteps in the stairs. She kept quiet.

Puri came in without knocking. He was dressed in clothes of snow-white khadi.

'Come! Come!' Nayyar welcomed him warmly. 'You gave us no time to telephone and tell you. We hadn't recovered from the surprise of her showing up unexpectedly when you rang.'

'It came as a surprise to us, why should he be surprised?' Kanta said lightly. 'Her heart must have telegraphed his heart that she was arriving. And for all we know, she sent him the news and came here first so that he may come with the car to take her home.'

Puri gave her a thin smile.

Kanak sat with her head bowed.

'Let's have tea now. Kanni told us to wait for you,' Nayyar said, giving

Puri's shoulder a playful whack. 'What's new?' He could not think of anything appropriate to say.

Puri wiped the sweat off his brow with a handkerchief, 'The sun gets scorching so early in the morning.'

Nayyar replied that at night it was so hot they could not sleep on their roof without an electric fan.

Kanta left the room, grumbling Nano would be late for school. Nayyar sat for a couple of more minutes, 'The hot spell will last for another two weeks. The monsoon clouds have only reached Bombay. The communists will now complain that the Americans have unsettled the weather by testing hydrogen bombs.'

Nayyar said when the servant brought tea, 'You both sit in my room. The servant will next dust this room. Mine's been dusted.'

Puri rose to his feet, but Kanak remained seated, her head bowed. Nayyar gave Kanak a pat on her back, 'Come on. Get up. After only six months at your parent's home you've begun to behave shyly just like a new bride.'

Kanak had to get up when Nayyar pulled her by her arm.

Nayyar took them both to his room. He took Kanak's arm and sat her on the bed. 'You both have a cup of tea. I'll have tea after I've had a wash.' He switched the fan on and smiled as he closed the doors, 'No one will disturb you.'

The room had a bedstead, a chair and a low stool. The servant boy put the tea tray on the stool.

Puri sat beside Kanak. Every nerve in his body was jangling on being alone with Kanak after such a long time. He said in a choked voice, 'You didn't even tell that you were coming.'

Kanak sat with her arms crossed and eyes downcast. She kept silent.

'Kanni!' He said in a soft, low voice and put his arm round her shoulder.

Kanak got up from the bed and sat on the chair.

Puri's ardour cooled and turned sour. He took a moment to gather his wits, and said, 'Kanni, I feel the same for you today as I did before and after our marriage. Come, let's go home.'

Kanak shook her head.

Puri said after a brief silence, 'Our house belongs to you, not me. I bought the house because you wanted me to. You should live there. Throw me out when you don't want me. I promise that I won't ever do anything against your wishes.'

Kanak again shook her head.

'Any particular reason why you don't want to live with me?'

Kanak said, 'It's not possible.'

'Why is it not possible?'

'It isn't.'

'I promise that the thing you disliked,' Puri said in pleading voice, 'it won't happen again. I'll never insist on a husband's right over his wife or that we have a relationship. It's your home and you live there.'

Kanak said 'no'.

'Why it's not possible when I am prepared to accept all your conditions?'

'There's no sense in doing that if there's no relationship between us.'

'You mean no other relationship is possible except physical?'

Kanak realized that Puri was trying to put her on the defensive and make her feel embarrassed by being deliberately obnoxious. She replied, 'That relationship is the most important between husband and wife.'

'I think there can be much more besides.'

'The much more part is also possible in other relationships.'

Puri had to shut up. He said after a brief pause, 'Do you really have that much loathing for me?'

'What's the point of such talk?' Kanak said, her gaze lowered.

'But why can't we live together when I am ready to accept anything you say?'

'There's no point in living together when there's no relationship.'

'You have no relationship with me?'

Kanak shook her head.

'I am the father of your daughter. I have a right over her.'

'You have no such right.'

'How can you say that?' Puri said, thinking that he had found a strong argument in his favour.

'She's my daughter.'

'She's your daughter, but I too am her father. She's also my child. A father has his rights and moral obligations to his children.'

'You suspected Urmila was pregnant when you threw her out. You had cried for that reason. What about your rights and obligations to that child?' Kanak looked at him waiting for an answer.

Puri said after a slight hesitation, 'I was guilty of not meeting my obligations because of the circumstances or my own weakness. But now I am willing to meet my obligations and I do have a right.'

'Mother's rights come first. I am not asking for a provider or a shelter for my daughter. I don't need it.'

'Kanni, what will we do in the future?'

'What we are doing now.'

'Is this the ruination of our marriage?'

'It was you who wrote to pitaji that you had lost your patience and wanted a divorce. I want the same thing and pitaji also thinks that it'd be the right thing to do.'

'I never wrote those words. I can't even think of divorce.'

'But I want it.'

'Kanni, what's happened to you?' Puri said, with a catch in his voice. 'We won't be able to face the world.'

'Why should we live in a world of make-believe? It's a matter of fact, we don't need to shout about it from the rooftops.'

Puri was silent.

Kanak also sat quietly with her eyes fixed on the floor. She heard what sounded like Puri attempting to hold back his tears. It's nothing but theatrics, she thought. She turned away her eyes and said, 'Can I go?'

Puri took a deep breath, 'Our relationship will not be broken no matter where you are and what you do. You won't get a divorce.'

'But I want it.'

'Why must we keep up appearances for the sake of people?'

'Pretending that we are together is keeping up appearances. Why should I hang on to the moulted skin of a dead snake?'

'You want freedom? You want to get married again?' Puri asked in a cold, hard voice.

'I'll do what I want.'

'Who do you want to marry?'

'It's none of your business.'

'Gill?'

'Mind your own business.'

'It *is* my business. You are my wife.'

'I am not. You yourself said that you wanted to give up your right to be my husband.'

'I said that because I felt sympathy for you. But you deceived me and you betrayed my trust.'

'I never deceived you,' Kanak said firmly. 'The day it became impossible for me to go on with the relationship, I told you plainly. Neither did I deceive you, nor do I intend to.'

'I'm not going to divorce you. I won't end our relationship so that you can be promiscuous.'

'You won't end the relationship because you want to take your revenge on me and to ruin my life!'

'I've never been revengeful or cruel to anyone. Urmila had to leave only because of you. It's you who has caused all this trouble.'

'I know how cruel you've been to Urmila, to your parents and to Tara. Whom have you not deceived and betrayed?'

'I've been cruel to Tara?'

'I know all about it.'

'Fine if you do,' Puri said, gnashing his teeth.

After a brief silence, Puri again said, 'You didn't say anything about divorce when you went away, or I would have thought along that line.'

'I had no such idea in my mind at that time.'

'Someone coached you in Delhi?'

'No one coaches me.'

'The person who coached Sheelo could have also coached you.'

'That's not true. It's a false accusation.'

Seeing that Puri was leaving, Kanak said, 'If you don't divorce me, I'll divorce you.'

Puri was going towards the stairs when Nayyar called out to him and took him into his office. Placing his hand on Puri's shoulder he asked, 'How did it go? Did you talk some sense into her?' Puri's face was flushed with anger. He was unable to speak. After a few moments he expressed his surprise, 'You told me not to think about divorce, but she's insistent on getting a divorce. She says that pitaji also wants the same thing.'

'That must be a recent development. She must have insisted and pitaji would have agreed with her. The whole idea sounds absolutely preposterous! What do you want, because she can't go against the family's wishes. Are you willing to be patient?'

Puri took a deep breath, 'I don't mind. You yourself said that it was a preposterous idea.'

'All right, then.' Nayyar said by way of reassurance, 'She can't do everything as she wishes. Let her stay in Delhi for now.'

Nayyar and Kanta wanted Kanak to give up her idea of divorce, but she did not relent. All three had long discussions and Kanak was told 'You live in Delhi, away from the problem of staying with Puri. Why do you want to break off your relations with him? Why can't everything stay as it is, for the sake of appearances? How will that restrict your freedom?'

'Why must I keep up appearances?' Kanak persisted.

'You said that the relationship was dead,' Nayyar reasoned with her. 'Since Puri doesn't run your life, what's your problem?'

'There are several problems to overcome,' Kanak replied, looking at her nails. 'By law, I am still his wife.'

'Why, are you thinking of getting married again?' Nayyar asked.

'The question is why should I hang on to a relationship that is dead.'

'You want to be free to marry a second time?'

'Maybe,' Kanak said, dropping her eyes.

Kanta was really angry, 'Damn you! Is that the real reason? Is it why you can't stand Puri any more?'

Kanak had to raise her head, 'That is totally untrue. I had no such idea when I left Jalandhar. Last time when you went back from Delhi, pitaji said to me that there was no point in continuing a meaningless relationship. Until then I hadn't even imagined that it could be possible.'

'You couldn't imagine it because you knew it'd be impossible. Deep in your heart, you must have wanted it,' Nayyar said rather coldly.

'Absolutely not. I never thought about it even in my dreams as long as I regarded him as my husband,' Kanak protested, her head erect.

'Listen, you got married to someone you wanted to marry. How many more times is a girl supposed to get married?'

'You all used to tell me that my marrying him was a mistake. If I made the mistake, don't I have the right to start a new life?'

'You must think of your situation, your relatives and about the future of your daughter even if you have the right,' Nayyar said softly.

Kanak was getting agitated, 'If you want to sacrifice me for the sake of avoiding an embarrassment to the family or a possible scandal, think of me as dead. Neither will I look to you for help, nor will my daughter be a burden on any of you.'

Kanak went to an inner room, threw herself onto a bed and covered her face with her aanchal.

After a while Nayyar called out to Kanak, and said to her when she came, 'Kanni, I know exactly how you feel. My heart goes out to you. It's good that you don't want to keep the pretence of being married and deceive people into believing things that are not true, but I won't be able to help you no matter how much I would like to. There are laws governing the divorce procedure. By law you may divorce your husband if you can prove that he is either impotent or has been violent and physically abusive or has had extramarital affairs or has some incurable disease that may be life-threatening to you or has deserted you for another woman or has turned you out of the house. And there's no way you could prove any of these charges.

'Puri, on the other hand, can have several valid complaints against you. For example, your unwillingness to live with him, and that he has never denied you the right to live in that house. The argument that you find it impossible to live with him has no legal significance. Puri's weird tendency, about which Kanta told me, surely could be intolerable for you, but it cannot be proven and therefore cannot be used as evidence in the court. The court can accept only verifiable information as evidence. Therefore, it might be useless for you to think of divorce.'

On her way back from Jalandhar, the thought that she had nothing definite to tell Gill filled Kanak with consternation.

Chapter 19

AFTER HE HAD TAKEN ON THE MINISTERIAL RESPONSIBILITIES, THERE HAD BEEN a gradual change in Sood's lifestyle. It had no longer been possible for him to manage with one room on the first floor of a small house in Mandi Bazaar. How could the minister's bodyguards and security personnel be accommodated in such a small place? And where would other government ministers and high officials sit when they came for consultation with Sood? A space large enough with furniture suitable for those visitors was needed, and a waiting area for those who came in the hope of meeting the minister with their grievances and petitions. These hopefuls came in such large numbers that, except for a few in Sood's inner circle, they sometimes had to wait two or three days before being able to see him. Sood had been given accommodation and an official car with the state flag on the bonnet in accordance with government regulation. A handful of guests would always be staying in his residence.

The residences of the ministers of the Government of Punjab had been in Simla in the beginning. After the capital was moved to Chandigarh, Sood had begun to spend most of his time in the new capital. There had been no marked change in his personal habits, despite his living in a big and grand residence. He had no time to wash his clothes any more, but his dress remained the same combination of thick khadi kurta-pyjama or kurta-dhoti with a Gandhi cap stuck over his closely cropped hair, and a pair of chappals for footwear.

Sood received his visitors in the mornings and evenings and on Sundays dressed in a vest and a pair of shorts. He would sit, knees drawn up, in the same attire on a large sofa in the living room running his hand through his hair or scratching his eczema, and talk with his visitors or berate secretaries and commissioners of various government departments. Bureaucrats, who saw themselves as the privileged class, had to bow their heads before this representative of the ordinary people of the country.

Sood had not built any bungalows or mansions for himself, and his bank balance was not worth talking about. He may not have cared to build a fortune for himself, but those who had been devoted to him had benefited greatly from their loyalty towards him, and continued to be confident and hopeful of doubling and tripling their gains. The recipients of his benevolence were not afraid of the law or of their actions coming under governmental censure. Big capitalists and industrialists, even those outside Punjab, acknowledged his power and influence, and were eager to become his friends. These magnates were willing to hire anyone at a monthly salary of one or two thousand rupees at the merest suggestion made by Sood.

Sood may not have amassed a fortune, but he was not unaware of the power of money in political and social arenas. He was at the helm of numerous organizations, which had accumulated over two crore of rupees in their coffers over the years. Sood was the only person with the authority to disburse these funds. Those employed at the schools and hospitals run by the organizations and those who sat on the management committees had to pledge allegiance to Sood, or fear being fired without due formality. A great many people hired in businesses and industries at Sood's recommendation or suggestion were loyal to Sood rather than to their employers.

Sood's nature and his behaviour, like his dress and rather spartan life, had remained unchanged: same straightforward manner, rigid political dogmatism, and an inability to accept or see the other side of an argument. As his power and influence increased, so did his arrogance and his bossy manner. He began using his strengths and abilities to defeat and destroy any political threat to his power. His intensity of purpose soon turned into intolerance for differing opinions and a desire to hear an echo of his own views. What he suggested or recommended was considered more important by government officials than an order from the chief minister. He was not yet the chief minister, but people called him the 'minister-in-chief'; everyone knew that Sood could become the chief minister whenever he wanted to.

When things grow bigger, so do their shadow. In the same way when the importance of a thing or the status of a person increases, so does the reaction to the increase in importance or status. Sood's popularity had grown not because of his political savvy, dedication to the country and his outspoken behaviour, but because of the favours people hoped to gain from his ever-increasing influence in the state. The number of Sood's supporters had grown, but even larger was the number of people hopeful of profiting through their association with him. Those who had not been able to—or had given up the hope of —gaining favours from him, had turned to criticizing him and accusing him of nepotism. Since only sycophants and yes-men had Sood's ear, he had little knowledge of such reactions against him.

If Sood showered riches on his favourites, he also made sure that those who opposed him bit the dust. He saw any disagreement with him as a potential threat to his authority and a ploy to dislodge him from his position as a leader of the party. Solis and Nath had ignored his suggestions to make changes in the Plan on the strength of assurance from the Prime Minister that they could count on his backing, and had retained the policy of large investments in the public sector despite the opposition from Sood and his group. The implementation of the Plan had begun in early 1956. Although big capitalists, business magnates and others alarmed by the growing menace of socialistic leanings of the Congress government were siding with Sood in numbers larger than before, eager to be in his good books, Sood had not forgiven Solis and Nath.

Sood's influence over Punjab politics had considerably increased in the past eight years, which had made many of Sood's political opponents and supporters of his rival Dr Radhey Behari join the Sood camp. Dr Prabhu Dayal had switched his allegiance to Sood in 1950. After the Partition, Prabhu Dayal had been appointed first as assistant surgeon in Ferozepur on the recommendation of Dr Behari. Since he was seen as Dr Behari's man, he had been promoted soon after to the post of assistant professor in the medical college. After joining Sood, Prabhu Dayal had gone to England on a sabbatical in 1955 for six months to complete a professional course. He had his eye on the post of professor of medicine in a new medical college. There were several MDs senior to him aspiring to the same post, but everyone knew that with Sood's blessing, even 'the lame could scale a mountain and the mute become garrulous'.

Sood had been suffering from eczema on his backside for a long time. He could not stop himself from scratching his bottom when it itched. The condition accentuated during the rainy season. A skin specialist from the medical college had got Sood's blood, urine, stool and the scales from his rash examined. The specialist had concluded, after trying out several treatments on Sood, that the itch was caused by a physical allergy. The fungal infection had penetrated deep into the skin and as long as there was physical allergy, there would be itching. Sood was advised to avoid sitting on his backside.

Prabhu Dayal had been travelling to Chandigarh twice a month, spending out of his own pocket, to treat Sood's eczema. He would carry the newest medicines and an ultraviolet lamp. He would himself apply the medicines and expose the infected area to rays from the lamp. He would give prophylactic treatment as a precaution even when the itch did not bother Sood. If Sood was busy, Prabhu Dayal would hang around listening and participating in political chit-chat and wait until Sood was free.

In the first week of August Prabhu Dayal again went to Chandigarh to give Sood his treatment. Sood was looking through some important papers slumped on the sofa in the living room. Prabhu Dayal sat down and waited, thumbing through magazines and newspapers stacked on a round centre table.

Sood finished with the file and dumped it on the floor. He was removing his reading glasses when Prabhu Dayal held out an opened illustrated magazine, 'Bhappaji, did you see this miracle?'

'What?'

'A girl who had died was found alive and became an undersecretary in the ministry of information. Doctor Pran Nath, member secretary of the Planning Commission got married to her.'

'When? Where?' Sood asked.

Prabhu Dayal said as Sood looked at the opened page, 'Nothing short of a miracle. Tara Puri had died in a fire. Bhappaji, she's the sister of our own Jaidev Puri.'

'If she had died in a fire, is this what's-its-name the photograph of her ghost?' Sood said throwing aside the magazine.

'What an odd coincidence, bhappaji,' Prabhu Dayal insisted. 'How can I not recognize her? I'll bet anything that she's Tara. Puri used to live across from our house in Bhola Pandhe's Gali and Tara was a close friend of my wife. It was I who put the dressing on the wound on her forehead. She had got married before the Partition. I remember the date, 29 July 1947. She was married to Somraj Sahni, that Somraj from Jalandhar. You helped him get the contract to build the boundary wall of the secretariat's garden. It was a Hindu marriage. You can ask Puri.'

'Hunh!' Sood said, picking up the magazine. 'How come she got married to what's-its-name Pran Nath?' He peered at the photograph, brought the page close to his eyes to read the caption, and said in surprise, 'The wedding was in Delhi, at the Naya Hind Press. Pandit Girdharilal owns what's-its-name the Naya Hind Press! What is going on? Somraj is alive and well.'

Sood lay prone on the sofa. Prabhu Dayal continued to talk about the mysterious event as he applied medicines and then ultraviolet rays to Sood's backside, 'There was some rumour before Tara's wedding that she didn't want to get married to Somraj. He's the same Somraj, who was involved in the Professor Deen Mohammed incident. Tara, in all probability, didn't die in the fire at Somraj's house and managed to escape. Poor Puri, he has no knowledge of all this. He and Somraj still think that Tara had died. Tara hasn't contacted her family. She was a bright girl. Wonder where she was all these years. Bhappaji, there's no doubt that it's her photograph, hundred and one per cent Tara.'

As soon as the treatment was over, Sood summoned the peon and ordered, 'Get Bahri Sahib.' When his personal assistant arrived, Sood ordered, 'Call Jaidev Puri at his house in Model Town in Jalandhar.'

Puri found it difficult to comprehend what had happened. Sood asked him to read the *Illustrated Weekly*.

Puri managed to find a copy of the weekly by afternoon. His brain reeled when he saw the photograph, 'Tara getting married when her first husband is still alive! And that too at the Naya Hind Press! This was done deliberately, just out of spite. And they had to publish the photograph! They are all in this together! Kanak wants to do the same thing whether I divorce her or not? This was meant to be a direct challenge to me.'

Puri wanted to hurt Tara and Kanak in a frenzy of rage and frustration. Then the thought crossed his mind that by doing that he'd be hurting himself, he'd be cutting off his nose to spite his face.

It was not possible for Puri to disregard Sood's orders. Sood gave an assurance to Puri and Somraj that it would be an official and completely confidential investigation. Doctor Pran Nath would be taught a lesson.

Puri felt a surge of anger and hatred towards Nath, 'What an example of cultured and gentlemanly behaviour! Wouldn't have been satisfied unless he had set his guru's home on fire! He used to call Tara his "younger sister". What a web of deceit he had spun to get Tara to come to his house and tutor.'

Nath and Tara wanted to get married in November 1955, but several things got in the way of their wedding. Nath had to go to England in the beginning of November with the minister of finance, as his advisor. Then he went to the USA with the minster of industrial development as his advisor. After that he and Tara could not find a suitable time before July 1956. Tara did not like the dreariness of a civil marriage, of going through a formal procedure only to make their marriage legal. At the same time, both were reluctant to have a full-blown wedding or an ostentatious ceremony at their age.

Nath's suggestion was to call a pandit or a granthi to his bungalow to perform the marriage rites, so that Tara could have the satisfaction of a traditional wedding. It was decided to have only twenty-five wedding guests, among them Dr Solis, Shyama, Prabha Saxena, Chaddha and Mercy, Kanak, Gill, Narottam and Kanchan, Sheelo and Ratan, and Mathur.

Kanak and Mercy were competing with each other to organize the ceremony. Both were against the wedding taking place at Nath's bungalow. Kanak made the decision, 'The bride will not go to the groom's house to get married. Doctor sahib will take her to his home after the ceremony in accordance with the custom.'

The ceremony took place at the Naya Hind Press. Pandit Girdharilal gave away the bride and Mercy, in the role of Nath's sister, welcomed Tara at Nath's bungalow.

Nath and Tara had arranged for three months' leave. They left for Switzerland a couple of days after the wedding. For Tara it was heaven on earth, and she wanted to enjoy her happiness and contentment to the utmost.

Tara had been back only for a week when the home secretary's peon came to her office and asked her to personally sign for a sealed envelope. On the envelope were her name and the position she was holding. The envelope was marked Very Confidential, which surprised Tara. She was in the middle of dictating some memos and letters to her stenographer. She finished giving the dictation before opening the envelope.

What she read in that very confidential letter left her aghast. She sat staring into space with her forefinger between her teeth, stunned as if she had lost consciousness for a minute. She sighed deeply and began to read the documents enclosed with the letter. Every word was like a blow to the head and every page she read made her feel as if she were sinking into a dark bottomless pit. She put the documents and letter on the desk after reading them and grasped the armrests to steady herself, staring blankly at her desk.

Tara took several deep breaths to bring herself under control. Her mind slowly registered the documents and the telephone on her desk. Her hand went to the phone, but she pulled it back, unsure if it were the right thing to do. Her head was flying off her shoulders. She clasped her forehead in her hands. In her agitation she wanted to smash her head against the desk. Memories of Banti banging her head on the threshold of her husband's home flashed through her mind. Bracing her arms she pulled herself upright and began to pace the room.

The phone rang. She did not want to answer it, but the persistent ring was unbearable. She thought she'd pick up the receiver and quickly hang up, but in a state of shock put it to her ear, 'Yes!'

Nath said, 'Listen, Tara. Perhaps you received a letter?'

'Yes, I did.'

'Don't let that upset you. I'll pick you up by 5 or 5.15.'

Nath receiving the same letter came as a terrible blow to her, 'I was doomed to suffer all my life and he has to suffer because of me.' She felt her legs buckle and held on to the desk to regain her balance, 'Does my fate await him too?'

Tara somehow found the strength to keep going, but that strength drained away when Nath put his arm round her; she just fell into his arms. Nath helped her get out of the car, took her to the bedroom and helped her lie down. He sat on the edge of her bed and asked her for the letter . He showed her the letter he had received and she saw that both the letters were the same. Attached to the letters were the testimonies that Puri, Somraj and Doctor Prabhu Dayal had given to the Special Police.

Tara pressed her head into Nath's lap and began to cry.

Nath put his hand on her head to console her, and asked, 'Who is Doctor Prabhu Dayal?'

Tara said, 'He used to live across from us in our gali. This is all bhai's doing. I don't know what grudges he's harbouring against me.'

'Puri alone can't do all this. He doesn't have the political contacts. Sood has a hand in this. This is not an attack on you, but the result of Sood's resentment towards me. Puri is nothing but Sood's puppet. You got dragged into this mess because of me. When grain is ground for wheat, the weevils are ground with it. Have you thought about replying to the letter?'

'I don't know what to say.' Tara took a deep breath. 'As far as the facts are concerned, those testimonies are correct, but you know I was never his wife. I have done nothing wrong. If I broke the law, I am responsible for the consequences. You weren't married before, so let them punish me. I don't care for this job.…'

'That's not the issue. The real issue is not your job, but clearing your name,' Nath said . 'I went into this marriage with my eyes open. I knew all about you. It was me who proposed to you. I have a moral responsibility to you. I'm sure that we did nothing wrong, but the charges against us are not on moral but on legal grounds. We'll have to take legal action to counter the allegations against us.'

'Huzoor, Gill babuji has come,' Parsu said from outside the door.

'I'll tell him I can't spend time with him today,' Nath said, and went to the living room.

Gill had been writing editorials for two Delhi newspapers twice a month on the national economy and the Second Five Year Plan. He often got some matter for his editorials from Nath. He had made an appointment with Nath for them to meet that day.

This was the first time Gill was meeting Nath after his return from Switzerland. The photograph and news of Nath's marriage had been published in their absence. Gill had brought along the magazine to show Nath. He opened the magazine at the page with the photograph and put it on a side table before Nath came into the living room.

Seeing Nath's long face and worried look, Gill asked, 'Doctor sahib, what's the matter? You are well?'

'I'm a bit worried.' Nath motioned Gill to take a chair, 'I'm sorry that you came from so far.'

'No. no, Doctor sahib, please don't bother about that. Is bhabhi all right?'

'No. She's also quite upset.'

'What's the matter, Doctor sahib? Please don't hesitate to tell me if I can do anything to help,' Gill said with sincerity.

'I don't know how to explain,' Nath said, taking a deep breath. He pointed to the magazine, 'There is the problem, thanks to Puri and Sood. People playing dirty politics. They want me removed from the Planning Commission. How can anyone sink so low?'

Nath briefly told Gill why he was worried and about the testimonies of Puri, Somraj and Prabhu Dayal. 'I'll show you the documents,' he said, and went to an inner room.

Nath made an attempt to smile when he returned, 'All this is because of your mischievousness. You couldn't resist getting the news published that the marriage took place at the house of Puri's father-in-law.'

'Huhn. That must be the main cause of his anger,' Gill acknowledged.

'We believe that we haven't done anything dishonest. We can face them with a clear conscience,' Nath said, 'but the charges against us have legal basis. The law is not concerned with truth and conscience. Legal issues are complex and open to interpretation. We must seek advice from a lawyer. We should attempt to stop this news from spreading.'

'If you want legal advice, wait till tomorrow,' Gill said. 'All offices will be closed tomorrow anyway due to the Dussehra holiday. Kanak's brother-in-law Nayyar is arriving tomorrow. He's serious minded and a successful lawyer. He knows Puri and Sood well. If the marriage was unlawful, Kanak and Panditji are also implicated in organizing it. After all Panditji gave the girl away. I'll go from here to Kanak's place and explain.'

Nayyar had come to Delhi for a different reason.

After Kanak had come back from Jalandhar at June end, Pandit Girdharilal had, after much deliberation, written another letter to Nayyar at the beginning of August, 'Try once again to convince Puri that there is more to married life than just keeping up appearances. Puri and Kanak both need to rid themselves of the bitterness and enmity that plague their relationship. Puri is a very sensible person. He should think of a compromise that allows both to do away with the acrimony in a dignified manner.' Panditji himself read the divorce law and suggested that if Puri wants he can divorce Kanak on the grounds of desertion, Kanak will not contest the charge and Puri won't get the blame. A request can be made to the court to conduct the proceedings in camera.

It was clear to Nayyar that Panditji was supporting what Kanak wanted. Since he didn't want to be blamed for the suggestion, he told Puri what Panditji had written in his letter.

Puri was very offended and angry that Tara's wedding ceremony was held at the Naya Hind Press. Without saying anything about his feelings, he told Nayyar curtly, 'Panditji is going senile. Kanak's just leading him on. She can't treat me as if I were a puppet in her hands. There are legal grounds for divorce, but I won't divorce her. I know what she's up to. I won't encourage promiscuity. What sacrifice did I not make for her? The relationship may be dead, but I won't give her the opportunity to get married again. If she decides to go ahead, she won't be somebody's lawful wife, her marriage won't be legal. I know how to get even with both.'

What could Nayyar say in reply and what could he tell Panditji. The thought of Panditji's mental state distressed him greatly. He supposed that Panditji wanted to hurry up only for the sake of Kanak. He wrote back that he had some work in Delhi and that he'd come to see Panditji during the Vijayadashami festival and discuss everything at that time.

Kanak had gone to the railway station to receive Nayyar. She began to fill him in on how Sood and Puri had conspired against Nath and Tara at the station. In the afternoon, Gill took Kanak and Nayyar to meet Nath.

Nayyar now knew the whole story. He was already full of praise and sympathy for Tara after what Kanak had told him earlier.

Nayyar examined the notices sent to Tara and Nath, and read the secret testimonies of Puri, Prabhu Dayal and Somraj to the Special Police. He thought for a few moments with a worried expression and his lower lip clenched between his teeth, then said in English as he stroked his eyebrows, 'There is no doubt that for all intents and purposes the first marriage was de facto dead. Those people wouldn't have been able to hound you if you only had taken the advantage of the new divorce law.'

'You are quite correct,' Nath admitted. 'First of all, who could even imagine that a situation like this would arise after nine years. Even to think about that inconsequential and unpleasant incident would have been humiliating. Legalities aside, what happened was not a marriage but a travesty of marriage. People think of going to law either when they need its protection or when they want to threaten someone with legal action.' Nath laughed.

'The law always means trouble,' Kanak said, glancing sideways at Nayyar. 'One should always be wary of it.'

Nayyar smiled lightly. He got the opening for getting down to business, 'In order to defend yourself, you will have to go to law. You'll need the protection of law to ward off this legal threat. Your case is rather unusual. This matter is neither within the purview of a court of law, nor is it a question of morality of actions or one that can be decided by common sense. This is not a simple legal action against you, but an attack on you with the help of the powers that be, under the guise of conducting a departmental inquiry. Had the matter been sub judice, Somraj himself could have been charged with plotting to kill Taraji by setting fire to the house. Charges could have been made. Questions could have been posed. Why was the news of her death believed and why were her last rites performed in such haste without ascertaining her death? Witnesses and evidence in support of such charges could have been found.'

Still stroking his eyebrows he asked Tara, 'Can we prove these testimonies to be false?'

Tara answered with her chin sunk onto her chest, 'The testimonies may not be legally false, but the fact is that I never accepted him as my husband. Never in the past nine years did I have any contact with him or live with him.'

Nath, 'Actually, Sood is angry with me. He wants to get me out of the way.'

Nayyar admitted, 'I know that, but I was talking about the accusations against Taraji.' He asked Tara, 'Did you ever receive a court notice that your second marriage was illegal, and that legally you were still the wife of Somraj?'

Tara shook her head.

Nayyar said, straightening his back, 'Then according to law the charges against you are completely baseless. Well, it is obvious,' he looked at Nath, 'as you said, it's not a complaint lodged by Somraj. If he had been the complainant, he would have prayed for your marriage to be declared illegal and for his right over Taraji. She should have been sent a notice about it. Somraj is only a pawn in this game. Sood is a lawyer, so he jumped at the chance of a possible legal loophole. But he judged it wrong because he has not practised law for a long time. I am surprised that your department overlooked this flaw. And why was a legal advisor not consulted? Maybe they wanted to charge you as a government official with an offence involving moral turpitude.'

Nayyar asked after a few moments' thought, 'You had no premonition of this notice? Granted, the decision to lay charges against you could have been confidential, but news does leak out here and there.'

'We returned to Delhi just nine days ago. We both were abroad.' Nath searched his memory, then said, 'Yes, I had heard that someone was out to get me. But I'd heard that so many times before.'

'I have my suspicions to the contrary, that the case against you was left incomplete and prepared half-heartedly. There are a number of weak links in the chain. Well, it's clear that the ministry has a two-sided approach in your case. Some influential people are definitely against you.'

Gill said, 'The whole affair stinks of political sabotage and political blackmail.'

Nayyar asked Nath, 'Are you reasonably sure that you can get a sympathetic departmental hearing?'

Nath expressed his doubt, 'The faction opposing the proposed nationalization under the Plan is quite powerful. Not everyone in the Cabinet is as enthusiastic about the Plan as the Prime Minister, but they have little say. Foreign experts offering unasked for advice have the ear of several top ministers, otherwise—as you said—the notices probably wouldn't have been sent. I'll incorporate the whole background to the case in my reply, including the conversation I had with Sood.'

'It won't be wise to leave the decision solely in the hands of the ministry. Isn't the Prime Minister the chairman of the Planning Commission?' Nayyar asked, crinkling his brow.

'Under the rules we both will send our replies to our respective ministries, and the decision will be in the hands of the minister in charge. It'd be against the rules to go directly to the Prime Minister,' Nath expressed his helplessness.

'But we are under no such obligation,' Gill and Kanak said almost simultaneously. 'We can appeal to the Prime Minister about this political blackmail.'

'I'll ask Gadiwala,' Gill said, 'about inquiring into this within the Congress party and asking questions in Parliament. He has faith in the socialistic economic policies of the Congress. In the House of Parliament, as you well know, there have been exposures of a conspiracy involving some big industrialists to sabotage the government's nationalization policy, and revelations about high government officials charged with bribery and corruption.'

Nayyar, his thumb and middle finger again holding his temple, motioned for others to listen, 'Doctor sahib and Taraji were subjected to political sabotage and blackmail under the pretext of following the rules precisely. They will have to use political means to defend themselves and to rebut the accusations by taking legal action against the ministry.'

Nayyar looked at Tara, 'It'll be necessary to prove that your so-called first marriage had become null and void before you got married again. For that you may enter a plea of desertion. We'll need evidence to suggest that you didn't desert that man, but he deserted you. The law requires such evidence. We'll need evidence or some proof that you tried to contact and keep your marital relationship with your husband, but your attempts were ignored. Will you be able to provide that evidence?'

Tara wagged her head slowly.

'Why'd that be a problem?' Nayyar said with a note of surprise.

'I never wrote to him. I never tried to contact his family, nor did I want to.'

Arching his eyebrows, Nayyar asked, 'The question is not what you wanted to do or what you didn't do. What I mean is evidence to support your plea. Listen, the testimonies of Puri and Prabhu Dayal constitute evidence that you were Somraj's wife. Is that true?'

'It's a false truth.'

'But there is evidence to prove that falsehood as truth. We also need evidence to refute their allegations. It's essential to show what's true and what's false. And we need evidence to support what's really true.' Nayyar raised his finger to give a warning, 'Don't take it to mean that I am telling you to lie. It's not an incident that is true or false; truth or falsehood depends on how we interpret its occurrence, and the intention behind that interpretation. We must make an effort to find out the facts to see if those facts help us ascertain the truth. We need evidence in ascertaining the truth.

'Puri's wife is a witness to the fact that Puri had known about you since 1949, and that for the past nine years both he and Somraj have been living in the same city. They are thick as thieves. Their relationship is so close that Puri is testifying in Somraj's favour against his own sister. Naturally, Puri was obliged to inform Somraj about you. He cannot say that he didn't. And Puri didn't call you to Jalandhar because he knew that Somraj had deserted you.'

Nayyar looked at Kanak, 'Won't Kanak give an assurance to testify that Puri ignored his sister's desire and her attempts to reunite with Somraj because he knew that Somraj didn't want to take Tara back?'

'I'll certainly do that,' Kanak leaned forward and said firmly. 'That *is* the truth. Somraj had been living with his bhabhi even before I came to Jalandhar. Puriji knew it, but tried to conceal it from everybody. I'll certainly admit that, in the court, in public, anywhere. That's not a falsehood, but the truth. It is absolutely true that Somraj and Puriji didn't want Tara to come to Jalandhar.'

Tara took a deep breath. She was amazed at this strange cause and effect that was gradually evolving into a logical answer to the false accusations against her. The fact that she despised Somraj and didn't want him as her husband had little significance.

Nayyar gestured for Kanak to listen and said to Tara, 'Your reply should be based on this type of evidence. There is another important point, that your reply should include a word of warning to your ministry that you will go to court if a now defunct marriage is used as an excuse for an unwarranted action against you. And should such a situation arise, you should not shirk from going to court. Their accusation can be proven false in court only on the basis of Kanni's testimony.'

It was decided after a long discussion that Tara and Nath would write out their statements and show them to Nayyar before he went back to Jalandhar. Kanak, in her role as Puri's wife, would write a letter to the Prime Minister and another to the president of the Congress party about this blackmail to sabotage the government's policy of nationalization.

Nayyar again gestured for everyone to pay attention, 'In the letter to the Prime Minister and the president of Congress it is imperative to draw attention to the anomaly that if the investigation has been undertaken to redress wrongs done to Somraj, the first step should have been making an application in the law court to annul Taraji's second marriage. Puri made no attempt to reunite his sister with her in-laws' family. What were Puri's motives behind his testimony against his sister? Was it a sense of duty or some other reason which prompted him to do so? Who filed the report that was the basis for action taken by the Special Police? Who gave the order for the inquiry? Is the investigation being carried out for purely political reasons? You should clearly state that both Puri and Somraj suck up to Sood to benefit from his influence and power, that they are just pawns in Sood's hands.'

When Pandit Girdharilal came to know about the malicious campaign against Tara and Nath, it filled him with pain and disgust. He talked gloomily for quite a while, 'What'll become of our country if party politics can descend to such a low level?' There was a lot of discussion on this topic for the next two days at the Naya Hind Press, but how could Panditji forget his daughter's problem. Panditji broached the subject in the afternoon of the day Nayyar was going back by the night train, 'Barkhurdar, what did you decide to do about Kanak's problem?'

Nayyar gave a brief answer, 'Pitaji, you have seen Puri's attitude. It seems pointless to expect him to make any concessions. But I've told Kanak to send a copy of her letter to the Prime Minister and the Congress president to Puri and add a note to it that Tara will go to court to fight the injustice against her. And that Kanak, as Puri's wife and someone who was in a position to have witnessed the ill treatment of Tara, would testify against the false accusations. Let's see what happens.'

Nath and Tara sent in their replies to the notices by the end of October. For Tara each day was an eternity of tension and suspense: What would the final outcome be? She was not so much worried about losing her job as she was about Nath feeling shamed and humiliated by the scandal. She had gone through hell, but suffering such ignominy after earning a respected reputation seemed intolerable.

Nath told the whole story to Dr Solis. Solis was also the adviser to the ministry for foreign affairs, a portfolio held by the Prime Minister, and met with him from time to time. The Prime Minister had a high regard and respect for Solis because of his international repute. Solis had it in mind to discuss Nath's problem with the Prime Minister, but didn't get a chance to speak to him.

The Prime Minister was so busy in the preparations for the coming elections and the selection of the Congress candidates that he could not find any time for Solis before the first week of January 1957. Solis reassured Nath and Tara afterwards that the Prime Minister had asked the decision on their case to be held in abeyance until he had reviewed it, and that he knew Sood and his shenanigans very well.

Solis's reassurance didn't make Tara's worry go away. She never considered herself guilty of doing anything wrong, it was the idea of a humiliating reputation that she loathed, but waiting for any verdict from the Prime Minister's Office meant more delay. The newspapers carried daily reports of the Prime Minister's whirlwind tours, of his statements and speeches about the elections. He said the same things most of the time, over and over again about the public's responsibility to the nation, 'We've got to move with the fast-changing times. Our country has been beset with grave problems, national problems as well as international problems, but the people are obsessed with their own small and personal problems. We must try to rise above all such petty, personal concerns.'

Tara had heard the same message from the Prime Minister soon after the country had become independent, when she was in the refugee camp, bereft of hope and with nothing to look forward to. On hearing the same message from him nine years later, all she could do was sigh deeply and hold her peace.

Everyone who came to meet Tara and Nath would talk about the elections. Election news from any state in the country becomes a topic of discussion in Delhi, the country's nerve centre. The Congress party's election strategy attracted a lot of criticism, 'The leaders still invoke Gandhiji's memory when asking people to vote for Congress, but can anyone see the ideals and principles of Gandhiji in the policies of the Congress or in the way the government administers the country? Gandhiji's ideals have been entombed with him in Rajghat.'

Tara would try to forget her troubles and take part in the conversation.

It was the third week of January, and bitterly cold. Gusts of chilly wind pierced the body like an arrow, and a light drizzle fell. Tara was a little surprised to see Kanak and Gill call on her after travelling so far in such weather.

Kanak was smiling and radiant with happiness, and trying to hide her blushes. After saying hello to Tara and asking after Nath, she said, 'I have received a notice from Jalandhar that he has petitioned for divorce on the grounds of desertion.'

Tara patted Kanak on her back and congratulated her warmly, 'You are at least out of your misery.'

Nath was busy in his study. Tara turned her face in that direction and called out, 'Listen, please come here for a minute.'

She said when Nath came, 'Give congratulations to Kanak.'

Nath took Kanak's hands into his and congratulated her. Then said as he took a chair, 'Do you know why Puri decided to divorce you? Should I tell you? For the fear that his reputation would be ruined if you testify against him. Now he'd be able to claim that you always bore him ill will, and were giving false testimony to smear his name.'

Kanak's face lost its radiance.

'Arey, don't worry about that!' Tara and Nath said together. 'A lie has no legs!'

Nath trusted Dr Solis to keep his word, but the sight of Tara wasting away was deeply upsetting to him. Nath tried to calm her fears, but Tara insisted she was not worried about anything.

Nath could see Tara's state for himself. Everyone had congratulated her on how well she looked after returning from Switzerland. Now she didn't look even half as good as before. Nath often felt her body to be abnormally warm. He brought a thermometer, and when Tara agreed to have her temperature taken after much cajoling, he found that her temperature fluctuated between 99 and 100 degrees.

Nath's anxiety knew no bounds. He telephoned Dr Solis, 'What do you want me to do? Should I resign if the Prime Minister cannot find the time to look into my case? I haven't done that only because I'll be playing into the hands of the conspirators.'

Dr Solis said helplessly, 'Had the Prime Minister been in Delhi. I'd have reminded him. As you know, yesterday he went back to Punjab. He's gone there to shore up the Congress candidate, which means Sood himself. That's politics for you. First Sood sabotages the Prime Minister and then asks him for his support. Well, I'll definitely try once he's back...'

In Jalandhar the counting of votes began at ten in the morning. The result was eagerly awaited in Delhi. The Congress supporters and opponents both knew that Sood would win; they were curious how many votes Sood's rival candidate would get? The counting was expected to be over by 6 p.m. Gill reached the bureau of the news agency at 5.45.

The bureau chief had left. The office was very noisy. Several freelance journalists were also present out of curiosity. Everyone was talking about the rumours they had heard about the situation in Punjab. All Congress adversaries had joined together in an attempt to defeat Sood, making it the first instance of a united front against the Congress. The public was curious whether such a coalition would work. One rumour had it that many Congress party members unhappy with Sood's nepotistic and dictatorial style had quietly supported his opponent. Congress seemed confident of getting the vote of government employees, but it was said that the government employees, fearful of Sood's goons, went to the Congress camp to get their voter slips, but for whom they actually voted was to be known only when the votes would be tallied. How many had done that was anyone's guess.

Sangal, an assistant editor at the agency, was teasing another journalist Munish, 'You hope that Sood will lose? Have a bet with me. One for ten wagers. If Sood wins you give me ten rupees, and I'll pay you one hundred if he loses. Want to bet?'

Munish was saying in a feeble voice, 'Arey, we'll find out in ten or fifteen minutes.' He didn't have the courage to place a bet.

They all continued to guess: The Congress has already won a majority in Punjab. There was little doubt that the party leader and the driving force behind the win would be easily elected.

Some journalists thought that Sood's opponent would lose his deposit. And that he must have had his petition challenging the result on the basis of irregularities in the polling and counting of votes all typed up even before the announcement of the final result.

Siddhu said, 'I was in Jalandhar just three days before the polling. Hey, it couldn't even be called a contest between him and Sood. As if some goat were taking on a water buffalo. The poor chap is sure to lose his deposit.'

Prasad refused to accept that Sood's opponent would be defeated by so large a margin. He said, 'Sood's opponents in Jalandhar didn't have motor cars, jeeps and trucks, but it was clearly evident that there was a great deal of opposition to Sood. I myself heard several Congresswallahs say that Congress must be saved from Sood. That they'd rather disobey party orders than vote for dishonesty. Packs of children went around shouting, "We hear in every pathway and lane, thieves like Sood and Puri are to blame." The feeling of discontent among the public was widespread. Sood's opponents were not very visible or vocal, but their whisper campaign is really working. My guess is Sood's opponent would at least capture ten to fifteen thousand votes.'

Sangal, standing next to a row of teleprinters, was flashing around a hundred-rupee note and challenging everyone to lay a bet, 'Any takers? Only ten rupees!'

The room resounded with the chatter of teleprinters spewing out ticker tape printed with news. Whenever a teleprinter began to print a new item, Sangal at once bent forward to check it. He straightened up without reading further the news from Nagpur, Calcutta, Bombay or Lucknow.

Singh and Chakravarty were working the phones to find out if any newspaper office had received news from Jalandhar by trunk call.

Sangal told them to stop, 'Let it go, bhai. If there is a trunk call, we too will receive it here. But who'd be able to get through to Delhi? The telephone lines must be jammed by hundreds of callers anxious to get news of Sood's election.'

Sangal held up his arm the moment he saw 'Jalandhar' on one machine and leaned forward to read it. The room suddenly grew quiet. Several others rushed towards the teleprinter with bated breath.

The agency office erupted into frenzy. Ignoring every rule of decorum, the journalists began to shout 'Inquilab zindabad!' and 'Down with dictatorship!' They hugged one another and jumped up and down and cheered. A burst of delighted enthusiasm left Sangal speechless.

Gill reached for the telephone. It was not free. Some people were already waiting to use it. He quickly went down the stairs and into a shop to telephone the news. But that telephone was also not free. He was so excited he could hardly contain himself. He went to a nearby mithai shop, and from there called the Naya Hind Press. A peon named Murali answered, 'Panditji just went out. Kanakji is not back yet.'

Gill wanted to telephone Nath, but the mithai shop gave him an idea. He bought five rupees worth of mithai and took a taxi to Nath's bungalow.

There was no one in Nath's living room. Gill called out loudly, 'Doctor sahib! Bhabhiji!'

Nath came in, eyes shining with pleasure. He saw Gill beaming with happiness and asked, 'Did you get the news?'

Tara followed Nath into the room. She too was glowing with joy.

'Hunh? You already heard the news?' Gill asked with surprise, noticing the expression on the faces of Tara and Nath.

'What news?' Tara, forefinger on her lips, wanted to know.

'First you tell me your news,' Gill said, holding the box of mithai close to his chest.

'We received letters this morning that we both have been exonerated,' Nath said.

Gill jumped with joy, 'Wah, wah! Congratulations!'

He shook hands with Nath and Tara, 'Here, have a celebratory mithai. I also have news for you. Now you feed me mithai to celebrate.'

'What news?'

'Sood lost by 17,000 votes!'

'What?' Nath's jaw dropped.

'Hunh!' Tara's eyebrows arched.

Gill repeated what he had said, and then, 'I read the news just a little while ago on the teleprinter in the news agency office. Newspaper specials will be out in about fifteen minutes. Let me phone Kanak.'

Nath, his face serious, said earnestly, 'Gill, now you'll believe, won't you, that our countrymen are not yet dead, that the voice of people can't be silenced for all time. It's the people, not politicians and government ministers, who hold the country's future in their hands.'